STAR TREK
DEEP SPACE NINE®
C O M P A N I O N

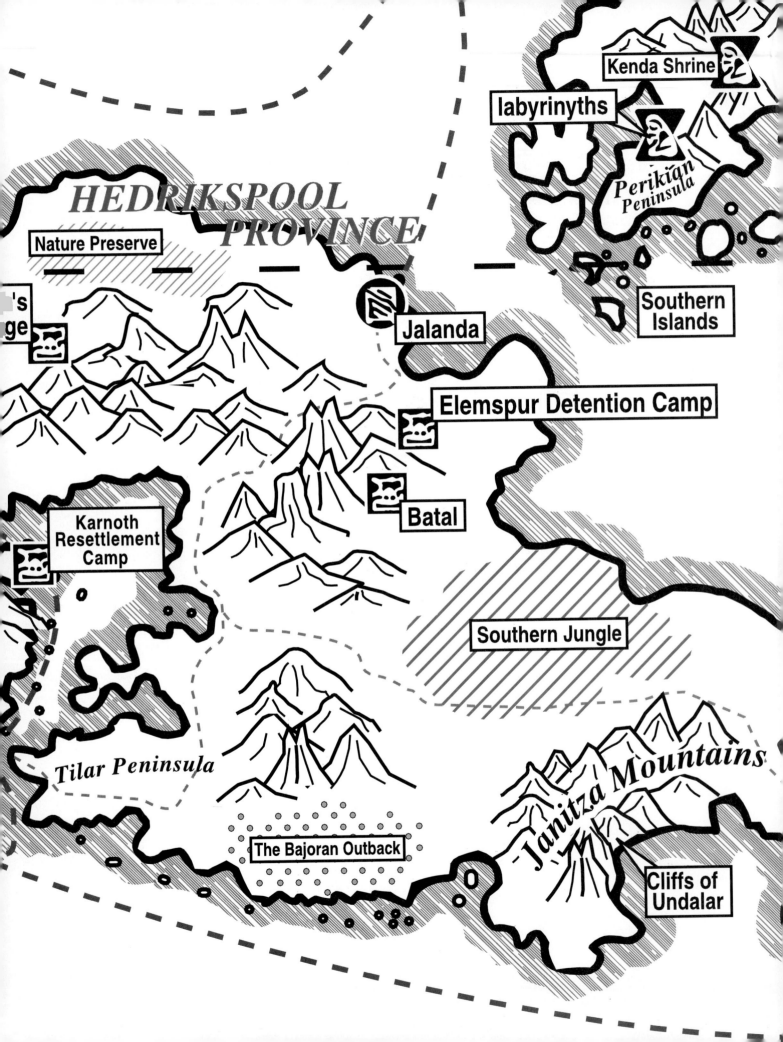

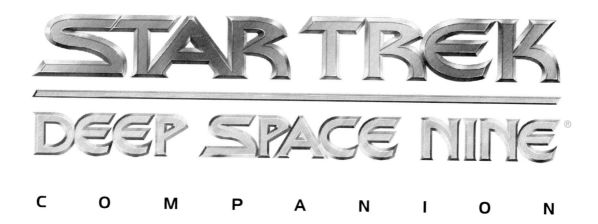

STAR TREK
DEEP SPACE NINE®
C O M P A N I O N

TERRY J. ERDMANN

with Paula M. Block

P O C K E T   B O O K S
New York   London   Toronto   Sydney   Singapore

An *Original* Publication of POCKET BOOKS

POCKET BOOKS, a division of Simon & Schuster Inc.
1230 Avenue of the Americas, New York, NY 10020

ISBN 0-671-50106-2

First Pocket Books trade paperback printing August 2000

Book design by Richard Oriolo

10 9 8 7 6 5 4 3 2 1

To Chet Priewe,

who pointed out the tonic,

subdominant and dominant;

and to Leo Fender,

who plugged them in.

—T.E.

To Joseph J. Brown,

who said, "You can't break the rules of grammar

until you learn the rules of grammar;"

and to Jeff Ryser, who said,

"Those editors in New York are not gods;

they're just jerks like you and me."

—P.B.

C O N T E N T S

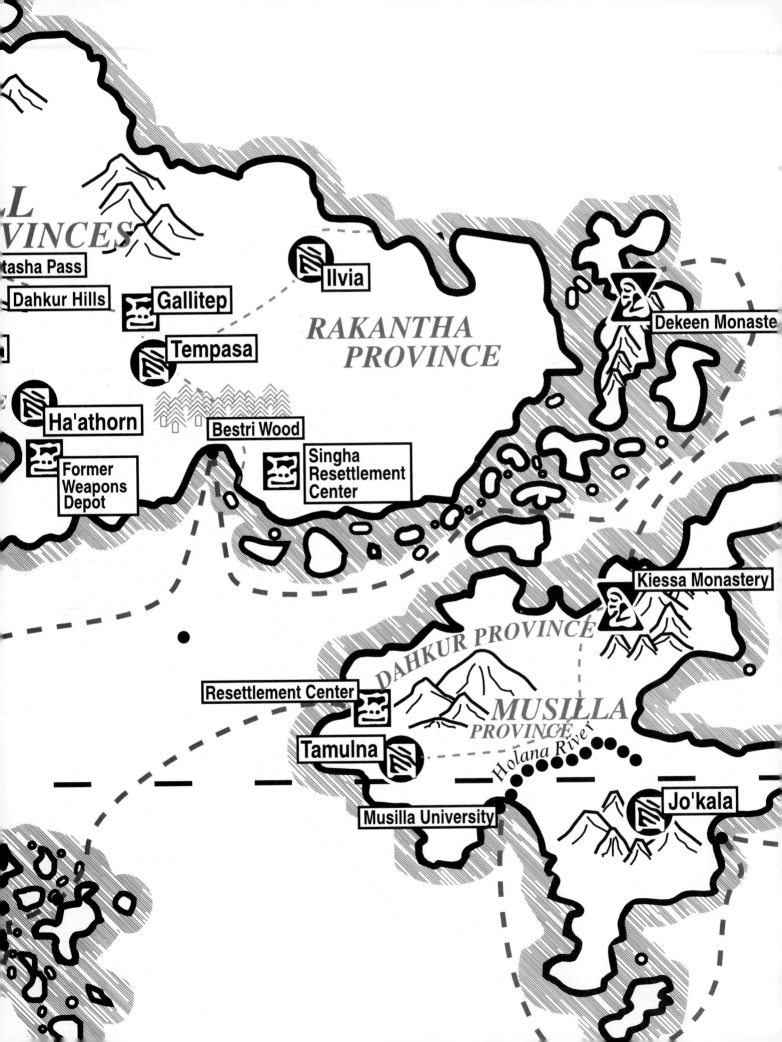

INTRODUCTION

In 1993, the producers of <u>Star Trek</u> took a chance. They opted to break free of the established—and admittedly successful—format that had sustained the series for twenty-seven years. The new show, *Star Trek: Deep Space Nine*, would not take place on a giant starship traveling through "space, the final frontier." Instead, it would be set in a frontier town located in space. The story would begin three years after the infamous battle of Wolf 359, with Commander Benjamin Sisko and his young son Jake warily arriving at their new home, a dilapidated space station located at the edge of the Alpha Quadrant. After making an astounding discovery about a previously undisclosed wormhole, the crew of Deep Space 9 settled in to await visitors from across the galaxy, visitors both friendly and ruthlessly aggressive.

The show's producers and writers were more than a match for the visitors, and for

viewers as well. They were capable of delivering action, drama, and light comedy. They also were up to the challenge of the *Star Trek* legacy, which is to say finding a palatable way to talk about subjects often considered taboo on the small screen. Religion, politics, war: those were staples of the series. Trusting in the intellect of their audience, the creators worked hard to entertain viewers with subject matter that no *Star Trek* series had delved into before. Those who stuck with the writers for all seven years will have no

trouble saying they succeeded beyond their own expectations.

They set the bar higher than ever before, blazing a trail for all future shows in the franchise. And I was lucky enough to have been there to see it all happen.

Near the end of 1993, Kevin Ryan, then senior editor at Pocket Books, contacted me about writing a companion book for *Deep Space Nine*. I had been working as a motion picture publicist for ten years, and was experienced in conducting interviews with actors and filmmakers and writing behind-the-scenes notes for press kits and marketing campaigns. I said yes, of course, having no idea of what I was in for. It takes a few dozen interviews and a few weeks of writing to produce a good press kit for a two-hour movie. When I started this project, it didn't occur to me that I would ultimately be compiling information for the equivalent of a 176-hour movie!

The series, and the writing process, lasted seven years. Along the way, Paula Block of Viacom Consumer Products became an integral part of it all, adding her exceptional way with words as well as her *Star Trek* expertise to the mix. Kevin moved on to other arenas and Margaret Clark became my editor—several times over. While I was working on this tome

for her, Margaret asked me to write *Star Trek: Action!* and *The Tribble Handbook*, and she loaned me out to fellow *Star Trek* editor Marco Palmieri for *The Secrets of Star Trek: Insurrection* (and then she asked me why I was taking so long on *this* book!). But it's finally done.

I truly hope you enjoy reading what follows a tenth as much as I relished researching and writing it. And if anything written herein inspires you to watch an episode of this amazing series a second, or third, or fifth time, then I've succeeded in my job.

As Vic Fontaine once said—this one's from the heart.

—TERRY J. ERDMANN

The new crew: from upper left to right: Rene Auberjonois as Odo; Colm Meaney as Chief Miles O'Brien; Cirroc Lofton as Jake Sisko; Avery Brooks as Commander Benjamin Sisko; bottom row: Terry Farrell as Lieutenant Jadzia Dax; Armin Shimerman as Quark; Nana Visitor as Major Kira Nerys; Siddig El Fadil as Dr. Julian Bashir.

FIRST SEASON
O V E R V I E W

Putting It All Together

What are the most important elements required in the development of a television series? A concept, certainly. A look. A tone. A personality, if you will. But in actuality, it's the people involved with the series, both on-screen and off, that form the skeleton upon which the entire production takes shape. And if the skeleton of the newborn television series *Star Trek: Deep Space Nine* were to resemble the space station itself, there is no doubt that Ops, the station's nerve center, could be represented in those first critical days only by co-creators Rick Berman and Michael Piller. It was late 1991 when Berman, executive producer of *Star Trek: The Next Generation,* received the clarion call from Brandon Tartikoff, then head of Paramount Pictures, to create a new science fiction television series for the studio.

"I was asked to create and develop a series that would serve as a companion piece to *The Next Generation* for about a year and a half, and then *TNG* would go off the air and this new show would continue," recalls Berman. "So I asked Michael Piller to get involved, and we put our heads together. I really never had the opportunity to discuss any ideas with Gene [Roddenberry]. This was very close to the end of Gene's life, and he was quite ill at the time. But he

knew that we were working on something, and I definitely had his blessing to develop it."

Tartikoff had mentioned the possibility of the new show being a kind of *Rifleman* in space—the concept being that if *Star Trek* was originally conceived of as a *Wagon Train* to the stars, then the new show would be *The Rifleman,* a man and his son living together in a frontier town. And the station itself, of course, would be a high-tech version of Fort

Laramie, or Dodge City, or any of a variety of classic American Western towns located at the edge of the new frontier.

Sounds simple enough—but remember, this wasn't to be just any science fiction series.

"The challenge of putting together a television show for the first time was especially intimidating because of the traditions and the expectations for *Star Trek*," admits Piller. "And yet, coming with the wind at our backs [from *The Next Generation,* where Piller also held the title of executive producer], it really felt as if we had figured out what made *Star Trek* work, and that we could bring all of the vision that Gene Roddenberry had about space and the future to a different kind of franchise. We didn't want to do the same thing again. We didn't want to have another series of shows about space travel. We felt that there was an opportunity to really look deeper, more closely at the working of the Federation and the *Star Trek* universe by standing still. And by putting people on a space station where they would be forced to confront the kinds of issues that people in space ships are not forced to confront."

In a series that focuses on a starship like the *Enterprise,* Piller explains, you live week by week. "You never have to stay and deal with the issues that you've raised," he says. But by focusing on a space station, you create a show about commitment " . . . about the Federation's commitment to Bajor and DS9," he notes. "About the commitment that people have to make when they go to live in a new environment, and have to coexist with other species who have different agendas than they have. It's like the difference between a one-night stand and a marriage. On *Deep Space Nine,* whatever you decide has consequences the following week. *So* it's about taking responsibility for your decisions, the consequences of your acts."

As they developed the bible for the show, Berman and Piller decided that the "town"—or rather the space station—would be a darker and grittier environment than fans of both the original series and *The Next Generation* were accustomed to seeing. And the inhabitants of the space station, while still reflecting all the best qualities of humanity, a factor that had been so important to Gene Roddenberry, would be. . . less than perfect.

"Everybody in the original series was heroic, but they weren't pure in the way that Gene Roddenberry decided to make the characters in *The Next Generation,*" explains Writer Joe Menosky, who served

on staff for *TNG* and freelanced several scripts for *DS9.* "It's a mystery to me as to *how* that worked on *TNG,* but it worked great. On paper you would think that these people have had every shred of human pathology that makes humanity interesting bled out of them, everything that makes one feel compassionate towards people, their weaknesses that make them human. And yet it worked."

But of the characters on *DS9,* notes Menosky, "You can see right away they're not the perfectly engineered humans of *TNG.* They seem more real. I don't know if that makes them as attractive to viewers or not. But they are really different, and they represent a different way to tell a story. And it was definitely a conscious choice to create that potential for conflict."

"Gene's major rule was to avoid conflict among his twenty-fourth-century human characters," says Berman. "But we needed this conflict for decent drama, and we didn't want to have to always bring the conflict into the stories from the outside. So the idea we came up with was, what if we create a cast of characters that have amongst them *non*-Starfleet people? There can be conflict amongst the non-Starfleet people, and there can be conflict between the Starfleet people and the non-Starfleet people. And then, what if we put it on a Cardassian space station that's very inhospitable, to say the least. So by having characters like Quark and Kira and Odo in this inhospitable setting, we were able to create a conflict with the environment, so to speak."

"We really set out to create conflict on every level of this show," says Piller, "conflict between the Federation and Bajor; conflict between Starfleet and the environment in the space station that was not particularly comfortable for humans; conflict with the religious aspects of the Bajoran people; conflict with the Cardassians and the beings our characters would encounter on the other side of the wormhole; conflict between us and the humanist values of Gene Roddenberry's futuristic humans. All of these things were to make life on this space station challenging."

The irony, of course, was that this concerted effort would create conflict with some of the most hardcore *Star Trek* fans, who didn't take kindly to the attempt to tinker with the magic formula.

"People talked about the show being 'edgier,' a word I hate," says Berman. "People talked about the show being 'darker,' which it really was never intended to be. But I think it's all because they didn't see that group of loving family members that existed on the first two *Star Trek* shows. You had a much more contemporary group of characters that had been plopped down in this space station. And I think that after a year or two, a lot of fans who appreciated what *Star Trek* was about saw that this series was *Star Trek* at its core, although it was also very unique."

It was Piller, primarily, who guided the writers in developing the facets of the characters' personalities at the initial stages. "Michael had a very clear voice for each of them," recalls Robert Hewitt Wolfe, who came aboard the series as story editor and departed (at the end of Season 5) as a producer. "He had a pretty good vision of what he wanted and then eventually the actors started to bring their own stuff in."

But unlike Athena, that vision did not emerge full-grown from Piller's mind. "When I got there, Michael was working on the pilot," says Peter Allan Fields, a veteran of the *Next Generation* writing staff who was brought in as co-producer during the pre-production period. "And I began trying to think up stories on this or that, and line up other writers, explaining to them what I thought we would want. But Michael would keep changing this character or fixing that detail, altering this and picking up the hem and changing the inseam. So I'd have to call up the same writers and say, 'Forget what I told you.' My first couple of months were unproductive because there wasn't that much for me to do until Michael had a firm grasp on what he wanted out of the show. He'd had a pretty good idea when I got there, but for Michael it wasn't good enough. He's got a wonderful knack of taking something and giving it just enough twist, something that we can still relate to but that's far and away alien. Or something that we haven't seen but have felt. Human emotion and character are . . . well, galaxy wide."

Like Fields, Ira Steven Behr was a *TNG* veteran, albeit a shell-shocked one. "I did not enjoy writing *TNG*," he admits. "I did not like the lack of conflict, the kind of stodginess, the tech solutions to a lot of problems." Behr's relationship with the *TNG* staff, particularly Piller and Berman, remained good, and when work began on their new "baby," he yielded to their requests that he return to the fold. "Mike said to me that 'the new show is going to have more humor, more conflict, it's going to be a little more bizarre.'"

Behr came on board as supervising producer. And like Fields, he found working with the outside writers during the preproduction period to be a difficult task, primarily because the thumbnail characterizations of the crew kept evolving. "I'm sending writers off, telling them to think Clint Eastwood for Odo.

Then they cast Rene Auberjonois, and it's not quite the same thing." Still, the final mix turned out to be even better than imagined. "Any time you cast a show, the actors bring in something different," Behr comments. "For example, Sisko was supposed to be a cross between Kirk and Picard. And Avery Brooks brought to it a much sterner air of authority. He's much more a military leader."

The friendship between Bashir and O'Brien was something that occurred to Behr only after Siddig El Fadil—who later changed his name to Alexander Siddig—was cast as Bashir. Behr had always liked Colm Meaney's character on *The Next Generation* and longed to do more with him. "Bashir was supposed to be this arrogant hothead, this young turk," he recalls. "But as soon as the role was cast, and I saw that Sid was this proper English gentleman, and we already had Colm as the Irish man of the people. . ." Behr knew instantly that he had a classic pairing, one that would provide great fodder for the writers.

Slowly, the skeleton grew, with many of the key crewmembers being solicited from *The Next Generation*. However, in tackling *Deep Space Nine*, their mandate was to create the look of something very different from their previous efforts. Marvin Rush, who had served as director of photography on Seasons 3, 4, and 5 of *TNG*, embraced the challenge of establishing the look of a brand-new series. "Even though I was already involved in a very successful show, it was clear to me that it was a good opportunity to do something new and different," Rush says. "I didn't start *TNG* and did not create the look of that show, although I had an effect on it. *DS9* was a chance to do something for which they wanted a very different vision. They wanted a darker, more sinister place. The station is, in fact, an alien design. So it had a different aesthetic and a different point of view."

Following some overall directives from Rick Berman, Production Designer Herman Zimmerman, who had worked on the first season of *TNG* and several of the *Star Trek* films, was largely responsible for carrying the Cardassian aesthetic originally established in the *TNG* episode "The Wounded" throughout the *DS9* production. The distinctive lines and shapes of the station ultimately would reward Zimmerman and his crew with an Emmy nomination, one of six for which the series was nominated during its first season.

"The marching orders for the station were to make it bizarre," recalls Zimmerman. "It was to be recognizable from a long way off. If, from the corner of your eye, you saw the station very small on a video screen across the living room, you were to know instantly that it was Star Trek: Deep Space 9 that was about to happen. Deep Space 9's shape had to be like no other."

The task of making the station's magnificent sets look terrific for the television camera fell to others, like Rush. "Deep Space 9 is a dark, shadowy place, and we had to find ways to introduce higher levels of contrast than we normally had on *TNG*," says Rush. That meant using both different lighting techniques—a lot of "blown-out practicals," or lamps exposed beyond their normal range to create an extreme style, as well as a lot of smoke and a lot of cold, blue light—and placing lights in unusual locations. Quark's bar and the corridors on DS9 are examples of sets designed with no obvious spaces for lighting. In both cases, Rush worked closely with Zimmerman to fashion something unique to complement Zimmerman's designs.

"Herman designed Quark's bar as a three-story set with no lighting grid and no real initial attempt to put in any specific lighting positions for me," Rush notes. "He wanted a set where we could shoot in every direction. And he came to me and asked what I could do with it. I thought it would be a great opportunity to do something that I've done a few times in the past, but on a much larger scale—which is to light the entire set from outside of the set, literally lighting through the steel grate floors." Rush's team created a grid of lights that were placed above the third floor, which shine through the floor down onto the set. "The entire set is lit from internal and external hidden sources, and you can literally pan a camera in every direction and not see a light," Rush says proudly.

The corridors were handled in a similar manner. According to Rush, the initial design called for blue fluorescent tubes to be a part of the set. In addition to giving the hallways a certain look, they would provide Rush with 80 percent of the lighting required to illuminate those scenes. "But when I showed Rick Berman some initial footage of the corridors with smoke and filtration on the camera, he thought it was a little extreme and we were asked not to use the neons."

This, again, meant that primary lighting would have to come from above, and that, in itself, was a problem. "Most stage sets, particularly for television, are ceilingless, because you're trying to work real fast and you don't want to be concerned with the intrica-

cies of getting low and seeing ceilings," explains Assistant Chief Lighting Technician Phil Jacobson. "But Mr. Berman had a very big concern about ceilings. He wanted them."

Rush discussed the problem with Zimmerman and the designer came up with some rectangular portholes—approximately two inches by six inches—in the ceiling for light to appear through. When that proved to be inadequate, Rush asked him to put some additional holes in the ceiling. The following day, Rush came in to find a series of circles, about three inches in diameter, cut into the ceiling. "We put lamps up there, aimed them very carefully and created this sort of polka-dotty kind of light," says Rush. "It looks alien."

A similar technique is used in lighting the crew quarters, which can obtain different looks via the use of mirrors placed above the ceiling to project light in different corners of the set. "You can't see them because they're up above the grid ceilings," Rush continues, "but the mirrors allow us to tilt the light in whatever direction we want. It's very fast and very easy and it looks unusual."

"O'Brien, Sisko, and Dax's quarters are all the same set," says Zimmerman. "That's a technique I developed when I did *The Next Generation*. We build five bays in a roughly circular format and divide the bays up, say three bays for a living room, one for each bedroom, according to the officer and rank. If you're an officer you may have a larger living room than a junior officer, or you may have two bedrooms. Then we literally redress the space with different wall treatment, furniture, and some architectural elements. Sisko's quarters are pretty much the same as O'Brien's, except for the props.

As hard as it sometimes is to shoot the space station, the veterans of *TNG* appreciate the contrast from the flat lighting that characterized sets like the *Enterprise* bridge. "The bridge is a very easy set to shoot," says David Livingston, supervising producer for *Deep Space Nine's* first three seasons. "It's a three-wall open set with a lot of room, big and cavernous. Ops, on the other hand, is a multilevel set with a lot of cramped areas and very contrasty lighting. It's more interesting visually and the directors have found ways around the pitfalls." In general, Livingston estimates that the extra complexity makes DS9's shooting day run about an hour or two longer than *TNG's*.

After the so-called creative decisions were out of the way, casting commenced, and eventually a mixture of well-known faces, newcomers, and people-who-might-have-been-familiar-except-they're-always-under-makeup were brought together. For Armin Shimerman, who was the first person called in to read for the role of Quark, the concept of acting anonymously under a lot of latex is something he's learned to live with, a fact he illustrates with an anecdote. "At the end of the first season, Rene Auberjonois suggested that some members of the cast go out for dinner," he recalls with a smile. "And we were eating in a restaurant when a little boy ran up to Rene and asked, 'Uh, are you Odo?' And Rene said, 'Yes, I am,' and told him that, in fact, we were all from *Deep Space Nine*. He pointed to Terry Farrell and said, 'That's the lady who plays Dax,' and then pointed to Nana Visitor and said, 'That's Major Kira,' and then pointed at me and said, 'And that's Quark.' And the little boy looked and looked at me and finally said, 'No way!'"

But Shimerman doesn't mind. "I consider myself a prosthetic actor," he says. "I've probably done as much makeup as any actor in Hollywood," including, as most fans know, a performance as the very first Ferengi seen in a *Star Trek* production, in the *TNG* episode, "The Last Outpost."

Fellow cast member Auberjonois hadn't done quite as much work under makeup, but he had played his share of oddballs over the years. Still, it was Auberjonois's stage background, rather than film or television appearances, that served him best in his transition to becoming a "prosthetic actor." As the look of Odo's "unfinished" face evolved, crew members worried how the actor underneath would be able to play the character without the advantage of having pliable features to convey a range of emotions. "But I'd done a lot of mask work over the years," says Auberjonois. "In fact, I taught mask at Juilliard. And once they saw that I was going to be able to be expressive with something that completely covered my face, they were able to move further in the direction they wanted." In fact, over the course of seasons, Odo's makeup would eventually go from several pieces to one whole mask face.

Auberjonois has nothing but praise for the makeup team who work on his alter ego: Makeup Department head Michael Westmore, who designed it, Craig Reardon, who developed the face, and Dean Jones, who applies it. Odo's makeup, which Auberjonois likens to "a pebble that's been rolled by the ocean on the beach for years, so that it's all sanded down," appears deceptively simple but is actually

an extremely difficult guise. "Most of the exotic makeups on *Star Trek* are very craggy and bumpy, with lots of places to hide the seams and the places where the makeup joins the face, like Cardassians and Klingons and Ferengis. But most people think that Odo's face is some sort of camera trick."

While Odo's makeup was to become more complex as it evolved, the look of the space station's beautiful Trill, Dax, was radically simplified from its original concept. "I shot for two days with a prosthetic forehead, like the original Trill [in *TNG* episode, "The Host"]," says Terry Farrell. "And then they kept reducing it with each test, until it really looked like someone had just hit me in the forehead. But Paramount didn't want to make me look strange." Eventually the producers chose to scrap the footage they had shot of Dax with a prosthetic and opted for a different look. "Finally we went to the spots," says Farrell, noting that they were influenced by the makeup created for Famke Janssen in the *TNG* episode "The Perfect Mate."

Janssen had, in fact, been offered the role of Dax prior to the casting of Terry Farrell. But the beautiful Dutch model-turned-actress turned down the role with a rationale that echoes Michelle Forbes's decision not to carry the character of Ensign Ro Laren over to *DS9* from *TNG*. "I wanted some kind of guarantee that I could do feature films on the side," remembers Janssen, who has since appeared in a variety of movies, including a memorable turn as Xenia Onatopp, the sexy villainess who tormented Pierce Brosnan's James Bond in *Goldeneye*. "Also, while I felt it was a great opportunity, I felt that I would get lazy as an actor if I didn't keep challenging myself with different parts," Janssen adds.

So it was Terry Farrell who inherited Janssen's spots, which, viewers may be surprised to hear, were not stenciled. "Michael Westmore did my makeup personally with two different colors of watercolor," she says. "The first season we experimented with art pens, but they would take me two or three days to get off of my skin—not pleasant!" The daily "tattooing" generally took a little over an hour, although Farrell allows that it would probably have taken less time if she and Westmore didn't have so much fun talking. "I love Michael to death," she says. "He tells the best stories."

Farrell was the last actor cast. By the time she made her first appearance before the camera, filming was well under way. It was, according to Unit Production Manager Bob della Santina, a time when the overall mood across the set was, "Damn the torpedoes, full speed ahead!" "It was a huge undertaking!" he says. The contrast to his sixteen-year stint working for Aaron Spelling Productions was, to say the least, noticeable. "I was accustomed to doing things quick and dirty. 'Let's get done. Let's make believe. How can we do this for seven dollars, on budget, under hours, and all that.' It was difficult for me to let go of that. But there is no question that the money spent here gets on the screen; it's never wasted."

Della Santina shakes his head when he thinks back to the filming of the pilot. "At the end of that experience, I was *enlightened*. I remembered being interviewed for the job and sitting in David Livingston's office. I don't think I really believed him when he talked about twenty and thirty makeup people and five-hour makeup sessions and an hour for makeup take-off and turnaround problems and the optical time involved in shooting the show and blue screen and how much second-unit work was involved. I said, 'Okay, fine,' but I really had no idea. David said, 'You're going to be overwhelmed, and you're going to remember this conversation.' And I do, often. And now I realize exactly what it takes to make this show and what makes it successful. It didn't just happen!"

All the effort paid off big time. Primed by the snowballing strength of *Star Trek: The Next Generation*, then in its sixth season, the launch of *Star Trek: Deep Space Nine* in January 1993 came on like gangbusters. The two-hour-long pilot scored a whopping 18.8 percent of the syndicated audience, and was, at the time, the highest-rated series premiere in syndication history. "Emissary" ranked number one during its time period in a number of key markets, including New York, Los Angeles, San Francisco, Boston, and Washington, D.C. The first season's ratings averaged out at a respectable 9.1 percent, or about 8.7 million households.

Deep Space Nine spent its entire first season in the top ten portion of the syndicated ratings chart and quickly became the darling of the much sought-after male 18–49 viewing audience.

But the show would find more and more competition in the once barren landscape of hour-long syndication that *The Next Generation* had pioneered. As a result, ratings would shift over the following six years.

Rick Berman shakes his head in bemusement. "In a way, *Star Trek* created its own competition, which affected everything that came after *The Next Generation*," he says. "At the point that *TNG* began to get really popular in 1989, we had virtually no competition. We were *it*. We were loved by a dozen million people a week or more."

But by the time *Deep Space Nine* made its debut, that position was being encroached upon by newcomers. *Hercules, Xena, Baywatch*. Suddenly syndication was *the* place to be. And so-called alternative networks like Fox and the WB also were coming up with new hour-long dramatic products. "You can probably sit down and name twenty television series, most of which did not succeed, that were in that same vein of science fiction or fantasy-adventure," says Berman. "And we were also competing with ourselves, with *The Next Generation* and the original series reruns, and later with *Star Trek: Voyager*."

For now, however, ratings looked very promising. Even members of the Television Academy seemed to be watching. With six Emmy nominations, the series garnered more nods than any other syndicated series during the 1992–1993 television season, receiving nominations for Outstanding Art Direction, Outstanding Sound Mixing, and Outstanding Special Visual Effects (all for "Emissary"), Outstanding Hairstyling (for "Move Along Home"), Outstanding Make-up (for "Captive Pursuit"), and Outstanding Main Title Theme Music. It won for Dennis McCarthy's title theme; the makeup designed by Michael Westmore and team members Jill Rockow, Karen Westerfield, Gil Mosko, Dean Jones, Michael Key, Craig Reardon, and Vincent Niebla; and a juried win for the special effects magic performed by Robert Legato and team members Gary Hutzel, Michael Gibson, and Dennis Blakey.

EMISSARY

Episodes #401-402

TELEPLAY BY MICHAEL PILLER
STORY BY RICK BERMAN & MICHAEL PILLER
DIRECTED BY DAVID CARSON

SPECIAL GUEST STAR

Picard/Locutus	PATRICK STEWART

GUEST CAST

Kai Opaka	CAMILLE SAVIOLA
Jennifer Sisko	FELECIA M. BELL
Gul Dukat	MARC ALAIMO
Gul Jasad	JOEL SWETOW
Nog	ARON EISENBERG
Tactical Officer	STEPHEN DAVIES
Ferengi Pit Boss	MAX GRODÉNCHIK
Cardassian Officer	STEVEN RANKIN
Ops Officer	LILY MARIYA
Conn Officer	CASSANDRA BYRAM
Vulcan Captain	JOHN NOAH HERTZLER
Transporter Chief	APRIL GRACE
Alien Batter	KEVIN McDERMOTT
Cardassian Officer	PARKER WHITMAN
Cardassian Officer	WILLIAM POWELL-BLAIR
Curzon Dax	FRANK OWEN SMITH
Doran	LYNNDA FERGUSON
Chanting Monk	STEPHEN ROWE
Young Jake	THOMAS HOBSON
Monk #1	DONALD HOTTON
Bajoran Bureaucrat	GENE ARMOR
Dabo Girl	DIANA CIGNONI
Computer Voice	JUDI DURAND
Computer Voice	MAJEL BARRETT

STARDATE 46379.1

The journey he has always been destined to take: A reluctant Sisko surveys the command center of his new post. DANNY FELD

Stardate 43997. The Federation starship U.S.S. *Saratoga* is among a number of Starfleet vessels attacked by the Borg at Wolf 359. The Borg are led by Locutus, known to Starfleet as Jean-Luc Picard, captain of the *Starship Enterprise*, who has been kidnapped and altered both physically and mentally by the Borg. Lieutenant Commander Benjamin Sisko, serving aboard the *Saratoga*, manages to get away in an escape pod with his young son, Jake, but a part of him will never leave that burning ship where he left his wife, Jennifer, who was killed in the attack.

Three years later, Sisko, now a commander, is assigned to oversee the Bajoran space station Deep Space 9, a former Cardassian outpost orbiting the planet Bajor. The Cardassians have recently withdrawn occupational forces from Bajor, leaving its inhabitants on their own for the first time in decades. At the request of Bajor's provisional government, Starfleet has agreed to establish a Federation presence in the system—hence, Sisko's assignment, which he has accepted with reluctance. This war-torn region is not an ideal place to raise Jake.

Upon his arrival, Sisko begins to meet his staff. His chief operations officer, Miles O'Brien, a recent transfer from the *Enterprise*, quickly apprises Sisko of the terrible state in which the Cardassians left the station. Major Kira Nerys, the Bajoran attaché assigned to the station to serve as Sisko's first officer, is a former freedom fighter harboring reservations about the Federation's presence. Sisko encounters Security Chief Odo, an alien with shape-shifting abilities, as the latter apprehends some thieves who've broken into the station's assaying office. One of the two criminals is Nog, a teenage Ferengi boy whose Uncle Quark owns the station's bar and gambling establishment.

Sensing an opportunity, Sisko uses Nog as a

pawn to force Quark to remain on the station and keep his business open. But in the midst of dealing with that situation, O'Brien informs Sisko that the captain of the *Enterprise* has asked to see him. It is an invitation that Sisko does not relish, a point he makes quite clear to Picard, whom he blames for the death of his wife. The meeting, which Picard had intended as a briefing regarding the Bajoran situation, is tense. Sisko lets Picard know that he will do the best job he can while he is there, although he is thinking of returning to Earth and resigning from Starfleet.

Back on the station, Sisko speaks to Kira about the conflicts among the disparate factions of the Bajoran people. Kira feels that only Kai Opaka, Bajor's spiritual leader, stands a chance of unifying her people, but the kai rarely meets with anyone. At that moment, an old monk approaches Sisko and offers to take him to the kai.

Sisko is surprised when the kai informs him that his arrival—or, rather, that of the "Emissary"—has been greatly anticipated. When Sisko says that he cannot help her people until they are unified, the kai responds that she cannot give him what he denies himself, and that he must look for solutions from within. She shows the commander a mysterious Orb, which seems to transport Sisko back in time to the day he met his wife. Sisko is emotionally shaken by the experience, which demonstrates the power of the Orb—a relic the kai says was sent to her people from the so-called "Celestial Temple." Eight other such Orbs were taken by the Cardassians during the occupation, and the kai fears that the Cardassians will invade the Temple in order to discover the secret of the Orb's power. She asks Sisko to warn the Prophets and gives him the last Orb in the hopes that it will help guide him to the Temple.

Not long after, Sisko greets two new members of his crew: Julian Bashir, a cocky young physician who will serve as the station's medical officer, and Jadzia Dax, the science officer. Sisko is especially pleased to see Dax, a Trill—a joined species that consists of a humanoid host and a wormlike symbiont that lives within the host's body. Sisko was good friends with the Dax symbiont's previous host, an older man named Curzon; discovering that the new host, Jadzia, is a beautiful young woman with all of Curzon's memories is somewhat bemusing for the commander. Nevertheless, he's grateful to have someone with her technological know-how around to help him analyze the Orb he received from Opaka.

Dax sets out to study the Orb—in the process

Sisko uses baseball as an analogy to explain the concept of linear existence to the wormhole aliens. JULIE DENNIS

experiencing a journey back to the day she received her symbiont from Curzon—while Sisko receives a visit from Gul Dukat, the Cardassian who once served as Prefect of Bajor. Dukat attempts to convince Sisko to "share" whatever information he may elicit from the last Orb, but Sisko denies any knowledge of the relic.

Dax's research indicates that the Orb may have originated in the nearby Denorios Belt, a plasma field that periodically produces severe neutrino disturbances. Sisko and she decide to investigate the region in a runabout and are startled when the small vessel passes through what appears to be a rip in the fabric of space. After a short, turbulent ride, they find themselves some seventy thousand light-years from Bajor, in the Gamma Quadrant. It seems they have passed through a wormhole—possibly the first stable wormhole known to exist. As they turn the runabout around and head back, their speed slows, and they eventually find themselves landing on something *inside the wormhole.*

Since sensors show that the region, contrary to all logic, contains an atmosphere capable of supporting life, the two emerge from the runabout to look

"I suppose you want the office": Kira doesn't hide her feelings about the Federation's involvement with her world. JULIE DENNIS

that there seem to be hostile entities inside the passage. But Gul Dukat is unimpressed.

Inside the wormhole, Sisko continues his confusing dialogue with the aliens. Just as he seems to be making some headway, Dukat's ship enters the wormhole. Alarmed by the intrusion, the aliens close the wormhole, trapping the Cardassian ship.

A few hours later, the space station arrives at Kira's position near the closed passage. Kira returns to the station to face the inquiries of several Cardassian warships, who want to know the location of Dukat's ship. When Kira's honest answer fails to satisfy them, they demand that she surrender the station or risk destruction.

In the meantime, Sisko tries to explain the nature of a linear corporeal existence to the aliens, hoping to prove to them that he and his kind mean them no harm. Again and again they look at key moments in his life, trying to comprehend. The one moment Sisko does not want to relive is the death of his wife, but when he asks the aliens to stop leading him there, they tell him that he is the one who keeps returning to that point in time. He *exists* there, they explain, and, as Kai Opaka told him earlier, they cannot give him what he cannot give himself; he must look within for solutions. Sisko finally reaches some common ground with the aliens when he comprehends that by remaining anchored to this terrible moment, he is not living his life in a linear manner—and that he must let go of it in order to continue his existence.

Outside the wormhole, Kira has managed to hold off the Cardassians for a time with O'Brien's help. But just as the escalating battle threatens to destroy the station or force its surrender, the wormhole reappears and Sisko's runabout emerges, towing the Cardassian ship. The battle is over.

A few days later, a changed Sisko reports to Picard. The life-forms in the wormhole have agreed to permit ships to travel to and from the Gamma Quadrant via the wormhole, which should improve Bajor's economic outlook. It also confirms the need for a permanent Starfleet outpost in the region—and Sisko assures Picard that he is now prepared to take on that responsibility.

around. But when Sisko attempts to communicate with whatever lives there, Dax is caught up in a ball of light and transported back to Deep Space 9. Left alone, Sisko again tries to communicate with the entities that inhabit the wormhole, a process made difficult by the fact that they have no concept of reality as Sisko knows it and that they are suspicious of Sisko's motives in coming there.

On the station, Dax attempts to explain the wormhole to the rest of the crew. They grow excited at the possibilities a stable wormhole leading into a new quadrant may represent for the future of Bajor, and when O'Brien determines that the Cardassians are heading for the Denorios Belt, Kira orders him to move the space station to the mouth of the wormhole before the Cardassians arrive. Bajor must stake a claim on the wormhole first, she says, and the Federation must also be there to back up that claim. A message is sent to Starfleet, requesting assistance. In the meantime, Kira takes a runabout with Dax, Bashir, and Odo—who was found in the Denorios Belt years earlier—to the wormhole. Once there, she attempts to warn Gul Dukat's ship away, explaining

Shooting a television pilot always requires a minimum of 110 percent of effort from everyone involved in the production, particularly a two-hour-long pilot. "In many ways, it's like shooting a feature film," explains Director David Carson. "You're creating and inventing the circum-

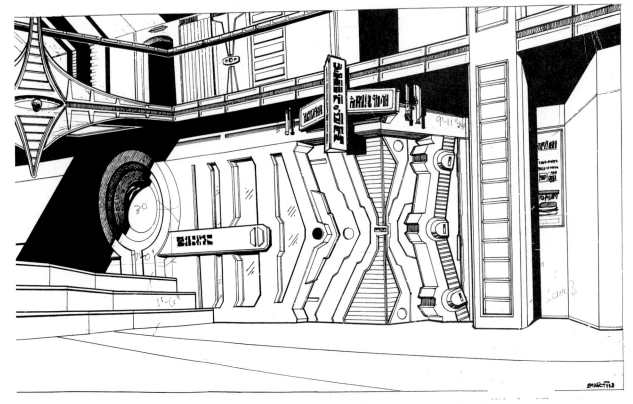

An early sketch of the Promenade. JIM MARTIN

stances in which the whole series is going to forward." But because the director of the pilot will not be responsible for the show after he completes his brief stint behind the camera, all of those creative aspects are developed in conjunction with the producers of the series, he says. "After you leave, it's their show, and you have to make absolutely certain that you don't leave them with people or things that they can't build on."

That mandate made Carson's duties in directing "Emissary," the pilot for *Star Trek: Deep Space Nine*, much different from his earlier assignments directing episodes of *Star Trek: The Next Generation*. "As a director on an established episodic show, you're very much a guest of the team that has been working and playing [together] for some time," he explains. "You try to interpret what the team has already established and contribute what you can to keep their show going; on schedule, on budget, and, at the same time, provide a bit of excitement. But with a pilot, you have to make sure that the sets are going to work properly for your camera. You have to deal with casting from scratch, and you're actually interpreting the script by your casting. The whole thing is worked out in rehearsals. It's like the alien land that Sisko finds himself in. It becomes a question of taking an interpreta-

Unlike Quark and Odo, long-time friends Armin Shimerman and Rene Auberjonois enjoy one another's company. KIM GOTTLIEB-WALKER

tion from the page and turning it into actuality, so all those things, like Sisko's command style, and Kira's temper, and the interaction of Odo and Quark were invented and developed from the germ of the idea that went from the script to the screen."

Fleshing out a character, or the relationship

The Promenade Directory, intended as background ambience, the Art Department felt free to be creative in naming places.

between characters, is an evolutionary process. Interviewed separately, Rene Auberjonois and Armin Shimerman have a remarkably similar take on the relationship between Odo and Quark, which had its seeds in a brief exchange that takes place in the pilot. During that scene, says Auberjonois, "Odo is very hard on Quark. I call him a thief, and there is very little humor, really. It's just a hard-nosed attack. But it evolved. It was probably something they had every intention of doing. In all television series, characters begin as a writer's vision, and then the actors are in place, and over the course of time, the actors become sort of unwitting collaborators by their personalities and the way they work. Armin and I have worked together on the stage. We've had the same kind of background as actors. We like to work the same way, and we enjoy each other immensely. So it just naturally evolved, and it is particularly gratifying to both of us that it became such a popular part of the show."

"The impetus for the relationship came from a very small moment in 'Emissary,'" recalls Shimerman, "when I'm talking to Sisko and Odo is there, and he calls me a thief, and I say, 'I am not a thief,' and he says, 'You are a thief.' That's where it started. The writers had set up some common comic elements: a

Terry Farrell on her first day of shooting. KIM GOTTLIEB-WALKER

Michael Piller on creating a cast of characters

Michael Piller is a co-creator of *Star Trek: Deep Space Nine*. He served as executive producer on the show's first two seasons and part of the third. He also co-created *Voyager*. Piller originally joined the *Star Trek* production staff of *The Next Generation* during the third season as co-executive producer.

"Once we decided that the show was going to take place on a space station, it became a question of who we were going to populate it with, what kinds of people," says Michael Piller. "Brandon Tartikoff had given Rick Berman the notion of a man and a boy in space. So when Rick and I sat down and began talking, we began with the notion of a man and a boy.

"As for the rest, we came to the table armed with great knowledge of the terrain that we had been working in over the past five years. It wasn't like, 'Scan the episodes and see what you can plunder from them.' It was more like, 'You know, that's a great alien race. Let's use one of those. The Trill, that's a great race. They had some interesting ramifications on *TNG*. A Trill character would provide great potential for dichotomy and paradox.

"We knew that we needed some kind of Data/Spock character who looks at the world from the outside in. And the idea that an alien entity would have to find some way to pass as human was fascinating, and seemed to give us an avenue into the kind of 'complexion of humanity' stories that we wanted to tell. But I think, frankly, that the technology contributed as much to the creation of Odo as a shapeshifter as anything else, the fact that the visual effects people were capable of creating someone like him.

"It was clear to me that having a Ferengi aboard Deep Space 9 would provide the show with instant humor and built-in conflict with the Federation guy in charge of the station, and also with Odo, who I'd always seen as the 'sheriff' of this town. The idea of Odo and Quark being at loggerheads was there from day one. I saw Quark as the bartender who is a constant thorn in the side of law and order, but who has a sense of humor about it. He'd be someone who could obviously throw lots of story dynamics into play.

"A doctor is always necessary in this franchise. You can't get away without it. We decided to create a flawed character, someone who was young and wet behind the ears, who was a little full of himself, a little arrogant, and who had a

tall man and a small man, a man who was emotionless and a man who was overly emotional. It's a natural affinity. And Rene and I had an affinity. I didn't know any of the other actors when we started, but Rene and I had worked together in the play *The Petrified Forest*. So there was already this chemistry. It's a little like Bogart and Bacall. And my teeth aren't Bogart."

It was a bit harder for Actor Terry Farrell to establish that chemistry with her costars during the pilot. While the rest of the cast and crew had been actively involved in preproduction rehearsals and camera tests since early August 1992, Farrell was not cast as Dax until filming was well underway. "She was the last character hired," recalls Casting Director Ron Surma. "Dax was a tough character to find. We needed a beautiful woman with the intelligence of all those accumulated lifetimes. It's not an easy role to understand, and we finally narrowed our choice down to Terry."

Farrell made her first appearance before the camera on September 1—officially, the eleventh day of production. "It was really hard for me," she says. "I was the last person in, and I was very intimidated. I got all my stuff the last few weeks of filming."

With no time to practice her lines with the other actors, Farrell suddenly found herself in the middle

lot to learn. He'd have to be brought down to size in order to grow. And we wrote him as kind of a jerk for much of the first season. But *Star Trek* fans don't seem to like their heroes *that* flawed. The input we got on Bashir was very negative at first. But we stood our ground and said, 'You have to give us time with this guy. He will grow and change.' And he did.

"I started using the character of O'Brien almost from the day that I got to *The Next Generation*. I gave him a little scene in 'Booby Trap,' the second script that I worked on there. It worked out great, so we started building more and more for him to do as the show went on, and one of his best episodes was 'The Wounded,' which introduced the Cardassians. After we decided that we were bringing him over to the new show, we thought, 'How do we use him?' We'd already decided to focus on Bajor, with this long backstory, establishing his bitterness toward the Cardassians, so it worked very nicely together.

"Kira was not in our plans. As a matter of fact, she was not in our first draft. Our inspiration was Ensign Ro. It was really Ro's character that had inspired us to put this show on Bajor, with all of the useful social problems that come of being on a warring planet. Her recurring character on *TNG* had been extraordinarily well received by the audience. And we liked the idea of having somebody working with the commander of the station who would be a thorn in his side, who would represent a different point of view. We knew we'd get conflict and interesting dynamics between the two characters. Ro came from a far more religious background, so the idea of the humanist versus religious conflicts was very attractive to us. But the actress who played Ro was not interested in doing another series, so we had to come up with a new Bajoran, one who was similar to Ro, but was not in Starfleet. I think that was better, frankly. Ro would have been wearing the same uniform as the commander and that would have given her a certain responsibility to him.

"As for Sisko's arc, every hero needs a journey. You want to take your leading man on a quest where he has to overcome personal issues as well as whatever space stuff happens to be out there. The idea of a man who is broken, and who begins to repair himself is always a great beginning for drama. Obviously, I was very familiar with the Battle of Wolf 359 from my work on 'The Best of Both Worlds.' To make that a backdrop to this man's life was not unusual, because it was a backdrop in *my* life, and in Rick's life. And we knew it would resonate with the fans. Furthermore, we hoped that Patrick Stewart would agree to do a guest shot. And the thought of putting our new hero in direct conflict with Picard because he blames him for the death of a family member just made us grin! It was a wonderful way to introduce this character, destroying all the viewers' expectations that Picard would come on and slap our new hero on the back and say, 'Good luck!'"

of a blocking rehearsal in Ops. "It's a complete set, and you really feel like you're in this huge room with all these people," she says. "It's not the intimacy that you usually feel on a set. And they'd all worked together for weeks by this point, so they were very comfortable with each other. But everyone was very overtired, and I was taking fifteen takes to get all this technobabble and they were getting frustrated and rolling their eyes. Every take made me more nervous. I was like, 'Please, fire me. I can't handle this.'"

Farrell got to play a scene with her predecessor—or rather, Dax's predecessor—for the scene in which Jadzia recalls receiving the symbiont from a smiling Curzon. However, the validity of her memory of that day would be called into question a few years later, ironically by the writers themselves, when they chose to reveal that Curzon had died while engaging in *jamaharon* with his old friend Arandis ("Let He Who Is Without Sin").

Robert Hewitt Wolfe, who cowrote the latter episode with Ira Steven Behr, does a bit of fancy footwork in explaining how Curzon could die on Risa, yet still be alive when he relinquishes the symbiont to Jadzia on Trill. "Well, we didn't exactly say he died *while* having sex with Arandis," he says with a grin. "He died *from* having sex with her. She killed him,

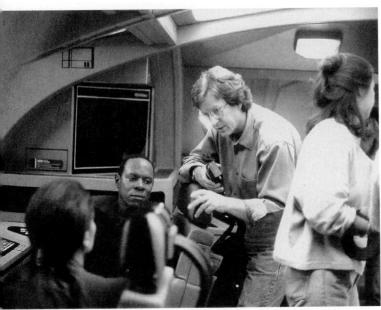

David Carson's skill with "Emissary" would win him the job of directing *Star Trek Generations*. KIM GOTTLIEB-WALKER

but it was a *slow* death. He had a heart attack and was hovering on the brink of death while they zipped him home to Trill. *Then* he died."

The pilot officially shot for twenty-eight days between August 18 and September 25, 1992; it was preceded by a preproduction period the week of August 11. As often happens, there were a few rough edges that would be smoothed out during the eleventh hour. Dr. Julian Bashir's character was still known as Julian Amoros during the week of preproduction, and the role of Gul Dukat would be recast after the producers determined that the original actor's performance lacked a certain presence. "It was either Mike Piller or Rick Berman who finally said, 'Let's get Marc Alaimo,' who had done a bunch of *TNG* episodes for them in the past," recalls Ira Behr. And, in fact, Alaimo had played a Cardassian—Gul Macet—in "The Wounded," the *TNG* episode that introduced the species to viewers. Adds Behr, "Marc came in and, of course, he *was* Gul Dukat."

In another interesting stroke of casting, an actor known as John Noah Hertzler was assigned the role of Sisko's Vulcan captain aboard the doomed *Saratoga*. It was a small role—the captain dies almost immediately—and not particularly noteworthy . . . except for the fact that it represents the first *DS9* appearance of the actor who would later be known to viewers as J.G. Hertzler!

"I can't stand the name John," Hertzler explains. "It was my dad's name, and it fit him very well, but it's the most common name in the fifty states. So for a while I used John Noah Hertzler, Noah being my grandfather's name, which I like. And then I went to J.G. Hertzler, using initials like my friend [actor] J.T. Walsh." Hertzler would continue to confuse *DS9* viewers by using yet another name—Garman Hertzler—when he appeared as Laas in Season 7's "Chimera."

There were dozens of carefully constructed scenes in the pilot episode, but for Marvin Rush, director of photography on *Deep Space Nine* for the first two seasons, picking a favorite is easy. In fact, he remembers it like it was yesterday, and in surprising detail.

"It was the very first shot of the very first day," he recalls. "David Carson and I designed the shot with a servo-remote-controlled camera crane. It's the first time you see Ops in the pilot. It starts in a pit, on a guy working on some fiber optics, and all the monitors are fritzing and frapping, and there's flashing lights and stuff's not working properly, because the Cardassians wrecked the place when they left. The camera starts on this guy and it comes up, catches an extra carrying some equipment, which pans the camera over to the left, toward the turbolift, where Sisko and O'Brien have just arrived. They come down the staircase, and the camera pans with them and it does a couple of little gyrations, which the audience probably doesn't notice. They pass very close to the camera, and it composes a two-shot, and then another two-shot, and then a three-shot, and then it takes them up the staircase and they go around one console, and it follows them around. It continues on and drives right into Sisko's office, where it sees Major Kira Nerys for the first time, yelling at this guy on a monitor in the office."

Rush pauses briefly. "That is really my favorite, because it is a very interesting, clever shot. It uses a very wide-angle lens because it photographs the entire set and shows every place that I could have possibly hidden a light, yet you never see a light. It was a great piece of work and very well-executed by my camera operator, Joe Chess, and my gaffer [chief lighting technician] Bill Peets." Rush notes that the first part of the sequence was cut a bit for time, but the rest of the shot is there, intact, on the screen, which made the amount of time invested all the more worthwhile. "We knew it would take all day to get it, and it did."

Rush's inspiration in dealing with that particular scene was mainly logistical. The Ops area of Deep Space 9 is comparable to the bridge of the *U.S.S. Enterprise* as a primary location on the series. The chal-

"The Prophets await you." A setup line for a later scene would prove prophetic by the series' end. DANNY FELD

lenge was to introduce that key area to viewers in an interesting manner, presenting them with all the details in a deceptively casual way that masks the complexity of the shot. But for other scenes, Rush's inspiration in his setups came from the world outside the studio gates, or as he himself puts it, "from being a patient and deliberate observer of the natural world."

The lighting for the scene in which Sisko meets Kai Opaka, for example, was triggered by a pleasant memory from Rush's past. "Years ago, I was sitting and talking with my wife in our backyard Jacuzzi, and suddenly I just quit speaking and began looking at her face," he says. "There was a fluorescent light on in the kitchen behind and above her that formed a perfect backlight that lit her hair, and the Jacuzzi had a light in it that was filtered through the water, casting a very soft diffused uplight on her face. And there was a tiny bit of moon out, and it was a kicker on her cheek. I realized I was looking at a perfect lighting setup, and I remember thinking to myself that I would want to use it someday.

"And I used it in 'Emissary,'" he says with a smile. "Kai Opaka is sitting next to Sisko by a pool of water, and she grabs his ear to explore his *pagh*." Observant

viewers will recall that in the scene, Opaka is backlit by bright light, with a softer source of illumination highlighting her face. A third source of light is provided by a mirror at the bottom of the pool, which bounces a light pointed in its direction up at the kai's face.

Not all of the setups were quite so idyllic. The conditions for Sisko's introduction to the wormhole aliens were positively hellish. The scene called for Sisko to look like "he was suspended in this limbo, but at the same time, was actually a part of it, almost attached to it," says Director Carson. "We wanted to bleed the edges of his image into the white space around him."

To accomplish that, says Rush, "we used these incredibly bright lights and overexposed the film like crazy. We needed an extremely large depth of field, because we wanted to go very, very tight on Sisko's face and yet have no focus depth at all, so that his ear was as sharp as his nose. That took a tremendous amount of light, and it was brutally hot," he admits. "Avery was a good sport about it. He put up with a tremendous amount of discomfort, and you would never know it from his performance. He knew what we were doing and why, and the fact that it was totally driven by the needs of the scene and the script."

The production traveled to San Marino's beautiful Huntington Gardens for Dax's perspective on the wormhole terrain. (Sisko's point of view, described in the script as "brutal terrain," was filmed on Paramount's Stage 18.) Pasadena's Oak Grove Park was used for the sequence at the baseball diamond. L.A.'s picturesque Leo Carillo Beach was the setting for the Orb-induced oceanside flashback scenes where Sisko encounters Jennifer. Finally, north to Newhall and the Golden Oaks Ranch, also known as the Disney Ranch, for two different scenes: Sisko's picnic with Jennifer, and the holodeck fishing sequence with Jake.

Although *Star Trek* fans considered themselves fortunate to be permitted at last to witness a portion of the infamous Battle of Wolf 359 (Only the aftermath of the battle was depicted in the *TNG* episode "The Best of Both Worlds, Part II," because the cost of creating the battle was deemed prohibitively expensive.), few of them realize that the scene was originally much more complex.

Robert Legato, then visual effects supervisor for *Deep Space Nine*, was instructed to shoot the battle sequence before live-action production had commenced on the pilot. "It was fun to do because I was allowed to make it up from scratch; there was no backlog of stock footage for it," he says. "The script said that they were right in the middle of this big fierce, ugly battle, and I had tons of debris in all the shots. Ships that were burning, on fire, flying past the camera. I made sure that all of the debris had the correct names on it, the names of the ships that were mentioned in 'The Best of Both Worlds' (The *Starships Tolstoy, Kyushu, Melbourne,* and *Saratoga* were among those described as lost in the battle), so the episodes would tie together."

But fate stepped in when the decision was made to shoot the live action as if the ships were *about* to enter into battle with the Borg, rather than joining them in mid-fray. "I had to go back and take all the extraneous ships out," he laments. "It was a heartbreaker, because it was a ton of work and very good-looking stuff—much bigger than anything seen on a *TNG* show."

There was distinct consolation, however. The aired pilot went on to receive the 1993 Emmy for Outstanding Special Visual Effects, an award that Legato shared with Gary Hutzel, Michael Gibson, and Dennis Blakey.

Odo's fate hangs in the balance as Bashir accelerates the development of suspicious DNA fragments. KIM GOTTLIEB-WALKER

A MAN ALONE

Episode #403

TELEPLAY BY **MICHAEL PILLER**
STORY BY **GERALD SANFORD AND MICHAEL PILLER**
DIRECTED BY **PAUL LYNCH**

GUEST CAST

Keiko	ROSALIND CHAO
Zayra	EDWARD LAURENCE ALBERT
Rom	MAX GRODÉNCHIK
Bajoran Man #1	PETER VOGT
Nog	ARON EISENBERG
Ibudan	STEPHEN JAMES CARVER
Old Man	TOM KLUNIS

STARDATE 46421.5

The shakedown period on the space station continues as its inhabitants come to terms with their new lives and each other. Dax attempts to refocus Bashir's amorous thoughts with meditation techniques, Jake tries to befriend Nog, the only boy his own age on the station, and Keiko wonders what she can do in her new home to feel useful. In the meantime, Odo makes a troubling discovery: Ibudan, a Bajoran that he once arrested for murder, is back on the station. Although Odo wants the criminal off the station, Sisko insists that he has no legitimate reason to make him leave. Not long after, Ibudan is found stabbed to death in a holosuite.

As Odo mounts his investigation, Sisko is distracted by a different problem. With too much free time on his hands, Jake has managed to get into trouble with his new pal, Nog. But Sisko's problem seems to provide a solution to Keiko's dilemma; she'll start a school on the station, thus giving Jake and the other children (and herself) something meaningful to do with their time.

The evidence associated with Ibudan's death seems to finger Odo as the prime suspect, and the Bajoran residents of the station become suspicious and hostile toward the shape-shifter. Although the station crew doubts the theory, Sisko reluctantly relieves Odo of his duty as security chief. In the meantime, Bashir analyzes some odd DNA fragments that he found in Ibudan's quarters, which seem to indicate that the Bajoran was performing some kind of medical experiment.

The tension aboard the station grows worse as angry residents vandalize Odo's office, and a volatile mob demands justice. But suddenly Bashir appears with startling news—the dead man was not Ibudan! He was a clone, created and later killed by Ibudan, in order to frame Odo for the crime. The real Ibudan is quickly discovered by Odo and arrested for the murder of his own clone.

"A Man Alone" was filmed prior to the episode "Past Prologue," despite its later air date, and contains much of the expository information that one would expect of a series' first regular episode. Viewers are provided with information regarding Trills, and Sisko's relationship with Curzon Dax, that didn't make it into the pilot, and the station school is started by Keiko, thus providing a fertile setting for stories featuring Jake and Nog. The two boys become friends in the episode. Little Molly O'Brien makes her first appearance on DS9, as does her mother, Keiko. Rom, who appeared in the pilot but was identified in the credits only as "Ferengi Pit Boss," is established as Nog's father and Quark's slow-witted brother.

"I originally read for the role of Quark," says Max Grodénchik, previously seen as a Ferengi in the *Next Generation* episodes "Captain's Holiday" and "The Perfect Mate." But Grodénchik thought that the reading went poorly. "I was so depressed that I went out and sat on the steps at the Gower Street walk-in entrance to the studio. And in a little while Armin came out and befriended me. He said, 'You know, I think it was between you and me for the role of Quark.' And I said, 'How do you know?' And he said, 'Well, we were the only two short people there.'"

The pair went on to discuss all things Ferengi, with Shimerman mentioning the planned character of Nog, and the fact that he'd heard that Nog would have a father. Shimerman suggested that if Grodénchik didn't get the role of Quark, that Nog's father might be a nice part. After Shimerman was cast as Quark, Grodénchik says, "Armin actually recommended me for Rom, and they gave it to me."

Drawing from a list of directors they already knew and respected, the producers scheduled Canadian-born Paul Lynch to direct five episodes for the first season of the series, beginning with "A Man Alone." Lynch had already directed five episodes of *TNG*, starting with the second installment, "The Naked Now." At that time, the director had predicted that *TNG* would air for at least five or six years, and when he began working at *DS9* across the lot, *TNG* was beginning its sixth season. "I guess they thought of me as a kind of good luck charm," Lynch laughs, "and my feeling was that *Deep Space Nine* would go seven years."

A comparison with the episode that aired a week earlier points up some differences in Odo's facial makeup and Kira's hair ("Past Prologue"), which had not yet made their evolutionary turn toward the look

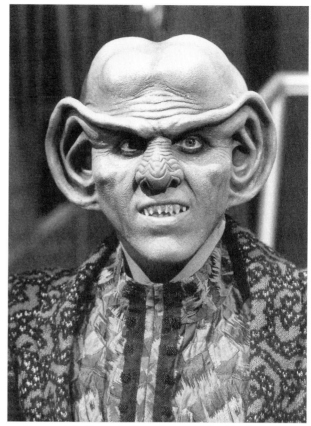

Once comic buffoons, the Ferengi were redefined by the writers on *DS9*. DANNY FELD

with which viewers are most familiar. On the other hand, from a makeup point of view, Quark came into his own—nose, that is! According to Makeup Artist Karen Westerfield, who was responsible for Quark's makeup throughout the entire series, the final face and nose for everyone's favorite Ferengi was being sculpted during the filming of "Emissary." As a result, Quark actually appeared in the pilot wearing a proboscis that had been made for Max Grodénchik. Quark received a nose of his own in "A Man Alone," but Armin Shimerman was disappointed that the first season's gallery shots—the product of a yearly photo session set up by Paramount's television publicity department—portrayed him in his brother's nose!

Shimerman admits he found a lot to worry about in the early days of the show. The fact that "A Man Alone" did not air until the week after "Past Prologue"—and that he did not appear in the latter episode—concerned him a great deal. "I thought, 'I'm not in the first episode to air after the pilot. Oh, they hate me.' I used to sit backstage with Nana [Visitor], and we'd talk about the fact that if we didn't do a good job they could fire us, because my contract said that if they didn't like me after the fourth or fifth episode, they could get rid of me."

The episode provides one of the *DS9* art department's first opportunities to indulge in the kind of behind-the-scenes in-joke humor that was such a trademark of *TNG*. An Okudagram (the term generally employed to describe a graphic turned out by the scenic art group, which is supervised by Michael Okuda) viewed by Odo in Ibudan's quarters aboard the Bajoran transport ship displays a number of interesting entries in Ibudan's personal calendar files. Among them are a reference to the ship's departure from Alderaan spaceport (the motion picture *Star Wars* is one of Okuda's favorites; Alderaan was the home planet for the film's Princess Leia); and a lunch date with "Della Santina."

The latter came as a surprise to *DS9* Unit Production Manager Bob della Santina, better known to those on the set as "Bobby D." "I frequently go into the art department and look at the graphics and signage they come up with," notes Bobby D. "The whole gang up there has a wonderful sense of humor, and I usually notice the stuff they do, like using the name of one of the executive producers or the prop guy or the guy who makes the coffee. And I've thought, 'It'd be nice if they used my name once, just for fun,' but I never verbalized that. But I didn't even know about this!"

The name "Zayra," given to the rabble-rouser portrayed by actor Edward Albert, previously seen in TV's *Beauty and the Beast*, is a tribute to Zayra Cabot, an assistant to Jeri Taylor, then serving as producer on *The Next Generation* and later becoming executive producer on *Star Trek: Voyager*.

"I think they decided to use the name Zayra because it was so odd," recalls Cabot. "When I started working here, everyone was talking about how 'Star Trek-ish' my name was." This fascination with Cabot's first name was apparently shared by the writing staffs of both series, as it was also used as the name of a planet in a sixth-season *TNG* episode.

PAST PROLOGUE
Episode #404
WRITTEN BY **KATHRYN POWERS**
DIRECTED BY **WINRICH KOLBE**

GUEST CAST

Tahna Los	JEFFREY NORDLING
Garak	ANDREW ROBINSON
B'Etor	GWYNYTH WALSH
Lursa	BARBARA MARCH
Admiral Rollman	SUSAN BAY
Gul Danar	VAUGHN ARMSTRONG

STARDATE UNKNOWN

A quiet cup of Tarkalean tea turns into an exciting encounter for Dr. Bashir when the station's last remaining Cardassian, a tailor named Garak, introduces himself to the physician in the Replimat. Recalling that the Cardassian is rumored to be a spy, Bashir rushes to Ops to inform Sisko of the meeting. But Sisko and the others are distracted by the appearance of a small Bajoran craft that is being pursued by a Cardassian war vessel. When

Kira and Bashir rescue Tahna Los from his damaged vessel.
DANNY FELD

the Bajoran requests assistance, O'Brien beams the badly injured pilot to Ops, and Kira recognizes him as Tahna Los, an acquaintance of hers from the Bajoran underground.

The captain of the Cardassian ship, Gul Danar, demands that Sisko turn over Tahna, whom he says is a member of the Bajoran terrorist group *Kohn-Ma*. But when Tahna claims to have renounced his association with the group, Sisko has no choice but to grant his request for asylum.

Not long afterward, Odo alerts Sisko to the fact that the Klingon sisters Lursa and B'Etor have arrived at DS9—and that they seem to be awaiting something—or someone. Sisko asks Odo to keep an eye on them, while at the same time, Garak hints to Bashir that the doctor should do the same. Disguised as a rat, Odo observes the sisters meeting with Tahna and demanding payment for an undisclosed item.

Sisko gives Kira approval to help two more *Kohn-Ma* members obtain asylum, but when Odo tells Sisko about the conversation between Tahna and the Klingons, the commander can't help wondering if there is a connection. In the meantime, the two sisters visit Garak to discuss what price the Cardassians might be willing to pay for the return of Tahna. And in Tahna's quarters, Kira is stunned to discover that her old ally is still loyal to *Kohn-Ma*, and that his purpose in coming to the station was to gain her assistance in a plan to free Bajor. Troubled, Kira turns to Odo for advice; their conversation makes her realize that she is no longer the person she once was, and that she must choose new loyalties.

Garak again goes to Bashir, this time alerting him to potential *Kohn-Ma* activity on the station. The Cardassian suggests that Bashir may find out more if he visits the tailor shop that evening. And that night, hidden from view, Bashir listens as Garak gets the sisters to reveal that they are selling Tahna a cylinder of bilitrium, a component required for the construction of a powerful bomb.

The command crew discusses the situation, and Sisko agrees to let Kira take Tahna to meet the Klingon sisters for their agreed-upon exchange. Sisko and O'Brien will follow in a different runabout. The exchange is made and Cardassian forces, alerted by Garak, appear and threaten to fire upon Kira and Tahna. In return, Tahna threatens to explode his bomb right there if either the Cardassians or Sisko approach, and they are forced to allow him to proceed. Tahna informs Kira that his real target is the wormhole, which he plans to destroy with the bomb,

thus diminishing Bajor's importance to both the Federation and the Cardassians, and forcing both groups to leave the planet alone. But Kira is able to delay the release of the weapon long enough so that the bomb is detonated harmlessly in the Gamma Quadrant. Tahna is arrested, and Kira is left to ponder if she made the right decision for her people.

Although "Past Prologue" was the first episode of *Deep Space Nine* to be broadcast following the pilot, it was actually shot after "A Man Alone," which helps to explain a few of the inconsistencies observant viewers may have noticed between the two episodes. Odo's makeup, for example, which would continue to metamorphose over the course of the series, went through a refinement between "A Man Alone" and "Past Prologue," as did Kira's hairstyle, which began to move away from the fluffy do of the pilot to a "no-frills-all-business" close-cropped style. "That was my doing," admits Nana Visitor. "I pushed for it. I just didn't feel that Major Kira would style her hair every day. She wouldn't care! I wanted a hairstyle that looked like she just woke up in the morning looking like that."

Of Odo's new look in the episode, then-

Visitor's new hairstyle added the right note to her portrayal of Kira Nerys. DANNY FELD

Co-producer Peter Allan Fields notes, "I remember [makeup department head] Michael Westmore turning to me and saying, 'Do you think it looks better?' and I said, 'Yes, absolutely.' I thought they did a superb job right from the beginning, but every job needs a polishing, a wax, and a finish."

"Past Prologue" featured a guest appearance by the popular Klingon sisters Lursa and B'Etor from *The Next Generation*, who were written into the story at Michael Piller's suggestion. It also introduced viewers to Starfleet Admiral Rollman, played by Actor Susan Bay. Bay, who would reprise the role in the second-season episode "Whispers," has worked as a director, a producer, and a development person in the entertainment industry, but she may be best known to fans as the wife of Actor Leonard Nimoy. Nevertheless, Bay believes that it was her long-standing relationship with Executive Producer Rick Berman (whom she met prior to his association with *TNG*) and a previous working relationship with Casting Director Junie Lowry-Johnson that got her the role on *DS9*, rather than her real-life role as "Mrs. Spock."

The episode is also notable for establishing the close relationship between Odo and Kira, which would become increasingly significant as seasons passed, and for introducing the character of "plain, simple Garak," the mysterious Cardassian tailor. Although Kathryn Powers received sole writing credit for "Past Prologue," both of those contributions have been attributed to Fields. It is well known that *Star Trek*'s producers are accomplished writers who frequently leave their mark on scripts that catch their fancy. Comments Fields, "It was terribly important to put in a scene between Odo and Kira that establishes trust between them, and the idea that she would turn to him when she didn't know where else to turn or what to do." Fields later would delve into the background of that relationship in the second-season episode "Necessary Evil".

And as for Garak, Fields recalls, "We needed a character whom Lursa and B'Etor would come to as a kind of go-between. But we didn't want to make him an out-and-out spy, because then what would you do with him after the episode? You'd have to put him in jail on Bajor. So we tread a pretty thin line."

The producers always liked the idea of making Garak a recurring character, although they weren't quite sure that they'd be able to justify keeping a Cardassian on the station. "We needed a Cardassian who didn't act like one, so I finally put him in a tailor shop, and nobody hit me, so we kept him there," Fields recalls with a chuckle. Of course, putting a possible spy in a tailor-shop setting was a natural for Fields, who started his writing career working on *The Man From U.N.C.L.E.*, a show that used Del Floria's Tailor Shop as the front for television's most famous spy operation ever, the United Network Command for Law and Enforcement. (Not so coincidentally, a store called "Del Floria's" is listed on the Promenade directory, a tribute to the earlier series by the Art Department.)

That the character of Garak clicked so well with viewers is due in no small way to the man behind the makeup, Andrew Robinson, who may be best known to audiences for a number of offbeat portrayals, including the Scorpio Killer in the first *Dirty Harry* movie and the title role of *Liberace* in an ABC-TV movie. "I have to admit, I thought it was really off-the-wall casting at first," recalls Director Winrich Kolbe. "Then I saw him go into the show, and suddenly the whole thing began to blossom. He's not what you expect of a Cardassian. They're the Prussians of the universe, always 'kill, kill, kill.' And then there's Garak, a little bit on the effeminate side, totally different from what you expect of a Cardassian."

Robinson was allowed to create his own characterization for Garak, according to Kolbe. "We agreed that he could push the envelope, but he couldn't leave the Cardassian platform. We had long talks about wardrobe and makeup, but we also talked about attitude, so that he would retain that stiffness that you see in all Cardassians."

Despite his initial reservations, Kolbe has nothing but praise for Robinson's performance. And Robinson, who works constantly in films and episodic television, was equally impressed with the quality of the material he was given to work with on *Deep Space Nine*. "You're only as good as the writing," the actor says modestly. "I wish there was more writing like this for television. I think we'd have a much healthier industry." The writing was so good, he explains, that Garak practically created himself. "From the moment I read Garak, I had an image in my mind. I could actually visualize the guy; he's all subtext," says Robinson. "If a smart guy like Garak says that he's 'plain and simple,' you realize that he's not plain and not simple. And that there is a lot going on. Regardless of how innocuous or simple each line is, there's always something going on underneath that belies the line. And his eyes and the tone of his voice say something different than the words he's speaking. It's not an easy thing to work with subtext, but when you do it well, you really get people's attention."

BABEL

Episode #405

TELEPLAY BY
MICHAEL McGREEVEY AND NAREN SHANKAR
STORY BY **SALLY CAVES AND IRA STEVEN BEHR**
DIRECTED BY **PAUL LYNCH**

GUEST CAST

Jaheel	JACK KEHLER
Surmak Ren	MATTHEW FAISON
Nurse Jabara	ANN GILLESPIE
Galis Blin	GERALDINE FARRELL
Asoth	BO ZENGA
Aphasia Victim	KATHLEEN WIRT
Aphasia Victim	LEE BROOKS
Bajoran Deputy	RICHARD RYDER
Businessman	FRANK NOVAK
Federation Male	TODD FEDER

STARDATE 46423.7

Plagued by a recent rash of mechanical breakdowns, O'Brien finds himself inundated with maintenance requests from every quarter, including Commander Sisko, who wants the station's replicators to provide palatable coffee. O'Brien wearily attends to a replicator, and, to his surprise, manages to coax it into producing a perfect cup of coffee. In the process, however, the chief unknowingly triggers a long-dormant device in the station's food replicator circuitry.

Not long after, Kira is startled when O'Brien, who appears sweaty and pale, begins to speak in gibberish. Bashir's examination of the chief is puzzling. He shows no signs of physiological damage but appears to be suffering from an unusual form of aphasia. When Dax is struck with the same malady, Bashir determines that both of his patients have contracted a virus that affects their neuro-synaptic pathways. On the heels of that discovery, two more crewmembers become aphasic, and Sisko places the station under emergency quarantine.

Odo's subsequent investigation of some suspicious activities on Quark's part leads to the discovery that the Ferengi has inadvertently been spreading the virus by illegally accessing station-crew food replicators to serve his customers. But when Bashir discovers that the virus has mutated into an airborne strain, it becomes clear that they will soon be dealing with an epidemic, and that no one on the station is safe.

As the virus continues to spread, affecting Sisko's son Jake, Kira finds the device that triggered the outbreak. Because it is based on Cardassian technology, they assume at first that the planned epidemic is an act of Cardassian sabotage. But Bashir's analysis of the virus's genetic structure proves it was actually part of a Bajoran plan to destroy the Cardassians who once controlled the space station. With the virus becoming more deadly by the hour, their only hope is to find the Bajoran who created the virus—and hope that he also created an antidote.

Kira discovers that Dekon Elig, the inventor of the virus, is long dead. However, Surmak Ren, who once served as Elig's medical assistant, is not. On a desperate hunch, Kira departs for Bajor, and beams the unwilling Bajoran aboard her runabout, in the process exposing him to the virus. Reluctantly, Surmak agrees to return to DS9 and help discover an antidote.

Back on the station, a panicky alien captain attempts to break quarantine by leaving the station without permission. His attempts to pull away from the station with the mooring clamps still attached doom his ship and endanger the docking ring. But with Sisko incapacitated by the virus, Odo is forced to rely on Quark to help him save the captain and release the ship from the clamps just before the vessel explodes.

In the DS9 Infirmary, Surmak follows up on Bashir's research and discovers the antidote, allowing life on the station to return to normal, and the coffee to revert to its previous nontoxic but impotable state.

O'Brien is the first to fall victim to the mysterious malady.
KIM GOTTLIEB-WALKER

Actor Armin Shimerman has fond memories of "Babel"; it was the episode in which he feels he truly hit his stride in his characterization of Quark. "It was the first time

The first glimmer of the strange and engaging friendship between Odo and Quark. KIM GOTTLIEB-WALKER

And I realized, 'Ah, this is the character, this guy who likes to have a good time, who enjoys life and who feels that no problem is insurmountable.' And that fun-loving spirit and delight became ingrained in my character at that moment."

The episode is notable for other moments of characterization, as well. Like "A Man Alone," it offers a tantalizing glimpse into the Quark/Odo relationship, so abrasive on the surface and yet clearly enjoyable to both characters at a deeper level. Both Shimerman and fellow performer Rene Auberjonois are pleased with the way the writers have employed this engaging chemistry in the scripts. "They basically use us as comic relief to heighten the dramatic effect of the story," observes Auberjonois. Over the course of the series, the writers would continue to employ the the relationship like ". . . a spice, or perhaps like Stilton cheese—a little bit of it goes a long way," laughs the actor. In the fifth season, however, he and Shimerman would finally be treated to a script that focused on their relationship for the entire episode ("The Ascent").

Sisko's deep bond with his son, Jake, is also well-conveyed in this episode, thanks to the tender phys-

that Quark was ever in Ops," recalls Shimerman, "and it was the first time that *Armin* was in Ops. I had passed it, but it wasn't really my home. My home was Quark's bar. And I remember just looking around and thinking, 'Yeah, I'm in control of Ops—I like this.'

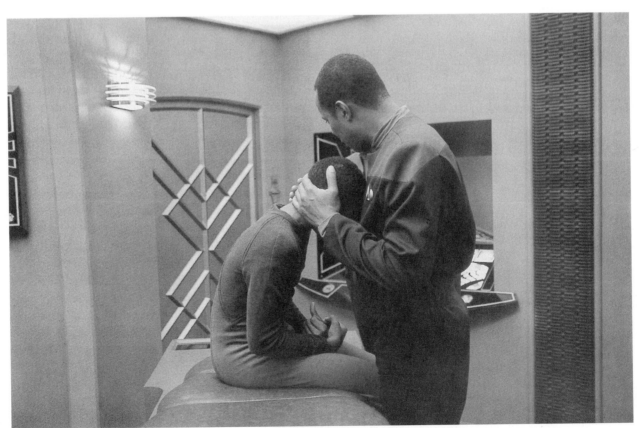

Avery Brooks's strong affinity for children helped shape his character's interactions with Cirroc Lofton. KIM GOTTLIEB-WALKER

Dan Curry aka Dekon Elig aka Visual Effects Producer.

icality of Avery Brooks's interaction with Cirroc Lofton. "I love seeing their relationship," comments Supervising Producer David Livingston, who sees a lot of his own relationship with his sixteen-year-old son in the portrayal. "Avery is so warm and connected with this kid. The Sisko character is not connected with many other people, in fact, maybe with nobody else. This man is out there alone with a lot of stuff going on inside of his head. The one person with whom he can reveal his emotional self on a continuing basis is his son. It makes for such a wonderful contrast with the rest of his character. And the two actors are so fabulous. The moments when Cirroc and Avery are together are just terrific. It's real and genuine, and it affects me because I'm in that same place with my son."

"It wasn't a thematic element," says Actor Avery Brooks. "I don't have any trouble being physical with my children. That's a part of *my* nature, as opposed to something they wrote about Sisko and Jake. The first day I met Cirroc, I hugged him. And I hug him every time I see him."

Close observation of the episode reveals, once again, a number of behind-the-scenes in-jokes and obscure references designed to amuse those in the know. "There are a lot of *Ren & Stimpy* jokes in the readouts and some of the character names," notes Mike Okuda. "Ira Behr is a big *Ren & Stimpy* fan."

Behr pleads guilty to the charge. "During the early days of the series, there was tremendous pressure on us. We were writing these shows, but we didn't know what the heck was going on with them. So to keep the writing staff together, I would do anything I could to break the tension." And one of those things was dragging members of the staff into his office to watch *Ren & Stimpy* episodes, which, notes Behr, "seemed like a wonderful comic find at the time."

Another subtle reference aimed toward fans—this one toward aficionados of the original *Star Trek* series—is found in the name of the cargo carried by Jaheel, the alien captain, who was transporting a shipment of Sahsheer to Largo V. Viewers with long memories will recall that Sahsheer was a term used by the Kelvans to describe a rapidly growing, beautiful crystal-like formation native to the Andromeda Galaxy in the original series episode, "By Any Other Name."

And the image of Dekon Elig, the creator of the aphasia virus (whose first name, not so coincidentally, bears a humorous resemblance to a certain brand of bug killer), is none other than Dan Curry, at the time visual effects producer for *The Next Generation* (he would become the visual effects producer for *DS9* in that series' second season). "They needed faces to put in, and Mike Okuda thought it would be fun to use me," says Curry. "I guess he thinks I have a nasty countenance." Actually, notes Okuda, "Dan really got into it. He even went down to Wardrobe to help pick out the clothes." Curry, who was in the process of prepping to direct the sixth-season *TNG* episode "Birthright, Part II," didn't need to waste time in the makeup chair to receive the traditional Bajoran wrinkles on the bridge of his nose; those were digitally added to his computer-scanned mug shot by *DS9* Scenic Artist Doug Drexler. Curry's image would be recycled for the second-season episode, "Necessary Evil," once again depicting a shady character—this time, Ches'sarro, a Cardassian collaborator apparently murdered by the Bajoran underground.

CAPTIVE PURSUIT

Episode #406

TELEPLAY BY JILL SHERMAN DONNER AND
MICHAEL PILLER
STORY BY JILL SHERMAN DONNER
DIRECTED BY COREY ALLEN

GUEST CAST

The Hunter	GERRIT GRAHAM
Tosk	SCOTT MacDONALD
Miss Sarda	KELLY CURTIS

STARDATE UNKNOWN

As Sisko patiently listens to a new dabo girl's account of sexual harassment by her employer, Quark, he receives a communication from Major Kira. A vessel is coming through the wormhole—and it's not one of the logged transports that originated in the Alpha Quadrant. DS9 is about to receive its first visit from an inhabitant of the Gamma Quadrant.

The alien vessel, which is damaged, contains a reptilian being who refers to himself as Tosk. Although initially suspicious, Tosk allows O'Brien to tow in the ship with a tractor beam. Sisko suggests that O'Brien greet the visitor at the airlock and, if possible, find out what Tosk is so nervous about.

With Tosk's life at stake, O'Brien must weigh his responsibilities to Starfleet principles against his personal sense of morality. JULIE DENNIS

Despite O'Brien's friendly overtures, Tosk continues to be wary, but he allows the chief of operations to initiate repairs on his vessel and hesitantly accepts the hospitality of the station. Through casual questioning, O'Brien learns that Tosk requires little in the way of sleep or nutrition, although he fails to determine whether the word Tosk is the being's name, species, or vocation. And while he senses no criminal intent in Tosk, it seems clear to O'Brien that his new acquaintance is on the run from someone or something.

Sisko decides to have Odo keep a watchful eye on their visitor, a precaution that pays off when Odo discovers Tosk tampering with a security grid in a remote corridor. Tosk refuses to explain his actions, and, to O'Brien's dismay, Sisko orders him confined in a holding cell, reasoning that someone may show up looking for Tosk.

Not long after, several someones do show up: three visitors from the Gamma Quadrant, who deactivate the station's shields and beam on board. The aliens easily fend off the station's security measures and strong-arm their way to the holding area. All fighting ceases, however, when the aliens find Tosk—their prey, according to the lead alien, who describes himself as a Hunter. Tosk's people, he explains, have been bred solely for the purpose of the hunt. It is their only reason for existence. And although Sisko is disgusted by the concept, he realizes that the Prime Directive will not allow him to interfere with this ritual.

O'Brien, however, has his own interpretation of "the rules of the game," and he rigs a security checkpoint to momentarily stun the Hunter, providing Tosk with an opportunity to get a head start back to his now-repaired vessel. After Tosk makes a narrow escape, Sisko gives O'Brien the obligatory lecture about his displeasure at the chief's manipulation of the rules. O'Brien accepts the dressing-down, then expresses curiosity that he was able to help Tosk get away, despite the fact that there were a few inherent weaknesses in his strategy that could have allowed Sisko and Odo to stop him. "I guess that one got by us," responds Sisko, poker-faced.

Out on the edge of the final frontier, Starfleet officers sometimes find themselves in situations where they have to make hard decisions about rules that no longer seem as clear cut as they were in the clean, sterile environment of a Federation starship. "Captive Pursuit," originally titled "A Matter of Breeding," brought such

The writers set another expectation on its end: a security officer who refuses to use a weapon. DANNY FELD

a decision to Miles O'Brien, pointing up many of the differences between *Deep Space Nine* and its predecessor, *The Next Generation*.

"In general, the *DS9* shows are not as squeaky clean as the *TNG* scripts were," observes Corey Allen, a veteran director who has worked frequently on both series. "The characters are allowed to be more flawed and that allows for more latitude in interpretation. In *TNG*, it always seemed to me that the people were wonderfully and heroically bent on the 'unbent'—they were straight arrows. But in 'Captive Pursuit,' there's this wonderful moment of realization—almost without words—when O'Brien is sitting at the bar with Quark, and he discovers the possibility that it's conceivable to break the rules of the Federation, which hitherto had been *inconceivable* to him. And suddenly he says, 'Of course—change the rules.'"

There were other breaches—and near breaches—of Starfleet etiquette in "Captive Pursuit" that never would have happened on the *Enterprise*, according to

Allen. At one point, the teaser was to have included some friendly repartee between dabo girl Miss Sarda and Sisko, implying that she was inviting the commander to "come by and see her some time." As Allen recalls, "We had long conversations on that and ultimately came down on the conservative side, but we'd never even had that kind of conference on *TNG*."

Sisko's decision to skip formal first contact procedures with the first alien visitor from the Gamma Quadrant was another break in protocol that Allen thinks Captain Picard would ever have been allowed to contemplate within the tighter structure of *Deep Space Nine*'s predecessor. Yet, as Allen points out, none of these breaks simply happened. They were thoroughly discussed by the director, writers, producers, and actors. And even as the *DS9* staff consciously chose to break with *Star Trek* tradition in some areas, they diligently reestablished touchstones that resonate in fans' collective memories in other areas, as when O'Brien recapitulates a familiar old proverb to Tosk, "As the Vulcans say, 'We're here to serve.'"

"Captive Pursuit" marks the first time viewers discover that Odo doesn't personally believe in carrying a weapon. The idea was there from the pilot, recalls Actor Rene Auberjonois, where Odo's first discussion with his new commander concerns the fact that he doesn't allow weapons on the promenade. Auberjonois was pleased when the writers carried that theme over into "Captive Pursuit," and had his character turn down a phaser offered by Kira, noting, "Thanks anyway, I don't use them."

"That's been the only reference to my never using a weapon," says Auberjonois. "I like that, and on the basis of it I've been very vigilant about following up on the idea. There've been a couple of times when the prop man innocently will start to stick a holster on me, and I'll say, 'Oh, no, no—I never carry a weapon.' And they take it away. I've only used a weapon once, and that was in 'Crossover,' where I'm really another character."

Does that mean Odo's a pacifist? While Auberjonois admits that he himself is by nature a pacifist, Odo isn't. "He's quite willing to really throw people around and use his own powers of morphing to his own advantage, but I guess it's just a point of pride with him that he doesn't use one. Using a weapon seems like such a humanoid thing to do."

The episode also featured some interesting special effects. The forcefield effect seen when the Hunter's ship blasts the station is reminiscent of an effect used in the pilot episode. "It was generated on

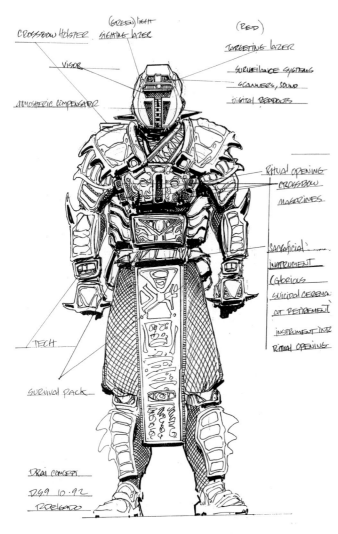

Labels on sketch:
CROSSBOW HOLSTER
(GREEN) LIGHT FIGHTING LAZER
VISOR
ATMOSPHERIC COMPENSATOR
(RED)
TARGETING LAZER
SURVEILLANCE SYSTEMS
SCANNERS, SOUND
DIGITAL READOUTS
RITUAL OPENING
CROSSBOW
MAGAZINES
SACRIFICIAL INSTRUMENT (GLORIOUS SUICIDAL CEREMONY AT RETIREMENT) INSTRUMENT INTO RITUAL OPENING
TECH
SURVIVAL PACK
DRAW CONCEPT
RG9 10-92
R.DELGADO

Ricardo Delgado's sketch for the proposed Hunters' costume.

a paintbox type system, combined with another type of effect that makes a 3–D globe that you can texture map," explains Robert Legato. "You can create a three-dimension object in the computer and take a skin, say an animating sparkle effect, and throw this skin on top of this ball, and then you superimpose it over where the station is and do some retouching. When you time it right, it looks like something gets hit, and has this sparkly animated effect around it."

The transporter effect used by the Hunter species was part of *Star Trek's* ongoing effort to always make alien technology look at least somewhat different from that of the Federation. In this case the effect, says Legato, was inspired by the scene in the classic science fiction film *Metropolis* where the "Maria" robot undergoes its transformation into humanistic form.

The character of Tosk was well played by actor Scott MacDonald, who would return to the series under Jem'Hadar makeup as Goran'Agar during the fourth-season episode, "Hippocratic Oath." Tosk's look—inspired by an alligator—won Michael Westmore's team an Emmy Award for Outstanding Makeup.

Q-LESS
Episode #407
TELEPLAY BY ROBERT HEWITT WOLFE
STORY BY HANNAH LOUISE SHEARER
DIRECTED BY PAUL LYNCH

GUEST CAST

Vash	JENNIFER HETRICK
Q	JOHN de LANCIE
Bajoran Clerk	VAN EPPERSON
Kolos	TOM McCLEISTER
Bajoran Woman	LAURA CAMERON

STARDATE 46531.2

Bashir's attempt to woo a pretty Bajoran woman with tales of his medical school travails is cut short when he receives word of an emergency at one of the station's landing pads. The *Runabout Ganges*, just returned from the Gamma Quadrant, is so low on power that its hatch cannot be opened, and its oxygen levels are also dangerously low. After O'Brien quickly jury-rigs a method to open the hatch, he is surprised to discover that one of the occupants is an archaeologist named Vash, whom he had previously encountered while serving on board the *Starship Enterprise*. O'Brien is even more surprised when Dax relates that the *Ganges* found Vash in the Gamma Quadrant, where she'd been living for over two years—dropped off by "a friend," Vash claims. Unknown to the station crew, that friend has also arrived on DS9. It's Q, the curious omnipotent being so frequently encountered by the *Enterprise*.

Despite persistent questioning by Sisko, Vash remains mysterious about her journey to the Gamma Quadrant. She stores some exotic artifacts at the station's Assay Office—which attracts the attention of the opportunistic Quark—and decides to take up an offer extended by the Daystrom Institute to travel to Earth and brief the scientists there on her recent exploits.

As O'Brien fills Sisko in on Vash's relationship with the *Enterprise* and Captain Jean-Luc Picard, the station is briefly struck by a sudden loss of power, which Dax points out is similar to the phenomenon that disabled the *Ganges*. Meanwhile, Q pays a visit to

Q, longtime nemesis of the *Enterprise* crew, pays a visit to
Deep Space 9. DANNY FELD

Vash and unsuccessfully attempts to revive their previous partnership. She is more interested in a proposition from Quark; he volunteers to stage an auction
of her artifacts for a percentage of the profits.

When O'Brien spots Q on the Promenade, the
anomalies aboard the station seem to make sense. But
Q denies creating the continuing power outages, and,
seeing an opportunity for an interesting method of
sizing up his new Starfleet adversary, places Sisko and
himself in a boxing ring to duke it out. Amazed when
Sisko decks him—after all, Picard never hit him—Q
withdraws from the action temporarily. Yet even in
his absence, the station continues to experience
power outages, followed by increases in the graviton
field that are causing increasingly dangerous breaches
in the hull. At his wit's end, Sisko allows Dax to flood
the station with a small amount of tridium gas to
trace the source of the power drain.

Q returns to taunt Sisko's efforts and suggests that
the real threat to the station may actually be Vash,
who is down at Quark's for the auction. The graviton
field continues to increase, to the point where the station is actually being pulled out of its normal position—and heading straight for the wormhole!

At last Dax manages to trace the power drain to
one of Vash's artifacts from the Gamma Quadrant,
and O'Brien beams it off the station just as the object

explodes in a brilliant flash of light. Then, out of the
flash emerges a winged energy creature, which soars
away toward the wormhole as the astonished inhabitants of DS9 watch.

With the life-form gone, everything returns to
normal at the station. Q reluctantly bids Vash farewell
and leaves her in only slightly more reputable hands
than his own, as Vash opts to forget about her trip to
Earth and strike up a partnership with Quark!

"**Q**-Less" brought several veterans of *Star
Trek: The Next Generation* to the *Deep
Space Nine* universe, most conspicuously, of
course, the popular character Q (John de
Lancie). Also returning was Captain Picard's old
flame, Vash (Jennifer Hetrick), who previously had
appeared in two episodes of *TNG*, "Captain's
Holiday" and "QPid," both penned by Ira Steven Behr
(the story for the latter episode is cocredited to
Randee Russell).

"At the beginning of the series, we were directed
to 'show that we're still part of the *Star Trek* universe'
by bringing over people from the other series," recalls
Behr. "By second season, though, we said, 'Hey, this
is a pretty good show. We don't need to bring anyone
over.' Although on occasion we'd do something really interesting, like bring over the three Klingons from
the original series" ("Blood Oath").

The story for "Q-Less" was written by another
TNG alumni, Hannah Louise Shearer ("The Price"
and "We'll Always Have Paris"), and the teleplay gave
yet one more *TNG* scribe-for-hire, Robert Hewitt

It seemed a natural pairing: the scheming archeologist and the
grasping Ferengi. DANNY FELD

Wolfe ("A Fistful of Datas"), a permanent position on *DS9*. "I wrote the first draft, they liked it, and put me on staff," Wolfe recalls happily. "I did the rewrite while they were negotiating my contract."

According to Wolfe, the original story by Shearer featured the character of Vash, but not Q. Wolfe was asked to add Q to the plot, which he found to be a mixed blessing. As other writers would discover during the first season of the series, it was difficult to write for the new characters, particularly because there was precious little episodic footage of them that the writers could study. "But I knew exactly what to expect of Q and how to write him," recalls Wolfe. But the bad thing, adds Wolfe, is that Q *is* so established, so *TNG*-oriented, and so Picard-specific, "that it's difficult to write stories about him and make him have relationships with the *DS9* characters. Here he is, an omnipotent being, running around causing trouble, but our characters just look at him as a pain, a nuisance. They don't have the emotional attachment that, in a way, the *Enterprise* crew did."

Ultimately, Wolfe hit upon the idea of using the character to demonstrate the *non*-similarities between Sisko and Picard, an aspect that Actor John de Lancie felt was the major point of his appearance. "Q's relationship with Picard had always been a battle of wits, but I come into *Deep Space Nine,* and Sisko just bopped me on the nose!" observes de Lancie. "From a character point of view, that's a very big difference."

Wolfe concurs. "Picard is an explorer, and in some ways, very much an intellectual. Sisko is a builder, a different kind of guy. He wears his heart a little more on his sleeve, and he acts on emotion, on instinct, more than Picard."

Although he was pleased with the way the episode turned out, Wolfe notes that he probably would have written it differently later on. "I'd concentrate less on Vash and Q and more on the regulars. It's not really good to center episodes on your guest stars."

A diminished emphasis on the relationship between Vash and Q might have made less obvious one of the elements that also troubled de Lancie. Q's interest in Vash has never really been explained, and his motivation in wanting them to remain together is unclear. Although the actor has speculated in the past that Q's interest in Vash might be connected to her relationship with Picard, that element wasn't relevant in "Q-Less," where Picard was nowhere in sight. "I think that Q is best used when he deals with large philosophical issues," states de Lancie. "And skirt-chasing just isn't one of them."

The script description read, " . . . in a blink of an eye, Q, changes outfits to match Sisko's, except that Q's has Captains' rank insignia." The skills of the actor and the production staff made it look seamless. DANNY FELD

Bringing characters from *TNG* to *DS9* might have made some viewers think they were watching *The Next Generation,* but it didn't feel that way to the director. "Shooting *TNG* was never as complex as this," says Paul Lynch. "Those shows were a breeze by comparison. I mean, we might have had some special effects makeup and the odd beam on or beam off, but on *DS9*, it's endless. There was one scene in 'Q-Less' where Q not only appeared and disappeared from one chair to another chair to a third chair, but he also changed costumes as he went. It looks effortless on film, but it took a great deal of time to shoot John de Lancie in different costumes, changing all the way around the bar.

"It's because Rick Berman wants everything to be the absolute best," Lynch continues, "and that's why the quality is so high. Everything has been planned to the last given point when we come in to shoot. It's just incredibly complex."

Although the guest stars received most of the attention, Wolfe did have the opportunity to let at least one of the regulars have a bit of fun with his character—even if it was at the expense of an American politician!

Is Quark's encouraging cry of "Bid high, bid often!" at the auction a deliberate evocation of the old line, "Vote early, vote often!" attributed to Chicago's late Mayor Richard J. Daley?

"Guilty," says Wolfe with a grin. "I just thought it'd be funny. You can do that with Quark—put words in his mouth that are definitely from other sources and then give them a little twist. And he can get away with it, because he's a comic character."

Then, could "Bid high, bid often," be considered an unofficial Rule of Acquisition?

"Definitely not," says Wolfe. "A Ferengi would never encourage another Ferengi to do something like that. An applicable Rule would be something like, 'Bid last, bid low.' Quark was just trying to encourage his bidders to do stupid things and pay more than they should. "

DAX

Episode #408

TELEPLAY BY **D.C. FONTANA AND PETER ALLAN FIELDS**
STORY BY **PETER ALLAN FIELDS**
DIRECTED BY **DAVID CARSON**

Jadzia Dax stands trial for Curzon Dax's alleged crime. DANNY FELD

GUEST CAST

Ilon Tandro	GREGORY ITZIN
Judge Renora	ANNE HANEY
Selin Peers	RICHARD LINEBACK
Enina Tandro	FIONNULA FLANAGAN

STARDATE 46910.1

As Lieutenant Dax returns to her quarters one evening, she is identified by a male Trill and then abducted by Ilon Tandro, a humanoid from Klaestron IV who is backed up by two Klaestron officers. Bashir intervenes in the struggle but is overpowered; nevertheless, he is able to alert the officers in Ops. As Sisko, Kira, and Odo attempt to locate and rescue Dax, they discover that the kidnappers have carefully planned their escape, avoiding the security-tracking grid, deactivating force fields, and disabling the station's tractor beam. Only Sisko's last-minute reactivation of the tractor beam allows the crew to force the return of their captured compatriot.

When Sisko and Odo face Ilon Tandro at the airlock, Tandro informs them that this is an extradition procedure and that he carries a warrant for Dax's arrest. The charge: treason and the murder of General Ardelon Tandro, Ilon's father, some thirty years earlier on Klaestron IV. It is clear to Sisko that the accusation must be against Curzon Dax, rather than Jadzia Dax, but Jadzia refuses to provide him with any information about the events on Klaestron IV.

Frustrated, Sisko plays the only card he can. Since the space station is technically Bajoran, Tandro cannot remove Dax without an extradition hearing. At the hearing, Sisko attempts to convince the Bajoran judge, Renora, that Jadzia is a different person than Curzon and cannot be held accountable for any crimes that might have been committed by her previous host. The judge rules that Tandro must prove the person named in his warrant is indeed the same person as the young woman seated before her, thus giving Sisko time to work on Jadzia's defense.

As Sisko, Kira, and Bashir attempt to build their case, Odo goes to Klaestron IV to research past events. He contacts Enina Tandro, widow of the general, who informs Odo categorically that Curzon was *not* responsible for the death of her husband. However, of the five people who might have been responsible for sending the transmission to the enemy that resulted in the general's death, Curzon is the only one without an alibi for the time period in question.

The hearing resumes, and the Trill who identified Dax for Ilon Tandro testifies that a crime committed by a joined Trill would be remembered by each new host body of the symbiont. Sisko parries by establishing that each new pairing of symbiont and host is essentially a different person, whether it carries the old memories or not. However, when Bashir is called to the stand, he reluctantly admits that he cannot determine whether or not the brainwave patterns of the Dax symbiont have changed since it was joined with its new host, Jadzia.

During a recess in the proceedings, Sisko receives word from Odo: he has discovered evidence that Curzon and Enina Tandro had an affair thirty years ago, which gives Curzon a motive for murder. When confronted with this information, Dax admits that Curzon participated in the affair, but will neither confirm nor deny his involvement in the general's murder.

Dax takes the witness stand, and Ilon Tandro attempts to establish that when Jadzia accepted the responsibility of becoming a joined Trill, she also accepted the consequences of criminal acts committed by Curzon. But he is interrupted by the appearance of his mother Enina, who has decided at last to come forward and clear Curzon's name. She knows that Curzon did not send the transmission that was responsible for her husband's death—because Curzon was in bed with her at the time the transmission was made. Curzon had sworn that he would never tarnish the Klaestron people's cherished memory of the general by revealing the indiscretion, but Enina has decided that her own reputation is not worth as much as Jadzia Dax's life.

"**D**ax" marked the return of writer D. C. Fontana to the *Star Trek* fold. Long known for her contributions to some of the best-remembered episodes of the original series ("This Side of Paradise," "Charlie X," and "Journey to Babel"), and for her involvement in the first season of *The Next Generation*, Fontana was brought to *DS9* by Peter Allan Fields because he wanted "a good science-fiction writer" to handle the teleplay for "Dax." Fields remembered Fontana from his days on *The Six Million Dollar Man*, where they both had worked with a future *Star Trek* affiliate, Producer Harve Bennett.

"I was given a very sketchy story," recalls Fontana.

"Dax" was an important turning point for both the writers and the actors in the exploration of Jadzia's character. DANNY FELD

"There wasn't going to be a lot of action. It was going to be all character revelation and interaction. That was what I liked about it."

Still, "it was a difficult script to write, as all early scripts in a series are," admits Fontana. "You don't have an ear for the way the actors deliver their dialogue, and you don't know the characters that well, and in some cases you're beginning to invent facts about them that may or may not work."

The fact that Fontana's teleplay was about a character as complex as a Trill didn't help. "Michael Piller came up with the idea that once they were joined, the symbiont and the host became as one, and you couldn't just cut a piece out of the pie, or rather, remove the symbiont, because they had become intermingled," explains Fields. "That's a pretty hard concept to express on the screen. And there was something more we wanted—heart, character—'Who is this Dax? Is she old? Is she young?' We were exploring it ourselves."

After Fontana worked on the teleplay, Fields had another go at it, "making it up as I went along," and received a partial credit for the teleplay in addition to the story credit. "It was awfully complicated to do," says Fields. "Originally the thought was to make Dax this complacent wise old owl with all these lives behind her/him/him/her. But then we realized, here's a soul who's got to be at war with parts of herself many times. And rather than making her a character [at peace with herself] like Guinan, why not make her a person who can have periods of turmoil based on the number of people inside of her?"

The challenge of portraying a character like that is part of what attracted Actress Terry Farrell to a role in a *Star Trek* series. "It's so exciting to be part of something where you can confront things in society and in human behavior that make us all feel a little uncomfortable." Case in point, says Farrell, was the scene in "Dax" where Enina and Jadzia say goodbye. "The first time we did the scene, there was a moment there where you didn't know if I was going to kiss her or not, or if she was going to kiss me. Then they decided that wasn't appropriate, so we did another take where we pulled back some. But it was an interesting moment, because it really would have worked. The Curzon personality in the worm must have missed her terribly, and Jadzia must have felt that and known exactly what was going on."

Both writers have expressed satisfaction with the way the scene was ultimately filmed. "I thought it said something about old relationships and some of the things you do for old relationships—the kind of love that carries forward, even though you can't physically carry it forward," observes Fontana.

"It's an affectionate scene," notes Fields. "Enina says, 'Live, Jadzia Dax. Live a long and fresh and wonderful life.' She touches Jadzia's cheek, and then Jadzia touches her own cheek where Enina's hand was. There's nothing wrong with it, whether the audience knows that Curzon was a lover of this woman or not."

The tantalizing theme of a character who only coincidentally conveys its physical desire in male or female terms—depending upon the body it occupies at the moment—is one that *Star Trek* writers have returned to again and again. From the first Trill episode, "The Host" (and, in a non-Trill but similarly themed episode, "The Outcast"), on *TNG*, to "Dax," the writers kept pushing the envelope of what they hoped viewers would be willing to accept. But it would not be until the fourth-season *Deep Space Nine* episode, "Rejoined," that *Star Trek* would break through its own steadfast limitations and permit expressions of desire—and kisses—between same-sex characters.

THE PASSENGER

Episode #409

TELEPLAY BY **MORGAN GENDEL** AND
ROBERT HEWITT WOLFE & MICHAEL PILLER
STORY BY **MORGAN GENDEL**
DIRECTED BY **PAUL LYNCH**

GUEST CAST

Ty Kajada	CAITLIN BROWN
Lieutenant George Primmin	JAMES LASHLY
Durg	CHRISTOPHER COLLINS
Rao Vantika	JAMES HARPER

STARDATE UNKNOWN

Returning from a medical mission in the *Runabout Rio Grande*, Kira and Bashir pick up a distress signal from a disabled Kobliad transport vessel. They beam over to discover an injured security officer, Ty Kajada, whose ship has been sabotaged by her prisoner, a murderer named Rao Vantika. Although Kajada warns them to stay away from Vantika, who has been badly burned, Bashir attempts to aid the criminal. Suddenly Vantika grabs Bashir by the throat, entreating the physician, to "Make me live." But Vantika dies a moment later.

Kira and Bashir take Kajada and the body of Vantika back to Deep Space 9, which, Kajada notes, was Vantika's original destination before she captured him. Despite Bashir's assurances, Kajada refuses to believe that Vantika is dead, and she insists he run tests to confirm his demise.

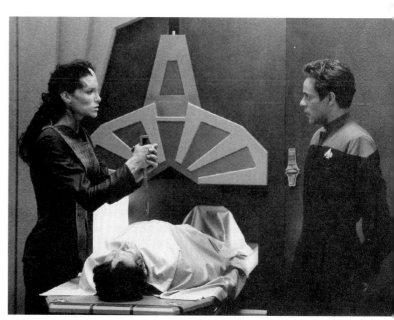

Ty Kajada refuses to believe that her prisoner, Rao Vantika, is really dead. KIM GOTTLIEB-WALKER

In the meantime, Odo is surprised to discover that a Starfleet security officer named Primmin has been assigned to the station to help oversee an anticipated shipment of deuridium, a rare substance that the Kobliad require for survival. It seems likely that Vantika was planning to hijack the shipment. But although the criminal is dead, it is probable that he had help planted on the station—thus the presence of the additional security personnel. Odo is offended by the implication that his services are not satisfactory for the assignment but is reassured when Sisko asserts that Odo is in charge of the operation.

When Odo finds that his security plan, along with everything else in the active memory of the station's computer system, has been accessed and purged, Kajada's belief that Vantika may still be alive no longer seems so farfetched. Dax's subsequent discovery that a complex map of the humanoid brain was among Vantika's belongings also raises suspicions. And that night, Quark has an encounter with a shadow-shrouded figure who claims to be Vantika. The figure tells Quark to follow through on Vantika's prior instructions to hire mercenaries to assist in the theft of the deuridium.

The next day, Dax tells Bashir that there is a possibility that although Vantika's body is dead, he may have found a way to transfer his consciousness to another person's brain. The pair speculate that Kajada is the most likely suspect and convince Sisko and Odo to leave her out of the security plans and keep an eye on her. Later, as Quark and the mercenaries he has hired haggle over payment in Quark's bar, they are interrupted by a scream, and Kajada falls from the third-floor balcony. In the Infirmary, barely conscious, Kajada tells them Vantika is responsible.

Uncertain what to believe, Sisko returns to Dax, who has discovered the method by which Vantika transferred his neural patterns: a tiny device hidden under his fingernails. They plan to scan Kajada for the telltale signs that will confirm their theory as soon as Bashir stabilizes her condition. Shortly thereafter, Quark and the mercenaries prepare to meet Vantika in person at a runabout to which the criminal has somehow managed to gain access—and are shocked to discover Dr. Bashir awaiting them.

As the freighter carrying the deuridium approaches the station, the crew is startled to see the *Rio Grande* heading toward it; at the same time, they discover that Bashir is missing. Bashir and the mercenaries commandeer the freighter, but the DS9 crew—who, thanks to Primmin, were able to deactivate a plan that would have shut down the station's defense array—lock a tractor beam onto the vessel before it can escape. Sisko contacts Vantika, who is indeed occupying Bashir's body, and the criminal threatens to destroy the freighter, along with the doctor, if the tractor beam is not released. Because the freighter's shields are up, the station cannot beam Bashir/Vantika off the vessel, but Dax is able to transmit an electromagnetic pulse through the tractor beam that disrupts Vantika's neural energy patterns just long enough for Bashir to regain control of his body and drop the shields.

Back on the station, Dax transfers the cells containing Vantika's neural patterns from Bashir's body to an energy-containment cell and Kajada destroys the criminal's remains at last with a single phaser blast.

"A lot of my stuff has to do with what's happening in the mind, as opposed to what's happening in reality," reflects writer Morgan Gendel. Gendel, who initiated the story for "The Passenger" and received a partial credit for the teleplay, delved into similar straits in the *Star Trek: The Next Generation* episode "The Inner Light," a fan favorite that won the 1993 Hugo Award for best dramatic presentation at the World Science Fiction Convention. "I don't really think about it, but at some subconscious level, it keeps trickling into my ideas. 'The Passenger' was a variation on that theme, that a [physically deceased] entity could continue to exist, could coexist in somebody's mind, to be reconstituted in a body at some later date."

Gendel's original pitch had an interesting twist that didn't make it into the final version of the story. "I really liked the idea of this cop from the future who's obsessed with chasing this one bad guy, and at the end it turns out that she herself really *is* that bad guy." While that possibility is hinted at briefly in the aired episode, Bashir ultimately is given the dubious honor of playing host to Vantika's consciousness.

The concept of the "transfer" gave the episode's writers a chance to touch upon viewers' memories of the motion picture *Star Trek III: The Search for Spock* in the scene where Bashir observes that he's never heard of synaptic pattern displacement being done by a non-Vulcan. According to Robert Hewitt Wolfe, who worked on the polish of the teleplay with Michael Piller, "We've seen Spock's consciousness influence McCoy, so we can't just ignore that." In any event, incorporating an established bit of *Star Trek* lore never is seen by the staff as diminishing an

Only eight episodes into the series, El Fadil is asked to portray Bashir as a ruthless killer. ROBBIE ROBINSON

floor, who is just inches away from this gas fire they've got going," recalls El Fadil. "These gas fires are very carefully controlled so they don't actually reach us, but they have to be put out after each take. So when they turn the tap, it always goes 'Whoosh!' and comes at you again. That was probably the hairiest of the special effects I had to do, because there was literally fire all around us; they didn't just draw it in afterward in postproduction. We did that scene about four or five times, and each time we were in there for about three minutes. It was a bit *Backdrafty!*"

MOVE ALONG HOME
Episode #410
TELEPLAY BY FREDERICK RAPPAPORT AND
LISA RICH & JEANNE CARRIGAN-FAUCI
STORY BY MICHAEL PILLER
DIRECTED BY DAVID CARSON

GUEST CAST

Falow	JOEL BROOKS
Lieutenant George Primmin	JAMES LASHLY
Chandra	CLARA BRYANT

STARDATE UNKNOWN

Following a disconcerting conversation with his son about the birds, the bees, and the Ferengi, Commander Sisko heads to one of the docking bays to officially greet a delegation from the Gamma Quadrant. The meeting with the Wadi, as the humanoid species is known, represents the Federation's first formal contact with representatives from the other side of the wormhole, and Sisko is determined that his crew give a good impression—even if Bashir has misplaced his Starfleet dress uniform.

However, the Wadi have no interest in either formalities or pleasantries. They're interested in games, and they've heard that Quark's bar is the place to find them. Disappointed, Sisko delivers the party to the Ferengi's establishment, and Quark, motivated by the promise of Wadi gemstones, introduces them to the game of dabo. When the Wadi win too often, Quark resorts to cheating. But the Wadi catch him at it and their leader, Falow, offers Quark the chance to engage in a Wadi game. Quark accepts and is introduced to the game of chula. Falow declines to tell Quark anything about the game beyond the fact that he must move his four game pieces through the various levels, or *shaps*, of the game board.

episode. "It's fun for the audience, the long-term audience," notes Wolfe. "It gives them the opportunity to say, 'Oh, yeah, I've seen that happen.'"

Appearing in an effects-laden series like *Deep Space Nine* frequently forces an actor to broaden his repertoire, an aspect of the job that comes to Actor Siddig El Fadil's mind when he recalls "The Passenger." "Anybody you see working well with effects is probably a consummate technician," he says. "You have to know when to get up, when to duck, what angle to have your head at, because sparks are flying and things happen, and you can't afford to do too many takes because you have one big explosion, and you can't afford to do another one."

El Fadil found the "technical" experience required for "The Passenger"'s teaser, in which Kira and Bashir enter Vantika's holding cell, to be rather harrowing. "Kira goes in with a fire extinguisher, and I've got to get past her and deal with this guy on the

Quark expects to make a quick profit from the visiting Wadi, but
he learns what happens when you forget the 203rd Rule.
ROBBIE ROBINSON

As Quark begins to play, a peculiar thing happens. The four station representatives who greeted the Wadi—Sisko, Dax, Kira, and Bashir—suddenly find themselves inside a peculiar maze, prompted to "Move along home" by the image of Falow. And each time Quark moves one of his game pieces to a new *shap,* the crew encounters a new challenge within the maze.

Alerted by Jake that the commander is missing, Odo soon discovers the disappearance of the other three senior officers as well. As he begins his investigation, Sisko and company encounter Chandra, a little girl who is chanting a rhyme while she plays a game that resembles hopscotch. Noticing that there is a door on the other side of the room, the four attempt to get to it, only to be bounced back by a forcefield. When Dax realizes that Chandra is able to pass back and forth through the field, they repeat her rhyme and emulate her movements, and successfully reach the door.

Back in the bar, Quark receives a nice pile of gemstones for reaching the third *shap,* and Falow tells him he can double his winnings by doubling the peril of his game pieces. Odo arrives to ask if Quark knows anything about the four senior officers. Remembering that he has four game pieces, Quark glances at Falow, and something in the Wadi's expression tells Quark that he is playing for more than gemstones. Alarmed, Quark chooses the safer path for his pieces.

In the maze, the four officers face another challenge and successfully reach the fourth *shap,* while in

the bar, Quark receives more jewels. Suspicious, Odo leaves the bar and has a security officer beam him over to the Wadi ship, where they have picked up a strange energy reading. But Odo has barely begun his investigation when he finds himself back in Quark's bar!

Certain that the Wadi game has something to do with the crew's disappearance, Odo orders the game stopped, but Falow states that stopping the game will cause Quark to "lose" the players. Quark continues, but an unfortunate roll of the dice causes Bashir to be swept away from the others by a swirling energy field. As Falow removes a game piece, Quark opts to take the remaining pieces on a shortcut, which he hopes will make the game end more quickly. But the move results in the loss of another game piece, and within a cavernous portion of the labyrinth, Dax injures her leg. Sisko and Kira refuse to leave her behind, despite the threat of an impending earthquake. The heroic gesture is to no avail, however; the three fall helplessly into an abyss—

—and find themselves at Quark's place, along with Bashir! Falow tells them that although Quark lost, his players were never really in any danger, since they were, after all, only playing a game.

Although it may strike viewers as a somewhat simplistic story, "Move Along Home" followed a tortuous path to the screen. Director David Carson, taking his second turn at the helm of a *Deep Space Nine* episode, recalls it as ". . . an extremely difficult show to do," primarily due to a variety of internal disagreements behind the scenes. "They'd basically designed this enormously complex and expensive show, which the writers, Piller included, wanted to do, and which the production couldn't afford," he says.

DS9's pilot, which Carson had also directed, had been very expensive; as a result, the production staff was charged with the unpleasant task of trying to save money throughout the rest of the first season. When the time came to film "Move Along Home," this policy led to a compromise that, in Carson's opinion, "watered the show down to such an extent that it didn't pack the punch it should have had." Carson describes the final product as "disappointing" and notes that it was the first such experience for him in working with *Star Trek.* Still, there were no hard feelings on either side. Just a few months later, Carson would be invited to direct the film *Star Trek Generations,* giving the British director his first opportunity to take charge of an American feature film.

"There was a lot of blood in people's boots by the

"Occasionally, there is an archway that reveals the depth and breadth of the continuing labyrinth . . . like looking across a courtyard in a New Orleans hotel." The concerns over budget scaled back the sets.
JULIE DENNIS

time that show was completed," says Ira Behr. "A lot of writers fought and failed, and the production staff had a hell of a time trying to make that thing work. But in its own cracked way, it's an okay show. You know—'Allamaraine!' For the rest of the season, anytime something got screwed up, or seemed inconceivable or insurmountable, somebody would peep up 'Allamaraine!' And you'd nod and know exactly what he meant."

Although the episode was not a big hit with viewers—it has the dubious distinction of ranking dead last in *Entertainment Weekly*'s evaluation of the series' first two seasons—it was noteworthy for several people. For Actor Armin Shimerman, "Move Along Home" offered a welcome character expansion. "It was the first time the writers allowed Quark to get somewhat serious," he says. "As Quark, I was once again screwing up, but they had given me a wonderful, almost heroic speech. They allowed Quark to, if not be a hero, at least have aspirations of doing something heroic. It's one of my favorite episodes."

The writing team of Lisa Rich and Jeanne Carrigan-Fauci contributed to the episode. According to Carrigan-Fauci, providing Quark with great dialogue was not a problem. "Armin's character is so delightful that it's fun to do stories where he's pivotal to things. It's wonderful to write the words that he says on the screen and especially exciting in this case because it was the first thing that we had written that was televised."

Prior to the launch of *Deep Space Nine,* Carrigan-Fauci and Rich had pitched to the writers of *TNG* several times. Their ideas went unproduced, but they were good enough to get both women spots as Writers' Guild interns, one on *TNG,* and one on its newly developed sibling. "We worked on the big storyboards for the shows, doing the whole beat breakdown on each episode, and we were there every time they'd brainstorm out a script," remembers Carrigan-Fauci. "We'd also read the scripts submitted to both series and do synopses and recommend the writers, yea or nay."

"Move Along Home," originally titled "Sore Losers," started out as a story idea by Michael Piller, who, according to Carrigan-Fauci, received at least partial inspiration from the old *Prisoner* episode "Checkmate," where residents of the Village were required to serve as human game pieces in a life-sized chess game. "The original idea was that the crew got caught up in sort of a 'Village'-like atmosphere, sort of surreal," she says. When the cost of building sets to suit that concept was deemed prohibitively expensive, alternatives were sought. For a while, Piller even considered shooting on Paramount's "New York Street," which had found occasional use in *TNG.* But that idea didn't pan out either.

In the meantime, the story began to evolve. "Michael gave the idea to one freelance writer [Frederick Rappaport, who shares teleplay credit], and then someone else had a go at it," recalls Carrigan-Fauci.

Rappaport, who would go on to write the teleplay for the second-season episode "Sanctuary," managed to introduce some of the personal touches to the episode, such as Jake's concern about his father. But other elements—the idea that the game was not just a gag—were lost. In an early version, "our people win the game" recalls Rappaport, "but they discover that Bashir has not been returned to the station. So Falow strikes a deal—Quark must return all his winnings if they want Bashir back."

Paul Coyle, who had worked with Piller on *Simon & Simon,* was the second person to tackle the teleplay. But ultimately his version—written when the producers still had those ambitious aspirations for the scale of the episode—was not used. Coyle, however, was given the opportunity to write "Whispers" during the second season.

Finally, Carrigan-Fauci and Rich worked up the courage to ask Piller if they could try their hands at a rewrite, incorporating an idea they had been discussing—setting the game in an unfamiliar (but easy to build) mazelike environment—and Piller agreed. Although the Wadi's favorite game, chula, seems to owe a debt to the popular role-playing game *Dungeons & Dragons,* Carrigan-Fauci says the game has far more ancient origins. "We did a lot of research into very old games, going back to Egypt and Rome, and some really early Elizabethan games, and we took some ideas from those." But the primary influence on the game came straight from childhood. "When we decided to make it a multilevel game, we made up a three-dimensional form of *Chutes and Ladders!*" laughs Carrigan-Fauci. "And that's where the name *chula* came from. I don't even think the people at *Star Trek* know that!"

Quark hopes to learn the financial secrets of the galaxy from the visiting grand nagus. DANNY FELD

THE NAGUS

Episode #411

TELEPLAY BY **IRA STEVEN BEHR**
STORY BY **DAVID LIVINGSTON**
DIRECTED BY **DAVID LIVINGSTON**

GUEST CAST

Rom	MAX GRODÉNCHIK
Krax	LOU WAGNER
Nava	BARRY GORDON
Gral	LEE ARENBERG
Nog	ARON EISENBERG
Maihar'du	TINY RON

AND

Zek	WALLACE SHAWN

STARDATE UNKNOWN

When Grand Nagus Zek, the elderly leader of the Ferengi business empire, comes to Deep Space 9 with his son Krax and his Hupyrian servant Maihar'du, Quark is more worried than honored by the visit. He fears that Zek, a Godfather-like figure, might just be there to make him an offer he can't refuse: the purchase of Quark's bar for a pittance of its real value.

As it turns out, Zek *does* want the bar—but only temporarily, for an important business conference concerning Ferengi interests in the Gamma Quadrant.

Meanwhile, Commander Sisko has problems of his own. Chief O'Brien has warned him that Quark's nephew Nog seems to be a bad influence on Sisko's son Jake. Sisko resists the temptation to split up the boys but can't help wondering if he's made the right

decision. Nog's father, Rom, has no such qualms when Zek expresses his disapproval of the Ferengi boy's attending the Federation school on the station. Stung, Rom orders Nog to stay away from the school.

Quark is surprised when Zek asks him to sit in on the gathering of powerful Ferengi businessmen. He's even more surprised when the grand nagus announces his retirement, and that his successor will be . . . Quark! But Quark has barely begun to relish the power that comes with the title when he discovers another attribute of the job: death threats from enterprising Ferengi who seek to enhance their own financial futures in the Gamma Quadrant.

Quark goes to Zek for advice, but the former nagus dies in the middle of their conversation. Quark makes Rom his bodyguard, laughing at his brother's desired preference to take over the bar. Not long after that, Quark narrowly escapes an assassination attempt. Although there are numerous suspects, Odo focuses on Maihar'du, who hasn't been seen since Zek's death.

While Odo conducts his investigation, Sisko worries about Jake's frequent absences; once again, Nog is to blame. When Jake misses dinner one night, Sisko follows Dax's advice to track the boy down. Much to his surprise, he finds Jake in an empty cargo bay, teaching Nog to read. Proud of his son, Sisko steals away without disturbing the lesson.

Another attempt is made on Quark's life, and the new nagus discovers that his foes are none other than

Zek's son Krax and his own brother, Rom! Just as the duo is about to eject Quark into space, Zek appears, along with Odo and Maihar'du. The nagus's "death" was a charade, assisted by Maihar'du and staged to test Krax's worthiness to be Zek's successor. Noting that Krax has failed miserably, Zek decides to remain grand nagus for a while longer. Quark, however, is impressed with Rom's part in the treachery, and rewards his brother by making him Assistant Manager of Policy and Clientele at the bar.

With a special effects-laden series like *Star Trek: Deep Space Nine*, it's easy for any single element to go over budget. "It's hard not to say, 'Oh, let's add just a few more optical effects, or add some more costumes or make the set a little bigger,'" notes Mike Okuda.

Ensuring that the filmmakers achieve the dramatic look they want in a fiscally responsible way was then-Supervising Producer David Livingston's day-to-day goal during the first three years of the series. (He would leave the staff positon after Season 3 to focus on his directing career.) "David's job was critically important in making sure the show is doable," says Okuda. "He took pride in his ability to be vociferous —that's how he described himself."

But what happens when the financial watchdog actually directs an episode, as he did with "The Nagus"? "Dr. Jekyll and Mr. Hyde," laughs Okuda. "Normally, in crowd scenes, when a director wanted twenty extras, David would let them have five. But of course in 'The Nagus,' David got a lot more!"

"Directing crowds is a lot of fun," admits Livingston. "But I've done scenes with just two people, say Avery Brooks and Nana Visitor, where they get into a conflict, just the two of them talking and relating to each other, and there're just as many sparks flying as with fifty people running around. But obviously, when you have a lot of extras, you feel like you're doing something."

"It's amazing how he was able to turn the hat completely around and be focused and work only as the director when he had to," confirms Bob della Santina. "It was good because he cared about the picture and forgot about what it would cost, because at that point, that wasn't really his job. His job was to make the picture better, and it became my job to go and fight with him and ultimately lose. He got more crowds and more effects and more stunts than anybody, but we love him dearly."

In addition to directing the episode, Livingston

The sculptor used a photo of Shimerman as Quark as the inspiration for the grand nagus's scepter. ROBBIE ROBINSON

also wrote the story for "The Nagus," originally titled "Friends & Foes," although he credits Ira Steven Behr with many of the teleplay's cleverest touches, including the introduction of the Ferengi Rules of Acquisition. "Little did I know that this episode was to change the course of my *Star Trek* life," sighs Behr, "so that I am now identified with the Ferengi as much as Ron[ald D. Moore] is with the Klingons. Who would have thunk it? Certainly not me!"

Behr recalls the fine-tuning he performed on Livingston's story. "David's story was about a Godfather-like meeting of a number of alien races that were going to use the station to hold a high-level crime summit. There was to be a Vulcan, a Klingon, a Romulan, and some players to be named later. But with all those characters, who was going to be the head of the syndicate? It didn't seem quite believable. I don't remember exactly why, but I came up with the idea of making it a Ferengi show, and it became a fun show to write."

The decision to turn part of the story into a not-so-subtle homage to Francis Ford Coppola's *The Godfather,* however, started at the top, with a suggestion from Rick Berman. "And we went for it *totally*," recalls Livingston.

The tribute is primarily confined to a scene in Act 4, in which the new nagus Quark holds an audience with Nava in his quarters. Everything about the scene was deliberately designed to parallel the opening frames of the classic film, from the dialogue (Quark's line, "Yet now you call me 'Nagus'") to the "pet" in

Quark's lap. The affectionate cat that sat in Godfather Don Corleone's lap has here become a Corvan *gilvos,* the endangered species that first appeared in the *TNG* episode "New Ground." The same puppet was used for both episodes.

Even the blocking, the set dressing, and the lighting were part of the effort. "Armin's posture, the way he sat, the actual focal length of the lens, the style of the shot, the venetian-blind effect behind him, it all completely aped *The Godfather,*" notes Marvin Rush. "It's an adoringly loving copy, with apologies to all."

Livingston chuckles, "The venetian blinds were kind of a hard sell to Rick [Berman] and Michael [Piller], but they finally bought it; they could justify that there might be something like that out in space."

Credit also goes to Actor Armin Shimerman, who, despite being sick during the filming, found the episode "a sheer joy." Livingston recalls sitting the actor down with a video of the movie and asking him to emulate Brando, then watching in delight as Shimerman translated a hand gesture of Brando's into a more Quark-like flick of the ear. "He nailed it totally," says Livingston.

We were having trouble finding the right person to play the grand nagus until someone brought up Wallace Shawn's name," Livingston recalls. "I thought he would be good for a different part, but Rick Berman said, 'No, what about him for Zek?' And, of course, he's been fabulous in the role. He's one of those actors who's totally fearless, and he just goes for it. Nothing holds him back. No inhibitions. He just bowls me over. Sometimes when I'm watching him I have to be careful, because I start to laugh during the take. He is just so . . . so much Zek."

But not, however, 100 percent Zek. "I did model the grand nagus on someone, but I'm not going to say who," Wallace Shawn says with a sly chuckle. "So when 'The Nagus' first aired, I didn't see the resemblance to me. But over the years I came to see the character more and more *as* me, and now I'm quite vain about Zek. I get upset if I see photographs of him that I find unattractive."

Shawn has appeared in over forty movies, from *Manhattan,* to *The Princess Bride,* to playing the voice of Rex, the nervous dinosaur in *Toy Story.* "I had never used an odd voice before," the actor states, "even when I did cartoons. And I hadn't planned to do it this time, but when I put in Zek's teeth and looked at myself in the mirror, the voice just came along with it. That was just on day one! I didn't know I was going to have to use that voice for seven years!"

Livingston's only regret about "The Nagus" is that audiences at home didn't get to enjoy the same version of the episode that he keeps in his personal collection. "I get tapes of all the shows, and I'm watching my copy of this at home, and all of a sudden this scene comes on, and the background music is the actual *Godfather* theme, played on the zither! I was ecstatic! And Rick [Berman] calls me up and says, 'How'd you like the show?' and I said, 'It's fabulous. I can't believe you got the rights to put the *Godfather* music in.' And Rick says, 'It's a joke.' Kind of a cruel joke, because it was so good! But at least my personal copy has that music on it."

VORTEX
Episode #412
WRITTEN BY SAM ROLFE
DIRECTED BY WINRICH KOLBE

GUEST CAST	
Croden	CLIFF DeYOUNG
Ah-Kel/Ro-Kel	RANDY OGLESBY
Rom	MAX GRODÉNCHIK
Hadron	GORDON CLAPP
Vulcan Captain	KATHLEEN GARRETT
Yareth	LESLIE ENGELBERG
Computer Voice	MAJEL BARRETT

STARDATE UNKNOWN

Odo is curious about the unexplained presence of several new patrons in Quark's bar: Croden, a quiet man who recently arrived from the Gamma Quadrant, and Ah-Kel and Ro-Kel, a pair of twinned Miradorns, whom Odo suspects of being raiders. When Quark insists that Odo is simply being paranoid, the shape-shifter decides to investigate, disguised as a glass that Rom delivers to a holosuite where the Miradorns are about to engage in a transaction with Quark. But the transaction goes awry when Quark attempts to back out of a previously agreed-upon arrangement for a valuable artifact of dubious origins and Croden enters, brandishing a Ferengi phaser and demanding the artifact.

A scuffle ensues, and Croden inadvertently kills Ro-Kel before Odo can intervene. Although Sisko suspects that the Miradorns were attempting to sell stolen merchandise, he has no proof, and therefore no reason to hold Ah-Kel, or, for that matter, Quark. But Croden is another matter, and Sisko and Odo

Odo's involvement with a fugitive rekindles his curiosity about his own origins. DANNY FELD

attempt to interrogate him. The alien refuses to discuss the failed robbery, although he makes some intriguing comments about the existence of shape-shifters like Odo in the Gamma Quadrant. Sisko decides to locate Croden's homeworld, Rakhar, to notify authorities.

In the meantime, following Ah-Kel's threats of revenge, Odo increases security around Croden's cell and quizzes the alien about his comments regarding shape-shifters. Croden offers to take Odo to a colony where some "changelings," as he refers to them, still exist, and he gives Odo a locket that supposedly came from that place. The locket, which fascinates Odo, contains a stone that has the ability to morph into an intricate metallic shape, then revert back to its original form.

Bashir's analysis of the stone indicates that it is an amalgam of organic material and crystal, perhaps a transitional stage between organic and inorganic matter. The only life-form bearing even a passing resemblance to the substance is Odo. Croden tells Odo that the stone came from an asteroid in an uncharted neb-

ula called the Chamra Vortex, and that only Croden can guide Odo to it. But when Sisko informs Odo that Croden's people have demanded his return to Rakhar, where he is wanted for myriad crimes, that option seems out of the question.

Odo and Croden leave for Rakhar in one of the station's runabouts. While en route, Croden seeks to gain Odo's understanding by disclosing the nature of his crimes on Rakhar, where he is considered an "enemy of the people," and, as a result, his family has been slaughtered. Odo remains impassive, but *the circumstances* change quickly when his vessel is attacked by another ship; Ah-Kel has followed the runabout from the space station and means to kill Croden.

Odo will not surrender his prisoner, but he knows he has little chance of evading the Miradorn ship. When Croden suggests that Odo allow him to pilot the runabout through the Chamra Vortex, Odo relinquishes the controls. Hoping to lose Ah-Kel, Croden lands on an asteroid, allegedly the home of the changelings he'd mentioned. But he soon admits that he doesn't know the true origin of the locket and that it serves as a key to the only thing that matters to him—a stasis chamber located in a cave on this asteroid. Inside the chamber is the only surviving member of Croden's family, his daughter.

Odo permits Croden to revive his daughter, but as the trio return to the runabout, Odo is knocked unconscious by the impact of one of Ah-Kel's blasts. Rather than trying to escape, Croden saves Odo, and when Odo awakens, he finds himself back on the runabout, with Ah-Kel's ship in pursuit. Taking control, Odo manages to trick Ah-Kel into destroying his own ship in the treacherous Vortex. After they leave the Vortex, Odo surprises Croden by allowing the Rakhari and his daughter to transport themselves to a nearby Vulcan science vessel. In return, Croden gives Odo the locket and wishes the changeling luck in finding his true origins.

"We wanted to do a show that was very much like one of those old Jimmy Stewart westerns, like the *The Naked Spur,*" says Peter Allan Fields, "where the good guy takes the bad guy from point A to point B." Recalling that the classic Western had been written by Sam Rolfe and Harold Jack Bloom, and knowing that Fields had a long association with Rolfe that dated back to their days together at *The Man From U.N.C.L.E.,* Michael Piller suggested that Fields call Rolfe and see if he'd be interested in writing a *Deep Space Nine* episode.

One of these glasses "was" Odo, a wonderful effect that outweighed any scientific concerns. DANNY FELD

"He'd written a script a few years earlier for *TNG* ("The Vengeance Factor")," recalls Fields, "and Sam was delighted that we had considered him for this. So we had a meeting, and he went to work. A wonderful man."

The quirky, circular nature of show biz makes the memory of this episode particularly poignant for Fields. It was Rolfe (who passed away shortly after "Vortex" aired) who had given Fields his first professional writing assignment, a rewrite on an *U.N.C.L.E.* teleplay. Three decades later, here was Fields looking over Rolfe's first draft on "Vortex," and discussing the changes that would be needed for the second draft. "I had sat at his feet on one side of the desk learning when I first started, and now I was behind the desk trying to tell Sam what to do," says Fields. "I was afraid he would be uncomfortable, but he thought it was terrific, and we both had a great time. He said, 'I taught you very well!' And that was a good compliment."

While inspired by the action/adventure genre, the episode takes time for the moments of humor that one has come to expect from a good *Star Trek* episode. The barfly Morn (whose name is reportedly a Fields-inspired anagram for a certain character from *Cheers*) is accused of talking too much, despite the fact that viewers have never heard him utter a word. "That became our standard running gag for Morn," explains Robert Hewitt Wolfe. "He's apparently a very loquacious, talkative guy who never shuts up. But we just never see him talk [on-camera]. It's a fun bit for people who watch the show closely."

Another fun bit is Odo's line, "I'm a security chief, not a combat pilot," which is a tribute to Dr. McCoy's running "I'm a doctor, not a (fill in the blank)" lines from the original series. "It's fun to do stuff like that," admits Wolfe. "And it was appropriate here."

The episode is noteworthy for two interesting points that it establishes about Odo—one that both the writers and Actor Rene Auberjonois have ingrained into the character, and the other a point of physics that the writers have chosen to dance around, depending upon the circumstances called for by a particular storyline.

"Vortex" introduces us to Odo's first on-camera smile—in response to a comment by Croden's daughter Yareth—and establishes the first hint to viewers that Odo likes children. "He does," confirms Auberjonois. "And he's nice to them, even though he's sort of harumphy and grumpy with Jake and Nog." The smile came about at Auberjonois's suggestion. "By the time 'Vortex' was being filmed, I had been experimenting with different things I could do with this rubber face," he says. "I never smile as a character, and I like that. But [by this time] I knew that I could, although it's sort of tricky to do and not look goofy. I don't want Odo to look totally goofy. But I liked the idea that a smile might be sort of a gift that Odo gives only on very special occasions. The smile was not called for in the 'Vortex' script, so I suggested to the director that we shoot it two ways, one without me smiling, in case Rick Berman and Michael Piller hated the idea. But they liked it, and now it is something that they actually write in when they want me to smile. They give me the cues to do it."

Because Odo's ever-evolving physical abilities are often an integral component in the writer's toolbox, it is unlikely that there will ever be a definitive treatise on Odo Physics 101. There is, for example, the question of just what his mass is, a point that can be debated within the confines of this episode. He's light enough to become a glass that is indistinguishable from the other glasses on the tray Rom easily carries, yet he's heavy enough in humanoid form that Croden remarks, "You're heavier than you look."

"This is a signature episode for that debate," admits Wolfe. "Obviously his mass changed during the course of the show. What I would say is that Odo exists on more than the normal four dimensions we are familiar with. He may not even be aware of this.

He turns into something like a glass or a rat, and shunts a portion of his mass into subspace, or some other dimension we don't know about. So when we look at Odo, we're seeing the four-dimensional part of a five-dimensional being. That's how I look at it."

Of course, that interpretation would be subject to change the next time the writers need to do something different with the character. Needless to say, no one ever dared broach the subject of what happens to his communicator when Odo morphs.

BATTLE LINES

Episode #413

TELEPLAY BY **RICHARD DANUS AND EVAN CARLOS SOMERS**
STORY BY **HILARY BADER**
DIRECTED BY **PAUL LYNCH**

GUEST CAST

Kai Opaka	CAMILLE SAVIOLA
Zlangco	PAUL COLLINS
Computer Voice	MAJEL BARRETT

AND

Shel-la	JONATHAN BANKS

STARDATE UNKNOWN

The crew is surprised when Kai Opaka, the spiritual leader of Bajor, pays a trip to Deep Space 9. Not only is it her first visit to the station, but also her first journey from Bajor. Although the kai says she is simply accepting Sisko's prior offer for a tour of the station, Sisko and the others can't help noticing that she seems strangely preoccupied. When the kai expresses an interest in the wormhole, Sisko offers to take her through it. Accompanying the pair on the *Runabout Yangtzee Kiang* are Kira and Dr. Bashir.

In the Gamma Quadrant, Kira picks up a narrow-band subspace signal, and the kai encourages Sisko to investigate it. Against his better judgment, Sisko acquiesces, and they follow the signal to a moon orbited by dozens of artificial satellites, one of which fires upon the runabout. Malfunctioning, the vessel crashes to the surface of the moon, and the kai is killed by the impact. Before Kira, Sisko, and Bashir can begin to assess their options, they are surrounded by a group of heavily armed battle-scarred humanoids.

The trio is captured and taken to a man named Shel-la, leader of the Ennis people, who informs

Sisko of the war between his group and the other inhabitants of the moon, the Nol-Ennis. Both sides of the battle are kept prisoner on the moon by the orbiting satellites. Sisko explains that he can take no sides in their dispute, but Shel-la says that won't matter to the Nol, who will assume by the crew's presence in the Ennis camp that they aligned themselves with him. Soon after, the Nol, led by Zlangco, invade the camp, killing Shel-la and many others. Kira uses her phaser to drive off the Nol, and they begin to attend to the wounded. Suddenly a newcomer arrives at the camp —Kai Opaka, returned from the dead!

Bashir determines that Opaka's physiology has been radically altered and that her metabolic processes are being controlled by a cellular-level bio-mechanical presence. Then, as the group witnesses the revival of Shel-la and the other "dead" Ennis, Bashir finds that their bodies have gone through the same kind of transformation, and, indeed, have died many times before.

Shel-la explains to Sisko that the Ennis and the Nol have been fighting for many generations. Unable to mediate a peace, their planet's leaders banished them to this moon, to serve as an example to the rest of civilization. Refusing to accept the hopelessness of the situation, Sisko suggests that Shel-la initiate a cease-fire with Zlangco, and stop the fighting long enough for the DS9 crew to be rescued. After that, Sisko promises he will transport both sides away from the moon and end the battle.

Shel-la agrees, but Sisko discovers that the Ennis leader went along with the plan only to lure Zlangco and the Nol out of hiding, so he could slaughter them. As the fighting begins anew, Bashir saves Sisko from a death blow and informs him that he has discovered that they can't afford to die on this moon— not even once. The alterations that occur after death force the "dead" to remain in the moon's environment. If they were to leave, they would truly die, once and for all—even the kai.

In a second runabout, Dax and O'Brien have been searching for the missing vessel and have traced it to the moon. Avoiding the attack that downed Sisko's ship, O'Brien manages to raise Sisko on his communicator. As Dax and O'Brien work on a method to get a transporter signal through the satellite net, Sisko prepares to tell Opaka that she cannot leave. But the kai seems to know that already, just as she knew that she was destined to come to this place, never to return to Bajor. The kai believes the Prophets have directed her to help the embattled

Sisko can find no way to resolve the irrational enmity between the Ennis and the Nol-Ennis. JULIE DENNIS

inhabitants of the moon begin a healing process. When O'Brien signals that he has found a way to divert one of the satellites and beam up the crew, Opaka bids her three friends good-bye and prepares to face her future.

For fans of the original series, the words "red shirt" meant more than an article of clothing. They were a classification. Trekkers knew that if a "red shirt"—a non-regular cast member garbed in a red Starfleet tunic—was assigned to a landing party with Captain Kirk, the odds were very much against him or her returning from that mission. "Red shirts" were the expendable members of the crew, and viewers were never really surprised if the poor innocents were snuffed by the episode's end.

Thus, when Hilary Bader, whose stories formed the basis for the *TNG* episodes "The Loss," "Hero Worship," and "Dark Page," first thought of sending a previously unseen *DS9* crewmember on a runabout mission along with several members of the regular crew, the staff writers shook their heads. The story called for the death of one of the people on the runabout, explains Bader, "and as with all episodes, if

you have a bunch of regulars and one expendable guest star, everyone knows in advance which person is going to die. So the staff thought, well, it'd be nice to surprise the audience by killing a regular, and suddenly someone said, 'We could kill Kai Opaka.'" It made sense, says Bader, because "she was the most expendable recurring character that they had, and it would make the story more effective, since no one would expect it."

The nut of Bader's story pitch—which originally concerned a battle between Cardassians and humans —was a tale of ongoing war between people who have been fighting for so long that they don't even remember why they're fighting. "It's a bit like Dr. Seuss's *Butter Battle* book—'Do you butter the top side or the bottom side?'" notes Bader. "There clearly must have been a more meaningful cause for this battle, but it's so long ago that it's not the issue anymore; it's not what they're fighting about. They're fighting about 'You're this and I'm not!'"

According to Bader, there was never any discussion as to whether or not to reveal the genesis of the war. "In the beginning, when the characters were humans and Cardassians, it was obvious, but as soon as we decided that we wanted these characters to

Making one of its earliest appearances, the cave set was used throughout the entire production of *Deep Space Nine*. DANNY FELD

worked on the teleplay based on Bader's story. "It takes viewers through the paces of seeing the sheer futility of it and gets into the mindframe of opposing forces so you can see how little provocation is necessary to reignite old hatred."

Like Lisa Rich and Jeanne Carrigan-Fauci ("Move Along Home"), Somers was a Writers Guild intern with the show when the opportunity came along to have a go at a script. "There's no better way for an unproduced writer to get launched," he notes. Somers had been around for every phase of the story, from the original pitch—which Somers recalls didn't have an ending—through its various drafts. Richard Danus is a skilled writer who had worked on *The Next Generation*, but the intern wasn't intimidated when the producers let him take the next turn at bat. "I knew I could do it," Somers says.

And his confidence was well placed. On the basis of his script for "Battle Lines," the producers brought Somers on staff for the rest of the series' first season. Although he was not renewed as a staff writer for Season 2, he was encouraged to come back and pitch—which resulted in two additional sales, the second-season episode "Melora" and the third-season episode "Meridian."

One interesting detail from the final teleplay is a definition of the Federation provided by Sisko, who states that the Federation is made up of over one hundred planets whose people have allied themselves for mutual scientific, cultural, and defensive benefits. In all of *Star Trek*'s thirty-year history, there have been few attempts to pin down just what the United Federation of Planets is.

have experienced an eternity of fighting, the people became a new species, and the original motivation disappeared." The staff realized then that "the less our people knew, the less important it would seem to them," Bader continues, "and the less tendency there'd be to take sides. And finally the point was that it didn't really matter why they fought. The act itself is more important than the issue that started it."

The notion of the resurrected kai being trapped forever in a kind of nether world surrounded by violence is not unlike the ending of the original series episode, "The Alternative Factor," wherein a character named Lazarus is trapped for eternity in an interdimensional corridor in combat with his insane counterpart from another universe. But while Bader is a longtime fan of *Star Trek*, she says the episode did not influence her concept for the *DS9* episode. Perhaps more relevant to "Battle Lines" is the original series episode "Day of the Dove," which, like the *DS9* episode, had embattled characters rising from the dead to fight again. "There are certain themes that reoccur in *Star Trek*, and the fact that war is pointless is one of them," observes Bader.

"The futility of war is definitely at the heart of 'Battle Lines,'" agrees Evan Carlos Somers, who

The first of many runabouts "destroyed." For this episode, only a portion of the exterior was built and "crashed."

According to Ira Behr, "We are always trying to push, to see what you can get away with, what you can't, what you can say about the Federation. Is it military? Not military? Rick Berman felt very strongly that it is basically a trading alliance. So we say that here, and now the viewers know. A lot of people think of the Federation in basically military terms, but that's not really what it is."

In addition to the loss of Kai Opaka, the episode marked the destruction of one of DS9's three original runabouts, all named after Earth rivers. The *Yangtzee Kiang* would be replaced by the runabout *Orinoco*—which makes its first appearance in the second-season episode "The Siege."

THE STORYTELLER

Episode #414

TELEPLAY BY **KURT MICHAEL BENSMILLER AND IRA STEVEN BEHR**

STORY BY **KURT MICHAEL BENSMILLER**

DIRECTED BY **DAVID LIVINGSTON**

GUEST CAST

Hovath	LAWRENCE MONOSON
The Sirah	KAY E. KUTER
Varis Sul	GINA PHILIPS
Faren Kag	JIM JANSEN
Nog	ARON EISENBERG
Woban	JORDAN LUND
Woman	AMY BENEDICT

STARDATE 46729.1

As Sisko plans his opening strategy to help defuse a potential civil war between two rival Bajoran factions, O'Brien faces a potentially unpleasant encounter of a more personal nature—a medical mission to Bajor that pairs him with Dr. Bashir. The two men depart in a runabout and the commander and Major Kira head for a docking bay to meet Varis Sul, the leader, or tetrarch, of the Paqu delegation. Because the Paqu avoid contact with outsiders, Kira explains that she knows little about the tetrarch—and she is as surprised as Sisko to discover that the leader is a fifteen-year-old girl.

They soon discover that while Varis is young, she is as tough and stubborn as her opponent in the dispute, Woban, the gruff leader of the Navot contingent. Sisko's attempt to bring the two together for an informal discussion of the issues they must resolve

Despite the villagers' confidence in him, O'Brien has no idea how to defeat the Dal'Rok. ROBBIE ROBINSON

quickly falls apart, and Varis storms away from the proceedings.

In the meantime, O'Brien and Bashir arrive at their destination and are met by Faren, the village magistrate. Although they have been advised that the entire village was in peril, they discover that only one man is ill—the Sirah, who serves as spiritual leader to his people. Bashir quickly determines that there is little he can do for the Sirah, who is dying of old age. Alarmed, Faren explains that the Sirah is needed to protect the village from the Dal'Rok, a terrible creature that attacks for five nights each year at the end of harvest. If the Sirah cannot face the Dal'Rok on this, the fourth night of the cycle, the village will be destroyed.

Back on the station, Jake and Nog spot Varis in the Promenade and the Ferengi boy is immediately infatuated. He convinces Jake to help him meet her, and the two soon show up on her doorstep and attempt to befriend her.

That night, against Bashir's advice, the Sirah goes to the village square to face the Dal'Rok, which appears to be a large, threatening energy cloud. Curiously, it doesn't register on O'Brien's tricorder. As the Sirah tells the story of the Dal'Rok, strange, stormlike conditions begin to whip the village. The villagers respond as a unit to the Sirah's words, and as he speaks of their strength, a white light arises from the villagers, pushing back the Dal'Rok. But then the sirah collapses, and the Dal'Rok begins to rage anew.

O'Brien and Bashir rush to the Sirah's side and the old man tells O'Brien how to finish the story; O'Brien repeats his words, and the Dal'Rok is driven away, after which the Sirah dies. To the cheers of the crowd and the befuddlement of the two crewmen, Faren declares O'Brien the new Sirah.

On the station, the negotiations between the Paqu and the Navot are not going well. Varis refuses to give up the land that Woban's people claim is rightfully theirs. When she shares her frustrations with Nog and Jake, Nog suggests that she can turn the problem into an opportunity if the Navot have something she wants in trade for the land.

In the village, O'Brien attempts to figure a way out of his predicament. He has no intention of remaining on Bajor, but he can't leave the villagers defenseless. In any event, he has no idea how to prevent the attack of the Dal'Rok. When he tries to speak to Hovath, a young man who served as the late Sirah's apprentice, Hovath attempts to kill him. Hovath knows that O'Brien is not meant to be the new Sirah—he is!

Calming Hovath down, O'Brien and Bashir learn that the Sirah's bracelet contains a piece of one of the orbs from the Celestial Temple. By using the power of the bracelet under the guise of storytelling, Sirahs over the years have periodically channeled the villagers' fears into the manifestation of the Dal'Rok, and similarly, their thoughts of hope into the defeat of the beast. The ritual has served to unite the villagers, Hovath explains, but only the Sirahs have known this secret. Hovath was in training to become the new Sirah, but his uncertainty during an earlier encounter with the Dal'Rok allowed several people to be injured. Now the people's lack of confidence in Hovath prevents him from taking over as the sirah.

That night, O'Brien awkwardly tries to tell the story in the village square, and although the Dal'Rok appears, he can't control it. As the villagers begin to panic, Hovath gains confidence in himself and steps forward to calm the people and tell the story. He succeeds in banishing the Dal'Rok, and O'Brien gratefully relinquishes his title.

At the station, Varis suggests an exchange—free trade access in return for the land—that seems as if it will work for both Bajoran factions. As she prepares to leave, she thanks Nog for his advice with a kiss on the cheek.

Kurt Michael Bensmiller's original script for "The Storyteller" was submitted to the staff of Star Trek: The Next Generation during that series' first season. "I think it was similar to something they had under development," says the writer, "so they didn't go ahead with it but instead asked me to pitch some other ideas," one of which became the second-season TNG episode "Time Squared." But the script for "The Storyteller" remained in the TNG offices, and after Michael Piller came on staff during the third season, he read it and liked it. "For a variety of reasons, it never got made for TNG," says Bensmiller, "but when DS9 came around, Michael remembered it. He said he had kept it in his mind and had me adapt it for the new show."

Bensmiller notes that the choice of O'Brien as the central protagonist in the new version was based on staff suggestions that the chief would be the character least likely to want to be proclaimed the new storyteller, "a techie elected to a position of leadership in a community," as Bensmiller describes it. Similarly, the decision to pair him with Bashir was also an in-house suggestion. "You have to understand that I wrote the episode around Christmas 1992, and the show didn't even premiere until January of 1993," says Bensmiller. "A lot of writing depends on seeing what the actors do with their characters, and there were no tapes to look at. In this case, I think they wanted a script that would focus on those two guys, to establish their relationship."

"It was a chance to do the Bashir and O'Brien thing, finally," says Ira Steven Behr, who shares the teleplay credit. "It was our 'The Man Who Would Be

Odo's bucket. ROBBIE ROBINSON

Colm Meaney and extras react to the "attack of the Dal'Rok."
ROBBIE ROBINSON

the edge. According to David Livingston, who directed the episode, Ira Behr had established that the Promenade was the boys' hangout, "but I felt that their standing up there wasn't right. They would have their place where they sat and would dangle their legs over. It's like guys in our century standing around the trash barrel doing doo-wop songs."

"The Storyteller" also gave a name to "legendary" baseball great Buck Bokai, who had been alluded to in the *TNG* episode "The Big Goodbye." (Bokai would actually appear on *DS9* in "If Wishes Were Horses" two episodes later.) And it gave viewers their first glimpse of Odo's bucket (which Odo would turn into a planter in the third-season episode "The Abandoned.") "We decided it wouldn't be real fancy," recalls Livingston, "because it's a bed, and Odo's not a guy with a lot of pretensions about him. He just needs a place to be able to rest."

Adds Behr, "Odo is a stripped-down man. He's as spare as a Samuel Beckett hero." And as for the idea of inflicting a character like this with the indignity of a bed—or rather, a bucket—full of oatmeal, Behr can only smile slyly and say, "We are shameless."

Curiously, the almost slapstick humor of some episodes of *Deep Space Nine* seems to have escaped many critics. "I hear people talking about how *Star Trek: Voyager* is so funny, and *The Next Generation* used to be so funny, but *Deep Space Nine* is dark and somber," complains Behr. "But there's never been a *Star Trek* show before or since that has as much humor as *DS9*. For some reason, the press has gotten into this 'We are the dark, dismal, slimy show of bad breaks in space!'"

The Bajoran village was created on Paramount's Stage 18, with the Sirah's living quarters set in the same room that had served as the meeting place for Sisko and Kai Opaka in "Emissary." Livingston was especially fond of shooting the village scenes there, because it gave him the opportunity to "feel like a director," he enthuses. "There were a lot of people—not enough people, actually, but we had a big set and it was exciting to shout through a bullhorn, because we had wind and lightning effects that created a lot of noise. I had no voice left by the end of the show."

King,'—and who else do you make king but O'Brien," a character whom Behr considers a quintessential man of the people. Behr notes that while he was somewhat disappointed with the finished episode's special effects, he was pleased with the relationship established between O'Brien and Bashir.

Actor Siddig El Fadil, who plays Bashir, was also pleased with that development, and even more pleased that the writers of subsequent episodes picked up on it. "O'Brien and Bashir didn't get along back then," he says. "They loved not getting along. Over the course of the episodes, Colm and I developed the relationship purely out of what we thought we'd most enjoy hating about each other. And after that we were forever doing the same stuff to each other off set as we did on set, making life hell for each other, in the nicest possible way."

The episode established a number of other elements. One—more visual than story-related—was Jake and Nog's habit of sitting on the floor of the Promenade's upper level and dangling their legs over

PROGRESS

Episode #415

WRITTEN BY PETER ALLAN FIELDS
DIRECTED BY LES LANDAU

GUEST CAST

Mullibok	BRIAN KEITH
Nog	ARON EISENBERG
Lissepian Captain	NICHOLAS WORTH
Toran	MICHAEL BOFSHEVER
Baltrim	TERRENCE EVANS
Keena	ANNIE O'DONNELL
First Guard	DANIEL RIORDAN

STARDATE 46844.3

Overhearing a conversation at Quark's bar, Jake and Nog discover that Quark has been stuck with a huge supply of Cardassian *yamok* sauce, which no one except Cardassians can stomach. Sensing an opportunity, Nog suggests that he and Jake can turn Quark's problem into a profit for themselves. Bewildered, Jake follows his friend's lead.

In the meantime, station personnel are making preparations to assist the Bajorans in a massive energy transfer by tapping the molten core of its fifth moon, Jeraddo. Kira and Dax make an orbital inspection of the moon from a runabout, hoping to confirm that all Jeraddo's inhabitants have been evacuated. But the sensors pick up signs of humanoid life-forms, and Kira beams down to investigate.

Materializing near a small cottage, Kira is confronted by a pair of Bajoran farmers brandishing

threatening-looking farm implements. From inside the cottage comes a third Bajoran, who appears to be the spokesperson for the group. When Kira attempts to point out that they all should have been evacuated by now, he puts her off by inviting her to supper, and Kira sees no choice but to send Dax on and accept the offer.

On the station, Nog makes some initial queries and discovers that a Lissepian freighter captain who has dealings with the Cardassians would be willing to purchase some *yamok* sauce. The captain counters Nog's request for five bars of gold-pressed latinum with an offer of a trade: one hundred gross of self-sealing stem bolts. Nog reluctantly accepts, and then he and Jake tackle the problem of obtaining the *yamok* sauce from Quark.

As Kira helps prepare dinner with the farmer, Mullibok, she learns that he and his two friends, who were both rendered mute by the Cardassians, fled to the moon years ago to escape the Cardassian Occupation of Bajor. Kira tries to explain to Mullibok that the three can now return to Bajor; what's more, if they remain on Jeraddo once the energy transfer begins, they will die. But Mullibok insists he'd rather die than leave his home.

After a clever exchange with his uncle, Nog officially takes possession of the *yamok* sauce, then exchanges it for the self-sealing stem bolts. He and Jake are at a loss as to what to do with them until it occurs to Nog that they can sell them—at a discount—to the Bajoran who initially ordered them from the Lissepian. Unfortunately, the Bajoran has no latinum either, and Nog and Jake are forced to accept seven tessipates of land in exchange for the bolts.

Kira explains the situation with Mullibok to Sisko and the Bajoran energy minister, hoping to find a compromise. But the minister is firm; the project must proceed on schedule. Kira returns to Jeraddo with two security guards and attempts to reason with the farmers. But the situation deteriorates quickly, and Mullibok is injured by one of the guards. Kira calls for medical assistance, and Bashir arrives to tend to Mullibok's wounds. With his two friends forcibly evacuated, Mullibok is the only remaining obstacle to the energy transfer project. Bashir offers to remove the Bajoran, but Kira declines and sends Bashir away. At last, Sisko travels to the moon and appeals to Kira as both her commander and her friend. Her career is on the line. Mullibok's fate is already decided—but hers isn't. That said, Sisko leaves her to her duty.

As Kira ponders her responsibilities, Jake and Nog overhear another interesting conversation at

Nog shows Jake how to turn *yamok* sauce into self-sealing stem bolts.
ROBBIE ROBINSON

Quark's bar. The Bajoran government wants to buy their land. Unfortunately, the government doesn't know that the owners are two young boys. They assume Quark is involved, and Quark makes it clear that he would *like* to be involved. Quickly, the two boys approach the Ferengi and offer to cut him in on a business opportunity that will cost him only five bars of gold-pressed latinum . . .

The next day, Kira makes her decision and tells Mullibok that he must leave Jeraddo. The Bajoran refuses, declaring that as long as his cottage stands, he'll remain. Kira sets fire to the cottage and tells Mullibok that it is time to get on with his life. But Mullibok says he'll die if he leaves. Kira assures him that he won't and reaches out to comfort him. But the old man shrugs off her hand. Saddened, Kira calls to the runabout above to beam them up.

Although the late Brian Keith's rich performance as Mullibok helped to make "Progress" one of the first season's more popular episodes, the well-known character actor would not have been Writer Peter Allan Fields's first choice for the role. "Brian Keith played Mullibok as a lovable old curmudgeon," says Fields. "But I didn't want that! I wanted a character who wasn't so lovable, someone who, when Kira puts her hand on his shoulder at the end, would look like he really means it when he shrugs her off and looks his own way. I wanted a strong guy who did not change at the end. There are too many old guys in television dramas who start out nasty and then get meek and gentle at the end. That's not what I wanted."

Mullibok's ultimate "meekness" is open to interpretation. The ambiguity of the ending—a Fields trademark—left many viewers wondering whether or not the old Bajoran would forgive Kira for her actions or even if she forced him to beam up with her! Nevertheless, Fields feels that the gentleness of Keith's interpretation worked against his personal vision of Mullibok throughout the episode. A number of details just didn't come across the way the writer intended: for example, Mullibok's use of Kira's first name, Nerys, which marked the first such usage in the series. To many viewers, this seemed to signify the warmth Mullibok felt for Kira. But according to Fields, "He said it because he was trying to con her." (And, in fact, the script for the episode clearly indi-

The producers decided that the Bajorans would lead a simple, almost rustic life, in contrast to the technological world on the station. ROBBIE ROBINSON

The set for Mullibok's homestead, constructed in the swing area on Stage 18. Note *DS9*'s familiar cave set in the background.

cates that many of Mullibok's seemingly charming lines are delivered in an attempt to manipulate—and even "sucker"—her.)

Fields is quick to note that he doesn't fault Keith's performance, only that it made Mullibok "less of an adversary than he ought to have been. He was less of a mountain for Kira to climb."

On a lighter note, in what would become a running motif in the relationship between Kira and Dax, "Progress" includes a scene where the two women discuss men—or at least males. Dax comments that though she recently turned down a dinner date with Morn, she finds the "seven or eight little wiry hairs sticking out of his forehead . . . kind of cute," much to Kira's amazement. While many viewers took that, and the subsequent conversations the two women had about the somewhat bizarre traits that Dax finds attractive in males, as an indication that Dax is drawn to the galaxy's more exotic types, Actor Terry Farrell says they're on the wrong track.

"The intention in that scene was to try to break into Kira's shell," explains Farrell. "I wasn't serious. I was trying to mess with her head, trying to get her to be herself around me. You haven't seen Jadzia with Morn, she doesn't date him. But as Jadzia, I think that Kira puts too much emphasis on what a guy looks like, so I'm teasing her about her youth, and her naivete about what people are really about. I'm trying to be funny, but I am also trying to get Kira to laugh at herself."

Although that may have been true during *DS9*'s first season, by Season 6 it was quite clear that her feelings for Morn were genuine, despite the fact that the feeling wasn't, alas, mutual ("Who Mourns for Morn").

Many of the terms used in *Deep Space Nine* were created by Peter Allan Fields—gold-pressed latinum, for example, which has the honor of being the first commonly used medium of exchange in the *Star Trek* universe. Establishing a Federation-wide standard of currency had been strenuously avoided for nearly thirty years, in part because creator Gene Roddenberry wanted to give the impression that the Federation is not profit-driven. The Ferengi, on the other hand, certainly are. "I had to have some kind of currency in the episode 'Past Prologue,'" Fields recalls. "I wanted something that sounded expensive. 'Gold-pressed latinum' just came out. And it stuck."

In "Progress," Fields gets credit for the invention of "self-sealing stem bolts," the commodity that Jake and Nog receive in exchange for Quark's *yamok* sauce. But don't ask Fields to tell you what they are or how they work. "I haven't the foggiest idea," he admits. "I just sat there and it came to me. Everybody on Earth has asked me what deep, dark place in my mind it came from, and the truth is, I just wrote the first thing I thought of."

"Pete gave us latinum, Pete gave us Garak, and he gave us self-sealing stem bolts," notes Ira Behr with affection in his voice. "And there's something about those things—the stem bolts in particular—that are the most indicative of the Pete Fields that I know. You just can't figure out what self-sealing stem bolts are—and Pete lives his whole life that way. We love throwing his ideas into the scripts." And, in fact, long after Fields retired from the show at the end of Season 2, the writing staff continued to throw in references to stem bolts, as well as create other terms that sounded "Fields-like," as an occasional tip of the hat to their former comrade.

Fields enjoyed writing the Jake and Nog subplot for the episode. "They are two young people who are alien to each other in every sense of the word," he says. "But, as young people go, they don't necessarily know that. They learn it as they go. When I wrote this, I was thinking that often when you see a situation like the one they get into, you naturally expect that the kids are going to lose everything and be in trouble. So I just flipped it, and they become incredibly successful without knowing gazooch!"

"Progress" and "The Storyteller" were episodes that marked the beginning of "an intense period of trying to turn Jake and Nog into the Laurel and Hardy of *DS9*" according to Ira Steven Behr. "It was a lot of fun to use those kids." Although Cirroc Lofton's ever-increasing height (by the fourth season the actor had grown taller than Avery Brooks) and Aron Eisenberg's age (thirty in *DS9*'s final season) forced a change in the types of stories that would work for the pair, Eisenberg always liked to think of them as "a futuristic Huck Finn and Tom Sawyer."

Still, even Huck and Tom eventually grew up, and once Nog made up his mind to join Starfleet in

Season 3 ("Heart of Stone"), light storylines for the pair became few and far between, with the exception of "In the Cards."

In a casting sidenote, Actor Terrence Evans (Baltrim) may not have delivered any lines in "Progress," but he would get to speak the next time he appeared. He would show up as the adoptive father of a Cardassian war orphan in second season's "Cardassians."

IF WISHES WERE HORSES
Episode #416
TELEPLAY BY NELL McCUE CRAWFORD & WILLIAM L. CRAWFORD AND MICHAEL PILLER
STORY BY NELL McCUE CRAWFORD & WILLIAM L. CRAWFORD
DIRECTED BY ROBERT LEGATO

GUEST CAST

Keiko O'Brien	ROSALIND CHAO
Buck Bokai	KEONE YOUNG
Rumpelstiltskin	MICHAEL JOHN ANDERSON
Molly O'Brien	HANA HATAE

STARDATE 46853.2

Taking advantage of a quiet day, Chief O'Brien reads the story of "Rumpelstiltskin" to his daughter Molly, Jake Sisko heads to a holosuite to play baseball, and Dr. Bashir indulges in a romantic dream about Jadzia Dax. In Ops, Commander Sisko, Major Kira, and Dax note unusually high thoron emissions registering from a plasma field outside the station. As they wonder if the emissions will create any problems, unusual things begin to happen: Rumpelstiltskin appears in Molly's bedroom, long-dead baseball player Buck Bokai follows Jake out of the holosuite, and Bashir is awakened in his quarters by an unusually affectionate Dax.

The senior officers gather in Ops, where they discover that the flirtatious Dax is one of the mysterious manifestations—all of which seem to have been conjured up by the imaginations of station personnel. While Odo attempts to deal with additional outbreaks of fantasy on the Promenade, the real Dax works against time to seal a rupture that she has discovered in the plasma field, one that she believes could destroy them all.

On the verge of annihilation, Sisko solves the mystery. Realizing that the threat to the station was first

Keiko and Miles entertain daughter Molly with a fairy tale that will soon take on a life of its own. ROBBIE ROBINSON

surmised by Dax, Sisko suggests that the rift in the plasma field, like the appearance of their "visitors," has been the product of their imaginations. Sure enough, as soon as they cease believing they are in danger, the rift disappears—along with Rumpelstiltskin, Bokai, and the amorous Dax duplicate.

The manifestation of Bokai returns later to explain his presence to Sisko. He and his companions have recently traveled through the wormhole as part of an extended mission exploring the galaxy. Apparently unfamiliar with humanoids, and struck by the uniqueness of their vivid imaginations, the aliens had been attempting to "figure out the rules" of their behavior by observing and interacting with the station's inhabitants. Although he declines to provide an explanation of his own species, "Buck" departs with the suggestion that he might return to do so in the future.

Although it could have been just another "mysterious-aliens-play-head-games-with-the-*Star Trek*-crew" story, "If Wishes Were Horses" metamorphosed into a delightfully whimsical episode thanks, in part, to some inspired behind-the-scenes discussions.

The *DS9* producers liked the basic concept of the story, "A race that didn't approach first contact like the Federation folk do, which is direct, friendly confrontation," recalls cowriter William L. Crawford. "They were a little more shy. And they would use their ability to reflect the fantasies or unconscious of individuals they ran into to bring out their good and bad points, so the aliens could make a decision if they wanted to go further." However, the original pitch offered by Crawford and writing partner Nell McCue Crawford placed a heavy emphasis on the use of a holosuite. When the producers pointed out that sister show *The Next Generation* was deep in development on "Ship in a Bottle," an episode with a similar emphasis, the holosuite aspect was drastically reduced. "The holosuite was actually a red herring anyway," says Crawford. "The characters on DS9 thought these beings were coming from the holosuite, that it was a malfunction, but they were really an alien race. In the end the stress was less on the holosuite and more on the aliens."

Some of the guises those alien characters took were dropped along the wayside as well, among them an Alice in Wonderland manifestation who was to interact with Jake, and a leprechaun. "There was a perception that, since this leprechaun was interacting

Rene Auberjonois's versatility at his craft is shown as he plays opposite this unusual costar. ROBBIE ROBINSON

with O'Brien, there might be some ethnic insensitivity there," recalls Crawford.

Actor Colm Meaney heartily concurs. "The American idea of Ireland is that it's rural and full of thatched cottages," he says. "And the reality of the Ireland that I grew up in was that seen in *The Commitments* (a gritty urban rock and roll comedy in which Meaney, coincidentally, costarred). It's not *Darby O'Gill and the Little People,* and from my personal point of view, enough of that stuff goes on—we don't have to reinforce it. Using caricatures or clichés of any nation is not something *Star Trek* is or should be into."

The character was replaced by the fairy-tale character Rumpelstiltskin and played by Michael John Anderson, a longtime *Star Trek* fan.

The appearance of baseball player Buck Bokai has a more complicated genesis. Although the Crawfords, Michael Piller (who also worked on the teleplay), Michael Okuda, and even professional model maker Greg Jein had a hand in his creation, the "Buck"

stops—or rather starts—at the desk of Ricardo Delgado, a junior illustrator during *DS9*'s first season.

According to Okuda, "Ricardo was coming up with ideas of decorative items that might sit on Ben Sisko's desk, and, being a big baseball fan, as is Sisko, he thought Sisko might have some kind of collectible baseball card on his desk." But who should the player be? Babe Ruth? Joe DiMaggio?

"I wanted it to be the [previously unnamed] shortstop for the London Kings, referred to in the *TNG* episode "The Big Goodbye," recalls Okuda, "but I suggested that he check with Michael Piller, since Piller's the one responsible for Sisko's interest in baseball."

Piller suggested a twenty-first-century baseball player of Asian descent. Remembering that they had photos of Jein on file, Okuda asked the model maker if they could use one for the card. But Jein did them one better, providing the art department with a roll of pictures of himself in a baseball jersey he had retouched to read "London Kings." Jein, a fan of the cult film *Buckaroo Banzai,* even gave the player a name: Buck Bokai. The card appeared on Sisko's desk in several episodes. When the time came to cast a real "Buck Bokai" for "If Wishes Were Horses," crewmembers were astounded by actor Keone Young's physical resemblance to Greg Jein. However, according to the show's producers, the similarity was a coincidence; they simply cast the performer with the best acting ability.

The tricky visual effects of the episode, which included duplicate Daxes and characters appearing and disappearing, presented no challenge to Robert Legato, a visual effects master who had switched hats to direct. But while Legato also wasn't a stranger to directing, having directed two episodes of *TNG* ("Ménage à Troi" and "Nth Degree"), he'd never directed creatures as stubborn as emus, who didn't particularly care to run, or do anything else, on cue.

"The only way you could get them to run was to actually push them, so you'd have to have someone in the scene pushing them across, and then they'd stop when no one was pushing them anymore," says Legato. Thus the avian actors required special motivation from their coperformers. One emu handler doubled as a Bajoran monk to help provide nonclerical inspiration. And Actor Rene Auberjonois was asked to improvise something that would trigger a more interesting performance from one of the birds. "He went out and did this little bit where he's just studying this bird, and he moves his head down and the emu moves its head down, and he moves his head up and the emu moves its head up," Legato

LEFT: **Greg Jein as Buck Bokai.** RIGHT: **The actor Keone Young as the "real" Buck Bokai.**

remembers with a smile. "It turned out to be a charming bit." Auberjonois reports that the scene reminded him of a peculiar character he played early in his career, in the motion picture *Brewster McCloud*. "I was a character who turned into a bird over the course of the story. It's a pretty special film."

Legato's special effects experience came in handy when setting up the alien appearances and disappearances. Hoping to avoid the telltale, so-called *I Dream of Jeannie*-jump caused when the camera is locked off, and the scene is shot with the actor present and then again with the actor not present, Legato tried something a little more creative for the scene where "Sisko" appears behind Jake.

"I wanted the two characters to be really close, so I shot it with Avery there behind Cirroc, and then we rotoscoped Avery out for the beginning of the scene. That way, he seems to pop on directly behind him without the usual jump in the film."

But is one to assume that the character who appears behind Jake is one of the aliens or his real father?

Legato admits that he's not sure himself; the episode was running a little short, and the scene was

added at the last minute. However, he chose to play it as if the character were one of the aliens, trying to learn more about how people are by playing devil's advocate with Jake. "That's why I have him positioned right over his shoulder, as if he were Jake's conscience, a Jiminy Cricket kind of thing," says Legato. "Avery wanted to play it standing up and towering over Jake, but that would have made it more like it was really his dad."

Special effects aside, Legato's greatest challenge in directing the episode may have been getting a performance out of his smallest cast member: little Hanna Hatae, who plays Molly O'Brien. According to Legato, four-year-old Hanna had a cold the day they were to shoot the scene in which she comes out of her bedroom to announce the presence of Rumpelstiltskin. "She didn't feel good, and she was tired, and she didn't want to play," recalls Legato. "And she simply would not do it. Her mother came in to talk to her, and the assistant directors and the studio teacher, and she still wouldn't do it. After forty minutes of absolutely nothing, I had a talk with her and told her if she didn't come out, I'd get in a lot of trouble. They'd be really mad at me. Then I told her that if she'd do the scene

So Would You Call It Art Deco?

Herman Zimmerman on the design of Deep Space 9

Herman Zimmerman has been the production designer for both *Star Trek: The Next Generation* and *Deep Space Nine*. He also has served in that capacity on the five most recent *Star Trek* motion pictures, starting with *Star Trek V: The Final Frontier* to *Star Trek: Insurrection*.

"I have a propensity for art deco," Herman Zimmerman states, "but I can't say that you could label the station *as* art deco. There *are* a number of those elements, in the sense that it's very geometric and art deco is a geometric kind of design idea. But the station really defines itself: It's Cardassian. I don't think you can call it anything else!

"Cardassians like an orderliness in all things. They prefer balance to symmetry, ellipses to circles, angles to straight lines. And they like things in sets of three. There are three concentric circles—the exterior docking ring, the middle habitat ring, and the center core—that make up the bulk of the station. There are three arms, or crossover bridges, that hold the three rings together. And there are three docking pylons that extend up and down off the docking ring."

It was Zimmerman who envisioned a curious assemblage of intersecting multiple rings, and Rick Berman who suggested making the shape of these hoops more alien by breaking them off at the tops and bottoms. According to Zimmerman, "no one person created the station. Rick Sternbach did a lot of the mechanicals on it. [Illustrator] Ricardo Delgado was responsible for much of the exterior plate detail. Mike Okuda came up with a terracing aspect that was incorporated into the lower core. And [Set Designer] Joe Hodges had a lot to say about how it eventually turned out. No one on the Art Department staff was the least bit afraid to accept an idea from somebody else. We are truly democratic, and the station is a very good example of that democracy in action. It's much greater than the sum of its parts, and not any one of us could have imagined what the end result would be until all of our minds were at work on it. We really are proud of Deep Space 9."

like she was supposed to, I'd be really appreciative and give her one of the nice toys in Molly's bedroom set. At that point, I didn't care how much they cost or if they were rentals or what!" Then, notes Legato, they crossed their fingers, set up the scene once again, turned the camera on, and called "Action!"

"The door opens up, she comes running out and says her line like a champ, and the camera man was so surprised that he blew the shot!" laughs Legato, who says they finally got the shot in "four or five takes"—and four or five toys later.

Lwaxana Troi offers Odo her affections. ROBBIE ROBINSON

THE FORSAKEN

Episode #417

TELEPLAY BY **DON CARLOS DUNAWAY** AND **MICHAEL PILLER**
STORY BY **JIM TROMBETTA**
DIRECTED BY **LES LANDAU**

GUEST CAST

Lwaxana Troi	MAJEL BARRETT
Ambassador Taxco	CONSTANCE TOWERS
Ambassador Lojal	MICHAEL ENSIGN
Ambassador Vadosia	JACK SHEARER
Anara	BENITA ANDRE

STARDATE 46925.1

When Deep Space 9 is "honored" with a visit by a delegation of Federation ambassadors on a fact-finding mission to the wormhole, Sisko places the assignment of shepherding them about in Dr. Bashir's hands. While three of the ambassadors pester Bashir with constant requests, the fourth, Lwaxana Troi, the Betazoid mother of *Starship Enterprise* Counselor Deanna Troi, proves to be far more self-sufficient, at least when it comes to finding her own entertainment. After Odo helps her to recover a latinum hairbrooch stolen during a dabo game at Quark's, Lwaxana is impressed—so impressed that she sets her sights on making the shape-shifter a close personal friend.

As Bashir escorts the other three ambassadors around the station, a frustrated O'Brien tries to deal with the station's uncooperative Cardassian computer. At the same time, Kira notes the arrival through the wormhole of an unidentified alien space probe. Cautious despite his curiosity about the object, Sisko has it towed to a position a few hundred meters from the docking ring and asks O'Brien to set up a computer interface that will allow them to download information from the probe.

Elsewhere on the station, Lwaxana, dressed to kill, tracks down Odo and attempts to flirt with him. Odo nervously puts her off and heads for Ops, where he tries to get Sisko to do something about the problem. Sisko, however, is amused rather than concerned, and he offers Odo only the advice to treat the situation "delicately." A short time later, Odo encounters Lwaxana on the Promenade. Although he tries to retreat in a turbolift, Lwaxana follows him. Suddenly the power to the pylon turbolift fails, as does the transporter, and the two are trapped together, which Lwaxana takes as the perfect opportunity to get to know Odo better.

In Ops, O'Brien is puzzled by the breakdowns and subsequent malfunctions all over the station. He points out to Sisko that the computer's personality seemed to change after they downloaded the information from the probe. It has become more obedient, but it seems to crave constant attention, like a child—or a puppy. The Ops officers discuss the possibility that they may actually have downloaded some kind of non-biological life-form into their computer. Unfortunately, there doesn't seem to be any way to communicate with it directly. And when O'Brien tries to upload the transmitted files back to the probe, the station's computer system balks and creates further breakdowns.

In the turbolift, a weary Odo—who is quickly approaching the point where he must allow his body to revert to its natural liquid state—slowly lets down his guard in response to Lwaxana's constant barrage of friendly chatter and shares some personal revelations about his past. Touched by his candor and vulnerability, Lwaxana shares some revelations of her own, convincing him that he can trust her enough to be himself, in every sense of the word. As Odo allows himself to liquify, Lwaxana catches him in her skirt, creating an improvised basin to safely contain him.

O'Brien continues to work on the computer problem, this time attempting to manually transfer the probe's data, but the effort triggers a plasma explosion in the station's guest quarters, trapping Bashir and the three ambassadors in a fiery corridor. Realizing that the alien life-form, which O'Brien is now referring to as the "pup," doesn't want to leave, O'Brien creates a subprogram that can safely house it—a "doghouse," so to speak. The strategy works, and the station's systems come back on line.

In the fire-scorched corridor, Kira and Sisko find that Bashir resourcefully managed to save himself and the ambassadors by leading them into a wall compartment to wait out the conflagration. Odo, once again in humanoid form, and Lwaxana are retrieved from the turbolift. As they part, Lwaxana suggests that they'll have more to discover about each other the next time they meet. And back in Ops, O'Brien promises Sisko that he will keep his new "pet" happy, busy—and out of trouble from now on.

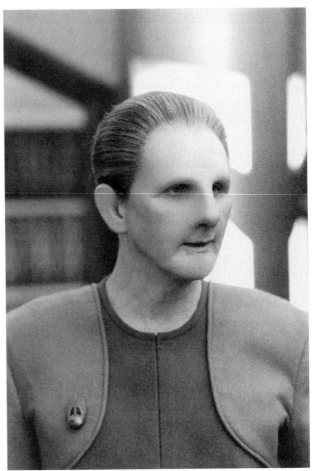

Majel Barrett's outgoing character proved a catalyst in revealing important insights into Odo's personality. ROBBIE ROBINSON

Originally called "Only the Lonely," after the classic Roy Orbison song, "The Forsaken" brought original series actress Majel Barrett into a recurring role in her third Star Trek series, as the character Lwaxana Troi. Of course, prior to her acting appearance in "The Forsaken," fans already had *heard* her on *Deep Space Nine*, as the voice of the Starfleet computers used on the runabouts. (Barrett also vocalized the Starfleet computers on the original series, *The Next Generation,* and *Star Trek: Voyager*).

Both Barrett and Actor Rene Auberjonois report that "The Forsaken" seems to be a favorite with fans, at least according to the feedback they've received at *Star Trek* conventions across the country. "In part, I'm sure that's because of Majel's popularity with the fans, and the popularity of her character Lwaxana," offers Auberjonois. "It was a real bonus for me to be paired with her in the show's first season. It helped to estab-

lish Odo and give him more dimension than he'd had up to that point. Through his relationship with Lwaxana, the audience was introduced to an aspect of him that made him endearing, and they really connected with him. And the script was wonderful."

Barrett concurs. "The episode was extremely well written. It brings out all sorts of new facets in Lwaxana's character, which, as an actress, I love, of course."

Auberjonois calls the episode "pivotal" in terms of Odo's characterization. "There are little odds and ends that I make up myself about Odo, but a lot of the important details I learn when I get my script," he admits. "For example, that I don't have a sense of smell or that I've never coupled before. And oddly enough, most of those things I tell Quark, who is supposed to be my nemesis, although it gives you an indication of what our real relationship is, that I tell him these incredibly personal things. And it isn't until 'The Forsaken' that I express anything that personal to anyone but Quark. I was glad when I heard they would be bringing Lwaxana back again." Ultimately Barrett would reprise her character in two more episodes, Season 3's "Fascination" and Season 4's "The Muse".

"The Forsaken" does indeed establish a great deal about Odo: that he doesn't have a real mouth, or, for that matter, an esophagus, stomach, or digestive system; that his early experiences in the Bajoran laboratory where he was studied for so many years made him loath to reveal his private side to outsiders; that the Bajoran scientist who "raised" him had a strong influence on him. (A theme that would be further developed in the second-season episode "The Alternate," and the fifth-season episode "The Begotten.") And that he can, in Sisko's words, "handle thieves and killers but not one Betazoid woman."

To comment on that last quality, Auberjonois relates a story: "Odo has this incredibly rigid and formal kind of assurance. When my dad, who lives in London and doesn't know *Star Trek* from Adam, first saw a picture of the character in a fan magazine I'd sent him, he wrote me a note that said, 'Why are you playing a fascist?' That's the way he looks to people. But the Lwaxana character allows me to do the kind of thing that I always try to do with a character. When I'm doing a tragedy or playing a serious character, I concentrate on finding as much humor in the character as possible. And if I'm playing a comic character, I look for the sad side. Because that's the way you get an audience's emotions going, by making the pendulum swing in as great an arc as you possibly can. So Odo's vulnerability is something that interests me a great deal."

The idea of putting Odo into a situation where he'd be forced to seek refuge in a woman's skirt came from story writer Jim Trombetta. "The bible for the show said that after x-number of hours Odo had to go into this tin bucket," says Trombetta. "But then you think about what would happen if he didn't have a bucket. That's the one thing another person could

help him with. It was a very female thing for Lwaxana to do, to make it safe for him."

The psychological implication of Odo's actions interests Trombetta. "It goes back to the Renaissance, and the characters referred to as 'gentlemen.' They had to be hard warriors with a hard shape, like armor. There's an anxiety if men become soft. They become helpless, babylike. Men don't like that. So here that caption works very vividly. Odo's a constable and a very tough guy, but he has to undergo that process and allow someone else to help him. He has no choice."

For those more fascinated with the physical than the psychological, the episode demonstrates for the first time what happens to Odo if he doesn't get to revert to liquid form in sixteen hours. Of the goop applied to his face as Odo begins to melt down in the turbolift, Auberjonois notes, "I asked Michael Westmore what it was, and he said, 'Oh, you don't want to know.' It's some sort of alginate, a natural foamy, tasteless substance that they use in fast-food restaurants to thicken milkshakes. They put my skin coloring into it, and then they sort of ladle it onto my face with a tongue depressor and let it drip off."

The slimy effect was limited to Odo's face and hands because the costumes are too expensive to mess up. But since Odo's clothes are apparently part of his body, isn't that an oversight? "We're talking about the willing suspension of disbelief here." Auberjonois laughs.

One other minor costuming note: "The Forsaken" establishes a small change in Kira's uniform, which loses the flap bottom of her tunic, thus turning the two-piece ensemble into a one-piece spandex jumpsuit, reportedly to better show off Nana Visitor's figure.

"The [original] uniform wasn't terribly becoming," admits Visitor, although the problem lay more in the fact that she'd recently had a baby than in Robert Blackman's costume design. "I had no idea I would be in a military uniform six weeks after giving birth!" she laughs.

DRAMATIS PERSONAE

Episode #418

WRITTEN BY JOE MENOSKY
DIRECTED BY CLIFF BOLE

GUEST CAST

Hon'Tihl	TOM TOWLES
Valerian	STEPHEN PARR
Guard	RANDY PFLUG
Ensign	JEFF PRUITT

STARDATE 46922.3

Kira balks when Sisko tells her to allow a Valerian transport to dock at the station. The Valerians had run weapons-grade dolamide to Cardassian forces during the occupation of Bajor, and she believes that they continue to supply the Cardassians with weapons. Sisko says he will intervene only if Kira provides him proof of such activities. But prior to the Valerians' arrival, a Klingon ship blasts through the wormhole and explodes. The vessel's first officer, critically injured, manages to beam aboard the station, but dies a few seconds later, uttering the word *victory*. Since the ship was known to be on a routine bio-survey mission, the crew is baffled both by the circumstances of the Klingon's death and the destruction of his vessel.

While Dax and O'Brien search for the Klingon ship's mission recorder, Kira and Sisko butt heads once again over the Valerian freighter. At Quark's place, Odo learns that the Klingons told the Ferengi they were

bringing something back through the wormhole that would "make the enemies of the Klingon Empire tremble." But before Odo can puzzle out the statement, he is struck by agonizing pain and his head briefly splits in two. Horrified, Quark calls for Dr. Bashir.

After Odo regains consciousness in the Infirmary, he's struck by an odd change in Bashir's personality, and is concerned when the doctor hints that the friction between Kira and Sisko is likely to intensify. At the same time, Sisko and Kira have a confrontation about the Valerians, and Kira discovers that Sisko doesn't intend to interfere with their affairs after all. O'Brien and Dax, still looking for the destroyed Klingon ship's mission recorder, also begin to show personality changes, and O'Brien questions Dax about her loyalties to Sisko. When Kira attempts to get Odo to go behind Sisko's back to help her cause, the security chief is certain that something is very wrong.

Dax and O'Brien present a nearly incomprehensible portion of the dead Klingon's journal to Sisko, Kira, and Odo; the report hints at mutiny aboard his ship and the presence of some alien energy spheres. Sisko is uninterested in the report but tells the others they can follow up on it if they want to—as long as they don't bother him. A short time later, Kira attempts to enlist Dax's allegiance against Sisko, whom she intends to eliminate. When she realizes Quark is eavesdropping, Kira attacks the Ferengi.

Quark complains about Kira's behavior to Odo, filling the security chief in on the conversation he overheard. Odo decides that it's time to have a conversation with Sisko, but when he gets to the commander's office, he finds that O'Brien seems to have settled in for the duration. Although he is working on piecing together the mission recorder's log entries, O'Brien seems more interested in Major Kira's activities. Odo finds Sisko in his quarters and expresses his concern over the behavior of the crew. But Sisko, engrossed in a clock he is designing, asks Odo to take his concerns to O'Brien.

Returning to his own office, Odo finds Kira waiting for him. She tells him that the Valerian freighter isn't leaving until she says it is—and that she plans to take over the station. After she leaves, Odo discovers that Kira and O'Brien have made it impossible for him to contact anyone outside of the station for assistance, so he turns to the now-reconstructed journal of the dead Klingon for a possible solution. The journal reveals that the Klingons found a collection of

Odo's suspicions about the senior staff deepen when Quark complains about Kira's violent behavior. ROBBIE ROBINSON

energy spheres that contained a telepathic archive; the archive described an ancient power struggle that destroyed a race known as the Saltah'na.

Playing upon the doctor's new political aspirations, Odo enlists Bashir's help in figuring out the rest of the pieces of the puzzle. They theorize that the energy matrix from the spheres could have caused the crew of the Klingon vessel to reenact the Saltah'nan power struggle and that the Klingon who made it to DS9 brought the matrix with him. Of the people who were present in Ops when the Klingon arrived, only Odo, with his nonhumanoid brain, was able to throw off the effects of the matrix. Convincing Bashir that the person who finds the way to control the energy matrix can control the station, Odo gets Bashir to work on a method of blocking the influence of the field from those affected.

Tensions rise to a head as Sisko foils an apparent assassination attempt, and Kira arrives with an armed guard. But O'Brien manages to beam himself and Sisko out of harm's way. When the two men seek Odo's assistance, the shape-shifter sends them to Docking Port 4, then directs Kira and Dax to the same area. Arriving with the doctor, Odo activates the interference signal developed by Bashir and forces the energy influence from the crew's bodies and into space, where it disperses harmlessly.

"**D**ramatis Personae," originally called "Ritual Sacrifice," was written by the "*Star Trek* Italian Bureau," otherwise known to his friends as Joe Menosky. After serving as executive story editor during *The Next Generation's* fourth season and writer/co-producer in the series' fifth season, Menosky decided to move to Italy for an extended period of research and study. Before he left, however, Executive Producer Michael Piller told him that he expected Menosky to function as a kind of branch office for the staff. So Menosky continued to do episodes for the last two seasons of *TNG* and also for Piller and Rick Berman's brand-new baby: *Deep Space Nine*. Eventually, he returned to the U.S. to join the staff of *Voyager* on a full-time basis.

Menosky describes the process of writing long distance as a "funny phone-fax thing. Since I was in Italy, I was separated from the follow through and the rewriting that normally goes on when you're on staff. I'd send them a first draft, and if it was close enough, they'd make whatever changes they needed during the week of preproduction. If it needed another draft, I'd do it and send it on to them. But no matter how it worked

This episode allowed all of the actors to step outside of the normal bounds of their characters. ROBBIE ROBINSON

out, there was always a fairly large gap between what I turned in and what was shot. And I can't even tell you what the differences were, because I never got to *see* any of the shows I wrote during that period!"

"Dramatis Personae" began with an "abstract intellectual idea," recalls Menosky. "I was thinking about behavior patterns and the idea that people tend to get trapped into certain ones that are common to everyone. Take, for example, falling in love. Everybody's gotten a phone call from someone who's just fallen in love, and they all tell you the same damn story. When you're in one of those behavior patterns, no matter how powerful and unique the feelings are, there's this feeling of doing something 'expected.'"

Menosky set out to put the whole idea of this "psychological/cultural programming" into *DS9* terms, which translated most logically as a space virus. "I wondered if there could be something like a telepathic virus, a little packet of telepathic energy containing something that works in the same way that a virus coopts the genetic code of a living cell and then changes its biology according to its design," says

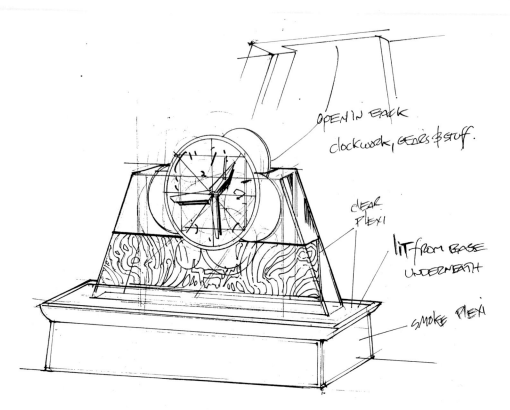

OPEN IN BACK
clockwork, gears & stuff.

CLEAR PLEXI

lit from BASE UNDERNEATH

SMOKE PLEXI

One of the countless designs for the Saltah'na clock.

Menosky. "This would do the same thing, but according to a kind of theatrical complex that it carried, transmit a little drama. Each one of these telepathic viruses represents a little play, containing a bunch of character dramatics and emotions and traumas that had happened. In this particular case, the little play was a power struggle that led to the fall of a race or a civilization."

The results of the virus allowed the cast—with the exception of Odo and Quark—to behave in some very nontraditional ways, which pleased the actors and the crew as much as the fans. "It's always fun for the actors when you give them a chance to do something out of the ordinary, when you let them put on a play within a play," says Menosky. "And the writers tend to think about that when they come up with an idea—'Oh, won't so-and-so have fun doing this!'"

"I had fun giving Avery Brooks the opportunity to dive away from his normal character on the show," concurs Director Cliff Bole, a longtime veteran of *TNG*, who had worked with Brooks previously on the series *Spenser for Hire*. "I remember going to him and saying, 'Here's a chance for us to dance and have some fun.'" Bole notes that the Sisko character, as originally conceived, was always under tight emotional control, quite unlike some of Brooks's earlier performances, including the character of Hawk that he portrayed in *Spenser*. As a result, he says, "the pub-

The actual clock that Sisko builds—with the help of Cliff Bole, Joe Longo, and members of the *DS9* Art Department. ROBBIE ROBINSON

lic didn't know the extent of his abilities for a long time. This man is awesome."

The manipulation of the characters' personalities was a challenge Ira Behr relished. "What I like about it was that it was a third-season show that we had the nerve to do in the first season," he enthuses. "Anybody else would say, 'You need to know the characters better before you twist them like this.' But seeing Kira come on to Dax—I don't care if it's first or third season, people are going to be interested in that! And

O'Brien as Iago and Sisko with his clock! All kinds of fun things!"

The episode also gave behind-the-scenes personnel the opportunity for some fun when it came to designing the Saltah'na clock, which Sisko works on in his quarters throughout the episode. "The point I was trying to make was that Sisko's 'persona' was an obsessive quirky Emperor Rudolf-type, one of those guys that you find throughout European history who were nuts, collecting weird little mechanical birds that they fussed over," says Menosky. "That was the idea."

From Menosky's original suggestion in the script ("I think what I initially had was an absurdly complicated huge, weird clock," he recalls.), the development of the clock fell primarily to Director Bole, Property Master Joe Longo and members of the Art Department, including Senior Illustrator Rick Sternbach and Junior Illustrator Ricardo Delgado. "We came up with all these different ideas of what this clock should look like and submitted them to Rick Berman," says Longo. "He liked one best, and we zeroed in on that."

Actually, three clocks were developed for the episode, each showing a different stage of construction. "In the show, we see Sisko drawing something, then we see him tinkering around with some pieces of something, then part of a clock, and finally a whole clock," says Longo. "We had all of the versions off to the side of the set while we were filming." The finished clock, which later became part of the permanent set dressing for Sisko's office, was constructed from pieces of brass and bronze. "I brought it over to Rick Berman's office when we figured it was done," notes Longo, "and Rick liked it a lot, but he wanted to know if there was a way that we could get the little carousel-type thing on it to turn. Of course I said yes, and then we went back and got it to turn!"

According to Bole, the clock doesn't really keep time, but he has faith that the crew could solve that problem. "Give Special Effects and the Prop Department a few more weeks, and they could do it. It's a treasure!"

DUET

Episode #419

TELEPLAY BY PETER ALLAN FIELDS
STORY BY LISA RICH & JEANNE CARRIGAN-FAUCI
DIRECTED BY JAMES L. CONWAY

GUEST CAST

Gul Dukat	MARC ALAIMO
Neela	ROBIN CHRISTOPHER
Lissepian Captain	NORMAN LARGE
Kainon	TONY RIZZOLI
Kaval	TED SOREL

SPECIAL GUEST STAR

Aamin Marritza	HARRIS YULIN

STARDATE UNKNOWN

When the captain of a Kobheerian freighter docking at the station requests medical assistance for one of its passengers, Kira's interest is piqued. The captain says his passenger is suffering from Kalla-Nohra, a syndrome that Kira knows is limited to the survivors of a mining accident at a Bajoran forced-labor camp that she helped liberate. She heads for the Infirmary and is startled to find that the survivor is a middle-aged Cardassian male—which means that he was part of the military operation at the Gallitep camp, and therefore, according to her, a war criminal.

After Kira has the Cardassian, who says his name is Aamin Marritza, arrested, Sisko visits him in a holding cell. Marritza denies he ever served at a labor camp and claims that he suffers from Pottrik Syndrome, not Kalla-Nohra. Dr. Bashir, however, disagrees; the ailment is Kalla-Nohra, which once again links the Cardassian with Gallitep. A short time later, Sisko is contacted by the Bajoran Minister of State, who says in no uncertain terms that if Marritza was at Gallitep, the Bajoran government expects Sisko to hand him over.

Sisko agrees to let Kira handle the investigation into Marritza's background, and Odo runs an initial background check that confirms at least part of the Cardassian's claims. Unconvinced, Kira interrogates Marritza, who eventually admits that he did serve at Gallitep—as a filing clerk under the camp's merciless leader, Gul Darhe'el. But when Kira refuses to back off, Marritza finds a chink in her armor, pointing out that she isn't interested in the truth—just vengeance.

Sisko allows the investigation to continue, despite a request from Gul Dukat that the Cardassian

Kira learns to see beyond her hatred of Cardassians and recognizes the worth of an individual. ROBBIE ROBINSON

there is one last bit of important evidence: records show that Gul Darhe'el was not at Gallitep on the day of the mining accident. Thus, the real Gul Darhe'el could not have contracted Kalla-Nohra.

The other pieces of the puzzle fall into place quickly. Marritza resigned from a teaching post several months earlier and put all of his personal affairs in order. He then specifically requested passage to the Bajoran station where Kira was posted. And Bashir, who has checked into Marritza's medical records, has discovered that the Cardassian has been receiving doses of a drug used by patients who alter their appearance. It is clear to everyone that the file clerk Marritza orchestrated the entire masquerade so that he would be arrested as a ruthless war criminal. But why?

Kira confronts Marritza with the information, and he breaks down at last. Marritza wanted to be tried before the Bajoran people as Gul Darhe'el, the Butcher of Gallitep, so that Cardassia would be forced to admit to the terrible crimes committed during the occupation of Bajor. But Kira refuses to let the blood of yet another innocent person be shed, and she releases him. As she prepares to send him back to his home, a Bajoran man breaks through the crowd on the Promenade to plunge a knife into Marritza, killing him instantly. When Kira protests that Marritza was not a criminal, the Bajoran claims that being a Cardassian was reason enough to take his life. Kira, shocked to recognize an attitude that was once her own, responds softly that it was not.

Ask a television series actor what his favorite episode is, and the odds are that he'll name an episode in which his character was featured prominently. The only time this rule ever seems to vary is when an episode airs that is of such high quality that it would be foolish to deny that it is, indeed, worthy of the highest praise—even if a cast member didn't play much of a part in the production.

"My favorite episode, ironically, is one that I had very little to do with," affirms Armin Shimerman. "And that's 'Duet.' That, I think, is a wonderful episode, with the writing and the directing and the acting all coalescing perfectly."

Understandably, the primary actor affected by the show was Nana Visitor. It was her favorite episode, too—but for an unusual reason. "I came away different," she reflects, "with a different perspective. I grew up in New York City, and racism is a subject that I'm familiar with, but I never had to deal with it in any real way."

—who has yet to be charged with a crime—be released. Odo obtains an image of Marritza from the Bajoran Archives, but the officers realize that it doesn't look anything like the prisoner. However, another Cardassian in the image *does* resemble him, and that man is identified as Gul Darhe'el.

When Kira confronts "Marritza" in his cell with this information, he gleefully admits that he is Gul Darhe'el, and then goes on both to brag about his countless atrocities and demean the efforts of Bajoran resistance fighters like her. Shaken, she discusses the conversation with Odo, who immediately picks up on one intriguing point. How did Gul Darhe'el, if that's who he is, know that Kira was in the Bajoran resistance?

As Odo checks into this detail, Kira returns to the prisoner to ask him herself. "Darhe'el" has an explanation, but it doesn't quite ring true. In the meantime, Odo discovers that an Aamin Marritza requested information on Kira Nerys several months ago. And the security chief finds out from Gul Dukat that Gul Darhe'el is dead and buried on Cardassia. And

The performances of Nana Visitor and Harris Yulin shone in what was widely considered to be the best episode of the season.
ROBBIE ROBINSON

Part of the rationale behind that decision was budgetary. "We'd spent a lot of money on the pilot and 'Past Prologue,' and we went hither and yon on location for several episodes," notes Peter Allan Fields, who wrote the teleplay based on Rich and Carrigan-Fauci's story. Thus, as the series approached the close of its first season, Fields understood that it was to everyone's advantage to create what's known as a "bottle show." "You stay right there," he explains, "and you don't spend a lot of money going hither and yon!"

With very little action and a lot of "talking heads" scenes, "Duet" could have been a very dull, if well-meaning, episode. But Director James Conway and key Actors Nana Visitor and Harris Yulin rose to the challenge, winning kudos from cast, crew, and critics alike. The casting of Yulin was a particular delight for Fields, who'd been a fan of the actor for years. "I'd always wanted to write for him," Fields says. "I was delighted that he wanted to do it."

Fields is quick to give credit to Ira Behr for his "really great input" into the script. "I'd be less than fair if I didn't say that without Ira's contribution, particularly in Marritza's reactions, I don't think I could have tricked it out like that."

Behr, speaking tongue-in-cheek, comments, "I gave as fine a performance as Harris Yulin up in Pete's office. We would go into those long monologues and stand and rant and scream, and actually a lot of it, word for word, is in there." It was the beginning, Behr adds, of what the writers now refer to as "Cardassian monologues." Says Behr, "Cardassians love to speak. Garak loves to speak, Enabran Tain loves to speak. Dukat loves to speak—very slowly—and certainly Marritza loves to speak."

Fields is also grateful for the fact that Director Conway didn't change the ending he had written. "Usually, no matter what you write, the director shoots the ending the way he wants to. And in this episode, I wanted that camera to pull up—and back—and just leave the characters there. And Conway did it. That tickled me."

Not that Fields has had particularly poor luck in that area. The hallmark of many Fields scripts is a quiet, yet emotionally resonant ending, sometimes deliberately ambiguous ("Progress" and "Necessary Evil") and sometimes hauntingly poignant ("Duet" and TNG's "Inner Light"). And that hallmark is clearly distinguishable on the screen in each of those episodes.

As a side note, this episode introduces the character of Neela, a Bajoran woman who works with O'Brien.

The writing started with a very simple story pitch by Lisa Rich and Jeanne Carrigan-Fauci, the same writers responsible for "Move Along Home." "The basic premise," says Carrigan-Fauci, "was, 'What would happen if you had to defend your worst enemy? What if you had to be responsible for his life?' There's so much conflict inherent in the concept. And of course it was only natural to use Kira and a Cardassian in that situation and to have them both learn something about each other."

While "Duet," originally known as "The Higher Law," clearly has its roots in dramas about the Holocaust—in particular Robert Shaw's powerful play, *The Man in the Glass Booth,* which the executive producers suggested the writing team look at before they got started—much of the episode's strength came from the decision to craft the show almost entirely around Kira and the Cardassian, Marritza.

Although viewers can hardly be faulted for overlooking her debut amid the heavy emotional threads of "Duet," Neela (Robin Christopher), would go on to play a far more significant part in the action of the season finale, "In the Hands of the Prophets." Interestingly, her character, or rather, that of a female assistant for O'Brien, was supposed to have appeared in three episodes, making her debut in "The Forsaken."

"We planned for O'Brien's assistant to be in two episodes prior to 'In the Hands of the Prophets,'" says that episode's writer, Robert Hewitt Wolfe. "We wanted to set her up way ahead of time and get the audience to think she was a new recurring character. Then, when she turns out to be the assassin in the finale, it would be a great surprise." Unfortunately, the actress who played O'Brien's assistant (then named Anara) in "The Forsaken" didn't work out, according to Wolfe. So the role was recast and the future assassin, now renamed Neela, made only one appearance prior to her denouement.

IN THE HANDS OF THE PROPHETS

Episode #420

WRITTEN BY **ROBERT HEWITT WOLFE**
DIRECTED BY **DAVID LIVINGSTON**

GUEST CAST

Keiko O'Brien	ROSALIND CHAO
Neela	ROBIN CHRISTOPHER
Vedek Bareil	PHILIP ANGLIM
Vendor	MICHAEL EUGENE

SPECIAL GUEST STAR

Vedek Winn	LOUISE FLETCHER

STARDATE UNKNOWN

A new day begins on Deep Space 9, and Chief O'Brien escorts his wife Keiko through the Promenade on her way to the station school. O'Brien pauses to purchase a snack at a kiosk and impresses Keiko with his knowledge of Bajoran *jumja* sticks, although not quite in the way he'd intended. The trivia about *jumja* came from his new assistant, Neela, and O'Brien is startled when he realizes that Keiko thinks he might be attracted to the pretty Bajoran. After a bit of teasing, Keiko heads on to the classroom.

As Keiko attempts to explain the scientific prin-

Commander Sisko meets Vedek Bareil in the tranquil setting of Bareil's monastery. DANNY FELD

ciples behind the construction of the nearby wormhole to her students, she is interrupted by the arrival of Vedek Winn, a spiritual leader from Bajor. Winn observes the lesson, then calmly states her opposition to Keiko's secular method of instruction, which does not touch upon Bajoran beliefs regarding the Prophets who reside in the wormhole. Keiko reports the incident to Commander Sisko, and Kira expresses some support for Winn's point of view. When Keiko rejects the idea that she incorporate religious beliefs into her curriculum, Kira suggests that there may be a need for a separate school for Bajoran children. Sisko doesn't like that idea either, since he wants to see Bajoran and Federation interests unified.

Uncertain how to resolve the matter, Sisko goes to see Winn, who warmly greets the "Emissary," as the late Kai Opaka referred to the commander. But Winn refuses to back down from her stance that Keiko has dishonored the Celestial Temple with her teachings. Winn informs Sisko that she won't be responsible for the consequences if the teacher does not recant.

Working with Neela, O'Brien is concerned to discover that one of his tools is missing. The tool can be used to access every critical system on the station. Curiously, an ensign named Aquino is also missing. A search of a power conduit leads O'Brien and Neela to the remains of both the tool and the unlucky ensign. The working theory is that Aquino had attempted to repair a plasma flow irregularity in the conduit and got caught in the power flow, but O'Brien is unsatisfied with that answer.

He is even more troubled when he finds out that Winn's veiled threat has come to fruition. Some of the Bajorans on the station have begun to treat Keiko with contempt. Winn continues to stir up the Bajorans with her superficially passive rhetoric and confronts Keiko at the door to the school. She will accept Keiko's decision not to teach the students about the Prophets if Keiko promises not to teach anything about the wormhole at all. Keiko can't accept that alternative, and she watches in dismay as Winn leads the Bajoran children and their parents away from the school.

Concerned, Sisko pays a visit to Vedek Bareil, the leading candidate to become the next kai, on Bajor. Sisko hopes that Bareil can help him arrange an audience with the Vedek Assembly so that he can discuss the school. But while Bareil's ideology is very different from Winn's, he does not want to risk his political future by appearing to take sides with Sisko. Frustrated, Sisko returns to the station, where he discovers that several Bajoran crewmembers have failed to report for duty. When Kira refuses to offer her support in resolving the situation, Sisko has some sharp words with her. A short time later, Odo and Bashir report the results of their investigation into Aquino's death; the ensign was killed by a phaser blast.

Odo has made an additional discovery. On the night he was killed, Aquino did not head for the power conduit, as his log indicates. He went to Runabout Pad C. O'Brien and Neela investigate the pad but find nothing. After Neela leaves, O'Brien runs an additional diagnostic on the other runabout pads, and finds that someone has placed a security bypass module at Pad A. He informs Odo and the shape-shifter quickly deduces that Aquino was killed when he interrupted someone tampering with the security net at Pad C. The murderer then switched his efforts to Pad A to avoid detection. As the pair attempt to figure out the motive behind the subterfuge, they hear an explosion and discover the empty schoolroom engulfed in flames.

Angered by Winn's insincere concern over the incident, Sisko accuses the vedek of instigating the animosity and resulting violence on the station in an effort to increase her following among the Bajoran people. But her attempt will fail, he tells her, because the majority of Bajoran people on the station have come to know that, for all their differences, the representatives of the Federation are not the enemy.

Later, Neela approaches Winn in private, and tells the vedek that the officers have found out about the runabout, leaving her no method of escape. But Winn suggests that it is the will of the Prophets that the plan continue, even if that means a sacrifice on Neela's part.

In the meantime, Sisko is pleasantly surprised when Bareil arrives at the station to help the commander "clean up" the situation. As Kira and Sisko escort Bareil through the Promenade, Dax and O'Brien find a mysterious subprogram in the computer that has created a series of forcefield overrides from the Promenade to Runabout Pad A—an escape route for someone. Other clues suggest that the weapon detectors on the Promenade have been disabled—by Neela.

Bareil and Winn address a throng of Bajorans outside the remains of the school, and Bareil counsels tolerance and acceptance of new ideas. After O'Brien alerts Sisko about the weapons detectors and his suspicions about his assistant, the commander spots Neela in the crowd with a phaser in her hand. He knocks her to the ground, causing her to miss her target: Bareil. Stunned, Kira realizes that all of Winn's activities were a ruse to bring Bareil to the station, where he could be assassinated before he became kai. But Neela insists that she acted alone, following the will of the Prophets. Later, a humbled Kira tells Sisko that she heard his earlier words to Winn and agrees with him, and Sisko happily observes that they've made some progress after all.

Guest appearances from distinguished stage and screen performers Philip Anglim (who originated the role of the Elephant Man on Broadway) and Louise Fletcher (winner of a Best Actress Oscar for *One Flew Over the Cuckoo's Nest*) highlight the first-season finale of *Deep Space Nine*, and set the stage for more political intrigue in the series' second season.

The explosion on the Promenade was an out-of-the-ordinary *live* fire effect. ROBBIE ROBINSON

a serious objection to people trying to impose their values on other people," states Wolfe. "And that's what this episode is about. No one has the right to force anyone to believe the things that they believe. That's one of the beautiful things about Gene Roddenberry's vision of IDIC (Infinite Diversity in Infinite Combinations), and that was one of the things that we really wanted to hammer home here. Sisko does everything he can not to impose his values on the Bajorans, but Vedek Winn is determined to impose her values on everyone."

The episode establishes the basis for much of what viewers have come to understand of the Bajoran political/religious system. Wolfe suspects that some of that came out of his Catholic upbringing but even more from his fondness for history. "The system isn't specifically Catholic as we think of Catholicism today," he observes. "It's fifteenth- and sixteenth-century Catholicism, when the pope held much more of a political office than now, and when the Medicis and the Borgias and the French kings and every other powerful family in southern Europe was fighting to get their guy to be pope."

The third of *Deep Space Nine*'s David Livingston–directed episodes, "In the Hands of the Prophets" once again shows the Livingston touch with its large crowd scenes. Explains Wolfe: "It was the last episode of the season, so we gave it a bigger budget, allowing David to be able to use more extras."

The larger budget also allowed Livingston to take the production on location for a day of filming at Fern Dell, a beautiful section of Hollywood's Griffith Park. "The series is designed budgetarily to have five or six location shoots per year," says Bob della Santina. "So we're very selective about the episodes, and rather than spend the money to go and just do something on location, we might prefer to build a small 'green' (as in foliage) set for one particular show and save the money for later on. And proximity is important, of course. Fern Dell is close to the studio, and it has a wonderful lush look to it."

"I had always thought it was a fabulous location," comments Livingston. "[Director] Corey Allen shot the first day of the pilot for *The Next Generation* there, and I wanted to go there for Bareil's sanctuary. Marvin Rush did a beautiful job of photographing it, and we added atmosphere and smoke to give it an ethereal quality."

Ethereal or not, Fern Dell isn't the easiest location for a director to work with. "It has a narrow path that restricts movement," points out della Santina. "That

The obvious quality of "Duet" led the writing team to struggle to top themselves in "Hands," according to Ira Behr. "All through 'Hands,' Michael Piller kept saying, 'It isn't good enough. It's got to be as good as 'Duet.' We've got to find more levels.' It was a challenge, and I think it is a terrific show. It gave us even more grist for the mill than 'Duet' did, and together they provided a great one-two punch to the end of the first season."

While it's easy to brand the tone of this episode "anti-fundamentalist," Writer Robert Hewitt Wolfe says the message is actually much simpler, and very much in keeping with Gene Roddenberry's philosophical mandate for *Star Trek* in all its various incarnations. "I have no argument with someone having a fundamentalist belief in Christianity or Islam or Judaism or Buddhism or anything else, but I do have

STATUE PANEL

STATUE PANEL IDEA
STAR TREK DS9
R DELGADO

01.92

This sketch by Ricardo Delgado was the basis for a statue used to dress Bareil's garden. Used many times over the seven years of production, its last appearance was in Kai Winn's residence in the final episode.

fireproof," says Gary Monak, who handles physical special effects on the series. "And then Odo and O'Brien come running in right after it blows up. It was already burning, and we had to do a big fireball explosion. We did that in full scale. That surprised them." But then, Monak and his crew had surprised the staff before. "On *Star Trek*, they're used to doing a lot of effects optically, and we're used to doing them live on camera. We'll be lighting a fire, and they're going, 'What are you doing? We don't do those. Is it safe?'" So Monak was prepared for the response when he set off the fireball. Still, Monak feels his fiery special effects, which are always carefully controlled, add something to the production. "It works better for the actors, because they can react to the effect."

Writer Wolfe gets the credit for at long last giving an official name to the peculiar Bajoran confection hawked on the station's Promenade. Long referred to by behind-the-scenes staffers as "glop-on-a-stick," Wolfe toyed with Yum Yum sticks and Jum Jum sticks before settling on the word *jumja*—which, as everyone knows, is made from the vitamin C–rich sap of the Bajoran *jumja* tree.

One aspect of the episode that Wolfe doesn't take credit for is Vedek Winn's peculiar headgear. Has he ever noticed that Winn's hat . . .

". . . Looks like the Sydney Opera House?" he concludes the query. "No, I didn't notice that." Following a burst of laughter, Wolfe notes that he is unsure as to whether or not the costume people intended Winn's hat to resemble the Australian landmark, but, he adds, "It *is* a cool-looking hat."

Costume Designer Robert Blackman is somewhat cryptic about the design. When asked if the resemblance to the opera house was intentional, subconscious, or a coincidence, Blackman responds, "Yes—to all of those," although he leans toward the coincidence factor. "You know, you're trying to come up with interesting and curious shapes that viewers haven't seen. It's about rhythm and other things. But I didn't sit down and say, 'Oh, the Sydney Opera House—let's make a hat out of it!'"

prohibits wider shots." What's more, the Fern Dell sequence was Livingston's first location shoot. "It was difficult," the director recalls. "But I got through it."

Also difficult—although for different reasons— was the explosion and subsequent fire in Keiko's school. "We had to drywall the entire Schoolroom, which has all these weird little corners that we had to

SECOND SEASON

O V E R V I E W

"**S**econd season was the end result of our own learning process," observes Executive Producer Michael Piller. "Every show has a shakedown cruise. That's just the way it is in television. And during the second season of *DS9*, we focused more clearly on what we felt was working for us: the stories we told and the characters we explored, and how the characters worked off one another."

"I think second season is where we found our stride," agrees Story Editor Robert Hewitt Wolfe. "Any success we have had in subsequent years was built on what we learned in the second season, with its successes and failures." Like Piller, Wolfe sees the contribution to the depth of the show's assorted characters as a highlight of the year. "We started to be comfortable with who the characters were," he notes, and that propelled many of the storylines.

Much of the credit for that goes to Piller, perennially an advocate for stories that spring from personality, rather than circumstance. "In all of my work, and the work that I try to inspire from the staff, you'll find that *character* is front and center," he says. "If you really write from the character's point of view, as opposed to the *writer's* point of view, it necessitates complex feelings about the action they're involved in. The way you make the crew accessible to the audience is to let them share those complex moments with the audience as they share them with the other characters on the show." Not only does that create compelling drama, Piller explains, but it also creates relationships that are "lasting and meaningful and that the audience can empathize with. That's a very critical part of the equation for me."

Piller's passion for shaping this character-driven drama occasionally triggered gripes from outside writers who saw their works transformed to that vision, but Piller is philosophical about such grousing. "The job of the head writer is basically misunderstood," he says. "A lot of rewriting goes on in the job. It was fundamentally my responsibility to make the scripts as good as they could be. You always hope there are staff members who can come up and really do the job and finish the scripts for you, because you can go crazy. That's really where we were in the second season. Ira [Steven Behr] and I were sort of going back and forth rewriting everybody's scripts."

In fact, the preproduction period was so fever-pitched that Behr—who ended first season as "supervising producer" and started season 2 as "co-executive producer"—didn't have any downtime. "I'd planned to spend two weeks in Santa Barbara with my family during the hiatus," he relates. "But after a week," he recalls, "Piller called me up from the office and said I had to come back to talk about the next season. I said **'What!?!'**" But back he went.

During the season, Behr would find himself turning to Wolfe as a sounding board for storylines with increasing frequency. Although they would not become the "Lennon and McCartney" of *Deep Space Nine*, as Behr—tongue-in-cheek—likes to put it, until the third season, the groundwork was laid here. For example, Behr provided uncredited input to Wolfe's script for "The Wire," while Wolfe performed a similar role in Behr's script for "The Jem'Hadar."

An increasing emphasis on character-driven storylines sat well with cast members, who enjoyed having their roles spotlighted in episodes such as The Circle trilogy, "Crossover" and "Necessary Evil" for Kira, "Melora" and "The Wire" for Bashir, and "Playing God" and "Blood Oath" for Dax. Quark's alter-ego, Armin Shimerman, was delighted to discover that Season 2 would establish him as quite "a ladies' man," with liaisons of one sort or another in "Rules of Acquisition" and "Profit and Loss" and numerous flirtations in between. "I believe Quark's had more relationships than anyone else on the show," Shimerman notes with pleasure.

Bashir, too, began to change, becoming a more action-oriented character (something Siddig El Fadil enjoyed), who was less infatuated with Dax, which allowed him to enjoy some midair smooching with Melora. He also began to establish the friendship with O'Brien that would be more fully played out in subsequent seasons, much to Writer Behr's satisfaction. "Some of the stuff I'm proudest of having done and being associated with is how we've taken Bashir and brought him so far in the episodes," he says. "His friendship with O'Brien is probably my favorite

relationship on the series right now. I love those two guys. They really care about each other, and in Season 1, nobody would have believed that could happen."

Season 2 also would introduce viewers to the first three "Let's torture O'Brien" episodes—"Armageddon Game," "Whispers," and "Tribunal"—a subgenre that would remain a perennial favorite of the writing staff.

Once again, Producer Peter Allan Fields would give Kira one of her best episodes, with "Necessary Evil." Writing for Nana Visitor, he explains, is no chore. "It's fun to write for somebody with depth, and from the beginning, I knew she had the talent." Still, knowing the character inside and out is different from knowing the actor playing the role. Fields had that point pressed home when he left his office to visit the *DS9* soundstage one hot day. Getting himself a Coca-Cola from the vending machine as he came inside the building, Fields spotted Visitor, whom he'd met before, relaxing in a chair between takes. "So I went up to reintroduce myself and said, 'Excuse me, Nana,' and she looked at the Coke and said, 'Oh, thank you so much'—very polite—and took my Coke and walked away. She wasn't being rude, she just had no idea who I was, and she was grateful that someone had thought to bring her a cold drink on a roasting hot day."

Fields might have forgotten about the encounter, which he thought was unobserved, if it hadn't been for a subsequent conversation with Rene Auberjonois, who chided Fields for not coming to the set more often—and then added, "By the way, the next time you *do* come down, I like *Diet* Coke."

By the second season, Auberjonois was "having a great time—I loved the character of Odo." But it was his love of the character that would lead him to ask Michael Piller to be a little more discerning in the use of the shape-shifter in various scenes. "I had a problem with episodes where I had almost nothing to do but where the writers felt obligated to use me," says Auberjonois. "It wasn't that I had nothing to do that disturbed me, because I'm getting paid anyway. But I was feeling like I hadn't had a full meal when I was seen in a show where there was no purpose in my presence."

Auberjonois left his feelings unvoiced until a scene in the second season's "The Collaborator" crystalized everything for him. "There was a tiny little scene where Odo makes a comment about humanoid behavior, and it got cut out of the script because the show was running long," he says. "I understood that, but I called Michael Piller to talk about it." Rather than doing the "usual actor thing" and trying to compel Piller to reinsert the scene, which was not his intention, Auberjonois pointed out that it was the kind of scene that the second season had been light on: scenes that provided Odo's unique perspective on humanoids, which are very much a raison d'être for his presence in the series. To Auberjonois's surprise, Piller agreed with him completely and had the scene put back in.

"For me, that was an important discovery, and I was particularly glad that my relationship with the writers and producers is such that I felt comfortable to go to them," reflects Auberjonois. "Because it's not in my nature to do that. I came out of regional repertory theater, and I always sort of assume that you take the parts you're cast in and play them to the best of your abilities."

Besides creating more character-driven stories, the mandate for the second season was to "establish bad guys in the Gamma Quadrant to give the Gamma Quadrant a face," recalls Wolfe. "We had meeting after meeting on what those guys would be like, before the word 'Dominion' was ever dropped into a script." Then, after the idea of the coalition of baddies was hammered out to everyone's satisfaction, "We sort of peppered mention of the Dominion into several episodes before we actually saw them," says Wolfe. "Basically, we were trying to build the idea that there was something big out there, something pretty tough."

Each mention illustrated a different way that the Dominion had an impact on society in the Gamma Quadrant, from the idea that if we wanted to trade in that area, we'd have to do business with this mysterious trading group ("Rules of Acquisition"), to the concept that the trading group had a military force that could come in and "kick butt" if necessary ("Sanctuary"), to the realization that the Dominion consisted of a complex society of cultural imperialists that were quite capable of taking over an entire world ("Shadowplay"). But the full details about the Dominion would not be revealed until the third season.

Besides plot-related changes, the second season also brought about some physical modifications to Deep Space 9, the most obvious of which was the addition of the second side of the Promenade, on the upper level of that set. "We never used to be able to have the characters go that way, because it didn't

physically exist," says Supervising Producer David Livingston. "[Production Designer] Herman Zimmerman had wanted to do it when we were building the permanent sets, but budget cuts made that one of the things we were forced to eliminate in the first season."

"It's the normal kind of teething pain that you have on any show," says Marvin Rush, who returned for a second year as director of photography. "You want set enhancements, so you make a laundry list: 'I'd like this and this and this . . .' in this case, reengineering that would make the walkways on top much wider and more efficient."

When the producers okayed the "laundry list" for the second season, Zimmerman had eighteen additional inches of space added to each side of the crossovers. "We initially had finished only the window side of the second level," says Zimmerman. "On the side with Quark's bar, there was just a blank wall. So we put a walkway over there and finished the entire area, with two turbolift entrances and two doorways to who-knows-where, and a second-level access to Quark's." The extra space, Zimmerman explains, allows directors to do "walk and talks" with two characters moving side-by-side.

Interestingly, by cutting down on the open space in the center of the Promenade—reducing it from fourteen feet to eleven feet to allow for the broadened walkways—the Promenade now appeared larger. "It's quite an illusion," Zimmerman says proudly. Viewers may not have noticed the expansion for the first few episodes of the season, which didn't focus heavily on action in the Promenade. But the change should have been apparent to all in "Rules of Acquisition," where a scene spotlights Zek seated at a cafe table in a spot on the Promenade where a few months earlier there had been neither table nor floor.

Additional set modification involved the creation of a new swing set and a Medical Lab; connected to the station's tiny Infirmary, which allowed producers to stage more complex scenes there, such as the symbiont transplant seen in "Invasive Procedures."

As is always the case in ongoing television production, there were comings and goings with the change of season. Hair Designer Josée Normand replaced the departing Candace Neal. Visual effects maven Rob Legato left to focus on motion pictures, ultimately receiving an Academy Award for *Titanic*. He was replaced by Visual Effects Producer Dan Curry, who had previously created the series' title sequence. Working with Curry as visual effects supervisors were Gary Hutzel and Glenn Neufeld. Each supervisor brings his own taste and distinctive sense of style to an episode. Thus, a battle sequence from one episode may look strikingly different from one in another. During the second season, Hutzel worked on the odd-numbered episodes with Visual Effects Coordinator Judy Elkins, while Neufeld worked on the even-numbered episodes with Coordinator David Takemura, who came over to *DS9* following *TNG's* sixth season, taking the place of Cari Thomas. Working as a series coordinator on even *and* odd episodes was Philip Barberio.

New to the credits roster, but not to the series, was Jim Martin, who had served as a production assistant in the Art Department during the first season. Known to all as "the incredibly prolific Jim Martin," because of his enthusiastic propensity for turning out more single pieces of art than anyone else in the department, he became the official illustrator after Ricardo Delgado chose to move on to features.

The end of the season found the Paramount *Star Trek* machine kicking into the highest gear ever. Gary Holland, Vice President of Advertising and Promotion for Paramount Domestic Television (and, coincidentally, cowriter of the teleplay for "The Collaborator"), recalls one week when "they were shooting 'Collaborator' on one soundstage, while doing scenes from 'Crossover' on another. On a third, they were shooting *Star Trek Generations* and on a fourth, they were wrapping up *The Next Generation*. At that point, you could just look around and go, 'It's amazing how much this engine drives the train of Paramount!'"

Deep Space Nine finished out the year with three Emmy nominations (as opposed to six the year before), for costume design ("Crossover"), hairstyling ("Armageddon Game"), and makeup ("Rules of Acquisition"). Unfortunately, like Casey at the bat, they struck out. But, as they say in Hollywood, it's the nomination that counts. And, as they say on Ferenginar, win or lose, there's always Hupyrian beetle snuff.

THE HOMECOMING
Episode #421

TELEPLAY BY **IRA STEVEN BEHR**
STORY BY **JERI TAYLOR AND IRA STEVEN BEHR**
DIRECTED BY **WINRICH KOLBE**

GUEST CAST

Li Nalas	RICHARD BEYMER
Rom	MAX GRODÉNCHIK
Borum	MICHAEL BELL
Gul Dukat	MARC ALAIMO
Freighter Captain	LESLIE BEVIS
Romah Doe	PAUL NAKAUCHI

UNCREDITED

Minister Jaro	FRANK LANGELLA

STARDATE UNKNOWN

When a Boslic freighter captain asks Quark to deliver an elaborate Bajoran earring to someone on the station "who'll know what to do with it," Quark knows exactly whom to contact. A short time later, the Ferengi barkeeper is at Major Kira's door, offering her the relic, which the freighter captain had brought back from Cardassia IV.

Recognizing the earring's significance, Kira goes to Commander Sisko and asks him for the loan of a runabout. The earring's design, she explains, is the insignia of Li Nalas, said to be Bajor's greatest resistance leader. The mysterious appearance of the earring obviously indicates that Li is not dead, as had long been rumored, and that he is being held as a prisoner of war on Cardassia IV.

Or at least, that's what Kira believes. Representatives of the provisional Bajoran government, whom Kira has already contacted, aren't so certain, and they definitely aren't willing to risk a war with Cardassia over an unfounded rescue mission. But Kira feels that Li could be the leader that her people, increasingly factionalized since the death of Kai Opaka, need to pull them together. Sisko agrees to consider her request for a runabout, but is soon sidetracked by a bigger problem. O'Brien and Odo have found disquieting signs that "The Circle," a Bajoran extremist group that wants to rid Bajor of all non-Bajorans, is gaining strength. With this fact in mind, and with some astute encouragement from Dax, Sisko agrees to let Kira have the runabout—if she agrees to take Chief O'Brien with her on her journey.

Traveling to a labor camp on Cardassia IV, the

Borum volunteers to stay behind while Kira gets Li Nalas away from the Hutet labor camp. ROBBIE ROBINSON

pair use Kira's feminine charms to get inside a prison forcefield and launch an attack against the guards. They find a somewhat bewildered Li, whose earring had been smuggled out by a friend who hoped to inspire just such a rescue, and make a valiant effort to extricate all of the Bajoran prisoners. Unfortunately, that proves to be impossible, and several of Li's compatriots, who comprehend his importance to Bajor, volunteer to stay behind and cover Li's escape.

Upon returning to the station, Kira immediately reports to Sisko, only to find him in midconversation with Gul Dukat. To Kira's amazement, Dukat is extending an apology on behalf of the Cardassian government for the existence of the Bajoran prison camp on Cardassia IV. Dukat assures her that all of the remaining prisoners will be released.

Neither Kira nor Sisko know what to make of this unusual behavior, but Sisko urges Kira to be grateful for the safe return of the Bajorans and congratulates her on the success of her mission. A short time later, Bajoran Minister Jaro also congratulates her, and welcomes Li Nalas home before an awestruck crowd on DS9's Promenade. Sisko notices that Li

seems uncomfortable with the reception, but, like everyone else, assumes that the hero is simply a humble man.

That night, Quark is attacked by three masked figures, who burn his skin with a branding device. While Dr. Bashir tends to Quark, Sisko, Kira, Odo, and Li discuss the assault. The mark the attackers left on Quark's forehead identifies them as members of The Circle. Li is aghast to hear that Bajorans would resort to such measures, and Sisko explains that The Circle is made up of people who have become impatient with the Bajoran government's inability to get anything done. What they need, adds Kira, is a strong leader who would speak out against extremist groups and unite the people. Li understands that Kira—and everyone else—considers him to be that leader.

A short while later, Sisko is alerted to the fact that Li Nalas has been caught trying to leave the station for the distant Gamma Quadrant. Alone with Sisko, Li reveals the tortuous truth. The bravery for which he is so renowned is the result of rumor and hyperbole. He was responsible only for killing an unarmed

Cardassian who was about to attack him. But the Cardassian turned out to be a vicious gul who had slaughtered many Bajorans, and Li's fellow resistance fighters somehow convinced themselves that Li had killed the gul in a "savage struggle." The story spread across Bajor and inspired equally outlandish tales about Li's courage, until his name grew to legendary status. The legend even followed him to the labor camp, where it became a source of inspiration to his fellow prisoners. Now Li hopes at last to escape the legend, because he is not the man Bajor thinks he is. But Sisko points out to him that Bajor does not need a man—it needs a symbol, and that's exactly what he is. He *is* the leader that Bajor needs, someone in whom the Bajoran people see the best of themselves.

It is hard to refute Sisko's logic. Li allows the Bajoran assembly to name him navarch, a brand-new title for whatever role he is to play in helping to determine the fate of his people. But no one at the station is prepared for Minister Jaro's subsequent announcement that Li will immediately replace Major Kira as the Bajoran Liaison Officer to Deep Space 9—and that Kira has been recalled to Bajor.

Inspired by the warm critical reception of the final two episodes of Season 1, Michael Piller directed the writing staff to focus on "the strength of the show" as they launched into Season 2. That meant letting go of the reassuring familiarities of the *TNG* universe and concentrating on the heart of what made *Deep Space Nine* unique. "We'd taken eighteen episodes and established the show, the concept, the franchise, and now it was time to dig deeper and see just how far we could go," says Ira Steven Behr. "So we decided to do a show that deals with Bajor, and the station, and the tenuous relationship between the Starfleet officers and this new environment they're living in: the station. We also thought it would be bold to do a three-hour show." Behr pauses to chuckle. "We're nothing if not bold—bold and stupid."

As the framework for their "bold" forage into the second season, Piller chose a Jeri Taylor storyline for *TNG* that he had snatched away from her the previous season. Recalls Taylor: "Michael saw it and said, 'You know, that's a much better story for *DS9* than *TNG*. I want it.' I said, 'You can't have it—it's *my* story. I need it for my series.'" But Taylor also understood the futility of arguing with one's boss and relinquished the story, only to see it sit, untouched, in the development pile during *DS9*'s entire first season. "So

Jeri Taylor saw Li as a reluctant hero; Ira Behr reshaped him into an unwarranted one. ROBBIE ROBINSON

I went to him and said, 'Michael, if you're not going to use that story, give it back.' And he said, 'No, no, no. It'll surface, I promise you.'"

Taylor's story initially focused on a Bajoran woman who was picked up by the *Starship Enterprise*. In later incarnations, that woman became Ensign Ro, although all versions contained the core idea of a Bajoran woman who "wanted to rescue the leader of the Bajoran resistance, someone who was held in deep respect by her people and who had been wasting away in a Cardassian prison," says Taylor. "When the woman finally burst in there and rescued him, he turned out to be someone who did not want to be a leader anymore, who really had wearied of all that. And somehow in the end, he became a hero once again."

Piller assigned the teleplay for part 1, "The Homecoming," to Behr. Peter Allan Fields would do the story and teleplay for part 2, "The Circle," while Piller himself would write the finale, "The Siege." The complex assignment required each of the three writers to be aware of what his two counterparts had in mind for their segments. "We broke the first two stories before I went off and wrote 'The Homecoming,'" recalls Behr. "But we broke the third one at the same time I was writing, so I'd run in, sit in the story meeting and then go back and write. We all knew what everyone else was doing."

There were several givens that were agreed upon at the very beginning: this was to be a show about the station being boarded, and Sisko and his officers forced to become guerilla fighters on their own station. It would delve deeply into Bajoran religion and politics, and include a lot of character development, relationships, and action. It would be, says Behr, "A nice canvas to begin the season, a nice way to say, 'Hey guys, look what we can do.'"

Behr's take on part 1 was to make Taylor's resistance leader less of a reluctant hero and more of a mistaken hero. "One of my favorite movies is *The Man Who Shot Liberty Valance,* and it deals with what happens when the hero really isn't a hero, but the legend is more important than the fact," says Behr. "That was the spin I wanted to put on it."

But even within that framework, "The Homecoming" certainly sets the tone the producers wanted for the season in terms of religion and politics, including a scene in the teaser that shows Kira worshipping before a personal Bajoran icon in her quarters. Although the spiritual realm is one that *Star Trek* has generally sidestepped in the past, Behr had no qualms about wading into potentially murky waters. "What I always say is, 'You do religion because you set people off,'" he says, with a wicked glint in his eyes. "That's the reason to do it. That's why writers are told *not* to do it, and that's why it's become tougher and tougher to do it on the series. That we did it at all was amazing, and I can't believe that no one [in the audience] seemed to notice. We were the only show on TV that consistently dealt with matters spiritual and no one seemed to care, which I find very strange."

Filming of "The Homecoming" began on July 7, 1993, in a working rock quarry at Soledad Canyon, north of Los Angeles. It was, by all accounts, one of the most hellacious location choices imaginable. The crew received plenty of advance warning about the hazards of the site, including notes on the call sheet that warned of extreme cold (in the early morning and evening hours), extreme heat (the rest of the time), bees, snakes, and unspecified bugs. Craft services personnel were advised to have on hand "tons of water and soda, rags, ice, and buckets of Sea Breeze," an astringent that takes the sting out of sunburn and bug bites.

Unit Production Manager Bob della Santina loved the "wonderful scope" of the site, and Director Winrich Kolbe appreciated its "total desolation." The first impulse, Kolbe admits, had been to ". . . go to Bronson Canyon, but that damn place has been shot so often, there's not a square inch that hasn't been filmed by somebody."

Nevertheless, the actors would have preferred to

risk the visual cliché of Bronson. "Soledad was brutal," recalls Colm Meaney. "The first day back in the second season, and you're slowly trickling back into it and then—boom—you're out there in this blazing heat, with no cover or vegetation anywhere. It was a very long day and by the end of it, we had been burned and blistered. For someone like me, with my background—well, I wasn't built for those conditions."

Concurs Nana Visitor: "Colm and I were sick to our stomachs. We were seriously wondering if we were going into heat prostration. It was the perfect location for Cardassia IV, because it was like hell."

Unfortunately for the cast, the producers liked the look of the location and would send them back to hell several more times over subsequent seasons ("The Ship," "Rocks and Shoals").

Although the visual effects producer's job often keeps him locked safely indoors, Dan Curry ventured into hell as well. It was "incredibly hot—unbearable,"

In what was to become a recurring nightmare, Colm Meaney and Nana Visitor face the hellish conditions of location shooting on *DS9*.
ROBBIE ROBINSON

he observes. Checking out the site firsthand allowed Curry to note the limitations of the quarry itself for the visuals he was required to produce, so he got the effects team working on a matte painting and miniatures that would create the illusion of the Cardassian settlement at Hutet.

Jim Martin's first assignment as junior illustrator was to design the Cardassian field control unit, a device that would deactivate the forcefield surrounding the Hutet labor camp. "I was really fired up, because this was the first prop that I was going to officially draw for the show," Martin says. He got what the producers wanted on his second pass, after receiving the comment that his first version looked like a garage door opener. "That broke me in," he laughs. "That's what it's about. You draw and draw until you nail what it is they're looking for."

Although David Livingston's job typically was to "make sure that all the production elements are in line and that we can make the budget that's been allotted for the episode," money wasn't as much of a concern as usual. "Everybody knew that we were going to spend some money on the first half-dozen shows, and we did go considerably over-pattern," he says. "But we wanted to come out of the box swinging, with really heavy production shows. We planned to make it up later on, and, in fact, I was one of the guys who had to direct the later shows when there wasn't any money left."

The casting for the episode, everyone agrees, was a godsend. "A terrific cast," enthuses Behr. "Frank Langella, Richard Beymer, and Louise Fletcher. They were a lot of fun to write for. Seeing Fletcher and Langella together was great."

Kolbe concurs, "Between the two of them, nothing could go wrong. We were bound for glory."

Langella's uncredited appearance was apparently a matter of the actor's own volition. "He wanted to do the show," says Kolbe. "He did it for his children, because they loved the show. It was not done for money or exposure."

Quark's new status as a ladies' man was established right in the teaser, where his relationship with the sexy Boslic captain hints at a great deal of sensual subtext. Even Kolbe's choice of the establishing camera angle on her entrance—positioned from Quark's point of view, gazing up the length of her body as she pauses on the stairwell—lets viewers know right away that this is a warm-blooded alien female. The casting of the captain gave amusing resonance to her beverage of choice. "We chose the name Black Hole because it just sounded like this mysterious drink," says Behr. "But we didn't know the Captain would be that sexy. She brought a whole different level to it!"

THE CIRCLE

Episode #422

WRITTEN BY PETER ALLAN FIELDS
DIRECTED BY COREY ALLEN

GUEST CAST

Li Nalas	RICHARD BEYMER
Krim	STEPHEN MACHT
Admiral Chekote	BRUCE GRAY
Zef'No	MIKE GENOVESE
Peace officer	ERIC SERVER
Cardassian	ANTHONY GUIDERA
Vedek Bareil	PHILIP ANGLIM

SPECIAL GUEST STAR

Vedek Winn	LOUISE FLETCHER

UNCREDITED

Minister Jaro	FRANK LANGELLA

STARDATE UNKNOWN

When Commander Sisko angrily confronts Jaro about the decision to send Kira back to Bajor, the Bajoran minister expresses his surprise, noting that it's no secret Kira's presence on the station has been troublesome for Sisko. Sisko denies the allegation and defends Kira, but it is his turn to be surprised when Jaro informs him that Kira's removal will mean a promotion for her, as thanks for rescuing Li Nalas. Jaro further placates Sisko by explaining that Li will be safer on the station than in Bajor's volatile capital. A short time later, Sisko is unpleasantly reminded of the planetside violence when he discovers The Circle's graffito insignia on the door to his quarters.

As Kira sadly packs for her departure, she is interrupted by the nonstop arrival of her friends from the station. Amid the confusion of several different conversations all taking place at once, Odo encourages her to fight for her job, but Kira is resigned to her fate. And when Vedek Bareil arrives with an invitation to spend some time at his monastery, Kira is delighted to accept. Before she departs, however, Sisko promises that he will fight to have her reinstated.

Vedek Winn allows her feelings for Minister Jaro and her desire for power to lead her astray, foreshadowing her ultimate fall from grace.
ROBBIE ROBINSON

At the monastery, Kira finds it difficult to occupy herself with "useless" pastimes. Nor is she sure of how to deal with her growing attraction to Bareil, which she senses is mutual. After an encounter in the temple garden, the young vedek leads Kira into a chamber within the monastery and shows Kira the Orb of Prophecy and Change. Left alone with the sacred relic, Kira experiences a vision. She finds herself in the Bajoran Chamber of Ministers, along with Dax, Vedek Winn, Jaro, and Bareil. The room appears to be in chaos, and Dax urges her to listen to the babel of legislators' voices. As she tries to comprehend them, Kira realizes she is naked, as is Bareil, who embraces and kisses her. The vision ends abruptly, leaving Kira both bewildered and intrigued.

On the station, Odo learns that the insurrection on Bajor is becoming more and more serious. According to Quark, The Circle is receiving weapons and explosives from the Kressari. Odo decides to investigate the Kressari, while Sisko goes to Bajor to discern whether or not Bajor's military will support the radical Circle movement over the planet's Federation-friendly provisional government. But the general with whom he meets—Krim—seems undecided. Before he returns to the station, Sisko visits Kira at the temple and warns her about the impending coup. A short time after he leaves, Kira is drugged and kidnapped by three masked men.

Odo's investigation leads to an odd discovery; the arms that the Kressari are supplying to The Circle are coming from the Cardassians! At the same time, Kira makes an equally shocking discovery: She has been kidnapped by Jaro, who is the power behind The Circle. Jaro believes that his efforts will unite Bajor with the power and strength it needs to survive, although first he must get rid of the Federation's presence. When Kira refuses to give him information about Sisko's plans, Jaro has her beaten.

Back at the station, Quark announces that he has discovered where The Circle's headquarters is. Sisko takes a small team to the location and rescues Kira. Odo reveals to Sisko and the others what he has discovered, and the group quickly discerns that the Cardassians are supplying the arms so that The Circle's coup will get rid of the Federation. And with the Federation gone, the Cardassians will be able to retake Bajor for themselves. On Bajor, unaware that he is a pawn in a larger scheme, Jaro congratulates Winn on their impending success, which is surely the first step toward her becoming the new kai.

Sisko attempts to put Li Nalas in touch with Bajor's Council of Ministers to tell them the truth, but communications with the planet have been severed. Contacting Starfleet, Sisko briefs Admiral Chekote on the situation. With a revolution about to begin and assault ships from Bajor headed toward DS9, the admiral orders Sisko to evacuate immediately. But Sisko has something a little different in mind.

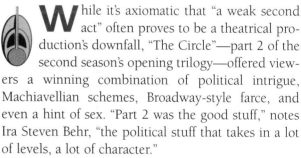**W**hile it's axiomatic that "a weak second act" often proves to be a theatrical production's downfall, "The Circle"—part 2 of the second season's opening trilogy—offered viewers a winning combination of political intrigue, Machiavellian schemes, Broadway-style farce, and even a hint of sex. "Part 2 was the good stuff," notes Ira Steven Behr, "the political stuff that takes in a lot of levels, a lot of character."

Writer Peter Allan Fields enjoyed participating in the endeavor, although he admits it wasn't easy. "We wrote them all at once," he says. "So whatever Ira put in his episode ("The Homecoming"), I would have to justify. I couldn't write an episode that was in diametric opposition to his." Nor could he alter a character's personality in midstream. "I had some trouble with Li Nalas. Originally he was supposed to be this regular guy, not a coward, but a regular guy who had fought some battles. And then by the time we got to the third episode ("The Siege"), this guy would stand up and be counted. But for various reasons, he never really changed his tune. He was an okay guy in part

Philip Anglim's portrayal of Bareil created an instantly memorable character. ROBBIE ROBINSON

1, part 2, and part 3. There was no arc in the character whatsoever."

Behr admits that Li's character was one element that was never used to its full advantage in the trilogy. "He did get a little lost in parts 2 and 3," he says. "Maybe if there had been one guiding hand through all three shows, his story would have paid off as well as I'd hoped [in providing the initial setup]."

But if there was no growth in Li's character, there certainly was growth in the relationship between Kira and Bareil, which pleased Fields, a fan of the Kira character since he began writing for the series.

Director Corey Allen also liked the strong Kira-focus of the episode. "Putting an actress as good as Nana Visitor together with Philip Anglim is a director's dream," he says. In fact, Visitor, Anglim, and several other members of the cast actually did contribute to one of the high points of Allen's career as a director.

"The opening section of Act 1 was one scene with seven people in it," recalls Allen. The scene—which Fields confesses to having based on the classic filled-to-capacity-and-then-some stateroom scene from the Marx Brothers' *A Night at the Opera*—"had all the cast coming by to say good-bye to Kira, with Philip Anglim coming in as the [visual] punchline," says Allen. In addition to putting the cast through lunchtime rehearsals, Allen notes that he stayed up until 1:00 A.M. the night before the scene was to be shot, prepping. "In the morning, we got the cast together while Marvin Rush was lighting the set and gave Marvin a run-through to let him see what the moves were," Allen says. "Then they went off and rehearsed it like the stage people that most of them are. I watched these marvelous actors take that thing and mold it into a scene with flashing hues and wonderful blocking, enjoying themselves and each other. Then we had one run-through on the lit set and filmed the whole thing in one take!"

Of course, that didn't mean that shooting was over for the day. Because *Deep Space Nine* isn't *Playhouse 90*, Allen was required to shoot the more traditional "coverage" that viewers who've experienced only post–"Golden Age" television have come to expect: assorted close-ups of characters' faces, reverse angles, and so on. If Allen had had the final say, which a television director seldom does, "I'd have broadcast the one-shot scene."

Still, he has his own private reward. "I asked for a

copy of the straight-through performance, because I'd never had the chance to do that in episodic television before," he says. "It was a marvelous experience."

Allen also enjoyed directing the Orb sequence. "It was terribly sexy," he says. "Dream sequences are always fun, because you can just go wild with your imagination." Allen recalls both Nana Visitor and Rick Berman being concerned with ". . . just how much bare flesh there would be."

And, in fact, while the aired version of the episode fades out as Kira and Bareil are about to kiss, Allen had filmed "a very hot and heavy kiss that was pretty torrid," according to Writer Fields. "You couldn't see below Kira's shoulders, but they were supposed to be naked and it was probably a little too on the nose. The producers wanted to maintain a little mystery about the relationship, and once you handed the characters that hot kiss, the mystery would be gone."

Considering the direction that the relationship between Kira and Bareil ultimately took, it's a good thing that Robert Hewitt Wolfe had revised his original concept of the vedek in "In the Hands of the Prophets." "When I created Bareil in that script, I saw him as a wise old guy, sort of a Gandhi figure. And Michael Piller said, 'No, he should be young and vigorous.' I think he always saw Bareil as a romantic hero, so the relationship with Kira was more his idea than mine."

Kira's recreational garb in the episode, and also her outfit from the mission to the Hutet labor camp in "The Homecoming," represent a deliberate shift in Bajoran costuming ennacted by Costume Designer Robert Blackman. "The color palette remained the same, the rust, green, and gold earth tones, but the textures changed," explains Blackman. "During the first season, the clothes on background Bajorans were flat-finished," a reflection of what the producers liked at that time. But as the show moved into its second season, says Blackman, "they felt that the clothing needed to have a rougher texture, that the wardrobe looked too sleek, like something you'd see at the Sherman Oaks Galleria"—a place made notorious in the 1980s by Frank Zappa's satirical song "Valley Girl." Thus, Blackman chose to use loose knits, crochets, and "things over things" for Kira's off-duty clothes, "so that you would get a kind of buildup of texture on a Bajoran background."

Blackman notes that the shift in costume design had synergy with changes in the look of the station's Promenade. "It became more bazaarlike, with ban-

The new textured, more naturalistic look of the Bajoran wardrobe plays well off of the familiar Starfleet uniform. ROBBIE ROBINSON

ners and more neon. It had been too utilitarian, too perfect."

In idyllic contrast to "The Homecoming"'s location shoot at the hellish rock quarry in Soledad, "The Circle" returned to Griffith Park's lovely Fern Dell section for the scenes in the temple gardens, previously seen in "In the Hands of the Prophets." "It's perfect for the monastery scenes, with that brook running through it—visually anyway," says Bob della Santina. "But soundwise, it's a disaster, so we ended up having to loop a lot of dialogue later on."

A visual effects sequence that must have looked simple on the page proved troublesome to Glenn Neufeld's team when just about anything that could go wrong did. The scene, which appears in Act 3, has Odo morph from the label of a cargo container into a rat that scuttles off to "investigate" the Kressari vessel. Among the problems were some carefully choreographed staging for the effects that failed to match up with previously shot footage, a variety of matte difficulties—furry animals like rats don't work particularly well when composited against greenscreen—and lighting mismatches between the various elements of the composite. If that wasn't enough to worry about, there's always the perennial difficulty of trying to direct temperamental rats. "You have to get it on the first or second take," observes Neufeld. "Because by the third, the rat is no longer hungry for peanut butter, and you can't make it do anything."

THE SIEGE
Episode #423
WRITTEN BY MICHAEL PILLER
DIRECTED BY WINRICH KOLBE

GUEST CAST

Keiko O'Brien	ROSALIND CHAO
Colonel Day	STEVEN WEBER
Li Nalas	RICHARD BEYMER
Krim	STEPHEN MACHT
Rom	MAX GRODÉNCHIK
Nog	ARON EISENBERG
Bajoran Officer	KATRINA CARLSON
Molly O'Brien	HANA HATAE
Vedek Bareil	PHILIP ANGLIM

SPECIAL GUEST STAR

Vedek Winn	LOUISE FLETCHER

UNCREDITED

Minister Jaro	FRANK LANGELLA

STARDATE UNKNOWN

Kira experiences a flash of déjà vu as she and Dax storm the Chamber of Ministers to reveal the truth about Jaro's scheme. ROBBIE ROBINSON

With less than five hours remaining before the Bajoran forces are due to arrive, Sisko evacuates Deep Space 9 of civilians and nonessential personnel. However, he has elected to remain behind to delay the station takeover and is pleased when his officers and Li Nalas choose to stay with him. Since all communications to Bajor are still jammed, Kira reasons that someone will have to go to the Chamber of Ministers to reveal the Cardassians' involvement in The Circle. With the runabouts tied up transporting evacuees, Kira and Dax arrange a ride to Bajor's Lunar V base, where several old subimpulse vessels have been hidden since the Cardassian Occupation.

When the Bajoran troops, led by Colonel Day and Over-General Krim, arrive at the station, it appears to be deserted, although Krim knows that appearances can be deceiving. He notes that the station's internal security net has been sabotaged, effectively preventing them from tracking the movements of anyone on board, which could mean that Starfleet has left a contingent behind. While Day and Krim argue about strategy, Sisko and his hidden teams prepare their own strategy and soon capture a small search party of Bajoran soldiers.

On Lunar V, Kira and Dax manage to get a dilapidated raider up and running, but their signal is intercepted by two more powerful Bajoran vessels. Kira takes her vessel into Bajor's atmosphere, hoping to outmaneuver the bigger ships, but the raider is disabled, and the women are forced to make a crash landing on the planet's surface.

Sisko lures Day into a holosuite, where the Bajoran finds himself trying to disarm holographic images. Sisko quickly seals the holosuite door and speaks to Day over the comm system, briefing him on the Cardassian plot. But Day doesn't believe it, and after Sisko releases him, he declines to pass Sisko's information on to Krim. Instead, he and Krim intensify the search for Sisko.

Knowing they may not have much time left before the Bajorans find them, Sisko appeals to a frightened Li Nalas, asking him to be the man that his people think he is. A short time later, Bashir creates a diversion, drawing away Day and providing O'Brien, Li, and Sisko with access to Krim.

On Bajor, Kira and Dax have survived the crash, but Kira is badly wounded and the two are quickly discovered—fortunately for them, by Bajorans from Bareil's monastery. Bareil helps to disguise them in religious garb, and they head for the Chamber of Ministers.

Interrupting the gathering of legislators, Kira finds herself in the midst of a chaotic scene very similar to the Orb vision she experienced days earlier. Although Jaro immediately attempts to have her arrested, Kira realizes that this will be her only opportunity to make the ministers listen. She hastily presents her evidence of the Cardassian plot that Jaro unwittingly helped to facilitate, and Vedek Winn, knowing that Jaro is finished, sides with Kira and the other ministers against her former ally.

On the station, Krim confronts Day about neglecting to brief him about Sisko's comments. Day protests that Sisko's words were lies, but Krim has received affirmation from Bajor. Noting that Bajor's provisional government has prevailed, Krim prepares to return command of Deep Space 9 to Starfleet. But Day refuses to accept the turnabout. Pulling out his phaser, he fires at Sisko but Li, reacting quickly, leaps into the path of the beam. Mortally wounded, Li expresses relief that he is "off the hook" at last. But Sisko knows that Li always will be remembered by his people as a hero, a role that, sadly, was more comfortable for him in death than in life.

W hile Ira Behr liked to refer to part 1 of the "Circle" trilogy as *The Man Who Shot Liberty Valance*, Michael Piller's action-packed conclusion was known among the staff as *The Alamo*, although the resolution of the story was much more upbeat than that historical epic. For one thing, most of the protagonists survived—with the exception of one key player.

"From the beginning [of plotting out the three episodes], we felt that we knew what the ending was going to be," says Behr, "although there was some disagreement about whether or not the character of Li Nalas would survive."

Ironically, though it was Piller who wrote "The Siege," the decision was ultimately made by Behr. Both Peter Allan Fields and Piller would have liked to see the character survive and possibly return in future episodes. "It seemed to me that killing him would just send us back to square one," states Fields. "Why go through three episodes with this guy, and then let him die? You're back as if he'd never been around. We could have written the whole thing without him."

But Behr had his reasons at the time. "I just felt that this was a man who was living a lie, and at the end there needed to be a form of redemption, one that involved some self-sacrifice," he says. "The character was so impotent in certain ways, so out of his depth, and so clearly miserable as this figurehead. I think death really was, at that point, a blessing for him."

A hero by happenstance who was undermined by the constraints of scheduling conflicts, deadlines, and budgets. ROBBIE ROBINSON

Then, too, as co-executive producer, Behr had practical matters to be concerned with. From a production standpoint, "We didn't know how easy it would be to get Richard Beymer back for however many times we would need him, or how much he would cost those times. That was an issue as well," he notes.

"Foolishly or not foolishly, it was my decision," says Behr, and he admits that it did leave the writers looking for a character who could fulfill a similar role on the series. "We were still looking for that character, oddly enough, in the fourth season," he says, which is why they decided to see if the character of Shakaar, introduced during the third season, could fill the shoes left behind by Li Nalas. He could, for a time. But eventually the producers would dispense with Shakaar as well. With the Dominion War in full swing by that time, there seemed little need for a man to unite and lead the Bajoran people toward a common goal.

Winrich Kolbe, who had directed "The Homecoming," returned to head the third part of the trilogy. On a dramatic level, he feels that "The Siege" suffers in comparison with the earlier episode. "'The Siege' was very action-oriented, with a lot of shooting and running and jumping," he says, "and what I remember most is that it took an awful lot of time to get it together. It really appeared to me at times almost like, 'Well, we've got two-and-a-half hours here—let's make it three.'"

For Nana Visitor, who carried the brunt of the scenes from all three hours on her shoulders, a two-and-a-half—or even two—hour epic might have been preferable. The hardest task she faces in the series,

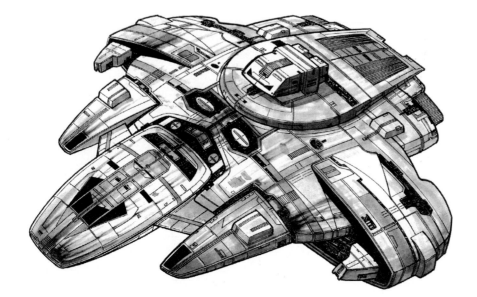

A concept sketch of a Bajoran impulse fighter. The realized ship was radically different, and a few years later, another starship would echo some of these lines.
JIM MARTIN

she says, "is maintaining the level of work I want to do in the twentieth hour of a day. It's very long hours, and if I do three shows back to back that are heavy on my character, it can feel like some kind of marathon." Thus, Visitor notes that she approached the assignment "like an athlete, thinking, 'How do I get through this and keep up the level of work?'"

Dan Curry enjoyed the challenges of presenting the in-atmosphere fight over Bajor. The sequence, orchestrated by Gary Hutzel's team, incorporated a matte painting of Bajor done by Illusion Arts's Syd Dutton with motion-controlled ship models. Astute viewers may note that both the little Bajoran fighter Kira is flying and the Bajoran pursuit ships cast shadows over the hillsides as they pass. "Gary took the ship matte, slid it over, and ran it inside a matte for the shadow," explains Curry, who points out that getting the backgrounds and the motion-controlled ships to work properly together was a painstaking job.

Similar care was taken in the sequence where the Bajoran assault vessels dock at DS9. "One of the things that makes motion control difficult when we have more than one ship in a scene is that no two ships are in scale with each other," says Curry. "So if you have a six-foot diameter model of Deep Space 9, and you have an eighteen-inch model of a ship, you have to keep in mind that in scale with the model, that ship should really be an inch and a half long. So you have to calculate the difference in the camera moves, and sometimes because of the limitations of how far the camera can move on its rig, you can't do the shot." Thus, says Curry, scale limitations on a two-ship shot sometimes can drive what viewers ultimately end up seeing.

The Bajoran moon spider, a *palukoo*, was built by Joe Sasgen.
ROBBIE ROBINSON

While Curry admits that going to computer animation would have eliminated some of those problems, the primary commitment on the series for most of its run was to miniatures. But eventually, the effects team would yield to the inevitable, with Season 7 finding them working almost exclusively with computer graphic imaging.

Kira's antique fighter and the Bajoran pursuit ships, all designed by Jim Martin and built by Tony Meininger, would very shortly find their way into the seventh-season *Next Generation* episode "Preemptive Strike." And *Wings* star Steven Weber joins the list of Paramount television series regulars (Bebe Neuwirth, Kelsey Grammer, Brian Bonsall) who've appeared in various incarnations of *Star Trek*. The usually likable Weber appeared in an unsympathetic role as Colonel Day, the sore loser who ultimately dispatches Li Nalas.

INVASIVE PROCEDURES

Episode #424

TELEPLAY BY **JOHN WHELPLEY AND ROBERT HEWITT WOLFE**
STORY BY **JOHN WHELPLEY**
DIRECTED BY **LES LANDAU**

GUEST CAST

Verad	JOHN GLOVER
Mareel	MEGAN GALLAGHER
T'Kar	TIM RUSS
Yeto	STEVE RANKIN

STARDATE 47182.1

When a violent plasma disruption hits the Denorios Belt, Deep Space 9 is temporarily evacuated, leaving behind only a skeleton crew to maintain the station. As O'Brien and Odo move through the station, sealing off airlocks, they find Quark hiding in one on the docking ring. Although Odo finds Quark's presence suspicious, he can't pin anything on the Ferengi . . . yet. A short time later, the station picks up a distress signal from a damaged cargo ship, and Dax uses a tractor beam to direct the vessel to the docking ring. Odo and O'Brien offer assistance to the crew, a humanoid female named Mareel, Klingon mercenaries T'Kar and Yeto, and a nervous male Trill named Verad, but find themselves greeted with weapons. At phaser point, Odo is forced to assume liquid form and to pour himself into a small box.

The group makes O'Brien take them to the Infirmary, where Bashir is ordered to put the box into a stasis chamber. The next destination is Ops, where the mercenaries take the rest of the crew hostage and disable the station's systems. Noting that the group had to neutralize the security grid in the docking ring in order to bring their weapons aboard, O'Brien deduces that Quark is involved in the situation. In the meantime, Quark discovers that what he had expected to be a harmless, though profitable, transaction for liquid data chains is something else entirely. The group has used him to gain access to the station and their true goal: Jadzia's symbiont, which Verad intends to make his own.

If the Dax symbiont is removed from Jadzia, Bashir points out, she will die in a very short time. But Verad says he has no choice. He spent his whole

Bashir is distraught when Verad forces him to remove the Dax symbiont from Jadzia. ROBBIE ROBINSON

life trying to qualify for symbiosis, only to be deemed "unsuitable." Once the symbiont has been removed from Jadzia and implanted in him, he plans to escape through the wormhole into the Gamma Quadrant. Jadzia attempts to reason with Verad to no avail, and Bashir refuses to assist in the procedure. Verad fires his weapon at O'Brien, injuring him, and states that he is prepared to kill the entire crew if Jadzia refuses to give up Dax. Resigned to her fate, Jadzia agrees, and convinces a reluctant Bashir to cooperate.

As Bashir performs the transplant, Sisko and Kira engage in a desperate attempt to retake Ops, but are quickly defeated. When Mareel attempts to explain her devotion to Verad, Sisko warns her that after the surgery, the man she cares for so deeply will be a different person: a blending of Verad, Dax, and all of Dax's previous hosts. Mareel declares that she always will love Verad—just as Verad Dax enters Ops.

Sisko engages the new Dax in conversation, reminiscing about good times he's shared with both Curzon and Jadzia. Then he appeals to Verad to save Jadzia's life by returning the symbiont, but Verad refuses. Sisko angrily tells him their friendship is over; Verad is not the Dax he knows.

But he is not the Verad that Mareel knows either, and Sisko tries to get her to admit to herself how much he has changed. In the meantime, Quark attempts to help his friends by attacking T'Kar, but he is overcome immediately and sent to the Infirmary with an injured ear.

As Verad Dax and Mareel finalize their escape plans, Mareel begins to believe that Sisko is right, and that Verad will not be meeting her at their rendezvous point. In the Infirmary, Bashir and Quark, who was feigning his injury, overcome their Klingon guard and release Odo from stasis. In Ops, after unsuccessfully attempting to contact Yeto, Verad realizes that Odo must be loose. He decides to leave immediately with T'Kar and takes Kira with him as a hostage.

Alone with Mareel, Sisko finds that it doesn't take much to convince her that by saving Jadzia's life, she will also get back the Verad she loves. Meanwhile, at the docking ring, Verad finds that Odo has released the clamps that had connected his ship to the station. A struggle ensues between Kira, T'Kar, and Odo, while Verad heads for a runabout airlock. There he encounters Sisko, armed with Mareel's phaser. Verad refuses to believe that Sisko would fire at him and risk harming Dax. But knowing that the alternative is Jadzia's imminent death, Sisko fires, dropping Verad in his tracks.

Soon after, Verad awakens in the Infirmary, and is inconsolable over the loss of the symbiont. And although Jadzia Dax has recovered completely, she can't help sharing some of Verad's pain. His memories and feelings will always be a part of her.

This episode presents viewers with another glimpse into the "Everything You Always Wanted to Know About Trills" handbook that pops into existence only when a script calls for previously unestablished information about the curious species. "We usually don't create more backstory for a character than is necessary for a show," explains Robert Hewitt Wolfe, who shares teleplay credit with John Whelpley for the episode; Whelpley also received story credit. "In this case, it was important to establish how difficult it was to get a symbiont. It said something about both Dax and the Trill culture that was interesting. If everybody was able to have one of these things, then Jadzia wasn't anything special. But the fact that she was one of the few people who qualified for it made her unique, in the same way that Spock was unique [on the original series]."

Of course, this was prior to the third-season

Avery Brooks's physical presence makes his realization of Ben Sisko a force to be reckoned with. CARIN BAER

episode "Equilibrium," which would reveal that it isn't as difficult to qualify for a symbiont as the Trill populace has been led to believe. But, as Ira Steven Behr points out, that's one of the relatively minor drawbacks of making it up as you go along. "It's dangerous but fun," he quips. "The whole Trill concept is very difficult, but 'Invasive Procedures' dealt very successfully with it, and it's one of my favorite episodes."

"Making it up as you go along" also applies to the look of the symbiont, which has evolved since its introduction in the *TNG* episode "The Host." At that time, says Makeup Department Head Michael Westmore, the symbiont looked something like a caterpillar "and there was a bladder inside of it that could be expanded and allow it to move a little." However, for *DS9*, the producers wanted a new look, "so we streamlined it and made it look more like a microbe, something you'd see under a high-powered microscope," he says. Westmore's team also made it pointed on one end "because it's a burrowing type of creature that has to be able to slide in and out," and gave it some small legs to propel itself. And for an extra touch of realism in "Invasive Procedures," Westmore inserted a mechanism from a gag item, a vibrating pencil that he found at Toys "R" Us, to make the Dax symbiont move around during the transfer sequence. The pouch that the symbiont crawls in and out of is a simple latex sheet that is glued to the actor's stomach.

As with a number of other episodes, the genesis for "Invasive Procedures" was a directive from Michael Piller. "It started out with Mike saying, 'Is there a way we can do *Key Largo*, with a bunch of people stuck in a closed-off environment because of the weather?'" recalls Behr. The writers rose to the challenge, even to the point of creating the *DS9* equivalent of bad weather: "a violent plasma disruption in the Denorios Belt."

Glenn Neufeld and David Takemura created the plasma storm by pouring liquid nitrogen onto flats of black velvet, producing a swirling pattern. Since the nitrogen dissipates rapidly when exposed to air, "We shot it at the highest speed we could on the motion-control rigs at Image G," says Takemura. The team then layered the various takes in a compositing bay.

The episode provided meaty roles for noted character actor John Glover and the other guest stars, among them Megan Gallagher, who would return for "Little Green Men" in the fourth season, and actor Tim Russ, whose face, sans Klingon makeup, would

John Glover, known for many a quirky turn on stage and screen, made Verad a "heavy" viewers could *almost* sympathize with. CARIN BAER

soon become familiar to *Star Trek* viewers. Russ was already well acquainted with the *Star Trek* universe. He had auditioned for the role of Geordi La Forge when *TNG* was being launched and later appeared as a villain in that series' sixth-season episode, "Starship Mine." But the best on *DS9* was to come after his turn as the Klingon mercenary T'Kar. Following a brief appearance as a crewman aboard the *Enterprise*-B in *Star Trek Generations*, Russ was cast as the Vulcan Tuvok on the third *Star Trek* spin-off series, *Star Trek: Voyager*. While his track record seems to indicate that there was a master plan in place, Russ humbly suggests that it was pure serendipity. "Rick Berman liked me," he says. "That's all there is to it. This business is so precarious—ten guys come in and read the hell out of a part, and the producers may like only one of them, and who knows what their reason is? The scenes I originally read for the *TNG* pilot were subtle, quiet scenes, nothing that gave me a chance to really get up and do some fireworks. But apparently there was just something about it that Rick liked."

The extraordinary circumstances set up by the storyline also gave regular cast members the opportunity to stretch the parameters of their weekly characterizations. "If this were a Howard Hawks movie, everybody would get the opportunity to do something cool," says Wolfe. "So we thought, 'Let's give everyone a chance to shine, the bad guys and the good guys. Everyone gets his cool moment.'" For the first time, Bashir demonstrates genuine affection for Jadzia. At the same time, Sisko embodies the powerful physical presence previously hinted at in "Dramatis Personae." "Sisko is a very formidable fighter," says Wolfe. "In many ways he's more convincing physically than either Patrick Stewart or William Shatner."

Some characters display previously undisclosed weaknesses, and others reveal outright flaws. The episode gave Terry Farrell her first chance to play Jadzia sans Dax's influence. "I approached [the scenes in the Infirmary] with the idea that Jadzia is scared, that she feels helpless," recalls Farrell. "She cares very deeply for everyone on the station and is afraid for them. That's why she's willing to say, 'Fine, I'll give my life for everybody, and you can have Dax.' But that had been while the strength of Dax was inside of her, telling her that everything was going to be okay. Once the worm is gone, she's only twenty-eight years old, and it's like, 'Wait, I haven't lived that much life yet.'"

In the meantime, Quark commits some unforgivable sins that weigh heavily on his alter ego's conscience. "I'm a little nervous about the fact that Quark has done some things that are truly punishable, this being one of them," says Armin Shimerman. "His allowing the takeover of the station is very close to treason. And although he helps rescue them at the end, he still initiated that takeover. I worry when Quark doesn't get punished for really sizable crimes. It makes the character less important [since his acts trigger no consequence], and it makes Odo look a little foolish, in that he's the law keeper and he can't get this little troll punished."

But while Quark may not have received his legal comeuppance, he didn't exactly receive a pardon, and never will if Kira has anything to say about it. "Nana Visitor and I had asked the writers to really beef up the conflict between our characters, and in this episode she had a wonderful speech where she told Quark that he had crossed the line, and that she would never treat him well again," Shimerman notes. "She pretty much kept her promise over the years, and the conflict between us grew. If you look through the episodes from second season on, you'll see that the friendship and cordiality of the first season disappeared for a while." By the end of the series, however, Kira had obviously decided to let Quark off the hook.

The episode marked the first use of Bashir's surgery, a new redress of a swing set that is attached to the Infirmary. "The Infirmary is a small set, and we found that in order to do scenes where people were sick or dying or turning into strange creatures, we needed a larger room," explains David Livingston. The swing set soon found use as the station's Schoolroom and Security.

Mareel's homeworld may be spelled "Khefka IV" in the script, but sharp-eared viewers who thought they were hearing "Kafka" weren't far off the mark; Robert Wolfe pleads guilty to the pun. Other in-jokes include a reference to "the cliffs of Bole," a tribute to frequent *Star Trek* director Cliff Bole, and a vessel known as the *Livingston*, possibly named for David Livingston, or perhaps for Picard's lionfish.

CARDASSIANS
Episode #425
TELEPLAY BY JAMES CROCKER
STORY BY GENE WOLANDE & JOHN WRIGHT
DIRECTED BY CLIFF BOLE

GUEST CAST

Keiko O'Brien	ROSALIND CHAO
Garak	ANDREW ROBINSON
Kotran Pa'Dar	ROBERT MANDAN
Proka Migdal	TERRENCE EVANS
Rugal	VIDAL PETERSON
Zolan	DION ANDERSON
Luson Jomat	SHARON CONLEY
Deela	KAREN HENSEL
Asha	JILLIAN ZIESMER
Gul Dukat	MARC ALAIMO

STARDATE 47177.2

Enjoying another cup of Tarkalean tea with Garak, the station's tailor, Bashir idly fishes for clues to the Cardassian's true vocation, to no avail. Their attention is drawn to two new arrivals at the Replimat, a middle-aged Bajoran man and a twelve-year-old Cardassian boy. Curious about the atypical pair, Garak approaches and begins speaking to the Bajoran, at the same time laying a friendly hand on the boy's shoulder. The boy responds fearfully, viciously biting Garak's hand.

Later, as Bashir relates the strange incident to the crew in Ops, Sisko is contacted by Gul Dukat, who already has heard about the encounter. Dukat claims to be concerned about the treatment of the boy, a war orphan raised by a Bajoran family, and asks the commander to investigate. The information, he says, may help in his effort to bring such orphans back home to Cardassia.

Sisko agrees, and begins by speaking to Proka, the boy's adoptive father. Proka tells him that while he has not raised the child to hate Cardassians, he has

Bashir's lunches with Garak were always part of the "tailor"'s atmosphere of intrigue. DANNY FELD

told him the truth about what they did to Bajor. As for himself, Proka no longer sees the boy, named Rugal, as a Cardassian; he loves him as if he were his own. But Proka's words are contradicted by an alien named Zolan, who claims that Rugal's Bajoran parents are abusive and that they consider their treatment of the boy to be their revenge against all Cardassians. Although Proka denies the charge, Sisko insists the boy be kept in protective custody until the truth is revealed, and he places Rugal with the station's schoolteacher, Keiko O'Brien.

Garak reacts oddly when Bashir tells him about Dukat's alleged efforts to help the Cardassian war orphans left behind on Bajor. He points out the incongruity of Dukat's involvement in a situation the gul himself helped to create when he was in charge of the Cardassian withdrawal from Bajor. Bashir heads immediately to Sisko, and finds him in the midst of a conversation with Gul Dukat about returning Rugal to Cardassia. Bashir boldly interrupts and questions Dukat about the decision to leave the war orphans on Bajor. Dukat explains that the decision was made by Cardassia's civilian leaders and that he was forced to comply. Uncertain who to believe, Sisko questions

Garak, who denies making any allegations about Dukat.

That night, Bashir is awakened by Garak, who says they must go to Bajor immediately. Bashir approaches Sisko for permission to borrow a runabout just as the commander receives another interesting communication from Gul Dukat. Dukat says he has discovered that Rugal is the son of one of Cardassia's most prominent politicians, Kotran Pa'Dar, and that Pa'Dar is en route to the station to reclaim the boy. Realizing that Garak's sudden desire to go to Bajor is more than a coincidence, Sisko allows Bashir to take the runabout.

On Bajor, Garak leads Bashir to an orphan resettlement center, where they are allowed to download the relocation records for thousands of children. As they return to the station, a suspicious Bashir questions Garak about what is going on. Garak points out that Pa'Dar was one of the civilian leaders who ordered the evacuation of Bajor, which caused Dukat to lose his job as prefect. The fact that Dukat is now leading an effort to reunite Pa'Dar with his son seems an odd coincidence.

When Pa'Dar arrives to meet his son, Chief

O'Brien warns him that the boy has strong negative feelings about Cardassians. And sure enough, Rugal angrily denies that Pa'Dar is his father, and refuses to go with him to Cardassia. What's more, Proka refuses to relinquish custody. But despite the fact that bringing the Bajoran-raised child home after giving him up for dead will expose Pa'Dar to public disgrace, he wants Rugal. The two fathers agree to allow Sisko to serve as an arbitrator in the matter.

Before the hearing can begin, Dukat shows up at the station, and Sisko realizes that they are all being manipulated to an unknown end. But he can prove nothing until Garak, analyzing the resettlement files, finds a clue that unravels the mystery. Bashir presents their findings at the hearing. Rugal was originally brought to the resettlement center by an officer who was attached to Terok Nor—the Cardassian name for Deep Space 9—and at the time, Terok Nor was under the command of Gul Dukat. The clear implication is that Rugal was separated from his father by a political enemy who hoped someday to humiliate Pa'Dar.

With the knowledge that both Pa'Dar and Rugal were the victims of a cruel conspiracy, Sisko knows that he has no choice but to separate the boy from his loving Bajoran parents and send him home to Cardassia with his real father.

The second appearance of Actor Andrew Robinson as "plain and simple" Garak was relished nearly as much behind the scenes as it was by viewers at home, although certainly no one was happier about it than Robinson. As a seasoned veteran of the Hollywood casting treadmill, Robinson had known better than to hold his breath when *DS9*'s producers told him, during the first season, that "they were really pleased with my work and they were going to have me back," says the actor. "In this business, people always tell you that the dailies were great and you're wonderful and so forth, but they often don't follow up by inviting you back. This is one of those rare occasions where they did, and Ira Behr actually apologized for not having me back sooner!"

"After 'Past Prologue,' we had planned to use Andy again, but we never did for the rest of the season," says Executive Producer Behr. "Then Season 2 came along and we said, 'We've got to use Andy Robinson, we really do.'"

But while it was one thing to *want* to bring Garak back, it was another to justify his appearance. That, acknowledges Behr, meant fleshing out his character.

The writers became enamored of Garak and with Andrew Robinson's wonderful take on the "plain and simple" tailor. DANNY FELD

"The first time he was just this tailor who was a spy, but you can only get away with that once," he says. "See him again and you have to start justifying everything, solidifying everything. When we were breaking the story for 'Cardassians,' it was like, 'How do we take Garak and lay pipe?' Any show he's in, anything he does, it's got to be some kind of characterization. And at the time, Dukat, who's changed a lot over the years, was such a diehard hateful villain that it seemed perfect to establish a link between these two Cardassians." The groundwork laid during "Cardassians" would resurface in the third-season episode "Civil Defense" and beyond. "It takes a while sometimes," says Behr. "You lay the pipe and then it'll take a year before you do another show where you can use it."

The show "laid pipe" in other directions as well, introducing the name Terok Nor, the designation for the station while Gul Dukat was in command, and some interesting bits of backstory about that era, which would find their way into later episodes. It also carried baggage from previous *Star Trek* episodes, most notably O'Brien's unresolved feelings about Cardassians, originally established in *TNG*'s "The Wounded," which led to a scene that spoke volumes with no words. As the O'Briens sit down to dinner with their houseguest, Rugal, the chief's discomfort with the situation continues to build until he pushes away his plate of Cardassian cuisine in disgust. There is a clink of china and O'Brien looks up to see that Rugal has pushed his plate away for similar reasons. As their eyes meet, the audience comprehends that the two have unexpectedly found common ground.

Although the script had dictated that the two characters move their plates at the same time, it was

Director Cliff Bole who created the subtle choreography of the moment, keeping the camera on O'Brien, with Rugal out of frame. "I went in that morning with it in my head," Bole recalls. "Then I had it designed and everybody went with it." He is quick to share credit with Marvin Rush and his crew, and Film Editor Tom Benko, whose choice of specific footage used in the final product—the plates touching, the meeting of the two characters' gazes—influenced audience reaction to the sequence.

What stands out most in Bole's memory of "Cardassians" was the opportunity to work again with Andrew Robinson. "I had directed him in episodes of *Vegas* and *Matt Houston*," he says. "Andy's a brilliant actor, with a range you can't believe." Despite the fact that the episode's title seemed to imply that it would be a harsh show about a species that had been, until that time, portrayed quite negatively, "Cardassians" was a story about humanist values, and Bole credits Robinson with strong contributions in that area. Although Garak is hardly a typical Cardassian, the script called for him to "go through a lot of little changes" that would eventually add more colors to Garak's intriguing palette, notes Bole. "In forty-two-and-a-half minutes [the actual length of an episode sans commercials, credits, etc.], I had to take Andy through three or four shades of character. We had great fun with it."

Robinson looks at changes in Garak's personality, in "Cardassians" and subsequent episodes, as "part of the actor's process. When you're working on a character that recurs over a period of time, what happens is kind of unconscious. In the very first episode, I was much more foreign and exotic than I later became. I think one of the reasons for that is the relationship with Bashir. What Garak gets from him is a certain humanization, which is not to suggest that he has become a human being—he's a Cardassian—but that there are certain kinds of human values that Bashir imparts to Garak." While Robinson feels the most obvious demonstration of that transference is in "The Wire," one can see the beginnings of it in "Cardassians," where Garak starts out viewing the situation with the orphans from one perspective, and then, in seeing the way Bashir reacts to it, "looking at it from another point of view and realizing, 'Yes, this is a very cruel situation.'"

And what does Robinson feel that Bashir receives from the exchange? "A certain political education," he responds. "Garak is someone who obviously has been

The wrenching aftereffects of war as seen by the writers: A Bajoran father with his adopted Cardassian son. ROBBIE ROBINSON

around and who's very well versed in the intrigues and the power politics of that world. I think perhaps that is what Bashir is learning from him."

"Cardassians" marks the beginning of *DS9*'s brief flirtation with "weird hats." They were part of an effort on the part of Costume Designer Robert Blackman to make the space station look like a place where ships from all manner of worlds would stop. Accordingly, Blackman's budget included a certain amount of money to develop costumes for extras who appeared in groups of two to five, and would look something like "sailors on shore leave," thus providing some background color. Beginning with "Cardassians," a number of those extras began appearing in "weird hats," notes Blackman, a trend that would run its course by the end of second season. "*Star Trek* has a great love/hate relationship with hats," he says. "We don't do a lot of them, because you draw them up, they like it, you do it, and then it's 'I hate it. Take that thing off. I can't see the face.'"

MELORA

Episode #426

TELEPLAY BY **EVAN CARLOS SOMERS AND STEVEN BAUM AND MICHAEL PILLER & JAMES CROCKER**
STORY BY **EVAN CARLOS SOMERS**
DIRECTED BY **WINRICH KOLBE**

GUEST CAST

Melora	DAPHNE ASHBROOK
Fallit Kot	PETER CROMBIE
Ashrok	DON STARK
Klingon Chef	RON TAYLOR

STARDATE 47229.1

Dr. Bashir is eager to meet Ensign Melora Pazlar, a cartographer assigned to chart the Gamma Quadrant. Because Melora is Starfleet's first Elaysian recruit, Bashir and O'Brien have been working overtime to make the station accessible to someone accustomed to a low-gravity environment. Melora requires a special wheelchair—which Bashir has replicated for her—and braces to get around in DS9's gravity. O'Brien has set up special ramps where possible and has modified living conditions in her quarters.

Melora's personnel files reveal an impressive woman, but one who won't tolerate being coddled, a personality trait that's verified with a vengeance when she arrives. Melora despises being considered a person with a "problem," and she is not happy when Sisko tells her that he does not intend to let her take a runabout to Gamma Quadrant alone. Dax is assigned to accompany her. Later, Bashir visits Melora at her quarters and successfully parries her attempts to put

Melora's prickly exterior slowly melts under the concentrated charm of Dr. Bashir. ROBBIE ROBINSON

him on the defensive. Taken aback by his pleasant determination to befriend her, Melora accepts an invitation to dinner.

Quark also is trying to get on the good side of a dinner guest, with far less success. Fallit Kot, an old business acquaintance of Quark's who served eight years in a labor camp for a deal gone sour, has made no secret of the fact that he's returned to Deep Space 9 to kill the Ferengi. When offers of wine and women fail to win over Kot, Quark appeals to Odo for help. Although the constable enjoys seeing Quark squirm, he agrees to look into the situation. However, as he points out, he has no reason to arrest Kot unless Kot actually attempts to harm Quark.

Just prior to leaving for the mission in the Gamma Quadrant, Melora suffers a fall, and Dax has to help her to the Infirmary. Melora's injuries are minor, but the incident leaves her feeling humiliated until Bashir reassures her that no one in space is completely self-sufficient and that it's all right to count on others. Melora's feelings for Bashir reach a turning point, and she decides that she can trust him on a personal level. She invites him into her quarters and turns down the gravity, allowing him to see her "fly" —and to learn to fly himself. The pair are soon entwined in a passionate midair kiss.

En route to the Gamma Quadrant, Melora allows herself to confide in Dax, and expresses concern over getting involved with Bashir. Dax encourages her to enjoy the moment and forgo thinking about the future. When they return to the station, Bashir has a surprise for Melora. He's been researching an old neuromuscular adaptation theory that he thinks could allow Melora to move around without her wheelchair or her braces. The therapy proves extremely promising. However, Melora's delight at her increased mobility is tempered by the knowledge that she will have to stop using the low-gravity field actuator in her quarters because it will confuse her motor cortex.

That night, Kot is prepared to make good on his vow to kill Quark, but the Ferengi manages to convince him that the 199 bars of latinum Quark is about to receive in a trade might be better than revenge. However, after Kot receives the latinum, he kills Quark's trader associate and takes the Ferengi hostage. Kot drags Quark to a runabout, the one in which Dax and Melora have just returned. Kot orders them to take it out again, but when they do, Sisko snares it with a tractor beam. Kot warns Sisko to release the ship, then fires his phaser at Melora to prove he's serious. Sisko, O'Brien, and Bashir beam to another runabout as Kira releases the tractor beam.

When Kot discovers he is being pursued, he orders Dax to fire on the second ship. Dax, who notes that Melora has regained consciousness, stalls long enough for the injured Elaysian to crawl over to a control that disengages the runabout's gravity. Kot is thrown off guard by his sudden weightlessness, which allows Melora to take advantage of the moment and disable him.

After they return to the station, Melora tells Bashir that she has decided to discontinue the treatments, which would have allowed her to be like the others, but would have changed who she really was.

Co-creators Rick Berman and Michael Piller had initially planned to include among the core crewmembers a character accustomed to living in a low-gravity environment. The character would have been confined to a futuristic wheelchair in the normal-gravity areas of the space station, but been able to "fly" in the customized conditions of her own quarters. Practical considerations like budget and setup time ultimately eliminated the character as a regular, but the idea of doing an individual episode revolving around a "wheelchair officer" remained, eventually catching the interest of Writer Evan Carlos Somers ("Battle Lines").

"It's very, very hard to sell to *Star Trek*," notes Somers, who served as a Writers Guild intern and later a staff writer during *DS9*'s debut season. "The chances are stacked against you. And I wanted to defeat the odds and immediately sell something." Although Somers's staff position had not been renewed for the series' second year, Executive Producer Piller had invited him to come back and pitch some story ideas. Armed with an insider's knowledge of which premises lingered on the storyboard awaiting development, Somers decided to go for it. "'Wheelchair officer' was prominent on the B-storyboard, so I just snagged it and told them that I'd be able to provide insight into this character."

For Somers, a paraplegic who uses a wheelchair, such insight comes all too readily. He had experienced many of Melora's frustrations firsthand, beginning with the difficulties in using a chair at a workplace that isn't designed for such devices. During his tenure at *Star Trek*, Somers worked in an older office building that was, at least initially, rampless, and that contained "one of the world's smallest elevators," particularly in relation to the size of his wheelchair. Melora found herself with similar problems, unable

Joe Longo transformed a standard wheelchair into Melora's twenty-fourth-century one with a few cosmetic changes. DANNY FELD

to use her high-tech antigrav wheelchair because of Cardassian architecture. "So Bashir has to replicate a much simpler wheelchair for her and she encounters all of the problems that I did whenever I went down to the *DS9* set to snoop around," says Somers.

Melora had some advantages over Somers, however, considering she had a highly trained crew on tap behind the scenes to make life easier for her. Her wheelchair, for example, was purchased by Set Decorator Laura Richarz and revamped by Prop Master Joe Longo, who recalls that he "added a control panel and some wheel covers to block out the spokes in the wheels, and changed the joystick. Basically, we tried to keep it as simple as possible, because of our experience in [the *TNG* episode] 'Too Short a Season.' We had made a big albatross of a moving chair for that, and it was bad. But this one worked great; the actress drove it everywhere."

Members of the crew also created the exoskeleton that provided Melora with limited mobility in

Daphne Ashbrook and Siddig El Fadil take a spin in a special flying rig. The actors say it looks like more fun than it is. DANNY FELD

metallic bands adjoining the pieces kept popping off, once right in the middle of a scene. Joe Longo never let me forget it."

Even Director Winrich Kolbe helped to ease Melora's passage through the station. "Obviously there are a lot of thresholds on the station that had to be removed [to ease filming]," he says. Kolbe also employed plenty of cuts to keep filming moving at its usual swift pace, but recalls one scene in which they decided to actually show how hard it was for Melora to move about. "We put ramps in the set, and it was a pain in the neck, because it's not easy to maneuver a wheelchair even under prime conditions. But going up ramps and making left turns and right turns in those corridors, well . . ." He sighs.

The flying sequences presented their own unique problems. Siddig El Fadil labels the scenes "great fun," but admits that the flying gear, which includes a "very thick wire corset, like a steel bathing suit," is extremely uncomfortable. "It has to be incredibly tight because when you're upside down, you tend to slip out," he says. "So they actually put their foot up on your spine and pull the strings tight, literally like an old-fashioned corset." But more difficult than the lengthy time spent in the air was the actual kissing. "It was hard to be romantic, kissing somebody longingly, like in some old movie, while you're spinning slightly and you don't know where you're going and you bump into each other's head." He smiles.

Composer Dennis McCarthy did his best to generate the appropriate mood, but he, too, had practical concerns to deal with. The soundtrack of every station-set scene of *Deep Space Nine* incorporates a low drone that is meant to convey, at a nearly subliminal level, the impression that the characters are on a piece of operational machinery. Although it adds atmosphere to the show, the sound often conflicts with portions of McCarthy's compositions. "'Melora' was one of the most romantic scores that I've had the chance to write and I really enjoyed it," notes McCarthy. "I made it more ethereal than usual, with less horns, letting the woodwinds play in the lighter areas while I tried to ignore that the station was continually rumbling."

Practical Special Effects Supervisor Gary Monak and Stunt Coordinator Dennis Madalone worked out the wire rigging and choreography for the sequences. While there are electrical flying rigs available, Monak's team built their own mechanical version, which Monak says made it "physically easier to get the action the director wanted," and allowed the crew

regular gravity situations. "I started with a basic framework for her limbs," says Jim Martin. "The producers didn't want any chest or waist pieces. They just wanted it to be around her arms, her neck, and her legs. And they didn't want regular hinges, because hinges aren't futuristic enough. So [Senior Illustrator] Rick Sternbach designed an expanding and contracting kind of hinge, something that pulls in rather than rotate, that I incorporated into my drawings. But the

to raise, lower, and move the "flyers" about to follow specific storyboarded moves. According to Monak, in the past, flying rigs had required a wire that was "just fine enough for the camera not to see, but strong enough to hold an actor." But in today's era of special effects, "a computer can 'remove' the wires, which simplifies things for us."

The process of eliminating those wires from the final footage so that it would look like Bashir and Melora were floating rather than dangling like puppets was done at Video Image by Glenn Neufeld and David Takemura. "We had to paint out the wires, frame by frame," recalls Takemura. "It wound up being fairly complex, because sometimes the wires got pretty close to the actors' faces."

For the photo of Melora and her brother that Bashir sees in her quarters, Dan Curry got up on a ladder and took a photo of the two actors, then took another photo of the beautiful Santa Susanna mountains on the west end of the San Fernando Valley. He then composited the two shots and painted in the light "so everything matched properly" with a Photoshop program. For all the time he put into it, however—and the subsequent amount of time it took to shoot the scene where Bashir picks up the photo and looks at it—it was on camera for only two or three seconds. But Curry doesn't mind. "Some of our shots may easily represent thousands of man-hours. But the audience recognizes the attention to detail. We always feel like 'good enough' doesn't cut it."

Although the writers never expressed a desire to bring Melora back to the station, Monak was prepared. "I thought maybe they'd use the flying rig again, so I left it up. And actually, that was as good a place as any to store it." The rig remained in place until the beginning of Season 5, when the *Starship Defiant*'s engineering set was deemed to be taking up much-needed space in the swing set area. The small—but tall—set was moved to an area on the stage where the top of the warp core competed for space with the overhead flying rig, which finally came down.

RULES OF ACQUISITION
Episode #427
TELEPLAY BY **IRA STEVEN BEHR**
STORY BY **HILARY J. BADER**
DIRECTED BY **DAVID LIVINGSTON**

GUEST CAST

Pel	HÉLENE UDY
Inglatu	BRIAN THOMPSON
Rom	MAX GRODÉNCHIK
Zyree	EMILIA CROW
Maihar'du	TINY RON
Zek	WALLACE SHAWN

STARDATE UNKNOWN

To a Ferengi like Quark, there's nothing more enjoyable than a lively game of *tongo*—unless it's a game of *tongo* that includes the participation of DS9's beautiful science officer Jadzia Dax, and, as a bonus, a bit of financially astute advice from the bar's new waiter, Pel. It's a perfect night that's made even better when Quark receives a call from Grand Nagus Zek, announcing that the Ferengi expansion into the Gamma Quadrant is about to begin. . . with Quark as Zek's chief negotiator.

A short time later, Zek arrives at the station and meets with Sisko and Kira to explain his desire to host a business conference with the Dosi, a species from the Gamma Quadrant, at DS9. Although suspicious of the nagus, Sisko agrees after extracting a promise that Zek will treat the Dosi fairly *and* donate fifty thousand kilos of brizeen nitrate to the Bajoran people. Zek then goes to Quark and instructs him to purchase ten thousand vats of tulaberry wine from the Dosi, a move that the nagus feels will provide the Ferengi with a substantial foothold in the Gamma Quadrant.

Quark is pleased with the opportunity, until Pel, again demonstrating her business savvy, points out that it is an opportunity for Zek, not Quark, and that Quark will be the recipient of all the blame if the negotiations fail. Realizing that he will need someone to serve as his consultant during the negotiations, Quark turns to Pel, leaving his brother Rom feeling betrayed.

The Dosi arrive on Deep Space 9, and Quark begins negotiations with Inglatu, a disagreeable male, and Zyree, an equally difficult female. Things don't start out well: first the Dosi say they'll sell only five thousand vats, then they insist they want to deal directly with Zek, not Quark. But Pel insists that Quark is the sole contact in the negotiations, and the Dosi retire to think about the deal.

The grand nagus accepts Quark and Pel's offer to go to the Gamma Quadrant and close the deal. KIM GOTTLIEB-WALKER

Uncertain that he'll be able to obtain the ten thousand vats the nagus has requested, Quark is floored when Zek tells him that he now wants *one hundred thousand* vats. However, Pel convinces a nervous Quark that he'll be able to successfully complete the deal. Curious about Pel's unusual (for a Ferengi) loyalty to Quark, Dax befriends him and is amazed to hear that Pel not only loves Quark, but is a female masquerading as a male! Pel had donned a pair of fake masculine earlobes in order to wear clothing, leave the Ferengi homeworld, and acquire profit, all activities that are forbidden to Ferengi females. Falling in love, however, is something that she never intended to do.

When Quark tells the Dosi about the increase in wine volume, the aliens leave the station without making a deal. But Pel has an idea. She and Quark will travel to the Gamma Quadrant and get the Dosi to sign a contract there. Once they arrive on the Dosi homeworld, however, the negotiations don't go any better, and Quark vows to stay there until he strikes a deal with Inglatu. Sharing a single bed in their Dosi quarters, Pel is overwhelmed by her feelings for Quark and kisses him. She's about to reveal her secret to her startled boss when Zyree enters the room and informs them that Inglatu doesn't have a hundred thousand vats to sell. There aren't that many vats on the planet. However, for the right price, Zyree is willing to put them in touch with someone who does have that much tulaberry wine: the Karemma, an important power in the Dominion. Quark has never heard of the Dominion, but it is suddenly clear to him that the nagus must know about this mysterious group, and that Zek is interested in something other than wine.

Returning to the station, Quark confronts Zek, who admits that dealing with the Dosi was a ploy to get in touch with someone in the Dominion. When Quark offers to set up a meeting between the nagus and the Karemma in exchange for a percentage of every Ferengi deal with the Dominion, Zek eagerly agrees. Unfortunately, at this point, Rom, who ransacked Pel's room in her absence, pulls Quark away from Zek and informs his brother of Pel's true identity. Realizing the implications, Quark promptly swoons.

Reviving in the Infirmary, Quark ascertains that Rom hasn't told anyone else about Pel's gender . . . yet. But Rom points out that Pel must be punished for her serious crimes against Ferengi society. Worried that Pel's secret will ruin his reputation with the nagus, Quark offers to give his brother the bar in exchange for his silence. Then he goes to Pel's quarters and offers her latinum to leave the station at once. However, Pel is no longer interested in latinum; she loves Quark, and she knows that Quark has feelings for her too. But after Quark convinces her that he never could be happy with a nontraditional Ferengi wife, Pel agrees to leave.

Unfortunately, before she goes, she can't resist revealing her true identity to Zek, who is appropriately horrified. The nagus promises to put Pel in jail, and when Quark protests, Zek threatens Quark, who is guilty of taking business advice from a female, with the same punishment. But Quark points out that the nagus is guilty of a bigger crime: allowing a female to represent him in a business negotiation. Zek agrees to keep Pel's identity a secret in exchange for Quark's Gamma Quadrant profits.

Pel invites Quark to accompany her as she leaves the station in search of new adventures, but Quark refuses, realizing later on that now he is poorer in more than lost profits.

"Rules of Acquisition," which marked Writer Hilary Bader's second turn at a *DS9* story, actually started out as a *TNG* pitch. "I had Pel involved with Riker to begin with, and then had Beverly Crusher find out, and some kind of sisterhood relationship developing," recalls Bader. The concept was ultimately deemed a better fit for *DS9*, a show populated by *lots* of Ferengi. Although the episode, originally called "Profit Margin," bears a resemblance to the motion picture *Yentl* and the Isaac Bashevis Singer story that inspired it, Bader cites childhood memories of being a tomboy as an equally strong source. "If you wanted to play baseball, you had to, if not pretend to

The game of tongo was introduced in "Rules of Acquisition."
BARRY SLOBIN

in places. [Some parts of the episode] became a bedroom farce and that's not how I'd envisioned it."

Some of the details were similarly. . . unsubtle. The idea of putting breasts on Pel so the audience would know she was a female, for example, did not originate with the writers. It came from Livingston.

"A director has to take what's in the script and then make sure that all of the intentions are realized visually," he says. "I asked them to give her breasts. Because just taking off an ear, to a human audience, doesn't necessarily signal a female."

Behr is philosophical about such fixes. "One of the problems in doing science fiction is you're ultimately dealing with human actors and human concepts and a TV show isn't a book where you can imagine all kinds of things. So, yeah, it's very important that the audience gets it, up front, right away."

Still, Behr is quite pleased with several aspects of the episode; *tongo,* for one. Although Hilary Bader created the name, Behr took the ball and ran with it. "My parents live in Las Vegas and my father's a gambler," he says. "This was a chance to invent a game that I thought my father would play under the right circumstances. I can't tell you the rules, but I'm sure someone will come up with them one day."

As for the creation of the Dominion, Behr notes that the introduction of that mysterious group served a specific purpose. The existence of the Gamma Quadrant next door to DS9 would not help the series if it just remained "unexplored space," he explains. "They did three years of that on the original series and seven years on *TNG.* We needed to define that space." And what better way than by creating an extremely pervasive villain?

Of course, he admits, there is an extra bonus to creating a good villain. "Villains are cool," he says honestly. "It's true I've done a lot of stuff with the Ferengi, but they're not really villains. I had this fear that my *Star Trek* tombstone would read, 'He really made the Ferengi work.' And there should be more to a man's life than that."

But trust a Ferengi to take credit even for Behr's moment of glory. "What I found really interesting about the episode," notes Actor Armin Shimerman, a strong promoter of Ferengi pride, "was that it was the Ferengi who made the first contact with the major power in the Gamma Quadrant. It was the Ferengi who discovered the Dominion, which I think is wonderful. For all of Starfleet's intelligence and technology, it was trading and merchandising that made the Dominion apparent to everyone!"

be a guy, certainly do everything that the guys did. Dress like a guy, talk like a guy, and sit like a guy, and then maybe they'd let you play," she says.

While the episode introduced a variety of interesting new details to the *DS9* universe—the game of *tongo,* the concept of the Dominion, and a whopping six-and-a-half new Ferengi Rules of Acquisition, to name a few—the executive producers reportedly felt that several aspects of the show were "over the top." Director David Livingston accepts at least partial blame for that, although he's still happy with the results. "The Dosi were written kind of silly, so I ended up directing them kind of silly," he admits. And Livingston also reveals that he was the one who decided to put bright red face makeup, inspired by a book of African tribal facial paintings, on the Gamma Quadrant aliens. Inglatu's resemblance to Arnold Schwarzenegger was intentional as well. "The Dosi were described to me as very 'buff' men and women, so that's the kind of actors we chose," says Livingston. "Hey, if they write it, you should go for it!"

"There's comedy and there's comedy," observes Ira Steven Behr, who wrote the teleplay for the episode. "Comedy should have truth in it, too. The tone was off

The episode sets up two bits of characterization that would be contradicted in later episodes. Zek is aghast at the idea of Quark having taken advice from a female, a charge that he, too, would be guilty of, following his introduction to Quark's mother, Ishka. And Rom is equally chauvinistic about Pel's pursuit of wealth but later would be the first one to defend Ishka for her beliefs.

Illustrator Jim Martin designed the case in which Pel carries her lobes, while Michael Westmore made the lobes themselves. Joe Longo's crew made the case from scratch, as well as the comb Maihar'du uses to comb Zek's ear hairs. Although viewers don't really see it on screen, the comb has a Ferengi head on it, similar to the one on Zek's staff.

And yes, those were Pakleds you saw walking around in the background on the Promenade. "I asked for them," laughs Livingston, who remembered the slow-witted species from his days on *TNG*. "We were doing a comedy and they're the funniest, goofiest-looking guys. I love the Pakleds."

An assault on Quark reawakens Odo's memories of the Occupation and an unsolved murder. CARIN BAER

NECESSARY EVIL

Episode #428

WRITTEN BY PETER ALLAN FIELDS
DIRECTED BY JAMES L. CONWAY

GUEST CAST

Pallra	KATHERINE MOFFAT
Rom	MAX GRODÉNCHIK
Trazko	ROBERT MacKENZIE
Gul Dukat	MARC ALAIMO

STARDATE 47282.5

When Pallra, a beautiful Bajoran woman who had lived on DS9 during the Cardassian occupation, summons Quark to her home, the Ferengi realizes she's interested in something other than discussing old times, although he's not sure what it may be. Pallra claims to want a favor, the retrieval of a strongbox from the shop she and her husband, Vaatrik, once operated on the Promenade. The contents, she insists, are purely sentimental. Although certain that there's more to the errand than she's willing to admit, Quark agrees.

Returning to the station, Quark and Rom break into the specified location and bring the box to Quark's bar. His curiosity getting the better of him, Quark opens the box and discovers a list of Bajoran names. Sending Rom to retrieve an imager so that he can copy the list, Quark senses that someone else is in the bar. It's a Bajoran named Trazko, who informs Quark that Pallra suspected the Ferengi would be unable to resist opening the box. Trazko fires his weapon at Quark and exits with the box, leaving Rom to discover the body of his dying brother.

While Bashir works frantically to save Quark, Odo questions a reluctant Rom about the robbery and the attack. After Odo accuses Rom of shooting his brother, the Ferengi quickly reveals all the details, including the information about the list of names and the location in which they found the box, once the site of a chemist's shop. The mention of the chemist's shop triggers strong memories in Odo, and he recalls the day the owner of the shop, Pallra's husband, was killed. It was also the day he was formally introduced to Gul Dukat; the Cardassian had wanted Odo to investigate the murder. Knowing that the alternative was the death of innocent Bajorans, Odo had agreed and soon found himself questioning Pallra. Pallra had informed Odo that her husband was having an affair, and suggested that his mistress had killed him in a jealous rage. She'd pointed the mistress out to Odo: a Bajoran woman named Kira Nerys.

As Odo's thoughts return to the present, it becomes clear to him that the assault on Quark is related to that still-unsolved murder. Returning to Rom, he urges the Ferengi to recall the names on the list, but Rom can recall only one: "something like Ches'so." Odo asks Kira if she recognizes the name, but she says she doesn't, and Odo again reflects upon the past, recalling his initial meeting with Kira. She had denied killing Vaatrik; the two of them had only been friends, not lovers. So why would Pallra think they were lovers? Odo had become even more suspicious a short time later when he spotted Pallra kissing Dukat.

That suspicion lingers as Odo's flashback ends, and he goes to Bajor to question Pallra, who claims to know nothing about the list of names. Nor does she recognize the name Ches'so. Odo notes that she recently obtained enough money to pay her overdue power bill, but Pallra declines to discuss the source of the money. A short time later, Kira figures out who "Ches'sarro" is, or rather was, since he died the previous evening. Sensing a link between his conversation with Pallra and the death, Odo takes his investigation further and finds himself thinking about his first meeting with Quark. He recalls that he had forced Quark to admit having accepted a bribe from Kira to say that she was at the bar the night Vaatrik was killed.

Odo's investigation of Pallra provides him with a re-creation of the stolen list. Every name on it represents a Bajoran who recently paid Pallra a great deal of money. Blackmail seems the likely reason, and wartime collaboration with the Cardassians the likely incentive, for that blackmail. He is close to solving the current crime, but the one from the past continues to haunt him, particularly his confrontation with Kira about her location during Vaatrik's death. She'd finally admitted to him that she was a member of the Bajoran underground, and that on the night of the murder she'd been sabotaging some equipment on the station. Since that in itself was a crime punishable by death by the Cardassians, Odo simply told Dukat that she was innocent of the murder.

When Trazko returns to DS9 to finish off Quark, Odo apprehends him. With both Trazko and Pallra in custody, and a link between the pair easily established, all the loose threads are tied up *except* for the murder of Vaatrik. Odo realizes that Kira had lied to him years ago, and that she *had* killed Vaatrik, who had walked in on her while she was trying to find the same list of collaborators that Quark eventually would unearth. The past is behind them, and Odo

admits that knowledge of the truth won't affect their friendship. But the two of them wonder if the bond between them ever will be the same.

Like the first season's much-acclaimed episode "Duet," "Necessary Evil" featured an extremely well-crafted script by Peter Allan Fields and an atmospheric directorial turn by James L. Conway. Little wonder the episode received similar kudos from all quarters.

"One of our best shows," enthuses David Livingston.

"Great show—extremely difficult show," comments Ira Steven Behr.

"One of the best episodes we've ever done," says Rene Auberjonois.

To convey the harsh conditions during the Cardassian Occupation, an elaborate redress of the standing sets was executed. DANNY FELD

"It was the easiest episode I ever shot," laughs Armin Shimerman, whose character, Quark, spent much of the episode lying flat on his back.

But if it was easy for Shimerman, it was far more complicated for everyone else associated with the episode. For Herman Zimmerman, the task was changing key details of the set to make the familiar station look as it had when it was known as Terok Nor. "We took out all of the nice things and made it much more spartan," he recalls, "and put atmosphere, smoke, into the air. And we actually built a physical barrier that ran down the length of the Promenade, making it look like a ghetto area on one side and the Cardassian business district on the other. It was an electrified high-tech wire thing, with neon lights on the top to simulate a force field, and a utility gate that slid back and forth on rollers."

For Marvin Rush, the challenge was creating a pervasive film noir atmosphere for all of the flashback scenes. Rush notes that he pulled out all the stops, using unusual camera angles and lighting to evoke the style of filmmaking popular in the '30s and '40s, à la *The Third*

The audience saw for the first time the conditions that drove the Bajorans to terrorist acts. DANNY FELD

Man, which Rush describes as "the prototypical film noir." "Marvin and Jim Conway created this fascinating look, all dour and dark and smoky, with a cold blue quality to it," says Livingston. "It was stunning."

Of course, the physical efforts to create a really stylistic episode would have been for naught if the writing hadn't been equally inspired. "It was a tough show to break," recalls Behr. "Peter did some nice stuff." And it didn't hurt, he adds, that Michael Piller, with his *Simon & Simon* background, had a lot of experience doing detective shows.

But if the show brings to mind any other television show, it's *Columbo,* a point that's particularly obvious when Odo questions Pallra, starts to leave, then turns and says, "One more thing . . ."

"Well, I wrote a lot of *Columbo*s," admits Fields, with a chuckle. Would he call the line a tribute to his old show? "I don't know," he says thoughtfully. "It's also part of Odo. You can't give tributes if it's out of character."

Although Rene Auberjonois hadn't been aware of Fields' *Columbo* connection at the time, he did recognize the reference. "When I read the script, I realized it was very much a *Columbo* sort of trick to do, so rather than play against it, I decided to do a little homage within the bounds of the particular reality that we establish for *Deep Space Nine.*"

Auberjonois wasn't the only actor to indulge in "a little homage." *Before* he wound up on the floor, Actor Shimerman got to as well, despite the fact that he was going against previous instructions. "When I first did the pilot, I got some notes from Rick Berman about what I should *not* do ever again." He smiles. "And one of the things he suggested was I was never to play a scene like Humphrey Bogart, because I sound a little like him. And I reminded Rick that it wasn't so much me as the overbite I have with the Ferengi teeth. But they wrote me a scene that was so obviously Humphrey Bogart! So I had the great pleasure of playing it as though it were a '40s Bogart movie, and the director was pleased with that particular take on it."

Even Max Grodénchik got to do an homage—to Armin Shimerman. "When I come to the Infirmary to see Quark, there's that guy about to kill him, and I do Armin's Ferengi scream. Of course, Armin is the best at doing those things, by far. He can get up higher and shriller than anybody." And, in fact, on the day Grodénchik shot that scene, the call sheet included a note for a copy of "Invasive Procedures" to be ready on the set, cued up to "SC. 57—Int. Surgery—Quark in pain" and "SC. 63—Quark groans horribly." Inspiration, no doubt.

The call sheets also indicate that many of Auberjonois's atmospheric voice-overs—format breaking enough that Fields was required to get special permission to include them in the script—were recorded during the actual filming of the episode, rather than on the looping stage during postproduction. "When we had time, I'd go with the sound crew to a quiet part of the stage and record," says Auberjonois. "That was mostly for editing purposes, so they'd know how long everything was going to be."

Once again, Dan Curry's countenance was employed to depict a bad guy. The image of Ches'sarro is a recycled photo of the visual effects producer taken for the first-season episode "Babel." To get in character for the original shot, Curry recalls "standing out in an alley at the studio and sneering and looking nasty." For the second use, he laughs, "They touched it up in Photoshop to give me even less hair than I have."

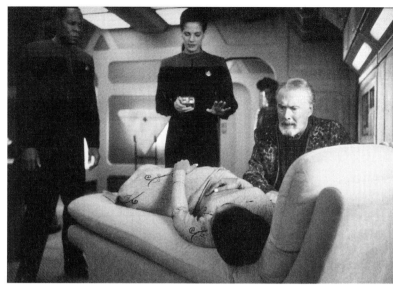

To Professor Seyetik's distress, Dax reveals that his wife, Nidell, will die unless she is rejoined with Fenna. ROBBIE ROBINSON

SECOND SIGHT

Episode #429

TELEPLAY BY **MARK GEHRED-O'CONNELL AND IRA STEVEN BEHR & ROBERT HEWITT WOLFE**
STORY BY **MARK GEHRED-O'CONNELL**
DIRECTED BY **ALEXANDER SINGER**

GUEST CAST

Fenna/Nidell	**SALLI ELISE RICHARDSON**
Lieutenant Piersall	**MARK ERICKSON**

SPECIAL GUEST STAR

Seyetik	**RICHARD KILEY**

STARDATE 47329.4

On the evening following the fourth anniversary of Jennifer Sisko's death, Benjamin Sisko takes a lonely late-night walk through the quiet Promenade and encounters a beautiful alien woman. The woman, who introduces herself as Fenna, engages Sisko in pleasant conversation, then, as he looks away for a second, disappears.

The next morning, Sisko and Dax meet Gideon Seyetik, a boastful terraformer who has come to the region to reignite the dead sun of Epsilon 119. Dax attempts to discuss details of Seyetik's mission with Sisko that night over dinner, but finds the commander strangely distracted. When Dax leaves, Sisko wanders over to the viewport where he met Fenna, and is delighted when she suddenly reappears. Fenna accepts Sisko's offer to show her around the station, and the two make plans to have a picnic together the next day. However, when Sisko begins to question her about herself, Fenna excuses herself abruptly and once again disappears.

Perplexed, Sisko asks Odo to find Fenna, although he has few clues to provide as to her whereabouts. A short time later, Dax approaches Sisko and asks him about the woman she saw him with the night before. But again, Sisko can provide few details. That evening, the senior staff is invited to dine with Seyetik aboard the U.S.S. Prometheus, where the professor bores them with endless accounts of his accomplishments. At last he introduces them to his wife, Nidell, a woman who looks exactly like Fenna, but who doesn't seem to recognize Sisko.

Sisko tells Odo to call off the search for Fenna, since he knows she's a passenger aboard the Prometheus. But Odo discounts that as a possibility, as his records prove that no one besides Seyetik has left the ship since it docked at the station.

Confused, Sisko returns to his quarters and finds Fenna waiting for him. When he mentions her resemblance to Seyetik's wife, Nidell, it is obvious that she has no idea what he's talking about. Sisko continues to press her for answers, but Fenna says only that she came to the station to find someone—him. She kisses him, but when Sisko returns the kiss, Fenna disappears right before his eyes.

Dax continues to prepare for her mission with Seyetik, and Sisko announces that he will accompany them, hoping that he will be able to unravel the Fenna mystery during the trip. As they head for Epsilon 119, Seyetik goes on and on about his exploits, including his first meeting with his future wife, Nidell, a Halanan. Later, Sisko goes to see Nidell but she claims to be too ill for visitors. Arriving at his own quarters on the ship, Sisko finds Fenna waiting for him. Sisko immediately summons Dax, who brings a tricorder to examine Fenna. The tricorder fails to read cellular structure or DNA patterns, reading only energy.

Determined to get to the bottom of the situation, Sisko and Dax bring Fenna to Seyetik's quarters, where they find Nidell unconscious on the floor, and Seyetik beside himself with concern. To everyone's surprise, Seyetik knows Fenna, and is not happy to see her.

Seyetik explains that Nidell is a psychoprojective telepath, and that Fenna is an illusion created by Nidell's unconscious mind, a condition that can occur in Halanans during periods of deep emotional distress. The same thing happened three years earlier, he admits, and it almost killed Nidell, just as it is killing her now. He admits that he is probably the cause of Nidell's condition, but since Halanans mate for life, she never will leave him, no matter how much she may wish to do so.

Returning to Fenna, Sisko convinces her that she must return to Nidell. Otherwise, Nidell will die, and Fenna will be unable to exist without her. Fenna is reluctant, but Sisko convinces her that their love is just a dream, Nidell's dream, even if Nidell will never remember that dream. As Fenna kisses Sisko goodbye, Dax summons him to the bridge. Seyetik has launched the shuttlepod designed to reignite the dead sun—with himself aboard.

Realizing that Seyetik intends to kill himself to free Nidell, Sisko contacts the shuttlepod and attempts to talk the professor out of it. But Seyetik refuses, intent on going out in a blaze of glory. His vessel explodes on impact, and the sun flares into new life. Standing next to Sisko on the bridge, Fenna slowly fades away.

Soon after, Nidell recovers, but has no memory of Fenna's experiences. She bids him goodbye to return to her homeworld, leaving only Sisko to remember the bittersweet experience for both himself and Fenna.

 or a number of reasons, "Second Sight" is not a favorite with the in-house writing staff at *Deep Space Nine*. "We wanted to do a romance," says Robert Hewitt Wolfe. "We'd

The writers saw the romance as a way to humanize the somewhat aloof commander of Deep Space 9. ROBBIE ROBINSON

never really done one for the show, and I don't think it worked as well as we hoped it would."

The pitch was brought in by Mark Gehred-O'Connell, who had previously provided the one-sentence concept that became the springboard for *TNG*'s sixth-season episode, "Timescape." Initially, it seemed to fit the bill, bringing to mind "one of those ethereal romances that they used to make in the forties and fifties about a magical love," says Wolfe. "A remake of *Portrait of Jennie*," comments Peter Allan Fields, a series producer at the time. "That's what I wanted to do."

And indeed, Gehred-O'Connell's initial pitch does bring to mind that 1948 film, which featured Joseph Cotten as a struggling artist inspired by his periodic encounters with an enigmatic woman played by Jennifer Jones. "Bashir meets this very mysterious, exotic woman, falls for her, and she disappears," the freelancer recalls. "Then he sees her again and she disappears again. He tries to get his crewmates to help him find her, and discovers that nobody has ever seen her, and they all begin to wonder, 'Gee, has Julian been working a little too hard lately?' So Bashir has to solve this mystery on his own."

Much would change from Gehred-O'Connell's pitch, not the least of which was, at Michael Piller's suggestion, the shift in focus from Bashir to Sisko. "During the second season, Michael kept saying 'Let's define Sisko,'" recalls Ira Steven Behr. "That's when he and I had conversations about making Sisko the builder, on establishing the difference between him and Picard, the explorer. Sisko is a builder, he stays with a project until the finish. That helped us to see

Sisko in a whole lot of different ways. He's a guy who's solid and real and human."

The decision was made to provide Sisko with a romantic encounter that takes place on the fourth anniversary of his wife Jennifer's death. "The basic idea was that this guy has been missing something in his life, and he finds it in this weird, magical way, and loses it again," says Wolfe.

The shift to Sisko lightened the film noir tone of the piece that Gehred-O'Connell had initially envisioned. With Bashir as the protagonist, the writer explains, the story was more of an adventure of the type popularized by the pulp crime novels of Cornell Woolrich, the author of the short story on which Hitchcock's *Rear Window* was based. "I developed the story before the series began to air, so I based my ideas on descriptions of the characters in the series' bible," he says. "And Bashir was described as being very naive, a real eager beaver looking for adventure. I thought this would give him an adventure, but one with a dark side to it, because it turns out that this woman is an abuse victim who projects a different version of herself to get away from her real life."

The abuse angle eventually disappeared as the character of Seyetik became more pompous than heinous. But casting ultimately played a greater role in undercutting the dramatic tension of the teleplay. "We wanted Sisko to like Nidell's husband, but we wrote Seyetik as kind of a jerk," laughs Wolfe. "He was an egomaniac, one of those consumed artists who's good at everything and knows it, but to make him likable, he had to be a larger-than-life John Huston type of character." The casting of Richard Kiley, unfortunately, did not serve that purpose. "I love Richard Kiley," states Behr, "but I felt that we only got one side of the character. We got his bigness but we didn't get his soul, this bitterness and boldness we tried to give him. For the show to work, Sisko had to respect Seyetik, and for whatever reason, there was never any current of understanding between Sisko and him. And for me, the show fell apart. The audience had to like Seyetik. He kills himself. How many times do we see a guy commit suicide on *Star Trek*? It was a great ending, an ending worthy of John Huston, but it just seemed like some other wacky thing that this character was doing. You didn't feel the sorrow."

The episode did have some memorable aspects, however. Dan Curry recalls a bluescreen-shot devised to accompany the scene in which Sisko shows Fenna around the station. "They go up to what is supposed to be the tip of one of the upper pylons and look

Regardless of Kiley's skills, the character of Seyetik was still less than likable. ROBBIE ROBINSON

down," explains Curry. The script describes the optical that follows as: "A view of Deep Space 9 that we've never seen before, a high angle shot looking down . . . The station is a vast glowing jewel against the darkness of space." The resulting shot, orchestrated by Gary Hutzel, one of *DS9*'s two visual effects supervisors, lived up to the challenge set by the writers and "was just a really cool shot." Curry smiles. "I'd like to see out that window more, and I'd like to see them go to a window, and see back through a window into a different part of the station. But it's very difficult for us to do, and it doesn't make the *story* better, so we don't do that a lot."

"Second Sight" included a tip of the hat to both the *Star Trek* movies and the original series. Seyetik's plan to use protomatter to ignite the dead star—originally a plan to use Genesis technology to rejuvenate a portion of Bajor's war-plundered terrain, according to Gehred-O'Connell—recalls the dangerous substance used by David Marcus in *Star Trek III: The Search for Spock*. "It was established Federation terraforming technology," confirms Robert Wolfe. "Of course, the Genesis device didn't work, but obviously Seyetik's work is built upon the research of previous scientists. And it was a nice way to work in a reference to the movies."

Wolfe's decision to name a bit of Klingon poetry "The Fall of Kang," after the character played by Michael Ansara in the original series' episode "Day of the Dove," seemed equally inspired at the time, but just ten episodes later, would come back to haunt him. "We didn't know we were going to bring Kang back in 'Blood Oath,'" laughs Wolfe. "I thought, 'It's been eighty years and he was a real cool guy; he probably went out in a blaze of glory.' And he did—but in a subsequent episode!" While Wolfe gamely offers the possibility that the poem was a reference to an ancient Klingon warrior who had the same name as Ansara's Kang, Ira Steven Behr has a simpler explanation. "This was Oscar Kang as opposed to Samuel Kang."

Haneek wants to bring her people to Bajor, which she believes is the Skrreeas's legendary home, Kentanna. ROBBIE ROBINSON

SANCTUARY

Episode #430

TELEPLAY BY **FREDERICK RAPPAPORT**
STORY BY **GABE ESSOE & KELLEY MILES**
DIRECTED BY **LES LANDAU**

GUEST CAST

Varani	WILLIAM SCHALLERT
Tumak	ANDREW KOENIG
Nog	ARON EISENBERG
General Hazar	MICHAEL DURRELL
Vayna	BETTY McGUIRE
Vedek Sorad	ROBERT CURTIS-BROWN
Rozahn	KITTY SWINK
Gai	LELAND ORSER
Cowl	NICHOLAS SHAFFER

AND

Haneek	DEBORAH MAY

STARDATE 47391.2

On a day when Kira finds herself increasingly frustrated by the foot-dragging tactics of Bajor's bureaucratic provisional government, she is sidetracked by the plight of four refugees rescued from a disabled vessel that has passed through the nearby wormhole. Although unable to communicate initially because of difficulties the station's universal translator has with their language patterns, the humanoid aliens seem to trust Kira, so Sisko assigns her the task of looking after their needs.

Kira keeps up a flow of dialogue with the group's apparent leader, a woman named Haneek, eventually providing the translator with enough data to make sense of the aliens' language. Haneek is quick to take advantage of this development by explaining that her people are in desperate need of aid—and that there are three million of them who must be brought through the wormhole to receive it.

In meeting with the senior crew to discuss the predicament of her people, the Skrreeas, Haneek expresses surprise at seeing men in positions of authority. All Skrreean leaders are women; men are considered too emotional to handle such responsibilities. Haneek explains that she is not a leader, just a farmer who was lucky enough to find the wormhole, which Skrreean myths have predicted will lead them to their legendary home, Kentanna, a "planet of sorrow where the Skrreeas will sow seeds of joy."

Sisko offers to help the rest of Haneek's people find their way to the wormhole and to find a new home. As most of the Skrreeas's leaders were killed by their conquerers, the T-Rogorans—who were themselves conquered by the mysterious Dominion—Kira suggests that Haneek greet the incoming Skrreeas as they arrive at the station. A short time later, the Skrreeas opt to make Haneek their leader, entrusting her with the task of finding Kentanna. Although she worries that she may not be up to the task, she sets about trying to locate the Skrreean homeland by using a chart of the Bajoran Star System.

In the meantime, not all of the Skrreeas are having an easy time assimilating into the station's milieu. There are thousands of them wandering about, enjoying their first taste of freedom, and, as Quark points out, they look at everything and buy nothing. In addition, their appearance is distasteful to some. They "flake," shedding little pieces of skin here and there. The overemotional nature of males like Haneek's son

Tumak, who reacts badly to one of Nog's practical jokes, doesn't make things any simpler.

When Sisko finds Draylon II, an uninhabited planet that looks ideal for resettlement, he expects the Skrreeas to be overjoyed. But the Skrreeas have made a discovery that excites them much more. Haneek's research indicates that war-ravaged Bajor, certainly a planet of sorrow, is actually Kentanna. Bajor's provisional government considers the Skrreeas's request for immigration but ultimately rejects it. Adding three million refugees to Bajor's already beleaguered population would be too much of a burden. Haneek argues that her people would take care of themselves, growing food in uninhabited regions of the planet that would feed both Skrreeas and hungry Bajorans. But the Bajoran minister reasons that if Skrreeas's crops were to fail, Bajor would have three million additional mouths to feed, a prospect the planet could ill afford.

Haneek turns to Kira for support, but Kira sides with the minister. Bajor is not Kentanna, she explains, hoping Haneek will opt to take her people to Draylon II. Later, Kira tries to explain her decision, but Haneek is not interested. She feels Kira has betrayed her. Their strained conversation is interrupted by a communication from Sisko. Tumak has taken a ship and is heading toward Bajor.

When Haneek arrives at Ops, Sisko asks her to talk her son into returning. His ship has a dangerous radiation leak. And if the leak doesn't harm him, the Bajoran vessels ordered to prevent Skrreeas's ships from landing on Bajor may. But Tumak refuses to respond, even to his mother. Instead, he fires on one of the Bajoran ships, which returns fire. The Bajoran weapons miss Tumak's ship, but ignite the radiation leak, blowing up the Skrreeas's vessel.

With no other choice, the Skrreea sadly prepare to depart for Draylon II. Kira wishes Haneek good luck, but the Skrreeas woman tells her that the Bajorans have made a mistake based on fear and suspicion. Ruefully, she admits that Kira was right—Bajor is not Kentanna—and departs, leaving Kira to ponder her words.

As marvelous an invention as *Star Trek*'s famous universal translator is, you will only occasionally hear the device discussed in any given episode, and you will never, ever hear how it works. "You don't want people to think about it," says Ira Steven Behr. "You just don't, for a million upfront reasons."

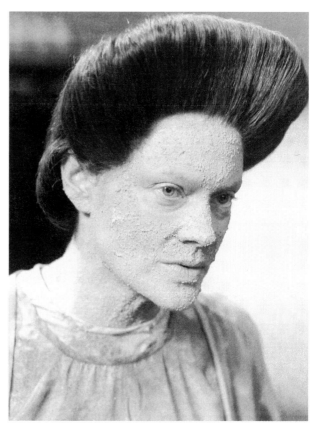

A simple descriptive line provided Michael Westmore with all the direction he needed in creating the makeup. ROBBIE ROBINSON

The universal translator is a crucial tenet in *Star Trek* dogma. It is the linchpin around which nearly every episode revolves, because when you seek out new life each and every week, you'd better be able to talk to it when you get there. But exactly how it works, how it manages to convey the illusion that people's lips actually move in sync with what is allegedly computer-translated verbiage, how crewmembers on away missions manage to speak to aliens even when they lose their communicators . . . well, don't ask.

All of which helps explain why the premise that DS9's universal translator initially had difficulty interpreting the Skrreea's language in "Sanctuary" was a story area in which the staff had to tread carefully. "It was a battle," says Behr, noting that the writers proceeded with similar trepidation in the fourth-season episode "Little Green Men." "But it was just too good [an opportunity] to pass up. It made the episode different. We meet aliens all the time, but these people were different."

The communication problem in "Sanctuary" provided the writers with a method of pacing the script. "We needed to delay the 'reveal' of what was going on," says Frederick Rappaport, who received the teleplay assignment after the producers bought a story pitch from Gabe Essoe and Kelley Miles. "Up until the end of Act 1, these are just pathetic aliens. We don't know there are millions more. And if we reveal that fact too early, we don't have a great 'act-out.'" (Television parlance for the way an act ends.) Understandably, the writers are always under pressure to create an act-out that will give viewers more to think about during the commercial break than "What's in the kitchen?"

The inability to communicate, compounded by their rather unappealing appearance (They are described in the script as scruffily garbed, with skin that is covered with "an off-putting mass of lumps and eczema-like scales."), also helped establish the unease between the Skrreeas and the Bajorans that would play a pivotal role in the episode's denouement. "The thing I liked about these aliens is that they flaked," notes Behr. "There's something to that old commercial that talks about 'the heartbreak of psoriasis.' It's something that people instinctively don't seem to like, so if you give this trait to a species, and you can't understand them, and then they say 'Help us,' you're automatically going to want to say 'No!'"

Michael Westmore found reaction to the makeup he created for the Skrreeas—finely ground pumice rock suspended in latex—similarly interesting. "When we were doing the makeup test on one, there were a lot of jokes about bad skin, 'What happened to you?' and so forth," he says. "But when you put it on groups of people, and suddenly you had twenty-five people standing around looking like this, then the perception was that this was a race of people, as opposed to an individual that you could make fun of."

The episode's downbeat ending and the voicing of anti-immigration sentiments that would soon become far more resonant to Californians with the passing of the state's Proposition 187, a controversial (and later overturned) law related to the rights of illegal aliens, pleased the producers. "It was a bold episode," says Behr. "It really walked the line with Kira, and pushed her into a very unattractive place, although we understood how she got there."

Rappaport credits Michael Piller with the idea that allowed the writers to move in a direction that made the normally sympathetic regulars a lot less sympathetic. "During the story meetings, we were all moving toward some kind of idealized ending, but it was Michael—he likes to rock the boat and I like that about him—who came in and said, 'No, let's not have

a pat ending, where everything is hunky-dory and we find a class-M planet for them and all is cool.' He said, 'Let's go darker here.'"

Rappaport turned in his second draft of the script. "Outside writers only get two shots at a teleplay, and you can only do so much in two drafts," he admits. And then the staff writers followed up on the path Piller had pointed out. It was Supervising Producer James Crocker who conceived Kentanna, the missing element that made the whole story come together, and, according to Rappaport, Ira Behr who wrote the powerful final line of the script, "Bajor is not Kentanna." "When I saw it," Rappaport says, "I was just blown away. It was such a lovely ending, and the way Les Landau directed it, where the airlock portals close on Kira, I couldn't have been more pleased."

On the lighter side, Aron Eisenberg gets to demonstrate a Nog version of the Ferengi grovel that Armin Shimerman, the master of all things Ferengi, taught him. And Dennis McCarthy demonstrates his sense of humor with the slow flute piece he wrote for Varani to play in Quark's bar. "This guy's supposed to

Aron Eisenberg does his tribute to the master groveler, Armin Shimerman. DANNY FELD

be hurting Quark's business, so I had him play something that would make you yawn, something that would annoy Quark—or me—like seven hours of 'new age' music." McCarthy laughs. "Aaaaghhh!"

"Sanctuary" includes yet another mention of the mysterious Dominion that would soon become so important to future developments on the series. And looking backward, rather than forward, a variety of guest stars with interesting *Star Trek* ties appear in the episode. Veteran character actor William Schallert—a guest star in the original series' episode, "The Trouble with Tribbles"—returns to the *Star Trek* fold as Varani, and Actor Andrew Koenig, son of Walter (Chekov) Koenig makes his *Star Trek* debut. The show also provides a role for Armin Shimerman's actress wife Kitty Swink as the Bajoran Minister Rozahn. (Swink would return as the Vorta, Luaran, in "Tacking into the Wind.")

The name of Koenig's character, Tumak, was originally "Turok," Rappaport's tribute to "one of my favorite comics when I was a kid," notes the writer. However, Behr, a longtime friend since they'd worked together on the television series *The Bronx Zoo,* knew his associate too well and "busted me on that immediately," according to Rappaport. "So I changed it to Tumak, which still is an homage. It was the name of Victor Mature's character in *One Million B.C.*" The name Varani, he adds, "was the name of the jinni in the film *The 7th Voyage of Sinbad.*"

At least a portion of the armada of Skrreeas's ships seen docking around the station was the result of a round of "kit bashing" by Glenn Neufeld and David Takemura. "We went out to a toy store and purchased dozens of models of airplanes and cars and tanks and so forth for the ships that would be seen in the far background," says Takemura. "Those don't need a lot of detail, so we can create little tiny spaceships out of the cannibalized parts."

The main Skrreean vessel has an interesting history, according to David Stipes, visual effects supervisor on *TNG,* who later would join the staff of *DS9.* The model, designed by Steven Berg (*The Abyss*) and painted by Ron Thornton (*Babylon 5*), had originally been built by Stipes's production company for an obscure movie called *Night of the Creeps.* This was the model's second appearance on *Star Trek*; it was the ship trapped in the asteroid belt in the *TNG* episode "Booby Trap." Although the model still belongs to Stipes, Takemura borrowed it for "Sanctuary" from science-fiction film memorabilia collector Bob Burns, who stores it in his vast museum of movie artifacts.

RIVALS
Episode #431
TELEPLAY BY JOE MENOSKY
STORY BY JIM TROMBETTA AND MICHAEL PILLER
DIRECTED BY DAVID LIVINGSTON

GUEST CAST

Keiko O'Brien	ROSALIND CHAO
Roana	BARBARA BOSSON
Alsia	K CALLAN
Rom	MAX GRODÉNCHIK
Cos	ALBERT HENDERSON

SPECIAL APPEARANCE

Martus Mazur	CHRIS SARANDON

STARDATE UNKNOWN

At a table in Quark's bar, Martus Mazur, a handsome humanoid man, lends a sympathetic ear to a matronly alien widow named Alsia. Alsia is about to invest her life's savings in a large mining concession, but she confesses that it hasn't been easy, planning all this on her own. Ever helpful, Martus offers to become her partner, and Alsia seems to be on the verge of accepting when Odo arrives and arrests Martus for swindling an elderly couple out of their savings. Martus shares a cell with an old, sickly alien who laments that he has lost everything he ever had because of the mysterious gambling device he owns. Activating the device, the alien exclaims in surprise when he sees that he's won—and then he dies, leaving the device in Martus's possession.

In a different part of the station, O'Brien is looking forward to playing racquetball in the new court

Con man Martus's unusual run of luck threatens to put his competitor, Quark, out of business. ROBBIE ROBINSON

he's built, until he finds out his primary opponent will be Bashir, a champion player who beats the chief game after game.

Now alone in his cell, Martus idly plays with the glowing device, winning game after game until Odo shows up and tells him the elderly couple opted not to press charges. Martus heads to Quark's for a drink. However, knowing that Martus is broke, Quark is unwilling to provide one until Martus offers to participate in the Ferengi's little game of chance. If he loses, says Martus, he'll give Quark his new "toy." Martus wins and Quark offers a modest sum to buy the device. But Quark's interest convinces Martus that the device is too valuable to give up. Not long after, Martus befriends Roana, a Bajoran widow who has decided to give up her shop on the Promenade. In no time flat, Martus has convinced her to reopen the establishment as Club Martus, a direct competitor to Quark's bar. To add insult to injury, Martus takes on Rom as a minor partner.

Martus's good luck seems to be growing. He's filled his bar with replicas of the original gambling device, and customers have flocked to Club Martus from Quark's to try them out. In the meantime, curious turns of luck are occurring all over the station. Dax finds a lost computer program, and Bashir continues to win in countless matches against O'Brien. At the same time, O'Brien is experiencing a streak of rotten luck, as is Kira, and, of course, Quark. Wondering if something physical is causing the odd fluctuations in luck, Sisko has Dax conduct a scientific investigation.

The competition between Bashir and O'Brien gives Quark an idea to win back his business, and as he puts together his plans, the flow of luck seems to shift. Suddenly Martus has to pay off a roomful of patrons who all simultaneously hit jackpots on his gambling devices. And Quark has managed to draw quite a crowd back to the bar to bet on an upcoming match between Bashir and O'Brien—a match that they are unable to get out of since Quark has promised half the proceeds to charity.

Now Club Martus is empty and Roana, suddenly seeing through Martus's charm, closes the business down. In a last-ditch effort to turn his luck around, Martus hands over his profits from the club to Alsia in exchange for a share in her investment.

Dax's investigation has led to the curious discovery that the solar neutrinos passing through the station are not spinning in accordance with the laws of probability. As she searches for an explanation, Bashir and O'Brien begin their match, only to discover that O'Brien can't lose and Bashir can't hit the broad side of a Plygorian mammoth. Acting on a hunch, Sisko and Dax head for Club Martus and conclude the gambling machines are to blame for everything. They destroy them over Martus's objections. Seconds later, Odo rearrests Martus on the earlier swindling charge. Back in the holding cell, Martus encounters Alsia, who he discovers has actually swindled *him*. But just as things seem darkest, Quark arrives to bail Martus out and send him away from the station to become someone *else's* competitor.

"People just didn't like it," Director David Livingston notes philosophically. "It was pretty much a piece of fluff, but it was fun. I had a good time doing it."

It's hard to put a finger on just what went wrong with "Rivals." The episode had a strong supporting cast, an interesting premise, and a fun action sequence with the station's odd couple, Bashir and O'Brien. But somehow, aside from some positive comments about the racquetball sequences, the episode seems to have struck out with both viewers and crew. "Our e-mail fans really liked the tight suit that Bashir wore in the matches." Robert Hewitt Wolfe grins. "They liked that a *lot*."

The initial story idea pitched by Jim Trombetta focused solely on the so-called butterfly effect (which was also an early name for the episode), which is "The idea that the flapping of a butterfly's wings in a tropical rain forest could make the stock market crash on Wall Street," according to Joe Menosky, who

Pairing Bashir and O'Brien allowed the actors to underline the characters' basic differences. ROBBIE ROBINSON

transformed ideas by Trombetta and Michael Piller into the final teleplay. "Basically, the concept that something can be linked by chaotic means in some weird causal way."

This wasn't the first time the *Star Trek* writing staff had heard a pitch related to chaos theory, notes *TNG* veteran Menosky. "Writers would come in and say 'What about chaos theory?' And someone else would say, 'Well, what about it?' Everyone would struggle but nobody would devise a story. It wasn't until Jim Trombetta pitched that Michael [Piller] saw a story."

The rivalry aspect of competing bars wasn't present in Trombetta's concept. His idea was that "Quark gets a device that gives him a lot of good luck, at the expense of other people," says Trombetta. "Someone had dug up this machine from an ancient civilization and was using it to gamble with. And Quark started having all this good luck, while everyone else was having terrible luck and things were falling apart."

Piller bought the concept and worked on it for a while, inserting the character of Martus, a Listener gone bad, initially conceived of as Guinan's wayward son (another idea that had been floating around since *TNG*, according to Wolfe). When Whoopi Goldberg proved unavailable for a guest shot, Piller decided it was no longer important to make Martus a relation of Guinan, although he did remain a Listener. Interestingly, the name of Guinan's species, El-Aurian, was first mentioned in this episode, not, as many people think, in the film *Star Trek Generations*. (Although it is obvious that early drafts of that film would have been in circulation around the *Star Trek* office by the time "Rivals" went into production in late 1993.)

Menosky enjoyed working on the story, which, he notes, had everything in there that he needed by the time Piller sent it to him. "A lot of times a writer is given a six-page story that isn't in very good shape, and you look at it and think, 'What the hell am I going to do with this?'" he says. "But 'Rivals' was a pleasure to work on, because Michael had a really strong idea about what he wanted to do with Martus as a rival for Quark."

But while the rivalry storyline would have seemed to allow for some nice character scenes, it "didn't quite gel," recalls Armin Shimerman. Shimerman was disappointed that the opportunity to work again with Chris Sarandon, with whom he'd appeared on Broadway over fifteen years earlier, didn't have the right spark. "Chris and I got along fine, but the one-upmanship that should have been there, these two

Ironically, the more the writers threw them together, the more the characters "learned" what they *did* have in common. ROBBIE ROBINSON

swindlers trying to outswindle each other, didn't really work." As a result, the character, conceived of as a recurring nemesis for Quark, didn't return.

The racquetball matches were staged on the holosuite set, a swing set for the series. "I had no time left to shoot it," says Livingston. "There was only six hours or so to do all of the scenes. So I had to plan it out really carefully and only shoot the absolute essential pieces that I needed."

The six hours probably seemed a lot longer to Siddig El Fadil and Colm Meaney. "The scenes were kind of bizarre because the racquetball court was such an odd shape that the ball would bounce wrong," says El Fadil. "It was designed in a sci-fi shape, with the walls at all sorts of oblique angles, and you'd hit the ball and you wouldn't know where it would go. So we were chasing these balls around like nutters, until they finally just staged us so we could look like we were shooting the ball where we wanted it to go." Because the set would have been expensive to put up and take down repeatedly, it wasn't used again on the series. "The dartboard was cheaper," notes, El Fadil, with a smile, "and we started using that in the third season."

If the fans liked Bashir in his racquetball gear, one has to wonder what they thought of O'Brien sans shirt. Meaney laughs at the idea that anyone might consider him a sex symbol. "It would seem to me that there are far more likely candidates for it!" he says. Nevertheless, there was some definite intention behind the scenes about having the chief strip off his shirt.

"I thought it was important," says Livingston. "He represents the common man on the show, and common men, when they get sweaty, take off their shirts. And so what if he doesn't look like Fabio. He looks *real*, like a human being. And later on, he has this nice loving moment with Keiko, where she hands him his shirt. I fought for that."

"I think it was an attempt to show he's sexy to his wife," observes Wolfe. "There's some sparks between the two of them. We don't see it all the time, but it's a real ongoing thing."

And sex symbol or not, it does give Meaney a "one-up" on El Fadil. "Bashir hadn't taken off his shirt yet," El Fadil says. "I reckoned they were going to send me to a gym for six months before they made me do a love scene." As it turned out, Bashir wouldn't take his shirt off for that love scene until the very last episode of the series, when he finally fulfilled his dream of sharing a bed with Dax—Ezri Dax.

Desperate to learn about his origins, Odo suffers the attentions of Dr. Mora. ROBBIE ROBINSON

THE ALTERNATE

Episode #432

TELEPLAY BY **BILL DIAL**
STORY BY **JIM TROMBETTA AND BILL DIAL**
DIRECTED BY **DAVID CARSON**

GUEST CAST

Dr. Mora Pol	JAMES SLOYAN
Dr. Weld Ram	MATT McKENZIE

STARDATE 47391.7

Odo is not terribly happy to see Dr. Mora Pol on Deep Space 9. Mora is the scientist who was assigned to the shape-shifter after the Bajorans found him, and the memory of the days when he was a "living experiment" makes Odo very uncomfortable. But Mora has come with news: Bajoran space probes have picked up signs of DNA similar to Odo's on a planet in the Gamma Quadrant. Mora would like to borrow a runabout to investigate. Sisko readily agrees and soon Odo, Mora, Dax, and a scientist named Weld are on their way. Along the way, Mora entertains Dax with stories of Odo's early days, much the way a parent would speak about his child . . . if that child had been a lab specimen.

The foursome beam to the surface of the planet and explore some stone ruins, finding a tiny life-form that may be related to Odo. As they prepare to transport back to the runabout, seismic activity rocks the planet and releases clouds of volcanic gas that incapacitate Mora, Dax, and Weld. But Odo, seemingly unaffected, acts quickly to get them back to the ship and then to the station. With Dax in the Infirmary, O'Brien attempts to classify the life-form the group has retrieved but tells Odo the computer is having a tough time because the organism keeps changing and reproducing. That night, Kira summons Sisko with disturbing news; someone or something has ransacked and almost demolished the science lab.

With the life-form missing and no sign of a break-in, O'Brien theorizes that the life-form itself may have caused the damage, and Sisko orders an intensive scan of the station to search for it. Guessing that the life-form exited via the ventilation ducts, O'Brien conducts a search in the conduits and ultimately finds the life-form, which appears dead, apparently unable to survive in the space station's environment. That evening, as Bashir studies the inert remains of the life-form, he is attacked by a large tentacled creature. He fends it off with a laser scalpel and the creature disappears into the ventilation ducts.

As Odo conducts an investigation, a recovered Dax compares the organic residue left behind by the creature that attacked Bashir to the remains of the planetary life-form. They're not the same. But Mora recognizes the DNA pattern from the new sample at once. Leaving Dax, he heads for Odo and informs the shape-shifter that the sample is from him. Odo protests that he was regenerating in his pail during both attacks, but Mora postulates that he wasn't. Searching for an answer, Odo suggests that perhaps the volcanic gas has affected him after all. Mora knows he's probably right, but he doesn't want to lose this fleeting chance to get Odo to come back to Bajor with him, once again to become an object of study. But that's the last thing Odo wants. At the peak of his panic and fury, Odo morphs into the creature and Mora flees in terror.

Realizing that in some ways he is responsible for the situation, Mora finds Sisko, explains that the creature is Odo and offers himself as bait to draw it from hiding. The plan works and the creature is captured, reverting to Odo. In the Infirmary, Bashir works with Mora to cure Odo, eliminating all traces of the gas from his cellular structure. Then Bashir leaves the two old acquaintances alone. Mora apologizes for the way he has treated Odo in the past and Odo, at last able to forgive, begins to form a genuine bond with his mentor.

"The Alternate" provides an intriguing look into Odo's psyche and a hint of how deadly an unfriendly shape-shifter can be. The story by Jim Trombetta and Bill Dial (the latter would go on to work with Michael Piller on the short-lived series *Legend*) morphed from one of several successful second-season Trombetta pitches.

Returning to terrain he had enjoyed exploring during the first season ("The Forsaken"), Trombetta's original story again focused on Odo, "a shape-shifting being who doesn't know much about himself," as the writer describes him. "I was thinking about multiple personality disorder," he recalls, "and it occurred to me that if a shape-shifter had such a disorder, not only would he go around exhibiting different personalities, but different bodies. That was the story; he lost himself, and found himself chasing a menace that was him. In doing so, he found something out about himself."

Not every self-discovery is pleasant, however. "This is something very scary—and it's you!" says Trombetta. "And it becomes a little like *Forbidden Planet,* with the revelation of the creature from the id."

The *Forbidden Planet* reference is apt, and although it's not deliberate, it's not entirely coincidental that the glimpse of Odo viewers get at the end

Showing the damage caused by the shape-shifting creature was easier than showing the creature. CARIN BAER

of the episode tends to bring to mind that film's famous id monster. "It didn't actually influence my sketches," recalls Dan Curry. "I'm such a big fan of that film—it's probably why I got into this business—that I intentionally tried to avoid it. My drawings are more like a taffy monster!" Still, the Odo-creature registered as the "Monster from the Id" with many people behind the scenes, and somewhere along the evolutionary trail his likeness began to live up to the moniker.

Glenn Neufeld found the realization of the creature more taxing than his work on the average episode. "I figured out that the way the script was written, by my timing, we'd be looking at the creature for a minute and a half of screen time," he says. "Thirty cuts between three and fifteen seconds each, at various times in the show. I was forced to point out that in the movie *Alien,* up to the moment where we really see it, there are really only a hundred frames of creature. And do we really want to see our creature all that time? And, of course, the answer was 'Yes.'"

The primary problem was time. "An episode gets shot in seven days," Neufeld explains. "My group has about a week of preproduction, and in that week we have to decide what the creature is going to look like, make artwork of it, make a deal with the visual effects house (in this case, Video Image) to do the work and create the creature in each of the shots. Then that work has to be finished and delivered to us so we can do the final composites into the production plates. So you go to the stage [during the week of actual filming] and people ask, 'What does the monster look like?' And you say, 'Well, it's big and gooey and about twelve feet tall and it goes Rrroowwlll!"

From that point on, the process becomes even more complicated, with Neufeld required to "stand with the director and tell thirty to forty people to stop what they're doing and start again because the actor didn't have his eyes at exactly the right eyeline, or whatever. I'm literally in everybody's way," he says. "The director rehearses it and says 'Okay, we're ready to go.' And I have to step in front of the camera and say, 'No, we're not because this next thing has to happen.' It's a big responsibility, because if you make a mistake, you not only face the scorn and derision of everybody who is trying to get the show done in seven days, but you force people to come back and reshoot at incredible expense."

To be fair, neither the actors nor the director have harsh memories of the effects crew's involvement in "The Alternate." Director David Carson, who proceeded directly from this episode to directing *Star Trek Generations*, notes philosophically that shooting scenes that incorporate special effects is always akin to "flying blind. You never really know how big a creature is, or how frightening it's going to be. So you shoot the scene in such a way that it can be cut in order to best enhance the effect. Then, later on, the producers can change the cut if they need to make it more frightening or less when the effect has been added. My whole job in effects sequences is to provide alternatives so the whole piece will be homogenous."

In scoring the episode, Dennis McCarthy took his cue from the special effects. "I treated it like a horror film," he says, noting that the arrangement was more synthesizer-heavy than the usual episode. "An orchestra can give you tremendous horror effects, but it can also sound dated. Adding the synthesizer pushes you into the era that we're in now."

The role of Odo's mentor, Dr. Mora, performed by frequent *Star Trek* guest actor James Sloyan, originally was to have been played by Rene Auberjonois in a dual performance. But, according to Auberjonois, "by the time the actual script came down, Mora's part

was too big. It would have taken two weeks to shoot the story with me doing both parts. It *is* possible, it's been done on the original series and on *TNG,* and even in our show. But in this case, I would have had to get out of my makeup, which takes two hours, and into another makeup. It wouldn't have been just a matter of changing costumes, as it was with, say, two Rikers. That takes just a few minutes."

The ultimate decision against using a heavily madeup performer in a dual role in "The Alternate" would influence the producers during the following season, when someone suggested Armin Shimerman play Quark's mother in "Family Business." "It was the same situation," says Shimerman. "The makeup makes it impossible."

ARMAGEDDON GAME
Episode #433
WRITTEN BY MORGAN GENDEL
DIRECTED BY WINRICH KOLBE

GUEST CAST

Keiko O'Brien	ROSALIND CHAO
E'Tyshra	DARLEEN CARR
Sharat	PETER WHITE
Nydom	LARRY CEDAR
Jakin	BILL MONDY

STARDATE UNKNOWN

On a munitions ship orbiting the planet T'Lani III, Dr. Bashir and Chief O'Brien work to help Kellerun and T'Lani scientists destroy their stockpile of harvesters, a deadly biomechanical weapon used by both worlds in a centuries-long war. With peace in the offing, this final step will ensure the future of the two races, and when at last Bashir discovers the correct procedure to neutralize the harvesters, there is much rejoicing among the research team. But as the last cylinder of harvesters is about to be neutralized, two Kellerun soldiers enter the lab and begin firing on the scientists. Bashir and O'Brien manage to kill their attackers, although they fail to notice that in the process, a small amount of the remaining harvesters material splashes onto O'Brien. With their return to the *Runabout Ganges* blocked, the pair take the only escape route available and beam down to the surface of T'Lani III.

A short time later, ambassadors from Kellerun

While the chief fights off a deadly disease, Bashir tries desperately to keep him alive and somehow signal for help. ROBBIE ROBINSON

and T'Lani arrive at Deep Space 9 and inform Sisko that O'Brien and Bashir were killed when O'Brien inadvertently tripped a security device in the lab. The ambassadors provide a visual recording of the incident, which convinces the command crew of their friends' deaths.

On the surface of T'Lani III, Bashir and O'Brien set up base in a deserted military command center and search for a way to contact DS9 or the T'Lani, whom they intend to inform of the Kellerun betrayal. With O'Brien focusing on repairing an old comm panel, Bashir attempts to occupy his own time by discussing with the chief the relationships between men and women. The discussion ends abruptly when Bashir hits upon a touchy area in O'Brien's relationship with his wife, Keiko, and only then does Bashir notice that O'Brien doesn't look well. A quick check with his medical tricorder confirms the worst: O'Brien has been infected by the harvesters.

In the meantime, Sisko goes to Keiko to present the bad news. Although stunned by the revelation, she asks to view the T'Lani recording of O'Brien's demise. After Sisko complies, Keiko points out a major inconsistency. The recording shows the chief drinking coffee in the late afternoon, something Keiko insists he never does. She believes the recording has been tampered with, and Sisko offers to travel to T'Lani III with Dax to find out why.

With O'Brien growing sicker, Bashir takes over the repairs on the comm panel, following the chief's instructions. As he works, they resume their earlier conversation about relationships, and Bashir reflects

on the one true love of his life, a ballerina whom he left behind on Earth in order to pursue his career in Starfleet. At last, the repairs are completed and Bashir sends out a weak distress signal, hoping that the T'Lani will find them before the Kellerun do. He realizes that whatever happens, it must happen quickly, for O'Brien's condition is becoming critical.

In orbit around T'Lani III, Sisko goes to the site of the accident while Dax checks out the abandoned *Ganges*. Her investigation reveals that someone has tampered with the runabout's computer log, attempting to erase a remote transport command that was made *after* the alleged accident at the T'Lani lab. The obvious conclusion is that Bashir and O'Brien might be alive.

But not for long. Bashir is relieved when the T'Lani ambassador arrives at the command center. But when the Kellerun ambassador and Kellerun soldiers follow, he realizes the truth; in order to secure the peace arrangement, the two governments conspired to kill anyone with any knowledge of the harvesters' technology. As the soldiers raise their weapons to obliterate the last two persons with that knowledge, O'Brien and Bashir dematerialize and find themselves on the *Ganges*, with Sisko and Dax.

Threatened by the T'Lani munitions cruiser, Sisko hails his assailants, but rejects their demands that he turn over Bashir and O'Brien. Instead, he cuts off communications and launches the *Ganges* at the T'Lani vessel, which responds by destroying the *Ganges*. As the T'Lani and Kellerun ambassadors prepare to take the second runabout in tow, they find that it has disappeared. Clearly, Sisko's attack was a ruse, and the Federation officers have escaped.

Although noteworthy for the second pairing of Ira Steven Behr's favorite duo, O'Brien and Bashir, "Armageddon Game" was another episode that would go through the writers' mill several times before the mix was palatable enough for production. "I liked it," says Behr, "but I'll tell you, it was a crunch show, where we were working weekends, that kind of thing. Not a good place to be."

Writer Morgan Gendel, back from the first season's "The Passenger," recalls that his initial pitch had to do with Federation personnel going to an alien civilization and insisting that the aliens get rid of a doomsday device. "And what the aliens do," says Gendel, "is encode the weapon onto O'Brien's DNA, so that if we want to destroy the weapon, we're going

Episode by episode the writers built a lasting friendship between these characters. ROBBIE ROBINSON

the weapon tries to kill everyone who had anything to do with getting rid of it.

"Really, the essence of my idea inspired him to spit back out the idea that became this episode," says Gendel, who would go on to become executive story editor on *Law and Order.* "That's just good collaboration. We had a good working relationship and he felt comfortable saying, 'Let's do it this way.' I felt good about it; that's the way it goes, whether you're on staff or not. You hope that every idea sparks another better idea."

But even after the basic framework was agreed upon, modifications continued. "Initially, the bad guys were supposed to be in a lab on a planet," says Gendel. "But if they were on a planet, then we had to have a ship for them to chase our guys at the end." And that, Gendel notes, bumped the budget up too high for the episode. So the ship and the lab became one and the same, a big space lab on the T'Lani munitions vessel.

Budgetary concerns also altered another idea: Piller's concept that the episode have an exciting *Midnight Run* or *North by Northwest* chase-movie kind of feel. After Gendel turned in his script, Behr and Jim Crocker would put in some long weekends making modifications when the chase sequences proved to be too expensive. "Ultimately it became a chase show on one set," comments Behr, with Bashir and O'Brien spending the bulk of the episode hiding out in one location.

What Behr likes best about "Armageddon Game" is the characterization. "It's a very important O'Brien/

to have to kill O'Brien. That's the idea: assuming that if digital memory is just an on-off switch, that what they do is either attach a molecule or not attach a molecule to each DNA strand, so O'Brien is, in effect, a walking floppy disk."

Unfortunately, notes Gendel, "there is another episode that uses a similar gimmick ("Dramatis Personae"), although I hadn't seen it at the time." But Gendel's pitch triggered some suggestions from Michael Piller as to how to reconfigure the storyline: an alien doomsday device that the DS9 crew helps to get rid of, whereupon the alien society that had possessed

The T'Lani and the Kelleruns. ROBBIE ROBINSON

Model of
the military
command
center on
T'Lani III.

Bashir show, and both the actors are great," he says. The bond established in the episode between the station's two British Isle natives is a small but important one. O'Brien may have shrugged off Bashir's notion that, "When two people face death together, it creates a bond that can never be broken." But the series' writers certainly didn't, as would become evident in subsequent episodes.

Relationships in general are emphasized in the script, be they the unearthing of bittersweet memories from Bashir's past (Bashir's old love, Palis, is named for a friend of Behr's wife, also a ballerina), or the well-crafted symmetry between O'Brien's reflections upon his sometimes troubled but rewarding marriage, and Keiko's passionate conviction that her husband is still alive.

Director Winrich Kolbe had no difficulty in extracting a touching performance from Rosalind Chao for the episode. "She knows her character a lot better than I do," Kolbe says. "I knew there was supposed to be tension between Keiko and O'Brien, and that obviously had to play into it. But I let her make the decision of how she would react. I said to her, 'What is your relationship with him? Do you give a damn? Do you have guilt, or remorse that maybe you should have tried harder?' We arrived at that particular conclusion, and it was her decision, and I just filmed it. Rosalind is a top-notch actress and she knew exactly what she had to do."

Behr is especially fond of the plot twist at the end where Keiko discovers that she's wrong about O'Brien's coffee habits. What counts, Behr says, is that she knows the truth that her husband is alive, not *how* she knows the truth.

But one of Behr's favorite moments was one that no one could have predicted during the scripting of the episode. Although the writers know what they have set down on paper, they rarely know how the details will be translated by the various production departments. Visual effects, for example, are always a surprise, as are the design of alien spaceships and costumes. Behr recalls that during the writing process of "Armageddon Game," the writers asked themselves, "Why are these two races at war?" The answer came to Behr abruptly while the staff was watching dailies from the episode and saw for the first time just what the Kelleruns and the T'Lani looked like. "It's because of the hairstyles," he recalls saying out loud. "Now we know what the war's about!" It was, he notes wryly, "the biggest laugh we ever had in dailies."

Ironically, Behr wasn't the only person who noticed the elaborate hairdos; the episode received an Emmy nomination for Outstanding Achievement in Hairstyling for a Series for Hair Designer Josée Normand and Key Hair Stylists Ron Smith, Norma Lee, and Gerald Soloman. The series lost the coveted award to *Doctor Quinn, Medicine Woman*.

The title to the episode came courtesy of Robert Hewitt Wolfe, who intended it as an homage to the original series episode, "A Taste of Armageddon." And the matte painting that provides the establishing shot of T'Lani III was a reworked version of one that originally had been created for the *TNG* episode "Legacy." According to Dan Curry, Illusion Arts's Robert Stromberg gave the matte different coloration and changed some of the buildings in the foreground. While such reworking is being done electronically more and more, this particular time Stromberg modified the painting in the old-fashioned way, with paint and brushes.

WHISPERS

Episode #434

WRITTEN BY PAUL ROBERT COYLE
DIRECTED BY LES LANDAU

GUEST CAST

Keiko O'Brien	ROSALIND CHAO
Ensign DeCurtis	TODD WARING
Admiral Rollman	SUSAN BAY
Coutu	PHILIP LeSTRANGE
Molly O'Brien	HANA HATAE
Computer Voice	MAJEL BARRETT

STARDATE 47552.1

Inside a runabout headed through the wormhole, Chief O'Brien ponders the bewildering events of the past fifty-two hours. His life, his relationship with friends and family, even his sense of reality—all has been turned on its ear. He can think of only one place to go, back to the Parada system to warn the inhabitants . . . although about what, he is unsure.

O'Brien records his impressions of the past two days in the runabout's computer, beginning with his return to DS9 from an assignment in the Parada system and his wife and daughter's subsequently distant behavior. The peculiar incidents mount up: Ensign DeCurtis is ordered by Sisko to realign the station's security net for upcoming peace talks, without first consulting O'Brien; Dr. Bashir insists on giving O'Brien a physical, and Sisko orders O'Brien to comply. Then, after questioning O'Brien about his recent experiences with the Paradas, Sisko instructs O'Brien to repair the station's upper pylons, rather than help the engineering crew to prepare security for the Paradas peace conference. Later, Ensign DeCurtis refuses to allow O'Brien to check the quarters assigned to the Paradas, explaining that only Kira has the access codes. When Sisko orders O'Brien back to the upper

Following his return from the Parada system, O'Brien finds that everyone on the station is acting oddly. CARIN BAER

pylons, the annoyed engineer pretends to leave, but lingers long enough to see DeCurtis enter the quarters without using any access codes.

Back in his own quarters, O'Brien is again confronted with the feeling that his wife isn't herself. But if she isn't herself, then who is she? After Keiko goes to bed, O'Brien searches the computer for any anomaly aboard the station that could be causing the crew to turn against him. He learns that he has been denied access to all logs dated after his return from the Parada system, and that his own logs have been analyzed by other crewmembers. In desperation, O'Brien turns to Odo, who has just returned from a trip to Bajor. But though initially sympathetic, Odo is eventually proven to be part of the same "conspiracy" as the rest of the crew. When Sisko, Kira, and Bashir attempt to corner and sedate O'Brien, the engineer grabs Kira's phaser and escapes, making his way to a runabout and leaving the station.

After a call placed to Starfleet fails to provide him with support, O'Brien decides to look for answers where his troubles began, in the Parada system. Closely trailed by another runabout from DS9, O'Brien manages to elude his captors, and when sensors indicate that his pursuers have beamed from their runabout to the surface of Parada II, he follows. There he finds Sisko and Kira meeting with Coutu, a Paradas rebel leader who tells O'Brien he can explain everything that's happened. But when Coutu makes an unexpected move, O'Brien raises his weapon to fire and is mortally wounded by Coutu's bodyguard.

As O'Brien lays dying, Bashir approaches, followed by another figure, another *Miles O'Brien*, identical to himself. Coutu explains that the real O'Brien had been captured several days earlier, and that the O'Brien who'd returned to the space station was a specially programmed replicant, designed to assassinate someone at the peace talks. Sisko had been warned of the possible substitution and taken precautions, but the replicant had had no way to comprehend the actions of the people he believed to be his friends. Even upon hearing the truth, he is true to the only memories he knows, and as he dies, he asks the real O'Brien to express his love to Keiko.

"I think 'Whispers' is a terrific show," enthuses Ira Steven Behr. "There's something about the way it was shot and the point of view that made it into an episode that was really special, and obviously Colm [Meaney] is one of the strongest actors we have."

Given a script that featured his character in every single scene, that's no small testimony to Meaney's capabilities. The decision as to how to play the replicant who usurps the real O'Brien's position, however, was relatively simple, according to Meaney. "In order not to give away what was going on to the audience, we tried to keep him exactly the same, even though it was a different O'Brien," he recalls. "I played it exactly the way I usually do. It was only the circumstances around him that were weird and gave you the feeling that something else was going on."

Writer Paul Coyle's initial spin on the story was quite different from the final product. "My original pitch to James Crocker involved O'Brien's waking up one day to find that Keiko and Molly were gone, and nobody on the station remembered him," he says. "There was no record that he had ever been there. And the computers reveal that there *is* a Miles O'Brien, but he's serving on the *Enterprise* somewhere far off."

The *Twilight Zone*–like quality of the pitch appealed to Crocker and Michael Piller, and Coyle was given the teleplay assignment. However, as often happens, story details began changing rapidly from that point forward. "When we got to the break sessions, the staff decided that they didn't like any of that amnesia business," says Coyle. "So everybody in the room brainstormed and somebody came up with the idea of doing *The Parallax View*, a Warren Beatty–starred suspense thriller from the 1970s, which was

One of the earliest "torture O'Brien" episodes. The writers loved to explore this motif year after year. CARIN BAER

highlighted by strong accents of political paranoia as the central character attempts to unravel a dangerous mystery. An earlier tale of paranoia, *Invasion of the Body Snatchers*, also influenced the tone of the episode.

"In a way, it's *Invasion of the Body Snatchers* from the body snatcher's point of view," observes Behr. "That's what ultimately makes the show tragic and interesting, that the body snatcher doesn't know it. It's unfortunate that the show ends so abruptly. I wish we'd had a little more time there."

Ironically, at one point in the development of the script, there was too *much* time left at the end of the episode. Coyle explains, "The episode came up short for one particular reason: we had to stick entirely on O'Brien for every minute. We couldn't cut away to any of the other characters because they'd obviously be saying, 'We don't think O'Brien is O'Brien.' So we could never open the story up for the audience and go to a B-story, or even linger on two characters after O'Brien leaves the room, because it'd be giving the story away."

After Coyle turned in his forty-nine-page draft, the in-house staff took over. "They were in a rush to shoot it," Coyle recalls, "so as a way to expand the story, they came up with the flashback structure, adding scenes in the runabout where O'Brien escapes from DS9 and goes through the wormhole." While such tinkering can sometimes come off as "padding," Coyle feels that the additions "worked well on the screen, added a nice pace to the show, and also emphasized the mystery: 'Why is O'Brien running?'"

The episode marks the second appearance of actress Susan Bay as Admiral Rollman ("Past Prologue") and introduces the *Runabout Mekong,* a replacement for the *Ganges,* destroyed in the previous episode, "Armageddon Game."

An apparent continuity slip in the third act of the final script, where the name *Rio Grande* is inadvertently substituted for *Mekong* in referring to the pursuing runabout, may have resulted in the loss of a touchstone back to *The Next Generation.* In that scene, O'Brien gives voice to a reprise of "The Minstrel Boy," last heard in *TNG's* "The Wounded." Coyle says that he noticed the runabout mix-up when he received his copy of the final shooting script (generally sent out to the writers after an episode is completed) and immediately notified Behr. Coyle later noticed that when the episode aired, most of that scene was gone; only the last few seconds of it remained. "I assume that [by the time I called], it was too late to go back and put in the right words," says Coyle. "After all that trouble to add scenes to pad the show out, here was a two-page scene they ultimately had to cut."

Science fiction buffs may have noted the use of the word "replicant"—a term most familiar to fans of the film *Blade Runner*—to describe the false O'Brien. The decision to use the word was motivated by the desire to use something other than android, which tends to bring to mind *TNG's* Data, or clone, which didn't have the appropriate connotation for the writers. With a nod toward *Blade Runner,* Coyle notes that he used the word precisely because the term hadn't been previously used in *Star Trek.* "Obviously this guy wasn't a clone or an android or a robot. So what's left? I used replicant and nobody objected."

PARADISE

Episode #435

TELEPLAY BY JEFF KING AND RICHARD MANNING & HANS BEIMLER
STORY BY JIM TROMBETTA AND JAMES CROCKER
DIRECTED BY COREY ALLEN

GUEST CAST

Cassandra	JULIA NICKSON
Joseph	STEVE VINOVICH
Vinod	MICHAEL BUCHMAN SILVER
Stephan	ERICK WEISS
Computer Voice	MAJEL BARRETT

AND

Alixus	GAIL STRICKLAND

STARDATE 47573.1

While surveying nearby star systems for Class-M planets capable of supporting new colonies, Sisko and O'Brien find a planet that already is occupied by humans. Efforts to contact the inhabitants from their runabout prove fruitless due to what appears to be a low-level duonetic field on the planet's surface. Curious, the pair beam down to investigate, and quickly find that none of their equipment will work. They are discovered by two men who tell them their colony has been stranded on this planet ever since they made an emergency landing over ten years ago. None of their technological systems have worked since then.

Sisko and O'Brien are taken to meet the rest of the group, who have constructed a makeshift village around their failed vessel, and to meet the colony

Alixus insists that Sisko accept the fact that he can never leave her world. ROBBIE ROBINSON

leader, Alixus. The colonists are eager to hear news of the realm beyond their planet, but Alixus is more interested in discussing the great strides the colony has made *despite* the lack of technology. And although some of the colonists have allowed Sisko and O'Brien's arrival to trigger thoughts of rescue parties, Alixus states proudly that she never will leave this world, even if the opportunity arises.

Invited to be guests of the colony as long as they help with the chores, O'Brien attempts to find equipment that might help them regain contact with the runabout. But Joseph, a colonist who was once the engineer of the downed ship, explains that Alixus had advised them to throw away the useless components long ago, so they would realize they had only themselves to rely on.

When Joseph is brought news that the illness of one of the colonists has taken a turn for the worse, he asks Sisko and O'Brien for help. But it is clear that they can do nothing to cure the sick woman. However, if they had access to the medical kit on the runabout, it would be a different story. O'Brien begins thinking of ways to use the duonetic field to their advantage, perhaps by modifying their communicators. Alixus abruptly pulls Sisko aside and tells him that he and O'Brien must stop talking about technology, because such talk is harmful to the morale of the community.

On DS9, Kira and Dax have realized that Sisko's runabout, the *Rio Grande*, is not responding to hails. They locate it flying aimlessly through space and set out to intercept it. In the meantime, Sisko and O'Brien join the workers in the fields and discover that life in the colony has a darker side, as they witness the release of a colonist from imprisonment in a small metal box. His crime: stealing one candle. Sisko has problems distinguishing the so-called discipline from torture, but Alixus insists that it is necessary for the good of the community.

That night, one of the female colonists comes to Sisko's room, with the clear intention of seducing him. Rejecting her advances, Sisko confronts Alixus, who admits to having sent the woman to ease his transition into the community. Angry and suspicious, Sisko wonders out loud at the apparent coincidence of a woman with Alixus's antitechnology convictions having crash-landed on a planet where technology is impossible. Alixus notes that sometimes fate delivers just what a person needs, and assigns Sisko to an additional work detail—an apparent punishment for his lack of cooperation.

The next day there is additional punishment, psychological in nature. Despite an adequate supply of fresh water, Sisko learns that Alixus is rationing water supplies to the colonists because they have failed to win Sisko and O'Brien over. Later, on the heels of an announcement that the sick colonist has died, Alixus reveals that O'Brien has been caught trying to activate his equipment, behavior that she declares wasteful and futile. Because Sisko is O'Brien's commanding officer, Alixus holds him responsible and puts him in the metal box.

In space, Kira and Dax catch up with the runaway runabout and manage to snag it in a tractor beam. Boarding the vessel, they find no signs of a struggle, but clear evidence that the ship has been tampered with. Taking the ship in tow, they begin to trace the *Rio Grande*'s path.

After a long, hot period in the box, Alixus releases Sisko and tells him that she will give water to him and the rest of the colony if he will bend and begin to adopt their ways. But despite his powerful thirst, Sisko rejects the offer and returns to the box.

Determined, O'Brien again sets out to find a way out of their predicament. Creating a compass, he finds the one piece of technological equipment on the planet that *does* work: a machine that creates a duonetic field. Deactivating it, he returns to the village, releases Sisko from the box with his now-functioning phaser and reveals Alixus's secret.

Caught, Alixus admits to having brought the colonists here deliberately, knowing they'd never be able to leave while her machine was functioning. She claims that her plan has allowed each person to live up to his full potential, but Sisko points out that it has also caused the deaths of several colonists, deaths for which she must take responsibility.

When Kira and Dax arrive, Sisko and O'Brien offer to remove the colonists, but although they have turned against Alixus, they are not prepared to abandon their home. Only Alixus and her son will be forced to leave Paradise.

"'Paradise' was a strong Sisko show," says Ira Steven Behr. "It was our *Great Escape*, with Sisko being Steve McQueen, the cooler king, not giving in. But in terms of what those people were doing, the message of the show always seemed a little unclear."

"Paradise" was another episode that went through many writers' hands before it made it to the cameras. The core idea—loosely patterned on the

Sisko's defiance resonates with every step Avery Brooks takes.
ROBBIE ROBINSON

beliefs of Southeast Asia's Khmer Rouge, with their view that technology has infected society and must be eliminated—originated with Jim Trombetta, in his third of four contributions to *DS9*'s second season. "I wanted to put these characters, who have humane ethics that are based on hardware, into a situation where you take the hardware away and see what happens to those ethics," he says. "If you have to fight a war and you have a phaser, you set the phaser on stun and knock the guy down. But suppose you only have a stick?"

Despite the fact that the episode strayed a bit from his original vision, Trombetta is happy with the result. "It's not a real action-packed thriller," he admits, "but all of the philosophical ideas get expressed and enacted in a very good way, almost in the sense of an old-fashioned drama."

Curiously, it was the philosophy of the episode that seems to have caused the most problems for the on-staff writers. "It was a show that worked well, but I don't know if we ever found it," reflects Behr. "We went back and forth over whether what these people were doing was a positive thing or a negative thing. *Star Trek* is such a tech show, and making these people antitechnology. . . it was almost like doing a negative show on Greenpeace."

Peter Allan Fields recalls working on a draft of the episode after Jim Crocker took the first pass at Trombetta's story. Other writers included Jeff King and the old *TNG* writing team of Richard Manning and Hans Beimler. The majority of the scripts didn't seem to have what Michael Piller was looking for,

according to Fields. Beimler would come on staff full time during Season 4, and would replace Robert Hewitt Wolfe as Behr's writing partner in Season 6.

Even after the teleplay was completed, there were questions about how dark to make the portrayal of "cult" leader Alixus, well played by Gail Strickland. "Gail and I worked very hard to make that character reasonable," recalls Director Corey Allen, "because her motives were right-thinking. She had created a paradise, and she needed to preserve it through discipline. We set out to let her be the reasonable and caring human being that she and I agreed she was, but we were swimming upstream. It didn't come out that way. But I think that it's to Gail's credit that in making the effort the character came out with more human traits."

The "puritanical outlook" of the episode guided Dennis McCarthy's hand in scoring the episode. "There's an eight-minute sequence at the end where Alixus is trying to get everybody to stay and as I watched it, I thought, 'What would Martin Luther have put in here?'" he recalls. "So I played it from a very Protestant viewpoint, using all the old church harmonies. It's subtle, but if I shortened the music and made it slightly more melodic, it could be used in a hymnal."

The Protestant sound of "Paradise" provides an interesting counterpoint to the type of music McCarthy tends to compose for Bajoran storylines. "Then I get very Old Testament," he admits, pointing to the first season drama "Duet." "The Nazi analogy in that episode made me think about cantors, and the kind of music that you hear in synagogues." McCarthy pauses and chuckles. "Of course, having a Jewish grandmother made it easy [to come up with that idea]. She always wanted me to be a cantor, but with a name like McCarthy . . . well, I don't think so."

In order to create the illusion that the *Rio Grande* is present in one scene without actually bringing in the heavy set piece, director Corey Allen framed his shot with only the runabout's "landing foot" in view. The design for the foot was created by Jim Martin.

The throwaway details peppered throughout the script include the information that runabouts were first commissioned two years before the episode takes place (apparently just prior to the show's debut); the fact that soccer still exists in this era, even if baseball doesn't; and the fact that at least some Starfleet officers wear boxer shorts under their uniforms. Costume Designer Robert Blackman notes that the shorts were made from the same fabric as O'Brien's T-shirt. Are we to infer from this that boxers are standard issue for

Starfleet personnel in the twenty-fourth century? "No," says Blackman. "In this particular instance, we chose to put the actor in boxer shorts. But for somebody else, it might be a different kind of shorts."

The scene in which O'Brien strips down to his shorts in order to set up a decoy with his uniform was filmed at Griffith Park's bird sanctuary, which may constitute hazardous working conditions, considering a warning in that day's call sheet noting the potential presence of poison oak at the location.

According to Behr, the mention of Jake's ever-increasing height was thrown into the script to reflect what might be referred to as a "technical necessity"—Actor Cirroc Lofton's continuous growth over the course of the series. While admitting that any other child actor would have gotten taller as the series progressed, "I don't know that any other child actor would be *that* taller, man!" laughs Behr.

SHADOWPLAY

Episode #436

WRITTEN BY **ROBERT HEWITT WOLFE**
DIRECTED BY **ROBERT SCHEERER**

GUEST CAST

Colyus	KENNETH MARS
Rurigan	KENNETH TOBEY
Taya	NOLEY THORNTON
Female Villager	TRULA M. MARCUS
Male Villager	MARTIN CASSIDY
Vedek Bareil	PHILIP ANGLIM

STARDATE 47603.3

Commander Sisko sends Dax and Odo on an assignment to the Gamma Quadrant to investigate an unusual particle field detected by the station's sensors. They track the field to a small unexplored planet, and when they beam down to pinpoint the source, they find a matter/anti-matter reactor standing in the middle of a valley. But even as Dax begins to study it, a small group of the world's inhabitants encircle them. They are taken into custody by a humanoid named Colyus, who serves as the Yaderan colony's Protector. Although he finds Dax and Odo have committed no crime, Colyus has a mystery on his hands. Since the previous fall, some twenty-two members of the village have disappeared, the most recent one just six hours earlier.

After Dax is able to convince Colyus that she and Odo are not connected to the disappearances, they

Although she's only a hologram, Odo feels a kinship with Taya.
ROBBIE ROBINSON

offer to help the Protector in solving the mystery. Colyus introduces them to Rurigan, an elderly man whose daughter is the most recent victim. When Odo hears that Rurigan's granddaughter, Taya, was the last person to see her mother, he asks to speak to her.

Taya is initially frightened by Odo's unusual appearance, but her curiosity soon does away with her shyness, and she begins to question Odo about his background. The spontaneous conversation, which touches upon the fact that Odo has been looking for *his* parents for a long time, creates a rapport between the two of them. As they discuss her mother's habits, Taya reveals that, like the rest of the Yaderans, her mother has never left the valley, a piece of information that intrigues Odo. Moved by Taya's sadness, the shape-shifter promises to do everything he can to find her mother.

Back on the station, Sisko gets his young son a job with O'Brien, in the hopes that it will prepare him for Starfleet Academy, which Jake later tells Sisko he doesn't want to attend. At the same time, Kira pays a visit to Quark to warn him that she'll be keeping an eye on him while Odo's gone, so he may as well forget any schemes he has in mind. Not long after, Kira receives a surprise visitor from Bajor, Vedek Bareil, who's been invited to speak at the station's shrine by Prylar Rhit. But it soon becomes apparent that Bareil is interested in more than a discussion of dogma.

On the other side of the wormhole, Odo continues his investigation, focusing on Rurigan, who helped to found the colony. The old man reveals that he is dying but isn't particularly helpful in providing clues. And like everyone else in the village, he has no interest in the area outside the valley and is convinced that none of the missing persons did either. Nevertheless, Dax and Odo decide to explore the edge of the valley, with Taya tagging along. As they pass some bushes, a Yaderan sensing device disappears from Dax's hand, and when Taya reaches out toward them, her arm disappears up to the elbow, only to rematerialize when she moves the arm back toward her face.

Returning to the Yaderan settlement, Dax investigates the reactor they first discovered and draws some swift conclusions. The device is actually a holographic projector that creates an omicron particle field from which all of the objects in the village, and all of the people, are formed. One of the machine's components is breaking down, which is why people have been disappearing. Although the villagers are shocked at the idea they're all holograms, Colyus convinces them that the only hope for their "survival" is to allow Dax to shut down the reactor system and repair it. There is a chance she may not be able to start it up again, but Dax points out that if she doesn't fix it, it will fail completely within a few months. Dax proceeds and the village vanishes, leaving only Dax, Odo —and Rurigan.

On DS9, Kira discovers that Prylar Rhit's invitation to Bareil was extended at Quark's suggestion, in the hopes that her budding romance with the vedek would take her mind off Ferengi affairs. The plan almost worked, but she takes particular delight in telling Quark that she's put an end to one of his illicit endeavors *and* enjoyed the time spent with Bareil!

The only real occupant of his village, Rurigan explains that when the Dominion took over his homeworld, Yadera Prime, they destroyed his whole way of life. So he left Yadera and came to this world, using a hologenerator to recreate everything he'd lost. In the thirty years he's been there, he's seen people marry, have children, and grow old, like him. The townspeople have taken on a life of their own. Although he feels that that small bit of happiness is behind him, Dax and Odo convince him otherwise, and Rurigan and Dax repair the system. When they reactivate it, the entire population of the village reappears, including Taya's mother and the other missing inhabitants. Dax and Odo take their leave, knowing that Rurigan will live out his remaining years in the presence of his loved ones.

"Shadowplay" featured three separate storylines and some memorable moments between Odo and a little girl who turns out to be a hologram. But if you ask crewmembers what *their* favorite part of the episode was, chances are you'll hear two words: Ken Tobey.

If the name is unfamiliar, you're probably not a baby boomer. Either that or you've missed out on a few classic science-fiction films.

"I love Ken," says Ira Steven Behr. "He's a sweet, sweet, sweet man. I've always liked his work and I've always wanted to use him. It was great to have him in a *Star Trek*, in a science-fiction thing."

Dan Curry seconds that emotion. "It was wonderful for us, because we're all science fiction fans and he was in the great ones, like *The Thing* and *It Came from Beneath the Sea.*"

As with most television series, the casting process for *Deep Space Nine* generally involves sessions where numerous actors read lines in front of the director and various producers. When Behr is involved in the casting sessions, observes Robert Hewitt Wolfe, odds are that the selection will include character actors who've been in the business for some time. "Ira's a big fan of actors who really have their craft down and have been in some of his favorite movies," says Wolfe, writer of the episode, initially known as "Persistence of Vision."

Wolfe's original take on the story focused much more on Rurigan—Tobey's character—than the aired episode, and it was also a good deal more downbeat. The spark that inspired that early version was a con-

The producer's privilege was exercised in casting a personal favorite, character actor Ken Tobey. ROBBIE ROBINSON

versation between Wolfe and Behr about virtual reality. "Ira said, 'How scary is it going to be in the future when you won't be able to tell what's real and what isn't?'" recalls Wolfe. From that conversation, Wolfe generated a story in which O'Brien and Dax get into a place that is a virtual-reality prison. They escape, but then realize they're still inside. "Then they escape again," says Wolfe, "and I wanted the tag to be where Keiko was telling O'Brien how good it was for him to be back, and O'Brien saying, 'I don't know whether I'm back or not. I'm never gonna know.' Fade out."

However, Michael Piller had a different take. "He wanted me to do the story about a relationship, and about those people who thought they were real, but weren't," says Wolfe. Wolfe resisted the changes at first, but ultimately found that he was very pleased with the results. "Michael forced me into it kicking and screaming, but I have to thank him for it now." He grins.

Behr agrees. While the final version of the script seemed "just okay," the filmed version had considerably more impact. "When we saw it, we said, 'You know what? You put Odo together with a kid and you've got a winner.' It worked. The whole idea of this man creating this world for himself was actually quite sweet. Every now and then, you have to do a nice, sweet episode, which *DS9* isn't known for, but now we've done it, and we'd do it again."

As for Wolfe's original concept, some of it got used the following season in "The Search," while the darker threads would show up in Wolfe's fourth-season teleplay for "Hard Time."

Besides the use of Ken Tobey (and another respected character actor, Kenneth Mars), the episode is noteworthy for being one of *DS9*'s few "A-B-C" shows, featuring not only a B-storyline (Kira, Quark, and Bareil), but a C-storyline as well (Jake telling his dad he doesn't want to attend the Academy). Although either of the subordinate stories could have been dropped if the production ran into timing problems, Wolfe points out that the three threads are thematically related. "They're all about the unreality of appearances. Everyone would think Jake would want to be a Starfleet guy, but he doesn't. You'd think Bareil was on the station to see Kira, but the truth is that Quark lured him there. And then there's the girl, who seems real, but isn't."

The teleplay includes some interesting revelations about the characters, including the fact that O'Brien played cello, but didn't follow up on it for a career. That gives him something in common with a number of the other station dwellers: Rom would

The father-son dynamic was captured eloquently in this scene.
ROBBIE ROBINSON

have preferred to pursue engineering over profit-making; Bashir wanted to be a tennis player, and "even Jake, who doesn't necessarily know what he wants to do, but knows what he *doesn't* want to do," reflects Wolfe, who admits that he wanted to be an astronaut.

O'Brien's designation as Senior Chief Specialist is one that hadn't been used before and was never used after. "We were attempting to come up with a rank equivalent to Chief Petty Officer, since no one liked that term," says Wolfe. "I actually called the Navy Information Office, and the problem is that he's been in Starfleet for a long time and probably is the second-highest ranking you can be and still be an enlisted guy. So we were trying to come up with a rank that sounds like that, and I don't think we were successful, so we just ignored it."

Odo's line "I don't do faces very well," triggers the eternal query, "Why not?" Since the writers hadn't pinned down a definitive answer, Rene Auberjonois devised one of his own. "If there's something for Odo to replicate that has a prototype, like a rat or a knapsack or a chair, he can replicate it exactly," says the actor. "But because he is searching for his identity, even beyond the fact that by third season he knows where he comes from, he cannot create a face for himself. It's an identity problem for Odo, because he is a character who believes, in the strictest sense of the word, in telling the truth. And I believe he could make a face like Paul Newman or Quark, but he can't create something that he doesn't understand, and he doesn't understand himself yet."

A figure of Odo provides scale in this sketch of the hologenerator. JIM MARTIN

The episode, partially shot in that reliable L.A. staple, Bronson Canyon, contains yet another mention of the mysterious Dominion, which Behr says was inserted deliberately. "It just seemed like the perfect place to keep it alive, and it served the purpose of explaining what had happened to Rurigan's people." It also telegraphed a lot about the nature of the Dominion, he adds wryly. "Ken Tobey is so likable and straightforward that you know if the Dominion killed his people and they don't like Ken Tobey, the Dominion's got to be a bad thing."

After facing numerous complications with sequences that probably looked pretty simple to viewers—such as making a tricorder vanish from Dax's hand and an entire village and its inhabitants disappear from the middle of Bronson Canyon—Glenn Neufeld thought that turning Odo into a spinning top at the end of the episode would be fairly routine. But no day is ever routine at *Deep Space Nine.*

"I had decided that I would have Odo make a dance move," recalls Neufeld. "He would step away from Dax, whom he's standing with, and then twist in one direction and put his arms out, and then spin himself in the other direction, lowering himself down as he spun. The real spin would then segue into the computer-animation spinning. Rene and I rehearsed it [while the episode was in production], and he actu-

ally got two or three spins out of it before he fell down. We shot reference plates so we'd know where to place our fake shadows and so on." The plan was to bring Auberjonois back during postproduction and film him performing the same move on a bluescreen. That way, Neufeld would have a matte of Odo that he could give to the computer animator "so that one matte could morph into the other matte, as well as the live action."

Unfortunately, on the day that Auberjonois came back to shoot the bluescreen, he had an inner ear infection. "Each time he would spin it was terribly painful for him, and he could only do three-quarters of a turn before losing his balance and falling down," says Neufeld. "He was really ill. So what originally was going to be a full turn before the animation cross began, turned out to be a partial spin just before Rene began to lower his torso."

The shot was completed, with the visual effects team making it work, "although it was pretty difficult to get the top spinning," Neufeld says. But the job wasn't over yet. After the producers reviewed the final effect, they decided that the top had to be larger. So the shot, which had taken three weeks to build the first time, was redone—in just two days' time— with the assistance of Josh Rose's team at VisionArt.

PLAYING GOD

Episode #437

TELEPLAY BY **JIM TROMBETTA**
AND **MICHAEL PILLER**
STORY BY **JIM TROMBETTA**
DIRECTED BY **DAVID LIVINGSTON**

GUEST CAST

Arjin	GEOFFREY BLAKE
Klingon Host	RON TAYLOR
Cardassian	RICHARD POE
Alien Man	CHRIS NELSON NORRIS
Computer Voice	MAJEL BARRETT

STARDATE UNKNOWN

Arjin, a young Trill who hopes to qualify for symbiosis, is nervous about meeting his field docent, Jadzia Dax, who will serve as his instructor in the next part of his training. Knowing about Curzon and Lela Dax's reputations for washing out initiates from the program, Arjin is taken aback by Dax's current host, Jadzia, who enjoys gambling, drinking, and wrestling, all traits that seem very inappropriate in a host. As they head toward the Gamma Quadrant in a runabout, Jadzia attempts to set the record straight, pointing out that she is not Curzon or Lela, and that Arjin doesn't need to worry about trying to impress her. But Arjin seems unconvinced.

When the runabout hits a subspace interphase pocket, it snags an unidentified bit of protoplasm on one of its nacelles. Returning to the station, Dax sends the specimen to a containment chamber in the science lab for further study. At dinner, Dax notes that Arjin is overly concerned with other people's expectations and doesn't seem to have aspirations beyond the prospect of being joined. She discusses her feelings with Sisko, admitting that she is reluctant to confront Arjin because Curzon was so hard on her when she was an initiate, to the point of recommending that she be dropped from the program. But Sisko insists that she isn't doing Arjin any favors by avoiding the truth.

A short time later, the specimen is inadvertently released from the containment chamber when a Cardassian vole—part of an infestation that is plaguing the station—eats through the security field energy lines. As Dax and Arjin attempt to analyze the protoplasm, Dax finally reveals her concerns to Arjin, who reacts defensively and leaves the lab in anger.

Dax completes her study and reports to Sisko that the substance is actually a rapidly expanding protouniverse. As it grows, it will displace their own universe. The most obvious alternative is to destroy it, but when Dax finds indications of life in the protouniverse, their alternative is no longer clear cut.

Sisko gives himself an hour to make a difficult decision: how to protect the station without destroying the living matter in the protouniverse, possibly an entire civilization of unknown beings. In the meantime, Jadzia finds Arjin drowning his sorrows in Quark's bar. She tells him how shy Jadzia made it through the program despite Curzon's opposition and found an inner strength and passion that she would never have discovered otherwise. Arjin must look inside himself to discover what he really wants out of life.

Sisko opts to attempt returning the protouniverse to the Gamma Quadrant, where it belongs. But that means a dangerous trip through the wormhole with the unstable substance. Knowing Arjin's excellent piloting skills, Dax invites the initiate to come along.

O'Brien creates the strongest containment field he can, but there is no way to anticipate how the field will react to the wormhole's verteron nodes. Sure enough, the field rapidly loses stability, and Dax suggests that the only way they'll make it through the wormhole is if Arjin can navigate manually through the veritable minefield of nodes. Although precision piloting through a wormhole has never been attempted before, Arjin manages to get them through and they return the protouniverse to where it belongs. A short time later, Arjin returns home, with a better understanding of the joined Trill known as Jadzia Dax, and of himself.

Arjin doesn't understand Jadzia's ways, including her boisterous enjoyment of the Klingon restaurateur's serenade. ROBBIE ROBINSON

While many *DS9* episodes have so-called A and B storylines, a few of them have a third plotline competing with the other story threads. In such cases, some elements are bound to receive short shrift in the final teleplay. In "Playing God," notes writer Jim Trombetta, there was a story about a Trill candidate for symbiosis, a story about voles on the station and a story about "this cosmic wonder that could fit in your pocket." It was the protouniverse storyline that fascinated Trombetta, but "because it was considered abstract, that part of the episode became secondary," he comments. And that, he felt, robbed the story of its emotional balance. Though it was obvious to anyone familiar with basic *Star Trek* philosophy that the crew couldn't destroy a subuniverse that contained life, Trombetta says he can understand if people didn't feel the ethical problem on an emotional level.

"It was a very difficult show," says Ira Steven Behr. When the tech premise that Trombetta brought in proved problematic, a succession of staff writers "struggled valiantly" reshaping the story until Michael Piller took the final pass at the teleplay. It was Piller, according to Trombetta, who asked that the emphasis shift to the Trill-initiate storyline, which allowed for the revelation of several titillating details about Dax's

Jadzia's lessons to Arjin taught the viewer how special and unique a being joined Trill is. ROBBIE ROBINSON

personal life, including her fondness for workouts with beefy alien wrestlers.

"I think Dax has a pretty healthy libido," smiles the episode's director, David Livingston. "When Arjin came to her door, I wanted her to look as sexy as possible. I wanted her to be a knockout—and she did look pretty spectacular." The choice of putting the science officer in a towel was calculated. "The audience is thinking, 'What's she doing with this guy?'" says Livingston. "Well, she was working out with him."

"Dax is trying to shock Arjin into trusting her," explains Terry Farrell. "Her job is to shock him into being himself because he's not ready to become a host. She even leads him to believe that she's slept with this wrestler, but she didn't. She was playing with Arjin's head." Farrell recalls that she had a long talk with Michael Piller about Dax's characterization for the episode. "Everything she does in the beginning of 'Playing God' is an attempt to get Arjin to react to her, to shake him out of his behavior. Because somebody who's really mature enough to be a host would have handled that treatment differently than Arjin did."

Dax's choice of drinks, in this case, a Black Hole, is also calculated, although Dax seems to genuinely like them. "I have the feeling they're very alcoholic."

"She looks out from the back room, dressed only in a towel . . . Arjin is uncomfortable . . . ." ROBBIE ROBINSON

A Cardassian vole.

Farrell laughs. "In the first version of the script, she requested a Bloody Mary," she recalls. The change clearly reflects the desire to create the greatest response in poor Arjin.

Tongo had been introduced earlier as well, in the episode "Rules of Acquisition," where it was described in the script as a cross between poker, mah-jongg, and craps. Although Actor Armin Shimerman notes that, "Nobody on the set really knows how to play *tongo*," he admits that there seem to be some obvious rules, and in "Playing God" the actors were instructed to mirror their actions from the earlier episode.

Shimerman liked the fact that the writers showed Dax engaging in another round of *tongo* with her Ferengi friends. "It enforces in viewers' minds that Dax is not 'all work and everything in its proper place' like most Starfleet characters," he says. "No other Starfleet character has a corner of his or her heart reserved for the playful Ferengi. But Dax does, and the writers have given her several speeches designed to convince the others of the Ferengi's good points. I'm very happy that Dax and Quark play *tongo* together."

One of Director Livingston's favorite elements of the episode resulted in some extra attention being paid to what might otherwise have been a throwaway detail. "I loved the voles!" he says. "I wanted to see those suckers and shoot them up close. Initially the script was written so that we didn't really see them as they scurried about. But I said, 'No, we've gotta see them!' So Michael Westmore designed this wonderful creature, and I shot big close-ups."

While most special effects sequences shot outside the station utilize either the main six-foot DS9 model or the similarly scaled half-model, the need for a unique view of a small section of the station occasionally arises. Then, budget permitting, a new model is built. Such was the case when "Playing God"'s script called for a visual to depict the proto-universe eating its way through a portion of the outer ring. Special Effects Supervisor Gary Hutzel oversaw the building of the appropriately scarred mock-up, which later would be placed in storage for the next time a ring section was required.

The episode features a second appearance (after "Melora") by Actor Ron Taylor, as the opera-loving host of the station's Klingon restaurant, and an appearance by Richard Poe as an annoying Cardassian officer who offers no useful information on dealing with voles. Poe would return a few episodes later as Gul Evek ("The Maquis, Part One"). Sisko finds out that Jake is in love with a dabo girl, referred to in the script as "Marta," and agrees to let his son bring her home for dinner "soon." But Sisko would not follow through on that offer until Season 3, in "The Abandoned," by which time the girl's name would change to Mardah.

PROFIT AND LOSS

Episode #438

WRITTEN BY **FLIP KOBLER & CINDY MARCUS**
DIRECTED BY **ROBERT WIEMER**

GUEST CAST

Natima Lang	MARY CROSBY
Garak	ANDREW ROBINSON
Hogue	MICHAEL REILLY BURKE
Rekelen	HEIDI SWEDBERG
Gul Toran	EDWARD WILEY

STARDATE UNKNOWN

When hails to a small damaged Cardassian vessel go unanswered, Sisko has it brought to DS9. Onboard are three Cardassians: Professor Natima Lang and her students, Rekelen and Hogue. Lang explains that the damage to their ship was caused when they were caught in a meteor swarm. Sisko offers the trio assistance with the repairs and suggests they head for the Promenade.

In Quark's bar, Bashir fishes for clues about Garak's past, while Odo tries to find out if Quark has acquired a small but illegal cloaking device. Suddenly, Quark recognizes Natima on the Promenade and tries to speak to her. But Natima says that she wants nothing to do with the Ferengi. Nevertheless, Quark manages to get Natima and her students to come into the bar for a drink. Quark makes it clear that he would like to renew their former relationship, but their

The return of Quark's old love, Natima, inspires the Ferengi to behave like Humphrey Bogart. ROBBIE ROBINSON

reunion is short-lived; Natima spots Garak, the only Cardassian resident of the station, and quickly takes her leave.

After O'Brien points out that the damage to Natima's ship was clearly caused by Cardassian weapons, Sisko confronts her. Natima admits O'Brien is right, and explains that her students are leaders of an underground movement that opposes the Cardassian military government. Their views have made them fugitives, and they are desperate to get off the station as soon as possible, particularly since they know Garak has seen them.

Their fears are well founded. A short time later, a Cardassian starship approaches DS9 and powers up its weapons. At the same time, Garak appears in Ops and tells Sisko that Natima's students are actually terrorists whom the Cardassian government wants returned. But Sisko refuses to turn over political refugees.

At Quark's bar, the Ferengi, who *has* indeed obtained a cloaking device, offers it to Rekelen and Hogue for their escape—*if* they convince Natima to stay behind on DS9 with him. Natima wants the cloaking device but rejects the conditions. She threatens Quark with a phaser and when he moves toward her, she inadvertently fires, dropping him in his tracks.

Alarmed, Natima kneels next to the stunned Ferengi and admits that she really loves him. Unfortunately, just as Quark finally convinces her to remain with him, Odo arrives to arrest her. Sisko unhappily informs them that the Bajoran provisional government has agreed to a prisoner swap with the Cardassians, and he is forced to abide by that decision.

The prisoner swap is the result of a suggestion to

Cardassia's Central Command by Garak, who hopes to restore himself to the government's good graces. A short time later, however, he receives a visit from a warrior named Gul Toran, who says he can arrange for Garak's return to Cardassia, *if* he assassinates the three fugitives before they leave the station. Meanwhile, Quark has convinced Odo to help him get the Cardassians off the station safely. The Ferengi escourts the trio to a cargo bay, only to find Garak blocking their only source of escape. Garak prepares to execute all four of them, and Quark attempts to convince him otherwise. Sensing Garak's hesitation, Toran appears from out of the shadows and announces that he will perform the execution himself. As for Garak, he is to remain a tailor on DS9 for the rest of his life; Central Command never did intend to restore his reputation.

As Toran takes aim at the fugitives, Garak fires at Toran, killing him. The two students head for their escape vessel, and to Quark's surprise, Natima says that she must join them and continue assisting the underground movement. Resigned to the fact that he can't stop her, Quark allows her to leave. He exits the cargo bay with Garak, two men who have each lost what they desired most in life.

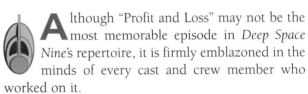

Although "Profit and Loss" may not be the most memorable episode in *Deep Space Nine's* repertoire, it is firmly emblazoned in the minds of every cast and crew member who worked on it.

Why? Does the date January 17, 1994, ring a bell?

If not, you probably weren't living in Southern California at the time. While the average American's memory of recent earth-shaking events is notoriously short, Angelenos are likely to remember that date. Earthquakes of magnitude 6.7 simply don't happen that often.

The crew call on January 17—the second day of filming on "Profit and Loss"—was set for 5:00 A.M., for a shooting start of 6:30. But because it takes several hours to bring out the natural beauty of characters like Ferengi and Cardassians, Armin Shimerman and a host of guest stars had arrived at the makeup trailer between 2:00 and 3:00 A.M. By 4:31 A.M., they were all well along in their makeup, at which point all hell broke loose . . . literally, according to director Robert Wiemer, a longtime veteran of *TNG* taking his first directorial turn on *DS9*.

"They all went running out to their cars in full makeup and raced home," he recalls. "And of course,

Neither earthquakes, nor extensive makeup, nor sharp Ferengi teeth could dissuade Mary Crosby from kissing Armin Shimerman. ROBBIE ROBINSON

since the power was out, there were no traffic lights, and every corner became a four-way stop." Which, he points out, gave everyone on the street a good chance to look at the other drivers stopped at each intersection. "The stories that must have been going around!" Wiemer laughs. "It must have seemed like the bowels of the Earth had opened and those creatures had come out!"

Not everyone at Paramount raced home, of course. As soon as the initial shocks began to subside, studio personnel began to inspect the lot for damage and structural soundness. And guest actor Mary Crosby, best known for her recurring role on the television series *Dallas,* impressed Armin Shimerman with her "cool under fire" demeanor in the makeup trailer. "We were all shook up but Mary waited patiently for several hours, through all the aftershocks, until they finally removed the makeup and sent her home." A member of the legendary Crosby clan that also produced both Bing and Denise (*TNG*'s Tasha Yar), Mary was not only a trouper, according to Shimerman, but, "a dear. I can't speak too highly about her."

Studio inspections continued on Tuesday the eighteenth and the production crew was given the okay to continue filming on Wednesday, setting everything on the episode back by two days. "I'll never know how we got done with it on time," reflects Wiemer. "In addition to everybody telling everybody else his or her personal earthquake story or experience—which took up a lot of time—we also had to deal with the aftershocks that rumbled through every minute and a half. All the lights would rattle and the sets would shake and everybody would catch his breath. Talk about breaking concentration!"

The original script for "Profit and Loss," as might be obvious from its working title, "Here's Lookin' at

You . . ." was a close parallel to the classic motion picture *Casablanca.* Although the producers initially liked the resemblance, it became a handicap when the potential for legal problems forced them to begin rewriting the script. "Everything that was really worthwhile on the show was borrowed from *Casablanca,* and we couldn't do that," notes Ira Steven Behr. "So then we had to find the show. And I thought that the idea of Quark involved with an alien, with a Cardassian, was an interesting way to go." However, Behr was unhappy with the ultimate direction of the episode, which he feels tipped into "soap opera." He was particularly unhappy with the treatment of Quark, who took on an atypically noble, romantic stature, à la Humphrey Bogart.

"I felt we didn't need another tough, sexy swashbuckling character on the show," he says. "We had enough of those. We needed our offbeat, interesting characters. It should have been *Beauty and the Beast,* or Woody Allen and every woman he's ever been with in films. You don't take Woody Allen and make him *into* Bogart. Yeah, you have Bogey *telling* Woody Allen how to behave, but he does it through his Woody Allen persona. The scenes with Quark drove me mad."

Of course, there are some people who thought they

Garak's unpredictable reactions to situations were explored by the writers with glee. ROBBIE ROBINSON

were just fine—Quark himself, for example. "It was great fun," says Armin Shimerman. "Mary Crosby was a sheer delight to work with. And the honest truth is I probably had a little bit of a crush on her during the week I worked with her. She put up with a tremendous amount of makeup that I don't think she expected, and she did it without complaint. And she allowed me to kiss her with my sharp teeth, which I have qualms about. I'm always terrified that I'll hurt someone."

How many takes were there on those kisses?

"I wish I could tell you," says Shimerman. "All of them were enjoyable, but I don't remember how many. After each one, we had to have our makeup touched up. The orange of my makeup mixed with the gray of Mary's makeup, and it wasn't a pretty sight. [Make-up Artist] Karen Westerfield was truly miffed at the damage that was being done."

One element of the show earned everyone's praise: the return of Andrew Robinson as Garak. "Every time Garak showed up, the episode got wonderful," says Behr.

"You can get away with wonderful stuff with Garak," adds Robert Hewitt Wolfe. "He can contradict himself left and right. Why does he kill Toran in the episode? He says it's because he loves Cardassia, but it's probably because he doesn't like Toran. That's reason enough for Garak. And have you noticed that Garak doesn't seem to know the meaning of the word 'stun'? We've seen the man fire a phaser about three times, and it's always been set to kill. I like that about him!"

Wolfe takes credit for one of the episode's best throwaway details: Odo's choice of reading material at the top of Act 5. Although the copy of Mickey Spillane's *I, the Jury,* that Odo is reading has been borrowed from O'Brien, Wolfe feels that Odo thoroughly enjoys that kind of pulp fiction, which led to some interesting discussions behind the scenes. Wolfe recalls, "Ira Behr wanted to know, 'What is it in that book that Odo likes? Is it the women? The violence?' Who knows? Odo's this alien creature, and we have no idea what he's bringing to the table when he sits down with *I, the Jury.* I think it's fun that he likes those books. I think the next thing he did was go out and find *Kiss Me Deadly.*"

"Profit and Loss" notes the first use of the name Cardassian Central Command. According to Wolfe, the staff realized that they needed a name for Cardassia's governing body, not only for this script, but for upcoming shows addressing Cardassia's relationship with the Maquis. "We'd always assumed that Cardassia was a military dictatorship," says Wolfe. "So we went back and forth with what we wanted, and finally came up with Central Command."

BLOOD OATH
Episode #439

TELEVISION STORY AND TELEPLAY BY
PETER ALLAN FIELDS
DIRECTED BY **WINRICH KOLBE**

GUEST CAST

Kor	JOHN COLICOS
Kang	MICHAEL ANSARA
Koloth	WILLIAM CAMPBELL
the Albino	BILL BOLENDER
Head Guard	CHRISTOPHER COLLINS

STARDATE UNKNOWN

The relative calm of Deep Space 9 erupts into "a Klingon afternoon," as Odo puts it, when the station is visited by three aged Klingon warriors: drunken, boisterous Kor, chilly weapons expert Koloth, and their proud leader Kang. The three have come to find Curzon Dax, and are surprised to discover that their old male friend is now a beautiful young female named Jadzia. Kang has brought news; he has found their greatest enemy, a man known as the Albino. More than eighty years earlier, the foursome had sworn a blood oath to kill him. However, Kang refuses to hold Jadzia Dax to an oath made by her former host, Curzon.

Knowing that a Klingon blood oath can never be broken, Dax tells Kira about her dilemma and the events of decades past. The Albino had been raiding Klingon colonies and her three friends had defeated him. But the Albino escaped and took revenge by killing the first-born child of each Klingon. When

Kor, Koloth, and Kang: Three aging warriors band together for one last glorious battle. DANNY FELD

Kang, Koloth, and Kor had taken their blood oath against the murderer, Curzon, who was the godfather of Kang's son, had taken it as well. Kira tries to talk Dax out of accompanying the Klingons on their mission, but Dax feels she has an obligation, both to her friends and to Curzon. Of course, first she will have to convince the Klingons.

Kor has no objections, but it takes a *bat'leth* match in which Dax proves she can hold her own to win Koloth's support. Kang is more difficult to convince; a battle of wits finally forces him to yield on the matter. Before Dax can leave, Sisko confronts her and reminds her of both her duty to Starfleet and the Federation's laws against murder, even the murder of someone as heinous as the Albino. But Dax tells Sisko she has to go, and that she'll face the consequences when, and if, she returns.

En route to the Albino's planet, Dax and Kang clash on what would be their best course of action. Dax wants to attempt a covert approach, while Kang prefers a bold assault in full view of the guards. Later, Kang confesses to Dax that he has been in touch with the Albino, who has grown tired of pursuit and offers the warriors a chance to die with honor. But Dax argues that an honorable victory would be far superior and she proposes a plan to increase their advantage. Impressed, Kang agrees.

The group puts the plan into action, surprising the Albino in his command post. Fighting fiercely, the four manage to overpower the guards before Koloth is killed and Kor injured. One-on-one with the Albino, Kang falls, mortally wounded, and Dax confronts their enemy alone. The Albino taunts her and Dax hesitates, uncertain if she'll be able to kill this man in cold blood. But suddenly the Albino falls forward, Kang's knife in his back. Thanking Dax for honoring him by allowing him to kill the Albino, Kang reflects that it is truly a good day to die, and does so. Dax returns to the station, ready to resume her everyday life, but changed by the experience.

A favorite with both fans and the *DS9* cast and crew, "Blood Oath" brought everyone's favorite Klingons back to the *Star Trek* fold. Writer Peter Allan Fields was already in the process of putting together a story about Dax and some old Klingon acquaintances of Curzon's when Robert Hewitt Wolfe, a fan of the original series, suggested using the characters of Kang, Kor, and Koloth.

"Once he mentioned it, it seemed a natural," says Fields. Although the producers were certain that Actors

Over the course of the series, the "warrior race" would take on an even larger role. DANNY FELD

Michael Ansara ("Day of the Dove"), John Colicos ("Errand of Mercy") and William Campbell ("The Trouble with Tribbles") were still alive, they weren't sure if they were still acting. The casting people quickly turned up Ansara and Colicos, but they couldn't find Campbell, at least not until someone pointed out that he was, "Right under our noses, doing the *Star Trek* convention cruises!" laughs Ira Steven Behr.

Michael Ansara, who would return playing Jeyal in "The Muse" during *DS9*'s fourth season, was delighted to reprise the role of Kang. "He was one of the best characters I've ever played," Ansara says. "I loved doing it, although I was surprised when they called us. Obviously, things have changed over the years, and the look of the Klingons has changed. We tried to get an explanation and they told us, 'Well, Klingons live to be very, very old and that's a natural physical metamorphosis!'"

The comment may have been tongue in cheek, but the look of the three Klingons actually was discussed behind the scenes. "We had all those conversations about 'Should they look like the original Klingons?'" recalls Behr. Ultimately, he says, they made a decision to keep to current Klingon makeup and assume they'd always looked that way.

Fields's story, originally called "The Beast," was patterned on a classic Kurosawa blend of revenge and redemption: *The Seven Samurai* or *The Magnificent Seven*. "I'm not sure if it came across," he says, "but if it did, I'm delighted. I sweated a lot while I was trying to write it. I wanted each of the old guys to be a

Stage 18 is filled with an elaborate gothic set. DANNY FELD

specific character. Koloth was the James Coburn character from *Magnificent Seven*, the craftsman who lives to slice and hack. And Kang was Yul Brynner."

As for Kor . . . "We weren't sure about him," admits Behr. "His character was a tougher nut to crack." Ultimately, Fields patterned Kor's persona not on a character from a Japanese or American Western prototype, but on Shakespeare's Falstaff, which mixed a few metaphors but certainly worked for the plot.

Actor Terry Farrell loved the vivid characterizations, which forced her own character to interact in a specific way with each Klingon in order to accompany the trio on their journey. "With Kor, I had to convince him that he was a hero, and that in my eyes he would always be a hero, so that was philosophical. With Koloth, I had to prove that I was strong enough to go to battle with him, so that was physical. And with Kang, I had to prove to him that my desire and need to be a part of this blood oath was strong enough that I could not imagine staying behind, that I was mentally strong and capable enough. So I had to exhibit the honor, the physical strength, and the mental perseverance to go with them."

The exteriors for the Albino's fortress were shot on location in Pasadena, at a large house designed by famed architect Frank Lloyd Wright. The interiors were constructed on Stage 18. An additional shot, showing the walls of the fortress being blown out, was a minature that Dan Curry's team did on top of Paramount's Van Ness parking structure. The fight scenes were choreographed by Stunt Coordinator Dennis Madalone and resident Klingon martial arts expert Curry. "Dennis and I get along very well, so there was no sense of stepping on anybody's toes," says Curry. "I'd go over and hang out while they were rehearsing and say, 'Maybe this move might be better.'"

Director Winrich Kolbe left the choreography to the experts, instructing Madalone to get maximum production value for the fight itself. "We were concerned that the two days we would spend in the Albino's hall would just kill us, in terms of work time," says Kolbe. "So my only instruction to Dennis was 'Don't go overboard, I'll handle the stuff up the steps.'"

Kolbe decided that Kang's death scene would be on the platform at the top of the stairs. "I loved that angle; it demanded to be staged up there," he says. "Very operatic."

According to Fields, however, the angle may have eliminated the one element he felt was missing from the scene. "They didn't go to a close shot of Kang dying," Fields says. "When a character is dying, you shouldn't be at a long shot. I really missed that close-up."

To get everyone into an appropriately "operatic" mood for the sequence, Kolbe requested that the sound department blast out the Wagner opera *Götterdämmerung*—a fitting epic about the twilight of the gods—on a cassette recorder "throughout the whole damn thing!"

Composer Dennis McCarthy scored the episode with similar verve. After discussing the tone of the show with Coproducer Steve Oster, McCarthy says he "decided to really kick ass, and make it a 'take-no-prisoners' kind of show." Dropping any attempt at subtlety, McCarthy instructed the orchestra to "play the battles *as* battles. We just went for it, and what I remember about the episode is the force of the music."

THE MAQUIS, PART I

Episode #440

TELEPLAY BY JAMES CROCKER
STORY BY RICK BERMAN & MICHAEL PILLER &
JERI TAYLOR AND JAMES CROCKER
DIRECTED BY DAVID LIVINGSTON

GUEST CAST

Amaros	TONY PLANA
Sakonna	BERTILA DAMAS
Gul Evek	RICHARD POE
Samuels	MICHAEL A. KRAWIC
Kobb	AMANDA CARLIN
Niles	MICHAEL ROSE
Guard	STEVEN JOHN EVANS
Gul Dukat	MARC ALAIMO
Cal Hudson	BERNIE CASEY

STARDATE UNKNOWN

Tension levels on the station rise when Dax determines that the explosion of the Cardassian freighter *Bok'Nor* while it was departing from Deep Space 9 does not appear to be an accident. Concerned with how the incident will affect Federation colonies in the newly established Demilitarized Zone, Sisko calls in an old friend: Cal Hudson, Starfleet's attaché to the colonies. Hudson confesses that the colonists, who, thanks to the treaty, have found themselves living in Cardassian territory, feel abandoned by the Federation.

Heading for his quarters, Sisko finds Gul Dukat waiting for him with a curious offer. Dukat is on the station in an unofficial capacity, and is prepared to help Sisko investigate the explosion of the *Bok'Nor* on that same basis. Dukat claims that Federation members caused the destruction, and he offers Sisko the opportunity to find and catch the culprits, *without* official Cardassian involvement.

Intrigued, Sisko agrees to accompany Dukat to the Volon colonies in the Demilitarized Zone. Once there, they encounter a Federation ship that is under attack by Cardassians, a clear violation of the treaty. Dukat determines that the offending ships must have come from Cardassian colonies in the Zone. He attempts to call them off but they refuse to respond. Suddenly another Federation vessel appears and fires on the Cardassians, destroying them. Sisko and Dukat are stunned; without the official knowledge of either of their governments, a war seems to be breaking out in the Demilitarized Zone.

Back on the station an attractive Vulcan woman named Sakonna approaches Quark with a business proposition. He is surprised when that proposition turns out to be a request for a supply of weapons.

Sisko and Dukat head for Volon III and attend a meeting that includes Federation colonists, Cal Hudson, and Hudson's Cardassian counterpart, Gul Evek. The group begins a volatile discussion of the recent skirmish, with accusations flying in all directions, including one by Evek that the Federation is engaging in organized terrorist activities against the Cardassians. When Sisko asks for proof, Evek presents the confession of the Federation colonist who blew up the *Bok'Nor*, a man whom Evek says committed suicide shortly after he made the confession.

Sisko is forced to wonder if Cardassian fears about organized terrorism are true. Hudson tells him that while he's aware of no such campaign, he wouldn't blame them if they did attempt to defend themselves.

When Sisko and Dukat return to the station, O'Brien has bad news. The explosion of the *Bok'Nor* was caused by a Federation device. As Sisko ponders his next act, Gul Dukat is kidnapped from the station by Sakonna and some of the Federation colonists. A short time later, the station receives a transmission from the Demilitarized Zone, where a group calling itself the Maquis claims to have abducted Dukat. Sisko, Kira, and Bashir take a runabout and attempt to follow the warp signature of the kidnappers' vessel, which leads them to a region along the Cardassian border known as the Badlands. Detecting lifesigns on a large asteroid, they beam down and immediately find themselves surrounded by a band of armed Federation colonists, apparently led by Cal Hudson.

Gul Dukat is as curious about the destruction of the *Bok'Nor* as
Sisko is. ROBBIE ROBINSON

Although "The Maquis" Parts I and II hold up on their own as strong, dramatic stories spiced with some good action sequences, their whole raison d'être was to lay some necessary groundwork for a new series about to be launched: *Star Trek: Voyager*.

"We knew that we wanted to include a renegade element in *Voyager*, and that the show would involve a ship housing both Starfleet people and these idealistic freedom fighters that the Federation felt were outlaws," explains Writer Jeri Taylor. "So in order to avoid having some burdensome backstory and exposition in *Voyager*'s pilot, we decided we could plant the idea of the Maquis in the shows that were already on the air."

The *TNG* episode, "Journey's End," aired first, establishing a group of Native Americans who had moved from Earth to preserve their cultural identity, only to find their new home threatened by the Federation's treaty with the Cardassians. That episode also introduced the character Gul Evek (Richard Poe), who soon would appear in both "The Maquis, Part II" and *TNG*'s "Preemptive Strike," the latter episode representing the third bit of seeding done by *Voyager*'s executive producers.

The use of Evek had a twofold purpose. It served as one of several solid links between the three pre-*Voyager* episodes (thus reinforcing the backstory), and

it also solidified the sense of continuity that *Star Trek* fans relish about all incarnations of the series. "You want to have the opportunity for crossover and continuity," says David Livingston, director of "The Maquis, Part I" and long-time vet of *TNG*. "It's fun to do that with a character when you find somebody that's good in the part, like Evek and Admiral Nechayev. The audience enjoys it."

The creation of the Maquis evolved from the *Voyager* creators' desire "to have some people who are quite different from the Starfleet human types we see all the time," says Piller. "The Maquis, which was a name used for French freedom fighters during World War II, are outlaws who are former members of the Federation."

Directing a piece of a multipart episode—not to mention a piece intended to set up a separate television series—can be a frustrating task, observes Livingston. "It was tough because it was a setup show," he says. "You know going into it that you're not gonna get all the goodies. You have to do all the work, all the exposition, all the character introduction, so it lacks something on its own. You can't really pay off anything you set up, because that's going to happen in the next part. The second hour's going to get the action. I got very little action, although I got to have Gul Dukat hit somebody!"

Still, Livingston had fun with some of the scenes, such as the teaser, which featured one of Dax and Kira's classic exchanges about the men Dax dates. "Nana and Terry are great together," Livingston enthuses, "especially when they're discussing sexual stuff, because although it's two women talking, it always ends up kind of bizarre. Kira is kind of macho, a very masculine kind of woman in a military uniform, who has a sexual side, but most of the time is running around acting really rigid. And Dax has been both a man *and* a woman several times, so the dynamics between the two are a lot more interesting than just two women talking."

Livingston also enjoyed the scenes with one of *Star Trek*'s more atypical Vulcans, the gunrunner Sakonna, whose garb was decidedly sexy for one of her species. "I had something to do with that," admits Livingston. "In fact, I wanted her even more provocatively dressed. I thought it would be a great contrast to put this woman in a really sexy dress. She needed to be sexy—she was putting the make on Quark!"

Robert Blackman found Livingston's suggestions of interest "because we've never had a clear view of a Vulcan's form. Robert Fletcher (the costume designer

Sisko's by-the-book mentality here is in sharp contrast to actions he will take later on. ROBBIE ROBINSON

Producers remembered Poe's performance in "Playing God" and invited him to reprise his role as a Cardassian gul. ROBBIE ROBINSON

for many of the *Star Trek* feature films) really developed a look for them in the films, but everyone's taste is different. I take certain things from that—the width of the shoulders, a kind of neckline—and then go on to do an interpretation that makes sense to me. But for Sakonna, it was going to be something else entirely: purple panne velvet dress right down to the ankle, with purple shoes. And we were already in the process of making it when we found out Rick Berman was opposed to it."

"It was very, very sexy, but Rick just didn't buy it for a Vulcan," confirms Livingston.

What Sakonna ended up with, says Blackman, was a kind of compromise: a form-fitting dress that shows off the character's figure quite well, and still breaks new ground as far as Vulcans go.

The top of Act 5 features Kira, Odo, O'Brien, Dax, and Bashir standing around in Ops, commenting on a conversation taking place between Sisko and a Starfleet representative via com in his office. They can't hear what he's saying, but the heated tone of the conversation is obvious. In fact, a scene was filmed and later cut, in which Sisko follows up on the close of the conversation by picking up his desk monitor and throwing it to the floor.

Wonder what got him so steamed? The addendum to Scene 47 is a scene that was never intended to be heard by the audience but was written to give Avery Brooks something to play against.

This is the dialogue Sisko is having with an admiral on the monitor in his office. We neither hear the dialogue nor see the Admiral on the monitor.

We do see Sisko trying to keep his temper while emphatically responding to the Admiral's heated inquiries. They are mid-conversation as the scene begins . . .

SISKO
(bristling)
I'm hoping I don't have to remind the admiral how many people pass through here during a week's time. It's not possible to keep tabs on every single person while they're on the station . . .

ADMIRAL
(hard)
If I didn't know you better, Commander, I'd think you were just making excuses . . .

SISKO
(heatedly)
I'm not making excuses! Would it be in keeping with Federation policy to frisk everyone who steps through our airlocks? To search through every room of every visitor during their stay?

ADMIRAL
(forcefully)
Of course not . . . but with two kidnappings and a ship being destroyed . . . all in less than a week's time . . . obviously your security measures leave something to be desired . . .

SISKO
Security on this station is by the book. Our security program and the officers who work in it are first rate.

ADMIRAL
Then what were they doing when all this was happening? We here at Starfleet are watching how you resolve this situation very closely, Commander. We think it might be prudent to replace this chief of security you have . . .

SISKO
Odo is both highly intelligent and extremely thorough. He's the most qualified person I have for the job.

ADMIRAL

Still, it would be a concrete example that you are taking active measures to resolve this situation . . . and to make sure it doesn't happen again.

SISKO

I stand behind my chief of security one hundred percent.

ADMIRAL
(with an edge)

That may be a mistake, Commander . . .

SISKO
(controlled fury)

Then it's <u>my</u> <u>mistake</u>.

ADMIRAL

Then let me make my point again. Starfleet is very unhappy this happened. We want this matter taken care of immediately. I don't have to remind you how this reflects on <u>your</u> position . . .

SISKO

We're doing everything we can to apprehend the kidnappers . . .

ADMIRAL

Don't bother me with details. Just clean up the mess, Commander. And quickly. Before this becomes a <u>permanent</u> stain on your record. Do I make myself clear.

SISKO
(angrily)

<u>Yes, sir.</u>

The Admiral's image disappears from the monitor.
(Then we will pick up at "In his office, Sisko drops his head . . ." in the script.)

THE MAQUIS, PART II

Episode #441

TELEPLAY BY **IRA STEVEN BEHR**
STORY BY **RICK BERMAN** & **MICHAEL PILLER** &
JERI TAYLOR AND **IRA STEVEN BEHR**
DIRECTED BY **COREY ALLEN**

GUEST CAST

Amaros	TONY PLANA
Legate Parn	JOHN SCHUCK
Admiral Alynna Nechayev	NATALIA NOGULICH
Sakonna	BERTILA DAMAS
Drofo Awa	MICHAEL BELL
Kobb	AMANDA CARLIN
Niles	MICHAEL ROSE
Gul Dukat	MARC ALAIMO

SPECIAL APPEARANCE

Cal Hudson	BERNIE CASEY

STARDATE UNKNOWN

Leaving Kira and Bashir surrounded by armed Maquis, Cal Hudson takes Sisko aside to explain his involvement with the group. Perhaps the Federation can turn its back on its colonists, but Hudson says he can't. As a result, he's turned his back on the Federation and joined the Maquis. He's certain that Cardassia is violating the treaty by smuggling weapons into the Demilitarized Zone, and says the Maquis and he will do whatever it takes to stop them. Sisko tries to convince him to use peaceful means, but Hudson refuses and stuns the three officers in order to slip away.

Dukat is forced to work with Sisko's crew to fight a common enemy.
DANNY FELD

Returning to the station, Sisko finds Admiral Nechayev waiting for him, and a Cardassian legate due to arrive shortly. Unaware that Sisko has already been in touch with the Maquis, Nechayev tells Sisko to contact them and convince them the treaty must be upheld. Hoping for the best, Sisko opts not to tell Nechayev about Hudson's involvement with the group. After Nechayev departs, Legate Parn shows up and informs Sisko that the Cardassian Central Command has discovered that there *is* a group of Cardassian officers smuggling weapons into the Zone. However, Parn claims that *Dukat* is their leader. In the meantime, Odo discovers that Quark helped supply Sakonna with weapons and puts the Ferengi into a holding cell until further notice.

Sisko manages to track down Dukat and confronts the Cardassian's Maquis captors in a tense standoff. When one of the Maquis opens fire, Sisko is able to gain control of the situation and rescue Dukat. He takes most of the group prisoner, including Sakonna, but leaves one Maquis behind to tell Cal Hudson that Starfleet knows nothing about his betrayal; he still has time to change his mind.

Back at the station, Sisko informs Dukat of Parn's accusation, and the fact that Central Command has turned against him. With few other options open to him, Dukat offers to help Sisko stop the Cardassian weapons-smuggling operation if Sisko will help him stop the Maquis. Sisko agrees and Dukat reveals that the Cardassians are probably using a Xepolite trader to transport weapons to Cardassian colonists in the Zone. With Dukat's help, Sisko captures a Xepolite ship loaded with arms.

With Sakonna now sharing his cell, Quark manages to apply his own brand of Ferengi logic to convince the Vulcan to reveal the Maquis's next step: an attack on a weapons depot hidden in a Cardassian civilian population center. While Dukat uses his contacts to find out at which colony the weapons are being held, Sisko tries one last time to persuade Hudson and the other Maquis to listen to reason. But Hudson says the Maquis are determined to fight and win.

After Dukat reveals the location of the depot, he joins Sisko and the station's senior officers in an attempt to head off the Maquis ships before they reach the Cardassian colony. In the initial skirmish, both DS9's runabouts and the Maquis ships take hits, eventually leaving Sisko and Hudson in a final face-off. Sisko lets Hudson know that he'll do whatever is necessary to stop the Maquis from taking action that could result in a full-blown war between Cardassia and the Federation. Although neither man wants to harm the other, Sisko finally manages to knock out Hudson's weapons, and Hudson concedes defeat, although he refuses to surrender. Sisko allows his old friend to escape, and returns to the station, wondering if he has really stopped a war or merely delayed the inevitable.

Part II of "The Maquis" features some exciting battle sequences, which were few and far between during the series' first two seasons. It also has a fascinating conversation in which Quark one-ups a Vulcan on the subject of logic, and the first appearance in *Star Trek* of a Cardassian with an atypical physique.

"We were afraid that the Cardassians were all becoming too alike," says Ira Steven Behr. "We wanted to see a kind of pear-shaped Cardassian, just to show that they're *not* all alike."

Thus, John Schuck, as Legate Parn, became the first actor to . . . push the Cardassian envelope. The original Cardassian uniforms, created for *TNG*'s "The Wounded," were extremely labor intensive, with a kind of "jigsaw-puzzle understructure made out of slightly rigid, flexible foam," says Robert Blackman. "We covered probably ninety-three percent of each

Creative photography made this small man-made jungle seem larger.
DANNY FELD

character's body in this foam, and then covered it with a very expensive polyester that looks like leather. I think there were three hundred and eleven pieces of foam that had to be glued together to do one suit. And the actor who wore it *had* to be like Marc Alaimo, who is an amazing fellow with zero percent body fat."

However, foreseeing the extensive use the costumes would receive in an ongoing series, Blackman began a series of modifications, eventually eliminating the foam. "The costumes are made now so that they can be adjusted to a body like John Schuck's, although that's about as far as they can go."

As always is the case when one director picks up an episode from precisely the point where the previous director left off, Part II's director, Corey Allen, had a conversation with Part I's director, David Livingston. Primarily they went over blocking for the characters as the episode opens. From that point, Allen was on his own. One of his challenges was an attempt to put some visual interest in a lengthy (six script pages) dialogue sequence between Sisko and Cal Hudson in the teaser. Allen's solution was to send them on a long walk through the jungle. "I don't know that it always works to 'walk–talk' a scene," says Allen, "but it's a pretty staple trick, to put it on legs."

Since the jungle sequence was actually filmed on Paramount's Stage 18, the walk had to be meticulously choreographed. "It was carefully planned out so they would take a circular route, making three ninety-degree turns as they walked," says Allen. "I used the same technique in 'Paradise,' setting the camera way back and having the actors take the longest possible walk in each direction."

For Behr, who would soon step into Michael Piller's executive-producer shoes when Piller left the series to oversee *Star Trek: Voyager* and *Legend*, "The Maquis, Part II" provided an opportunity to sow a few seeds of his own for future use. Kira's previously all-negative feelings about Dukat begin to show some ambivalence here, as she is forced to begin seeing him as the multifaceted being he is. "That was the beginning of their whole complicated relationship, which would become more and more complicated during third and especially fourth season," Behr says. By the fifth season, however, Kira and the viewers at home would be allowed to despise Dukat all over again.

Dukat's throwaway line, "On Cardassia, the verdict is always known before the trial begins," immediately was recognized by the producers (particularly Michael Piller) as ample fodder for an entire story, inspiring the season's penultimate episode, "Tribunal."

But Behr would most enjoy taking one of Gene Roddenberry's long-established tenets and giving it a unique twist, thus setting the stage for some of *DS9*'s most ground-breaking efforts. The creator of *Star Trek* had frequently postulated that the Earth of both Kirk's and Picard's times was a paradise, with no poverty, crime, or war. While Behr took care not to contradict that view, he began having the characters take a closer look at it, as when Sisko points out that, "It's easy to be a saint in paradise."

"I've been waiting to say that line in *Star Trek* for a long time," says Behr. "We need to dig deeper and find out what, indeed, life is like in the twenty-fourth century. Is it this paradise, or are there, as Harold Pinter supposedly said, 'Weasels under the coffee table?' Sisko's speech in this episode, and Quark's speech to Sisko about the Federation in 'The Jem'Hadar' was the beginning of our really starting to question some of the basic tenets of *Star Trek* philosophy. Because, yes, it's a paradise—but so what?"

The ripples from that question would create hard-hitting episodes like "Past Tense," "Homefront," and "Paradise Lost" in *DS9*'s subsequent seasons.

THE WIRE
Episode #442
WRITTEN BY ROBERT HEWITT WOLFE
DIRECTED BY KIM FRIEDMAN

GUEST CAST	
Garak	ANDREW ROBINSON
Glinn Boheeka	JIMMIE F. SKAGGS
Jabara	ANN GILLESPIE
AND	
Enabran Tain	PAUL DOOLEY

STARDATE UNKNOWN

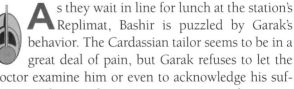

As they wait in line for lunch at the station's Replimat, Bashir is puzzled by Garak's behavior. The Cardassian tailor seems to be in a great deal of pain, but Garak refuses to let the doctor examine him or even to acknowledge his suffering. When Bashir attempts to press the point, Garak abruptly breaks off their lunch engagement.

Later that day, Bashir is suspicious when he overhears Garak asking Quark to obtain some merchandise for him. When questioned, Quark insists that Garak requested a sizing scanner for his shop. Bashir forgets about the incident until he receives an urgent call from Quark, asking the doctor to come to the bar.

A drunken Garak refuses to admit that there's anything wrong with him. ROBBIE ROBINSON

He arrives to find Garak extremely drunk and clearly suffering from something other than liquor. Again Bashir attempts to get the Cardassian to the Infirmary, and again Garak refuses, only to collapse from the excruciating pain.

Examining Garak at last, Bashir discovers the Cardassian has a small implant in his brain. While neither Odo nor he can identify it, Bashir informs the security chief that Quark may have some insight. Knowing that the Ferengi had recently been sending messages to Cardassia Prime, Bashir and Odo meet that evening to monitor Quark's outgoing transmissions. They hear Quark order a piece of Cardassian biotechnology, only to be told that the item has been classified by the Obsidian Order, an intelligence agency within the Cardassian Empire. When Odo and Bashir return to question Garak about their discovery, they find out he's left the Infirmary.

Bashir tracks Garak to his quarters and finds the Cardassian in agony, still unwilling to discuss the cause of his pain until Bashir reveals that he knows about the implant. Garak explains that the device, which Bashir had thought was designed to punish Garak, does exactly the opposite—or rather, it *did*.

The implant was devised to stimulate the pleasure centers of Garak's brain in the event that he was ever caught and tortured for certain information. But Garak admits that he has been using it to cope with his exile on Deep Space 9, and now the implant is breaking down. Addicted to its effects, Garak would rather die than have the device removed.

Bashir insists that he wants to help Garak, but the Cardassian only claims that he isn't worth the effort. During the Occupation, he explains, he had ordered a shuttle carrying escaped Bajoran prisoners, dozens of innocent Cardassian civilians, and his own aide, Elim, shot down. The incident was the cause of his exile, he tells Bashir.

Although surprised by the revelation, Bashir insists on working to find a way to help Garak. His first step is to turn off the implant. Then comes the harder part: helping Garak through the "cold turkey" phase of his addiction, which has pushed the Cardassian into a semilucid verbal attack on everything, particularly himself. Ranting, Garak tells Bashir that he was once the protégé of Enabran Tain, head of the Obsidian Order, with a bright future that he stupidly threw away. Contradicting his earlier revelation,

Garak now says that he actually helped the Bajoran prisoners escape, and it was *that* act which caused his exile and Elim's execution. Suddenly, Garak has a seizure and collapses. To his dismay, Bashir finds that turning off the implant has not halted the deteriorating effect on Garak's cellular structure; the Cardassian's biochemistry has actually become dependent on the high endorphin levels caused by the implant.

Bashir considers reactivating the implant long enough to find a cure, but Garak, reviving, asks him not to. Believing that he is dying, Garak tells Bashir yet another story. Elim was not Garak's aide; he was his closest friend. When a scandal rocked the Obsidian Order and Garak seemed likely to be blamed, he planted evidence to shift the blame to Elim, only to discover that Elim had done the same to him. And *that* was the cause of his exile.

Bashir surmises that Enabran Tain, now living in retirement, is the only man who can save Garak. The doctor travels into Cardassian territory to find Tain, and discovers that Tain knows all about him, and about Garak's condition. Tain quickly agrees to provide Bashir with the information to save Garak's life, claiming he likes the idea of Garak surviving to live out the rest of his miserable days in exile. Before he leaves, Bashir asks Tain whatever happened to Garak's friend Elim. Laughing, Tain reveals that Elim is Garak's first name. When Garak recovers, Bashir asks him which of the stories he told were true. Smiling, Garak tells him they *all* were, *especially* the lies.

A bottle show is a show deliberately written to require a minimum number of special effects, actors, and new sets. "We knew we were going to be spending money on 'The Maquis,' and we'd already spent a lot of money on a variety of other episodes in the second season," says Robert Hewitt Wolfe. "That's how I sold this episode. I'd had it rejected before, and I came back and said, 'We're broke and we need a bottle show. We have to use this.'"

But bottle shows don't mean sloppy seconds, Wolfe is quick to point out, "A lot of these small shows turn out to be pretty good. 'Duet' was one of our best shows ever, and it was conceived to save money!"

Though "The Wire" garnered nearly as much internal praise as "Duet" from cast and crew, it was not nearly so well received by fans, a fact that surprised Ira Steven Behr. "The fans said they were disappointed because they did not learn anything about Garak," says Behr. "That's such a misreading, a real refusal to see what the show was supposed to be about. So their reaction to the show disappointed us."

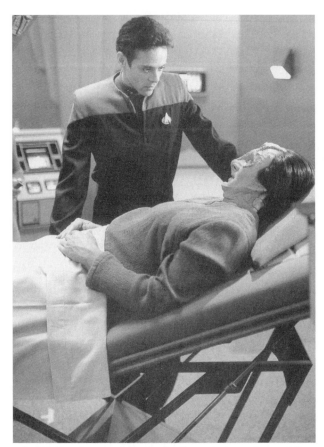

Establishing that everything Garak tells you is the truth, especially the lies, gave the writers tremendous freedom with future stories.
ROBBIE ROBINSON

Although fans would learn a bit more about Garak in subsequent seasons, they never would learn the complete truth. And that's the way Behr felt it should be about an individual whose characterization hinged on never knowing what was real about him and what wasn't. But wasn't that also true of Odo, whose background was kept a secret until *DS9*'s third season?

"I felt we needed to land on the truth about Odo," says Behr. "I didn't feel the same need with Garak. Sometimes we'd seem to write ourselves into a corner and have to say, 'Okay, we'll tell you this about Garak.' But then we'd find a new tributary, something else to take it off that. So it wasn't about, 'Oh God, now we know about Garak,' but 'Oh, now we know *this* about Garak, but what about *that*?' We kept dodging the bullet. For most of the series, I had no idea what he was. And personally, I don't know that I ever wanted to know."

Which didn't mean that every now and then we

wouldn't find out a bit of the truth about the infamous tailor. "When I was writing the story, the movie *Schindler's List* had just come out," says Wolfe, "and Ira was saying, 'Maybe he was Schindler; maybe he was the guy who let the prisoners go.' And then it was, 'Maybe he wasn't; maybe he was the Butcher of Budapest.' So we just kept telling all these lies, and I think the truth lies somewhere in there. Maybe he did let people go. Maybe he did shoot the ship down. Who knows? He *wasn't* a gul; he wasn't in the military. He *was* in the Obsidian Order, and his first name *is* Elim. Those things, I would say, are the truth."

Whatever Garak is, Actor Andrew Robinson couldn't have been happier with the role. "I love this show," he says. "The fact that it has writers who are willing to write a character who tells one story, and then another, and then a third, and then have Bashir ask, 'What was the truth?' and have Garak respond, 'It's all the truth—especially the lies.' I have tremendous respect for writers of that caliber, who are willing to create a relationship between characters like Bashir and Garak that is built on the kind of exchange that happens in all really solid relationships. And then to follow through to a payoff like 'The Wire.' I wish there was more writing like that for television. I think we'd have a much healthier industry."

Interestingly, Wolfe's original idea for the episode —the one the producers did *not* buy—didn't focus on Garak at all. "I've experienced some drug abuse among people close to me," he says thoughtfully, "and the truth is, you never really expect to find out some person is a drug abuser. I originally pitched the idea that Kira was addicted to some substance, like battle stimulants, and she had been ever since she was in the Resistance, and she would be for the rest of her life. And I got shot down. I mean, I know why. That's not an easy episode to do and then walk away from. So we got to do it with Garak."

The episode marks the first time a female director has worked a *DS9* episode. The producers liked Kim Friedman's work on "The Wire" so well that they quickly signed her up to do the final episode of the second season ("The Jem'Hadar") and the first episode of the third ("The Search, Part I"), as well as subsequent episodes. Friedman, a science-fiction buff who, curiously, had never directed for a science-fiction series until *DS9*, loved the experience. "I learned so much," she says. "The Special Effects and Optical Departments are just wonderful. A great group of men and women, very smart and very talented."

Her biggest challenge on "The Wire," however,

This episode laid some tantalizing hints about Garak's past and his relationship with Enabran Tain. ROBBIE ROBINSON

wasn't effects sequences. It was the multitude of two-person scenes. "It was written that way intentionally," she explains. "But it's very difficult to sustain a level of interest with just two persons the whole time. I used a lot of handheld camera shots to heighten the drama, particularly in some of the scenes where Garak is going crazy and Bashir is trying to stop him."

Siddig El Fadil didn't mind the fact that the episode wasn't action-packed. "It was great to do something this dramatic," he says. "It was just old-fashioned acting, which is always fun."

Behr is a stong advocate of so-called talk episodes. "It's drama, *drama*," he says emphatically. "It's not about special effects, or scientific quirky ideas that may or may not ever come to realization in our world. It's about the human heart in conflict with itself. So, yes, sometimes we dare to be talky, but good talk, I think, makes great TV."

In addition to learning Julian Bashir's middle name (Subatoi), we are introduced to many terms and names, some of which will mean far more in subsequent episodes. We learn that the Cardassian homeworld is referred to as Cardassia Prime, that the Obsidian Order is the eyes and ears of the Cardassian Empire and that Enabran Tain *is* the Obsidian Order, or was, until he retired. But Tain proved too good a character to use only once. "The scene between Bashir and Tain became a favorite of ours, because we wanted to find out more about that guy!" admits Behr. Tain would return during *DS9*'s third season and fifth season. His final appearance would reveal one of Garak's biggest secrets ("In Purgatory's Shadow").

As for the Obsidian Order, Robert Wolfe notes that it most likely would have been referred to as "the Gray Order" if he hadn't turned on an episode of *Babylon 5* and discovered that the governing body of one of the alien species was called the Gray Council. "I thought, 'Damn!,' and then I made up a huge list of different kinds of metals, gems, and colors, and finally came up with obsidian, which I actually like better than gray!"

CROSSOVER

Episode #443

TELEPLAY BY PETER ALLAN FIELDS
AND MICHAEL PILLER
STORY BY PETER ALLAN FIELDS
DIRECTED BY DAVID LIVINGSTON

GUEST CAST

Garak	ANDREW ROBINSON
Telok	JOHN COTHRAN JR.
Klingon #1	STEPHEN GEVEDON
Human	JACK R. OREND
Marauder	DENNIS MADALONE

STARDATE UNKNOWN

Returning from a hospital facility at a new Bajoran colony located in the Gamma Quadrant, Kira and Bashir encounter some unusual operational difficulties as their runabout passes through the wormhole. The rough ride leaves them a little dizzy, and even more disoriented when they discover that the space station seems to have been moved back to its previous position orbiting Bajor. As they approach DS9, the runabout is boarded by two hostile Klingons, whose attitude abruptly becomes deferential when they see Kira. Things become much stranger as they step aboard the station and are confronted by a no-nonsense Garak and a mirror image of Kira, who refers to herself as the station's "intendant."

With Bashir hustled away to the station's ore mines, Kira finds herself escorted through a very different DS9, one in which Terrans provide slave labor, Klingons and Cardassians are united in a brutish "Alliance," and Intendant Kira controls all. Intrigued with her double, the narcissistic intendant informs Kira that she is in a different universe, one that a dif-

Kira learns that the mirror version of Sisko isn't a very nice guy—and he doesn't like being a slave to the Alliance. DANNY FELD

ferent Terran from her side—Captain James Kirk—had crossed over to years earlier. Kirk's appearance had a profound effect upon the mirror universe, the intendant explains, ultimately triggering a shift in power that allowed the allied Klingon and Cardassian Empires to become the predominant power, and Bajor to become a major player. Although protocol calls for the intendant to kill anyone who comes from the other universe, Kira is able to convince her to spare both her life and Bashir's while she searches for a way to back to her own universe.

In the ore mines, Bashir discovers a downtrodden counterpart to O'Brien and a cruel version of Odo serving as an overseer to the workers. After Kira fills him in on what's happening, Bashir attempts to enlist the mirror O'Brien's aid in getting home, but O'Brien doesn't want to risk the punishment. In the meantime, Kira almost succeeds in obtaining the mirror Quark's help, but the Ferengi is arrested and put to death for helping Terrans to escape the station. Later, Kira is approached by Garak, who tries to convince her that her only hope for escape is to cooperate with him. Garak plans to have the intendant killed. If Kira agrees to impersonate the intendant, then resign, allowing Garak to take over. He will then help Kira and Bashir get off the station. On the other hand, if she *doesn't* choose to cooperate, Garak will have Bashir killed.

Knowing that the mirror Sisko works for the intendant, Kira lets him know about Garak's plan, hoping that Sisko will be grateful for the information and help her get her runabout back. But Sisko is unfazed by Garak's plan, and uninterested in Kira's plight. Meanwhile, in the ore mines, Bashir takes advantage of an accident to get hold of a weapon. Killing Odo, he makes his escape and encounters O'Brien, whom he finally convinces to help him. Unfortunately, the pair are apprehended a short time later and brought to the intendant, who is hosting a large party at Quark's bar.

The angry intendant prepares to have Bashir and O'Brien put to death. Suddenly, Sisko, tired of being the intendant's tool and inspired by the knowledge that *somewhere* Terrans live a life of dignity, turns against her. Sisko and O'Brien join forces against the Alliance and help Kira and Bashir get to their runabout. Pursued by Klingon ships, the pair return to the wormhole and manage to cross over into their own universe in the nick of time.

Nana Visitor works with her double. Each scene in which she played against herself was shot twice, creating long, intense days. DANNY FELD

The classic original series episode "Mirror, Mirror" has remained such a favorite with viewers that it seemed only natural that another incarnation of *Star Trek* found its way back to that fascinating universe. "We'd been talking about the episode for a while, and finally we thought we could do it right and have some fun with it," recalls Ira Steven Behr.

The teleplay for "Crossover" (originally called "Detour") was cowritten by Peter Allan Fields (his final script as a *DS9* staff member) and Michael Piller. However, it was Robert Hewitt Wolfe (affectionately referred to by Behr as "one of our resident *Trek* nerds") who provided the historical details that served to link "Crossover" to "Mirror, Mirror." Wolfe says, "I came up with some of the backstory, the idea that the mirror Spock took over after our Kirk left, and how that turned out to be a mistake. Empires aren't usually brutal unless there's a reason. There are usually external or internal pressures that cause them to be that way. So I just thought that if the parallel [mirror] Earth [we saw in Kirk's time] was that brutal, there had to be a reason. And the reason was that the barbarians [the Klingons and the Cardassians] were at the gate."

As Intendant Kira points out, the rest was history. With the Terran Empire no longer interested in keeping things in check, the Klingons and the Cardassians joined forces to form a coalition that took the Empire's place in dominating the galaxy.

With the story in place, it was now up to the people behind the scenes to convince the audience that they were back in the mirror universe. Changes to established sets proved less complicated than they had been for "Necessary Evil," according to Herman Zimmerman. "It was more lighting and costuming than anything physical that we needed to do," he says. "It was still the same place, but in an alternate universe."

The mining sequences were shot in the cargo bay set on Stage 4, with the addition of some atmospheric smoke and unusual lighting. "I wanted a feeling of searchlights always panning across the room," Director David Livingston recalls. "It gave the scenes a really weird, interesting look."

Weird was also the operative word for many of the camera angles Livingston chose. "I talked to [the producers] about the look of the movie *The Third Man* and got them to approve canted angles," he says. "I started off in the runabout and went as far as possible, putting the camera on the floor and using incredible angles. It looked unusual and immediately told the viewer he was in another world." Livingston continued to tilt the camera in subsequent scenes but "didn't get quite as outrageous."

As for costumes, just as in the original episode, many were variations on the ones the characters normally wear. Odo's, for example, was similar to his traditional outfit, except that it was gray and had a high collar and belt. Actor Rene Auberjonois liked it so much that he asked Robert Blackman if his regular uniform could be modified to look more like it. Rick Berman approved the change, and Odo received his new uniform just in time for the start of third season.

While Intendant Kira's uniform has caused many a jaw to drop, Blackman swears that it isn't all that different from Major Kira's traditional jumpsuit. Being stretch vinyl, it conforms to her body a bit more, he admits, and the three-and-one-half inch heels on the boots make her taller. But other than that, says Blackman, "If you were to put the two uniforms together, you'd say, 'Well, it's kind of a shiny gray version of the rust.' It's not that I've exposed more of her body—it's exposed pretty much the same way it always is. What's the difference? *She's* the difference. It's how Nana wears it. It's what she does. She walks like a provocative woman, with her legs crossing in front. She uses her hips, and a whole other kind of body English than she normally uses. She's a trained dancer, so it's partially due to that, but frankly, when you go from a flat shoe to a three-and-one-half-inch heeled shoe, a woman walks differently—period."

According to most of the people who know her, the coy, coquettish intendant is much closer to Nana Visitor's real personality than the tough-as-nails major, something that Visitor herself confirms. "It's very much me. I mean, I hope I don't send people to their deaths or anything like that, but, yeah, that is more of who I am." She laughs. Visitor arrived at the persona by thinking about Kira's core personality and then "messing with her ego a bit, and messing with a few key elements in her life that would have changed its direction. She's a spoiled brat with an ego gone awry."

While Siddig El Fadil didn't get to play a different role in this particular mirror outing, he reports that it was "great fun to see everybody being different. It was fun to interact with people acting that way. And shooting Odo was one of the pinnacles of my career. I got to shoot him about eight times. It was great!"

Judy Elkins was responsible for adding one crucial element to that sequence: a wax sculpture of Odo that the effects team rigged to explode. The scene was

Nana Visitor's coquettish performance came from within—but the costumes provided additional inspiration. DANNY FELD

first shot with Rene Auberjonois, and then Elkins did a freehand sculpture based on his appearance in a frame from the footage.

Why did the phaser blast blow Odo up rather than melt him? "Because he melts anyway," explains Dan Curry, "so you wouldn't be able to tell if he was just morphing into his liquid state or not. So in order to show that he was "history," they blew up this wax replica, and in that moment of intense heat, the wax splattered just like shape-shifter goo."

The episode went a day over schedule in filming, primarily because of the time that went into setting up the split-screen photography. A typical scene between Kira and the mirror Kira, as described by Livingston, called for him to "decide which side we wanted to shoot first, and then Nana would act it out facing her stand-in, so that the eyeline was right. Then we'd decide which take was best and while the camera was still locked off, have Nana change her makeup, hair, and costume, and get into the other position, moving her stand-in to the position Nana had been in before. Then we'd play the tape back so that she could talk to herself, so the timing would be correct." Livingston notes that for the scene where

David Livingston worked closely with Marvin Rush to create this hellish look. DANNY FELD

the intendant touches Kira's face, the hand of the stand-in was used. "You'll see that her hand actually comes from the bottom of the frame; you never see it connected to her body."

While Visitor found the split-screen sequences something of a challenge, she'll remember the milk-bath sequence a lot longer. "I'm very shy and I was not about to do a real nude scene," she says. "So I asked for these cone things they have. They were horrible, made like the ones they put in the street. And my makeup artist, Camille Calvet, gives me this bottle of glue to put them on, and when I come back she says, 'Where's the bottle?' I tell her I used it all. And she says, 'You're only supposed to use a few drops. We're never gonna get that stuff off!'

"In the meantime, our crew is great, they make the bath nice and hot for me and tell me they put

orange oil into the water so it will smell nice and soften my skin. So I get in and we start rehearsing, and all of a sudden I feel the cones starting to pop off. And Camille's nearby, so I whisper, 'Camille, what takes the glue off?' And she says, 'Orange oil.'"

Visitor says she's "pretty sure" the crew didn't know about orange oil removing glue, but the scene was shot in record time.

The tub Visitor soaked in was a holdover from *The Next Generation*, and would show up again in the feature *Star Trek: Insurrection*. Stunt Coordinator Dennis Madalone served double duty in the episode, coordinating stunts as well as playing a character called "Marauder," a role he would reprise in each of the mirror sequels. An early version of the script included Worf among the complement of nasty Klingons serving the Intendant. When Michael Dorn proved unavailable, many of Worf's lines went to the mirror Garak. But Dorn would get the opportunity to play in the mirror universe after all. He'd show up as the Regent in "Shattered Mirror" and "The Emperor's New Cloak."

THE COLLABORATOR

Episode #444

TELEPLAY BY **GARY HOLLAND** AND
IRA STEVEN BEHR & ROBERT HEWITT WOLFE
STORY BY **GARY HOLLAND**
DIRECTED BY **CLIFF BOLE**

GUEST CAST

Vedek Bareil	PHILIP ANGLIM
Kubus Oak	BERT REMSEN
Kai Opaka	CAMILLE SAVIOLA
Eblan	CHARLES PARKS
Prylar Bek	TOM VILLARD

SPECIAL GUEST STAR

Vedek Winn	LOUISE FLETCHER

STARDATE UNKNOWN

 t is a difficult time for Vedek Bareil. In two days, the Bajorans will elect a new spiritual leader and, as the late Kai Opaka's personal choice, it seems certain that Bareil will be chosen. But Bareil is troubled by the disturbing visions he has seen in the Orb of Prophecy and Change, visions that imply his involvement with the suicide of a Prylar named Bek. Not even the feelings that he has for Kira, who has become his lover, can bring him inner peace.

Winn's accusations regarding Bareil's involvement in the slaughter of Bajorans sow the seeds of doubt in Kira. ROBBIE ROBINSON

Following a visit to the station by Bareil, Kira encounters Vedek Winn, Bareil's opponent in the upcoming competition. Knowing of Winn's likely involvement in the attempt on Bareil's life months earlier ("In the Hands of the Prophets"), Kira is suspicious of her presence on DS9. Not long after Winn's arrival, a Bajoran named Kubus is spotted on the station. Known as a Cardassian collaborator, Kubus is quickly surrounded by a mob, then arrested by Odo, as Winn watches nearby.

Kubus, who was exiled from Bajor after the Occupation, tells Odo and Kira that he wishes to live out his remaining years on Bajor. Kira refuses, but soon discovers that Vedek Winn has offered Kubus sanctuary, and plans to take him home. As Kira and Odo try to figure out her motivation, Odo recalls that prior to coming to her decision, Winn had used his computer. They learn that Winn was researching the Kendra Valley massacre. Forty-three Bajoran freedom fighters, including Kai Opaka's son, were killed by Cardassians when the alleged collaborator, Prylar Bek, betrayed their location. Bek committed suicide shortly after the incident.

Major Kira refuses to allow Winn to leave the station with Kubus. Winn then reveals that in exchange for sanctuary, Kubus has agreed to provide the name of the real collaborator: Vedek Bareil. It was Bareil who ordered Bek to reveal the information to the Cardassians, Winn explains.

Kira doesn't believe the accusation, so Winn offers her the opportunity to prove Bareil innocent before the accusations become public. Kira questions Kubus and learns that Bareil came to see Bek the day before he hung himself. Bareil claims he came only to coun-

sel the prylar, whose guilt over the massacre was overwhelming. But Odo reveals that the communications records between Bek and the Vedek Assembly for the week prior to the Kendra incident have been sealed, something only a vedek like Bareil could order.

Odo and Kira get Quark to bypass the seal, and they learn that the transmissions have been erased. O'Brien can't recover the data with the speed that Kira needs, but he can identify the person who erased it: Bareil.

When Kira confronts Bareil, he explains that Bek was ordered to reveal the location of the resistance fighters. Otherwise, the Cardassians would have killed every resident in the vicinity, taking some twelve hundred lives versus forty-three. Disillusioned by his involvement, Kira prepares to inform Winn, only to discover that Bareil has already withdrawn from the election. This surprises Kira. She knows that if Bareil were guilty, he would have revealed his culpability to the people, rather than sidestepping the issue. Kira goes back to her investigation and discovers the truth.

Returning to Bajor on the day Winn is declared the new kai, Kira again confronts Bareil. He reluctantly confirms her findings: Kai Opaka was the collaborator who ordered Bek to reveal the information, not him. She had sacrificed the life of her own son to save the lives of twelve hundred people. Bareil has sacrificed his career in order to protect Opaka's memory.

If you weren't adverse to using clichés, you might call Gary Holland's sale of "The Collaborator" a case of "local boy makes good." Holland, who was in charge of advertising and promotion for *Deep Space Nine* at Paramount for the entire run of the series, had been aching to write a *Star Trek* script ever since he'd first seen the classic episode "The City on the Edge of Forever" as a boy in Baltimore. "It literally was one of the things that motivated me to want to become a writer," he says, "and it started me doing little *Star Trek* comic books and stuff like that at the age of seven."

Holland grew up reading that tome of media-oriented science fiction, *Starlog* magazine, which inadvertently led to his first brush with Hollywood. "*Starlog* had a synopsis of a new series, *Logan's Run,* which was going to debut on television in the fall," he remembers. "I thought, 'Let me try to write a script.'" At age fourteen, Holland's spec script was good enough to get him an agent, although the actual series came and went so quickly that he never had the opportunity for a sale. Still, it did sig-

The fervor Visitor brought to her performance in defense of Bareil justified establishing an intimate relationship between the pair.
ROBBIE ROBINSON

nal the fact that selling a script was not an impossible dream.

Ultimately, he got on a career track that drew him into the entertainment industry, albeit not through the door he'd originally envisioned. Nevertheless, when he accepted the position at Paramount, he couldn't help thinking, "I'm on the lot, I've *got* to get in there now." Common sense kept him focused on his primary reason for being there, his 9-to-6 job, and he got to know the people behind the scenes. By this time, Holland had racked up a number of writing credits, including one for an Emmy-nominated half-hour dramatic film. He'd also gotten an agent, "who happened to be with the same agency as Harlan Ellison [writer of "The City on the Edge of Forever"]." Then, toward the end of *DS9*'s second season, Holland was invited to come in and pitch.

Holland pitched three stories, two of which were quickly dismissed by the "catchers," Ira Steven Behr, Robert Hewitt Wolfe, and Peter Allan Fields. They didn't seem to like the third one, either—a downbeat story about a Bajoran who'd been living on Cardassia, and who showed up on the station, wanting to go home to Bajor—but they talked about it for ten minutes, which is a long time at a pitch session.

Recalls Behr, "Gary Holland came into the room with a story that was barely a story, one of those things that happens a million times. And as he was talking, things started coming into my mind. About Bareil. And about making the crime be one of collaboration. And I just started spewing."

"'My' Bajoran had a past and a secret that Kira had to discover," says Holland. Initially, that secret concerned a murder, and the victim was Kira's father, with the ultimate twist being that the man was actually covering for his little daughter. But, under Behr's prodding, the secret turned to collaboration with the enemy, and the twist became something with far greater repercussions in the ongoing *DS9* storyline.

"We were all sitting in the room," recalls Wolfe, "and it occurred to us, 'God, we could do this story and make Winn the kai. That's a scary idea!'"

"We had talked all year about Bareil becoming the next kai," says Behr. "*All year!* And during this conversation, we started talking about a collaborator, and I suddenly realized, 'We don't want Bareil as the kai. What the hell good is that going to do us? He's a friend, and he's not going to cause any trouble for the Federation.' The trick to drama is to find the person who's going to cause the most conflict and put him in the most powerful position."

Back at his office the next day, ironically in the Gene Roddenberry Building, Holland was surprised when Behr phoned and said, "Well, I took your collaborator story to Michael Piller right after you left and he likes it too, so we want to buy it."

"Gary said, 'It's not what I pitched, really,'" relates Behr. "But I told him, 'Do this show. You sparked it. No one was even thinking about it until you walked into the room. Go off and do it.'" Two days later, Holland and Behr had a very brief story meeting, during which they hatched the idea that Bareil was actually covering for Kai Opaka. Holland returned four days later with a first draft that earned kudos from the staff. Behr then told Holland they'd decided to let him write the teleplay. "Gary wrote a very good script with very little time," says Wolfe. "A lot of his input was left in the final version, more so than most freelancers."

Holland is responsible for some of the more interesting elements in "The Collaborator," including establishing an intimate relationship between Kira and Bareil. "My feeling was that for Kira to really care about what's going on with Bareil, we had to show just how close they had become," he says. The producers ultimately agreed, and the intimate aspects of the relationship that had been dropped from early versions of the script were reinstated.

Other scenes that Holland argued for included the

Orb sequences and the scene in which Kira is forced to ask Quark for help in bypassing the security seal on the communication files. The scene served two purposes: It injected a flicker of humor into what actually was a very dark episode, and it provided a "Deep Throat"–type character to a story with a number of Watergate parallels; think of Prylar Bek as John Dean. The name of Bek was an homage to Don Beck, whose company produces the promos for both *DS9* and *Voyager.*

TRIBUNAL

Episode #445

WRITTEN BY **BILL DIAL**
DIRECTED BY **AVERY BROOKS**

GUEST CAST

Keiko O'Brien	ROSALIND CHAO
Makbar	CAROLINE LAGERFELT
Raymond Boone	JOHN BECK
Gul Evek	RICHARD POE
Cardassian Voice	JULIAN CHRISTOPHER
Computer Voice	MAJEL BARRETT

AND

Kovat	FRITZ WEAVER

STARDATE 47944.2

Vacations don't come easily to Chief O'Brien. Before he leaves the station, he must fuss with dozens of minor details in Ops. Running late, he hustles to join his wife Keiko at the runabout they've borrowed for their trip. But on the way, he runs into Boone, a former crewmate from the *Rutledge.* They exchange a few pleasantries and then O'Brien continues to the runabout, oblivious to the fact that Boone has surreptitiously recorded their conversation.

On his way at last, O'Brien finally begins to relax —just as the runabout is intercepted by a Cardassian patrol ship manned by Gul Evek, who arrests O'Brien for an unnamed crime. Taken to Cardassia Prime, O'Brien is brutally stripped and processed, then taken before Makbar, the chief archon, who will represent the state's case against him. Makbar informs O'Brien that the court has appointed a Cardassian named Kovat as his attorney, but she refuses to tell him what his crime is.

Makbar contacts Sisko to inform him of the legal proceedings to come, but bluntly explains that the trial will serve only to reveal *how* O'Brien's guilt was established; both the verdict and the punishment— execution—have been determined already. Although Makbar will not allow Sisko to attend the trial, she will permit O'Brien's spouse to attend. And, after he establishes his credentials as an officer of the court who once served under Gul Dukat, Odo is granted permission to accompany Keiko and to serve as O'Brien's nestor, an advisor to the offender.

After Odo and Keiko depart, Sisko turns up some disquieting information. Two dozen photon warheads have been smuggled off the station by a transporter expert. Worse, security logs contain a recording of O'Brien's voice, requesting access to the weapons locker. It seems likely that the weapons were destined for delivery to the Maquis, probably via O'Brien's runabout. Sisko informs Odo, who questions O'Brien about the warheads, but O'Brien denies knowing anything about them.

Back on the station, Dax finds evidence that the recording of O'Brien's voice was probably a fabrication. At the same time, Kira establishes that a man named Boone, a possible member of the Maquis, talked to O'Brien before he left on vacation. Sisko has Boone brought in for questioning, but Boone will admit nothing. Sisko's investigation seems to be at a dead end until a member of the Maquis approaches Bashir and tells the doctor that Boone is not one of them, and that the Maquis have no knowledge of the crime. Suspicious, Sisko has Bashir give Boone an extensive medical examination.

At the trial, Gul Evek testifies regarding ongoing Maquis attempts to terrorize and murder innocent Cardassians, connecting such events to the warheads found in O'Brien's runabout. Makbar and Kovat try to convince O'Brien to confess, but he refuses. Unwilling to allow Odo to introduce evidence that would help clear O'Brien, the court is about to declare its guilty verdict when Sisko arrives in the courtroom with Boone. Seeing Boone, Makbar abruptly announces that although O'Brien is guilty, she will release him to Sisko's custody "in the spirit of furthering Cardassian/Federation relations."

Returning to the station, Sisko explains that Bashir's examination had revealed Boone was actually a surgically altered Cardassian; the real Boone had died years earlier. The trial had been an attempt to discredit the Federation by proving the Maquis had its official sanction. When Sisko showed up with Boone, however, Makbar knew he had the evidence to publicly embarrass Cardassia's High Command. Deeply relieved, the O'Briens are at last able to go on their delayed vacation.

O'Brien is processed in the standard fashion by his Cardassian captors. ROBBIE ROBINSON

When Ira Steven Behr wrote the line "On Cardassia, the verdict is always known before the trial begins," in the teleplay of "The Maquis, Part II," he not only inspired a subsequent episode, but etched the ground rules of the entire Cardassian legal system in stone. "That one line gave them the concept for the whole episode," notes Behr.

It also provides a good example of the way members of *DS9*'s writing staff occasionally use each other's scripts as springboards into new stories, a practice that's generally encouraged on the series. Any fact that the viewers find out in an episode, for instance, that O'Brien has a brother, or that Dax has been a mother three times and a father twice, could become the thread of a future episode. Not in every case, of course, but certainly where the producers think they smell a good story. "Some things are best left mysterious, but there's a whole lot of filling in the blanks in good writing," says Behr. "I love filling in the blanks, especially when it comes to characters. We all do." In this case, the blanks were primarily filled in by Writer Bill Dial.

The cold, even grinding, hand of the Cardassian justice system was embodied by the character of Makbar. ROBBIE ROBINSON

First-time director Avery Brooks made compelling use of the "dark . . . multilevel but spare" set. ROBBIE ROBINSON

The story itself, one of many over the course of the series that would pit everyman Miles O'Brien against *DS9*'s equivalent of the trials of Job, is reminiscent of one of Kafka's dark tales. However, the look of the episode, from the stark "processing" room to the Big Brother–like monitors scattered throughout Cardassia Prime, was inspired by George Orwell's *1984,* according to Herman Zimmerman. "Cardassia is a military state, made up of a lot of factions that are against each other," he says. "Spartan, uncompromising and merciless are all adjectives that you could use to describe Cardassia."

Contributing to the sterile Cardassian cityscape was a matte painting by Syd Dutton and Robert Stromberg of Illusion Arts, the company that does many of *Star Trek*'s impressive "establishing" matte shots. Some forced-perspective miniatures were created by Tony Meininger, owner of Brazil Fabrication & Design; his company also built the massive six-foot model of the DS9 space station.

The intimidating Cardassian courtroom was constructed on *DS9*'s holosuite set, which has also served as a science lab and a racquetball court. The courtroom's design details were unique and hair depart-

ment head Josée Normand incorporated some of them into Makbar's hairstyle. "It was one of those times that I went over to the set for inspiration," says Normand. "Sometimes when I see the surroundings these people live and work in, the weird shapes of the furniture or whatever, it gives me ideas."

The episode marked Actor Avery Brooks's first turn behind the camera as a *Deep Space Nine* director. "I was glad that Colm was in it, because I enjoy working with him and watching him work," says Brooks. "And it was the first time that *DS9* had gone to Cardassia, so there were new things for me to consider, like what the temperature was likely to be, and that kind of thing."

It was also Colm Meaney's first turn in front of the camera sans wardrobe. O'Brien's harsh treatment in the processing cell reinforces *Star Trek* continuity by inviting comparison with a similar scene in *The Next Generation* episode "Chain of Command, Part II." In that episode, Captain Picard was also stripped naked and suffered the pain and humiliation of a Cardassian interrogation. Other links to *TNG* are another mention of O'Brien's old ship, the *Rutledge,* and the massacre at Setlik III.

THE JEM'HADAR

Episode #446

WRITTEN BY **IRA STEVEN BEHR**

DIRECTED BY **KIM FRIEDMAN**

GUEST CAST

Captain Keogh	ALAN OPPENHEIMER
Nog	ARON EISENBERG
Talak'talan	CRESS WILLIAMS
First Officer	MICHAEL JACE
Second Officer	SANDRA GRANDO
Computer Voice	MAJEL BARRETT

AND

Eris	MOLLY HAGAN

STARDATE UNKNOWN

Quark and Sisko are taken captive by a group of vicious soldiers known as the Jem'Hadar. ROBBIE ROBINSON

Hoping to whet Jake's educational ambitions and to invest some time in father-son bonding, Sisko offers his son a trip to the Gamma Quadrant as a "working vacation." But the best-laid plans begin to take a turn for the worse when Jake invites Nog to come along, and Quark invites *himself* along, ostensibly to supervise his nephew.

Arriving at an uninhabited tropical world in the Gamma Quadrant, the odd foursome set up camp. While Jake and Nog begin surveying the planet, Quark unsuccessfully attempts to talk Sisko into allowing him to engage in a new business scheme on the station. Later, Quark and Sisko exchange heated words, and an embarrassed Nog runs into the woods with Jake hot on his heels. Suddenly, a frightened alien woman races out of the forest, her pursuers only seconds behind. Before they know it, Quark, Sisko, and the woman are taken prisoner by a group of soldiers known as the Jem'Hadar.

Returning to the abandoned campsite, Jake and Nog begin searching for Sisko and Quark, who have been imprisoned with the woman, Eris, in a cave sealed by a force field. Eris tells Sisko about their captors, the Jem'Hadar. She describes the Jem'Hadar as the most feared soldiers in the Dominion, a name that both Quark and Sisko have heard before. According to Eris, the Dominion runs much of the Gamma Quadrant, controlling its inhabitants through negotiation and, should that fail, the force of the Jem'Hadar. Eris claims that her planet was forcibly taken over by the Dominion; she was pursued to this world because of her family's outspoken opposition to their conquerers.

Although Eris has telekinetic abilities, the Jem'Hadar have placed a collar around her neck that prevents her from using them to get through the security barrier outside the cave. Sisko decides their first order of business should be to remove the collar, but before he can do so, Talak'talan, one of the Jem'Hadar, enters the cave. He informs Sisko that the Dominion will no longer tolerate the presence of ships from the Alpha Quadrant on their side of the wormhole.

In the meantime, Jake and Nog find the cave, but they realize they have no way to get past the guards. Returning to their runabout, Jake discovers he can't beam the prisoners aboard, and he can't return to the station until he disengages the *Rio Grande*'s autopilot. But once he does that, he learns that he'll have to fly the ship back manually—and he's never operated a runabout.

Back at Deep Space 9, the crew is startled when a Jem'Hadar ship comes through the wormhole and Talak'talan beams through the station's shields to appear in Ops. The soldier informs Kira that her

CLOSE-UP: It Starts with a Pitch . . .

An insight into the scripting process

Joe Menosky served as executive story editor during the fourth season of *Star Trek: The Next Generation*, and as writer/coproducer during that series's fifth season. After working as a freelance writer with *Deep Space Nine*, he joined the staff of *Voyager* during their third season, serving first as producer and later as co-executive producer.

"It starts with a pitch from a writer to a producer," says Joe Menosky. "The pitch is a verbal concept of what the story is, and it can be really short. I pitched 'Dramatis Personae' over the phone to Michael Piller in about a minute: the idea of a telepathic virus and everybody getting infected and getting yanked into this sort of drama that they then execute. And Mike said, 'Okay, I'll buy it.' That constitutes a sale.

"You then go off and write a six-page double-spaced story about what basically happens, but not blow-by-blow. It's your pitch plus whatever comments the producer offered when you made your pitch. For example, he might have said, 'You should emphasize Quark instead of Odo when you write up the story.' So you do that and then you turn it in and the staff looks at it, talks about it, and gives you feedback: 'This works and this works and this doesn't work.' It's always an iterative process, where you go off and write independently and then it gets pulled back into the mix and this collaboration happens.

"Then you do what's called a beat sheet, which means that you take their comments on your story and do a blow-by-blow description, literally scene by scene. It's very shorthand; it'll say teaser, fade-in, exterior space station, to establish commander's log. Then maybe interior, Ops, Kira, Dax, whoever is there, and then a very short description of what happens in that scene, maybe only two lines. And it goes on like that. It's a road map for the teleplay. You know where all the scenes are, you know whether it's going to be too expensive to produce, you know whether or not you're servicing enough of the actors.

"What you can't tell, ironically, is how it's going to work. So you get to the next step, which is the hairiest part of the process, where the entire staff gets together and looks at the beat sheet. There's a big board up on the wall, like a blackboard, and on it you start rebreaking the beat sheet. It's always sort of interesting how much of the beat sheet you've done is followed beat by beat until finally someone in the room says, 'Well . . .,' and it just takes off in another direction. The most I've ever gotten through is Act Three, and I was really lucky. These meetings can go for days. The average to break a story is six hours the first day and six hours the next, although I've heard of week-long break sessions. But while it's the

---

commander is being detained for questioning by the Dominion. He repeats his threat about Alpha Quadrant ships violating the Dominion's territory and provides proof of the ships and colonies the Dominion has destroyed. Then, easily defeating the station's tractor beam, Talak'talan beams back to his ship and returns through the wormhole.

A short time later, the *Starship Odyssey* arrives at the station under the command of Captain Keogh, who's been ordered by Starfleet to handle the situation and rescue Sisko and the others. Kira, Dax, Bashir and Odo volunteer to assist, and follow the *Odyssey* through the wormhole in two runabouts. The first thing they encounter is the *Rio Grande*, with Jake in command—sort of. O'Brien beams over to help the two boys and discovers that Jake's tinkering has left many of the ship's systems inoperative. Separating from the other two runabouts and the *Odyssey*, which are about to engage the Jem'Hadar in

combat, the *Rio Grande* heads for the planet in the hopes of rescuing Sisko and the others.

As the battle begins to rage above, Quark finally manages to remove Eris's collar and she deactivates the force field. The three captives escape, and a short time later, are beamed up to the *Rio Grande*. With Sisko recovered, Keogh orders a retreat back to the wormhole, but before they can leave the area, a Jem'Hadar ship destroys the *Odyssey* in a kamikaze-style attack.

The three runabouts somberly return to the station, where Quark informs Sisko that he has analyzed Eris's collar and discovered that it was a fake. She could have used her powers to get out at any time. The fact that she didn't makes Sisko realize that Eris is a spy for the Dominion, and that she was meant to return to the Alpha Quadrant with Sisko. But before they can arrest her, Eris beams off the station—where to, no one knows—leaving the crew with the uncom-

JULIE DENNIS

hardest part, it's also really fun and invigorating because there's all these intellectuals sparring and sometimes there's violent arguments, and joking and laughing.

"Then the writer goes off again, this time with the new beat sheet, so he can write the teleplay. At that point, you're turning a three-page road map into a sixty-page script, and each one of those little two-line descriptions that say, 'So-and-so and so-and-so in a bedroom,' gets turned into, say, a sex scene done artfully and with humor. Doing a teleplay is fun when you've got a good beat sheet. You finish it and turn it in, and there's another meeting and everyone gives you notes on the teleplay and you argue for your points, but, again, it's really collaborative. Most of the time when scripts get changed, it's for the better.

"The writer then does a second draft and by that time you're getting really close to preproduction, called prep. Ideally, when you turn in the script this time you'll get notes, but it's always a process of tuning it finer and finer. By this time, if you're a freelance writer, you'll have passed the script to whichever staff writer is going to shepherd it through the rest of the process. The staff writer will have to start dealing with comments from the production staff, as well as continued comments from the other writers. Stuff like, 'We can't afford ten phaser blasts in this show, make it five!' Or 'This actor is sick this week, give him less lines.' Really specific production needs that the script has to reflect. At this point, you're doing a polish. And the writing part of it gradually pulls back until production takes over entirely."

fortable realization that their dealings with a new enemy have only begun.

The second season of *Deep Space Nine* was "a really fun, very creative time," reflects Ira Steven Behr. "Robert Wolfe, Jim Crocker, Peter Allan Fields, and I would go to lunch together every day. And I remember saying one day, 'Okay guys, we're gonna come up with villains, not one but *three* sets of villains. And we're gonna make them as scary as any villains you can possibly find.'" As part of this mandate, Behr assigned the group some homework: read Isaac Asimov's *Foundation Trilogy*. "Don't ask me why." Behr laughs. "I don't know what the hell I thought they'd find. But everybody read it, except Pete."

Time went by, the villains were created, and the season wrapped on April 25, 1994, with the completion of the episode "The Jem'Hadar." In February

1995, well into the third season, Behr received a fax from Fields, who had retired after Season 2. In its entirety, the fax, which remained pinned to Behr's bulletin board for the rest of the series run, read: "To Ira Behr, *Deep Space Nine*. I've finished reading *Foundation Trilogy*. Please advise. Fields."

Tardy homework assignment aside, Fields admits that he had little to do with the episode "The Jem'Hadar." "If I had, frankly, it would have been called something else," he says. "'The Dominion' (the original name of the episode, as well as the group name the writing staff chose for the villainous coalition) was a pretty good name," Fields adds. "But 'The Jem'Hadar' sounds like 'mah-jongg,' or some kind of card game!"

Depending on your point of view, the credit or blame for the name Jem'Hadar falls to Wolfe, who also originated the concept of this particular faction of the Dominion being a fierce warrior race with skins like rhinos.

Viewers get their first glimpse of a Vorta, played here by Molly Hagan.
ROBBIE ROBINSON

the same feel and meaness by putting little horns all around his face. It makes them dangerous—if you bump into one, you're going to bleed. So you know automatically that you never get close to the Jem'Hadar."

The idea of the Jem'Hadar, a vicious group of warriors who would carry out the Dominion's threats, was always part of the villainous trinity, notes Wolfe. "Basically, the idea was that the Dominion was the Carrot-and-Stick Empire. The businessmen, the Vorta, were the negotiators, the friendly guys who show up with the carrot. 'Hey, we're your friends. Have some phaser rifles, or space travel, whatever the hell you want. We'll arrange it. All you'll have to do is owe us.' Then, if you don't toe the line, they kick your ass with the Jem'Hadar."

Interestingly, one of the carrots that the writers speculate has been offered to Gamma Quadrant residents is the genetically engineered Tosk ("Captive Pursuit"). Confirms Wolfe, "Sure, you want to be genetically engineered, no problem. You want some Tosks that you can hunt, the Vorta will provide them for you." In fact, the script for the episode includes some expository narrative that was written not for the viewers at home, but for the internal staff's education. As the four Jem'Hadar shimmer into view in Act 1, the script notes: "This is the same kind of invisibility effect used by Tosk in 'Captive Pursuit.' The thought behind this is that the same people who breed the Tosks as gifts to the hunters, breed the Jem'Hadar as well . . ."

That the stick wielded by the Dominion is a powerful one is brought home in a number of ways. For one thing, the Jem'Hadar seem to have the ability to transport right through raised shields. The energy weapons on their scarab-shaped ships can also penetrate shields. The threat of those ships, based on one of Senior Illustrator Rick Sternbach's Egyptian-influenced designs and built by model maker Tony Meininger, is powerful enough to convince Starfleet that Sisko will need a powerhouse like the *Defiant* to deal with them ("The Search"). A *Galaxy*-class starship is clearly not a match for the Jem'Hadar, a fact that the writers came up with to demonstrate that "these guys are not to be taken lightly," says Behr.

"We wanted to show the long-term fans how dangerous these guys were," adds Wolfe. "And it's my belief that if that had been the *Enterprise* and not the *Odyssey*, and Picard rather than Keogh in command, that it still wouldn't have survived. [Veteran *TNG-*

"We wanted warriors, businessmen, and a dark force that was controlling it all," says Behr. "At the beginning, we thought the Vorta were going to be big burly kinds of humanoids that looked like Brian Dennehy or Bob Hoskins. But it didn't work out like that." Instead, the Jem'Hadar became the muscle behind the Dominion, although the initial description of their rhinoceroslike appearance bothered Rick Berman, who didn't want them to look too "comic-booky."

However, with a makeup master like Michael Westmore in charge of developing the look, that was never a danger. "I get a lot of inspiration from nature books and magazines," he admits. But there are ways to avoid the pitfalls of creating something too close to a familiar Earth creature, he says. "You start with the concept of the rhinoceros hide for the Jem'Hadar, and you give them a nose that's based on a rhinoceros nose, but without a horn. If you'd put a horn on it, viewers would say, 'Oh—rhinoceros.' But what makes *Star Trek* so interesting is that you give the creature

Quark's character allowed the writers a way to take a hard look at the Federation's values. ROBBIE ROBINSON

Writer] Ron Moore may not agree, Patrick Stewart probably wouldn't, but it's my belief that Keogh had just as good a ship, just as good a crew, and he got smoked."

The battle sequences between the three Jem'Hadar ships and the *Odyssey*, orchestrated by Glenn Neufeld's visual effects team, resulted in an Emmy nomination for the episode. They were, fittingly, very complex, according to David Takemura. However, a bit of clever recycling helped convey the destruction of the *Odyssey*, with Takemura making use of a portion of one of the fiberglass *Enterprise*s that had been blown to bits for the *TNG* episode "Cause and Effect." "Someone had the presence of mind to save the pieces and store them," says Takemura. "I took a piece of the bottom of the cigar section of the *Enterprise*, did some kit bashing, and made a demolished version of the bottom of the ship."

For the actual explosion, the team shot the intact four-foot *Enterprise* model, which stood in for the *Odyssey*, then shot the piece that Takemura had "customized," positioning it so it would match the previ-

ous footage of the intact ship. After that, it was up to Animator Adam Howard to "marry" the two models. The model of the Jem'Hadar kamikaze ship was composited into the scene at Digital Magic, after which Howard added the explosion elements and the hull of the *Odyssey* turning into molten metal.

The episode, shot in part at Griffith Park's bird sanctuary, was directed by Kim Friedman, returning after her recent stint on "The Wire." One of Friedman's favorite sequences in "The Jem'Hadar" is the confrontation between Quark and Sisko regarding the latter's "prejudices" against the Ferengi. "Armin, Avery, and I talked about it a lot, how far Quark could go here, because this is the commander he's talking to and Quark is in a rather precarious position on Deep Space 9," she recalls. "But we felt that Quark realized there was a chance that he could die, and that would give him the courage to say things he would never say back at the station."

According to Behr, "We were going into the end of the second season and it was time to lay to rest this long-time feeling that the Ferengi were the 'failed villains' of the *Star Trek* universe. I wanted people to see them as something else. And if we could show that Sisko, whose character has a lot of weight, would take what Quark says [about the positive differences between Ferengi and humans] seriously, then the audience would take it seriously."

Of course, Sisko still didn't let Quark initiate his plan to sell merchandise over the station's monitors. But Quark obviously considered that to be only a temporary setback. He would launch a stationwide ad campaign via monitors and replicators in the fourth-season episode "The Quickening."

Eris's apparent telekinetic powers would never be employed by another Vorta. Considering that the typically obsequious species weren't really known for their truthful nature, it's likely that Eris had faked those powers here. In any event, as the writers put more thought into the function of the Vorta, telekinesis was set aside as a misstep that Behr and the others hoped viewers would forget.

THIRD SEASON
O V E R V I E W

With its older sibling (<u>The Next Generation</u>) out of the house, and a new baby (*Voyager*) on the way, the third season of *Deep Space Nine* saw the series thrust out of the nursery and into adulthood. And like any parent, Paramount had hopes and expectations for *DS9*, now the only first-run *Star Trek* series on television. The third season was, after all, the year that *TNG* had come into its own, winning over the last of the die-hard Trekkers who still missed Kirk and crew, while garnering higher and higher ratings from the general public.

As it set out on its own, the series received a "birthright" of sorts from the studio. *DS9* would inherit the entire backstory from the original series and *TNG*—all the species and plotlines that one could find in the Alpha and Beta Quadrants (as well as the Gamma Quadrant), whereas *Voyager*, restricted to the Delta Quadrant, could not

use them. And the first ten episodes of the new season would air without competition from *Voyager*. This would give *DS9* a chance to further hone its own unique identity and capture the hearts of those viewers who hadn't accepted it with the same devotion they demonstrated for *TNG*.

Given the success of its famous older sibling, the pressure on *DS9*'s producers and writers must have seemed daunting at the close of the series' second season. And the input that was coming in from fans across the country couldn't have eased the stress level, particularly not against the backdrop of the hoopla surrounding the highly publicized airing of the *Next Generation* finale, "All Good Things . . ."

Among other points, the producers were hearing that young male viewers (a key group to most advertisers) felt *DS9* did not yet measure up to its sister show, particularly in terms of action and excitement. Viewers, in general, expressed a desire for the crew to have more interaction with outsiders, more travel away from the station (which was considered confining), and situations that generated more of a feeling of jeopardy. The two highest regarded characters were Odo and Quark. Commander Sisko, although well liked, seemed to come across as a rather low-key presence. Stories that dealt with intellectual and philosophical subject matter, e.g., religion and politics (Bajoran, of course), were not embraced by viewers on the whole.

Viewers would definitely see more of what they wanted during the coming season, although the changes were driven by something more powerful than a desire for higher demos. "Bringing in the *Defiant* was based on our own internal perceptions of something that would make the show better," states Robert Hewitt Wolfe, who was elevated to executive story editor for the third season. "It was not based on ratings."

In fact, Wolfe and Ira Steven Behr, who would move up to executive producer by the end of the season, had been talking about giving the crew the ability to leave the station en masse for some time. Although a reliable staple, runabouts had their limitations, particularly if a scene called for more than two people. "We wanted a ship in which we could send more people out on an adventure," says Wolfe, "and we'd never really figured out how to do it."

An even greater impetus was triggered by plot developments in "The Jem'Hadar." "They'd just blown up a *Galaxy*-class starship," says Behr. "We'd created villains who were that powerful, and all we had floating around as the thin red line of defense against this possible invading army were three runabouts."

Behr and Wolfe approached then Executive Producer Michael Piller and suggested creating a ship to defend the station. Knowing that the studio was already making preparations to launch *Voyager*, Piller told them to talk to Rick Berman, who might have concerns about throwing a second ship into the limelight at the same time.

Berman did indeed have concerns. Behr says he countered by explaining that, "It's a different show, it's a different ship, and we need something cool, something *DS9*-specific." Oh, and one last thing: they wanted this ship to have a cloaking device.

A cloaking device! Berman was initially opposed; Gene Roddenberry always had held that Starfleet did not employ cloaking technology because the Federation "did not believe in sneaking around." But eventually, the writers composed an explanation that everyone felt honored the spirit of Roddenberry's philosophy. "Gene knew a lot of things," says Behr. "He

knew about television, and he knew how to keep a shark moving in the water."

So the ship was in, and new Supervising Producer Ronald D. Moore, fresh from *The Next Generation*, was given the honor of writing the teleplay for her—and his—maiden voyage. Moore had a few concerns of his own about the assignment. "They told me, 'We've got this ship!' And I said, 'You've got *what*? But this show's about a *station*. I just *left* a ship!'" Behr and Wolfe explained that this would be a tougher kind of ship, not a big exploratory vessel with babies on board. "And you're gonna have to introduce it in this opening episode," they concluded.

"One of the first things I had to do, as I started working on the episode, was come up with the name for the ship, which they'd graciously left to me," says Moore. "And my first choice was *Valiant*, after one of the original series starships." But the producers nixed the name because it was too close to *Voyager*. "They didn't want another 'V' name," explains Moore, who quickly came up with the name of a different ship from the original series: *Defiant*, a vessel that had been swallowed up by interspace in "The Tholian Web."

It was, Moore thought, a cool name, but one which would necessitate a bit of backstory. "Why would you name a ship the *Defiant*?" he recalls thinking. Obviously, because it was brought in to defy someone or something. The writing staff soon came up with an appropriate backstory about the ship having been built to fight the Borg. *Defiant* was conceived of as "a unique little warship that was overpowered and overgunned"—elements that the writers realized could lead to dynamic plotlines in future episodes.

Another major change in the series was the decision to reveal the secret of Odo's past. While this, too, seemed to address viewers' desires (A large percentage of the more vocal fans stated that Odo was the *DS9* character they wanted to learn more about), it was, again, a plot twist that had been in the making for some time. Not long after the writers devised the three-pronged nature of the Dominion (consisting of sleazy Vorta, brutal Jem'Hadar, and mysterious Founders), Behr and Wolfe began to theorize about the masterminds behind the coalition. "Ira and I had this private theory that the Founders, whom we figured we'd never see over the course of five years or whatever, would turn out to be shape-shifters," recalls Wolfe.

"We joked around all second season about the Founders being Odo's people," says Behr, "but we never thought they'd go for it in a million years. And then we were talking to Michael [Piller] one day, and Michael said, 'I have this crazy idea and you're going to think I'm nuts, but what if the Founders were Odo's people?' We just cracked up, and Michael said, 'What's so funny?'" Informed that they'd had the same idea for several months, Piller responded with some colorful references to their immediate lineage, then concluded that great minds obviously think alike. Piller and Behr took the concept to Berman, who agreed that it was a great idea. And then they called Rene Auberjonois and invited him to lunch.

When an actor is invited to lunch by his producers, it can mean any number of things, from the very positive to the very negative. In this case, the discussion was a very positive one, although there were some troubling aspects to it for Auberjonois, at least initially.

"Up until that point," says Auberjonois, "I'd always joked that the day we find out where Odo is from is the day that they will be writing me out of the show. Because that was always the most interesting aspect of Odo's character, that search for who he was. So Michael Piller and Ira Behr called me before the third season started, and we got together, and the first thing they did was to reassure me that they had no intention of writing me out of the show. But I still had some concerns, because I thought if we solved that mystery about Odo's character, I didn't know where we'd go with him.

"But it quickly became clear to me that these writers are very shrewd and very clever," Auberjonois admits, "because what they did was to make the character more complex. This just added to Odo's angst and to his depth, and it made him more challenging and interesting to play. And then they added into the mix his feelings about Kira. And the fact that he ultimately comes to understand that he can't go back to his people, that he can't go home again. They opened up more avenues for me to travel as an actor."

The producers also opened up more avenues for Auberjonois and several fellow thespians to travel as directors during the third season, with Auberjonois breaking into that side of the biz by directing "Prophet Motive," and "Family Business"; Avery Brooks then following up on the previous year's "Tribunal" to direct "The Abandoned," "Fascination," and "Improbable Cause." And, now free of the pressures of acting in a weekly dramatic series, TNG's Jonathan Frakes came over to DS9 to guest star in one episode ("Defiant"), and direct three others ("The Search, Part II," "Meridian," and "Past Tense, Part II").

Besides Moore, other former TNG staffers to join the series on a permanent basis included Writer René Echevarria, who came on as producer, and Director of Photography (DP) Jonathan West, along with Camera Operator Kris Krosskove. Echevarria recalls that at the conclusion of TNG, Berman and Piller suggested that Brannon Braga go to Voyager, and Moore and he go to DS9. "At first I said, 'I donwanna,'" he laughs. "I didn't know anything about Voyager at the time, but I thought it would be fun to be involved in a new show from the beginning. But Michael asked me to do DS9 for a while, because he thought I would benefit more as a writer by going to work for Ira Behr. He said, 'You've already worked for me, and you've worked for Jeri Taylor, but you've never worked for Ira and he has a lot to teach you.' He even gave me the option to go to Voyager after the first season if I still wanted to. As it turns out, I would never even think of doing that. I love it here, and I'm having a great time, and I think Michael was right on target."

Jonathan West had served as DP on TNG for that show's final two years, taking Marvin Rush's place when Rush left the series to do DS9. When Rush subsequently left at the end of DS9's second season to start up Voyager, West was asked to pick up the reins once again. "I said 'Sure!'" quips West. "I love the people here." Regular viewers of DS9 need not feel remiss if they didn't notice a change in lighting technique with the start of West's tenure. "I'm not known for a specific style," admits West. "I can do hard light, soft light, whatever is needed by the project. I always approach the work from the same standpoint, trying to create texture and dynamics in keeping with what's appropriate for the spacecraft, or, in this case, the station."

However, he *did* change the look of the show via camera lenses. "Prior to third season, a lot of telephoto lenses and longer lenses were utilized, which isolated the characters from their environment, and kept the environment out of focus. In the pilot, for example, you never really saw the station in its entirety. So I backed off in the use of these wider lenses, and all of a sudden we saw more of the station, and got more information on the screen." Considering the fact that the third season was the year that many of the characters, such as Jake and Ben, began to feel more at home on the station, the change fit in well with the tone of the show.

Like several of the series' actors, West, too, would be given the opportunity to direct, beginning with the third-season episode "Shakaar." By DS9's fifth season, confidence in his skills was so strong that he was entrusted with directing the extremely complicated (and extremely popular) episode, "Trials and Tribble-ations."

Behind the scenes, Robert della Santina now carried the title line producer in addition to unit production manager. In front of the camera, Sisko finally was promoted to captain, and Nog expressed the desire to put himself on a more *hew-mon* career track by joining the Academy. New recurring characters, such as Kasidy Yates, Shakaar, and Lieutenant Commander Michael Eddington, were introduced, while one established character, Kira's lover Bareil, was dispensed with, much to the distress of several fan groups.

Of the new characters, the evolution of Eddington, played by actor Kenneth Marshall (who played the lead in the 1983 fantasy epic *Krull*), would prove to be the most interesting. Initially brought in, at least in part, to fill in as another regular whenever Colm Meaney went off to do a film, Eddington was first depicted as a by-the-books Starfleet type in competition for Odo's job. But throughout Season 3 the writers seeded doubts about him in viewers' minds. He sabotaged the *Starship Defiant*, albeit at Starfleet's request, and later it was all too easy to believe that he was a changeling. Despite the fact that he told Sisko he was content to wear the gold of security rather than the red of command ("The Adversary"), somehow you didn't quite believe him.

Perhaps that was inevitable, given Ron Moore's inspiration for the character. "I named him after the character of Paul Eddington, who was a protagonist in one of my favorite movies, *In Harm's Way*." In the 1965 film, Eddington, played by Kirk Douglas, is an executive officer to a character played by John Wayne, and, although heroic, he's not a terribly nice guy. "He rapes a girl and then eventually goes out in a B-25 and crashes into the enemy," says Moore. "For some reason, I thought, 'Yeah, that's Eddington.' It just created a tone in my head."

It's hardly surprising, therefore, that the *DS9* character also revealed a darker side to his personality in subsequent seasons of the series, and ultimately dies in a "Blaze of Glory."

Ratings proved to be a mixed bag during Season 3, with the show winning the number-one slot for all syndicated series in key adult and male demos nationally during the critical November and February sweeps periods. The introduction of Warner Brothers' action spoof *Hercules: The Legendary Journeys* did not initially have much of an impact on *DS9*'s ratings, but the one-two punch of *Hercules* and *Xena: Warrior Princess* would begin to take a greater toll in subsequent seasons. At the time, however, the studio was pleased to note that *DS9*'s third-season average was twenty per-cent higher than that of its nearest competitor, *Baywatch*.

In the yearly Emmys race, *DS9* was nominated for two awards (compared to three the previous year), for hairstyling ("Improbable Cause"), and makeup ("Distant Voices"). This time, Makeup Supervisor Michael Westmore and his team brought home the gold.

THE SEARCH, PART I

Episode #447

TELEPLAY BY **RONALD D. MOORE**
STORY BY **IRA STEVEN BEHR &
ROBERT HEWITT WOLFE**
DIRECTED BY **KIM FRIEDMAN**

GUEST CAST	
Founder Leader	SALOME JENS
T'Rul	MARTHA HACKETT
Ornithar	JOHN FLECK
Michael Eddington	KENNETH MARSHALL

STARDATE 48212.4

Alarmed by the outcome of the Federation's initial run-in with the Dominion ("The Jem'Hadar"), Kira runs simulations to determine Deep Space 9's ability to defend itself against a possible attack by the Jem'Hadar. The prognosis seems grim until Sisko returns to the station in the *U.S.S. Defiant*, an experimental Federation starship originally designed to fight the Borg. Starfleet has provided Sisko with the warship so he can travel to the Gamma Quadrant and locate the "Founders," the mysterious leaders of the Dominion. Sisko's assignment is to convince the Founders that the Federation doesn't represent a threat to them. By using the *Defiant*, however, Sisko will also demonstrate that the Federation has the might to defend itself, if necessary.

Sisko has returned from Starfleet with two additional surprises: a Romulan named T'Rul, who will operate the *Defiant*'s cloaking device—on loan from the Romulans for the mission—and Lieutenant Commander Michael Eddington, who is to replace Odo in matters of Starfleet security. Offended by Starfleet's lack of faith in his skills, Odo resigns his position as chief of station security. However, Kira convinces a reluctant Odo to join the mission to the

Sisko engages in hand-to-hand combat with a Jem'Hadar when the *Defiant* is boarded. ROBBIE ROBINSON

Gamma Quadrant as an official Bajoran representative. At the same time, remembering Quark's previous contacts with the Karemma ("Rules of Acquisition"), who are part of the Dominion, Sisko coerces the Ferengi into going along.

Entering the Gamma Quadrant, the cloaked *Defiant* narrowly escapes detection by scouting Jem'Hadar ships, then continues on its way to contact an official of the Karemma named Ornithar. Under the guise of trade negotiations, Quark and Sisko attempt to get Ornithar to reveal the location of the Founders. Ornithar says his only contact with the Dominion is through the Vorta, but eventually he reveals the location of a relay station in the Callinon system, where the Vorta have told his people to direct communications for the Dominion. Studying a star chart of the region, Odo's attention is drawn to the neighboring Omarion Nebula.

His role fulfilled on the mission, Quark departs for DS9, while Sisko and the others head for Callinon. Dax and O'Brien beam down to the unmanned relay station, where they discern the coordinates for the majority of the station's outgoing transmissions. Suddenly, a shield appears around the outpost, and three Jem'Hadar ships move in. Unable to rescue Dax and O'Brien without revealing their presence to the Jem'Hadar, the cloaked *Defiant* leaves the pair behind and heads for the coordinates O'Brien provided.

Seeking Odo's input on the next stage of their mission, Sisko is disturbed when Odo reports that he's "indisposed." When Kira confronts Odo in his quarters, the shape-shifter confides that he feels compelled to leave the ship immediately and travel to the Omarion Nebula, although he is uncertain why. As Kira attempts to dissuade him, the *Defiant* is attacked by the Jem'Hadar. Despite putting up a fearsome fight, the ship is boarded by Jem'Hadar soldiers, who overwhelm the bridge crew. Down below, Kira and Odo defend themselves from the soldiers, but Kira is hit by a phaser blast and passes out.

She revives on board a shuttlecraft that Odo is piloting to the Omarion Nebula. The *Defiant*, he tells her, was dead in space when he left; he doesn't know about survivors. Before she has time to fully digest that information, they discover an odd Class-M planet that isn't a part of any star system. Landing the shuttle, Odo and Kira step outside and walk to the edge of a gelatinous lake. Suddenly, a portion of the lake begins to morph, transforming itself into four humanoids who resemble Odo. A female in the group steps forward and smiles at Odo, welcoming him "home."

While writers Ira Behr and Robert Wolfe were the ones who initially conceived of a ship that would serve to expand *Deep Space Nine*'s horizons (both figuratively and literally), the *Defiant* was the child of many parents.

She got her basic looks from Illustrator Jim Martin, whose first sketches reflected the producers' request for "a beefy runabout," he recalls. Four or five designs later, however, the word came down that the vessel was going to be a starship, and not a runabout. So Martin and Production Designer Herman Zimmerman submitted a variety of new drawings, including one that Martin had rendered the previous season. "It was an unused drawing of a cargo ship, crude and a little meaner [than the ultimate design], and that's the one they responded to," Martin reports.

The sketch of the turtlelike vehicle featured weapons in what would later become the *Defiant*'s engine cowlings. "They didn't want it to look like the other starships," says Martin. "That's why the nacelles and engines are internal." A cockpit located in the front of the cargo vessel eventually became a hood on the *Defiant*. Martin says, "It's not actually where the bridge of the *Defiant* is, but it works well as a frontal array in the design."

The approved drawings went to Model Maker Tony Meininger, who gave *Defiant* her "bone structure." "Tony is a master at turning two-dimensional drawings into three-dimensional miniatures," says Visual Effects Supervisor Gary Hutzel. "And in this case, he got a chance to really contribute to the design." Because the ultimate goal was to come up with something that "looks like it's moving, even though it's sitting still," according to Hutzel, photos of high-powered sports cars like Lamborghinis and Ferraris were tacked to the walls of the studio as inspiration. "We wanted an overpowered hustler of a machine," says Hutzel.

The final look of the four-foot model pleased Martin. "It looked muscular and very thick-shelled, like it could handle a lot of action."

The writers, of course, were responsible for *Defiant*'s feisty personality. Cost concerns contributed to her raison d'étre. A bridge was a necessity, of course, and the budget also allowed for construction of a corridor and one example of the crew's tiny quarters. But that was it. Engineering would not be built until the season finale. "At the time," says René Echevarria, "we thought we might never be able to build all the sets that the audience would expect to see on a starship, like sickbay, for example." In order to justify the

Starfleet Security Officer Eddington becomes a recurring character, while the Romulan, T'Rul, appears only in the first two episodes.
ROBBIE ROBINSON

stripped-down nature of the vessel, the writers decided to make it a kind of starship that viewers had never before seen. The concept of making *Defiant* a warship seemed to be in keeping with the grittiness of the series. The backstory that it was built to fight the Borg "was a fair enough justification," says Echevarria.

Science Consultant Andre Bormanis concurs, for typically rational reasons. "I liked the idea of getting away from the concept that all Federation technology was squeaky clean and perfect," Bormanis says. "The *Defiant* has its problems because it's a prototype. It was hastily put together in the face of the Borg threat."

As fans of the *Star Trek* motion pictures are aware, Starfleet vessels are often equipped with spotlights that serve to highlight their glorious names (think, for example, of the introduction to the refitted *U.S.S. Enterprise* in *Star Trek: The Motion Picture*, or that ship's successor in the conclusion of *Star Trek IV: The Voyage Home*). But because individually photographing those specialized lighting elements requires more shooting time than is generally available in television production, the producers had decided against putting spotlights on the *Defiant*. But it's hard to deny a debutante her one moment of glory in the spotlight. So just for her debut, the feature practice was implemented.

"We did a separate light pass from outside the ship," says Gary Hutzel. "We hooked a mag light on a C-stand arm that was connected directly to the camera head, so that it rocked and rolled with the model. Then we designed the shot to display some of the ship's better angles as it backed away and turned around." As the little fighter leaves DS9 for its first trip through the wormhole, the name *Defiant* is brightly illuminated.

With the mandate that the new vessel would have a cloaking device, teleplay Writer Ronald D. Moore contributed one more component to the *Defiant*, at least for the season's opening two-parter: a Romulan crewmember. "We had a notion that we were going to keep the Romulan engineer on board as a permanent fixture to operate the cloaking device," Moore says. But the producers quickly realized that the new character would not offer enough story material to justify making her permanent. So T'Rul left *DS9* after "The Search, Part II" (which left her alter ego, Actor Martha Hackett, free to sign on to *Voyager* as the villainous Seska).

Ironically, although the producers had fought hard for the right to install one on the new ship, "by the time we ended the two-parter, we had given up the cloaking device," laughs Moore. "We thought we wouldn't ever see it again. It wasn't until a few episodes later that we decided to say it was still there."

This would create some long-term problems for Jonathan West. "Our sets are built with a lot of the lights permanently in place," explains West, and the new *Defiant* set was no exception. In his script to 'The Search,' Moore cued West's input by describing the cloaking sequence, indicating that "a lighting change happens on the bridge . . . [becoming] darker, moodier, giving the bridge an eerie, 'submarine' quality." Given the established lighting, this necessitated a lot of manual changes prior to the actual sequence, but West recalls that he was assured that "we'll never be cloaked again; this is just for the first show."

Famous last words. "Since then," West reminisces, "we've cloaked a number of times and we really haven't adapted the sets [to accommodate the effect]. Each time, we have to start from scratch and send people up into the grids to put diffusion on the lamps and turn off a lot of instruments."

Finding a place to "berth" the *Defiant*—or rather, the *Defiant* sets—was another problem. At the beginning of the series, notes Robert della Santina, "We were assigned three sound stages. We built Ops, the station's corridors, and the cargo bay on one of them, the Promenade set on another, and the third was supposed to be reserved for our planet surface and cave set, plus a lot of open square footage to build loose sets. Then we discovered that we needed to create a holosuite set, which we ended up using a lot, and a place to park the

runabout. And finally, the *Defiant* came along, and that was it for space, and *then* we built the engineering portion of the ship," della Santina moans.

Every ship has its "shakedown" period, and the *Defiant* was no exception. As the crew began shooting "The Search, Part I" on the new set, they immediately began to discover design flaws. "It was all flat," notes Assistant Director B.C. Cameron. "There was a raised platform in the middle, with the commander's chair on it, and a raised platform in the front with the helmsman's seat on it. Everything was permanent, so there was no place to lay the dolly track, which meant that we couldn't move the camera around," she says.

"Initially, it was very hard to shoot in the *Defiant* set," confirms Director Kim Friedman. Friedman says she resorted to watching old World War II movies featuring "people sitting in cockpits" in the hopes of increasing her familiarity with the art of shooting in very constricted places. "Since that first episode, the *Defiant* has been modified," she adds, "making it much easier to shoot in."

Although the series' new inanimate "cast member" demanded a great deal of time, *DS9*'s flesh-and-blood crew also received its share of attention in the season opener. The station's commander, Benjamin Sisko, was portrayed as a man who had finally begun to think of "this Cardassian monstrosity as home." The scene in which he and Jake discuss this new feeling is brief, but Ira Behr believed it to be a defining moment. "It was *really important*," he asserts. "We strongly felt that we had to establish that 'what once was is no longer true.' When Sisko came to the station he didn't want to be there. That worked in the beginning, but we didn't want people to think that the lead character still didn't like where he was. He's now committed to Bajor and committed to his job."

Odo, too, has an epiphany about "home," although it is not as pleasant as the one Sisko experiences. In allowing Odo to resolve his external quest to find his people, the writers realized that they would need to give him a new quest, one that was internal. "Odo expected that finding his people would give him all the answers," says Robert Wolfe. "But [in the episode], we were basically saying, 'It's not that easy. Finding out who your people are doesn't tell you who *you* are.' It's like somebody who doesn't know who his parents are finding out that his dad is Adolf Hitler. Finding the answers doesn't turn out to be such a wonderful thing, and now he has to figure out, 'am I my father's son, or am I my own person?'"

Odo is additionally troubled by a new "sibling"

Jadzia Dax's new hairdo would be retired after the initial two-parter.
ROBBIE ROBINSON

"Terry Farrell liked the look," Normand says, "but apparently half of the fans liked it and half didn't. So we went back to the ponytail, but it was a different ponytail, a little more elevated. And the barrette didn't come back." At least, not during the third season.

A prop from earlier episodes made an appearance in "The Search, Part I," sans the character who had previously used it. Zek's scepter was, of course, created for the first-season episode "The Nagus," but it was featured far more prominently here, in a scene where Quark is required to kiss it. For the shot, Friedman brought the scepter's head right up to the camera's lens to reflect Quark's uncomfortable point of view.

But if Quark was uncomfortable, so was Actor Armin Shimerman, who sees eye to eye with his Ferengi counterpart on a variety of issues. "Despite the Federation's lip service to their Prime Directive, which says they're not supposed to apply their standards to any culture's attitudes, it seems to me that this was another example of the Federation making fun of, taking advantage of, and ridiculing the Ferengi way," Shimerman observes. "So kissing the scepter was a bit irksome to both the actor and the character."

Ironically, while the scepter belongs to the fictional grand nagus, its appearance, designed by Sculptor Dragon Dronet, is pure Shimerman. When the assignment to create the prop was issued, Dronet says, he wasn't told it was for the grand nagus. "I thought it was for Quark," he says. "I was given a photograph of Armin in makeup, and I searched through my collection of *Starlog* magazines until I found a picture of the back of Quark's head. I sculpted it to look like him, but I never had a chance to tell that to Armin." Dronet laughs.

The sequence at the end of Part I contains Friedman's favorite shot in the episode. "It's when Odo is looking at the changeling lake for the first time," she says fondly. "I kind of pushed the camera toward his face and on it was this mixture of awe and fear and wonder and joy, all at the same time. Rene is an incredible actor, and he created a truly heartbreaking moment."

And speaking of the planet, just how scientifically plausible is a so-called rogue Class-M planet? "It's right at the limit of what you might consider credible," admits Bormanis. "Suppose you had a planet that was created in orbit around a star and had then been ejected from its solar system by a close encounter with another object. You might have total loss of life, but that's not to say life couldn't subse-

within his adoptive family at *DS9*: the enigmatic Michael Eddington. His ambiguous personality (Is he a good guy or a bad guy?) was established from the start, with this first appearance. "Kim Friedman took great care in introducing the character," observes Actor Kenneth Marshall. "She was very specific about how Eddington should handle himself with the crew." For example, Friedman directed Marshall not to behave in an unfriendly manner toward Odo, because "the fact that he was there was threatening enough."

Eddington would be around for some time, but some additions to the show were far less permanent: Dax's new hairdo, for instance, which disappeared after the opening two-parter. "The producers wanted to give Dax a different look for the season," comments Hair Designer Josée Normand. "They didn't know if they wanted short hair or long hair," so Normand found a style where the length was indistinguishable.

quently arise again million of years later." Or, as Odo's species apparently did, arrive in spaceships and establish squatter's rights on the strange world. Life-forms *could* survive without a radiating sun, insists Bormanis. "There wouldn't necessarily be a lack of heat if the planet was geologically active internally," he says. "Even the Earth's core is molten, largely because of radioactive decay."

THE SEARCH, PART II

Episode #448

TELEPLAY BY **IRA STEVEN BEHR**
STORY BY **IRA STEVEN BEHR &**
ROBERT HEWITT WOLFE
DIRECTED BY **JONATHAN FRAKES**

GUEST CAST

Founder Leader	SALOME JENS
Garak	ANDREW ROBINSON
Admiral Nechayev	NATALIA NOGULICH
T'Rul	MARTHA HACKETT
Michael Eddington	KENNETH MARSHALL
Male Shape-shifter	WILLIAM FRANKFATHER
Jem'Hadar Officer	CHRISTOPHER DOYLE
Jem'Hadar Soldier	TOM MORGA
Jem'Hadar Guard	DIAUNTÉ
Computer Voice	MAJEL BARRETT

AND AS

Borath	DENNIS CHRISTOPHER

STARDATE UNKNOWN

Informed by the female shape-shifter that this rogue planet in the Omarion Nebula is his homeworld, Odo is filled with questions, and not entirely comfortable with the answers he receives. The female tells him that he, and the others of their kind, are all part of the Great Link, described as the very foundation of their society. Merging her hand with Odo's, she allows him to briefly experience the link, convincing him that he is, indeed, home.

Kira, however, is a solid, and as such, she is not wanted on this world. Noting that she won't be there long, Kira announces her intention to try to contact Sisko from the shuttle, but the female shape-shifter will not allow it. The shape-shifters value their isolation and cannot risk transmissions being traced to their world. But Kira lets Odo know that she plans to try contacting Sisko anyway, using techniques that will not reveal the source of the transmission.

Garak dies a heroic death in the Founder's psychological experiment with the crew. ROBBIE ROBINSON

For his part, Sisko, along with Bashir, is traveling toward the wormhole in a shuttle, having been forced to abandon the *Defiant* during the Jem'Hadar attack. They are intercepted by Dax and O'Brien, who were released from captivity after meeting with the Founders. Dax informs Sisko that big changes are taking place back at DS9, and Sisko soon finds that this is an understatement. At the station, Admiral Nechayev fills Sisko in: The Founders want to establish peace with the Federation, and a treaty will be signed at the station within days.

Although it sounds good, Sisko is suspicious. There are Jem'Hadar soldiers all over the station, serving as security for the Founders, and Borath, who claims to be a male Founder. However he is a member of the same species as Eris, the duplicitous woman Sisko encountered in the Gamma Quadrant. That fateful meeting culminated in the destruction of the *Starship Odyssey* ("The Jem'Hadar"). When Sisko discovers that the Romulans are to be excluded from the peace talks, it is just one more discordant note, but Admiral Nechayev dismisses his concerns.

On the other side of the wormhole, Kira discovers that a hidden power source on the rogue planet is preventing her from transmitting a signal. When she tries to track down the source of the interference, she finds a locked door—something for which shape-shifters would have no need. In the meantime, Odo receives lessons in shape-shifting and shape-shifter history. He asks the female shape-shifter, or changeling, as her people refer to themselves, why they dislike humanoids. She explains that long ago the changelings roamed the stars to expand their knowledge of the galaxy, only to be met with savage persecution by the solids they encountered. Eventually, the changelings retreated to this secret planet, but sent out infant shape-shifters to gain the knowledge for which they still longed. Ultimately, the infants were to bring that knowledge home to the Great Link. Odo is the first to return. Hoping to show Odo his place within their society, the female merges completely with him, providing yet another tantalizing taste of the Great Link.

On the station, O'Brien is badly beaten by a Jem'Hadar soldier. Bashir complains to Eddington, who refuses to get involved, saying his orders are to leave the Jem'Hadar alone. Shortly thereafter, Sisko discovers that members of his crew have been transferred without his consent, and that the Federation is pulling out of the sector, leaving Bajor to the Dominion. The price of peace is too high, Sisko tells Nechayev. But it's too late; the peace treaty has been signed.

After the unarmed Romulan T'Rul is killed by the Jem'Hadar, Sisko decides enough is enough. With the help of Garak, Bashir, Dax, and O'Brien, he plans a suicide mission to steal a runabout and collapse the wormhole, thus keeping the Dominion out of the Alpha Quadrant. Garak is killed in the effort, but the others escape and follow through, destroying the intergalactic passage to the Gamma Quadrant.

In the Omarion Nebula, Odo tells Kira that he plans to stay with his people, and Kira asks him to help her get to the hidden power source before she departs. Agreeing, Odo unlocks the door and finds Jem'Hadar soldiers within. The soldiers lead them to an interrogation room, where they find the command crew of the *Defiant* seated with their eyes closed, technical devices attached to their heads. Also present is Borath, who reveals that Sisko, Dax, O'Brien, Bashir, and T'Rul have been engaged in a little experiment to see how much they'd be willing to sacrifice to avoid war with the Dominion. Unfortunately, from the Dominion's point of view, the price is a bit too dear.

As the female shape-shifter enters the room, Odo discovers the awful truth: The changelings are the Founders, who decided years earlier to impose order on a threatening and chaotic universe through forceful means. Borath's people, the Vorta, serve the Founders, as do the Jem'Hadar. Unable to sanction the behavior of his people, Odo makes a decision. He prefers to be linked to the solids he's known his whole life rather than join the Great Link. The female shape-shifter

reluctantly allows Odo to take his friends and return to Deep Space 9 in the *Defiant*. As they depart, Odo realizes that he forever will be an outsider in the world of solids, but he also knows that his decision is the only one he can live with.

Standard story structure, particularly as utilized in episodic television, traditionally opens with a personal story, then moves into a situation of jeopardy, which culminates in a fight scene. But standard structure generally doesn't please the writers of *Deep Space Nine*, particularly when they're working on a two-parter. "We like to use the first part to set something up and then totally subvert the audience's expectations in part two." Ira Behr smiles. Thus, the first half of "The Search" was conceived of as "the big action show," and the bulk of Part II was devoted to Odo's personal story.

Of course, not everyone seemed to interpret Part II as Odo's story. Certainly not the viewers who got

Piller, Behr, and Wolfe all came to the same conclusion—that the Founders were Odo's people. ROBBIE ROBINSON

entirely wrapped up in the perils (apparently) experienced by Sisko and the others back on the station. However, once again, they can blame those sneaky writers for attempting to subvert their focus. "It was a perverse need to have some fun with the audience," admits Behr, who wrote the teleplay. "We were going to show them their worst nightmare as the only way out of that second episode." And then, suddenly, with the finesse of a magician opening a box to reveal that the contents had vanished, they would reveal to viewers: "'Hey, that's not what the show is about! It's about Odo! That's the storyline you should be watching,'" says Behr. "The plot is not important; it's all just fireworks and mirrors!" Behr sighs in resignation. "We wanted to make a point that this was a drama about people and conflict on a much smaller level. But no one seemed to get it, so maybe it wasn't such a great idea."

Instead, some viewers grumbled that it was just another take on the worn "it was all a dream" scenario. Obviously, Behr had something different in mind. "I never thought of [the experiences of Sisko and company with the Vorta and Jem'Hadar] as a dream," says Behr. "It was implanted thoughts." And that, he notes, had much more serious overtones. "If the Founders are capable of *playing* with us like that, how much worse could they be in reality? That was our intent, to show that these guys were so ahead of us that they were literally playing with us."

"Taken as a whole, the episodes showed both sides of who the Founders are," comments Robert Wolfe. Odo's interactions with the changelings showed the public face of his people, while the crew's interaction with the Founders, via the implanted thoughts, adds Wolfe, "showed their secret face, the dark truth."

A history maven, Wolfe likens the Founders to the Roman Empire. "They would rather take over someplace without firing a shot, but they're *going* to take over. So the whole thing was a test for them. 'Can we take over by diplomacy? Can we offer a treaty, get our foot into the Alpha Quadrant and slowly absorb them through cultural imperialism?' And Sisko basically said, 'You're not getting us without a fight.'"

If there was no cooperation between the Founders and the Federation, there certainly was some between Kim Friedman and Jonathan Frakes, the two directors of "The Search." In fact, they actually shared a scene. "Kim and I shot one scene together," reports Frakes, who made his *Deep Space Nine* directorial debut with this episode. "It was the end of her show and the beginning of mine, and by DGA rules, we both had to be there to see where the cut went."

With only a verbal description of what the link will look like, the actors must draw on their skills to make it believable.
ROBBIE ROBINSON

For Frakes, who had previously directed episodes of *The Next Generation*, stepping into *Deep Space Nine* was, as they say, the same, but different. "From the camera back, it felt like I was home," he explains, "because there were people like Jonathan West and others who were part of the old *TNG* crew. But from the camera forward, it was all new faces, new characters, and new sets, except for Colm, whom I knew quite well from *TNG*; and Armin, whom I knew from New York's Impossible Ragtime Theatre on 28th Street, between Sixth and Seventh!" And, of course, Natalia Nogulich, who reprised her role as the icy Admiral Nechayev from *TNG*. By an odd quirk of fate, Frakes also knew another one of the guest stars, although he may not have recognized her without her character makeup. Salome Jens, who would go on to reprise the female changeling throughout the series, had appeared under a similar amount of latex in the *TNG* episode "The Chase," which had also been directed by Frakes.

Every director has a so-called signature shot, a camera-move or setup or angle that he is fond of

The producers were not happy with the realization of the Founders' world. ROBBIE ROBINSON

employing. Frakes demonstrated his in this episode, when he positioned Kira by herself in the rogue planet's garden. By placing the camera high up on the wall of the cave set, he emphasized visually how alone she felt on this planet where she was the outsider, where even Odo wasn't there for her. Frakes wasn't even aware that he had a signature shot until Editor Bob Lederman, who cowrote the stories for third season's "Improbable Cause" and fifth season's "The Assignment," pointed it out to him. "Bob has edited a lot of my shows [on *TNG* and *DS9*] and he told me that I'm big on peeking over walls into rooms." Frakes laughs. "I was the first director to take the camera up outside the observation lounge on *TNG*. I shot into the room as if it were way up. Obviously, I knew I did that shot," Frakes says, with an amused smile. "But I didn't realize that I repeated it on other shows until Bob mentioned it."

"The Search, Part II" introduces a new Vorta to viewers, although he is initially referred to as a Founder, part of the real Founders' intent to stay behind the scenes as long as possible. The producers wanted to bring back Actor Molly Hagen as Eris, the duplicitous Vorta seen in the previous season's "The Jem'Hadar." Unfortunately, says Behr, Hagen was unavailable, so Dennis Christopher, known to moviegoers for his role as the sweet, Italian-obsessed son of Paul Dooley (Enabran Tain) in *Breaking Away,* stepped in as Borath.

While the Jem'Hadar would continue to make regular appearances in *DS9,* the Vorta seemed to disappear for quite some time after "The Search, Part II." Was there a falling out between them and the Founders? "After 'The Search' we had our hands full with so many other things," Behr laughs, "that we didn't get back to the Vorta." But because they were essential to future storylines, they were finally brought back late in the fourth season. "To keep the Founders as mysterious and aloof as we wanted them to be, it was necessary to see the Vorta again, as the conduit between them and the Jem'Hadar," says Behr. That concept led to the idea that there might be some animosity between the Vorta and the Jem'Hadar, which led to their return in "To the Death."

Although Behr and his staff had hoped to create a planet that was as strange and mysterious as its inhabitants, he was greatly disappointed with the end result. "Some of the ideas that we came up with sucked!" Behr states emphatically. "For instance, the dark planet with the weird things on it—that set never worked."

However, it was not for want of trying. "The optical shots that were involved in our first view of the Founders' planet were very complicated," says Producer Steve Oster. "There was a lot of interfacing between what the director was planning and what the Art Department was doing. The planet needed to be fairly dark in order for us to see the glowing, gelatinous sea that makes up the Great Link."

The Great Link itself involved a collaboration between Model Maker Greg Jein, who created a miniature of the changeling sea and the surrounding area, and the visual effects department. First Jein's team built a perspective landscape that was ten feet long and twelve feet deep. The look of the miniature landscape was influenced by a visit to the cave set, where the Founders' planet would be created, and some sketches provided by the art department. Jein said the sketches left him with an impression of "a lot of weird colors and rocks." He then began carving urethane foam into rocks and painting "funky florist flora with wild colors so it looked like an alien glade."

"We all joined in to help paint rocks and put in the miniature plants," agrees Visual Effects Coordinator Judy Elkins. "The plants looked a lot like they came from the original series, in bright pinks and blues and greens. We called it 'The Planet of the Odos.'"

The use of those Easter egg–bright colors would quickly come back to haunt them, however. "Greg had to build the miniature three weeks before the actual set was built." Special Effects Supervisor Glenn Neufeld laughs. "We went to the set one day, expecting to see it looking one way, and it didn't. So we ran to the phone and told Greg, 'You know those purple and yellow trees? Well, paint them orange or rip them out. We don't care which!'"

Computer Animator Adam Howard rotoscoped the changeling sea at Image G. Then the elements were sent to VisionArt's Josh Rose, who pulled a matte for the inside of the lake, and "rendered a plane of Odo goo for the entire sea's surface," Rose notes. It's supposed to be the same material as Odo's body." To help create the effect of Odo's brethren rising out of the sea of goo, DS9's other visual effects supervisor, Gary Hutzel, shot the glow of a mag light against a board. Rose animated that element inside the goo, so that it looked as if "little lights were rising to the surface, and then rising out of the liquid as a monolith, a column of goo, which then formed into a goo body." As the goo bodies walked out of the sea and reached land, they were transformed into previously bluescreened images of the live actors.

In the end, despite the ignored subtexts and miscalculated sets, Behr liked the episode. "It was a wonderful showcase for Rene Auberjonois, and in terms of the issues raised, it worked."

It also contained one of those wonderful throwaway lines that serve to inspire future episodes, the female shape-shifter's comment that, "No changeling has ever harmed another." That platitude would be rendered obsolete in the season's final episode, "The Adversary," when Odo inadvertently kills a fellow shape-shifter. However, Odo's sentence for this terrible infraction would not be paid out until Season 4's final episode, "Broken Link."

THE HOUSE OF QUARK
Episode #449
TELEPLAY BY **RONALD D. MOORE**
STORY BY **TOM BENKO**
DIRECTED BY **LES LANDAU**

GUEST CAST

Keiko O'Brien	ROSALIND CHAO
Grilka	MARY KAY ADAMS
D'Ghor	CARLOS CARRASCO
Rom	MAX GRODÉNCHIK
Gowron	ROBERT O'REILLY
Tumek	JOSEPH RUSKIN
Kozak	JOHN LENDALE BENNETT

STARDATE UNKNOWN

With business in the bar being especially slow, the last thing Quark needs is a customer who's out of money. But discussing a line of credit with a drunken Klingon is risky business, as Quark discovers when Kozak, the Klingon, attacks him with a knife. The brawl is brief but deadly. Kozak trips over his own feet and lands on Quark, fatally impaling himself on his own knife in the process.

After Quark inadvertently kills her husband, Grilka demands restitution. ROBBIE ROBINSON

Quark is unharmed in the incident. In fact, he finds that the bar is suddenly filled with bystanders consumed with morbid curiosity—all potential customers. Capitalizing on their interest, Quark brags that he killed Kozak in self-defense, despite Odo's warning that Kozak's family might retaliate. And sure enough, soon Kozak's brother D'Ghor shows up, demanding the truth about the death. A frightened Quark is prepared to admit his deception, but D'Ghor stops him, explaining that if he were to find out that his brother died dishonorably in an accident, he would have to kill Quark. If, on the other hand, D'Ghor died honorably, in personal combat . . .

Quark gets the message and continues to play the role of "Quark, slayer of Klingons."

In a quieter part of the station, O'Brien is surprised when his wife Keiko informs him that she has closed the station's school; there aren't enough students to justify keeping it open. Although she acts as if she isn't troubled by the closing, O'Brien knows that without the school, Keiko can't help feeling that she has no role on DS9.

Kozak's death, and Quark's alleged role in it, have made a big difference in business at the bar. One evening, as Quark happily counts the day's proceeds, Kozak's widow Grilka arrives and inquires about her husband's demise. Although Quark spins the same lie that appeased D'Ghor, Grilka quickly gets to the truth of the matter and kidnaps the Ferengi.

On the Klingon homeworld, Quark learns that his lie may have cost Grilka the chance to head the House of Kozak. The Klingon laws regarding inheritance sometimes grant special dispensation to a female whose mate dies in an accident. But if, as Quark told D'Ghor, Kozak died in an honorable fight, there would be no dispensation. Since there was no male heir to their union, Kozak's House would fall, allowing D'Ghor, an enemy of Kozak's for years, to take over. To prevent that from happening, Grilka forces Quark to marry her, which would allow Kozak's slayer to take his place, and his wife.

Grilka presents her new husband to the Klingon High Council, just as D'Ghor attempts to stake his claim on the title and property of the fallen Kozak's House. Gowron, the head of the Klingon Council, declares that the Council will need some time to make a final decision on the matter. In the meantime, the House of Kozak will be known as the House of Quark.

Discovering that Grilka hasn't a clue as to what to do next, Quark volunteers to go over the financial records of the House. He quickly finds that D'Ghor has been systematically attacking Kozak's family assets for years, weakening the House in order to prime it for a takeover. When Quark and Grilka present their findings to the High Council, D'Ghor denies the charges. He brings forth evidence to prove that Quark lied about the manner of Kozak's death: Quark's brother Rom, who witnessed the accident. D'Ghor demands vengeance through personal combat.

With his life on the line, Quark decides to leave, rather than face D'Ghor in battle. But when the time comes for Grilka to face D'Ghor, Gowron, and the High Council, she discovers she is not alone. Quark has returned, *bat'leth* in hand, ready to answer D'Ghor's challenge, but in his own unique way. As D'Ghor advances on him, Quark flings aside his weapon and tells the Council that pitting an unarmed Ferengi against a Klingon isn't a competition; it's an execution—and there's no honor in that.

Unmoved, D'Ghor raises his own weapon to finish Quark off, but Gowron intervenes, shamed by D'Ghor's lack of honor. Dismissing D'Ghor in disgust, Gowron grants Grilka the dispensation she had sought to lead the House on her own. A grateful Grilka grants Quark the divorce he requests.

Back in Quark's bar on Deep Space 9, O'Brien makes a tough decision and tells Keiko about an upcoming agrobiology expedition on Bajor. Although they would be separated for six months, the expedition offers the opportunity to perform important research in botany, her chosen field.

As Keiko and O'Brien kiss, Rom asks Quark to tell him about facing D'Ghor one more time. And for once, Quark finds that there's as much pleasure in a brother's admiration as there is in latinum.

Although Ron Moore had already tested the unfamiliar waters of his new job by taking on the teleplay of "The Search, Part I," the third episode of the season briefly returned him to subject matter that was infinitely more familiar.

"I got tagged with being 'the Margaret Mead of Klingons' right after I did 'Sins of the Father' for *TNG*," Moore observes. "It was kind of a landmark show in terms of portraying their culture. After that, in story meetings, people started talking to me about the Klingons, like I knew them or something. When I came to *Deep Space Nine*, I didn't miss them. But, of course, one of the first shows in the bunch [that I worked on] was 'The House of Quark.'"

The concept pitched by *DS9* Editor Tom Benko was irresistible: "Quark kills a Klingon and gets a rep-

An unlikely pairing of the Klingon and the Ferengi facilitated exploring interesting aspects of both races. ROBBIE ROBINSON

utation as a gunfighter," recaps Moore. "We started talking about it more and more, about how it gave us the ability to revisit the Klingons and their culture, and do it with some fun and humor. That was one thing we always pulled back from on *TNG,* enjoying ourselves and having a romp. But the Klingons were ready for some kind of comedy episode, so this was a great opportunity."

It also gave the writers the opportunity to find a new venue for Gowron, one of *Star Trek* fans' favorite recurring characters, now that *TNG* was history (as an ongoing television series). "It wasn't a conscious decision to have Gowron make the transition from *TNG* to *DS9,*" says Moore. "It was more the fact that on this show you feel all of the *Star Trek* universe is fair game because it's all part of the same franchise. So any element that I want to borrow legitimately seems fine."

Ira Behr has a more tongue-in-cheek rationale. "I think that Ron and Gowron have a secret pact," he comments. "They've never been seen together. I think Ron might *be* Gowron."

Whatever the reason, Actor Robert O'Reilly couldn't have been more thrilled. "Although I suspected it was possible, I didn't know anybody was going to make the transition from *TNG* to *DS9,*" he says. "A lot of us thought we wouldn't. So I was very pleased.

"I tend to be a little nervous when I move to a new show," says O'Reilly. "I don't know anybody, and when I first meet people, I'm a little bit of an introvert. So the first couple days of filming would have been a little difficult if it hadn't been for Armin "

Shimerman, an old friend of O'Reilly's from several stage presentations they'd done together, "took care of" O'Reilly, making sure he was comfortable during a week of particularly grueling weather. With the temperature hovering around 100 degrees, working conditions on the smoke-filled soundstage, particularly in heavy Klingon gear, were not particularly pleasant. Shimerman could easily empathize with the overdressed Klingons; he was wearing a heavy Klingon robe himself. The air conditioning on Stage 18 was not in use because of the smoke, deemed necessary for atmosphere, and it certainly created a dramatic entrance for one guest to the set.

"I remember I turned, and the smoke seemed to part, and there was [eminent theoretical physicist] Dr. Stephen Hawking, visiting the set with Rick Berman," says Shimerman. He recalls murmuring to a member of the crew, "I never thought I would see him on the set," only to hear the coworker respond, "Yeah, and he brought Hawking with him."

Shimerman laughs at the memory, although he notes that it was "one of the high points of my life." He now has a photo of himself with Hawking in his den.

The Great Hall sequences with Gowron were important to the episode. Moore knew that the Hall gave an "almost Shakespearean" aura to dramatic sequences in *TNG's* best Klingon episodes. So he pushed for the setting in "The House of Quark." "I knew it would be great to put Quark in there," he says. "It was something you *wanted* to see."

But the two-part season opener hadn't been cheap, and the producers were being asked to rein in the budget a bit for the episode. Supervising Producer David Livingston found a way to satisfy everyone by cutting the blueprint for the Great Hall in half. He instructed Director Les Landau first to shoot scenes in one direction, then the set dressing was changed and sequences were shot that would represent the opposite side of the room.

Although Moore and Benko have the only official writing credits on the show, everyone contributed bits and pieces to the episode. "I have to say that I came in with the basic concept, but these writers are so frickin' good," enthuses Benko. "You go into story meetings with three, four, or five guys to flesh out the

The strong persona the writers established for Quark allowed him to retain his dignity. ROBBIE ROBINSON

something as incongruous to them as a basic accounting system. However, it was Robert O'Reilly who inserted a bit of business that he borrowed from Charlie Chaplin as he tossed aside his calculator. Armin Shimerman also credits O'Reilly with suggesting Gowron's parting comment to Quark: "A brave Ferengi . . . who would have thought it possible?"

"That meant a lot to me," says Shimerman, "because usually Quark is at the butt end of the jokes. But here was a chance to do something, still comedic, but also heroic."

Not that Quark is a weak character. Indeed, according to Behr, "Sometimes he's too strong, or strong in the wrong places." But the beauty of Benko's story, Behr says, was that it pitted Quark against the strongest beings in the galaxy. "The surprise of the show is that he can hold his own."

Writer Benko has the unique distinction of being the only person who has written, directed (*TNG* episodes "Transfigurations" and "Devil's Due"), and edited *Star Trek*. In fact, he says, it was "great to go over to the set and watch them shoot a story that I came up with." After it was shot, he still had to put on his other hat, and put the thing together in the editing room.

The episode, originally known as "Fight to the Death," has resonances from the original series. Bashir orders a bowl of Vulcan *plomeek* soup, last seen on the wall outside Spock's quarters in "Amok Time." Tumek is played by veteran character actor Joseph Ruskin, who appeared in "The Gamesters of Triskelion." Ruskin would return to do a voice-over later in the season, and then reprise the role of Tumek in Season 5's "Looking for *par'Mach* in All the Wrong Places."

"The House of Quark" marks Keiko's departure from the station for some time. Her hiatus served two purposes. It freed up time for Colm Meaney to work in some film projects, and it also gave the writers the opportunity to explore the Bashir-O'Brien relationship, long a desire of Behr's.

Although it was only the third episode of the season, refinements in makeup and hair were already underway. Odo's makeup went from several large appliances to a one-piece mask appliance. Dax's hair returned to the more familiar ponytail.

story, and, as Ira says, 'We all check our egos when we come into the room,' including him." So everyone has a chance to throw in ideas, and if they work, they become part of the final script. Thus it was Robert Wolfe who came up with the idea that Quark would throw down his *bat'leth,* rather than fight to the death, because, as Wolfe observes, "He's a Ferengi, and Ferengi values would say that's a terrible way to go—so distasteful!"

Moore came up with the wonderful visual image of a group of ferocious Klingons utterly baffled by

EQUILIBRIUM

Episode #450

TELEPLAY BY RENÉ ECHEVARRIA
STORY BY CHRISTOPHER TEAGUE
DIRECTED BY CLIFF BOLE

GUEST CAST

Dr. Renhol	LISA BANES
Joran Belar	JEFF MAGNUS McBRIDE
Timor	NICHOLAS CASCONE
Yolad	HARVEY VERNON

STARDATE UNKNOWN

While attending a friendly dinner gathering in Sisko's quarters, Jadzia is attracted to a keyboard that belongs to Sisko's son, Jake. Although musically unskilled, Jadzia is compelled to experiment with the instrument, and soon begins to play a melody that she seems to remember from somewhere. The melody continues to haunt her after the meal, and she begins to exhibit peculiar behavior, demonstrating unusual fits of temper toward her friends, and experiencing vivid hallucinations. After an unnerving "encounter" with a menacing masked figure, Jadzia realizes something is wrong, and she goes to Bashir for help.

Bashir discovers that her levels of isoboramine—an organic neurotransmitter that mediates synaptic functions between host and symbiont—are dangerously low. The condition is serious enough for Bashir to recommend a trip in the *Defiant* to the Trill homeworld for an examination by the doctors at the Symbiosis Commission. There, Dr. Renhol begins a treatment to raise Jadzia's isoboramine levels. But Jadzia experiences another frightening hallucination, accompanied by the same haunting music. In this vision, she finds herself attacked by members of the Symbiosis Commission, although the uniforms they wear date back nearly one hundred years.

Confused, Jadzia goes to see one of the guardians, a group of unjoined Trill who care for the symbionts in the caves of Mak'ala. The guardian, Timor, tells Jadzia that the hallucinations she's been experiencing are memories from one of Dax's previous hosts. Later, Sisko reveals that the *Defiant*'s computer has analyzed the music that has preoccupied Jadzia: it's a composition

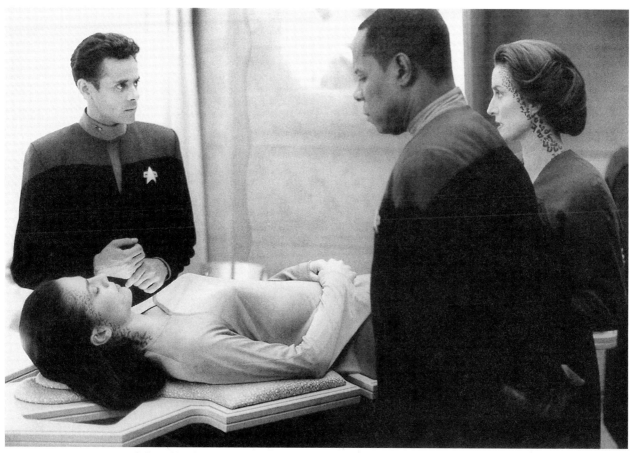

Dr. Renhol would rather let Jadzia die than allow the truth about joining to be exposed. DANNY FELD

that was written by a Trill named Joran Belar eighty-six years earlier. As Jadzia is shown a picture of Belar, she experiences another memory flash and witnesses the murder of a Trill doctor by the masked figure she saw before. When the figure is revealed as Joran Belar, Dax has a seizure and goes into neural shock.

Back at the Commission, Dr. Renhol is alarmed by how low Dax's isoboramine levels have fallen. If the levels don't rise within forty-eight hours, she warns, she will have to remove the Dax symbiont from Jadzia, a procedure that will kill her. Sisko and Bashir go to Timor for help but find him nervous and evasive. Realizing the key to this mystery may be in records related to Joran Belar, Sisko and Bashir conduct a computer search, but discover Joran's files have been purged. A cross check of information, however, reveals that Joran died the same day that the Dax symbiont was put in Curzon.

Contacting Joran's brother, Yolad, they learn that Joran was killed attempting to escape after he murdered the Commission doctor who recommended he be dropped from the symbiosis initiate program. But Yolad also reveals that his brother had told him some six months prior to the incident that he was *already* joined.

Sisko and Bashir confront Dr. Renhol as she prepares to remove the Dax symbiont from Jadzia, and they force her to admit the truth. Prior to being joined to Curzon, the Dax symbiont was joined to Joran, an unstable Trill with violent tendencies. By all established Trill lore, which indicated that only one in a thousand Trill were capable of symbiosis, a joining with such an unsuitable host *should* have resulted in the quick death of both host and symbiont. But it didn't, which revealed to the Commission that many more Trill were capable of joining: nearly half the population. The release of that information would have triggered chaos among the Trill, as there weren't nearly enough symbionts to fulfill every eligible person's desire to be joined. Thus, the Commission suppressed all information about Joran's joining, and even blocked the knowledge from the Dax symbiont's memory. Now, that block is deteriorating, and Dax is beginning to remember Joran.

By threatening to reveal the Commission's secret about the symbionts to the Trill populace, Sisko forces Renhol to divulge the necessary steps to save Jadzia: They must stabilize synaptic functions between host and symbiont by allowing Joran's memories to surface and reintegrate with Dax's other memories. Jadzia returns to Timor, who has her enter the pool of unjoined symbionts. There the energy discharges of

the symbionts awaken all recollection of the Joran persona in Dax. Jadzia emerges from the experience intact, with a whole new lifetime of memories to sort through and reflect upon.

René Echevarria's first teleplay for *DS9* had its genesis in a magic show seen by Executive Producer Michael Piller. The show featured performance magician Jeff Magnus McBride, who appears in "Equilibrium" as both the unstable Joran Belar and his masked metaphorical representative in Dax's nightmares. (Joran would later be played by Avery Brooks, in "Facets," and by Leigh J. McCloskey, in "Field of Fire.") "McBride has a very impressive magic show," explains Echevarria, "a great act, much of which involves a series of masks that he wears and removes, one after another. It's very Kabuki, very theatrical."

Unfortunately, the act wasn't a ready-made *DS9* story. So when a pitch utilizing the magician's skills was purchased from Christopher Teague—a mutual friend of Piller and McBride's—members of the series' writing staff were perplexed.

"I just kept wondering, 'What's this thing with masks?'" says Ron Moore. "We went downtown and saw a performance of McBride onstage, and I remember sitting there and thinking, 'What are we gonna do with this? I have no idea what this show's going to be.'"

"It was hell to break," concurs Ira Behr. "We had the actor and the masks and that was it."

Moore recalls that the original storyline had something to do with "the circus coming to Deep

While Sisko reminds us that Dax has many lives, by calling *her* "Old Man," this episode reminded viewers of that fact. DANNY FELD

The effects for this sequence may have been limited, but the use of a pool provided the many layers of symbolism the writer was seeking.
ROBBIE ROBINSON

Space 9, and this magician was in it, and we thought, 'Well, we're not gonna do *that*.'"

So the writers began to sweat through what they *could* do with it. "Initially, it was an Odo show," says Echevarria, "about Odo's dreams, or a figure that he was chasing. And then Ron Moore realized that the masks were a better metaphor for Dax, a Trill who's had many hosts. And that's how it got rolling."

From that point on, things slowly began to fall into place. The circus story became a what's-happening-to-Dax show, Echevarria says. "And then it became a mystery, a show about a deep, dark secret."

Echevarria notes that the usual financial constraints limited some of the ideas. What the episode called for, he says, were scenes with "Dax walking through a town and seeing a spire over a hilltop, going to investigate, and being drawn to images and places and not knowing why." Instead, the mystery was to be played out in more "produceable" settings, such as the *Defiant*, and the much-used cave sets on Stage 18.

While memories of the arduous writing process aren't particularly pleasant, the staff was relatively pleased with the final product, which established a variety of interesting details about the Trills and their society (including the fact that their homeworld is called Trill). We hear more about Sisko's chef father,

whom we would meet the following season. And, for those who wonder if Starfleet officers sleep in regulation Starfleet jammies, we find out that Bashir and Jadzia have much more fashionable bedroom attire, courtesy of Bob Blackman.

We also learn that Bashir doesn't like beets, although writer Echevarria does. "It was supposed to be rutabagas," says Behr—his small tribute to a song by Frank Zappa and the Mothers of Invention—"but René didn't think rutabagas were funny enough."

On the tech side, visual effects were limited primarily to the electrical flashes that pass for communication among symbionts, and a bit of computer-graphic magic orchestrated by Glenn Neufeld and VisionArt's Josh Rose for the scene in which Jadzia finally sees Joran's face beneath the mask. Audio embellishments were supervised by Steve Oster, at the time a co-producer under Peter Lauritson, responsible for overseeing postproduction elements. "The music was important in 'Equilibrium,' so we had to get with the composer [Jay Chattaway] ahead of time and get him to write a theme for us, because Dax needed to hum it throughout the show," Oster says.

Another challenge for him was the scene where Jadzia walks through the Promenade and goes into one of her fugues. "Soundwise, that crossover piece was rather crucial," he says. "Suddenly all the sounds on the station change and become very weird. Designing all the elements and arranging them so we got a smooth transition was important in making it clear to the audience that Jadzia was walking into the dream situation." The aural transition was handled at Modern Sound, where the series' sound was mixed.

The theatricality of the masked figure's appearance gave the episode an interesting dramatic signature, somewhat reminiscent of Peter Shaffer's play *Amadeus,* where the recurring visits of a mysterious masked figure hasten the death of an ailing Mozart. But for Echevarria, the episode brings to mind a different Shaffer play. For the penultimate scene, where Jadzia symbolically accepts Joran's memories, Echevarria decided to set the encounter at Mak'ala, so that he could make use of the symbionts. "It was a key story point," he says. "Only the symbionts can unlock the mystery and allow Jadzia to *abreact*; that's a psychological term for reliving a trauma. I got it from *Equus.*"

SECOND SKIN

Episode #451

WRITTEN BY **ROBERT HEWITT WOLFE**
DIRECTED BY **LES LANDAU**

GUEST CAST

Garak	ANDREW ROBINSON
Entek	GREGORY SIERRA
Yeln	TONY PAPENFUSS
Yteppa	CINDY KATZ
Gul Benil	CHRISTOPHER CARROLL
Alenis Grem	FREYDA THOMAS
Ari	BILLY BURKE

AND

Legate Ghemor	LAWRENCE PRESSMAN

STARDATE UNKNOWN

Kira is shocked when she is presented with proof that she had been incarcerated at Elemspur, a Cardassian prison, ten years earlier. Recalling that she had spent that period with the Shaakar resistance group hiding in Bajor's Dahkur Hills, Kira contacts an alleged cellmate from

Elemspur, who claims to remember her, even though she doesn't remember him. Puzzled, Kira departs for Bajor to learn the truth, but a short time later Sisko receives a transmission from Bajor, informing him that Kira never arrived.

Kira awakens on Cardassia to discover that she's been kidnapped. As her captors attempt to explain that they've brought her home, Kira catches sight of herself in a mirror and is horrified to see that she now looks like a Cardassian. A Cardassian man named Entek informs Kira that she is really Iliana Ghemor, a field operative of the Obsidian Order who went undercover ten years ago. Her assignment was to infiltrate the Bajoran resistance, disguised as a terrorist named Kira Nerys, whose memories and appearance she was given. At the time, Entek was her supervisor. Unfortunately, he explains, his organization's infiltration methods may have been too thorough; the altering of Iliana's memories to carry out her assignment may have made her reintegration into Cardassian society difficult.

Kira refuses to believe Entek. She rebuffs the man that Entek introduces as her father—Legate Tekeny Ghemor, a member of Cardassia's Central Command —despite the fact that his feelings for his daughter seem quite genuine. Frustrated that Iliana's memory is not returning, Entek attempts to jar her by showing her the cryogenically preserved remains of the "real" Kira Nerys, who he says died ten years ago. Kira believes the body is a fake, but is shaken when Entek speaks to her of experiences she's never told anyone. He claims the "experiences" are artificial memories the Obsidian Order implanted in Iliana for her mission.

Back on Deep Space 9, Garak says that he has received information that Kira may have been taken by the Obsidian Order. Although he insists there is nothing he can do about the situation, Sisko thinks otherwise, and forces Garak to accompany Odo and him to Cardassia.

Determined to get away, Kira overrides the force-field confining her in Iliana's room, but Ghemor, knowing she will be captured if she leaves, gets her to reconsider. When Entek returns, he puts Kira through a grueling interrogation as he attempts to recover the information Iliana was to provide to the Obsidian Order. Concerned for his daughter's safety, Ghemor invokes his authority within the Central Command and insists that Entek leave. Comforting the exhausted and confused Kira, Ghemor admits that he can't bear the thought of his daughter being interrogated to

Kidnapped and surgically altered to resemble a Cardassian, Kira realizes that the devious scheme is aimed directly at Legate Ghemor.
ROBBIE ROBINSON

the point of harm. He offers to help her escape from Cardassia through his secret connections.

Kira realizes Ghemor is a dissident who no longer believes in the Obsidian Order or the Central Command, and suddenly she understands what's been going on. Entek wasn't interested in the information "Iliana" had; he was interested only in capitalizing on Kira's resemblance to Ghemor's daughter. By torturing someone who appeared to be his daughter, Entek knew Ghemor would attempt to save her and reveal his connection to Cardassia's dissidents.

His plan an apparent success, Entek and two agents of the Obsidian Order enter the room with raised weapons, capturing Kira and Ghemor. But Entek's victory is short-lived as Sisko, Garak, and Odo arrive and liberate the prisoners. When an angry Entek attempts to stop them from leaving, Garak kills him. Ghemor returns with Kira to Deep Space 9, where medical tests prove that she is Bajoran, and that she has been surgically altered to appear to be Cardassian. Ghemor vows to find his real daughter, who he believes may still be living undercover on Bajor. They part with genuine affection, Ghemor telling Kira that until he finds Iliana, she's the closest thing he has to family.

Becoming a "rubberhead" gave Nana Visitor new respect for those actors who go through the process on a regular basis. ROBBIE ROBINSON

Prior to obtaining his staff position on *DS9*, Robert Hewitt Wolfe recalls pitching a story idea to the *TNG* producers about several members of the *Enterprise* crew becoming Romulans for the course of an episode. The pitch didn't sell, although, notes Wolfe, the sixth-season episode "Face of the Enemy" uses a similar theme. And Wolfe filed away the basic idea in the back of his brain for future use. "I thought a lot about people who didn't turn out to be who we thought they were when we were young," he says. "I think everyone's parents turn out to be different people than you thought they were when you were six."

Eventually, Wolfe began to spin a *DS9* story around the theme. The story ultimately became "Second Skin," but it went through a major change in personnel before it reached production. "My original idea," he recalls, "was that O'Brien was a Cardassian, but he didn't know it. He'd been replaced during that Cardassian battle he was in twenty years earlier (*TNG*'s "The Wounded"). The replacement was a deep-cover agent who'd been given O'Brien's memories."

This radical concept would have meant that the Miles O'Brien fans first met in "Encounter at Farpoint" wasn't human, that his shipmates had un-

knowingly been working with a Cardassian, and that his loving wife Keiko had conceived a child with . . .

That threw a wrench into Wolfe's plot. "O'Brien has this kid, and I couldn't figure out how to explain this human-looking baby," Wolfe admits. "So then I thought—Kira—Kira could be a Cardassian."

Like O'Brien, Kira had a long antagonistic relationship with the Cardassians, which would emphasize the irony in the revelation that she herself was a member of the species she despised.

As the story moved forward, however, the probability that Kira was actually a Cardassian faded. Wolfe notes that his original ending for the episode had Bashir telling her that he really couldn't tell if she was Bajoran or Cardassian. The aired ending is much more definitive, with Kira explaining that Bashir has confirmed her genetic structure is entirely Bajoran. Observes Wolfe, "It really doesn't matter whether she's a Cardassian or not. She's Kira Nerys and that's who she believes she is. That's what's important."

Kira isn't the only victim of deception in the episode, Wolfe points out. "Without sounding pretentious," he says, "the theme of the entire episode could be 'You can't judge a book by its cover.'"

The writers liked to remind viewers that Garak is an unknown factor. ROBBIE ROBINSON

Everyone, it seems is wearing a "second skin," according to Wolfe. "So Kira is both who she is *and* she's Iliana Ghemor," he explains. "Legate Ghemor is both a very staunch supporter of the Cardassian government *and* an opponent of the Cardassian government. The *Defiant* appears to be a Kobheerian freighter, but it's really a warship. Garak looks like a tailor, but he's really a spy. Sisko looks like a Kobheerian captain (courtesy of stock footage from "Duet") and Odo looks like a bag. There's many levels of deception throughout the show."

The concept of placing memories into someone's head is a classic science fiction theme, admits Wolfe, who cites the film *Blade Runner* and literary works "We Can Remember It for You Wholesale" and *Nimbus*. By using a semi-familiar science fiction motif, Wolfe was able to sidestep a more traditional *Star Trek* cliché. "I wanted to avoid revisiting the other times that we made our people look like aliens," he says. "I wanted to make Kira believe she *was* an alien. The best way to do that was to make her believe that they'd stuck memories in her head."

Kira's worst nightmare, waking up to find herself

a Cardassian, could easily pass for one of Nana Visitor's. "It's the longest I've ever been in the make-up trailer," she moans. "It was absolute torture to come in at two-thirty in the morning, do five hours of makeup, and *then* start the work day when everybody else comes in."

Visitor, whose usual time in the makeup chair as Kira is limited to about one and a half hours, says her experience as a Cardassian has increased her respect for the other aliens in the series. "When I see Cardassians starting to get into a little bit of a state of panic after eighteen hours, I know exactly what the problem is," she reflects. "It's very, very hot when you're covered in rubber in the head area. You can't sweat, and when you're doing it in hundred-degree weather, it can be tough. I'm so glad I'm not a full rubberhead!"

Acting in all that latex can be distracting, but Visitor followed the advice of the other "rubberheads" as she plunged into the episode. "The most important thing is to get over the fact that you have makeup on your face, and not let that do your work for you," she says. However, Visitor's own feelings of makeup-inspired claustrophobia—she notes that her Cardassian makeup covered "over my nasal passages and every other place a claustrophobic doesn't want to be covered up"—may have helped her to generate the correct frame of mind for Kira in the episode. The normally straight-shouldered major exhibited an uncharacteristic slouch while she was imprisoned on Cardassia. Visitor explains that the posture shift was a conscious effort on her part. "I was a prisoner," she says, "I was caught and trapped, and I automatically went back to the times that I had been a prisoner not so long ago."

The episode introduces several new technological concepts, all in the spirit of "making it up as we go along," laughs Wolfe. The transporter-suppression field, for example, came about "because we needed it!" he says. "We needed Kira, Ghemor, and Ari to be unable to beam away." On the other hand, O'Brien's modification to the shield harmonics of the *Defiant* was based on knowledge of existing technology, according to Andre Bormanis. "We know that different classes of submarines will generate different acoustic signatures that some underwater microphones can detect and recognize," he says. Similarly, *Star Trek's* writers hypothesize that a starship's shield, or force field, is generated at a specific frequency, which differs from those generated by ships of different alien technology. What O'Brien does, he explains, is to cause an amplitude shift in a wave, imposing a different frequency over the *Defiant's* shield signature. "It's like altering the acoustic signal coming out of a submarine's propeller."

Was similar technology used to alter Sisko's appearance on the viewscreen in the same episode?

"No," says Bormanis. "That's just monkeying with the comm signal to project a different image. The other ship thinks it's locked onto your viewscreen, but it's just picking up your manipulated com signal."

The production team was pleased with the episode's guest actors. Lawrence Pressman made such a good impression as Ghemor that he was brought back at the end of the season as the fake Krajensky in "The Adversary." He would reprise Ghemor in the fifth-season episode "Ties of Blood and Water."

Television veteran Gregory Sierra, who played Entek, was such a good villain that the producers considered making him a recurring character. "But we killed him off," shrugs Ira Behr. "And it was great to have Garak be the one to kill him."

"We don't want to take Garak's fangs away," explains Wolfe. "In some ways, when Ghemor tells Kira not to trust Garak, he's also talking to the audience. Just because he came in and saved the day this time doesn't mean you can trust him."

THE ABANDONED
Episode #452
WRITTEN BY D. THOMAS MAIO & STEVE WARNEK
DIRECTED BY AVERY BROOKS

GUEST CAST

Teenage Jem'Hadar	BUMPER ROBINSON
Mardah	JILL SAYRE
Boslic Captain	LESLIE BEVIS
Alien High Roller	MATTHEW KIMBOROUGH
Jem'Hadar Boy	HASSAN NICHOLAS

STARDATE 48214.5

On a busy evening at Quark's bar, Jake is surprised when his girlfriend, a dabo girl named Mardah, reveals that Commander Sisko has invited her to their quarters for dinner. At the same time, Quark is surprised by a visit from a sexy Boslic captain, who wants to sell him some salvage from the Gamma Quadrant. Ever susceptible to her seductive charms, Quark makes a deal and finds himself the owner of a newborn alien infant that had been trapped inside the twisted wreckage of a crashed ship.

Disgruntled, Quark turns the baby over to Bashir, who notes that the child has an unusually high metabolic rate. The baby makes Sisko nostalgic for the days when Jake was younger. A teenager is an entirely different animal, one whose choices in female companionship can be somewhat unsettling. But not as unsettling as Bashir's revelation that the mysterious baby is developing so rapidly that it has matured from an infant to what appears to be an eight-year-old boy in just a few hours.

Odo tries in vain to help a young Jem'Hadar escape his genetic destiny. ROBBIE ROBINSON

Although the child is no more than two weeks old, he already has the ability to speak and reason. Bashir suspects that his advanced skills, which seem artificially enhanced, are the result of complex genetic engineering. A short time later, he discovers exactly what the end result of that engineering is meant to be when the boy matures into a teenaged Jem'Hadar, violent and barely under control. Only Odo, whom the teenager recognizes as a changeling, is able to control him, since the Jem'Hadar are bred to serve the Founders. Starfleet wants Sisko to send the boy to a starbase for study, but Odo, who spent years as a similar "lab specimen," asks Sisko to let him work with the boy and prove he's not just a genetically programmed killing machine. Sisko agrees to let him try.

Later, Mardah joins Sisko and Jake for dinner, and Sisko learns quite a bit about Mardah, whom he likes, and even more about his son, the poet. At the same time, Odo makes progress in winning the trust of his "ward," whom he allows to move in with him in his new quarters on the station. Odo teaches the boy about the Jem'Hadar and attempts to find a way for him to channel his desire for violence. But battling against ferocious holosuite opponents only seems to intensify his bloodlust, leaving Odo to consider Kira's advice that a being engineered to kill may not be able to change just because Odo wants to give him a chance for a different life.

The point quickly becomes moot when Sisko tells Odo that Starfleet considers studying the boy a top priority and is sending a starship to pick him up within hours. The teenager has other ideas about his fate. He pulls a phaser on Sisko and demands a runabout, so that he and Odo can return to the Gamma Quadrant to be with their people. Odo offers him a different option: to explore the galaxy together and make a new life. But the boy wants only to be with the Jem'Hadar.

When Sisko attempts to stop him from leaving the station, Odo intervenes, explaining that if Sisko forces him to wait for Starfleet to arrive, the boy will either kill some innocent people or be killed himself. Sisko allows Odo to take the teenager to his people in the Gamma Quadrant. Later, a sadder but wiser Odo tells Kira that she was right.

Teenage angst could well be considered the theme of this episode, the first of three that were directed by Avery Brooks in the third season ("Fascination" and "Improbable Cause"), which explores some interesting variations on "the

The future as envisioned by *Star Trek*: Mardah is judged by the content of her character. ROBBIE ROBINSON

generation gap." Sisko realizes that his relationship with his son is changing and looks back on Jake's infancy with bittersweet longing. At the same time, Odo acquires a charge of his own—the quintessential alienated alien teenager—and makes his own move toward a new kind of maturity as he moves out of his bucket and into his own quarters on the station.

Director Brooks also found a deeper level of resonance in the script. "For me, it was very much a story about young brown men, and, to some extent, a story about a society that is responsible for the creation of a generation of young men who are feared, who are addicted, who are potential killers," he says. Brooks admits that the comparison is a metaphorical one. The Jem'Hadar are, after all, the deliberate product of a species with calculated motives, while the young men of the twentieth century are the product of an uncaring society. But the metaphor was useful to him in directing the episode.

Brooks is a man who cares deeply about youth, as well as youths in trouble, and his feelings here are like those expressed by Odo. "Odo knows that this is still a child," the director says. "And for him to give up and just let the boy go—what kind of a statement would we be making? That these people are expendable, that we don't really care about them? Those are the hard questions to answer."

Although we'd heard about Mardah (née Marta) the dabo girl in second-season's "Playing God," we meet her here for the first time. And unfortunately, though she seems a good match for Jake, and provides viewers with the first clues as to Jake's literary

This Jem'Hadar weapon was created by Dan Curry, who also created the Klingon *bat'leth*. ROBBIE ROBINSON

career path, their relationship would be over within four episodes ("Fascination").

One of the interesting things about the pairing is that while Sisko is concerned with Mardah's profession and the age difference between the two, no mention is made of their racial difference. "That's *Star Trek*," notes Ron Moore philosophically. "If you can accept cross-species relationships, everything else just sort of pales in comparison."

Ira Behr concurs, "If there's anything about *Star Trek* that is worthwhile beyond its being an hour's entertainment, it's that in some narrow way it postulates positive things about the future. And this is one of them: If we can't be color-blind in the twentieth century, for God's sake, let's be color-blind in the twenty-fourth."

For the dinner scene, Costume Designer Robert Blackman provided some new duds for Jake that he describes as "oversized twenty-fourth-century hip-hop clothing." According to Blackman, Jake's new attire, which debuts in this episode, helps to show that he's growing up. "He's out of the Doctor Dentons and into two-piece clothing," says Blackman. As for

Sisko, Blackman took note of Jake's worries that his dad might embarrass him at dinner, so he put the older Sisko in a three-piece outfit. "I thought it would be nice for Sisko to look dignified, even more than he would be for a date of his own."

Regarding Odo's change of venue, while the changeling may not have had qualms about giving up his bucket, Actor Rene Auberjonois did. "You get used to things and you think, 'I don't want to give that up—I love the bucket!'" he recalls. "So my initial impulse as an actor looking out for his character was to be disturbed by it. But you have to trust the writers, and nine times out of ten they really come up with a way of opening it up for more possibilities. The bucket was really a very limiting kind of concept. After that I had my own quarters, which were quite fascinating."

Auberjonois also liked the touch the writers included about Kira bringing Odo a plant, which Odo decided to keep in his bucket. "It was a sweet moment, and it paid off a year later in 'Crossfire,' when Odo has his tantrum," he observes. In that scene, Odo trashes his quarters when he is forced to accept that his feelings for Kira are unrequited. "Only really hard-core *Star Trek* fans would notice," Auberjonois says, "but I pick up the bucket with the plant in it and hurtle it against the wall." The actor added that unscripted bit of business to the scene, lending resonance to one of those random details established by the writers.

Another random element from an earlier episode found its way into "The Abandoned" when the sexy Boslic captain from "The Homecoming" returned to give Quark more unprofitable goods. Leslie Bevis reprised the role, as she would yet again in the fourth season's "Broken Link."

The cargo the Boslic palms off on Quark is a Jem'Hadar child (played at various ages, by the infant Chew twins, Hassan Nicholas and Bumper Robinson). Because there are severe restrictions on what materials can be applied to a baby, makeup designer Michael Westmore limited the infant's look to a tiny appliance that was —lipped onto its forehead with a little KY jelly. "You can't use makeup," he says. "You can't use paint. You can't use glue." There were fewer restrictions on the boy the infant grew into, and none at all by the time they got to Bumper Robinson.

Bumper's first appearance, his escape from the Infirmary, was the main effects shot of the episode, as the teenager leaps through Odo's morphed body. The scene goes by so quickly that most viewers don't even think twice about what they've seen. But the effects team, supervised by Glenn Neufeld, agonized over getting it exactly right. VisionArt Design & Animation was responsible for building the Odomorph, and Neufeld coordinated the live-action work that would be combined with the animation. Neufeld rehearsed a stunt person barreling through the scene so that he could time it and block Rene Auberjonois's bluescreen action accordingly. Then he switched to a photo-double for the actual shot. Unfortunately, says Neufeld, "the double didn't dive far enough, so his foot didn't quite go through [Odo], even though the animation made him splash and a hole opened up around him."

To repair the gaffe, Animator Adam Howard painted a shadow on top of the Odo animation that looked as if it were inside Odo, creating the illusion that the two elements were intersecting. In addition, notes Howard, they shifted the matte lines so that the exit point of the youth was a little vague. "It looks like he's falling off to the side, rather than falling straight," explains Howard.

The weapon the youth uses to dispatch his opponents in the holosuite is based on actual fighting cleavers that Dan Curry purchased in Tibet. For the episode, Curry redesigned the weapons, making them somewhat larger, and improved the handles. The original pair, notes Curry, had "ceremonial handles—you'd hurt yourself if you actually fought with them. So I improved the ergonomics by putting a handle on them almost like a German Luger."

The episode introduces a bit more information about the Jem'Hadar, including their need for ketra-cel-white, although the substance had not yet been named. In an apparent contradiction to later information that the Jem'Hadar don't eat ("To the Death"), the boy-sized Jem'Hadar claims to be hungry, although that could be due to the fact that he was not at that point ingesting the white, which may eliminate the need for food.

CIVIL DEFENSE

Episode #453

WRITTEN BY MIKE KROHN
DIRECTED BY REZA BADIYI

GUEST CAST

Garak	ANDREW ROBINSON
Gul Dukat	MARC ALAIMO
Legate Kell	DANNY GOLDRING

STARDATE UNKNOWN

While deleting some old Cardassian programs from the computer in Deep Space 9's ore-processing unit, Jake and O'Brien inadvertently trigger an automated Cardassian security program, which seals Sisko and the pair in the recently unused facility. Throughout the station, computer monitors display a prerecorded message from Gul Dukat, warning of a Bajoran worker revolt that is in progress in the unit. The Ops command crew attempts to beam the three out, only to find that the station's computer systems have responded to the so-called emergency state by refusing to function without Cardassian authorization codes.

Faced with the prospect of being exposed to lethal neurocine gas, Jake crawls through a narrow conduit in the unit and releases the hatch to the ore chute, allowing all three men to escape from the room just in time. Unfortunately, their escape triggers a stationwide counterinsurgency program, trapping

Sisko, O'Brien, and Jake try to extricate themselves from the clutches of an automated Cardassian counterinsurgency program. JOSEPH VILES

inhabitants of the station into whatever section they happen to be.

From Ops, Dax attempts to regain control of the main computer, but instead she activates level two of the counterinsurgency program, which is designed to release neurocine gas throughout the station's habitat ring. Garak arrives at Ops, and his access code allows him to step through the protective forcefield, but not to shut down the security program. He does have a suggestion on how to prevent the release of the gas; destroy the station's life-support system. That will give them twelve hours to regain control of the station before everyone suffocates. In destroying the system, the crew discovers that they now have activated level three of the program, initiating a self-destruct sequence that will destroy the station in two hours.

Working at a terminal in Ops, Garak determines that only Gul Dukat can deactivate the security program, so he attempts to convince the computer that he is Gul Dukat. The computer doesn't buy it, however, and initiates level four of the program, triggering phaser blasts that force everyone in Ops to take

cover. A few minutes later, Gul Dukat, responding to an automated distress signal from the station, actually shows up in Ops. But he refuses to deactivate the program unless Kira makes a few unacceptable concessions. Offering Kira some time to think about it, Dukat attempts to beam back to his ship, only to discover that he can't. A recording of Dukat's old superior, Legate Kell, appears on the monitor, stating that Dukat has obviously attempted to flee his post during the revolt. His access codes have been rescinded, meaning Dukat can neither leave the station, nor stop the self-destruct.

The goal now is to shut down the reactor, but that can't be done from Ops. Together, Dukat and Dax come up with a plan to short out the forcefields, thus allowing someone to reach the reactor room before the self-destruct sequence begins.

Down in an ore-processing bay, Sisko, O'Brien, and Jake manage to blast open the doors and escape to the docking ring. Dukat and Dax deactivate the forcefields, and Kira tells Sisko of their plans. Realizing that they are much closer to the reactor room than anyone in Ops, Sisko and the others head down there to disengage the fusion initiator. But with only five minutes remaining, there may not be enough time. Sisko opts instead to direct the explosion into the station's deflector shields. Crawling through a burning conduit, Sisko gets to a reactor control junction and makes the necessary modifications just in time. The shields channel the explosion into space and the station is saved.

What started out as an interesting idea for another bottle show quickly evolved into, as Ira Behr puts it, "one of those backbreaking, horrible, horrible experiences — but it was terrific at the end."

The story, pitched by writer Mike Krohn, was clever enough: your basic man against machine plotline. What was hard, says Ron Moore, was finding a way "to make the jeopardy intriguing, and to find the inner story."

By the time the script was completed, virtually every writer on staff had had a hand in it, although the episode is credited solely to Krohn. Krohn, everyone agrees, did a nice job on the first draft, but due to other commitments, he didn't have a great deal of time to work on it. So various staff members came up to bat on the numerous rewrites, only to be sent back to the dugout by Michael Piller.

"He hated it, he hated it, he hated it," states Behr,

Television magic: Smoke, controlled fire, and eerie lighting.
ROBBIE ROBINSON

likening the tortuous experience to one he and the other staff writers on *TNG* went through to turn "Yesterday's *Enterprise*" into a solid script. Typical of the ulcer-inducing pressure was an 8:00 A.M. phone call that Behr received on a Monday morning via car phone on his way to work. "'I hate to say this, Ira, but I ain't buying any of it—it's not working,'" Behr recalls hearing Piller saying. "I began wondering, 'Why did I get out of bed?'"

Still, it wasn't as if Piller had forced them into the situation. "We wanted to do a show where we could say, 'Let's forget *Deep Space Nine* the drama, or *Deep Space Nine* the comedy of manners,'" admits Behr. "'Let's just do an action show where every time you think you hit a solution to the problem, something else happens.' And that's a tough thing to create in the midst of a weekly TV series." The writing staff was already behind for the season, according to Robert Wolfe, who notes that a show had dropped out and been moved, and a lot of other undeveloped ideas "kept moving around."

"[The writing process] turned out as painful and disgusting as we thought it would be," says Behr, "but it turned out solid, with some nice twists and some great stuff for Garak and Dukat, and the paired up teams."

The episode cleverly follows up on what could have been throwaway lines regarding the bad blood between Garak and Dukat established in Season 2 ("Cardassians"), and establishes connections to future episodes concerning Dukat's feelings about Kira.

The latter development was not something that

Nana Visitor was happy to see in the script, at least, not in the way it was handled. "I would have liked my character to make the point that only a few years earlier, Dukat's wanting me would have meant that he would have *had* me, and I wouldn't have been able to do a thing about it," says Visitor. "So it shouldn't have been seen as a 'cute' moment. It was actually a horrifying moment, one that would make Kira feel disgust and panic."

After the episode, Visitor made her feelings known to the writers, and subsequent episodes dealing with the pair, such as the fourth season's "Return to Grace" and the fifth season's "By Inferno's Light," have better reflected her take on the subject. Throughout the run of the show, Visitor held firm in her conviction that there never should be a hint of romance between Kira and Dukat. "To Kira, Dukat is Hitler. She's not ever going to get over that," the actress stresses. "She can *never* forgive him, and that's important to me. Kira may have started to see Cardassians as individuals, but she will *always* hate Dukat."

Throwing the key crewmembers into circumstances where they were forced to interact in small units was an attempt on the writers' parts to "reinforce some of the relationships we already had," explains Wolfe. "We wanted to revisit some of them."

Actor Armin Shimerman enjoyed being paired once again with Rene Auberjonois but was disappointed that nothing new was revealed in their relationship. "We found out that Quark's cousin Gaila (whom we'd hear of again in the fourth season's "Little Green Men" and meet in the fifth season's "Business As Usual") has a moon, and a few other things about Quark, but nothing much about Odo. Rene and I had hoped that some new element would have been added to the relationship because they were forced to stay in the same room together, but that didn't happen." Shimerman's hopes would be fulfilled in the following seasons, with episodes like "Crossfire" and "The Ascent."

The low lighting required for most of the scenes caused some headaches for Jonathan West. "The sets are built with a lot of the lamps and lights already in place, shining through gratings and graphic areas," he says. "When we have to lower the light level, it's quite a job. The sets aren't built for that, so we more or less have to start from scratch and send people up into the grids to put diffusion on the lamps and turn off a lot of instruments."

Gary Hutzel's visual effects team had its share of

problems as well, primarily with the scene in which the Ops replicator creates a phaserlike weapon that fires upon everything that moves. "It was phaser hell," Hutzel says, "because they had about two-and-a-half pages of dialogue while it's shooting at everyone. There were somewhere in the neighborhood of sixty phaser blasts. Now, a phaser blast has relatively short screen time, but it's expensive. So we spent a lot of money doing that sequence. And it was complicated, matching the beams moving across the sets and making sure the timing looked right, particularly when you had a series of rapid edits."

A different effect, the green fire that surrounds Sisko and O'Brien as they crawl through the maintenance conduit, was relatively simple. Noting that creating the effect physically would have necessitated burning dangerous materials that produce toxic fumes, Hutzel says creating the color change in postproduction was a snap. "The A-64 switcher that we use to composite our visual elements has the ability to target colors and change them into whatever we want," he says. In this particular case, it changed a run-of-the-mill traditional yellow-orange fire into a hellish green plasma fire.

The episode marked the first time veteran television director Reza Badiyi, well known in the industry for his work on such classic shows as *Mission: Impossible* and *Mannix*, took on the world of *Star Trek*. Badiyi credits his daughter Mina, an avid *Star Trek* fan, for providing him with intensive tutoring sessions on the *DS9* characters. Badiyi would later repay Mina with a small role in the fourth season's "Paradise Lost."

"Civil Defense" also marks a wardrobe change for Odo: the sudden disappearance of his new belt. "I didn't like it," Auberjonois admits. "It was my personal decision and my fault that it was there in the first place." Although Auberjonois had liked the entire outfit when Blackman came up with the design for "Crossover," he eventually came to feel that the belt, "made it look a little too 'Buck Rogers'-y, so I suggested that we drop it." The writing staff later worked the change into a little in-joke in the fourth-season episode "Crossfire," when Kira finally notices the change.

Finally, the actor playing Legate Kell was Danny Goldring, who would return to play Burke in the fifth season's "Nor the Battle to the Strong."

MERIDIAN

Episode #454

TELEPLAY BY **MARK GEHRED-O'CONNELL**
STORY BY **HILARY BADER** AND
EVAN CARLOS SOMERS
DIRECTED BY **JONATHAN FRAKES**

GUEST CAST

Deral	BRETT CULLEN
Seltin	CHRISTINE HEALY
Tiron	JEFFREY COMBS
Lito	MARK HUMPHREY

STARDATE 48423.2

On an exploratory mission in the Gamma Quadrant, the *Defiant* picks up some peculiar gravimetric readings in the nearby Trialus system. They arrive for a closer look just in time to see a planet inexplicably appear near the Trialan sun. The ship is hailed by Seltin, a representative from the planet, who offers to answer Sisko's questions about her world if he and his crew will join the inhabitants for a meal.

During the meal, Seltin explains that her planet, Meridian, exists in two separate dimensions; for some unknown reason, it periodically shifts from this physical dimension to another, where the planet and its inhabitants become noncorporeal. When they return to this dimension, it is as if no time has passed for them, even though decades have gone by. They aren't sure what causes the shifts, although a Meridian named Deral has done some research on the phenomenon. According to Deral's studies, the periods that they spend in the corporeal dimension are be-

Jadzia begins a doomed relationship with Deral on Meridian.
ROBBIE ROBINSON

coming shorter and shorter. This particular appearance, for example, will last only twelve days, after which they will shift back to the other dimension for sixty years. Eventually, Deral theorizes, the intervals spent in the corporeal realm will be so short that the planet will become too unstable to shift, and will cease to exist in both dimensions. Sympathetic to their fate, Sisko volunteers to help find a way to stabilize the dimensional shifts.

Back on Deep Space 9, Kira deflects the advances of an amorous potential suitor by claiming that Odo is her lover, but her admirer, Tiron, isn't easily put off. If he can't have the real thing, he'll have the next best, and he offers Quark a large amount of latinum for a holosuite fantasy featuring the major. However, to create a program based on Kira, Quark must record her image with holoequipment—not an easy task since she hates the holosuites. An attempt to lure her into one fails, as does an attempt to make a scan with a portable holocamera.

In orbit around Trialus, Dax notices an anomaly in the sun's fusion cycle. It could be an important clue, but they need more data, so a probe is sent to scan the core of the sun. While they wait for the results, Dax spends some time with Deral on Meridian, where the two give in to a growing mutual attraction.

When the data returns from the probe, Dax realizes that an imbalance in the sun's fusion reactants is what triggers the dimensional shifts. If that reaction can be stabilized, Meridian will remain in orbit much longer, perhaps thirty years. Further research determines that the *Defiant* can stabilize the reaction, but not within the five days Meridian has left remaining in this dimension. Unwilling to be separated from her for sixty years, Deral decides to return to the Alpha Quadrant with Dax. But the decision leaves him feeling torn; he knows that his world needs him to build its future. Dax presents an alternative; she will use the transporter to alter her molecular structure so that she can remain with Deral on Meridian when it goes through its dimensional shift.

On the station, Quark finds a way to illegally access Kira's personnel files for his program, but Odo discovers what the Ferengi is up to. Kira comes up with a unique way to foil his plan. When Tiron activates the program Quark has provided, he encounters a seductive figure with a sexy woman's body—and Quark's head!

Her structure modified, Dax awaits the shift with Deral. But as the shift begins, it becomes apparent that something is terribly wrong. Dax's presence is interfering with the process and destabilizing the planet's quantum matrix. In essence, she is functioning like an anchor, holding the planet between the two dimensions. As Meridian's gravity and atmosphere disappear, Dax is in serious danger—but the crew aboard the *Defiant* realizes her plight and manages to beam her onto the ship just in time. Once Dax is transported, the planet shifts safely into the other dimension, but that is bitter consolation for Jadzia, who knows that Deral is gone from her life for the next sixty years.

In every season of a television series, there is at least one episode that causes the people who worked on it to wince when you mention its name. They may not know exactly what went wrong, but each and every one of them agrees on one point: It just didn't work.

"Of all the stories I've done for *Star Trek*, 'Meridian' is my least favorite," reflects Hilary Bader, who shared story credit with Evan Carlos Somers.

"I don't think anyone likes the show," comments Ron Moore. "I don't think *we* liked the show. This one just went wrong. It never jelled."

"A classic case of making it up as we go," says Visual Effects Supervisor Glenn Neufeld. "I don't want to talk about it."

"[Basing the episode on] *Brigadoon* was my idea, my idea, I'll give it to you," admits Ira Behr. "I love *Brigadoon*, so I'm idiot enough to say, 'Let's do *Brigadoon*!' I am a moron."

A lot of people love *Brigadoon*, the wistful musical about a mysterious village in the Scottish highlands that appears only once every hundred years. And there have been far stranger inspirations for *Star Trek* episodes. So Bader ("Battle Lines," "Rules of Acquisition," and "Explorers") wasn't particularly surprised when she heard that the producers of *DS9* were "thinking about doing a *Brigadoon* story, that kind of magical story," she recalls. She brought in an idea that would eventually become the A-story of "Meridian," although she admits that the aired episode contains very little of her original concept. A secondary storyline of hers disappeared altogether, replaced by a humorous B-story from Somers ("Battle Lines," "Melora"), an old friend of Bader's. The teleplay was written by Mark Gehred-O'Connell ("Second Sight"), although there were many last-minute changes during both the prep week and the actual filming period.

An interior set looks like the outdoors, thanks to the expertise of the production staff. ROBBIE ROBINSON

An obvious question comes to mind: Isn't there a point in story development where the producers can decide to cut their losses on a script that simply refuses to come together?

The answer isn't that simple. "The schedule is unforgiving," explains Moore. "Something has to be shot tomorrow. It's always moving. So it has to be a major disaster to move a script back into development, and even then, you have to have something else ready to drop into its place, which usually isn't the case."

More often, the producers will make a decision during prep (the seven days prior to filming) to throw out the old script, rebreak the story, and rewrite the script. In extreme cases, says Moore, "We'll be up late writing stuff that's shooting the next day, and trying to refashion the entire story at the same time. It's madness," he admits, but that's what happened on "Meridian."

"Those were the dark days," observes Behr, recalling long, long hours and many cigarettes (he has given up smoking since then). "It was just horrible."

Neufeld's effects team didn't have an easier time, with a horrendous session of rotoscoping to make the inhabitants of Meridian disappear and reappear and disappear again. "We knew who we would need in bluescreens, and we knew we would need roto. We'd decided that ahead of time," says Neufeld. "We had a generalized idea of how we were going to make them vanish, what elements we needed, what we were going to do with the mattes, and how we would achieve it. And we did it and it didn't look like *anything*, and we just kind of went, 'Oh, dear,' and started again." Despite all the careful planning, Neufeld says they wound up making up most of the effects as they went along, "playing with settings and other elements, roto-ing on top of roto, over and over. Thousands of frames."

The team had happier results with the effects sequence that topped off the B-story focusing on Quark's sleazy holoprogram. The scene called for Tiron to enter the holosuite and see Kira lying in a bed wearing a sexy negligee, her face obscured from Tiron by a strategically placed pillow. As Tiron moves closer, Kira lifts her head to look at him, and Tiron realizes it's not Kira's head at all—it's Quark's!

Initially, Nana Visitor was scheduled to appear in the scene as the Kira-construct's body. But the sequence required her to wear a foam rubber head, as shape, size, and position reference for the insertion of Quark's head (via bluescreen) later on. Unfortunately, Visitor, a confessed claustrophobe, had not quite recovered from her "rubber head" experience in "Second Skin" a few weeks earlier. "I was still in a state from that," she says. "My makeup artist Camille [Calvet] tried to put the head on me, and I panicked and couldn't do it."

Enter Leah Burrough, the body double who got to show off Kira's legs and torso. Burrough was shot with a motion-control camera while wearing the head, with one smooth pass flowing up her body. Then Shimerman was shot in street clothes, with his Quark makeup on. All told, there were "ten or twelve bluescreen elements there to make that gag work," recalls Steve Oster. "It was great fun to shoot."

While most of the fun aspects of the episode seem to revolve around the B-story, there were gratifying moments in the A-story for some members of the crew. Director Jonathan Frakes took the crew to San Marino's beautiful Huntington Gardens for some of the Meridian sequences. However, the beautiful open air meeting hall and eating area was filmed on Stage 18, although you would never know it from Jonathan West's warm, natural lighting.

The set—the basic structure of which was a reuse of Masaka's temple from the *TNG* episode "Masks,"

Auberjonois's unscripted reaction to Kira's demonstration of affection
led the writers to explore the changeling's unvoiced feelings.
ROBBIE ROBINSON

became a recurring role when the producers decided
to bring Combs back as Weyoun's clone during fifth,
sixth, and seventh seasons.

DEFIANT

Episode #455

WRITTEN BY RONALD D. MOORE
DIRECTED BY CLIFF BOLE

GUEST CAST	
Gul Dukat	MARK ALAIMO
Korinas	TRICIA O'NEIL
Kalita	SHANNON COCHRAN
Cardassian Soldier	ROBERT KERBECK
Tamal	MICHAEL CANAVAN
Computer Voice	MAJEL BARRETT

SPECIAL GUEST STAR	
Tom Riker	JONATHAN FRAKES

STARDATE 48467.3

On a day when nothing seems to be going right, Kira is intrigued by the appearance of William T. Riker, a commander on the Starship Enterprise, who's visiting DS9 en route to shore leave on Risa. Although she claims otherwise, Kira is not invulnerable to Riker's charm, and she offers him a tour of the station, including, at Riker's suggestion, the Defiant. After rebuffing the friendly greeting by O'Brien, his old shipmate aboard the Enterprise, Riker gets Kira to authorize activation of all of the Defiant's bridge consoles. Suddenly, he stuns her with a hidden phaser. Seconds later, he beams a waiting man and woman onto the bridge.

On the station, Sisko receives a message from Riker, claiming that an onboard accident has injured Kira and left the warship just seconds from a warp core breach. Sisko orders the docking clamps released so that Riker can get the ship away from the station before the explosion. But as O'Brien prepares to beam the pair out of danger, the clearly undamaged ship puts up its shields and leaps into warp. Safely out of range, Riker and his allies set course for the Badlands.

Consulting Starfleet records, Sisko figures out the truth. The man who was masquerading as Will Riker is actually Thomas Riker, a transporter duplicate who was created inadvertently nine years earlier. Tom

was also used in DS9's "The House of Quark" and "Blood Oath." It consisted of a partially enclosed building that had a skylight where the sun would beam down into the room. Outside the building was a 270-degree backdrop with trees painted on it, rented from Walt Disney Studios, where it had originally been created for the film *Mary Poppins*. With those elements, West's job was to "recreate what nature would have done on a planet." So he brought in a large, intense lighting unit for the sun, and had it set up on the ceiling grids. Then he added some 20 x 20 light grip bars and bounced the light from them into the setting to create the ambience of a bright sky. "Too often, when you're shooting exteriors on a soundstage, you forget that the sky itself creates some sort of an illumination or reflection on people," says West. "It was one of the most interesting lighting situations I've done in a while."

The episode marked Composer Dennis McCarthy's return to duties on *DS9*, after having taken time off to score *Star Trek Generations*. McCarthy created a sad, gentle theme to play up the romantic aspects of the show, adding more strings than usual to the makeup of the orchestra, and taking away some brass.

Tiron's last line to Quark, promising to return to "ruin" the Ferengi, actually came true. The producers were so pleased with the performance of Jeffrey Combs (best known for his roles in *Re-Animator* and *From Beyond*), that they brought him back as Quark's archenemy Brunt. The following year, Combs got a third role, as the Vorta Weyoun. This ultimately

Not even Kira is immune to the renowned Riker charm.
ROBBIE ROBINSON

Riker is an exact replica, with most of Will's memories, but also some important differences. Tom Riker is believed to be a Maquis, meaning the *Defiant* is now in the hands of dissidents. Fearing that Cardassia's Central Command will assume Starfleet actually *wanted* the Maquis to have the warship for their skirmishes with Cardassians in the Demilitarized Zone, Sisko briefs Gul Dukat on everything he knows. When Dukat suggests that destroying the *Defiant* may be the only way to head off a war between the Federation and Cardassia, Sisko reluctantly agrees and offers to help.

After traveling with Dukat to Cardassia Prime, Sisko is quizzed by Korinas, an observer from the Obsidian Order, on the *Defiant's* strengths and weaknesses. Sisko reveals that while the ship has a Romulan cloaking device, it may be detectable with an antiproton beam.

In the meantime, Tom Riker meets a group of waiting Maquis ships and heads for the Cardassian border. Using a decoy vessel to lure patrol ships away, Riker slips into Cardassian territory and attacks an out-

post. But before he can move off to inflict damage at a different location, Kira sabotages some of *Defiant's* systems, temporarily disabling the cloaking device. While the Maquis crew repairs the damage, Kira lambastes Riker for risking a war just to participate in the fray in the Demilitarized Zone. Riker tells Kira that he's after bigger prey. The Maquis believe that certain factions of the Cardassian government are behind a secret military buildup in the distant Orias system. Not even Central Command knows about this base, but Riker means to stop its completion.

Back on Cardassia Prime, Sisko studies the pattern behind the *Defiant's* attacks within Cardassian space. Suddenly he discerns Riker's strategy. He is drawing Cardassian ships away from the Orias system, which is clearly his real target. Dukat is puzzled, as he believes the region to be uninhabited, but he agrees to send a warship to investigate. Alarmed, Korinas warns Dukat to keep his ships out of the Orias system; any ship sent in will be destroyed by the Obsidian Order.

While Dukat waits for Riker to make the next move, Kira warns Tom that if he makes a run for Orias, the Cardassians will be able to track him. Sure enough, nearby ships pick up a phase shift in the *Defiant's* neutrino signature as it heads for Orias, and the chase is on. As the *Defiant* approaches the system, three warships suddenly appear in front of it, blocking its path. Dukat is more surprised than Riker; the ships don't belong to the Cardassian military, which means they have been sent by the Obsidian Order. And the Order, Dukat reveals angrily, is explicitly forbidden to have military equipment of any kind.

Tom Riker refuses to back down until Kira points out that it's the only way to save his crew. ROBBIE ROBINSON

As they are caught between the three ships in front of him and Dukat's ships behind, Kira asks Riker to back down from his self-appointed mission, which seems doomed to failure. But Riker refuses and engages the Obsidian Order ships in battle. The odds get worse, as sensors reveal more ships approaching from the Orias system. Suddenly, the *Defiant* receives a message from Cardassia Prime conveying a compromise that Dukat and Sisko have worked out. Dukat will allow Riker to surrender and turn the *Defiant* and her crew over to the Federation, *if* Riker turns over the *Defiant's* sensor logs and himself to the Cardassians. That way, Central Command will be able to see what the Obsidian Order is hiding in the Orias system *and* they will have a scapegoat to punish for terrorist Maquis activities.

Realizing that it's the only way to save the lives of Kira and his Maquis crew, Riker reluctantly agrees and beams over to a Cardassian vessel that is under Dukat's authority. Saddened by Riker's fate—life imprisonment at a Cardassian labor camp—Kira takes command of the *Defiant,* and sets course for Federation space.

"**W**e had talked about picking up the character of Tom Riker [from *TNG's* "Second Chances"] and making him the leader of the Maquis," recalls Ronald D. Moore. "The initial notion was that the Maquis were getting tougher, but we didn't know why. And then we'd discover that their leader was Tom Riker."

Moore discussed the as-yet-undeveloped story concept with Ira Behr, who suggested that it might be a good idea to bring Riker to the station and let him interact with the characters, and play some dabo before revealing his connection to the Maquis. Moore agreed and sat down to start writing, only to face a key question: What would the Maquis want at DS9? The answer came to him quickly: the *Defiant.*

The first few pages of Moore's original story were easy. Riker comes aboard the station and, as Moore puts it, "He's groovin' on Kira; he's the old Riker-as-the-galaxy's-Lothario, putting the moves on our major. He maneuvers her onto the ship, stuns her, and takes off in the *Defiant.* Then he pulls off the beard and it's Tom. I thought, 'That's a cool opening.'"

But after that, Moore admits, he didn't have much at all. "Then some interesting stuff happens and we chase him down and get him." He laughs. The story regained its momentum in the break session with DS9's other writer-producers, who pointed out that, "We needed Sisko. What was Sisko going to be doing while Tom and Kira were out running around?" Someone brought up the film *Fail Safe,* the taut '60s cold war thriller. The idea clicked for everyone. "Put Sisko in the Cardassian's war room, looking up at that big board, and having to help the enemy shoot down one of his own ships," recaps Moore.

Adding to the realism of the sequence was some behind-the-scenes magic performed by Gary Hutzel and his effects crew. When Hutzel read the script, he knew he was facing a challenge. "What you have is Sisko and Dukat in the Cardassian nerve center, directing traffic, as it were," he says. "And any time you try to tell a ship story with graphics on a viewscreen, it can get real, real boring. So during the preproduction meetings we discussed spicing it up and doing more with it than our normal graphics." The producers complied and even hired additional personnel to help the Art Department get the extensive graphics work done quickly.

But there was still the problem of how to do the Cardassian's large main viewer. "It wasn't going to be very spectacular," recalls Hutzel, "because they could not build a large screen. They could only take an existing one that wasn't very big." So Hutzel suggested going in the opposite direction. "I offered to do it as a miniature. The whole main screen wall in the episode is a miniature built by Tony Meininger. It's wonderful. No one ever knew." To maintain the illusion, Hutzel took several shots of Avery Brooks walking in front of a bluescreen and combined them with the miniature, so that Sisko appears to be looking up at an impressively large Cardassian screen.

On the nontech front, the episode reveals some interesting nuances in the characterization of Dukat and Tom Riker. The revelation of Dukat's feelings about missing his son's birthday, for example, contribute to the temporary softening of his character that transpired through third and fourth seasons. "I wanted a moment in that scene where we see that Dukat has better things to do than participate in this particular mission. That he has some humanity and a life outside of that war room—and that this kind of sucks for him, too," says Moore. "He's not getting any joy out of what they're doing."

As for Tom Riker, Kira's caustic speech to him about the difference between heroes and terrorists, a gem of a scene-stopper in Act 4, came as the result of some long soul-searching on the part of the writing staff. "One of the things that we knew we had to find in the episode that was difficult was Tom Riker's *rai-*

The Federation extends an offer of assistance to the Cardassians; however, Brooks's body language conveys Sisko's feelings about the offer. ROBBIE ROBINSON

son d'être for doing all this," recalls Behr. "That whole 'hero/terrorist' thing took some getting to. It actually got clarified during the successive drafts."

The episode's title is a bit of double play that Moore felt suited the turncoat Starfleet officer as much as the ship he steals. But even more insight into Tom's core persona is provided in Act 5, when he finds himself on the receiving end of another psychological jab from Kira. "Tom is insecure," confirms Frakes. "He's much less confident than Will. But he's also kinder and sweeter. I think I like Tom better!"

The intriguing situation involving the Obsidian Order's secret operations in the Orias system would be fully revealed in "Improbable Cause" and "The Die Is Cast" later in the season. At the time of "Defiant," however, those plot threads were undeveloped, according to René Echevarria, who wrote the teleplay for "Improbable Cause." "We didn't know we were going to do the two-parter when we did 'Defiant.' There was a vague idea of a first strike, but that was it. When the later show came up, we said, 'Why not use it?'"

One plot thread remains dangling, particularly in one actor's mind. "I keep thinking Tom is coming back," says Frakes. Did the producers say anything to suggest that? "No," Frakes admits. "But don't you think that it makes sense for them to send Kira over there to free Thomas? It's a no-brainer," he says with a smile.

The producers may have had something in mind, but if so, they never got around to it. In their pre-

Left unanswered: What happened to Tom Riker? ROBBIE ROBINSON

fourth season pitch letter to freelance writers, Tom Riker appeared on a short list of subjects the staff was *not* interested in hearing pitches about (which sometimes means they are already working on a story of that type), along with stories about the mirror Jennifer (an in-house story about her would turn up not long after), Nog at the Academy (ditto), and Dax or Odo getting pregnant.

Jadzia confesses her "love" to Benjamin when a bout of Zanthi fever brings out unusual feelings aboard the station. ROBBIE ROBINSON

FASCINATION

Episode #456

TELEPLAY BY **PHILIP LAZEBNIK**
STORY BY **IRA STEVEN BEHR & JAMES CROCKER**
DIRECTED BY **AVERY BROOKS**

GUEST CAST

Lwaxana Troi	MAJEL BARRETT
Vedek Bareil	PHILIP ANGLIM
Keiko O'Brien	ROSALIND CHAO
Molly O'Brien	HANA HATAE

STARDATE UNKNOWN

The space station's Bajoran inhabitants are preparing for the yearly Gratitude Festival, but Jake is in no mood to celebrate. His girlfriend, Mardah, has been accepted to the science academy on Regulus III, some three hundred light-years away. His father encourages him to go to the festival, where he may find someone new.

In the meantime, O'Brien nervously awaits the arrival of Keiko and Molly on a shuttle from Bajor. Kira looks forward to seeing Bareil, who is coming to share the holiday with her. But while Kira's reunion is sweet, O'Brien's is somewhat strained; Keiko is exhausted from the trip, and Molly is sick from all the candy that another shuttle passenger—Lwaxana Troi—has given her. Officially, Lwaxana has come to serve as the Betazoid representative to the festival, but she's really there to see Odo, much to the changeling's chagrin.

Bareil is interested in spending time alone with Kira before the festival begins, but Kira is too busy completing the preparations. Similarly, O'Brien would like to share some intimate moments with Keiko, but she's too tired to be enthusiastic about anything besides sleep.

As the festival begins, Lwaxana experiences a brief headache, which Jake and Bareil feel simultaneously. From that point on, life on the station becomes a little topsy-turvy. Suddenly Jake is compelled to tell Kira that he's discovered the love of his life: her! The teenager's confession surprises Kira, but it can't match Dax's astonishment when Bareil tells her that he'd like to get to know her a *lot* better. Later, Lwaxana has another headache, which Dax feels. A short time later, the Trill confesses to Sisko that she's always been in love with *him*!

The evening progresses, and romance refuses to rekindle between the O'Briens, particularly after Keiko tells Miles that her botany survey on Bajor is likely to take two months longer than they'd anticipated. The two argue and Keiko stalks off in anger, leading bartender Quark to offer O'Brien some Ferengi advice on making a marriage work. The advice is useless, but the conversation makes O'Brien realize just how much Keiko means to him, and he leaves the bar determined to make things right with his wife. Speaking to Keiko through the closed bedroom door, O'Brien says that he is prepared to resign so that he can be with her and Molly on Bajor. But Keiko asks him to give her some time to think.

Finally free of her duties, Kira finds Bareil, only to learn that he is no longer interested in her, except as a friend. Bareil goes off to look for Dax, who, at Sisko's request, is being examined by Bashir. Bashir can find nothing wrong with the Trill, and Dax convinces him her supposed infatuation with Sisko was a practical joke. Sisko is relieved, until, outside of the Infirmary, Dax kisses him and says that she loves him.

A short time later, Kira runs into Odo, Lwaxana, and Bashir, who are headed for a party that Sisko is hosting. When Kira mentions Bareil's behavior, as well as Jake's sudden case of undying love, Bashir wonders if he missed something in Jadzia's tests. Lwaxana experiences another headache, and then she and Odo head for the party, while Kira and Bashir go to the Infirmary to look at Dax's scans. Once there, however, the two immediately fall into a passionate embrace and begin kissing.

At the party, a perplexed Sisko observes Jake mooning over Kira and Bareil chasing after Dax, who still has eyes only for Sisko. Unable to contact Bashir, Sisko sends Odo to find him. Odo interrupts Bashir and Kira's heated clinch and brings the doctor back to the party, where Bareil is getting more persistent in his pursuit of Jadzia. When Jadzia presents Sisko with a bracelet that Bareil gave her, Bareil attacks Sisko, and Bareil is decked by Jadzia. Keiko arrives at the party and tells O'Brien not to resign. Suddenly, Lwaxana has another headache, and Quark makes a pass at Keiko.

All of the components of this chaos finally click in Sisko's mind and he has Bashir examine Lwaxana. Sure enough, Bashir diagnoses Zanthi fever, a virus that affects the empathic abilities of older Betazoids. The fever causes Betazoids to project their emotions, in this case her unrequited feelings toward Odo, onto others in close proximity. Bashir gives Lwaxana an injection that cures her, and effectively cures everyone else as well. As Lwaxana leaves the station after the festival, she confesses to Odo that she knows about his feelings for Kira, and promises not to reveal his secret. The two part as friends.

As every literary-minded fan knows, *Star Trek* has many ties to the works of William Shakespeare. In that noble tradition, "Fascination" was an attempt by the producers to bring the humor and charm of *A Midsummer Night's Dream* to the station. "We felt we needed a light show, because we were coming up on 'Past Tense,'" says Ira Behr, who cowrote the story for this episode with Jim Crocker. "In some ways, it works very nicely. And in some ways," he pauses and shrugs, "you know."

"I guess it was over the top," admits Director Avery Brooks. "But what is over the top, after all? If you're having a pint of Guinness and you see the foam pouring over the top, you think, 'That's great!' But in a television episode, there's this concern about action being too large. It all comes down to rhythm, and whether a scene has it or not."

Still, it was one of those shows where the producers chose knowingly to go, as Behr is fond of saying, "dangerously wacky." No one is quite sure where

Part of Jadzia's charm was her willingness to see beauty in its many forms. ROBBIE ROBINSON

the idea came from, although Behr thinks it originated with Michael Piller some time much earlier. "I do remember that we all sat down to watch the 1935 film version of the play, with James Cagney, Mickey Rooney, and Joe E. Brown," Behr says. "But then we never found a way to do it."

Not until the third season. At that point everyone attempted to give the episode his all. Jonathan West lit the show differently, brightening the sets, highlighting more color, and bathing the characters in pink light to change the mood. He also made use of reflective material to create a feeling of magic. "In the background of a lot of the close-ups, there are little pieces of balloon foil and glittery stuff," says West. "We put those in so that subliminally you'd get this kind of sparkle every once in a while." West notes that the series' color palette was also expanded for the episode. "We brought in a few colors we generally do not use, like purple, which is a no-no because it's too reminiscent of old science fiction artificiality."

Robert Blackman relished the short vacation from the restrictions of traditional episodes. "It was a nice opportunity we hardly ever get," he says. "Everybody gets nice dress-up stuff. They're all so

The foolishness and folly of a Shakespearean glen is transported to the Wardroom of DS9. ROBBIE ROBINSON

intoxicated with love that my goal was to make them as attractive as possible. We put an amazing outfit on Terry [Farrell]—a beautiful outfit on a beautiful woman. And Kira had on a great outfit when she was up on the podium, opening the festivities—a very tight body stocking topped with transparent chiffon. It looked both Bajoran—appropriate for the ritual she was performing—and provocative at the same time."

Dennis McCarthy also had fun with temporarily lapsed limitations. "It gave me a chance to compose a little bit of humorous music," he says. "On the *Star Trek* shows, we're normally leery of doing comic music." McCarthy notes that he usually has to be careful "not to get too silly. You can have tongue-in-cheek humor, but not over-the-top humor. If you're in a *Tiny Toons* mode, and you see a character like Quark, there's a tendency to say, 'Yo! Let's go for it—where's my xylophone!'"

Not everyone had fun with the show. "It was a very silly episode," comments Armin Shimerman, who teaches a Shakespeare class during his downtime from the series. "I thought it was embarrassing for us to be acting out of character and doing love scenes with people who are supposed to be our friends."

"The episode is memorable for not quite pulling off what it attempted to do," notes Siddig El Fadil, although he admits he did enjoy his juicy scenes with Nana Visitor. "We didn't rehearse them at all," he says. "I was really nervous about them, but it was tremendous fun."

The teleplay for "Fascination" was written by Philip LaZebnik, a comedy writer who also did some work on *TNG* ("Devil's Due" and "Darmok"). Behr feels that the best part of the episode was the focus on

the relationship between O'Brien and Keiko. "I think it's the most real example of married life in the history of the *Star Trek* series," he says. "It's about expectations, trying to live up to them and trying not to have too many, and about bonding with your spouse and not being able to bond with your spouse, about being on different wave-lengths." One of those realistic scenes, however, led to a reshoot on the final day of filming. An argument between Keiko and Miles "got too nasty," says Behr. "Keiko was too nasty to O'Brien and we didn't want it to be quite so overt." So, just as in lasting real-life relationships, where partners frequently have to hold back for fear of saying something that could cause irreparable damage, the actors were asked to replay the scene, reining in some of the hostility.

The episode includes one of Behr's fondest moments from the third season, which focuses, not so coincidentally, on his favorite *DS9* relationship. "Miles is at the docking ring, saying goodbye to Keiko, and he turns around and a racket is thrown into his hand, and there's Bashir waiting for him," says Behr. "And off they go." The scene points up the fact that O'Brien's friendship with Bashir flourished in Keiko's absence. The thread would be further developed when Keiko returned to the station the following year.

"Fascination" establishes some interesting background details, the fact that Bajor has a twenty-six-hour day, for example. And it openly reveals a plot point that only had been hinted at previously: the fact that Odo loves Kira. Interestingly, this was a case where an actor's performance strongly influenced the producers. "There was a moment in 'The Collaborator,'" Behr recalls, "where Rene [Auberjonois] does a take with Nana that we hadn't been expecting. And we all looked at it and said, 'Odo loves her. That's what he's playing!'" Recognizing the rich story possibilities, Behr's team took the ball and ran with it, giving Auberjonois plenty of material to play with in the coming seasons.

Of somewhat lesser importance, but equally tantalizing, was a bit of information cut from the episode's first act that would have explained how Lwaxana learned that Odo's people were the leaders of the Dominion. In the shooting script, Lwaxana claims to have friends in high places—including Admiral Nechayev, whom she says she thinks of as "the sister I never had."

An amusing in-joke in the second act did remain. Quark attempts to sell "genuine latinum-plated renewal scroll inscription pens . . . sure to become collector's items," each engraved with a "lovely portrait of the station by Ermat Zimm." The line is a tip of the hat to the man responsible for much of the station's look, Herman Zimmerman.

PAST TENSE, PART I

Episode #457

TELEPLAY BY **ROBERT HEWITT WOLFE**
STORY BY **IRA STEVEN BEHR &**
ROBERT HEWITT WOLFE
DIRECTED BY **REZA BADIYI**

GUEST CAST

Chris Brynner	JIM METZLER
B.C.	FRANK MILITARY
Vin	DICK MILLER
Bernardo	AL RODRIGO
Lee	TINA LIFFORD
Michael Webb	BILL SMITROVICH
Male Guest	HENRY HAYASHI
Female Guest	PATTY HOLLEY
Danny Webb	RICHARD LEE JACKSON
Stairway Guard	ERIC STUART
Gabriel Bell	JOHN LENDALE BENNETT

STARDATE 48481.2

An unusual transporter accident sends Sisko, Bashir, and Dax several hundred years into the past when O'Brien attempts to beam them from the *Defiant* to a Starfleet symposium on Earth. All three officers wind up in San Francisco in the year 2024. Jadzia is found and assisted by Chris Brynner, a wealthy businessman of the era, but Sisko and Bashir are apprehended by the police and taken to a "Sanctuary District." This is a gated part of the city where the homeless, the unemployed, and the mentally ill are locked away from the rest of society.

At Brynner's office, Dax is able to obtain an ID card, and he offers to help her find her missing friends, whom he ultimately discovers are being kept in the Sanctuary District. In the meantime, Sisko and Bashir wind up in a processing center, where Sisko learns the date. Alarmed, he explains to Bashir that it is just days before the onset of the Bell Riots, one of the most violent civil disturbances in American history. If they can't get out of the District soon, they'll be caught right in the heart of it. What's more, warns Sisko, they can do nothing to interfere with the event—in which hundreds of innocent people will be killed, and a man

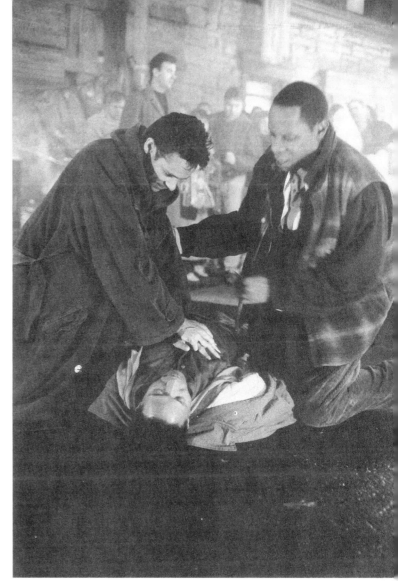

Dr. Bashir tries in vain to save the life of Gabriel Bell. DANNY FELD

named Gabriel Bell will sacrifice his life to stop the massacre—or they risk changing history.

On the *Defiant*, O'Brien determines that the trio has been transported back in time, but cannot pinpoint the exact date. There is a chance they may be able to retrieve them if they pick the correct time period, but the ship will be able to make a total of only five or six attempts.

As Sisko and Bashir search for a place to live in the District, they encounter a homeless man named Webb who tries to talk them into helping out in the community. They decline the request because of their fear of altering the past. Later, when the pair end up in a fight with some of the District's more violent residents, they are helped by a bystander who steps in to even the odds. Unfortunately, the man is stabbed to death for his efforts, and Sisko is horrified to discover that the deceased was Gabriel Bell. Sisko comes to the reluctant conclusion that Bashir and he will have to help play Bell's part in the impending riots if the future as they know it is to be salvaged. Returning to Webb, the two offer to participate in an upcoming rally.

Sisko's fears prove to be well founded. With the death of Bell, the future quickly begins to unravel. On board the *Defiant* in the twenty-fourth century, Kira and O'Brien discover that Starfleet Headquarters has disappeared, along with every other sign of its influence, except for the *Defiant* itself.

On Earth, the events leading to the Bell Riots are taking shape. When the processing center is stormed by residents of the District, Sisko steps forward to provide a cool head amid the chaos. He identifies himself as Gabriel Bell—and the die is cast.

As the staff of *DS9* prepared to launch its third season, the plight of the ever-expanding homeless population of America weighed heavily on Robert Hewitt Wolfe's mind. It was, as he states, "difficult to turn a blind eye to the sight of people living on the streets in unprecedented numbers." And that vision could be seen throughout urban Los Angeles. But nowhere was it more conspicuous than in Santa Monica, a region of mild temperatures and ocean breezes, and beautiful parks filled to capacity with people who had—and have—nowhere else to go.

Wolfe was not alone in his observation. "In Santa Monica the homeless have become living sculptures," comments Ira Behr. "People literally walk over them." So Behr was not unsympathetic when Wolfe began "bugging him" about a story in which Sisko comes to Santa Monica in the 1990s. But, he also knew that it had to be something more than a passive lament about the state of the twentieth century.

Wolfe's first crack at the subject was a script called "Cold and Distant Stars." Behr says, "It just didn't work for me." The title had to do with the plight of Sisko as a homeless man, looking up at the sky and knowing that was where he belonged.

"I wanted Sisko to be saying, 'I'm the captain of a starbase in the year twenty-three-whatever, and I don't belong here,'" says Wolfe. "And everybody's telling him, 'You're a homeless schizophrenic, take your Thorazine.' But that never quite worked," he admits.

Then Behr came up with an angle that he thought would serve the story well. "I was driving home one evening, and I suddenly thought, 'Attica,'" he recalls. Behr's 'Attica' insight was based on his rec-

The vivid staging of these two very different scenes was to underline the prejudice of *both* centuries. DANNY FELD

ollection of the severe riots that had broken out in upstate New York's Attica prison in 1972. The riots were triggered by living conditions in the prison that had degraded to the point where the prisoners were almost being stripped of their humanity. "I came in the next day and told Robert, 'I hope you like it, because I think this is the way we have to do it—we're gonna do concentration camps,'" he says.

The timing on the episode couldn't have been more appropriate. Only a few days later, the writing staff was shocked to read the headline on the front page of the *Los Angeles Times:* "Homeless Camp Weighed in L.A. Industrial Area." The article described a plan proposed by the city to "make downtown Los Angeles friendlier to business . . . by shuttling homeless people to an urban campground in a fenced lot in the city's core industrial area." Dissenters quoted in the article claimed that ". . . building a large fence would make it nothing but a prison."

"The article came out as we were planning the episode, literally when we were breaking the story," René Echevarria recalls.

"We were amazed," concurs Behr, noting that people who knew about his and Wolfe's "concentration camp" story kept approaching them and asking if they'd known about the government's plan. "I said, 'I didn't know about it until I read it in the paper,'" says Behr. "It was scary. It was really scary."

"I hadn't realized the country was so depressed as to need it," comments Siddig El Fadil, "but the episode was almost a cinematic version of that statement by the L.A. Council."

In the time-honored tradition of *Star Trek* episodes, the politics were concealed within the fabric of the storyline. "We didn't have a big political agenda on any level," Behr states. "But we wanted to deal with how *Star Trek* arrived at this great Gene Roddenberry vision of the future. Well, this is one of the things that happened: To get there you have to go through hell."

While the plight of America's forsaken middle class, who in Behr and Wolfe's vision will join the destitute and mentally challenged to become tomorrow's homeless, was at the forefront of the story, the two writers also worked in a subtle statement about prejudice. Jadzia, although found in essentially the same straits as Sisko and Bashir, is quickly ushered into the world of the "haves." However, the two men are immediately dumped into the Sanctuary District. As Behr puts it, "The simple fact [is] that a beautiful white woman is always going to get much better treatment than two brown-skinned men. That's the reality of life."

Although it is one of *DS9*'s more serious efforts, there was still some room for the writers to have a bit of fun, primarily in the names that they came up with for the assorted dims, ghosts, gimmies, and other residents of the twenty-first century. Quite a few of the monikers were lifted from the movie *The Magnificent Seven.* Says Wolfe, "It was a little in-joke for ourselves, to go along with others, like naming the angel who comes in and saves the day Gabriel. And, of

course, B.C." That name was a tip of the hat to the episode's first assistant director, B.C. Cameron.

To take their characters back to the twenty-first century, the writers were required to come up with some form of time-travel. They preferred one that they hadn't employed before, and one that wouldn't require a lot of exposition. "For some reason, whenever we go back in time on *DS9*, it has to be different," says Wolfe. "We had never used the transporters to beam people back in time, which I thought would be kind of a neat way to do it. My belief is that the less you explain it, the better off you are. We like to get in and get out as quickly as possible for the sake of the story, because the story's not about chroniton particles." In any event—Wolfe laughs—"It's all approved by our science guy."

Ah, yes—the "science guy," otherwise known as Andre Bormanis, who is charged with, among other things, examining the recurring questions about time travel from all sides. "There is no real physics of time in the sense that there is a physics of matter. But some physicists spend a little bit of time talking about whether or not time is quantized," Bormanis explains. "They wonder if there is some small, fundamental, indivisible unit of time, just as there is an indivisible unit of matter. On *Star Trek*, we assume that in the future there will be a stronger physical basis for understanding time, and that there will be a quanta of time, like 'chroniton particles' or things of that nature. Of course, I don't know why they worry so much about rationalizing it. It's just sort of a *Star Trek* science-fiction staple that we occasionally do time travel."

With that kind of casual attitude, it's surprising that we never heard about "Starfleet's temporal displacement policy" until this episode. "Well, there's certainly been enough of it." Wolfe chuckles. "You'd think they'd have developed a policy by now!" Since no one else had, Wolfe and Behr did. While the writers didn't bother to go into much detail about this policy for "Past Tense," the reference would provide the humorous basis for the existence of Starfleet's Department of Temporal Investigations in the episode "Trials and Tribble-ations."

As if taking the crew of DS9 into a different century wasn't risky enough, the episode also took the cast and crew of the series into unfamiliar terrain: the "New York Street" section of Paramount's back lot. But at least they took along an experienced guide. "Just a few months prior to making 'Past Tense,' I had directed a *Cagney and Lacey* movie-of-the-week on

Organized chaos. DANNY FELD

Cameron. "We did interviews and picked specific people out from groups of two or three hundred," she says.

It's a good thing they were all cast as humans. "We only had to dirty them down," recalls makeup guru Michael Westmore, "so I was able to hire ten makeup artists as opposed to the twenty-five we'd have needed to put alien appliances on them."

As for garbing the poor unfortunates, Robert Blackman notes that his wardrobe staff, "Just beat everything, bleached it, dyed it, burned it, and painted it until everything was kind of a sludge color. They all had to wear a lot of layering. Thank God it was in the winter, so it was cool enough."

Badiyi's efforts were appreciated by El Fadil. "Reza set a tone with almost a feature-film type of cinematography," he states. "Catching all those background actors who managed to perform when it was boring and cold was extraordinary. And, of course, the children, who were all filthy, really helped to create an atmosphere."

Also contributing to the atmosphere of Part I was Dennis McCarthy's score. Composer McCarthy states that he was able to bring something to the soundtrack that he's seldom been allowed to employ: silence. "Those wonderful silent moments that we all love in music are usually a no-no on *Star Trek*," McCarthy says. "I knew that this show required some of that and I used it. Steve Oster listened and said, 'Great.' There are only about seven minutes of scoring on that whole episode."

Thanks to the tremendous amount of preparation, all of the exterior shooting went smoothly. Well, almost all of it. "The first night out on the street we had a huge crane shot," says Cameron. "We had to pull back to reveal this big street with all these boxes and people sleeping on the street with dirt and smoke and steam. I remember the producers making a big issue about making sure that there were no legible names on the cardboard boxes. So the crane pulls back and it's gorgeous, with all the extras and set decoration and the extraordinary lighting. Everybody was so impressed. The next day the producers watched the dailies—and right in the middle of the shot is this huge refrigerator box with 'Amana' written in huge letters across it! No one had seen it. I couldn't believe it! How could we have missed it?"

that back lot," notes Part I's director, Reza Badiyi. "I'd also shot there years ago, on shows from *Mission Impossible* to *Mannix*. But no one had ever used it for *Deep Space Nine*."

In fact, aside from a few trips a year to such scenic locales as L.A.'s Griffith Park, "*Deep Space Nine* hardly ever goes outside of the sound stages," observes Badiyi. "So I took Jonathan West out there and we talked. It really worked. It gave us much more freedom."

"We had to create a gritty, dirty look for the city," comments West. "A lot of that was accomplished in art direction, dirtying down the sets on New York Street by painting them in earthy tones so they didn't reflect too much color. Half of good photography is in the art direction. The other half is in lighting and composition.

"We did a lot of night work," West continues. "I used real fire in some of the scenes, and I put lamps into flicker boxes near the trash cans. I also had two xenon lamps on eighty-five-foot-high cranes to simulate helicopter search lights. I shot it all four or five stops overexposed so the light was really intense. It suggested that Big Brother was watching."

"'Past Tense' was one of our largest exterior shows," relates Steve Oster, "especially in terms of the number of extras we used. We had eighty or ninety people, which is very unusual for us."

Up to that point, it was the largest number of extras they'd used on the series, according to B.C.

PAST TENSE, PART II

Episode #458

TELEPLAY BY **IRA STEVEN BEHR &**
RENÉ ECHEVARRIA
STORY BY **IRA STEVEN BEHR &**
ROBERT HEWITT WOLFE
DIRECTED BY **JONATHAN FRAKES**

GUEST CAST

Chris Brynner	JIM METZLER
B.C.	FRANK MILITARY
Vin	DICK MILLER
Detective Preston	DEBORAH VAN VALKENBURGH
Bernardo	AL RODRIGO
Grady	CLINT HOWARD
Danny Webb	RICHARD LEE JACKSON
Lee	TINA LIFFORD
Michael Webb	BILL SMITROVICH
Swat Leader	MITCH DAVID CARTER
Henry Garcia	DANIEL ZACAPA

STARDATE UNKNOWN

Posing as the late Gabriel Bell, Sisko takes charge of the volatile hostage situation in the processing center as rioting begins within San Francisco's Sanctuary District. Outside the District, Jadzia sees news coverage of the event and realizes that she must get into the District to help Sisko and Bashir.

On the *Defiant*, Kira and O'Brien begin searching the past via a series of transporter trips, knowing that they have only a limited amount of chroniton particles to facilitate the endeavor.

At the processing center, Sisko convinces Webb, a decent family man, to act as their representative in dealing with the outside world. They try to communicate via an interface terminal, but are quickly cut off by the police. However, Detective Preston, a police negotiator, offers to speak to Webb in person. Sisko accompanies Webb to the meeting and states their demands: Close down the Sanctuaries and reinstate the Federal Employment Act. Preston agrees to present their demands to the governor. She returns a short time later with the governor's response; he'll reduce the charges against "Bell" and Webb if they release the hostages. Sisko and Webb reject the offer.

Dax manages to find her way into the Sanctuary District, and although her combadge is stolen by some of the residents, she is reunited with Sisko and Bashir at the processing center. Bashir helps Jadzia recover her combadge and sends her back to her friend Brynner, whom she convinces to help restore the processing center's computer access. Once that is done, many of the District residents are given the opportunity to tell their stories to the millions of people monitoring the situation over the computer interface. Unfortunately, the governor is unmoved by their plight and orders Preston to send troops into the District.

Kira and O'Brien realize they've hit the correct time period when they manage to contact Dax on her combadge. In the meantime, Sisko and Webb try to keep the hostages safe as SWAT teams move in. In the inevitable hail of gunfire, Webb is killed along with a number of others, and Sisko takes a bullet in his shoulder protecting a hostage named Vin. As the National Guard takes control of the situation, the grateful Vin, a guard in the District, allows Sisko and Bashir to escape and switches their cards with two of the dead. Thus, as before, it appears that Gabriel Bell died while trying to help the hostages. With Vin's promise to tell people the truth about the incident, history is restored to its normal course and the crew of the *Defiant* return to their own time.

When Michael Piller saw the story for an early version of "Past Tense," he had one major suggestion. "He said, 'You could do a hostage drama for an entire episode, and here you don't even get into the hostage situation until Act Four,'" recalls René Echevarria. Piller suggested that the writers turn the story into a two-parter, which not only allowed them to flesh out the drama but also helped the producers to amortize the costs over the combined budgets of two episodes. "Which helps

Sisko, in the persona of Gabriel Bell, keeps watch as Webb attempts to negotiate with Detective Preston. ROBBIE ROBINSON

The well-crafted characterization of B.C. lifted him above the simple label of murderer. ROBBIE ROBINSON

when you're going for something big," observes Echevarria.

Echevarria wrote the first draft of Part II, after which "Ira jumped in for the rewrite," he says. "He was very passionate about it."

Behr doesn't deny it. "I got obsessed about it." He laughs. "And there were things that I got more and more obsessed about, like B.C., the character that Frank Military plays."

It would have been easy to allow "cold-blooded murderer" to be the sole extent of B.C.'s portrayal. "In Part I, B.C. kills Gabriel Bell," Behr points out. "He's a murderer, and then in all of Part II we never mention that he's a murderer." Why? Because there were reasons that B.C. became a killer, reasons that tied in with the central theme of the two-parter. "We didn't want the crux of the thing to be, 'Sisko trapped with a murderer,'" explains Behr. "He wasn't inherently a murderer. If you treat people like animals they become animals. If B.C. had not been homeless, what would he have been? We created his backstory, stuff that would never appear on the screen, and decided he probably would have been a garage mechanic or something. Even though he's obviously a threatening, scary character, and he's on-the-edge-crazy all through the shows, we didn't define him as a murderer. Those are the kinds of touches that I'm proud of."

And then, of course, there was "The Hat." Behr got stuck on that, too. "I got obsessed with this hat thing B.C. had," Behr admits, "and started writing until his hat became his whole personality!"

Character schtick aside, Behr's obsession with the hat ultimately helped the wardrobe department

define the various inhabitants of the Sanctuary District. "The kind of hat they wore distinguished which gang they were in," says Robert Blackman, "We called them 'the fedora people' and 'the beret people.' The ghosts all wore the weirdest hats."

The director's hat was passed on to Jonathan Frakes for Part II. "It's the episode that helped me to get the job of directing *Star Trek: First Contact*," Frakes states happily. In order to be considered for his first film-directing assignment—a very important film to the studio—he had submitted a copy of "Past Tense, Part II," along with the *TNG* episode "Cause and Effect," to the studio. Apparently, the two episodes demonstrated the right mix of dramatic pacing and action.

As is typical with multiparters, Frakes followed the tone set by the director of Part I. "Reza and I didn't share any scenes," Frakes notes, "and he did most of the casting, but I got to cast Clint Howard."

Like only a handful of other actors (including Charles Napier, Charlie Brill, and William Schallert), this would mark one of the few times a guest actor from the original series had returned to play a role on *Deep Space Nine*. Howard's initial appearance in the *Star Trek* universe was a memorable turn as the youthful-looking Balok in "The Corbomite Maneuver."

"Clint was quite funny and he did a wonderful job," comments Behr. "But we originally wrote the part for Iggy Pop. I'd been trying to cast Iggy for years, twice when I was working on *Fame,* and then on *DS9*." At the time "Past Tense" was going into production, "Pop was touring in Spain or someplace, so

Visitor's one-of-a-kind bandage. DANNY FELD

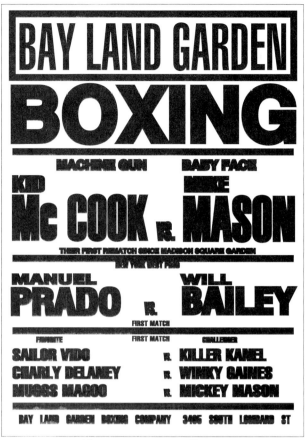

Ripped from a San Francisco wall, circa 1930.

The producers get their due in Jim Martin's psychedelic tribute.

he was unavailable," sighs Behr. "It's always something. I was crushed when he couldn't do it."

Behr took personal delight in a different one of Frakes's casting choices. "Deborah Van Valkenburgh was great," he enthuses. "I was very excited about having her on the show because she was in one of my favorite movies, *The Warriors*."

Frakes loved the contemporary feel of the episode. "It was great to be out of the period and come back as close to the twentieth century as that," he says. The scenes in the processing center number among his favorites. "The one with Dick Miller and Avery was dynamite! When Avery got Dick up against the wall—whew! That was *one* of the best things I've ever seen Avery do."

On the other hand, confesses Frakes, "I wasn't crazy about the hippie sequence and the thirties sequence. We didn't have time to do anything unique. We just stood there and watched people come out of the van and the speakeasy."

Visitor's most important piece of costuming in those scenes, a futuristic bandage that covers Kira's distinctive Bajoran nose ridges, created headaches for her and the props department, although Visitor admits it

was all her fault. "The first time we finished one of those scenes, I took the bandage off and threw it away," she moans. "And, of course, when they found out, they were like, 'Oh no! You didn't!' Somehow I'd thought they'd have a box of these bandages, but apparently there was only one, and it was specially made. We had to go through a couple of Dumpsters!"

The sequence with Kira and O'Brien beaming into the 1930s gave the Art Department, known for its small but stalwart contingent of *Star Trek* trivia experts, a chance to have some real fun recreating a piece of set dressing. The lovingly rendered facsimile, a 30s era boxing poster, was used as set dressing for the scene with Kira and O'Brien. "As we were reading the script to 'Past Tense, Part II,' it occurred to us that it was almost the same scene [as the one in "The City on the Edge of Forever"]," explains Scenic Artist Doug Drexler. "In fact, I could have believed it if they'd all bumped into each other in the alley: Kirk and Spock and O'Brien and Kira. We had a good reference for the boxing poster, so we re-created it and stuck it in there."

The sixties sequence also featured a poster contrived by the Art Department. This poster was a pseudo-psychedelic notice suitable for black-light viewing, advertising a rock act known as "Berman's Rainbow Dreamers" at the "Behr Theatre." The poster, courtesy of Jim Martin, refers, of course, to Rick Berman and Ira Behr. "Someone pointed that poster out to me on the set," recalls Behr. "Talk about self-referential." Behr doesn't always appreciate such in-joke material, but recognizes the driving force that creates it. "Everyone on the show is a Trekker," he shrugs. "You can't kill them with a stick."

For the climactic mayhem near the end of the episode, Stunt Coordinator Dennis Madalone made use of equipment that is seldom employed on *Deep Space Nine*. "We did some squib hits instead of fake phaser hits," he says, referring to the tiny pyrotechnic devices used to simulate bullet wounds. "We normally only use sparks, but these were blood hits. And we were using real shotguns with half-loaded blanks. That's a real rarity on our show. We had to be very safety-conscious coordinating all of that."

The episode put David Takemura into the front seat as special effects supervisor for the first time, after serving as special effects coordinator for many years on both *TNG* and *DS9*. One of Takemura's tasks was to render a shot of the *Defiant* orbiting the Earth. "I used an eight-by-ten NASA transparency of the real Earth to create the footage," he says. Takemura designed a motion control move that had the transparency panning in one direction while the motion control camera itself panned in the other direction. The shot resulted in an image of the Earth that did not look static. "I thought it was a nice shot," he says modestly.

"Past Tense" also marked an important transition in the characterization of at least one of the regulars. "This show was the end of the old Bashir and the beginning of the new, more responsible Bashir," comments Siddig El Fadil, noting that "Bashir proved to everyone and himself that he can handle very tricky situations with almost no backup and no gizmos, not even a shotgun like Sisko had. It became conceivable that Bashir would be your first or second choice on an away team if you were going on a combat mission. I think that they were a renaissance pair of shows for Bashir."

Behr notes that the episodes took some heat from reviewers and from fans on the Internet for being too "liberal" and "soapboxy." Behr shrugs. "I suppose we could have shown the 'positive aspects' of concentration camps," he notes wryly. "But I hope we presented a lot of different attitudes. For a two-hour television show that also had to talk about chroniton particles and all of the usual information that people expect from *Star Trek*, I thought we did a pretty good job.

"We're not going to solve anything with two hours of TV," Behr observes. "The homeless are still there. The problem hasn't gone away. But maybe just one person saw this and started to see the problem in a different way. In 1995, *Forrest Gump* was the feel-good movie of the year. Yes, it's important to feel good and I'm not putting that down. But in reality, in 1995, Forrest Gump would be homeless. I just thought it was important to show the other side."

LIFE SUPPORT
Episode #459

TELEPLAY BY **RONALD D. MOORE**
STORY BY **CHRISTIAN FORD & ROGER SOFFER**
DIRECTED BY **REZA BADIYI**

GUEST CAST

Vedek Bareil	PHILIP ANGLIM
Nog	ARON EISENBERG
Leanne	LARK VOORHIES
Nurse	ANN GILLESPIE
Legate Turrel	ANDREW PRINE
Riska	EVA LOSETH
Bajoran	KEVIN CARR

SPECIAL GUEST STAR

Kai Winn	LOUISE FLETCHER

STARDATE 48498.4

A new romance seems in the offing for Jake when he discovers that Leanne has just broken up with her old boyfriend. The only hitch is the dom-jot game with Nog that he'll have to cancel in order to go to dinner with Leanne. As he considers his next move, his thoughts are disrupted by a commotion on the Promenade. There's been a serious accident on a Bajoran transport and the wounded are being brought aboard the station, included the badly injured Vedek Bareil.

As Bashir tends to Bareil, Kai Winn, another passenger on the vessel, reveals to Sisko that she and Bareil were en route to a secret meeting that would have initiated peace talks between Bajor and Cardassia.

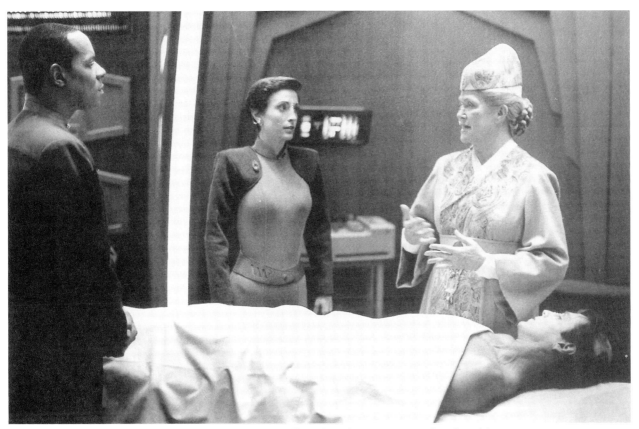

Knowing that Bareil's political savvy is vital to the peace talks with Cardassia, Winn can't allow the vedek to rest. ROBBIE ROBINSON

It was Bareil, however, who was the driving force in the preliminary discussions between the two worlds. Unfortunately, Bashir is unable to save Bareil, and he declares the vedek dead, only to discover a short time later that Bareil still has some faint signs of brain activity. Acting quickly, Bashir is able to resuscitate Bareil, and pronounces that he should be back on his feet within a few weeks. However, Winn will need his assistance in the peace talks sooner than that. Reluctantly, Bashir agrees to allow Bareil to advise Winn from his bedside.

Elsewhere on the station, Jake manages to break his dom-jot appointment with Nog, only to find himself agreeing to a double-date with the Ferengi, Leanne, and a female friend that Leanne will bring along. Predictably, the date goes dreadfully, with Nog insulting the two females and embarassing Jake. After the women leave, the two youths part on angry terms. But to Jake's surprise, his father defends Nog, saying that he was acting naturally for a Ferengi, and suggesting that the incident isn't worth breaking up their friendship.

Bareil's recovery does not go as Bashir had hoped. The treatment Bashir performed in order to revive him has damaged Bareil's circulatory system. The doctor recommends an indefinite period of time in a stasis field while he researches the unusual condition. The vedek refuses; he won't delay the peace talks.

Forced to choose a less satisfactory alternative, Bashir puts Bareil on a dangerous experimental drug that will allow him to function normally for a few more days. However, the drug begins to cause irreversible damage to his internal organs. Bashir notes that he can replace the damaged organs with artificial ones, but warns that Bareil will suffer additional damage if he doesn't allow Bashir to put him in stasis. Bareil refuses because Winn needs him. Bashir appeals to Winn, asking her to release the vedek from his responsibility to her, but Winn, afraid to negotiate on her own, declines.

Not long after, Bareil suffers massive synaptic failure in his left temporal lobe. As before, the damage is irreversible, which means Winn will no longer be able to seek his advice, unless the doctor replaces some portions of Bareil's brain with implants. Bashir resists the suggestion from Winn, but when Kira, too, suggests that it's what Bareil would want, he gives in.

As Bashir conducts the procedure, Jake sets

about repairing his relationship with Nog by getting the two of them thrown into DS9's holding cells under some contrived charges. As he had hoped, the enforced period of time together allows the two to work out their differences.

A dispassionate Bareil, his emotions essentially removed along with the damaged portions of his brain, helps Winn finish the talks and the Cardassians sign a peace treaty with Bajor. When the other half of his brain begins to fail, Kira begs Bashir to keep him alive with another artificial implant. The doctor gently refuses, unwilling to reduce Bareil to a machine. Kira sadly accepts Bashir's advice, and remains with the man she loves for the last few hours of his life.

Meet Ronald D. Moore, professional hit man.

"I've killed a lot of recurring characters in my day," he says. "K'Ehleyr. Kirk. Then I killed Bareil."

There's always a motive for murder. Revenge. Jealousy. Ratings. But Moore's bloodlust is usually triggered by dramatic necessity. The story reaches an emotional dead end, and something needs to be done to give the audience a reason to care about the action. In such cases, death can be a powerful catharsis, particularly the death of a character the audience has come to like.

"Life Support" began as a pitch by Christian Ford and Roger Soffer about Bashir as "Frankenstein." Initially, the story concerned a Federation ambassador who is traveling to the station to negotiate peace with the Romulans. He's involved in a shuttle accident and arrives at DS9 in critical condition. Although Bashir makes a valiant effort to save him, the ambassador dies. But treaty negotiations are at a critical point; this opportunity may never come again. Bashir figures out a way to bring the ambassador back to life to continue the negotiations.

"He's just slowly dying for the rest of the show, and descending into madness," says Moore. "He becomes this monster that Bashir has to let die."

During the break sessions, it became clear that two aspects of the show just weren't working. "One was, 'Who is this guy?'" Moore recalls. The other went hand in hand with the first: 'Who really cares what happens to him?'"

The Romulan aspects of the story weren't particularly compelling either. "Peace with the Romulans is not a big thing in *Deep Space Nine*-land," observes Moore. "All the negotiations were happening off-

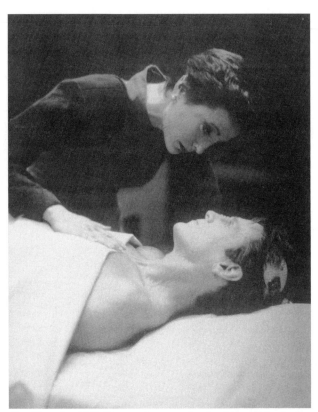

Ron Moore has "killed" many characters, but he claims all the deaths were driven by story needs. ROBBIE ROBINSON

camera anyway. And yeah, we were trying to make it a Bashir show, but in reality everything focused on the ambassador, and nobody cared about him."

The obvious solution was to make the dying character someone the audience knew. At the time, rumors were flying around that Colm Meaney might be leaving the show, so for a short period the writers toyed with the idea of killing O'Brien. "Obviously, we wanted Colm to stay," says Ira Behr, "and we didn't want to do anything that would drive him away. And that's when Ron said, 'What about Bareil?'"

The suggestion made sense. The writers weren't particularly happy with the way the Bareil/Kira relationship was working out and weren't certain where it should go. There was no sense in the production offices that Bareil was a huge favorite with the fans. Ironic, because after the episode aired, the producers received lots of mail from a fan organization they'd never previously heard of or from: The Friends of Vedek Bareil.

"We got letters," confirms René Echevarria. "We got pictures of a bunch of people at a memorial service for Bareil. Very somber. Angry letters."

Whether an awareness of fan interest in Bareil would have granted the vedek a stay of execution is a moot point. The episode did gain the measure of humanity the producers were looking for, and the substitution of Cardassians for Romulans worked. "It became more of a *Deep Space Nine* story," says Moore. "Suddenly we had some real stakes."

Bringing in Kai Winn, of course, raised the ante even more. The caliber of Louise Fletcher's contribution was appreciated by all, perhaps even more so as, according to Behr, she was extremely ill with the flu while they were filming her scenes. "In some of the dailies, we would look at her and say, 'Jesus, she has no business being up. She should be in bed,'" he recalls. "But she was a real trouper."

There were, however, far worse discoveries to be made in viewing the dailies. "I wish there had been cameras here when the writing staff sat down to watch." Behr smiles grimly. "You could just feel this sensation going around the room: *'What the hell have we done?'* We were appalled."

The appalling problem was in how the A (Bareil) and B (Jake and Nog double-date) story lines played off each other—or rather, how they *didn't* play off each other. "I'll take the blame for it," Moore volunteers. "I said to everyone, 'This is such a grim episode, we should have a light B-story, maybe let Jake and Nog do some fun stuff.' It sounded great in concept, and I enjoyed writing the scenes, but, man, such a mistake!"

Writers of episodes heavy in scientific jargon generally find their way to the door of science consultant Andre Bormanis, but Bormanis credits his friend John Glassco, a pathologist who works at St. Joseph's Hospital in Burbank, for much of the tech assistance in "Life Support." "He helps me out with the heavy medical stuff," says Bormanis.

"The question that arises," Bormanis says, "is how much of you can you replace and still be you. Especially when it comes to replacing parts of the brain. It's a great science fiction question, because we are getting to the point where we're going to be able to tap into the optic nerve and create ocular implants." From there, he asks, " 'How far away are brain implants?' Someday, the question will be, 'How much of your gray matter can you replace with circuitry and still be a human being?'" At that point, he adds, you're not far from being considered a cybornetic organism, like *Star Trek*'s Borg.

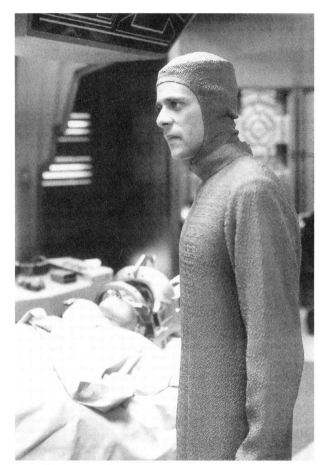

The writers explore the physician's role in maintaining the quality of life. ROBBIE ROBINSON

Speaking of technical components, Jim Martin designed a "brain scanner" and a "brain operator" for Bashir to use in treating Bareil. "One was a lightweight thing that you could set down over your head so it would look like it was scanning your brain," Martin explains. "The other was a big heavy thing that encased the head, but allowed you to operate on the patient from the back." In Martin's mind, the difference between the two devices was clear, but apparently it wasn't to Director Reza Badiyi. "When I saw the episode," grins Martin, "Bashir was examining Bareil with the operating device and operating with the scanner." He shrugs resolutely. "But you know, what gets filmed is what's ultimately real, so from now on in that universe, the scanner is actually the operator, and vice versa."

HEART OF STONE

Episode #460

WRITTEN BY **IRA STEVEN BEHR &
ROBERT HEWITT WOLFE**

DIRECTED BY **ALEXANDER SINGER**

GUEST CAST

Rom	MAX GRODÉNCHIK
Nog	ARON EISENBERG
Computer Voice	MAJEL BARRETT

SPECIAL GUEST STAR

Founder Leader	SALOME JENS

STARDATE 48521.5

En route from an assignment near the Cardassian border, Odo and Kira learn of a Maquis attack on a Lissepian supply ship and opt to pursue the Maquis vessel. They follow it to a deserted moon in the Badlands, where the Maquis appears to make a crash landing. Although they find the damaged vessel, the occupant is nowhere to be seen, so Kira and Odo split up to search the inhospitable cavernous landscape. A short time later, Odo receives a distress call from Kira. Returning to her side, he discovers that she has been immobilized by a strange crystalline formation that has attached itself to her foot. Worse, the crystal is growing rapidly. Odo's efforts to remove it are futile, as are his attempts to either analyze the odd crystal with his tricorder, contact the station, or beam Kira back to their runabout.

Back on DS9, Commander Sisko is surprised by an unusual request, accompanied by a traditional Ferengi bribe, from Rom's son, Nog. The young Ferengi wants Sisko to write him a letter of reference to get into Starfleet Academy. Curious about what kind of scheme may be motivating this odd behavior, Sisko decides to test Nog by having him inventory the contents of one of the station's cargo bays. The Ferengi does an excellent job in record time, but still Sisko doubts the sincerity of his request.

In the caverns of the seismically unstable moon, Kira's situation grows dire. The crystal steadily continues to encase her body, making it difficult for her to breathe. Despite Kira's suggestion that Odo leave the dangerous environment and head back to the station, Odo stubbornly remains, bent on finding a

Odo finally manages to confess his love to Kira. ROBBIE ROBINSON

method to remove the substance. He brings an ultrasonic generator from the runabout and waits for it to find the right frequency to shatter the crystal. However, he knows that Kira may not have enough time left for that to happen.

To help distract her from her plight, Odo shares some personal revelations with Kira: He enjoys spending time with O'Brien in one of the holosuite programs. His name, Odo, is actually an abbreviation of the Cardassian word *odo'ital*, which means "nothing," and his life only became more than nothing when he became acquainted with Kira and the others on DS9.

As the violent tremors on the moon grow worse, Kira fears that the cave will collapse, killing them both. She orders Odo to leave, but he refuses, admitting at last that he is in love with her. To his surprise, Kira responds by saying she is in love with him as well.

On DS9, Sisko tells Nog that he has decided to turn down his request. He fears that the Academy's workload and the discipline would be too much for the Ferengi, particularly if this newfound desire is just a whim. Nog denies that it's a whim or a scheme. Sisko pushes him until he gets the truth. Nog doesn't want to end up like his father, a mechanical genius who could have been an engineer, but for Ferengi tradition, which demanded he go into business despite the fact that he has no talent for making a profit. Nog doesn't have the instinct for business either and feels Starfleet will give him opportunities his father never had. Touched by Nog's disclosure, Sisko agrees to recommend him to the Academy.

In the cavern, Kira's revelation makes Odo ponder a number of unusual coincidences that surround their enforced stay on the moon. This leads him to the conclusion that Kira has been lying to him on several points, including the fact that she loves him. In fact, Odo no longer believes that the woman he is speaking to *is* Kira, because Kira would never lie about her feelings, even for the best of reasons. Odo levels a phaser at her and demands to know where the real Kira is. Suddenly the crystal-encased image of Kira morphs into the form of the female shapeshifter whom Odo had previously met on the changeling homeworld.

The female changeling reveals that there never was a Maquis hiding in the caverns; it was her all along. Suspecting that Odo's reason for remaining with the "solids" was connected to his affections for Kira, the changeling had planned to convince Odo that Kira was dead. With his link to the solids severed, she'd hoped that Odo would then return to live among his own people. But the plan has failed, and Odo forces her to reveal the location of the captured Kira, after which the female changeling beams away. Odo rescues Kira, and the two leave the moon, with Odo revealing part of the changeling's scheme, but not the key to her rationale. His deepest feelings will remain a secret from Kira.

The teleplay is done. One storyline concerns a dramatic situation fraught with physical danger, a personal revelation, and a surprise payoff. The other focuses on some humorously atypical behavior on the part of a recurring character. The episode is filmed and aired, and it turns out that that audience responds more strongly to the humorous vignette than to the compelling dramatic story.

So which one was the A-story?

"That's a really good question," admits Ira Behr, who cowrote "Heart of Stone" with frequent collaborator Robert Hewitt Wolfe. "When we conceived it and broke the story, it was definitely the Odo/Kira storyline. But although we didn't realize it when we wrote it, the little B-story took on such resonance in the playing that it was the story that drew most of the fan reaction. Aron was wonderful. Avery was wonderful. Max was wonderful. And *they* didn't have that horrible, horrible prop of a rock."

Nobody liked the rock, or rather, the crystalline formation that traps and threatens to encase Kira in the episode. Once more a literary reference had inspired a plot point: in this case, a scene in the book *Sometimes a Great Notion* in which a character gets caught under a log and drowns when water rises above his head. "We thought, 'That would be sort of cool—we could do that,'" recalls Wolfe.

But nothing about the rock worked out the way they'd hoped. For one thing, the person who was to be encased in the crystal was Nana Visitor, a self-described claustrophobe who'd already been tortured by Wolfe earlier in the season ("Second Skin"). This time, notes Visitor, "they drilled me to the floor."

That's not much of an exaggeration, according to Glenn Neufeld. "We strapped her feet to the floor before we put the crystal on."

"It was extremely uncomfortable for Nana," says Director Alexander Singer, a veteran of such *TNG* episodes as "Relics." "We arranged for there to be a kind of seat inside that she could relax her body in between takes. Otherwise, she would have been on her feet for hours and hours."

The glamorous art of acting: spending an entire day "trapped in rock."
ROBBIE ROBINSON

That might not have mattered so much if the final product had looked better on camera. "It didn't look like I'd imagined when I read the script," says Visitor. "I thought it was going to look like my body turning to stone. Instead I looked like a big old hot fudge sundae, and my head was the cherry on top."

Visitor wasn't alone in her opinion about the aesthetics of the rock. "It presented almost insurmountable problems for production in terms of getting it really interesting, getting it really right, without postproduction highlighting, and working on it without computer graphics," says Singer. "We kept fighting to get angles and light on it." But nothing made the pinkish lavender rock look more realistic. "It was the kind of special effect that, had this been a feature, they would have spent months in preparing, and shooting tests and so on," Singer notes. "As it was, we got it and shot it, and then had to improve on it in postproduction."

And even the postproduction process proved arduous. Glenn Neufeld worked closely with Singer to set up the shots in such a way that the computer-generated effects done by VisionArt would be a snap. They weren't, of course. "There's a shot where Odo morphs into a canopy, and rocks are bouncing off of him," says Neufeld. "But how long does it take for

him to become the canopy, and how long is he the canopy with the rocks falling? I need to know this so I can tell Nana, 'Rocks are gonna crush you and you look away, but then you don't get crushed. Now look up!' Too fast. 'Now look up really slowly.' Those things have to be choreographed."

The scene where "Kira" turns into the female changeling (played by Salome Jens, who graciously allowed the producers to hold her guest-starring listing until the end credits, so as not to spoil the surprise) was also choreographed carefully, says Neufeld, "and pretty much none of that worked, and VisionArt fixed all the problems."

Rocks aside, the A-story had some moments of great poignancy that would influence Odo/Kira storylines throughout the rest of the series. "The reason Odo realizes it's not Kira is because she says she loves him," observes René Echevarria, who participated in the story break sessions. "If you consider the thought process that he must have gone through to realize that she's lying, it's really heartbreaking."

No one is closer to Odo's pain than actor Rene Auberjonois, whose admission of love to the fake Kira is accompanied by body language that speaks more of physical torture than the baring of one's soul. "It sprang from my sense that Odo knows the incredible investment and pain involved in admitting this," says Auberjonois. "It's fear of rejection and his fear that by admitting it, any hope that it could ever come to fruition will evaporate. So there's a tremendous sense of loss and fear, and it physically manifested itself the way you saw it."

Another secret was disclosed to station personnel in the more upbeat B-story about Nog. The storyline was inspired by Wolfe's fanciful thought, "Of Wesley, Jake, Alexander, and Nog, wouldn't it be funny if Nog were the one to end up a Starfleet captain?"

"It was an idea that had such fun about it, and such verve," notes Singer. "And when you added Quark and Rom, the whole thing began to take on a wonderful balance."

But fun was the farthest thing from Aron Eisenberg's mind when he got the script. "My first feeling was, 'Oh, God—I'm off the show!' I thought they were writing me out until Rick Berman actually pulled me aside and told me that definitely wasn't the case."

Relieved, Eisenberg reappraised the script and noted that Nog had experienced a shift in thinking that he hadn't seen coming. "[Up to this point] I always had respected Quark more than my father," he says. "I was a true Ferengi and my father was a failure at that." But the strength of Behr and Wolfe's writing helped to bring him around to the correct mind-set. "The part where I talk to Sisko about my father is my favorite scene ever, in all the acting I've done—telling Sisko my father could have been an engineer, given the opportunity. I realized just how proud I really was of him, and how I wished that he'd gotten his chance. And now I was going to have my chance, knowing he fully supported me." At that point, Eisenberg, along with Nog, switched his loyalties from Quark to Rom. "Now I'm more irritated than impressed by Quark, because I feel he could be a better . . . well, not a *hew-mon* being, but a humanitarian," he laughs.

If it was the writing that helped sell Eisenberg on the appropriateness of Nog's new aspirations, it was personal experience that gave him the emotional impetus to sell it to the viewers. Born with only one kidney, which functioned inefficiently, Eisenberg received a kidney transplant at sixteen. He likens the choice Nog makes in "Heart of Stone" to the one he made when he graduated from high school. "It was either go to college or try to be an actor," he says. "I didn't know where I'd be in four years, I didn't know if my new kidney would fail. So I went for it. And for Nog, it was a big gamble, too. It would have been easier to go into the bar business, like his uncle, and not do what he really wanted."

Although conceived as one of the season's "save money" shows, there were no budgetary constraints on imaginative dialogue. Viewers find out that O'Brien's predilection for holo-kayaking, introduced during the third season of *TNG* is still strong, and that Odo is still enjoying O'Brien's detective novels. There are probably a number of viewers who would question Odo's comment that the classic pop ditty "Louie, Louie" is an innocent sea chanty, but Robert Wolfe swears it's true. "We wanted to have Odo sing it, but we couldn't get the rights," smiles Wolfe.

Although he's never seen, we hear of the fascinating Ensign Vilix'pran, whose unique physical condition makes for one of the most bizarre throwaway scenes in *Star Trek*. "One of the frustrations with doing television is that it's very difficult to portray nonhumanoid aliens," says Wolfe. "Really weird, totally strange aliens. And we needed a scene for Bashir, and Ira and I just started ripping, making this guy weirder and weirder."

"We wanted something that would never have been done on *TNG* or any other series," adds Behr. "So here you have your two male stars talking about a baby shower. That seemed like an interesting way

of showing the twenty-fourth century really is different. Then we said, 'Well, why not make it a male giving birth . . .'"

". . . Then we decided he didn't actually give birth to the babies, they grew off his body like buds," continues Wolfe. "And then we added that O'Brien was building him a hatching pond, so obviously the babies, after they drop off his body, have to live in water for a while. We actually went so far as to say that he had wings, but that didn't make it into the final draft. That was the one step too far."

For obvious reasons, Vilix'pran was never seen, but we hear of him again in the fifth season's "Apocalypse Rising" when Bashir announces that he's in the family way once again, and in "Business as Usual" where Jake mentions that he sometimes baby-sits the ensign's offspring.

DESTINY

Episode #461

WRITTEN BY **DAVID S. COHEN & MARTIN A. WINER**
DIRECTED BY **LES LANDAU**

GUEST CAST

Gilora Rejal	**TRACY SCOGGINS**
Ulani Belor	**WENDY ROBIE**
Vedek Yarka	**ERICK AVARI**
Dejar	**JESSICA HENDRA**

STARDATE 48543.2

In the wake of the recent peace treaty established between Bajor and Cardassia, Sisko oversees preparations for the arrival of two Cardassian scientists who will assist station personnel in deploying a subspace relay in the Gamma Quadrant. If successful, the project will allow communication through the wormhole for the first time. However, before the scientists arrive, a vedek named Yarka warns Sisko that an old Bajoran prophecy predicts "three vipers" will return to their "nest in the sky" and cause the "temple" to burn and cast open its gates.

To Yarka, the meaning is clear. The Cardassians en route to DS9 will somehow bring about the destruction of the wormhole. But Sisko points out that only two Cardassians are coming to the station, not three, and that the project is too important to Bajor's future to cancel.

When the two scientists, Ulani and Gilora, arrive,

Cardassian scientists, though somewhat reptilian, are *not* the three vipers of Bajoran prophecy. BARRY SLOBIN

their friendly manner immediately puts the crew at ease —until they are informed that another Cardassian scientist is expected, which Yarka interprets as the third viper. He begs Kira to convince Sisko to send the Cardassians away, but Kira refuses to let her faith interfere with her duties.

Dejar, the third scientist, is stiffer and more traditional than her two counterparts, and it is clear that Ulani and Gilora aren't comfortable around her. However, the project gets underway with no complications, with Gilora and O'Brien remaining on the station to receive the signal from the Gamma Quadrant, and Dejar and Ulani traveling in the *Defiant* with Sisko, Kira, and Dax to set up the relay on the other side. As soon as they get there, Dax spots a large rogue comet with a brilliant tail.

Alarmed, Kira realizes that it could be the "sword of stars" that Yarka claimed would destroy the wormhole. She tells Sisko that she believes the prophecy is coming true and that it's up to him, as the Emissary of Bajoran lore, to make the decision that will affect the outcome of the chain of events. But Sisko sees himself as a Starfleet officer, not a religious figure, and without scientific evidence to substantiate the prophecy, he won't stop the experiment.

When all is ready, Sisko has Dax send the first transmission through the wormhole, but it doesn't work. Dax then sends a transmission of a different frequency, and this time the wormhole reacts violently, opening and experiencing a brief, drastic shift in gravity. Although Sisko orders the carrier wave terminated at once, the gravitational surge has altered the

course of the comet; it is now headed directly toward the wormhole. If it enters the anomaly, the silithium in the comet's core will collapse the passageway forever, seemingly fulfilling the prophecy.

The *Defiant* returns to the station, where O'Brien and Gilora modify the ship's phasers in order to vaporize the entire comet at once. But when the *Defiant* returns to the Gamma Quadrant to implement the plan, the weapons relay malfunctions. The ship fires a standard phaser burst, which splits the comet into three fragments that are still on course for the wormhole. O'Brien is at a loss to explain the accident until Gilora reveals that Dejar is a member of the Obsidian Order, and that she probably sabotaged the equipment in order to prevent any peaceful joint ventures between Bajor and Cardassia.

Dejar is confined to her quarters while the others plan a strategy for about saving the wormhole. They decide the best course of action is to send out a shuttlepod, maneuvering it between the comet fragments so that the small ship's warp drive creates a subspace field around the pieces as they travel through the wormhole. Sisko and Kira perform the dangerous flight successfully, with just a miniscule amount of the silithium leaking into the wormhole. To everyone's surprise, those silithium particles interact with the wormhole's ambient radiation to create a filament that allows the subspace signals from the Gamma Quadrant to travel through. The project is a success, and it was all predicted by the ancient Bajoran prophecy that Yarka had misinterpreted. The three vipers were actually the comet fragments, which permanently wedged open the temple gates of the wormhole. Sisko comes away from the experience with a new respect for Bajoran prophecy, and for his own role in Bajor's future.

"It was stubborn," says Ira Behr. "It was a very difficult show. It's amazing it ever got made."

"Destiny" was meant to be a second-season episode. The story idea had been pitched and purchased from freelancers David S. Cohen and Martin A. Winer, who were also allowed to do the teleplay. But somehow, it didn't quite work, and the script remained unproduced until the middle of *DS9*'s third season.

Recalls René Echevarria, "The early draft had a lot of nice stuff in it. It was done very lyrically and the writers had a lovely poem concerning Trakor's prophecy." Unfortunately, the prophecy that they'd

A Bajoran space station where Cardassians are honored guests, a reminder to viewers that everything cannot be seen as black or white. ROBBIE ROBINSON

come up with was one of happiness and light, according to Echevarria, "a wonderful thing that was going to happen, a miracle, and Sisko was told that he was going to be a part of it."

And while that may have been a wonderful thing for the Bajoran people, it wasn't great for episodic drama. "A miracle was happening," says Echevarria. "So why was that bad? Why would Sisko not want to be a part of it?"

So the staff writers rebroke the story and allowed Cohen and Winer to take another shot at it. The new version was closer, but still merited no cigar. Finally, recalls Echevarria, "One of us—I think it was Ron Moore—said, 'Jesus, this should be a prophecy of *doom*.'"

Suddenly, the story made sense. A prophecy of doom, but Sisko still wants to go forward with the plan that could trigger the prophecy, "because he's a Starfleet officer, because he doesn't believe this 'Emissary' stuff," notes Echevarria. And suddenly there was dramatic tension galore: Sisko versus the Bajoran people, Sisko versus Kira, Sisko versus himself."

Echevarria helped shepherd the story through the final stages, right down to making up Rule of Acquisition #34 ("War is good for business") and #35 ("Peace is good for business"). "I did write those," he admits, adding with a chuckle that Ferengi Meister Behr has to approve each new rule.

As in "Heart of Stone," viewers were reminded of the Cardassian peace treaty (established in "Life Support"). They were introduced as well to two more sympathetic Cardassian women (following Mary Crosby's Natima in "Profit and Loss"), which Robert Wolfe

claims is less a matter of softening the Cardassians than it is a way of showing there are "different kinds of Cardassians. At the height of the cold war with the Soviet Union, there were sympathetic scientists, people we could work with and talk to."

Although Jake and Nog got rid of all of Quark's leftover *yamok* sauce in the first season ("Progress"), the Ferengi bartender seems to have a fresh supply for the station's Cardassian guests. They can thank Ira Behr's fondness for names coined by former producer Pete Fields. "Two of the things he gave us were *yamok* sauce and self-sealing stem bolts," smiles Behr. "They're silly names and I like silly names, so every now and then we just like to bring them back."

One of the sets created for the *Defiant* during its maiden year is a generic crew cabin that can serve as quarters for, say, Sisko, Dax, or Bashir. In this episode, it's the cabin where Sisko and Kira go to discuss "the sword of stars" in private. And while it appears at first glance to be a rather limited set, it has a number of possible looks, thanks to three movable (or "wild") walls. "There's only one wall that isn't wild," explains Robert della Santina. "It's the one that includes the doorway. That's a double-faced wall that also serves as part of the corridor." But a director can pull out any of the other walls to give the room any one of three different looks, he says.

For the episode's sword of stars, the prophesied comet, Writers Cohen and Winer consulted with Andre Bormanis to make sure they didn't have the comet do anything out of character. "They knew what a comet was, but they were a little shy on details," recalls Bormanis. "Things like, 'How big is a typical comet? What is it made of? How do they travel

Yarka's prophecy forces Sisko to examine his role in the Bajoran faith.
ROBBIE ROBINSON

through space? And how fast and in what kind of orbit?' And they wanted one sort of unusual effect associated with this comet, so we came up with an invented name of a substance that was found in the comet, the 'maguffin,' as they say."

The comet the visual effects team developed for the episode is a model built by Tony Meininger, and not a computer-generated image, as one might think. The artistic challenge, according to Gary Hutzel, was determining what the inside of a comet looks like. "A lot of people describe a comet as a big chunk of dirty ice," he says, "so we took it that way. It had a rocklike surface but the inside was transparent, like ice or crystal."

Hutzel also reveals that the episode's all-important transmitter is actually the solar observatory from *Star Trek Generations*. "In the feature, it has extremely long extensions on it," says Hutzel. "So basically, I took a saw to it! We cut off the extensions and redesigned a couple of elements and did a new paint job."

The "fiery trial" prophecy that Yarka begins to tell Sisko at the end of the episode is actually Cohen and Winer's original prophecy from their first draft.

A non-profit–driven Grand Nagus Zek, reshaped by the wormhole aliens, horrifies the traditional, profit-driven Ferengi Quark and Rom.
DANNY FELD

PROPHET MOTIVE

Episode #462

WRITTEN BY IRA STEVEN BEHR & ROBERT HEWITT WOLFE
DIRECTED BY RENE AUBERJONOIS

GUEST CAST

Rom	MAX GRODÉNCHIK
Emi	JULIANA DONALD
Maihar'du	TINY RON
Medical Big Shot	BENNET GUILLORY

AND

Zek	WALLACE SHAWN

STARDATE UNKNOWN

Quark is in heaven—figuratively speaking, that is. He's about to make a killing on the sale of some self-sealing stem bolts and enjoy his *oo-mox*, too. Suddenly the Grand Nagus Zek and Zek's servant, Maihar'du, pay him a visit. Before he knows it, the pair have moved into his quarters, displacing Quark to his brother Rom's messy quarters. After holing up at Quark's for some time, Zek reveals that he's been rewriting the Ferengi Rules of Acquisition, and he invites Quark and Rom to be the first to read them.

To their horror, they discover that Zek has revised the rules to reflect qualities of kindness and generosity, rather than the traditional Ferengi virtues of profit and greed. Initially they assume that the new rules are part of a clever money-making scheme the nagus has contrived. They soon find out he's serious about them—serious enough to tell Quark's client where she can purchase self-sealing stem bolts at a much lower price than Quark was asking!

Elsewhere on the station, Dr. Bashir is startled by the news that he has been nominated for the Carrington Award, a highly prestigious award presented yearly by the Federation Medical Council. Although his friends expect Bashir to be thrilled, the doctor is anything but, since he knows his chances of winning are nil; the award generally goes to recipients for a lifetime of medical achievement. Thus, the waiting period before the awards are announced is akin to slow torture, with Bashir being the uncomfortable recipient of friendly teasing by Dax, O'Brien, and even Odo. When the winner finally is announced, losing is a relief.

In the meantime, Quark grows more and more worried about the nagus, who has established something called the Ferengi Benevolent Association, with Rom as senior administrator of the project. With all his talk of "moving beyond greed," Quark fears there is something seriously wrong with the nagus, something that will get him killed by Ferenginar's bewildered populace when he returns home to announce his New Rules of Acquisition.

At Quark's request, Bashir examines Zek, but can

find no medical clues to his change of behavior. Not long after, Zek reveals that he plans to present a gift to the Bajoran people. Since he won't tell Quark what the gift is, the bartender and his brother break into Zek's personal shuttle to find out for themselves. They discover one of the missing Orbs of the Bajoran Prophets, and when Quark is exposed to the sacred object, the vision he experiences makes everything clear. The new rules didn't originate in Zek's mind; they came from the wormhole aliens, who have somehow transformed the nagus into this new enlightened variety of Ferengi. But when would Zek have been in communication with the aliens?

After perusing Zek's personal logs, Quark concludes that the nagus had initally gone to the wormhole with thoughts of making use of the aliens' ability to see the future, thus allowing him to anticipate economic changes throughout the galaxy. Obviously, something went wrong, and Quark realizes that he must get to the bottom of the situation if Ferengi society is to continue along its normal course. So he kidnaps the nagus and takes him back to the wormhole to confront its occupants.

The wormhole aliens tell Quark that their encounter with Zek disturbed them; they found his goals adversarial and aggressive. However, in examining his species' history, they discovered that the Ferengi were not always so, and they "restored" him to an earlier, less adversarial state of existence. When Quark protests this action, the aliens threaten to do the same to him. Quark manages to convince them that if they restore the nagus to his original profit-hungry self, he and all other Ferengi will leave them alone. The aliens agree, and Zek is returned to normal. When the pair return to the station, every last copy of the revised Rules of Acquisition is destroyed, and the Ferengi way of life is saved.

Actor Rene Auberjonois always will remember "Prophet Motive" as the episode in which he went from being a DIT to a full-fledged director of hour-long television drama. He'd started the ball rolling some four months earlier, at the beginning of *DS9*'s third season, when he approached Rick Berman and expressed interest in becoming a DIT (the tongue-in-cheek acronym for *Star Trek*'s unofficial "director in training" program, coined by David Livingston).

"Rick was incredibly supportive, and from that time on, I proceeded to go to production meetings and editing, casting, and dubbing sessions," says

The well-rehearsed interactions between Shimerman and Grodénchik made Rene Auberjonois's first-time directing a joy. DANNY FELD

Auberjonois. "I watched the whole process, and talked to the directors at length."

Auberjonois was not exactly a neophyte; he'd had experience directing theatrical productions and had even directed some sitcoms, but never a film production (as opposed to the video medium used on many sitcoms), and never a one-hour drama. So he was hesitant when Berman ran into him a few months later and asked, "So, are you ready?"

"I said, 'Uh, uh, uh, no, not yet,'" recalls Auberjonois. But when Berman called him a few weeks later and said, "I think it's time to put you in," he accepted the challenge, and by the luck of the draw, was assigned to "Prophet Motive."

"It was a wonderful show to start with for a lot of reasons, key among them Armin and Max," he says. Unlike some of the other actors in the series, who prefer to be spontaneous in their performances, Armin Shimerman and Max Grodénchik like to rehearse their scenes together. "That really suited a novice director like me," says Auberjonois. "They gave me unlimited access to themselves. We came in

As the actors see it, without all the wizardry of visual effects. ROBBIE ROBINSON

on weekends and rehearsed on the sets, so that when filming began, the scenes were already totally rehearsed and ready to go."

"A glorious experience," confirms Shimerman. "We worked everything out and we were solid, all three of us. We were all in harmony. That's the beauty of rehearsal: the richness you can get from working together with extra time so that you can develop something good."

Some of the richness came through in the bits of business they worked out together, as with Rom following the path of Quark's finger, as Quark describes being thrown from the Temple of Commerce. Some of it came through in Auberjonois's whimsical staging, for example, framing the two brothers in the large oval window of Quark's quarters, while Rom reads from the revised Rules of Acquisition. The script had suggested that Rom was seated in the middle of the floor while Quark paced around him, but the onstage rehearsal sessions had allowed Auberjonois to spot a better visual.

"I began to envision the scene as a Maxfield Parrish illustration," says Auberjonois. "I've always found the Ferengi, although they can be quite grotesque, to be like fairy-tale characters." And indeed, placing the two gremlinlike brothers in front of the window with the large book made it look, as Shimerman comments, "like a picture from some children's book, with two trolls sitting on a moon somewhere, because of all the stars behind us. A beautiful shot."

Auberjonois had to fight for those stars. "The starfield behind that window was not one that moved," he explains. One of the unwritten laws of *Star Trek* filming is that you never place a stationary camera in front of a window that looks out into space, unless the stars are moving. It's one of the little touches that give all *Star Trek* series a subliminal feeling of "reality." "It was the only time that I said, 'I have to have that!'" says Auberjonois, "and they built a moving starfield for that window."

Auberjonois did stick to the tried and true for other scenes, however, particularly Quark's Orb trip. "I screened 'Emissary' frame by frame," he says. "It was the first time that we'd gone back to the wormhole with an Orb, and I felt it was my responsibility to evoke [Director] David Carson's wonderful sequence as much as I could."

That meant going back into the "white limbo"—type of lighting and sets that Carson and Marvin Rush had worked out two years earlier. Jonathan West overexposed the action by several stops and used diffusion filters "so that the white bleeds across the image, giving you this sense of being in a fog."

The Visual Effects Department also had to emulate the look of sequences created for "Emissary" by Rob Legato's effects team, according to "Prophet Motive"'s Visual Effects Coordinator David Takemura. "All of those shots in the wormhole fantasy sequences are actually composites," he says. "Each individual shot consists of an out-of-focus layer and then a clean version of the shot mixed on top of the out-of-focus layer." Takemura explains that the composite causes certain elements, say the highlights on a person's face, to bloom out as though they were overexposed.

In some cases, an exact match with scenes in "Emissary" wasn't possible. The path of Quark's flight into the interior of the wormhole in the Ferengi shuttle could have been precisely matched to that of Sisko's runabout in the pilot, except that the motion control data had been lost. So Glenn Neufeld's team used videotape references to program the Ferengi shuttle into the shot.

Animator Adam Howard provided a variety of contributions to the visual effects sequences. They range from painting the light elements that stream from the Orb whenever Quark opens its cabinet to helping convince the audience that Zek's head was floating in the cabinet for one gag.

Although the episode seems quintessentially *Deep Space Nine*, with its Ferengi-oriented notions of greed being the prime motivator in the galaxy, its origins are surprisingly Earth-bound. They can trace their roots back to a spec script penned by Ira Behr years ago to impress Hollywood producers with his writing abilities. Behr's uncommissioned script, titled "Uncle Sylvester," was an episode of the comedy series *Taxi*, coincidentally another Paramount show. "Sylvester was Louie's uncle," waxes Behr fondly, "a con man whom Louie idolized and had built his whole life around, the biggest SOB womanizer of all time. And he was coming to visit Louie, who was dying to impress his uncle by doing every nasty, vicious thing he could think of. Sylvester comes and he's a changed man; he's had a revelation and all he wants is to get back with his wife. Louie is so disappointed; the man who set him on this path has gone off it, and Louie doesn't know what anything is about anymore."

If you substitute Louie for Quark, it's not hard to see the relationship between the two scripts. Behr notes that he never sold the *Taxi* episode or worked on a sitcom.

Ironically, many of the changes that Zek was prepared to set into motion on Ferenginar were only temporarily delayed by Quark's trip into the wormhole. By Season 6, Quark's mother, Ishka, would push Zek's thoughts into that direction, and this time there was nothing Quark could do to stop the tides of change.

In a strange way, the inspiration for the B-story about Bashir's nomination for the Carrington Award also sprang from a television series sister show: *The Next Generation*.

"We wanted to do a show about Bashir knowing he wasn't going to get an award," says Robert Hewitt Wolfe, who cowrote the episode with Behr. "Not because he doesn't deserve it, but because it's the kind of award they only give to someone at the end of his career. So he's sitting there going, 'I'm not going to get it.' But everyone on the station gets involved with whether he'll win or not, and talks him up and gets him sort of starting to wonder if it might be possible . . ."

The storyline, Wolfe confesses, was a staff in-joke related to the nomination of *Star Trek: The Next Generation* for an Emmy Award as best dramatic series in its seventh and final year. "Everyone knew that *TNG* was not going to win," says Wolfe. "It's not the kind of show they usually give awards to.

"Everybody thought *NYPD Blue* was going to get it. Everyone on staff was certain *Star Trek* would not get it. And then at some point they began to convince themselves that maybe it actually would."

The anticipation lasted to the bitter end. The envelope was opened. There was that split-second pause before the name was announced, and then the heart-pounding realization that it wasn't *NYPD Blue*. But it wasn't *TNG*, either—it was *Picket Fences*.

Tied in with the B-story was the introduction of a brand new pastime for Bashir and O'Brien: darts. Although they start out playing the game in a cargo bay, they would soon move the board to Quark's. Either locale was cheaper than a return to the holosuite handball court created for "Rivals." "We couldn't go back there because it was too expensive," explains Behr. "And we'd heard that a pool table was going to be used on *Voyager*, which was our first choice. And they'd already done cards [on *TNG*]. So what was something that two guys could do and talk while they're doing it?" Given the options, darts seemed the best choice. The fact that the pair were both from the British Isles, where the pastime is a favorite in pubs, was icing on the cake.

Darts at last headed Bashir and O'Brien down the road to friendship that Behr had foreseen from the beginning, although the extent to which it facilitated their bonding surprised Siddig El Fadil. "We had no idea at that point that darts would turn the relationship into this extraordinary camaraderie," he says. "It's quite fun, and mischievously so, because it's one of the only places an Irishman and an Englishman would get on so well: in space, in the twenty-fourth century."

Darts also opened the door for an extra named James Lomas, who went from a one day stand-in job on the series to a semiregular role as *DS9*'s official darts advisor. Generally, when you see a dart hit the board at Quark's, it's been tossed by Lomas (or Lomas's back-up, Shawn McConnell, who fills in when Lomas gets booked for extras' work on other shows).

VISIONARY

Episode #463

TELEPLAY BY **JOHN SHIRLEY**
STORY BY **ETHAN H. CALK**
DIRECTED BY **REZA BADIYI**

G U E S T C A S T

Ruwon	JACK SHEARER
Karina	ANNETTE HELDE
Morka	RAY YOUNG
Bo'rak	BOB MINOR
Atul	DENNIS MADALONE

S T A R D A T E U N K N O W N

When an accident gives O'Brien a mild case of radiation poisoning, the engineer agrees to follow Bashir's advice and take it easy for a few days. However, the next few days are to be anything but relaxing.

A Romulan delegation arrives at the station to study intelligence reports on the Dominion—part of the arrangement for allowing the Federation to use a Romulan cloaking device on the *Defiant*. Sisko asks Odo to step up security for a while, in order to avoid any trouble while the Romulans are around. In the meantime, following doctor's orders, O'Brien heads to Quark's to play a game of darts. However, in the midst of the game, he finds himself transported to a different part of the station, where he sees a duplicate of himself talking to Quark. Before he can say a word

A case of radiation poisoning sends O'Brien on a series of leaps into the future, including one where he finds himself in the middle of a brawl. ROBBIE ROBINSON

to the pair, O'Brien finds himself back in the bar, where he doubles over in pain.

Bashir examines the chief and pronounces both the "hallucination" and the pain to be normal side effects of radiation poisoning. But some five hours later, O'Brien finds himself engaged in the same conversation with Quark that he had witnessed during his hallucination. What's more, he sees *himself* standing on the other side of the Promenade, where he recalls he initially observed the exchange. Dax determines that O'Brien's exposure to the radiation could have caused him to experience a temporal shift. But even as she comes up with the theory, O'Brien experiences another timeshift, and finds himself in the middle of a brawl between the Romulans and some Klingons at Quark's.

When O'Brien returns to his normal time, Bashir examines him again and determines that the timeshifts are a threat to the engineer's life. Some five hours later, O'Brien is at Quark's, awaiting the events that he foresaw in his vision. Sure enough, a group of Klingons arrive and instigate a fight with the Romulans in the bar. O'Brien finds himself engaged in the brawl, and sees his past self appear in time to help him out in the fight, and then vanish. Then, seconds later, the present O'Brien experiences another shift, this time to a corridor on the station, where he seems to be investigating a wall panel. To his horror, he sees his future self killed by a blast from a phaser device that has been hidden in the wall.

When he returns to the present time, he leads Sisko and Odo to the panel, but they find nothing. However, Dax has found something: the presence of low-level tetryon emissions on the station. The emissions seem to be interacting with the radiation in O'Brien's system and causing the time jumps. The source of the emissions, though, is a mystery. While Bashir attempts to neutralize the remaining radiation in O'Brien's body, Kira reveals that she has moved the Romulans to new quarters, right near the wall panel O'Brien pointed out. That explains the potential sabotage, but not who will commit it. It could be the Klingons *or* the Romulans. A short time later, the weapon appears behind the wall panel; Odo suspects that the Klingons, who wish to spy on the Romulans, are the culprits.

With the discovery of the device, it seems as if O'Brien has avoided the death he foresaw, but suddenly he shifts forward in time to find himself viewing his own dead body in the Infirmary. Fortunately, he also encounters the future Bashir, who gives him medical information to pass on to the Bashir of O'Brien's correct time frame. When O'Brien returns, the information allows Bashir to prevent O'Brien's imminent death. By this time, Dax has determined that the source of the tetryon emissions is a quantum singularity that is orbiting the station, periodically affecting the radiation in O'Brien's body. Seconds later, O'Brien shifts again, and finds himself aboard a crowded runabout that is evacuating personnel from the station. As the future O'Brien tries to fill him in on the little he knows about the situation, the present O'Brien sees DS9 explode and the wormhole collapse.

Realizing that there is only one way to get to the truth of the situation before the station explodes, O'Brien volunteers to use a device that will send him on a more controlled trip into the future; unfortunately it may also give him a potentially lethal dose of radiation if he doesn't return in time. Leaping three hours into the future, O'Brien joins forces with his future self to unravel the mystery. They quickly discover that the quantum singularity orbiting the station is the warp core of a cloaked Romulan warbird that will attack and destroy the station. If O'Brien can return to the past and convey this information, they'll be able to protect the station. But the radiation has taken its toll; O'Brien is too ill to make the return trip. He gets his future self to take the timeshifting device and return to the past in his place.

After O'Brien fills Sisko in, the commander deduces the rest. The Romulans had been planning to destroy the wormhole to prevent the Dominion from entering the Alpha Quadrant. Knowing Sisko would never allow this to happen, they'd also planned to destroy

the station. But now that Sisko knows the truth, the attack will never take place. Foiled, the Romulans depart, and the "future" O'Brien resigns himself to being the "present" O'Brien.

 A complicated episode on every front, "Visionary" bent a few rules, made more than a few people crazy and had the biggest explosion you didn't ever quite see.

The episode began with a pitch that René Echevarria took from Texas schoolteacher Ethan Calk (who also would pitch a story for "Children of Time"). "It struck me as a very different, clever science fiction premise with a twist," says Echevarria, "a story that had a nice built-in clock element."

Ira Behr thought the teleplay might be suited to the skills of a friend who was well-versed in complicated science fiction concepts, author John Shirley. "He hadn't written for television, and he wanted to take a shot at it," says Behr. He warned his friend, "You're gonna hate it by the time it's done, and let's hope you don't hate me as well." Although the two are still friends, Behr says he was right on at least one count. "I won't say it was the most pleasant experience he ever had in his career," Behr concludes.

While the general feeling is that Shirley did a nice job of keeping what could have been an extremely confusing plot clear and comprehensible, Behr was not entirely happy with the episode. "It was good, but it seems like a show that could have been done on *TNG*."

And this is a bad thing?

Typical of the directions provided in the script, "Future O'Brien sits bolt upright. Future O'Brien nods, then takes a closer look at the obviously ill Past O'Brien. They both frown at this confusing notion." ROBBIE ROBINSON

The natural home for a dart board—Quark's bar. ROBBIE ROBINSON

gone to the trouble of hollowing out a space inside the wall for the object and then used a very carefully tuned transporter beam to get it there," says Bormanis. However, the idea that someone had modified a replicator to accomplish the job was a bit more of a stretch.

"It wouldn't be a simple modification," Bormanis observes, "because one of the things we've established about replicators is that they have only molecular level resolution. You can replicate simple objects, such as food, very easily, but replicating objects of real complexity requires what we call quantum-level resolution, because your copy has to be perfect. You have to go beyond molecular level, right down to the last little quantum or quark of whatever it's made of." Because replicators don't have that level of sophistication, it would take quite a technician to complete the upgrade. The level of skill required to realign the matter-energy conversion matrix is fleetingly covered in Odo's observation that the culprit had performed a "very sophisticated, very professional job," meaning that Atul, Morka, and Bo'rak were obviously smarter than they looked.

Taking technical contrivances to a more personal level, it's no wonder that both versions of Miles O'Brien hate temporal mechanics, since it was the death of one of them. The idea of killing the present O'Brien and replacing him with the future one was reportedly the idea of Ron Moore, part of TNG's writing staff at the time that team considered killing off the familiar William Riker and replacing him with his transporter duplicate ("Second Chances"). This time, the writers decided that the idea of an O'Brien who was identical to the first, with the exception of having a few more hours of experience in our timeline under his belt, wasn't a terrible thing.

The scenes where the two O'Briens interact come across quite convincingly in the completed episode, but they weren't easy, according to Gary Hutzel. "It's always very confusing for the actor," he says, "because although the director and I have extensive discussions, until we arrive on the set, we don't know ourselves exactly what's going to happen."

Colm Meaney's attitude toward the highly technical nature of such sequences is typical of many of the actors. Hutzel says, "Colm is just like, 'Listen, don't explain. Don't explain. Just tell me what to do.'" Nevertheless, he adds, Meaney's performance in the episode worked beautifully.

The biggest effects sequence of the episode, however, didn't involve any cast members, unless you consider the space station itself to be a "regular."

"I prefer our shows be Deep Space Nine–specific. 'Visionary' is kind of a tech mystery, and it's more TNG's kind of show."

Behr is not a big fan of plots that rely heavily on elements like quantum singularities and tetryon particles. "I think that both TNG and Voyager go too far with it," he says, noting that such reliance was one area about which he tended to get into disagreements with Michael Piller. "I really wanted to take the tech out of DS9, and you'll see that in the first two seasons there was a lot more tech than in Season 3 forward." This is when the baton was passed from Piller to Behr as executive producer.

As usual, heavy technical explanations fell to Andre Bormanis, who, in this case, had to devise both a good explanation for why O'Brien was jumping about in time, and how the Klingons managed to beam surveillance equipment into a bulkhead.

The time jumps were relatively simple, a matter of coming up with "a description of what mechanism might allow O'Brien to do what he's doing," says Bormanis. The trigger, exposure to a certain type of radiation, "was a little on the campy side," he admits.

As for the Klingon equipment, there was nothing very implausible about the idea that "somebody had

Blowing up the station, says Hutzel, "was a very, very big deal. We'd decided that the station *had* to blow up, and it *had* to be particularly spectacular. So it was a very elaborate deal."

For the gag, Special Effects Master Gary Monak had Model Maker Tony Meininger pull two new castings from the station's original six-foot mold. The duplicates, Monak says, were very similar to the original in terms of detailing, although they lacked the lighting elements.

"We rigged it so that it would go off in about ten stages: ten separate explosions that had to go off within a half a second," says Monak. The explosions were shot with a high-speed camera at ten to fifteen times normal speed; the half-second multiblast took up five to seven seconds of film. Monak and his partner R. J. Hohman rigged the two models somewhat differently so that they could decide after filming which explosion looked better.

"They think it out just like animation storyboards," comments Judy Elkins. "They're amazing pyrotechnicians."

When questioned as to what goes into such explosions, Monak rattles off assorted ingredients like a chef recounting the soup of the day. "There's a little bit of everything: glitter, black powder, rubber cement, sparkle flash, sometimes a little high explosive primer-cord–type stuff." Although models are often cast out of fiberglass, Monak instructed Meininger to make the two stations out of a brittle plastic, which would be much more breakable (and therefore more spectacular) than fiberglass.

While more and more effects are being rendered via computer graphics these days, explosions are still done live. "You can't get the same effect with a computer," explains Elkins. "You don't get the fireballs, the fire effects, the shards, the pieces flying away. When you're working on a big scale like this, there's nothing like blowing up a big model. It's just beautiful."

By all accounts, the two explosions, filmed on Stage 12, went flawlessly. Unfortunately, the producers ultimately chose to include only a small bit of the station's devastation in the episode's final edit, no doubt disappointing fans of loud, spectacular conflagration.

Fans of continuity, however, were probably pleased with Bashir's choice of hyronalin as an appropriate treatment for radiation poisoning, another tip of the hat to the original series ("The Deadly Years") from Ron Moore. "There's a lot of references from the original series rattling around in my head, because I watched it fanatically as a kid," he says. "Somehow it's easier to remember those references than the stuff I worked on a few years ago on *TNG*."

As noted previously, Bashir and O'Brien's dartboard receives a permanent home at Quark's bar in this episode, which came in handy for some of the episode's plotting. "It gave us a way to establish that O'Brien's time jumps weren't taking any time [in the present]," says Robert Wolfe. "He could throw the dart, go through a five-minute experience in the future, and then return to see the dart hit the wall."

Jack Shearer, who plays the Romulan Ruwon, also played Vadosia in *DS9*'s "The Forsaken." He would return to the *Star Trek* fold in two different parts: as Admiral Hayes in *Star Trek: First Contact,* and as Admiral Strickler in the *Voyager* episode "Non Sequitur."

DISTANT VOICES

Episode #464

TELEPLAY BY **IRA STEVEN BEHR &
ROBERT HEWITT WOLFE**
STORY BY **JOE MENOSKY**
DIRECTED BY **ALEXANDER SINGER**

GUEST CAST

Garak	ANDREW ROBINSON
Altovar	VICTOR RIVERS
Bajoran Nurse	ANN GILLESPIE
Dabo Girl	NICOLE FORESTER

STARDATE UNKNOWN

While lunching with Garak at the Replimat and gloomily pondering his impending thirtieth birthday, Dr. Bashir is approached by a Lethean named Altovar. The threatening-looking alien wishes to purchase some biomimetic gel, a restricted substance. Bashir refuses to provide the gel, pointing out that its sale is prohibited in the Federation. Later, Bashir finds Altovar ransacking his Infirmary and attempts to apprehend him, but the Lethean renders Bashir unconscious with an electrical discharge.

When Bashir revives, he finds that his hair is turning gray, and the station is dark and apparently deserted, with few of its systems operational. But the station is not completely abandoned; he hears the sound of distant whispering and periodically runs into his closest acquaintances. The first is Quark, whom he finds cowering behind his bar, terrified of

An aging Bashir has a conversation with different components of his personality, embodied by his friends. ROBBIE ROBINSON

but again Altovar appears. Capturing Sisko, the Lethean tells Bashir that he will kill each part of his personality, leaving the doctor a "withered shell," whom he will then destroy.

Fleeing through the station, the rapidly aging Bashir finds Kira dead and Odo dying. He enlists O'Brien's help, but the pair keep getting sidetracked before they can reach Ops. They wind up at Quark's, where a crowd is betting on how and when Bashir will die. Moments later, O'Brien has died and Quark is killed by the Lethean. Attempting to escape, Bashir falls and breaks his hip. Once again, Garak appears, and despite the Cardassian's continued suggestions that he give up, Bashir convinces him to help him get to Ops.

Now about one hundred years old, Bashir finds Ops decorated for a birthday party: his. But Bashir ignores the party and tries to get to the computer controls while Garak continues to dissuade him. Bashir realizes that Garak actually is the Lethean, but he refuses to give up his struggle to stay alive. He returns to his Infirmary, which, as the center of Bashir's world, is obviously the location from which he must make the repairs. Ignoring the Lethean's threats, Bashir works calmly to restore the various systems, and then to trap and destroy Altovar. After he does so, Bashir revives in the real world, surrounded by his friends.

an unnamed something. When Quark runs off, Bashir attempts to follow, but loses him in the Promenade. In Odo's security office, Bashir finds Garak, who offers to help the doctor search the station. The two split up and Bashir explores the habitat ring, where he is stalked by Altovar. He narrowly escapes via a turbolift. When Bashir exits the lift, he encounters Dax, O'Brien, Odo, and Kira, who are engaged in a heated argument.

As he attempts to get a straight answer out of them, Bashir realizes that he's aged some twenty-five years since his first encounter with Altovar, whom the foursome insist is attempting to destroy the station. O'Brien manages to partially repair the communications relay, which can now receive but not send. To Bashir's surprise, the relay is picking up the same whispers that he's been hearing all along. For the first time, he can make out the voices—which turn out to be those of the real crew of DS9, who pronounce that Bashir is in a telepathically induced coma. Worse, if he doesn't revive within three hours, he'll die.

After scanning O'Brien, Kira, Dax, and Odo and failing to pick up any lifesigns, Bashir understands. He is indeed in a coma, and each of his friends represents a different aspect of his personality, while the Lethean attacking the station represents the telepathic damage to Bashir's mind. But just as Bashir reasons that "repairing" the damaged station will allow him to revive in the real world, the Lethean captures Dax. Bashir finds himself back with Garak, who directs the doctor to Ops to repair the damage. On the way, Bashir encounters Sisko, who he hopes will help him,

"**D**istant Voices," originally titled "Too Many Rooms," was another story pitched by DS9's "Italian bureau," aka Joe Menosky. According to Ron Moore, the story sat untouched in the production office for quite some time. "Everyone was terrified of it"—Moore laughs—"because it was insane." In that sense, one might say it was not unlike the writer, whom Moore describes, tongue-in-cheek, as, "A brilliant guy who had gone slowly mad in Europe. Joe is drawn to culturally rich shows with a lot of symbolism," Moore explains. "But here he had circlets of gold on people's heads, and metaphors and symbols from mythology. Everyone was saying, 'What is this show? What are we going to do with this show?'"

There were other problems, notes Robert Wolfe, who cowrote the teleplay with Ira Behr. Menosky's original story didn't utilize the regular cast in Bashir's coma fantasy. Instead, Wolfe says, the archetypal images in Bashir's brain were portrayed by different actors, "So we would meet, say, Bashir's 'youth' and Bashir's 'age' as separate people. As we were fiddling

Westmore's design for the Lethean would be used again in
"The Sword of Kahless." ROBBIE ROBINSON

with the story, Ron Moore came up with the idea of setting it on the station and having our people portray different parts of Bashir's personality. It was a good solution, a way to make a very difficult story work. So Ron figured out how to save it, and Ira and I ended up writing it."

Not that the job was suddenly a piece of cake. "It started as a vague tech mystery," says Behr. But to get the audience into the show, Behr and the others knew they had to reduce the emphasis on tech and turn it into a character piece. "We knew that when we got past all the exposition, there would be enough wacky stuff going on to keep the audience interested," he says.

Moore wrote a memo suggesting that they make the story "Bashir-specific; we can't get lost in the doodads around him." That was fine with Wolfe. "I identify more with Bashir than with any of the other characters on the show," he says. "We're the same height, the same age, and I think that we have some of the same personality traits, in that he's got a lot of insecurity underneath that public persona, despite the fact that he projects a lot of cockiness to the world."

At the time he was working on the episode, Wolfe had just turned thirty. So, as it happens, had Siddig El Fadil. Neither Wolfe nor El Fadil claim the birthday had much impact on them in their personal lives, but both were aware of the fact that thirty is a landmark in some people's lives. "Some things won't change in 350 years," states Wolfe. "Major milestone birthdays will still kind of freak people out."

"It worked out perfectly for me." Siddig smiles.

"[As Bashir] I got to rant and rave about it, which I hadn't done in real life."

But if he didn't have to cope with a single traumatizing day, he did have to put up with, as Behr puts it, "a bitch of a week. With all the makeup, and his being in every scene, Sid had a very tough time. But sometimes the show just called for it."

"I was in everything except one small scene that was just a quarter of a page," Siddig notes. "That's every single moment of the episode except for possibly fifteen seconds. It was hard work, but it gave me a certain degree of control. It's a simpler kind of work than having to wait for other characters to give you what you need so you can react. I quite enjoyed it."

While the burden of effort was on Siddig, the episode still gave some of the other actors interesting challenges. "[Director] Alex Singer said to me, 'You have to be really frightened,'" relays Armin Shimerman. "And I said, 'Well, yes.' And he said, 'No, you don't understand. The other people [in Bashir's mind] can't be frightened. So *you* are the only one the writers will allow me to have be frightened.' So I was really over the top when Quark was cowering under the bar."

Shimerman also took advantage of the unique setup, portraying Quark as a facet of Bashir's personality, to do some different things with his performance. "Later in the episode, when they came back into the bar, I took it upon myself to do Quark with a British sort of accent. The character was inside of Bashir's head, after all, so I made him a lot more suave, a lot more British. It was my attempt to push the envelope on the character."

For Rene Auberjonois, it was not so much a matter of "pushing the envelope," as it was reaching into the past to his theatrical training. For the shot where Bashir finds Odo melting into a big pool on the corridor floor, Auberjonois realized that "this was a place where the actor could help the director. They didn't know how they were going to do the shot, so I suggested sliding. I have a certain amount of mime training, so I was able to make it look like I was melting. We put a pad under my butt so I could slip easily. Then they just erased me as I went down."

The task of "erasing" the actor fell to the staff at VisionArt, under the guidance of Josh Rose, who first animated a "ripple" on the computer and then used an image-processing effect to distort the lower part of Odo's live-action uniform before compositing the ripple over it. "We transitioned the rippling distorted uniform into a computer-graphics goo element that was the color of the uniform, and then transitioned that into another CG element that was just goo colored," says Rose. "We ended up with an animated soft-edged morph that slowly crept up Odo."

Not even optical effects can save sequences that are heavily weighted with dialogue. Such exposition may be necessary, but it can be deadly in the wrong hands. But Ira Behr credits Director Singer with finding a unique way to deal with those scenes. "He brought them to life by keeping the camera moving," says Behr.

"I was intrigued with the show," says Singer. "There's a scene where Bashir walks into the conference room and finds the crew involved in a nasty argument. They proceed to talk, can you believe it, for *five* pages! There was no indication in the script on how to shoot it, so it represented an appalling problem: How do you do five pages of people talking about disagreement?"

With remarkable finesse, Singer choreographed the actors' movements and the camera's movements so that the scene could be done in one long master shot. "We had a flow of images that would never be the same in more than one frame," explains Singer. "The camera had to move very rapidly, to pan very rapidly, and to adjust its frame very rapidly. It was more rapid than a Steadicam's gyroscopic stabilizer would allow, so we made it a handheld shot." With Cinematographer Jonathan West handling the camera, Singer rehearsed the actors "five or six times." Then the actors sat down to continue rehearsing their lines.

"An hour and a half had gone by and not one foot of film had been shot," laughs Singer. "That's unheard of." But with five pages of interacting dialogue, much of which overlaps, Singer realized that such preparation was a dire necessity. "The actors' patience in this was very special," he lauds the group.

Finally the film was rolling. "We did five or six takes," Singer recalls. "Some of those takes went almost to the end of the sequence and then collapsed. I knew that [in the editing process] I would cut away to a close-up of Sid from time to time, but I wanted one perfect master for the whole shot. We got it about the fifth try."

Singer is justifiably proud of the shot, despite the fact that it probably went unnoticed by the majority of viewers. "That scene probably took longer than anything that I have done for any of the *Star Trek* shows," Singer says. "I've since used it as an illustration to my classes in editing and film directing. It's a tour de force."

Jonathan West also did something with the

The writers felt that Garak would be the persona the Lethean would assume in order to mislead Bashir. ROBBIE ROBINSON

lighting that he never had done before on *DS9*. "I turned everything off," West says, including the ambient lighting that is permanently installed on the Promenade set. "We started with a black stage, and then I went in and put individual lights around pillars and corners," notes West. "I lit it only with white and blue."

The results surprised even the experienced cinematographer. "There are some warm coppery tones in the set that we never really see. When we lit it with this raking light, all of a sudden the whole Promenade took on a completely different quality. I didn't know it was going to look like that when we first started out. It caught me off guard." Predictably, the special look also took longer to light. "It was the most time-consuming episode," West observes, "because we couldn't just say, 'Turn on that bank of lights over there.' The only thing still on was the starfield."

Makeup also was an area that took more time than usual. "Getting the aging makeup worked out for Bashir became a scheduling problem," says Steve Oster. "He was four different ages on the show and some of those ages took three hours to create. We tried to shoot all of his similarly aged scenes on the same day, but they occurred on different soundstages. So we had to weigh losing an hour out of the day by moving the crew to a different soundstage, versus changing the makeup."

"Three hours!" recalls El Fadil with a shiver. "I never want to have prosthetics again. I don't know what the other actors do to deal with it, but they

Evolution of a Supporting Character

Max Grodénchik on Rom's incredible journey

Actor Max Grodénchik has appeared throughout the seven seasons of *Deep Space Nine* as Rom. Grodénchik was one of the originators of the Ferengi in two episodes of *The Next Generation*. He has performed in productions from television's *Doogie Howser, M.D.* and *thirtysomething*. His feature film work includes *The Rocketeer* and *Apollo 13*.

"When this series started," says Max Grodénchik, "Rom had no prospects. He was under his brother's thumb. He had no real sense of self, and he felt that he was a failure as a Ferengi. He was frightened, a scared little guy. But with the influence of all the different races that have come through the station—the Bajorans, the humans, the Klingons, and so on—he began to think about other ways of life and to reshape his own. He began to stick up for his son and then for himself, and to separate what was important to him in life, and what wasn't. And he developed to a point where he wanted to share with someone else. He fell in love and married Leeta and felt worthwhile.

"I think it all began back in Season 1, when Rom returned a purse and Quark asked, 'Why did you do that? The First Rule of Acquisition says once you have their money, you never give it back.' But it made sense to Rom. He was trying to do a good thing, the right thing. And somehow that led him to the point where the guy who felt less like a Ferengi than any other Ferengi was suddenly head of the Ferengi Alliance!

"It's just like an American kid wanting to grow up to be President. I'm sure every Ferengi boy wants to grow up to be the grand nagus. If you're an American kid and somewhere along the line you start getting bad grades, you tell yourself, 'Well, maybe I'll just settle for being a fireman.' Your dreams get whittled down over the years. So I'm sure for Rom it's the last thing he ever expected. It's just been an amazing journey!

"Over the years, I've tried to outguess the writers. I've tried to imagine what's next for Rom, and think of what's best for Rom. But they always come up with something better than I could ever imagine. I certainly can't complain and I've learned that maybe it's not my job to think about it. I should just leave it to the Blessed Exchequer!"

---

manage. I hated it entirely. It was the most horrific experience of my life."

The horror was worthwhile, though. The episode won an Emmy Award for makeup. "I think that the old-age makeup was the selling card to winning," says Michael Westmore, "Although Altovar, the Lethean, was really interesting because his makeup was different from anything we had ever done before."

As is all too typical when creating a new alien, Westmore got his information about Altovar very late

in the schedule. "Because of last-minute casting, I didn't have time for sketches, so the headpiece is converted from another alien. I would have needed about three days to build a mold of his entire head, and I didn't have three days. I had one sculptor doing the hands, one doing a separate thumb on the hands, another doing the face, and a fourth doing the lower part of the face on a separate mold. The rubber literally was coming out of the oven and going right to the set." Westmore sighs in resignation. "It'd be wonderful to have the luxury of knowing about things soon enough to be able to sit around twiddling your thumbs."

One subtle bit of makeup magic is employed in a scene in the Infirmary. It's unlikely that even the sharpest eyes can tell that O'Brien, lying dead on a gurney, isn't actually Colm Meaney. For the scene, the actor, who had the afternoon off, was replaced by a life mask of O'Brien (provided by the makeup department) and a dummy of O'Brien (provided by the wardrobe department).

The moody atmosphere created by the script and West's lighting inspired Composer Dennis McCarthy to write what he terms "a very dark score. It was such an 'out there' show that it called for really 'out there' music. So I got experimental with it, very twentieth-century, with (Hungarian minimalist composer) Ligeti sorts of sounds and a (contemporary Polish composer) Penderecki sort of thinking. And then, just to break it up because it was so dark, when the tennis balls flew out of the storage compartments, I actually played a little humor."

The tennis balls were one of the few humorous elements in the episode, along with the sexy dabo girl. "At the end of the story break we started thinking about Marilyn Monroe singing 'Happy Birthday' to JFK," says Ira Behr. "We said, 'What's in the mind of Julian Bashir?' Well, the mind's a chaotic thing, and we've always played Julian as a bit of a rake, so we felt we needed a pretty woman. At such a serious moment, a life-and-death moment, it was nice juxtaposition."

Credit Robert Wolfe's wife Celeste for resolving a gaffe that may have bothered medically minded viewers as much as it bothered her. "Celeste was pre-vet," notes Wolfe. "And every time she saw 'Emissary' or heard Bashir's line about mistaking a pre-ganglionic fiber for a post-ganglionic nerve, she'd say, 'They're nothing like each other! No one would make that mistake!'"

This was, of course, before anyone knew that the mistake was symptomatic of Bashir's lifelong struggle to hide his genetic enhancement. Nevertheless, Wolfe, via Altovar, introduced the suggestion that the then-medical student had intentionally missed the question in his final exams because he didn't want to be number one in his class. "Altovar is correct," says Wolfe. "That's my way of saying, 'Well, okay,' to Celeste."

IMPROBABLE CAUSE
Episode #465

TELEPLAY BY RENÉ ECHEVARRIA
STORY BY ROBERT LEDERMAN & DAVID R. LONG
DIRECTED BY AVERY BROOKS

GUEST CAST

Garak	ANDREW ROBINSON
Retaya	CARLOS LaCAMARA
Informant	JOSEPH RUSKIN
Romulan	DARWYN CARSON
Mila	JULIANNA McCARTHY

AND

Enabran Tain	PAUL DOOLEY

STARDATE UNKNOWN

After hurrying through a lunchtime meal with Garak, Bashir pauses to talk to Kira before returning to the Infirmary. Seconds later, the two respond to an explosion on the Promenade. Garak's shop has been completely destroyed, although the tailor himself is unharmed.

The incident appears to be the result of an accident, but Odo points out that no incident concerning Garak should be taken at face value. Sure enough, they soon find proof that the explosion was caused by a bomb, and that the bomb's triggering device is of a type known to be favored by Flaxians. As there just happens to be a Flaxian on the station, Odo now has a suspect. But talking to the Flaxian reveals nothing, and Garak is similarly uncooperative about suggesting a motive for the botched assassination attempt.

Lunch with Garak is part of Dr. Bashir's daily ritual.
ROBBIE ROBINSON

Garak's decision to rejoin Enabran Tain leaves Odo in an uncomfortable position. DANNY FELD

Hoping to increase the Cardassian's cooperation, Odo gives the Flaxian permission to leave the station and cancels the security detail that has been protecting Garak. When Odo boards a runabout to track the Flaxian, he finds Garak waiting for him, anxious to participate in the chase. But the Flaxian ship blows up soon after they initiate their pursuit, and they return to the station.

The clues behind the second explosion point to the Romulans, who Odo surmises may have hired the Flaxian to kill Garak in the first place. But why would Romulans want to kill Garak? When queried, members of the Romulan Tal Shiar group admit to having executed the Flaxian, who was wanted for crimes against their empire. However, they claim to know nothing about the Flaxian's attempt to kill Garak.

Odo resorts to contacting a Cardassian informant for answers. The informant believes that the attempt on Garak's life is a very small piece of a larger puzzle. In recent weeks, Romulan ships have been gathering at the Cardassian border, possibly in preparation for an invasion. What's more, Garak isn't the only former operative in Cardassia's Obsidian Order to have been the victim of a recent assassination attempt; five others perished the same day that Garak's shop blew up.

Returning to the station, Odo confronts Garak with his theory that the tailor blew up his own shop when he saw the Flaxian assassin on the station, knowing that Odo would launch an investigation. Garak admits that both he and the five dead operatives were all associates of Enabran Tain, the former leader of the Obsidian Order. Garak doesn't know

why the Romulans might want all of them dead, but Tain might know.

Garak attempts to contact Tain, but learns that his former boss abruptly left his home a day earlier. Concerned, Garak asks Odo for a runabout. Odo agrees to give him the runabout, but only if he accompanies the tailor. Once under way, Garak directs Odo toward a planet near the Cardassian border, where he knows Tain has a safe house. But before they arrive, they are intercepted and captured by a Romulan warbird. On board the vessel, they are brought before Tain, who reveals that it was he who ordered the attempt on Garak's life.

Confidently, Tain tells the pair that the Tal Shiar and the Obsidian Order have joined forces to take a fleet of warships into the Gamma Quadrant, and stage a first-strike attack against the Founders, the power behind the Dominion. Because Tain plans to come out of retirement after he eliminates the Founders, he felt it necessary to get rid of his former associates, all of whom knew things that could be used against him.

After Garak points out that he came looking for Tain in order to save him, Tain offers his former protégé the opportunity to join him in his moment of glory. Despite Odo's warnings about Tain's deceptive nature, Garak jumps at the chance, leaving Odo to face an uncertain fate at the hands of the coalition that would destroy his people.

Like a number of other *DS9* episodes, "Improbable Cause" sprang from the imagination of a writer who was inspired by an event in an earlier episode. Film Editor Robert Lederman, a veteran of *TNG* who'd moved to *DS9* with "Emissary," recalls that while he was working on editing "Second Skin," he spotted an idea for a Garak story. "There was a scene at the end where Garak shot a guy from the Obsidian Order," says Lederman, "and as I was sitting there working on it, I thought, 'The Cardassians can't just let him live in exile without any problems.'"

Lederman and his writing partner David R. Long quickly devised a story about the Cardassians' retaliation against Garak. "In our original pitch," notes Lederman, "Garak felt that someone was trying to assassinate him, so he blew up his tailor shop himself." Lederman and Long's story didn't involve the character of Enabran Tain, the intriguing Cardassian introduced in the previous season's "The Wire." "That came from the writing staff," admits Lederman.

But only after Lederman's pitch lit a fire under

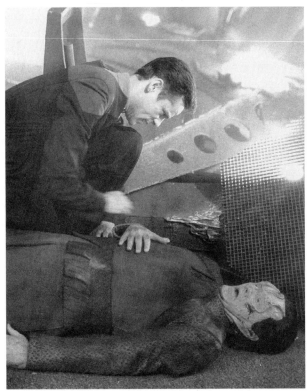

As the personification of an enigma wrapped in a riddle, Garak offered many possibilities to the writers. ROBBIE ROBINSON

them. "We all immediately sparked to the idea of Garak blowing up his own shop," says René Echevarria, who wrote the teleplay for "Improbable Cause." "We all said, 'Why would he do that?'"

As they discussed Garak's potential motivation, the producers, like Lederman, came up with a plot-point touched upon earlier in the season, this time in "Defiant." In that episode, they'd established that the Obsidian Order was involved in a military buildup so covert that even Cardassia's Central Command was unaware of it. And they'd left the purpose of that buildup a mystery. Was that a deliberate move?

Well, no. "I can't say that when we did 'Defiant' we knew we were going to do this," Echevarria admits. "We had a vague idea of a first strike, but I don't think we knew more than that. When the idea for this Garak show came up, we said, 'Why not? Why not make it that?'"

The staff broke a new story and Echevarria completed the first four acts. But Act 5 proved especially elusive, with a weak denouement totally dependent upon the opening scene of Act 4, where Echevarria had Garak leave a "damning piece of information" with Dr. Bashir. In this early draft, Garak said, "Doctor, behind a panel in my quarters is an isolinear rod. If I don't come back, tell Sisko about it." As it originally

worked, Act 5 found Odo and Garak trapped on the Romulan warbird, where Garak wound up telling Tain, "If you don't let us go, the information [in the isolinear rod] will be released."

"That's all they had," sighs Echevarria. "And Tain goes, 'Oh, damn.' That's kind of an old gag, and that's what the show had built to. It was terribly anticlimactic."

But weak as it was, it was the only device the staff writers could come up with that would safely get Odo out of that room on the warbird. "Everything we tried was just a writer's device or a cliché or a convenience or a cheat," notes Ronald D. Moore.

That's when Michael Piller, serving for the last time as executive producer on the series, came to the rescue. "Michael said, 'Don't get Odo out of the room,'" says Moore. "'Keep him there and go fight the Dominion, and make up a second part.'"

"We'd painted ourselves into a corner so far that we had to kick out the wall behind us in order to get out." Moore laughs. "We'd really never done that before. It was frightening." Aside from creative concerns, the decision to go to a second part triggered some technical complications. "We were already in prep on 'Improbable Cause' and the sets were being built when Michael approved the idea to leave Odo on the ship," says Moore. At the same time, he notes, Ira Behr and Robert Wolfe were wrapping up the script for "Through the Looking Glass," which was scheduled to go into production as soon as "Improbable Cause" was completed. It was clearly too late in the production schedule to insert the newly green-lighted "Improbable Cause, Part II" in between the two.

"'Through the Looking Glass' was getting ready to go," says Moore. "So we talked to postproduction and asked them if we could shoot the episodes out of sequence and then flop the airdate order." This is somewhat more complicated than changing a few dates on the call sheets. It necessitates asking guest actors like Paul Dooley to work a day one week (for Part I), and then hold his schedule open to return nearly three weeks later (for Part II). The Fates, however, were kind. Moore notes that the next obvious question became, "Where does the story go now?"

"We needed to make sure that Part I set up Part II," explains Echevarria. "So Ron and I very quickly rewrote Acts 4 and 5 of 'Improbable Cause,' and then Ron moved on to write 'The Die is Cast.'" Some of the rewritten material took on new life. For example, the once-clichéd conversation referring to the isolinear rod in Garak's quarters was reconfigured as a sly joke the Cardassian plays on Bashir ("If I don't return

Garak's unwavering support of Tain, despite everything, created a mystery that would not be solved until the fifth season. DANNY FELD

within seventy-eight hours, I want you to take that rod and eat it."). The fact that the revised scene works naturally as a bit of humorous by-play between the two characters is fortuitous; there was no time to rewrite it from scratch.

By this time, the writers had figured out why Garak had blown up his own shop—and they'd also found a clever way to explain it. Despite the fact that Garak enjoys mocking Bashir when the doctor relates Aesop's famous fable about "The Boy Who Cried Wolf," he can't deny that the truth behind the fable is exactly why he blew up the tailor shop. Garak, the consummate liar, couldn't simply ask for Odo's help when he knew his life was in danger."You couldn't be sure that I'd take you seriously," the security chief concludes. Although the writing staff considered putting Odo's revelation that he knew Garak's motives in Part II, "it just leapt out and worked in that scene [in Part I]," says Echevarria.

Not that the Cardassian would admit that he'd learned anything from his experience. "I don't think Garak was all that interested, at that point, in keeping his lies straight," Ira Behr states seriously. "The thing with him was just to keep bobbing and weaving."

"Improbable Cause" marks the appearance of some new Tal Shiar uniforms. "That was a personal crusade of mine," asserts Ron Moore. "I hated, underline hated, the Romulan costumes. Big shoulder pads, the quilting, I just loathed it. I begged, insisted, screamed, pleaded." It's not that Robert Blackman was in love with the square-shouldered uniforms. His predecessor, William Theiss, had come up with them for the first season of *TNG*. When Blackman later stepped

into Theiss's role on that series, "I was happy not to have to design something, because they were already made," he says. "Of course we've made tons of the original square-shouldered costumes since then, and we still have about fifteen of them [in storage]."

For this episode, notes Blackman, "we made eight new Tal Shiar uniforms. We used the same fabric [as the old ones], but we dyed it down slightly, and then we made them much sleeker and a little more menacing."

The planned destruction of Garak's shop brought Herman Zimmerman and the Art Department to the front lines. "We needed an explosion and fire," notes Zimmerman, "so we built a special wall for the set." It was this architectural "stand-in," explains Zimmerman, that was used for the actual explosion, "ending up with the melted metal and torn circuitry."

Although they didn't actually blow up the entire set, Garak's shop was completely destroyed in order to shoot the important sequence, explains Gary Monak. His crew began by using an air-mortar so that the overhead camera shot would show the door blowing out, followed by Styrofoam and rubber debris. "We used fireballs and a series of small explosions to make it look big for the camera," he says. "And after we did the initial explosion, we went in and really wrecked the set. We melted things down and then they painted it out so it looked all black."

Of course, this was not the first time Monak had blown up that part of the stage. "In the first year we blew up the schoolroom ["In the Hands of the Prophets"] in that same area," Monak laughs. "They figured out that we could do it safely, so they let us do it again."

Although he couldn't take advantage of an actual fire to light his shots, Jonathan West did take his inspiration from it. "After the initial explosion, we had gas jets set up for the fire effect," he says, "but since fire doesn't give you all the illumination you need, I set up a half-dozen fire flicker boxes. Some of them bounced off of white cards and others were shot direct, and we set some of the boxes to be flickering rhythmically and the others to be inconsistent. That way the boxes gave off a whole variety of impulses."

On the other end of the scale, an absence of light was used to color the mood of the scene in which Odo meets his informant. If you thought the informant's rich voice sounded familiar, you're correct. He was played by Joseph Ruskin, who appeared earlier in the season as the Klingon Tumek in "The House of Quark" and as Galt in the original series episode "The Gamesters of Triskelion."

THROUGH THE LOOKING GLASS

Episode #466

WRITTEN BY **IRA STEVEN BEHR &**
ROBERT HEWITT WOLFE
DIRECTED BY **WINRICH KOLBE**

GUEST CAST

Garak	ANDREW ROBINSON
Jennifer Sisko	FELECIA M. BELL
Rom	MAX GRODÉNCHIK
Cardassian Overseer	JOHN PATRICK HAYDEN
Marauder	DENNIS MADALONE

SPECIAL GUEST STAR

Tuvok	TIM RUSS

STARDATE UNKNOWN

Sisko's trip to the mirror universe pushes him into a difficult relationship with the mirror version of his late wife, Jennifer.
ROBBIE ROBINSON

Sisko is caught off guard when the man he takes to be O'Brien turns out to be the engineer's double from the mirror universe that Kira and Bashir visited a year earlier. The mirror O'Brien transports himself and Sisko onto a ship in the alternate universe, where he explains that after Kira and Bashir left ("Crossover"), the mirror Sisko started a rebellion against the Klingon / Cardassian Alliance. But the mirror Sisko was killed in the midst of a mission crucial to the survival of the rebellion. The mirror O'Brien wants Sisko to complete that mission: halting the work of a Terran scientist who is developing technology that will allow the Alliance to track down all the rebel bases.

Sisko is uninterested in helping until he finds out that the scientist is the mirror version of his deceased wife Jennifer—and that the rebels will be forced to kill her if Sisko does not convince her to join the rebellion. Reluctantly, Sisko agrees to masquerade as his deceased counterpart to aid the plan.

On Terok Nor, the mirror version of DS9, Kira, the station's intendant, tells Jennifer that her estranged husband is dead and urges the scientist to complete her device. Only then, she says, will the bloodshed against the Terran rebellion cease. However, Jennifer is unaware that Kira has little interest in preventing bloodshed; she is coldly capable of killing *whoever* stands in her way.

Posing as his double, Sisko is introduced to the other rebels, which include mirror versions of Bashir, Rom, a Vulcan named Tuvok, and Jadzia, who is Sisko's mistress in this universe. The rebels are more interested in killing Jennifer than converting her to

their side, but Sisko manages to convince them that her scientific skills will be valuable to them. Later, the mirror Rom, who is loyal to the intendant, shows up at her quarters to inform her that the man they believe to be the mirror Sisko is alive. He reveals what the rebels are planning, which allows Kira to capture Sisko and the mirror O'Brien before they can sneak aboard Terok Nor.

Kira sends O'Brien to work in ore processing with the other slaves but has Sisko brought to her quarters. After deciding that she's not ready to execute him—yet—she allows him to meet with Jennifer. But Jennifer despises the man she believes to be her husband; the mirror Sisko was an egotistical womanizer who she believes fought the Alliance simply because he loved to fight. Allowing her to think that he is her deceased husband, Sisko apologizes for his previous behavior and reveals that he has come to Terok Nor to rescue her. Her real enemy shouldn't be him, he explains; it should be the Alliance, which will kill the rebels as soon as her device reveals their hiding places. Although she can move around the station freely, he says, she's as much a slave to the Alliance as the workers in the mines.

Sensing that he is making some headway in convincing her, Sisko signals O'Brien down in ore processing. In turn, the mirror O'Brien triggers a malfunction in some equipment, allowing him and the other Terran prisoners to escape. Up in the habitat ring, Sisko breaks out of his quarters and Jennifer agrees to leave with him. The two meet up with O'Brien and head for a waiting ship, only to discover that Kira is on to their plan and has blocked their escape. But rather than surrendering, Sisko retreats to the ore-processing center with his group. When Kira and her troops force their way in, Sisko calmly reveals that he has activated the station's self-destruct sequence, and only he can deactivate it. With no alternative, Kira allows Sisko, Jennifer, and the rebels to leave the station in exchange for the access code to halt the sequence.

At the rebel encampment, Jennifer admits that she knows Sisko is not her husband; he's too kind. Thanking him for rescuing her, Jennifer kisses him goodbye, and the mirror O'Brien fulfills his promise to return Sisko to his own universe.

Logically, Vulcans would be part of the rebellion, so a part was created for Tuvok, from *Star Trek: Voyager*. ROBBIE ROBINSON

Everyone working on *Deep Space Nine* enjoys the "Crossover" episodes, which is how they generally refer to stories that take place in the mirror universe established in the original series. Writers, actors, and directors alike enjoy the opportunity to take their characters in a direction that can be as much as 180 degrees from their norm.

The temptation, of course, is to go as far afield as possible, but there seem to be limits that are contingent upon the character. In the original "Mirror, Mirror" episode, Spock's mirror alter ego had much more in common with his "real" universe counterpart than the other members of the landing party, and it's true here as well. The mirror Tuvok, played by *Voyager*'s Tim Russ in his second *DS9* appearance ("Invasive Procedures"), is apparently the same as the real Tuvok. The mirror Jadzia, while a very sexual being, may not be all that different from our Jadzia. "If *Deep Space Nine* were a movie," quips Ira Steven Behr, who cowrote the episode with Robert Hewitt Wolfe, "Dax would probably be sleeping with all of the characters and it would be okay. She's a 'free spirit,' as they said in the sixties." And the mirror Jadzia's relationship with Sisko doesn't seem nearly as surprising as it might have, considering the latent attraction the real Jadzia revealed in "Fascination."

On the other hand, characters like Rom can go totally opposite in the mirror universe, according to Director Winrich Kolbe. And while the Sisko in the episode was not actually the mirror Sisko, he was trying to act like him, the director notes. That allowed Avery Brooks to leave behind "this clammed-up head of the space station he normally plays and become a swashbuckler," says Kolbe.

It also gave Sisko the opportunity to see more bedroom action than he's had in at least three years. The viewers can be fairly certain that Sisko bedded the mirror Jadzia, but Robert Wolfe says the suggestion is also there that he had a dalliance with Intendant Kira. "He had to," says Wolfe. "It was part of his cover, wasn't it? In all of those movies [with people pretending to be other people], you have that scene. He doesn't *have* to sleep with the person, but he has to get out of the situation. So . . ."

"The episode was all one continual sexual encounter or chance for a sexual encounter for Sisko," says Behr. "Going to bed with Dax, the obvious sexual tension between him and Kira, and the sexual tension between him and Jennifer."

The real femme fatale of the episode is Intendant Kira, whose overt sensuality is part of her power, according to Nana Visitor. "All of the appetites that [our] Kira has and keeps to herself, the intendant has and uses for her own profit and good," says Visitor. "So her sexuality is very self-satisfying and she's not above using it with anyone, man or woman."

Achieving that sexy smolder is no mean feat of acting, considering the fact that the intendant's rubberized costume, according to Visitor, "feels like a diver's suit—it doesn't breathe at all." Between takes, Visitor stood in front of huge fans to keep her from sweating, which, Wardrobe discovered, would discolor portions of the outfit.

As in the first "Crossover" episode, differences in the mirror Terok Nor were literally established with "smoke and mirrors." The lighting was more contrasty, recalls Jonathan West. "We used more cross-lighting and stronger back-lighting," he says. "I changed the white fluorescents in Sisko's office to red by covering them with a red gel. And in the ore-processing facility we used a mix of blue light and darkness, and more smoke than usual."

The smoke was provided at Kolbe's request. "I like to use smoke, because it gives an interesting visual," says Kolbe. "Plus, I think it takes the edges off sets that have been shot ten thousand times. The cave set (locale for the rebel base), for instance, has been shot over and over in both *TNG* and *DS9*."

The mounting body count of familiar characters who've been eliminated in the mirror universe was a standing joke with the writers, who only occasionally worried about running out of characters to populate that realm. "It's a brutal universe." Wolfe laughs. "As of this episode, we'd lost Rom, Sisko, Quark, and Odo." He ticks them off. "I guess that is pretty bad. We kept saying we'd have to bring people back who we'd killed in *our* universe so that we could kill them again in the other one."

For the intendant character, the end is justified by any and all means. ROBBIE ROBINSON

The harsh realities of the mirror universe seemed to be most dangerous for the Ferengi. ROBBIE ROBINSON

Still alive, however, was the one-eyed rebel marauder played by Stunt Coordinator Dennis "Danger" Madalone. He managed to convince David Livingston (director of "Crossover") and the producers to let him play the character in the first mirror episode. When the second story came around, Madalone eagerly read the script but was disappointed at the lack of specifics regarding certain members of the cast. "There's a scene in the caves where Sisko walks in and the rebels all welcome him back because they thought he'd been killed," says Madalone. "So, I went to Rick Kolbe and said, 'You know, Rick, I played one of those rebels in part one, and I think I should be in the room with the one eye.'" The producers and writers agreed, and Madalone returned, complete with on-screen credit, as he would in Season 4's "Shattered Mirror."

One question that seems to worry some viewers—why did it seem so easy to get in and out of the mirror universe—isn't so easy to answer. "Well, the choice was this," sighs Behr. "Every time we wanted to do a mirror universe show, we had to come up with tech [to explain how they got there]. It came down to, did you want to spend half an act finding ways, or did you want to get in there and have fun? So, we made it easier to get in. But at least our people didn't come up with the way to do it. The mirror universe people did."

Adds Wolfe: "I would say that it *was* probably extremely difficult to do, but the mirror O'Brien worked it out, with lots of preparation." In other words, the viewers just didn't see it happen.

THE DIE IS CAST

Episode #467

WRITTEN BY RONALD D. MOORE
DIRECTED BY DAVID LIVINGSTON

GUEST CAST

Garak	ANDREW ROBINSON
Lovok	LELAND ORSER
Michael Eddington	KENNETH MARSHALL
Vice Admiral Toddman	LEON RUSSOM
Romulan Pilot	WENDY SCHENKER
Enabran Tain	PAUL DOOLEY

STARDATE UNKNOWN

Tain's plan is perfect—except that his Romulan ally is actually a changeling. ROBBIE ROBINSON

On the station, Sisko and his crew are shocked when a huge fleet of Romulan and Cardassian vessels decloak near DS9 and then enter the wormhole. On board one of the lead vessels, Tain and Garak reminisce fondly about old times. Then Tain gives Garak his first assignment: Interrogate Odo and find out any useful information about the Founders.

On DS9, Sisko and his senior staff learn the full details of Tain's plans from Starfleet Security's Vice Admiral Toddman. Although Sisko wants to take the *Defiant* into the Gamma Quadrant to locate Odo, Toddman refuses. He wants the *Defiant* to stay where it is, ready to defend Bajor if the Jem'Hadar decide to take revenge on the Alpha Quadrant for Tain's actions. Risking a potential court-martial, Sisko opts to defy Toddman's orders and takes the *Defiant* out.

On the warbird, commanded by the Romulan Colonel Lovok, Tain reveals that the Obsidian Order has developed a device that should aid Garak's interrogation of Odo. Garak protests that Odo doesn't seem to have any information that will assist in their attack. But when Tain suggests that Lovok can perform the interrogation, Garak realizes his loyalty to Tain is on the line. Reluctantly, he goes to fulfill his assignment.

En route to Dominion territory, the *Defiant's* cloak fails, leaving its crew vulnerable to attack by the Jem'Hadar. Eddington confesses to sabotaging the cloaking device to prevent Sisko from pursuing the Romulan/Cardassian fleet. Undeterred, Sisko orders O'Brien to repair the damage so they can press ahead.

Garak discovers the Cardassian device emits a quantum stasis field that prevents a changeling from altering its form. Pushed well beyond the time when he would normally have returned to his natural liquid state, Odo is in agony. Garak cannot bear watch-ing the changeling suffer, and begs him to tell him something—*anything*—so that he can turn off the device. Finally, Odo admits something he hasn't told anyone; he wants to return to his people and join them in the Great Link. It's not the secret that Garak anticipated, but he understands that it's the deepest, most personal secret Odo has. He turns off the machine and allows Odo to revert to a liquid.

Garak reports to Tain that he was unable to break Odo. With no further use for the changeling, Tain wants him terminated, but Garak concocts a reason to spare his life. Surprisingly, Lovok supports Garak in his desire to keep Odo alive.

The fleet arrives at the Omarion Nebula and launches its attack, only to discover that the Founders have deserted the planet already. As one hundred fifty Jem'Hadar fighter ships quickly surround the twenty vessels in the Romulan/Cardassian squadron, they realize they've been set up. The Founders apparently knew about the invasion from the beginning.

Garak takes advantage of the ensuing chaos to release Odo. Once again Garak is caught off guard when Lovok shows up to help them get to their runabout. Lovok reveals that he is a changeling, and the reason for the failure of the attack is clear. The changeling found out about Tain's plan and then helped to facilitate it, knowing that in the end they would be rid of a threat to the Founders. Now, only the Klingons and the Federation pose a threat, and Lovok confidently states that even they won't be a threat for much longer. Lovok invites Odo to return with him, and to join the Great Link. Odo refuses.

As Odo and he prepare to escape from the war-bird, Garak attempts to rescue Tain, but Tain refuses to leave the fleet, despite its imminent destruction. Its cloak repaired, the *Defiant* appears just in time to rescue Odo and Garak's runabout from the attacking Jem'Hadar. Returning to DS9, Sisko is relieved to hear that Toddman has decided not to press charges. In the meantime, Odo thanks Garak for not revealing his secret, and the two tenuously skirt what could be the start of something akin to friendship.

"I'd never been in a situation where we'd completed a single episode's screenplay and then decided to do an entire sequel afterward," says Ronald D. Moore. "There was a real sense of challenge to it."

The challenge was to decide what the focal point of the sequel should be. There were a number of strong plot points to choose from, and the prospect of a monumental space battle. But at the emotional core, Moore realized, was the relationship between Garak and Odo. "That relationship was the primary thing in 'Improbable Cause,'" he observes, and that was what would drive "The Die Is Cast."

The relationship is *not* one of warm fuzzy feelings and noble sacrifice. This is Garak we're talking about. "Garak is not a nice guy," Ira Behr grins, "although sometimes he is. The first show ended with an offer being dangled in front of him. And Garak has to make a moral decision. We wanted to show what he's capable of, even when he doesn't want to do it. Could you torture someone, if you had to? Garak can do it."

The producers also had some bloodthirsty desires of their own. "We wanted to show a regular character in pain and being tortured," admits Behr. "And we knew Rene would sell the hell out of it with his acting."

Actor Rene Auberjonois was a willing victim, although it meant spending even more time than usual in what some cast members view as *DS9*'s own little torture chamber, the makeup trailer. "It was wonderful for me, because it was the first time I really got to work closely with Andy Robinson, who is an old friend," comments Auberjonois. In fact, during the sequence in which Garak interrogates Odo, the two worked so closely that they were literally nose to nose on the floor.

They can thank Director David Livingston for the intimate blocking during what Livingston refers to as the melting scene. "My basic direction to both actors was, 'Go for it,'" says Livingston. "I told them that I was going to do it in one shot by pushing the

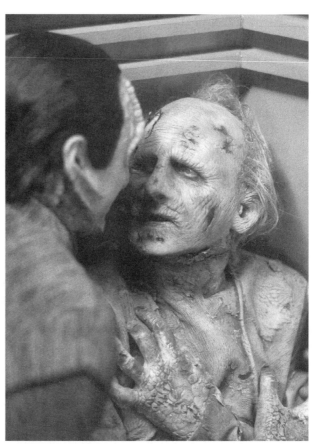

True to his own moral code, Garak can do evil. ROBBIE ROBINSON

camera in very close, using a very wide-angle lens, pressing them up against the wall to make it as intense as possible. And they did go for it. I think the scene is the best in the episode. It's very intense, very dramatic, very powerful."

Auberjonois agrees. "I felt like some character from *King Lear*," he says. "The acting mechanism I used there was very Shakespearean."

Helping to sell the tragic aspects of the interaction was Dennis McCarthy's moving score. "I had to express the horror of what Garak was doing to Odo, and yet still put some shred of humanity into the music to show that Garak was suffering, too," says the composer, "because Garak was having a hard time doing this. It was an opportunity to get very atonal, musically. I don't believe that we ever heard a major chord on that show."

Describing the scene was Ron Moore's job. "I thought, 'How do you torture a guy made out of goo?'" says Moore. "'He has to recharge every sixteen hours, so what would happen if he couldn't? If that's how they torture him, what would we see?' I wanted it to be very visual, so I thought it would be an interesting image if he was turning to dandruff. So I wrote that he was desiccating, as if the moisture were being sucked out of his body and pieces of him were flaking off."

How feasible was Moore's selected method of torture? Feasible enough that Andre Bormanis was able to provide some rationalization for the producers. "I invoked some morphogenic enzymes that allow Odo to shape-shift or revert to his natural gelatinous state," says Bormanis. "And then I provided a little language about the mechanism by which we might inhibit the activation of those morphogenic enzymes."

And how do you figure out what would inhibit the activation of a fictional substance? Bormanis has an answer for that as well. "An electromagnetic field can inhibit certain kinds of chemical reactions. If you assume there is something going on at a biochemical level inside Odo when he shifts, then, in principle, you could inhibit that process, either through chemistry or through application of some kind of electromagnetic field."

Now that the writers had a feasible method of doing away with changelings, they could have had a real problem. Why couldn't their enemies activate a series of morphogenic enzyme–inhibitor machines around the Founders' planet to end the Dominion threat? It also pays to have quick-thinking writers. "As you recall," says Moore, "we said in the episode that the machine was a prototype. They had only one copy of it. And then we destroyed the entire fleet and the plans to the machine were lost." Moore grins. "We're usually good at leaving ourselves trap doors to get out."

To portray Odo on his "bad skin day," Auberjonois spent two days in tatters. "The makeup took longer to put on because the whole uniform had to be made of stuff that was disintegrating, and that was very uncomfortable," admits Auberjonois. "I always wear a mask on my face, but I'd never really sympathized with the actors who wear the big, heavy costumes, like the Cardassians. Their costumes are built over wet suits, and can you imagine wearing a wet suit under hot lights on the soundstage all day? Well, [the tattered uniform] was a rubber version of my regular costume. And it was hot!"

Although the special garment was produced by *DS9*'s Wardrobe Department, some unusual contributions from Makeup gave it that certain je ne sais quoi. "We had to design a whole new face for Rene that had all the cracks and crustiness required," explains

"We should feel as if Odo is about to collapse into a pile of dust . . ."
ROBBIE ROBINSON

Michael Westmore. "I sculpted up the new face with all these cracks in it, and then we glued little flakes over it, so they were hanging off the face. And then we made a sheet of this stuff so Robert Blackman could cut it up and glue it onto the uniform." After that, Blackman notes, Westmore painted the latex to make it look like Odo's uniform.

Completing the illusion was the work done by the visual effects crew, who, for a change, were able to shoot a morphing sequence without resorting to the use of a bluescreen plate. "We used the first unit live-action plate," notes Josh Rose. "They had done a bunch of shots, and they had little Odo flakes on the floor, like little pieces of latex that had come off of him. We were able to use a shot of those little pieces and morph them to goo. Then, after they came together, they were sucked into the big pile of Odo. As he transformed, we made the color of the goo a little darker than usual so he didn't look as pretty as he normally does, and he kind of crawls into the bucket."

In the episode, the upshot of the torture sequence is that Odo finally does reveal a secret to

Garak, admitting that he wants to go home to his people. While that may seem a little anticlimactic to some, it provided real emotional weight for Odo's future development. "That was an important beat," says Moore. "We wanted to reestablish that even though he's discovered that his people are, in a metaphorical sense, Nazis, he really wants to be with them. So that scene set up the internal character conflict that would guide us on Odo and the Founders from then on."

"The Die Is Cast" set a precedent for future episodes that would portray clusters of ships on a truly grand scale. "It was a big two-parter and we knew it had better pay off," says Moore. "I thought, 'Wow, this could be cool, because we're telling the audience that there's an invasion fleet that's going to do this massive thing.' So we wanted as many warbirds as we could see, and a lot of Jem'Hadar ships, and we wanted the *Defiant* in the middle of them all."

"We had more ship shots on that show than on any other single episode up to that point," confirms Steve Oster.

With the traditionally tight budget of episodic television series, it is no small deal to make such an opticals-heavy event happen. "It was the first time we did a fleet," says Gary Hutzel. "Traditionally, any kind of multiple-ship shot is considered prohibitively expensive. But this show totally broke the mold."

Hutzel's task was to break the mold without breaking the budget. One way of doing that was an inexpensive but effective cheat. "I shot transparencies of the Cardassian and Romulan ships on light boxes, and we 'flew' those in the background," Hutzel explains. "We kept the camera in contant motion so the audience wouldn't concentrate on them."

For the biggest shot of the sequence, there were no holds barred. "I needed something that would break apart," Hutzel says. "We wanted the scene to say that Sisko is really turning it on, so we designed the shot to have the *Defiant* fly right through a Jem'Hadar ship."

Hutzel chose a model that had originally been built for the second-season episode, "The Jem'Hadar." Then Tony Meininger cast a series of small sections from that ship's molds. In the motion-control studio,

Hutzel aligned the sections to match up with corresponding sections in the footage of the full model. He then photographed them individually, and when the *Defiant* "collides" with the Jem'Hadar vessel, those are the pieces that actually break away and fly off into space. But, when you look at the final shot—Hutzel laughs—"you see a Jem'Hadar ship blowing up, because that's all you're supposed to see."

The episode sets precedent in another way, as it marks Ira Behr's first show as *DS9*'s full executive producer, moving up from co-executive producer to fill Michael Piller's slot when he left the series to produce *Legend* for UPN. The change would give Behr a bit more rein to orchestrate the kinds of moments he loves, for example, indulging in a scene between a couple of gray guys sittin' around talking.

"'The Die Is Cast' starts out talky as hell, with a scene between Garak and Enabran Tain," says Behr. "Ron and I really worked on that because it was hard to make it come alive. Neither one of the characters was a regular on the show, and here they were, chatting away about all their backstories and their feelings about one another. I love doing that because it's not your traditional storytelling."

The fact that Behr and the rest of the writing staff are fond of both Garak and Tain plays a role in the amount of screen time they command. "Writers tend to fall in love with their work all the time, just in order to be able to do it." Behr laughs. It wasn't surprising, therefore, that after apparently killing off Tain in this episode, the writers would bring him back for one final appearance in the fifth season ("In Purgatory's Shadow"), revealing at least part of the truth about his relationship with Garak.

A single line in the final act of the episode would trigger a sea change in *Deep Space Nine's* direction. Lovok's comment that, "After today the only real threats from the Alpha Quadrant are the Klingons and the Federation . . ." was, according to Behr, just a throwaway line at the time. But that single unassuming comment was ultimately responsible for the Federation's problems with the Klingons in Season 4, and for Worf's transfer to *DS9* ("The Way of the Warrior").

EXPLORERS

Episode #468

TELEPLAY BY **RENÉ ECHEVARRIA**
STORY BY **HILARY J. BADER**
DIRECTED BY **CLIFF BOLE**

GUEST CAST

Gul Dukat   **MARC ALAIMO**
Dr. Elizabeth Lense   **BARI HOCHWALD**
Leeta   **CHASE MASTERSON**

STARDATE UNKNOWN

At Quark's bar, all of Dr. Bashir's romantic intentions toward the new dabo girl, Leeta, evaporate when Dax informs him that the *Starship Lexington* is expected to dock at DS9. The *Lexington*'s medical officer is Elizabeth Lense, valedictorian of Bashir's graduating class at Starfleet Medical. Her posting on the *Lexington* was considered the choicest assignment at the time. Although Bashir preferred being sent to DS9, he's never gotten over the feeling that his accomplishments will always rank second to hers.

Meanwhile, Sisko returns from a trip to Bajor with the blueprint for an ancient solar-sailing vessel. Legend has it, he explains to Jake, that the Bajorans used such ships to explore their star system eight centuries earlier, and may even have traveled all the way to Cardassia. Enthralled with the idea, Sisko decides to build one of the vessels, using the same types of tools and materials as the ancient Bajorans.

Over the next few weeks, Sisko painstakingly re-creates the vessel. He then invites Jake to accom-

pany him on a voyage to test the ship's mettle. Jake initially declines, but later changes his mind, much to Sisko's delight. As they prepare to depart the station, Sisko receives a transmission from Gul Dukat, who warns him about the hazards of his journey. But Sisko suspects Dukat's concern is more related to the thought that Sisko may prove the Bajorans developed interstellar travel before the Cardassians.

Setting sail, Jake finds himself getting caught up in his father's excitement. The voyage provides him with the perfect venue to share an important revelation with Sisko: He's been offered a writing fellowship at the Pennington School in New Zealand. Sisko is proud of his son's achievement, but he's not sure how he feels about the prospect of Jake leaving the station. Before they can discuss it further, one of the mast supports gives way, and the pair are forced to struggle for control of the vessel. Finally, Sisko jettisons one of the sails, solving the problem for the moment.

Sisko is concerned about continuing the voyage, but Jake reminds him that the ancient Bajorans probably ran into similar problems and didn't give up. Buoyed by his son's confidence, Sisko opts to press on. As they prepare to get some rest, Jake reveals that he plans to postpone accepting the scholarship for a year because he doesn't want his father to be alone. He'd feel better if Sisko had someone else in his life who was special, like a girlfriend.

Just as Jake admits that he has made the acquaintance of a very attractive woman who'd like to meet Sisko, the ship lurches violently, caught in an eddy of light that inexplicably takes it to warp speed. After a wild ride, the ship is released by the current. Sisko realizes that they were carried by a stream of tachyon particles, which travel faster than light. Unfortunately, he has no idea where the eddy carried the ship, as their navigational instruments were destroyed during the ride.

While father and son await a response to their distress call, Jake fills his father in on the freighter captain he wants Sisko to meet. Just as Sisko agrees to a meeting, they spot three Cardassian ships heading toward them. Although initially apprehensive, they find out that the ships, under the command of Dukat, are there to congratulate them because the pair has made it all the way to the Cardassian system! By a strange coincidence, Dukat also brings word that a "recent" archaeological discovery on Cardassia has revealed that Bajoran legends were accurate and that an ancient Bajoran sail ship apparently made it all the way to his world.

The captain sees their trip aboard the reconstructed Bajoran solar ship as a way to reconnect with his son. ROBBIE ROBINSON

Back on the station, Bashir finally meets up with Dr. Lense. To his surprise, he discovers that Lense is envious of the long-term research work that Bashir is doing at DS9.

If you can envision Norwegian explorer Thor Heyerdahl setting sail on a voyage across the stars, instead of the Pacific Ocean, then you have a good idea of the inspiration for the *DS9* episode "Explorers." "I was talking with friends about the fact that the Federation is based on ships," says Hilary Bader, then an intern on *Deep Space Nine*. "Someone mentioned exploring, and the old ways of doing things and people trying to prove things. And as soon as you start thinking along those lines, you see the parallels to *Kon-Tiki*. I thought, 'Wait a minute, that would be a good story.' So I went in and pitched it."

The *Kon-Tiki* was the name of a raft that Heyerdahl sailed from Peru to Tahiti, substantiating his theory that ancient sailing boats could have and had crossed the Pacific Ocean. His subsequent book inflamed the fantasies of a generation of baby-boomers.

Avery Brooks was able to give Sisko a different look. ROBBIE ROBINSON

Bader found an avid audience in René Echevarria, who would write the teleplay based on her story. "We immediately started kicking ideas back and forth," says Echevarria. "'Would the ship travel between Bajor and Cardassia?' 'What if it was a sailboat?' I'd always wanted to do a sailboat story, so I talked to Andre Bormanis about the possibilities."

Bormanis was on top of those possibilities. "You could take advantage of just the radiation pressure from the sun," he explains. "Photons carry a small amount of momentum—a very, very tiny amount—but enough that if you had a couple of square kilometers of a really thin Mylar material facing the sun, radiation pressure would eventually impart acceleration on that. Solar wind particles hitting the material would add to that. The sails would be highly efficient, but very, very slow. The price you would pay is speed, but, in principle, we could sail among the planets.

"Solar sails have already been designed and seriously considered by NASA and the Jet Propulsion Laboratory as a mechanism of interplanetary transport," observes Bormanis. The episode caught the attention of some of those designers, and netted *DS9* the 1995 "Best Vision of the Future" award from the Space Frontier Foundation, an organization dedicated to opening the space frontier to human exploration and settlement. The award was presented by JPL's Robert Staehle. "He's a guy who actually works on solar sails!" recalls Echevarria proudly.

While the theories behind the story were sound, the series did take a few liberties in depicting Sisko's vessel. "A real solar sailing vessel would look substantially different from the one in the show," Bormanis admits. "It would have to be much larger relative to the size of its payload, but a five-kilometer sail would have been a little bit hard for our special effects team to pull off. René's conception had kind of a Jules Verne look, a wooden cabin outfitted with some brass."

To help bring that fanciful, poetic look into reality, Illustrator Jim Martin consulted with Herman Zimmerman and Dan Curry before creating interior and exterior designs for the vessel and its accoutrements. "Designing ancient brass navigating devices is a lot different from doing high-tech fighters," says Martin, "and a lot of fun. All of the props were antique bronze."

The Verne-esque quality carried over to lighting the ship as well. "I felt like I was shooting *20,000 Leagues Under the Sea*," laughs Jonathan West. "The ship was all done in copper and silver tones, so it had many textures. I used a lot of warm light on the actors' faces to help provide a hue to the sense of adventure." West found that the ship's small interior wouldn't accommodate his usual camera equipment. "We were cramped, and in many shots we were turning to see all parts of the ship at once. We used a remote camera on the arm of a fifteen-foot crane sticking through the window. We started deep and then dollied back, right out the window."

Shooting the outside of the ship turned out to be even more complicated, although you'd never know it to judge by the grace of the vessel sailing away from the station. Finding new angles to shoot the circular Cardassian station is a constant challenge for the visual effects crews, but the angle Glenn Neufeld chose in "Explorers" impressed Dan Curry. "It's just great," enthuses Curry. "Glenn did the shot looking up at the deck so you see the arms of the station like a huge ceiling."

In devising the shot, Neufeld recalls that he walked around the six-foot station model for two hours. "I made a one-inch paper mock-up of what the computer-animated *Kon-Tiki* ship was supposed to look like and put it on a stick," he says. "Then I took the stick in my hand and walked around getting into bad positions. The people over at Image G were forced to watch me stand on apple boxes and hang over this two-hundred-thousand-dollar station miniature with my five-cent mock-up. I finally found the one place where we could put the full camera rig inside the station when it's right side up. It gives an underside view that's actually inside the outer ring. We actually drove the camera in there, with a quarter inch to spare on one side of the camera and a half inch on the other. When we panned and tilted, we had to pull the camera back out a little, and at the end of the tilt it came within a quarter inch of touching the model. The motion-control operator said, 'You want me to put the camera where?'" Neufeld laughs. "Because if you make a mistake and you load the wrong information into the motion-control computer, the camera is going to whip around and smash the model to pieces. It was all a very tense situation."

Jim Martin's design of the ship's exterior was sent to Industrial Light & Magic's visual effects supervisor, John Knoll, who was in the process of completing his work on *Star Trek Generations*. At the same time he was supervising the effects on the theatrical version of *Mission: Impossible*. "I was going to turn the work down because I didn't think I had the time," recalls Knoll. "But they'd already faxed me a bunch of Jim's drawings. When I got home and looked at them, I said, 'Oh, wow, this is a cool ship! Maybe I can *find* the time.'"

Knoll had two months to do twelve shots of the ship's exterior. "The ship is entirely computer generated, and the most difficult aspect was the sails," Knoll says. "I animated them using a procedural software written by Habib Zargarpour (also at ILM) and myself." The software treated the sails as though they were a springy fabric, and gave them properties that the real material would likely demonstrate, such as viscosity. It also created the motion of the sails, their propagation rate, their hardiness and resilience. "I animated what the masts were doing and the sails would sort of come along with it, thanks to the procedural software," Knoll explains. "It was a great deal of effort to get that all together and working. I did about half of the episode in England, where I was working on *Mission: Impossible*. I rendered the shots in the hotel on my computer."

Known internally as "the butterfly episode," Dennis McCarthy "decided to compose what I saw. It was light and airy and wonderful, so that's the score I went after." The episode afforded McCarthy the freedom to be experimental in his composition, and he took great delight in "creating something that was *soaring*, because that was the visual." Typically, the composer finds himself scoring scenes that take place on a starship or a space station, where his instrumentation is constantly fighting against the low atmospheric rumble of equipment that is added in postproduction. In the quiet unmechanized sailing vessel, there would be no such rumble, which allowed McCarthy to free up instruments he normally couldn't use. "I used a *harp* on this one," he reports happily.

Although the idea of father and son sharing in an adventure seems like a natural, Bader's original story concerned O'Brien. "I didn't pitch it as a Sisko story," she says. "It was the producers who told me that they were looking for a way to put Jake and Sisko in a close moment."

The teleplay provided that and more, following up on the idea that Jake was growing up. At the same time, it softened any potential separation anxiety his father might experience by revealing that Jake didn't plan to leave his old man all alone. The episode lays the seeds for the introduction of a new semiregular character, Kasidy Yates, with Jake's enthusiastic

Chase Masterson's first audition was a failure but it led to a
recurring role. ROBBIE ROBINSON

endorsement of the freighter captain. (Kasidy would
not be mentioned by name, however, until the following episode.)

Jake's specified career goals initially were just
grist for the mill. "The episode gave us an opportunity to focus on what Jake wanted to do with his life,"
notes Ira Behr. At the time, Behr didn't give any serious thought to following up on Jake's aspirations as a
writer. But the following season, the series' writing
staff would return to the idea with episodes like "The
Visitor" and "The Muse."

Meanwhile, on the space station, the B-story also
had a curious connection to "The Abandoned": Chase
Masterson. "We had first auditioned Chase for Jake's
girlfriend Mardah, the dabo girl." Ira Behr laughs.
"Avery was directing that episode, and when Chase
came in, he was like, 'For *my* son?! For *me*, maybe!
But for my *son*? Get her out of here!' Chase had
played it full throttle, with kittenesque sexuality. But
we kept her in mind, thinking she could make a fun
character. When we cast her as Leeta in 'Explorers,'
we didn't know if we were going to continue her

character right away. We just wanted to see how it
would work." It worked just fine, with Leeta appearing not only a few episodes later in "Facets," but
intermittently throughout the rest of the series, cul-
minating in her marriage to Rom.

A more significant aspect of the B-story, in Behr's
mind, is the scene where Bashir and the chief get
drunk and establish once and for all that they have
become friends. "That was a scene that I pushed for,"
admits Behr. "Every couple of shows I'll have a scene
that becomes the baby that I nurture. This one was
just so human. It had friendship. It had vulnerability.
It was funny. It was sloppy. It's that stuff that *Deep
Space Nine* has helped bring back into the *Star Trek*
universe."

Pausing, Behr's tone grows more serious. "*The
Next Generation* was very serious at times, and I
understand that it did a lot of wonderful things, but
it had a very self-important air to it. Finding things
that work against that is very important to me, and
has become more and more important as I've taken
over the day-to-day aspects of running the show. And
so that scene became really important. It was both
entertaining and a breath of reality."

Contributing to that reality was Bashir and
O'Brien's enthusiastic rendition of the British standard, "Jerusalem," a song chosen after the producers
discovered that obtaining the rights to warble initial
picks "Louie, Louie" or "Rocket Man" would be too
expensive. "'Jerusalem' was Colm and Sid's idea,"
notes Behr.

"'Jerusalem' was very familar to both of us," confirms El Fadil. "It's like an anthem in England, and
something that drunk people might very well sing."

The song, as Behr notes, "worked like gangbusters," despite the fact that Siddig was nervous
about playing a drunk on-camera. "I'd never done it
before," he reveals. "It was terrifying. To be drunk, to
die, or to make love are the most terrifying things for
an actor to perform. But we just got into it. Of
course," he grins mischievously, "to Colm, drunk acting wasn't hard at all. It was second nature to him."

FAMILY BUSINESS

Episode #469

WRITTEN BY **IRA STEVEN BEHR &
ROBERT HEWITT WOLFE**

DIRECTED BY **RENE AUBERJONOIS**

GUEST CAST

Kasidy Yates	PENNY JOHNSON
Rom	MAX GRODÉNCHIK
Brunt	JEFFREY COMBS
Secretary	MEL GREEN

SPECIAL GUEST STAR

Ishka	ANDREA MARTIN

STARDATE UNKNOWN

On a busy night at the bar, Quark thinks the only thing he has to worry about is the fact that Nog is studying for his Starfleet exams instead of bussing tables, until he receives a visit from Brunt, F.C.A. (the Ferengi Commerce Authority). An agent of what is essentially Ferenginar's equivalent of the I.R.S., Brunt has come to DS9 to serve Quark with a Writ of Accountability for improper supervision of a family member; Quark's mother, Ishka, has been accused of earning a profit, an illegal activity for females. As the family's eldest male, Quark is being held responsible for Ishka's actions. It's up to him to travel home and get Ishka to confess to her crimes. Against Quark's better judgment, he allows his brother Rom to come with him.

When Quark arrives, with Rom and Brunt in tow, he finds things are worse than he'd imagined. Not only is Ishka unrepentant about her transgressions, but she has also taken to wearing clothes, another serious violation of Ferenginar's laws. Brunt leaves, warning Quark to get his house in order within three days or his mother will be placed in indentured servitude, and Quark will be forced to make restitution for her crimes. But Ishka refuses to imprint the confession Quark offers, infuriating her oldest son. Later, Ishka tells Rom that she can't imprint the confession because it would mean that she admits what she did was wrong. This is a matter of pride, she explains; she knows that she is as capable of earning a profit as any male.

In the meantime, Jake hasn't forgotten about Sisko's promise to meet the female freighter captain ("Explorers"). Captain Kasidy Yates is currently on the station, and Jake is eager to put her and Benjamin together. When Sisko finally goes to one of the cargo

By Ferengi standards, Quark's mother Ishka is out of control—a clothes-wearing, profit-earning *female!* ROBBIE ROBINSON

bays to meet Kasidy, he discovers that she is an attractive, self-confident individual. Intrigued, he agrees to meet her the next day for coffee.

On Ferenginar, Quark discovers that his mother's transgressions are more serious than even Brunt knows. Ishka has been conducting business transactions under dozens of aliases all over the Ferengi Alliance. There's no way he can pay back everything she's earned, which means that he's financially ruined. After angrily confronting his mother with this information, Ishka accuses Quark of being jealous of her financial acumen, just as her late husband was. Quark storms off, intending to tell the F.C.A. all about Ishka's financial empire. But as he waits to see Brunt, Rom rushes up to him with the news that Ishka will split her profits with Quark, fifty-fifty. Suddenly seeing the entire affair in a different light, Quark returns to his mother's house to take Ishka up on her offer.

However, Ishka has made no such offer. Rom lied to get the two of them together in one room. Quark and Ishka talk, and she reveals that she loves Quark as much as she loves Rom; after all, it's clear that Quark inherited his lobes for finance from her. Reconsidering her position, Ishka agrees to imprint the confession and give back the money she earned, for Quark's sake.

On DS9, Sisko and Kasidy's date seems to go well, but he's disappointed when she reveals that she has to rush off to another engagement. After Kasidy reveals what the engagement is, Sisko is tickled. Her brother, a colonist on Cestus III, is sending her an audio transmission of a baseball game in which his team recently participated. The subspace transmission has taken two weeks to travel to the station, but it will be like listening to the game as it happens. Sharing the fact that he, too, is an avid baseball fan, Sisko is invited to listen to the game with Kasidy. The relationship is off to a good start.

After Ishka fulfills her promise, a relieved Quark bids her farewell, but sentimental Rom lingers to give Ishka a private goodbye and to chuckle over a shared secret. Brunt and Quark may be satisfied with the way things turned out, but only Rom knows that Ishka turned over only a third of her immense profits!

"There's a lot more to it than just the yucks," notes Robert Hewitt Wolfe of "Family Business." "Underneath it all, it's a story about family."

On this point, nearly everyone associated with this episode concurs. During preproduction, Wolfe's cowriter Ira Steven Behr joked, "This is the *Long Day's Journey into Night* of Ferengi stories," because of the Eugene O'Neill–like *sturm und drang* that resonated beneath the otherwise broad comic scenes. Before long, Director Rene Auberjonois and Actor Armin Shimerman had taken the gibe to heart and translated it into the filming process.

"That was much more serious than the usual Ferengi story, even though there was a lot of comedic stuff in it," says Auberjonois. "It's about a very painful thing, a son who has totally lost any sort of relationship with a parent. You realize that Quark left home as a young man and has never returned until this point, and that his estrangement is very difficult for him and his mother."

"It was a very heartfelt psychological study," agrees Shimerman. "I don't know if the writers were aware of this, but there is a great deal of similarity between Quark's relationship and my own relationship with my mother. A lot of it rang true for me when I read it, so I worked out some of my own problems, or at least explored them while doing the script."

Behr admits that there was an equally powerful incentive in coming up with the story. "We wanted to do a show about the Ferengi that was more serious," he says. "The Ferengi just get *ripped* by people. There are people who love them, and a lot of people who hate them. They just find them silly." This could be because of the way the species was first portrayed on *TNG*.

Behr came up with the idea to do a show about

The creation of Moogie, a female who could hold her own against *any* male, was another step in the "evolution" of the Ferengi.
ROBBIE ROBINSON

brothers. "I'm fascinated by sibling relationships and male bonding," he says. "I wanted to look deeper into that. And I also thought it would be fun to see a Ferengi woman who did not fit the supposed stereotype."

The concept was that Quark's moogie would be a women's libber, but one who went beyond the actions of a stereotypical protester. If all she did was sit around "screaming to end profit," comments Wolfe, she wouldn't have been a true Ferengi. Ishka had no desire to put an end to the financial aspects of the Ferengi way of life. She just wanted in on them, being a female who wanted the opportunity to out-earn the men.

As with "Prophet Motive," Auberjonois found that rehearsing his principal actors prior to the start of production was very useful, particularly in working out the physical comedy. During some of those rehearsals, Shimerman and Max Grodénchik were joined by Andrea Martin, whom Shimerman calls "a delight to work with, and a great sport," particularly considering the amount of time she had to spend in makeup.

Martin was cast at Auberjonois's suggestion. "I admired her and thought she would have the right take on it," says Auberjonois. "It needed to be a comic performance, but by a really good actor. We had a lot of trouble finding the right balance in the people we saw." Finally, Auberjonois mentioned Martin's name to the producers, and "Ira just went for it," he recalls.

"I love her from *SCTV*," acknowledges Behr. "We all do. The public loves *Saturday Night Live*, and everyone else, I think, loves *Second City*."

Martin may have wondered just how much they loved her by the time she realized the true meaning of prosthetic acting, which dictated three hours in the makeup chair every day. And as an older Ferengi, Martin's makeup called for extra care. "To make her head a little more wrinkly," says Makeup Designer Michael Westmore, "we made a thin skin that went over one of our stock Ferengi heads. Then we made a new face for her, wrinkled, and did the backs of her hands." And because Ishka was to be nude in several scenes, they also had to create makeup for body terrain previously untraveled in Ferengis. A take over Ishka's shoulder had to be reshot because the producers didn't feel that Martin's supple skin matched the rest of Ishka's appearance. "So we literally took Kleenex, wrinkled it up and rubberized it, and covered her back and shoulders," recounts Westmore. "She wasn't thrilled."

Ishka's nude scenes created some technical problems for Auberjonois as well. "It was very limiting, having to hide her behind things," he says. For the scene in which Ishka finally imprints her confession, for example, Auberjonois blocked parts of her anatomy with a bowl of Ferengi fruit.

The fruit bowl came in handy for a different scene as well, one that Auberjonois is particularly happy with. As he blocked the scene in which Rom and Quark tussle on the floor in Ishka's living room, Auberjonois placed the bowl where it would be sure to fall to the ground during the tumult. By luck, the impacted fruit flew directly at the camera, as if on cue. "I didn't know it would turn out so wonderfully." He grins. "If it had been in 3-D, it would have been great!"

As an interesting side note, brothers Rom and Quark were stunt doubled in the fight scene by Stunt Coordinator Dennis Madalone and his brother-in-law, George Colucci.

Despite the quasi-serious nature of the Ferengi storyline, Writers Behr and Wolfe had a great deal of fun making up details for viewers' first glimpse of Ferenginar, right down to the scene descriptions that no one but cast and crew would read. In Act 2, for example, we are told that "Ferenginar, the home-

Planning is everything, but sometimes a director gets lucky.
ROBBIE ROBINSON

world of the Ferengi, is a fetid dismal swamp, subject to a near endless downpour."

Why does it always rain there?

Responds Behr, "Because Robert had this feeling that given the way Ferengi look, the style of body with big heads and ears and little eyes and no hair, that they would live in a moist climate."

Adds Wolfe: "We've never really seen rain on the planets we've gone to. We tend to do desert a lot. Vulcan: hot and dry. Cardassia: hot and dry. We wanted something different for Ferenginar."

It also gave them the opportunity to do more Ferengi-oriented shtick, such as providing towels at the door for people to dry off, for a price.

In addition to naming the Ferengi homeworld for the first time, "Family Business" introduces the term slips, which joins strips and bars in the latinum lexicon. Personnel-wise, the episode is notable for the introduction of the recurring characters of Brunt, F.C.A. (played by Jeffrey Combs, a favorite of the producers from "Meridian," and later to be seen as the Vorta Weyoun), and Kasidy Yates (Penny Johnson, who'd also appeared in the *TNG* episode "Homeward," as Dobara). Kasidy's brother lives on Cestus III (last mentioned in the original series' episode "Arena"), which is evidently no longer claimed by the Gorn, and he plays baseball for the Pike City Pioneers.

"Yeah, it was named after Christopher Pike." Wolfe smiles. "We wanted to come up with a cool name for a town and we figured, hey, for all we know, Pike was the one who discovered that world in the first place."

SHAKAAR

Episode #470

WRITTEN BY **GORDON DAWSON**
DIRECTED BY **JONATHAN WEST**

GUEST CAST

Shakaar	DUNCAN REGEHR
Lupaza	DIANE SALINGER
Furel	WILLIAM LUCKING
Syvar	SHERMAN HOWARD
Lenaris Holem	JOHN DOMAN
Security Officer	JOHN KENTON SHULL
Trooper	HARRY HUTCHINSON

SPECIAL GUEST STAR

Kai Winn	LOUISE FLETCHER

STARDATE UNKNOWN

Kira and Shakaar convince Colonel Lenaris that there's a better way than fighting to end their conflict. DANNY FELD

Kira is not happy when she learns that Kai Winn has been appointed to take over the duties of the recently deceased first minister of Bajor's Provisional Government. Although there will be a formal election in a few weeks, she knows that no one is likely to oppose Winn. The idea of placing both Bajor's spiritual and political future into Winn's hands is disquieting.

Equally disquieting is the subsequent visit Kira receives from Winn, who has come to ask the major to intervene in a dispute in her home province of Dahkur. A group of farmers, led by Shakaar, the head of Kira's resistance cell during the Cardassian occupation, refuses to give up government-provided soil reclamators needed for Bajor's recovery efforts.

For the good of Bajor, Kira agrees to talk to Shakaar about returning the agricultural equipment. However, she is surprised when she hears her old friend's side of the story. The Dahkur farmers only recently received the reclamators, after waiting three long years for them. They were promised that they could keep them for at least a year, but with the death of the first minister, the promise was withdrawn. The government's new project is geared toward food production for export, while Dahkur needs the equipment to feed the local community.

Kira feels a compromise may be possible if Shakaar speaks with the kai, and she arranges a meeting, which Winn agrees to attend. But instead of meeting with Shakaar, Winn sends two security officers to arrest him. Infuriated by the deception, Kira helps Shakaar subdue the guards and offers to help him fight the kai.

Back at DS9, O'Brien is experiencing an epic winning streak at the dart board in Quark's bar. Recognizing the financial value of the chief's luck, Quark begins setting up matches, without O'Brien's knowledge. The chief is keen to take on all comers, until he injures his shoulder, forfeiting the game to his opponent. The sorriest person at the match is Quark, who'd placed a mountain of latinum on O'Brien.

Now fugitives, Shakaar, Kira, and their supporters hide in the mountains where they once eluded the Cardassians. The longer the pursuit goes on, the more word of the conflict spreads among the Bajoran people, and many of them begin to side with Shakaar. Realizing that she is fighting an increasingly unpopular battle, Winn turns to Sisko for the Federation's assistance in bringing in Shakaar. Sisko refuses to intervene, and instead suggests she withdraw her troops. But Winn sees the conflict as a personal test by the Prophets and presses on.

As Bajoran troops close in, the exhausted fugitives realize there is no option but to stop running and fight. Reluctantly, Shakaar leads them into a canyon to set up an ambush. But when the time comes for them to fire on fellow Bajorans, many of them former resistance fighters like Shakaar, they can't do it. Shakaar and Kira drop their weapons and confront the pursuing troops. After a tense conversation, a cease-fire is called, and Shakaar is escorted to Winn.

To Winn's surprise, Shakaar announces his intention to oppose the kai in the upcoming election for first minister. Realizing that a public competition will expose all of the details of the conflict to the public, including the fact that Winn was willing to risk a civil war over farm equipment, the kai opts to drop out of the race.

Director of Photography Jonathan West finally made his directorial debut in "Shakaar," after having planted the seed in executive producer Rick Berman's mind during *TNG*'s final season. West felt he was up to it. "I'd been an actor and I'd worked in theatre, so I knew actors and I understood the story-telling process," he says. "I'd also taken part in the Television Academy's directorial workshop, and that was a great learning experience."

West's assignment to "Shakaar" was the luck of the draw, although luck may not be the best word for at least part of the shooting experience. Steve Oster recalls that the location filming in Bronson Canyon was so cold (Call sheets for the week stressed the need for space heaters, warm clothes, and boots for mud.) that the producers decided not to film everything that had been scheduled for the setting. "We just got the establishing shots of Shakaar's house up there, and rebuilt the house on Stage 18 for close-ups," Oster recalls. However, the temperamental March weather did allow production to take advantage of the famous Bronson caves for one of the scenes. Notes West, "The schedule changed so much because of the rain that we wound up with some empty time on location, so we got into the real caves," rather than use the artificial ones that would have been created on the soundstages.

As would happen again in subsequent episodes directed by West, Kris Krosskove moved to the position of director of photography on "Shakaar," with Ray Stella filling in for him as camera operator. West credits Krosskove with designing some strikingly realistic effects meant to emulate Bajor's harsh sunlight and cool blue moonlight for scenes where Shakaar's house was recreated on interior soundstages.

After seeing "lots of people," according to Ira Behr, Duncan Regehr, previously seen in the *TNG* episode "Sub Rosa," was cast in what was to become the recurring role of Shakaar. Envisioned as a Clint Eastwood–type, the actor had to convey the qualities that would make him both "a good leader and a good killer; we had to give him that edge," says West.

Used since the very early days of filmmaking, Bronson Canyon is the site for this location shoot. DANNY FELD

Duncan Regehr was cast as Shakaar, with the belief that the character and actor could hold their own against Visitor's Kira. ROBBIE ROBINSON

There was also the thought that this man might turn into a love interest for Kira, and, per West, who served as director of photography on "Sub Rosa," Regehr definitely had "a romantic flare about him when he played the ghost." Accordingly, the script included "a couple little subtle beats to play, just to see if we could gain some chemistry between the actors," recalls Ron Moore. "And it seemed to work."

The script is credited to Gordon Dawson, a close associate of Sam Peckinpah, and the man who gave Ira Behr his first episodic television assignment (on *Brett Maverick*). "It was great to give an episode to the guy who gave me my first episode," comments Behr, although he admits the script went through a number of changes before it finally made it into production. Both Moore and René Echevarria recall that the script already existed when they transferred from *TNG* to the *DS9* writing staff.

"To be fair," says Echevarria, "they had sent Gordon off with a structure that, in a lot of ways, didn't work." And production of the episode was delayed when the studio and the producers decided to move stories further away from Bajor and Bajoran politics. Late in the season, the decision finally was made to revive "Shakaar." The internal writing team ended up rebreaking the story—several times. "Three different times with three different takes," recalls Moore. At one point, he says, "it was going to be about a museum on Bajor that was being reopened for the first time since the occupation. They were putting efforts and funds into opening this great cultural relic from their past. And Shakaar and his people were upset because they needed the resources for their farming equipment to feed people. It became this debate about culture versus survival that just didn't go anywhere."

Kai Winn was a latecomer to the mix and the script's dramatic salvation. It was only after the writers envisioned Winn's role in the Bajoran/Cardassian peace treaty ("Life Support") that things began to click. "We thought, 'What if she goes all the way and becomes leader of the planet? That will really set the stakes and bring Kira into the story,'" says Moore.

Cast and crew alike have nothing but praise for Louise Fletcher. "Working with her is great fun," says Nana Visitor, but she admits that Kira's feelings toward Winn take center stage when they act together. "I think of how much I hate this woman," she says. "I think of what she's done. I think that my lover is dead because of her. I think of the ill-intentions toward our people."

The Bajoran language in the script comes courtesy of *DS9*'s unofficial staff linguist Moore. "I just make it up," he chuckles. "I do it phonetically so it has a certain rhythm and sound in my head that I can tag as the way Bajorans sound." He also provides an English translation for the benefit of the actors. Kira's prayer in "Shakaar"'s teaser, for example, is a request that Bareil be guided and protected on his journey to the gates of heaven.

But surely Moore, nominally the "Klingon guy" on the writing team, doesn't also make up the Klingon language he uses? Well . . . yes. "Marc Okrand's *Klingon Dictionary* sits on my desk," Moore states emphatically, "right here. But I use it very infrequently. To be honest, Marc baffles me. I'm not a linguist. I failed languages. Rules of grammar and syntax just put me away. So I just make it up and make it sound as cool as I can."

FACETS

Episode #471

WRITTEN BY **RENÉ ECHEVARRIA**
DIRECTED BY **CLIFF BOLE**

GUEST CAST

Guardian	JEFREY ALAN CHANDLER
Rom	MAX GRODÉNCHIK
Nog	ARON EISENBERG
Leeta	CHASE MASTERSON
Computer Voice	MAJEL BARRETT

STARDATE UNKNOWN

Quark's annoyance at his nephew's intention to attend Starfleet Academy is mollified when Dax invites him to attend a "very important meeting" for the station's senior staff. In the wardroom, Dax asks the group, as her closest acquaintances, to participate in her *zhian'tara*, the Trill Rite of Closure. If her friends agree to loan her their bodies for a few hours, Jadzia will have the opportunity to actually meet each of Dax's previous hosts. The ritual consists of the telepathic transfer of each host's memories into a temporary host's body, a procedure accomplished with the assistance of an unjoined Trill Guardian.

Sisko, Kira, Bashir, Odo, Quark, O'Brien, and Leeta each agree, and Kira is chosen as the recipient of Lela, Dax's first host. During this initial transference, Jadzia is put at ease by Kira/Lela's friendly man-

The transfer of Curzon's memories into Odo's body produces unexpected results. ROBBIE ROBINSON

ner, and she discovers that a number of personality traits she had always interpreted as unconscious habits actually originated with Lela. She makes similar discoveries about Dax's next host, Tobin, embodied by Chief O'Brien, and Leeta/Emony. Quark isn't happy about sharing his body with Audrid, a female, but he manages to get through the experience, and Bashir, speaking as Torias, expresses regret that his life was cut short by an accident.

Jadzia is apprehensive about meeting Dax's next host, Joran ("Equilibrium"). Sisko has volunteered to host the essence of this unbalanced murderer, al though not without the precaution of having Odo lock him in a holding cell. But although he is physically confined, Sisko/Joran manages to use his intellect to shake Jadzia's confidence in herself, and to trick her into lowering the cell's force field. When he attempts to strangle her, Jadzia manages to drop him with a few well-placed Klingon-style blows, and Sisko wrests control of his body from Joran.

His participation in the *zhian'tara* completed, Quark simmers while his nephew goes through exercises to ready himself for the Academy Preparatory Program, six weeks of classes that could be vital to Nog's getting into Starfleet Academy. Quark's brother Rom optimistically commissions a cadet's uniform from Garak for his son, but Quark ominously warns him that he's wasted his money. Later, when Nog fails one of his exercises, a suspicious Rom surmises that Quark had something to do with it.

Jadzia's experience with Joran has left her feeling insecure; she realizes that she may have delayed participating in the *zhian'tara* because she feels she doesn't measure up to Dax's other hosts. After all, her previous host, Curzon, had tried to wash her out of the Trill Initiate program, and Curzon is the final host that she will encounter.

Curzon's joining with Odo is something of a surprise to everyone. With the changeling's morphing abilities, the combined entities wind up looking like a cross between Odo and Curzon, right down to the latter's spots. Rather than engaging in conversation with Jadzia, the joined being immediately seeks out Curzon's old friend Sisko. Although Sisko would love to spend time with the old man, he brings him back to Jadzia. However, when Jadzia attempts to discuss her days as an initiate with Odo/Curzon, he initially changes the subject. Pressing the point, Jadzia asks why he didn't object when she was reinstated into the program. Reluctantly, Odo/Curzon notes that he just felt sorry for her, which does nothing to diminish

Jadzia's insecurity. But she's really thrown for a loop by his next statement: Curzon and Odo love being joined and have decided to remain together permanently. Dax will have to do without Curzon's memories!

Intimidated by Curzon, Jadzia seems prepared to accept his decision. But Sisko points out that Curzon, for all his charm, can also be manipulative and self-ish. He urges Jadzia to confront him, just as Sisko did in the past whenever Curzon crossed the line in their friendship.

In the meantime, Rom, too, has a confrontation. He accuses his brother of reconfiguring the holo-suites so that Nog would fail his test. Quark admits that it's true, although he claims he did it for Nog's own good. Furious, Rom tells Quark that Sisko is going to let Nog retake the test, and if Quark wants to keep his bar standing, he won't interfere. Cowed by his brother's atypically courageous behavior, Quark backs down, and Nog passes his tests.

When Jadzia faces Odo/Curzon and demands that he return her memories, Curzon tries to intimi-date her once again. This time, however, he fails, and finally admits that the reason he had her dropped from the intitiate program was that he fell in love with her. Guilt-ridden over his actions, he was grate-ful when she decided to reapply. But because he still loves her, he is too ashamed to rejoin with Dax. A sympathetic Jadzia tells Curzon that she loves him as well, which is why they *should* be rejoined: that way, Jadzia and Curzon can be together, through Dax. Curzon agrees, and allows his memories to be trans-ferred back to Dax, leaving Jadzia feeling more cer-tain of herself than ever before.

If Jadzia Dax thought she had a tough time in Season 3, she's not alone. The writing staff had an equally difficult time working with her storylines. The three shows in which she played the most prominent role—"Equilibrium," "Meridian," and "Facets"—"were all difficult to bring off," according to Ron Moore. That might have some-thing to do with the fact that each of them was based on a rather abstract story concept into which the character of Dax was inserted, from "A magician comes to DS9" to "Let's do *Brigadoon*" to "Let's do *Sybil*."

For "Facets," it was Ira Behr's idea to do an episode based on *Sybil,* the stirring psychological study of a woman with multiple-personality disorder, says writer René Echevarria. But although *Sybil* had worked as an engrossing book and a memorable tele-

Auberjonois lends Odo's face to Curzon. ROBBIE ROBINSON

vision movie, it didn't translate smoothly into a Jadzia Dax story. "I just kept bumping into the fact that doing *Sybil* necessitates coming up with a deep, dark secret that explains why this phenomenon is happen-ing [to Dax]," says Echevarria. "But I felt that we had already done that with her in 'Equilibrium' and we couldn't do that again."

Finally Echevarria framed an idea about a bizarre Trill ritual that would invoke all of Dax's hosts. That seemed to work, except for the fact that it would essentially turn the episode into a one-person show, which wouldn't be very dynamic. When all of the activity focused on watching Jadzia change into each host, "it just didn't give us anything," comments Moore. "Once she became each host, it was kind of 'Okay, let's sit back and watch Dax be *this* person now.' There was no true interaction between Jadzia and that host. So we ultimately decided to throw the hosts into our other cast members and set up scenes with them all."

That got the ball rolling, although it certainly didn't make plotting the course simple. "I had to research what had been established in the series, how many hosts there were and who, and track them to the number of male and female characters we had available," says Echevarria. It quickly became appar-ent that there weren't enough women among the reg-ular and recurring cast members to play all of Dax's female hosts. "That's how we came up with the idea of Quark being trapped into being Audrid," adds

Echevarria. "If any male was going to pretend to be a woman, it had to be Quark!"

That bit of "sub-casting" made sense, even though Armin Shimerman played the part a little differently than his coworkers had assumed. "Before I shot it, everyone said to me, 'This is going to be hysterical, you playing a woman,'" recalls Shimerman. "They thought I was going to do Milton Berle. But I thought that was too easy a choice. I never saw it as a comic scene. Instead, I found as much of my *anima*, my female side, as I could and played it as straight as possible," with the exception of the point where Quark's personality emerges to complain. That, admits Shimerman, was played for comedy, because "the woman wasn't a comic character, but Quark is."

A different bit of female subcasting made less sense, but only because the writers didn't have time to set it up properly. With two female hosts left to place, choices were limited. As Dax's first host, Lela would be the first alternate to appear, and her scene with Jadzia would be longer than those of the others (with the exception of Joran, whom Echevarria had always intended to link with Sisko, and Curzon, who would carry a major portion of the plot). Kira was the obvious choice for Lela's embodiment. But what of Emony, the gymnast?

The initial plan had been to bring Keiko O'Brien to the party, and allow Keiko to be Emony. But as it happened, Actress Rosalind Chao was not available the week of filming. So they turned to a character introduced to the *DS9* audience only a few weeks earlier: the dabo girl Leeta. "We thought, 'Why *not* Leeta?'" says Echevarria. "So we tossed off a line in the teaser about she and Dax having spent 'quite a bit of time together.'"

The line served its purpose, but Ira Behr doesn't blame viewers if they didn't entirely buy it. "It didn't make any sense," he says. "We paid lip service [to the relationship between Dax and Leeta], but it never really paid off again. It was just one of those things. Sometimes you've just gotta shoehorn ideas into an episode to keep it going."

The other embodiments were easier to fabricate. "I just had to make them up," says Echevarria. "Like Tobin, a little nebbishy guy, a nervous Nellie, would be fun for O'Brien." Apparently it was also fun for Colm Meaney, who performed the role in convincingly nerdy style, complete with a flat, nasal American accent.

As the aggressive Torias (of whom we would hear more in the fourth season's "Rejoined," Siddig El Fadil also got the opportunity to do a different accent,

Science fiction offers actors unique opportunities: Shimerman plays the female Audrid, one of Dax's hosts. ROBBIE ROBINSON

although it wasn't his idea. "On the spur of the moment, right before the camera rolled, the director (Cliff Bole) asked me for a swaggering John Wayne-y/Humphrey Bogart-y kind of American accent," notes Siddig. "I couldn't quite come up with it. If it sounded a bit bizarre, it's probably because it wasn't really very true."

Conversely, the way that Avery Brooks portrayed Joran was so convincing that the producers opted to reshoot that scene. "Avery was *too* wicked," says Gary Hutzel, who worked with Bole to stage the sequence's force field effect. "He talked in this very quiet voice that was really creepy and literally sent shivers up your spine. The producers decided it was too much."

The scenes with the various hosts were written to play longer than the versions the audience ultimately saw, according to Echevarria, and they all included little transitional moments that had been carefully worked out by Echevarria and Director Bole. "In the first one," Echevarria explains, "Lela got a pot of clay and poured it, and Cliff did a close-up of the pot. Then he had Jadzia come over and take it from Lela's hand and move away, and when he widened the shot [to follow her], we saw that it was now Jadzia and Tobin talking, and so forth. The transitions were really great, but they got cut for time."

Echevarria also wrote the Trill language used by the Guardian in the *zhian'tara* ritual. "It's all gobbledy-gook, although I used little roots that I repeated throughout, and I used the names of the people involved," he explains. "I tried to track them with something melodic, but I should have talked about it to the actor playing the Guardian, because he certainly didn't read the words the way I'd imagined them."

Although the preliminary script had its clever moments, it never caught fire until the writers hatched the idea of focusing on Curzon and his impact on both Jadzia and Odo. Toward that end, Echevarria now admits that the episode might have been stronger if he'd gotten to that part of the script a little faster. "Ira strongly recommended that we get to Curzon's full act quicker and not see all of the hosts," he says. "But I wanted to see them all, and finally Ira said, 'Okay, see how it looks.'"

Curzon's fully realized persona came as something of a surprise to his creators. "If I had it to do over again, I would have been more careful about his character," comments Echevarria. "He was almost always drinking or talking about drinking in those scenes." (At one point, Curzon requests *tranya* at Quark's bar, the drink served by Balok in the original series episode "The Corbomite Maneuver.")

"The way Curzon came across was by no means the way I saw his character," states Behr. "I saw him as kind of a bon vivant. Instead, he was like Shecky Curzon, a wacky, funny guy."

But Rene Auberjonois had a good time playing him. "It was a little complex, because I had to be both Odo and Curzon Dax. That was tricky, but it was fun." However, Auberjonois thought of Curzon as "swashbuckling, almost a Cyrano character. His nose was so prominent, and he was such a rake."

Auberjonois points out that the episode marked "the first time that Odo got to morph into another kind of humanoid." That means it was also the first time that Michael Westmore had to create a kind of hybrid look for the changeling. (He would later create other hybrids such as Odo-as-Klingon in "Apocalypse Rising," and Odo-as-Odo-with-a-lot-more-practice in "Children of Time.") "The prosthetics piece was thicker because it had more features laid into it," notes Auberjonois. "It was still Odo's makeup, with features that were more delineated. And, in a weird way, it was closer to my own face than usual."

To achieve that look, Westmore cast a new plaster form of Auberjonois's face and sculpted a new face onto it. "We got a picture of the original actor (Frank Owen Smith, who played Curzon in "Emissary") and put a little bit of his face into Odo's face," says Westmore. "Then I put Trill spots on him."

For Odo/Curzon's flashy new outfit, the Wardrobe Department also drew inspiration from the pilot episode. "I recall going back to 'Emissary' and reworking who Curzon was," says Robert Blackman. "He was a very hedonistic and very sensual man." Blackman designed a garment that resembled the Trill-wear previously seen on the series, "but I made it out of these amazingly tactile fabrics, like velour brocade."

Putting Odo/Curzon into his new outfit was somewhat more complicated than the changeling-Trill made it appear. The seamless effect, jointly created by Bole's first unit team and Gary Hutzel's visual effects crew, involved locking down the camera and shooting three different plates: one with Auberjonois in Odo's traditional uniform, one of the empty set, and one of the actor wearing the new Trill design. The magic was completed in the compositing bay.

Actor Aron Eisenberg also received a new wardrobe item in "Facets," even though it wasn't yet official: the uniform of an Academy cadet (newly redesigned for this episode). "It was really great for Nog because it made him feel that he was achieving his dream," Eisenberg says. "Putting on the uniform gave him a sense of, 'I'm not a troublemaker, I'm part of Starfleet.'" Eisenberg, who began to figure more prominently in the series during its fifth season, couldn't help feeling a little of that awe himself. "Now I'm a part of the core of the show, and that was really cool."

Nog's decision to go to Starfleet Academy, and Rom's ferocious defense of that decision here, also represented a turning point for Actor Max Grodénchik. "When the series started, Rom was very adamant about keeping Nog away from Keiko's school," he says. "And here, years later, Rom was going to bat for his son to go to Starfleet to get an education, doing exactly the opposite of what he started out believing. The writers allowed Rom to grow, which was just fantastic. And after standing up for his son, the next logical step for him was to stand up for himself when he has to fight for something he believes in strongly. And that," Grodénchik emphasizes, "made the union episode ("Bar Association") possible."

To go along with Nog's more mature role, the producers decided that it was time to "age" his makeup accordingly. "We added cheekbones," says Westmore. "Aron used to wear just a head piece and a nose. But starting with "Facets," we made a new prosthetic appliance so the nose is now enjoined with the cheekbones. It made Nog look a little bit older, but we still left the freckles on," he adds with a grin.

THE ADVERSARY

Episode #472

WRITTEN BY IRA STEVEN BEHR &
ROBERT HEWITT WOLFE
DIRECTED BY ALEXANDER SINGER

GUEST CAST

Krajensky	LAWRENCE PRESSMAN
Michael Eddington	KENNETH MARSHALL
Bolian	JEFF AUSTIN
Computer Voice	MAJEL BARRETT

STARDATE 48959.1

The mood in the wardroom is decidedly upbeat as Sisko receives a fourth pip for his collar, signifying his promotion to captain. At the subsequent celebration party, Federation Ambassador Krajensky injects a "business-as-usual" atmosphere when he tells Sisko about a coup that has taken place on the Tzenkethi homeworld. Sisko is to take Krajensky and the *Defiant* to that sector to "remind" the Tzenkethi of the Federation's presence on nearby colony worlds.

Not long after departing, the *Defiant* receives a distress signal from a colonist on Barisa Prime, stating that the planet is under attack by the Tzenkethi. When contact is abruptly cut off, Sisko sets course for the colony world and attempts to brief Starfleet Command about the incident. However, the ship's communications system is malfunctioning. O'Brien and Dax discover that strange alien devices have infiltrated the ship's critical systems; their placement is obviously the work of a saboteur. Since the saboteur would have been exposed to trace amounts of tetryon particles when he placed one of the devices, Dax scans each member of the crew for signs of the particles. Within minutes she discovers that Krajensky is the culprit, and also that he is a changeling, who morphs before their eyes and escapes through an access hatch.

It quickly becomes clear that the changeling has taken control of the ship. The crew can do nothing to prevent him from activating the cloaking field and arming the *Defiant*'s weapons. Sisko realizes that Krajensky's visit to DS9, his information about the Tzenkethi coup, and the transmission from Barisa Prime were all faked. It seems likely the Dominion is hoping to start a war between the Federation and the Tzenkethi that would destabilize the Alpha Quadrant and make it easier for them to move in. With the *Defiant* primed for battle and just a few hours from

Odo takes the dying changeling's words to heart. ROBBIE ROBINSON

the Tzenkethi border, it is imperative that they locate the changeling.

They've barely begun their search when O'Brien finds Dax unconscious in the engine room; he'll have to make the repairs alone. Sisko decides that if O'Brien can't regain control of the vessel before they get to the Tzenkethi border, he'll have to destroy the *Defiant*.

Because the changeling can look like anyone, Sisko has his officers pair up, with instructions to keep their partner in sight at all times. But in the course of hunting down the shape-shifter, Sisko, Odo, Eddington, Kira, and a Bolian officer are each separated from their partners, and suspicion grows among the crewmembers. Odo points out that Sisko, who has been wounded in an encounter with the changeling, is not a shape-shifter; he's bleeding. If the substance had been fake changeling blood, it would have reverted to gelatinous goo after it was separated from his body.

Now armed with a way of locating the changeling

via simple blood tests, Sisko has Bashir test everyone. When Eddington's blood seems to morph into orange goo, he is taken into custody. But moments later, they discover a second Bashir, the real Bashir, and realize they were duped by the shape-shifter. The changeling escapes again, just as the *Defiant* enters Tzenkethi space.

Grimly, Sisko initiates the auto-destruct sequence, giving O'Brien only ten minutes to find a way to gain access to the ship's sabotaged systems. But as he works, Odo appears . . . and then another Odo. Unwilling to be sidetracked by playing "choose the changeling," O'Brien manages to drop the force fields that had kept him from repairing the saboteur's work. The false Odo changes form and attacks O'Brien and Odo. In the course of fending him off, the real Odo inadvertently causes the changeling to fall into the ship's warp core, fatally injuring him. O'Brien completes his repairs, returning control of the ship to Sisko. The captain deactivates the self-destruct. Back at DS9, Odo conveys some disturbing news; the dying changeling's last words were, "You're too late. We're everywhere."

Hunting for the changeling in the narrow confines of the *Defiant* ratcheted up the anxiety factor. J. VILES

"'The Adversary' really appealed to me in this sort of visceral John Wayne level," comments Ron Moore. "There's a monster on the ship, it's after us, and we're gonna hunt it down and kill it. We're not gonna negotiate with it, we're not gonna worry about whether it's sentient, we're not gonna play any of the usual *Star Trek* games with it. It's just, 'Find and kill the monster.' There was something very pure about that show."

Scratch the surface of anything that sounds simple, and you'll discover that it's complicated. Case in point, the fact that the producers of *Deep Space Nine* initially planned to end Season 3 with a cliff-hanger that would be resolved in the opening episode of Season 4.

"We had been talking about this big, very political two-part story with shape-shifters," recalls René Echevarria. "We'd decided that the scariest thing would be to set the story at home, with people we care about." That idea quickly evolved into a story that involved "meeting Sisko's dad, seeing his restaurant, and learning that shape-shifters were on Earth, and had infiltrated the very heart of . . ." Echevarria pauses. "That was the cliff-hanger ending."

But for some reason, the studio didn't want a cliff-hanger that year. To say that this initiated a change of plans is putting it mildly. "We had to find a premise!" Ira Steven Behr says. "We had one week to

actually write a script before preproduction started." With nothing more promising on the horizon, the writers decided to keep their focus on shape-shifters. "We knew that we wanted to do something with the Dominion and we wanted to do paranoia," says Behr. "That's the thing we held on to: paranoia."

But what to do with the shape-shifters? The producers opted to hold onto their concept for the shape-shifter threat on Earth for some time in the fourth season "Homefront," and "Paradise Lost." So what else could they do with only one episode? "We knew that for just one episode, we couldn't justify building the sets for the Founder's planet," says Robert Hewitt Wolfe. (It would have to be a whole new planet, since the Founders had abandoned their old home in the Omarion Nebula in "The Die Is Cast"). "We needed to do something more contained," he continues. That's when the idea of *Defiant* "heading inexplicably toward destruction, like the death machine that she really is, being all locked down and going like a runaway train, became the basic hook that everyone really liked." That, and the idea of "shape-shifters running amok," he adds.

A few more elements went into the conceptual pot. "We thought, 'What about *The Thing*?'" says Behr, invoking the name of the classic 1951 film of paranoia at an isolated encampment. Finally, they began to consider the line they'd come up with at the beginning of Season 3: "No shape-shifter has ever harmed another." "We took that line and made the whole episode about it," says Behr, who shared the writing chores for the episode, originally known as "Flashpoint," with frequent partner Wolfe. "We wrote the script very fast."

Turning the *Defiant* into a "runaway train" wasn't as simple as it sounded, nor was it as cheap. "We wound up building the ship's engineering room because we needed to have a place where we could play out this thing," sighs Behr. "It became a huge, double-level set, the kind of a set that normally would be built over the show's hiatus and with a budget that could be amortized over the course of the subsequent season. But it was the end of the season, and believe me, it just grew out of nowhere."

With its glowing warp core and expansive graphics, the engineering room is one of the most distinctive sets ever built for the series, much to the dismay of Bob della Santina, who is under an eternal mandate to conserve soundstage space. "The Art Department is wonderful about designing sets that we can utilize portions of [for other sets]," says della Santina. "We can use the *Defiant*'s mess hall as an infirmary and a transporter room, so we get mileage out of that. But there's nothing we can do with engineering. You can't disguise it."

The episode also gave the Art Department the opportunity to create several new props, including a new phaser rifle, which was the last design submitted by Artist Jim Martin before he left the show to work on the feature *The Phantom*. Martin designed the rifles with a new feature: triggers. "They're buttons, actually," explains Joe Longo. "Ira said that when he was watching people shoot, they hadn't been activating anything, so we made them more realistic. It gives the actors something to do."

The glowing wormlike fibers that entangle the *Defiant*'s circuitry may look like computer animation, but, in fact, they were a physical effect supervised by Gary Monak. "We projected a high intensity light through some fiber optics. Unlike regular optics where the light comes out of the end, this was side-lit, so the whole tube threw off light," Monak explains. "And we put a color wheel inside the projector to make the fibers look like they were alive and pulsating."

"The episode was filled with visual effects that we hadn't used before," notes Steve Oster. "There were more morphs than in any other single episode, and the final battle between Odo and the changeling involved a lot of complicated bluescreen work."

"Complicated" doesn't begin to tell the story. "Everything in that final confrontation had to be choreographed and relayed to the visual effects people," says Director Alexander Singer, who set aside his usual habit of using storyboards on such scenes. "It was so difficult that we had the actors walk through the scenes while the effects people and I watched them and decided, 'We're gonna have to do so-and-so; this is a matte shot; this is going to be done by a stunt man.'"

"It was very, very complex," concurs Rene Auberjonois. "After we completed the first-unit photography, the season wrapped and everyone went away, except for the crew and Larry Pressman and me. During the regular shooting, we had this whole struggle holding on to each other, but then we had to reenact it separately, looking at a monitor and lining up our bodies correctly when the other actor wasn't there anymore. I had to put my hands up until they were in exactly the same place [as they'd been before] and act the scenes without Larry there, and then he had to do it the same way."

Josh Rose got a charge out of working on the fight sequence between the two changelings. "This was the first time where [joining] 'goo to goo' wasn't a slow process," he says. "It had to appear violent. To make the action realistic, the animators imitated real life. When you hit your hand, it jolts and there's a reaction. So in the computer, when the goo models impacted, the animators sent out a little ripple to make it look real. Then they had to meld them together. There's never a line where they meet, they just instantly mesh."

Glenn Neufeld has two favorite moments amid all the episode's morphing. "The first is when Dax scans Krajensky and realizes he's the changeling," Neufeld says. "We made an incredibly quick transition, with Lawrence Pressman going from live-action goo to crouched goo. There are only *four frames* of animation."

Neufeld's second-favorite bit of action occurs just seconds later, as "Krajensky" makes his escape through an access hatch in the ceiling. "The actors all look up at the ceiling, and its 'Oh, oh, tableau (a theatrical moment where the cast onstage freezes)!' I mean, it was *supposed* to be tableau, but as a locked-off 17-millimeter shot, it just didn't play." Singer and Neufeld removed a wall to create some working space, and restationed the equipment above the actors for a shot that would provide room to show the liquefied changeling moving out. "I wasn't sure

Finally Sisko achieves captain's rank. ROBBIE ROBINSON

how it was going to work," Neufeld admits. "I told the animators at VisionArt to have the tube of goo go out, and to put a tail on it. Of course, I was just expecting to see the tail a little bit as it goes out of frame. But they animated it so that the tail comes up and actually whips around in front of the camera. I saw it and said, "Yes! That's exactly what we needed.""

Rose, too, has a favorite moment. "We did a shot where this computer-generated goo arm comes out and grabs an actor by the neck and throws him against the bulkhead." He laughs. "It was great. The interaction between the actor and the goo really resembled live action."

The actor that got bashed by the changeling in that shot was actually Dennis Madalone, and getting cast as the character once again was part of his personal master plan. Having played Marauder, the guy with one eye in the "Crossover" episodes, Madalone felt that it was only logical that his character exist as station personnel in the "regular" universe as well, probably as a guy with both eyes. "I brought it up at the production meeting for 'The Adversary,' and I didn't think that Ira was gonna buy it, but he said, 'That's right. This is where Dennis is the other guy.'"

Madalone played his role with gusto, which resulted in his convincing interaction with the CG apparition. "To this day, people who saw the dailies think I broke my neck. But I obviously had to sell it so that it looks like the character eats it!"

The director appreciated Madalone's special qualifications for the role. "I would never have done that with an actor, because he could bash his brains out!" Singer laughs. "Dennis did the stunt with his usual enthusiasm, and *my* brains were rattled by it. Of course, we had discussed it well in advance, and rehearsed it, but it was a very difficult shot to do."

Another character that Singer chose to emphasize was Eddington, who played a prominent role in the episode. "It was obvious that he should be covered with close-ups," notes Singer. "Beyond this episode I couldn't say, but for the course of this show, I treated him like a regular member of the cast."

Although Eddington is proven innocent, there had always been an edge to his character from his first appearance in "The Search," and the episode made good use of that quality. "When we created Eddington, we wanted Joe Professional on the station," says Behr. "He didn't have to be a villain, he was just another professional who didn't have to be a nice guy."

Actor Kenneth Marshall appreciated this potential to stand out. "The way Eddington is written always presents the idea that he's a threat in some way," he says. "He had sabotaged the ship ("The Die Is Cast"), and in "The Adversary," they made it look like he was the changeling. Eddington has been trained to take command eventually. I think he's a natural commander, like an actor who can play Hamlet but doesn't have the box-office name, so he plays Horatio. But he's going to be the best damned Horatio you ever saw."

"After 'The Adversary,' everyone on the Internet was convinced that Eddington was a changeling, even though we went out of our way to show that he wasn't," says Behr. The fans' steadfast refusal to accept the obvious had a predictable effect on the DS9 staff, who are equally stubborn. "We all looked at each other and said, 'There's no way this guy is *ever* gonna be a changeling!'" Behr laughs at the memory. "We

said, 'Let's make him a Maquis.'" And, of course, a year later, they did ("For the Cause").

One more character experienced a great change: Sisko got promoted to the rank of captain. "I said to Rick Berman, 'Why don't we just make him a captain?'" says Behr. "And he said, 'Okay.' So he just became a captain, and I was very excited."

"It's kind of silly that he hadn't been a captain before," observes Robert Wolfe. "Whenever people would do articles about *Star Trek* they would talk about the three captains: Kirk, Picard, and Janeway. We were like, 'Screw that! Sisko's just as much a star of the show, and he's saved the Federation's cookies often enough that he deserves the title.' Personally," he confesses, "I wanted to make him an admiral."

The episode, and the season, ends on the note of paranoia that the staff had been looking for, and nicely sets up both Odo's ultimate trial by his people ("Broken Link") and the Season 4 two-parter about the changelings making it to Earth. Initially, says Wolfe, the producers thought they would launch the new season with the former cliff-hanger. But it got delayed once again when the staff got wind of the imminent arrival of a new—but very familiar—crewmember to Deep Space 9. Worf, son of Mogh, was on his way.

Star Trek: The Next Generation veteran Michael Dorn joins the cast as Lieutenant Commander Worf. JEFF KATZ

FOURTH SEASON
O V E R V I E W

Considering that the edict from the studio at the end of Season 3 had thrown plans for the immediate course of the series completely out the window, it was no small victory that *Deep Space Nine*'s fourth season was received as a resounding success on many fronts. The show boasted some of its most popular episodes ever, ranging from the action-packed "The Way of the Warrior" to the heart-string-tugging "The Visitor" to the all-out comedy of "Our Man Bashir" and "Little Green Men." It then went where few television series, network or syndicated, dared to go. In the public's opinion, at least as espoused by *TV Guide* magazine, *Deep Space Nine* may have been the "Rodney Dangerfield of the billion-dollar *Star Trek* franchise" (meaning, it "don't get no respect"), but the writers chose to focus their efforts on doing episodes that *they* were proud of, rather than pulling weekly stunts for the sake of ratings.

That held true even with the one episode that the studio had, more or less, requested: "The Way of the Warrior."

"We were asked by Paramount to do something in the fourth season that would shake up the series," relates Executive Producer Ira Steven Behr. "We were *not* told, 'This is what you have to do.' We had to figure out what to do, and Rick Berman and I didn't really know."

In fact, all they did know at the time was that the cliff-hanger that eventually would become "Home-front" had to move out of its third-season slot. That done, Behr put his mind to the problem at hand, and a few days later found himself thinking about a line from Ron Moore's third-season script for "The Die Is Cast."

"A shape-shifter in that episode says something like, 'In the future, all we have to worry about is the Klingons and the Federation, and that won't be for much longer,'" says Behr. "I'd said to Ron at the time,

'You know, we could do a whole show about that if we wanted to, how the Dominion would want to get between the Klingons and the Federation.' But the earth didn't move. Nothing shook."

Still, the idea stayed with Behr, so he casually tossed the notion at Berman, who had a much more spontaneous reaction. "Rick said, 'The Klingons—*that's* the way to go,'" recalls Behr. "'Everybody loves the Klingons. And if we bring in the Klingons, why don't we bring back Worf?'"

The suggestion gave Behr pause. Bring in a new character, or rather, a new *old* character? From another show? But he had to admit, it made a certain amount of sense. "Of all the *TNG* characters, probably the one who would fit in the best [on *DS9*] would be Worf," he says.

Berman saw even deeper possibilities for the character. "Worf went from being the only Klingon in Starfleet to being the only Klingon in a Starfleet that was no longer on a friendly basis with the Klingon Empire," Berman explains. It was a storyline ripe for development.

Word of Michael Dorn's impending arrival spread quickly, so quickly that the fans learned about it early in the seasonal hiatus, long before the actors had returned to the Paramount sound stages.

"I was in Australia doing a convention," recalls Rene Auberjonois, "and someone in the audience asked me what I thought about the fact that Michael Dorn was going to join the cast. It was a big piece of news to hear ten thousand miles from home, from a fan. But I'm sort of used to having the fans tell me what's going to be coming up next, because they read it on the Internet, and I can't turn a computer on."

Although the revelation surprised him, Auberjonois took it in stride. "I said at the time, 'If it's true, I think it's fabulous,'" he comments. "I knew Michael—not all that well, but I thought he was a terrific guy, and it seemed to me that Klingons were very popular characters, and anything that would strengthen our show would be great."

The other cast members felt similarly, although some were uncertain what the addition of Worf would mean to their own characters. "I started the season not really knowing where Kira would fall," says Nana Visitor. "I thought her position on the station wasn't so sure. I thought she might be reduced by it, because there would be another fierce warrior and it would change the dynamic. But the fact was, she was still the loose cannon, more so than Worf, so while they were each warriors, they were

very different, and the things I was worried about didn't happen."

Visitor did correctly predict one change, however. "I felt there would be probably be less of a focus on Bajoran activity, and I understood that was the point," she notes. "There's a hard-core group of people out there who are interested in Bajor and then there's a lot that aren't."

But even where the orbits of characters didn't seem to conflict, there was a bit of tension. Does the addition of one character to the roster mean that everyone else gets a little less screen time? Ira Behr sighs. It's a question with which he's obviously familiar. "At the time, people were saying, 'Worf is gonna come along and it's gonna screw up all these other characters,' but it wasn't that way at all," he comments. "The thing of it is, seasons just take on a life of their own, and people get lost in the shuffle sometimes. In Season 4, we weren't using Bashir enough for a while, but we ended up with a couple of nice Bashir shows in the second half of the season. In Season 6, O'Brien got a little lost in the shuffle, partly because of his film schedule, but often it's just who generates what shows."

Actors are a notoriously insecure lot, and when they begin to notice that they haven't had a juicy scene for, say, three or four weeks running, they can get a bit antsy. Some of the group handle the down time by looking for things to fill their time; Colm Meaney, for example, does at least one film per year. Armin Shimerman has taken care not to let the grass grow beneath his Ferengi feet.

"It was during fourth season that I began to realize I was always going to have long periods of time off, so I went to my agent and asked him to find me some other work," he says. The actor began showing up in recurring roles (sans prosthetic makeup) on *Buffy the Vampire Slayer* and *The Practice*.

The changes initiated with "The Way of the Warrior" would resonate for almost an entire year, according to Behr. "We only recovered our equilibrium in the middle of fifth season," he says, "following another meeting with the studio in which we said, 'How about making the Klingons our friends again? You'll see them as much as you want, but we want to get back to the Dominion.' While I like having brought Worf onto the show, and I love some of the things that he brought along, I think it had a fairly substantial impact that wasn't all for the good. It took us way off from where we'd intended to go, and it was slow going getting back."

Not every change initiated during the fourth season had something to do with Worf or Klingons. There was a complete makeover for the show's opening credits sequence, including a new arrangement of Dennis McCarthy's haunting score. Then there was the matter of Avery Brooks' hair. Or rather, the *lack* of Avery Brooks' hair. Brooks already had added a goatee to Sisko's look during the last few episodes of the third season. But going bald was a more serious physical statement, at least in the producers' collective opinion.

"That was another one of those things that required Rick and I to have a meeting with Paramount," says Behr, straight-faced. "Before we did it, he and I talked strategy, about how we were going to convince these guys to let us do it. How it meant a lot to Avery. We did a test tape of how Avery looked [with his head shaved]. We got ourselves all psyched up for this meeting. We went in and popped in the tape. And they looked at it and said, 'Fine. Okay.'"

Berman and Behr looked at each other a moment, somewhat nonplussed. "It was like, 'Okay! Fine, then! That's what we'll do!'" recalls Behr. After all that rehearsal, no performance had been required. "We had geared ourselves up for this big fight and there was no fight. Paramount was fine with it. And Avery was very pleased."

That much was instantly apparent to everyone. "It was a terrific idea," says James L. Conway, who directed "The Way of the Warrior." "I was shooting the episode and I happened to look at some of the reruns of the earlier shows and I said to Avery, 'It's like a different actor.' And Avery said, 'I *feel* like a different guy.' And you can see it in his performance. With his head shaved, I think he feels much freer, much more himself."

Then there was a new costume for Major Kira. Costume Designer Robert Blackman says, "Her old uniform was a bit more mannish. We reduced the shoulder pads and opened the neck a little, made the color darker. We just made it more body conscious." Behr notes that the change instigated a flurry of negative comment on the net, accusing the producers of attempting to turn Kira into "a *Baywatch* babe." "It had nothing to do with that," insists Behr. "This is all I know about the costume change: we'd been talking to Nana Visitor about lightening Kira up a little bit. She'd been on the station for three years and we felt it was time for her to take a less adversarial relationship with her coworkers. In the course of the conversation, Nana mentioned that her current uniform with all the corduroy padding made it tough for her

to move. And that was the last I heard about it until I saw this new uniform, which included high heels."

And in perhaps one of the few instances in recorded history where an actor has voluntarily moved his credit to a lower position in the cast roster, Actor Siddig El Fadil officially changed his name to Alexander Siddig, which moved his name to the penultimate spot in the alphabetical actor credits, right before Nana Visitor's.

Had the actor grown tired of hearing his name mispronounced on a daily basis? "My name was a little confusing to people," Siddig says with a smile. "And not just the audience. Casting directors are much more incapable of remembering one's name than the audience. And producers can be handicapped in that too. The name said too much about what I wasn't," he continues. "Siddig El Fadil is an important name. It is *my* name, officially, on my passport and all that, and one that I will keep. But for an actor it really wasn't so suitable. So I started again, with half and half, which is more reflective of my character. As for Alexander, that was just a name out of a hat."

Moving his name closer to Visitor's was somewhat portentous. During the season, close friends Siddig and Visitor would fall in love. When the couple revealed they were expecting a child, the writers hatched a unique way to work Visitor's pregnancy into the show.

Among the crew, changes in titles and status were slightly less dramatic. Line Producer Robert della Santina moved up to Coordinating Producer and continued to serve as unit production manager. Former Executive Story Editor Robert Hewitt Wolfe made it to the producers' ranks with the title of Co-producer, while Co-producer Steve Oster became Producer and Producer Peter Lauritson became Supervising Producer.

New faces were, in many cases, actually familiar old faces. Writer Hans Beimler, who'd worked with writing partner Richard Manning on several seasons of *TNG*, joined the writing staff with the title of producer, following a stint on William Shatner's *Tekwar* television series. Another *TNG* veteran, David Stipes came onboard with "For the Cause," taking the place of departing Visual Effects Supervisor Glenn Neufeld. And LeVar Burton joined the rotation schedule for *DS9* directors after he wrapped the CBS series *Christy*.

The series wracked up four nominations at Emmy time, with two for "Our Man Bashir" (for hairstyling and musical score), one for "The Visitor" (makeup) and one for "The Muse" (costume design). Unfortunately, the gold went elsewhere.

THE WAY OF THE WARRIOR
(Parts I & II)

Episode #473/474

WRITTEN BY IRA STEVEN BEHR &
ROBERT HEWITT WOLFE
DIRECTED BY JAMES L. CONWAY

Serving as the Federation's advocate, Worf meets with Chancellor Gowron. ROBBIE ROBINSON

GUEST CAST

Kasidy Yates	PENNY JOHNSON
Gul Dukat	MARC ALAIMO
Gowron	ROBERT O'REILLY
Martok	J.G. HERTZLER
Drex	OBI NDEFO
Kaybok	CHRISTOPHER DARGA
Huraga	WILLIAM DENNIS HUNT
Weapons Officer	PATRICIA TALLMAN
Station Computer Voice	JUDI DURAND

SPECIAL GUEST STAR

Garak	ANDREW ROBINSON

STARDATE 49011.4

The dying changeling's boast that his people were "everywhere" ("The Adversary") has rattled the Alpha Quadrant. On Deep Space 9, Sisko's crew conducts grueling drills to prepare themselves for potential infiltration by an enemy that can wear any face. On Cardassia, borders have been sealed as a precaution against similar threats. But no one seems quite as worried about a Dominion invasion as the Klingons, who, under the command of General Martok, have flocked to DS9 to fight at the side of their Federation allies, despite the fact that the Federation has not requested their aid. They are convinced that an attack is imminent, and they are prepared to face it head-on.

Sisko is taken aback by the Klingons' unusual paranoia, even more so when the Klingons begin picking fights with people they perceive as possible enemies. On the station, Morn is harassed and Garak beaten for no apparent reason. In space, a Klingon bird-of-prey captures Kasidy Yates's freighter in a tractor beam and demands that she allow the Klingons to inspect it for shape-shifters. Sisko brings the muscle of the *Defiant* to Kasidy's defense and forces the Klingon commander, Kaybok, to back down. Later, Martok lets Sisko know that he has had Kaybok executed for disobeying orders.

Unable to comprehend the Klingon rationale, Sisko sends for someone who might be able to get to the heart of the matter: Lieutenant Commander Worf,

formerly of the *U.S.S. Enterprise*. As Starfleet's first Klingon officer, Worf seems the ideal man for the job, until Sisko learns that Worf is considering resigning his commission. Worf has spent most of his life with humans and is no longer certain where he belongs; still, he promises to help Sisko in any way he can.

Knowing that Sisko can't get Martok to provide the real reason DS9 is surrounded by a Klingon task force, Worf starts a fight with Drex, Martok's son, to get the general's attention. But Martok will say only that he is acting under Chancellor Gowron's orders. In order to find out the truth, Worf calls in a favor from a Klingon officer indebted to Worf's late father.

The truth is disturbing. The Klingons believe Cardassia has been infiltrated by the Dominion, and that the new civilian government has fallen under the influence of the Founders. As a result, the Klingons are planning a major assault on Cardassia. Since the Klingons have no proof of any of this, Sisko asks Martok to call off the impending invasion and points out that the Federation will not support it. But instead of delaying the attack, Martok tells his troops to begin immediately, and the fleet heads for Cardassia.

With orders from the Federation to remain neutral, Sisko cannot directly warn the Cardassians about the coming invasion. But there are other ways to get word off the station, and Sisko makes sure that Garak hears about the attack. Garak, in turn, quickly warns Dukat on the Cardassian homeworld, allowing his old enemy to mobilize the Cardassian fleet prior to the Klingons' arrival.

As the battle begins, the Federation takes a stand and officially condemns the invasion, causing Gowron to dissolve the peace treaty between the Klingon Empire and the Federation. But the Chancellor is willing to give his friend Worf one last chance to redeem himself by joining him in the assault on Cardassia. Worf reluctantly tells the Klingon leader that he cannot betray his word; he has sworn his loyalty to Starfleet and the Federation. Gowron responds by severing all of Worf's Klingon ties: His lands will be taken, his brother removed from the High Council, his House stripped of its titles. He will be left with his honor alone.

But Worf doesn't feel honorable. He has become an enemy to his people, and his position in Starfleet is no consolation. He tries to resign his commission, but Sisko refuses to accept it during this critical period. The Klingons will hit Cardassia Prime at any minute; it's time to take a more active stance.

Contacting Dukat, who is now chief military advisor to Cardassia's civilian government, Sisko offers to help escort the ruling council out of harm's way. Dukat quickly accepts the offer, and Sisko takes the *Defiant* out to meet him.

By the time they arrive, Dukat's ship is under heavy fire by the Klingons. The *Defiant* decloaks and fires on the attacking ships, effectively ending two decades of peace between the Federation and the Klingon Empire. The *Defiant* briefly drops its shields to beam the Cardassians aboard, then heads back to the station with the Klingons in hot pursuit. But when they arrive at DS9, they realize their problems are just beginning. Several dozen Klingon ships are approaching, including Gowron's vessel.

Martok and Gowron contact the station and demand that Sisko surrender the Cardassian council members. Sisko argues that he's had Bashir test the Cardassians. They aren't changelings, and the attack is a mistake. But Gowron refuses to listen to reason, and observes that the Alpha Quadrant will be safer with Cardassia under Klingon control. Then, despite Sisko's warning that the station's defenses have been upgraded to fend off a Dominion attack, a battle begins.

Sisko isn't bluffing. As the Federation's first line of defense against the Founders, DS9 boasts a full complement of powerful weapons. The Klingon fleet takes a beating, but manages to knock out some of the station's shield generators, allowing Gowron to send in Klingon boarding parties. Still, the station crew manages to hold its own long enough for Federation reinforcements to arrive.

Sisko's decision to help rescue Dukat brings an end to the Federation–Klingon alliance. ROBBIE ROBINSON

As Gowron considers continuing the attack, Sisko points out that seeing the Klingons fight the Cardassians and the Federation fight the Klingons is probably just what the Founders want. And Worf notes that destroying an empire to win a war is no victory. Gowron opts to stand down, but tells Sisko that he will not forgive or forget what has happened. The battle is over . . . for the moment.

As the crew makes repairs on the station, Sisko convinces Worf that Starfleet is his true home, and Worf decides to remain on DS9 as the station's new Strategic Operations Officer.

"The premise was that the Klingons had finally gone nuts, basically," says Actor Michael Dorn. "They'd been at peace too long and a bunch of them had gotten together to say, 'This is not the way we're supposed to be. We should be fighting.' Then they finally decided and they went to war."

Thus began Season 4 of *Deep Space Nine*, a season that would bring a great deal of change to the residents of wormhole junction.

Number one among the changes, of course, was the addition of Worf, son of Mogh, to the station's complement. In preseason publicity materials, Ira Behr described Worf as "the kind of dysfunctional character who will fit right in at the station." He chuckles when reminded of that later on. "Well, it's true," he says. "Worf is a character whose [*Star Trek*] throughline is basically one of exile and failure and confusion and uncomfortableness, and I felt that he would fit in very well."

Worf, always an outsider, was a natural fit to *DS9*. ROBBIE ROBINSON

Everyone was aware that Worf had been an extremely popular character in his prior incarnation on *TNG*, so it would have been easy to let him remain that same Klingon. But Behr was more than willing to look a gift horse in the mouth and go for more. The break session for "The Way of the Warrior" was "fairly straightforward," according to Ron Moore, except for the fact that the writers spent a sizable amount of time plotting out Worf's future trajectory on the show, beyond the episode at hand.

"We were in the process of figuring out who he was going to be and who his relationships were going to be with among the cast," says Moore. "We had to give thought to how he'd fit in with the group before we even knew for sure that he was confirmed for the show. That would inform the first episode. When he comes to the station, who's he coming to? What are the initial relationships he establishes, who are his friends, who are the people he won't get along with? How will he react to Bashir as opposed to Odo? All those kinds of things had to be discussed immediately, and that took up the body of time."

Worf had been a security officer on the *Enterprise*, but if he was going to make DS9 his new home, he'd need to find a new vocation. "One of the very first decisions was that Worf was going to change to the command track," says Moore. "That was something I suggested: 'Let's put him in red, not gold. We have a security officer and we don't need another one.' He'd spent seven years on *TNG* as this character, and we needed to make him evolve into *our* character. What are the differences? What is going to make our Worf a little different from the other Worf, and make it worth watching week after week?"

"That was one of the things we felt obligated to do," concurs Behr. "We had to give the audience a *Deep Space Nine* Worf. We had to move the character away from where he was before. All the characters on *DS9* grow, and we always try to take them farther than where they began."

But while the producers were plotting out Worf's future, his alter ego was planning his own take. "They talked about how Worf was really going to learn a lot from the people on the station," says Dorn. "But I kind of felt that everybody was going to learn a lot from Worf. That's the ego in Worf, and that was my spin."

Over the next few years, there would be a little give and take on both sides, but Worf *would* learn a thing or two.

Curiously, the season opener, which focused so heavily on Klingons, was written not by Ron Moore—a man who'd already spent years creating stories about Klingons in general, and Worf in particular—but instead by Behr and frequent collaborator Robert Hewitt Wolfe. But Moore didn't mind "losing out" on the honor. "I had written the opening episode the season before ['The Search'], and I can say that being first on the firing line is a difficult thing," he says. "This was to be a two-hour episode, and it introduced a new character. It was natural that Ira would want to handle it."

The episode opened with a tribute to Gregg Duffy Long, one of the writers' assistants, and Ronald W. Smith, a hairdresser on the show, both of whom recently had died. "We were all really hit hard by both of those passings," notes Behr somberly. "It was a tough way to begin the year."

The script itself, however, was full of energy and studded with a variety of little gems: amusing sight gags (Odo "drinking" himself, and our first view of some of the outlandish holosuite costumes that the crew apparently store in their quarters); a verbal tip of the hat to the original series (the Tholians, whom

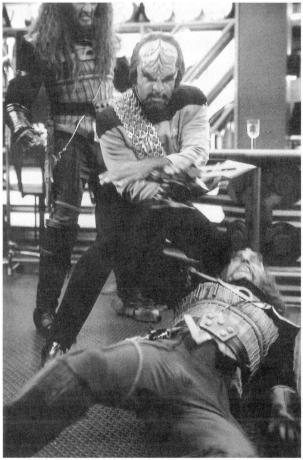
The *DS9* writers brought out different parts of Worf's character to make him more their own. ROBBIE ROBINSON

admits Wolfe. "Jim Conway directed the whole episode with a very nice, crisp pace, which means he ate up more pages than usual and we ran a few minutes short."

Actor Armin Shimerman was pleased to get the additional scene, but was perplexed by its content. "I read it and I got kind of angry because it's at a point where everything is going to hell in a handbasket and Garak comes into the bar and we begin discussing *root beer*. On the face of it, it looked like sheer foolishness," Shimerman notes. "Andy [Robinson] and I got together and rehearsed the scene the day before it was shot, and we decided that the only way to play it was to play *against* what was written. That it should be a major subtext scene."

But when they performed the scene for Conway, the director was concerned. "Jim had interpreted it as comedy and he felt we had to play it for laughs," says Shimerman. "And we spent about forty-five minutes discussing it, which is a long time to take out of a shooting day. They brought the producers down and Andy and I showed them our version of the scene and Ira immediately said, 'Yes. Shoot it that way.'"

"The scene was never meant to be a joke," comments Behr. "It was two aliens giving their individual viewpoints about what it was like to live under the Federation. They have serious problems with the whole Federation philosophy, and the fact that it's such a big behemoth organization. But at the same time, we wanted to end it on a somewhat positive or realistic note, so even though they question the giant, they want the giant there on their side when they're in trouble."

the writers love to mention but never get around to showing); and a fascinating philosophical discussion about root beer between Quark and Garak.

"The root beer conversation was one of several padded scenes that we added late in the process,"

Bringing back the Klingons to the *Star Trek* fran-

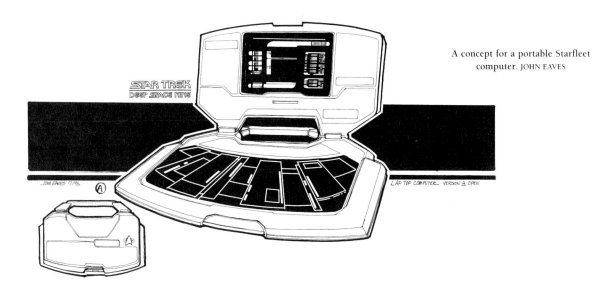
A concept for a portable Starfleet computer. JOHN EAVES

"Klingons beaming in and us shooting 'em, and then even more Klingons beaming in," Dennis Madalone remembers. "It was a fun day." ROBBIE ROBINSON

chise required a lot of prep work prior to filming the episode. While there was a features-era Klingon bird-of-prey in storage, it required modifications to make it more suitable for television. "The set goes all the way back to *Star Trek IV: The Voyage Home*," says Production Designer Herman Zimmerman. "We've rebuilt it several times, because we've used it in almost every feature picture. For 'The Way of the Warrior,' we took all of the platforms out of it and made it level to the stage floor, except for the captain's chair platform. We'd done the same thing with the *Defiant*'s bridge after the first few episodes of the third season. It makes it a lot easier to photograph. And we put everything on wheels so it can be moved around and we can get the camera where we need to in a hurry."

"The simplification made it affordable for us to take it down and put it up again," says Producer Steve Oster, "because the whole thrust of this episode was to say that the Klingons are here to stay."

Aside from the sheer volume of Klingons, makeup wasn't a huge challenge. "Michael [Dorn] came in the way we'd more or less left off with him in *Generations*," says Makeup Supervisor Michael Westmore. "We made a few adjustments on the sides of the face to make the prosthetic a little thinner, but we didn't do anything to the top of the head or the wig."

Although at the time no one knew he would become a recurring character, Martok was given a distinctive look. "He has a scar across his cheek and on his lip," says Westmore. "I made the teeth for him and tried to do something a little different with them. All the teeth are from different molds, and they give a certain curl to the lip depending on which teeth I select."

The Costume Department, naturally, had to make additional Klingon uniforms, which aren't the most comfortable outfits in the universe, according to Assistant Director B.C. Cameron. "They're really hot," she says. "The first day of filming we had the Klingon ship full of smoke, and all these guys in these heavy outfits, and it was ninety degrees outside." Cameron rolls her eyes. It's not her favorite memory, although it's clearly more fun in retrospect.

The two-hour production was indeed loaded with stunts, and for once, Stunt Coordinator Dennis Madalone found himself working with a director who had the same amount of passion for action as he did. "Normally I'm leading the way, in terms of setting things up, but Jim Conway was coming up with all this stuff that wasn't in the script," grins Madalone. "It was like, 'Okay, we're gonna kill your guys here, and then again over here, and on and on.' He was doing a Madalone special! It looked like nonstop Klingons everywhere, but it was just four or five guys that we made look like fifty!"

"I *love* action," enthuses Conway. "I've done many, many action sequences over my career, and when I have a chance to do a big one, I just have a lot of fun. I like to sit down with a script and prepare it shot by shot, from the first scene to the last scene. I can visualize the camera moving and see different things, different shots, and decide which ones I like best before I shoot. An action scene takes more time, but by the time we were ready to film, I'd dreamed up some shots, talked to Dennis about those and others, and walked the sets with him. We knew how we wanted to do it."

After directing two of *DS9*'s most popular episodes, "Duet" and "Necessary Evil," Conway had left directing for a year to executive produce two short-lived series: *Burke's Law* and *University Hospital*. "Then I came back," he says. "I really love *DS9*, because on *DS9*, everything doesn't have to turn out okay."

The producers showed the prodigal director their appreciation by offering him the two-hour season opener, no small compliment to Conway's skills, because a two-hour show is . . . different. For Steve Oster, whose recent promotion meant that he now had to deal with more than just postproduction. It was "a trial by fire," he admits. "I had to jump in there and do this big episode right off the bat. And I was working with a group of people in a different way than I'd worked with them before. But basically it was a great first experience."

Part of that experience was keeping the episode's larger-than-usual budget under control. But one thing that worked to his advantage was the fact that he was allowed to combine two one-hour episode budgets for the effort.

"I originally budgeted the show at seven times pattern," says Visual Effects Supervisor Gary Hutzel, "and we ended up spending more. But we got a lot of bang for our buck." The effects work on the episode was so extensive that the producers assigned both

The writers preferred the new look Brooks favored for Sisko. "He's more striking without hair," says Wolfe. "I was always in the pro-beard, pro–shaved head camp." ROBBIE ROBINSON

Hutzel and Supervisor Glenn Neufeld to the job. It was a unique situation, since the pair normally alternate on episodes. "There was no choice," says Neufeld. "There was over double the work of a normal show, including Klingons attacking the station and extended sequences where the *Defiant* rescues Gul Dukat and the diplomats. And the producers expressed a desire for there to be *zillions* of ships involved in the attack scenes."

"We read the script and saw terms like 'fleets of ships,'" says Visual Effects Coordinator Judy Elkins, "which is always enough to strike terror into our hearts. Usually we're shooting one model, and if you see something about a fleet, it means you have to shoot that model a hundred times! Luckily, these were Klingon ships, so there were toys, models, and Christmas ornaments for us to use."

The relationship between the Effects Department and Paramount's licensing department is a symbiotic one. The licensing department frequently borrows blueprints and sketches in order to insure that *Star Trek* merchandise is detailed exactly like the professional models. The Effects Department periodically will request batches of licensed paraphernalia so they can enhance action sequences and create spectacular explosions without destroying their valuable models. Case in point: "The Way of the Warrior" utilized some Playmates toys ("We had to take out the sound effects," says Elkins sadly), Ertl model kits (which blew up *real* good), and Hallmark's bird-of-prey Christmas ornaments.

"Judy and her team detailed about twenty of the

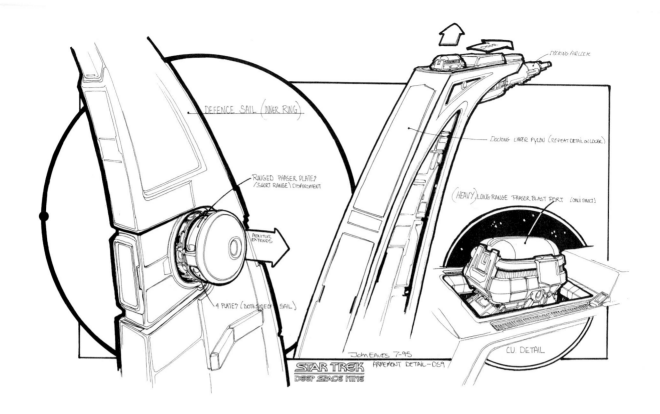

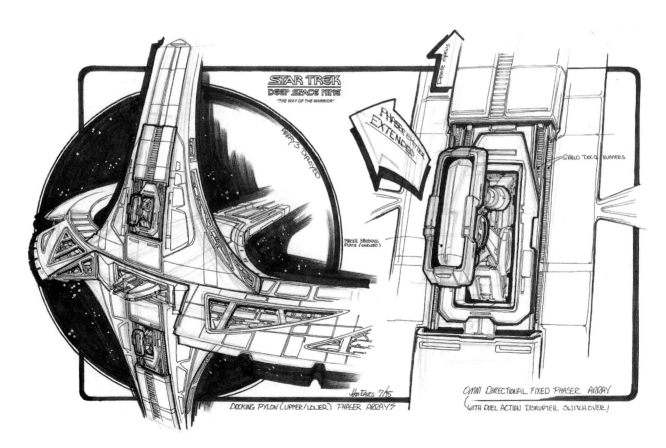

Suggestions to the effects team for the placement of new weapons and where they can be located on the station. JOHN EAVES

Playmates ships to make them look less like plastic toys," says Hutzel. "And they set up an assembly line to put together and paint seventeen of the model kits." The kits were then passed on to Special Effects Manager Gary Monak, who carefully packed them with explosives and party store glitter (which resembles pulverized bits of ship flying through space as the explosion goes off).

The battle sequence in the last twenty minutes of the episode was, at the time, the most elaborate ever produced for *Deep Space Nine*, but the single most expensive shot of the show was never seen in its entirety. "It was right after what we called the *Wheel of Fortune* shot [so named because the angle gives the station a passing resemblance to the big wheel on the game show]," says Hutzel, "where we're shooting straight down at the station and the birds-of-prey are swooping through the frame, and ships are exploding like popcorn all over the place. Sisko says 'Weapons stations—fire at will!' We cut to the inside of a tube and follow the point of view of a photon torpedo as it blasts out into space."

"In the original shot as we built it, the torpedo is sitting in there and you see all the struts and mechanisms inside the tube, which is a matte painting that I did," says Adam Howard. "Then we animated a blast pushing it through, and went to a shot that Gary had done where you're literally sitting just behind the torpedo as it's ducking and weaving and finding its way. But that ended up getting cut into two separate shots that start just *after* it gets fired out of the station," sighs Howard.

The shot was a little *too* showy for the producers' taste, calling too much attention to itself in the midst of some very heated action. "I think the phrase that was used was, 'That took me right out of the show,'" says Hutzel, who kept a personal copy of the intact sequence.

The studio had asked for a knock 'em dead season opener, and the two-hour debut of "The Way of the Warrior" delivered, easily slipping into the number one slot for action weeklies. The show ranked first in its time period in four different markets, beating out all network shows in St. Louis, Sacramento, Hartford, and San Diego. It placed second in nine other markets, including key cities like New York, Chicago, and Boston.

HIPPOCRATIC OATH
Episode #475

TELEPLAY BY LISA KLINK
STORY BY NICHOLAS COREA AND LISA KLINK
DIRECTED BY RENE AUBERJONOIS

GUEST CAST

Goran'Agar	SCOTT MacDONALD
Arak'Taral	STEPHEN DAVIES
Meso'Clan	JERRY ROBERTS
Temo'Zuma	MARSHALL TEAGUE
Regana Tosh	RODERICK GARR
Jem'Hadar #1	MICHAEL H. BAILOUS

STARDATE 49066.5

Old habits die hard, and Worf, the station's new strategic operations officer, finds it difficult to wean himself from his previous role as a security officer. Spotting a known smuggler in Quark's bar, Worf can't understand why Odo won't arrest the alien, or at least question Quark about his likely involvement. Odo's apparent lack of concern leads to the Klingon's decision to do some investigating of his own.

Elsewhere, Bashir and O'Brien conclude a bio-survey mission in the Gamma Quadrant and set course for home. Along the way, the runabout picks up signs of a downed ship, and when the two men investigate, their vessel is hit by a plasma field, triggering a crash landing on a remote world. On the planet's surface, they are immediately taken captive by a small group of Jem'Hadar.

When Goran'Agar, the Jem'Hadar leader, learns that Bashir is a doctor, he decides to let the humans live, for the time being. Bashir is taken to a makeshift lab, where he is told he must conduct scientific research, or die. The object of his research is to discern why Goran'Agar is no longer addicted to ketracel-white, a substance that the Dominion had genetically engineered his species to require for survival. Goran'Agar wants all of his men to be similarly free of the addiction so they can escape the tyranny of Dominion rule. Bashir is told that he has five days to find the cure; after that, the supply of ketracel-white will run out. Then, Goran'Agar's men will die, but not before killing Goran'Agar, the doctor, and O'Brien.

Bashir enlists O'Brien's help, and the pair begin to work on a device that will help them to escape. But a Jem'Hadar soldier discovers the device's true purpose and attacks O'Brien. Goran'Agar orders the soldier to spare O'Brien's life, to the surprise of his men and

The fact that Goran'Agar survives without ketracel-white gives Dr. Bashir hope that he can cure the Jem'Hadar addiction.
ROBBIE ROBINSON

right in the middle of the transaction. In doing so he derails Odo's plan to get to the heart of the smuggling operation, a plan in which Quark was assisting the constable. Chagrined, Worf confesses his error to Sisko, who assures the Klingon that he will adjust to the somewhat nonregulation lifestyle aboard the station over time.

In the Gamma Quadrant, O'Brien returns to the camp on his own and tries to convince Bashir to escape. But the doctor is on the verge of a scientific breakthrough and refuses to leave. Certain that Bashir will be killed even if he comes up with a cure, O'Brien destroys his research. Goran'Agar returns and sees the damage, comprehending that it seals his fate. He tells the two humans to take their ship and leave; he will kill his soldiers in combat, rather than subject them to the pain of a slow death as the drug runs out. Bashir and O'Brien return to the Alpha Quadrant, each disagreeing with the other's actions, but at least coming to an understanding.

This episode was a blend of two separate story pitches. The first, from Nicholas Corea, was about a group of Jem'Hadar who wanted to free themselves of the addictive "white"; the second, from Lisa Klink, was about Bashir and O'Brien taking opposite sides in a struggle between two different groups, one native and one not, on an alien world. Klink had first pitched her idea prior to taking part in a Writers Guild internship on *DS9* during the show's third season. No sale, but the producers were encouraging, so Klink was allowed to pitch again. And again. "I repitched it several times," she admits. "They thought there was something interesting about it, but the story wasn't quite right. So each time I came back I pitched a different version, and they said they'd think about it."

The producers did think about it, referring to it occasionally as *The Bridge on the River Kwai* story because of the similarities between the colonel played by Alec Guinness in that film, and Bashir, who effectively helps "the enemy." Eventually, they bought Klink's story, but faced some problems developing it. "We were having trouble coming up with what Bashir was trying to do for these aliens that are on the 'wrong side,'" says René Echevarria. "What was the measure of the conflict between Bashir and O'Brien? If this was *The Bridge on the River Kwai*, what was 'the bridge?'"

Echevarria recalls pointing out during the break session that the story by Nicholas Corea, which also had been purchased, would merge well with Klink's.

Bashir. The leader's apparent compassion makes an impact on Bashir, who now believes that if all the Jem'Hadar were freed from the white, it might ultimately reduce the Dominion threat to the Alpha Quadrant. But O'Brien doesn't share Bashir's sentiments, insisting that the Jem'Hadar have been bred to kill and nothing will change that. He flatly refuses to help Bashir's efforts, but the doctor pulls rank on him and orders him to comply. Not long after, O'Brien engineers his own escape into the planet's dense jungle.

Goran'Agar orders his second to bring back O'Brien alive. When the order is refused, the Jem'Hadar leader realizes his men no longer will obey him. Bashir asks Goran'Agar to rescue O'Brien himself, and promises to continue working on the cure while the commander is gone.

On the station, Worf's investigation has led him to the conclusion that Quark is about to purchase some illegal Tallonian crystals from the shady alien. It seems clear that Odo is not going to do anything about the situation, so Worf steps in to make an arrest

The writers did not hesitate to put Bashir and O'Brien at odds.
ROBBIE ROBINSON

"Nobody seemed to think I was right at the time," he smiles, "but later on I said it again." And this time the idea clicked with everyone.

The recent addition of Worf to station personnel called for the insertion of an additional storyline, this one designed to give viewers some insight into the Klingon's period of adjustment in his new settings. The B-story, which dealt with Worf's attempts to do Odo's job, "was our way of saying, 'Okay, he used to be a cop, more or less, on the *Enterprise*, but it's not going to be like that anymore," says Ron Moore. "We wanted to keep emphasizing, 'this is not *TNG*. The station doesn't work like the *Enterprise*. Worf is going to have some troubles fitting in, but he's going to learn.'"

Klink wrote two drafts of the hybrid teleplay, which the *DS9* producers were so impressed with that they passed it on to the writing staff at *Voyager*, where they knew there was an opening. Klink was hired on staff for *Voyager*'s second year and remained there until the end of that series' fourth season.

"Hippocratic Oath" marked Rene Auberjonois's third time behind the camera, and the episode that made him understand fellow actor/director LeVar Burton's comment that "the third show is the one where you really hit the wall."

"He told me that the first couple of shows are almost like a free ride, because you're so overprepared and you work so hard and everybody's so supportive," explains Auberjonois. In his case, his first two shows had been the closest *DS9* gets to light

comedy. Shooting went smoothly, predictably. "But this was entirely different," he says. "It was a very difficult experience. I really came face-to-face with my own mortality as a director."

There were any number of problems. Auberjonois, who was next up on the directing schedule, initially been told that he was to helm "The Visitor," but Colm Meaney's work schedule threw a wrench into that plan. "Colm was leaving to do a film and they had to do one of his shows before he left," says Auberjonois. So "The Visitor" was moved to the next director on the list, David Livingston, while Auberjonois was hastily given a script that featured O'Brien. "It wasn't quite ready to go, and I wasn't ready to go, because I was still thinking about the other script," he says.

Although much of the action takes place on a jungle planet, the episode was filmed entirely onstage. "That was difficult," says Auberjonois. "It really should have gone on location. We didn't have enough space on the stage and that made it very hard to shoot and I didn't have enough experience to handle that."

It could have been worse, though. The production company doesn't have a full-sized runabout because the vessel is rarely shown on the ground. "Doing it with a model for this show would have constricted the director too much," says Steve Oster, "because there were too many scenes where people were entering and exiting the runabout." So, following the advice of Herman Zimmerman, the crew used the existing interior of the vessel, which has been seen in many episodes, and built only a portion of the exterior to continue the illusion that viewers were seeing all of the ship. The missing sections were covered with trees and foliage from the jungle crash.

"It was a great thing to do visually," says Oster, "and logistically, it was the only way we could do it because we wouldn't have been able to fit a runabout within the small stage area where we built the jungle."

Casting was one bright spot in the experience for Auberjonois. "Robert Foxworth came in to read," the actor says. "He's an old friend of mine; we went to college together and his son is my godson." Unfortunately, Foxworth was *too* good. The producers wanted to save him for an episode where he would get a bigger part: "Homefront" and "Paradise Lost." So Scott MacDonald, previously seen as Tosk in first season's "Captive Pursuit," received the role of Goran'Agar.

"Scott was terrific," comments Auberjonois. In

The magic of Hollywood—it looks like a full-sized crashed runabout.
ROBBIE ROBINSON

Moore allows that the writers simply forgot about Goran'Agar's comment when they got to the later episode, Ira Behr prefers to think of it as an example of Goran'Agar being "metaphorically stupid, as the Jem'Hadar so often are."

THE VISITOR

Episode #476

WRITTEN BY **MICHAEL TAYLOR**
DIRECTED BY **DAVID LIVINGSTON**

GUEST CAST	
Adult Jake Sisko	TONY TODD
Korena	GALYN GÖRG
Nog	ARON EISENBERG
Melanie	RACHEL ROBINSON
Computer Voice	MAJEL BARRETT

STARDATE UNKNOWN

On a dark and stormy night in the early twenty-fifth century, an old man gazes around his home, taking in the artifacts of a lifetime. As he injects himself with a hypospray, he hears someone at the door and opens it to find a young woman drenched by the rainstorm. He invites her in to dry off and discovers that the woman, Melanie, is an aspiring writer who's come to find out why *her* favorite writer, Jake Sisko, stopped writing before he reached the age of forty.

An elderly Jake Sisko smiles and decides to share an untold story with the stranger. It begins long ago, he explains, back when he was eighteen. His father, Benjamin, had taken him to the Gamma Quadrant to watch the wormhole go through a subspace inversion, a rare occurrence that happens only once every fifty years. During the voyage, the wormhole's fluctuating gravimetric field had destabilized the *Defiant*'s warp core, and his father had repaired it. But just as the danger seemed to have passed, a bolt of energy shot out from the warp core, striking Ben Sisko full on and knocking Jake backward with the discharge. Jake had watched in horror as his father dematerialized, presumably lost forever.

Months later, as Jake struggled to move forward with his life, he awakened to see his father appear in his room. But within seconds, Sisko again dematerialized. The incident was dismissed as a nightmare, until, after several more months had passed, Ben Sisko again materialized before his son. This time, Jake was able to summon help and get his father to

fact, MacDonald is an actor the producers really appreciate in a role that requires a lot of latex. "When we cast him, we were looking for someone who could really talk through a lot of makeup, because Goran'Agar was going to require a full-face prosthetic, and that's a difficult thing for an actor," observes Moore. "Some actors just get lost in the makeup, while others pop right through it. And Scott had already done that as Tosk, so we knew he could again."

There's more to the Jem'Hadar than latex. There's also the pump, that is, the device that delivers the ketracel-white. "Tiny pumps that came out of copy machines seemed to work the best, in terms of the speed and the sound," notes Special Effects Master Gary Monak. "The first time we had to do a bunch of Jem'Hadar, we got twelve of these pumps from a surplus place, and they all worked fine. But the next time it came up and we needed more, they no longer existed. We had gotten the last twelve pumps that work." Monak smiles. "It might be touch and go if they ever send thirty of these guys to us looking for neck pumps."

There is another apparent continuity glitch presented by Goran'Agar's comment that his crew has "eaten the same food" that he has. Later in the season ("To the Death"), viewers would learn that the Jem'Hadar don't eat, sleep, or have sex. While Ron

Melanie receives more than she anticipated when an elderly Jake Sisko tells her the story of his lifelong quest to save his father.
ROBBIE ROBINSON

the Infirmary, where DS9's senior officers determined that the captain's temporal signature had been altered by the warp core accident, thrusting him into subspace. Unfortunately, before they could figure out a way to realign his signature, Sisko dematerialized into subspace once again.

For several more months, Dax and O'Brien tried to find a way to locate Sisko, but eventually the unrest between the Klingons and the Federation forced Starfleet to evacuate the station. Jake was sent to Earth, where he became a published writer, fell in love, and married. Then, when he was in his thirties, he received another brief visit from his father, this time at his home in New Orleans. But Jake's joy in seeing him was overwhelmed by his reawakened obsession to help bring him back.

Working with Dax, Jake learned that the accident had created a subspace link between his father and himself, and that there was a pattern to the older Sisko's appearances. The next one, Dax calculated, was likely to occur when Jake was an old man. Hoping to find a way to help his father, Jake abandoned his writing to study subspace mechanics. His wife, Korena, could not compete with his obsession, and he ultimately lost her.

Fifty years after the original accident, Jake returned to the Gamma Quadrant in the *Defiant*, with Dax, Bashir, and Captain Nog. As the wormhole again began to invert, Jake awaited his father's rematerialization, hoping this time to free him. But, instead, he was pulled into the same region of subspace as his father.

The reunion was brief, but long enough to convince Ben that Jake's obsession had taken a terrible toll. He begged Jake to let go of his futile quest and rebuild his life. Then, the two were separated once again, with Jake returned to the *Defiant*.

Jake finishes his account to Melanie and presents her with a copy of his latest book, a collection of short stories that he wrote to honor his father's request. Before she departs, he explains that he has learned at last how to save Ben. If he dies while his father is with him, the "cord" that has been pulling Sisko through time over the years will be cut, and Sisko will return to the moment of the original accident.

Later, when Sisko materializes at Jake's house, he is gratified to learn that Jake has gone back to writing. But he is stunned when he discovers that Jake has poisoned himself and why. But Jake's sacrifice is not in vain. As he dies, Sisko finds himself back on the *Defiant*, where he successfully avoids the original accident and the two Siskos receive a second chance to live out the rest of their days together.

"The Visitor" was "that certain kind of *Star Trek* episode that appeals very strongly to certain people," as Ira Behr puts it. "It's a whole 'heart-on-the-sleeve,' sentimental, emotional, personal story."

"It was wonderfully written, wonderfully performed," observes Steve Oster. "But I think everyone was surprised at the audience reaction. No one expected it to have the emotional impact that it did."

That impact first became apparent to Behr when he saw fan-generated commentary on the episode. "There were people actually theorizing that Michael Taylor (the writer of the episode) must be a pseudonym for Michael Piller and Jeri Taylor collaborating on a *Deep Space Nine*," he chuckles. Piller and Taylor are, of course, both *Star Trek* writers known for stories with a lot of heart, whereas freelancer *Michael Taylor* was someone the fans had never heard of up to now. (He would go on to become a staff writer on *Voyager* during that series' fifth season.) Behr decided to take the reaction as "a positive response," a conviction that was borne out when the episode was nominated for a Hugo Award, the science fiction literary community's version of the Oscar, for the best dramatic presentation. Both "The City on the Edge of Forever" and "Inner Light" were previous recipients of this award. But the Fates denied the privilege to "The Visitor," which, Taylor notes, "was trounced by *Babylon 5*." However, the episode did receive the dis-

Writing, acting, and directing mesh to create the emotional high point of the season. ROBBIE ROBINSON

tinction of being voted the best *Star Trek* episode *ever* by the readers of *TV Guide*. "*TV Guide* called it a '*Star Trek*' shocker," recalls René Echevarria with a chuckle, "the fact that 'the least popular incarnation of *Star Trek*' had produced the most popular episode."

What was it about the episode that hit home for so many viewers? "We always like to think *Star Trek* has this quality of universality, but this time we *really* had it," says Behr. "The idea of losing a parent. A love that spans a lifetime. A love stronger than death. Usually that's romantic love, but for this show, this series, we chose the love between a father and son. And it worked like gangbusters. Everyone could relate to it."

Taylor's story was inspired by the father/son relationship that the series has portrayed so well since its beginning. "I'd been thinking how remarkable Sisko's interaction with his son Jake was in television, the idea of a committed black single dad who sticks around and raises his kid."

That's an idea that is particularly important to Avery Brooks. "I'm glad that relationship is there," the

actor says. "It is, even in the most naive mind, a sin of omission that we have not looked at this side of people raising their children [in other television shows], and having some cultural resonance other than that of white Americans. It's something that we have to see more often, the relationship of a brown man and his son. Because historically that's not how it began in this country for brown families who didn't have the freedom of their own will and volition, let alone the ability to hold their families together."

Although Taylor's story focused on the special bond between Sisko and his son, it applied a wicked twist. "What if Sisko was forced into the more stereotypical situation, where he couldn't be there for his kid," says Taylor. He initially thought his story would focus on Sisko, who is thrown forward in time and catches only brief glimpses of his son growing up. But as he began to write up his ideas, the focus shifted to Jake, "because he's the guy who's left behind," he says.

Although Taylor received the sole writing credit on "The Visitor," he freely praises Echevarria's behind-the-scenes contributions to the script. "He made it twice as

Jake's lavish home on the edge of a Louisiana swamp. JOHN EAVES

good," says Taylor. "He made lines of mine into better lines, and deepened the relationship between Jake and the young woman interviewer. It was a lesson to me how to really make the most of a good story."

It was Ira Behr, however, who came up with the frame for the story. "We were all a little concerned about trying to tell a story that took place over a period of sixty years, in sequence," says Echevarria. "So Ira said, 'What if we start cold, in the future, with Jake older,' and we all responded to that because we could see how that would really free you up in the narrative sense."

It also was Behr's idea to have Jake tell his story to someone who'd come to see him. As Taylor searched his imagination for the appropriate person, he remembered that young Jake had aspirations to become a writer. And that, in turn, made Taylor think of the famous interview that reclusive writer J.D. Salinger once had granted to a high school student. "That's why I chose to have a young woman approach Jake," he says.

Echevarria helped Taylor deepen the connection between Melanie and Jake, the young writer who hadn't yet committed herself to print and the old

writer who had left words behind. Rachel Robinson, daughter of Andrew Robinson (Garak), won the role of Melanie. "We saw a *lot* of young women," says Director David Livingston, "but she blew everybody away. She had an innocence and an intelligence and an enthusiasm, all qualities that I thought made the character very rich."

"She gave a very lovely performance," observes Behr. "I know Andy was very proud, and he had every reason to be. I'm sure Tony Todd's dad was very proud of him, too, because he gave a terrific performance as well."

Todd was awarded the role of adult Jake after a long casting process that had included Cirroc Lofton, the actor most comfortable in Jake's shoes. "He did a really nice job with the character emotionally," says Echevarria, but the decision was ultimately made to use someone older who would have an easier time bridging the gap between eighteen and eighty. Livingston notes that Todd studied Lofton's work in various episodes in order to get a feel for the younger actor's mannerisms and speech patterns. "I don't know if anyone else noticed it, but there were some

The uniforms and communicators resembled those seen in the final episode of *TNG*. ROBBIE ROBINSON

things that Tony did where I'd think, wow, that was just what Cirroc would do," the director comments. "And yet Tony made it his own as well. I was very moved by his performance. He cried on almost every single take. In fact, I had to tell him, 'Okay, you *can't* cry here, Tony.' He was so emotionally invested that he was exhausted by the end of each day. He had a lot of long speeches and a lot of different makeup changes and we shot really long hours."

"It was a very hard makeup to put on, as well as maintain," admits Makeup Artist Camille Calvet. "It was early in the season so we didn't have much time to prepare. He had a bald cap, cheek pieces, nasal labials, a nose and some different earlobes for the oldest look. Tony's great in makeup. One day he shot for almost eighteen hours and the prosthetics started breaking down and pulling on the back of his neck." Calvet's expression is understandably sympathetic. It's not easy shooting long days, in or out of makeup, in front of or behind the camera. Particularly not in the middle of a monsoon . . .

There was no monsoon in the script during preproduction, at least not until David Livingston made a fateful suggestion. "I thought that the setting for the opening should be 'a dark and stormy night,'" grins Livingston. "I knew it was the right way to start, that rain and thunder and lightning was the most powerful image."

The producers had a few reservations. Steve Oster notes, "It's a big megillah to do rain, because it takes a lot of time and can create a lot of extra work." Finally they agreed that it *would* make the scene more atmospheric. Livingston could have his rainstorm. "Except it ended up becoming more like a hurricane than a rainstorm," notes Oster.

"It wasn't rain, it was a *typhoon!*" observes occasional rainmaker Gary Monak.

"Oh my God, it was a mess," moans First Assistant Director B.C. Cameron. "The stage was flooded."

It was, by all accounts, a difficult day (and night) of shooting that still triggers emotional reactions from all involved. Time does add perspective. "It was an interesting experience," says Oster good-naturedly, "because David was previously my boss, the person who sat behind what is now my desk." The job of the person behind the desk, he explains, is to keep the reins taut during production, which meant, in part, that it was his job to "keep rein over rain—no pun intended."

Yet Oster admits that, despite all the trouble, Livingston's instincts were correct. "The first day we watched the dailies for those scenes, I realized it was worth it," he says. "It was just as David said in our production meeting: the storm can become a character. And it did just that. So while there were moments at two in the morning when we had water pouring out of the overflow tanks under the stage, and we were waiting to refill the rain machines, when I thought, maybe this was a bad idea. But I forgot all about that when I saw it on the screen."

For Science Consultant Andre Bormanis, the episode is memorable for a different reason, one more pertinent to his job. "It was one of the first episodes where we started to establish that subspace was a *place*," he says. "For years we'd talked about 'subspace radio,' and how warp drive generates a 'subspace field.' But, here we established that it was a real thing, another domain, another dimension that exists, which warp drive gives us access to. Sisko gets caught in some sort of little pocket in subspace that is created when they have the accident in the engine room of the *Defiant*. And because time proceeds at a much different rate within that subspace domain than it does outside, he was only in there for what appeared to be to him a few minutes, or maybe an hour or so, while Jake experienced sixty years."

During that period, fashion marched on, as demonstrated by the Starfleet uniforms worn by the aging characters of Dax and Bashir. If they looked familiar to viewers, there's a reason. "They're basically the ones we used in the future sequences of 'All Good Things. . .'," says Costume Designer Bob Blackman. "The time frame was similar so we decided we could use that design again."

INDISCRETION

Episode #477

TELEPLAY BY **NICHOLAS COREA**
STORY BY **TONI MARBERRY & JACK TREVIÑO**
DIRECTED BY **LeVAR BURTON**

GUEST CAST

Kasidy Yates	PENNY JOHNSON
Dukat	MARC ALAIMO
Razka	ROY BROCKSMITH
Ziyal	CYIA BATTEN
Heler	THOMAS PRISCO

STARDATE UNKNOWN

A Bajoran smuggler informs Kira that he has found a piece of metal that may belong to the *Ravinok*, a Cardassian ship that disappeared six years earlier with a group of Bajoran prisoners. Although the lead is a slim one, Kira feels she must investigate, in part because she had a good friend among the lost prisoners. She isn't pleased when she learns that a Cardassian representative is to accompany her on her journey, less so when it turns out to be Gul Dukat. Dukat explains that since the *Ravinok* was under his general command, it is his duty to find any remaining troops, just as it is Kira's to find her friend.

As the pair leave the station, Sisko finds himself in a good news/not-so-good news situation. His relationship with Kasidy Yates is growing more serious, and while he's pleased to hear that her potential new job with the Bajoran Ministry of Commerce would keep her closer to DS9, he's not quite sure how he feels about her taking up residence on the station. It is, as he explains, "a big step"—which turns out to be the worst thing he could say to Kasidy. Angered by Sisko's apparent lack of commitment, Kasidy says that she will turn down the job, leaving Sisko's feelings more jumbled than ever.

Kira and Dukat follow the lead on the *Ravinok* to

Kira and Dukat search for the wreckage of the *Ravinok*.
ROBBIE ROBINSON

the Dozarian system and land on the only Class-M planet. There they find the wreckage of a downed ship and twelve graves. But Dukat reveals the *Ravinok* had fifty people aboard, which means that there could be some survivors. First, however, there is the task of identifying the bodies, which Dukat volunteers to do, noting it is a Cardassian tradition that they bury their own dead. In the meantime, Kira tries to figure out what happened to the ship. The ship's computers reveal the *Ravinok* was attacked by unidentified warships, Kira returns to inform Dukat. She finds the grief-stricken Cardassian sitting next to the grave of a Bajoran woman, Tora Naprem, his mistress. Kira recognizes the name from the ship's manifest and notes that there was an obvious relation—a "Tora Ziyal"—listed as well. Dukat admits that Ziyal is his daughter, and that if he finds her alive, he'll have to kill her. The existence of a half-Bajoran child would threaten his marriage and his position in the government.

As they begin a search to find the survivors, Kira warns Dukat that she will not allow him to kill the girl. Within a day they find a Breen encampment, where the *Ravinok* survivors are being forced to mine dilithium ore. Among the workers is a girl of obvious mixed heritage, part Bajoran and part Cardassian: Tora Ziyal.

Disguised as Breen, Kira and Dukat overcome the guards and round up the prisoners. Kira learns that her friend is dead, but Dukat finds his daughter and prepares to kill her. Kira tells the girl to run, but Ziyal explains that the thought of her father coming to save her is all that has kept her alive. If she can't leave with him, she would rather die. She moves forward to hug him and Dukat's resolve shatters. He will take her home with him, no matter what the cost.

On the station, Sisko receives unsolicited advice from Dax, Bashir, and Jake regarding the situation with Kasidy. At last he takes his son's counsel and goes to see her, apologizing for his earlier behavior. He tells her to take the job and is surprised to discover she already has.

The pitch he took from Texas freelancers Toni Marberry and Jack Treviño struck an immediate chord with René Echevarria. "They basically said, 'We find out that Gul Dukat has a half-Bajoran daughter and he asks Kira to help him find her. Later in the story we realize that he intends to kill her.'" The plot was clearly reminiscent of John Ford's classic Western, *The Searchers*, and utterly irresistible to the producers of *DS9*, who bought the pitch for "Indiscretion" and gave the teleplay assignment to Nicholas Corea ("Hippocratic Oath").

Although the story of Dukat's ill-fated daughter, Tora Ziyal, would prove increasingly important to future storylines, "Indiscretion" also served as the launch pad for other important aspects of the continuing saga of *Deep Space Nine*. It was here that viewers heard about Cardassia's "new civilian government." The political system was spawned in the wake of the Founders' decimation of the planet's ruling militia ("The Die Is Cast") and devastating attacks by the Klingon Empire. The parallel, notes history buff Robert Hewitt Wolfe, is the late twentieth century's Soviet Union during the period after the fall of the Berlin Wall, when communism waned and capitalism reared its head.

"We were kind of going down that road with Cardassia," reflects Wolfe, "where this military dictatorship tries to go civilian and falls on hard times. But, we always intended to go back," he stresses. "We *always* planned to make them go military again." The writers did orchestrate a turnabout just a year later ("By Inferno's Light").

On a more personal level, Dukat and Kira began to undergo some changes. "The thing that was most appealing to me about the episode," says Director

Though the introduction of Ziyal would blunt some of Dukat's edges, the writers never lost track of his essential nature. ROBBIE ROBINSON

LeVar Burton, "was that it focused on these two characters, characters who had an adversarial relationship and who had to reevaluate who they were to each other and how they viewed each other."

"It was an important episode for me," says Hans Beimler. "It really started to define their relationship in a new way, taking it to a different place. And that was meaningful for me, because I ended up writing the 'next chapter' of that relationship in 'Return to Grace.'"

"Indiscretion" did indeed take Dukat and Kira to "a different place," but not necessarily a romantic one, and it's best demonstrated in the scene where Dukat has an unfortunate encounter with a thorn. "There are moments in life," explains Ira Behr, "when you can be with someone with whom you have nothing in common, who you have nothing but disdain for, and then something happens: a moment of shared experience, or shared laughter, and it just changes the playing field. And it doesn't mean that you become friends afterward, it doesn't mean that you've broken through to a new level of understanding that'll be with you for the rest of your lives. But something has changed."

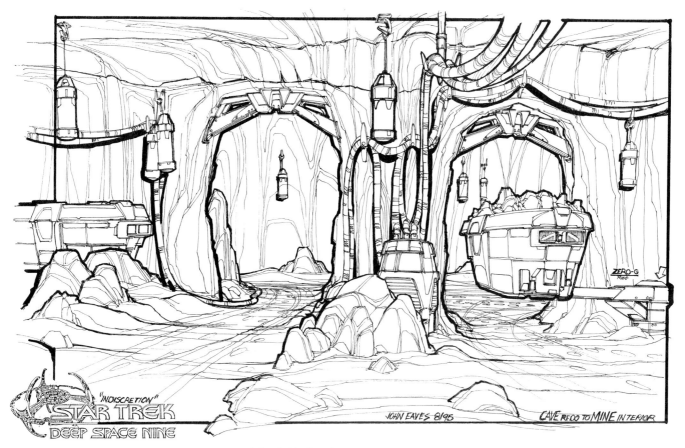

A detailed look at the Breen mine. JOHN EAVES

The shooting script says much the same thing after the incident: "This is a bonding moment. And though it's probable that neither of them would ever discuss it, after this, their relationship will never be quite the same again. They've started to see each other as people." But was there ever a chance of a deeper relationship?

"No," says Wolfe emphatically. "Never. It was always more about Dukat than Kira. If you put a gun to her head, I don't think Kira would ever consider it." Nana Visitor confirms this: "Playing Kira, I can't even entertain the thought. It's too disgusting."

"I think it's only in Dukat's mind that there was any hope of a relationship," summarizes Behr. "And maybe in Marc Alaimo's mind. Certainly Kira never thought so, and certainly *we* never thought so. But Marc was so insistent in playing that hope in the way he treated her that it became a fun thing to follow up on, although we knew there was no way in hell it would ever happen."

To add insult to injury in the episode, Kira tells Dukat, "Captain Sisko's right; you *are* in love with the sound of your own voice." It's a bit of an in-joke. It was

Behr who came up with this defining aspect of Cardassians, the so-called "big Cardassian monologue."

"Ira characterizes the race as a bunch of people who talk like the people in Russian novels," says Wolfe. "They talk a *lot*."

"And no one can milk it like Marc Alaimo," adds Behr, "even though there are times when you just want him to get on with it. So there may have been a little . . . editorializing in Kira's line."

The B-story, in which Kasidy's announcement that she'll be spending a lot more time on the station evokes an unfortunate response from Sisko, is also attributed to Behr. "That was Ira's take on the whole thing," says Wolfe. "That Sisko would say that stupid thing."

"We weren't sure what the B-story was about when we sat down at the break session," Behr says. "And suddenly 'It's a big step,' just crystalized into this whole male/female thing. Talk about putting your big male foot in your mouth! That line spoke volumes to me."

Location filming for the episode at hellish Soledad Canyon ("The Homecoming" and "The Ship") proved the usual mixed bag. "Anytime we go

The tradition continues—unbelievably hot shooting locations. It's no wonder Visitor comments, "I loooovve working on the soundstage."
ROBBIE ROBINSON

there, we can always bet that it will be one hundred degrees-plus," says Producer Steve Oster. "It can be beautiful the week before, but when we're shooting, it's over a hundred."

"It was brutally, brutally, brutally hot out there in the rock quarry," admits Director Burton, who was helming his first episode of the series. "But it was fun. It was real movie making. We had a huge crane. We had a Steadicam. We had all of the toys. Everything that you ever dream about in directing, we had on that episode."

They also had some unique problems, resolved, as usual, by Herman Zimmerman. "We had to imply that something the size of a Cardassian freighter could actually be located in this quarry," he says. "And we had taken some big set pieces with us that we'd painted, not knowing what, if anything, we were going to do with them. They were about ten feet square, painted like the color of the hull of a ship. And one of them was just laying against this very fine gravel that looks like sand, and I thought, that looks like a piece of fuselage that's been uncovered while the rest of the ship is covered with sand. So we inten-

tionally buried just those two pieces of ten by ten, side by side, and covered the edges with sand, so it looked like the side of a ship sticking out. We added a couple of wings and that helped a lot."

Burying the pieces required a unique approach as well. "There was this huge, three-story mound of gravel in the quarry, and if you went up to the base of it and put your foot in it, part of it would come

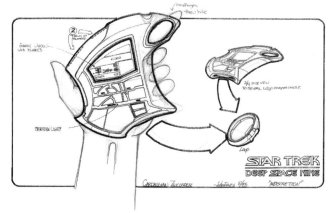

This Cardassian tricorder is designed to fit the user's hand.
JOHN EAVES

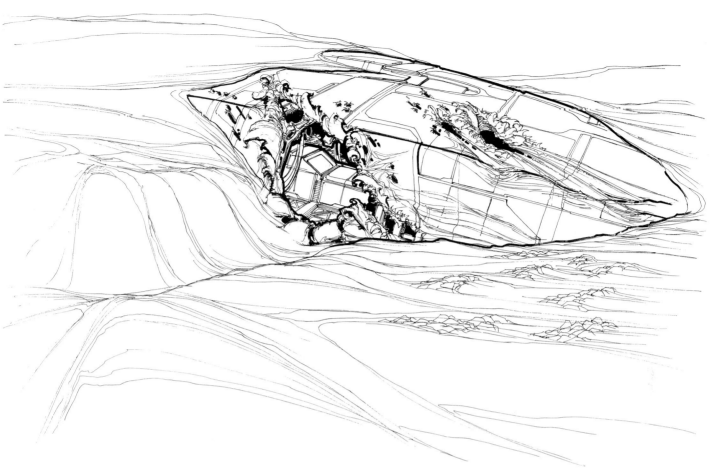

Production design for the crashed *Ravinok*. JOHN EAVES

down," says Oster. "There was a lot of concern about that, and while construction was going on, we were constantly aware of it. We ended up building the ship on flat ground away from the hill and then just tapping the hill down onto it. They put the pieces as close as they dared get and then filled the mountain in behind it."

The possibility of landslides made the producers decide to film Nana Visitor's interiors inside the ship back at Paramount, rather than in the quarry as originally planned. "Construction said, 'We're not putting *anybody* inside this set,'" notes Oster. "'Because if the mountain goes—" Although the mountain behaved itself, no one regretted filming the interiors back at the cool soundstages in Hollywood, along with the dilithium mine sequences that introduced viewers to the mythic Breen.

"They'd been red herrings since *The Next Generation*," says Wolfe. "They were these people who

were out there who were dangerous but were never really responsible for any of the trouble going on. Sort of a running joke. But we needed bad guys in this particular episode, and we just struck on the idea to use the Breen."

But even though we finally get to see the Breen . . . we don't. Timing was partially to blame. Coming on the heels of episodes featuring many Klingons and many Jem'Hadar, Behr says, "I wasn't really in the mood to come up with a new alien race. So I said, 'Let's not see them. Let's just put them in costume because they normally live in the cold.'"

A decision to provide the visual suggestion that the Breen are a snouted species, like an arctic wolf, resulted in a headpiece with room for a muzzle. The costume would see additional use the following year in "By Inferno's Light," where viewers learn why it is important never to turn your back on a Breen, and would be featured in the series' final season.

REJOINED

Episode #478

TELEPLAY BY **RONALD D. MOORE &**
RENÉ ECHEVARRIA
STORY BY **RENÉ ECHEVARRIA**
DIRECTED BY **AVERY BROOKS**

GUEST CAST

Lenara Kahn	SUSANNA THOMPSON
Dr. Bejal Otner	TIM RYAN
Dr. Hanor Pren	JAMES NOAH
Michael Eddington	KENNETH MARSHALL

STARDATE 49195.5

Lenara Kahn and Jadzia Dax try to resist the feelings that they had for
each other when their symbionts were joined to prior hosts.
ROBBIE ROBINSON

The news that a group of Trill scientists are coming to the station to conduct tests related to the creation of an artificial wormhole isn't earth-shattering, but the fact that the team leader is a joined Trill named Lenara Kahn has the potential to rock Jadzia Dax's world. One of Kahn's previous hosts was a woman named Nilani, wife of Torias, former host to the Dax symbiont. Their relationship ended tragically when Torias was killed in a shuttle accident, and Dax was placed in another host. In the Trill society, "reassociation," or engaging in a relationship with a lover from a past life, is strictly forbidden and punishable by exile from the Trill homeworld. This ultimately would mean the death of the symbiont after its current host dies. To the Trill, who consider protecting the life of a symbiont more important than anything, such a fate is worse than capital punishment.

Nevertheless, Dax opts to remain on the station during Lenara's visit, believing that she can control any feelings she may still have for her former wife. During a dinner reception for the scientists, the two Trill engage in casual conversation, noting with amusement that they are the focus of every guest's attention. But after they separate it is clear to each of them that an attraction definitely remains.

The Trill team, made up of Lenara, her brother Bejal Otner, and Dr. Pren, begins to work on the tests, which will be monitored aboard the *Defiant*. As science officer, Dax is involved in the experiment, putting her in close proximity to Lenara. Although their discussions initially are work related, the past keeps bubbling to the surface. Dax invites Lenara to dinner, and then quickly coerces Bashir into joining them as a chaperone. The two women reminisce for most of the evening, leaving Bashir feeling like a third wheel until a minor medical emergency gives him the excuse to leave. The two women agree that it is good to see each other, even in different bodies. Dax gives Lenara's hand an affectionate squeeze that is overseen by Pren.

When work resumes on the *Defiant*, the closeness between the two women is apparent to Pren, although Otner chooses to ignore it. However, after the first phase of the experiment proves successful, Dax hugs Lenara enthusiastically and Bejal feels that he can no longer pretend. He confronts his sister, who denies that anything is happening between Dax and her. Upset by the accusation, Lenara goes to Dax's quarters, where the two finally admit to each other that something *is* happening. Yielding to the moment, the two engage in a passionate kiss. Then Lenara forces herself to go, leaving Dax to struggle with her own mixed emotions.

The next day, Jadzia seeks Sisko's advice. Sisko gently reminds her of her responsibilities to the Dax symbiont inside her and counsels her to be very sure of feelings before she throws her future away. Then, during the second phase of the experiment, an accident nearly takes Lenara's life, and the two women realize that they don't want to lose each other again.

Ultimately, only Dax is willing to make the sacrifice that reassociation would call for. Lenara doesn't think she has the strength to break the Trill taboos and give up her life's work; perhaps she should go back to Trill for a while to think it over, she suggests. But Dax predicts that if Lenara leaves, she will never return. Not long after, as she watches Lenara board a departing transport, Dax knows in her heart that she has lost Lenara forever.

Although the inappropriately labeled "lesbian kiss scene" made this one of the most controversial *Star Trek* episodes ever, "Rejoined" didn't stir up quite as much of a reaction in the "outside world" as that *other* kiss, some thirty years earlier, between Kirk and Uhura in "Plato's Stepchildren." However, it did get its share.

"Some of the response was pretty angry," says Ron Moore, who cowrote the teleplay with René Echevarria. "Some felt betrayed, didn't want to see this in their homes. An affiliate down south cut the kiss from their broadcast. I remember thinking, it's been a long time since *Star Trek* was banned in the South. Maybe it's time that we get banned again."

"My mother was absolutely scandalized by the episode," says Echevarria. "Shocked and dismayed. She told me, 'I can't believe you did that. There should have been a parental guidance warning.' But it's exactly what I wanted to happen, to sneak it right into the living room."

"We got a lot of phone calls and letters," recalls Steve Oster, "probably more than any other episode I can recall. Interestingly, most of the phone calls were negative, while most of the letters were positive. Our staff all took turns fielding the calls, and the reactions were all over the place. One that I will always remember was a call that one of our production assistants [p.a.] took. A man said, 'You're ruining my kids by making them watch two women kiss like that.' And our p.a. said, 'Let me ask you a question. Would you have been okay if one of the women had shot the other to death with a phaser and the kids watched that?' And he said, 'Yes, of course.' And the p.a. said, 'Well, maybe you'd better think about who it is that is ruining your kids.'"

While every member of the staff will proudly stand behind the episode, they freely admit that "Rejoined" was not really a story about gay issues, any more than "Plato's Stepchildren" was a story about interracial relations. "It was a story about love," says Director Avery Brooks, "and the consequences of making choices out of love. The kiss was irrelevant." More important to Brooks in crafting the episode was the concept behind the story. "You have found the person that you want to spend the rest of your days with, the rest of eternity with, and that person is taken away from you," he explains. "And then years later that person returns and you have another chance. Now, that's an extraordinary story! Because when we lose people, there's always recrimination about what we said last. 'If only I'd had a

Director Avery Brooks did not allow still photography of the kiss because he didn't want it to be sensationalized. "People want to hype stuff like that," he says, "but I wasn't going to have it."
ROBBIE ROBINSON

chance to say . . . ,' you know. I think about that almost daily."

In fact, Echevarria's original concept for the episode was that a former *male* lover from Dax's past shows up at the station. "It was the same kind of story," says Moore. "They're still in love after all these years but they're forbidden to be involved with each other anymore." The Trill taboo against "reassociation" was something cocreator Michael Piller had suggested early on in the series. "He felt they'd have to have a very strict taboo in order to avoid an aristocracy of the joined," says Echevarria. "Otherwise, they'd all only want to hang out with each other, their dear old friends from five hundred years ago, and it would become a really screwed-up society. The existence of the taboo meant that we could do a tragic love story. But it was Ron who had this inspiration to make the ex another woman. We could tell the same story and the taboo about reassociation would track with our own taboo about homosexuality. We could tell the story without ever talking about the fact that they were two women."

And that was the way the episode ultimately played out. Viewers saw Sisko and Kira question Jadzia about the wisdom of getting involved with an ex-spouse, but never heard a discouraging word about the fact that the ex was female. "It deals with homosexuality and sexual orientation and tolerance, but I'm very proud of the fact that nowhere in the episode does anyone even blink at the fact that these are two women," says Moore. "That's the part that sails by everyone on the show. It's in the audience's face, but nobody is saying, 'That's a big deal.'"

Ironically, the *Star Trek* episode that first introduced Trills to viewers could have made that same statement a few years earlier. In *TNG*'s "The Host," Beverly Crusher falls in love with a joined Trill. The symbiont's host, a male, dies and the symbiont is temporarily placed in the body of Will Riker. Crusher comes to accept her former lover in that body, but when the symbiont is transferred to its permanent host, a female Trill, the doctor decides that romance with a Trill is too unpredictable and ends the relationship.

Times change, even in the world of the future. This time around, the relationship was run all the way up the flagpole, and everyone approved it, from Ira Behr to Executive Producer Rick Berman to the studio executives. "They questioned us closely about our intentions, and why we were doing it, and how it would work in the story, and how far we were going to go," says Moore. "They saw that we were sincere, that it was a good story, that we could say something with the show, that it was what *Star Trek* stood for and that it would actually be something to be proud of. They went for it."

The story required an unusual amount of exposition to explain Trill customs to the audience. "That was for viewers who don't know the characters intimately," explains Moore. "It's always a tough balance to strike. You have to write for the people who watch every week as well as for the people who watch intermittently. Not everybody knows Dax's family history, or what Trill society is all about."

"We can't just ignore backstory and expect people to know what we're talking about all the time," adds Behr. "A lot of times I think we leave our viewers in the dark, except for the real hard-core fans. In this case, we just wanted to make it clear that 'This is why this is going to happen, because we're not doing a show about *lesbians,* we're doing a show about *Trills,* and to make sure you know that, we're going to tell you what Trills are.'"

The B-story, Lenara's creation of an artificial wormhole, was admittedly "just a maguffin to get us through the tale and to explain why Lenara was coming to the station," says Moore. "It had to be a science project so that Lenara and Jadzia would need to work together."

"This is the epitome of an episode where the tech was the last thing that anyone cared about," says Behr. "It was a thread to hang the story on. It worked okay, but it's the least interesting part. Who gives a damn about the wormhole—there are female Trills kissing!"

Nevertheless, the people whose job it is to care about such threads gave it their all. It was a big deal for David Takemura, who switched hats from Visual Effects Coordinator to Supervisor for both "Rejoined" and "The Visitor" while the regular supervisors, Gary Hutzel and Glenn Neufeld, cosupervised the long and arduous postproduction work on "The Way of the Warrior."

Takemura had two major effects sequences in "Rejoined." The creation of the artificial wormhole was his first challenge (along with some related scenes of a probe being fired into the anomaly's center), and Dax's walk across the top of a force-field to save Lenara's life. The fact that the wormhole was "artificial" was a saving grace for Takemura. "That meant it could look different from the regular *DS9* wormhole," he says. "If I'd had to recreate that one it would have taken me weeks to even get close. But this one was man-made and not quite as organic. So we came up with a triangular design that followed some of the same design pathways as the regular wormhole, with particles spinning around the center. After I figured out how I wanted it to open and collapse, VisionArt actually did it on their computers, under Josh Rose's supervision."

The force field sequence combined physical effects, computer graphics, and carefully planned choreography. A wooden ramp was constructed and painted "ultimatte blue," then set against a similarly colored bluescreen wall. Terry Farrell was directed to "sort of skate down it," says Takemura. Gary Monak added "robofog," a mixture of nitrogen and hot water that creates an eerie ground fog effect, to the scene. The crew then shot plates of Farrell, which were combined with previously shot plates that showed the empty engineering room. VisionArts next added the computer-generated force field, and Computer Animator Adam Howard added the plasma glow that appeared around her feet as she moved.

STARSHIP DOWN

Episode #479

WRITTEN BY **DAVID MACK & JOHN J. ORDOVER**
DIRECTED BY **ALEXANDER SINGER**

GUEST CAST

Hanok	JAMES CROMWELL
Muniz	F.J. RIO
Stevens	JAY BAKER
Carson	SARA MORNELL

STARDATE 49263.5

Sisko and his officers bring the *Defiant* to a remote system in the Gamma Quadrant to discuss the Karemma's trade problems with the Federation, problems that are due to Quark's involvement as the middleman. Before Sisko can rectify the situation, the crew spots two approaching Jem'Hadar warships, which target the ship of the Karemma representative, Hanok. As Hanok watches from the *Defiant*, his ship flees into the atmosphere of a nearby gas giant, a dangerous move that could kill the Karemma crew. Sisko orders the *Defiant* to follow, and the ship immediately is buffeted by high turbulence while its sensors are rendered virtually useless. To pinpoint the other ships, the *Defiant's* crew employs an old echo-location technique. Unfortunately, the pulses emitted by the ship also give away their presence to the Jem'Hadar, who fire upon them and cripple the vessel.

With the *Defiant* rapidly losing altitude, the ship's hull is in danger of cracking like an eggshell in the gas giant's heavy gravity. Dax heads for a Jefferies tube to try to restore impulse power, but a hull breach develops, endangering her and the others on that deck. An emergency force field puts off the inevitable just long enough for Dax to finish her repair work, but it collapses before she can get clear of the area. As the poisonous nitrogen atmosphere of the gas planet rushes in, Sisko orders Bashir to seal off the area. Bashir complies, but steps into the gas-filled corridor just before the door closes behind him. Finding Dax,

Sisko plunges the *Defiant* into dangerous straits when he tries to stave off the Jem'Hadar attack on a Karemma vessel. ROBBIE ROBINSON

the doctor drags her into a turbolift, where they find momentary refuge.

On the bridge, the engines come back to life as Dax's work pays off. O'Brien arms two atmospheric probes with quantum torpedoes and the *Defiant* continues its search for the Karemma vessel. Echo-location picks up a nearby Jem'Hadar ship, and Sisko orders one of the torpedoes launched. It hits its mark, but not before the enemy vessel causes severe damage to the *Defiant,* leaving Sisko with a life-threatening concussion. With all systems on the bridge dead, Worf leaves for engineering, hoping to gain control of the ship from there. In the meantime, Kira attempts to keep Sisko from slipping into a coma, while Dax and Bashir await assistance in the turbolift and Quark unsuccessfully attempts to make peace with Hanok in the mess hall.

Worf sets to work with O'Brien's crew in engineering, only to realize that the remaining Jem'Hadar ship has fired two torpedoes at *Defiant.* They successfully evade one, but the other embeds itself in the mess hall bulkhead, where it is still primed to explode.

With no other options, Quark and Hanok work together to defuse the torpedo. Hanok discovers the true meaning behind the Ferengi rule "The bigger the risk, the bigger the win," which puts their dispute on the road to resolution. In engineering, O'Brien's team comes up with a plan to fire the phasers by using the deflector array, which will be good for only one shot. Worf makes the shot count and eliminates their pursuer. The *Defiant* rescues the Karemma ship, makes repairs, and returns to DS9. A grateful Sisko treats Major Kira to her first baseball game.

On a cold February morning in 1995, John Ordover, senior editor of *Star Trek* at Pocket Books, and his writing partner, David Mack, were trying to make their way into Manhattan. "We were stuck in traffic on the Brooklyn-Queens Expressway," Mack recalls, "when I looked over at John and said, 'I'd like to sink the *Defiant.*' Those were my exact words." Ordover, aware that the prior evening Mack had watched the award-winning German submarine drama *Das Boot,* immediately knew what his friend had in mind. "Okay, what's the story?" he asked.

"For the next twenty minutes we just rattled it out," Mack says. "We came up with the high concept of the *Defiant* getting into a conflict in orbit over a planet, being damaged, and plunging down into an

As this still photograph points out, the gas effect was not as effective as the water could have been. ROBBIE ROBINSON

alien sea where it sinks like a rock. From there it was sort of *The Poseidon Adventure,* with the crew trapped and trying to get out before the ship runs out of power and the structural integrity field collapses, and the ship is crushed like an egg and everybody drowns."

"We thought of it as a bottle show," says Ordover, referring to the producer-favored practice of using only regular cast members on existing sets. "We figured that that way they'd have more money to spend on special effects."

The pair worked on the story for several weeks before pitching it, in writing, to the producers. "Our initial idea was that while the crew is trapped underwater, Odo arrives with a rescue team," Mack explains. "He says, 'Just drop me in the water. I'll sink down to the ship, find a damaged spot in the hull, and seep in with the water.' They say to him, 'But it's hundreds of kilometers down—you'll be crushed.' And Odo says, 'I can't be crushed. I'm liquid.'"

Mack still likes the plan. "We had an idea for a great visual with the water seeping through a cracked bulkhead and then this gold viscous fluid flowing with it, then Odo just stands up and reforms out of the water. We thought it would have been the coolest thing to ever come down the pike—and if it weren't for the fact that water ended up not figuring into the episode at all, it might have been."

"We had to pare it down," says Steve Oster, "because underwater stories just aren't shootable on the television route. My first comment after reading the first draft was, 'It's a wonderful script and when you make the movie I'd love to see it.' It was written as a huge show, as they sometimes are, because good writers like to give you the bang for the buck. We had to figure out what we could throw away."

With an expensive underwater show deemed out of the question, the writers came up with the next best thing. "We always knew that if they liked the core story we could find a way to do it cheaper," Ordover says. "So we changed the location to the atmosphere of a giant gas planet."

"The principle is the same," says Director Alex Singer, an enthusiastic lay astronomer. "The atmosphere of Jupiter is the analogy that I kept in my head, because it is roughly equivalent to water under pressure."

"Actually, we ended up using Neptune as our model," notes Andre Bormanis. "I looked up some of the parameters for the rate at which pressure increases to make sure that we were accurate and credible. Gases at the core of a gas giant planet can become a hundred times as dense as lead, but it's still a gas because it's moving randomly."

Transforming water to gas didn't work on every level. The flooding of the ship, for example, was far less dramatic than originally envisioned, notes René Echevarria. "Shutting a hatch [against an incoming rush of water] is straight out of a submarine movie," he says. "But when we tried to do that classic scene with gas instead of water, it was hard to translate."

Gary Monak tried his best, again creating an atmosphere out of robofog. "We installed a piece of Plexiglas for the camera to shoot through, and then we yanked the hatch so it opened like a trapdoor," he says. "That let the robofog come in at them real quick, as if the bulkhead was bursting open. Then they used opticals to finesse it.

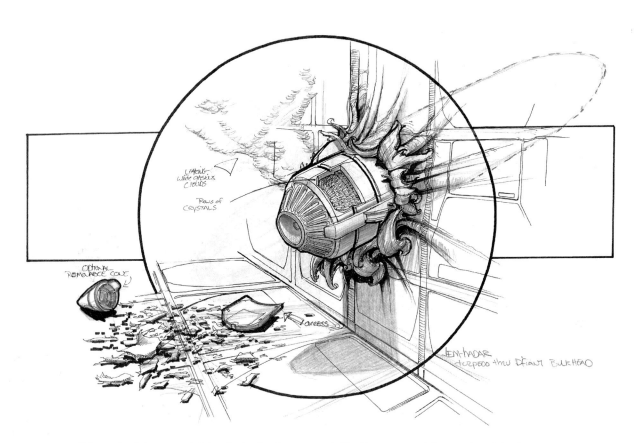

Before a sketch is approved, it is submitted to key personnel. The director wanted the torpedo to "glow." JOHN EAVES

"It could have been a set piece viewers would never forget: shutting the hatch and killing your own people!" Echevarria sighs. "We did the best we could, but there was no tension."

"For the rest of the series, we had a joke," confirms Ira Behr. "We'd say, 'You know, we could still do that submarine movie, and we could do it right this time!'"

If the show wasn't successful in some ways, it did work in others. "It was great fun for me," observes Armin Shimerman. "I got to play comedy, although there's a lot of seriousness involved in the situation. And I got to work with Jamie Cromwell, who's my old friend."

Cromwell had previously appeared on *TNG* ("The Hunted" and "Birthright"), so he felt perfectly at home during the shooting of the *DS9* episode. "I knew Michael Dorn and a number of the crew people from *TNG*. Armin and I had done a television movie together (an air disaster drama titled *Flight 451*)," he says. "But the makeup was pretty dominating. I don't know how an alien feels about any particular thing, so I just played him as a human character and tried to handle the makeup."

Cromwell was already known as a character actor when he was cast in the role of Hanok. Still, no one knew that his career was literally on the verge of taking off. "He had finished *Babe*," laughs Shimerman. "I hadn't seen it yet, so I wasn't aware of the major step that he had taken." The Oscar-nominated *Babe* would soon put Cromwell in demand for more high-profile parts, including, ironically, a major role as Zefram Cochrane in *Star Trek: First Contact*.

As in "Hippocratic Oath," the writers found ways to demonstrate that Worf's "period of adjustment" wouldn't be all that easy, in this case, with a B-story that had O'Brien educating Worf on how to work with the crew. Director Singer gave this storyline as much attention as the A-story. "I was drilled on Worf's development by Ira and Steve Oster," he says. "And Michael Dorn certainly understood the usefulness of these scenes. It was terribly important to his

introduction to the series that we make him more accessible as a character [than he had been on *TNG*]. This was a different view of Worf. Suddenly he had to deal with the psychology of human behavior at a level to which he was unaccustomed."

Kira, too, is forced to do some psychological introspection. She tries to reconcile her impressions of Sisko as her commander and her friend, as well as an important religious icon to her people. The vehicle for the Kira storyline is a peculiar Bajoran fable that took on a life of its own. "We initially wrote that Kira was just babbling, saying anything that came to her mind," Ron Moore says. "Then I think we kind of outsmarted ourselves and started telling a story that actually needed a resolution. But we never wrote the resolution. The audience wasn't supposed to be listening to the story so much as noticing that she was babbling."

Singer understood the intention, if not the story itself. "Telling a story to keep someone alive is the ultimate storytelling," he says. "Nana understood that beautifully, despite the fact that the story had this interminable village dopiness about brothers and *kava* farmers. The first time I saw her do it, I got chills. She just choked me up. We did several takes and every time she did it I was profoundly moved."

"I decided that Kira has very little sense of humor," comments Nana Visitor, "so she wouldn't be a great storyteller. But even if she were, considering the circumstances, her words still would have come out in that flat way because of what was overwhelmingly on her mind and tearing her heart out. Her captain was dying and she couldn't do anything about it. She was in a fury to not let it happen."

Beyond *kava* farmers, one of the things Kira babbles about would actually come to fruition in an episode later that season. Although her suggestion that the station set up a four-shift crew rotation schedule seems little more than a throwaway line here, Sisko must have been paying close attention, because the plan is put into effect in the episode "Accession."

LITTLE GREEN MEN

Episode #480

TELEPLAY BY IRA STEVEN BEHR &
ROBERT HEWITT WOLFE
STORY BY TONI MARBERRY & JACK TREVIÑO
DIRECTED BY JAMES L. CONWAY

GUEST CAST

Nurse Garland	MEGAN GALLAGHER
Denning	CHARLES NAPIER
Rom	MAX GRODÉNCHIK
Nog	ARON EISENBERG
Carlson	CONOR O'FARRELL
Wainwright	JAMES G. MacDONALD

STARDATE UNKNOWN

When a young Ferengi goes out on his own, he raises capital by selling his boyhood treasures. Thus, as Nog prepares to depart DS9 for Starfleet Academy, Rom conducts a traditional auction for his son. Suddenly, Quark arrives with news that his ship has come in, or rather, the shuttle Cousin Gaila has owed Quark for ten years has arrived. Demonstrating uncharacteristic generosity, Quark offers to take Nog to the Academy, with Rom along for the ride. To make sure the trip is profitable, Quark brings along some valuable contraband to sell.

As the shuttle enters Earth's star system, Rom realizes the warp drive has been sabotaged, no doubt by Gaila, who never really liked Quark, and that there is no way to stop it. Fortunately, Rom figures out a way to use Quark's illegal cargo of kemacite to get them out of warp, after which he hopes to make an emergency landing on Earth. His plan works, but it also throws them back in time to 1947. The three Ferengi awaken in an observation room on an Army Air Corps base in Roswell, New Mexico.

The team of military and science personnel who have captured the Ferengi believe them to be Martians. The three Ferengi can do little to convince them otherwise, since their universal translators aren't working. Nog, who has been studying about Earth, recognizes their captors' uniforms and realizes that they've in landed in Earth's past.

Rom borrows a hairpin from attractive Nurse Garland, who's been studying them along with her fiancé, Professor Carlson, and fixes the translators. Once communication is established, Quark attempts to interest the humans in doing business; he's decided that he can make a financial killing by selling technology to the primitive *hew-mons*. While Quark

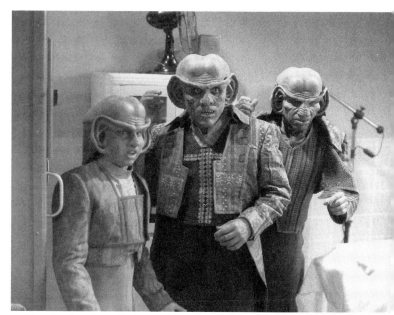

Nog, Quark, and Rom inadvertently wind up in the year 1947 at Roswell, New Mexico. ROBBIE ROBINSON

and the others await the U.S. government's response to his business proposition, they discover that what they had assumed to be a military guard dog is actually Odo. The changeling had stowed away on the shuttle to catch Quark red-handed in his smuggling scheme. Odo tells the Ferengi where their ship is hidden, in Hangar 18, and heads back to repair the engines.

Rom thinks he may be able to get the ship back to their own time, but Quark decides he doesn't want to leave. He's sure he can manipulate this primitive culture and become the richest man in the galaxy. He doesn't have any qualms about altering history to do it.

However, he's underestimated just how primitive, and paranoid, humans of the twentieth century are. Certain that Quark is hiding something, the base's commander has him repeatedly injected with truth serum. The drug has no effect on Ferengi, so one of the officers switches to physical threats. At this point, Nog speaks up and claims that they are advance scouts for an invasion fleet with plans to take over Earth. Despite the fact that this is a lie obvious enough for Garland and Carlson to discern, the officer believes it and drops his guard long enough for Nog to deck him.

Garland and Carlson, unhappy with the way the extraterrestrial visitors have been treated by the military, step in to help the Ferengi escape to the hangar, where Odo is waiting. The shape-shifter and the three Ferengi take off and head for a nearby atomic bomb test site. The radiation from the blast interacts with the remaining kemacite to engage the shuttle's warp engines, and the ship winds up back in the twenty-fourth century.

"This was more of a public service than anything else," Ira Behr states emphatically. "There had been so much talk about Roswell lately that we just felt it was time to tell the truth once and for all." Actually, the idea for the episode had been with the *Star Trek* producers for some time. "I took the original pitch when I was on staff with *The Next Generation*," says René Echevarria. "I think it was about Toni Marberry and Jack Treviño's fifteenth pitch. They said, 'We've got a *Deep Space Nine* story.' And I said, 'Well, I can't take that.' And one of them said, 'Quark is the Roswell alien.' I said, 'I love it.'"

Echevarria told the idea to *DS9*'s producers, but at the time Michael Piller didn't respond to it. During the series' fourth season, as the fiftieth anniversary of the infamous New Mexico incident was approaching, someone brought the pitch up. The response was immediate. "We all said, 'It's insane, so let's do it,'" grins Echevarria.

Ferengi episodes generally provide the series with a bit of comic relief, and "Little Green Men" was certainly no exception. But the writers also tend to sneak in some statements of social relevance, which are usually conveyed by Quark. In this case, Armin Shimerman was quite happy to speak Quark's mind. "He has speeches about atom bombs and cigarettes, which is our way of commenting on situations that we find in our lives today," observes the actor. "Granted, Americans don't smoke as much as they used to, but they smoke a lot in the rest of the world."

Behr felt he couldn't make an episode that aped the style of fifties movies that *didn't* use cigarettes as a key prop. The pinnacle of such excess, in his opinion, was a 1951 dinosaur island movie called *The Lost Continent*. "You see smoking in fifties movies all the time, from war movies to bug-eyed monster films, but *Continent* took it to an art form that is just jaw-dropping to watch," recalls Behr with a chuckle. "Every time there is a problem, everyone starts handing out cigarettes."

Although it worked atmospherically, Behr ultimately wasn't quite happy with the messages about the evils of nicotine that he and co-writer Robert Wolfe inserted into the script. "Knocking cigarettes is such an easy target," he sighs. "We thought it would speak for itself, but we actually verbalized it and I

"I loved the idea that we could have people in a *Star Trek* episode acting like twentieth-century human beings, smoking cigarettes, cigars—the whole deal," grins Ira Behr. ROBBIE ROBINSON

wish we hadn't. We got a little self-righteous and it was like shooting ducks in a barrel." Upon due reflection, Behr wishes he had taken another tack altogether. "If I had anything to do over again with 'Little Green Men,'" he says, "I'd have Quark come back to the twenty-fourth century with a cigarette jones. I would love to have had him puffing on them like mad."

Although atomic bombs are at least as harmful as cigarettes, Behr chose to comment on their use in a more subtle, ironic way. Once again, his feelings were influenced by a motion picture. "I was *incensed* by the movie *True Lies*, where they used an A-bomb as the background for a kiss between Arnold Schwarzenegger and Jamie Lee Curtis," he says. "The difference in movie-making between *Dr. Strangelove* and *True Lies* exemplifies a culture that has lost its way, where the blast of an atomic bomb literally seems to have lost its meaning. I thought that if the everyday coded message of 'what things mean' has become so tainted, and so lost that we are no longer able to identify the world clearly and understandably because of our inability to use the language and the visualization of things, then let's just take it and make it even stupider."

Thus, the twentieth century's ultimate destroyer of all things was employed as the *deus ex machina* that saved the day for Quark and company, returning them to their own time.

Although it would send them on a time-consuming chase, the Visual Effects Department relished the fact that the script called for an authentic atomic bomb blast. "The writers wanted a classic piece of footage that you've seen over and over, so we started looking though atomic bomb footage from stock film companies," says Glenn Neufeld. "We saw hundreds of incredible pieces of film, with houses disintegrating, and aerial views of moving shock waves." But Neufeld's team immediately encountered some problems: most of the footage was in black and white, and the negatives for most were long gone.

After assembling four hours of potential clips, each ranging from five to thirty seconds long, they decided on one from the Nevada Test Range. "Because it's fifty years old, the negative had a lot of scratches and tears. We really had to clean it up," says David Takemura. "And the footage had to be steadied because the frame was shaking considerably. The poor soul who shot it probably has radiation poisoning by now."

Sticking with the fifties theme, the producers threw open the casting session to actors known for their work in "classic" B-movies of that decade. "It was one of the best casting sessions ever," grins Behr. "It gave me a chance to have every character actor I had ever wanted to see. We had everyone, Jonathan Haze from *Little Shop of Horrors*, Gregory Walcott from *Plan 9 from Outer Space*. I was having a blast! And when Charles Napier came in, he had the jaw *and* the attitude." Behr loved the fact that Napier had done a slew of Russ Meyer sexploitation movies in the fifties, sixties, and seventies. But could he do the job as the ultra-macho base commander? "I told him that I wanted someone who wasn't afraid to have a cigar in his mouth, and he said, 'Give me barbed wire and I'll smoke it for you,'" Behr laughs. "I love this guy."

There was an extra bonus in Napier's casting for fans of the original series; he had played Adam, one of the space hippies in "The Way to Eden" nearly thirty years earlier. Napier's character in "Little Green Men" was General Denning, a hint that the writers apparently let the fifties influence the *names* of their characters as well as the casting. The general's name suggests that of veteran B-movie star Richard Denning, who appeared in such films as *The Creature from the Black Lagoon* and *The Day the World Ended*. Similarly, Nurse Garland (played by Megan Gallagher, who had previously appeared in "Invasive Procedures") recalls leading lady Beverly Garland, who starred in countless fifties B-movies. And Professor Carlson undoubtedly is a tribute to actor

Cold war–era ambience extended even to the episode's lighting.
ROBBIE ROBINSON

Richard Carlson, who starred in *The Magnetic Monster* and *It Came from Outer Space*.

Because the characters would be twentieth-century humans, the Hair and Makeup Departments also got a voice in casting the episode. "If someone didn't want to get his hair cut in a fifties style, he didn't get the job," laughs Michael Westmore. "Of course, for the women we only needed to get red lipstick and stylize the eyebrows."

Although the assignment of directors to *Star Trek* episodes generally follows a firm schedule of rotation, Director James L. Conway broke tradition when he heard about the upcoming "Little Green Men." "I was talking to Ira about the stories they had coming up," Conway says. When Conway heard about the "Hangar 18 episode," the director expressed his interest in no uncertain terms. "I'd directed a movie called *Hangar 18* in 1980," he admits. "It was a modern-day dramatization of the Roswell incident. So directing this was like coming full circle."

As most science fiction aficionados know, Hangar 18 is the Air Force hangar where an alien spacecraft is reputed to be stored. The production crew was happy to go outside of the claustrophobic sound-stages to recreate it, but the budget dictated they not go far. Luckily, they needed only to travel a few feet, to a location, coincidentally, just outside of Para-mount's Stage 18. "Our original concept was to use the outside of Stage 18 for Hangar 18, but when we looked at it, it just looked too much like a sound-stage," says Steve Oster. "But while we were looking

Hangar 18 is actually Paramount's Mill, home to the
Construction Department. ROBBIE ROBINSON

THE SWORD OF KAHLESS
Episode #481
TELEPLAY BY HANS BEIMLER
STORY BY RICHARD DANUS
DIRECTED BY LeVAR BURTON

GUEST CAST

Kor	JOHN COLICOS
Toral	RICK PASQUALONE
Soto	TOM MORGA

STARDATE UNKNOWN

The Klingon Empire's strained political relationship with the Federation does not
extend to the boisterous Klingon warrior Kor.
He has returned to Deep Space 9 to lure his
friend Dax on another quest ("Blood Oath"). Kor is on
the trail of the Sword of Kahless, the legendary weapon
of the Empire's first leader, lost for a millennium. The
pair invite Worf to accompany them on their mission
to find the artifact, then Dax goes to bed while the two
Klingons drink late into the night. When Kor finally
retires, he is attacked by a Lethean, who renders Kor
unconscious and then lifts information regarding the
location of the sword from the Klingon's mind. In the
morning, Kor remembers nothing of the incident.

Hoping that the recovery of the sword will help
restore Federation/Klingon relations, Sisko allows the
trio to borrow a runabout. They travel to a planet in
the Gamma Quadrant where Kor believes the sword
to be located. Kor's directions lead them to a large

at it, we turned around and saw Paramount's construction mill. We went, 'Hey, that's a cool building.'
So there it was."

Beyond being a very funny show that was clearly
a labor of love for all involved, "Little Green Men" is
noteworthy in the ever-growing *Star Trek* annals for
the introduction of two important elements. The
episode gives viewers their first opportunity to hear
the Ferengi language. The task of writing it fell to
Robert Wolfe. "I sort of thought things through and
tried to make the words fairly consistent," he says.
"But frankly, it's a lot of goofy sounding stuff. I tried
to use a lot of silly sounds, like p's. P's are funny," he
laughs, "so there's a lot of them." The second contribution to *Star Trek* lore is the introduction of the term
"waste extraction," quite possibly the first mention of
a toilet in *Star Trek*. "When we first wrote the words
'waste extraction,' we didn't even want to *think* of
what the hell *that* was. *Extraction?* Whoa!" Behr
laughs. "That's taking twenty-fourth-century technology a little far. It takes you one step past replicators.
I just hope it has nothing to do with sharp pincers."

The writing staff began inserting waste extraction
jokes in subsequent scripts, "one right after another,"
says Behr. "I even saw a mention of waste extraction in
one of the licensed *Deep Space Nine* comic books. Finally
we had to stop because it was getting ridiculous."

Kor, Dax, and Worf travel to the Gamma Quadrant in search of the
mythical Sword of Kahless. ROBBIE ROBINSON

underground facility, and they succeed in defeating a force-field that protects the central chamber. Once inside, they find that the chamber has been looted. But Worf discovers a second hidden chamber, and within that one is the Sword of Kahless.

As the trio leave the chamber, they are confronted by the Lethean and a group of Klingons, led by Toral, Worf's old enemy from the House of Duras. Toral wants the sword for the political power it will bring him. A fierce battle ensues. Dax, Kor, and an injured Worf manage to escape with the sword. Unfortunately, contact to their orbiting runabout has been blocked by the Klingons; they'll have to climb to the surface in order to transport off the planet.

The journey is troubled from the start. Kor learns that Worf had previously spared Toral's life, and accuses the Starfleet officer of being too human. Worf finds the respect he had felt for the old warrior waning, particularly when Kor suggests that rather than giving the sword to the emperor, it would be better if *he* retained the sword and used it to unite the troubled Klingon Empire. Later, Worf reveals to Dax that he feels it is his own destiny, not Kor's, to possess the sword and lead his people.

Tensions rise as the journey continues. Kor nearly falls to his death when he refuses to briefly relinquish possession of the sword to Worf in order to save himself. He is convinced that Worf wants him dead, although Worf argues that his priority was to make sure that the sword was returned to the Klingon people. With the two men literally at each other's throats, Dax takes possession of the sword. Even so, she can't prevent an eventual standoff between the two, although the arrival of the Klingons and the Lethean can. Still, their belief in the power of the sword helps in the ensuing battle, and the three manage to defeat their attackers. Kor and Worf then turn on each other.

Angry and frustrated, Dax stuns each of the men with her phaser, then at phaser point convinces Toral to turn off the jamming device that has been blocking communications to the runabout. Once they are all safely aboard, Worf and Kor realize that if the sword was able to turn them against each other, it will serve only to further divide the Klingon people. Reluctantly, they beam the weapon into space, knowing that it may be lost for another millennium, but believing that it will be found when destiny deems it appropriate.

"This was the beginning of our finding our stride with Worf," reports Ira Behr. "It was the first episode where we even scratched the surface of the character." Until this point in the fourth season, Behr continues, they'd been working with stories that had been green-lighted prior to word that Michael Dorn would be joining the show. As a result, he says, "Worf had no connection to them, because we just didn't know how to fit him into those scripts."

The story for "The Sword of Kahless" is by Richard Danus, executive story editor of *The Next Generation* during its third season. Danus also wrote the episode "Déjà Q," and contributed to the teleplay for "Booby Trap" and befriended then-newcomer-on-staff Ira Steven Behr. "Richard was the one person who actually made my life bearable during that terrible season," Behr says. "He knew that he was on the way out, and he made sure that he helped me to get my foot in as much as possible." Several years later, Danus visited Behr at *Deep Space Nine*, "and we gave him a story," the very appreciative Behr says, smiling.

"The Sword of Kahless" turned out to be much

Dan Curry refined the Sword of Kahless, taking only some of the features from Eaves's renderings and adding the triangular point in the center. ROBBIE ROBINSON

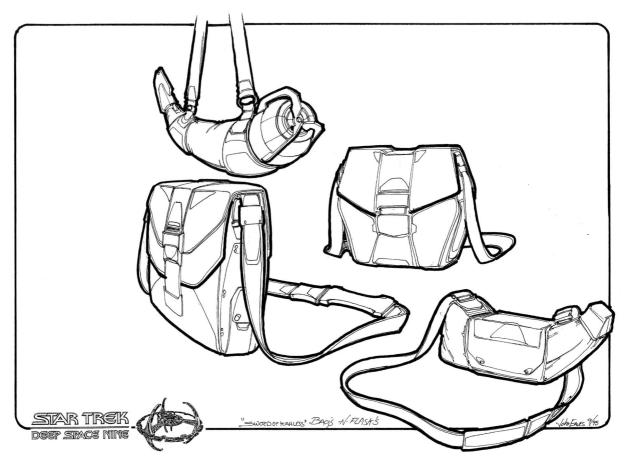

Each piece of equipment must be designed. JOHN EAVES

more than a simple story, however. It drew on mythology, from both Klingon culture and ancient human culture as well. "It's the search for the Holy Grail," says Director LeVar Burton, "and it's about how the importance placed on the end of the quest, or on the object, affects who we are. The truth is that life is not about the destination, it's about the journey." The potent mixture of philosophy and legend is, Burton says, "just one of the things that I thought about while I was directing."

Over the centuries, the Grail has generated tales of almost supernatural power, but Hans Beimler, who wrote the teleplay from Danus's story, resisted the impulse to give the *bat'leth* miraculous powers. "The idea is that the sword itself doesn't have any magic," he says. "It's the *concept* of the sword that has the power. We could have said that some technology or magic gave the Klingons a feeling of power, but that would have been a cheap way to go. We wanted to explore the notion that there were some dark streaks to be revealed within these characters. The minute anyone starts talking about the sword it starts infect-

ing them, so Worf gets caught up from the very beginning, back at the bar."

But the writing staff was disappointed to learn that some viewers couldn't accept that premise. "A lot of fan reaction was that there must be a tech explanation, that the sword was emitting something," says René Echevarria. "I was astonished. And it didn't seem to be one of the more popular shows of the season. Of course, it was hurt a little bit by the production values."

Although Beimler had created details like booby-trapped tunnels and other surprises in his first draft, they were killed for scheduling purposes and the quest sequence was shot within Stage 18's very limiting cave set. "It wasn't so much that the gags would have cost too much money as that they would have taken up time," explains Steve Oster. "Depending on what the gag is, it can add two hours of production time, and if you have four or five of them, you've just added a day to the schedule." On most episodes, time can be conserved by shooting scenes with some actors while others are being made up. In this case, that wasn't possible, because, as Oster points out, "Dax, Worf, and Kor were in almost every scene. What with getting them into and out of their make-up, it would have become a logistical nightmare."

Making the caves interesting, therefore, became Burton's quest. "It was supposed to be a labyrinth of caves, so it was really a matter of being as clever as I could, giving this limited set several different looks to convey different locations," he says. "But one of the things that I love about filmmaking is that it's a process of problem solving, and you get to work with very inventive, clever people." Burton points out Director of Photography Jonathan West as one of those people. "Jonathan's contributions were immeasurable and very specific. He kept urging me to think about creating depth in the staging of the scenes, and with his prodding and prompting, that's exactly what we did. We found depth and dimension instead of shooting right up against flat walls," Burton grins.

As an example, Burton cites a scene in which Dax, Worf, and Kor find themselves on a precipice. First the director shot the actors on the second level of the cave. Then Gary Hutzel built a miniature duplicate of the cave from 'black wrap,' a heavy-duty

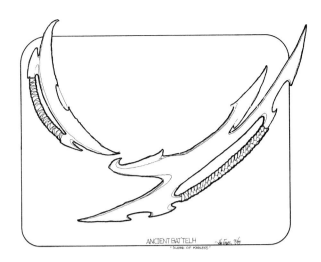
One of the countless sketches for the title prop. JOHN EAVES

aluminum foil used extensively by cinematographers to wrap or deflect lights. "The miniature was eight feet long and five feet tall," Hutzel reveals. After filming the miniature from a low angle, Hutzel's team simply "matted the footage of the actors onto the miniature."

The titular object, the Sword of Kahless itself, deserved special attention. As Worf picks it up for the first time, Composer David Bell's music rises in an almost religious mode. "I saw these characters as very Wagnerean," notes Bell. "So I used Wagner opera vocabulary in the orchestrations, and I actually used Wagner tubas in the score." The Wagner tuba, a brass instrument devised at the request of the German composer for his opera series *Der Ring des Nibelungen,* is a unique instrument not often heard in Hollywood. Was the music a cue suggested by the script? "Absolutely," responds Behr. "If that scene doesn't work, the whole show doesn't work. If the audience isn't made to understand the spiritual importance of that weapon, then we have no episode."

The Klingon *bat'leth* has been established for a number of years, so Kahless's *bat'leth* clearly had to be something special. Starting with drawings supplied by the Art Department, Joe Longo ordered a new *bat'leth* made of hardened aluminum with a leather-wrapped handle. The prop then was given to freelance sculptor Dragon Dronet, who etched designs into the blade using a handheld dental bit. "The producers wanted the designs to look old and rather like Damascus," says Dronet, referring to the Syrian style of decorating blades with wavy patterns. "I decided to do a combination of Damascus and a topographical map, so that it would look as if you're staring down at mountains. Then I wrote Klingon names

Sand spread out across the floor gives the much used set a different look. ROBBIE ROBINSON

down the side." Dronet designed a stand for the weapon from scratch. "I made the base out of one-inch-thick Plexiglas and engraved the pattern into it, and then sprayed on platinum paint to make it look metallic," he says. Then he added his own unique touch. "I carved the legs to make them look like *targ* feet," he laughs, "because that's what Klingons have on their homeworld."

Director Burton really put Farrell through her paces for the episode. "It was necessary for her to be aggressive and absolutely grounded in her dealings with both Worf and Kor," he says. "So my conversations with Terry had to do with really rooting her performance way down in the belly and not in the head." Farrell pulled out all the stops, and established a mode of performance for Dax that Burton and Farrell humorously dubbed "Action Barbie."

OUR MAN BASHIR

Episode #482

TELEPLAY BY RONALD D. MOORE
STORY BY ROBERT GILLAN
DIRECTED BY WINRICH KOLBE

The real spy accompanies the make-believe spy on an unexpectedly dangerous adventure in the holosuite. ROBBIE ROBINSON

GUEST CAST

Rom	MAX GRODÉNCHIK
Michael Eddington	KENNETH MARSHALL
Caprice	MELISSA YOUNG
Mona Luvsitt	MARCI BRICKHOUSE

SPECIAL GUEST STAR

Garak	ANDREW ROBINSON

STARDATE UNKNOWN

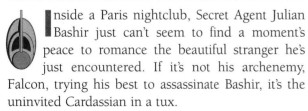

Inside a Paris nightclub, Secret Agent Julian Bashir just can't seem to find a moment's peace to romance the beautiful stranger he's just encountered. If it's not his archenemy, Falcon, trying his best to assassinate Bashir, it's the uninvited Cardassian in a tux.

Dr. Bashir isn't at all happy to see Garak in the middle of his holosuite fantasy, which centers on Bashir's exploits as a glamorous spy during Earth's 1960s. But the Cardassian, fascinated by this insight into Bashir's personality, convinces the doctor to let him stick around and watch.

At the same time, Sisko and several members of his senior staff are approaching DS9 in the *Orinoco* when a sabotage attempt by a Cardassian separatist group causes the vessel to malfunction. Acting quickly, Eddington attempts to beam them off the ship, but the explosion blows out the transporter before the crew can rematerialize. Their patterns wind up in the transporter's buffer, but Eddington must act quickly to find a more permanent place to store them. With seconds to spare, he instructs the station's computer to wipe all computer memory necessary in order to save the patterns. The computer complies and the crew is saved—but no one knows where their patterns have been stored.

Whisked to Bashir's "Hong Kong apartment" by the holoprogram, the doctor and Garak are provided more casual attire by Bashir's personal valet, Mona Luvsitt. A noise in the room alerts them to the presence of an unexpected visitor: a Russian spy named Anastasia, who looks exactly like Major Kira. Bashir attempts to freeze the program, but is informed that computer control has been disrupted due to a stationwide emergency. When Bashir calls Ops for clarification, Eddington realizes that the transporter patterns have been placed in the holosuite memory core. He warns Bashir not to shut down the program or leave the holosuite, since it could end his crewmates' lives. Then Eddington, Odo, and Rom try to figure out how to restore the crew.

Bashir returns his attention to the program. Anastasia informs him of a series of artificial earthquakes and the not-so-coincidental disappearance of one of the world's leading seismologists, Professor Honey Bare—a dead ringer for Dax. Bashir deduces that he'll have to save Bare if he wants to keep Dax alive, but before he can do anything, he receives another unexpected guest.

It's Falcon, the hired assassin—but this time he looks just like O'Brien. Bashir, Garak, and Anastasia overpower Falcon and his henchmen. They travel to a club in Paris, where, Anastasia says, a man named Dr. Noah may be connected to Bare's disappearance. At the club, they meet Duchamps, a Worf look-alike who works for Noah, and ask him to set up a meeting. Duchamps does better than that; he drugs the three of them and delivers them to the doctor, who resembles Sisko.

Noah can't resist telling the trio about his diabolical plan to kill everyone on Earth by producing earthquakes that will release molten lava from its core. After the lava is released, the tectonic plates will settle, the surface of the planet will shrink, and Earth's oceans will cover all of the land masses—with the exception of Noah's refuge, a complex on the top of Mount Everest that will become an island. There, Noah will start a new society. Unfortunately, Noah isn't interested in having Bashir join that society, so he has Falcon lock him and Garak in a cave that will fill with lava shortly. Anastasia, he assures them, will make good breeding stock for the new human race.

As in all good spy stories, the hero is able to turn the head of one of the villain's lackeys. In this case, it's Dr. Honey Bare, who can't bear to see Bashir die. She provides them with a key, and they escape from the cave just in time. Bashir wants to get back to Noah's control room, but Garak has had enough of their exploits. He wants to end the program and get out. When reason fails to sway Garak, Bashir is forced to shoot him, convincing the Cardassian that he's not leaving.

They return to the control room, where Bashir learns from Eddington that he needs two more minutes to complete the preparations required to remate-

rialize the patterns. Bashir passes the time by trying to convince Noah he's come over to his side. Noah doesn't believe him. He's surprised when Bashir is the one who activates Noah's super weapon, launching the destruction of the world. Nevertheless, Noah decides to kill Bashir anyway, but before he can fire his gun, he dematerializes, along with Falcon, Duchamps, Honey Bare, and Anastasia. Seconds later, the five officers rematerialize on the transporter pad of the *Defiant*, where Rom has improvised a way to integrate their physical and neural patterns.

Back in the holosuite, Bashir finds that Garak has changed his mind about not participating in his holoprogram. In fact, the Cardassian suggests that they change the location of their next lunch engagement from the Promenade to Bashir's penthouse apartment in Hong Kong.

Although it's not one of the no-nos included on the official tip sheet the *Star Trek* offices send out to inquiring freelancers, one thing the staff writers prefer *not* to hear is a pitch about a funny (or dangerous) holosuite (or holodeck) malfunction. "You can't just go into a holodeck and have it malfunction again," says René Echevarria. "It's happened too many times. We

"I wanted viewers to pay attention to the holosuite story," says Ron Moore. "'Who's Dr. Noah and what is he doing?'" ROBBIE ROBINSON

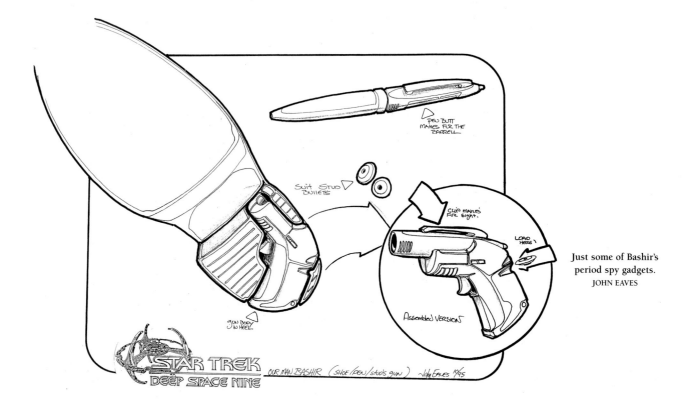

Just some of Bashir's
period spy gadgets.
JOHN EAVES

haven't heard a new holodeck story for years." Of course, given the right circumstances, rules are likely to be broken.

"We'd been waiting for someone to come up with a holosuite story or program that is uniquely *Deep Space Nine* for four years," says Ira Behr. "As opposed to doing *TNG*-type detective stuff. I mean, yes, if we could do the Battle of Britain with Bashir and O'Brien in the holosuite, we'd do it in a second. But it's too expensive. You can't have them in the planes and all that. You can't do William Wallace [of *Braveheart* fame] or any of that stuff. But *this* we could do."

Echevarria thought the same thing as he listened to the story pitch of *DS9*'s Assistant Script Coordinator (and typist) Robert Gillan. "I knew immediately that this would work," he says. "I told it to Ira and it was, 'Done—sold!' Right there. He went downstairs and gave Bob a big hug."

Gillan didn't have every aspect of the story worked out when he pitched. All he knew was that he wanted to do a holosuite story that focused on some heroic fantasy of Dr. Bashir's. But what caught Echevarria's fancy was the fact that Gillan had a rationale for the story that went way beyond the tired "the holosuite technology screwed up" plotline. "My thought was, what if something went wrong with the *transporter*, and the computer had to decide where to

store the people using it so they wouldn't die," says Gillan. "The computer would put the physical patterns in the holosuite, a place where complex patterns are stored all the time.

"That was the basic premise," he continues with a smile. "That Bashir was already in there with a program running and the holosuite doesn't realize that these new patterns don't belong in the lineup of characters that are already in the story. So it just uses one of the patterns as the next male or female character in the story. Then Bashir realizes that the people he thinks are Sisko and O'Brien and Worf are actually characters from his story. He has to keep them from *dying* in there, because if they do, the computer will phase out their physical patterns and they'll really be dead. And he can't shut it down, because it'd be like turning off your computer without hitting 'save.'"

It was Ron Moore's idea to make Bashir's program a '60s-era spy saga. "We were sitting in the break session trying to figure out what Bashir's holosuite fantasy would be," he recalls. "I'd always thought that he was a bit of an enigma, and it occurred to me that he was friends with Garak—a *spy*! So maybe in the holosuite he's into sixties spy thrillers." While James Bond is the most obvious example, Moore, an admitted buff of the genre, says the teleplay owes as much to other films and TV shows of the era as it does to Ian

Fleming's famous creation. "It's an homage to *James Bond, The Man From U.N.C.L.E., The Wild, Wild West, Our Man Flint,* and *Matt Helm,* he says. "I loved all of them as a kid. They had a certain style to them, panache. I loved writing the episode."

Although Moore tried to avoid direct references to any of his childhood heroes, some names and turns of phrase skated a little close to the edge, and MGM/UA, the studio that produces the 007 films, reportedly did *not* find imitation to be the sincerest form of flattery. As a result, a later episode that featured Bashir's spy holoprogram ("A Simple Investigation") was far more generic in its references.

Like "Little Green Men" and "Trials and Tribble-ations" the following season, "Our Man Bashir" was an episode the entire staff fell in love with. Moore may have gotten the teleplay assignment, but his coworkers felt pleased with their own contributions. For example . . .

"I came up with some of the goofy names," says Robert Wolfe. " 'Komananov' was mine."

Behr lays claim to "Mona Luvsitt," which, according to Moore, was "Suzie Luvsitt" until Behr pointed out that the name "Mona" was much more "appropriate." Behr also takes credit (and blame) for "Dr. Noah," which, upon later reflection, wasn't as good an idea as it seemed at the time, although it jibed with the madman's plan to flood the world.

"I tossed in the idea of the champagne cork that hits Falcon in the forehead," states Hans Beimler proudly. "I never thought that would make it to the screen!"

"That was me, throwing the cork from off-camera," offers Dennis Madalone. "I got him on the first shot!"

The trick that preceded Madalone's contribution wasn't quite as simple, but Glenn Neufeld knew just how to pull it off. "They wanted Bashir to see the reflection of Falcon in the bottle of champagne," he explains. "But they hadn't discussed how they were going to do it in advance." Realizing that the filmmakers had scheduled time in the middle of the hectic shooting schedule to set up the shot with the real bottle, Neufeld pointed out that he could do it later on, in much less time, *without* the bottle. "I told them, 'We'll shoot a plate of the guy walking toward the camera and then I'll take the plate and warp it onto the bottle later.' It took them a beat to realize I was saying, 'Okay, you really don't have to do anything now.' Then it was, 'Oh! Okay. We'll go to another shot then. Moving on.'"

Terry Farrell was given the name "Dr. Honey Bare."
ROBBIE ROBINSON

But if they saved an hour or two that day, they lost it over the long haul. While most *DS9* episodes shoot for seven days, and an occasional one shoots for eight, "Our Man Bashir" went a record-breaking nine days. "I think that show had the longest production schedule of any single episode," says Steve Oster. "There were a lot of sight gags: people smashing through glass, beds hidden in walls, all kinds of stunts."

Creating all those gags was a lot of fun. "We needed to be big with this show," says Director Winrich Kolbe. "And when I read the script for the first time, I felt we should really come in with a bang."

Hence the shot where Falcon, played in the opening scene by stunt person Mark Yerks, is sent flying through a glass window. Although "candy glass" is frequently used for such situations, the filmmakers were going for a realistic look in this scene, so tempered glass, which shatters differently but requires much greater care, was used. "There is some danger in doing a stunt like this, but it was timed so that the glass would be shattered by a rig right before he fell back into it," says Oster.

"We don't normally use tempered glass," admits Madalone, who supervised the activity. "But I knew I could make it safe. I knew we would have the guy in a leather jacket so we could have the collar up. And he was going to be put in a wig and go through the glass backward. The chances of him getting hurt were one in a million."

No one ever begrudges taking the time to make sure a stunt will be performed safely. But other time-consuming details were a bit maddening. "There were a *lot* of sets, and every time you go into a new set, everything has to be set up from square one," says Oster. "Any time we deviate from the norm, where we lose the familiarity of where we are, there are a lot of things that can happen. Like the morning we got to the set with Noah's lair, up in the Himalayan mountains. We checked the backdrop that was supposed to go outside the windows and we discovered that the mountains had no snow on them. So here we are, on top of the world, on top of Everest, if you will, and there's always snow on Everest." Oster had the show's scenic crew rush over and add snow to the mountains—which cost time and money, since the drop was a rental that would have to be restored to its original condition later on.

Set design, from Bashir's Hong Kong penthouse to Dr. Noah's aerie, may have been "a decorator's nightmare," as Garak puts it in the episode, but it looked impressive on the small screen. The Special Effects Department devised an elegant sideboard that rotated *and* flipped over to reveal a shiny aluminum control panel covered with working blinky lights for Noah's earthquake machine. "We put a mechanism under the floor to make it rotate," grins Herman Zimmerman. "And the device that flipped the top of the sideboard was like a bicycle-sprocketed chain drive, powered by electricity."

The tapestried wall that rises up behind the sideboard to reveal Noah's backlit map of the world was counterweighted and operated by several grips. Similarly, the turntable that held Bashir's rotating bed was also manually operated. "Everything that *could* be manually operated *was*," says Zimmerman, "because the brain is still smarter than most computers and you can still do some things faster by hand."

The '60s look (and sound) was lovingly duplicated by the Makeup Department (Michael Westmore's research gave him a leg up for the look he'd later create in "Trials and Tribble-ations"), music (Jay Chattaway's brass-heavy John Barry-ish score was nominated for an Emmy), hair (also nominated for an Emmy), and the Costume Department. Costume designer Bob Blackman enjoyed putting the characters into period garb, from Noah's Nehru suit to Anastasia's slinky nightgown. "You can't see any body

parts, but you can see the *hint* of a body part," he says. "You can see the side of a breast and the shape of a nipple—and that's how far we can go and still have it shown on Sundays at five P.M." Although Bashir's tux and suit could be "off the rack" ("He's got a narrow body so you don't have to worry about putting him in a suit with peg pants," says Blackman), Garak's gear had to be recut so that it would sit properly around the character's thick Cardassian neck. "His body is a 42, but with a 22-inch neck!"

While everyone has fond memories of the episode, none are quite as sentimental as Nana Visitor's. "'Our Man Bashir' was the first episode we did after Sid [Alexander Siddig] and I got together as a couple," she says with a smile. "It happened very fast for me." Ironically, although the two had been friends for years, Visitor had been unaware that Siddig's feelings for her ran far deeper. The irony of the situation doesn't escape her. "Just as Odo carried around his secret about Kira for all that time, Sid had those feelings for me and I never knew."

HOMEFRONT

Episode #483

WRITTEN BY IRA STEVEN BEHR & ROBERT HEWITT WOLFE

DIRECTED BY DAVID LIVINGSTON

GUEST CAST

Admiral Leyton	ROBERT FOXWORTH
Jaresh-Inyo	HERSCHEL SPARBER
Erika Benteen	SUSAN GIBNEY
Nog	ARON EISENBERG
Head Officer	DYLAN CHALFY

AND

Joseph Sisko	BROCK PETERS

STARDATE UNKNOWN

On DS9, an unexplained phenomenon that is causing the wormhole to open and close at random occupies most of the crew, with the exception of Odo, who has a bone to pick with Dax. It seems the Trill takes "perverse delight" in bringing chaos to Odo's regimented lifestyle by periodically moving his furniture. Such petty concerns are soon forgotten when Sisko receives news of an explosion at a Federation/Romulan diplomatic conference on Earth. Twenty-

Sisko attempts to convince Federation President Jaresh-Inyo of the changeling threat to Earth. ROBBIE ROBINSON

seven people were killed in the incident. Worse yet, all evidence points to the bomb having been set by a changeling, which means that Odo's people *have* reached Earth. The implications are frightening.

Sisko, along with Odo, is summoned to Earth. They confer with Admiral Leyton, head of Starfleet Operations and Sisko's former commander, about Dominion activities. Sisko is surprised when Leyton immediately puts him in charge of Starfleet Security on Earth.

Sisko makes time to visit his father Joseph, who runs a restaurant in New Orleans. Both Sisko and Jake, who has accompanied his father to Earth, are concerned about Joseph's health, but the old man refuses to admit to any problems. Jake has a pleasant reunion with his friend Nog, who later admits that he's having problems getting along with some of the upperclassmen at the Academy, particularly the ones in Red Squad.

The next day, Sisko and Leyton go to see Federation President Jaresh-Inyo. The President balks at their recommendations for extreme precautionary measures against the changelings, judging the tactics overly paranoid. But when Sisko's briefcase abruptly morphs into Odo, thus providing a graphic demonstration that Dominion infiltration could be widespread, the President agrees to allow Sisko to increase security on Earth and conduct blood-screening tests on Starfleet officers and high-ranking Federation officials.

Later, Odo encounters Leyton and his adjutant, Commander Benteen, on the grounds of Starfleet Headquarters. A curious comment by Leyton makes

Odo suspicious, and he forces the admiral to reveal himself as a changeling. The real Leyton is alarmed by the news, and Benteen suggests that perhaps the increased security measures they've instituted aren't strong enough. Leyton voices the opinion that it's unlikely they'll convince pacifist Jaresh-Inyo to do more. The conversation is interrupted by an urgent call from Jake, informing Sisko that Joseph's been arrested.

Arriving in New Orleans, Sisko learns that his father refused to submit to a blood screening, something now required of all family members of Starfleet personnel. Sisko tries to convince him to listen to reason, but Joseph angrily retreats to the kitchen, where he begins chopping vegetables. As the two continue to argue, Joseph inadvertantly cuts his finger, and Sisko can't help studying the blood on the knife. His father is furious, but his words make Sisko begin to doubt the paranoid rationale he has been operating under.

That night, Earth's entire power-relay system goes off-line. The only explanation is sabotage, and everything points to the Dominion as the culprit behind the dirty work that has left Earth defenseless. The unusual behavior of the wormhole now makes sense. Sisko speculates that it may have been caused by a cloaked Dominion fleet entering the Alpha Quadrant, and heading for Earth. Although he is deeply disturbed by the thought of filling the streets with armed troops, Sisko and Leyton convince Jaresh-Inyo to declare a state of emergency on Earth. In New Orleans, Jake and his grandfather observe the results with alarm, as groups of soldiers begin to beam down. It's clear to them that Earth is preparing for war.

One brick changes the shape of a building. Paramount's decision to do something in *DS9*'s fourth season—ultimately resulting in making the Klingons enemies of the Federation and bringing Worf on board the station— did more than bump "Homecoming" out of its slot as *DS9*'s third season cliff-hanger. It actually changed the scale of that episode, along with that of its second half, "Paradise Lost," which would have been the fourth-season opener.

"If it hadn't been for 'The Way of the Warrior,' we would have had the necessary money to spend on this two-parter," sighs Robert Hewitt Wolfe, who cowrote the teleplays for both parts with Ira Steven Behr.

Not that anyone regretted "The Way of the Warrior;" it was extremely popular with viewers. But

The inspiration for Leyton's character, interestingly, was the actor who played him. ROBBIE ROBINSON

it *did* shove the "shape-shifters on Earth" storyline out of the limelight, into something more akin to limbo. "It wasn't in sweeps," says Wolfe. "It came in the middle of nowhere."

There really wasn't any other choice. "We couldn't do it earlier," explains Ira Behr. "The studio doesn't like us to do two-parters up front." So the producers waited until they were a third of the way into the season before they relaunched the story, at which point they immediately ran into budgetary concerns.

"That's kind of the way the seasons work," admits Steve Oster. "You spend a lot of money up front on the big season openers and the big November sweeps episodes. Then you get to a point where you're looking at a deficit and the fact that you've got fourteen shows left. So this is where you start thinking, 'Do we really need X?'"

If the show came up a bit short in terms of budget, there was no shortage in terms of creative input. "We always try to make the two-parters as rich as possible, in terms of characters and storylines," says Behr.

And the storyline *was* rich, nothing less than "an attempt to make the audience complicit in believing that a threat is imminent, and that by any means nec-

essary, it must be dealt with," says René Echevarria. "We go out of Part I saying, 'There's going to be a big battle, and we're going to stop them. Martial law— yes! Clamp down on rights—yes! Blood tests—yes! No civil rights—yes!' And then in Part II we find out that the real point of the story is how dangerous this feeling is."

"The moral motto of the whole story is that paranoia is ultimately the end," adds Wolfe. "There are only four Founders on Earth, but whatever *they're* doing, *we're* doing more damage to ourselves than they are."

Although the paranoia theme was inherent to all versions of the plot, one of the earliest versions discussed during third season had an even more complex political plot, according to Ron Moore, who wrote the story for Part II. "The changelings come to Earth, infiltrate the populace, and cause near civil war within the Federation," he relates. "We were going to have Vulcan start to break away from the Federation as a result of what was going on on Earth, and a confrontation in Earth's orbit where a Federation starship is about to fire on a Vulcan transport."

But as the writers began breaking the story,

Moore notes, "We realized that the whole thing with the Vulcans wasn't quite selling it. So we started talking about a military coup of the Federation by Starfleet, à la *Seven Days in May*," he says, referring to the 1964 film about a military scheme to overthrow the U.S. government. "We thought that was actually more interesting, and more unexpected in the *Star Trek* universe—that Starfleet would take over the government out of fear and paranoia. What the fear of the other, of an enemy, could drive even Starfleet to do."

Drawing the audience into that paranoia was definitely part of the plan. Indeed, it was essential to selling the story. "We wanted to make people think we were doing a different story," says Wolfe. "The whole thing is a total misdirection. Part I is a total misdirection of Part II."

That kind of doublethink also is incorporated into some of the subplots. Case in point: Nog's attempt to get into Red Squad, which initially seems to be a B-story, and a familiar one at that. "That was another piece of misdirection," grins Wolfe. "We wanted people to think that this was just, 'Oh, yeah, Nog is encountering prejudice. We've seen that on television a million times. We know that story.' And then we turned it into something else."

Behr and Wolfe's enthusiasm for *their* story helps to explain the unusually high level of character description included in their teleplays, particularly the one for "Homefront." Television scriptwriters frequently provide useful background details in the nondialogue sections of their teleplays for the benefit of staff persons responsible for creating the look of the show and actors searching for the correct emotional tone. But "Homefront" provides two full paragraphs of backstory on Joseph Sisko when his character is introduced, including the fact that years earlier he'd "fought a debilitating battle against a severe illness, barely surviving . . . . Unfortunately, the years are starting to run out, a fact he's determined not to reveal to his son."

Similarly, we learn that Leyton "is a veteran of conflicts with the Romulans, Tholians, Cardassians, and Borg," and that President Jaresh-Inyo "is a Grazerite, a willowy, contemplative, humanoid alien . . . Grazerites are evolved from herbivorous herd animals and as such loathe violence and confrontation."

Unfortunately, sometimes even backstory doesn't help to sell a character. Jaresh-Inyo's look didn't go over particularly well with the staff or the audience. "I don't think the makeup or the characterization or

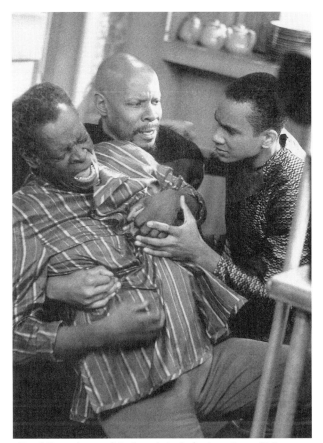

"Brock Peters is one of the legends in the business," says Livingston.
ROBBIE ROBINSON

my contribution to his performance worked very well," admits Director David Livingston. "He came off too soft to be the leader of the Federation."

"The casting decision didn't particularly work," notes Behr simply.

"I was a little disappointed," says Wolfe. "We wanted him to be somewhat antelopelike. We hoped that the idea that Jaresh-Inyo comes from a pacifistic, herbivorous-based culture, that he was the kind of guy who doesn't inherently fight, would make Leyton's point of view more understandable. Basically, [Jaresh-Inyo] is Jimmy Carter, a very good man." But a good man who doesn't do well in the public's eyes when it comes to dealing with hostiles.

Casting of the other guests was far more successful. Susan Gibney had made such an impression in her guest appearances on *TNG* that she was a leading candidate for the role of *Voyager*'s Kathryn Janeway, and Robert Foxworth had been spared from the rigors of "prosthetic acting" in "Hippocratic Oath" to allow him to take a leading role (sans latex) here. Ironically, "Robert *wanted* to be in makeup. He *loved* the idea!" says Foxworth's good friend Rene Auberjonois.

The episode also introduced Brock Peters, who'd played the traitorous Admiral Cartwright in *Star Trek VI: The Undiscovered Country,* as Ben Sisko's father, Joseph. Just the mention of Peters's name inspires a sigh of delight from Casting Director Ron Surma. "It was a *pleasure* to be able to use Brock Peters," he says emphatically. "I remember being very young and watching him in *To Kill a Mockingbird* and just being amazed at his performance. Which is not to say that we didn't look at a number of people, but when it came down to it . . . ." Surma makes a gesture with his hands that implies, "How could we find someone better than Brock Peters?"

"He clearly was the best person for the role," Robert Wolfe agrees wholeheartedly.

While "Homefront" is straightforward drama, the writers threw a bit of humor into the episode, with early scenes focusing on O'Brien and Bashir's holosuite exploits and Odo's reaction to one of Dax's pranks. "We knew the show wouldn't have a lot of laughs, so we needed the scenes," says Behr. O'Brien and Bashir's fur-collared bomber jackets and leather headgear did the trick here, and started a trend of increasingly outlandish costumes for *DS9*'s odd couple. "It was great fun for a while," says Alexander Siddig. "Although I think it must have been frustrating not to be able to actually see them do their stuff in the holosuite, flying the planes and fighting [with] the Irish warriors and all that."

Colm Meaney is just as happy that budgetary constraints eventually limited the number of holosuite costumes the pair were thrust into. "It's very hot!" he says. "Sometimes, the way they write these things, it seems like they think we're ten years old, playing 'Biggles flies to war!'" But just like Biggles, he's learned to take it with a stiff upper lip. "These things come out of the blue," he says with a shrug, "and you just try to make the best of them."

The scene with Odo and Dax actually has more serious underpinnings. Although it can be taken lightly, the writers meant it to convey something significant about *DS9*'s resident changeling. "Odo's an obsessive-compulsive control freak, which is what the Founders are," says Wolfe.

"The scene sets up the rigidity of the Founders," confirms Behr. "Even Odo. Definitely Odo. He's one of them. They are so anal retentive, so paranoid, so set in their ways. Ultimately, that will be their downfall."

PARADISE LOST
Episode #484
TELEPLAY BY IRA STEVEN BEHR & ROBERT HEWITT WOLFE
STORY BY RONALD D. MOORE
DIRECTED BY REZA BADIYI

GUEST CAST

Admiral Leyton	ROBERT FOXWORTH
Jaresh-Inyo	HERSCHEL SPARBER
Erika Benteen	SUSAN GIBNEY
Nog	ARON EISENBERG
Riley Shepard	DAVID DREW GALLAGHER
Security Officer	MINA BADIE
Academy Commandant	RUDOLPH WILLRICH
Security Chief	BOBBY C. KING

AND

Joseph Sisko	BROCK PETERS

STARDATE UNKNOWN

With Dominion sabotage blamed for a planetwide power outage, Starfleet stations troops all over Earth to prepare for an invasion. But the more Sisko and Odo read Starfleet's reports on the sabotage, the more questions they have. Sisko can't see how the Dominion could have gotten the necessary computer codes to initiate the outage. And Odo finds a curious report indicating that while most units were being mobilized after the outage, one unit, the Academy's Red Squad, was actually *demobilized*.

Sisko contacts the commandant of Starfleet Academy to point out the discrepancy. The commandant misunderstands Sisko's intent and confesses that the report should have been erased; he's grateful that Sisko caught the embarrassing mistake before it fell into the wrong hands. The commandant also implicates Admiral Leyton in Red Squad's covert activities.

Knowing of Nog's interest in Red Squad, Sisko forces him to reveal the name of one of its members. Then Sisko tricks the Red Squad cadet into revealing what happened the night of the outage. As he had feared, the squad was responsible for shutting down Earth's power relays; they were even provided with the appropriate access codes by their superiors. Reluctantly, Sisko goes to Federation President Jaresh-Inyo and reveals that Admiral Leyton is leading a group of Starfleet officers in a plan to overthrow the Federation government and replace it with military rule. Jaresh-Inyo finds it hard to believe that Starfleet officers would commit sabotage. However, if

Sisko is arrested after Leyton and Benteen "prove" that he's a changeling. B.J. COHEN

Sisko can bring him hard proof linking Leyton to the sabotage, the president will force the admiral to withdraw his troops and resign.

Before Sisko can begin gathering his evidence, Leyton confronts him and tries to convince his former executive officer that martial law is the only way to deal with the Dominion threat. But Sisko refuses to participate in what he considers treasonous behavior, so Leyton relieves him of his post in Starfleet Security and tells him to go back to DS9.

As Sisko tries to decide what to do, he is approached by a changeling in the guise of O'Brien. The shape-shifter reveals that he is one of just four changelings presently on Earth. It's only taken those four, the false O'Brien explains, to create havoc on the planet. The fear and paranoia the changelings inspire ultimately will destroy the solids, he arrogantly asserts.

Sisko contacts Major Kira at DS9 and sets a plan in motion. He then returns to his former office at Starfleet Headquarters, where Odo has downloaded some pertinent classified files. They surmise that Leyton's coup is scheduled to take place the day before the president's upcoming speech. But when Sisko goes to Jaresh-Inyo's office with the information, he finds Leyton, Benteen, and four security guards waiting for him. Forcing Sisko to submit to a blood test, they "reveal" to the President that Sisko himself is a changeling.

A short time later Leyton visits Sisko in his holding cell and admits that he faked the blood test. He assures Sisko that he'll be freed—*after* the coup. After he leaves, Odo helps Sisko escape and confirms that

the *Defiant* is on its way with the proof Sisko needs. Sending Odo to inform the president, Sisko goes to Leyton's office with a phaser and a demand for his resignation. Lieutenant Arriaga, who made it look as if a cloaked Dominion fleet were coming through the wormhole, will arrive on the *Defiant* and admit to acting on Leyton's orders. But Leyton says the *Defiant* will never arrive. He's sent Benteen out on the *Lakota* to intercept what the *Lakota*'s crew believes is a ship full of changelings.

The *Lakota* attacks the *Defiant*, which is forced to defend itself. When Benteen, in command of the *Lakota*, reports that she can't stop the *Defiant*, Leyton orders her to destroy it. But Benteen can't bring herself to kill her fellow Starfleet officers and powers down her weapons, allowing the *Defiant* to proceed to Earth. Faced with the knowledge that his most loyal officer has rejected him, Leyton realizes he has lost, and removes his admiral's pips. With the status quo restored on Earth, Sisko prepares to return to DS9, grimly determined not to let fear conquer the Federation.

Some people remember the Alamo. Some remember the *Maine*. But the note scribbled on the wall reads: "Remember Paradise Lost."

Why?

"That was in my office before I moved to the third floor," says Ira Behr. "And it was to remind me how we'd screwed up." In Behr's opinion, the episode was cursed with the same devil that plagued "Homefront": the budget. "We hurt the show," he

The Tillman Water Reclamation facility is the location used for Starfleet Headquarters. ROBBIE ROBINSON

says. "We cut down on opticals in the final space battle, which was a mistake. And we cut down on extras, in terms of showing the occupying Starfleet force [on the streets of Earth]. To this day, I can't tell you how aggravated it makes me. It just drives me crazy."

Money is always a problem in producing a weekly series. There are people on staff at every television show whose job it is to watch the bottom line and help the show reach the end of the season without dipping into the red ink. This doesn't mean that writers can't argue against the financial decree, and sometimes the battle is won. But writers have to pick their battles, and Behr wishes he'd fought this one a little harder. "It was a case where I could have either stared the beast down or blinked," he says. "I blinked, and it hurt the show. I should have said, 'We're gonna do it and save money some other time.'"

The crew did their part to stretch the budget, with Glenn Neufeld reusing and recompositing a three-second shot of the *Defiant* from "The Way of the Warrior" for part of the sequence where it fights the *Lakota*. But the rest of the battle was all original footage shot with the *Defiant* model and the studio's eight-foot *Excelsior* model, back from a stint in *Star Trek Generations* as the *Enterprise*-B. The *Excelsior* was, in fact, still decked out as that ship, courtesy of ILM, which had done the effects for *Generations*. "We had to take off all the detailing, the numbers and names, and make new ones," says Neufeld. "[Scenic

Art Supervisor] Mike Okuda was instrumental in cutting us new decals and actually showing us how to get the old ones off without destroying the paint job. We did a lot of hand rubbing with water."

The Art Department helped to make sure that every dollar that went into the episode was on the screen. Herman Zimmerman gave Joseph Sisko a restaurant that twenty-fourth-century New Orleans would be proud of. "We were going on Nick Meyer's [director of *The Wrath of Khan* and *The Undiscovered Country*] assumption that in the future, there are a lot of things that won't change," says Zimmerman. "So this restaurant is typical French Quarter New Orleans, to pay homage to the idea that people of the twenty-fourth century will still want the romance of that era. We had an ersatz lincrusted ceiling—made of fiberglass, rather than actual embossed tin—which was very popular in the late nineteenth century."

Zimmerman's able staff provided a lot of material for the two-parter, particularly for the exterior shots of Starfleet Headquarters. They helped design the Starfleet Command building model, inspired, in part, by the General Motors pavilion in the 1964 World's Fair. Although it's nearly impossible to see them on a television screen, the front of the building is detailed with statues of famous starships. (Galoob *Star Trek* toys were used for this aspect of the composition.) Visual Effects Supervisor Gary Hutzel oversaw the creation of a matte painting combining that model and several other miniatures, along with a shot of the Golden Gate Bridge taken by Dan Curry.

Starfleet Command, like Starfleet Academy, is located in San Francisco; however, the parklike grounds and one of the foreground buildings are located in Van Nuys, California, at the Tillman Water Reclamation plant, which was also used for the *TNG* episode "The First Duty." The tram in the foreground, the Art Department's tribute to the tram in Gene Roddenberry's unsuccessful pilot *Earth II,* was based, says Okuda, on "a couple of CD holders and a hummingbird feeder bought at a gardening shop." (The same feeders were used in some of the Borg sequences in *First Contact*, which went into production shortly after this episode was shot.) The tunnel that the tram moves through wasn't actually a tunnel, according to Judy Elkins. "It was just a bunch of metal arches," she says. Computer Animator Adam Howard was the man who sold that particular effect by painting reflections and highlights that made the area between the arches look like Plexiglas. "He even animated a blinking light to the 'tube,' to make it look

The model of Starfleet will be composited into a shot of the Tillman plant. GENE TRINDL

as if a yellow light went on and off when the tram came through," says Elkins.

Although monetary resources may have been limited, the intellectual resources of the writers were not. They made carefully considered decisions in scripting. For example, the scene where a changeling comes forward to Sisko and reveals that there are only four of them on Earth, not hundreds or thousands as Leyton would have everyone believe, was written with Colm Meaney in mind, rather than an additional guest star or a visual effect.

"Colm's just a terrific actor," enthuses Behr. "We love using him, and I have to say that because of the budget restraints, we had a lot riding on that scene, and I think it worked pretty well. It was my favorite scene to write in the show. The paranoia of the entire two-parter was to be summed up at that point, which is a heavy weight to put on any scene, especially when the character is not a monster, not an evil person coming out of the shadows. It's someone you recognize, and we were hoping that would add to the eeriness of it. Your friend is your enemy."

Another clever bit of writing that saved some money was Odo's rescue of Sisko, which has the changeling use what looks suspiciously like a Vulcan nerve pinch to knock out a security officer. "We needed a way to disable the guard and we ran out of money for the morphs, frankly," says Wolfe, laughing.

Where did Odo learn a Vulcan nerve pinch?

"I don't know," says Rene Auberjonois thoughtfully. "I have no idea. But, obviously, Odo is a man of many talents."

The script also produced a gem of a line for Sisko: "Paradise has never seemed so well armed." It's a variation on one of Behr's favorite contributions to the script for "The Maquis," "It's easy to be a saint in paradise."

"Ira likes to show that paradise isn't easy," says Wolfe. While *Star Trek* creator Gene Roddenberry was fond of describing the world of the future as paradise, the *DS9* writers are more interested in showing just how hard it is to *maintain* that paradise. "You don't just *get* paradise," Wolfe explains. "You need to work your ass off to have it."

CROSSFIRE

Episode #485

WRITTEN BY RENÉ ECHEVARRIA
DIRECTED BY LES LANDAU

GUEST CAST

Shakaar	DUNCAN REGEHR
Sarish	BRUCE WRIGHT
Jimenez	CHARLES TENTINDO

STARDATE UNKNOWN

For Security Chief Odo, only one thing is more important than his deeply ingrained need for "order": his relationship with Major Kira. He particularly enjoys the time they spend together each week going over station business, and he goes out of his way to make her feel at home in his office during those meetings. But when First Minister Shakaar arrives at the station to negotiate for Bajor's early admittance into the Federation, Odo finds himself losing control over the most important aspects of his life.

Shakaar's visit begins peacefully enough, but Odo soon receives word that The True Way, a Cardassian extremist group, is planning to assassinate the First Minister. Shakaar, Kira's former leader in Bajor's resistance movement during the Cardassian Occupation, refuses to cancel the conference and capitulate to terrorists. Odo beefs up security and becomes Shakaar's personal shadow, which puts him in a somewhat awkward position when the First Minister begins spending a lot of time with Kira.

Odo realizes that he's the odd man out when Shakaar and Kira begin a romantic relationship. DANNY FELD

Things get worse when Shakaar confides in Odo that he has strong feelings for Kira, and wonders if she might feel similarly. The confession disturbs Odo, and when Kira shows up late for their weekly meeting, he can see that she is distracted. The attraction between Kira and Shakaar is clearly growing stronger, and Odo's thoughts about the couple soon begin to distract *him* from his responsibilities. Escorting them onto a turbolift, he receives a communication from Worf stating that the lift must be rerouted. Following established procedure, Odo requests Worf's security code prior to releasing the controls on the lift. But the changeling is so wrapped up in the conversation between Kira and Shakaar that he neglects to wait for Worf's response, and the turbolift abruptly goes into free fall.

With their communications cut off, only Odo's morphing abilities save them from the assassination attempt. But nothing can save Odo from the embarrassment of admitting to Sisko that his distraction almost allowed The True Way to succeed. Realizing that he must resolve the situation, Odo goes to Kira's quarters, only to be informed by the guards that Shakaar has been inside with her since they returned from dinner three hours earlier. Odo relieves the guard outside Kira's door and takes his place. Shakaar doesn't leave until morning, and when Kira sees Odo, she is overjoyed to tell him about her new relationship with Shakaar.

Devastated, Odo goes to his office, only to find that Worf has apprehended the would-be assassin. In an uncharacteristic fit of rage, the shape-shifter tears apart his quarters, destroying everything, including a plant that had been a gift from Kira. Quark, who lives directly below the constable, shows up to complain about the noise, and finds Odo sitting in the wreckage. Quark gives him some sage advice: tell Kira how he feels or forget her and get on with his life. Odo goes to Kira and tells her he's canceling their weekly meetings because of scheduling conflicts. Surprised, Kira can see there's more to Odo's decision, but she decides not to push him.

"**P**oor Odo," says Rene Auberjonois, laughing. "The most miserable things happen to him. I was at a convention recently and a woman came forward to ask a question. She asked, 'Why do they always do this to Odo? Why can't they give him a break?!' The audience was just screaming and applauding, because they knew exactly what she meant, and so did I."

Auberjonois didn't need to look any further than

Rene Auberjonois improvised the destruction of Kira's gift plant to symbolize Odo's estrangement from her. ROBBIE ROBINSON

his own past for Odo's pained reaction when Kira hugs him after spending the night with Shakaar. "It's mostly an adolescent thing," he says. "If an actor really analyzes, beat by beat, moment by moment, where he draws his emotional recall from, it is always from childhood and adolescent experiences. That's where we really come face-to-face with the majority of our emotional situations. There certainly are other things that happen as we get older, but Odo's such an unfinished character that I find myself drawing from my youth."

It really wasn't René Echevarria's sole intention to torture *DS9*'s resident shape-shifter when he began working on "Crossfire." "Robert Wolfe just threw out the idea of doing *The Bodyguard,* with Odo protecting Kira and falling in love," he recalls. "That's how it got started." As the episode began to evolve, Echevarria's draft took what he describes as a wrong turn. "I'd structured the story so that everything builds to this 'big moment' where there's an explosion and a fireball is coming [at Shakaar and Kira]," the writer explains. "Odo has to decide which one to protect. Does he do

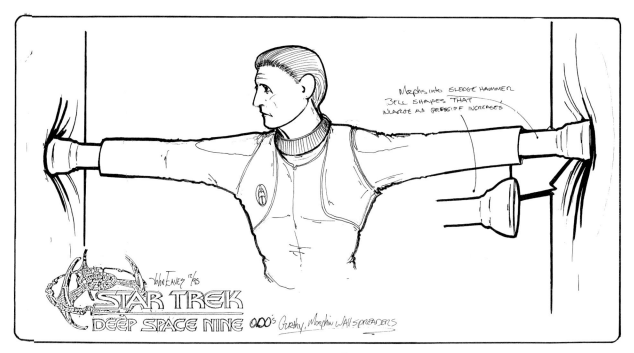

Reference drawing for the visual effects team. JOHN EAVES

his job, or protect his love? I had him morph and envelop Shakaar, and the blast almost kills Kira. But the overriding message was that Odo [made his choice] out of spite and it just didn't work. So we massively overhauled the story and made it a much more gentle show."

By the time the decision was made to overhaul, there were only six days left prior to the start of principal photography. That's cutting it *very* thin, because a massive amount of preproduction work is accomplished during that period, and it's difficult to finalize details when the script isn't complete. But rather than feeling like "poor, poor René" under the gun, Echevarria threw himself into his work with a sense of gusto. "The fact that you can leave a story session with so much work ahead of you and instead of being depressed that nobody liked your first draft, you're excited because it's going to be better, is a tribute to Ira Behr and the passion we all feel for the show. I knew this was a better story and I dove into it with that passion. That's the way it is around here."

As Echevarria worked on the rewrite, he inserted an amusing conversation between Odo and Worf about order and friendship into the script for utilitarian purposes, but it helped set the stage for later developments. "The script was a little short," says Echevarria, "so I came up with that little riff between

the two of them. It just hit me that they are alike in certain ways. And also, we were trying to set up that Worf was going to move to the *Defiant* ("Bar Association"), and I wanted to nudge him in that direction."

One major change, of course, was finding something equally exciting to replace the fireball sequence. The writers came up with a falling turbolift. "The piston in the elevator trick!" laughs Gary Hutzel. "Now that was a firecracker!" Although Hutzel enjoyed working on the scene, he's not sure that it was true to Odo's character. "I've always been of the mind that Odo is not Superman, or a member of the Fantastic Four," he says. He's not a superhero; he's an alien with some unusual abilities that the producers have taken care not to overexploit. And Hutzel, too, is protective of Odo. "Once you establish that Odo can change himself into anything, then why should he ever be afraid of anything? I've always fought against that type of stuff."

The writers initially wanted Odo to become "some type of a hook that would latch onto the side of the shaft," says Hutzel. "Then somebody suggested that he should push out on the sides of the elevator to stop it and I glommed onto that. Of course, if he just stands there in his own form and pushes it out, then it's Superman all over again. I wanted him to become some sort of a device, but the director was

A piece of improvisation from Auberjonois dismayed the producers.
ROBBIE ROBINSON

very adamant about seeing Odo's face in the sequence, so we ended up with this hybrid."

Duncan Regehr's second appearance as Shakaar was a bit of a disappointment to Behr, although it had nothing to do with the actor's performance. "I think we mishandled his character in the episode, and he never recovered after that," Behr says regretfully. "The first time we saw him he was Clint Eastwood, the foreigner, the man of few words, the terrorist. He became way too sensitive here. It just wasn't [the same] Shakaar." It was inevitable that the writers would begin thinking of ways to split up Shakaar and Kira, giving Odo new hope for his unrequited love.

Odo's unspoken feelings for Kira are, strangely enough, counterpointed in a scene that displays another kind of unspoken love: that between Odo and Quark. "The rule of that relationship is that neither of them can admit to the other the type of love

that they have," says Echevarria. "So when Quark comes to Odo to give him the best advice he can, Odo asks why he's there and Quark gives him a cockamamie reason."

Armin Shimerman had mixed feelings about the scene. "It's really serious, really touching," he says. "It's a scene about one person trying to help another person out of simple affection." But Shimmerman was annoyed by the wardrobe choice made for his character.

"Pajamas are kind of like Doctor Dentons," admits Robert Blackman, "those one-piece footed pajamas that kids wear. That was my image. The cut is kind of a sack with legs and arms on it." Despite the fact that Quark has demonstrated a distinct predilection for being smartly dressed during daytime hours, "we all have our weird comfort clothes," says Blackman. Although shaped like a sack, the material Blackman used was very "smart." "The pajamas were made of an antique brocade," he notes, although he deliberately used the wrong side of the material to create a certain look. "They were expensive. If I'd really wanted to take it one step farther, they would have been flannel, but I didn't go that far."

One detail in the sequence surprised everyone who viewed the finished episode. As Quark comes in to talk to Odo, he (and the audience) can't help but observe that a bit of Odo's normally well-kept "hair" has fallen out of place. Although it's a minor detail, it's an important one. Since the shape-shifter doesn't really have hair, it's rather startling to see it behave like . . . well, hair. It serves as a fascinating visual metaphor: Odo literally can't keep himself together. However, such a style choice is generally approved from the top down, and in this case, it wasn't. "Decisions like that go through a chain of command," explains Michael Westmore. But Westmore knows it didn't come from the makeup staff who normally tend to Odo's upkeep.

Nor did it come from the producers. "We were amazed by it," says Behr. "When we saw that scene in dailies, I couldn't look at anything else except that friggin' hair." So who's the culprit? "I did it," admits Auberjonois. "I just pulled some strands, because I was trying to evoke an image from a Japanese print I'd seen of a warrior in defeat." He smiles calmly, as if unaware of the ripples his artistic decision made in the production pond.

RETURN TO GRACE

Episode #486

TELEPLAY BY **HANS BEIMLER**
STORY BY **TOM BENKO**
DIRECTED BY **JONATHAN WEST**

GUEST CAST

Dukat	MARC ALAIMO
Ziyal	CYIA BATTEN
Damar	CASEY BIGGS
K'Temang	JOHN K. SHULL

STARDATE UNKNOWN

At First Minister Shakaar's request, Kira prepares to travel to the Cardassian outpost of Korma to share Bajoran intelligence about the Klingon Empire. She is surprised to discover that the captain of her Cardassian escort ship, a battered old freighter called the *Groumall*, is Gul Dukat, whose circumstances have changed radically since the last time she saw him. His decision to bring his daughter by a Bajoran mistress back to Cardassia has cost him both his high-ranking position and his Cardassian family. Now, Dukat and daughter Tora Ziyal live together as exiles, with the freighter their only home. But Dukat keeps his spirits up by running the ship in a military manner and plotting his return to grace.

At Korma, Kira and Dukat find the outpost destroyed and all of the Cardassian and Bajoran diplomats dead. When a Klingon ship decloaks near-by, they realize that it's responsible for the carnage. Despite the fact that the *Groumall* is nowhere near a match for a bird-of-prey, Dukat fires on the Klingon ship. Completely unscathed, the bird-of-prey ignores the freighter and leaves the area.

Angry and humiliated, Dukat is quick to take Kira's advice that they salvage a disruptor from the outpost, install it on the *Groumall* and pursue the Klingon ship. While the freighter's weapons are being upgraded, Kira gives Ziyal some basic military training and forges a friendship with the girl. Later, Kira and Dukat deduce that the bird-of-prey's next target will be Loval, a Cardassian weapons research installation. As the ship nears the planet, they strategize a plan to draw the Klingon vessel into firing range. The plan works and they fire a disruptor blast, crippling, but not destroying, the bird-of-prey. Kira and Dukat beam over to the Klingon ship, commandeer it, and transport its crew onto the *Groumall*, while beaming the Cardassian crew to the Klingon ship. In a final touch of vengeance, Dukat fires upon his former vessel, killing the Klingons aboard.

Knowing that his achievement will clear his name, Dukat contacts Cardassia's government to report the capture of the Klingon ship and the valuable information its computer holds. Kira assures Dukat that the information could help Cardassia to launch a major counterattack against the Klingons. But a disillusioned Dukat reports that Cardassia's Detapa Council prefers to look for a "diplomatic solution" with the Klingons. Although the government is prepared to restore Dukat to his previous post as military advisor, Dukat wants no part of it. After all, what's the point of being a military advisor to a government that won't fight?

Taking his lead from the Bajoran resistance, which beat the odds against them to defeat their Cardassian oppressors, Dukat decides that he will fight the Klingons on his own. He asks Kira to join him aboard the bird-of-prey and return to the life she knows best. Kira is tempted, but she knows that that life is behind her. What's more, she knows that it is not a life for a young girl like Ziyal. She talks Dukat into allowing his daughter to return with her to the space station until Dukat's private war is concluded.

Kira and Dukat find themselves fighting on the same side against a common enemy. ROBBIE ROBINSON

D*S9 Editor Tom Benko's succinct story pitch, the Jews and the Nazis forced to work together after the war, triggered "Return to Grace." This was a sequel, of sorts, to "Indiscretion" that provided new insight into Gul

Even when the character seemed to be redeeming himself, the writers always believed that Dukat was at his core an evil being.
ROBBIE ROBINSON

Dukat's personality, but drew the line at making him seem lovable.

"There are so many facets to Dukat," says Hans Beimler, who wrote the teleplay. "He's a very complicated character. But he's always been a Nazi, *always*. In this episode, you're aware of different shades to his personality. But, if you think about it, they're all very self-serving. This is not a pleasant man. He's done a lot of terrible things."

It's no surprise, then, that while Kira can put aside the past long enough to fight alongside Dukat, as she did in "Indiscretion," she never will submit to being the object of his affection. No matter what kind of veneer he takes on, notes Ira Behr, "Dukat is not a nice man. He is not a sensitive man. He likes to *act* like a sensitive man, but he's a man of appetites to whom public image is very important, much more important than the truth. He wants to be liked *by* Kira as much as he likes Kira. I find him reprehensible myself," summarizes Behr.

Behr also finds him a compelling character to build episodes around, one whose motivations occasionally mirror those of historic figures. In this case,

Behr likens him to the legendary Sioux leader Sitting Bull. "In one of the treaty negotiations," explains Behr, "Sitting Bull stood up and refused to sign. He was told, 'All of the other Indians have signed,' and he said, 'What other Indians? There are no Indians left but me.'" In "Return to Grace," Dukat reaches the same conclusion. "He literally says, 'What Cardassians? I am the only Cardassian left,'" Behr says, adding that the episode left Dukat in a place where he could have chosen to truly grow as a man or to take the easy way out and go back to what he knows. And, as viewers who followed his storyline into the next season are aware, he would wind up choosing the latter.

Although essentially a two-person show, the episode brought back Cyia Batten for her second and final appearance as Ziyal and introduced Casey Biggs in a small role as Dukat's first officer, Glinn Damar, a character whose importance would increase dramatically over the course of the next three years. "When I went in to read for the role, I thought to myself, 'What's the big deal? They could have gotten one of the extras to play this part.'" Biggs recalls. "But I guess

Casey Biggs's inauspicious debut as Glinn Damar belies his larger role in future story lines. ROBBIE ROBINSON

the writers had this whole arc planned in their heads, because the first day of the shoot, Jonathan West came up to me and said, 'I don't want you to get nervous or anything, but they have big plans for this character.' I said, 'Why did you have to tell me this

right *now*—just before my first shot, my first day in all this makeup!'"

"Casey was a really good actor and I was happy that he took the part," comments Jonathan West, who relinquished his usual position as director of photography in order to take another turn as director. "He knew that it was not a big role, but I let him know that he wasn't just a background person. I gave him close-ups and took the time to get reactions from him, almost as if, from the audience's point of view, he was registering the value judgments on what was going on."

The episode had no real B-story, although there initially was a short scene where Quark attempts to engage Kira's services as a collection agent (she declines), which was shot and later cut from the episode for time. And the ending would have been quite different if it hadn't been for the concerns of West and Assistant Director B.C. Cameron. The story focused, in part, on Kira's attempts to teach Dukat that he couldn't always go head to head with his enemies, and that sometimes it's better to use guerrilla tactics and do the unexpected. Thus, it struck West and Cameron as odd that the denouement of the

Her expression says it all. Visitor felt that her character would never become involved with Dukat. ROBBIE ROBINSON

script had Dukat and Kira beaming onto the bridge of the bird-of-prey and overpowering its bridge crew in hand-to-hand combat, while Ziyal and Damar accomplish much the same in a different part of the Klingon ship.

"There were sixty people on the bird-of-prey," says West. "And in the script, these four people beat them up and kill a lot of them." From a practical perspective, West wondered how he would shoot all the bodies littering the deck. From a creative perspective, he wondered how he would convince the audience that a handful of people could take over a bird-of-prey with a large crew.

West credits Cameron with the solution. "She said, 'What if they get onto the ship, but instead of overcoming them, they beam the Klingons back to the freighter?'"

Wondering if they could support such a premise, West and Cameron looked through the script and found an early scene that mentioned Kira's knowledge of Klingon technology. Suddenly, everything began to fall into place. There was only one snag. How would one approach the writers?

"We were four days into prep when we came up with the new concept," recalls West. "I was scared to death because B.C. and I aren't writers; we're hired to do what we do. So after our production meeting, I went up to Ira and Hans and started beating around the bush until Ira finally said, 'Just say it already!'"

West said it and the writers listened thoughtfully, then promised to think it over. "They were reluctant to completely let go of the hand-to-hand combat," recounts Cameron, "because they liked the excitement it gave the show." Eventually Behr and Beimler decided that Kira and Dukat would fight a *few* Klingons when they arrived at the bird-of-prey, and the new ending was adopted.

"They were more than gracious; they were wonderful about it," says West of the writers. "They said it was a good idea and they thanked us. Bringing up that change was the hardest thing in the world for me to do, but it solved everything."

SONS OF MOGH

Episode #487

WRITTEN BY RONALD D. MOORE
DIRECTED BY DAVID LIVINGSTON

GUEST CAST

Kurn	TONY TODD
Noggra	ROBERT DoQUI
Tilikia	DELL YOUNT
Klingon Officer	ELLIOT WOODS

STARDATE 49556.2

Worf is stunned when his brother Kurn arrives at the station and asks him to perform the ritual of *Mauk-to'Vor*, restoring his honor by killing him. Kurn is a ruined man; Worf's stand against Gowron in the Klingon leader's war against Cardassia has brought disgrace on the House of Mogh. Gowron has stripped the family of its seat on the High Council and its most valuable possessions. Kurn informs Worf that providing him with an honorable death is the least that he can do. Forced to agree, Worf goes through the ritual, plunging a knife into Kurn's chest just as Dax and Odo arrive at his quarters.

Dax quickly has Kurn transported to the Infirmary, where his life is saved by Dr. Bashir. In the meantime, Worf is put through the wringer by Sisko, who will not abide Klingon murder rituals on his station. Worf must find another way to resolve Kurn's difficulties.

While Worf tends to his brother, Sisko turns to another troubling problem. Just what are the Klingons doing in a region near Bajoran space, under the guise of "military exercises"? With no immediate answers, he orders Kira and O'Brien to take the *Defiant* to the area and run a sensor sweep. During the sweep, there is a huge explosion and a cloaked Klingon ship is badly damaged. Following Kira's offer of help, the Klingons reluctantly ask *Defiant* to tow their vessel to DS9 for assistance.

On the station, Worf tries to help Kurn find a new life and a new purpose. He convinces Odo to take him on as a deputy in the station's Bajoran security force. Kurn initially does well in the job, but during a confrontation with a smuggler, he allows himself to be shot. While Bashir patches up Kurn once again, Odo informs Worf that he cannot employ a man with a death wish. A despondent Kurn tells Worf that his life is in his older brother's hands.

An examination of the damage suffered by the

Worf has effectively destroyed his brother's life—and now Kurn wants him to end it. ROBBIE ROBINSON

This was to be no simple homicide. Moore was thinking fratricide, committed by one of *Star Trek*'s favorite characters, the eternally conflicted Worf. For a series that often is considered too deep and intellectual for the general viewing public, *Deep Space Nine* has offered its share of violent episodes. Three of them aired during the fourth season: "The Way of the Warrior" and "To the Death," both of which have ferocious battle sequences, and "Sons of Mogh," which features one of the most graphic displays of violence by a lead character.

Concern over the impact of that act did, in fact, lead Moore to discuss it with Rick Berman, who could have vetoed the scene. But the fact that Kurn's life ultimately is saved and the manner in which Director David Livingston shot the action convinced everyone that it was the right choice. "You don't actually see anything," says Livingston. "You don't see blood spurting or the insertion of the knife into the body or anything like that. But the camera angles were forced and very strong, making it seem as if

Klingon ship suggests that the vessel was laying a minefield of cloaked explosives, presumably to cut off DS9 and the Bajoran system from the rest of the Federation. Sisko needs the coordinates of the mines, and Worf and Kurn are the only ones who can get them. Bashir disguises their appearance and gives them temporarily altered DNA codes so they can pass a cursory scan.

Once on the disabled Klingon vessel, they quickly find what they need, but they are discovered by a Klingon officer. When the officer threatens to kill Worf, Kurn kills him first, allowing the brothers to succeed at their mission, but pushing Kurn deeper into depression. He has murdered a soldier of the Klingon Empire who simply was doing his duty; Kurn's dishonor is complete.

Faced with the prospect of his brother committing suicide and *not* entering *Sto-Vo-Kor* with the honored dead, Worf chooses an alternative that will keep Kurn alive. He asks Bashir to wipe his brother's memory, and an old friend of their father's will provide Kurn with a home and a new identity. Worf witnesses Kurn's rebirth as Rodek, son of Noggra, bitterly aware that he has saved his brother, yet has lost him forever.

The police blotter on Ronald D. Moore gets thicker all the time.

"Ron came to me and said, 'You know, we must stab him. We have to kill him,'" confesses executive producer Ira Behr. "And I said, 'You're right.'"

"I don't recall how graphically the scene was written, but we told the director, 'Don't hide the magic,'" states Behr. ROBBIE ROBINSON

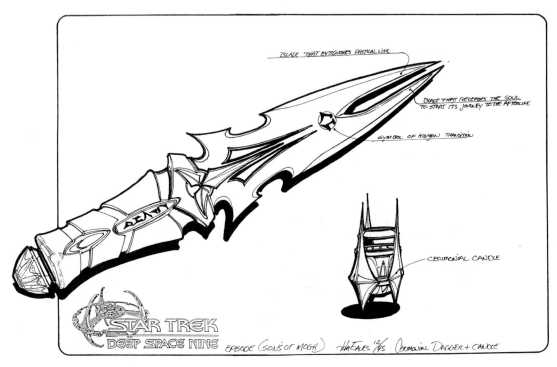

The Klingon ceremonial dagger and a candle that was not created. JOHN EAVES

something terrible was happening. We played the actual impact on Kurn's face."

Interestingly, Worf's attempt to kill Kurn didn't seem to bother most viewers. It made sense, just as it made sense to Moore when he sat down to write the story covered in the beat sheet. "I started looking at it and after a while I realized that the original structure wasn't working," says Moore. "Kurn comes to the station and wants Worf to kill him, but Worf won't do it. Worf struggles through the whole episode to find a job for Kurn but keeps failing and failing. It was just kind of flat. You knew Worf wasn't going to kill his brother and the rest was all very by-the-numbers stuff. That's when I went to Ira and we began talking about, 'What if he really *did* try to kill his brother?' That's *really* what this character would do, if we're being honest with ourselves. He's a Klingon. His brother makes his case and has a good point. Okay. Take out the knife and stick it in this guy's chest and the audience will sit up and go '*Whooaa!*'"

What *did* bother viewers was Worf's final solution to Kurn's dilemma. "A lot of people objected to Worf robbing his brother's memories, kind of killing him on a certain level, yet not," recalls René Echevarria. "The fan reaction was pretty strong. They really seemed to hate that." But while Moore admits that the merits of

wiping Kurn's memory may be debatable, he feels they're justified. "Worf tried to kill him and it didn't work," he says. "Then, through the course of the show, Worf realizes that he's more human than he's really wanted to admit to himself. [Given a second chance] he wouldn't be able to kill him again. So in that sense, what course is open to his brother? Commit suicide and not get into *Sto-Vo-Kor*? It's Worf's responsibility to take the decision off his brother's shoulders, and to give his brother a new start."

If Worf was the mastermind behind Kurn's fate, it was Dr. Bashir, alleged firm believer in the Hippocratic oath, who performed the dirty deed, just as he had consented to turning poor Bareil into a talking vegetable during *DS9*'s third season. It was around this time that the writing staff began affectionately referring to the Infirmary as "Dr. Bashir's House of Horrors," Moore chuckles. "It's like, '*Bring me a body!*'" cries Moore, imitating Bashir-as-Frankenstein. "*I will kill Bareil for you! And I will wipe Kurn's memory!*"

"I'd be very, very cautious before I sent someone into Dr. Bashir's Infirmary," quips Behr. "Unless I wanted a guy dead."

"People asked, 'Why would Bashir do this?'" says Moore. "But it's not too hard to envision Worf going to Bashir, explaining the situation, and Bashir saying,

The chemistry between the actors encouraged the writers to expand their characters' relationship. ROBBIE ROBINSON

Designed to fit the length of Dorn's forearm—the new weapon—a *mek'leth*. ROBBIE ROBINSON

'Okay, it's your belief system.' I just wasn't interested in writing that scene."

On the more upbeat side, the episode, originally called "Brother's Keeper," marked the earliest suggestion of an attraction between Dax and Worf. "We started talking about putting Dax and Worf together as soon as Worf was brought into the show," notes Behr. "But we weren't sure it would work, so we gave them just this little thing [in the teaser] to see how it would work, and it convinced us. It was pretty clear they had chemistry."

But what of poor Troi, Worf's former flame? "My thinking was that the relationship with Troi somehow broke up after the destruction of the *Enterprise*-D [in *Star Trek Generations*]," says Moore. "It was probably amicable. But I never found a place where it felt natural to mention Troi without turning it into a big scene of exposition."

The teaser sequence also includes a debate about the merits of Worf's new weapon, the *mek'leth*. While the weapon would be featured prominently in *Star Trek: First Contact*, it actually was introduced to viewers nearly a year earlier on *Deep Space Nine*, thanks to a request by Actor Michael Dorn, according to visual arts producer and martial arts expert Dan Curry.

"After Michael signed for *DS9*, I got a phone call at home and heard this deep familiar voice say, 'Daniel, I need a new weapon,'" recalls Curry. "Michael wanted a one-handed weapon that would be smaller than the *bat'leth* [which Curry designed for *The Next Generation*], recognizing that in martial arts, particularly in Asia, the smaller the weapon you use,

the cooler you are. So that a guy who can use a dagger against somebody with a broadsword is certainly the badder of the martial artists."

Curry invited Dorn to his home and showed him his collection of Asian and Himalayan weapons. "One of my favorites is a Himalayan cavalry sword that has very unusual but practical ergonomics. The blade of the *mek'leth* is similar to this Himalayan blade, but the handle has grappling features so you can deal with pole weapons and larger blades. It's designed for use forward, like a sword, or backhand, like a dagger, and the ergonomics rest perfectly on the forearm and then extend just beyond the elbow, so that you can block a heavy blade without endangering yourself."

A master of low-tech as well as high-tech, Curry made a prototype from "cardboard reinforced with Popsicle sticks held on by hot glue," which Dorn tested in Curry's backyard. After the design had been blessed by Dorn, Behr, and Berman, Joe Longo cast several out of aluminum and had others manufactured from rubber reinforced with steel. The difference in materials, of course, is dictated by how close the prop is intended to come to the flesh-and-blood actors and stunt personnel.

BAR ASSOCIATION

Episode #488

TELEPLAY BY ROBERT HEWITT WOLFE &
IRA STEVEN BEHR
STORY BY BARBARA J. LEE & JENIFER A. LEE
DIRECTED BY LeVAR BURTON

GUEST CAST

Rom	MAX GRODÉNCHIK
Leeta	CHASE MASTERSON
Grimp	JASON MARSDEN
Frool	EMILIO BORELLI

AND

Brunt	JEFFREY COMBS

STARDATE UNKNOWN

Union leader Rom keeps would-be patrons of Quark's away by bribing them. ROBBIE ROBINSON

After suffering from an ear infection for several weeks, Rom collapses in Quark's bar and is taken to the Infirmary. As Bashir treats the Ferengi, he asks why Rom didn't stop by earlier. Rom admits that he couldn't get time off from work; Ferengi employers don't provide sick time, vacation time, or paid overtime. Bashir suggests that Quark's employees need a union to prevent them from being exploited, but even the mere mention of the word terrifies Rom.

Upon returning to the bar, Rom learns that Quark is cutting his employees' salaries to compensate for flagging profit margins. Rom tries to talk his brother out of the decision, but Quark's mind is made up. Recalling Bashir's words, Rom calls a secret meeting of Quark's staff and encourages them to fight back by forming a union. The other Ferengi are aghast; Rom's suggestion alone is probably enough to get them in serious trouble with the Ferengi Commerce Authority (FCA). But Rom points out that they have nothing to lose and rallies them together; a union is born!

Rom finds encouragement from an unexpected quarter. O'Brien comes from a long line of working-class heroes, and he fills Rom's head with the exploits of his martyred ancestor, Sean Aloysius O'Brien, who led a successful coal miners' strike in the early twentieth century. Inspired, Rom gathers his "Guild of Restaurant and Casino Employees" and presents a list of demands to Quark, who laughs them off. But Rom refuses to back down and calls a strike against the bar. Desperate, Quark tries replacing the workers with holowaiters.

But Rom's strategy begins paying off. Quark's bar is nearly deserted, although that's partly due to the fact that Rom is paying customers to stay out. And following Sisko's orders, Odo refuses to disperse the strikers who are blocking the entrance to the bar, even after O'Brien, Bashir, and Worf wind up in a strike-inspired brawl.

Still, Sisko doesn't want the strike to last forever; he tells Quark to settle the matter or pay up on back rent the Federation has never collected from him. After Quark's attempt to end the strike by offering Rom a bribe fails, FCA Liquidator Brunt arrives and promises Quark that *he'll* end the labor dispute quickly—by any means necessary.

Brunt crashes a union meeting and threatens the workers with financial ruin if they don't return to their jobs. But after Rom gives them an inspirational pep talk, the employees rededicate themselves to the strike. Concerned that Brunt will hurt his brother if he doesn't capitulate, Quark tries to talk Rom into giving up. But Rom holds firm, and Quark learns to his dismay that Brunt feels the most effective way to threaten the union leader is to hurt someone Rom cares about: Quark!

When Rom comes to visit a badly beaten Quark in the Infirmary, he discovers that his employer has contrived a way to let everyone save face. Quark will honor the demands of the strikers secretly if Rom disbands the union and pretends that Quark has won. Rom agrees and everyone returns to work—*except* for Rom, who tells Quark that he's quitting his job as waiter to become one of the station's diagnostic and repair technicians. His experience has proven to him that he can survive on his own, and that he's better off with Quark as his brother than as his employer.

"People think of this as a comic episode," Armin Shimerman states. "And it is, of course. But in truth, it's really about union-management problems." The subject is a serious one to Shimerman, who sits on the Board of Directors of the Screen Actors Guild. "The irony of it is that I play *management* in the episode," he says. "So I thought that to make Rom have a reasonably hard job as a union organizer, I would have to be tough about it, to show the struggle to the audience. Although you don't see it on TV very often, this is something that goes on in America all the time."

Playing Quark "tough" also went a long way toward putting Shimerman's character "back on track" in the minds of viewers. "I've gone to conventions and heard people say that Quark is becoming too nice," the actor laughs. "And he *has* come a long way since the pilot, so they were right. He's not the Ferengi he was before. He's lost a lot of the harshness. And 'Bar Association' was a way to remedy that."

Of course, even as it reestablished that Quark is *not* the nicest guy in the world, it provided viewers with another glimpse of the Ferengi's softer side. "We've always known that Rom cared about Quark," Shimerman says. "But I think we got a better idea of how much Quark cares about Rom. When Rom quits the bar at the end of the episode, I purposely played that with no emotion, *tabula rasa* [a clean slate], so

"I don't think of Rom as just a comic character," says Max Grodénchik. "It just comes out funny because of the way his mind works." ROBBIE ROBINSON

that the audience has to decide for themselves how devastated Quark may be. I let them fill in the blanks."

Director LeVar Burton loved the mixture of tones. "The execution of the idea was whimsical, but the situation was absolutely serious, particularly to Rom," he says. "There were two terrific scenes in the midst of all the comedy. One was when Rom and Quark are in the corridor and one throws the other up against the wall. The other is after Brunt crushes Quark's eye socket and Rom comes to talk with Quark in the Infirmary. That's serious drama, a power struggle between two brothers. And that's family ties."

The pitch for the story came from Barbara and Jenifer Lee, "two sisters who pitched about eighteen ideas in an hour," reports René Echevarria. "They were so sweet that I was able to listen to them all, although at first there was nothing interesting. They were down to one-liners, and it was literally their *last* one-liner: 'Rom starts a union.' I said, 'I love it.'"

Although the writing staff originally thought they'd use the story as a B-plot in either "Rejoined" or "Crossfire," their growing fondness for the idea soon ruled that option out of the question. This was too good to relegate to a secondary position. "There was so much to mine there," Echevarria notes, "we knew we were only scratching the surface. So we made it an A-story."

Which is not to say there were no concerns, Echevarria continues. "At the time, it bothered us that the story about Rom and Quark was almost as serious as the story about Worf and Kurn ['Sons of Mogh,' which had aired only the week before]. "We thought, 'Gee, we're doing brothers too much.' But when you become a slave to the idea that you have, it ultimately doesn't matter that they bump up against each other. You can't help that."

"We thought it was an opportunity to let Rom come forward," observes Robert Hewitt Wolfe, who cowrote the teleplay with frequent partner Ira Behr. "You could see it from Quark's point of view, the fact that Rom is causing all these problems for him. But it's really more a story about Rom than Quark. He's the one who goes on strike, so he's the protagonist driving the story."

Of course, if it were up to Max Grodénchik, his character wouldn't have driven quite so far. "The thing we found most interesting about the show was that Max didn't want to do it," comments Ira Behr. "He was totally freaked out about having Rom leave the job in the bar."

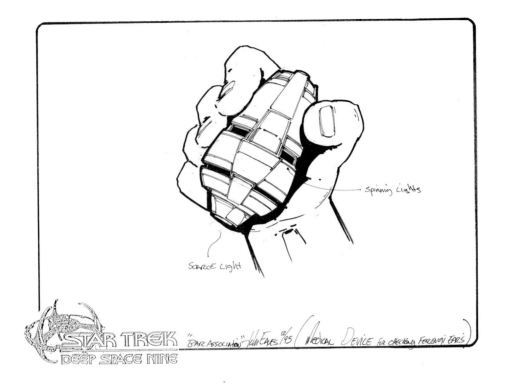

Bashir's high-tech ear
examination instrument.
JOHN EAVES

"Max was terrified of this episode," Shimerman confirms. "After he read the script, he called me almost in tears. He said, 'They're changing my character. They're taking him out of the bar.' Max was devastated, because he felt that it was the death knell for Rom. I told him that the best thing that can happen to a character is change, and Rom was changing for the better."

Grodénchik soon found that out for himself. "Dr. Bashir is the hunk of the show, and Leeta left him for *me*," he says, grinning. "That made me feel really good. And that was my first on-screen kiss." Grodénchik laughs at the memory. "I told Chase [Masterson], 'Keep your mouth closed!' Because you haven't been kissed until you kiss with those [prosthetic] teeth. She went right for the teeth, but on the second take she didn't. By the second kiss I think she'd learned her lesson."

The writers also learned a lesson from the scene. "There was just something *Beauty and the Beast* about them that we liked, so Ira said, "Let's marry Leeta and Rom." It would take until the end of Season 5 ("Call to Arms") for those vows to be pledged. But, Moore notes, "The scene in 'Bar Association' where she gives him a kiss was the beginning of that whole strain."

Grodénchik also came to appreciate the character growth opportunity that was being provided by the writers. "Rom does this big thing, forming a union, and then he realizes that he has to leave his job," the

actor says. "He has to end his working relationship with his brother to retain his family relationship with him. He doesn't want to jeopardize the love between them." Grodénchik chuckles softly. "Rom's a better man than I am."

The show includes more than one tip of the hat to previous episodes of both *DS9* and its predecessor, *TNG*. The tooth sharpener that Worf bought from Nog in "Little Green Men" is stolen by a Dopterian ("The Forsaken"). Odo recites a litany of "security breaches" that occurred on the *Enterprise* under Worf's watch (the incidents are drawn from the episodes "Rascals" and "A Matter of Time"). And Behr managed to insert his own tribute to one of his favorite films, *Fort Apache* (another John Ford classic), in the scene where Sisko chews out O'Brien, Worf, and Bashir for brawling in the bar. Although the scene is reminiscent of one in "The Trouble with Tribbles," Behr claims that he had in mind Victor McLaglen, Dick Foran, and Pedro Armendariz, not Chekov and Scotty.

"We'd actually written the brawl and we weren't able to film it, for time or money or something," says Behr. "But the part that had really interested us was the image of the three guys standing there at attention, being harangued, like the brawling sergeants in *Fort Apache*. I just loved the idea."

Another throwback to *TNG* was the use of the Nausicaan heavies who beat up Quark. Once again, an older *Star Trek* element was given a new twist to match the unique atmosphere of *DS9* as viewers were treated to a very special game of darts.

"LeVar Burton wanted the worst guys they had to use as strikebusters," recalls Dart Adviser James Lomas. "So he asked for the Nausicaan masks and uniforms from *TNG*." Lomas and fellow dart expert Shawn McConnell inherited the uniforms, which now were specially cushioned with thick, tough foam, and had the fun of throwing darts into one another's chests. It was just a typical day, apparently, in the life of a Nausicaan.

"Bar Association" provided the writers with another opportunity to expand on Worf's adjustments, or nonadjustments, to station life by moving his quarters to the *Defiant*. Dax's feelings about Worf, suggested in numerous episodes throughout the season, continue to simmer. "We were setting up a sort of flirtation," says Wolfe. "Ever since 'The Way of the Warrior' we'd thought that Dax might be cool enough to keep Worf off balance and give him someone to relate to."

Filming of the episode went smoothly, despite a number of difficult shots. "I'm enormously proud of one of them," enthuses Burton. "It begins on the Promenade, with some people picketing, and then Rom comes out and gives the 'thumbs up' sign to O'Brien, who's up on the second level with Worf, and then the shot continues while we do a page and a half 'walk-and-talk.' We did it all in one take, with a Steadicam operator on a crane. He actually stepped off the crane's platform onto the second level, which means that we had to counterbalance the crane off-camera after he stepped off. It was very complicated, and very, very complex to get it all to work, but when I read the script, I saw it immediately," he says, snapping his fingers. "We rehearsed it several times and finally got it after four or five takes."

Complication was the name of the game for the scene where the script called for numerous "Quarks" walking through the bar at once. "Sometimes when you read the script you see what they've written and you go, 'Oh my God, how the heck are we gonna do this one?'" laughs B.C. Cameron. "I've learned not to panic, because somehow, we always bring it around to a point where it's doable."

As usual, the filmmakers utilized both simple methods (a photo double of Armin Shimerman in the distant background) and extremely high-tech meth-

"The [dart] game consists of one of them taking a dart and flinging it at his companion . . . [they] seem to find this endless fascinating . . . ."
ROBBIE ROBINSON

ods (bluescreen, split screen, and multiple layer compositing) to achieve their goals. "That was by far our busiest bluescreen shot ever," says Glenn Neufeld. "All of the elements had to be synchronized when they were shot. We very carefully matched up our secondary shots to keep the perspective, because if anything had looked odd, it would have given away the fact that it's a trick."

In truth, one problem discovered in postproduction nearly had them stymied. Odo approaches a holographic Quark, who then "fritzes out" and drops his tray. But it turns out that various reflections from the set (reflections of activities that viewers would *not* expect to see in the bar) were visible on the drinking glass at the bottom of the frame. Having the glass redrawn by an animator seemed the only solution, but it would be a time-consuming, tedious, and costly solution. But ultimately the filmmakers found a simpler fix. "We blew the film up about three percent until the affected portion of the glass went out of frame," Neufeld says with a smile.

The arrival of Akorem, who claims *he* is the Emissary, threatens to disrupt the advancements Bajor has made.
ROBBIE ROBINSON

ACCESSION

Episode #489

WRITTEN BY JANE ESPENSON
DIRECTED BY LES LANDAU

GUEST CAST

Keiko O'Brien	ROSALIND CHAO
Vedek Porta	ROBERT SYMONDS
Kai Opaka	CAMILLE SAVIOLA
Molly O'Brien	HANA HATAE
Onara	DAVID CARPENTER
Ensign Latara	GRACE ZANDARSKI
Gia	LAURA JANE SALVATO

SPECIAL GUEST STAR

Akorem Laan	RICHARD LIBERTINI

STARDATE UNKNOWN

Every day brings dozens of routine arrivals to space station Deep Space 9, but this will not be an ordinary day. Returning at last from a lengthy botanical research project on Bajor, Keiko O'Brien has surprising news for her husband: she's carrying their second child. The shuttle from Bajor also brings to the station a pair of newlyweds, who wish to obtain the Emissary's marriage blessing. Although Sisko still feels uncomfortable in the role, he graciously performs the ritual.

And then comes the most startling arrival. A Bajoran lightship emerges from the wormhole, carrying Akorem Laan, a legendary poet who's been missing for two hundred years. Akorem reveals that he had an accident in space and was saved from death by the inhabitants of the wormhole. Akorem believes their intervention was part of a divine plan, that they returned his life to him so that he could serve as the Bajoran Emissary. Sisko feels this makes sense, and volunteers to step aside, allowing Akorem to assume the revered position of Emissary.

Although he claims to feel relieved by this decision, Sisko begins to have qualms about it when Akorem tells the Bajoran people that the Prophets wish for them to return to the old ways. This means they must again adhere to their *D'jarras*, a caste system that restricts families to prescribed occupations. The *D'jarras* fell away during the Cardassian Occupation, when every Bajoran had to become a soldier in order to survive. But Akorem believes it is time to reinstate them, even if it means that the Federation, which has rules against caste-based discrimination, will deny Bajor the membership status for which it has petitioned.

Late that night, Sisko awakens from a nightmare and goes for a walk on the deserted Promenade. There he encounters a vision of Kai Opaka, who declares that he does not know himself. Sisko is troubled by the experience, although Bashir has a quasi-scientific explanation. It was an "orb shadow," a hallucination occasionally experienced by people who've been exposed to the Bajoran orbs. Bashir can block the physical cause of the symptoms, but he notes that the Bajorans believe these shadows occur only when the subject has ignored the advice the Prophets provided during the orb encounter.

In the meantime, Kira, too, suffers from conflicted feelings. She tries to follow her *D'jarra,* which demands that she be an artist and not a member of the military, but she has no aptitude for it. Nevertheless, she feels she must follow the demands of the new Emissary, and tells Sisko that she will resign her commission as soon as the captain finds a suitable replacement. For Sisko, who already believes that he has failed in his mission to bring Bajor into the Federation, this is a crushing blow. It is followed by yet another one when Sisko learns that a Bajoran vedek has murdered a monk. The monk was of an unclean *D'jarra,* the vedek explains calmly. Since he would not resign from the Order, the vedek felt he had no other choice.

Appalled, Sisko requests a meeting with Akorem and declares that giving up his position as Emissary was a mistake; he is challenging Akorem's claim to the title. With no other way to prove who is the real Emissary, Sisko suggests the two of them go to the wormhole and ask the Prophets. Akorem agrees.

In the wormhole, the alien inhabitants quickly disillusion Akorem by revealing that he was saved and sent into the future for Sisko's benefit, not Bajor's. Akorem's presence makes Sisko realize that he is the true Emissary. Since Akorem has no further role to play, Sisko asks that the aliens return him to his own time, to live out his life with his loved ones, without any memory of the future. The aliens comply and Sisko returns to the station, understanding at last that he, like the Prophets, is of Bajor.

"This story was pitched to me by a free-lancer named Jane Espenson, and I championed it," Hans Beimler relates enthusiastically. "She pitched 'the other Emissary' and the minute I heard those words I knew it was a show. So I told Ira [Behr], and he saw it immediately too."

Beimler wasn't Espenson's only champion among the writing staff. "I use this as an example of a *great* pitch to people who come in and try to tell me too much," says René Echevarria. "Her idea was that someone appears, whether magically or whatever, who claims to be the Emissary. Sisko says 'Great.' Then he realizes that he has to fight for the thing he's always tried to get rid of. Now that's how you pitch a

Nana Visitor's powerful performance raised the level of the episode. ROBBIE ROBINSON

story. Jane Espenson is very smart, and I thought that this was an important show."

That doesn't mean that the writers felt it would be a piece of cake. "Shows about religion, the alien religion and the Prophets, are extraordinarily difficult," notes Beimler. Not because they're hard to produce, but because they're not proven ratings winners. As a result, the studio tends to be happier when *DS9* is doing action stories.

"The studio doesn't like Bajor stories in general," adds Echevarria. "And Bajor's religion is one aspect of Bajor to which they *really* don't respond." Although the quasi-ecumenical nature of episodes like "Accession" is central to the series, Behr continues to be surprised that, outside of the studio gates, few people have noticed. "We do religion as part of the show," states Behr. "It's a continuing theme and the source of storylines." But when *TV Guide* did an article about religion on television, he points out, *Deep Space Nine* was lumped together with twelve other shows where the magazine writer really had to stretch to find a religious connotation. "The fact that we were just thrown into the mix amazes me," he says. "I would have expected it to be more controversial."

Ultimately, though, "Accession" is as much about

people as it is about the nature of religion. "The arc with Sisko as Emissary is something that's very dear to my heart, and this story touches specifically on a Sisko level," says Echevarria. "But it's an odd episode, because it starts as a Sisko show, sort of becomes a Kira show for a while, and then it goes back to Sisko."

And speaking of Kira, Echevarria gives high praise to Actor Nana Visitor for providing much of the show's dramatic impact. "Nana gave an amazing performance," he says, "and at one point I thought she was truly astonishing. We were all very worried that the speech about bringing back the *D'jarras* was just a little odd, that it wasn't going to sell. Hans kept asking what we could play there, so we added some mixed reaction from the crowd and said that some people were applauding, some weren't. And Nana, by herself, sold that, just by the way she started applauding, slowly, and then building, as if thinking, 'I've got to clap. I must. I have to support him.' That just told you everything you needed to know about the Bajorans. You can always count on Nana. I would give her any story, any role. She's really good."

While writing the first draft of the script, freelancer Espenson included a B-story that would have ramifications later in the series: Keiko's pregnancy. Her motivation for creating the pregnancy had more to do with Worf's presence on *DS9* than O'Brien's, as demonstrated by the Klingon's reaction to the news. Viewers who'd seen Worf deliver baby Molly in the *TNG* episode "Disaster" understood immediately. "That was Jane's gag," says Echevarria. "There was a lot of good stuff in the draft that she wrote." The B-story played right into one of Behr's favorite areas: Miles O'Brien's personal life. "Because of the Bajoran religion, it was a heady show," Behr explains. "So the O'Brien stuff brought us back to lighter emotions and feelings. I think that was necessary for the episode."

But was it necessary to say that the engineer couldn't keep his quarters clean? "I don't know that he can't take care of himself, but I think that any little recognizable human trait that we can exhibit in our characters is a triumph," Behr says. "For many years, *Star Trek* seemed to want to take its characters beyond ordinary humans. There was a whole 'Twenty-fourth century people are better' thing, and it's a little vague as to why. I think that it's great to show that, yes, we go into the future and, yes, all this positive stuff happens, and, yes, we're going to achieve so much of what we aspire to. But nevertheless, when the wife's away, we kind of let it all go to hell in a handbasket. And that's great." Colm Meaney,

A line so simple, it *could* have just been a throwaway. "You are of Bajor." ROBBIE ROBINSON

who had to play the scenes, disagrees, to a point. "It was expedient to have some sort of what's considered humor in the script," Meaney says, "but I object to saying this guy's incapable of keeping his apartment tidy when his wife's away. That's a cliché."

Although it hadn't been planned, Keiko's fictional pregnancy provided a unique way to deal with an unexpected, real-life development a short time later, when Nana Visitor became pregnant with her second child in real life. Eight episodes later, in "Body Parts," Kira would become an integral part of O'Brien's family in ways that no one had imagined.

The episode also revealed ideas about the Prophets that had not been imagined previously. "The scene with the wormhole aliens wasn't quite working in the final draft," says Behr. "We were going over it and finally I said, 'We are of Bajor. You are of Bajor.' And René said, 'What does that mean?' And I said, 'I don't know, but boy, it really sells it home, doesn't it?' I remember that everyone had the same reaction: 'Oooh. What does that mean?'" And, as with many of *DS9*'s best lines, it led the way to some truly dramatic revelations.

The show presented some equally stunning visuals, particularly the image of Akorem Laan's exit from the wormhole. "When we got the 'Accession' script, we all thought, wouldn't it be great if this guy was on one of those nice solar sail ships from 'Explorers!'" says Andre Bormanis. "We said, 'We've got the model. Let's use it.'"

Actually, the model existed only as a computer graphic, inside designer John Knoll's workstation at

ILM. "I created two new shots of the vessel for the show," says Knoll. "It wasn't supposed to be the exact same ship. It was supposed to be one like it, that comes tumbling out of the wormhole, with the sails all torn up. So rather than the controlled flight that we'd done previously, I got to make it look more like a derelict. I had to draw shredded sails and have it tumbling end over end. Of course, I used the same model, and only made superficial changes to it."

The end credits of the episode may have surprised astute viewers, as a number of staff members suddenly seemed to be playing musical chairs. Fritz Zimmerman replaced Set Designer Ron Wilkinson (Zimmerman would alternate in that position with Peter Samish), and Art Director Randy McIlvain's credit switched positions with Herman Zimmerman's in the scrolling roster (the latter's title also changed from production designer to visual consultant). The reason for all the changes was *Star Trek: First Contact*, which had just gone into production; a number of *DS9* and *Voyager* staffers would be helping out with the movie during the last portion of *DS9*'s fourth season.

Klingon advocate Ch'Pok confronts Worf, who is accused of causing the death of innocent civilians. ROBBIE ROBINSON

RULES OF ENGAGEMENT
Episode #490

TELEPLAY BY **RONALD D. MOORE**
STORY BY **BRADLEY THOMPSON & DAVID WEDDLE**
DIRECTED BY **LeVAR BURTON**

GUEST CAST

Ch'Pok	RON CANADA
T'Lara	DEBORAH STRANG
Helm Officer	CHRISTOPHER MICHAEL

STARDATE 49665.3

Accused of destroying a civilian Klingon transport ship, Worf faces a hearing to determine whether he should be extradited to the Klingon Empire for trial. The facts are not in dispute: While in command of the *Defiant,* which was under attack by two Klingon warships, Worf ordered the crew to fire on a vessel that suddenly decloaked in front of them. As a result, 141 Klingons were killed. But whether the incident was a tragic, unavoidable mistake, as Sisko states, or the result of Klingon bloodlust, as Ch'Pok, the Klingon advocate would have it, is not clear. The representative from the Judge Advocate's office, a Vulcan admiral, T'Lara, allows witnesses to be called to determine Worf's state of mind.

A frequent sparring partner in Worf's holosuite combat simulations, Dax is the first to be questioned. She testifies that Worf can always control his most violent instincts. Ch'Pok forces her to reveal that the day before the attack, Worf participated in a holosuite battle in which the character he plays ordered the destruction of a Klingon city filled with civilians. Next, Ch'Pok questions Sisko, who states that he had no qualms about placing Worf in charge of the humanitarian mission protecting a convoy of Cardassian medical supply vessels, despite the potential danger of Klingon attack. Later, Quark testifies that prior to leaving, Worf admitted that he hoped the Klingons *would* attack the convoy, presumably so he could retaliate with the *Defiant.*

Sisko has Odo investigate the background of the dead Klingon transport captain, hoping to establish that the man wanted to take on the *Defiant* in battle. When Odo finds nothing incriminating, Sisko presses the constable to continue his investigation by checking out the dead passengers.

Back in the courtroom, Kira offers the opinion that Worf made the right tactical decision in firing on the transport. However, Ch'Pok points out that during the Cardassian Occupation, Kira was a terrorist who carried out an attack that resulted in the death of innocent Cardassian civilians. A few minutes later, under tough questioning, O'Brien admits that had he been in command, he wouldn't have given the order to fire. Although things are beginning to look bad for Worf, Sisko refuses to concede defeat to Ch'Pok.

When it's his turn to testify, Worf stands by his decision to fire on the transport, stating that it was the only appropriate course of action. But Ch'Pok goads Worf by bringing up the fact that he is an outcast among his own people. He suggests that Worf might have destroyed the Klingon ship because it was filled with his enemies, and that he would kill innocent children just to prove his courage. Provoked beyond reason, Worf attacks Ch'Pok, who uses the incident to point out that Worf *would* knowingly attack an unarmed opponent. Satisfied, Ch'Pok rests his case.

While the admiral deliberates, Odo finally brings Sisko the information he needs. Apparently, every passenger that Worf allegedly killed was a passenger on a vessel that crashed several months earlier. Somehow, each passenger "survived" that crash, only to "die" on the transport Worf destroyed. With Ch'Pok on the ropes, Sisko forces him to admit that it's possible the entire affair could have been staged to discredit Starfleet's only Klingon officer, forcing Starfleet to stop providing escorts for Cardassian ships and allowing the Empire to take over more Cardassian space.

With the charges dropped, Worf admits to Sisko that Ch'Pok had a valid point: he *did* have something to prove, and the appearance of the transport ship gave him an opportunity for vengeance that he craved. Beyond that, in order to protect his crew, he made a decision that put civilians at risk—behavior Starfleet considers unacceptable. Sisko allows Worf to stew in his guilt, but he softens the blow by expressing his honest belief that despite his recent failings, Worf will make a good captain someday.

By this time it should come as no great surprise to regular viewers of *DS9* that Ira Steven Behr is a passionate fan of certain Hollywood filmmakers, chief among them director-screenwriter Sam Peckinpah. And that's why, in 1994, when Behr read a newly published book titled *If They Move . . . Kill 'Em: The Life and Times of Sam Peckinpah*, he immediately sought out the author, David Weddle.

"Ira invited me to lunch at Paramount and gave me a tour of the sets," Weddle says. "He was just super nice to me." Weddle recognized an opportunity at hand. "So I said to him, 'Do you think I could pitch to your show?' And Ira said, 'Sure.'"

Weddle contacted Brad Thompson, a friend from film school with whom he'd written a screenplay, and suggested renewing their partnership. At the time,

"The characters said some compelling things about Worf," Moore notes. ROBBIE ROBINSON

Thompson was reading about computer failures, or rather, "what happens when computers fail, and when computers provide too much information." One noteworthy case was the Persian Gulf incident, in which an American cruise missile shot down an Iranian airliner because a computer display indicated that the plane was in the wrong place, and the airline pilot was not listening to the channel upon which the Americans broadcast their warnings.

"That inspired us," Thompson says. "What would happen if someone in Starfleet shot down a ship full of people because they were in a combat zone? We pitched it as a Sisko story and the twist in the end was that it had all been faked."

"We had the Klingons put out a little drone that created a holographic image of a fake ship," Weddle adds. "When we pitched it to Ira, he said that it wasn't right for Sisko, but they had Worf coming on the show the next season and it sounded like a great show for him, putting him in a command situation that he could learn from. So Ira stood up and wrote it in grease pencil on a board."

"What he wrote was, 'Worf kills a bunch of people,'" Thompson laughs.

"Then he said, 'I think this might be a very good show, but if we do it, it'll be toward the end of the year,'" Weddle continues. When the executive producer finally called, months later, he asked the partners to provide a written version of the story. "We wrote a nineteen page story document. They liked it, and Rick Berman liked it, so we were really happy."

"It was a good premise," says Behr. "We'd wanted to do a trial show, and we liked the idea of a Klingon attorney."

"A courtroom is a crucible for a lot of drama," notes Ron Moore, who wrote the teleplay. "Even on *The Next Generation*, I'd always been angling to do a courtroom show, but I never had the chance. They've always intrigued me. I'd liked 'Court Martial' from the original series, and when I was younger I'd wanted to be a lawyer." Moore laughs at the memory. "Sometime in undergraduate shool I realized that I didn't want to be a lawyer so much as I wanted to be Perry Mason!" The show also provided, as Moore puts it, "a chance to slap Worf around. 'Sons of Mogh' had told him, 'You're not as Klingon as you thought you were, and you're not going back to the Empire.' But inside, Worf thought, 'Well, I've got Starfleet.' Now I wanted to put *that* into question, to shake up the character and really make him question where he was, who he was, what he wanted, where he belonged. This was a chance to do it."

But Behr didn't want to do something that was "just a trial show." He wanted something that would stand out from *TNG*'s "The Measure of a Man" and *DS9*'s first-season episode "Dax." "We had to come up with a different way," Behr says. "I had seen the movie *Clockers,* which I quite liked. There was one scene during a kind of flashback where Harvey Keitel was talking to the camera. I said, 'Why don't we do that?' and Ron just flipped for it."

Moore had seen the technique used with great effectiveness in the British film *Testimony.* "It's a cool stylistic device," he says, "sort of breaking the fourth wall, but sort of not, because the actors aren't talking to the audience, they're actually talking to someone in the courtroom."

Unfortunately, that was the point where everything began going wrong, according to Behr. "We got totally focused on structure, and how it was gonna work, all the nuts and bolts," he laments. "Big mistake, but it happened, and now it's a show that just didn't work. We did a show that is based on the intent of the defendant, just as the American legal system is, but we left the defendant out of the show. Worf just sits there, staring into space."

Although he feels it was a flawed episode, Moore enjoyed the courtroom scenes. ROBBIE ROBINSON

"We got blinded," Moore agrees. "I was really intrigued by the writer's device. What went by the wayside was Worf. Worf doesn't speak for chunks of the show. The guy on trial is barely in the episode."

And that, for Behr, ultimately negated the power of the show. "It's clever on a certain level, but ultimately it's pretty hollow as drama," he says, clearly disappointed. "When we watched the final cut, our collective jaws just dropped. Our basic response was, 'So what?'"

Structural problems or not, Director LeVar Burton threw himself into the episode, starting by viewing "a lot of episodes of *LA Law,*" he says, smiling. "Elements of 'Rules of Engagement' are like *Rashomon,* with everybody having a different spin on events, and it was important to me to have a different look and feeling for the telling of each tale," Burton notes. "We shot all of the courtroom scenes pretty much in sequence, so I planned a progression of fluidity and motion as the story unfolded. We started fairly static with the camera and then moved the camera more and more. By the time that Sisko was finally driving the action, we were totally using Steadicam."

Burton's wish to have a different look for each version of the story was picked up by Glenn Neufeld. "It was *Rashomon* in Klingon ship land," he says, "so we tried to tell the story each time from a different perspective in the battle. We shot the column of ships moving in one direction, and then after Worf has turned and flown around we shot it from the other end. The trick was in keeping all the lighting elements straight, because when the convoy is moving one way, the light always comes from a certain point. Then three days later I would light the bird-of-prey and I had to recreate the same lighting. The detail was necessary because what we were seeing was not just a space interlude, it was part of the storytelling."

Burton also found an opportunity to work with an old friend, Ron Canada, whom he cast as Ch'Pok, the Klingon attorney. Burton had worked with Canada in the *TNG* fifth season episode "The Masterpiece Society." Notes Burton, "I fought really hard for Ron. His role was very dialogue intensive, and he got sick during the episode. It was a superhuman effort on his part to get through it. He did a terrific job."

The fact that everyone worked so hard is appreciated by Behr. "When you're trying to do something different, and special, and truly '*off* the nose,' time works against you," he points out. "In the week that we had to break the story, and the two weeks that Ron had to write it, there wasn't enough time. So we rushed, and—" invoking a lyric from "MacArthur Park," Behr sighs—"we left the cake out in the rain."

Miles O'Brien is obsessed with "memories" as false as the specter, Ee'Char, who haunts him. DANNY FELD

HARD TIME

Episode #491

TELEPLAY BY **ROBERT HEWITT WOLFE**
STORY BY **DANIEL KEYS MORAN & LYNN BARKER**
DIRECTED BY **ALEXANDER SINGER**

GUEST CAST

Keiko O'Brien	ROSALIND CHAO
Rinn	MARGOT ROSE
Molly O'Brien	HANA HATAE
Muniz	F.J. RIO

AND

Ee'Char	CRAIG WASSON

STARDATE UNKNOWN

A devastated Miles O'Brien returns to Deep Space 9 from his visit to Argratha, where his curiosity about the native technology had resulted in false charges of espionage. Before his fellow crew members could come to his aid, the Argrathi had carried out O'Brien's punishment, placing the manufactured memories of twenty years of brutal incarceration into his mind. Although O'Brien understands that these memories are false, he finds it impossible to forget them, particularly those regarding his cellmate, a kindly man named Ee'Char.

An examination by Bashir confirms the worst. The Agrathi put O'Brien through a time-compressed simulation of the prison experience, which makes the chief feel as if he actually lived through every day of imprisonment. The memories are real, and there's nothing Bashir can do to help him. He prescribes counseling to help O'Brien live through the psychological fallout of his experience.

At home with his loved ones, O'Brien has a difficult time readjusting to the daily routine. His memories of the hardships he experienced are all-pervasive. During those imagined ugly years, his only link to humanity was his relationship with his friend Ee'Char. But O'Brien never speaks of Ee'Char to his friends or family. Instead he lies and says he was always alone in the cell. But Ee'Char refuses to disappear from his mind. The chief begins to see him around the station, although he knows the apparition can't possibly be real.

As weeks go by, O'Brien's psychological condition does not improve. Nerves frayed, he begins snapping at his friends and skipping his counseling sessions. Ee'Char appears more and more often, urging him to seek help. After Bashir reports O'Brien's behavior to Sisko, the station commander relieves O'Brien of duty and orders him to return to counseling. Furious, O'Brien confronts Bashir and lambasts him for informing Sisko. However, Bashir and Ee'Char, the latter of whom only O'Brien is aware of, patiently plead with O'Brien to accept the help that's being offered to him. As O'Brien storms back to his quarters, Ee'Char warns him that sooner or later he will have to tell someone the truth about what happened in the cell. But O'Brien ignores him and goes home, where he flies off the handle at his daughter and shakes her. His alarmed wife pulls the child away from him. O'Brien, horrified by his own behavior, flees to the cargo bay, intending to kill himself.

O'Brien prepares to shoot himself with a phaser, but Bashir arrives and attempts to engage his friend in conversation. At last O'Brien begins to talk about Ee'Char and the secret that has been tearing him apart. For most of the time in the imaginary cell, Ee'Char and he were close, sharing their scant rations and keeping each other's spirits up. But toward the end, on the verge of starvation, O'Brien mistakenly believed that Ee'Char was withholding food from him. In a fit of rage, he killed his friend. A short time later, he was "released" from his psychological incarceration. But the guilt-stricken engineer could not forgive himself for murdering Ee'Char. He felt that the act proved he was no better than an animal, an animal that might harm Keiko or Molly.

Bashir contradicts him, pointing out that an animal would never feel this much guilt over its actions, and that his pain proves his humanity. The Argrathi did everything they could to strip away that humanity, he explains, and for one moment they succeeded. But if the chief allows that one moment to define his entire life, they will have won.

O'Brien sees the sense of Bashir's words, and his vision of Ee'Char fades away for the final time, bidding the chief to "Be well." O'Brien is at last on the road to recovery.

"Hard Time" became an episode only because Robert Hewitt Wolfe had a passion for the story. "Dan Moran and Lynn Barker had pitched a story to us in the very first season of *Deep Space Nine*," Wolfe explains. "The

The director trusted the actors who have played their parts for years to find the emotional center. ROBBIE ROBINSON

concept was a guy given twenty years of prison by implanting ideas in his head, and he has to deal with those ideas because they're real to him. I tried to get Michael Piller to buy it then, but he turned it down." Wolfe suggested the story again during *DS9*'s third season, and again had the idea shot down. "Finally, I managed to convince them to do it in the fourth season," Wolfe says happily.

"Michael didn't think the story was a show," says Ira Behr. "He felt that all the drama happened in the past and there was no real ground to cover in the present. So we didn't do it. But Robert really liked it and so did I." So when the story concept resurfaced once again, Behr notes, "I said, 'Okay. I can green-light shows now, so I'll green-light it.' So we did it and it was a real interesting show."

Because several years had passed since the story had been pitched, the first hurdle to producing it was to find the freelancers. "It took weeks for us to find them," Wolfe says. "Dan was a published writer, so

"Because we shot out of continuity, we had to pay a great deal of attention to detail," recalls Singer. ROBBIE ROBINSON

we went to his publishing company and they told us who his agent was. But his partner and he weren't working together anymore, so it was hard."

Once they'd purchased it, they found that breaking the story was equally difficult. "This was a pretty contentious show among the staff," Ron Moore notes. "We were fighting about how much to use the hallucination character. Robert wanted flashbacks, just flashbacks. I was fighting for no flashbacks, just the guy as a hallucination, coming and talking to O'Brien. Basically, we came to an agreement on using both, and I think that was the best decision. Neither one of us was really right, but it was difficult to get to that place."

The "hallucination character," Ee'Char, hadn't been in the original pitch. Wolfe created him from scratch. He also added to the mix some elements of a different story pitch: a sequel, of sorts, to the popular *TNG* episode "Lower Decks." The story focused on the plight of Ensign Sito Jaxa, who had been captured (and presumably killed) by Cardassians in "Lower Decks." The original take was that Sito had been imprisoned under less than humane conditions, and, although now free, was suffering from post-traumatic stress disorder.

Wolfe played with the story for a while. No solid motivating incident for Sito's condition had been established, so Wolfe settled on the idea that Sito had killed her cellmate, a person to whom she'd become very close. The story was never produced, but it resurfaced in Wolfe's mind as he thought about the O'Brien episode. "I took the end of the Sito story and threw away the rest," Wolfe says. "And I incorporated that ending into 'Hard Time.'"

Wolfe's wife, Celeste, a psychotherapist and licensed family counselor, provided additional input that upped the episode's authenticity. "I made a real effort to give as realistic a report as possible of what O'Brien was going through," Wolfe says. "The only thing that's fantastical is the Ee'Char hallucination. But I tried to keep the emotional part as close to real psychology as I could while still making the story work."

Director Alex Singer recognized that the success or failure of the episode was contingent on the performance of the lead character. "What happened to him was so complex and terrible, with so many levels of memory and material buried in his psyche, that the performance of the actor was the key element for

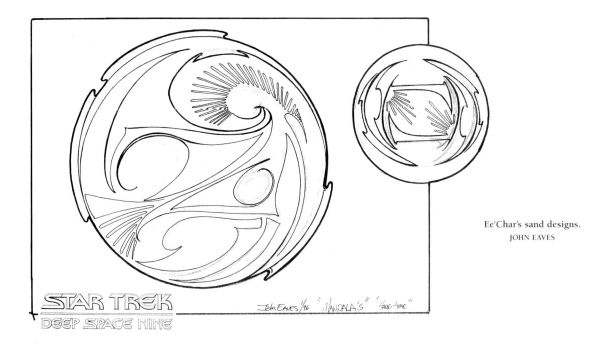

Ee'Char's sand designs.
JOHN EAVES

me," says Singer. "All of it was possible because Colm Meaney is the actor that he is."

The actor, meantime, took it all in stride. "It was hard work, although it wasn't oppressive," Meaney says. "There was a lot of makeup, a lot of highly pitched emotions and the typical physical wear and tear. The fact that it *was* so emotional made me have to go to the top of my range, really, so it was an interesting change."

Meaney doesn't like to define acting techniques. "I'm really text oriented," he says. "What the text gives me is what I play. I think that every actor draws from all sorts of experiences, and you're not necessarily conscious of what you're doing. I don't believe you can pin acting down and say that this is how you arrive at point A or point B."

Like many directors, Singer often leaves basic characterization to the actors, who have been wearing the skin of their screen personae for some time. But in this case, he felt impelled to enter that arena. "I was very concerned that the relationship with O'Brien's wife and daughter be believable and meaningful, so I spent a lot of time on that," the director says. "The little girl, Hana Hatae, who's adorable and very bright, was only about seven years old then, and we were asking her to be an actress in a situation she probably didn't even grasp. She had to be frightened of Colm, whom she adores, and believe that he was scary and that he could hurt her. Colm worked with her, and I worked with her. One of the worries in the back of my head was, 'What am I doing to this kid?

Am I embedding something in her psyche that is damaging?'"

Staging presented a challenge for the scenes filmed in O'Brien's cell. "We had two people in a cell for a lot of the show," says Singer. "It was necessary to be very inventive, to work out patterns that weren't too repetitive." Lighting helped in this effort, redefining the look of the room from scene to scene. "The shafts of light shining down from above provided contrast with the darkness of the cell. That was very effective," Singer observes.

"The fight was one of the most interesting physical things I've ever done," he continues. "I enjoy problems when they're novel, and this was very novel. It was a fight to the death between two men who were dying of hunger, so they're enormously weak. Our stuntmen are guys in marvelous shape with enormous energy, and we had to go against that to give the feeling of two old men battering each other helplessly. This was uniquely difficult, and in thirty-seven years of directing, I've never had a problem as weird as that."

Another weird problem had to do with the sand on the floor. "It was maddening," Singer laughs. "It made me crazy. The footsteps, the impressions made in the sand by the cast and crew, were an incessant problem."

The sand was necessary for a "decontamination" scene, where a beam of light enters the cell and smooths a drawing O'Brien has done on the floor. "We had a shot of O'Brien drawing pictures in the sand, and another of clean, smooth sand," explains Judy Elkins, who served as visual effects supervisor. "And we had a computer-generated light element that Adam Howard animated to make a wipe that took one sand shot away and put the other on. We just needed to replace one sand shot with the other, but the camera had to be locked down to make them match. Then we just covered up the transition with a dancing ray of light."

In the script, Dr. Bashir says of O'Brien, "He's been through some terrible things in his life," and lists a catalogue of misfortune that serves to remind the viewer of how the character has been tortured over the years. Of course, that is all in the producers' overall plan. "Every year we like to drive O'Brien totally mad," laughs Behr. "We did it with 'Whispers,' we did it with 'Tribunal' and 'Visionary,' and we did it again the following season in 'The Assignment.' We just like to hammer him because he's such a great character. And he's so accessible. You feel his pain, and even though it's a TV show and you figure he's gonna come out all right at the end, you're still compelled to root him on."

Sisko won't allow himself to relate to the mirror version of Jennifer as if she were his wife. CARIN BAER

SHATTERED MIRROR

Episode #492

WRITTEN BY IRA STEVEN BEHR & HANS BEIMLER
DIRECTED BY JAMES L. CONWAY

GUEST CAST

Jennifer Sisko	FELECIA M. BELL
Nog	ARON EISENBERG
Klingon Officer	CARLOS CARRASCO
Helmsman	JAMES BLACK
Guard	DENNIS MADALONE

SPECIAL GUEST STAR

Garak	ANDREW ROBINSON

STARDATE UNKNOWN

Staring down at the bustling Promenade, Jake Sisko loiters in his usual spot on the second level. In the past, with Nog at his side, this was the spawning ground for hundreds of exciting dreams and schemes. But now that his Ferengi friend has gone to Starfleet Academy, it's just not the same.

A melancholy Jake returns to his quarters to look for his father. But the senior Sisko is not alone; he's with Jennifer Sisko, a double of Jake's mother from the mirror universe. Jake is thrilled to meet her, but his father is uneasy with the visit, even though Jennifer brings good news: the Terran rebels have driven the Alliance off the mirror space station.

Sisko leaves the two of them alone while he attends a meeting, but when he returns, they're gone. On the table is a small device that Sisko recognizes; it's the same kind of mechanism the mirror O'Brien once used to transport him to the alternate universe. Anxious to recover Jake, Sisko accepts the implicit "invitation" and uses the device to travel to the mirror version of DS9. He's met by "Smiley" O'Brien, who informs Sisko that neither his son nor he is leaving until Sisko helps them out.

Smiley explains that when he last visited Sisko's DS9, he downloaded the plans to the *Defiant*. The rebels have built their own version of the ship to defend their station, still called Terok Nor, against the tyrannical forces of the Alliance. They need Sisko's help to make the powerful warship operational. Smiley expects the Alliance fleet to arrive at Terok Nor in four days. Sisko has until then to get the ship running, after which Smiley promises to return Jake and his father to their own station.

Sisko finds Jake, along with Jennifer, in the station's bar. Jake apologizes to his father for following Jennifer to the mirror universe. But Sisko knows that it was Jennifer's idea in the first place, and he takes her to task for preying on his son's feelings about his dead mother. Jennifer reminds Sisko that it was he who converted her to the rebels' point of view during his previous visit; Jake's involvement was an unfortunate necessity.

On the flagship of the Alliance fleet of Klingon and Cardassian ships, the regent, Worf's mirror counterpart, lashes out at the mirror version of Garak for losing Terok Nor to the rebels. Garak blames Intendant Kira for the defeat and swears his loyalty to Worf as the fleet presses on to wreak vengeance against the rebels.

On the station, Sisko throws himself into preparing the *Defiant* for battle while Jake spends time with Jennifer, who discovers that it's hard not to think of the youth as the son she never had. But there's no time to enjoy the bond; word arrives that the Alliance fleet has stepped up its pace and will arrive within eight hours.

Desperate for assistance from any quarter, Sisko goes to Intendant Kira, who now is a prisoner of the rebels. Kira isn't keen to assist Sisko. He reminds her that when the Alliance fleet arrives, they aren't likely to be any friendlier to her than they will be to him; after all, she's the one who lost the station. Kira tells Sisko that the targeting systems on Alliance ships can be fooled by warp shadows. This information is conveyed to the mirror Bashir and Dax, who, in turn, provide a diversion that delays the arrival of the fleet.

As Jennifer helps Sisko with the final adjustments to the *Defiant*, she tells him that she's decided it would be best to send Jake back to Deep Space 9 now, so that he'll be out of harm's way. Her feelings toward Jake make her wonder if there's a similar connection with Sisko, but Sisko won't give Jennifer any encouragement. He finishes the work on the ship just in time, but when he sees that Smiley is unfamiliar with its operation, he volunteers to lead the attack on the Alliance fleet.

Meanwhile, Jennifer finds Jake on the Promenade, where he's learning that the mirror Nog is nothing like his old friend. After Jennifer and Jake leave him, Nog frees Kira from her holding cell, only to be rewarded by a deadly disrupter blast from the treacherous intendant. Unfortunately, Kira's escape path intersects directly with that of Jake and Jennifer. Kira decides that taking Jennifer hostage might return her to the regent's good graces, but she has no use for Jake. She fires her weapon at him, but Jennifer jumps into the line of fire. When a grieving Jake inadvertently reveals he is Captain Sisko's son, the intendant spares his life, but tells Jake to inform his father that she will collect on the debt some day.

With the help of Bashir and Dax, Sisko and the

Defiant force Worf and the Alliance fleet into retreat. Sisko returns to Terok Nor to find Jake holding vigil at Jennifer's bedside. Jennifer reaches out to take Sisko's hand, saying that she knew there was a connection between them. Sisko allows that it's true, and she dies at peace, leaving the two Sisko men to deal with the loss of Jennifer Sisko a second time.

To the writers of *Deep Space Nine*, a trip to the mirror universe is like a vacation. "We'd just come through a couple of very serious episodes and we wanted to have some fun," says Ira Behr. "Not that there weren't some serious things happening on an emotional level in 'Shattered Mirror,' but basically this was a chance for us to have some fun." Behr is talking about his writing staff, of course, but the element of fun couldn't help but spill over to the actors who got to play what the writers had conceived.

"I've been trying to make the mirror Bashir meaner," Alexander Siddig says with a smile. "I want him to be the inverse of Dr. Bashir, like a doppelgänger [a ghostly counterpart of a living person], the animus to his anima. Bashir wouldn't hurt a fly, but this guy is unstable, difficult, and stupid." Siddig found clues as to what would be plausible for his character in specific scenes in the script, for example, the scene in which the scruffy mirror Bashir squabbles with Sisko. He also opted to make a physical change in his character. "I grew a beard for the episode," he says, "but then I

Siddig enjoyed playing a bad guy. "I had the opportunity to be really sadistic and horrific," he says cheerfully. CARIN BAER

Behr's idea to put the mirror Garak in a dog collar amused the writing staff, but didn't particularly please the actor. BARRY MCLAUGHLIN

intendant, "as Kira exactly. I mean, they are exactly the same person. But the intendant's ego has been warped, so that everything that Kira would do for her people, the intendant does for herself. She's self-serving with a capitol S!"

"It's great to have these actors be able to free themselves up and play completely different people who are semibasically the same," Director James Conway says. "Of course, Michael Dorn hadn't done the mirror universe before, so I told him, 'Think of yourself more as Gowron than Worf, in terms of being outlandish.' And he did that very well."

As for the mirror version of Nog, Aron Eisenberg chose to base his persona on a nearby mentor. "Nog had to be obnoxious and rude," he says, "so I played him like an edgy Quark." Eisenberg loved his first (and last) trip to the other side, which gave him the opportunity at long last to utilize his martial arts training and do his own stunts, supervised by Dennis Madalone. One of those stunts was the fall he took after Intendant Kira blasted him. "It was sad that I got killed by her, but it was a good episode," he says good-naturedly.

"I had a good time doing that," Visitor laughs.

"We cracked ourselves up writing that scene," admits Behr. "There was something so wonderful about it. We placed just the tiniest little bug of doubt about Nog in the intendant's mind, just that little disquieting 'He knows something that he should not know,' and she kills him. It's the big response to a small irritation." Behr laughs at the memory. "In my opinion there is very little that's gratuitous in *Star Trek,* so I just thought that the whole gratuitous nature of that scene was kind of juicy."

Nog was the third Ferengi character killed in as many mirror episodes, a fact that isn't quite coincidental. Prior to the start of the series' seventh season, Behr began to consider doing another mirror show. "If I were Brunt, I'd be getting very nervous about now," he said at the time.

Conway had nearly as much fun as the actors he was directing, particularly in setting up the scene in which Nog is flanked by two beautiful dabo girls. "I had planned that as a two-shot (Nog and one girl), to just pan over," the director explains. "But when I saw the wardrobe, I decided to come in close with a wide-angle lens and shoot upward a little bit. It was just too delicious a shot not to have. And it also sold the joke of little short Nog being with two beautiful, *tall,* well-endowed women.

"That's what the mirror universe is about," Conway continues. "It's dark and it's sexy, so you can't

had to shave it off early because we had to do a reshoot on an earlier episode. There's actually one scene where they had to paint one on me."

Colm Meaney also has an interior image of his mirror counterpart, who is more pleasant than Bashir's doppelgänger. "I picture Smiley as being a bit dirty, and scuzzier than the regular O'Brien, just because of what he's had to go through," Meaney says. "He's a trickster, and there's something sort of seedy about him. Miles, on the other hand, is straight as an arrow."

In contrast to her fellow actors, Nana Visitor claims that she sees her sexy counterpart, the

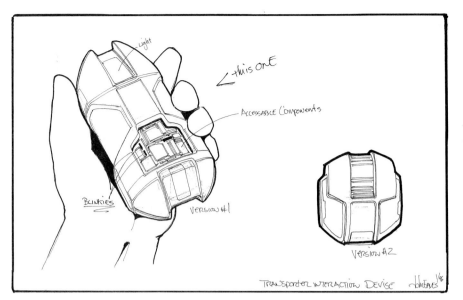

The producers chose to change this object into an agonizer. JOHN EAVES

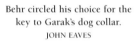

Behr circled his choice for the key to Garak's dog collar. JOHN EAVES

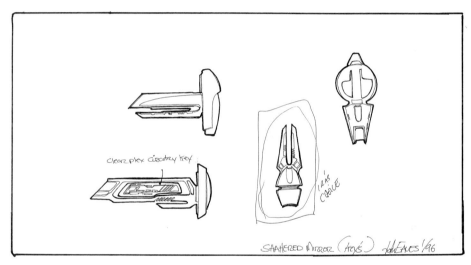

be afraid of that in those shows because you'd miss opportunities. There's no subtlety over there."

That might explain a rather peculiar exchange between Worf and Garak about the Cardassian not being the Klingon's "type." "Just having fun," says Beimler. "The alternate universe is a sexually charged place, and who does what to whom is a matter of great interest to us."

But for all the fun and games the alternate universe inspires, there are a few rules the writers have to follow. "We can't just go over there and interfere with their culture just because we can," notes Beimler. "That's not a good enough reason. Ira's very specific about this. He wants the crossover shows (as the DS9 writers refer to them) to have what he calls

'bond,' which means there must be a reason to do them. The crossover universe has a kind of heightened reality. It's a swashbuckling kind of place. But we can't go there just because we're in a swashbuckling mood. We must go there for a specfic reason." In this case, the story about Jennifer, her impact on Jake, and the emotional pulls on Sisko provided a solid reason. "Shattered Mirror" was the first collaboration by Behr and Beimler, who would go on to become regular writing partners when Robert Wolfe departed at the end of Season 5.

The episode called for huge space battles; Glenn Neufeld and Gary Hutzel again joined forces to complete the work. "It was a very big show for a single episode," Hutzel says. "If you compare them, it was

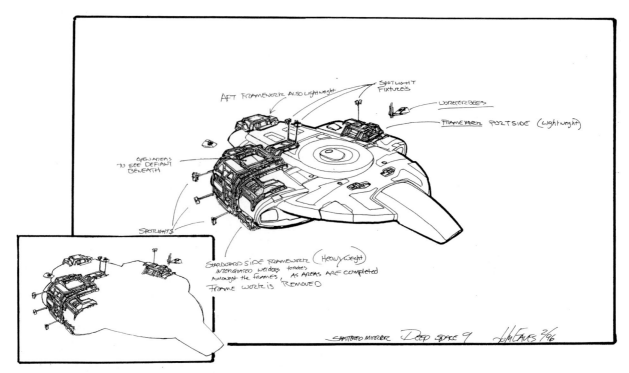

The following labels appear on the rendering:

AFT FRAMEWORK ALSO LIGHTWEIGHT

SPOTLIGHT FIXTURES

WORKERBEES

FRAMEWORK PORTSIDE (lightweight)

OPEN AREAS TO SEE DEFIANT BENEATH

SPOTLIGHTS

STARBOARD SIDE FRAMEWORK (Heavy Weight) INTEGRATED WELDERS torches Amongst the frames, AS AREAS ARE completed Framework is REMOVED

SHATTERED MIRROR DEEP SPACE 9 John EAVES 3/96

A rendering of the mirror *Defiant* under construction. Both the ship and the scaffolding were created in CGI. JOHN EAVES

actually larger than 'Way of the Warrior,' because that was two hours. I mostly did motion-control photography on it, but it was all Glenn's design. 'Shattered' had five-times the regular effects budget." In order to accommodate the numerous cuts—meanwhile back on the Klingon flagship . . ." as Neufeld calls them—the effects team produced "three flavors of each shot." This would give the editors a variety of angles that would keep the battle exciting. Of course, that tripled the time allotted to each shot, again adding to costs.

But a writer's directive caused Neufeld the biggest concern. In the script, the Klingon flagship was described as "much larger" than usual. Behr's reasoning that "it's the alternate universe, it can be anything it wants" and "Klingons are crazy so they might build a ship that size" didn't help the effects team. The simple fact is that only one appropriate Klingon cruiser model existed: the *Negh'Var*, originally built for *TNG*'s "All Good Things . . ." and modified for "The Way of the Warrior," and that model was the same size as the *Defiant*, two and a half feet long. "To have the *Defiant* dive and strafe and move in as tight on the *Negh'Var*

as described in the script, the Klingon model would have had to be twenty-five times larger than the *Defiant*," Neufeld notes. And he couldn't shoot close-ups of the *Negh'Var*, enlarge them, and composite the *Defiant* over them, because the detail on the Klingon model wouldn't hold up to scale.

That's when Neufeld made a decision. "I called the producers and said, 'I'm going to change your battle sequence a little bit, so that the *Defiant* will attack the top of the cruiser only from far away. But when it attacks the bottom of the cruiser, I can get in there close up." The producers approved the proposal, and Neufeld contracted model maker Tony Meininger to build a twenty-foot mock-up of "the underbelly only" of the Klingon cruiser.

Despite the high cost of the episode, Behr admits to being pleased with the results. "We all loved the space battles in 'Shattered Mirror,' so I can't knock it," he says. "Glenn was leaving the show, and that was his parting shot. It was, 'You can't stop me, I'm gonna do it.' And it was just great. I loved those scenes."

THE MUSE

Episode #493

TELEPLAY BY RENÉ ECHEVARRIA
STORY BY RENÉ ECHEVARRIA &
MAJEL BARRETT RODDENBERRY
DIRECTED BY DAVID LIVINGSTON

GUEST CAST

Lwaxana Troi   MAJEL BARRETT
Jeyal   MICHAEL ANSARA

SPECIAL GUEST STAR

Onaya   MEG FOSTER

STARDATE UNKNOWN

From his usual perch on the second level, Jake Sisko observes as the passengers of a recently docked Bajoran transport ship step onto Deep Space 9's Promenade. He's looking for inspiration for future stories. He finds just what he needs in the arrival of an exotic alien female, who meets Jake's gaze and then mysteriously disappears.

In the meantime, Odo is perplexed by the arrival of a different visitor. It's Lwaxana Troi, Federation ambassador and would-be close friend of the shapeshifter. Lwaxana has come to Odo for his assistance. She's pregnant with the child of her new husband, a Tavnian named Jeyal. Although she is pleased with the imminent birth of her son, she is heartbroken over his likely fate. Jeyal insists that they follow Tavnian tradition, which calls for their son to be raised only by men. Accordingly, Lwaxana has abandoned Jeyal and hopes to remain on DS9 for the birth, close to the only person she feels can protect her from Jeyal: Odo. The security chief initially is not pleased with this responsibility. But he soon grows comfortable with it, and with Lwaxana's presence, both on the station and, ultimately, in his quarters.

Jake finally meets his mystery woman, who introduces herself as Onaya. He is surprised and flattered by the interest she takes in his writing. When she offers to show him techniques to heighten his skills, he leaps at the opportunity. Jake bows out of a trip that he, his father, and Kasidy were planning together so he can remain with his potential muse.

In her quarters, Onaya gifts Jake with an old-fashioned ink pen that once belonged to another of her protégés, and urges him to write a new story on paper, something he's never done before. As Jake writes, Onaya massages parts of his head and neck, noting that it will stimulate his creativity. Soon, Jake

Jake's involvement with a mysterious older woman heightens his writing talents—and nearly ends his life. ROBBIE ROBINSON

finds himself engrossed in his story, so engrossed that he fails to notice Onaya is drawing energy from him and pulling it into her own body, as if it were sustenance. As their sessions continue over the next few days, Jake discovers that his writing abilities have never been so strong. His physical condition, however, is another matter. Onaya literally is draining his life away.

Odo and Lwaxana's peaceful idyll soon is interrupted by the arrival of Jeyal, who demands the return of his unborn child. Odo counters by announcing that he intends to marry Lwaxana at once, which will annul her marriage to Jeyal and make Odo, and not Jeyal, the legal guardian of the child. Jeyal insists on attending the wedding ceremony. His motivation, Lwaxana explains, is based on the fact that the marriage will be deemed valid only if all present are convinced that the new groom sincerely wants his betrothed.

Odo's friends and Jeyal gather for the ceremony, where he must openly proclaim his feelings. Although his initial attempt isn't very convincing,

CLOSE-UP: No Longer Alone

Re-creating the main title sequence

Dennis McCarthy began composing for *Star Trek* starting with *The Next Generation*'s pilot, "Encounter at Farpoint." Trained as a classical pianist, McCarthy toured with the rock 'n' roll band The Hondells, followed by a nine-year stint with Glen Campbell. He segued into arranging on *The Glen Campbell Hour* television show and later became composer on *Dynasty* and *The Colbys*.

Composer Dennis McCarthy recalls a conversation he had with Rick Berman in 1992. The subject was Deep Space 9— the station, not the series. And the goal was to set a mood. "'This is a lonely outpost,'" McCarthy recites Berman's words from memory. "'There's no activity going on. They're going to discover this wormhole and make something out of the place, but at the moment, it's like being sent to Montana in the winter. It's a place you probably don't want to go.'"

For the next three years, McCarthy's main musical theme for *Deep Space Nine* reflected that conversation, creating a vivid audio portrait of a proud, isolated fortress sitting on the edge of the final frontier.

Then came Season 4, and the once desolate station suddenly was buzzing with activity. Nowhere was that more evident than in the series' refurbished opening title sequence, where viewers were treated to brand new visuals that showed ships gracefully maneuvering around the station, tiny people in environmental suits working outside the towering pylons, and the mighty *Defiant* pulling away from the docking ring, en route to a trip through the wormhole.

The music, too, was different. Bigger, richer, more energetic.

What changed?

"We weren't lonely anymore," says McCarthy with a grin.

The composer is happy to be responsible for both versions of *Deep Space Nine*'s memorable theme. "Originally, the theme was going to be written by Jerry Goldsmith," he explains, referring to the award-winning film and television composer who had penned the rousing theme used in *The Next Generation*. Fortunately for McCarthy, Goldsmith was busy with a motion picture score. "So Rick called me up and said, 'Hey, the ball's in your court,'" McCarthy relates.

Following their initial discussion, McCarthy recalls that he had one question. "I said, 'Do you want to use any of the old Alexander Courage theme [from the original series]?' And Rick said, 'No. This is new territory.'"

As Berman had suggested, the main visual of the station was "this thing, just sitting out there by itself in the vastness of space, very lonely," McCarthy notes. "I came up with the idea of just using this single French horn, doing this rubato [changing the duration of notes slightly, playing some a little faster and others a little slower] slow-paced piece that goes for about thirty, forty seconds, and then gets into the actual theme itself. That's about as lonely as you can get without being maudlin."

Odo soon gathers his resolve and speaks from the heart. His feelings for Lwaxana are sincere; she's the only being he's ever met who seemed to relish how "different" he was from humanoids, rather than fear that difference. Her presence in his life has made him feel less alone, and he wants her to be part of it forever. All present are touched by Odo's words, particularly Lwaxana, and Jeyal relinquishes his claim on both her and the child. Not long after, Lwaxana tells Odo that she is going home to Betazed to have the baby. She is pleased that he cares for her, but she knows that he doesn't love her. Odo is taken aback, but he realizes that she's right and allows her to leave.

After one of his sessions with Onaya, Jake collapses in the Replimat and is taken to the Infirmary. Bashir informs Jake's father, who has just returned to

the station, that something has been stimulating the youth's cerebral cortex to the point of near synaptic collapse. Bashir begins to treat Jake, but during the night, Onaya appears in the Infirmary and takes him away, saying they must finish what they've started. Tracing a mysterious trail of psionic energy, Sisko finds the pair in a small conduit junction, where Onaya has been pushing the dying Jake to keep writing. Phaser in hand, Sisko forces Onaya to move away from his son. Onaya proudly defends her actions, noting that she has touched many minds in her lifetime, all legendary men whose creative potential she helped to unlock. The fact that their immortality came at the cost of their lives is, to Onaya, a fair trade.

Although Sisko attempts to stop her, Onaya takes her leave, transforming herself into an energy being

Dan Curry's elegant visual was equally spare. "I wanted to do a ballet around the station, since that's all we really had to work with," Curry says. Under Curry's supervision, effects house Santa Barbara Studios created a comet, sweeping slowly through the vastness of space. "The camera pans over it," Curry explains, "and then our eyes find the station in the distance. A runabout sweeps by in the foreground, and its trail wipes onto the screen the title *Star Trek: Deep Space Nine*."

Curry hand-inked the title, despite the fact that even in 1993, when the sequence was completed, computer graphics easily could have handled the job. "I still hand-ink a lot of the stuff that I do," he admits, "just to prove to myself that I can do it that way, and to give myself a medieval sense of accomplishment."

The runabout in the original sequence, like the station itself, is a motion-controlled physical model. The fourth season update, however, features *three* runabouts: the original one, and two brand-new computer-generated ships created by VisionArt. The *Defiant*, too, is a CG effect by VisionArt.

"At the time we were working on the new title sequence, Gary Hutzel was supervising the visual effects on 'The Way of the Warrior,'" explains Curry. "There wasn't enough access time to the model for both of us to use it. I let Gary have it and I worked with VisionArt. I pushed pretty hard on issues of lighting and stuff like that, and they were able to create a CG *Defiant* for us that's mixed with the physical model of the space station. I'm positive that most people don't know it's CG. Even people in our Art Department didn't know until I pointed it out to them. VisionArt did a wonderful job of matching the lighting where the ship comes out of the shadows behind one of the pylons. And using CG allowed me to do a couple of moves with the *Defiant* that we couldn't have done with a model, because when a model rolls beyond a certain point, you wind up seeing the model mount."

ILM's John Knoll, responsible for the solar ships that appeared in "Explorers" and "Accession," contributed the little worker bees and the tiny welders toiling on the pylons. 'I made about half a dozen little bits and pieces for the sequence," says Knoll, including, he notes with a smile, 'a generic alien ship with blue glowy engines."

"'Make it bigger, make it stronger,' that's what we talked about," McCarthy says. "We weren't lonely anymore, and the new visuals showed a lot of activity. They were welding and doing stuff and there were a lot of ships running around. One French horn no longer made a lot of sense, so I put all six French horns in. I also added a counterpoint to the bottom end, just put more movement into it in total, and I did some power-chording in all those new downbeats."

The visuals determined the tempo, McCarthy observes. "The original was very slow, and I thought, rather majestic," he says. "This needed to be a little faster. For example, I wanted to hit a very important musical point as the *Defiant* pulls away, and that affected the tempo. But I think it's a bit too fast now, and given the choice, I would slow it down a little bit. I like everything about the new piece, except it doesn't have quite as much *majesty* as it did in the earlier version. The tempo took away some of the depth. That's just my personal taste."

that easily escapes the station. With Onaya gone, Jake begins to recover and allows his father to read his uncompleted manuscript, which he names *Anslem*. Sisko is impressed, although Jake worries that Onaya deserves the credit. His father points out that Jake wrote the words, not Onaya; she may have used her powers to draw them out, but they always were inside him, and still are. When he feels ready, Sisko assures his son, he'll be able to find them for himself.

Just mentioning this episode causes great consternation among members of the *Deep Space Nine* staff. Director David Livingston, for instance, readily confesses, "I think it's one of my poorer efforts. I let the material down, because I just didn't know what to do with it."

"The script had problems," admits Ira Behr, "It went through many permutations. I mean this one went through a *lot*."

It all started when Majel Barrett Roddenberry pitched an idea to several of the principals. "Majel told me that she had an idea about Lwaxana coming back to the station pregnant and that she would claim it was Odo's baby," recalls Rene Auberjonois.

"Majel came up to me at the third-season wrap party," Behr notes. "She said, 'Lwaxana's pregnant.' That started us thinking about a set of stories about love on the station, and about different aspects of desire."

"We began the story break not knowing what the B-story would be, or even if there should be a B-story," says René Echevarria, who wrote the teleplay

The return of Michael Ansara to *DS9* was a treat for viewers and the production staff. ROBBIE ROBINSON

and shared story credit with Roddenberry. "Then we decided to do a very soft show about different romances: Rom and Leeta, Sisko and Kasidy, O'Brien and Keiko. And the fourth romance would be Odo and Mrs. Troi."

"We usually break a story in two days," adds Behr. "A really tough show will take three days, and that's a *really* tough show. This one took at least five days, maybe six. It was the toughest story break of the year."

"I did a story about the four romances and it just didn't gel," says Echevarria. "Nobody was very excited. We decided that the plan was a little *too* soft. Then we started kicking around things to do and somehow a space vampire came up." Echevarria laughs. "I was horrified. I said, 'No! No! I'm not doing space vampires!' But they liked the idea and someone said, 'What if it's Jake's story and she sucks creativity?'"

"We'd wanted to do a Jake story, something about his being a writer," states Ron Moore. "After Majel pitched her idea, we thought about Jake getting involved with a woman (as a subplot). Then we decided that wasn't interesting enough, so we thought, 'Well, we could get him involved with an alien woman who's interested in him because he's a writer.'"

The idea stuck, and the planned four romances became two. "We thought the idea of this muse was an interesting idea, and it started to take over," says Behr. "It was about the dark side of creativity," he notes. "The need to express oneself creatively does tend to have a dark side. Just ask Ernest Hemingway. Ask F. Scott Fitzgerald. Ask Jack Kerouac. Ask Phil Ochs. The list is virtually endless."

But somehow it never quite worked. "The notion of this exotic, beautiful, older woman who comes to you and gets excited by watching you write is like the most *ridiculous* idea!" says Moore in retrospect. "Only a *writer* would come up with that." Moore breaks into laughter at the image. "Think of it. You're sitting there writing away and she's just entranced. We watched that scene in dailies and we thought, are we insane? What are we doing? How did we get *here*?"

Echevarria sighs. "I had no feeling for either story. I just buckled down as a professional and did the best I could. I thought, 'Is this going to seem really silly?' But Ira kept telling me, 'It's gonna work, it'll be fine.'"

About the only thing everyone on staff liked about the muse storyline was the casting of Onaya. "Meg Foster was perfection," Echevarria states. "When we sat down for precasting, Ron Surma

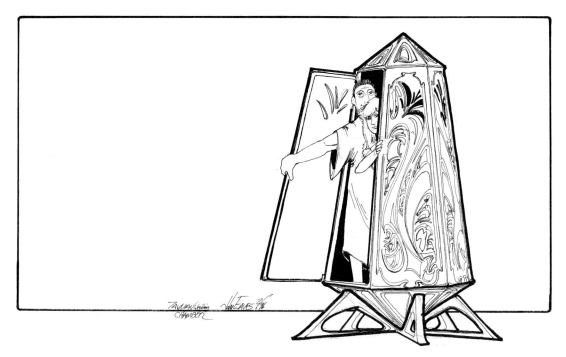

The Tavnian wedding chamber or the box. JOHN EAVES

asked, 'Who do you see as the character?' and I said, 'Meg Foster. I want Meg Foster.' And he said, 'She's available.'"

"She came in and read, and that's always nerve-wracking because sometimes the actors will come in and they don't read well or they have a different take on your words," says Behr. "But Meg came in and she was so seductive and interesting. You know, you can fall inside those eyes."

"Her eyes are a pale, intense blue, and they've probably been a drawback to her," observes Michael Westmore. "They work for her when she plays aliens because it looks like somebody else is behind her face."

Westmore's makeup gave the actress what he describes as an "unhealthy look," which worked well with the wardrobe designed by Robert Blackman. "When we first see the character, she's dying," says Blackman. "She's very frail and very pale. We put her in this dark dress to emphasize that. About halfway through, that dress changes to a lighter color, but you're really not aware of it because her makeup changes, too. It's exactly the same dress, but I lightened it up about four beats so that she appears to change as she sucks the life out of Jake."

The writers had fun creating the muse's "credits." "I knew Rick [Berman] would say to use only one Earth name and two alien names, but after I put in Keats, Robert Wolfe suggested Catullus, which sounded like an alien name, but actually was a Roman poet," Echevarria laughs. "The third one was Tarbolde, which was Ron's suggestion. Tarbolde supposedly wrote the poem that Gary Mitchell recites in 'Where No Man Has Gone Before.' We thought that was kind of fun."

Robert Wolfe, however, was disappointed in the end. "Catullus was a Roman poet in the first century A.D.," he says, "and the Muses were a part of the mythology of that time, so it really *was* a tie-in. Unfortunately, Foster mispronounced the name so now it does sound like some wacky alien."

Many aspects of the Lwaxana Troi plotline changed. "The original notion was that this wedding involved her and Odo having to be together in a box for sixteen hours, standing in a closed casket kind of thing," says Echevarria. "We wouldn't see it, but we'd just know that they did it." The point was that somehow the experience would force Odo to realize he *did* have feelings for her. But Echevarria didn't buy it.

"I remember calling Ira on a Sunday afternoon and saying, 'This is just ridiculous,'" he says. "Why doesn't he just declare his love? What if it's in the ceremony?' And Ira said, 'Okay, forget the box.' The construction department already had started building the box, but we got rid of it and I tried to write something sweet."

But no matter what they did, ultimately, neither

storyline pleased the staff. "We always start with good ideas," asserts Ron Moore. "And there's always a reason why we try something, but they just don't always come out right."

The title for Jake's novel came from René Echevarria. "I wanted something that would imply it was autobiographical, so *Anslem* was the name of the protagonist, who was a young man like Jake," he says. "There was this funny moment at the production meeting for 'The Muse.' David Livingston said, 'I need some lines from the book in case I want to show the pages Jake is working on.' So I told him I'd write something quick and get it to him. And a few minutes later he said to me, 'What is *Anslem* about?' And I said, 'Uh, uh, I'll write that too and get back to you.'"

As it turned out, the lines weren't needed, so Echevarria never bothered to write them. "I still don't know what it's about," he laughs.

Not even Constable Odo knows that the head of Starfleet Security on DS9 secretly works for the Maquis. ROBBIE ROBINSON

FOR THE CAUSE

Episode #494

TELEPLAY BY RONALD D. MOORE
STORY BY MARK GEHRED-O'CONNELL
DIRECTED BY JAMES L. CONWAY

GUEST CAST

Kasidy Yates	PENNY JOHNSON
Michael Eddington	KENNETH MARSHALL
Ziyal	TRACY MIDDENDORF
Brathaw	JOHN PROSKY
Lt. Reese	STEVEN VINCENT LEIGH

SPECIAL GUEST STAR

Garak	ANDREW ROBINSON

STARDATE UNKNOWN

In the station's Wardroom, Starfleet Security Officer Eddington reveals to the senior staff that the Klingon offensive has taken a large toll on the Cardassians. To help them get back on their feet, Starfleet is providing a shipment of industrial replicators that will pass through Deep Space 9. Eddington notes that Starfleet Intelligence believes the Maquis may try to stop the shipment, so Sisko orders Eddington and Odo to tighten up security on the station. The pair then reveal to Sisko that they have reason to believe there's a Maquis smuggler aboard DS9—the evidence points to Sisko's lover Kasidy Yates. The evidence is slim, but convincing enough for Sisko to allow them to contrive a reason

to search her ship. In the meantime, life continues as usual on the station, with the crew watching a springball match between Kira and another Bajoran. However, Garak spends more time watching a member of the audience than he does the game. He's fascinated by a new resident on the station: Ziyal, the half-Bajoran daughter of Gul Dukat.

Because there are old scores to settle between Garak and Dukat, the tailor is not quite sure what to make of his enemy's daughter. His suspicion is piqued when Ziyal invites him to join her in a holosuite program: a reproduction of a Cardassian sauna. But curiosity gets the best of him and he agrees.

When Kasidy tries to leave for her next delivery, Odo insists on making an emergency health inspection of her vessel. Kasidy complains to Sisko that the delay will cause her to miss a scheduled rendezvous. Sisko grants her permission to leave, but immediately after sends the *Defiant* out to follow her ship and observe her actions. While under cloak, the crew of the *Defiant* sees Kasidy's ship change course and head for the Badlands. A short time later, she meets with a Maquis raider and beams over her cargo. When the *Defiant* returns to DS9, Eddington and the others brief Sisko, whose heart sinks at this news of betrayal. A plan is made to follow Kasidy on her next trip out and to arrest her crew and that of the Maquis ship, if they conduct another rendezvous in the Badlands. With the replicators set to arrive at the station shortly, Eddington suggests that he remain on

DS9 to oversee security procedures, and that Sisko man the *Defiant*.

Before Kasidy leaves the station, Sisko makes one last-ditch effort to stop her, suggesting they go away together for a few days. Although she is tempted, Kasidy turns him down, stating that she has to honor her commitment.

With Sisko in command, the *Defiant* follows Kasidy's ship into the Badlands, where it awaits the rendezvous. But when no Maquis ship arrives, Odo suggests that they may be victims of a ruse to draw Sisko away from the station. Sisko orders the *Defiant* to decloak and beams over to Kasidy's ship to question her about her mission. He discovers that Kasidy, too, has been duped—told to bring urgently needed supplies to this location despite the risk of exposing herself as a Maquis. Too late, Sisko understands the motives behind the elaborative scheme and rushes back to the station, leaving Kasidy behind.

Eddington, who himself is a Maquis, eliminates the only potential opposition to his plan by stunning Kira with a phaser. With all of the station's security personnel under his command, he easily takes possession of the replicators and removes them from the station. By the time Sisko returns, he's long gone. Later, Eddington contacts Sisko to let him know that the Maquis's quarrel is with the Cardassians, not Sisko or the Federation. But the communication only serves to increase Sisko's cold anger at the turncoat, and he vows to see him court-martialed.

Sisko's reaction is warmer when Kasidy turns herself in at the station. Although she could have escaped when he left her in the Badlands, she's returned to tell Sisko that she loves him and is willing to face punishment for collaborating with the Maquis. Sisko promises her that he will be waiting for her when she returns from prison.

A happier interlude occurs in the holosuite, as Garak cautiously meets Ziyal, uncertain as to the young girl's motives. She could, after all, be planning to kill him. But Ziyal reveals that she has no interest in her father's vendetta against Garak; she merely wants to share his company. Garak decides to trust her, and the two take the first steps toward friendship.

Over the years, many of *Star Trek*'s twenty-third- and twenty-fourth-century story-lines have been inspired by twentieth-century events. While the phrase "ripped from today's headlines" doesn't exactly apply to *Deep Space Nine*, writer Mark Gehred-O'Connell has no difficulty pinning down the exact news story that inspired "For the Cause."

"The impetus was actually the Oklahoma City bombing," he recalls. "What struck me about it was that for the first few days after the event, everyone was so sure that it was foreign terrorists. Anyone who appeared Middle Eastern suddenly was under suspicion for no reason at all. The explosion itself was terrible enough, but to have that sort of reaction made it even more awful." A few weeks later, Gehred-O'Connell, who has contributed several stories to *DS9*, transformed his feelings about the experience into a story pitch regarding a terrorist attack on the station. "In a situation like that, who would they immediately suspect? What if it turned out to be the last person in the world to come to mind? I just wanted to play with that idea. And it ended up being a story where Kasidy Yates turns out to be the number-one suspect."

The story went through some changes. The terrorist attack went away and the focus of the piece became the level of trust between Sisko and Kasidy, and how Sisko would react to being told that the woman he loved seemed to be a criminal. "Once you sit down and actually start turning an idea into a five-act story, it can very quickly lose all resemblance to the initial idea," admits Gehred-O'Connell. The final product may not appear to have a lot to do with the Oklahoma City bombing, he says, "but that's what got the wheels turning in my head."

The freelancer pitched the story to Ron Moore, who ultimately wrote the teleplay. "Ron liked it," says Gehred-O'Connell, "but he wasn't sure if they'd be able to use Actor Penny Johnson again in the near future." Some seven or eight months would pass before he got the phone call from Moore confirming their interest in the story. "I thought it was an opportunity to really put Sisko into a vice," says Moore. "I wanted to make it as hard as possible on him. Start him out in bed with the woman he loves. He's a happy man. And then those guys come to him and say they suspect this woman is in the Maquis. He doesn't want to believe it, but as soon as they've said it, it throws suspicion into the relationship."

Was it risky taking an established character into an unanticipated direction? Not really, according to Ira Behr. "We knew we had to give the audience something they wouldn't expect, and that's Kasidy. The story also involved revealing Eddington as a member of the Maquis, and it seemed to us that people would expect that."

"Sisko loves Kasidy and he tries to give her a way out," says Ron Moore. ROBBIE ROBINSON

So, was Kasidy's established personality thrown out just to keep viewers guessing for a bit longer? "It may *seem* like we just take characters and do with them whatever we want," says Behr, "but Kasidy's character made it totally believable; a strong independent woman like her could break the rules."

What seemed more risky, surprisingly, was setting a scene with Sisko and Kasidy together in bed. "It became an issue," comments Behr, aware of the irony. After a season that had featured what may have been the hottest kiss between two female characters in the history of television, there were concerns over allowing a male and female to do what comes naturally. But Behr got the scene through, noting that Gene Roddenberry certainly had been one of the strongest proponents for open sexual behavior in the future. And after all, this clearly wasn't a case of sex for sport. "No one was going to believe that of Captain Benjamin Sisko and Captain Yates," notes Behr.

There was more to the story than the Sisko/Kasidy relationship, however. Gehred-O'Connell attributes much of the rest to Ron Moore, who had requested that the freelancer flesh out his tale with a few additional twists. One involved adding a "Klingon threat" of some sort to the plot. The other concerned unmasking Eddington as the new leader of the Maquis. "The series hadn't done anything with the Maquis all season," explains Gehred-O'Connell, "and the producers wanted to reintroduce them. This seemed like a good episode for that."

The Klingon subplot, which would have established that the Maquis were now in cahoots with our temporary enemy, eventually was dropped. The Eddington storyline, however, came to fruition, fulfilling the spark of an idea that had come to the writers during the scripting of "The Adversary."

"Eddington was supposed to be a benign adversary for Odo," says Behr. "He was supposed to be the greatest security officer that Starfleet had, and he was going to step on Odo's toes. But frankly, by the time of 'The Adversary,' they were just so alike, and it was constricting them both. And then there was that speech where Eddington congratulates Sisko on being made a captain, and how that's what everyone wants to be."

The subtext to that scene implied that for some reason Eddington was aware that he would not be get-

"Garak is a dangerous man," Moore explains. "And yet there's something about him that Ziyal is attracted to." ROBBIE ROBINSON

ting that same opportunity. And with that subtext, the writers found a new direction to take the character. "We started to see more about him," says Behr. "What if this guy who we originally conceived to be as true blue as possible suddenly realizes that there's something better out there? So we took the character to the point where he's capable of doing questionable things to achieve some greater morality." Behr and the others saw Eddington as "a farther side of Sisko," someone who at some point found his loyalty torn between some clear, admirable goals and something else.

Beyond the Maquis plotline, the episode featured a B-story concerning Garak and Ziyal, this time played by Tracy Middendorf in the same foam latex facial prosthetics originally created for Cyia Batten. And although viewers had heard of springball before, they finally got to see it. In addition to the expense of building a new set (and taking the time to shoot something approximating a game), the crew had to come up with some rules of play.

"We had to determine how you get a point, how you beat your opponent, what the scoreboard does when the ball hits a certain part of the wall and more," says Steve Oster. "Those are the things you do by sitting down with the special effects guys who are operating the scoreboard and saying, 'Okay, when the ball hits that red square there, let's put up this yellow stripe here.'"

"We decided it was sort of like full-contact handball," says Director James L. Conway. "Theoretically, there's a force field between the court and the audience. So we had to design shots, sometimes with a real ball and sometimes with an optical ball, so it'd

hit the back wall and we could see a little light effect and then it could bounce back in."

Kasidy's freighter, located on Stage 18, was built, at least in part, from pieces of Sisko's old ship, the *Saratoga*. As usual, the Art Department added a special touch. "There had been references about how the *Xhosa* was an old ship," says Scenic Art Assistant James Van Over. "So we mimicked the old blinking lights from the original series on the ship's control panels. [Scenic Artist] Doug Drexler and Mike Okuda made me watch episodes of *Star Trek* over and over again to make sure the timing was right on how they blink."

Another casual tribute to the original series was Ron Moore's line regarding Tholian punctuality (first noted in "The Tholian Web"). And Ira Behr added a tribute of his own to two of his all-time favorite baseball teams: the 1961 Yankees and the 1978 Red Sox.

THE QUICKENING
Episode #495

WRITTEN BY **NAREN SHANKAR**
DIRECTED BY **RENE AUBERJONOIS**

GUEST CAST

Ekoria	ELLEN WHEELER
Epran	DYLAN HAGGERTY
Norva	HEIDE MARGOLIS
Attendant	LOREN LESTER
Tamar	ALAN ECHEVERRIA
Latia	LISA MONCURE

SPECIAL GUEST STAR

Trevean	MICHAEL SARRAZIN

STARDATE UNKNOWN

While on a bio-survey mission to the Gamma Quadrant, Kira, Dax, and Bashir pick up an automated distress call from a planet in the Teplan system. When they beam down to investigate, they discover the planet's entire populace is inflicted with a deadly plague. A woman asks them to help her get to the hospital, but when they arrive, they realize that it is more of a hospice than a hospital, and that the facility's healer, Trevean, does not cure people. Instead, he eases their suffering by poisoning them when they "quicken," or reach the final stage of the blight.

Bashir feels there must be a way to save the inhabitants, but Trevean assures him there is not. The

His discovery of a terminal disease sets Dr. Bashir on an apparently
hopeless quest. ROBBIE ROBBINSON

the years, there have been too many false promises of a cure, followed by a far more painful death than Trevean offers. Finally, a young man named Epran agrees to allow Bashir to study him, and he convinces several others as well.

Bashir sets up a makeshift clinic and injects everyone with an antigen that he hopes will be a cure. At first there seems to be some improvement, but then Epran and the others get much worse. Bashir discovers the virus is mutating from the electromagnetic field generated by his instruments and he shuts everything down. But it's too late; the damage is done. Epran dies a horrible death, and the others beg Trevean to end their agony with his poison. The caretaker complies while Bashir looks on, devastated by his own inability to end their suffering.

With Kira due to return shortly, Bashir thinks the best thing he can do is to leave the people in peace. But after he finds out that Ekoria has quickened, he gains new resolve and tells Kira and Dax to go back to the Alpha Quadrant without him.

With Ekoria his only patient, Bashir continues his studies. He is disappointed when he notes that her bloodstream shows no trace of the antigen he's given her; he assumes that her immune system has rejected it. Although she grows weaker every day, Ekoria hangs on to life for a few more weeks, just long enough for Bashir to induce labor and deliver her child. She witnesses a miracle before she dies; the child is born without any trace of the blight. The antigen had been absorbed through the placenta, which means that the offspring of other pregnant women can be innoculated within the womb. Thanks to Ekoria, a new generation will be born without the blight, and the suffering on her world finally will end.

blight always is incurable, and has been for two hundred years, ever since the Jem'Hadar decided to make an example of the planet by contaminating it with the terrible disease. All of the people are born with it. Some die young, some live long enough to bear children. The distress signal they heard was initiated two centuries earlier; no one remembered its existence, and no one expects to be saved.

Realizing they are unwanted, the landing party prepares to leave, but Ekoria, a young pregnant woman, approaches and asks for their help. She wants to live long enough to deliver her child. Will they help? Bashir and Dax agree to stay and try, while Kira is sent away with the runabout so as to avoid detection by the Jem'Hadar.

With Ekoria as a volunteer, Bashir begins to study the disease. He quickly isolates the virus that causes the blight, but because Ekoria is still in the dormant phase, he finds himself at a dead end. Bashir needs to study some victims who have quickened, but at first he finds that no one will volunteer. Over

The 1995 motion picture *Restoration*, about a seventeenth-century doctor torn between his duty and debauchery, struck a chord with Ira Behr. Shortly after seeing it, he suggested to his staff that they write an episode about "Dr. Bashir on a plague planet."

"I wanted to do a show about a man who thinks he has the answer and who is humbled," Behr recalls. In addition, one of the show's office assistants, Gregg Long Duffy, recently had died of AIDS. "And," says Behr, "my wife Laura works closely with AIDS Project Los Angeles. The whole AIDS thing was on all of our minds, so we just wanted to come up with a disease that breaks your heart."

The writing staff was busy, so Behr contacted

Auberjonois cites the influence of Renaissance painters in his placement and positioning of actors. BARRY McLAUGHLIN

and rookie. Small things like that help me to focus when I'm creating characterization."

The title, however, had to go. "Naren's title gave away that somehow Bashir would solve this problem," says René Echevarria. It was Echevarria who came up with the new title after he noted the double meaning of the word "quicken." "When the disease becomes active, it 'quickens,'" he explains. "And, of course, 'to quicken' also means 'to come alive,' and that's what the show ultimately is about. It's a neat word, because it means both things. Bashir does heal them; the children will not have the disease."

While the finished show contains imagery that is almost ecumenical in nature, Behr, Shankar, and Echevarria insist that none of it originated in the writing. Actor Alexander Siddig recognized it in the aired episode, but notes, "It didn't occur to me while we were shooting. That was Rene Auberjonois's subtle thematic touch." Director Auberjonois made some of his stylistic choices when he realized that Bashir's healing people in the streets was not unlike Jesus performing miracles. "In fact," Auberjonois says, "Ekoria was a bit like the Virgin Mary, so I tried to place her where she would look like a holy picture. She stands in front of a rounded arch window, which almost looks like a halo around her head. With my grandfather being an artist, and my father being a poet, I'm very influenced by visuals like that. Jonathan West shot it beautifully. We tried to get a sort of Vermeer look to it," he says, referring to the Dutch painter's work.

While Behr occasionally feels disappointed with the way a promising episode turns out, this time he was very pleased. "A lot of things really came together in 'The Quickening,'" he says happily. "I mean, the sets were unbelieveable. The production values did not let us down. So much of it worked!"

Because the series' regular production designer, Herman Zimmerman, was at work on *First Contact*, the task of building those wonderful sets fell to Art Director Randy McIlvain. It was hardly a pleasant experience. In fact, it was much more difficult than anyone had anticipated. Key among the problems was some uncooperative weather, which caused a number of delays at the mountaintop location site in the northwest corner of the San Fernando Valley. "We trekked everything up to Rocketdyne [a U.S. government shuttle rocket testing facility] and created this city with twenty-foot walls," says McIlvain, "and then it started to rain." The water-based paint washed off, he laments, "and we couldn't use any electrical saws

freelance writer Naren Shankar, who previously had been science advisor and story editor on *The Next Generation*. After the story break sessions, Shankar wrote a script that he titled "The Healing Touch," which dealt with "a race of people who are doomed to get this horrible disease from the day they're born," the writer says. Shankar opted to modify the AIDS parallel to a certain degree. "I didn't give the sense that the people were outcasts or pariahs, which is how AIDS patients are often perceived."

Shankar's script would be modified extensively before shooting got under way, but a number of his pet details remained, including some interesting word play. "Trevean is an anagram for 'veteran,'" Shankar points out. "I wanted him to be a grizzled old vet, the guy who has seen more than anybody else." And his original name for Ekoria was Ekorio "That's an anagram for 'rookie,'" he notes. "Veteran

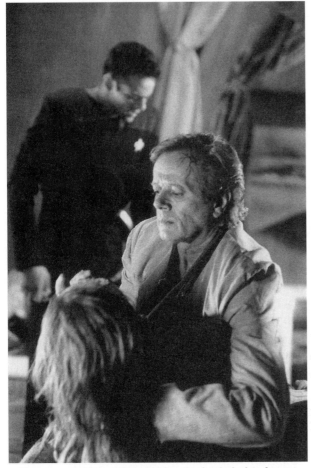

"You can see in Michael Sarrazin's face that he's had a lot of experiences in his life," notes Auberjonois. BARRY McLAUGHLIN

or equipment. "It was raining so hard that we couldn't see—for three days!"

The shooting company had to wait for the sets to be rebuilt, which put Auberjonois off schedule. "The set was destroyed by rain, I had seventy extras, I had never shot on location before, I was working on a crane, *and* we had to turn the schedule around," the director says. "You'd think that's where I'd fall apart, but this was, for me, my breakthrough as a director. It's the first time I really had a handle on it.

"I was very interested in the conflict between Trevean, who I saw as a sort of Dr. Kevorkian figure, and Bashir," Auberjonois continues. "What I loved about it was the ambiguity. I didn't take sides. The doctor's whole purpose is to preserve life at whatever cost, and this man was helping people to die with dignity, so you saw each man's point of view."

"For Bashir, this story was a lesson in abject arrogance and how blinding it can be," says Siddig. Prior to this episode, he observes, "Bashir had only suc-

ceeded. He always won. He always got his man. So it was very interesting for him not to be able to do that."

Bashir's "benign arrogance," as Behr puts it, comes from his Starfleet mentality. "It's that 'we can fix the problems of the world' thing," Behr says. "Like the Peace Corps. We're not only the cops of the world, we're the doctors of the world. Our morality will save the world. We really believed that during the Kennedy era. It was a national illusion."

Bashir believes in the Starfleet philosophy, although the reality of the situation soon set him straight. One thing that can be said about Bashir, notes Siddig, "is that he usually keeps a positive outlook on a situation. Even within that horror, he kept on plowing along."

"It *was* a horror story, basically," comments Behr. "It's about this genetically engineered plague and the hubris of a doctor who thought that he could just come in and be a hero. Of course," Behr says, thinking of the fifth-season episode "Doctor Bashir, I Presume," "had we known then that *he's* genetically engineered, it would have been really cool."

Even a genetically engineered human has his soft side, and viewers were introduced to one aspect of Dr. Bashir's: his teddy bear Kukalaka. The bear itself wouldn't be seen until a year later, in "In the Cards," but we learn his unusual name. The genesis of the name is somewhat embarrassing to Echevarria, who came up with it as a tribute to an old friend. "He once told me that as a child he had an invisible friend, and I *thought* its name was 'Kukalaka.' So I showed him a tape of the show, thinking he was going to be delighted." Unfortunately, Echevarria's memory had been faulty. Kukalaka turned out to be the name of a cat belonging to his old friend's ex-flame.

More painful than an unintentional faux pas, of course, was the illness on the planet, particularly when it reached the "quickening" stage. The producers wanted the quickening effect to look horrendous, and, thanks to the wonders of postproduction computer multilayer compositing, it did. That may not have been quite as apparent to the actors on the set, who saw people like Actor Dylan Haggerty, as Epran, performing with white dots stuck to his face. Strange, perhaps, but not quite horrendous. "The spots were used to track in the burning elements, the blisters," explains Gary Hutzel. Hutzel's team made the pseudo blisters by spraying a mixture of baking soda and vinegar onto a sheet of Plexiglas against a black background. The effects team then replaced the white

John Eaves's rendering of the blighted city.

dots with the bubbly "spritzes," and followed up by animating veins that followed the actor's facial contours.

"The technique was relatively new," points out Judy Elkins. "Previously we would have had to do a lock-down shot and get the actor to stay still and do all these cross-dissolves like in the old werewolf movies." With the new method, says Elkins, "An actor can be moving around and it won't interfere with the effect, because the computer program can track the points on his face."

Although "The Quickening" was a particularly somber episode, Behr feels that every episode should have at least a bit of humor. "In this one, we knew we had to do it right at the beginning," he says. But what would be fun? Robert Wolfe threw out the suggestion that Quark could be doing some kind of advertising, and Echevarria actually wrote a fake commercial for the teaser. Unfortunately, it went on for too long. "Rene Auberjonois said, 'This is funny, but I think it

Early version of Quark's merchandise. JOHN EAVES

should be just a silly little jingle,'" recalls Echevarria. "Then he improvised what he meant. He literally said the words, 'Come to Quark's. Quark's is fun,' and that was what wound up being used."

"I thought that it should be something totally inane and annoying," confirms Auberjonois with a smile, "and we just made it up on the spot. Armin [Shimerman] made up the tune."

TO THE DEATH

Episode #496

WRITTEN BY IRA STEVEN BEHR &
ROBERT HEWITT WOLFE
DIRECTED BY LeVAR BURTON

GUEST CAST

Toman'torax	BRIAN THOMPSON
Virak'kara	SCOTT HAVEN
Weyoun	JEFFREY COMBS

SPECIAL GUEST STAR

Omet'iklan	CLARENCE WILLIAMS III

STARDATE 49904.2

Sisko forms an uneasy alliance with the Jem'Hadar. ROBBIE ROBINSON

Returning from an arduous face-off with Breen privateers at a Bajoran colony world, Sisko finds that Deep Space 9 has been ravaged by a Jem'Hadar strike force. Although his crew is exhausted, Sisko knows he must take the *Defiant* in pursuit of the station's attackers.

As they track the strike force, they come upon a badly damaged Jem'Hadar warship and beam aboard its survivors: six Jem'Hadar and a Vorta named Weyoun. The Vorta tells Sisko that his vessel was attacked by the same marauding Jem'Hadar that hit DS9, and he offers to lead Sisko to them—*if* Sisko will help Weyoun "eliminate" the renegades.

The rebellious Jem'Hadar are a threat to the Dominion as well as the Federation, Weyoun reveals in private. They are trying to restore a recently discovered Iconian gateway, an ancient transportation device of immense power. Whoever possesses the gateway can move instantaneously across great distances, without the use of a starship, and ultimately employ it to overpower both the Dominion *and* the Federation. Reluctantly, Sisko agrees to help Weyoun destroy the gateway.

Sisko's officers are skeptical about the plan, which hinges upon keeping Weyoun's Jem'Hadar, who know only that they are pursuing some traitorous Jem'Hadar, in the dark about the gateway and its implications. But, as Sisko points out, there is no alternative. He meets with the Jem'Hadar first, Omet'iklan, to make sure he understands that while on the *Defiant*, and on the mission to destroy the traitors, Sisko is in charge. Omet'iklan agrees to accept Sisko's authority temporarily. After the mission is over, however, there are no guarantees.

Sisko conducts a drill to prepare his team for the attack, but it doesn't go well. Omet'iklan suggests they fight in mixed teams, but Weyoun refuses, fearing they will learn about the gateway and join their rebellious brethren. Omet'iklan reveals that his men already know all about the gateway, but their loyalty to the Founders is absolute.

With mixed teams there are mixed results, which culminate in a deadly match between Worf and Toman'torax, the Jem'Hadar second. Sisko and Omet'iklan break up the fight, and the first punishes his officer, in a manner befitting Jem'Hadar discipline, by breaking his neck. But Sisko would never inflict the same punishment on Worf. Omet'iklan observes that Sisko should die in Worf's place, and promises to see that he does when the mission is over.

Prior to arriving at Vandros IV, where the gateway is located, Weyoun approaches Odo and tells him that his people still wish him to return to the Great Link. The Vorta offers to make that possible for Odo, but the changeling refuses.

The *Defiant* reaches its destination, and Starfleet and Jem'Hadar teams beam down. But they quickly discover that their phaser weapons and combadges have been rendered inoperative by the gateway's damping field. Hand-to-hand combat with bladed weapons is the only alternative. A group of the renegade Jem'Hadar attack. They enter into a bloody battle, slowly making their way into the Iconian ziggurat that houses the gateway. As they near their target, Sisko is wounded when he gets between an enemy blade and Omet'iklan. The First can't understand why Sisko would risk his life to save a man who has sworn to kill him, but there is no time to ponder; O'Brien has set an explosive that is about to go off, destroying the gateway.

With the gateway gone, all weapons resume functioning, and Sisko's crew uneasily faces their armed Jem'Hadar counterparts. They are joined by Weyoun, who has noted their success from the ship and beamed down to inspect the site. Suddenly, Omet'iklan turns his phaser on Weyoun and disintegrates the Vorta—payment, he explains, for questioning the loyalty of his men.

As for Sisko, there is no payment to be exacted. Omet'iklan has decided to put an end to the killing for the day. But as the *Defiant* team departs, the First warns Sisko that the next time they meet, they will be enemies once again.

Casting Clarence Williams III, explains Behr, "[gave us a] wonderful actor to help us explain a little bit about the Jem'Hadar, and who they are." ROBBIE ROBINSON

"**O**ur main purpose in 'To the Death' was to give more dimension to the Jem'Hadar," says Robert Wolfe, who wrote the story with Ira Behr. "Our intention was to show that the more you learn about them, the less you *want* to be around them." Wolfe notes. "If you meet the Borg on a one-on-one basis, they're kind of cuddly, and when you get to know the Klingons they're not so scary anymore. But the Jem'Hadar, when you really get to know them, are damn scary guys."

Director LeVar Burton had to learn about the Jem'Hadar during preproduction, because he'd never before encountered the species. "I had to look at previous episodes to understand who they were and what their relationship to the Founders is," he admits. The research inspired him to call on Clarence Williams III, known for his role on the sixties series, *The Mod Squad*. "He's an old friend of mine, but we'd never worked together before," Burton smiles. "This was just an opportunity to say, 'Hey, CW, you want to come and do this thing?'" Burton's casting was perfect, not only with his Jem'Hadar choice, but with his Vorta choice as well. "We had a hard time casting the character Weyoun," he says. "We read a lot of people and it just wasn't gelling." Then inspiration struck. "It was like, 'You know what? Jeffrey Combs!'" Burton smiles. "We all just knew that he could do it."

Combs, of course, was known for his portrayal of Brunt. He'd recently completed the episode "Bar Association," directed by Burton, and he was set to play the Ferengi again in the upcoming episode "Body Parts." So when Ira Behr paid him a visit, Combs didn't immediately believe what he heard.

"Ira said, 'We really like what you're doing with Brunt, but we also want you to come back as a character who's more identifiable as you,'" Combs recalls. "I thought, 'Yeah, right.' I mean, this is Hollywood, and I thought that was just his way of complimenting me, not really anything that I would hold any substance to. But sure enough, they called and asked me to do this new character, Weyoun. That is the highest compliment an actor can be paid, to hear that they believe in your versatility to the point that they'll let you do two characters in episodes back to back, and that they trust you'll be different."

"With the ubiquitous, inimitable, multitalented Jeffrey Combs, we finally had a Vorta who sold the Vorta," Ira Behr enthuses. Unfortunately, the character died at the end of the script, but he was so good, they decided to bring him back as a clone the following season.

It's clear that Combs enjoys playing the Vorta. "Weyoun is the snake of the universe," he laughs. "He's the smiling car salesman who'll tell you anything to make you feel as if you're the most important thing in his life just to get you to buy his product."

Where did Combs find the inspiration that makes his Vorta portrayal outshine all previous attempts? "I'd seen a great movie, Stanley Kubrick's *Barry Lyndon*," he says. "There's a sequence at the court with all the proper sort of etiquette. Everyone has it out for everyone else, but they say things with such grace and kindness! That's the way I wanted to approach Weyoun, half car salesman and half court fop."

"It's a wonderful performance," says Behr. "Jeff took every moment of threat and made it jaunty, and every moment he was supposed to be suave, he was crazy. The scene between him and Rene Auberjonois is one of my favorites."

While Burton enjoyed many aspects of the production, he admits that it was an extremely tough episode for him. "We had a day of location shooting that was my worst day as a director, because there was so much work and so little time," he says. "There was a huge number of people on location, including all of these Jem'Hadar who require major makeup and two major fight sequences to stage. All were elements that felt like they conspired to just bite me in the ass."

B.C. Cameron felt the same pressure. "LeVar and I went out to Griffith Park's bird sanctuary the night before and walked the sets," she says. "I remember thinking, 'There's no way we're gonna get all this work done. We had twenty-five Jem'Hadar stuntmen who had three-o'clock makeup calls.

"We spent the whole day at the top of the bird sanctuary, and the only way up and down was by golf cart," Cameron continues. "The cast trailers and the honeywagon [restrooms] were way down below. So if anyone went down, we had to wait and wait to get them back up again. Logistically, it was a nightmare."

Some of the location work wasn't finished during daylight, including several close-ups that would be completed later on in front of trees stationed on the soundstage. But one other shot *had* to be done on the hill, no matter what. "Jonathan West had said to me, 'When the sun drops behind that ridge, we'll lose the light and we're done,'" says Cameron. "We just kept pumping along and he kept saying, 'We're losing the light, we're losing the light.' Finally it was pitch black and I do mean *pitch* black. We had to do a single on Avery, so Jonathan lit him with a huge silk beside him, reflecting a blue light shining from behind the trees. Suddenly it looked like broad daylight against a blue sky. "I said, 'Jonathan! I will never believe you again,'" Cameron laughs.

The fight scenes, by all accounts, were phenomenal, but some of them never aired. "This is the first

The nature of syndicated television required the level of violence to be scaled back. ROBBIE ROBINSON

episode of *Deep Space Nine*, and maybe the first *Star Trek* ever, that was edited for violence," Ira Behr states. "Close to forty-five seconds of the hand-to-hand combat was cut, and I think that really hurt it. We built up to this battle and now it's just too perfunctory." Making matters worse was the fact that the audience sensed the edits. "The fans who wrote letters on the Internet saw that the rhythms were thrown off," he says.

"This episode should have been the biggest action show ever," Stunt Coordinator Dennis Madalone laments. "We had all the manpower, and LeVar got it all on film. We made it violent and rich just like 'Battlelines' and 'Blood Oath.' In the first edited version, fifty-two Jem'Hadar had been killed. Dax had killed ten and Sisko had killed seven. But when the censors got hold of it, they took out thirty-two Jem'Hadar deaths."

A lapse in memory by the writers caused a rush of corrective activity just before shooting. The final script mentioned that the creators of the 'gateway' were from the Tkon Empire, first seen in the *TNG* episode "The Last Outpost," so the Art Department based all of their graphics on established Tkon designs, including a large Tkon symbol mounted on a wall. "The day before it was shot, they changed the script to say it was the Iconians," reports Denise Okuda. The Art Department staff hastily duplicated a design that had been used for the Iconians. The replacement material made it to the set just in time for filming.

"We'd picked the wrong empire," Robert Wolfe laughs. "We knew that there was this ancient empire from *TNG* that had gateway technology, and we wanted specifically to reference it. We just picked the wrong one."

BODY PARTS

Episode #497

TELEPLAY BY **HANS BEIMLER**
STORY BY **LOUIS P. DESANTIS &**
ROBERT J. BOLIVAR
DIRECTED BY **AVERY BROOKS**

GUEST CAST

Keiko O'Brien	ROSALIND CHAO
Rom	MAX GRODÉNCHIK
Molly O'Brien	HANA HATAE
Brunt	JEFFREY COMBS

SPECIAL GUEST STAR

Garak	ANDREW J. ROBINSON

STARDATE UNKNOWN

As O'Brien anxiously awaits the return of his pregnant wife, Keiko, from a botanical expedition to Torad IV, Quark returns from a two-week trip to Ferenginar, where he closed a vole belly deal, visited his mother, did some shopping, and received the results of his annual insurance physical. Unfortunately, those results indicate he has a rare affliction known as Dorek syndrome, leaving him less than a week to live and very little time to pay off his debts. His brother Rom urges him to list his desiccated remains on the Ferengi Futures Exchange to raise capital. Quark doubts anyone will buy them, but realizes he has little to lose.

When the *Runabout Volga* returns, O'Brien hears that it took severe damage in an asteroid field, and that Dr. Bashir has had Kira and Keiko beamed directly to the Infirmary. Rushing over there, O'Brien is stunned to learn that Kira is now carrying Keiko and his baby in her womb. Bashir explains that Keiko suffered serious internal injuries in the accident, and he had to quickly find a new home for the baby or risk losing it. The transfer has been a success, but Kira will have to carry the baby to term, rather than Keiko.

Meanwhile, Quark finds that he was right about his remains, which aren't exactly a hot commodity. But suddenly he receives an anonymous bid of five

Arriving at the Divine Treasury, Quark learns a new way to interpret the Rules of Acquisition from Grand Nagus Gint. ROBBIE ROBINSON

hundred bars of latinum—a generous offer—and he quickly accepts it before the bidder can change his mind.

Not long after, Bashir delivers a message from Quark's physician: Quark doesn't have Dorek syndrome after all. He's not dying. Before the bartender has the opportunity to fully enjoy his "recovery," he receives a surprise visit from his nemesis Brunt, liquidator for the Ferengi Commerce Association and, not so coincidentally, the anonymous bidder for Quark's remains. Quark explains that the diagnosis was a mistake, but Brunt doesn't care. He wants Quark's desiccated body and doesn't intend to leave without it, because, as a Ferengi Rule of Acquisition states, a contract is a contract is a contract. Quark has only two choices: he can die within six days, thus fulfilling his contract, or he can break the contract, comiting an unforgivable sin in Ferengi society that will render him a pariah among his people.

While Quark struggles with his decision, Keiko and Miles make a decision of their own. They ask Kira to move into their quarters until the baby is born, so that they can be close to their unborn child. After some thought, Kira agrees.

Quark makes what is, for him, the easier decision. He'll fulfill the contract by dying. To assist him in that effort, he enlists Garak, who uses a holosuite program to show him a variety of assassination options. Quark doesn't like any of them—too loud, too smelly, too savage. Finally, he admits that he'd like his death to be a painless surprise, and Garak assures him that option can be arranged. That night, as Quark returns to his quarters, he anticipates death at every turn. He enters his quarters nervously, then lies down on his bed . . .

. . . only to find himself in the Divine Treasury, the Ferengi equivalent of the afterlife. Quark assumes that Garak has killed him, but he is quickly set straight by an ancient old man who claims to be Gint, the first Grand Nagus, but who bears an odd resemblance to Rom. Gint reveals that Quark isn't dead, he's dreaming, and that he should break the contract with Brunt.

Quark is horrified; how can he break the precepts upon which all Ferengi society is based? But Gint points out that the Rules of Acquisition are nothing more than *suggestions* as to how the Ferengi should live their lives. Then Brunt appears to remind Quark of the consequences of breaking the contract. Quark awakens in a panic, overjoyed to discover that he's still alive, but sobered by the realization that he must make a decision.

Later, Quark confronts Brunt and returns his five hundred bars of latinum (plus interest), effectively breaking the contract. Brunt proceeds to seize Quark's assets, and slaps a notice on the wall of the bar, warning all that no Ferengi can do business with Quark. The bar is systematically stripped of every bottle, every piece of furniture, every glass.

As Quark sits in the empty bar, pondering his depressing future, Bashir arrives with a case of brandy that he doesn't want. Then Dax arrives with glassware she hates, and Sisko comes by to see if Quark is willing to store some extra furniture in the bar. Before long, the bar is once again filled with assets, and he is forced to accept the fact that possessions aren't the only valuable commodity in the universe.

The writing staff of *Deep Space Nine* always strives to reach what Ira Behr refers to as "the bottom of the show." What Behr means, of course, is an episode's *substance*, or the illusive quality of "what an episode ultimately is about." "Body Parts," according to Hans Beimler, "is a classic case of what Ira is always looking for. The substance is that Quark has a line that he will not cross. He has a very clear ethical code and he lives by it." And, of course, the Ferengi is pushed to the very edge when the code he lives by threatens his life. "This is a com-

"No one's ever asked me to play 'John Boy,' but that's actually closer to my real personality," chuckles Jeffrey Combs. GREGORY SCHWARTZ

edy, but it deals with some very serious business," Beimler says. "Quark is a very complicated guy with a lot of complicated issues. He's not just a silly Ferengi. The more you explore the character, the more you see that he's very sophisticated and complex."

"The original pitch [by Boston-based freelancers Louis P. DeSantis and Robert J. Bolivar] sounded like a B-story joke," comments René Echevarria. "It was, 'Quark thinks he's going to die and presells his body parts. Then he finds out he's not going to die.' We really dug down to find what it was about, and in the process, we managed to find out who Quark is, and how Ferengi he is."

"Quark has always believed that he's an outsider on the space station, and that the only thing that's his own are his Ferengi ways," Armin Shimerman expounds. "He believes in the Ferenginess of himself. So to give that up—because a contract is a contract is a contract—is a major moral dilemma. And that's what I tried to play, although within the context of humor. I also tried to make it an 'everyman' sort of lesson, because it's my belief that Quark is the most human of characters, and I feel that hidden away in the writer's minds they have the same belief."

Shimerman is always ready and willing to share insights about his character, particularly when he's asked to play against his own instincts. He cites as an example his decision in "Body Parts" to show no reaction in a scene where Brunt insults Quark. Director Avery Brooks was puzzled by Shimerman's choice. "Avery took me aside and said, 'Hey this guy's just insulted you,'" recalls Shimerman. "'Aren't you going to react?' And I said, "'Avery, *your* character would take umbrage if he was insulted. But my character is insulted every episode, every day. If he's to survive in this particular environment, he must slough off insults, otherwise he'd be in fights every day.' And that was a surprise to Avery. Once he was aware of that, his bent on my character went a slightly different direction."

Brooks sees the give-and-take of such discussions as a normal function of directing. "Any preconceptions that I have," he says simply, "can be completely erased once I've watched what two actors will do." Brooks notes that his method of handling dialogue, whether delivering it or directing it, is to "talk about what's underneath it. You can't play the words," he says, "because there's nothing to play. You've got to play something else. There's something else that motivates us to speak, that motivates us to do things. To make decisions. To act." And that's the directorial imperative that guided him with Shimerman's performance.

"Body Parts" gave Actor Jeffrey Combs the opportunity to push the developing character of Brunt. "I wanted him to be really delighted in being bad," laughs Combs, "I wanted him to be lascivious and just relish his own evil intent." Just as Behr is interested in finding "the bottom of the show," the actors are interested in finding the "bottom" of their characters. "I don't take on a character and say, 'OK, I'm going to be funny,'" Combs comments. "I look at the character and ask what it is about the character that *is* funny or that can be funny. Whatever comedy there is comes out of who this person is, not necessarily something that's laid on top merely for the sake of humor. I'm not interested in that. The comedy of Brunt comes out of his joy of causing harm to Quark, and just tormenting him."

As the scriptwriter for the episode, Beimler, too, examined Brunt's heart and soul in order to produce a realistic portrayal. "Brunt is intolerant," Beimler says. "Quark grates him because Quark has been able to do things that Brunt doesn't think of as pure or quite right. It's the way certain people view expatriate

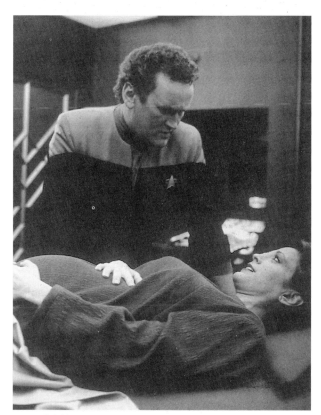

While the actors took Visitor's pregnancy in stride, Meaney's character seems not to. GREGORY SCHWARTZ

Americans who may have traveled and had a different life experience. They say, 'How could you leave America?' So he spent fifty-five years in Africa, that doesn't mean he stopped being an American, he's an American experiencing another life. And that's what Quark is. He's gone out of the Ferengi world, but it doesn't mean he's stopped being a Ferengi. But people like Brunt are envious and jealous of him."

The B-story in "Body Parts" would have a more resounding impact on the series than the A-story. "We had learned shortly before we got to work on this show that Nana was pregnant," Ron Moore explains. "By happenstance, we had just made Keiko pregnant ('Accession'), and we didn't want two pregnant women walking around the station. So we wondered what we were gonna do. Gates McFadden had been pregnant during one season of *TNG*, and it had meant sticking her behind a desk in a lab coat all the time. We sure didn't want to do *that* to Nana."

"We didn't know what to do," admits Ira Behr, "especially after we'd just had an episode about Lwaxana being pregnant ('The Muse')." Behr discussed the problem with Rick Berman, but neither of them liked the idea of going with the obvious: having Kira's pregnancy be the result of her relationship with

Shakaar. But nothing else immediately came to mind. Finally, Berman told Behr to go home for the night and think about it. Behr did what most married men do when they get home: he told his wife Laura about his day. "And without batting an eyelash, Laura said, 'Well, why don't you just take the baby out of Keiko and put it into Kira.' And I said, 'Baby, you're the greatest!' And I kissed her and the music came up." Ralph Kramden impression aside, Behr was so taken with the suggestion that he immediately called Berman at home and the creative wheels started spinning. "I want Laura Behr to get full credit, in print, for the idea," Behr states.

After Behr called Berman, one of his next calls was to Andre Bormanis, the man who could, presumably, devise a credible way to make Laura's idea work. Bormanis was a bit nonplussed by the call. "I said, 'Oh my God, don't make me do this. I don't know nothin' about birthin'—or transportin'—no babies.'" Bormanis chuckles at the memory now, but at the time he wasn't sure what to do. Nevertheless, he made a phone call to his pathologist friend John Glassco, who'd helped him out before with medical queries. "After he stopped laughing," Bormanis says, "John said that we should transport the whole fetal placental complex, and that there'd have to be certain things done for the blood chemistries." But given the technology, Glassco thought it *might* be possible. Of course, you can't please everyone. "My uncle the surgeon thought it was pretty ludicrous," admits Bormanis.

But it was much more relevant what Kira's doctor, and coincidentally the baby's real father, thought of the solution. "Teleporting the baby was a great idea," Alexander Siddig says happily. "And if it were really possible, think of all the noninvasive transplant procedures one could do!"

Nana Visitor was tickled by the whole thing. "Suddenly my baby was part of the plot!" she says, laughing. "I was very grateful that they thought of such a clever way to allow me to be pregnant on the show and not just be filmed from the neck up, which really would have limited everything I could do. I'm hugely grateful for that," Visitor smiles. "The writers took it completely in their stride, that their warrior was going to have a baby. And they made it work brilliantly."

"Body Parts" marks the first time that Andrew Robinson began using a middle initial for his official credit. "My middle name is Jordt, in honor of my grandfather," Robinson reveals. "He was a guy that I loved and to whom I owe a lot. So I just decided that it was the right time in my life to make the change."

BROKEN LINK

Episode #498

TELEPLAY BY ROBERT HEWITT WOLFE & IRA STEVEN BEHR
STORY BY GEORGE A. BROZAK
DIRECTED BY LES LANDAU

GUEST CAST

Founder Leader	SALOME JENS
Gowron	ROBERT O'REILLY
Aroya	JILL JACOBSON
Freighter Captain	LESLIE BEVIS
Amat'igan	ANDREW HAWKES

SPECIAL GUEST STAR

Garak	ANDREW J. ROBINSON

STARDATE 49962.4

 Responding to a summons from Garak, Odo arrives at the tailor's shop to find no sign of criminal activity, only a Bajoran woman whom Garak wants to introduce to the constable. After Odo explains to the Cardassian that he has no interest in entering into any "mating rituals," he turns to leave and abruptly collapses in pain.

An examination by Dr. Bashir determines that Odo's mass and density are in an abnormal state of fluctuation, but not the reason behind the malady. All Bashir *does* know for certain is that moving around seems to increase the fluctuation, so he orders Odo to remain in the Infirmary. Odo grudgingly obliges, until Kira brings him the day's criminal activities report and the security chief notes an item of interest. He arrives at the cargo bay just in time to intercept the shady Boslic freighter captain and her crew. But before he can arrest them, he again is stricken down by the mysterious affliction, and the captain escapes.

Odo's condition deteriorates rapidly, and Bashir admits that there's nothing he can do for him. They both come to the conclusion that Odo's only hope is to return to his people, so Sisko volunteers to take the changeling to the Gamma Quadrant on the *Defiant*. Once there, he will transmit a subspace signal explaining the purpose of the visit . . . and hope for the best. At the last minute, Garak asks to accompany Sisko's crew, hoping to find out if there were any survivors of Cardassia's ill-founded attempt to attack the Dominion the year before ("The Die Is Cast").

The crew doesn't have long to wait. Soon the *Defiant* is surrounded by a half dozen Dominion warships, and the ship is boarded by a group of three

The female shape-shifter temporarily relieves Odo's suffering.
ROBBIE ROBINSON

Jem'Hadar and one changeling: the same female that Odo has encountered in the past.

The female informs Sisko that she's come to take Odo home to her world; only the Great Link, she says, can restore him. Protective of his friend, Sisko refuses to allow her to leave with Odo, so the Founder permits the *Defiant* to continue its voyage, albeit "blindfolded," as it were, by a device that prevents the ship's navigational computers from recording the route. The female then meets with Odo and stabilizes his condition by linking with him briefly. The effect is only temporary, she points out; he must join with the Link or die.

Odo realizes that the Founders caused his illness so he'd be forced to return home and enter into the Great Link. Once there, he will be judged for having killed another shape-shifter ("The Adversary"), the first of his kind to have ever done so. As she leaves Odo to ponder his fate, the Founder is confronted by Garak, who inquires about Cardassian survivors. The female contemptuously informs Garak that there were no survivors, and that all Cardassians were doomed the moment they attacked her people.

When they arrive at the Founders' planet, Sisko informs the female shape-shifter that he and Bashir will accompany Odo to the surface and await the results of his "judgment." After they beam down, they watch Odo and the female melt into a sea of goo and disappear. This is the Great Link, the united whole of Odo's people.

On the *Defiant*, Worf forcibly prevents Garak from attempting to destroy the Founders' planet with the ship's formidable weapons, despite the fact that it would save the Alpha Quadrant from the growing Dominion threat. Later, Sisko and Bashir watch in amazement as the Great Link expels Odo from its midst. Bashir's tricorder readings indicate that the security chief is now *human*, and the female changeling explains that this is Odo's punishment. He chose to align himself with the solids, she says, so he has been transformed into one. His face, however, will remain as it always has been, smooth, unfinished, and not quite human, to remind him of who he was and what he has lost.

Returning to the station, Odo realizes that it will take some time to get used to being human, and he realizes something else, as well. While he was in the Link, he sensed that the changelings were attempting to hide certain things from him. Observing Gowron, the Klingon chancellor, delivering an inflammatory speech via the station's monitors, Odo understands what one of those things was. The head of the Klingon Empire, which is now poised on the verge of war with the Federation, is a changeling!

The original series has Spock, *The Next Generation* has Data, and *DS9* has Odo: the outsider, the other, the entity who can comment on the foibles of humanity precisely because he *isn't* human. But there the similarity ends, for Spock was the half-human who wished to be a pure Vulcan, and Data was the android who wished to be a human. "Odo is the anti-Pinocchio," quips Robert Hewitt Wolfe. "He's the wooden boy who wants to be a better wooden boy. He wants to be a better changeling. He wants to be the best shape-shifter he can be. He never had any real desire to become a human, which is why becoming one is actually a tragedy. But then, it *is* a punishment."

Punishment was the central theme of freelancer George A. Brozak's pitch for "Broken Link," the idea that the Founders would take Odo to be judged for commiting what was, to them, an unthinkable crime: killing another changeling. Thus, exactly a year after that killing occurred ("The Adversary"), Odo would at last receive retribution. To the staff writers, it was clear what Odo's punishment should be. "The only appropriate punishment would be to make him a solid," says René Echevarria. "So we thought, okay, let's do that for five or six episodes."

Actually, it would be more like twelve episodes

The writers wanted to establish Odo's importance to the Founders, so they sent the female shape-shifter. BARRY McLAUGHLIN

before they got to "The Begotten," the episode in which Odo regains his powers. But that gave the writers time to fully explore Odo's deepest emotions, something Ira Behr, who cowrote the teleplay with Wolfe, had wanted to do for some time. "I think that there has been in Odo's personality a strong strain of wanting to overcome his fascist Founder tendencies," Behr says. "His isolation. His sense of self. His sense, dare we say it, of superiority. And the desire to commit and connect to those around him. I think he has that inside him and has always been a bit afraid to do it. But now suddenly we take the primary barrier away from him. And there's positive and negative things about it."

But although Odo is transformed in the episode, one thing that doesn't change is his face. And there's a reason for that.

"Taking away the powers of one of the most popular characters on the show was a bold thing to do, especially since we don't give them back to him in the

next episode," says Behr. "And we knew it was going to be tough [to convince the powers that be]. But to take away that face, which to me, is Odo, you'd not only take away the powers, you'd take away the character." The rationalization provided in the script is that they leave that face to remind Odo of how much he's lost, something that Behr claims is just one of "the many ways, both macro and micro, of making the Founders deliciously evil and calculatingly clever. Odo can never forget what he's left behind for a second."

The illness that forces Odo to travel to the Founders' new homeworld was nearly as much punishment to Actor Rene Auberjonois as it was to DS9's resident changeling. "We made a series of latex appliances that had a drip effect, which we then glued onto his original prosthetic face," explains Makeup Artist Dean Jones. Then we went back and put Methicil, a drippy, slimelike substance, on top of that." The melting effect was done in stages: "First we had just a little bit of drip with the prosthetic, and by

The isle on the Founders' world where Bashir and Sisko await Odo's judgment. JOHN EAVES

the time we got really heavy into the 'meltdown,' we added the Methicil, which runs and drips. It's normally clear, but we added some pigment to it so that it would look Odo color."

"Makeup and Wardrobe each came up with various ways to make it look like he was dripping and melting," says Steve Oster. "We assigned them to do various stages, like 'Here he's in stage one, here he's in stage two, here he's in stage three.' In the final stage we'd goo him up and tell him, 'Just lie there.' Rene, bless his heart, was very patient with us. In the scene where the female shape-shifter comes to see him in the *Defiant* sickbay, he's barely able to hold his shape and he looks like a big wax candle that's been melted. Rene was just lying there with all this goo in the hair and the goop on the face—he was just dripping. The things we do to actors!"

Auberjonois also had to perform a "near-nude" scene for the episode. "I wasn't completely naked," he admits. "I was in what they call a posing strap. It was flesh-colored and I might as well have been naked. That sure taught me something. We take it for granted that when women have to be naked or very

exposed in plays or movies that it's all part of the business. But suddenly I really understood it. I'm a middle-aged man who has to lie there practically naked and I was very uptight over whether I would look all right. I remember lying there and I sort of looked around to see what everybody was doing. Nobody was at all interested. There were guys over at the craft services table getting a doughnut, a cup of coffee. The camera people were talking. No one was looking! If it had been Dax or Kira," Auberjonois concludes, sounding a little miffed, "it would have been quite another thing."

But although appearing nearly nude wasn't exactly his cup of tea, Auberjonois did love performing the scene. "I was trying to convey Odo's amazement," he says. "All these emotions that are going through him, what it must be like suddenly to have a body and feel things inside him and outside him, and all the senses, like smelling and tasting, which he's never had before." He compares Odo in that scene to a newborn, "but not an infant," he says. "I was a newborn adult. It was wonderfully challenging, trying to communicate all these feelings. It was exhilarating for

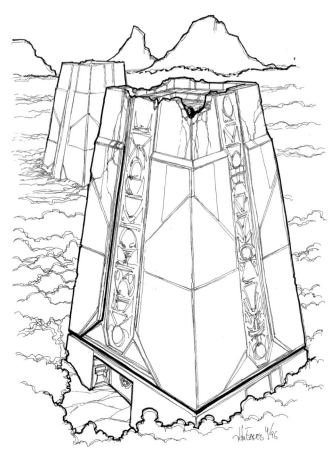

The proposed new Founders' homeworld. JOHN EAVES

concurs Behr. "It goes with the whole 'sense of order' concept of the shape-shifters."

Other elements the writers originated in the script weren't quite as "emotionally impactful," but they were there for a reason. The character of Chalan Aroya, for example, may have seemed a mere bit of window dressing to viewers. But according to Ira Behr, her introduction, at least initially, had a more basic purpose.

"It was our first effort in the path to get Odo involved," he says. "We thought, 'Wouldn't it be great if he has a relationship when he's a human?'"

Unfortunately, the producers ultimately decided that Chalan Aroya wasn't the right woman for Odo. "She was totally sweet," says Auberjonois of Actor Jill Jacobson, who played Chalan. "But as good as she was as an actress, the writers felt that her character wouldn't work for an ongoing relationship." The writers eventually did get around to their plans for Odo in "A Simple Investigation." However, they chose "a much more businesslike, efficient person for him," comments Auberjonois. "She's sort of in the same business as Odo."

In a lighter vein, the episode also establishes that pregnant Bajorans experience sneezing fits rather than morning sickness. The humorous interlude was there, of course, to give Major Kira some business in an episode that would take most of the rest of the crew away from the station. But it also gave the writers the chance to have a little fun. "We didn't want her to have the same pregnancy symptoms as humans," Behr explains. "Robert [Wolfe] wanted her to stink! It was a *great* idea, that she'd give off this aroma, but it was just too much. I was afraid that neither the powers that be nor the feminists would understand our sense of humor. So we went with the sneezing thing. Sneezing is incredibly annoying, and it's also somewhat silly."

This meant that Nana Visitor has to perfect her "method" sneezing techniques. "It didn't work out too bad," she giggles. "I never know if I can do something like that until I do it." By this time, Visitor was into her second trimester of pregnancy, and experiencing many of the same feelings as her alter ego. "It was difficult when the rest of the team would go off on the *Defiant* and I'd be stuck at home because I couldn't do the physical activity. It wouldn't make sense for Kira to be able to go along, and I got as antsy as Kira would have gotten. I felt left out."

Fortunately, it was the last episode of the season, and following the summer hiatus, Visitor would only

him, yet at the same time he was terrified, filled with a great sense of loss. He's lost something of himself, but he's gotten something else."

Auberjonois liked playing another scene almost as much: Odo's walk through the Promenade. As the script explains, "the last thing he wants to do is show weakness in front of the people he's sworn to protect." Auberjonois took that to heart. "My image for the walk was Alec Guinness in *The Bridge on the River Kwai,*" he says, referring to the sequence in which Guinness, although suffering terribly, holds his head high as he walks past his men and his captors. "That's what this scene was about to me," Auberjonois notes. "A person trying to hold himself together."

While it might have been easier to simply beam Odo over to the *Defiant,* the writers very much wanted Odo to take that walk. "We explained that they couldn't beam him because his state would be disrupted," says Wolfe. "But that was because we wanted to show Odo's pride."

"The grandeur and emotional impact of it was the image of this man who was going to hold on,"

have to appear in a few more episodes before the birth of baby Django (named for famed jazz guitarist Django Reinhardt).

But the most significant detail the writers inserted into the episode was its very brief tag: the idea that Gowron, chancellor of the Klingon Empire, is a changeling. Odo's revelation handily set up the plot for the fifth-season opener, "Apocalypse Rising," in which the crew ventures into Klingon territory to find out the truth. "It's funny," says Behr. "We wrote that Gowron was a shape-shifter in 'Broken Link,' but we ultimately decided to change it to Martok, because we wanted to protect Gowron, so that we could continue to use his character. But then we saw J.G. Hertzler again and said, 'He's really great. We've got to find a way to use this character and actor again.'" That led, of course, to some of the events in fifth season's "In Purgatory's Shadow."

The Klingon plotline was important to the writers. "We were in the process of realizing how we could change the situation with the Klingons, and essentially bring an end to the Klingon war," says Echevarria. "We wanted to close the chapter on it and get back to what the franchise had been, which was Cardassians and Bajorans. It hadn't occurred to us yet to ask the question, 'What if the Cardassians joined the Dominion?'"

FIFTH SEASON
O V E R V I E W

Season 5 found the human machinery that powers <u>Deep Space</u> *Nine* pounding away on all cylinders, turning out episodes of increasing dramatic power— and funny stuff, too. In front of the cameras, there were pyrotechnically dazzling space battles, Klingons itching for a good fight, tribbles looking for a good home, duplicitous changelings, traitorous Cardassians, intergalactic war, a new baby . . . and Captain Kirk and Mister Spock. Behind the scenes, there was the thirtieth anniversary of *Star Trek,* new directors, new writers, new technological advances, new casting, a new baby, and an attempt to maneuver the series back toward the road it had been on when fate had forced a detour away from an inevitable confrontation with the Dominion. "Season 4 threw us for a loop, with the whole Klingon thing, and bringing Worf into the show," states Executive Producer Ira

Steven Behr. "So the seminal thing about our fifth season opener was that we wanted to get back on the track we'd anticipated being on a year earlier. We were moving back toward making the shape-shifters and the Dominion our enemies. Not the Klingons. I didn't want to have the Klingons as our enemies."

But at the same time, Behr didn't want to give people the wrong impression about the series, that it was flip-flopping on its true heading, nor did he want to negate the writing staff's efforts over the past year.

"We wanted to let people know that we didn't switch horses in midstream," he explains. "So 'Apocalypse Rising' was an important episode. By having that shape-shifter in there, we were saying, 'Season 4 wasn't a mistake. It wasn't the Klingons [turning against us]. There was a shape-shifter behind it all along.' And that's why we *had* to do that episode." Even as they began making plans for this major change at the end of fourth season by setting up the "Gowron as changeling" premise in "Broken Link," fate once again intervened, with the decision to make an episode celebrating the thirtieth anniversary of *Star Trek* ("Trials and Tribble-ations"). Everyone on staff quickly fell in love with the premise the writers conceived, a visit to the original series episode "The Trouble with Tribbles."

"Coming into year five, the 'Tribbles' show dominated our thinking," admits Ronald D. Moore, who started the year as supervising producer and moved up to co-executive producer at midseason. "It really influenced everything that was happening in the first few episodes, because we constantly had preproduction meetings about the 'Tribbles' show." Even in the writers' meetings that *weren't* related to "Tribbles," the subject somehow always came back to the "Tribbles" show, he notes. "It overshadowed everything for a while. Word would come back from someone's office about some detail, and we'd start talking: 'I don't think we're gonna be able to do it; I don't think we're gonna get the money; I don't think so-and-so's gonna sign off.' Just one thing after another. 'I don't think we can build the sets; I don't know if we can track this thing down; maybe you should try something else.'"

Once the producers received the green light to proceed with "Trials and Tribble-ations," a new complication arose: should 'Tribbles' be the first show of the new season? The producers discussed the pros and cons of that option. "We originally wanted to open the season a week earlier than usual and air 'Tribbles,' which would have tied us closer to the thirtieth anniversary [September 8, 1996]," notes Behr. "Then after that, we would catch up [with the established continuity] and show 'Apocalypse Rising.'" Instead, the decision was made to hold the episode for the fall sweeps period, which would give the word on the show more time to build.

The decision paid off, with 'Tribbles' providing *DS9* with its highest household ratings in three years. The episode ranked number one for its time period in New York and number two in the key markets of Los Angeles, Chicago, and San Francisco. But although it garnered critical raves and a number of award nominations, "Trials and Tribble-ations" was unable to bring home the gold at either the Emmy awards (where it lost out in Outstanding Visual Effects, Art Direction, and Hairstyling for a Series) or the World Science Fiction Convention's Hugo Awards (where it was beat out for Best Dramatic Presentation).

In retrospect, Behr has no regrets about the time and energy expended by everyone on "Trials and Tribble-ations." "It was a terrific show, terrific on every level, from the writing to the acting to the production, and terrific in the way that we were able to salute the original series," he says. "The only thing that bugs me about it is that it feeds off the myth of the franchise, and the fact that it's so popular saddens me in a way, in the sense that I wish that a show that is *Deep Space Nine* intensive didn't have to lean on the history. But it is a great show."

With all the hoopla over "Tribbles" and the thirtieth anniversary, another landmark event received considerably less fanfare. The series' one hundredth episode, "The Ship," aired the week after "Apocalypse Rising," and three weeks before "Trials and Tribble-ations."

Ironically, the season's less publicized offerings would have far more impact on the storylines carrying into later seasons. "Looking for *par'Mach* in All the Wrong Places" would launch the relationship between Worf and Jadzia, "The Ascent" would bring Nog back to *DS9*, while "Rapture" would do the same for Kasidy Yates. "Doctor Bashir, I Presume" would reveal that the good doctor is genetically enhanced, and "Call to Arms" would launch the war against the Dominion. "In Purgatory's Shadow" and "By Inferno's Light" would give the producers the opportunity to resurrect Martok, or rather, to introduce the "real" version of the character who'd been impersonated by a changeling, and also to add J. G. Hertzler to the series' growing repertory of recurring guest actors. The events of "The Begotten" not only would restore Odo's shape-shifting abilities, but also see Kira give birth to the O'Briens' son, Kirayoshi.

The latter element gave Nana Visitor the opportunity to shed the pregnancy pad she'd been wearing since the birth of son Django a few weeks earlier, which was a mixed blessing. "It was time to go back to the one-piece uniform that would show all the late-night baked potatoes I'd had," sighs Visitor. "But [costume designer] Bob Blackman and I decided that it was kind of nice for women to see that there's an aftereffect to pregnancy. So many times on television, women are pregnant and then—boom!—they're back to a size eight. And I know in real life that happens to some women, but certainly not *all* women and certainly not me!"

While Visitor was pleased with the way the writers had worked her real-life pregnancy into the show's ongoing plotline, in retrospect she feels they missed out on one important aspect of the situation. "During the whole baby span on the show, I just wished that there were more scenes between Keiko and myself," she says. "My oldest son, Buster, has a stepmother, and the dynamic between us is fascinating. It's such an important thing, two women being responsible for a child and sharing that child. I suppose if you haven't lived through it, it would be a hard thing to perceive. And also, it's not 'The Kira Show,' after all. It's about going out on the *Defiant*, and doing battle."

Behr likes to think it's about a bit more than that. "We always talk about the characters, and what's the most interesting, dramatic way to tell a story," he says. "None of the writers want easy answers. We try not to go too much by the book, not to create too much white noise. I mean, we're working in a medium that is guilty of many things, and that's never far from my mind. We want the shows to have something *to* them."

One way of keeping people interested was Behr's decision to recruit new directors. After using many of the same reliable people for years, suddenly Behr and Beimler were bringing in people that no one had heard of before, at least not in association with *Star Trek*: Allan Kroeker (*Tekwar*), Victor Lobl (*Beauty and the Beast, Max Headroom*), John Kretchmer (*Buffy the Vampire Slayer, Charmed*). and Jesús Treviño (*NYPD Blue, Chicago Hope*). There also were a few names from the *TNG* era: Gabrielle Beaumont, responsible for such shows on that series as "Booby Trap," "Disaster," "Face of the Enemy," and "Lower Decks," and Michael Vejar, who had directed "Coming of Age" in the first season of *TNG*. And there were a few new members of the production's director-in-training program, namely, Andrew J. Robinson, Michael Dorn, and Alexander Siddig.

The new directors seemed to relish the challenge that *Deep Space Nine* represented. "Ira said they wanted new energy and fresh thinking," recalls Victor Lobl, director of "For the Uniform." "So that made it fun, to come in and be given a certain amount of latitude to bring my own style to a show that was already sort of on autopilot." Allan Kroeker confesses that he knew little about *Star Trek* when he began working on the show ("The Assignment"), but that didn't stop him from becoming one of the producers' favorite directors, with helming duties on the all-important season finales for the next three years. It must have been something in his style, he guesses. "I get a lot of inspiration from jazz, which someone once said is rehearsed improv," he says. "You work, work, work on the scales and then you get there and you improvise. But you can't really improvise unless you've done the homework and gone through the arduous work of planning the whole thing in your head."

Another new face was Visual Effects Supervisor David Stipes, who had filled in for departed Supervisor Glenn Neufeld on fourth season's "To the Death" and "Broken Link," and became his official replacement in Season 5. If Stipes's name seems familiar, it should; he worked on the sixth and seventh seasons of *TNG*. Visual Coordinator Adam Buckner followed Stipes aboard.

Over in the producer's office, the departure at the end of this season, of Robert Hewitt Wolfe—who'd been elevated from co-producer to producer at the start of the season—left an opening that would be filled by writers Brad Thompson and David Weddle, who had successfully completed a number of freelance assignments. Wolfe, who left for a production deal at 20th Century Fox, departed without severing his friendship with the staff. He would contribute one last episode to *Deep Space Nine* during the series' final season: "Field of Fire." There were other changes among remaining staffers. Producer Beimler was elevated to cosupervising producer at the start of Season 5, and Supervising Editor J.P. Farrell—no relation to Terry—became coproducer. Art Director Randy McIlvain continued to fill in for Production Designer Herman Zimmerman while Zimmerman completed his work on *First Contact*.

In the executive offices, both Rick Berman and Ira Behr signed development contracts with Paramount at the end of the season. Berman's five-year deal charged him with developing and producing feature films, television series, and telefilms for network, syndication, cable, pay TV, and new media ventures. Behr's three-year overall development deal with Paramount Network Television focused on drama series and long-form projects for television.

On the awards front, in addition to the three Emmy nominations for "Trials and Tribble-ations," *Deep Space Nine* received two additional Emmy nods, for Outstanding Makeup and Outstanding Cinematography for a Series (both for "Apocalypse Rising"). The show lost on both counts, but picked up esteemed awards from different organizations. "Call to Arms" received the International Monitor Award for Best Electronic Visual Effects in Film and Television Media, from the International Telemedia Society. The Society of Motion Picture and Television Art Directors presented an inaugural award for excellence in production design to Herman Zimmerman for his work on the series.

APOCALYPSE RISING

Episode #499

WRITTEN BY IRA STEVEN BEHR &
ROBERT HEWITT WOLFE

DIRECTED BY JAMES L. CONWAY

GUEST CAST

Gowron	ROBERT O'REILLY
Martok	J.G. HERTZLER
Gul Dukat	MARC ALAIMO
Damar	CASEY BIGGS
Burly Klingon	ROBERT BUDASKA
Head Guard	ROBERT ZACHAR
Towering Klingon	JOHN L. BENNETT
Drunken Klingon	TONY EPPER
Young Klingon	IVOR BARTELS

STARDATE UNKNOWN

Dukat sneaks the disguised Sisko, Odo, Worf, and O'Brien into Klingon space. ROBBIE ROBINSON

Starfleet Command takes Odo's revelation that Gowron has been replaced by a Founder ("Broken Link") very seriously. With the battle between the Klingon Empire and the Federation heating up, Starfleet decides that an infiltration team must be sent into Klingon territory to expose the truth. Their choice for the dangerous mission: Captain Sisko. They provide him with four small polaron emitters designed to project a field that will cause a changeling to revert to its natural gelatinous shape. All Sisko has to do is get himself and three members of his senior staff past the large enemy fleet surrounding Klingon military headquarters on Ty'Gokor, avoid detection long enough to set up the emitters, and get Gowron to walk into the field.

Getting past the fleet is the easy part. Dukat can take Sisko and company to Ty'Gokor in his bird-of-prey ("Return to Grace"). The Cardassian also can create Klingon identities for them and add their names to a list of candidates for the Order of the Bat'leth, a ceremony that Gowron will be presiding over on Ty'Gokor in just a few days. Before they leave DS9, Bashir surgically alters the captain, O'Brien, and the now human Odo so that they all look like Klingons. The doctor also modifies Worf's appearance, so the other Klingons won't recognize him.

En route, Worf attempts to drill the team on Klingon behavior and finds it an uphill battle. When they arrive at Ty'Gokor, Dukat leaves the four "Klingons" on their own. They attempt to fit in as best they can until Martok—Chancellor Gowron's most trusted advisor—arrives, meaning the chancellor himself isn't far behind. It's time to set up the

emitters. After several close calls in which members of the team narrowly avoid detection, the emitters are in place. But just as Sisko is about to activate them, he hears Gowron call out his name—or rather, the name of his Klingon cover identity. He steps forward to receive the Order of the Bat'leth from the chancellor, then returns to his place, where he once again prepares to trigger the emitter.

Suddenly, he is struck from behind. Martok has recognized him! All four men are imprisoned and the polaron emitters destroyed. Later, Martok comes to their cell, troubled. He's angry that Sisko's mission failed, because Martok, too, has had doubts about Gowron. Perhaps the Klingon leader *has* been replaced by a changeling. However, without the emitters, there's no chance of establishing the truth—unless someone kills Gowron. Once he's dead, he'll revert to his natural form and eliminate all doubt. Worf suggests that Martok could challenge the chancellor to honorable combat and kill him. But Martok says that it should be Sisko and the others who dispatch Gowron, and he helps them to escape. When Worf attacks Gowron, the chancellor's guards move in to help him, but Gowron insists on fighting Worf alone. This is the behavior of a true Klingon, who values honor above his own life. Sisko and his men understand that and hold their fire. Surprisingly, Martok does not understand, and Odo suddenly realizes that it is Martok, not Gowron, who is the changeling infiltrator.

Odo exposes the traitor, and Sisko fires on the changeling, as do others in the room. The fake

Martok explodes in a mass of burning changeling protoplasm. The Founders' plan becomes clear to all: They misled Odo into thinking Gowron was a spy, hoping the Federation would destroy the Klingon chancellor and leave changeling Martok in charge of the Empire and the Empire at the Federation's throat. Sisko urges Gowron to call off the war that the false Martok helped to instigate, but Gowron notes that Klingons never turn back from battle once it has begun. Still, he agrees to call a temporary cease-fire and has Sisko and the others returned safely to DS9.

"**N**ow that we had Worf aboard, and we'd made a commitment that the Klingons were part of *Deep Space Nine*, we had to find out what their role was and try to use them effectively," says Ron Moore. "'Apocalypse Rising' was our first major attempt to do that." But although Moore ostensibly was *Star Trek*'s "Klingon guy," Ira Behr and writing partner Robert Wolfe took on the chores for the season opener. "I like to do the first and last episodes of the season," Behr acknowledges. "I think that the guys like to come back to a new season and not have to jump right in and be the ones on the firing line to get that first show up. And I want to be sure that the first show has a good chance of being something that I can live with, so it's just easier if I'm involved. The buck stops here."

Moore didn't mind. He was about to get started on his own Klingon saga, a new twist on *Cyrano de Bergerac* ("Looking for *par'Mach* in All the Wrong Places"). Besides, he notes, "I may have the *reputation* of being the Klingon guy, but other people have good takes on them, too. And it's good to have more than one writer developing an entire culture. They bring something else to the party, and ultimately that enriches the whole franchise." Moore did provide input for the episode. Audiences learn in the teaser that although station command falls to Kira when Sisko is away, Worf commands the *Defiant*. "That didn't just *happen*, it wasn't just something that Ira and I wrote down," laughs Wolfe. "That was a *huge* discussion."

"It's something that Ron felt was important," admits Behr. "We haven't really played it up all the time on the series, but it's there. It came about when we were in the process of defining Worf's duties. In real command situations, the captain would not always go on dangerous missions, so Worf commands the *Defiant*, in deference to Sisko."

"Essentially, he's the first officer of the ship, while Kira's the first officer on the station," adds Wolfe.

"Michael's had nine seasons of putting up with me," grins Robert O'Reilly, "and we play off each other very well." ROBBIE ROBINSON

"That gave Worf something specific that he did as tactical officer."

Behr also attributes to Moore the fact that Martok, rather than Gowron, ultimately was revealed as the changeling in the Klingon government. "I think Ron's loyalty to *TNG* made him a little bit nervous about killing off Gowron, which is what we thought we'd have to do with the guy," says Behr. "He came to me after the story was broken and said, 'You know what? Can we make it Martok instead of Gowron? We ended Season 4 saying that Gowron was the changeling. And if we do a whole episode about going to kill Gowron the changeling, there's no surprise for the viewers.' Which was true, so I said, 'Yeah, sure. Why get the [*TNG*] fans freaked out.'" Of course, in an interesting bit of irony, Moore himself would ultimately contribute to Gowron's death in the series' seventh season ("The Dogs of War").

So Behr and Wolfe went back and added the Martok twist, "which turned out to be the best thing we could have ever done," Behr states emphatically.

O'Reilly feels that on *DS9*, Gowron was more of a political animal, almost Machiavellian. BARRY MCLAUGHLIN

"Because I really think J.G. Hertzler is great, and it paid off in dividends."

"This is the show where we fell in love with J.G. Hertzler as an actor," explains René Echevarria. "It was like, 'Hey, this guy is terrific. And here we are *killing* him.' But actually, we were killing a changeling, which started us thinking, 'If he's been replaced, where's the real guy? Maybe he's not dead. Maybe we can find him.'" And they would, soon enough, in "In Purgatory's Shadow."

Although "Apocalypse Rising" was, in essence, the sequel to "Broken Link," Behr and Wolfe originally planned the season opener as a two-parter. "We broke it that way," confirms Wolfe, "but I can't remember why. And when it became a one-parter, we had to squeeze together everything that we'd planned on doing in two. We'd have been a lot better off if we'd been able to budget the sets and makeup and costumes over two episodes, but it *was* action-packed," he laughs. "There was a lot of plot to cover that we just slashed mercilessly. There was supposed to be a lot more with Dukat. In fact, most of part one would have been about their adventures on Dukat's ship while he takes them to Ty'Gokor. Then, at the end, we would have made a much bigger deal about them getting into their 'Klingon look.'"

Giving Sisko, Odo, and O'Brien the Klingon look may have delighted the fans, but it didn't delight the actors. "It was a rocky start [to the season]," sighs Behr. "It was one of those things that you just have to get past, because it's just different points of view. We, being the ridiculous writers that we are, thought the actors would be amused by it. But they were extremely unhappy, although they wound up doing fine."

"Oh, it was *hideous*," laments Colm Meaney. "When they put that forehead prosthetic piece on me, I couldn't close my eyes. It's like they were glued open! It was driving me crazy. I was bitching and moaning so much. And then my final major...uh, tantrum, you could say," he chuckles, "was about my nails, because they'd darkened down my hands and I thought my nails were ruined. I remember that Michael Dorn was very much looking forward to the fact that we would get to experience what he has to go through every day and he would get to gloat. But after two days of experiencing *me* in that makeup, he was saying, 'Never put Colm in that makeup again.'"

Dorn wasn't the only one who took pleasure in his fellow actors' discomfort. "It was gratifying to see them so miserable," observes Rene Auberjonois with more than a touch of malevolent glee. "Colm usually gets to wander into makeup five minutes before it's time to shoot and they put a little powder on him and out he goes. And here he was just whining and carrying on, and it made me happy as a Cheshire cat." Ironically, Auberjonois *liked* being in the Klingon makeup. "It absolutely validated my contention that *my* makeup is the most uncomfortable," he snorts. "That Klingon stuff was a piece of cake! It was completely comfortable. The only mildly uncomfortable aspect about it was the teeth, which I could pull out between takes."

Auberjonois was equally effusive about the makeup while on the soundstage, which made Steve Oster's job a little easier. "Our principals who are not usually Klingons had suddenly *become* Klingons," says Oster, "and some of them had issues with putting on heavy makeup. Then Rene comes onto the set and begins gushing about how *wonderful* this Klingon makeup is, because he's so used to having full rubber on his face, and this leaves half of his face free. And I went over to him and said, 'I couldn't have paid you to have had better timing on that.' With all of his gushing, suddenly no one could say anything negative about it, because Rene was saying how great it was compared to what he normally goes through."

"They didn't particularly like the wardrobe either," chuckles B.C. Cameron. "They'd put off getting dressed until the last possible moment because they didn't want to stand around waiting in those heavy costumes."

Not that it was any easier preparing or shooting all of the episode's Klingon extras. "We had so many

Brooks and Meaney were not comfortable in the Klingon makeup. ROBBIE ROBINSON

Klingons we couldn't get everybody in the makeup trailer," recalls Makeup Artist Camille Calvet. "Only the principals got time in the trailer. I believe there were upwards of forty a day who came through. And they were there all week. People came in waves."

"Each of those Klingon extras had a makeup and hair person work on them," says Oster. "And we had to bring in extra wardrobe people for all the Klingon accouterments. We had an army of support people on that episode, people who came in at three in the morning to start applying makeup."

Fortunately, Michael Westmore's department has been fitting prosthetics to Klingons for years, so the situation wasn't quite as chaotic as it might seem. "The extras all got standard foreheads that were made out of the many molds we have on hand for Klingons," states Westmore. "We've got somewhere between thirty-five and forty different heads. We haven't had to sculpt new molds for years—we're able to adapt what we have, matching and changing them around, maybe making a little plate to glue over a section that will make it seem totally different. "But they did have their own teeth cast up," he continues.

"Each one had his own individual set of brand-new custom-molded teeth that I made out of acrylic."

The makeup team's work was rewarded with an Emmy nomination (although not a win), as was Jonathan West's exemplary work in cinematography. "It was an extremely challenging show," notes West. "It had a lot of visual possibilities, with all the extras and the big set, the fire gags, and the smoke. We did some split-screen work, trying to make the forty to sixty Klingons look like one hundred fifty and two hundred. On some of the wider shots, we divided the group into three and sometimes four segments, locked off the camera, and shot pieces of the group. Then the visual effects guys worked their magic and each of the four pieces were seamlessly integrated into one shot, making it look like there were four times as many people."

With Production Designer Herman Zimmerman still working on *First Contact*, it was up to Art Director Randy McIlvain to oversee the creation of the huge Klingon Hall of Warriors set. The most memorable components were the twelve-foot tall statues of Klingon heroes that supposedly supported

Some of John Eaves's designs for the statues in the Hall of Warriors.

the hall's ceiling. "We actually went back and picked out Klingon characters that had been mentioned in the past," says McIlvain. "Then John Eaves drew them and they were carved out of Styrofoam."

"We were going to have eight, but we cut back to four," says Laura Richarz. "The guys that made them carved them right from John's illustrations. They did a wonderful job."

The statues, of course, were to be the repositories of the polaron emitters that Sisko and company brought to Ty'Gokor to detect the changelings. The rationale behind the emitters was the responsibility of Science Consultant Andre Bormanis. "We didn't really need to get into the details of the technology," he says. "It was simply a sensor array. We wanted to sell the idea that detecting a changeling via sensors was a very difficult thing, and that you'd require some sort of system where you have several elements working together to create some sort of resonance. If we made it easy to detect a changeling, then the changeling ability is no great advantage."

On a different tech front, Bormanis suggests that techniques of surgically altering people so they can pass as aliens of some sort have probably improved

"The writers told me about the joke in advance," smiles Visitor.
BARRY McLAUGHLIN

since Jim Kirk had his ears bobbed to pass as a Romulan in "The Enterprise Incident." In those days, a simple scan from a tricorder could "see through" superficial alterations. "We saw a great example of that in 'The Trouble With Tribbles,'" he says. "The second McCoy scans Arne Darvin, he notices that his heartbeat is this, his blood pressure's that—'This man is a Klingon!' So clearly, if Sisko's men are going to go into a secured facility, where they're bound to have the equivalent of biological metal detectors, you have to be able to literally alter a person at a cellular level. Maybe not down to the very last cell, but internally enough that a standard sensor sweep would not notice that they weren't really Klingons. Of course, if someone did a serious scan, like on a bio-bed, well, forget it."

The episode brought back one of the producers' favorite directors, James Conway, for one final turn at the *DS9* helm. "It was a terrific script and I was honored to be able to do it," he says graciously. "I'd just been hired as Executive Vice President of Spelling Productions, and Ira and Rick Berman begged me to hold off going over there long enough to do the episode. I loved the script so much that I talked to the people at Spelling and they agreed to let me report later." Although the producers found a host of talented new directors for the show that year, they hated letting Conway go. "I miss him a lot," says Behr. "I can't believe he became a *suit!*" Which is to say, Conway became a member of the corporate establishment.

The script included the usual light moments, including another reference to the never seen alien crewperson, Vilix'Pran, who was "budding" again, and a joke that came close to breaking the fourth wall of the show, when Kira pats her own budding tummy and tells Bashir that it's all *his* fault. "We did do that on purpose," admits Behr. "That was strictly for the audience. We thought it would be nice [to acknowledge the relationship]." By this time, of course, Nana Visitor and Alexander Siddig had gone public with the news that they were expecting a child together—they even did a small pictorial about it in *TV Guide*—and they had no qualms about in-jokes that focused on the subject. "So we started finding ways to put Nana and Sid together in episodes, giving them little moments that we were aware would seem to have double meanings," Behr says with a smile. "We got a kick out of it."

THE SHIP

Episode #500

TELEPLAY BY **HANS BEIMLER**
STORY BY **PAM WIGGINTON & RICK CASON**
DIRECTED BY **KIM FRIEDMAN**

GUEST CAST

Kilana	KAITLIN HOPKINS
Muniz	F.J. RIO
Hoya	HILARY SHEPARD

STARDATE 50049.3

While evaluating possibilities for a mining operation on uninhabited Torga IV, Sisko and his crew witness the crash landing of a Jem'Hadar warship. The ship survives the impact, but its Jem'Hadar crew does not. The ship itself is a valuable prize that might give the Federation a tactical advantage over the Dominion. Sisko sends for the *Defiant*, which, unlike the runabout that Sisko and his team traveled in to Torga IV, has the requisite muscle to tractor the Jem'Hadar vessel off the planet. On DS9, Kira receives Sisko's message and heads out with the *Defiant*, leaving Bashir behind to resolve some questionable business dealings with Quark.

On Torga IV, Sisko has most of his crew working to bring the ship's systems on-line, while a few others remain in the orbiting runabout to keep watch for unexpected visitors. Suddenly a second Jem'Hadar warship drops out of warp and destroys the runabout. Sisko and his remaining crew hustle for the comparative safety of the downed ship as Jem'Hadar troops begin appearing on the planet's surface. In the scuffle that follows, Muniz, one of O'Brien's men, is injured, but he manages to make it into the vessel with Sisko, Dax, Worf, and O'Brien.

Knowing that the Jem'Hadar can transport through just about anything, Sisko and the others wait for the brutal soldiers to beam in and continue the fight—but nothing happens. Instead, Sisko is contacted by a Vorta named Kilana, who suggests a meeting to discuss their "situation." Sisko agrees, but while Kilana tries to talk him into relinquishing the ship, a Jem'Hadar soldier beams into the vessel. He places a sensor device on board, which is discovered by O'Brien, along with the Jem'Hadar himself. Muniz manages to kill the intruder, but by the time O'Brien takes a closer look at the device, it has shut down.

Muniz's condition worsens, and it becomes obvious to all that he is dying. Still, O'Brien angrily resists

Sisko and his team search for the secret hidden aboard the Jem'Hadar ship. ROBBIE ROBINSON

remove from the ship, and it's also the reason why the Jem'Hadar couldn't launch an outright attack on the vessel.

The changeling attempts to attack Sisko and Dax, but it no longer can hold its shape. It emits a piercing, keening sound that is heard throughout the ship, and by Kilana and the Jem'Hadar outside. When the sound stops at last, the changeling turns to dust, and the bombing outside the ship stops. Seconds later, Kilana materializes inside the vessel, reporting that the Jem'Hadar are dead. They've killed themselves because they were unable to save the Founder's life. Sadly, she and Sisko ponder the fact that the lack of trust between them has cost the lives of both the Founder and Muniz.

Sisko allows Kilana to remove the Founder's remains. The *Defiant* arrives to pick up the crew and the Jem'Hadar ship. On the way home, Worf finds O'Brien in the cargo hold, where the chief is sitting with the casket that holds Muniz's body. citing an old Klingon tradition that calls for friends to protect the dead against predators, Worf joins the chief for the remainder of the journey, erasing the remains of any discord between himself and O'Brien, his old companion from the *Enterprise*.

In a perfect world . . .

But it isn't, of course. It's the world of television, where something always makes production hard. With "The Ship," the difficulties weren't within the script or the acting or any of the things you'd normally expect. It was the intrusion of nature. For the exteriors, it was the torrid temperature of the location. And for the interiors, it was, of all things, gravity.

"Ah, yes," Steve Oster sighs. "Another one of those famous 'DS9 goes on location' occurrences. This was out at our famous gravel pit at Sand Canyon [north of Los Angeles], where we'd shot before several times. We had to build this huge Jem'Hadar ship. Once again, whenever we go on location, we get an unseasonably hot day. The surface material of the ship rose to one hundred twenty-four degrees, so the decals that we had put on to make it look real just peeled off from the sun. Much of the action played on top of that ship, so we had a baked crew by the time we got done."

"I'll never forget it," says Director Kim Friedman. "The air temperature was a hundred and seventeen when you were standing on top of that ship. We had bottles of water to pour over our heads. I'd call,

Worf's advice that they tell Muniz the truth. As tensions rise aboard the ship, Kilana requests another meeting with Sisko. This time, she offers to let him keep the ship if he'll allow the Jem'Hadar to retrieve an unidentified item that's on board. But Sisko refuses to endanger his crew by going along with her plan.

With negotiations at an impasse, the Jem'Hadar begin firing on the ship, making conditions aboard nearly intolerable. Nerves frayed, Dax and Worf desperately search the ship in an attempt to find whatever it is that Kilana wants, while O'Brien tries to get some of the vessel's systems on-line. At last he manages to restore main power, giving rise to the hope that they can get the ship to lift off. But as they power up, the reactor containment fields begin to overload. With a warp core breach imminent, Sisko orders O'Brien to shut the engines down.

Disappointment turns into despair as they discover that Muniz has died during the attempt. As Sisko contemplates the loss, Dax notices liquid dripping from the ceiling of the ship's command center. Looking up, they realize that it's an injured changeling. Clearly, *this* is what Kilana sought to

In retrospect the writers would have "ratcheted the tension up one more notch," according to Hans Beimler. ROBBIE ROBINSON

'Action,' and by the time the take was over and I'd call 'Cut,' our clothes and hair were totally dry." But that was only the crew, of course, not the cast, who obviously couldn't pour water over their wardrobe or makeup. "I felt sorry for the actors," the director laments. "The rest of us were wearing shorts and almost nothing, and *we* couldn't stand it. About five o'clock someone said, 'Oh my God, the temperature's gone down a little bit.' It was like ninety-nine or one hundred, and we'd noticed!" Friedman laughs.

Assistant Director Lou Race joined the series with "The Ship," after having been tested on two *Voyager* location episodes, "Basics, Parts I and II." "I was used to working outside, so I didn't realize how unusual it was for *Deep Space Nine* to go on location," Race says. "That sort of ignorance probably served me well, because I just expected people to get up and go. They weren't used to working that way, but I was, and it probably helped me to move the show a little bit faster to get it done.

"We were in that quarry," he adds, "so we had some real light and shade problems. The optimal shooting time was about ten A.M. to about four P.M.,

so we had to figure out what to shoot from seven to ten and after four."

The exterior set used in the gravel pit was quite unique. "I remember the angle of the upside-down Jem'Hadar ship," says Friedman. "We shot it from many different weird aspects, looking down, looking up, from the side. The designers had very craftily buried it and angled it in the sand."

"A real Jem'Hadar ship would have been the size of a football field," notes Oster. So we built only a section of it, just the back end. And we gouged the ground as if it had gone down and hit the sand."

Back at the soundstage, the set designers were doing their part to make the interiors of the flipped Jem'Hadar ship match the exteriors. "The hardest part was figuring out what they looked like right side up," says Laura Richarz. "We had John Eaves do a lot of drawings to show how the actors could walk on the ceiling and not break any lights. Of course, the director wanted it to look as if the ship was at an angle, but we couldn't build it like that, so she canted the camera."

"That was interesting," Friedman says, "designing

A scene shot in a quarry, and yet another unbelievably hot day on location. ROBBIE ROBINSON

the sets to be built upside down, and then walking through them and shooting them. They put metal grates over the lights so we could have something to walk on. That was a fun set."

Deciding what images would convey to the audience that the cast was on the ship's bridge was a challenge. "Usually, what tells you that you're upside down is familiar shapes," Richarz explains. "But since it's established that the Jem'Hadar don't sit, there were no upside-down chairs, which made it hard to indicate that the bridge was upside down.

Since the set itself didn't convey the appropriate clues, they added "props" of a sort: dead Jem'Hadar bodies. "We used prop house dummies, like you would throw off a cliff," Richarz says. "They're soft and kind of articulated. It was a joint effort between costume, makeup, and set decoration. Michael Westmore made new heads for them, complete with realistic glass eyes. Unfortunately, the feet didn't real-

ly fit in the boots. We had to make new ones so that the dummies wouldn't fall out of the boots when they were secured to the top of the set. We also had to remake the arms, because they looked too short hanging straight down. We added four inches to them. Now, despite the fact that we were on a ship we'd never seen before, we had something to tell us that we were upside down."

The premise for the episode was pitched to Hans Beimler by freelancers Pam Wigginton and Rick Cason. "It was the notion that we capture a Jem'Hadar ship," Beimler says. "The contents of the pitch were quite different from the final show, but I remember being excited the minute I heard, 'Jem'Hadar ship.' I knew that was a show, so I sent it to Ira and he agreed."

"The whole point of doing that show was that we wanted to make everyone tense," says Behr. "We wanted to see our people hot, and uncomfortable,

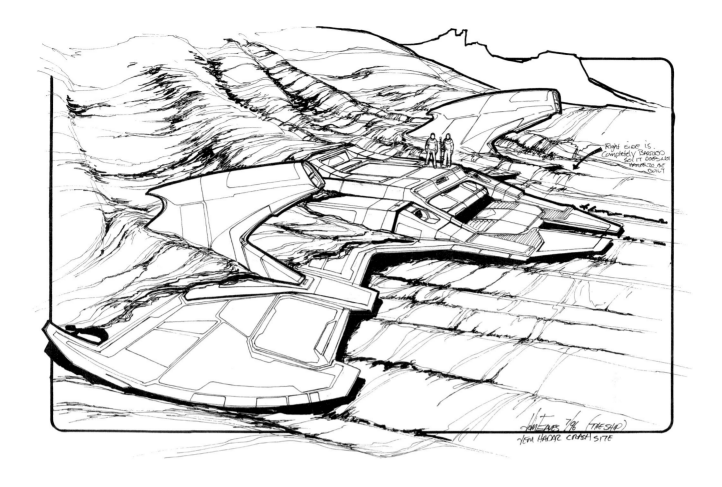

The Jem'Hadar ship: The sketch showed more than the producers would build. JOHN EAVES

but it didn't come off quite as well as we would have wanted. We wanted to do the Alamo thing, thirteen days of constant bombardment gets your nerves on edge, but somehow we weren't doing it. We weren't rocking the boat enough."

"I think that the most successful element of the show is when the pressure is getting to everybody and nerves are starting to fray," says Beimler. "Worf gets pissed off, and O'Brien, and that whole evolution. The one thing I think we shouldn't have done was go outside the ship. I would like to have stayed inside and just kept the female Vorta as a voice, saying, 'Come out, Captain, you've got to trust me. You've got to trust me.' The pressure, the steam, would have built up a little more in the ship. But in the episode Sisko actually beams out and has a confrontation with the female Vorta, causing the tension to dissipate."

The choice to bring back Muniz, last seen in

"Hard Time," was important to the writers, although it didn't work out quite the way they'd hoped. "Ira wanted to establish that there was an inner circle amongst the engineers, guys who hung out together," adds Beimler, "and that there was a special place in the heart of O'Brien for his engineering guys. Muniz was one of those guys. We tried to build a relationship between the two of them at the beginning."

"The whole idea was to show that the engineers, the tech guys, have a brotherhood that's different from just the old Starfleet brotherhood," says Behr. "We wanted to bond O'Brien with this guy and have it mean something. But the scenes didn't play the way they should have. They didn't play like two guys who were really comfortable with each other. It wound up being about O'Brien and a guy who's dying. The audience never came to care enough about Muniz because they didn't see O'Brien's investment in Muniz." Nevertheless, the writers would revisit the concept of

A corridor from the normal perspective. In the final version it would be turned upside down. JOHN EAVES

the "unity of the engineers," as Behr refers to it, three episodes later, in "The Assignment."

While Actor Kaitlin Hopkins gave the female Vorta a distinctive personality, it was hard for the producers to avoid comparing her to her Vorta predecessor, Weyoun. Behr admits that this was a problem. "There's not an actor among our many actors who is more beloved by the writing staff than Jeff Combs," he says. "Jeff can do no wrong. He plays a fabulous Brunt, and he plays a fabulous Weyoun. So every time it comes to casting a Vorta, we want to put Jeff in there. And it's really tough not to put Jeff in there, and it's really tough to find actors who can play the many colors that he gives it. Rick Berman suggested that we try another female Vorta, so we looked for the actress we'd used the first time [Molly Hagen, 'The Jem'Hadar'], but she wasn't available." As they looked for alternatives, the actresses who came in had trouble hitting the right tone. "They tended to play it straight and obedient, or too strong," Behr says. "Kaitlin gave it a very game try," Behr says. "She tried very hard."

Sharp-eyed viewers may have noticed a familiar-looking alien species with an unfamiliar difference. Yes, Hoya was a blue-skinned Benzite. And no, she didn't have the breathing device her people sported on *TNG*. The Makeup Department decided to phase out the small apparatus, which used a small quantity of dry ice to simulate the atmospheric vapors that Benzites require. "Apparently there's been some advances in Benzite medical technology," comments Mike Okuda.

Hans Beimler is proud of "The Ship" for a variety of reasons, not the least of which is a scene in which Sisko discusses the lives that have been lost and the cost of war. "It's amazing that in all these years of *Star Trek* no captain had ever sat down and talked about those consequences," he says. "In the *Star Trek* universe, where we blow people up cleanly with phasers, war seems almost antiseptic. But I think it's nice to periodically remind ourselves that the casualties are real people, and that when our characters discuss them, they're talking about people who exist for them. That, to me, was one of the most important moments in that episode, and a great moment for the series."

"The Ship" was the one hundredth episode in the series. "It wasn't the beginning of a season, it wasn't the end of a season," points out Ron Moore. "It was the second show of the year and we were in preparation to do a big celebratory episode, 'Trials and Tribble-ations.'"

"We did take out an ad, and I actually have it hanging in my office," Beimler says with a smile. "It was kind of fun to have written the show that's the hundredth episode. It was my turn in the rotation, so it was just a coincidence, but it was kind of nice."

"We were very proud that we got there," adds Behr.

In an attempt to win the beautiful Grilka, Quark takes on Thopok.
GALE M. ADLER

LOOKING FOR PAR'MACH IN ALL THE WRONG PLACES

Episode #501

WRITTEN BY RONALD D. MOORE
DIRECTED BY ANDREW J. ROBINSON

GUEST CAST

Keiko O'Brien	ROSALIND CHAO
Grilka	MARY KAY ADAMS
Tumek	JOSEPH RUSKIN
Thopok	PHIL MORRIS

STARDATE UNKNOWN

It's a typical day at the Replimat, with Jadzia and Worf sharing drinks but *not* the same point of view about Klingon opera, when suddenly Worf's attention shifts to an attractive Klingon female entering the Promenade. As the woman heads for Quark's, accompanied by Tumek, an elderly male retainer, and Thopok, a muscular guard, Worf is unable to take his eyes off her. He is horrified when he sees her embrace Quark warmly. How could a woman *that* beautiful be a friend of Quark's? But he's even more alarmed when Jadzia tells him that it's not just Quark's friend—it's his *ex-wife*, Grilka ("The House of Quark"). Grilka's visit is inspired by financial need. The hostilities between the Federation and the Klingon Empire have been detrimental to the financial health of the House of Grilka. Quark generously offers to look over her records, and it seems as if Grilka will be equally generous with her gratitude.

However, Worf can't believe that a magnificent

Klingon female would be interested in a mere Ferengi. After Jadzia teases him about having a bad case of *par'Mach*—the Klingon word for love—Worf decides to throw caution to the wind and woo the lady himself. He attempts to capture her attention by challenging Thopok. Before the fight can begin, Tumek intervenes and privately informs Worf that he's wasting his time; Grilka cannot mate with the son of Mogh, whose house is dishonored among all Klingons. Tumek observes that it's just as well, since Worf's human upbringing has ill prepared him for pursuing a Klingon woman.

To add salt to the wound, Worf learns that Grilka has invited Quark to a "private dinner." When Quark asks Dax for some tips on courting Klingon women, Worf can't resist adding some advice of his own. The evening is a big success, and Quark returns for more advice. Worf sees it as a way to prove that he knows as much as any Klingon about winning the heart of a female, and soon Dax and he are vicariously involved in the budding relationship. They teach Quark to enact the great battle fought by Emperor Kahless and the Lady Lukara against hundreds of fierce warriors at Qam-Chee, an encounter that was prelude to a night of intense passion.

In the meantime, the O'Briens are adjusting to having Kira as a live-in houseguest ("Body Parts"). With the pregnant Bajoran carrying their unborn child, Miles has become as proprietary about her welfare as he is about Keiko's. He tries to limit what he sees as overly strenuous activities, takes charge of her medications, and massages her aching muscles. The

"Worf is a big, stoic, ultra-serious warrior, and Dax is a woman who just refuses to take him seriously," says Ron Moore. "She can look him in the eye and say, 'Sheesh, are you kidding?'" GALE M. ADLER

increasing intimacy of their relationship has predictable side effects, and the two are surprised to find themselves attracted to each other. Kira decides that the best way to alleviate the sexual tension is to take a short holiday on Bajor. But when Keiko hears about it, she insists that Kira can't travel alone, and since *she's* busy, Miles must accompany the Bajoran.

Worf and Dax's efforts with Quark are again successful, and the battle ritual with Kahless and Lukara kindles increasing passion between the Ferengi and Lady Grilka. But Thopok cannot stand to see Grilka's house "dishonored" in this manner, and he challenges Quark to a fight to the death. Quark figures he's doomed: he can either fight Thopok and die, or avoid the fight and be branded a coward. But Dax comes up with a third alternative: a virtual control device that will allow Worf to control Quark's moves in the upcoming match with Thopok. In essence, Worf will fight for the Ferengi.

Rehearsal goes well, but Worf tells Jadzia he regrets putting all this effort into a plan to win Grilka

for Quark, instead of for himself. Jadzia suggests that Worf should set his sights on someone more fun *and* attainable, meaning herself, but Worf doesn't get the hint.

The next day, the real battle begins, and with Worf hidden in a holosuite controlling Quark's every move, the Ferengi performs admirably. Until Worf inadvertently damages the virtual control device, leaving Quark defenseless. As Dax struggles to repair the mechanism, Quark vamps for time by proclaiming his love for Grilka in language as poetic and verbose as he can muster. At last, the device is repaired, allowing Quark to knock his opponent to the floor. But rather than killing the defeated Klingon, Worf has Quark take Thopok's *bat'leth* to Grilka. In turn, Grilka hands the weapon to Thopok and discharges him from her service, thus allowing the warrior to retain his honor.

With victory his, Quark claims his prize, as he and Grilka fall upon each other in passion. In the adjoining holosuite, a similarly worked up Worf has no outlet for his emotions until Dax addresses him in terms he can't help but understand. After a brief physical standoff, the pair fall into one another's arms like a pair of ravenous wolves.

O'Brien and Kira are about to leave for Bajor. Kira mournfully describes their destination: it's one of the most romantic locations she knows. If the two of them go there together, something they'll both regret is *bound* to happen. At last, Miles puts his foot down and refuses to go. He'll tell Keiko that there was a misunderstanding and Kira left without him. Relieved, Kira agrees, and opts to go visit her friend Shakaar.

Later, Dr. Bashir is unnerved when his Infirmary suddenly is filled with patients who look as if they've been through the battle of Qam-Chee—which, in a way, they have. Catching on as to the source of Quark's, Worf's, and Jadzia's scratches, fractures, and contusions, Bashir decides that sometimes it's better not to ask any questions.

Again the writers pit Quark's wiles against the might of the warrior race. ROBBIE ROBINSON

Andy Robinson decided to strike while the iron was hot. The actor that viewers of *Deep Space Nine* know as Garak has another entertainment business persona: theatrical director. In fact, in 1995, he won two Los Angeles Drama Critic Awards for directing, and the material he helmed was not easy stuff: Samuel Beckett's *End Game* and Harold Pinter's *The Homecoming*.

"I knew that these awards were going to be published in the newspaper," Robinson says with a grin, "so I made sure that I called Rick Berman, with the hope that he'd been reading the paper with his morning coffee. It turned out that he had, and that's when I pitched him on the idea of my directing a *DS9*."

Robinson spent a part of the show's fourth season as a student of *Star Trek*'s unofficial "director's school," following other directors through their paces. Then at the beginning of Season 5, his name was placed on the show's director rotation list. "I don't think directors ever get a choice as to which episode they get to do," he says. "It's the luck of the draw." Robinson considered himself very lucky when he was assigned to *"par'Mach,"* since the teleplay was inspired by yet another great theatrical piece, Edmond Rostand's *Cyrano de Bergerac*. In the orginal play, two men, Christian and Cyrano, both long for the love of the beautiful Roxanne. Cyrano, an unattractive man with great wit, is employed by the handsome, but less intelligent Christian to woo the lady on his behalf.

The idea of translating *Cyrano* to *Star Trek* origi-

nated with Actor Michael Dorn, according to Ira Behr. "He wanted to do it with himself as the title character," Behr says.

"That idea kicked around the halls for a while," reports Ron Moore. "Then we decided to do it with Quark, and that became the Cyrano setup: Worf, Quark, and Grilka. But as soon as we started looking at it more seriously, we realized that it was an opportunity to put Dax and Worf together." The concept of a Dax/Worf relationship had been germinating for some time, ever since the writers noticed the flirtatious way that Terry Farrell played her scenes with Dorn. Notes Moore: "We could see the chemistry working on camera, especially when she was taking the steam out of Worf and he was reacting to her. There was obviously something to play there, so we started to write to it, and the more we wrote, the more we liked it." With the addition of yet another beautiful female protagonist to the mix, the tragic Cyrano story took on a whole new level of romance and led it away from the initial source material.

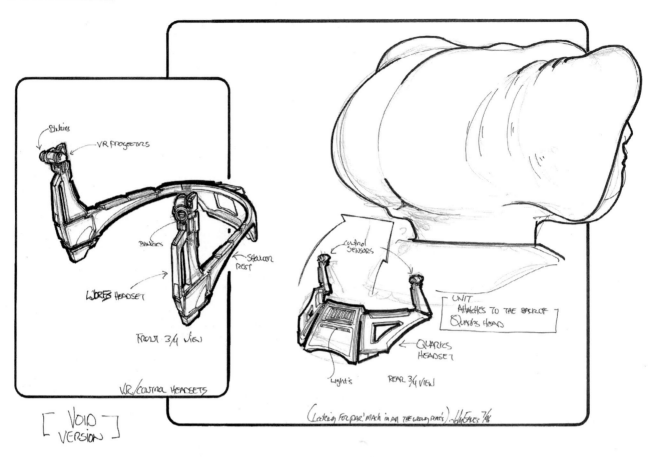

Artist's concept for one of Quark's holographic gizmos. JOHN EAVES

"*Cyrano* is the main character, and since Worf plays Cyrano, that makes this a Klingon story," remarks Armin Shimerman. "I approached it as if I were playing Christian, but probably the most bizarre Christian ever! He's the one who's a little bit naive and unintelligent, and as for the gorgeous creature that Christian is, well, Quark is not."

As one might imagine, moving a story from seventeenth-century France to twenty-fourth-century deep space required a few changes. "The most famous scene in *Cyrano* is when he's hiding in the bushes giving Christian the lines to relay to Roxanne," Moore says. "I didn't want to do that literally. I wanted something that we could do in a science fiction context. We talked about putting a transmitter in his ear, but that had been done in the movie *Roxanne*. Actually controlling the guy seemed like the next step, and we felt we could get a lot of mileage out of it."

"We needed to come up with a way that Quark could do his fighting and survive," says Robert Wolfe. "In 'The House of Quark,' we had him throw down

his weapon and decline to fight. So we needed to come up with something different from that. And that's when I came up with the idea of the holographic puppeteer."

"That was one of the best tech gags we've done," Moore states. "We didn't explain it very much. You just see that Worf has some kind of a gizmo on, pointing into his eyes, and that Quark has a device on him. So somehow Worf is seeing what Quark sees and can control his body. Dax has invented it, and I wasn't interested in explaining it to the viewers. We just buy the premise and move on."

He did, however, hash out the idea with Andre Bormanis, to see if the basic concept was sound. Happily, it was. "We described the puppet suit as a web of sensors and actuators that would allow Worf's movements to be translated to Quark instantaneously, so that he would be manipulated into mimicking Worf's skills with the *bat'leth*," Bormanis says. "That sort of remote control is pretty sophisticated even today," he adds. "It's like the technology that effects people are using to create digital animation. You put on a kind of sensor suit that tracks the position of your body from moment to moment, and a computer stores that as digital data that it then uses to create an animated wire-frame model."

Andy Robinson credits the success of the fight sequence to the choreography that he worked out with *Star Trek*'s resident martial arts expert and Klingon blade master, Dan Curry. "Dan is the *bat'leth* specialist, and he was enormously helpful," Robinson enthuses. "He has a really good film sense, so he actually helped me visualize and design some shots."

Armin Shimerman also had reason to thank Curry. "I knew that Quark wouldn't be good with weapons, but he had to *look* good in the battle because Worf was manipulating him and Worf is a maestro," Shimerman says. "So I went to Dan, and he gave me lessons. I borrowed a *bat'leth,* took it home for ten days, and worked on the maneuvers that he'd practiced with me. So most of the fight actually is *me* fighting," he notes proudly. "I got pretty good with the *bat'leth,* actually."

Because the scene required some very specific physical pantomime, Shimerman also sought the advice of another expert to help sell the shot where Worf prevents Quark from lopping off his opponent's head. "I hired a mime, and worked with him on how to make it look as though the *bat'leth* had a mind of its own," he says. "I'd never done any mime work before, so that was an interesting part of the homework."

Actor Phil Morris, who played Quark's opponent Thopok, is the son of the late Greg Morris, who played Barney on television's *Mission: Impossible* series, like *Star Trek* a Desilu (and later Paramount) production. The younger Morris has a long-term affiliation with *Star Trek*. At the age of seven, he appeared in the original series episode "Miri." "The producers got a bunch of children from the pool of talent then working on the Paramount lot," he recalls with a grin. "They got me, my older sister Iona, two of William Shatner's daughters, John McEveety's [director of 'Miri'] kids, and more. It was *cool*, man, working with Michael J. Pollard, and it was a lot of fun until my foot got run over by a camera dolly— which made it both the highlight *and* the lowlight of my career to date!" But Morris's *Star Trek* career wasn't over yet. "I was one of the cadets in the beginning of *Star Trek III: The Search for Spock,*" he says proudly. "I had a brief *moment* with Admiral Kirk,

asking him if we were going to get a reception when we got back to Earth."

Years later, Morris returned to Paramount to play the son of Barney Collier on the new version of *Mission: Impossible*. That series ended as *Deep Space Nine* was starting up, and Morris tried out for the role of Commander Sisko. "I was too young at the time," he admits. "He was supposed to have a kid who was thirteen. But I jumped at the chance when they asked me to play a Klingon in '*par'Mach*' a few years later."

Today, Morris is best known to the viewing public for his recurring role as lawyer Jackie Childs on *Seinfeld*. Morris would be back in sixth season's "Rock and Shoals" as the Jem'Hadar Remata'Klan, as well as appearing on *Voyager*'s "One Small Step."

A little foresight on the part of the producers allowed "*par'Mach*" to feature the very expensive Klingon Hall set, which here serves as the holographic backdrop to the fight scenes. Fortunately, the episode was already on the schedule when production began on "Apocalypse Rising." "With that bit of forewarning, we decided against ripping out the Klingon Hall," says Steve Oster. "That way we would be able to save on building a new set *and* defray some of the expenses of the earlier episode." Thus, the Great Hall was constructed on Stage 30, an area not usually used for *Star Trek* production. Following its debut in "Apocalypse Rising," it sat untouched for several weeks while shooting continued undisturbed on the traditional *DS9* stages. "When we came back to shoot it for '*par'Mach*,'" says Laura Richarz, "we changed a few things. We took out the statues and the platform, and turned it into an ornate empty hall so they'd have room for the fighting."

The title, a play on Eddie Rabbitt's country hit "Looking for Love in All the Wrong Places," may have seemed a little frivolous to some viewers, but it said it all to Moore, who upped the ante by creating a B-story that focused on an attraction that springs up between Kira and O'Brien. "Then it became this whole thing of *everybody* looking for love in all the wrong places," smiles Moore. "The trick of that was to take it as far as we thought the characters would go, with both of them tempted but neither one of them willing to do anything about it. I think that was one of the more *real* storylines we've ever done. They were flesh-and-blood people in a very believable situation, reacting believably."

NOR THE BATTLE TO THE STRONG

Episode #502

TELEPLAY BY **RENÉ ECHEVARRIA**
STORY BY **BRICE R. PARKER**
DIRECTED BY **KIM FRIEDMAN**

GUEST CAST

Kirby — **ANDREW KAVOVIT**

Kalandra — **KAREN AUSTIN**

Bolian — **MARK HOLTON**

Nurse — **LISA LORD**

Ensign — **JEB BROWN**

Female Guard — **ELLE ALEXANDER**

Male Guard — **GREG "CHRISTOPHER" SMITH**

AND

Burke — **DANNY GOLDRING**

STARDATE UNKNOWN

Jake Sisko's first professional writing assignment is not turning out exactly the way he'd hoped. He's been asked to do a profile of Dr. Bashir, but from the budding journalist's point of view, his trip accompanying the doctor to a dull medical conference has been a waste of time. As they return to the station, Jake listens to Bashir babble about prion replication and wonders how he can possibly turn the experience into something more exciting.

Suddenly, his prayers seem to be answered. A Federation colony on Ajilon Prime has been attacked by Klingon troops; they desperately need medical assistance. Although Bashir is concerned about bringing an eighteen-year-old civilian into a battle zone, Jake convinces the doctor to go, certain that a story about "Surgery Under Fire" is just what his readers will want. Once they arrive at Ajilon Prime, however, Jake nearly forgets about his story. He's surrounded by scores of casualties, Starfleet officers fighting for their lives. This is triage, where overburdened doctors and nurses must make instant decisions that determine who will live and who will die. Jake has never experienced anything like it, but he has no time to process his emotions as he's quickly recruited to lend a hand.

Back on the station, Sisko worries about Jake, but convinces himself that the young man will be all right for the two days it will take the *Farragut* to move in with a relief team. But not long after, he gets word that the *Farragut* was destroyed on its way to Ajilon

Jake gains the experience to apply the old adage, "Write about what you know." LYNN McAFFEE

Prime. Sisko's next course of action is clear: he must take the *Defiant* there.

On the besieged planet, Jake helps Kirby, a young orderly, move patients throughout the makeshift medical facility, becoming bloodied and exhausted in the process. There's little time to rest, and now it looks as if the facility itself may be attacked by Klingon ground forces. Jake is rattled by the prospect, and when the Klingons take out the facility's reactor, he is nearly overwhelmed with dread. With only emergency power available, the patients are in grave danger. Bashir recalls that there is a portable generator in the runabout and asks Jake to help him retrieve it. But before they reach the ship, explosions begin to go off all around them. Jake flees in a blind panic, leaving Bashir to fend for himself.

Jake finds himself in the midst of a landscape littered with the bodies of Starfleet soldiers. In his haste to escape this wasteland, he skids down a hill and collides with what seems to be another body. But this "corpse" is still alive—and dangerous. Initially mistaking Jake for a Klingon soldier, the injured Starfleet officer strikes at him, knocking Jake to the ground. Jake is determined to save the man, thinking that somehow this act will atone for his abandoning Bashir. But the officer is too badly wounded to survive, and he dies before Jake's horrified eyes. Eventually, Jake finds his way back to the medical facility, where he learns that Bashir made it back in one piece, suffering only some plasma burns. He goes to see Bashir in the intensive care ward, but is filled with guilt when the doctor tells him how worried *he* was about Jake. Ashamed of his own cowardly behavior, Jake finds that now he can understand the actions of a patient in the ward, a young ensign who phasered himself in the foot to escape the horrendous battle.

Talk of the imminent Klingon invasion only adds to Jake's fears, and the gallows humor employed by the rest of the group triggers an angry outburst from him. Concerned, Bashir tries to get Jake to tell him what's wrong, but Jake can't.

The Klingon force finally attacks, and the medical team prepares to evacuate the wounded via a long underground tunnel. Paralyzed with fear, Jake hangs back, hiding, explosions going off all around. A guard defending the tunnel entry is shot and killed by two Klingons, who next turn their fire on Jake. In a panic, he grabs the dead guard's weapon and begins firing wildly in the direction of the Klingons. His blasts bring down the entrance to the cavern in which the facility is located, and also trigger an avalanche of debris that envelopes Jake.

When he comes to, Jake sees his father and Dr. Bashir hovering over him. They tell him that the Klingons are pulling out and that Jake's efforts to seal the entrance may have saved the lives of all the patients. But Jake doesn't feel like a hero; he knows that his actions were motivated by fear, not courage. Wanting to come clean, he writes a piece about his behavior on Ajilon Prime—observing that the line between courage and cowardice is thinner than most people know—and allows both Bashir and his father to read it. Later, he takes comfort in his father's comment that it takes courage to look inside oneself, and even more courage to write about it for other people to see.

You can't tell a book by its cover, but sometimes you can find the right title for an episode there, case in point, "Nor the Battle to the Strong." Initially referred to as "Portrait of a Life," René Echevarria hadn't thought of anything better by the time the teleplay was completed. "I didn't know what to do," he says. "So somebody said, 'Look at *Bartlett's Familiar Quotations*,' a book I'd never learned how to use. So I picked it up and looked at it, and flipped it over, and there, listed on the back cover, was a sample quote: 'Nor the battle to the strong, nor the race to the swift.' I thought, 'Well, that sounds kind of interesting, *and* it has the word *battle* in it!'" The quote from *Ecclesiastes* worked for Echevarria and the other writers, so he didn't have to

The writers wanted Jake to experience the horrors of war.
ROBBIE ROBINSON

delve any deeper. "Very fortuitous," he says with a chuckle, "but I still don't know how to use the book, really." Beyond the biblical title, the episode's other allusions are literary, as in classic American literature. "It was *The Red Badge of Courage* in Bronson Canyon," smiles Laura Richarz.

True enough, admits Ira Behr. "I love *The Red Badge of Courage*, and I wanted a show about Jake," he states. "Nor the Battle to the Strong" was another one of those episodes that attempted to move the production farther afield from *The Next Generation*'s "clean, Teflon image," Behr says. "Just getting down into the mud and the horror of death. We tried to make it mean something." The attempt was noteworthy here, and the writers would try again, to even greater effect, two years later, in "The Siege of AR-558."

The pitch purchased from freelancer Brice R. Parker was essentially "Jake, behind-the-lines, journalist," according to Echevarria. "It began as an episode set in a Cardassian hospital, where the Klingons were attacking," he recalls. "There were a lot of intercultural misunderstandings between Jake and the Cardassians, who were primarily females, since we've established that Cardassian women are the scientists and the doctors. But we'd learned from 'Apocalypse Rising' that it's cost-prohibitive to have that many extras in alien makeup. And since we were trying to save money for 'Trials and Tribble-ations,' we decided that we didn't really need to build a set. We could just say that they'd moved out of the damaged hospital and into caves underneath the complex." So the Cardassian hospital became a makeshift

Gary Monak's special-effects crew set off over three hundred explosive charges. RON TOM

artillery," says Lou Race. "We were blowing up things in front of him, beside him, behind him. We made it look more dangerous than it actually was, but the explosions had to be timed with Cirroc's running so he wouldn't get injured."

A scene where Jake had to cross a battlefield of dead soldiers was less hazardous . . . and more decorative. "We had a lot of extras out there," says Race, "about fifty percent extras and fifty percent dummies. We spent a lot of time 'Martha Stewarting.'" Draping the dead with custom-made linens? Arranging flatware in strategic military patterns? Lou Race shakes his head. "Arranging the bodies around the mountain so that they'd look dead in the most effective way," he explains with a grin.

Alexander Siddig enjoyed being paired with Cirroc Lofton for an entire episode, but was disappointed that nothing came of it later on. "I thought it was going to be the beginning of a friendship between Bashir and Jake," he says. "Perhaps Bashir saw himself in Jake and could begin passing on his experiences to him. That's how I approached it, that I was acting as a young mentor for Jake, as opposed to a somewhat older one, like his father. But it turned out not to be that way."

While Jake was devastated by the battle going on around him, Siddig isn't surprised that Bashir, who actually hasn't experienced much more than Jake in the way of combat, was ready to do what it takes in the situation. "Bashir's pretty reckless that way," Siddig smiles. "He gets almost myopic at times, just goes ahead and tears through whatever he needs to tear through. He's a bit like a Doberman under those circumstances." In many ways, Bashir is a different breed of doctor than his predecessors in *Star Trek* and *The Next Generation.* "He's not a pacifist," says Siddig. "He's a soldier. It would be unthinkable for him to act like a Beverly Crusher, having philosophical qualms about whether or not she could pick up a gun. He'd have no problem at all picking up a weapon and shooting someone if they're a threat, and I expect any company commander would want that from his doctor in the field, because it's a dual role."

Siddig was ably assisted in the fast-paced triage sequences by Director Kim Friedman, who had experience directing episodes of *ER.* And, so was Echevarria. "Kim gave me a couple of *ER* scripts to show me the format of how they do the inner cutting in those frenzied scenes," Echevarria says. "It was a great experience for me to spend time with her down on the stage, actually blocking and saying, 'I need

Federation medical facility, populated mainly by humans. "It didn't hurt the show, actually," says Echevarria. "It reminded you every minute that they were in an extraordinary situation. And I tried to come up with some interesting characters, including a very droll Bolian and some hard-bitten, made-cynical-by-life people."

The focus of the episode is Jake, a fact that's emphasized by his voiceover narration, unusual for *Star Trek* in that it's not done as a log entry. Also, Dennis McCarthy reused the theme that he'd created for Jake in "The Visitor." Even when Jake isn't present, he's the subject of conversation, as in the scenes between Sisko and Odo on the station, and Sisko and Dax on the *Defiant.* Being the focus of the episode meant that Cirroc Lofton got more of a physical workout than he normally does. "We laid out a huge group of mortars in Bronson Canyon for the scene where Jake comes running through the Klingon

something here and then I want to whip over here, and then I want to go here.' It helped to get across that sense of urgency."

Things moved so quickly that Friedman whipped through the material in less time than expected and the episode wound up short, some eight to ten pages short, according to Echevarria. Fortunately, the show's script supervisor, Judi Brown, who times each scene, gave the producers a heads-up on the situation far enough in advance for Echevarria and the other writers to be able to expand the story to fill the minutes. "One of the things we added was a second scene with the young man who shot himself in the foot," Echevarria says. "It's a pivotal scene where he talks to Jake about what he did, and for Jake, who already has had his experience outside with the dying soldier, it brings it all home to him."

The scene with Burke, the dying soldier, represented Echevarria's greatest hurdle in completing the episode. "I originally had written that Jake falls into a foxhole with a Klingon warrior, not a Starfleet soldier," he says. "The warrior has been blinded in battle, and he decides that he needs Jake to help him survive, so he forces Jake to stay with him. In that permutation of the script, they were there for days, and they come to have this strange admiration for each other. Eventually, Jake tells him how he came to be there, and the warrior is so appalled that he throws Jake out of the foxhole, because he doesn't want to die with a coward. I was very attached to the scene, and Ira and I had a bit of a tussle about it."

"One of the biggest arguments we ever had," confirms Behr. "I kept telling him that we couldn't do it because the whole show was predicated on the idea that the Klingons, the enemy out there, were what's frightening Jake. And once you humanize them and empathize with them, the fear level comes down too much."

"Looking back on it, I can see he was right," Echevarria admits. "The end of the story has to do with this relentless, unstoppable enemy coming in, and we would have just spent eight pages with one of them who we liked a little too much. So the Klingon became a Starfleet guy who's as tough as a Klingon."

TRIALS AND TRIBBLE-ATIONS
Episode #503

TELEPLAY BY **RONALD D. MOORE &**
RENÉ ECHEVARRIA
STORY BY **IRA STEVEN BEHR & HANS BEIMLER &**
ROBERT HEWITT WOLFE
DIRECTED BY **JONATHAN WEST**

GUEST CAST

Dulmer	JACK BLESSING
Lucsly	JAMES W. JANSEN
Arne Darvin	CHARLIE BRILL
Waitress	LESLIE ACKERMAN
Engineer	CHARLES S. CHUN
Lt. Watley	DEIRDRE L. IMERSHEIN

ACTORS FROM THE ORIGINAL STAR TREK EPISODE

Captain James T. Kirk	WILLIAM SHATNER
Mister Spock	LEONARD NIMOY
Doctor Leonard McCoy	DeFOREST KELLEY
Montgomery Scott	JAMES DOOHAN
Lt. Uhura	NICHELLE NICHOLS
Ensign Pavel Chekov	WALTER KOENIG
Cyrano Jones	STANLEY ADAMS
Ensign Freeman	PAUL BAXLEY
Mister Lurry	WHIT BISSELL
Arne Darvin	CHARLIE BRILL
Korax	MICHAEL PATAKI
Bartender	GUY RAYMOND
Guard	DAVID ROSS
Nilz Baris	WILLIAM SCHALLERT

Based on the original Star Trek episode "The Trouble With Tribbles" by David Gerrold

STARDATE UNKNOWN

It's not every day that *Deep Space Nine* receives a visit from agents of the Federation Department of Temporal Investigations. But when it does, the inhabitants treat it as seriously as their ancestors once took an audit by the Internal Revenue Service. Queried about the *Defiant's* recent trip back in time, Captain Sisko is cautious as he recounts the details.

It was an accident, he explains. The ship was returning from Cardassian space with the long-lost Bajoran Orb of Time. Also aboard was a hitchhiker of sorts, an elderly human merchant who went by the name Barry Waddle. However, Waddle's chance passage proved to be anything but. When the crew of the *Defiant* suddenly found themselves over two-hundred light-years from their prior location and more than a century in the past, it quickly became appar-

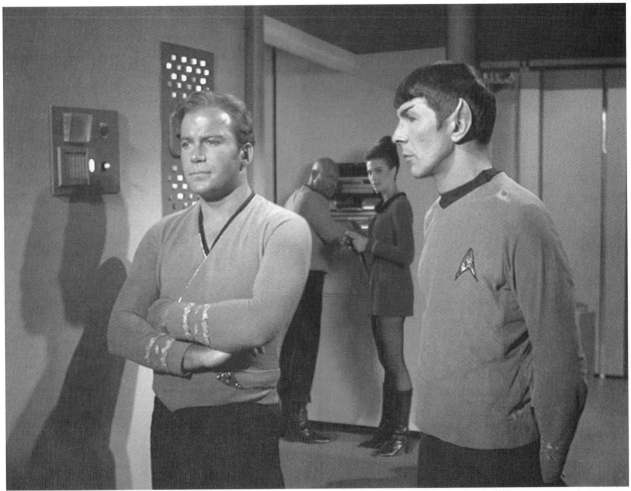

Sisko and his crew travel back in time, to prevent the assassination of Captain James T. Kirk.

ent that Waddle—and the Orb of Time—were to blame.

Computer records revealed that Waddle, or Arne Darvin, as he'd once been known, was actually a Klingon spy who'd been surgically altered to resemble a human. His manipulation of the Orb had landed the crew within transporter distance of Deep Space Station K-7 and the ship that was orbiting it at the time: the original *U.S.S. Enterprise*. But why?

The computer had some clues. One hundred five years ago, Darvin had been posing as a Federation official visiting K-7. His real mission was to derail Federation colonization efforts by poisoning a shipment of grain stored on the station. But the captain of the *Enterprise*, James T. Kirk, had exposed Darvin's plan and had him arrested. As a result, Darvin's career with Klingon intelligence was destroyed. Clearly, his trip back in time was intended to change history, perhaps by killing Kirk.

Sisko and the others realized they had to stop

him. Dressing in period Starfleet uniforms, Sisko, Dax, Bashir, and O'Brien beamed over to the *Enterprise* to search for Darvin, while Odo and Worf, disguised as civilians, went to the station. Although Sisko's crew encountered a few minor mishaps in getting used to twenty-third-century technology, they managed to pass the scrutiny of Starfleet's finest. Unfortunately, there was no sign of Darvin on the ship.

In K-7's bar, Odo learned that Darvin *had* been there earlier in the day. Hoping the culprit might return, Odo remained in the bar and observed a chance encounter between the *Enterprise*'s Lieutenant Uhura and a trader selling tribbles—small, fuzzy, benevolent creatures that were irresistible to humans. Not immune to their charms, Odo obtained one, much to Worf's disgust. Klingons, it seemed, were mortal enemies of the furry pets.

The search for Darvin was interrupted briefly when a Klingon battlecruiser arrived at the station.

In his search for the explosive device, Bashir examines tribbles.

Although Kirk and the station manager expected the worst, the Klingons only wanted shore leave privileges, which reluctantly were granted. The decision led to predictable results, with the Klingons and humans getting into a brawl in K-7's bar just as O'Brien and Bashir arrived to join Odo and Worf's search efforts. The two humans were drawn into the rowdy free-for-all, but Odo and Worf spotted the elderly Darvin in a corridor and took off in pursuit. Bashir and O'Brien wound up being hauled off with members of the *Enterprise* crew for a dressing down by Kirk himself, while Odo and Worf managed to bag their prey, learning in the process that Darvin had planted a bomb in one of the tribbles.

But which tribble? As Kirk had discovered, tribbles were incredibly prolific. Not only was the station covered with them, but, thanks to Uhura's one little pet, the *Enterprise* as well. Using the *Enterprise's* internal sensors, Sisko and Dax managed to ascertain that the dangerous tribble wasn't on the ship. That left only the million-plus tribbles on the station as suspects.

Overhearing Kirk's comment that there probably were tribbles in the station's storage compartments, Sisko and Dax investigated the area and managed to find the "assassin" just before *it* found Kirk. The timeline saved, Sisko and company used the Orb to return the *Defiant,* and Darvin, back to their own era.

Satisfied that no temporal infractions have taken place, the agents pack up and leave the station, leaving Sisko and company with only one remaining problem: what are they going to do with all the offspring, now populating DS9, of the one tribble that accompanied Odo to the twenty-fourth century?

Spring of 1996. The thirtieth anniversary of *Star Trek* was a few short months away. *Star Trek: First Contact*, the second motion picture based on *The Next Generation*, was going into production. *Voyager,* the newest kid in the *Star Trek* franchise, had been given the go-ahead to do a special episode featuring one of the seven actors from the original series. The studio was planning to produce a prime-time television special saluting *Star Trek*. But none of this activity involved the staff at *Deep Space Nine.*

Not yet, anyway.

"We had already heard some of the plans for the thirtieth anniversary," recalls Ira Behr. "And we kind of figured, being *Star Trek's* middle child, we were going to miss out on this whole thing." Then came the fateful phone call from Rick Berman, asking Behr if his writing staff would be interested in doing something for the anniversary. "I think my exact words were, 'Let me talk it over with the guys,'" relates Behr, the guys being the other members of *DS9's* writing team.

The team had some concerns. If they did come up with a special episode, they wondered if it would air during the week of September 8, the actual

To insert Meaney and Siddig into the lineup, the effects crew filmed them on a motion-controlled turntable in front of a green screen.

That's Jim Rider, a motion-control photographer, on the
Enterprise bridge.

ters into scenes that fans were familiar with already,
for example, one of the *DS9* crew being inside the
storage compartment bin in "The Trouble with
Tribbles," tossing out tribbles and hitting Kirk on the
head with them. Everybody liked that idea. From the
top of his head, Moore began spitballing additional
ideas from the same episode: the *DS9* guys getting
involved in the famous bar brawl, getting chewed out
by Captain Kirk in the lineup sequence, and so on.
Moore even came up with the idea of a bomb being
planted in one of the tribbles, which would become
a main plot point of "Trials and Tribble-ations." Behr
took the basic idea to Berman. "He liked it," reports
Behr, "but he was very unsure about whether we
could ever do it."

Technology was a concern. After all, there was no
point in doing it if it wouldn't look great. "So we
called up Gary Hutzel and asked, 'Can we do this?'"
says Moore. "And Gary got very excited." So excited
that he went off and shot some test footage to show
the producers. Moore chuckles at the memory. "Gary
comes in and shows us this clip," he says. "It's the
scene from 'Tribbles' where Kirk comes out of the
bridge turbolift, and the camera tracks with him as he
comes down to the second level and sits down on the
tribble. And Gary says, 'Well, what do you think?'
And Ira and René and I look at each other, like,
'What?' Gary laughs and runs the tape back to the
beginning. And as Kirk comes out of the turbolift
again, Gary freezes the clip, and he says, 'See this
security guy standing next to the turbolift? Well, he
doesn't belong there. He's one of *our* guys!'"

The producers were floored. "It was so good, that
we hadn't even seen it," says Moore. "And that was
what we were looking for, something that we could
do so subtly that it wouldn't draw attention to itself.
We wanted to be able to put Dax into the back of that
shot and track Kirk in, and if you weren't looking for
her, man, you weren't going to see her, because she
wasn't standing out. Gary had shown us that we
could do it."

anniversary of the original series' debut. If so, would
it be considered the opening episode of Season 5?
How would that affect plans to use the season premiere to follow up on several of the plot elements
from "Broken Link," the fourth season closer? These
concerns were outpaced by a perceived opportunity
to do something really special, once they figured out
exactly what that might be. Ron Moore once had
done his own tribute to the original series, by resur-
recting Scotty and bringing him to Picard's *Enterprise,*
in *TNG*'s "Relics." But with *Voyager* using Sulu in *their*
episode, it would have seemed derivative to bring
someone from Kirk's crew to *DS9.* For a while, Moore
played with the idea of sending Sisko and the others
to Sigma Iotia II, the planet visited by the original
Enterprise in "A Piece of the Action," but that idea
didn't pan out.

Then René Echevarria suggested sending the *DS9*
crew into the past, where they could sneak aboard
the *Enterprise* and interact with some of the classic
characters via clips from the original episodes. "We
started talking about it and everybody immediately
realized that it would be incredibly difficult, probably
very expensive," says Echevarria. "It really didn't go
very far." But somehow Echevarria couldn't let go of
the idea, and he soon converted Moore to his line of
thinking. "Ron told Ira, 'We should look into it,'"
Echevarria says. "'Maybe it's not that expensive.
Maybe we can do it.'"

Moore then suggested inserting the *DS9* charac-

Once the studio had given the producers the
green light to proceed with the episode, Moore and
Echevarria set to work on the teleplay. As they wrote,
they consulted extensively with Jonathan West,
who'd been chosen to direct. Recalls Echevarria: "We
would look at a video of the 'Tribbles' scene we were
writing into, then rewind and watch and ask, 'Is the
perspective right? Can we put the character there? If
that camera angle becomes their point of view, then
where would they be sitting?'" Because of all the intri-

The detailed overhead graphics and plant-ons were meticulously reproduced by the Art Department.

cate lighting situations the episode would present, it had been clear to the producers that whoever directed the episode would need to have an in-depth understanding of cinematography, past and present. West, cinematographer on the series from its third season forward, as well as the director of several *Deep Space Nine* episodes, was the obvious choice. "There were several directors we were considering, but because of the meticulous nature of the assignment, Jonathan was the perfect candidate," says Steve Oster. "A director of photography automatically thinks in terms of specific shots and how to integrate a scene together." West even had worked with *Star Trek*'s original director of photography, Jerry Finnerman, who had, in recent years, shot some second-unit photography for *DS9*.

"We had some very specific things to match," says West. "I tried to approach the visuals very similarly to what was done in 1967, with lens choices and shot style. We used a different lighting style and a finer grain of film, which had a different color saturation."

"If you look at the flawless matching of the light-

ing of the new material to the original material, you can't even spot a mood difference," marvels Visual Effects Producer Dan Curry, who directed some of the episode's second-unit photography. "Thirty years ago, lighting styles were quite different. Jonathan and Kris Krosskove, who was cinematographer on the episode, did an amazing job."

But while producing an exact visual match to the original episode was essential to the success of "Trials and Tribble-ations," the same wasn't true of the musical soundtrack. "We had quite a bit of discussion about that show," says Dennis McCarthy. "I had an idea of taking the original Jerry Fielding score and using his themes verbatim, at the same time taking advantage of the fact that we now have this large orchestra and advanced electronics to bring it up to the scale that we've been using on *Deep Space Nine*. But the producers felt that this was *Deep Space Nine*, not the original *Star Trek*, and they wanted to keep this episode within that context. I understood their thinking, so as I wrote a new score I tried to do it as if I were Jerry Fielding writing it today, using the parameters that we've developed over the years at

The lovingly recreated model of the *Enterprise*. GREGORY JEIN

Deep Space Nine. I was very happy with the result. I think Fielding would have liked it."

McCarthy notes that he did get to rerecord one important musical element of the original episode: "We rerecorded the Alexander Courage fanfare," he says. "The guys in the orchestra and I listened to the original so we could get as close as possible to the feel of that sound." To duplicate the distinct tenor of the theme, McCarthy used six French horns, among a total of forty-five musicians.

More than any other department, the *DS9* art team was almost gleefully maniacal in their obsession with detail. "When we found out that it might really happen, we were just completely beside ourselves," says Scenic Artist Doug Drexler. "For a lot of us in the film industry, the original *Star Trek* was one of the motivating factors that got us into the business."

"The excitement was contagious," observes Art Director Randy McIlvain. Getting close enough wasn't good enough, because they always felt they could get a little closer if they tried harder. They duplicated more than reasonable facsimiles of wall intercoms, turbolift controls, surface textures, and backlit graphics galore. The distinctive moiré-patterned graphic that appeared on the overheads in the *Enterprise*'s corridors was recreated in Scenic Art Supervisor Mike Okuda's computer. The gaudy red and yellow plantons that grace the corridor walls were painstakingly redrawn by Drexler and then lathed out of wood.

Even people who weren't full-time staffers on *Deep Space Nine* caught the fever. Professional model maker Greg Jein, who periodically does work for *Star Trek,* was delivering a model of the *Excelsior* that he'd built for *Voyager*'s "Flashback" episode when he caught a glimpse of Gary Hutzel's test footage for "Trials and Tribble-ations." He recalls being informed, "Yeah, we'll probably do a model of the *Enterprise,* but we don't know when, and we probably *won't* know till the last minute." Nevertheless, "being a crazy kind of guy," says Jein, "I decided to start work on it anyway!" Jein's craziness paid off. He and his friends went on to complete the five-and-a-half-foot-long recreation of the famous starship, as well as Deep Space Station K-7 and a D-7 Klingon battle cruiser for "Tribble-ations."

Costume Designer Robert Blackman had to recreate the original series Starfleet uniforms from scratch. The designer lucked out on the old-style Klingon uniforms, when he found four original costumes and a fifth shirt and vest stored away in "ratty old boxes." "That was a godsend," he notes, "because there was no way to duplicate any of that very specific metallic fabric that they'd used, and I was in a cold sweat."

Makeup Supervisor Michael Westmore's efforts in matching the look of the sixties weren't nearly as harrowing. "I already had been working in television during the sixties, so I had used those same makeup colors," he says. "There wasn't a huge variety in Hollywood at the time, and a lot of it is still available. All of the *DS9* makeup artists really enjoyed themselves."

Hairstyles provided a source of amusement on the set. Terry Farrell received a towering beehive. Alexander Siddig was the lucky bearer of a traditional "Scotty wave," modeled after the side-parted hairdo associated with the *Enterprise*'s chief engineer. "The hairdos were hysterical, especially Bashir's," Rene Auberjonois chortles. "And I had a great hairdo. With my hair all greased back, I looked like Jerry Lee Lewis!"

After all the behind-the-scenes work was completed, the actors got to strut their stuff on the soundstages. "It was like visiting somebody's family reunion and being a guest," gushes Farrell. "What was great was that we were supposed to react to the sets like, 'Wow, we're on the *Enterprise!*' And it was easy because it *felt* like, 'Wow, we're on the *Enterprise!*' It looked so real!" The writers couldn't have been happier with Farrell's enthusiasm, since they had inten-

Brooks and Farrell were photographed in front of a panel that did not exist in the original episode. ROBBIE ROBINSON

THE ASSIGNMENT

Episode #504

TELEPLAY BY **DAVID WEDDLE &**
BRADLEY THOMPSON
STORY BY **DAVID R. LONG & ROBERT LEDERMAN**
DIRECTED BY **ALLAN KROEKER**

GUEST CAST

Keiko O'Brien	ROSALIND CHAO
Rom	MAX GRODÉNCHIK
Molly O'Brien	HANA HATAE
Jiyar	PATRICK B. EGAN
Tekoa	ROSIE MALEK-YONAN
Station Computer Voice	JUDI DURAND
Computer Voice	MAJEL BARRETT

STARDATE UNKNOWN

As Rom enjoys a *hew-mon*-style breakfast in Quark's bar and tells his brother how much he loves working for Chief O'Brien, the chief himself is having a rather strange morning. He's been looking forward to Keiko's return from a trip to Bajor's fire caves, but when he greets her transport, he discovers she's not herself. Literally.

O'Brien listens in growing horror as the being that appears to be his wife calmly informs him that it is an entity who has taken possession of Keiko's body, and that it will hold the body hostage until O'Brien completes an assignment. If O'Brien fails to follow her instructions or attempts to reveal the truth to anyone, the entity will kill Keiko.

"Keiko" doesn't *seem* to want much from O'Brien. All he has to do, she explains, is reconfigure some of the communication and sensor relays on the station. It won't harm the station or the people on it. Seeing no other alternative, O'Brien reluctantly agrees.

The entity seems to enjoy playing the role of housewife. She sees no reason to cancel the birthday dinner Keiko had planned for O'Brien, despite the chief's obvious unease. The next morning, she orders him to recalibrate the impulse response filters in the subspace communication emitters. O'Brien worries that the work might harm the station, despite what the entity told him, and decides to talk to Sisko. But the entity knows O'Brien as well as Keiko does. Before he can approach the captain on the Promenade, "Keiko" draws the engineer's attention to the second level, where his wife is leaning precariously over the railing. Before he can do anything, Keiko plummets to the level below.

O'Brien is relieved when he learns that Keiko,

tionally positioned the character of Dax as a surrogate for themselves. "Dax was basically a stand-in for René Echevarria and me," admits Ron Moore, "because we were such big fans of the original series. So Dax spends a lot of the episode wandering around the *Enterprise,* just grooving on the whole thing."

The filming experience was a celebration in every sense of the word. "I remember the first day that we went over to the soundstage where the recreated interior of the *Enterprise* was," says Editor Steve Tucker. "It was like a giddy party was going on. Everybody was in these new costumes and the sets were so exciting."

"This episode was just an amazing, amazing amount of work," Ira Behr states proudly. "The crew, the technical people, the actors—they just threw themselves into it. They all were having fun. Just sitting on those sets, being on that bridge, it was a hoot, a real hoot."

And, more than that, "Trials and Tribble-ations" was, in every sense of the word, a gift from those people who participated in its production to their counterparts on the original series. "We got to reach back thirty years and shake hands, almost physically," says Siddig. "And I think that's a beautiful thing."

The chief fears for the lives of his loved ones when he realizes that his wife's body has been inhabited by a Pah-wraith. DANNY FELD

brief confrontation with Odo in which the engineer is forced to knock out the former shape-shifter. O'Brien then contacts the entity and tells her to meet him at one of the runabout pads. Together, they take off, and the entity instructs O'Brien to target the center of the wormhole. Using his remote comlink to the modified station controls, the chief activates the beam—but instead of firing into the wormhole, it blasts the runabout. The currents of energy flow through Keiko's body, destroying the Pah-wraith and leaving his wife unharmed. The reunited O'Briens return to the station, where the chief explains his bizarre behavior to the crew and rewards Rom for his help.

"The Assignment" is a show of firsts. It marks the first *Star Trek* episode for Canadian director Allan Kroeker, who would go on to helm many key episodes over the next few years, including the finales for Seasons 5, 6, and 7. It was the first produced teleplay for freelance writers David Weddle and Bradley Thompson, following a successful story pitch the previous year ("Rules of Engagement"), and the first *Star Trek* television score for Composer Greg Smith. And, of course, the episode marks the first on-air mention of the Pah-wraiths, the powerful banished life-forms that would become an integral part of the series' ongoing storyline. At the time, however, their creation was more a matter of convenience than an epiphany.

Weddle and Thompson's teleplay was based on a story submitted by Robert Lederman and David R. Long, who previously had done the story for Season 3's "Improbable Cause." "In our original pitch, Keiko was on a biological expedition on a planet that was inhabited by noncorporeal beings," recalls Lederman. "Keiko returned to the station along with one of those beings, under its control. After the producers bought the pitch, Lederman notes, "they changed it in a very positive way. Only the title stayed the same."

The task of developing the story fell to René Echevarria. "The entity in the original story used Keiko as its hostage. It was separate from her, but could do things to her," Echevarria recalls. The first thing that occurred to him was to turn it into a possession story, "because that added a creepiness to it," he says.

Ron Moore agreed. "I pushed for that, because the closer the character was to the Keiko we recognized, the more she spoke and acted like Keiko, the creepier it would be. There's something scary about saying, 'You're in my wife's body,' and then she just

although seriously injured, will recover. But the entity still possesses her body, and it warns O'Brien not to try any more tricks. He has thirteen hours to complete his task, but O'Brien doesn't see how he can make the changes in that amount of time. When Rom volunteers to take on some additional duties, O'Brien swears him to secrecy and puts him to work on the project. But late that night, a worried Dax approaches O'Brien. She's inadvertently come across signs of O'Brien's alterations and come to the conclusion that the station has a saboteur.

Sisko calls an emergency meeting, where an uncomfortable O'Brien must pretend to be as baffled as the others. Urged to come up with possible candidates for the saboteur, O'Brien directs them to Rom, who is brought in for questioning. O'Brien secretly continues the Ferengi's work until he is summoned to Security by Odo. Rom wants to talk to him—alone. As he had promised the chief, Rom has kept mum about his work. But he needs to know one thing: Why are they recalibrating the deflector grid to kill the wormhole aliens?

Suddenly, O'Brien understands what the entity wants. The specified recalibrations will focus a chroniton beam at the wormhole. While harmless to humanoids, the beam would be deadly to the wormhole's inhabitants. Rom tells O'Brien about the Bajoran legend of the Pah-wraiths, who dwelled within the wormhole until the Prophets cast them out and imprisoned them in Bajor's fire caves, the same fire caves Keiko recently visited.

O'Brien manages to finish his work, despite a

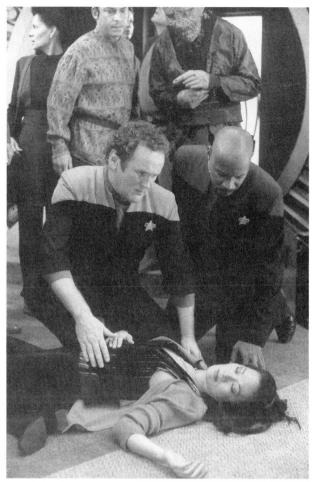

While it lays the groundwork for the finale, the premise of this episode was, according to Behr, "Let's make O'Brien miserable . . . again." DANNY FELD

says, 'OK, let's go to bed,' just like every night, and she knows all your little habits and the furl of your brow and all the little things that only a wife would know. That makes your flesh crawl on a certain level, and I think it's why the episode works."

"My other thought was to tie this entity into our show in some way," Echevarria adds. "So I said, 'What if there are evil entities in the wormhole?' and Robert Wolfe really grabbed on to that. He had a lot of interest in fantasy and mythic storytelling, and he saw the potential of it as something we could play on."

"I just liked the idea of evil Bajoran gods," Wolfe says, with a grin. "I remembered that in the very first season we'd come up with the fire caves, because Jake and Sisko were going there on vacation ['The Nagus'], and we had someone say, jokingly, 'Watch out for the Pagh-wraiths' [sic]. At the time I was thinking, 'What's a cool gobliny kind of thing that superstitious people might believe could be hiding in the fire caves?'" While that line of dialogue didn't make it

into the final version of "The Nagus," Wolfe never forgot it, and now he saw an opportunity to resurrect the concept. "We knew we wanted something evil to be inhabiting Keiko's body, and I remembered those Pagh wraiths of long, long ago."

With the entire writing staff occupied with the very complex "Trials and Tribble-ations," Ira Behr assigned the teleplay to freelancers David Weddle and Bradley Thompson. "We couldn't make heads or tails out of what we were gonna do with the story," Weddle admits. "But when we got into the break session, we found out what the producers really were going for. It was the annual 'Let's torture O'Brien' show. Hans Beimler said something like, 'You know, it's like a nightmare of a relationship. Everyone comes over for a party when you're having a huge fight with your wife and she acts as if everything is perfectly normal.'" The example struck home for the freelancers. Thompson was married and Weddle was soon to be wed. "As soon as we heard that," Weddle laughs, "we said, 'Oh, this is great! We can write this!'"

Interestingly, the motivation for the party changed in midstream. "Kira was staying with the O'Briens at the time," notes Brad Thompson, "so the party was going to be some sort of Bajoran religious holiday. It would establish the Pah-wraiths as well as put O'Brien on the spot with the Pah-wraith wife." That's when reality, in the form of Nana Visitor's extremely advanced pregnancy, came into play. "After we had turned in our final draft of the script, they found out that Nana would not be available for the episode," Thompson says. At that point, the staff writers did a last-minute rewrite of some of the scenes, and invented another reason for the party, namely, the chief's birthday.

And then there's the Pah-wraiths. Regardless of Wolfe's enthusiasm for them, no one, least of all the freelancers, suspected the magnitude to which the importance of the entities would grow within one brief year. The name of the entities took a slight turn in the script from Wolfe's original notion. Back then, he says, "it was *Pagh*. 'Pah' is a misspelling, from my point of view."

"Not if it comes from Ancient Bajoran," Weddle counters with a laugh. "The g's were added centuries later, when the seventh hemisphere became more influential."

René Echevarria has a simple explanation for how "*Koss'moran*" (in this episode it means "to be banished," according to Rom) had become "Kosst Amojan" by the time of "The Reckoning." "I changed

The sense of menace was heightened by the superb work of Meaney and Chao. ROBBIE ROBINSON

allow Keiko to seem sinister in Miles's eyes. I love when they write stuff that has an edge to it so I can play against the sweetness and light that they normally write for Keiko."

"This was a very cerebral show," notes Composer Greg Smith. "It was all on the inside. Only O'Brien and the alien Keiko were aware of the situation, so the music had to be ultra subtle. And things are much scarier when they're underplayed, as Chao's performance was." To support that subtlety, Smith chose to use "passive sounds, like French horns and strings," reducing the use of instruments that might draw attention to themselves. In fact, he had only one trumpet playing on the score.

" 'The Assignment' was a breath of air, frankly, for everyone," Steve Oster comments. "The first five episodes of the season were all big shows, so after that, from a production point of view, it was very nice to have a relationship story between Keiko and O'Brien."

it," he says with a laugh. "I heard it pronounced *Koss'moron,* and I didn't want that. Then when Ira saw the change he said, 'No, change it back.' I said, "*Moron?* You want it to be *moron?*" In the end, Behr approved the new spelling and pronunciation. Spelling concerns aside, the freelancers proved themselves more than capable with their first assignment. "When Ira gave it to us," Thompson recalls, "he said, 'Now, there's no chance you're gonna get to do the rewrite.' He also said, 'I hope you'll continue to talk to me after this experience.' And I thought, 'Oh. Thanks for the confidence!'"

"After we turned in the first draft," Weddle continues, "they called us back in for a meeting with all the guys and told us, 'This is a good thing. This almost never happens. You guys are going to get to write the next draft.'" Weddle grins. "The teleplay still was rewritten substantially after we did our rewrite, but we were pleasantly surprised that they let us do it."

"They took a shot and it was a good episode," Ira Behr concludes. "They were intelligent guys and they weren't kids." At the end of the season, the two writers were brought on staff, and the following year they found themselves doing a sequel of sorts, with "The Reckoning."

Actress Rosalind Chao found the episode reminiscent of "Whispers," from Season 2. "In the earlier one, [the fake] Miles isn't sure if Keiko is possessed or not, and in this one, *I* definitely was possessed," she laughs. "Those episodes were fun because I could give my performance a sort of double meaning and

LET HE WHO IS WITHOUT SIN . . .

Episode #505

WRITTEN BY ROBERT HEWITT WOLFE & IRA STEVEN BEHR

DIRECTED BY RENE AUBERJONOIS

GUEST CAST

Pascal Fullerton	MONTE MARKHAM
Leeta	CHASE MASTERSON
Bolian Aide	FRANK KOPYC
Risian Woman	BLAIR VALK
Risian Woman	ZORA DEHORTER

SPECIAL APPEARANCE BY

Arandis	VANESSA WILLIAMS

STARDATE UNKNOWN

When Worf and Jadzia hit a rough spot in their burgeoning relationship, the pair decide to take a vacation and share "some time alone together." Although Worf would prefer to go elsewhere, Jadzia talks the Klingon into going to Risa, a beautiful, climate-controlled pleasure planet.

The trip starts out poorly, with Bashir, Leeta, and Quark opting to tag along, and goes downhill from there. Worf does not care for the sybaritic lifestyle encouraged by Risa's inhabitants. Nor is he happy to

The New Essentialists choose a startling way to convince vacationers on Risa that Federation citizens are becoming too complacent and self-indulgent. ROBBIE ROBINSON

discover that Dax has an old friend on the planet: the beautiful Arandis, chief facilitator at the Temtibi Lagoon resort. Arandis is a former lover of Curzon Dax's; in fact, their lovemaking brought on Curzon's death.

As Worf mulls over his feelings, he is approached by Pascal Fullerton, chairman of the New Essentialists Movement. Fullerton and his group are on a crusade to shut down Risa, which they see as a symbol of the kind of self-indulgence that's eroding the foundations of Federation society. Although few of the vacationers are interested in Fullerton's preaching, he finds a receptive audience in Worf, much to Jadzia's dismay.

That night, a group of Essentialists storm the facility's solarium, armed with phaser rifles. But the attack is just a stunt to convince the vacationers how vulnerable they are. Dax is incensed, but Worf sees some logic in the group's behavior. Later, in their room, Worf accuses Dax of not taking their relationship seriously and Dax accuses Worf of taking everything *too* seriously. A potentially romantic evening is ruined.

Dax spends much of the next day with Arandis, first helping her and the Risians clean up the damaged solarium, and later, relaxing together. When Worf catches a glimpse of the two of them together, he comes to the wrong conclusion about their activities and storms off in a jealous rage. He winds up at Fullerton's quarters and tells the Essentialist he knows a way to drive the guests from Risa.

Soon, a galelike rainstorm hits Risa, putting an abrupt end to the resort's outdoor activities. Since the weather grid normally prevents rain from falling over the area, Arandis and Dax realize there must be a

problem with the grid. But before they can check into it, Fullerton and his Essentialists arrive, followed by Worf, who explains that he has modified a tricorder to disrupt the grid. For the next few days, Risa will experience its natural weather cycle, which means rain, rain, and more rain.

Dax is furious. She accuses Worf of destroying the vacations of thousands of people just to punish her for her alleged irresponsibility and unfaithfulness. When Worf mentions that no Klingon woman would act the way she does, Jadzia points out that Worf doesn't exactly behave like any Klingon she's ever met. He has no passion for life, no ability to cut loose and enjoy himself.

Her comments strike a nerve, and Worf reluctantly reveals the reason for his behavior. As a young teenager, while enjoying the full extent of his Klingon physical prowess in a sports competition, Worf inadvertently killed a human boy. The incident made him realize that if he was to live among humans, he must learn to practice restraint. That resolution has colored every moment of his life.

The pair are close to reconciliation when the region is struck by a powerful earthquake. Realizing that Fullerton is still in control of the jury-rigged tricorder, Dax and Worf head for his quarters. Sure enough, they find that the Essentialists have disrupted the planet's tectonic stress regulators with the device. Worf takes it away from Fullerton and switches it off. Worf believes that people will return to traditional Federation values on their own, without the Essentialists' "help."

A few days later, with the planet's beautiful weather restored and Worf's trust in Jadzia firmly entrenched, the pair take time to enjoy what's left of their vacation by skinny-dipping in the Temtibi Lagoon.

A less open and honest group than the *Deep Space Nine* filmmakers probably would heed the advice that Thumper's mother has the little bunny repeat in front of Bambi: "If you can't say something nice, don't say nothin' at all."

But since this is a group of individuals who readily accept responsibility for their actions, they all tell the truth, even when asked to talk about "Let He Who Is Without Sin . . ."

"Must we?" asks Ira Behr, one half of the guilty writing team.

"The worst episode I ever wrote," admits Robert Wolfe, the other culpable party.

"Markham is another one of the old pros who gave us a really nice performance," says Ira Behr. ROBBIE ROBINSON

"It's a show we all wish we had a second crack at," states Ron Moore.

"It was not my happiest time as a director," comments Rene Auberjonois.

The road to "Sin" was paved with good intentions. The writers had been discussing the themes of Eugene O'Neill's *A Moon for the Misbegotten,* a play in which the characters allow drunkenness, sex, and religious fervor to carry them to tragic endings. "The idea," Behr explains, "was to do a show that would rattle the audience, that would show sexuality and push the envelope about Risa." It was fitting, somehow, that Behr personally would take on this challenge. After all, he'd created Risa in the *TNG* episode "Captain's Holiday." (It also featured a Ferengi named Sovak, played by Max Grodénchik.) Behr notes that he was primarily interested in exploring the notion, "Once you get past the titillation, is this a lifestyle that people in the twentieth century can approve of?" But even as the show was being produced, Behr discovered that the answer was an unmitigated "No."

"Kids watch this show, and in some markets it airs at five o'clock," he sighs. "That meant we couldn't show skin, so there was no sex. It became a totally asexual show, and once that happened the whole thing got flushed down the toilet because none of it made sense anymore." Wolfe had sensed doom early on. "We wanted to do something fun and sexy as a follow-up to 'Trials and Tribble-ations,'" he says. "Ira and I came up with the story and wrote the first draft, but it just wasn't working and by then we were really short on time. I wanted to take the guys with the

weather-control satellites and change it into more of an action thing like *Die Hard.* But it was too late—the ship had sailed."

Although the script answered some interesting questions about a few of the characters—how Curzon met his end, and why Worf is such a stick in the mud—no one was happy with it. Sometimes a weak script can be salvaged by other elements of a production. However, this time, the atmosphere was pregnant with distractions. "Nana was having her baby, so Sid was pretty unfocused," Auberjonois notes. "He wanted to be with her and the baby."

"My mind really wasn't on the show very much," Siddig admits, albeit with a happy smile. "That's the week that I became a father. Nana had gone into the hospital in the middle of the show, and she had Django at eleven o'clock at night. Obviously a late-night birth meant I stayed up all night with the baby and Nana. Then at five-thirty I got in my car, bleary eyed, and drove to Malibu, to break up with Leeta." Siddig laughs at the juxtaposition of events. "It was all very surreal. I still don't know how I managed that except that having seen Nana give birth the night before, I figured I should be able to manage any number of things."

Other actors had their own unique problems as well. "Terry Farrell cannot be in the sun, and the producers had not taken that into account," Auberjonois says, "even though I'd mentioned it at the production meetings. So I personally was running around building a tent that she could stand under so we could shoot her scenes." While a number of tents had been brought to the location to be used as distant background pieces, bringing one forward, not to mention devising an awning for it, had not been on the already tight schedule.

The abridging of the script. The birthing of the baby. The burning of the sun. Perhaps all of those situations could have been anticipated. But no one expected the tackburrs. "Up to that point we'd been in really good shape, timewise," says B.C. Cameron. "But then we were rushing to get the work done before the light went away and we couldn't shoot. I was scrambling, trying to get all these elements pulled together. The beach sort of rolled up onto a little bank where there were some plants, and that's where Rene wanted all the background characters to be standing while they listen to Monte Markham's speech. We got the people up there and all of a sudden they were going, 'Ouch, ouch, ouch, ouch.' They were picking tackburrs out of their feet, because

The final matte painting would only use parts of this sketch— the palm trees and the giant *Horga'hn*. JOHN EAVES

those plants on the bank were all tackburr plants and the tackburrs were all in the sand. And of course, everyone had sandals and thongs on. So we just told them, 'Just stand real still!'"

In contrast to everyone else's problems, Armin Shimerman had a pleasant experience making the episode. "My best friend was one of the guest stars," he says. "His name is Frank Kopyc and he played the blue Bolian who's an assistant to Monte Markham's character. Frank is the man I modeled Quark after," Shimerman reveals. "He was my inspiration for Quark, so it was nice to have him right at my elbow. He's a fun-loving, sort of self-inquisitive type of guy who enjoys life, but at the same time always is worried about being *first*. And I don't mean that in a *bad* way," Shimerman grins. "That's the way I like to play Quark. He's very human, and his problems are definitely serious ones and human ones. It's just that Quark sees the world from Frank's point of view."

Actor Vanessa Williams's presence also was a pleasant aspect of the show. "The episode was set to air during sweeps week, and the studio wanted a 'name' for the role," explains Auberjonois. "I was surprised that Vanessa accepted it, but she did it with tremendous grace. She was a complete and total professional."

A day at the beach, and since this is a *DS9* location shoot things must go awry. ROBBIE ROBINSON

eye and came right over," Robert Blackman recalls. "I'd made several cover-ups and wraps for her, so we tried them on and she was fine. The fitting was over in twenty-five minutes and off they went to work. She was great." Finding unique costumes for the episode was a bit of a challenge for the costume designer. "There were bikinis and swimsuits with big cut-outs here and there," Blackman says. "When you get down to a bathing suit, it's really hard to find variety. They're either one piece or two piece. Unless," he adds with a chuckle, "you do a Rudi Gernrich topless suit—and that's never gonna happen on *Star Trek!*"

Which is not to say that a minimum of fabric was used on the show. In fact, the opposite is true. "The Risa show was all about pillows, drapery, and carpeting," notes Laura Richarz. "The Drapery Department people outdid themselves for this huge interior set where the walls are made of drapery in three or four colors. They were all quadrupled in material for fullness, and some of them were as high as fourteen feet. But the coolest thing I did were the loungers," Richarz smiles. "I went to Modern Props [a rental house] and found some radar scoops that they had put legs on." Radar scoops are large metal dishes built by the military to receive radar signals. "They were just sitting there, looking like giant loungers," Richarz says. "So I went up to Drapery and found this really great deco fabric that had been there for years. We made pads for the scoops and they made just really bizarre loungers." And then there were the tents. "The Property Department had them in storage," Richarz comments. "They were left over from those 'knights-in-shining-armor' movies. It was fun to see the tents go up," she says with a chuckle, "because we wondered if this was the weirdest production they'd ever been used in."

When the episode was over, the writing staff had to admit something they'd long suspected. "Romance is not one of our strong suits," says Robert Wolfe. "We try to do them and generally they don't work as well as we want them too. Even when the scripts are working, the episode doesn't always crystallize. People don't turn on *Deep Space Nine* looking for romance, or if they do they're looking for it in the background, as a flavor. When we made it central, it just didn't work."

"There's something called 'stunt casting' that the publicity department and the stations like," says Steve Oster. "We're always looking for opportunities to stunt cast. Vanessa Williams had expressed an interest in the show, and it all came together in the last minute." Because of her active schedule, Williams arrived in Los Angeles the same morning that she was needed to appear on camera. "She flew in on the red-

THINGS PAST

Episode #506

WRITTEN BY MICHAEL TAYLOR
DIRECTED BY LeVAR BURTON

GUEST CAST

Dukat	MARC ALAIMO
Belar	VICTOR BEVINE
Soldier	BRENAN BAIRD
Okala	LOUAHN LOWE

SPECIAL GUEST STARS

Garak	ANDREW J. ROBINSON
Thrax	KURTWOOD SMITH

STARDATE UNKNOWN

Something is troubling Odo as he returns from Bajor with Sisko, Dax, and Garak. The four have just attended a conference that provided a historical perspective of the Cardassian Occupation of the planet, and Odo's role received quite a bit of attention from the Bajorans. Assigned by the Cardassians during that period to keep order on the station, Odo earned the trust of both the captors *and* the captives, the Bajorans say, because he served only justice. But Odo was not comfortable with the depiction, and he's not comfortable with the follow-up discussion on the runabout.

As the ship approaches Deep Space 9, the crew in Ops is alarmed to note that the runabout is on autopilot and the life signs of the four persons on board are very weak. Bashir beams onto the vessel and finds the crew comatose, each with an unusually high level of neural energy in their cerebral cortex. The runabout's computer reveals that the ship was irradiated by a plasma storm during its trip, but Bashir can't understand why that would create this reaction. Their conscious minds are active, but he can't revive them.

From the crew's perspective, they *are* awake. However, rather than finding themselves in DS9's Infirmary, they see themselves in the Bajoran ghetto section of Terok Nor during the height of the Cardassian Occupation. Although they recognize each other, everyone else sees them as Bajorans. Confused, they decide not to dissuade others of this apparent illusion. For his part, however, Odo is more than confused; he's deeply agitated by their situation, haunted by recollections that none of the others have.

The quartet notice Gul Dukat, then commander of the station, talking to a man that Garak recognizes

Sisko, Garak, and Dax are forced to experience a troubling memory from Odo's past. ROBBIE ROBINSON

as Thrax, Odo's predecessor as chief of security on Terok Nor. They conclude that somehow they've traveled back in time at least nine years. As they try to make some sense of this, two Cardassian soldiers arrive and take away Dax, who has been chosen to be a special "friend" to Dukat. Although the men are helpless to do anything about the Trill's predicament, Garak's theft of a Cardassian comlink allows them to figure out what their identities are in this reality.

Sisko is an engineer named Ishan Chaye, Garak an artist named Jillur Gueta, and Odo . . .

. . . but Odo already knows. He's a bookkeeper named Timor Landi.

How does he know? Sisko inquires. Odo explains that he recognized the other two names and guessed at the third. They were Bajorans who were falsely accused of an assassination attempt on Dukat. All three were executed, as *they* may be if the scenario continues. What he doesn't reveal is the fact that he has actually seen the ghostlike corpses of the three Bajorans, walking the Promenade, staring at *him*. He's seen other things, too, including visions of blood on his hands.

In checking the comlink again, Garak notices something odd. They've traveled back only seven years in time. But by that time, Odo had taken over for Thrax. So where is the Odo of this time period?

Odo says he doesn't know, but he *does* know they'd better get off the station if they want to survive. Sisko agrees and contacts the Bajoran resistance for help. But his efforts are too late. The attempt on Dukat's life occurs just as Odo said it would, and Sisko, Garak, and Odo are arrested. When Thrax comes to their cell to tell them of the charges against them, Odo points out that all the evidence is circumstantial. If Thrax digs a little deeper, he'll see that they're innocent. But Thrax is too overworked to pay heed. Sisko begins to suspect that their predicament somehow is connected to Odo, but the former changeling insists that he has no clues.

The arrival of Dax, who has escaped from Dukat, interrupts the conversation. She breaks them out of the cell and they head for an airlock, only to find their escape route blocked by Thrax and his guards. The guards are dispatched, but just as they're about to get the better of Thrax, the Cardassian morphs into changeling-type goo and slithers into a vent.

Nonplussed, they press forward, but suddenly find themselves back in the holding cell, where they are informed their execution will take place in two hours. The other three press Odo for answers, realizing that somehow he is at the center of this dangerous mystery. But before Odo can answer, Thrax returns and removes Odo from the cell. Odo pleads with the security chief to see the truth, to use his investigative expertise to dig deeper. But Thrax speaks only of the way the Bajoran people fight against "order" and "the rule of law," phrases that chill Odo with their familiarity. As a last refuge, Odo admits he and the others have come from the future,

that they don't belong here at all. But, surprisingly, Thrax already knows. And it doesn't make any difference.

Suddenly the pair are on the Promenade, watching as the execution of Sisko, Garak, and Dax is about to take place. Odo exclaims that he won't let the execution happen again, and tells Thrax that the Cardassian doesn't even belong here—it's *Odo* who should be supervising the execution, for he was the one who served as security chief during this period.

Suddenly, Thrax disappears, and Sisko, Garak, and Dax are standing with Odo. On the other side of the Promenade, an execution is taking place. It's the real Timor, Ishan, and Jillur—and the Odo of that time period is watching them die, while the Odo of DS9's present looks on in shame.

It's true, he tells his friends. He was security chief at the time. He allowed three innocent men to die because he was too busy, too concerned about maintaining order, and the rule of law.

Odo awakens in DS9's Infirmary, along with Sisko, Dax, and Garak. Bashir has an odd theory. Although Odo is now a solid, the plasma storm activated residual morphogenic enzymes in his brain and initiated a telepathic response. His mind reached out instinctively to find other changelings to form the Great Link, but only Dax, Sisko, and Garak were nearby. Since Odo had been thinking about the executions just before the accident, the Link experience forced him to relive it and face the truth. Later, when Kira asks him to assure her that this was the only time he allowed the innocent to die on his watch, Odo admits painfully that he can only hope that's true.

"I call this episode 'Nightmare on Odo Street,'" laughs LeVar Burton, director of "Things Past." It's an apt title for an episode that primarily takes place in the former shapeshifter's subconscious. "We'd wanted to do a 'Back to Terok Nor' show for a long time," comments Robert Wolfe, "and we'd heard a lot of time travel ideas that would have allowed us to do it, but Michael Taylor came up with this idea of everybody getting stuck in Odo's dreams and we thought, 'Why not make it one dream, the dream of Terok Nor and Odo's guilty memories?'"

Guilty memories?

"One of the things that always drove the writing staff nuts," says Ron Moore, "was the idea that Odo had been a policeman during the Cardassian Occupation, but never had gotten his hands dirty, that he had

The writers were pleased with this dark look into Odo's psyche.
ROBBIE ROBINSON

been above it all, and that everybody had trusted him. We never bought that. It seemed to me that if I were a Bajoran, I wouldn't trust the *cop* who's still on duty from the Occupation. Somewhere along the line something bad went down on Odo's watch," Moore asserts. "And 'Things Past' was the show to say it."

Ironically, Michael Taylor's pitch had little to do with this theme. "It was a circular structure based on the old theme of waking up from a dream only to realize you're still in the dream," Taylor says, "except that I had the characters waking from dreams into *other* characters' dreams. Only at the end did the characters realize they were all in an Odo 'master dream.'" The writing staff liked the premise, although they urged Taylor to make it darker, and more night-marish. Taylor went to work on a revision, which the then–New Yorker completed right before he flew out to Los Angeles to meet with the writers. "It was sort of like *DS9* meets *Friday the 13th*," he chuckles. "When I got there, we all read the thing and every-body looked up and said, 'Okay, what are we *really* going to do?'"

"Dream stories are notoriously difficult to make work on *Deep Space Nine*," Moore says. "We've tried quite a few, and to make this one work we finally refocused it into one big shared experience that's not really a dream but is more of an odd telepathic con-nection."

Establishing a "telepathic connection" in a char-acter that viewers know isn't a telepath forced the writers to come up with a bit of technobabble about "residual traces of morphogenic enzymes" in Odo's brain. "It felt authentic," says Moore. "It justifies why, if Odo's human, he has the ability to telepathically do something. And it's also a hint that Odo's being a solid might not be a permanent condition," he adds.

The story development and script rewrite process was an eye-opener for Taylor. "I got my first lesson on how television really works," he says, laughing. Obviously, the freelancer paid attention; after writing "Resurrection" and the teleplay for "In the Pale Moonlight" in Season 6, he was hired as a staff writer on *Voyager*.

"I loved the script," enthuses Rene Auberjonois. "Odo's a character whom we've come to believe always tells the truth. In fact, in the pilot he says to Dukat, 'There's one thing that you know about me— I never lie.' We've tried to be consistent with that. But that doesn't mean that he doesn't lie to himself. He is this wonderfully contradictory character, in that he's made of liquid, but he's very rigid."

Unfortunately, Auberjonois's fondness for the script sabotaged his performance, at least in his opin-ion. "Quite candidly, I loved not wisely, but too well," he chuckles, comfortably paraphrasing Shakespeare. "I played it a little too intense. The emotional line of the script got to me and there's a danger in that. You can do the audience's work for them instead of letting them find it with you.

"LeVar, however, did a wonderful job directing," the actor adds.

Cast and crew alike are fond of LeVar Burton, and they've come to appreciate his skill on the soundstage. "He's a very capable director, so when he's working, we don't need to be on the stage a lot," says Steve Oster. "That was fortunate for me during 'Things Past' because the next episode up was 'The Ascent.' That was a location show and we all went location scouting up on Mount Whitney while we left LeVar here to deal with the show."

Burton is a hands-on director who likes to do as much of the needed work as possible on the stage. "My approach is, 'I have this idea, how can we do it?'" he says. "So I go to the experts to find out. I go to Jonathan West and [Key Grip] Steve Gausche to get their advice on whether something is doable. And you know what? They are *game*. After so many years of doing this stuff, day in and day out, it gets every-body's juices flowing to do something that's a little out of the ordinary. So when I asked for it here, they just said, 'Yeah, let's go for it.'"

To capture his "Nightmare on Odo Street," Burton used what he calls "a few horror picture

"The story's a little unconventional for *Deep Space Nine*," admits Ira Behr. DANNY FELD

tricks. For instance, when this phantasm is following Odo around the station, we did some 'in camera' tricks," he explains, meaning that the filmmakers performed some effects maneuvers live, on the spot, rather than leaving them to be created in postproduction. In this case, that meant "looking away and then having the person appear where he hadn't been a moment before," Burton says.

Revisiting Terok Nor was revisiting "Necessary Evil," to recreate the dark and depressed look of the station during the occupation. The production designers decided to fill the Promenade with fog, so Gary Monak and his crew set up a dry-ice fog generator and blew it into the set where "it would be held like water in a pan," explains Lou Race. "We got the fog to about four feet deep, and from above it seemed like we were looking down into a huge white cloud. At lunch time," he admits with a grin, "we'd all go down and dive into it and disappear."

The writers are fond of coming up with ways to pair characters that haven't been paired before, and even at this late date in the series' run they found an opportunity. After tossing Jadzia and Dukat together,

they treated audiences to one of the Cardassian's patented laments about what a lonely and complicated kind of guy he is. "That's how Dukat sees himself," says Moore. "He wants to be loved. He's the kind of dictator who thinks, 'It's not enough that I put my foot on the throat of the people I'm oppressing, I want them to *love* me for it.' Dukat believes he's the hero of his own story."

Moore personally had fun introducing the audience to a term the staff had been using behind the scenes for years, when he had a Bajoran resistance fighter refer to the Cardassians as "spoonheads." The reference goes back to Michael Westmore's original inspiration for the Cardassian makeup design—a painting in a Thai restaurant that portrayed a woman with a spoon in the middle of her forehead. "I put it into the script," admits Moore. "They're gonna call them names. People just do that. And it was a nice in-joke, too."

"We got a little criticism for 'Things Past,'" Taylor reports. "The fans wondered why we didn't just do the episode in straight flashback. They thought that having it take place in Odo's head was somehow superfluous. But to me that was what was interesting. It was the crux of the story, because the nature of science fiction is that these things aren't just gags. Odo wouldn't tell anybody about his secret by choice. The only reason he'd tell is if he was *forced* to tell. He was put into a position of vulnerability through this strange science fiction incident that linked him to his friends." If they had done it in flashback, Taylor concludes, "it wouldn't have been science fiction."

THE ASCENT

Episode #507

WRITTEN BY **IRA STEVEN BEHR &**
ROBERT HEWITT WOLFE
DIRECTED BY **ALLAN KROEKER**

GUEST CAST

| Rom | MAX GRODÉNCHIK |
| Nog | ARON EISENBERG |

STARDATE UNKNOWN

It's not easy for Ben Sisko to accept that his son is moving out—even if he's only moving to his own quarters on the other side of the habitat ring. But Jake couldn't be happier. Nog is returning from Starfleet Academy to fulfill his sophomore-year field study by serving on Deep Space 9. The two friends are going to be rooming together. Rom also is happy that Nog is coming home. As he expresses his excitement to the less-than-excited Quark, the two are interrupted by a surprise visit from Odo. He's come to take Quark to testify before the Federation grand jury on Inferna Prime, despite the fact that Quark claims he has no idea what he is to testify about.

The long trip to Inferna Prime is a strain on Quark. Odo isn't a particularly good companion, not that the security chief feels inclined to be a better one. Then, halfway to their destination, things take a turn for the worse as Odo and he discover that there's a bomb planted in the runabout. They attempt to beam the device out of the ship, but it explodes before it fully dematerializes and the runabout is badly damaged. After they manage to survive a crash-landing on a nearby planet, they make a few more distressing discoveries. The explosion destroyed the communications system, the replicator, and most of the rations. The planet's local vegetation appears to be poisonous and its climate is unbearably cold. It ini-

Quark tends to Odo's injury after an argument results in a nasty fall down the mountain. ROBBIE ROBINSON

tially appears that their only available choices are starving to death or freezing to death, but Quark comes up with an idea. Although the signal booster for the runabout's subspace transmitter is shot, they might be able to use the transmitter, *if* they move the heavy piece of equipment to the top of a distant mountain.

Back on the station, Jake is unpleasantly surprised to learn that Starfleet has turned his old friend Nog into a straight-laced physical fitness freak who cleans his quarters for recreation. Nog isn't exactly thrilled with *his* roommate, either. Jake won't exercise or pick up his clothing or return a dirty dish to the replicator. As the Ferengi puts it, Jake is a "slovenly, undisciplined, unfocused *writer*," a description even his father is hard put to disagree with.

The situation finally explodes when Nog returns from a hard day's work and finds their quarters looking like a war zone. The two friends exchange harsh words, and the Ferengi decides to move out. Jake lets him know that's fine with him, but neither is really happy about the solution. Nor, frankly, are their fathers, particularly Rom, with whom Nog has moved in. Sisko goes to his son and tells him he'll have to move out of his new bachelor pad *unless* he gets a roommate. The captain follows up by sending Nog back to his old quarters. He orders the two young men to work things out, and, not surprisingly, they find that doing so is not as hard as they'd thought. Concessions are made on both sides, and they decide to try again.

On the frigid planet, Quark and Odo set out

toward the mountain, sharing one set of cold-weather gear between them. It's an arduous, exhausting trip, made worse by the lack of food, but they take some comfort in the fact that the top of the mountain seems only hours away. Until, of course, they come to the edge of a cliff and discover that they will have to climb down a steep incline and cross a wide valley before they can even *begin* to tackle the mountain. As days pass, the bickering between the pair gets sharper. It escalates into a juvenile shoving match that results in the two losing their balance and sliding down the mountainside. Quark comes through the accident unscathed, but Odo suffers a broken leg.

With no other choice, Quark builds a travois so that he can drag both Odo *and* the transmitter up the mountain. Finally, Quark is too exhausted to go another step. Odo encourages Quark to take the transmitter and leave him behind, but the Ferengi claims to be too tired even to do *that.* Unwilling to give up, Odo attempts to crawl up the mountain, pushing the transmitter as he goes. Quark recognizes this as an attempt to shame him into resuming his own climb, but he resumes the climb anyway.

Day gives way to frigid night, and Odo reaches the conclusion that Quark failed to reach their goal and died. Knowing that he won't last much longer, he begins recording his final log entry, which is interrupted when he's transported up to the *Defiant.* Quark *did* make it, and Odo is faced with the unpleasant thought that his old nemesis saved his life. But, he is reassured that nothing will change between them when Quark confesses that he *still* hates Odo, and Odo happily admits the same.

"Jake wrote *all* the episodes," jokes Wolfe. "We don't actually write anything. He even wrote 'Let He Who Is Without Sin. . . .' It's one of his less effective works, but we couldn't skip it." ROBBIE ROBINSON

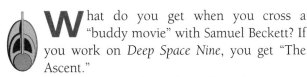**W**hat do you get when you cross a "buddy movie" with Samuel Beckett? If you work on *Deep Space Nine,* you get "The Ascent."

"I've read *Waiting for Godot* at least thirty times since I was fifteen years old," says Ira Behr. "And I wanted to do *Waiting for Godot,* with Quark as Estragon and Odo as Vladimir. And just have them . . . waiting. They're waiting for Sisko by a runabout and they don't know why they're there or how long they've waited. I just wanted to do it. But I never had the nerve."

It's hard to believe that Behr lacks the nerve to do much of anything. Then again, to expect the television viewing public to sit through a twenty-fourth-century version of an existential Samuel Beckett play that few critics claim to honestly understand is a pret-

ty daunting idea. This is *Star Trek,* after all: populist entertainment with a high-tech edge. But when the writing staff decided it was time to do an A-story about Quark and Odo, rather than the occasional B-story subplot, Behr had, at last, found what seemed to be a good opportunity to do a spin on *Godot.* "We've wanted to put Odo and Quark together in a story that took place off the station ever since first season," says Ron Moore. "But Ira had the wisdom to wait until a lot of stuff had happened to the characters, which gave us more to play with."

The moment also seemed right to do the kind of story they had in mind. "We wanted to do an episode emphasizing Odo's human frailty, showing the effects on him of not being able to shape-shift," says Robert Wolfe, who cowrote the episode with Behr. "But we didn't want them to be fighting bad guys because we'd done stuff like that already. We wanted to have them going somewhere that would have been easy for Odo to get to if he could morph. So we put him and Quark up against the elements and had them climb a mountain."

"It was a joy," says Rene Auberjonois. "For years, whenever Armin [Shimerman] or I went to events like conventions, or even to the supermarket, people would say, 'I love it when you and Quark . . .' And Armin and I always had answered, 'But we hardly ever get to do anything together.' It's a tribute to the writers and a tribute to Armin and me that there's such a strong reaction even though the show hasn't really addressed it all that much. So it was particularly fun to do a whole episode together, although it was hard on Armin," notes Auberjonois. "The altitude was very, very tough."

Shimerman typically has no problem wearing the prosthetics that make Quark the handsome Ferengi he is, at least, not on a soundstage at sea level. But moving those prosthetics into the Sierras produced some unforseen reactions. "I'd felt fine until we got up into the heights, and then I was nauseous, and I had no energy and I couldn't focus," recalls Shimerman. "The pressure inside the rubber head normally is tolerable. But not up there. And since most of the show was going to be shot at that location, I was afraid that we'd have to pull the plug." Fortunately, the production company's medic was prepared for altitude reactions. "Actually," Shimerman comments, "he's the hero of that episode, because if he hadn't given me something, I don't think I could have done it."

Before long, Shimerman was feeling better—except for the part where he was being pummeled by his friend Auberjonois in a scene that called for Odo to shake Quark awake. "Rene really beat on me!" Shimerman exclaims. "I remember thinking, 'You know, this is beyond acting now.' It's partially my fault, because I told him, 'I have a rubber head on so you can't hurt me.' But apparently I was wrong."

Obviously a script titled "The Ascent" suggested altitude, and it was Steve Oster who made the decision as to how *much* altitude; 14,495 feet, as it turned out. When he heard an early description of the required topography, he knew exactly where to go. "I do an annual trip to Mt. Whitney," he says, "so I know the area well."

The mountain had all the prerequisites for the assignment: it was big, the highest mountain in the lower forty-eight states, and it was close, located in central California, a relatively simple trip from Los Angeles. Nevertheless, the majority of the crew never had been there before. "It was funny taking them up there on the first location scout," Oster says, "because the nearby city of Lone Pine [where the crew spent their nights] is in the high desert, and the Sierras are just off in the distance. They don't look like anything. So when we stopped there for gas, everybody looked at me like, 'Uhhh, Steve . . . we're supposed to be in an Alpine location?' Then we drove the last ten miles. It's not until you turn into the last curve that you look up at Mt. Whitney and realize you're in the Sierras."

Oster knew the region so well that he saved the company the cost of a matte painting for the scene

All of the location filming on Mt. Whitney was shot within a radius of two hundred yards. ROBBIE ROBINSON

where Quark and Odo come to a high precipice and realize that they'll have to climb down to get over to the big mountain. Oster brought the crew to an old U.S. Forestry Service road that led to the exact visual the writers had in mind. "[Director] Allan Kroeker dubbed the spot 'Steve's Rock,' because anyone who didn't know the area wouldn't have found it," says Oster proudly.

As for Kroeker, he had a grand time. "It was a charmed episode," he says. "Everything just went *right*."

Although for a while, some of the crew had their doubts. "When we were scouting the location, Allan

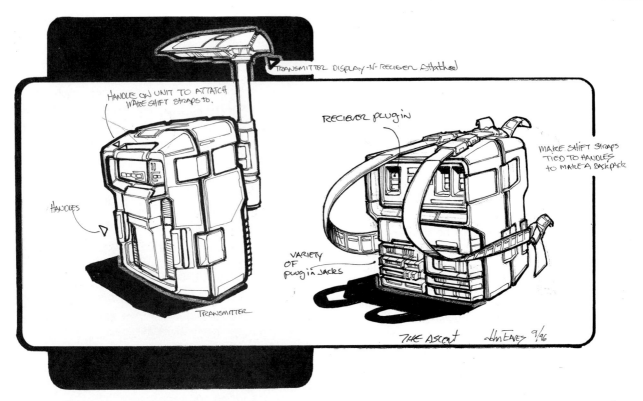

Transmitter display -n- reciever attachment

Handle on unit to attach make shift straps to.

Handles

Transmitter

Reciever plug in

Make shift straps tied to handles to make a backpack

Variety of plug in jacks

The Ascent   John Eaves 9/96

John Eaves suggested some modifications to a backpack left over from *TNG*. The same prop would be modified for a distress beacon in "Waltz."

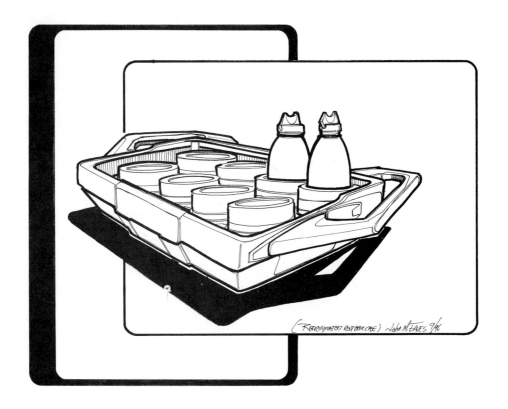

(Refrigerated root beer case) John M. Eaves 9/96

Concept for a root beer tray.
JOHN EAVES

went over to where water was sliding down over the rocks into this waterfall, and he had his hands up like directors do when they're framing up what they want the camera to see," First Assistant Director B.C. Cameron says. "I was thinking, 'What is he doing? How the heck are we gonna get the camera up there? Somebody's gonna have to rein this guy in, 'cause he's getting out of control.'"

"I was looking at the most interesting places to put the cast," Kroeker laughs. "I remember looking at B.C. and she was shaking her head. But I go on the premise that if *I* can go there, *anybody* can go there." Luckily, Steadicam Operator Rusty Geller was game for the challenge. "We got a lot of good angles," laughs the director.

"That was the first shot we did the morning we started there," Cameron says, shaking her head still. "Up on the side of that waterfall."

During the three days on the mountain, the weather was kind to the filmmakers. A little too kind, in fact. The script indicated that the climate of the alien planet was freezing cold, but in reality, the crew was treated to temperatures of 60 to 65 degrees each day, Cameron recalls. "The actors got all hot and sweaty because they were having to trudge around the hills carrying all this stuff the script called for," she says.

And the cold weather gear they were required to wear certainly didn't help. Observes Shimerman, "We were hotter than hell . . . "

". . . But we were shivering as if it were cold," Auberjonois completes the thought.

So how do you make a warm autumn outing look like a bitter winter trek? Use a good cinematographer and a big wind. Kris Krosskove, *Deep Space Nine*'s gifted camera operator, temporarily moved into the director of photography position while Jonathan West stayed in Los Angeles prepping to direct "Rapture." "I used wide lenses and a filter that tends to give the film a very icy feeling," Krosskove explains. "Then in the afternoon, when the sun was lower in the sky and we lost the warmth, I switched to a filter that neutralizes the light. And I also used a polarizing filter that makes the blue sky seem bluer and the clouds look puffier."

Krosskove sent special instructions to the telecine lab where the film was transferred to tape for editing. "We kept the color spectrum on the blue side," he explains. "That kept it cool and very frosty looking."

Gary Monak was responsible for the other weather-modifying equipment. "At one point Quark gets hammered by a storm," Monak says, "Normally we would use some big wind fans for that. But just before leaving L.A., we decided that it might be better to use a compresser and some 'air movers,' these big cones that are used for ventillating ships. It turned out to be a good decision, because we would have needed a fifty-ton crane to get the fans up to that ridge."

Back on the station, the writing staff solved a problem of their own making by having Nog assigned to Deep Space 9, despite the fact that he was only a second-year cadet. "It does seem a little soon, I grant you that," Behr comments. "But we like Aron and we like the character of Nog. At that point, we didn't know if we were going to continue for seven seasons, so we wanted to use his character while there still was time." The writers created the idea that an Academy student's sophomore year consisted of "field studies." They established that Sisko had spent his at Starbase 137—although they would fail to explain why Nog's field studies wound up lasting three years. One can assume, though, that with the war on, Nog probably learned more at the station and in battle that he would have in a classroom.

Behr and Wolfe clearly had a great deal of fun writing "The Ascent." They took the bold step of suggesting that the game of fizzbin, invented by Captain Kirk in the original series, had become a real game. "We figured that the people on Sigma Iotia II were clearly very smart, so they were able to extrapolate a game from the little bit that Kirk told them," Wolfe explains with a twinkle in his eye. "Now it's the national game of Iotia and Quark knows how to play it."

They took the even bolder step of writing a small section of the steamy romance novel that Odo attempts to read on the runabout. "We had a blast writing that," laughs Behr. "We could have gone on for pages! Actually, it was kind of a dry run for the story of Shmun and the Vulcan love slave in our book *Legends of the Ferengi*."

And Behr even found a subtle way to pay tribute to his favorite play when he had Nog call Jake "a slovenly writer." "The characters in *Waiting for Godot* keep on insulting each other, and the worst thing they can think to say is, 'Critic!'" Behr smiles. "So I just thought, 'Writer!'"

RAPTURE

Episode #508

TELEPLAY BY **HANS BEIMLER**
STORY BY **L.J. STROM**
DIRECTED BY **JONATHAN WEST**

GUEST CAST

Kasidy Yates   PENNY JOHNSON
Admiral Whatley   ERNEST PERRY, JR.

SPECIAL GUEST STAR

Kai Winn   LOUISE FLETCHER

STARDATE UNKNOWN

After Sisko sees the painting of B'hala, Bajor's lost city, he becomes strangely obsessed with finding the legendary site. He has the painting scanned into the computer so that he can study it more carefully. He later transfers the image into one of Quark's holosuites. After manipulating and enhancing a three-dimensional version of the painting's central obelisk, Sisko thinks he may have found some clues. But as he tries to save the program, the holosuite system shorts out and Sisko receives a shock that knocks him unconscious.

Bashir pronounces Sisko fit, but notes that the plasma burst has left him with post-neural shock syndrome, which will make his senses seem more pronounced for several days. The doctor suggests the captain take it easy for a while, but Sisko remains obsessed with the ancient puzzle and soon returns to the holosuite to continue his research. He's interrupted by a

message from Admiral Whatley: Bajor's petition to join the Federation has been approved. Sisko is pleased—this is what he's been working toward for five years—but before long he is caught up again in B'hala.

When Kira goes to find him, he is lost in a trance, experiencing a vision of Bajor's past and future. Kira is respectful of Sisko's obsession; an old prophecy states that only someone touched by the Prophets can find B'hala's ruins. But others aren't as understanding. No one can distract Sisko from his quest, not the arrival on the station of Kai Winn, nor the return of Kasidy Yates, who has just been released from a Federation prison ("For the Cause"). Sisko greets the latter with an odd invitation: join him on an immediate trip to Bajor. Although puzzled, Kasidy accompanies him to some caves that travel deep beneath the planet's surface. Sisko is briefly incapacitated by an excruciating headache, but he presses on and soon finds the lost city.

The Bajorans are awestruck by Sisko's discovery; even Winn, who often has opposed Sisko's actions, now is convinced that he is truly the Prophets' Emissary. But Admiral Whatley is concerned about Sisko's apparent distraction. This is a time when Starfleet will need to rely on the station commander's leadership abilities more than ever, but Sisko is reluctant to leave B'hala and return to DS9. Eventually, Sisko agrees to return to the station the next day and submit to another examination by Bashir.

When Sisko returns, he surprises the station's inhabitants with his apparent powers of psychic insight. But the visions have come with a price. Bashir believes that Sisko's unusual neural activity will kill him if he doesn't allow the doctor to operate. But the operation will also put an end to the visions, and Sisko feels he can't let that happen. Kasidy and Jake are appalled, as is the admiral and most of the crew. But Kira feels the Prophets will take care of Sisko, and Winn allows him to consult with the Orb of Prophecy to focus his visions. Worried that the Orb experience may last for days, Whatley decides to proceed with the planned ceremony celebrating Bajor's admission into the Federation. But partway through the event, Sisko appears, exhausted and in obvious pain. He warns the assembled that if Bajor joins the Federation at this time, it will be destroyed. Then he collapses.

Rushed to the Infirmary, Bashir declares that Sisko is on the verge of death. He needs to operate immediately, but since Sisko had refused surgery, the captain's closest relative must make the decision.

Admiral Whatley is stunned when Sisko reveals something about his personal life. ROBBIE ROBINSON

Unwilling to let his father die, Jake grants permission to operate.

When Sisko revives, he learns that Bajor's Chamber of Ministers has voted to delay Federation membership. Whatley asks Sisko to change their minds, but Sisko refuses. The visions may have faded, he says, but he knows that what they showed him was right. Returning to his quarters, he faces a warm welcome from Jake and Kasidy. Although he is devastated at the loss of the visions, he understands that he also retained something equally important.

"'Rapture' was a pretty wacky show for television," declares Ron Moore. "To have your lead character suddenly hearing the voices of the gods and believing in visions and going out on this whole weird tangent until it's taken away from him is . . ." he pauses, laughing, ". . . rather unusual."

Viewers already knew that Starfleet wasn't wild about Sisko's role as Bajor's Emissary, but that theme is played out in spades here. "It's almost a Prime Directive issue," Moore notes. "It's a classic example of what not to do: the Starfleet captain who encounters the primitive culture and declares himself a god. That *has* to be something they teach Starfleet Academy students in their first year," he says. "So certainly when they start hearing that somewhere out on the frontier Ben Sisko is now being revered as a spokesperson for the Prophets, it probably would raise a lot of eyebrows back at Headquarters."

The limited availability of new mother Nana Visitor shifted the story to Kasidy. ROBBIE ROBINSON

Despite the fact that the episode was, in many ways, the antithesis of what one normally would consider *Star Trek,* it was a fan favorite, according to Ira Behr. "I was surprised at the response it generated," he says. "They really seemed to take to this, to the spirituality, the faith. There's such a lack of faith in today's society. We're all so desperate to find something to believe in. This is the episode that made me realize just what we had created, in terms of the Bajoran faith and the Emissary. I knew that it was going to become a more and more important part of the show, and that a part of the audience was going to love it."

Hans Beimler's teleplay, based on a story pitch by L.J. Strom, "went through a real evolution from the original idea," says Beimler. "It became a whole new story that gave us a chance to revisit some of the themes that had been planted in the pilot episode. It's one of the shows that turned out to be a cornerstone in the series, because of the effort that was put into it by everybody on the staff."

"I don't know if Rick [Berman] and Michael [Piller] had any idea that the Emissary concept they established [in the pilot episode] was going to grow into the thing it did," says Behr. "I have to give René Echevarria credit for it, because he was very much into these stories and he pushed for them."

Echevarria was the writing staff's strongest advocate for shows like "Destiny" and "Accession," and his work behind the scenes on those episodes helped to establish a solid line of continuity between them and "Rapture." "'Destiny' was the first story where we really started to investigate what being the Emissary meant," he says. "It was the first crack in Sisko's resistance to holding that title. Then in 'Accession,' Sisko finds himself fighting for this thing he claims he never wanted."

Then came "Rapture," which gave Sisko "a glimpse of what it could be like to be a Prophet," says Echevarria, a plot twist that was eerily prophetic when one thinks about the final episode. "Here we actually *did* know what we were doing," he laughs. "We did know where we were going. And we were able to seed in a lot of stuff that the fans really appreciated."

Take the locusts: a rather biblical reference, to say the least, with far-reaching symbolic meaning. "The Prophets are telling the Bajorans, 'Don't join the Federation, because if you do you will be embroiled in this war,'" explains Echevarria. However, the locusts also had a more arcane meaning to the writ-

With this episode, Sisko moved from a grudging acknowledgment to accepting his role as a religious figure to the Bajorans.
ROBBIE ROBINSON

ing staff. "They're from this idea for a show that we never did—about space locusts," says Behr. "These things like locusts were going to come to Bajor and destroy everyone, and the Bajorans refused to do anything about it because it was something that had been predicted in the Prophecies. So they were willing to die. And Sisko was trying to figure out how to deal with these superstitious, spiritual people. We never did it because we couldn't figure out a way to do 'space locusts' that would make some sense and wouldn't look goofy. But we finally got to mention the locusts in 'Rapture.'"

"Rapture"'s B-story, regarding Kasidy's return to the station after serving a brief sentence in prison for assisting the Maquis, is closely tied to the main plot. In fact, there's only a brief discussion about the circumstances of her absence, and no time is wasted in pulling her into the A-story.

"The idea was, 'Don't go with the expectations,'" comments Behr. "I love Penny Johnson. She's just so straightforward, an actress in the tradition of Jean Arthur or Barbara Stanwick. A woman who's her own person, who's not just there for the man, but is totally supportive of the man she's involved with—a great relationship. If she was back, I wanted her to just get back to that relationship. Sisko isn't a dummy. He's a mature man. He understands what she did. I'd never want to make him seem petty or small. That would compromise his character."

So Kasidy was back in Sisko's life. However, Johnson's commitment to her ongoing role on *The Larry Sanders Show* would prevent her from making any additional appearances on *Deep Space Nine* for the rest of the season.

Louise Fletcher made her first appearance of the season, and, as Kai Winn, delivered a speech to Kira about how she spent the Occupation, which served to add some admirable qualities to her normally unsympathetic character. This, too, was an example of the writers' fondness for standing expectations on their heads. "We like to allow the audience to hate people like Winn," says Behr, "and then give her a speech that is basically just for Kira and the audience [that contradicts their expectations]. It's a perverse thing to do."

Perverse, but necessary if one wishes to create a realistic persona. "The kai is a really important character on the show," says Beimler, "and she's not one-note. She's complicated, multifaceted. That's because one of the things that Ira always has emphasized with us is to make the characters three-dimensional."

"The intention was to make her a bit less of a villain, and to force her, because of the magnitude of what Sisko was doing, to reassess her feelings about him," adds Echevarria. "He's not just a foreigner out to usurp her people. But as the show progressed, we eventually needed to get her back to another area, back to the older Kai Winn. So a moment of redemption was in her grasp, but her venality wins out in the end. And she loses."

As often is the case in a Sisko-oriented episode, a home-cooked meal plays a role in the story. Although the *Star Trek* franchise has popularized the notion that humanity of the future will receive its meals from slots in the wall, the *Deep Space Nine* staff works overtime to show that even in the twenty-fourth century, there are exceptions. "I'd like to lose the replicators," rails Behr. "They're my least favorite thing in *Star Trek*. A society that uses replicators is a doomed, finished society."

Philosophical motivation aside, cooking often serves a story purpose as well. Sisko's interest in cooking, says Beimler, evolved out of his brief first-season passion for clock building ("Dramatis Personae"). Hobbies, Beimler notes, are therapeutic, and it was clear from that early episode that Sisko liked tinkering. "But clock building means spending quiet time by yourself. Cooking is something you do for other people. It's more nurturing, and it addresses who the character is a little better."

In "Rapture," it's Jake who wants to do the nurturing, so for a change he cooks for his father, although Sisko is more preoccupied with the melon and the strange shapes that he's carved from them.

B'hala would be revised by a number of people: John Eaves, Doug Drexler, Mike Okuda, and Herman Zimmerman. JOHN EAVES

The similarity to the famous mashed potato scene in *Close Encounters of the Third Kind* isn't entirely coincidental. "I wish we could have done it as well," sighs Behr. "It was an homage scene, but we wanted it to be a cool moment of itself, and it just didn't make it."

"Rapture" was the first episode to run after *First Contact* opened at theaters, but the only crossover impact was the appearance of the new Starfleet uniforms designed for that film. Bob Blackman had had them, ready and waiting, over in wardrobe for some time. "We couldn't use them until we had an episode where we knew the airdate would be after the movie premiere," says the costume designer. But nothing ever is wasted in television production, particularly not something as expensive as a Starfleet uniform. The old *DS9* jumpsuits were sent over to *Voyager*, "where they were sorely needed," Blackman says.

A rather tongue-in-cheek method of drawing attention to the new costumes found its way into the script for "Rapture," when Bashir asks Sisko, "Does my uniform look a little brighter to you?" But this was as far as the writers went in terms of incorporating references to *First Contact* into the episode. Despite the fact that viewers probably would have

appreciated something as simple as a mention of recent repairs to the *Defiant,* which supposedly was badly damaged in the film, Behr wanted to forget about the use of *Deep Space Nine*'s beloved battleship in the project. "I didn't see the point in bringing it on just to kick the crap out of it," he says. Behr notes that the line "Tough little ship" was added to the movie's script after he had voiced his concerns.

Recreating the lost city of B'hala proved to be a demanding but rewarding task for the folks behind the scenes. Two versions of the obelisk were created: a model that was approximately nine feet tall, for the holosuite; and the much larger, full-sized obelisk that's unearthed in the cave.

Director Jonathan West had to fight for the big obelisk. "The producers originally planned that it would be only partially seen, maybe a foot and a half of it that was imbedded in the cave wall," he says. "They didn't want to reveal it in its full height. But both Herman Zimmerman and I took issue with that, because the discovery needed to be much more grand. Cost is always a factor in episodic TV, but sometimes you need to stand up for what you believe in. And I think that having it there added to the awe and inspi-

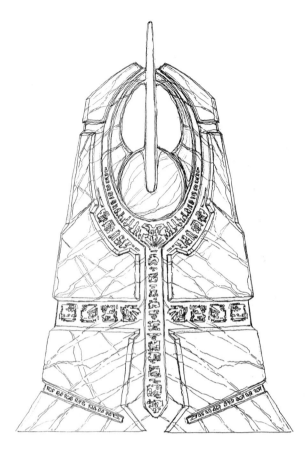

An early version of the *bantaca* spire. JOHN EAVES

episode, so her friends took the image of B'hala and had it transferred onto a T-shirt, which was further embellished with the words, "My friends all went to B'hala and all I got was this lousy T-shirt." The shirt was signed by Okuda's coworkers and sent to her as a get-well gift.

THE DARKNESS AND THE LIGHT

Episode #509

TELEPLAY BY **RONALD D. MOORE**
STORY BY **BRYAN FULLER**
DIRECTED BY **MICHAEL VEJAR**

GUEST CAST

Silaran Prin	RANDY OGLESBY
Furel	WILLIAM LUCKING
Lupaza	DIANE SALINGER
Trentin Fala	JENNIFER SAVIDGE
Nog	ARON EISENBERG
Latha Mabrin	MATT ROE
Brilgar	CHRISTIAN CONRAD
Guard	SCOTT McELROY
Station Computer Voice	JUDI DURAND

STARDATE 50416.2

Dr. Bashir gently chides Kira as he examines the Bajoran and the human baby growing inside of her. She hasn't been taking her *makara* herbs, he says. Kira protests that the vile-tasting herbs counteract the sedatives he provided to help her sleep. But Bashir is firm—take the herbs—and Kira reluctantly agrees. As Bashir completes the exam, Odo arrives with some unhappy news. Latha Mabrin, one of the members of her old resistance cell, has been murdered. There appear to be no clues, until Kira returns to her quarters and finds a bizarre message waiting for her, a distorted voice reciting, "That's one."

Kira reports the message to Odo and Sisko at once, and they conclude that it might be a threat against all former members of the Shakaar resistance cell. Although Kira wishes she could travel to Bajor to look for suspects, she knows that at the moment her primary responsibility is to the unborn baby.

A short time later, she is contacted by Trentin Fala, an informer for her old cell. Fala is terrified that she will be the unknown assassin's next victim. Kira

ration that Sisko and the audience felt when they saw it, a lot more than if it had been a little chunk!"

To create the painting that Sisko studies in the teaser, John Eaves worked on initial designs, and then Doug Drexler reconstructed the basic pieces in a 3-D computer program. Mike Okuda refined that image in Photoshop, adding the people, shading, and the obelisk's reflection in the water. The illustration was outputted and then rendered as a painting. Because the script called for the painting to be on "an eighteen-by-twelve-inch weathered piece of parchment," Herman Zimmerman took on the responsibility of hand-singeing the edges. "No one else was willing to do it," chuckles Scenic Art Assistant James Van Over. "This way, if it went up in flames, the production designer would get the blame!"

Van Over got the task of creating the enlarged portions of the reflected digital image that Sisko studies in an effort to find out what's on the missing side of the obelisk. "The detail didn't exist in the initial computer models, so we had to recreate all that," he says. "In the end, the whole Art Department worked on the effect." Well, nearly the whole department. Denise Okuda was out ill during the making of the

Silaran Prin, a Cardassian driven mad by injuries he received during the Occupation, seeks revenge. ROBBIE ROBINSON

O'Briens' quarters, where they can help protect Kira and the baby.

Going to Ops, Kira works with Nog and Dax on the only tangible lead. Together, they unscramble the distorted messages she's been receiving, only to find that the distorted voice is Kira's own. But before they can take in the implications, an explosion goes off in the habitat rang—specifically, in the O'Briens' quarters. Furel and Lupaza are dead.

Kira takes some comfort in the fact that the O'Briens weren't there when the explosion went off, but she is emotionally devastated. Odo reveals that with the help of his sources on Cardassia, he has compiled a list of possible suspects, but he refuses to show it to Kira. He knows that she would head off on her own to find the killer. But Kira retrieves the information from Odo's computer file and erases his copy of the names so she can't be followed.

Traveling alone in a runabout, Kira rules out several of the suspects before arriving at a remote planet near the DMZ, home to a Cardassian named Silaran Prin. As she investigates his stark living quarters, Prin surprises Kira and renders her unconscious, then places her in a restraining field. When she comes to, Prin, who is horribly disfigured, informs her that she is going to die, punishment for what she and the others did to him.

Prin considers himself an innocent. He wasn't in the Cardassian military. He was a servant to the commandant of a weapons depot. Kira and the others were responsible for the explosion at the depot that injured him and killed or crippled dozens of others. However, Prin has decided that the baby Kira is carrying is not guilty of any crime, so he will surgically remove it before he puts the guilty Bajoran to death.

Kira begs Prin to show some compassion and give her a sedative before he cuts her open. Prin agrees and injects her. Kira seems to pass out, but as soon as he switches off the restraining field, she comes to life. The *makara* herbs have counteracted the effects of the sedative, just as she knew they would. Kira kills Prin to save her own life. When the *Defiant* arrives to rescue her, Sisko, Odo, and Bashir find Kira undamaged by the ordeal, reflecting ruefully on the true nature of innocence and guilt.

calms her and arranges for Dax and Worf to bring her back to the station, where she'll be safer. But when the two officers attempt to beam Fala up to their runabout, something goes horribly wrong with the transporter and the Bajoran is killed. Odo deduces that the accident was, in fact, murder. Fala was killed by a device that had been hidden on her person, scrambling the transporter beam during rematerialization. Another message comes in, coded for Kira. This time the voice says, "That's two." And before Odo and she have time to consider the evidence at hand, another message comes through. A Bajoran named Mobara is the third victim.

Tense and exhausted, Kira goes to bed, a guard posted outside the door of her bedroom. But before she can fall asleep, she hears a loud crash from the outer room. Phaser in hand, she exits and finds Furel and Lupaza, two close friends from her cell, who've disarmed Kira's guard. The pair are looking for information so they can hunt down the assassin, but Kira convinces them to stay put. They opt to remain in the

This episode marked the first story sale for fledgling scriptwriter Bryan Fuller, who would later go on to become a member of *Voyager*'s writing staff. "My agent submitted it to *DS9*'s producers as a spec script, and they said that

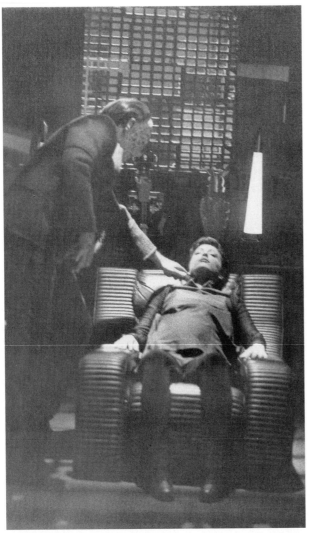

Although her son Django had been born several weeks earlier, Nana Visitor continued to wear padded maternity garb. ROBBIE ROBINSON

victim, that he wouldn't kill Kira because she's holding an innocent life inside her. And that became the crux of the story."

Ron Moore received the teleplay assignment for Fuller's story. "I'd never written in that genre before," he says. "It was a challenge and it was a lot of fun. Of the shows I've written on *DS9*, I have to say that it's one of my favorites. It really came across as I intended it, and in some ways, much better, a powerful, dark piece of television that ends in a really unexpected way."

Moore gives much of the credit to Director Michael Vejar, who was taking on his first *Deep Space Nine* episode, and to the performance of Nana Visitor, tackling the first full-force Kira-focused episode since the birth of her baby. "Nana just did a wonderful job," says Moore. "She just really shined, particularly during that long monologue in the Infirmary, where she tells Odo how she joined the resistance."

Long monologues can be deadly dull on-screen, but Moore knew there was a lot of valuable information to be conveyed in this one, so he was grateful for Visitor's thespian skill. "It tells us a lot about Kira, young and scared and biting her fingers in the cold, but coming through for them," he says. "And it tells us a lot about the resistance, that they would take this thirteen-year-old girl on a combat mission because they had to. That's how desperate the situation was for these guys.

"It also sets up the ending," he continues. "It tells us Kira's side of the story. Because eventually, we're going to hear Silaran Prin's side of the story, and you have to kind of balance it. You have to put Kira in a context in order to be fair, so that it's not all slanted against her."

The scene where Prin conveys his story and Kira parries his accusations was another tour de force for Visitor, one that couldn't have been easy for the new mother. "It takes physical stamina," she admits. "It's like being an athlete, in that you have to pace yourself and not give too much during rehearsals, but not give so little that it surprises you when you actually do a full take. You just have to control it so you don't exhaust yourself. And you *can* get very exhausted. Some days I go home and I can't get rid of it. I'm still in Kira's world."

Moore is pleased that he was able to allow Kira to remain Kira in a scene that did not paint her in the most complimentary light. "Typically when you get into a scene like this in television or even film," he says, "your heroine is confronted by the man from

they liked the writing, and that I was familiar enough with the series to come in and pitch," recalls Fuller. "They passed on the script itself, but when I came in I pitched the story again, and eventually they bought it," he laughs.

A variation on Agatha Christie's classic mystery *Ten Little Indians,* Fuller's pitch concerned the methodical assassination of members of Kira's former resistance group, and her efforts to figure out what was happening. The producers encouraged Fuller to reshape the story as an escalating thriller, with Kira being the main target of an individual who had been the innocent victim of a terrorist act by the group during the Occupation. "I thought it would be interesting if we could come up with a reason why Kira wasn't being offed with everyone else," says Fuller. "I thought since the killer saw himself as an innocent

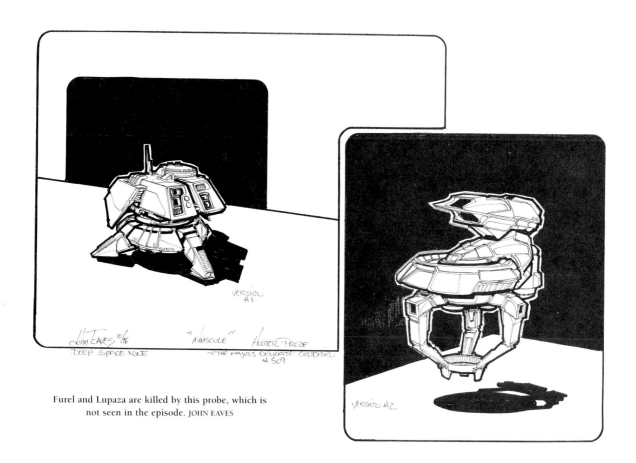

Furel and Lupaza are killed by this probe, which is
not seen in the episode. JOHN EAVES

her past who's been wronged by her in some way, and
usually she'll say, 'You know what? I feel bad, too.
You're right. I wish I didn't have to do those things
that I did. Can't we all just get along?' But that would
have been so phony, especially in this situation. So I
respect the fact that Kira looked up at Prin and said,
'Screw you! You expect me to feel bad for *you*? Fifteen
million Bajorans died in the Occupation. You people
were on our land, you didn't belong there, and you
were *all guilty*!'" Moore catches his breath and laughs.
"I mean, that's pretty bold. You can't say whether
that's right or wrong—it's the stance of a terrorist. But
it's what I felt Kira absolutely believed at the core of
her being."

Prin's beliefs are equally complex. Although
clearly a madman, his rationale for killing is no less
valid than Kira's. He executed only the guilty, Prin
points out, while Kira killed indiscriminately. "It's
messy," says Moore. "The moral lines that people
draw from a distance, or after the fact, are very facile.
It's very easy for people who weren't there to make
those distinctions. In a certain sense, both people in
that room are right and both of them are wrong."

"We all like to think we understand the realities

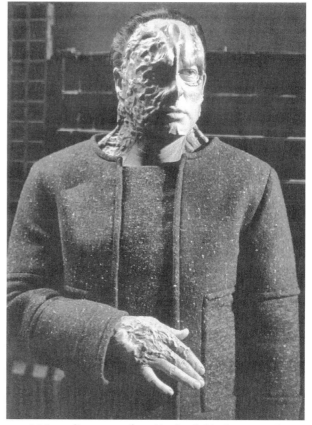

Prin's peculiar manner of speaking "made him fun to write,"
says Ron Moore.

By killing people close to Kira, the writers provided motivation for her to take desperate actions. ROBBIE ROBINSON

of life, but reality is shaky and truth is elusive," Behr says. "We're all victims and we're all perpetrators. It's difficult stuff to come to grips with."

Although many of the more serious *DS9* episodes include lighter B-stories, Kira's dark mystery takes up the whole of "The Darkness and the Light." Jay Chattaway's music for the episode is fittingly sober and thoughtful. There is just an occasional hint of a sad refrain from the "Bajoran hand flute," most noticeably in the sequence where Kira reminisces about her early days with the resistance. Sharp-eared listeners have heard this instrument before, although it's unlikely they knew its name. While its sound resembles the breathy tone of a wooden flute, it's actually a custom-made device known as an electronic wind instrument (EWI). "I've developed my own theory of the Bajoran culture," says Chattaway, "and whenever there's a sensitive scene about the Bajorans, the EWI is there. The performer blows into a mouthpiece, and it looks kind of like he's playing a clarinet, although the instrument itself makes no sound. It's only the controller of a computerized musical instrument digital interface. What he's doing, in fact, is using air currents to trigger a whole bunch of syn-thesized tones that will sound like a wooden flute. His voice, his breath control and his nuances of bending notes can create sounds that resemble those of a woodwind instrument."

The episode marks the return, and unfortunate demise, of Furel and Lupaza, last seen in "Shakaar." Although the writers sometimes enjoy killing off a character, no one was particularly happy about getting rid of Kira's friends. "It was something we talked about extensively during the break session, whether to do it or not," admits Moore. "But it was just so right. The vedek dies at the beginning and it's just sort of a surprise. Then this woman Fala dies and it's gruesome, even though you've only gotten to know her in the smallest way. We needed it to build. We needed somebody to die that Kira really cared about."

Behr views the deaths philosophically. "Part of the problem with doing episodic television is that it's hard to get the audience to feel genuine loss, because they know we're not going to damage anyone," he says. "We're only going to bring in redshirts. But this was a chance to bring in two good actors and make you care that they die. We very rarely have that opportunity, so we just decided to take it."

Visitor views the deaths even more philosophically. "Because it's *Star Trek,* you're never quite sure that you won't see someone again," she smiles. "There's all kinds of interesting devices [the writers come up with] so that we can see people again." We would see one of the pair again later that same season, when William Lucking returned as Furel in a flashback sequence from "Ties of Blood and Water."

The final visual of the episode, an unusual shot that features the underside of the *Defiant* passing before the camera as the ship slowly clears Prin's planet, came about in a bit of serendipity. "That was a curious thing," says Gary Hutzel. "I was planning on just doing a standard fly-by for that shot when we ran into some technical problems with the motion control rig. The pan/tilt wasn't operating properly; it was locked off at a downward angle as the camera drove past the ship. I looked at it and said, 'Fine. Sold. We'll shoot that.' It became the shot—and it looked good. Thank goodness for technical problems!" he laughs.

THE BEGOTTEN

Episode #5IO

WRITTEN BY RENÉ ECHEVARRIA
DIRECTED BY JESÚS SALVADOR TREVIÑO

GUEST CAST

Keiko O'Brien	ROSALIND CHAO
Shakaar Edon	DUNCAN REGEHR
Y'Pora	PEGGY ROEDER
Dr. Mora Pol	JAMES SLOYAN

STARDATE UNKNOWN

A visit from Quark distracts Odo from the aches and pains of his now-human body. The Ferengi has just purchased something that he's sure Odo will want: a vial of dead changeling goo. He's right about Odo's interest, but wrong about the changeling's condition. It's not dead, it's sick. What's more, it's an infant. One of the hundred such infants that Odo's people sent out into the galaxy to learn about other races. It knows nothing about what it is or what it has the potential to become, but Odo would very much like to teach it. Sisko grants permission. After Dr. Bashir treats the infant, Odo takes over, vowing not to make the mistakes that Dr. Mora, the scientist who discovered Odo's sentience ("The Alternate"), made with *him*.

However, Odo has barely begun the education of the baby changeling when Dr. Mora shows up on the station. He's heard about the discovery and wants to offer his expertise. Odo doesn't want Mora's help. He remembers all too clearly the invasive nature of the tests that Mora put him through. But like any parent, the scientist excels at manipulating his former charge, and he soon convinces Odo to let him stay to "observe."

Elsewhere on the station, another infant is about to come into the universe. Kira is in labor with the O'Briens' child ("Body Parts"). But for Bajoran women, giving birth is all about being relaxed, and between the chief's obvious discomfort with the birthing ritual and the tardy arrival of Kira's boyfriend Shakaar, the delivery room is anything but peaceful. After several hours, it becomes apparent the baby will not be born this day and all parties are sent home.

After several days of rejecting Mora's methods of stimulating the changeling, it seems clear that gentle encouragement alone won't work, and time suddenly is at a premium. Sisko informs the pair that Starfleet Command wants Odo to establish commu-

Odo's mentor Dr. Mora arrives at the station to observe the baby changeling. ROBBIE ROBINSON

nication with the changeling as soon as possible. Otherwise, they'll take over the project themselves.

Using Mora's equipment, Odo submits the infant to minor electrical shocks, designed to make it move about and take different shapes. The technique works, to Odo's obvious delight. Mora reveals that he felt the same sense of elation when he was working with Odo, until, of course, he realized that the shapeshifter had grown up to resent him for his efforts. Almost against his will, Odo begins to feel a sense of empathy with his former mentor. He understands that Mora views him not as a successful experiment, but as a parent views a child. Now that they're working together, the development of the young changeling moves forward rapidly. One amazing day it forms a face that is reminiscent of Odo's, and uses newly created eyes to peer curiously at the former shape-shifter.

Mora admits that he was wrong; Odo's gentle approach to communication obviously has paid off. The young being was reaching out toward Odo, curious about him. Mora notes that he never made that connection with Odo. Suddenly, Odo is inspired to defend Mora. He understands now that the scientist helped him far more than he ever harmed him.

As Odo reflects on the fact that the presence of the baby shape-shifter has allowed him once again to experience what it's like to be a changeling, he receives devastating news: the infant is dying and there's nothing anyone can do to stop it. He takes it into his hands, and as he expresses sorrow that he'll never be able to teach it how to become a Tarkalean hawk, the entity dies and is absorbed into Odo's hands. Odo suddenly realizes that he's been transformed; he can morph. He turns into a Tarkalean hawk and soars above the Promenade. He is a changeling again, but his elation is tempered by the price of this gift: the loss of the infant.

Odo bids a sad farewell to Dr. Mora and runs into Kira, who is also in a melancholy mood. She's delivered the O'Briens' baby at last—and having turned over the infant, now feels its loss more deeply than she'd imagined. The two friends go for a walk together, united by the knowledge that they've both been through an experience that has changed their lives forever.

"**S**omeone's *always* pregnant," Robert Hewitt Wolfe states definitively. During their tenure with *Deep Space Nine*, a number of the writers became fathers, and nature took its course here and there among the rest of the crew as well. Production Associate Robbin Slocum worked throughout her pregnancy in Ira Behr's office; Nana Visitor carried her baby through parts of the fourth and fifth season, and Actor Robert O'Reilly, who plays Gowron, became the father of *triplets*! It's no wonder that the subject of babies seemed a fertile topic in the minds of certain members of the writing staff.

"I'd wanted to do a 'baby changeling comes to the station' story for months,' says René Echevarria. "But I didn't want it to become a child because we'd already done that with a Jem'Hadar ['The Abandoned']. My idea was that it wouldn't do much of anything, and yet Odo would invest an enormous amount of time into it." Ultimately, Echevarria's idea came to term when he realized that the baby somehow could provide the means to "cure" Odo.

"René came up with the idea of reabsorbing the changeling," Ira Behr says. "He thought that would be the perfect way [to reestablish Odo as a shapeshifter]. But we didn't know when it should play out, so we just decided to have Odo remain a solid for twelve episodes," approximately one half of the season. "Now we had two story arcs going, the O'Brien baby in Kira, and Odo as a solid." Recognizing that thematically tying the ends of the two arcs together seemed a natural step, Behr concludes, "We just followed both of the arcs though half the season and then we brought Odo back."

"'The Begotten' is certainly one of my favorite episodes in the entire run," Rene Auberjonois says. "Of course, actors always like scripts where their character is the whole A-story," he adds with a smile.

The baby changeling was "played" by many substances, including solutions of gelatin, plastic, and Murphy's Oil Soap. ROBBIE ROBINSON

Of course, Auberjonois had some able assistance from his co-stars, one human and one . . . not. "There was a limit to what we could do with a story about Odo spending time with goo that can't do anything," chuckles Echevarria. "It really came together when we decided to bring Dr. Mora into it. Then it became a father/son story in which Odo relives the stresses and strains of his own childhood and comes to understand Mora a little better."

Behr was happy to bring the doctor back. "Mora was a bit one-note in 'The Alternate,'" he observes, "so we wanted a chance to make him a little more interesting." Behr notes that the more he himself

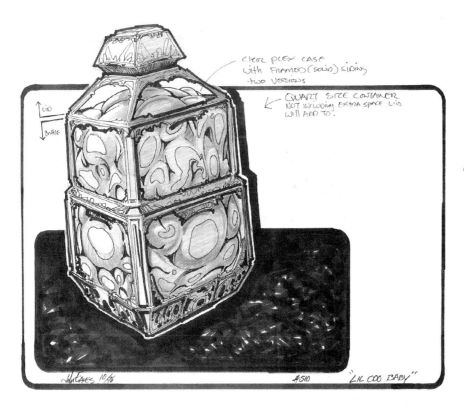

clear plex case
with framed (solid) siding
two versions

QUART SIZE CONTAINER
NOT including EXTRA SPACE LID
will add to.

LID

BAFFLE

JEaves 10/96   #510   "LIL COO BABY"

Quark delivers the "li'l goo baby" to Odo in an ornate container inspired by this rendering. JOHN EAVES

experiences parenting, the more he realizes how complicated it is. "It all comes down to point of view, and this time I wanted to give Mora *his* point of view. I think the show was better for it."

Considering its inherent limitations, the acting ability of the baby changeling proved exemplary. "Morphing sequences are expensive, so we had to be judicious as to when we really needed to use a morph," says Steve Oster. "In some situations, we wanted to use a practical goo," that is, a goo effect created on set during filming, as opposed to the post-production visual effect. "Then all we'd need is for the Visual Effects Department to add a ripple to it rather than having to create it all from scratch."

Although it may not seem that way, goo, apparently, is pretty complex stuff. "We did several weeks of research and development," says Oster. The "goo tests" constituted some of *Deep Space Nine*'s most bizarre casting sessions. "Gary Monak and his crew had to come up with goo of the right color and consistency that would hold its form for a moment and then fall down and ooze around," Oster continues. "We spent many a night sitting here with different textures and viscosities of goo, trying to decide what would work for what." If it sounds just a bit like fun, it was. "We had a good time coming up with the right consistency," comments Echevarria. "We'd sit there pulling on and tugging at the different batches, and in the production meetings we'd hand it all around."

They *did* have a reference point to work from. Odo's natural appearance had been established in the first season. What many people don't know is that Odo's liquid form is a common floor-care product. Gary Monak reveals the truth behind the mysterious substance: "When we first started the show, the producers knew they wanted Odo to retire in a bucket," Monak relates. "But no one could agree on a color. So I went to the market and just looked at the shelves to see what they had around. And I found Murphy's Oil Soap. When I showed some of that to the producers, they liked the color and the translucence of it, and even the texture of the gelatinous state. So that's what we've gone with the whole seven years. I didn't tell them at the time that it was just Murphy's Oil Soap," he laughs, "but any time Odo would morph we'd pour a little puddle of it on the floor." And cleanup was, no doubt, a snap.

Of course, like any actor, the baby changeling needed to demonstrate its range, so it couldn't always appear as a simple puddle. Monak found additional products to enhance its performance. "In 'The Begotten,' for the beginning stages, we used gelatin mixed with some other stuff," Monak explains. "We also used a plastic that's referred to as a 'hot melt vinyl,' which you can heat up and mold. And we made up some goo that's basically like the stuff they pour on people on Nickelodeon television."

Joe Longo joined into the process by finding

Handwritten notes on image: "ODO FACE MORPH", "...RE OF A BUST DESIGN SO AS NOT TO RESEMBLE THE ABYSS TENTICLE", "John Eaves 96", "THE BEGOTTEN #510"

A concept of how to show changeling baby morphing. JOHN EAVES

what might be considered wardrobe for the little character. "I made ten different containers for it," he says. "They were all different geometric forms that supposedly helped the baby learn about shapes. We put lights in the bottoms of the containers to give the goo a glowing effect." One of those containers, a flat circular Plexiglas piece in which the infant was supposedly shocked to initiate movement, was irreverently dubbed "the frying pan" by the set decorators.

At one point, the baby changeling was required to stretch forward and morph into a semblance of Odo's face. Accomplishing the effect required the cooperation of several departments. Makeup Artist Dean Jones first carved a mold that looked like Odo's face. Into that mold, Monak's crew then poured a resin that was colored like Murphy's Oil Soap. After it hardened, the result was a two-foot-tall sculpture which primarily was used, Monak says, by the Visual Effects Department to line up the shot. The changeling's actual movement in the scene was actualized in computer graphics.

Every good actor has a stand-in, of course, and the goo baby was no exception. When first time *DS9* Director Jesús Treviño decided that he wanted an unbudgeted over-the-shoulder shot from behind the changeling toward Odo and Mora, the crew wasn't quite sure how to achieve his desire, until Lou Race stepped in with a suggestion. "I said, 'Why not do it practical?'" Race recalls. "'Why not put some goo on somebody's hand and use that?'" It was an amazingly simple solution, and since no one else had thought of

On Kira's feelings after she delivers, Visitor notes, "There's no way that my holding a baby wouldn't be tempered with my own experience." ROBBIE ROBINSON

it, Race was rewarded by being "cast" as the baby. "They put a stocking over my hand, covered it with this goo and did the shot," Race giggles. "For that one angle, I was the little changeling. That's my hand's fifteen minutes of fame."

"That shot would have cost thousands of dollars in postproduction, but those guys did it for nothing," notes Echevarria. "It was just a great moment in guerrilla filmmaking."

For Rene Auberjonois, spending long periods of time talking to containers of liquid soap and gelatin "was complex, but actors have this willing suspension of disbelief," he says. "The childlike capacity for play that actors hang on to actually makes that sort of thing easier. And René Echevarria really has a handle on Odo. I found the episode so wonderfully written that what I had to say was very evocative to me."

The script inspired a special new set: a Bajoran birthing room, a place filled with soft, comfy pillows and tapestries that hopefully would reflect the spirit of the relaxation ritual. "We wanted to take Bajoran birth as far away from human childbirth as we could," says Echevarria. "So we came up with the idea that you'd have to be very, very, very, very relaxed." However, Nana Visitor was ready to get out of the relaxing delivery room and back into Kira's normal lifestyle on the series. Although she had, in reality, delivered her baby six episodes earlier, she'd been required to continue to act and dress as if she were still pregnant. At last, in "The Begotten," she was able to leave her delicate condition behind.

"I'm so grateful that the writers hadn't tried to hide my pregnancy or cut me out of episodes completely," she says. "But I was furious that I wasn't allowed to go into battle while I was pregnant. The other actors teased me that I was taking it all too seriously, but I felt so left behind for all those interesting shows. I mean, the *tribble* show! I was barely there. Then, for the last two weeks of my pregnancy, they said, 'That's it. You're not working anymore.' I was *furious,"* she says breaking into a huge laugh. "I was like a caged animal. I just wanted to be at work going off on missions with everybody else."

But although Visitor's baby was happy and healthy at home, the actress was able to bring an element of sadness into her performance here. "Kira realized that she had to let the baby go," she says. "I can't imagine that being easy. Originally, it had been written that she was okay with it, but I have experience with carrying a child and even before love kicks in, this huge maternal instinct kicks in. I imagine that

Kira also would have that instinct. Even if she had told herself that she's not going to love the child as her own, the chemical things would happen in her body. So I fought to get them to show that it was a difficult thing for her."

While the birth of little Kirayoshi meant that Visitor could return to work, it augured the opposite for Rosalind Chao. "When they made me pregnant with the second child on the show, I knew you wouldn't see much of Keiko," she says. "From then on, I was cooked." Between her filmmaking schedule and the fact that working with children, especially very young ones, is fraught with work law regulations and scheduling restrictions, Chao knew there wouldn't be many episodes with her and Yoshi. And true to her fears, Chao would appear in only two more episodes before the series' end: "Time's Orphan" and "What You Leave Behind."

FOR THE UNIFORM

Episode #511

WRITTEN BY PETER ALLAN FIELDS
DIRECTED BY VICTOR LOBL

GUEST CAST

Michael Eddington	KENNETH MARSHALL
Sanders	ERIC PIERPOINT
Nog	ARON EISENBERG

STARDATE 50485.2

Sisko visits a refugee camp in the DMZ, hoping to obtain information about Maquis activities from a Starfleet informer. Instead, he finds Michael Eddington, the former DS9 officer who betrayed Sisko by leaking Starfleet information to the Maquis ("For the Cause"). Eddington warns Sisko not to come after him and beams aboard a waiting Maquis raider, but Sisko is unwilling to let him get away. He returns to the *Defiant* and gives chase, but when the ship fires on Eddington, it suffers a massive computer failure, compliments of a computer virus planted by the former security chief. Although the *Defiant* is helpless, Eddington allows an angry and humiliated Sisko to leave the fray unharmed. The starship is towed back to DS9 by the *U.S.S. Malinche*.

Adding insult to injury, Sisko learns that Starfleet has assigned the *Malinche*'s Captain Sanders to apprehend Eddington, since Sisko hasn't been able to

Sisko is confronted by Eddington when he attempts to infiltrate a Maquis camp. DANNY FELD

accomplish the job in the eight months he's been trying. Sisko receives word that Eddington has attacked a Cardassian colony in the DMZ with a biogenic weapon—and that no other starship is in the vicinity. He sees the chance to get back in the game, despite the fact that only half of the *Defiant*'s systems are working.

As the *Defiant* follows what appears to be the warp signature of a Maquis ship, Sisko receives a "gift" from Eddington: a transmitted copy of *Les Misérables*. Eddington taunts Sisko by noting the similarities between the captain and the book's villain, Javert, a man who spent decades chasing the noble Valjean over an inconsequential infraction. Undaunted, Sisko closes in on the Maquis ship, only to find that it's not anywhere in the vicinity. Suddenly, a distress call comes in from the *Malinche*, which has just been ambushed and disabled by Eddington.

Sisko determines Eddington's next Cardassian target, but is too late to stop him from releasing his biogenic weapon into the atmosphere. The *Defiant* gives chase to Eddington's fleeing raider, but the raider disables a transport vessel that is evacuating Cardassians from the planet. Sisko is forced to break off his pursuit to rescue the helpless civilians.

Trying to get one step ahead of the wily Maquis, Sisko turns back to the gift Eddington sent him. Just as the traitorous former officer sees Sisko as a villain, it becomes clear to him that Eddington sees *himself* as the hero, Valjean. And all great heroes are willing to make a melodramatic sacrifice for the values they hold most dear.

Sisko sends a message to the Maquis; in retaliation for their recent attacks, he plans to poison the atmosphere of a Maquis colony world. He warns them to evacuate. Eddington responds to call his bluff, but is shocked when Sisko actually follows through on it, sending the planet's inhabitants scrambling. Sisko tells Eddington that he is prepared to eliminate every Maquis colony in the DMZ. As Sisko had hoped, Eddington makes a heroic gesture and turns himself in to save the colonies, putting an end to Sisko's bitter vendetta.

If "Rapture" brought Kasidy Yates's character full circle from the events of "For the Cause," "For the Uniform" attempted to do the same for Starfleet traitor Michael Eddington. But Eddington's storyline wasn't quite wrapped up; he would return one last time later in the season, in "Blaze of Glory." Explains Ira Behr: "We liked 'For the Uniform' so much that we decided to do it again and finish Eddington off."

"For the Uniform" also brought retired staff writer-producer Peter Allan Fields back to the fold. "If Peter asks to do an episode, Peter does an episode," comments Behr fondly. "He's still part of the family and always will be." Although no longer an active participant in plotting the course of DS9's future, Fields's occasional freelance input would continue to add layers of depth to characters that viewers thought they knew everything about. Sisko's obsession with capturing Eddington in this episode was something of a revelation, and it set the stage for the day when he would betray his principles for a greater good in "In the Pale Moonlight," for which Fields again provided the story.

The episode included tips of the hat to two classics, one in a rather conspicuous manner, the other more sly. The overt nod is to Victor Hugo's *Les Misérables*, which provided some useful dramatic shorthand in conveying Eddington's personality, and gave viewers a concise literary analysis of the novel. It's not the first time *Star Trek* has wielded the classics to make a point; Shakespeare, Melville, and Dante, to name but a few, have all had their day. Actor Kenneth Marshall, who played Eddington, points out that by the time the episode first aired, the well-publicized hit musical production of *Les Misérables* had made the public quite aware of the themes of the original novel. "So it's not as if they picked something a little more obscure," Marshall says.

The more subtle classics reference was to *Robin*

With one look, Brooks conveys the heavy burden of command that Sisko feels. ROBBIE ROBINSON

Hood, or, more specifically, to a scene in the 1938 theatrical version of *The Adventures of Robin Hood* in which Errol Flynn's Robin takes Olivia de Havilland's Maid Marian to see the starving masses. It's not hard to envision Eddington as Robin when he forces Sisko to look at the hungry, bedraggled Maquis. The Flynn film is "another favorite movie of all time," admits Behr. "We talked about it in the break session."

On the technical side, "For the Uniform" marks the first time viewers got to see Starfleet's new holocommunicator in action. "That's something I had been pushing for," says Ron Moore, "because I just think it's so absurd that in the twenty-fourth century they have holodeck technology that allows them to recreate the Roman Empire, but everybody talks to each other on television monitors. It's just so lame. The viewscreens have been around for over thirty years. Can't we move to something a *little* more interesting? But it's like pulling teeth."

Moore's frustration is understandable. Brannon Braga and he made a similar attempt to "stretch the envelope" in *First Contact,* when they introduced a holographic viewscreen to take the place of the ever-

present widescreen monitor that's become a permanent fixture on every *Enterprise.*

Behr supported Moore's rationale for the holocommunicator. "Viewscreen scenes are always difficult to pull off," Behr notes. "The longer they are, the more boring they are, and having a character talk to someone on a viewscreen is very distancing." Moore sold the idea by discussing "the beauty of having people together in a room [while they're communicating], how it would be so much more dynamic," Behr adds. "And it did work in this episode. We never could have had Eddington on the viewscreen for all of his scenes. It would have been [dramatic] death."

Still, the holocommunicator's debut was not perceived as particularly effective. The setup came across as a bit static, particularly in the scenes between Sisko and Captain Sanders. "It was new territory for everybody," says Director Victor Lobl, who was working on his first *Star Trek* episode. "We talked about it at great length, where to put it, how to position the people." There was some concern that blocking it in a certain way would lock all future directors into a constricting formula, so Lobl finally had one

The holocommunicator as seen on the set. ROBBIE ROBINSON

The filmmakers ultimately set up the holocommunicator device behind the captain's chair. "John Eaves designed a boxy little border, just a frame, that would sit on the carpet and ostensibly be the source of the hologram," explains Laura Richarz.

As for the effect itself, "the tricky part about it was to come up with a way to give it a different look, visually," says Steve Oster. "As a practical effect, I mean. If we had unlimited funds, we could shoot a blue screen and then shoot the plate with other people talking [to the hologram] and then insert them à la Princess Leia in *Star Wars*. But that would be expensive to do for each shot, and we tried to split the difference here. I'm not sure how successful it was."

If the holocommunicator didn't make television screens sizzle, the episode gained a lot of energy from the sequences in which the crew was required to operate the *Defiant* manually. "Great idea," says Behr happily. "I loved it. We wanted it to feel like a submarine movie, and we kept talking about *Run Silent, Run Deep,* for those scenes." As Behr admits sheepishly, they realized later on that none of the writers had viewed the 1958 film recently enough to know if the scenes paid appropriate homage or not.

The *Defiant*'s trip into the Badlands allowed the visual effects team to give the region a new look. "The Badlands originally were done for *Voyager* as CGI and no one really liked them," says Hutzel. "They'd been reworked a couple times, but when it fell upon me to do the Badlands for this episode I decided to throw out everything that had been done and start over." Hutzel's team created "For the Uniform"'s roiling plasma fields by laying out a twenty-foot-square piece of black velvet on the floor of Image G and climbing up into the facility's eighteen-foot catwalks. Pails of liquid nitrogen, which boils furiously at room temperature, were poured from the catwalks eighteen feet above down to the velvet surface, and photographed at one hundred twenty frames per second. "It splattered real good," grins Hutzel. "We needed that much force to get the violence of the effect."

The casting of Eric Pierpoint as Sanders was Behr's idea. Audiences may best know Pierpoint as George, the amiable Newcomer from the television series *Alien Nation*. Behr knew him as a regular on the television series *Fame,* on which Behr served as a producer. "I thought he did a great job [in "For the Uniform"], and we always talked about bringing him back, but we never did," Behr laments. "He would have been a perfect person to kill off."

character stand (the projected hologram) and one sit (Sisko). "We figured that left it a little looser for the future."

"It was difficult to find a spot on the *Defiant*'s bridge to do it," recalls Moore. "Originally, I had foreseen doing it in front of the helm, but that would put the hologram in front of the viewscreen, and because the ship was in motion, we'd have to put something *on* the viewscreen anyway," adding an optical *to* an optical. "The Visual Effects Department loathed it," he concedes.

"It was a terrible idea from the git-go," comments Gary Hutzel. "The idea was to create this amazing 3-D image, but TV's a 2-D medium, so it's hard to show that it's 3-D. So you move the camera around so the audience can see that it's 3-D, but then it could look to them like the guy beamed in. So you have to find a way to deal with that. It created all these problems that the writers hadn't thought about, and it missed the whole point of why Gene Roddenberry wanted a viewscreen: so you could avoid unnecessary expense."

IN PURGATORY'S SHADOW

Episode #512

WRITTEN BY ROBERT HEWITT WOLFE &
IRA STEVEN BEHR
DIRECTED BY GABRIELLE BEAUMONT

GUEST CAST

Garak	ANDREW J. ROBINSON
Gul Dukat	MARC ALAIMO
Tora Ziyal	MELANIE SMITH
General Martok	J.G. HERTZLER
Ikat'ika	JAMES HORAN
Romulan	CARRIE STAUBER
Jem'Hadar Guard	JIM PALLADINO

AND

Enabran Tain	PAUL DOOLEY

STARDATE UNKNOWN

Worf and Garak finally meet the *real* General Martok.
ROBBIE ROBINSON

The station picks up an encrypted Cardassian message from the Gamma Quadrant, and Sisko calls in Garak, the station's resident expert on Cardassian codes, to break the code. Garak dismisses the transmission as an old planetary survey report. Later he admits that it's actually a call for help from Enabran Tain, the former head of the Obsidian Order, who was presumed killed in an attack on the Founders ("The Die Is Cast"). Sisko reluctantly agrees to allow Garak to take a runabout to investigate, with the stipulation that Worf go along to keep an eye on him.

When Worf realizes that the source of the transmission they've been tracking originates deep in Dominion territory, he is reluctant to continue. Garak convinces him to press on, but before long they run into a large fleet of Jem'Hadar ships. Worf realizes that a massing of enemy ships this close to the wormhole can only mean one thing: an invasion of the Alpha Quadrant. He transmits a warning to DS9 just before they're captured.

On the station, an angry Dukat confronts Kira about allowing his daughter Ziyal to become friendly with Garak, but Kira ignores his veiled threats. After Worf's hasty transmission is received by the worried crew, Dukat tries to get Ziyal to leave the station with him, but she refuses. Sisko and his senior staff discuss their options, which include the drastic measure of sealing the wormhole to prevent the Dominion fleet from coming through.

Worf and Garak are taken to a Dominion internment camp. The Jem'Hadar have been holding an elite group of prisoners, including Martok, the Klingon general and close aide to Gowron, who had been replaced by a changeling ("Apocalypse Rising"). Martok takes the pair to Tain, who is gravely ill. Upon hearing that his summons brought only two rescuers, Tain expresses deep disappointment in Garak. A short time later, Worf and Garak are stunned when they encounter a prisoner who's just been released from solitary confinement: it's Julian Bashir, which means that the doctor back on DS9 is a changeling.

Although wounded by Tain's remarks, Garak decides to make amends with his former mentor before the old Cardassian dies. Tain asks Garak to make a final promise: to escape . . . and avenge Tain's death. Garak asks a favor in return—that Tain acknowledge Garak as his son. Tain complies and dies peacefully. His personal mission completed, Garak joins the others in looking for a way to escape. On the other side of the galaxy, time has run out. Sisko gives the command to close the wormhole, but discovers that the equipment that would have accomplished the task has been sabotaged. As the Jem'Hadar fleet begins pouring into the Alpha Quadrant, Sisko calls for battle stations.

"It was that time of the year, when it seemed right to do a two-parter," says Ira Behr. "Basically the same spot where 'Past Tense' was in third season, and where 'Homefront' and 'Paradise Lost' were in fourth. And after doing 'Apocalypse Rising' to open the season, we knew we *had* to get the changelings back into the show, and to get the Dominion back on the playing field."

A favorite film influenced the plot to come. "We'd been talking since the end of Season 4 about doing *The Great Escape* on the station," Behr notes, recalling the classic "good guys escape from a Nazi prison camp" movie. For a long time they had considered doing the episode from Eddington's point of view, "with him in the brig and showing how he breaks out, forcing the audience to kind of root for the guy," he says. "It never worked out, because we weren't confident that the fans were really behind the character. But, we still had this thing about someone being in a prison, and there being a prison break."

Other ideas were floating around in the creative ether. "We wanted to bring back Martok," says Robert Wolfe. "We really liked him. And we wanted to put Dukat in bed with the Dominion." And then there was "the Tain thing," as Behr refers to it. "I got into this thing about Enabran Tain being Garak's father, which is something we'd talked about since we'd introduced him ['The Wire']. I wanted to put the button on that."

The two-parter was, as Wolfe notes, "A way to tie up a lot of loose ends and sort of propel us into the war." More and more ideas made their way into the mix: the thought of pairing Garak and Worf in an adventure, a bookend to the interaction between the pair that had been established in "Broken Link"; Worf finally getting his opportunity to battle it out with the Jem'Hadar, suggested by "To the Death"; boosting the paranoia level that there were changelings among us. "People kept pointing out to me that 'changelings on Earth' was a great concept, but it's really not part of our franchise," says Behr. "Earth isn't our franchise. So instead we put the changeling threat in one of our people."

The "Bashir as changeling" storyline came up in the midst of the two-parter's break session. "We thought, 'Okay, we've got prisoners of the Dominion,'" says Wolfe. "'But we need a surprise. Something we don't expect. And suddenly we learn that Bashir's a prisoner too. He's been replaced on the station.'" Members of the viewing audience weren't the only ones surprised by that twist. "Apparently I'd

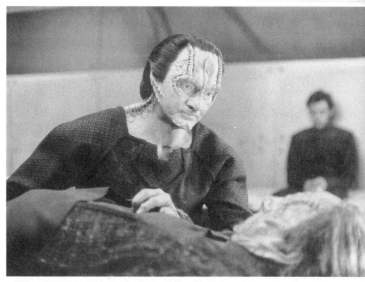
Although it ties up one story point, this episode launches many others. ROBBIE ROBINSON

been a changeling for the previous three or four shows before this fact was revealed in 'In Purgatory's Shadow,'" says Alexander Siddig. "But I didn't know it until the last minute. So obviously it had no impact in how I'd played him in those earlier episodes. Once I *did* know, I had a chance to do something about how the other Bashir behaved. But what a shock!" Siddig initially thought the writers might have withheld the information deliberately. But he later changed his mind. "They rarely know things very far in advance," he says. "So they probably didn't know he was a changeling for the earlier shows either!"

That's not surprising. Although some plot machinations are planned well in advance, others are far more serendipitous. "At the time we were working on these two shows, we had no idea that Bashir was going to turn out to be genetically engineered," admits Behr. "So even though it was the very next episode . . ." He shrugs. It was the beginning, he adds, of "the double pumping of Bashir. For a long time he was just this guy, but suddenly he was a prisoner of the Dominion *and* he was genetically engineered. Which is why we did the show the following year ['Inquisition'], which asked, 'Is he really a Dominion agent?'"

Although reintroducing Tain, and establishing him as Garak's father, was something everyone on the writing staff wanted, Behr confesses that there was another motivation. "I am a *huge* fan of Andy Robinson, and I wanted to give him an emotional scene. What better way to do that than to have his

From the gee-whiz greenhorn seen in the pilot, Bashir evolved into a man who could hold his own against the Jem'Hadar. ROBBIE ROBINSON

estranged father dying before him, with him desperately wanting acknowledgment."

It's one thing to play an angst-filled scene once. Hitting the right emotional mark, over and over again, is "one of the hardest things about film acting," confesses Robinson. "Whatever internal choices you make to get to a genuine emotional place have to work take after take. And they have to work in situations that are very technical and artificial, with people setting up lights and cameras and sound equipment. You have to really push it all to the side and keep that emotional focus." Behr is very pleased with the way the deathbed scene turned out. "At first we thought we had to be much more on the nose about it," he says. "But then I fell in love with the idea of Tain giving Garak what he wants, but in this left-handed way, talking about this little tiny moment from years ago, and saying, 'I was very proud of you that day.'"

The episode also reintroduced the character of Ziyal, this time in the person of Melanie Smith, the third and final actor to play Dukat's daughter. Behr takes a left-handed turn of his own in explaining how

The Dominion internment center, described as a facility for "people the Dominion is especially curious about." JOHN EAVES

Background Artist Mark Shepherd performed the role of resident barfly Morn on the series *Star Trek: Deep Space Nine*. Away from the set, Shepherd creates computer-generated artwork.

"Back in 1992, I heard that there was going to be a casting call for regular extras on a new show called *Deep Space Nine*, and I decided that I would try to get in on it," recalls Mark Shepherd. "I finally got through to the casting director, who asked what I was trying out for. I said I wasn't sure; could he recommend something? He suggested I try out as a humanoid doctor type, and I thought that was great.

"The following day, I went to this open call, and there had to be at least a hundred people trying out as aliens, Bajorans, Starfleet personnel, and so forth. I was one of the last people to be interviewed. They took my picture with a Polaroid camera, and after a while I got called upstairs into this room where they had the snapshots set up on a table. Behind the table were four people, and they looked at me for a split second and then told me to go back downstairs. After ten minutes, they called my name and told me they had some good news and some bad news. The bad news was that I didn't get picked for the thing I came in for, but the good news was they wanted me to play an alien for them. Would I mind if they put appliances on me? I told them that was great, and they sent me off to the Wardrobe Department for an initial fitting. Then they said they'd be in touch in about a month.

"Almost a month later I got a call to come in for another fitting, and this time I saw the Morn mask for the first time. It hadn't been painted yet, and it reminded me of a Dr. Seuss character. They asked me to put it on along with this big bulky piece of wardrobe that became the official Morn suit. It's kind of like wearing one of those pads that are used for moving furniture, and it's got these imitation leather breastplates on it, like body armor. Before I left, I asked when I'd get to work and they told me it would be the day after Labor Day.

"Labor Day rolled around and I hadn't gotten a call so I was a little worried. But I made up my mind to be there first thing in the morning. I didn't have a car so I had to take a bus, and the only way to do that was to catch a bus at ten P.M. the night before. I got to the Paramount lot at three-thirty in the morning and went to the Wardrobe Department, but nobody was there yet, so I took a nap for an hour. Then I went over to the soundstage and the people there began telling me I wasn't supposed to be there that day. But then I ran into Michael Westmore, and he said he *was* expecting me to be there; my makeup was all set up and ready to go. I guess it was just one of those things, and after that, everybody was real nice to me."

the show came to have three different women playing the same character. "When I was nine years old, my mother took me into the Bronx to see *Doctor No,* and Jack Lord played Felix Leiter," he says. "A few years later, I saw *Goldfinger,* where Felix Leiter was played by Cec Linder. And then David Hedison played Felix Leiter, and then Bernie Casey. It changed my life! From then on, I always wanted to have the opportu-

nity to just play with the audience's minds. Because it really doesn't matter on a certain level. And so, for various reasons, we changed the part once, and then we had to change the part again." In a perfect world, he smiles, "I would have changed the role of Ziyal *every single time*—just to keep reminding the audience that this is all a construct."

Although the title "In Purgatory's Shadow"

sounds as if it could have come from Milton, it's actually just something that Robert Wolfe made up. "He *loves* titles," sighs Behr. The episode invokes a few *TNG*-oriented references: a disparaging mention of Earl Grey tea—Picard's favorite brew—by Garak; and Sisko's comment about "the latest Borg attack," a nod to *First Contact*. "That's the 'imp of the perverse,'" grins Behr. "I tend to rail against any connection between the movies and our show, but every now and then, when no one's looking, we'll put in our own reference, just for the hell of it."

On a more somber note, "In Purgatory's Shadow" opens with a dedication card to Derek Garth. The card honored a *DS9* grip who'd died in an auto accident on his way to work during the filming of the episode. "That was a bad thing," says Behr. "A really bad thing. Derek was just the most positive guy on the set."

The writing for both "In Purgatory's Shadow" and "By Inferno's Light" went as smooth as silk, according to Behr. "By the fifth season, Robert and I were so in sync—we were writing *Legends of the Ferengi* for Pocket Books at the same time—that it's really hard to tell who thought of what," he says. "We would just come in and knock off an act a day, like ten pages every day." Astute viewers may have noticed that the writing team had, by this time, begun alternating whose name came first in the episodes on which they paired. "In Purgatory's Shadow" was by Wolfe and Behr, while its successor, "By Inferno's Light," was by Behr and Wolfe. "The young whippersnapper said, 'Can I have my name first?'" Behr recites in a whiny, nasal voice. "And I said"—and here he switches to a long suffering sigh—"'Oh, *okay*.'"

Wolfe grins at the memory. "I was like, 'Hey, this sucks. My name's always second. I don't want to be second all the time. Why don't we start moving it back and forth?' And Ira did it. And of course, then that decision bit me on the ass because it was my turn to come first on 'Let He Who Is Without Sin . . .' So there is no justice," he concludes with a chuckle.

BY INFERNO'S LIGHT
Episode #513
WRITTEN BY **IRA STEVEN BEHR &
ROBERT HEWITT WOLFE**
DIRECTED BY **LES LANDAU**

GUEST CAST

Garak	ANDREW J. ROBINSON
Gul Dukat	MARC ALAIMO
Tora Ziyal	MELANIE SMITH
General Martok	J.G. HERTZLER
Deyos	RAY BUKTENICA
Ikat'ika	JAMES HORAN
Romulan	CARRIE STAUBER
Gowron	ROBERT O'REILLY
Jem'Hadar Officer	BARRY WIGGINS
Jem'Hadar Guard	DON FISCHER
Station Computer Voice	JUDI DURAND

STARDATE 50564.2

Sisko and the others wait for the attack to begin, but to their surprise, the enemy fleet turns away from DS9 and heads for Cardassia. Dukat's ship breaks away from the station to follow the fleet, and he reveals that he's negotiated a pact that will make Cardassia part of the Dominion—with himself as Cardassia's leader.

At the Dominion internment camp, the prisoners come up with a plan to reconfigure Tain's hidden transmitter so that it will signal the runabout and activate its transporter. The plan requires Garak to spend hours in a tiny crawlspace while the others keep Jem'Hadar attention occupied. The primary source of diversion is Worf, who participates in match after match with Jem'Hadar soldiers so that the Jem'Hadar can learn more about Klingon combat techniques.

In the Alpha Quadrant, Sisko convinces Chancellor Gowron to reinstate the treaty between the Federation and the Klingon Empire so they can unite against the joint Dominion/Cardassian forces.

Worf continues to win his brutal matches against the Jem'Hadar, ignoring the physical damage he's doing to himself. Meanwhile, Garak's claustrophobia comes to a head, and he suffers a severe panic attack that endangers the escape attempt. At DS9, Sisko receives a message from Dukat, demanding that he surrender the station, but Sisko refuses and prepares to defend it. As Starfleet, Klingon, and even Romulan vessels join forces to face the enemy, the changeling Bashir steals a runabout and heads for Bajor's sun.

Jem'Hadar warriors entertain themselves by engaging Worf in fight after fight. ROBBIE ROBINSON

At the camp, Worf prepares to face his toughest opponent, the Jem'Hadar first. Garak rallies himself to finish his task, but he's barely had time to get started when some guards arrive to look for him. They find the crawlspace, but Bashir and the other prisoners overcome the guards before they can get to Garak. A weakened Worf has difficulty meeting the challenge of the first, but he won't yield. The first admires Worf's courage and refuses to kill him, but the camp's Vorta has no such compunctions. He orders a guard to kill the Klingon, but in the nick of time, Garak completes his work and the prisoners are beamed up to the runabout, where they send a message to DS9 and make a clean getaway.

Sisko and company are startled to receive a transmission from Bashir that originates in the Gamma Quadrant. They realize that *their* Bashir is about to send his explosive-rigged runabout into the sun, creating a blast that will wipe out the combined Federation forces *and* Bajor. The *Defiant* stops him just in time, and the changeling is destroyed. When the real Bashir and the others return from the Gamma Quadrant, Martok is made commander of the Klingon forces that will henceforth be stationed on Deep Space 9. There is little time for celebration as Dukat sends a message to Sisko, warning him that the battle isn't over.

"I'm not sure if this worked as well as it could have as a two-parter," confesses Ira Behr. "It might have been better as a two-hour block. Or even as a ninety-minute show. We didn't really gain anything by splitting them up. The second hour moves like a house on fire. Events are happening at such an accelerated pace. If we'd had the hour or forty-five-minute buildup immediately precede it, I'd have liked it better."

From a purely dramatic standpoint, the events of "By Inferno's Light" *might* have been more effective as the tail end of an extended episode. There's no denying that the hour was jam-packed with enough action and suspense to keep the most jaded viewer attentive, right from the opening teaser. In the best tradition of old-time serials, the audience learns that it's been duped. The vicious-looking Dominion fleet that was pouring through the wormhole at the conclusion of "In Purgatory's Shadow," poised to attack, doesn't attack. Instead, it moves on to Cardassia, accompanied by the new head of the Cardassian government, Gul Dukat.

After teetering on the brink of respectability for a

DS9's producers enjoyed the character of Martok, and made him a semiregular. DANNY FELD

year and a half, Dukat makes his choice. "You and I on the same side," he tells Kira. "It never seemed quite right, did it?" The comment could easily sum up the feelings of the producers toward *DS9*'s favorite villain; they never foresaw him becoming one of the show's heroes. "Dukat is a self-deluded, opportunistic, egomaniacal sadist," says Behr. "In other words, he is the Richard Nixon of *Deep Space Nine*. He will do whatever it takes to come out on top."

Dukat's motivation in making a deal with the devil was "pure desperation," says Robert Wolfe. "Cardassia was losing," he explains. "They were getting their asses kicked by everyone's forces. It was over." Wolfe gives Cardassia's situation a historical perspective, likening it to the Weimar Republic, Germany's government between 1919 (following its defeat in World War I) and 1933 (the threshold of Hitler's rise to power). "People were trading buckets of deutsche marks for a loaf of bread. It was cheaper to burn deutsche marks than to buy wood. Hitler's reign was a horror story, but there were people who didn't see the alternatives. And Dukat felt he was doing the only thing he could do to save his culture and his people." Although Dukat's rise to power in the Cardassian government may seem a bit abrupt to some, Wolfe notes that "Hitler's rise happened pretty quickly, too. So did Caesar's. It was a coup."

Although "By Inferno's Light" works essentially as a single-track story, with no separate B-story line, the events in the Dominion prison do serve to drive the action on DS9. Without Bashir's imprisonment, the fake Bashir would have been unable to sabotage the station's graviton emitters. Without Garak's efforts to free the prisoners, the real Bashir never would have been able to send the message that alerted Sisko to the presence of the changeling, thus preventing the destruction of Bajor's sun. Two plot points would resurface in later episodes, the more conspicuous of which was the apparent ease of the prisoners' escape from the Dominion prison camp. Why *was* that runabout left in orbit anyway? That's what Section 31's Sloane would want to know in the sixth-season episode "Inquisition." As for the other point, well, by seventh season it was pretty easy to understand why one wouldn't want to turn his back on a Breen.

Unlike the previous episode, this time around, Alexander Siddig *knew* in advance that the Bashir on the station was a changeling. As a result, he was able to shade his performance. "My angle on the changeling was that he managed to create a very good copy of Bashir, but that it somehow lacked Bashir's

Chattaway translated Garak's mounting fears into a cacophony of sounds. DANNY FELD

sense of humanity," says Siddig. "Bashir has a lot of levels. He has a sense of humor and he's very mercurial, laughing at the drop of a hat, or getting very angry. So I stripped him of all that. It would be hard to tell unless you were someone who was very close to Bashir." And the changeling spends little time around Bashir's closest friend, O'Brien, in this episode, and no time at all with Garak.

As for Garak, he may have had a more emotional scene in the prior episode, but here he nearly gets to climb the walls as the victim of severe claustrophobia. How does an actor prepare for scenes of that nature? "That was an easy one," laughs Andy Robinson. "For two reasons. First, I *am* somewhat claustrophobic. The very first time I put on the Garak makeup and the wet suit that they build the Cardassian costume on, I thought that I was going to die. I wanted to get out of it and not do this job. I had to really cool myself down. So that's always there, to some degree. But the other thing was, the day we shot the scene in the crawlspace, I had the flu. So I was feeling about as horrible as a person could feel. And then on top of that, having to get into that makeup and the director, Les Landau, putting that camera right up to my nose . . ." His voice trails off. "I didn't have to act. I was already there."

Adding to the grim, claustrophobic look of the Dominion prison were Herman Zimmerman, Laura Richarz, Tom Arp, Joe Longo, and others. The main portion of the prison camp was a huge set built on

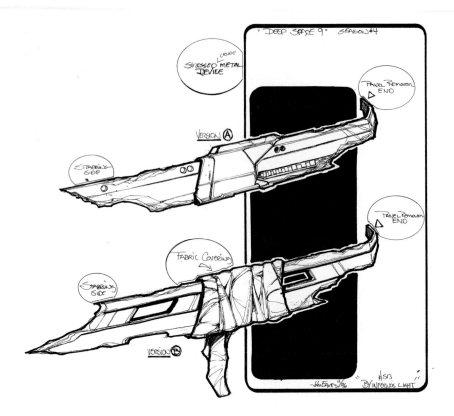

The tool used to open the cell's access panel. JOHN EAVES

Stage 18. Garak's tiny crawlspace area was located on that set as well, adorned with fiber optics lights and a variety of tubes, and painted in suitably depressing colors. "It was very grim. Everything was dark gray and kind of dirty," says Richarz. As usual, the team came up with some innovative uses for everyday objects, turning CD racks into light fixtures to hang over the beds in the prisoners' barracks, and plastic Christmas tree stands into plant-ons for the walls.

Bringing about the return of Martok was something in which the producers took great delight. "We didn't have any particular plans for him," says Behr. "We just liked him." But having permanently stationed him at DS9 by the end of the episode, it was inevitable that they *would* come up with some plans for the character. "We thought it would give Worf someone from his own people that he could like and admire," notes Behr, which would represent a definite change for the Klingon who never had lived among Klingons.

Actor J. G. Hertzler understood at once. "Worf finally had a friend, somebody that he could communicate with," Hertzler observes. And unlike some of Worf's previous relationships with Klingons, "Their agenda is not one of scheming or plotting or politicking. It's warrior to warrior. I think that's what the writers liked about Martok. Plus he's a crusty old bastard!" Martok's return called for a few changes in makeup. Michael Westmore opted to eliminate the

prominent scar that ran through the character's lip in "The Way of the Warrior." Hertzler has an explanation for what happened to it. "That scar was caused, it was determined, by Martok's biting through his lip with the tooth that sticks out, during some sort of combat situation, and it healed," he says. "I think Michael figured that after they'd ripped out his eye, Martok had so many scars that they should get rid of some of them."

Martok lost an eye in the Dominion prison camp, which gave Michael Westmore the opportunity to create an interesting prosthetic. "We decided not to show an empty socket," comments Westmore. "So we did it as if the skin had been pulled down and sewn." Martok rejects Bashir's offer of an ocular replacement for the missing eye in "Soldiers of the Empire," a decision that Hertzler believes may have grown out of a conversation he had with Ira Behr earlier in the season. "He told me backstage, 'We're going to bring you back, and you can get your eye back, of course.' And I said, 'Well, you know I have a feeling that Martok may want to maintain it as a badge of honor. It's an ever-present, constant reminder to him of how much he hates the Jem'Hadar for what they did to him and what they stand for.'"

The prosthetic proved to have its drawbacks. "It totally closes up that one eye," says Westmore, "which made it impossible for him to do his own stunts because he no longer had any depth perception." Hertzler has learned the limitations of Martok's get-up. "There are two dangerous spots for me," he says. "One is when the camera moves in for a close shot, especially a handheld camera. I remember doing a scene with Worf, and we'd rehearsed it—I had to run through this area to one side of me—and of course, the camera wasn't at rehearsal. So when we actually shot the scene, I ran right into the camera. *Bam!* Because they forgot I couldn't see on that side."

What's the other dangerous spot?

"Oh, the craft services table," he laughs. "People can be blown into the recesses of the stage if I turn left in a hurry, because this costume is massive!"

DOCTOR BASHIR, I PRESUME?

Episode #514

TELEPLAY BY **RONALD D. MOORE**
STORY BY **JIMMY DIGGS**
DIRECTED BY **DAVID LIVINGSTON**

GUEST CAST

Richard Bashir	BRIAN GEORGE
Rom	MAX GRODÉNCHIK
Leeta	CHASE MASTERSON
Amsha Bashir	FADWA EL GUINDI
Rear Admiral Bennett	J. PATRICK McCORMACK

SPECIAL GUEST APPEARANCE

Dr. Zimmerman	ROBERT PICARDO

STARDATE UNKNOWN

It's a routine day in Quark's bar, with Rom trying and failing to build up the nerve to ask Leeta for a date, and Bashir and O'Brien enjoying a game of darts. But things take a turn for the strange when Dr. Louis Zimmerman, Director of Holographic Imaging and Programming at Starfleet's Jupiter Research Station, arrives to inform Bashir that he's been chosen as the human template for Starfleet's new Longterm Medical Hologram (LMH). Zimmerman explains that he will need to learn everything he can about Bashir, from childhood quirks to adult interpersonal relationships, and he'll need to interview Bashir's family, friends, and coworkers. Bashir asks Zimmerman to refrain from talking to his parents, noting that he hasn't been close to them for years. Intrigued, Zimmerman immediately invites Bashir's parents to the station.

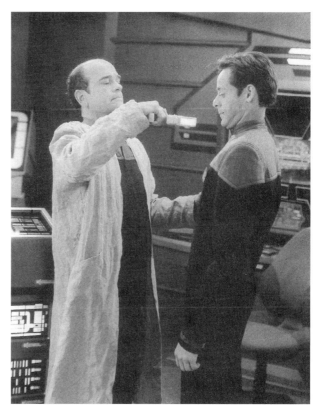

Dr. Louis Zimmerman scans Bashir for a template he'll use to create a new Longterm Medical Hologram. ROBBIE ROBINSON

Zimmerman begins the task of interviewing the crew about Bashir, taking note of all their observations, good and bad. He takes a particular liking to Bashir's ex-girlfriend Leeta, and asks her out on a date, much to Rom's dismay. Bashir receives an unpleasant surprise when his parents, Richard and Amsha, arrive to be interviewed. Bashir warns them to be careful when they speak to Zimmerman, particularly in regards to their "little secret," which, if revealed, could destroy Bashir's career *and* send both parents to prison. Richard takes offense at the inference that they're not bright enough to know this already, and father and son exchange angry words.

The next day, Rom is floored when Leeta tells him that Zimmerman has asked her to return to Jupiter Station with him. She's secretly hoping that Rom will give her a reason to turn Zimmerman down, but Rom is too shy to provide it. In the Infirmary, Richard and Amsha approach Bashir to apologize, and to assure him that they never would reveal that he'd been genetically enhanced as a child. They depart, unaware that they were addressing the holographic Bashir. O'Brien and Zimmerman had been testing it, and the two men have unintentionally eavesdropped on their conversation.

O'Brien immediately goes to tell his friend what happened. Bashir is devastated. DNA resequencing of the type he went through is illegal in the Federation, and genetically enhanced beings are barred from serving in Starfleet or practicing medicine. His only option, as he sees it, is to resign from Starfleet before Zimmerman files the report that will reveal the truth. Bashir tells his parents his intentions, but when he goes to see Sisko in the morning, he discovers that Richard and Amsha already have explained the whole situation. Sisko, in turn, has discussed the matter with Rear Admiral Bennett, Starfleet's top legal officer, and they've "cut a deal." Richard will spend two years in a minimum security prison for subjecting his son to illegal genetic engineering. In exchange, Bashir will be allowed to retain his commission and medical practice.

When Bashir realizes that his father truly wants to take responsibility for the situation, he reluctantly but gratefully accepts Richard's sacrifice. Elsewhere in the station, Rom stops Leeta from leaving with Zimmerman by admitting, at long last, that he loves her.

If *Star Trek* gave out awards for "the most memorable freelancer we've ever met," Jimmy Diggs would be in the running for top prize. He has sold numerous story ideas to *Star Trek: Voyager*—including "Elogium," "Rise," "Concerning Flight," "The Omega Directive," "Infinite Regress," and "Gravity." But not so long ago, Diggs, who's a Vietnam veteran, notes that he had a lot in common with jack-of-all-trades-but-master-of-none Richard Bashir, father of *Deep Space Nine*'s Julian. "I've had my problems," he admits. "I was a fireman for a while, and I worked as the guy backing up planes at airline gates. I was an electronics technician in the Navy. I was a security guard and an occasional actor on the syndicated TV series *Renegade* when someone from that show gave me the break that led me into writing."

A chance meeting with one of *Renegade*'s producers at a seasonal wrap party turned into an opportunity to pitch some story ideas. The producer expressed an interest in one of them and told Diggs to write it and come back. Unfortunately, by the time Diggs completed the script, the producer had lost his job at *Renegade*. Still, the sympathetic producer felt he owed Diggs a favor, so he sent the script over to Jeri Taylor, who was then at *The Next Generation*. Taylor liked the script enough to bring Diggs in as a writing intern. "And that's how all this madness started," he concludes with a grin.

"I decided to make Doc Zimmerman kind of a slob," says Robert Picardo, "so he slouches and his hair is a little messy."
ROBBIE ROBINSON

After Diggs pitched the story for "Doctor Bashir, I Presume?" a year and a half went by, so he was skeptical when he received a phone call from someone calling himself Ron Moore, saying that he wanted to buy his story. "I thought it was a practical joke," he says, "one of my friends fooling around." After grilling Moore for a few minutes, Diggs realized that this was indeed the man—and that he had three days to pull his notes together and turn in the story.

The idea that Moore wanted was actually the B-story of one of Diggs's pitches. "They decided it was worth an A-story," Diggs says happily. "It was a simple high-concept piece. Dr. Louis Zimmerman, creator and template for the original Emergency Medical Hologram [EMH], comes to DS9 to use Dr. Bashir as a template for a more personable, user-friendly Longterm Medical Hologram [LMH], ostensibly because he's been getting complaints from all over Starfleet about the irascible nature of the EMH."

Moore had liked the idea, but filed it away for future reference, until he had a chance conversation with friend Robert Picardo, who expressed an interest in doing an episode of *Deep Space Nine*. "Having managed to make a brief appearance in *First Contact*, I thought that clearly *Deep Space Nine* was the next arena for the ubiquitous Doc to conquer," Picardo says with a chuckle. "So I was very happy to hear that they were considering a story about just that."

Moore obtained Diggs's story, thinking, he recalls, "'All right, this will be a fun show, and we'll get a lot of comedy out of Bob. But what will the show *really* be about?'"

"While we were breaking the story, Ron was really struggling," says René Echevarria. "His instinct was that there needed to be some big secret that Zimmerman uncovers, and we couldn't, for the life of us, think what it would be."

"Up to this point in the show, Bashir's background was a big question mark," says Diggs "Everybody else had these incredible backgrounds. Kira Nerys was a former terrorist and freedom fighter. Sisko had been in the battle of Wolf 359. Worf was the mighty Klingon warrior disgraced by the Empire; and even O'Brien had fought tooth and nail against the Cardassians. But Bashir's background was layered in fog, which made him incredibly intriguing. So here we had a chance to delve into that background. There was a feeling that he was a very private individual, which meant that it would be interesting to put him into an embarrassing situation."

"I kept saying, 'What's the secret of Bashir's past? What's the thing that this guy, Zimmerman, is going to find that's so interesting?'" says Moore. "I remember that René and I started talking about genetics, and René pointed out that genetic engineering is one of the things that is oddly missing in the *Star Trek* universe. It's a concept that's very much out there in science fiction, and even in the real world of science, but in *Star Trek*, it's virtually never discussed, aside from the fact that there was this thing called the Eugenics Wars at some point, and Khan came out of it."

"And then Ron just had this bolt of inspiration," says Echevarria. "What if Bashir had been genetically engineered?"

"It really explained a lot about the character to me," continues Moore. "He'd had some strange jigs and jags in his profile over the course of the first four seasons. We have this guy with a lot of arrogance, who almost became a tennis player, who has all these different tales of why and when he went to medical school, and why he didn't become valedictorian of his class, and who has something about his past on Earth that he doesn't want to talk about. When Odo was going to Earth ['Homefront'], he asked Bashir, 'Is there anybody you want me to look up?' and Bashir says, 'I have nobody there I want to talk to.' There was something in this guy's backstory that was interesting. And it suddenly all made sense if this was a guy who'd been genetically engineered to be very, very smart but who'd had to hide it all his life."

Alexander Siddig, too, always had felt that there was something odd about Bashir's childhood. "I had a feeling that it was troubled," he says, "and early on in the series, I told the writers that there must be a reason for why Bashir had become so multilayered. It seemed like there might be some sort of abuse associated with his parents."

It was Moore who came up with a rationale for Bashir's parents' behavior when he was a child, an emotional explanation as to why they would allow their son to be the subject of highly illegal technology. At the time it just seemed like a good, solid plot point. But it hit amazingly close to home for Jimmy Diggs. "It really caught me off guard when Jimmy called me after reading the script," Moore relates. "He was very emotional, and he told me that it meant a lot to him. I had no idea that there was a personal connection."

"My daughter has this learning disability," explains Diggs. "She's the sweetest, kindest, most loving child that you could ever imagine. She works hard to get the grades that she does. Bashir's parents obviously had an option that I didn't, and I had to wonder if I'd really consider that. If I did, would she blame me, saying, 'Wasn't I good enough for you the way I was?' And then there's those other points that parents who have a child with a learning disability agonize over: 'Was it something that I did wrong?'"

Bashir's parents, particularly his father, are very different from any civilians that we've previously encountered in the future that *Star Trek* represents. As longtime fans know, and as Ron Moore recites by rote, "The-Federation-is-a-very-nice-place-to-live. *But—*" he pauses "—that doesn't mean you can't be a loser and you can't screw up. In the twenty-fourth century, everybody seems to have a job, and everybody's taken care of and everybody has food," he explains. "But there are people who are just not going to make it. And Bashir's dad is like that, the kind of guy who's always posturing himself as a success, but never has succeeded at anything."

The casting of Actor Brian George as Bashir's father actually served to assist Siddig's image of his own character. "The mother and the father are very different from one another," he says. "She's very clearly ethnic, while he's almost white. That was useful to me, because it muddies the waters of Bashir's heritage a bit more. I liked that because I didn't want Bashir to have any particular heritage or cultural identity that he had to live up to. And the chap who played my father did it as a sort of middle-class Londoner, by contemporary standards, that is, and that provided a class difference between the two of them too. It's clear that Bashir had some choices to make in his life, and he took on a very high-class accent that neither of his parents have. Basically, all of Bashir was manufac-

The casting substantiated Siddig's belief that his character's parents were different from Bashir. RANDY TOPPER

tured, either by some scientists or by himself over the years. I quite like the notion that he's a completely assimilated person, not someone who's inherited any particular traits from his family."

But it was when the producers began looking for someone to play Bashir's mother that they ran into real problems. "We wanted Arab-Americans to play both parents," says Director David Livingston. But it proved impossible to find a female Arab-American actor. "That's because there are none," points out Siddig. "Arab actresses are an oxymoron. Most Arabs are Muslim, and Islam frowns upon acting. No one outside of the family may see a woman without a headdress on, or see her cry or laugh. In the Islam world, you won't see a woman acting, except in a place like Egypt, where the rules are more liberal, and even then there are very strict definitions of what a woman may or may not do. But the woman they found did an amazing job."

Credit Casting Director Ron Surma for finding Fadwa El Guindi, a social anthropology professor at the University of Southern California. "Ron had heard something about a woman who'd done some community theater in town," says Livingston. "She had a real genuine empathetic quality about her when we brought her in to read, and we decided to go for it."

"It was such a marvelous moment," smiles Ira Behr. "She was as nervous as can be, but she had tremendous class. We told her to just be herself, and she was great."

With the previously "fun" Bashir plot now quite serious, it was up to Zimmerman to up the humor factor, and he was ably assisted by a strong subplot featuring Rom and Leeta. "We knew that we could hit the genetically engineered thing only so much in the course of the episode," says Behr. "We had to have something else. We already had Picardo, who is a terrific actor . . ."

". . . and we had to have something for Zimmerman to do when he wasn't working on his LMH," continues Moore. "And wouldn't it be fun if he was after the same girl that Rom was?"

"We'd been thinking long and hard about pairing up Leeta and Rom ever since 'Bar Association,' and we knew it was a funny idea, but we wanted to get the audience to root for it," Behr states. "So how do you do that? Well, you pair her up with someone you hope the audience won't want her to go with, making Rom seem a much better alternative. Sweeter, nicer, kinder."

Although he winds up losing the girl, Picardo loved his turn on *DS9*. "What was nice about it was that I didn't have to just be a jerk the whole episode," he says. "I mean, Dr. Zimmerman's attitude is that everyone, except him, of course, is an idiot." However, his infatuation with the voluptuous Leeta allowed him to show another side. One additional side of Zimmerman, a rather negative one, was left behind in an early draft of the script. "Early in the show we established that the LMH has some problems and lots of bugs," says Moore. "And O'Brien finds out that the problem is that Zimmerman is deliberately screwing up the program because he doesn't want it to replace the existing EMH. It's an ego kind of thing. Then, when O'Brien realizes that Zimmerman is going to expose Julian, he stops it by blackmailing Zimmerman, telling him that he'll expose him and tell Starfleet that he's been screwing up his own program to keep the project from ever getting off the ground."

"It worked on a certain level," reflects Echevarria, "but Sid was very distraught over it. He said that he had a big problem with this thing remaining a secret that he, as an actor, would have to live with for the rest of the series, that it would affect every scene that he was in, that he had this deep, dark secret. And that set us back on our heels. So we finally came up with the idea of amplifying Bashir's relationship with his father, so that his father ultimately decides to take the fall. And it actually became a stronger story, of healing between Julian and his father. It answered what Sid wanted and it made the show much, much better."

Star Trek fans love to scour episodes for gaffes and bloopers, and "Doctor Bashir, I Presume?" has a fairly conspicuous one. Admiral Bennett refers to the Eugenics Wars of two hundred years ago. But as every fan worth his salt knows, the Eugenics Wars took place during the 1990s—and *Deep Space Nine's* fifth season takes place in 2373.

Ron Moore sighs. "As I was writing the scene, I was thinking about the line Khan delivered in *Star Trek II,* how on Earth two hundred years ago he was a prince. And I just wrote down two hundred." Moore laughs. "It was wrong. It was a mistake. I just didn't do the math."

Odo bids a sad farewell to Arissa, the mysterious woman who won his affections. WREN MALONEY

A SIMPLE INVESTIGATION

Episode #515

WRITTEN BY RENÉ ECHEVARRIA
DIRECTED BY JOHN KRETCHMER

GUEST CAST

Arissa	DEY YOUNG
Traidy	JOHN DURBIN
Sorm	NICHOLAS WORTH
Idanian #2	RANDY MULKEY
Tauvid Rem	BRANT COTTON

STARDATE UNKNOWN

Bashir holds court at Quark's and reveals details about the latest installment of the "Julian Bashir, Secret Agent" holosuite program to his friends. Dax will play the part of a beautiful socialite, O'Brien the bad guy, and Odo a dashing fellow agent. But when Odo hears that his character must steal the heart of a beautiful woman, he opts out of the game. As he passes through the bar, he notes the presence of a striking human woman, who mentions that she's waiting for someone. He's intrigued by her, although he denies it to Quark.

The next day, the woman, Arissa, is arrested for attempting to break into the station's computer. She claims to have been looking for information about the man she was waiting for at Quark's, an Idanian

named Tauvid Rem, who never did show up. Arissa tells Odo that Tauvid has information about the daughter she gave up fifteen years ago, and Odo offers to take her to Tauvid's quarters. There, they find that Tauvid has been murdered.

Later, Odo catches Arissa retrieving a data crystal that Tauvid hid in the station's assay office prior to his death. She admits to Odo that she doesn't have a daughter, but that she *does* need the information on the data crystal, which Tauvid had told her would help her break her ties with the notorious Orion Syndicate. Arissa believes that Draim, her boss in the Syndicate, probably had Tauvid killed to keep him from giving her whatever information is on the crystal.

Odo places Arissa in protective custody in his quarters while Dax and O'Brien try to access the encrypted data crystal. As they spend time together, Arissa begins to trust Odo, and she tells him how she came to work for Draim, and how she quickly found out about his deadly business practices. Odo encourages her to testify against Draim and reclaim her life. The changeling pays a visit to Bashir for advice about how to judge a woman's romantic interest. Odo returns to his quarters, where he gives in to his growing attraction for Arissa.

After spending a passionate night with Odo, Arissa sends a message to Draim proposing an exchange: the crystal for her freedom. Draim agrees, but orders the two hit men responsible for Tauvid's death to kill her after the crystal is retrieved. In the meantime, an Idanian arrives at the station and tells Odo that Arissa is an intelligence agent who works for his government. Her assignment was to infiltrate Draim's organization, but she's unaware of that fact, because the government had supplied her with a new identity; her previous memories are stored on the data crystal that Tauvid, another agent, was bringing her.

Odo tries to take the Idanian to Arissa, only to find that both she and the crystal are missing; Arissa has taken it for her meeting with Draim's henchmen. Odo and the Idanian save her just in time, and the memories of her past are reimplanted. When she and Odo meet again, she tells him that she's married, but she lets the brokenhearted changeling know that what she and Odo shared was real, and that she'll never forget him.

The single-minded determination with which Odo protects Arissa is driven by more than his changeling need for order. ROBBIE ROBINSON

Although a relationship with Chalan Aroya ("Broken Link") hadn't been in the cards, Odo finally found the opportunity to get intimate in "A Simple Investigation." Ironically, it didn't happen the way anyone had foreseen. Odo wasn't exactly a virgin, as he explains to Arissa. He'd previously experienced a joining on his homeworld that one "might consider sexual" ("The Search, Part II"), but an intimate coupling with a humanoid was definitely new territory for him. The writers had envisioned the event when they had turned him into a human at the end of Season 4, but the right opportunity didn't come along until *after* Odo regained his shape-shifter status in "The Begotten."

"I wish we'd done the show while Odo was still human," admits Ron Moore. "If he had been human, the relationship with this woman would have carried a little more weight."

As it turned out, however, the fact that Odo *wasn't* human became an important aspect of writer René Echevarria's script. "Something I really wanted to convey in this episode was that what touched Odo about this woman was that she wasn't spooked by his alien nature," says Echevarria, a point that the writer would explore again in Season 7's "Chimera." An early draft of "A Simple Investigation" highlighted Arissa's comfort level in a scene that had her come out of Odo's bedroom, where she'd been sleeping alone, to find Odo regenerating in the next room. "He's sort of this gooey thing draped all over his jungle gym, a strange but beautiful, glistening thing," recounts Echevarria. "Ordinarily Odo would be embarrassed to be seen like this, but she comes up and gently touches him and then he sort of morphs onto her

and she lets him. I was very attached to the idea, but Ira felt it was important here that Odo make love as a man. And looking back on it, I'm glad we did it that way, because I was able to save that special moment for Kira, where it was more important."

Not that having sex as a man made the scene any less complicated. Director John Kretchmer masterfully orchestrated his approach to the "afterglow" scene, where Odo and Arissa are cuddling in bed, shooting it as one seamless sequence, without the benefit of cuts or close-up insert shots to cover potential missteps. "It's a very subtle shot, and if you look at it, you don't really understand how complex it was to choreograph and shoot," says Kretchmer. "This was my first *Star Trek* episode, and I didn't want to blow it. I couldn't have done it if Rene [Auberjonois] and Dey [Young] hadn't been comfortable with each other, or if they hadn't been able to remember three and a half pages of dialogue! That's a long scene."

With the help of Jonathan West, who carefully lit all the angles that Kris Krosskove would cover with a remote camera head attached to a dolly-mounted crane arm, Kretchmer managed to perfect the scene in just eight takes. Why bother with all the extra effort? "The first two-thirds of the story are about Odo and Arissa getting together," Kretchmer explains, so he deliberately avoided doing any two-shots (shots that include two actors in the same frame) with the pair early on. "I felt that once they *were* together, we should do the scene in a way that made it stand out. We needed a shot where they were both on-camera for the duration. It just seemed appropriate after they'd made love."

Doing it "as a man" was a little uncomfortable for Auberjonois for a rather personal reason. The official aesthetics for Odo dictate that he's smooth. *Really* smooth. *All over*. "They even thought about covering my nipples," Auberjonois recalls, although they ultimately decided against it. But when it came to body hair, he wasn't so lucky. "I had to shave my body," he sighs. "*Every hair*."

This was the second time the actor had been asked to "take it off," as he puts it. "I had to do it for 'Broken Link,' too," he recalls. "Whenever my body is exposed they ask me to shave the backs of my arms and my armpits and my legs. It itches like crazy coming back!"

As with several other *DS9* episodes, this one can trace part of its inspiration to an old movie, in this case a 1952 film called *The Narrow Margin*, a well-regarded B movie directed by Richard Fleischer. "Charles McGraw is this tough cop who has to take this tough dame played by Marie Windsor on the train to a trial," Ira Behr says of the film. "They go through all of this stuff together, with his partner getting killed and him falling for her, and at the end of the movie it turns out that she's a cop, too, a decoy for the real woman. It's a great movie that everybody has stolen from over the years."

Like the Julian Bashir, Secret Agent riff in the episode, the plot threads borrowed from *The Narrow Margin* were meant to provide a little "window dressing" for what essentially was "a love story that needed a little help," says Behr. Aside from the solid relationships that developed over the years between characters like Sisko and Kasidy, Dax and Worf, and Odo and Kira, Behr says wryly, "I think we do crappy romances. But in terms of romantic shows, this wasn't a bad one."

Ironically, Auberjonois thought that the romance with Arissa was meant to lead his character *away* from the ever-looming relationship with Kira. "We knew that it hadn't originally been the writers' intentions to put Odo and Kira together, and yet it sort of kept happening," he says. "I think both Nana [Visitor] and I felt this episode was a way to graceful-

"Dey Young was the person with whom I felt I had wonderful chemistry," says Rene Auberjonois. WREN MALONEY

ly move away from that idea." However, just a few episodes later, in "Children of Time," Odo would confess his love for Kira. Although it took a year for the writers to follow up on it, the inevitable match did occur at last, in "His Way."

This time around, Julian's secret agent subplot wasn't given much screen time, and was written carefully to avoid treading on the toes of any current or past secret agent franchises. The scene in the limo where Odo visits Bashir for romantic advice was shot on the last day of filming, much to the dismay of Alexander Siddig, whose mind was in another place altogether; he was busy prepping to direct his first episode, "Business As Usual," set to begin the following day.

"They had trouble finding just the right vehicle," says B.C. Cameron. "But finally they found *half* of a limousine. The whole front half was cut off, so we just had the back doors."

For those who are wondering, yes, confirms Echevarria, the secretive Idanian race introduced in this episode is indeed the same race that's responsible for Idanian spice pudding, a tasty staple of the station's Replimat since the series' first season.

BUSINESS AS USUAL

Episode #516

WRITTEN BY BRADLEY THOMPSON &
DAVID WEDDLE
DIRECTED BY SIDDIG EL FADIL

GUEST CAST

Regent	LAWRENCE TIERNEY
Gaila	JOSH PAIS
Farrakk	TIM HALLIGAN
Customer	ERIC CADORA
Talura	CHARLIE CURTIS

SPECIAL GUEST STAR

Hagath	STEVEN BERKOFF

STARDATE UNKNOWN

Quark submits an elaborate banquet to the scrutiny of Hagath, as
Cousin Gaila holds his breath. DANNY FELD

Although Quark is up to his lobes in debt, he's not exactly thrilled when his rich cousin Gaila comes to him with a business proposition. For one thing, the last time Gaila offered him something, Quark was nearly killed ("Little Green Men"). For another, Gaila makes his living selling arms, a business Quark always has avoided. But Gaila is offering Quark five percent of his sales, and all Quark has to do is handle customer relations: show prospective buyers a good time and allow them to test harmless replicas of Gaila's weapons in his holosuites. It sounds good to Quark. He wouldn't technically be breaking the law, and he'd be able to pay off his massive debts within a month. Gaila introduces Quark to his business associate, Hagath, who is impressed with Quark's holosuite facilities. As they agree to do business together, Hagath casually warns Quark never to cross him.

In the meantime, O'Brien deals with baby Kirayoshi, who has been left in his care while Keiko attends to a botanical emergency on Bajor. Yoshi is going through a crying phase that subsides only when the chief holds him, which puts a serious crimp in O'Brien's work and leisure activities, and gives him a kink in his neck. The problem is resolved when Sisko insists the chief take a few days' leave to give Yoshi his full attention.

Quark's lucrative new career nearly is cut short when Odo tries to arrest him for helping Hagath deal arms. But to Quark *and* Odo's surprise, the Bajoran government asks Sisko not to interfere in the shady business, because Hagath supplied arms to the Bajoran resistance during the war against the Cardassians. Quark rejoices over his victory, but he soon learns that it's come at a cost. The word has spread about his side business, and Federation citizens are avoiding his bar, even close friends like Dax. To make matters worse, he discovers that Hagath is quite serious when it comes to dealing with people who cross him; he's just had an associate killed for "letting him down" in a business transaction.

The pressure builds when the Regent of Palamar arrives to do business with Hagath. The regent wants weapons that will quash a rebellion led by his nemesis, General Nassuc, weapons that will kill twenty-eight million people. Gaila and Hagath immediately begin discussing which lethal items would do the most effective job, but Quark is aghast. He confesses his reservations to Gaila, who reminds Quark of the money that's involved and the fact that Hagath will kill him if he prevents the deal from going through. Nevertheless, Quark's conscience gets the better of him, and he decides that he has to stop Hagath, even if it means sacrificing his own life.

Quark stalls the transaction with the regent and brings General Nassuc to the station, allegedly to sell viral weapons to both sides and double their profits. Instead, he arranges for Nassuc to "accidentally" encounter the regent in the station's cargo bay, which leads to predictable fireworks. Gaila and Hagath flee from the station, with Nassuc's troops in pursuit, and the regent is killed. In one fell swoop, Quark has managed to eliminate his problem *and* save twenty-eight million lives. Knowing that the Ferengi honestly was trying to put an end to the arms arrangement, Sisko lets him off with an agreement that Quark will pay for repairs to the cargo bay—which should take quite some time.

It seems fitting that an episode about the master salesman of Deep Space 9 should find its origins in a classic sales pitch. "It was during our first pitch session," recalls Bradley Thompson. "We'd just gone through this incredible list, pitching one-liners and stories and stuff that just didn't fit the show's needs, and Ira [Behr] was so patient. And then finally David came up with the brilliant question: 'What are you looking for?'"

"I come from a family of salesmen," explains Thompson's writing partner, David Weddle. "That's what you do. You ask the customer what he's looking for. And Ira told us some of the things he was interested in, one of which was a story where Quark runs up against the limits of his greed. So *boom*, off we went to start developing a story."

It's a subject that the producers had felt was rife with possibilities. "Quark is a Ferengi businessman," comments Hans Beimler. "That's something he's proud of, that has significance to him. He's not a weasel. 'Business As Usual' is a great story, because it tells us how far Quark has been pushed, and to what

Though the characters were angry at Quark, the actors obviously had great affection for Shimerman. ROBBIE ROBINSON

Placing the baby in the pit meant there was no need for the infant to be present during shooting. ROBBIE ROBINSON

depths he's willing to go, that he would take the role of an arms dealer. And he's never completely comfortable with it. He kids himself for a while. He's in denial, but when they start talking about killing twenty-eight million people, he becomes a man in tremendous turmoil."

"What I like about this episode is that there's a real, actual problem that Quark has to face, a true dilemma," says Quark's alter ego, Actor Armin Shimerman. Although his cousin Gaila has no difficulty dealing in weapons of mass destruction, Quark begins to learn a hard truth about himself, a truth that will raise its head with increasing frequency before the series ends. "Having lived with Starfleet for so many years, Quark's begun to acclimatize to their culture, as anyone would who lives in a foreign culture," conjectures Shimerman. "Because as you live in that culture longer and longer, you begin to take on its characteristics. And certainly, Quark's feelings of remorse and justice and morality are beginning to loom larger and larger in his life."

Following that early pitch session, it took a while for Thompson and Weddle actually to come up with the story that would become "Business As Usual." In the meantime, they sold the story idea for fourth season's "Rules of Engagement," and were tapped to write the teleplay for fifth season's "The Assignment." The eventual pitch for "Business," like "Rules," drew its inspiration from current events. "We'd heard that Russian scientists were pulling plutonium out of warheads and selling it," says Weddle. Knowing that Cardassia was, at this point in the series, falling apart, the pair wondered what would happen if the planet decided to sell off its weapons.

"That was the first idea," says Weddle, "and it evolved from there." After they sold the pitch, they went in to discuss the potential direction of the story with the show's writer-producers. The subsequent story document they delivered was so well received that a number of key scenes ended up in the final teleplay, including Gaila's speech to Quark about the millions of stars in the sky, and whether or not anyone would notice if "one of those twinkling little lights suddenly went out."

The B-story, about O'Brien's problems with Kirayoshi, was another sequence that made it through the scripting process virtually intact. "After we wrote those scenes, they changed very little," says Thompson. "In the break session, Ira came up with the idea of everybody whispering in Ops so they wouldn't wake the baby. The scripted version is pretty much verbatim what Ira said."

"That's about me being a dad," Behr grins. "I just wanted to do something really human. They did a great job on it."

A short but sweet scene in which Worf gently cradles baby Kirayoshi in his arms would lie fallow in the writers' minds until the following season, when

Weddle and Thompson would assign Worf to baby-sitting duty for Yoshi in their teleplay for "Time's Orphan." And that minor plot point itself would be expanded into an entire B-story when "Time's Orphan" wound up running a bit short.

Behr liked several other things about "Business As Usual," particularly its guest casting. "Steven Berkoff is an excellent villain, actor, and all-around interesting dude," he says happily. "We were glad to get him as Hagath. He's an excellent writer, too. A renaissance man. He writes very, very, very strange and wonderfully crafted plays."

As for veteran tough guy Lawrence Tierney, "It was one of the highlights of my year to have him on the show," notes Behr. "He's one of my icons." Best known as the lead in the 1945 version of *Dillinger,* and, more recently, *Reservoir Dogs,* Behr is almost as impressed by Tierney's reputation off-camera as on. The actor's frequent brushes with the law are legendary and have been publicized widely over the years. "I think his rap sheet is longer than his filmography," Behr chuckles.

Unfortunately, Tierney, who turned 80 in 1999, arrived on the set disabled by a stroke he'd suffered in recent years. Although he was able to deliver lines, he had some difficulty remembering them. This

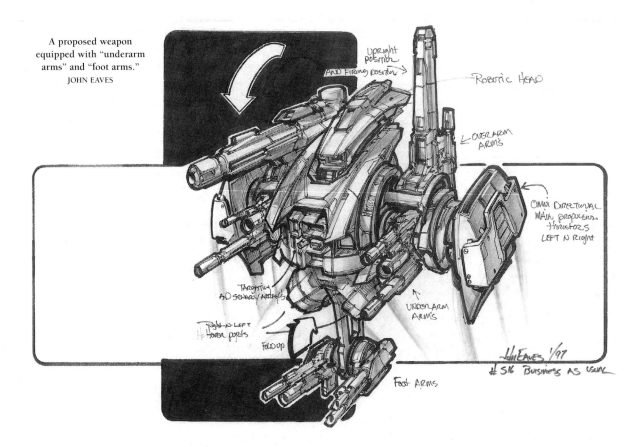

A proposed weapon equipped with "underarm arms" and "foot arms."
JOHN EAVES

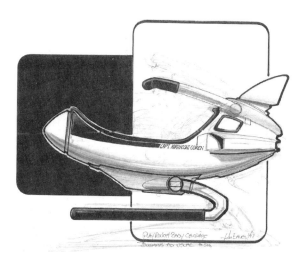

Yoshi's baby carriage. JOHN EAVES

proved especially trying for Alexander Siddig, who was directing his first *DS9* episode. "It was a real challenge for Sid," observes Lou Race. "But he and the other actors all hung in there with Lawrence. In the end, Sid and I agreed that he really came there to deliver one line: 'I'm here to buy weapons; are you here to sell them?' And he delivered that line like somebody calling to you from the other side of death. It was just chilling. So when the guy had to deliver, he did, and when he did his close-up, nobody stayed in their trailers. They all came over to watch."

Such difficulties aside, Siddig enjoyed the experience, which was his first venture into television directing. "I've directed several plays in England and loved doing it," he says. Siddig went through the now established training course, which he describes as "many weeks of watching people doing things, only some of which is of real use to anybody," he laughs. "To me the most useful stuff is being on stage and acting, and keeping your ears and eyes open."

DS9's holosuite set temporarily was expanded by an extra fifteen feet to accommodate both the impressive display of weapons that Quark presents to Hagath and for a backdrop that would allow the visual effects team to add the scene's attacking target robots. The weapons came courtesy of Prop Master Joe Longo and Laura Richarz. "Some of them were rented, some of them we built," says Richarz. "Some of them were from *The Warlords: Battle for the Galaxy*. Their stuff was a little more organic than ours is. And we even made one weapon out of something we'd used on a Jem'Hadar ship."

With truly heavy villains like Hagath and Tierney's regent on hand, Quark's cousin Gaila couldn't help but seem like more of a pussycat. "I don't think the fans would accept a Ferengi heavy at this point," says Behr. Even Brunt, who probably came closest to being a Ferengi villain over the course of the series, was "only a heavy to other Ferengi," he adds. Quark ultimately would find it possible to forgive his untrustworthy cousin the following season, in "The Magnificent Ferengi."

As for Quark himself, would he have wanted to pull out of that lucrative deal with Hagath quite so fast if the regent had wanted to kill a few less people? "I don't know," says Shimerman thoughtfully. "One would think that Quark's old Ferengi instincts are still there somewhere and that money still makes a difference to him, assuming the number of dead were much smaller."

Concurs Thompson, "We just found one line to Quark's greed that he wouldn't cross. We haven't found the bottom line yet."

TIES OF BLOOD AND WATER

Episode #517

TELEPLAY BY ROBERT HEWITT WOLFE
STORY BY EDMUND NEWTON & ROBBIN L. SLOCUM
DIRECTED BY AVERY BROOKS

GUEST CAST

Legate Ghemor	LAWRENCE PRESSMAN
Gul Dukat	MARC ALAIMO
Kira Taban	THOMAS KOPACHE
Furel	WILLIAM LUCKING
Weyoun	JEFFREY COMBS
Gantt	RICK SCHATZ

STARDATE 50712.5

Kira is looking forward to an official visit from Tekeny Ghemor, a Cardassian who is well known as the leader of a dissident movement against the planet's former government. Now that Dukat and the Dominion have taken over Cardassia ("By Inferno's Light"), she is hoping that Ghemor will lead the opposition against the new regime. Kira first encountered Ghemor when she was kidnapped and surgically altered to look like Ghemor's missing daughter ("Second Skin"). The experience left the two nearly as close as father and daughter. She's saddened, therefore, when Ghemor reveals that he's too ill to take up the cause; he's dying of Yarim Fel syndrome. Nevertheless, he does have something that may be of use to her: confidential

Kira cares for Ghemor, who has come to the station to die with the only family he has. RON TOM

information about the Cardassian government. He tells Kira of a Cardassian tradition in which the dying give their secrets to their family to use against their enemies. Ghemor is willing to tell his secrets to Kira, who is the closest thing he has left to family. Sisko points out that this is an incredible opportunity to gather intelligence on the enemy, and Kira reluctantly agrees to the task.

As she spends day after day at the Cardassian's deathbed, Ghemor struggles against agonizing pain to share his secrets, while Kira struggles with painful memories of her own father's lingering death during the Occupation. Determined to remove Ghemor from the station, Dukat arrives with his Dominion cohort, Weyoun, a clone of the Vorta that Sisko had seen killed by the Jem'Hadar a year earlier ("To the Death"). When Dukat can't get Ghemor to leave of his own volition, he attempts to poison Kira's mind about him by providing proof that Ghemor participated in a notorious massacre at a Bajoran monastery during the Occupation. Kira angrily confronts Ghemor with the accusation, and the dying man doesn't deny his involvement. Despite his genuine remorse over his actions, Kira cannot forgive him and she stops visiting him. Later, Odo reminds Kira that Ghemor was only one of four hundred Cardassian soldiers involved in the event. He wonders if Kira isn't really upset about something else. She goes back to her quarters and thinks again about her father's final days, and how she had left his side to fight Cardassians rather than stay and watch him slowly slip away.

The memory is interrupted by Bashir, who's come to tell her that Ghemor will be dead within the hour. Kira refuses to return to the Cardassian's bedside, and an angry Bashir points out that no one deserves to die alone. Kira recalls that her own father died calling her name, with no one to comfort him. Suddenly, she goes to Ghemor's room and takes his hand, and the old man dies in peace. Freed from the regrets of the past, Kira takes Ghemor's body to Bajor and buries him next to her father.

The idea for "Ties of Blood and Water" originated in a pitch by husband-and-wife team Edmund Newton and Robbin Slocum, a *Deep Space Nine* production associate. The story held deep resonance for Robert Wolfe, who wrote the teleplay. "Their pitch was that Tekeny Ghemor, from 'Second Skin,' comes to the station to die and he wants Kira to take care of him." But when Wolfe sat down to write the teleplay, "it was about the death of my mother," he says thoughtfully. "This was a very personal script."

It was personal for Nana Visitor as well. "I know a bit of the realities of caretaking," she says. "It's not easy. I have a family member who has a very difficult illness. And no matter how much you know intellectually or emotionally what you want to do for that person, it's one of the hardest jobs. I take my hat off to anyone who takes care of a disabled person or someone who is critically ill. It's truly unconditional love. It is draining, physically, and along with that, the person who is ill isn't always in a state to be grateful or reasonable."

Visitor likes that the writers were willing to expose Kira's failings and shortcomings. ROBBIE ROBINSON

A Bajoran grave marker. JOHN EAVES

When her character, Kira Nerys, is thrust into that role, finding herself the sole source of emotional support to Ghemor as he dies, "Kira doesn't do well," Visitor says. "But I like playing the *truth* of things. I love that they did this with my character, that they wrote that Kira isn't Miss Perfect Saint. It wasn't about her not loving the person she cared for. It was about 'This is tough.' And that it required more of her than she had at the moment. And it was a learning experience for her."

"The whole point of the story is that Kira had missed her own father's death, and she doesn't know what that was about," observes Wolfe. "This experience tells her what it was like, and now she's able to close the door on that."

How did Visitor prepare for the wrenching scenes? "I told the truth," she says. "My preparation for something like that is to live the moments as they happen and then tell someone about it. And whatever happens, happens." Director Avery Brooks provided an additional assist by sharing a personal story with her about a relatable situation, Visitor notes. "And that's all I needed," she says.

"We did talk about watching someone die," Brooks affirms. But he did not give her specific instruction about where to go from there, or how far to take her reactions. "I never talk about degrees [of emotion] in that way." For the dialogue-free sequence in the middle of the episode, where the viewer sees Kira caring for Ghemor, the director drew on the reality of a bedside death watch. "There is a suspension of time," Brooks observes. "Time is kind of irrelevant." But even though you're looking at the same things in a room, there are ways to make the shots look different. "That's why there was one shot that I did from the ceiling," he points out. "Looking at them straight down like that. Because in a way, psychologically, that's what Ghemor is looking at."

Brooks was pleased with the final look of the sequence. "There's no real tight angles. Each shot in the montage sequence was, for me, like a portrait. I was very interested in creating portraits, in terms of composition and lighting. Still portraits. Not photographs, but paintings."

Although she's often seen as the strongest charac-

A hero worthy of her own bubble gum card. RON TOM

figure . . . first officer of one of the most important military installations in the Quadrant."

"So much stuff has happened on Deep Space 9 since everyone got there," notes Ira Behr. "I would think these guys would be the heroes of the galaxy. There'd be Bajoran bubble gum cards of them. It's not like the *Enterprise* that keeps moving on. They're here, right here. And I would think that even the people on the station would be whispering, '*Look, that's Worf.*' '*That's Dax.*' They'd know everything about them."

And Kira, most likely, would hold a particular fascination for the Bajoran people. "They can't identify with the Emissary," explains Wolfe. "He's too mystical. And he doesn't look like one of them, he doesn't have a ridge on his nose. So popular imagination is likely to seize on the Bajoran standing next to him in all the pictures. '*Who's she? She's doing all these great things. She's saved our planet.*' It's inevitable that someone like that is going to become famous. She's a hero in her own right."

Besides bringing back respected character actor Lawrence Pressman as Ghemor, "Ties of Blood and Water" is noteworthy for returning one of the producers' (and fans') favorite characters back to the fold: Weyoun. "When we first saw Jeff [Combs] do the role in 'To the Death,' we were wishing we could find a different ending to the episode, because we really didn't want the character to die," comments Behr. "But we just couldn't think of anything. The next thing you know, they're out there in Griffith Park, shooting the fight, and he's dead. I knew immediately that he had to come back. There was no way he couldn't."

The cloning solution ("It seemed like a viable way of doing it," Behr observes.) fit in perfectly with the concept of the Founders' skill with genetic engineering, and it ultimately led to the running gag of introducing Weyoun 5, 6, 7, and so forth. Actor Jeffrey Combs saw a chance to insert a little of his own personality into the show when he reintroduced the character. When the new Weyoun first appears, he seems to be hiding behind Dukat. "I was having fun," Combs says about his choice of position. "That was an acknowledgment of, 'Oh, you thought I was dead, but here I am.' I take a great joy in unsettling people," he adds with a laugh.

ter on the station, in many ways, Kira also is the saddest. The scene where Kira introduces Ghemor to Kirayoshi points that up nicely. "This is her family," says Wolfe. "The father that is not her father. The baby that is not her baby. That's Kira's family."

It's details like that which add to the character, making it real. "There are some people who say to me, 'You know, I miss the Kira from earlier in the series, who's a fighter and quick to argue,'" Visitor smiles. "And I cite shows like this, that make Kira mature and emotionally sophisticated, more complex, more ready to react a different way other than viscerally." The episode also clues in the audience as to Kira's increasing "celebrity" to both the Bajorans and the Cardassians. As Ghemor says, she's a "public

FERENGI LOVE SONGS

Episode #518

WRITTEN BY **IRA STEVEN BEHR & HANS BEIMLER**
DIRECTED BY **RENE AUBERJONOIS**

GUEST CAST

Ishka	CECILY ADAMS
Rom	MAX GRODÉNCHIK
Leeta	CHASE MASTERSON
Maihar'du	TINY RON
Leck	HAMILTON CAMP
Brunt	JEFFREY COMBS

SPECIAL GUEST STAR

Zek	WALLACE SHAWN

STARDATE UNKNOWN

Between his recent blacklisting by the FCA (Ferengi Commerce Authority) and the fact that his bar has been temporarily closed down due to a Cardassian vole infestation, Quark feels his life couldn't get much worse, until Rom informs him that he's getting married to a dabo girl, Leeta. Rom suggests that a visit to their mother Ishka, on Ferenginar, is probably just what Quark needs to cheer him up. When a needy Quark shows up at her door, Ishka seems uncomfortable with the idea that her oldest son will be living with her for an unspecified period of time. Quark quickly learns why when he finds Grand Nagus Zek hiding in his closet. But why is he here? The scandalous truth is that Ishka and Zek have fallen in love, but the nagus demands that Quark keep the relationship a secret. Quark agrees, thrilled that his mother is now the beloved of the most powerful man on his homeworld.

Back on Deep Space 9, there's trouble in paradise. Although Rom didn't *think* that he minded the fact that Leeta was a nonFerengi, he's having second thoughts about his wife-to-be. He decides to have her sign a traditional Ferengi Waiver of Property and Profit, which calls for the female to give up all claims to the male's estate should the marriage end. O'Brien counsels him against it, but Rom is insistent. Predictably, the marriage is called off, leaving both parties feeling miserable.

With Zek practically in the family, Quark hints that he'd like his revoked business license reinstated. But Zek refuses, noting that it's up to the FCA. An unhappy Quark goes to his room and once again

Brunt tricks Quark into destroying the relationship between Zek and Ishka. ROBBIE ROBINSON

finds a visitor in the closet. This time, it's Liquidator Brunt, the FCA agent who had Quark blacklisted.

Brunt quickly comes to the point: he's deeply concerned about Zek's relationship with the free-thinking Ishka, and he wants Quark to break it up. In return, he'll give Quark a new business license. Quark agrees and sets out to poison Zek's mind with doubts about Ishka's true feelings for him, and with thoughts about her dangerous feminist leanings. The plan works and Ishka is heartbroken, and, for some reason, very worried about Ferenginar. Quark feigns sympathy, then contacts Brunt, who keeps his word and gives Quark the business license.

Quark can't help but feel that things are looking up when Zek offers him the position of first clerk, a reward for warning him about Ishka. He soon realizes that Zek is not the financial wizard he used to be, and, in fact, his memory is shot. By day's end, the Ferengi market exchange has experienced a drastic slide, and a stunned Quark returns home, where he realizes that Ishka was more than Zek's lover; she was the brains behind the throne. In turn, Ishka realizes that the breakup with Zek was due to Quark's inter-vention—at Brunt's behest. When Quark goes to work the next day, he runs into Brunt, who's sizing up the grand nagus's throne. Brunt gleefully reveals that he got Quark to destroy Zek's relationship with Ishka so that *he* could become grand nagus when the Board of Liquidators throws Zek out of office!

Quark considers going home to Deep Space 9, but his newfound conscience convinces him to first put right what he's put wrong. With careful coaching from Quark, Zek convinces the Board that he's still on top of things. Then Quark reveals to Zek that all the brilliant financial advice actually came from Ishka, and that everything he told Zek about her was a lie. The two lovebirds get back together, and Quark heads for DS9, where Rom has reconciled with *his* true love by giving all of his money to the Bajoran War Orphans Fund.

"**W**e still carry the scars and wounds of the first couple of seasons when everyone said we were 'too dark' a show," Ira Behr complains. It's something the general public and even the general *Star Trek* audience never got past. They were convinced that *Deep Space Nine* episodes were deep, dark, and depressing. Yet the series regularly did some of the wackiest, wildest hours in the entire *Star Trek* franchise. And that's something Behr is proud of. "All I wanted was a show

"I'm younger than both Armin and Max," Cecily Adams says, "so it's fun to play their mother." ROBBIE ROBINSON

where we'd take chances," he says. "We went where we wanted and damn the consequences."

So Behr has no one to blame but himself if "Ferengi Love Songs" (known up to the eleventh hour as "Of Love and Profit") is a bit too cartoonish even for his tastes. "It was never meant to be that way," he says. "We weren't doing a cartoon. I saw the tone more along the lines of a Howard Hawks *Bringing Up Baby* kind of a thing. But we pitched it at too high a level, and I think it's the first time that Zek got away from us. It was a show that worked well in dailies, in little snippets, but put it all together and you're saying, 'Enough already!'"

"It was very much a cartoon," Armin Shimerman says, recalling the comical double takes that he did when he found Zek hiding in his room. "I mean, the idea that the richest, most powerful man alive is in your bedroom closet boggled my imagination. So my response to it *had* to be cartoony. How else can you respond to something like that? How could you take that seriously?"

That's the way Director Rene Auberjonois saw it

as well. "I've always thought of the Ferengi as cartoon characters," he states. "A few years ago, the *TV Guide* summer issue had Quark on the cover, wearing a Hawaiian shirt, and at the time I commented to Rick Berman how funny that was. Rick said, 'Yes, it's the only character on *Star Trek* that we can do that with.' You could never do that with Odo or Worf. You can't make fun of them that way without somehow diminishing the strength of those characters. But with the Ferengi you *can*."

The concept for the show was a natural, according to Behr. "Right after 'Family Business' we thought, 'Let's put Moogie and Zek together.' It seemed like a gimmick that you just *had* to do. There was no way we *couldn't* do it." Unfortunately, Andrea Martin, who'd made such an indelible impression as Moogie, was unavailable to reprise the role. But the producers got lucky when casting called in Cecily Adams.

Adams is no stranger to episodic television, although she's never played an alien before. "I get cast a lot as secretaries," she says. "I played one named Muffin Goldstein on *Simon and Simon;* I played one of Murphy Brown's temps. Moogie was an amazing departure for me."

The daughter of *Get Smart*'s Don Adams, the new Moogie admits she wasn't really familiar with *Deep Space Nine*. But she did know that Quark's mother had been established in an earlier episode, and she was friends with Actress Kitty Swink, the wife of Armin Shimerman. "So I called Armin to tell him I was up for the role and he was kind enough to lend me a tape of the show that Andrea Martin had done," she says. "I watched it and got an idea of the tone, the comedy, and the relationships." A natural mimic, Adams was well versed in Moogie's melodic intonations when she arrived at the studio to audition. "She came in and said, 'Do you want to hear this the way Andrea Martin would do it?'" Behr recalls. "And then she just *did* Moogie. We all looked at each other and said, 'Why the hell not!'"

But while she had the voice down, Adams had a more difficult time with Moogie's vocabulary. "It was like reading in another language," she laughs. "During the audition, I didn't know what the character was talking about! The name 'Maihar'du' was in there and I had no idea how to pronounce that, or what the 'Tongo Festival' was. I felt like I was literally walking into another universe."

But if she thought Moogie's universe *sounded* odd, she was even more stunned by its visual requirements. She never had worn prosthetics. "I was excit-

"Wally and I would get out of makeup and have no idea who each other was," laughs Cecily Adams.

ed when I came in that first day, but then they put the headpiece on and glued it to my eyelids, and in that first moment I knew I was in for it," comments Adams. After three hours in the makeup chair, she continues, "they put me in wardrobe, and put me on the set. We did one rehearsal and then they said, 'Roll camera.' It was sink or swim, and I had no idea how to move my face with all that makeup on."

But Adams was fortunate. Both her costar and her director were *extremely* well versed in prosthetic acting. "Armin said, 'Cecily, it's all in the eyes,'" she relates. "'If you're doing your work on the inside, it will show on the outside.' And Rene encouraged me to go a lot farther with the character and trust that it wouldn't look like overacting. I said to him at one point, 'I'm just afraid that I'm gonna look like a cartoon character,' and he said, 'Cecily, have you looked in a mirror? You *are* a cartoon character!' I was like, 'Oh. Yeah. Okay.'" She laughs at the memory. "It was the best of both worlds, having one of them on either side of me."

Creating the sets was a relatively simple task. Ishka's house had been established in the earlier episode, so the Art Department basically had only to assemble and redress it. Zek's Chamber of Petitioners in the Ferengi Tower of Commerce was the only new set. Although one never would suspect that the very wealthy grand nagus would place his bottom on a secondhand throne, the truth must be told. "We'd built an oversized captain's chair for the Romulan ship's bridge in 'The Die Is Cast,'" admits Laura Richarz. "But we never shot it because it was way too big and very clunky. However, it *was* thronelike, so

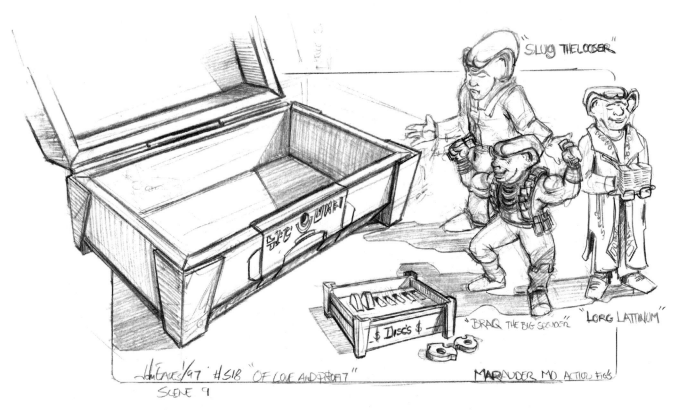

The complete Marauder Mo™ action figures included Slug the Loser™, Lorg Latinum™ and Braq™ the Big Spender. JOHN EAVES

we reupholstered it in a silly way and turned it into Zek's throne." However, Richarz's favorite bit of set decoration was the Marauder Mo action figures. "John Eaves designed them and made a whole box full. They were so cool, everybody wanted one."

Beimler reveals that Ishka's chiding comment to Quark about not saving the original packaging was a gentle jab at Behr. "Ira's one of those guys who buys all these toys and *never* opens them. And God forbid *you* should open one because it'll make it less valuable."

The fun wasn't limited to the production staff. Dennis McCarthy notes that he had a great time composing the score, which he describes as "Carl Stalling meets Prokofiev." Stalling, as aficionados of film music may recall, is the much-loved composer of the Warner Brothers classic *Merrie Melodies* cartoons. And Prokofiev, whose large body of work includes *Peter and the Wolf,* also wrote a well-known piece called "Humerous Scherzo for Four Bassoons."

"The bassoon," McCarthy explains, "is a fast-playing, low instrument, like a clarinet on steroids. For some reason its sound always makes me want to laugh or to cry. If you think of Stravinsky's opening to *The Rite of Spring,* you hear how beautiful the instrument can be. But in Carl Stalling's works, you hear the bassoon and you fall out of your chair laughing. So for 'Love Songs,' I brought in extra woodwinds. I featured the bassoon in Ishka's theme and used a contrabassoon for Zek's theme. And there's also an E-flat contrabass clarinet that's playfully running around in there. That all contributed to a sense of Prokofiev-type humor."

Humorous music in *Star Trek?* What gives? It's true, admits Associate Producer Terri Potts, the usual line the composers follow is, "We don't do comedy, we're *Star Trek.*" But at some point during the run of *Deep Space Nine,* Potts says, "we got everybody on board and said, 'If we're gonna do comedy, we've got to commit. We do it or we don't.'"

SOLDIERS OF THE EMPIRE

Episode #519

WRITTEN BY **RONALD D. MOORE**
DIRECTED BY **LeVAR BURTON**

GUEST CAST

Leskit	DAVID GRAF
Kornan	RICK WORTHY
Tavana	SANDRA NELSON
Nog	ARON EISENBERG
General Martok	J.G. HERTZLER
Ortikan	SCOTT LEVA

STARDATE UNKNOWN

General Martok receives orders from the Klingon High Council to search for the *B'Moth*, a Klingon battlecruiser that has disappeared near the Cardassian border. The mission aboard the *Rotarran*, the bird-of-prey that Martok's been assigned, will be his first since his confinement in the Dominion prison ("In Purgatory's Shadow"). He invites Worf to share in the glorious adventure by serving as his first officer, and Dax volunteers to join them as science officer.

After they come aboard, the two DS9 officers discover that their fellow crewmates are not the proud Klingon warriors they'd expected. It is an embittered crew whose morale has been destroyed by a punishing series of losses at the hands of the Jem'Hadar. Worf advises Martok that the best way to restore morale would be to score a decisive victory against their enemy, but Martok feels they shouldn't enter into combat before the crew is ready. In the meantime, Dax shares some bloodwine with the crew in an attempt to lighten their spirits, but her efforts are met with doom and defeatism.

The ship's crew spots a lone Jem'Hadar patrol ship, and they cloak before it can detect them. Although the crew is itching for a fight, Martok orders the *Rotarran* crew to ignore it and continue toward their goal. The decision brings spirits even lower. Dax warns Worf that the mood is creating a dangerous atmosphere aboard the ship, but Worf continues to support Martok's cautious behavior. Later, when some frustrated members of the crew take out their pent-up anger on each other, a young Klingon nearly is killed.

Sensors pick up a distress call from the crippled

Worf challenges General Martok in order to save his honor. ROBBIE ROBINSON

B'Moth, and the crew wants to rescue the survivors. However, Martok fears that the Jem'Hadar have left the ship as a trap, and he refuses to let the *Rotarran* cross the Cardassian border to investigate. Realizing at last that Martok's brutal experience in the prison camp has left him afraid to face the Jem'Hadar, Worf decides that he must challenge Martok for control of the ship, even if that means he must kill the general. The two men pull out their knives and engage in a fierce fight. The crew can't help but get emotionally involved in the battle, first cheering Worf, and then Martok. As the fight reaches fever pitch, Worf sees that Martok has regained his nerve and remembered his duty as a Klingon warrior. He drops his guard, and Martok wounds him and wins the fight. Just then, a Jem'Hadar ship approaches, and Martok leads the revitalized crew to victory over the enemy vessel. After rescuing the *B'Moth* survivors, the *Rotarran* returns to Deep Space 9, spirits restored, and Martok expresses his gratitude to Worf by inviting him to become a member of the House of Martok.

"I said to Ron Moore the words he so longed to hear," Ira Behr relates. "'Give me *Star Trek: Klingon*—a story that we could do as a *Star Trek* episode, but with all Klingon characters.'" Write an episode of an imaginary series that's all about Klingons? Moore automatically loved the idea. "It was very cool," he says. "I wanted to do a whole episode that would stay with the Klingons and not once cut back to the station."

Approaching the assignment with perhaps a bit too much enthusiasm, Moore immediately began writing a story of mythic proportions about Worf and Martok taking a bird-of-prey to a Klingon outpost that the Empire has lost contact with. When the pair arrive at the outpost, located on a strange planet, they find that all the Klingons are missing. Near the outpost is a fog-enshrouded lake, upon which a boatman appears. Worf and Martok give some coins to the boatman, who rows them across the lake . . .

"Basically, it was the River Styx," Moore says. "There was going to be a friend of Martok's on the other side that they wanted to bring back, and Worf's father was over there, too. I was really intrigued by it."

However, when Moore turned in his story document to Behr, the executive producer was forced to point out an unfortunate reality. "I was trying to show the inner life of the crew of a bird-of-prey *and* do this big, out-there kind of piece," Moore admits. "It was

Life aboard a bird-of-prey offered Moore a microcosm of Klingon society to explore. ROBBIE ROBINSON

just too much to do in one episode. And, as Ira said, it was the wrong point in the season to do a big meditation on the metaphysics of Hell and Life and Death," relates Moore. Everyone in the cast and crew was a little too tired to grapple with such big issues.

That's a real concern for the producers, who always must keep timing in mind when scheduling big shows. "Late in the season, people are worn out, so a big show is difficult," confirms Steve Oster. "It's hard on the crew when they're beginning to wind down."

"Ira said, 'Let's just go with *Star Trek: Klingon* and tell a story,'" says Moore. "So we cut all that loose and it became a show about Martok and Worf on the bird-of-prey, going out on a mission. I knew that Dax had to come along because I needed another voice. But what was important to me was giving that ship an inner life, in the sense that you walk in and each of the people there would have his own specific character and backstory and relationships. We'd find out how a bird-of-prey works, what the things are that make it run."

Moore hit upon the idea that this was "a beaten crew, one that had gone through some tough times and seen some horrible things." That gave him the resources to focus on their specific characteristics. "One of them thinks they're cursed, and one of them is a female engineer who doesn't want to give up. And then there's the troublemaker who just enjoys making the situation worse and worse in a perverse desire to destroy them all." Giving each Klingon crew member a distinctive personality *and* a distinctive look was important to Moore, who was aware of a problem perceived in previous "heavy makeup" episodes. "On some of the shows where we've had a lot of Klingons on camera, even *I* get them confused. So we wanted more visual distinction here, and as a result, one was given short-cropped hair and one had no sleeves. Tavana's hair is red, and there was even a blond Klingon. I just wanted variety." To emphasize their different personalities, Moore wrote a speech for Dax about there being "strong Klingons and weak Klingons." Moore explains, "I wanted to say that Klingons are people too. Some are good, some are bad, some are strong, some aren't. They're not Jem'Hadar."

Getting Worf released to go on a Klingon mission while he's still on duty as a Starfleet officer took a special dispensation. "In an early draft, I had Sisko saying, 'Starfleet is a little dubious about this. Why do you really want to do it?'" says Moore. "But then I figured that Sisko had the authority to grant that sort of thing. I didn't see any purpose in kicking it higher up the chain." The executive producer, of course, has a simpler explanation: "The military precedent was cited by Admiral Behr and approved by Vice-Admiral Moore!"

Just the mention of "Soldiers of the Empire" makes Director LeVar Burton break into song—Klingon battle song, that is. "We had a great time!" he says enthusiastically. "And Michael Dorn, who has a terrific voice, really got into that song." That song, ironically, came from an interactive CD-ROM game that actually *was* titled *Star Trek: Klingon*. Moore had served as a consultant on the CD-ROM, which was directed by Jonathan Frakes. Moore remembered the song, cowritten by *DS9* freelancer Hilary Bader and Keith Halper, one of the game's producers. "I decided that I wanted to show the crew going into battle singing," he says. "It's just the kind of thing that Klingons do. They're [like] Vikings, and they sing in battle." Reprising the song for the episode saved Moore some time and energy. "*I* didn't want to have to write a song!" he laughs.

Bader, who also wrote the script for the CD-ROM, was tickled when she heard the song in "Soldiers." She'd originally written it for a scene "where the Klingons were going off to become warriors," she says. "I just thought, 'Let's write a song for them to go out on.' So I wrote a poem in English, and we called it 'The Klingon Warrior Anthem.'"

The poem was duly translated into Klingon by linguist Marc Okrand, known to fans as the father of the Klingon language and author of *The Klingon Dictionary*. But here, for the first time in English, is the song's opening stanza:

> *Hear Sons of Kahless*
> *Hear Daughters too*
> *The blood of battle washed us clean*
> *The warrior brave and true.*

Coincidentally, the CD-ROM was the first project in which J.G. Hertzler made an appearance as a Klingon—however, not as Martok. "I played a character known as 'Elderly Klingon,'" recalls Hertzler. Dorn, too, had appeared in the game, which gave the two men an advantage over their co-stars. "J.G. and Michael had recorded the song before," Burton says. "So they kind of knew it. But none of the others had. We pulled them all aside during the lighting setups and brought them up to speed."

"*Everybody* sang," notes B.C. Cameron, laughing at the memory. "All the background players, the extras, the crew. We had big cards with these Klingonese words written on them for the actors to read. For days, that's all you'd hear on the stage: people singing this battle song."

The sequence inspired Burton to ask for a concession that's rarely granted in *Star Trek*. "I wanted to go exterior of the ship [by cutting to a visual effects space shot] and carry the sound of the song from the interior out with us," he says. "We hardly ever do that. It's a hard-and-fast rule, but I felt it really was appropriate in this instance. I pushed pretty hard for that, and Rick Berman went for it," he says happily.

Laura Richarz also had fun elaborating on Klingon detail. "'Soldiers of the Empire' was the first *DS9* show where we saw a Klingon mess hall," she says. "We had to have a table and chairs. We'd originally made chairs for 'Appocalypse Rising' because the script said they were there. But then later the producers changed their minds and said that Klingons wouldn't sit around." She smiles. "Of course, we kept the chairs." According to Richarz, Herman Zimmer-

Farrell seems to enjoy her role. ROBBIE ROBINSON

man contributed a design for "this really cool table that steps up as you get more to the middle," she relates. "The only problem was that the chairs were all the same height, so that some of the diners looked like this." Here Richarz slides down low in her seat, peering over a desk with only her head visible. "I wound up putting three-inch cushions on some of the chairs, to give them extra height."

In spite of all the hard work and good intentions, the episode didn't quite work for Behr. "'Soldiers' is an episode that *almost* made it," he laments. "LeVar is one of the strongest directors we have when it comes to working with actors. But the casting process was difficult, and I don't think the makeup always helped the actors. None of it went far enough."

Behr points out a scene in Act 1 that sums up the problem, in his mind. We meet two members of this "cursed ship," part of the nastiest crew in the Klingon Empire. But somehow, that's not the impression you get. "The scene at Quark's really was depressing," groans Behr. "These were supposed to be the baddest guys. One of them has teeth around his neck. And people in the bar talk about them like they're bad guys, but they're not badass at all. Throughout the

entire show, without a doubt, the toughest man on the ship is Martok. And that totally screwed up the show in my mind." In retrospect, Behr feels that it was the *Star Trek* mystique that watered down the episode. "Unless you're really pushing people, what you always end up with is another episode of *Star Trek*. People aren't really nasty looking, people aren't really scary, people aren't really sexy. It's like what happened to 'Let He Who Is Without Sin,'" he sighs. "The twenty-fourth century can be bland unless you really stay on it."

CHILDREN OF TIME

Episode #520

TELEPLAY BY RENÉ ECHEVARRIA
STORY BY GARY HOLLAND AND ETHAN H. CALK
DIRECTED BY ALLAN KROEKER

GUEST CAST

Yedrin Dax	GARY FRANK
Miranda O'Brien	JENNIFER S. PARSONS
Lisa	DAVIDA WILLIAMS
Molly	DOREN FEIN
Brota	BRIAN EVARET CHANDLER
Parell	MARYBETH MASSETT
Gabriel	JESSE LITTLEJOHN

STARDATE 50814.2

As the *Defiant* heads back to Deep Space 9 from a reconnaissance mission in the Gamma Quadrant, Dax is intrigued by the strange energy barrier that surrounds a nearby planet. Although everyone would prefer to go straight home, Dax talks Sisko into allowing her to get close enough to the barrier to investigate. But the barrier's quantum fluctuations wreak havoc with the ship, and as various systems short out, a tendril of energy from one of the consoles strikes Kira. She recovers quickly and seems fine.

As the crew evaluates the extensive damage, the ship is hailed from the planet's surface. A man and a woman welcome Sisko by name and invite him to visit their world, Gaia. Intrigued, Sisko, Dax, Worf, and O'Brien beam down and are greeted by the pair they saw on the viewscreen, Miranda O'Brien and Yedrin Dax. The away team's puzzlement over the familar names turns into astonishment when Miranda tells them that the settlement on Gaia was founded by the crew of the *Defiant*, which crashed on the planet two centuries ago. Two days from now, Miranda explains,

Sisko and his crew meet their own descendants, including Miranda O'Brien and Yedrin Dax. ROBBIE ROBINSON

the *Defiant* will try to leave Gaia's orbit, and when it passes through the energy barrier, it will be thrown two hundred years into the past and crash. Miranda and Yedrin are the descendants of Sisko and his crew.

Jadzia scans the pair and confirms the truth. The symbiont inside Yedrin is indeed the same Dax symbiont she carries within her, and Miranda definitely is related to the chief. Although the Gaians' tale of survival is heartening—there are eight thousand people thriving on the planet today—there also are disturbing aspects, key among them the fact that Kira's injury from the energy discharge is more serious than anyone knows. Without treatment from the medical equipment on Deep Space 9, she'll die, as she did two hundred years ago.

Sisko points out that now that they know about the impending accident, they can avoid it, and get Kira back to DS9 in time to save her. Unfortunately, by altering history in this way, the timeline that Miranda and the others live in will cease to exist. Not necessarily, says Yedrin. He believes there's a way to duplicate the *Defiant* as it passes through the barrier. That way, one ship will get back to the station, while the other fulfills its destiny by traveling into the past and crashing on Gaia. Sisko tells Jadzia to evaluate Yedrin's plan. If it's sound, they'll begin implementing it immediately.

On the *Defiant*, Odo is confined to a stasis device because he can't hold his shape within the barrier. While Bashir goes down to visit the settlement, Kira digests the information they've received about the Gaians. She's surprised when Odo—a very different looking Odo—walks into sickbay. This is the changeling who's been on Gaia for two hundred

years, and he's learned a number of things in that time, such as how to hold his shape despite the barrier's quantum fluctuations. He's also gotten better at making himself look human. This future version of Odo has come to the *Defiant* to see Kira, and to tell her something he's wished he could say for two hundred years: he loves her and always has. He invites the stunned Bajoran to come down and see Gaia with him before she goes back to DS9.

Jadzia's initial analysis of the information Yedrin provides is very promising, but she later discovers that he has faked the data so that history will repeat itself and the *Defiant* will meet with the same accident as before. There is no way to save Kira *and* the eight thousand inhabitants of Gaia. Sisko refuses to sacrifice Kira's life or ask people like O'Brien to give up their families on DS9. However, Kira feels that she can't run away from destiny; if the Prophets mean for her to die so that the others can live, then that's what she wants. As the crew helps their descendants plant a crop on what presumably will be the Gaians' last day of life, they make a joint decision: they'll repeat the accident so they can keep these people alive.

The Gaian Odo is aghast. He doesn't want Kira to die again, particularly now that she knows about his true feelings for her. Perhaps there is a chance for the two of them back on Deep Space 9. But Kira's mind is made up, and the crew returns to the *Defiant* to meet their predestined fate. However, at the crucial moment the ship is to hit the barrier, the vessel's autopilot veers away from the anomaly, and the *Defiant* emerges into normal space. Someone changed the ship's flight plan so that it wouldn't crash—but who? The crew scans the surface of the planet and discovers that all eight thousand inhabitants have vanished.

As the crew heads for home, the Odo that Kira always has known comes to see her. He reveals that it was his future self who changed the ship's course. He knows because that Odo linked with him before the *Defiant* left Gaia's orbit. Kira is shocked; the future Odo sacrificed the lives of eight thousand people in order to save hers. "He loved you," Odo explains. And the two part, uncertain as to what their own future will be.

By day, Gary Holland is the Vice President of Advertising and Promotion for the Domestic Television division of Paramount Television Group. During his off-hours, however, he's just another struggling freelance writer trying to sell story ideas and scripts to producers in

The Gaian Odo's makeup, while different, took the same amount of time to apply as his present mask. ROBBIE ROBINSON

old, he realizes that in fact they haven't, and that it was an attempt to escape from the planet that threw them into the past and set the whole chain of events into motion. "The final twist confused the heck out of everybody," Holland says, laughing. "In fact, it confuses me now just telling it. But I had only made up the whole convoluted tale so that Odo could say what he had to say to Kira."

Holland pitched the story to Ron Moore in October of 1994, during the series' third season. Moore liked the basic idea, so he repeated the bare bones to Ira Behr. Behr was interested in the idea of the crew meeting their own descendants, but he pointed out that they already had received a number of time travel pitches ("The Visitor"). So Holland was in the same boat as a lot of other freelancers, where the producers didn't say "yes," but they didn't say "no," either. It was more of a "not now." "Ron would call me every six months to say, 'We really want to do this,'" Holland recalls, but as time went by, he began to lose hope for his story.

So, in January of 1997, Holland was surprised to receive a call from René Echevarria, who told him that the producers had heard a pitch that was very similar to his, from a Texas schoolteacher, Ethan Calk (who also wrote the story to Season 3's "Visionary"). "That kind of freaked them out," Holland says. "And it made them think that maybe it was time to do it. So my thanks to Ethan Calk for getting the guys going!"

"The two stories were so nearly identical that it was frightening," laughs Robert Wolfe. The entire writing staff was intrigued by the similarities, although Calk's story, unlike Holland's, was a straightforward time travel tale. They purchased both stories, and told each freelancer to write a story proposal.

Before starting on his document, Holland discussed the story with Ron Moore one more time. "I brought up the fact that when I'd originally pitched this story, I'd framed it around Odo telling Kira that he loved her. But Ron told me, 'We think we've really taken the Kira/Odo thing as far as we can on the series.' They just didn't think that it was worth pursuing any further. But I decided to write it out anyway."

Five days later, both Calk and Holland sent in their proposals. "There were elements of each that we liked," Wolfe notes, "so we combined them in a blender, mixed well, and René wrote a really nice script."

The writers decided that maybe they were wrong about their star-crossed lovers, and Echevarria played up that angle in his teleplay. "This was an important

Hollywood. Holland is luckier than many. He came up with the DS9 episode "The Collaborator" in Season 2, and he also is responsible for Voyager's "Dreadnought." In between those two sales, however, there was a second story that he had pitched to the DS9 producers that had continued to haunt him for two and a half years.

It all sprang from the way Actor Rene Auberjonois played a scene in "The Collaborator," explains Holland. "There was a snippet of a scene where Kira tells Odo that she loves Bareil, and Rene gave this very odd reaction," he says. "At that moment, you realize that Odo's in love with Kira." After a friend suggested that it would be intriguing to take that premise to another level, Holland's mind began to race. "I thought, 'We have no idea how old Odo is, so if he's in his early development, it might be a long time before he can admit to those kinds of feelings,'" recalls Holland. "So I wondered, 'How can I get an older Odo into a story?'" The answer, as he saw it, was time travel.

Holland soon formulated a mystery in which the Defiant crashes on a planet and the crew finds their own descendants. They assume that they've traveled seventy-five years into the future, but as Sisko grows

show for Odo and Kira," comments Echevarria. "For the first time, Kira finds out how Odo feels about her. Odo had put aside his obsession with her in 'Crossfire,' and then, because of Shakaar, he never had a chance to be with her after we'd made him human. But he did have this 'training-wheel' relationship with a woman during that period ("A Simple Investigation"), which convinced him he could be a man. Now, because of these unique circumstances, he finds that it's all on the table again." But while the producers ultimately were happy with this development, the two principal actors weren't quite sure what to make of it.

"I'm not a huge fan of that whole romantic storyline," Nana Visitor states. "I think it's much more interesting to have a real deep friendship without it becoming physical. I would have liked Odo and Kira to stay like that. I did think this episode was brilliant," she adds. "But it isn't one of my favorites, because I just wasn't crazy about my part in it."

For Auberjonois, the episode didn't signal that much of a change, since his character had loved Kira for many years. But he wasn't entirely happy with the way the Gaian version of Odo demonstrated the depths of his love. "It's a very difficult and complex thing," Auberjonois says. "He allows an entire civilization to just disappear in a blink. He could rationalize it because of his love, but it's a big thing. It's tricky. I'm still not sure about it, or about what kind of message it sent to the audience."

Ron Moore feels he can address that. "It tells the audience how deeply this man can love. He can love to the point that he will sacrifice an entire world for a woman. It's the opposite of James Kirk, if you want to look at it in those terms," he points out, referring to Kirk's doomed relationship with character Edith Keeler, from "The City on the Edge of Forever." Kirk sacrificed his love for the future of the galaxy.

In this sense, Odo's behavior serves to show the audience that not all *Star Trek* leads are cut from the same cloth. Perhaps more of a realist than a romantic, Behr saw Odo's behavior as the only way to give the story some ballast. "During the story break, it was going to be Yedrin who causes the colony to be wiped out," says Behr. "But halfway through it, I said, 'We can't do it this way. Nobody will care. There's no story here. We've *got* to make it Odo.' And the others said, 'Whew, that's a biggie.' I said, 'Yeah, but it's not worth doing otherwise.' On *Star Trek* or *TNG*," Behr adds, "they probably would have made it the scientist and there'd be no harm, no foul. Everyone's hands would

have remained clean. But that wasn't a consideration here."

Interestingly, it isn't the love story that Behr liked best about the episode. His favorite scene was something that he initially envisioned as an epic moment from the golden age of filmmaking. Unfortunately, for a variety of reasons, it just didn't end up the way he imagined. Director Allan Kroeker vividly remembers the day Behr told him about the scene. "Ira and his gang were just getting back from lunch," he smiles, "and I saw them walking side by side, looking like *The Wild Bunch,* with their goatees and dark glasses and black clothes. They'd just wrapped up this script, and Ira grabbed me by the shoulders and said, 'You're gonna *love* this movie moment! It's a crane shot, and these people are *harvesting*. You're gonna be cutting down these *plants* . . .'"

"I wanted extras!" states Behr, with a glint of Cecil B. DeMille in his eyes. "I wanted sixty more people than we had there! I wanted to see *Gone with the Wind* action. I wanted a *movie* moment. What I *got* was a TV moment." He pauses a second. "But it was a *good* TV moment."

"It took a long time to convince Ira and the others that there was nothing to harvest up in Ventura (where they shot the location scenes for the episode)," sighs Kroeker, sorry to be the one to burst Behr's bubble. "Absolutely nothing. So we went to the idea of planting instead of harvesting. But the writers were never as happy."

"It *had* been written as a harvesting scene," confirms Lou Race. "But, unfortunately, the real world invoked its authority over the *reel* world. There were

Events, time, and cost changed this scene. ROBBIE ROBINSON

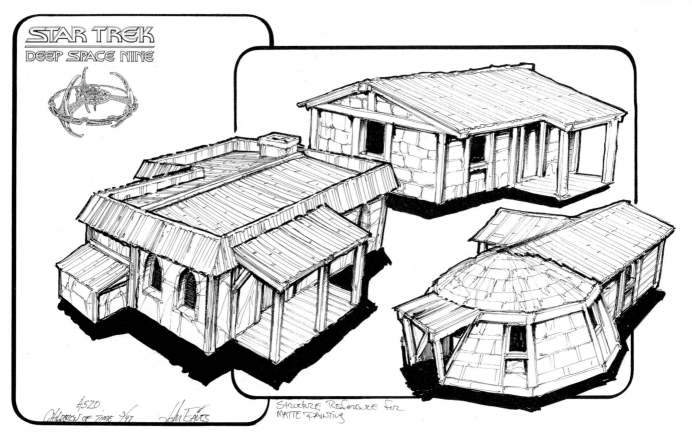

STAR TREK
DEEP SPACE NINE

#520
CHILDREN OF TIME 3/97   John Eaves

STRUCTURE Reference for MATTE PAINTING

The Gaian village. JOHN EAVES

no plants ready to be harvested at the time, and we weren't about to fly to Kansas and go for cornfields. So we did the planting scenes, which actually worked better for the story, because these people were preparing to die, and they were putting something into the ground to live beyond them."

Even with the decision made to do epic planting rather than epic harvesting, the scene was difficult to actualize. "We went to Ahmanson Ranch, out near Ventura, California," says Steve Oster. "And it looked wonderful during prep. Of course, this being *DS9* on location, the weather was awful during the days we were shooting. We had unseasonable high winds, and we had to move the equipment trucks around all day to provide wind blocks for the sets. It was sunny, but just bitter cold. I had a snow jacket on, but the extras in their sleeveless shirts were supposed to be toiling in the fields, and we had to spray them to make them look as if they were sweating."

Complicating matters was the fact that they had to shoot the sequence backward in order to catch the best light for the most panoramic portion of the shot (for tighter shots, the filmmakers knew they could rig artificial lighting). "Allan planned for bigger and big-

ger sweeping shots toward the end of the sequence, and we wanted to do those at the beginning of the day," notes Race. "So we started at the end of the shot, with all the plants in, and then we selectively pulled them out so that the actors could put them back into the ground on camera. It was kind of like unpainting a wall." And what were the Gaians planting in the scene? We had to use what we could get in real quantity at that time of the year," admits Laura Richarz, "so we used mums."

At least they didn't need to plow up an entire field. "There was a knoll where someone had recently done a commercial shoot, creating an African savanna look," Oster relates. "They'd left a dirt area that hadn't been replanted yet, so we plowed only that, hoping that the audience would infer that the fields continued down and around the slopes."

The quaint village sets, later reused for "Blaze of Glory," proved inspirational to the people responsible for set decoration. "Village shows are complicated," Richarz states. "We had a lot of stalls for people to sell things, so we had to decide what they'd be selling. I went to a hobby store and bought the trees and grass and sand meant for model train layouts. Then I bought dried flowers and took them apart. When we put all that in bowls, it looked like spices." Race fell in love with one of the props provided for the village, and used it everywhere he could. "It was a freestanding wooden ladder," he says. While there's nothing particularly unusual about a ladder—the average production company has dozens of them standing around—this was an *on-screen* ladder, something Race couldn't recall having seen on *Star Trek* before. "Nobody climbs up on a freestanding ladder in *Star Trek*," he notes. "So I said, 'That ladder's gonna be in every shot!' And wherever I had the chance, I stuck that ladder in, and put somebody on it!"

Although Odo's "future look" made him appear very different, that actually was recycled, too. "We used the life mask of Rene Auberjonois that we'd created for Curzon in 'Facets' and added some appliances to it," explains Dean Jones, the makeup artist who is responsible for turning Auberjonois into Odo. "We called the mask 'Neo-Odo.'"

Neo-Odo differs from traditional Odo in several ways. "Odo doesn't have any nasal labial folds, so when the new face was sculpted, we put them in," Jones says. "We gave some character to the chin and the squint lines between the eyes. But we were careful not to take it all the way to the human form."

Auberjonois had a good time playing his future self. "I made him a lot more relaxed and more confident in himself," he says. "His emotions are more upfront. It's strange, because even though he's hundreds of years older, the maturity and growth actually make him seem younger and more sexual. He had an open-chested, more casual way of dressing, and that affected the way he moved." Viewers didn't get to see all of Neo-Odo's scenes with Kira. "A lot of that material was cut for time," admits Echevarria, "including a long walk together where Odo talks about his life on Gaia. He says, 'I lived with the colony until my friends died, and their children died, and I got tired of watching people die. I lived a hundred years as a tree, and then I migrated and lived as a cloud.'" Echevarria smiles. "I hated to lose that dialogue, but I found a way to use it later. I gave it to Laas, in 'Chimera.'"

BLAZE OF GLORY

Episode #521

TELEPLAY BY **ROBERT HEWITT WOLFE &**
IRA STEVEN BEHR
DIRECTED BY **KIM FRIEDMAN**

GUEST CAST

Michael Eddington	KENNETH MARSHALL
General Martok	J. G. HERTZLER
Nog	ARON EISENBERG
Rebecca Sullivan	GRETCHEN GERMAN

STARDATE UNKNOWN

A peaceful dinner with Jake and Nog is interrupted when Martok brings Sisko a disturbing message intercepted from the Maquis. The members of the rebel group who have survived slaughter by the Cardassian/Dominion alliance have found a way to even the score. They've launched deadly missiles against Cardassia, missiles that are cloaked and undetectable. The weapons conceivably could kill millions, which no doubt would lead to retaliation by the Cardassians' Dominion friends, and possibly to an all-out war against the Federation and *its* allies. With no other alternative, Sisko turns to the only man who might be able to stop this tragedy before it takes place: Michael Eddington, the jailed Starfleet turncoat who led the Maquis until Sisko captured him ("For the Uniform").

The only way to stop the missiles, Eddington tells Sisko, is to transmit the deactivation code from the launch site, assuming Sisko can find it. The

Sisko makes it clear that Eddington is going to help him whether the Maquis wants to or not. ROBBIE ROBINSON

embittered Maquis refuses to help his former commander, despite the captain's offer of a pardon. Sisko isn't taking no for an answer, and he forces the handcuffed prisoner to accompany him in his search for the missile base. As they enter the Badlands, Sisko makes Eddington, who knows the area well, take the controls in order to avoid several pursuing Jem'Hadar warships. Shaking them, Eddington finally agrees to take Sisko to the launch site and to help deactivate the missiles. But before they reach their destination, the Jem'Hadar return, compelling Eddington to take a riskier tack, one that requires Sisko to make some dangerous modifications to the runabout's impulse flow regulators. The plan works, and they lose the Jem'Hadar.

Back at Deep Space 9, Nog tries to figure out how to make the rowdy Klingons respect his authority as a representative of station security. Sisko had counseled the Ferengi to stand up to them, but that's a difficult prospect, since Nog is half their size. At last, he screws up his courage and confronts Martok, who is impressed with the cadet's combination of bravado and foolishness. After that, Nog is able to walk a little taller on the station.

Sisko and Eddington arrive at their destination, Athos IV, but they quickly discover that two Jem'Hadar also have found the site. They manage to overpower them, but know that more are bound to show up. As they move toward the command center at the Maquis settlement, they discover the dead bodies of many of Eddington's compatriots. Inside the bunker, they find a dozen Maquis prisoners who are alive, including Eddington's wife, Rebecca.

Now Eddington reveals the truth: there never were any missiles. The message that Martok intercepted was Rebecca's way of letting Eddington know that the other remaining Maquis and she had made it to the Athos base. They counted on Sisko receiving the message and "coercing" Eddington to take him to the base, after which they planned to enlist Sisko's help in evacuating them to safety. Unfortunately, no one had anticipated the Jem'Hadar finding the base as well. Sisko is angry about being manipulated, but he's relieved that there won't be a galactic war. Now they need worry about one battle only—the one they'll face in escaping from the base. Sisko and Eddington hold off the Jem'Hadar as the other Maquis head for the runabout, but Eddington is wounded in the firefight. The Maquis leader sends Sisko on to the ship, while he faces the Jem'Hadar. As the ship escapes, Eddington dies fighting for the principles he believed in to the end.

Alas, poor Eddington . . .

"I liked him," says Robert Wolfe. "And I like Ken Marshall. He's a really good guy. And we killed him."

"We tried to give him a heroic death," comments Ira Behr, who cowrote "Blaze of Glory" with Wolfe. "I told Ken we'd give him a 'Steve McQueen' death. Right out of *The Sand Pebbles*. You know: 'You let the woman go and you stay behind.'"

Although viewers may think that Eddington's death was brought about by the Jem'Hadar, the simple truth is that he was a victim of timing. More than any other year, Season 5 laid the groundwork for many of the plot threads that would carry *DS9* forward over the next two years. With all that story material building up underfoot, "we were just desperate to finish something off," says Behr. "We had to finish the thread. It was necessary. We just had so many things. So I told them, 'We are going to end something and then not hear about it again!'"

Behr wanted to go even farther than killing off Eddington. "I wanted to kill every Maquis in the galaxy, but I was reminded, 'Well, you know, just in case *Voyager* comes back, we'll need some, so don't say they're *all* dead,'" Behr chuckles. He had to settle for merely excising them from *DS9*. Following "Blaze of Glory," as far as Behr and his writing team were concerned, "they'd been wiped," he says.

"It's funny," says Marshall. "Kim Friedman, who directed this one, was talking to the actors on the set about what she wanted, and she said, 'Think Shakespeare in space.' And it's true, in a way. One of the things I like about *Star Trek* is that they take a great deal of care about what they're writing. There

Eddington died heroically to tidy the storyline. ROBBIE ROBINSON

were something like nineteen different rewrites on some of my episodes, and it drove me crazy as an actor, having to unlearn the stuff I'd learned, and learning the new stuff the night before shooting. But because of [that kind of care], you get something good. You get something to sink your teeth into as an actor. They're not afraid to really use language."

Even though it was to be Eddington's final appearance, the writers still felt compelled to add a few humanizing brushstrokes to his characterization, for example, the fact that he's married, a bit of statistical information that surprised Marshall when he read it in the script. "That was strange," he says with a laugh. "They give me a wife and then they immediately take her away from me. I liked it, though. It was a way of deepening his commitment to the cause, to show that he's not just doing it because he sees himself as Valjean." Marshall and the viewers also learned that Eddington was Canadian, a fact the writing staff threw in on a whim. Hans Beimler has worked on two different television series in Canada, and frequent *DS9* director Allan Kroeker is Canadian. "Allan tends to do Canadian jokes," Behr says. "And the fact that of all the semiregulars, it's poor Eddington who buys the farm just seemed like a very Canadian thing."

"You just know he's going to die because he doesn't have his 'lucky loony' with him," adds Wolfe, referring to the old keepsake Eddington mentions in the script. "It's a very cool coin. Very distinctive. I've spent a lot of time in Canada, and the show has a lot of Canadian fans. So we thought, what the heck."

Raising vegetables, particularly tomatoes, apparently is one of Eddington's passions, one that he shares with Wolfe's mother. "She tried to grow tomatoes in San Francisco," relates Wolfe. "You can't do it. There's not enough sun. She could grow zucchini, but not tomatoes. It was a big deal to her, but San Francisco is not tomato country. Judging by what we saw of the planet the Maquis were living on, that wasn't tomato country either," adds Wolfe. To create the tomato-unfriendly environment of Athos IV, the special effects crew used an environmentally friendly smoke concoction that fills the air like fog. The crew generally is accustomed to the presence of smoke on the soundstage, where it's used to create mood as often as it is to emulate smoke or fog. But the scenes at the Maquis base took three days to complete, and the smoke level was kept high to accommodate the action dictated by the script.

"They had so much smoke on the set, because it had to seem like you couldn't see the Jem'Hadar coming out of the fog," recalls B. C. Cameron. "Usually the smoke doesn't bother people, but the stunt guys who were playing the Jem'Hadar had a hard time."

Thanks to the efforts of Gary Hutzel and Gary Monak, one of the original visual concepts for the Badlands finally appeared on-screen in this episode. "There were always supposed to be these whirling fires inside the Badlands," says Hutzel. After Hutzel reconceived the basic look of the region in "For the Uniform," according to Hutzel, "The producers began asking, 'Where's our pillars of fire?' So I went to Gary Monak and asked him to create one for us. He made a box with a powerful fan at the bottom that would create a vortex."

"The boxes were over eight feet tall," continues Monak, "and we made a couple different kinds to experiment with. The most effective one was an octagonal box made out of drywall that had been painted black. We left one side of the octagon off and filmed through that opening. Once we shot some nitrogen in there and got it rotating in a counter-clockwise direction, we injected fire with a propane burner. The heat made the flame rise so we got this finger of fire going. The hotter we made it, the higher the flame would rise in the box." After the pillar was photographed, it was a simple matter for Hutzel to add that element to the other footage of the Badlands that he'd created.

The Maquis base was situated on Stage 18, the location of the Gaian town built for the preceding episode, "Children of Time." "We took that same little village, painted the walls black, turned the lights out, and filled it with smoke," comments Steve Oster. *Voilà:* Athos IV. Well, not quite that simple. "We pulled out all the detail of the Gaian village, removed one of the center buildings, changed out some walls and added the well," amends Laura Richarz, who refers to the new set color as "dismal gray." Richarz says they also reused the community room from "Children of Time," converting it into the command center, where the Maquis are held hostage by the Jem'Hadar. "It can save a lot of time and money when you can reuse a set, particularly in back-to-back episodes," she observes.

In addition to wiping out the bulk of the Maquis, the writers managed to dispense with a loose thread that had been dangling ever since the episode that established the group in the series' second season ("The Maquis"): the fate of Sisko's old friend Cal Hudson. "We never were going to bring him back

Eisenberg's balancing act was a nod to Henry Fonda's Wyatt Earp in *My Darling Clementine*. ROBBIE ROBINSON

anyway," says Wolfe. "So we find out that Cal Hudson is dead, and by the end of the episode, Eddington is dead."

Although he did give Eddington his *Sand Pebbles* moment, Behr remains uncertain as to whether the scene was as emotionally fulfilling as it could have been. "If we could have had more production time, I'd have made the sequence longer," he suggests. "But I had to deal with the fact that A, he wasn't a regular character, and B, there'd have been a part of the audience we couldn't sustain with an elongated scene. And, of course, your head is spinning with those unanswered questions about how we feel about Eddington. I still haven't figured that one out. Do we like him? Do we not like him? Was he good? Bad? Was he a pain in the ass?" Behr shakes his head. "I'm not sure."

Sisko experiences the same problem at the end of the episode, when he discusses Eddington's demise with Dax. "I felt that it was very important to Sisko to try to make sense of the man Eddington was," Behr explains. "We owed it to Sisko to give him some kind of closure, some kind of understanding. On top of everything else, he let the guy die, basically."

By and large a serious episode, "Blaze of Glory" does include its lighter moments. "We tend to hit the humor where we can," says Behr. Morn's off-camera moment of unclothed hysteria, provoked by Quark, was yet another of the staff's attempts to build up the mythos surrounding the taciturn barfly. "It sounded funny," smiles Behr. "You never see it, but you talk about it. Keep Morn alive. Lord knows that when you

see him, he's barely alive. He's more alive in story and song than he is in actuality."

The B-story, concerning Nog's attempt to gain the Klingons' respect, served several purposes. It added to the young Ferengi's characterization, certainly; but more important, "It kept the Klingon presence alive, which I thought was important to do at this point," says Behr, "because we wanted to see Martok on the station, to show that he'd survived 'Soldiers of the Empire.'"

EMPOK NOR
Episode #522

TELEPLAY BY **HANS BEIMLER**
STORY BY **BRYAN FULLER**
DIRECTED BY **MICHAEL VEJAR**

GUEST CAST

Garak	ANDREW J. ROBINSON
Nog	ARON EISENBERG
Pechetti	TOM HODGES
Boq'ta	ANDY MILDER
Stolzoff	MARJEAN HOLDEN
Amaro	JEFFREY KING

STARDATE UNKNOWN

Parts to facilitate repairs on Deep Space 9 aren't always easy to come by. Case in point: a plasma distribution manifold that can't be replicated, and it is *highly* unlikely that the Cardassians will supply one to Starfleet. O'Brien suggests sending a salvage team to Empok Nor, an abandoned Cardassian space station, for some badly needed components. Sisko okays the mission, and O'Brien pulls together a team of two engineers, two security guards, and one Cardassian, Garak. Hopefully, he will be able to spot any booby traps the departing Cardassians may have left behind. The chief also brings along Nog, who's proven a noteworthy intern in engineering.

After landing their runabout at a docking bay, Garak activates life support, and the team enters the deserted station. They split up to find the parts on O'Brien's "wish list." When Garak checks out the Infirmary, he's disturbed to discover that two stasis tubes have been activated recently. A short time later, Nog notes that their runabout no longer is docked; he's shocked to see it start to drift into space, and then explode!

When Garak tells the team about the stasis

O'Brien is forced to return to the role of soldier, as he warily moves past the bodies of his dead crew. ROBBIE ROBINSON

chambers, they realize that two recently revived Cardassian occupants of the chambers must have disengaged the docking clamps and destroyed their vessel. With the runabout gone, the team must find a way to contact Deep Space 9 for help. O'Brien devises a way to use the station's deflector grid to send an SOS, which requires the team to split up. Not long after, one of the guards and an engineer are murdered. After the rest of the team discovers the bodies, Garak offers to track down and "neutralize" the Cardassians, while the rest of the team finishes the work on the deflector.

Garak quickly finds and executes one of the men, then reports to O'Brien that the dead Cardassian was under the influence of a psychotropic drug that amplified his aggressive tendencies. He speculates that the soldier might have been the subject of a military experiment, and O'Brien guesses that if so, it might have been an experiment that went wrong; they probably were left behind in stasis because they were uncontrollable. As Garak prepares to look for the other Cardassian, O'Brien uneasily notes that something is different about the tailor's behavior.

The wary group returns to work, but a short time later one of the two-man teams is attacked by the Cardassian soldier. One man is quickly killed, but Garak manages to eliminate the Cardassian before he gets the second. Just as the survivor is about to breathe a sigh of relief, however, he's viciously stabbed by Garak. He lives just long enough to reveal to O'Brien that it was Garak who assaulted him.

The chief understands at once that the Cardassian drug somehow has affected Garak, and that he and Nog are in grave danger. O'Brien shifts gears and falls back on his training as a soldier, one who was forced to kill a number of Cardassians at the Battle of Setlik III, to find Garak before he finds them. But Garak is a clever opponent; he manages to separate the chief and the cadet, and takes Nog hostage. Unwilling to play games, O'Brien demands that Garak meet him in the Promenade and put an end to this. Garak agrees. Soon the two men are face-to-face in a dangerous standoff, with a bound Nog watching helplessly. Putting down their weapons, they enter into hand-to-hand combat. Garak's superior strength and strategic skills seem to tip the outcome of the fight in the Cardassian's direction, but as the chief points out, he's an engineer, not a soldier. At a crucial point in the struggle, O'Brien taps his combadge and triggers an explosion in a rigged phaser that he's left near Garak. The explosion knocks Garak against a bulkhead, rendering him unconscious, but leaving him alive. The three are rescued, and the parts salvaged. Garak's system is purged of the deadly drug, leaving him restored, but repentant about the violence he committed under its influence.

At the end of "Empok Nor," the audience finds Garak in DS9's Infirmary, feeling remorse over the drug-induced madness that had so recently pushed him to mayhem and murder. And while Actor Andy Robinson bears little resemblance to his Cardassian counterpart, he can't help feeling a bit of that same remorse over Garak's behavior in the show. "That episode," he sighs. "It turned out okay, but it made me so uneasy to do that character." Robinson has spent many years trying to escape an unfortunate legacy of his film debut as the Scorpio killer in the first *Dirty Harry* movie. It was a break-out role; no one who saw the film could forget Robinson's riveting performance as the crazed serial killer—and that's precisely the problem. In Hollywood, there's a practice known as typecasting. Once an actor makes a particularly vivid impression on audiences and casting agents, it's difficult for him to parlay roles of a different nature. Although Robinson wanted to continue to earn his living as an actor, he didn't want to do it by playing only a series of wacko killers. "After you've done a psychotic, and you've gone to that well, it's very hard to go back there," he says. "At least for me."

Yet here he was, twenty-five years later, reading a script in which Garak turns into a psychopathic killer. "After I finished that first draft, I thought, 'Ugh.' I felt like the writers were intruding on Garak. He's such a multidimensional character, such a mysterious character." But Robinson, who's considered practically a regular by cast and crew, decided to wait a bit before he voiced any complaints. "I've learned to trust Ira [Behr]," he says. "He has good sense when it comes to Garak. He understands the character. And sure enough, when the next draft came through, a lot of the stuff I hated was gone."

Behr wasn't a big advocate of "Garak as psychopath." "It's a less interesting Garak, in a way," he says. "Turning him into a killing machine isn't exactly multidimensional." Understandably, Behr wasn't happy with the original script. "The first draft came in from Hans [Beimler]," he recalls, "and I told him, 'This doesn't work. Not even close. There's no char-

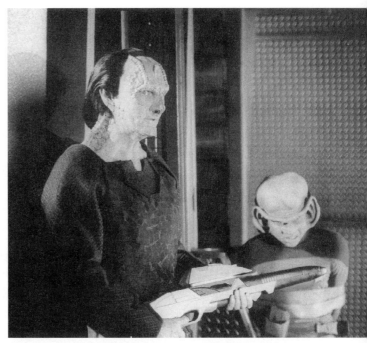

Robinson was disappointed by the choice to turn Garak into a crazed killer. ROBBIE ROBINSON

acter, no meaning. It's just a series of events and none of it makes any sense.' We had to go back and rebreak the story and find all the characterization stuff between Garak and O'Brien. Later on, I talked to Andy and he said, 'I never could have done that first script. We were vacuums. There was nothing in my character. It made no sense.'"

Beimler didn't mind going back to square one; it happens all the time in television writing. "I thought it was there after I did the first draft, but there was no bottom to the story," he says. "The second draft got into the relationship with O'Brien and Garak, and that really gave it some substance and content."

It's no secret that O'Brien is one of Behr's favorite characters, and he felt it was important for this story to add dimension to the Irishman's personality, rather than subtract it. "The thing I've always felt about O'Brien is that there's something very sweet about him," Behr notes. "The fact that he has this soldier background has always puzzled me. We inherited that from *TNG* ['The Wounded'], so we tried to make it work. It's not the most important part of O'Brien's character, but I do like the fact that it's there, and we try to bring it out. And Colm is such a good actor that he was quite believable in this show as the kind of solider who knew what needed to be done. Although ultimately, it's the O'Brien that we're familiar with

The suggested redress of the spacesuit first seen in *Star Trek: First Contact*. JOHN EAVES

rather than the O'Brien [with the combat history] who gets them out of the situation."

As often happens on the series, the other writers joined in to hammer out the troubling plot points. René Echevarria recalls "picking our way through an all-new take, but we had fun doing it. We focused on O'Brien, and the limits of violence, how far he'd go. The intimations are that he used to be a soldier who had to kill, and he doesn't want to be that way anymore. And he's put in this situation where he's going to be forced to do it, but ultimately he's able to outsmart Garak without killing him. If it's about anything, it's about that line where O'Brien tells him, 'You're right, I'm not a soldier anymore. I'm an engineer.'"

"The story came from a pitch from Bryan Fuller," recalls Beimler, "and from the get-go, you could see it would be a really nice scary piece. I think it might have been the first time in *Deep Space Nine* where we were really trying to scare people. Science fiction is

more our bailiwick than horror, but it was interesting to do something dark and foreboding."

"I pitched it five days after I'd found out that they were going to buy 'The Darkness and the Light,'" Fuller relates. "It was originally a Worf and Garak story, where they board a derelict Cardassian ship that used to belong to the Obsidian Order. It had all these bodies on it that were infected with this 'Blue Sunshine'-type drug."

Blue Sunshine?

Fuller grins. "That was a big cult movie in the '70s, about these normal, functional people who start taking drugs and become psychopaths who start killing people," he says. "It's sort of freaky."

Clearly, Fuller's list of top films differs somewhat from Ira Behr's.

"I thought it would be fun to see Garak, who has kind of a borderline personality anyway, go back to his old devious ways through the device of this drug,

With lighting, intercutting, and music, the hope was to evoke the same nuances as a horror film. ROBBIE ROBINSON

"Empok Nor," she says, "we did an overlay of this boring gray carpet to give it a cold look, because it was supposed to be frozen."

Richarz also supplied the stasis chambers, which were borrowed from *Voyager*. (They'd been created for "The Thaw.") "They were shown at an angle on *Voyager*, and we changed that, and repainted them and added interior blue lights," Richarz says. A rather unusual aspect of the episode's set decoration was the positioning, or rather the suspension of some of the props, and personnel, in midair. "We wanted to suggest that there was no gravity on the station when we first arrived," says Race. "So we suspended all this space junk that we could drop on cue when Garak threw the switch to activate the station's power."

"It was kind of a last-minute decision," points out Gary Monak. "If we'd had more time, we could have done a better job. But it was like, 'Camera's ready—oh, by the way, we need some items floating in space.'" Monak's team hung flotsam and jetsam from monofilament wire to make them look weightless. Some were suspended from the rafters and released at Director Michael Vejar's command with the touch of a switch, and some were manipulated by crewpersons positioned above the set, holding fishing poles. And then there were the living props. "They decided that we had to actually *see* the characters Garak had killed hanging all around the Promenade, and for an extensive period of time," Monak relates. "We put the actors in flying suits, which are like parachute harnesses, not very comfortable, and hung them about a foot off the ground with cables." It was a lot of work for relatively little screen time, but it could have been worse, Monak points out. At one point, they'd planned on hanging up the two dead Cardassians as well.

A different bit of audio embellishment startled the producers when they viewed the episode. "In the sequence where Garak is stalking the second Cardassian soldier, we hear the two Starfleet officers, Boq'ta and Amaro, talking to each other in the background," says Echevarria. "We added a bunch of dialogue that we were told wasn't really going to be heard, that it would just sound like, 'murmur, murmur.'" The writers came up with Amaro's short soliloquy about his dead partner, Stolzoff, ending with his comment about wanting to kill the "spoonhead" who got her. But they were surprised when the line turned out to be clearly audible on the soundtrack. "I mean, here was a Starfleet officer basically making a racist slur, without it being commented on or corrected,"

and to have this one-upmanship contest between him and Worf on the ship," Fuller explains.

However, just as the macho contest between the Klingon and the Cardassian changed, so did the setting of the derelict ship, which became a Cardassian space station. The redress, obviously less expensive than construction of an entirely new set, was effective, transforming the familiar station into "a haunted house," as Lou Race puts it. It wasn't the first time the crew had transformed the familiar DS9 into a grimmer version of the station. But there were differences this time around. "We stripped it down, Spartan," says Laura Richarz, "because Cardassian stations are no-frills. And we also changed the carpet." The most distinctive thing on the DS9 Promenade, especially for the wide shots, she notes, is the carpet, an artful patchwork of geometric shapes and colors. For

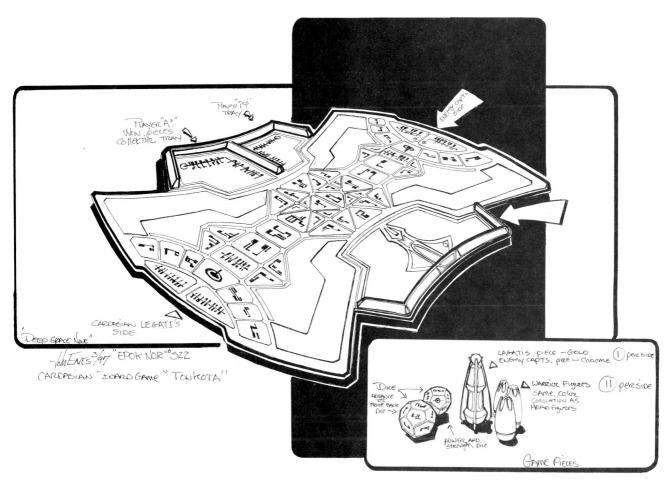

Garak's kotra board. Originally *towokta*, it was envisioned as a cross between chess and Stratego. JOHN EAVES

says Echevarria. "He just kind of tosses it off. But it was intentional."

Ironically, if the line actually had been scripted, it might not have survived into the episode. Although the expression had been introduced to viewers earlier in the season ("Things Past"), it had, in that episode, been used by non-Starfleet personnel, specifically, a member of Bajor's underground resistance movement. Knowing Gene Roddenberry's strong feelings about the lack of racial prejudice in that august organization, someone on staff was bound to have called the slur into question, had they known about it in advance. However, "when we add background dialogue, it doesn't go through the usual channels," Echevarria says. "Ira didn't read it. Rick didn't read it. Because it wasn't meant to be heard. It was done on the looping stage." Once they *did* hear it, the decision was made to leave the line alone. Although not "appropriate," it was understandable, given the context. "Amaro's been through a bad day at the hands of the Cardassians, so you sort of forgive him," says Echevarria. "It was racist. But it was also very real, so I'm glad that it was in there."

IN THE CARDS

Episode #523

TELEPLAY BY **RONALD D. MOORE**
STORY BY **TRULY BARR CLARK & SCOTT J. NEAL**
DIRECTED BY **MICHAEL DORN**

GUEST CAST

Weyoun	JEFFREY COMBS
Dr. Elias Giger	BRIAN MARKINSON
Nog	ARON EISENBERG
Leeta	CHASE MASTERSON

SPECIAL GUEST STAR

Kai Winn	LOUISE FLETCHER

STARDATE 50929.4

Bartering with Dr. Elias Giger for a baseball card turns out to be a whole lot harder than Jake and Nog expected. ROBBIE ROBINSON

As the Dominion threat to the Alpha Quadrant intensifies, Jake Sisko can't help but notice how depressed station personnel have become. Even his father, who normally is the person who tries to lift everyone *else's* spirits, is feeling low. When he hears that Quark is about to auction off antiquities that include a baseball card of Willie Mays from his rookie season in mint condition, Jake knows that it would be the perfect gift to cheer up Sisko.

After Jake talks Nog into giving him his life's savings, five bars of latinum, to use in bidding, Jake heads for the auction, prepared to claim his prize. But he hasn't counted on the competing interest of another man at the auction. Dr. Elias Giger bids a whopping tens bars of latinum and wins the lot containing the baseball card.

Unwilling to accept defeat, Jake and Nog approach Giger and offer to buy the card, but Giger is uninterested until he researches their backgrounds and discovers they may be able to help with something of more value to him than latinum. He gives them a list of peculiar medical supplies and scientific equipment that he needs to complete an invention he's been working on for fifteen years: the Cellular Regeneration and Entertainment Chamber that will stave off mortality by keeping a body's cells from dying of boredom. If Jake and Nog can get him the items on the list, they can have the card.

It seems clear that the problems bothering Sisko aren't going away. He discovers that Kai Winn has come to the station to meet with Dominion representative Weyoun. The captain fears this can represent only bad news for Bajor. Sure enough, Winn reveals that Weyoun wants Bajor to ally itself with the Dominion by signing a nonaggression treaty. Sisko feels this would be an unwise move, and he advises her to stall the proceedings.

As Jake and Nog begin their quest, they find that it won't be as easy as they'd hoped. For example, Chief O'Brien *might* know where to find the neodymium power cell that they need, but since Jake doesn't want to tell him why he needs it, the chief's incentive to help is low. Once Nog teaches Jake a lesson in "incentive-based economics," performing some drudge work for O'Brien that allows him to go to the holosuite, things begin to flow more smoothly. They meet with similar success in dealing with other crew members. Rescuing the doctor's kidnapped teddy bear from ex-girlfriend Leeta nets five liters of anaerobic metabolites; adjusting the subharmonic balance of Worf's Klingon opera recordings gains two meters of electroplasma conduit; and so forth. But just as they obtain all the goods, they discover that Giger has disappeared from the station, along with the precious card.

Jake's imagination leaps to some odd conclusions about Giger's disappearance. After seeing the kai talking to a vedek who bid against them at the auction, Jake assumes the frequently duplicitous Winn had the scientist kidnapped. Nog and he confront the kai with the outlandish accusation, and wind up being called on the carpet by an angry Sisko. Although Nog wants to tell the captain the truth, Jake is determined to keep the baseball card a secret. He tells his father that the incident happened because they were drunk. Furious, Sisko orders them to confine themselves to their quarters, but on the way there, the two are beamed off the station into a Jem'Hadar interrogation room and confronted by Weyoun.

At last, Jake admits the truth, but Weyoun refuses to believe the story about the baseball card. He's observed their behavior over the past few days: their clandestine meetings with the station's senior staff, Kai Winn, *and* the mysterious Dr. Giger, whose peculiar experiments took place right below Weyoun's quarters. As it turns out, it's Weyoun who was responsible for Giger's disappearance. He's certain that Giger, Jake, and Nog are conspiring against the Dominion.

Desperate, Jake fabricates a new story, telling Weyoun that Nog and he work for Starfleet Intelligence. The fate of the galaxy depends on their tracking down Willie Mays, and every mention of him, hence their efforts to obtain the card. The tale is so preposterous that Weyoun decides he believes the first story, about the card being a present for Sisko. He's also interested in Giger's invention; immortality appeals to him. Weyoun allows the pair to leave, *with* the baseball card, and the boys return to a station where morale has been restored, thanks to the favors they did for the appreciative crew, and the wonderful gift that has given Sisko a moment of joy.

The writers wanted another scene between Weyoun and Winn, but time ran out. ROBBIE ROBINSON

"We had a very simple little premise for a show," recalls Ron Moore. "Jake and Nog chase a card around the station, trying to give it to Sisko. That's really just where we started. We figured we could do the show right before the season finale and it would be fun and funny and contained and cheap, and after that we'd send them out on this big war story."

In lesser hands, "In the Cards," which represented Michael Dorn's first go at directing a *Star Trek* episode, could have been a throwaway show. The premise *was* pretty simple, and at first glimpse it looked like nothing more than a throwback to the fun but lightweight B-stories that featured Jake and Nog in the series' first season. ("The Storyteller" or "Progress"). "It was show number twenty-five in the season," says Ira Behr, "which usually is a buried show. It's not in sweeps (television's key ratings' sampling period), and it's not show number twenty-six, which gets publicity because it's the last show of the season. It's kind of a lost show, which means you can have fun with it and not worry about how many people are going to see it."

Writer Ron Moore definitely had fun with the

story contributed by Truly Barr Clark, a former intern on the series, and Scott J. Neal, from his silly throw-away lines of dialogue ("Sold to the blue man in the good shoes!") to tongue-in-cheek social comment ("I'm Human. I don't have any money.") to bizarre historical detail (the flag for the first Martian colonies was inspired by a black velvet painting of a matador).

"That was a *lot* of fun for me," chuckles Moore. "I just thought that was a hysterical bit, about it being the inspiration for the Martian flag. Unfortunately, the line is kind of buried under the music. I had a black velvet Elvis, complete with a tear rolling down his cheek, in my office, and I really wanted to use that in the episode, but I knew that would never fly. So I just settled on 'a rare example of a twentieth-century *hew-mon* art form, acrylic on black velvet,' and Joe Longo did the rest."

You wouldn't think that it would be difficult to find a black velvet painting. But for some reason, they *are* rare today. "I figured I would go down to Olvera Street and find one," says Longo, referring to the historical area that is known as the birthplace of Los Angeles, and the site of stores that sell some of the tackiest artifacts on the planet. But to Longo's surprise, none of the vendors had what he was looking for. "I finally found one at an art dealer's and *rented* it for the episode," he says. The painting, which supposedly is purchased by the station's resident barfly, would resurface in a larger role a year later ("Who Mourns for Morn").

But although the rest of the staff was inclined to go along with Moore in the pursuit of fun, the sheer audacity of one of the exchanges between Jake and Nog had them all aghast. "Everybody looked at me as if I was out of my mind, and they all said, 'You're not serious, are you?'" recites Moore. "And I said, 'Yeah, I love it.' And Rick [Berman] was like, 'You really want to do this?' They kind of expected me to take it out, and I refused. After they shot it, the editors came back to us and *they* wanted to take it out, and Peter Lauritson said, 'I suggest we lose this,' and I just said, 'No, no, *no!* I love this joke! It's one of the best stupid jokes I've every written and *it's gonna stay in the script!*'"

It did. Which is why the episode's mad scientist received a name change fairly late in the game. "I'd gotten all the way to Act 4, where Jake sees the kai," Moore says, "when I wrote the line, 'We're going to beard the lion in its den,' and I wanted a joke to follow. From 'lion,' my mind went to the bear, the teddy bear that I'd already established in the script and then I realized that I needed to find something that rhymed with tiger . . . tiger, miger, giger—*Doctor* Giger!"

After that, capping Nog's disgruntled "Lions and Gigers and bears . . ." with Jake's "Oh my!" was a piece of cake.

It is clear that Moore's coworkers love him very much.

René Echevarria, on the other hand . . .

"Whenever I want to get at René, I just mention 'Kukalaka,'" Behr states drolly. "I also quote lines from the Koran: 'There's a first time for everything—and a last time too.'" Which is Behr's way of saying he *hates* the name Echevarria came up with back in Season 4 for Bashir's teddy bear.

"It was just this dopey name that showed up in 'The Quickening,' and I can't believe I let it go through," sighs Behr. "It was bad enough Bashir had a bear. But *Kukalaka.* It just took Bashir one step into dopiness. And then it came back to haunt us in 'In the Cards.'"

"Kukalaka's been a running joke among the writing staff ever since René gave the bear that preposter-

On the surface it's a story about a baseball card, but beneath, it's about friendship and family. ROBBIE ROBINSON

ous name," laughs Moore. "We all said, '*Kukalaka?*' And I just wanted to put it in this script someplace so we could hear it again."

That decision finally gave viewers a chance to see Bashir's favorite childhood playmate, following a search nearly as complicated as the hunt for the matador. "It was Denise Okuda's," says Longo of the physical personification of the previously unseen stuffed animal. Then he changes his mind. "No—wait! It wasn't. Denise brought hers in and we didn't end up using it. Laura Richarz went out and found four old bears. And I found four myself. We brought them all into a meeting so the producers could take their pick. Then B.C. Cameron said, 'I've got one that I'd like to use because I've had it since I was a little baby.' And she brought hers in." And the winner? "B.C.'s bear," smiles Longo.

But as fun as "In the Cards" was, there was a strong dramatic theme at its core: Jake's love for his father and his desire to give something back to him for all that his father has given him. "All the plot

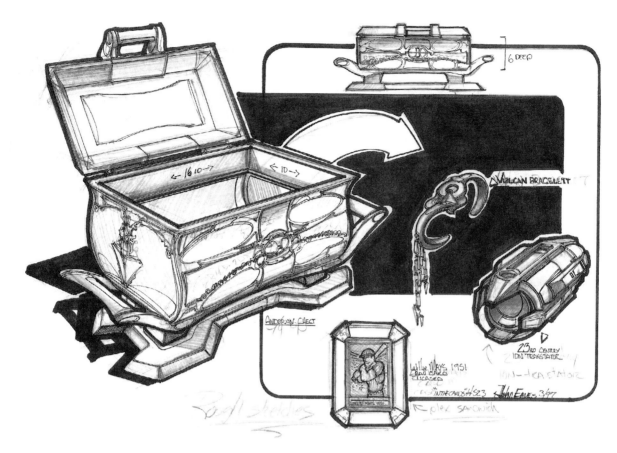

"Lot forty-eight." JOHN EAVES

machinations, all the humor, all the tech talk, everything, it ultimately comes down to simple human emotion of trying to make someone you care about feel better," states Behr. "It's very simple, and very nice."

And although that theme isn't quite as potent here as it was in "The Visitor," it still had more than enough resonance to make the end of the episode truly satisfying on an emotional level. "I was just playing on something that has been in the show since the very beginning," Moore says. "One of the things this show is about is a very strong family relationship. The father and son are really tight, and they really do love each other. It's a family that *works*, and that's important to us. In this particular episode, Jake's feelings ground everything, and it makes you actually care about all the ridiculous stuff. There's heart to it."

Jake's gift to his father, of course, is a 1951 Willie Mays rookie card, a card that Steve Oster estimates is valued at $20,000. "Probably worth even more in the twenty-fourth century," grins Moore.

There are, of course, more valuable baseball cards. "Right now a Mickey Mantle card is way more

valuable on the market," notes Behr. "I mean, there's no comparison." But considering the personal nature of the gift, and the emotion behind it, the Mays card somehow made more sense. It was the one that Michael Piller recommended when the producers solicited his opinion.

Being Hollywood, the card pictured on the show was, of course, a stand-in for the real thing. "The last thing I wanted laying around the set was a $20,000 baseball card!" laughs Oster. "But Joe Longo found a company that specializes in producing replicas of baseball cards. Who knew there was a company that did that? They made one for us. It had tiny, tiny wording on the bottom that says 'Duplicate' but you never see it because the camera's never close enough to the card. But other than that, it looks exactly like the original."

Dr. Giger's marvelously named Cellular Regeneration and Entertainment Chamber was a rented personal sauna. "I saw it three or four years ago at Modern Props," says Laura Richarz. "Just this big egg-shaped thing. It was so weird, I took a picture of it, and it was one of those things I kept in my head because it was so unique. I knew that someday we'd find the perfect use for it."

As for the inspiration behind the chamber invented by Dr. Giger, played by Brian Markinson, a veteran of *Voyager* episodes "Cathexis" and "Faces," Moore comments, "I had to figure out what the insane obsession of the mad scientist was. Ira had come up with the idea that perhaps he was trying to bring his wife back to life, and all he had was her nose or her ear and he was going to recreate her from that." Moore tried the premise but found that it wasn't working. "As René [Echevarria] later pointed out, if this guy really was trying to bring his wife back to life, the audience would start to sympathize with him on some level," explains Moore. "You'd want him to succeed, and that would make this a different story."

Echevarria suggested going for the traditional mad scientist grail, immortality, but Moore wasn't sure where to go with that. He went back and discussed the problem with Behr, who counseled the writer to come up with something that would initially sound plausible, but which would quickly begin to sound crazy. Moore again considered immortality, and this time he hit upon the theory of "cellular ennui," the concept that one literally can be bored to death. "And that worked!" relates Moore. "He starts talking and you buy into it for a little while, and as you're listening it begins to sound kind of wacky, but you hear a lot of wacky stuff on *Star Trek,* but then eventually you start to think, 'Wow, this is really twisted.'"

But perhaps the biggest surprise of the episode is the fact that the B-story is an ultra-serious plotline that will lead directly into the start of the Dominion War. "That was interesting," smiles Moore, "to make the A-story this romp and have as the B-story something that really is serious, that has big implications for the series. That's the reverse of our normal structure, but it worked better this way."

Behr notes that despite the palpable drama of the Winn/Sisko plot, the writers didn't have quite enough content to make it an A-story. However, it did work nicely to set up the season finale, says Moore, "and that, in turn, set up the next season."

CALL TO ARMS
Episode #524
WRITTEN BY **IRA STEVEN BEHR** &
ROBERT HEWITT WOLFE
DIRECTED BY **ALLAN KROEKER**

GUEST CAST

Garak	ANDREW J. ROBINSON
Weyoun	JEFFREY COMBS
Gul Dukat	MARC ALAIMO
Rom	MAX GRODÉNCHIK
Nog	ARON EISENBERG
General Martok	J.G. HERTZLER
Leeta	CHASE MASTERSON
Tora Ziyal	MELANIE SMITH
Damar	CASEY BIGGS

STARDATE 50975.2

Rom and Leeta attempt to make a decision about the bride-to-be's attire for their upcoming nuptials, while Sisko and O'Brien note with dismay that yet another convoy of Jem'Hadar ships is coming through the wormhole, their destination: Cardassia. It's clear they're witnessing a buildup to some form of Dominion aggression, but there's not much they can do about it, other than order the crew's loved ones out of harm's way. O'Brien has already shipped off Keiko and the children to Earth, and Sisko wishes he could do the same with Jake. Unfortunately, Jake has other ideas; he's become an official correspondent for the Federation News Service.

The atmosphere around the station gets a little grimmer when Starfleet Intelligence reveals that the

The Dominion war escalates, and Sisko prepares to leave Kira and the station to the expected Cardassians. ROBBIE ROBINSON

Romulans have signed a nonaggression pact with the Dominion. The Miradorn and the Tholians have signed similar treaties, and the Bajorans are being pressured to sign. The Dominion is making impressive inroads in the Alpha Quadrant. But Starfleet Command has decided to put an end to the incursion. Sisko's been ordered to prevent additional Jem'Hadar ships from entering the Alpha Quadrant, and he plans to mine the entrance to the wormhole, a move that could lead to war.

Rom, Dax, and O'Brien hatch a plan to create a batch of cloaked, self-replicating mines. The only drawback is that the entire minefield will need to be in place before it can be activated, which means there's a good chance that it will be discovered, and they'll be attacked before the job is done. Since Starfleet has informed them that it cannot send reinforcements to help defend the station, they'll be on their own. In the midst of all this, Kira and Odo meet and agree to put on hold any potential romantic overtures until the current crisis is over.

A short time after they start positioning the mines, Weyoun arrives and delivers an ultimatum to Sisko: Remove the mines or the Dominion will take over the station and remove the mines. The conversation ends in a stalemate, but Sisko is sure that a Dominion attack will be forthcoming. The minefield must be finished immediately.

Sisko sends General Martok to patrol the border and watch for Dominion ships. At the same time, he tells Kira to call a meeting with Bajor's Council of Ministers; he's going to recommend that they sign the nonaggression pact with the Dominion. Kira opposes the decision, but Sisko feels it's the only way to guarantee Bajor's safety. After ordering all Bajoran personnel off the station, Sisko officiates at a private wedding service for Rom and Leeta. Moments later, Rom ships Leeta off to Bajor as Sisko receives word that Dominion forces will arrive within the hour.

The battle is joined. As Sisko defends the station, Martok and his troops keep Dominion forces away from the *Defiant* until Dax and O'Brien finish deploying the minefield. After the two officers activate the mines, they head back to the station. Sisko announces that the time has come for Starfleet personnel to evacuate. Dax bids a warm farewell to Worf, who's been assigned to Martok's ship, and promises to marry him when they reunite.

Sisko provides some inspiring words to Kira, Odo, Quark, and the few others who will stay behind on DS9, noting that the Federation fleet has not been

sitting idle; they've just destroyed the Dominion shipyards on Torros III. With a solemn promise to return to the station, Sisko beams to the *Defiant*, which leaves the system, sans Jake, who has decided to stay on Deep Space 9 to report on the coming events.

Kira deliberately triggers a booby trap that Sisko left behind, disabling much of the Federation equipment on the station, then "welcomes" the Dominion troops. As the *Defiant* rendezvouses with a huge combined Federation/Klingon fleet of ships, Dukat takes over the station commander's office, where he finds Sisko's baseball waiting for him. He understands the message; Sisko will return.

"They dragged me off, wounded," says Robert Hewitt Wolfe. "I've got blood on my face." A casualty of war? Sort of. After five years writing *Deep Space Nine* episodes, Wolfe couldn't help feeling a bit worn around the edges by the time he got to "Call to Arms." But that isn't what caused his injuries. "I was one of the crewmen being helped off the station in the scene where they're evac-

Robert Hewitt Wolfe (left), bloodied—by the Makeup Department— but not bowed, makes his departure from Deep Space 9.
ROBBIE ROBINSON

The cast of *Deep Space Nine* tapes a (sad) farewell to the departing Wolfe. ROBBIE ROBINSON

uating," he says with a grin. "But I wasn't wounded by the series. It paid for my house!"

The writing staff had known that Wolfe was leaving them long before "Call to Arms" was written. "I told Hans [Beimler] halfway through the season that Robert was going to leave," says Ira Behr. "I could just sense it. There were a lot things going on in his life."

Wolfe was moving on to a production deal at 20th Century Fox, where he'd snagged a contract to write a television movie for Wesley Snipes (*Futuresport*, which aired on ABC in 1998). But there were other reasons for moving on. "I had pretty much done all I could do with the characters, I thought," says Wolfe. And although he would provide one last episode as a freelancer in the final season ("Field of Fire"), "five years was enough," he states. "Thirty-some-odd episodes. I didn't want to keep doing it and not do it well."

The majority of those episodes were written with Behr, with whom he also partnered on the book *Legends of the Ferengi*. While Behr would miss his presence, he was stoic about his friend's departure. "Robert needed to do what he had to do, and I didn't say one single thing to try to change his mind," Behr admits. "It had worked really nicely, but to have anyone here against his will was only gonna screw up the mojo."

"René [Echevarria] wrote a little piece for the actors to perform during one of the scenes in the wardroom, about 'what are we going to do about Robert leaving?'" says Behr. "We had the cast film it for him, and then they all turned and waved, 'Goodbye, Robert.'" The personal tribute was pre-

sented to Wolfe on cassette, no doubt with a copy of the episode itself, including the scene with the injured officer, which *did* make the final cut, although Wolfe didn't get a good close-up. In the scene where Worf and Jadzia say goodbye, Wolfe passes behind them, a limping, dark-haired crewman, wounded and bloody, hanging onto the arm of a blond male medical officer.

"Call to Arms" is an episode about goodbyes. "I was very proud of this episode," says Behr. "Because we dealt with something like seventeen [regular or semiregular] characters in forty-two and a half minutes. We gave literally everyone a moment, gave everyone their shot." Over the course of those forty-two and a half minutes, viewers got to see a little of everything: romance, special effects, Rom having a truly brilliant idea.

"I just loved that," chuckles Behr. "I'd made Rom an idiot in 'Babel,' with Quark railing, 'My brother couldn't fix a straw if it was bent!' And now I decided to make him a genius. The truth is, I wanted him to be a bit of both. He's an idiot savant, basically, brilliance *cum* panic."

As for the goodbyes, the script included Sisko's moving farewell to the people remaining on the station, Dax's romantic farewell to Worf, Rom's hurried farewell to Leeta, and Garak's sweet farewell to Ziyal. According to Behr, the farewells were steeped in more than sentiment. "It was the big hint to the audience," says Behr. "I knew that we were going to do something very bold the following season, and I wanted to prepare people for it, because we already were thinking of having this multipart episode the next year that was going to turn the show around."

"We needed the crew to wind up scattered all over the place so that we could work different stories with them in the sixth season," says Wolfe. "We needed a station group and a fleet group that we could contrast down the road." Wolfe, of course, wasn't going to be involved with that. "Yeah, but still, you have to set up the next year," he explains. "You want to get the ingredients in place. That's the neat thing about the endings that we do. It's like setting a table for yourself. You're not setting up a cliffhanger where you have to solve a certain problem. You just have to put out some beetlesnuff." He laughs. "You know, something to set up the solution."

One minor component of the setup was the matter of Odo and Kira, now that the changeling's future self had spilled the beans about his feelings for her in "Children of Time." "We just felt that it was time for a change," says Behr. "We'd pulled on this thread for so long without really doing anything with it, that it was time to say, 'Hey!' And 'Children of Time' basically gave us the impetus to do it."

All well and good, but the action taken by the pair in "Call to Arms" was, basically, *inaction*. "Kira's feeling at that point was, 'Okay, it's out in the open,'" says Nana Visitor. "'We've said it, but we're agreeing not to deal with it while we've got this problem on the station.'"

Rene Auberjonois confesses that he had no idea where the writers intended to take the two characters beyond the episode. "Odo tells Kira that he's going to put his feelings aside during the 'current crisis,'" he recalls. "But I didn't know where it would ultimately go. To tell the truth, I think it was a writer's device to allow them to *not* deal with it for a while, because in Season 6, Odo is drawn to what appears to be the dark side, drawn in by the female shape-shifter. In a sense, he betrays Kira, which creates a real schism."

While Wolfe wouldn't be around to help the couple get past that schism and to make sure that everything was in place, the other writers would. "We didn't go directly into vacation that year when we stopped filming," says Ron Moore. "The writing staff stuck around for another three weeks, and we worked. And we were working toward an end, the idea that we would get the station back by the sixth or seventh episode."

Moore's final episode of Season 5 had been "In the Cards," but members of the writing team always contribute to episodes that don't bear their names. It was Moore who added one of "Call to Arms"'s most compelling dramatic details. "I just had this image of Sisko's baseball," he recalls, "and I walked in and told [Ira and Robert] about this idea that Sisko leaves it behind as a message to Dukat that he'll be back." The baseball, or rather, its absence, would provide a very different message the following season, at the conclusion of "Tears of the Prophets."

Drama aside, for some viewers, a season finale ain't a season finale without some battle scenes—the bigger the better. "Call to Arms" certainly didn't disappoint on that count. "That one just about killed Dan Curry, [Visual Effects Coordinator] Adam Buckner, and me," says Visual Effects Supervisor David Stipes. "We were on that thing for weeks shooting motion control photography, and just running into trouble right and left, struggling to get the shots the way I wanted to get them."

The episode starts out with a shot of a large

Dax's promise to marry Worf when they reunite served as a not-so-subtle hint that big things were on the way. ROBBIE ROBINSON

group of Dominion reinforcements flying through the wormhole. Although *Deep Space Nine* tends to do most ship shots with motion control models, this particular one was done as CGI. "We started with a stock wormhole and composited in a ton of computer images," says Buckner. "It was a difficult stunt because of the material versus the size. The producers wanted us to build a whole fleet. But when you do that many ships, they have to be so small. It gets really hard to see them on television. So we had to find a good middle ground where we could get a sense of the huge volume of ships and still convey the scale of how big those ships were. We started with a full-resolution computer model and then scaled it in three sizes, far away, mid-ground and close-up."

But if that brief shot was difficult, it was nothing compared to the final sequence in the episode, where the *Defiant* and Martok's bird-of-prey fly out to meet the Federation fleet. "This was the show that really drove home to me the fact that motion control, although a wonderful technique, has real limitations," says Stipes. "We had to have the *Defiant* and the bird-of-prey fly away from the camera so we could see the back and the top of the ships, and then they had to turn around, so we had to see the front and the bottom. Well, where do you put the mount [the attachment that holds the model to a stand]? And where do you lay all the dolly track that you need?" No motion control sound stage is that large.

Ultimately, the two ships were done as CGI, as were a number of the vessels in the fleet. "We ended

The explosions that greet Dukat's arrival were easy, according to Monak. "Don't tell the producers," he chuckles. ROBBIE ROBINSON

up with a combination of both motion control practical models, both full-size and smaller kit-built ships, and computer generated ship models that had been built by ILM for *First Contact*," notes Buckner. "They'd made a number of new ships for the Borg attack at the beginning of the movie."

"Part of what we had to deal with in staging the shot was showing the scale," continues Stipes. "We needed to show that the ships were big and powerful, and that there were a lot of them. So we showed them in the distance and had them coming toward the audience. And the *Defiant* comes in and it's like, 'Here we are. We've joined the fleet and now we're gonna come back and kick fanny.'"

That final shot looked terrific, and certainly served to set the tone for the coming season. Unfortunately, it did the job a little too well. "What we'd written for that scene was, 'Lots of ships, two little ships coming to join them,'" relates Behr. "But what the effects people shot was, '*Lots of ships,* two little ships coming, turning around, joining them, and

then coming *back* together.' Whoops!" Although the producers loved the shot, "it went much farther than we wanted," Behr comments. "It told the audience that we were attacking *now,* like, 'Okay, we're marshaling our forces and here we are to join up,' which was never the idea. That changed the entire opening to Season 6. We'd already written the opening of the first show, and René said, 'Guys, this doesn't work, because the effects people have made the audience think that something a lot bigger has happened. We have to address that.'"

"We'd asked what the fleet should be doing," says Buckner, "and we were told that the fleet was massing and moving toward Deep Space 9." When the *Defiant* approaches the fleet, it's going in the opposite direction, he points out. "We felt that it ought to be flying along with the fleet, that it would join it in the fight to retake the station. Otherwise, essentially, it would have sort of chugged up to the fleet and said, 'Hi, I'm here!' That's a little less aesthetic," he laughs.

Behr sighs. The producers *had* approved the shot,

after all. "Anyway, we changed the opening of Season 6 to have all those ships we saw in 'Call to Arms' battered and beaten and leaking plasma."

From small details, like the self-replicating mines that in reality are composters Laura Richarz ordered from a gardening catalogue, to great big scenes, like the final shot, "Call to Arms" seems to have something for everyone, and it easily ranks as one of the writing staff's favorite episodes. Although he didn't have much to do with it, prior to the series' final season, Ron Moore stated categorically that "Call to Arms" might just be his favorite season-ending episode of *any* incarnation of *Star Trek*. "The crew has to leave their station, it's taken over by the bad guys, they split up, they join this massive fleet, the war is on," he ticks off the high points. "You can say that the first half of 'The Best of Both Worlds' is a better *cliff-hanger*," he admits. "It's hard to beat that. But this isn't a cliff-hanger. It's just a great ending."

SIXTH SEASON

O V E R V I E W

"I've said this many times," declares Executive Producer Ira Steven Behr, "but I can't say it enough. We want to make good television. We want to do shows that can stand as decent hours of television. One of the things I have to do as 'leader of the pack' here is to make sure that everyone working on the show, especially the writing staff, knows how seriously I take it, so that *they* will take it seriously as well."

Behr had his work cut out for him in Season 6, *DS9*'s most ambitious year to date. For the first time ever, the writers would create a contiguous arc for a group of episodes—in this case, the first six. It was, they felt, the only way to do justice to a story as large and complex as the one they wanted to tell.

Although it was an unprecedented move in *Star Trek*, it wasn't entirely unforesee-

able. "I think that the potential for the serialization—or *near*-serialization—of the show was always there," Rick Berman observes thoughtfully. "If you're on a spaceship, as in *Voyager* or *The Next Generation* or the original series, you have your family of people who go off and meet new aliens every week. But *Deep Space Nine* was conceived as a stationary show. It took place on a space station, and we found ourselves developing dozens of ancillary characters, secondary characters, and recurring characters. And

because we remained there, those characters kept coming back. Ira and I once sat down and we came up with over thirty characters who'd appeared on the show that the average fan would be very familiar with. That's unheard of on other *Star Trek* shows. So once you had the tapestry of all these different characters, and you had all of these different stories that were kind of weaving in and out, I think it sort of begged for more of a serialized format. And the fact that the Dominion War became such a major part of the last two seasons really contributed to the feeling of serialization."

It was a learning experience for everyone. "We broke the six episodes together," says Co-executive Producer Ronald D. Moore, "but as everybody went off and worked on writing them, things would start to change or shift. It became a much more interactive process than it ever had been before. Because each detail had a domino effect. We'd had that happen before, to a certain extent, but we'd never done this many episodes with this many continuing storylines as a *single piece*. We weren't used to the rhythm. It was definitely challenging!" he grins.

By the time they reached the end of the arc, the feeling around the office was, "'Season's over—let's go home!'" chuckles Behr. "It was like, 'Well, isn't that *enough*? Let's go on vacation!'"

The arc may have been over, but that didn't mean there was time to catch a collective breath. "They're *all* difficult episodes to write, so we *never* catch our breath," Behr comments. "It's an amazing thing. Many TV shows do the same basic episode every week. But with *Deep Space Nine*, we were always thinking about what *kind* of show we wanted to do, and *where* in the season it would be best to put it. We always tried to give our audience a multidimensional kind of experience."

There had been no guarantee that a six-episode arc would hold the audience's attention, but once they were committed to it, they were there for the whole ride. "We were so worried about how they would work," he says. "But in a way, it really helped us. Because it made *us* work like the dickens. And after that, we kept painting ourselves into corners, promising the audience future results from the things we were putting together."

In Behr's opinion, that internal pressure paid off, both in personal satisfaction and in quality of product. And it gave them the confidence to tackle more and more complicated shows, like the season's two most lauded episodes, "Far Beyond the Stars" and "In the Pale Moonlight."

While "In the Pale Moonlight" garnered the most approval from the fans, "Far Beyond the Stars" drew the most attention in "the outside world." When the annual Emmy nominations were announced, "Far Beyond the Stars" received nods in Art Direction, Costume Design, and Hairstyling, but none for the outstanding writing, directing, or acting. Still, kudos are kudos—and that year the series tied in the number of nominations with such respected shows as

Homicide: Life on the Street and a remake of *Twelve Angry Men*. In addition to the three for "Far Beyond the Stars," the show also was recognized for achievements in Makeup ("Who Mourns for Morn"), Music Direction ("His Way"), and Special Visual Effects ("One Little Ship"), but, unfortunately, no statuettes went home to sit on the mantel.

Character development, as always, was a priority with the writing staff. Sisko's connection to the Prophets, no longer relegated to an occasional mention of his status as the Emissary, became more and more direct ("Sacrifice of Angels," "The Reckoning"). The producers also began to set up the startling revelation that his connection with Bajor was far more than a coincidence. Odo's long unrequited feelings for Kira were finally returned by the object of his desire, sealed with a very public kiss ("His Way"). Worf and Jadzia Dax were joined in matrimony ("You Are Cordially Invited") . . . and separated by untimely death ("Tears of the Prophets"). Quark risked his life over the very unprofitable commodities of friendship and family. And the once callow Dr. Bashir, his long-suppressed secret revealed to all in Season 5's "Doctor Bashir, I Presume," became much more mature. "It was a great opportunity for him to shed his skin, so to speak," says Alexander Siddig. "I was all prepared to fully revamp the character, to change him totally," he says, but the producers kept the changes subtle. They allowed Bashir to drop his veneer of naïveté, and his previous tendency to babble ("The Sound of Her Voice"), but resisted the temptation to totally overhaul the character. However, his new status as Starfleet's only officially sanctioned genetically engineered officer introduced the character to two new storylines—counselor and friend to his less fortunate, unenhanced brethren ("Statistical Probabilities") and potential candidate for the mysterious Section 31 ("Inquisition").

The series' recurring characters received almost as much attention as the regulars, with Nog really coming into his own. "We'd already turned the corner on Nog when we got him involved with Starfleet Academy," notes Moore. "He became interesting to us at that point, the Ferengi who wants to be like the big guys, the Starfleet characters." Nog kept his cool under fire and was rewarded with a promotion to ensign in "Favor the Bold."

At the other end of the military food chain was Admiral Ross, introduced in "A Time to Stand." The producers were so impressed with Barry Jenner's portrayal that he was quickly brought into the fold.

Although tremendously flattered by the producers' interest, Jenner humbly insists that he only was doing what he feels an actor is supposed to do. "It's too easy for someone in my category to come in and play Mister Stern, Mister Disciplinarian, Mister Admiral," smiles Jenner. "And there are plenty of actors who can deliver the lines, where the words are direct and spoken correctly, with the delays in the correct spot. But I gave him a backstory. As an actor, I tend to give everybody I play some sort of previous life. In Ross's case, he was obviously a line officer who'd seen a lot of combat, seen a lot of people killed, and he's got a lot of memories. And that really tied into the way I did the audition scene, where he was talking to Sisko about sending young men and women off to battle, knowing that some of them won't come back."

Jenner was gratified when Ira Behr told him, "We've had a lot of other admirals on this show. We're glad we found you. Sorry it took five years!" But other supporting characters were highlighted only to meet a less fortunate end. Ziyal, for example, was marked for death.

"Killing Ziyal served our needs," says Hans Beimler. "We understood the ramifications on all the characters. We'd built up her relationship with Garak. The girl who always told the truth had fallen in love with the guy who never tells the truth—or all of the truth. It made for a nice tragic love story, and her death served to motivate Garak in his future actions."

Although still a shadowy character, Garak would henceforth devote himself to doing whatever he could to put the blocks to Cardassia's involvement in the war. Ziyal's death also had a profound impact on Dukat, pushing the already unstable leader of Cardassia into madness ("Waltz").

One more recurring character was introduced to the series during Season 6: Las Vegas lounge singer Vic Fontaine. The concept of Vic certainly went beyond anything viewers expected from a *Star Trek* show. Some loved him. Some, to put it mildly, didn't. But that really didn't matter, because it was pure fun for Behr. And who says that executive producers aren't entitled to a little fun?

With the exception of Terry Farrell's exit from the series at the end of the season, life was relatively stable. The writing team of Bradley Thompson and David Weddle came on staff as story editors, filling the gap left by the departure of Robert Hewitt Wolfe.

"The sad news was that Robert was gone," says Beimler, who moved up to the position of supervising producer in the sixth season, dropping the "co-" from his title. "Although for me, that was *good* news too," he giggles. "He was a terrific writer and we missed him. We all missed his voice in the room. But his departure did give me an irresistible opportunity, which was to be Ira's writing partner," he adds. "We did ten scripts together during the season, and close to ten in the next."

Other promotions included that of John Eaves, from illustrator to senior illustrator; Terri Potts, from associate producer to co-producer; Steve Oster, from producer to co-supervising producer; and René Echevarria, also from producer to co-supervising producer.

One of the responsibilities that Echevarria took on during Season 6 was to play a den mother to Thompson and Weddle. "When I started at *The Next Generation*," Echevarria explains, "Jeri Taylor was very hands-on and worked with me very closely. As I would write a first draft and then rewrite it, I would talk to her about the scenes and think them out. Like, 'I have an idea—this is what I'm going to do,' and she would say, 'Yeah, why don't you try this?' It was a *big* learning experience, and I had the chance to share that experience with Brad and David. I think we all got a lot out of it. I know *I* got a lot out of being in that role, being the senior person in the room and making decisions. Sort of being Ira," he laughs, "listening to people talk and argue and then finally saying, 'My instincts are telling me that this is what we should do.'"

Echevarria worked particularly closely with Weddle and Thompson on "Inquisition," "The Reckoning," and "Time's Orphan." "They were doing me the favor of filling in for me on those episodes during a difficult period, while my mom was very ill. Every chance I got, I flew home to Florida to be with her. And the guys would do the drafts and then we polished them together."

The season closed on a particularly dark note, with the disappearance of the Prophets, the death of Jadzia, and the despondency of Sisko, the show's strong central character. Yet, no one could predict the amazing twists and turns the series would take in its final season.

A TIME TO STAND

Episode #525

WRITTEN BY IRA STEVEN BEHR & HANS BEIMLER
DIRECTED BY ALLAN KROEKER

GUEST CAST

Garak	ANDREW J. ROBINSON
Weyoun	JEFFREY COMBS
Gul Dukat	MARK ALAIMO
Nog	ARON EISENBERG
Martok	J.G. HERTZLER
Damar	CASEY BIGGS
Admiral Ross	BARRY JENNER

AND

Brock Peters	JOSEPH SISKO

STARDATE UNKNOWN

Three months into the war against the Dominion/Cardassian alliance, the Federation has little to show for its efforts. Having abandoned Deep Space 9 to enemy forces, Captain Sisko's crew now operates from the *Defiant,* taking on the enemy from the tough little battleship. But the crew is growing demoralized following endless bouts of "engage and retreat" with attacking vessels. After news arrives that the Seventh Fleet has been almost wiped out, the *Defiant* is ordered to report to Starbase 375 for reassignment. Admiral Ross relieves Sisko of the *Defiant's* command. Ross gives a new assignment to the entire crew, including the Cardassian "civilian," Garak: destroy the main Alpha Quadrant storage facility for ketracel-white. Without the white, the genetically addicted Jem'Hadar will die. Sisko wonders how they'll be able to infiltrate Cardassian territory without the *Defiant's* cloaking capabilities, but Ross reveals they'll have something better, a Jem'Hadar attack ship—the same ship that Sisko captured a year earlier ("The Ship").

Learning to control the alien vessel proves to be difficult—and uncomfortable. There are no chairs, no food replicators, no sickbay, and no viewscreen. The ship is designed to be piloted by one person who must wear a virtual headset to navigate, and the headset is not compatible with human physiology, as Sisko discovers. Incapacitated by severe headaches, Sisko accepts Garak's offer to share piloting duties. Cardassian physiology is more compatible with the technology.

Back on DS9, Major Kira attempts to adjust to her new Jem'Hadar and Cardassian co-workers,

Traveling undercover in a Jem'Hadar ship, Sisko faces a tough decision when he realizes he must fire on a Federation vessel.
ROBBIE ROBINSON

which include her old nemesis Gul Dukat. About the only comforting note is the fact that Dukat's forces have not yet been able to dismantle the self-replicating minefield that prevents additional Dominion forces from coming through the wormhole. Kira worries that Dukat plans to avenge himself against the Bajoran people, who once drove Cardassian forces from the region. Odo assures her that the presence of the Vorta, Weyoun, who is determined to demonstrate that the Dominion is Bajor's ally, will keep Dukat in line. However, after a private meeting in which Dukat makes no secret of his desire to have a closer relationship with the major, Kira has her doubts. She encourages Odo to ask Weyoun to reinstate the changeling's Bajoran deputies and to restore his responsibility for security on the Promenade. Weyoun complies and asks Odo to join the station's newly established Ruling Council, giving him a voice in station policy. This is more than Kira expected and it makes her uneasy, but Odo dismisses her fears.

As Sisko and his crew near their destination, they run into an unexpected complication. Their Jem'Hadar ship comes under attack by the *Centaur*, a Starfleet vessel captained by Charlie Reynolds, an old friend of Sisko's. The *Centaur*'s weapons knock out communications, so Sisko can't let Reynolds know that he's firing on allies. Sisko is reluctant to use his own weapons on a Federation ship, but finally realizes he has no choice. After taking a few carefully aimed shots at the *Centaur*, Sisko is relieved but surprised to see the vessel head back toward Federation space. He soon understands Reynolds's motivation; three Jem'Hadar ships are approaching. The enemy ships ignore Sisko's vessel to pursue the *Centaur* and Sisko continues toward his target.

Arriving at the ketracel-white facility, O'Brien beams down eighty-three empty canisters and one that's full of explosives. In return they receive eighty-four canisters loaded with the white. With only three minutes until detonation, they prepare to leave the vicinity—only to be trapped when the facility raises its security net and tells the ship to stand by. Sisko realizes that the explosion will disable the security net before the impact hits them, which means that if they move quickly enough, they should be able to ride the "wave" of the blast to safety. The plan works, and the Jem'Hadar ship is able to move out of harm's way as the explosion destroys the facility. Unfortunately, the blast has knocked out a number of the ship's systems, including the warp drive—and without warp speed, the ship is seventeen years from the nearest Federation starbase!

SONS AND DAUGHTERS

Episode #526

WRITTEN BY BRADLEY THOMPSON &
DAVID WEDDLE
DIRECTED BY JESÚS SALVADOR TREVIÑO

GUEST CAST

Alexander Rozhenko	MARC WORDEN
Gul Dukat	MARC ALAIMO
Martok	J.G. HERTZLER
Tora Ziyal	MELANIE SMITH
Damar	CASEY BIGGS
Ch'Targh	SAM ZELLER
N'Garen	GABRIELLE UNION

STARDATE UNKNOWN

Following its rescue of Sisko's crew, the Klingon bird-of-prey *I.K.S. Rotarran* travels to Starbase 375 to drop off the Starfleet officers and to take on much-needed Klingon reinforcements. General Martok is disappointed: he had requested fifteen replacements but has received only five, and it doesn't look as if there's a warrior among them. The *Rotarran*'s first officer, Lieutenant Commander Worf, is shocked to discover that one of the inexperienced recruits is his estranged son, Alexander.

Worf explains to Martok that he had sent the boy to live with his own foster parents, the Rozhenkos, on Earth after he had determined that Alexander showed no inclination toward becoming a warrior. Puzzled by Alexander's decision to join the Klingon Defense Forces, Worf admits he hasn't spoken to his son in several years. Martok urges him to mend fences with his son, but the ensuing effort quickly deteriorates.

Alexander unwisely challenges Ch'Targh. ROBBIE ROBINSON

On Terok Nor, Kira is surprised but pleased to see Tora Ziyal. Dukat's illegitimate daughter has returned from Bajor to live on the station with her father. Although Kira despises Dukat, she agrees to have dinner with him and Ziyal. To her surprise, she has a pleasant evening; her feelings for Ziyal put her on unfamiliar common ground with her old enemy.

In the *Rotarran* mess hall, Alexander has a less enjoyable meal. He responds to the taunts of Ch'targh, a seasoned warrior, by pulling out his knife. Knowing that inexperienced Alexander cannot win, Worf puts an end to the battle, humiliating and angering his son. As Worf leaves the room, Ch'targh reminds him that he won't be able to come to Alexander's aid when the boy is fighting the Jem'Hadar. Later, Martok gently chides his first officer for stepping in, but the conversation is interrupted by alarms heralding an apparent Jem'Hadar attack. When the attack fails to materialize, Worf realizes that Alexander forgot to erase a battle simulation from his sensor display. Members of the bridge crew laugh about the incident and welcome Alexander to the ranks. But Worf feels that they have accepted him as the ship's fool, rather than as a fellow warrior.

Determined to make a warrior out of his son, Worf attempts to teach Alexander to defend himself against a Jem'Hadar weapon. Alexander's skills are lacking, and the practice session turns into an angry confrontation. Later, Martok informs Alexander that he will be transferred off the *Rotarran* at Worf's request. Alexander challenges his father, accusing Worf of trying to get rid of him again, just as he had before when he'd discovered that Alexander wasn't the kind of son he wanted. Worf is stung by the truth of Alexander's words, but he has no time to consider them; the ship has come under Jem'Hadar attack.

On the space station, Dukat invites Kira to a celebration he is hosting for Ziyal; several of her drawings are to be exhibited at the Cardassian Institute of Art. Pleased at the news, Kira accepts, but she reconsiders when Dukat sends her a gown to wear. Kira returns the dress and tells Dukat that she wants nothing to do with him. Later, she apologizes to Ziyal for missing the reception, but she makes it clear that her feelings about Dukat will never change.

The *Rotarran* sustains heavy damage during the Jem'Hadar attack and begins leaking plasma from its primary impulse injector. With his sensor console destroyed, there is nothing that Alexander can do on the bridge, so he volunteers for the hazardous duty of sealing the leak. Ch'targh offers to accompany him. In the heat of battle, Worf has no time to dwell on his son's fate, but after the *Rotarran* destroys the enemy vessels, he looks for Alexander. He discovers that Ch'targh and Alexander have completed their task successfully, but the awkward young Klingon has locked himself in a corridor. The crew is amused, but this time Worf takes no offense at their good-natured response.

He escorts the boy to his quarters and, at long last, has a much overdue conversation about their relationship. Worf explains that he cannot change the mistakes he made in the past, but he promises to behave differently in the future. He will teach Alexander to be a warrior, and Alexander will teach Worf to be a father. To seal the pact, Worf and Martok perform a ritual ceremony to welcome the youth into the House of Martok.

ROCKS AND SHOALS

Episode #527

WRITTEN BY **RONALD D. MOORE**
DIRECTED BY **MICHAEL VEJAR**

GUEST CAST

Garak	ANDREW J. ROBINSON
Remata'Klan	PHIL MORRIS
Keevan	CHRISTOPHER SHEA
Nog	ARON EISENBERG
Limara'Son	PAUL S. ECKSTEIN
Vedek Yassim	LILYAN CHAUVIN
Neeley	SARAH MacDONNELL
Gordon	JOSEPH FUQUA

STARDATE UNKNOWN

Chief O'Brien's attempts to repair the crippled Jem'Hadar warship are interrupted when the ship is beset by two Jem'Hadar fighters. Hoping to elude them, Sisko orders his vessel into an uncharted nebula. The warship takes several hits, one of which causes a console to explode, severely injuring Dax. The damaged vessel plummets down toward a nearby planet and crashes into its ocean. Sisko's crew is able to evacuate the warship before it sinks, and they make it to shore with a few supplies.

On the station, Kira awakens to another day as an "ally" to the Dominion. She gets dressed and heads to work, paying little attention to the Cardassian and Jem'Hadar faces that surround her. In Ops, she accepts her morning cup of *raktajino* from a Cardassian soldier. It's just a routine day at the office—almost. Later, Jake informs her that a vedek

Sisko and O'Brien prepare to engage the Jem'Hadar. ROBBIE ROBINSON

named Yassim is organizing a demonstration to protest against the Dominion's occupation of the station. Kira notes that she'll talk to Yassim, and bristles when Jake asks if she's abolishing the right to protest on the station.

Kira's meeting with Vedek Yassim doesn't go the way she'd hoped. Yassim feels that it is every Bajoran's responsibility to oppose the evil that the Dominion represents. The major feels that it would cause problems for other Bajorans, and she counsels the vedek to be patient. But the vedek sees only that Kira has become an apologist for the enemy. The next day, Kira and Odo are prepared to step in if things get out of hand at the protest, but neither of them are prepared for Yassim's wake-up call to the Bajoran people. "Evil must be opposed," the vedek addresses the crowd, an instant before she commits suicide by hanging herself on the Promenade.

Thousands of light-years away, at a makeshift base camp, Bashir stabilizes Dax's condition while Sisko sends Garak and Nog to look for fresh water and food. Unbeknownst to the crew, one of the Jem'Hadar fighters also has crash-landed on the planet, killing several Jem'Hadar and incapacitating Keevan, the Vorta in command. Nog and Garak are captured by Jem'Hadar troops and brought to Keevan, who asks if they have a doctor in their unit. Garak reveals that they do. Keevan sends Remata'Klan, the Jem'Hadar third, to locate the Starfleet unit, assess their strength, and then report back—without engaging them.

In the meantime, Sisko notes that Garak and Nog haven't returned, and he organizes a small search party. They run into Remata'Klan's group, which, contrary to the third's orders, begins firing on Sisko and the others. Remata'Klan orders his men to lower their weapons and to return to base camp. Although Keevan is angry at the group's disobedience, he gives Remata'Klan a new assignment. Soon afterward, the third shows up at the Starfleet camp and informs Sisko that Keevan will trade prisoners Garak and Nog for Sisko and Bashir. Sisko agrees after Remata'Klan assures Sisko that Bashir and he will be unharmed and allowed to leave the Jem'Hadar camp after they meet with Keevan.

Sisko and Bashir arrive at a specified point, Garak and Nog are released, and the captain and the doctor continue on to Keevan's camp. Once there, Bashir conducts emergency surgery on the Vorta. When Keevan revives, he reveals that his hold over the Jem'Hadar soldiers is tenuous at best. Although the soldiers don't know it, Keevan has only one vial of ketracel-white left to divide among the ten Jem'Hadar. The addicted troops already are suffering from the effects of withdrawal. Once the drug is gone, Keevan knows that his control over them will end and they will become irrational and violent. They'll kill him, Sisko's group, and finally each other, *unless . . .*

Keevan reveals his scheme. He will send the Jem'Hadar to attack Sisko's camp, but he will provide Sisko with their precise plan of attack. This will allow Sisko to ambush and kill them all. Then, Keevan will surrender to the captain as a prisoner of war, allowing Sisko to take his damaged communications system (which can be repaired by O'Brien), and contact Starfleet.

Sisko is disgusted at Keevan's lack of compassion for his own men, but he sees no other choice. However, the next morning he makes a last-ditch effort to save the lives of Remata'Klan and his men. Sisko offers to sedate the Jem'Hadar until they can obtain a new supply of the white. But Remata'Klan refuses, stating that he has no choice but to follow the orders of the Vorta and proceed to his death. Reluctantly, Sisko orders his crew to open fire. After the Jem'Hadar are eliminated, Keevan comes forward to keep his end of the bargain. Disgusted, Sisko has the Vorta put under guard and tells O'Brien to repair the communications equipment.

The morning after Yassim's suicide, Kira gets dressed and heads to work, once again accepting her morning cup of *raktajino* from a Cardassian soldier. It seems like another routine day—but suddenly Kira looks around and sees her surroundings as if for the very first time. She is a Bajoran in a station that is filled with Bajor's enemies. Unsettled, Kira tells Odo that Yassim was right: she must begin fighting back. Collaborating with the Cardassians makes her no better than the people she hated during the Occupation. Although Odo's concerned that it might be a mistake, he agrees to help Kira plan a new resistance movement.

BEHIND THE LINES

Episode #528

WRITTEN BY RENÉ ECHEVARRIA
DIRECTED BY LeVAR BURTON

GUEST CAST	
Weyoun	JEFFREY COMBS
Gul Dukat	MARC ALAIMO
Rom	MAX GRODÉNCHIK
Nog	ARON EISENBERG
Damar	CASEY BIGGS
Admiral Ross	BARRY JENNER

AND	
Female Shape-shifter	SALOME JENS

STARDATE 51145.3

At Starbase 375, crew members from the *Defiant* celebrate their successful return from another mission against the Dominion. During the festivities, Admiral Ross arrives to inform Sisko that Starfleet Intelligence has discovered why their enemies have been outmaneuvering them at every turn. The Dominion has a sensor array hidden at the edge of the Argolis Cluster; the massive device can monitor ship movements across five sectors. Ross orders Sisko to formulate a plan to put the array out of commission.

The next day, Sisko tells Ross his plan. Dangerous conditions within the cluster dictate that all ships heading in that direction must go around the phenomenon, giving the Dominion array plenty of time to spot their approach. But if a ship were to go directly *through* the cluster, it would gain the element of surprise necessary to get close enough to destroy the sensor device. The plan is risky, Sisko admits, but

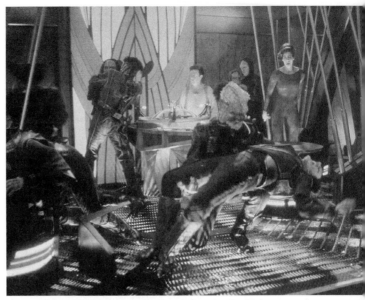

Kira's small resistance cell creates chaos in Quark's bar.
ROBBIE ROBINSON

Dax feels she can navigate around the cluster's treacherous gravimetric distortions.

Ross approves of the plan, but he informs Sisko that he won't be heading up the mission. The admiral is making Sisko his adjutant—an important job, but one that will take him away from his duties as captain of the *Defiant*. Ross doesn't see this as a problem; Dax will command the starship in Sisko's place. The captain worries the whole time the *Defiant* is gone, but both the ship and the crew come through unscathed, their mission a success.

Back at Terok Nor, Kira has formed a small resistance cell, consisting of herself, Jake, Rom, and Odo. Their first act—a plan to foster ill will between the Cardassian and Jem'Hadar allies—appears to be working. *Somehow*, a memo that Glinn Damar had been working on concerning the growing shortage of ketracel-white has fallen into the hands of the Jem'Hadar. Damar feels the soldiers stole it; the Jem'Hadar don't like that accusation *or* the information in the memo. A fight breaks out in Quark's bar. By the time Odo arrives to break it up, several men on each side are dead. Kira is delighted with the outcome, but Odo feels that her scheme was foolhardy. She wonders if Odo's new position on the station's Council ("A Time to Stand") has made him more interested in maintaining the status quo than in helping the Federation win the war. Stung, Odo asks if she's questioning his loyalties. Before the conversation can go any further, Odo receives an unexpected visitor: the female changeling whom Odo last saw when the Founders removed his shape-shifting abilities ("Broken Link").

Trapped in the Alpha Quadrant by the minefield deployed at the entrance to the wormhole ("Call to Arms"), the female shape-shifter tells Odo that she's come to the station to be with one of her own kind: him. Odo finds that odd, considering their last encounter, but she tells him that he has been forgiven for killing a fellow changeling. Knowing that only Odo's unrequited feelings for Kira have kept him from returning to the Great Link, the Founder appeals to Odo's desire for the peace and clarity that the Link seems to provide. She offers to link with him, and Odo yields.

When Kira finds out, she's concerned; the female shape-shifter has lied to Odo, tricked him, and sat in judgment of him. Yet Odo refuses to consider the possibility that in offering to link with him, the Founder may be trying to manipulate him. Still, he promises Kira that he will refrain from joining with the female shape-shifter again until the war is over.

Later, an inebriated Quark barges in on a meeting of Kira's small resistance group. He's been plying Damar with alcohol and has received a major payoff in information: the Cardassian claims to have figured out a way to deactivate the mines by using the station's deflector array. Rom knows how to sabotage the deflector, but he'll need someone to disable the alarms so that his efforts go undetected. Odo offers to run a security diagnostic the next morning, which will take the alarms off-line for five minutes and provide a window of opportunity for Rom.

But the next morning finds Odo deep in conversation with the female shape-shifter when he should be in Security. He wants so badly to learn about his people that he ignores his promise to Kira and yields again to the Founder's invitation to link. When Kira realizes that Odo isn't going to disable the alarms, she tries to warn Rom—but it's too late. Rom is arrested and thrown into a holding cell.

Furious, Kira goes to Odo's quarters and demands an explanation. He calmly explains that he was in the Link, and that Rom's predicament, the war, and even his friendship with Kira suddenly seemed irrelevant. Stunned by the admission, Kira realizes that for the first time in their relationship, they're now on different sides. As she storms out, the female shape-shifter enters from another room and allows herself a small smile of triumph.

FAVOR THE BOLD
Episode #529
WRITTEN BY IRA STEVEN BEHR & HANS BEIMLER
DIRECTED BY WINRICH KOLBE

GUEST CAST

Garak	ANDREW J. ROBINSON
Weyoun	JEFFREY COMBS
Gul Dukat	MARC ALAIMO
Rom	MAX GRODÉNCHIK
Nog	ARON EISENBERG
Martok	J.G. HERTZLER
Tora Ziyal	MELANIE SMITH
Damar	CASEY BIGGS
Leeta	CHASE MASTERSON
Admiral Ross	BARRY JENNER
Bajoran Officer	WILLIAM WELLMAN, JR.
Admiral Cobum	BART McCARTHY
Admiral Sitak	ERICKA KLEIN
Jem'Hadar Soldier	ANDREW PALMER

AND

Female Shape-shifter	SALOME JENS

STARDATE UNKNOWN

The crew of the *Defiant* experiences a moment of triumph over the Dominion as it takes out two Jem'Hadar ships with the *Rotarran's* help, but victory is short-lived. Starfleet Command has ordered all ships in the sector to fall back to Starbase 375. It's not the first time Starfleet has called for retreat, and morale is sinking fast. The Federation needs a major victory to rally the troops. Sisko devises a plan to achieve that victory: a combined Starfleet-Klingon fleet will attack and retake Deep Space 9 from the Dominion.

On the station, Kira and Quark attempt to get Odo to release Rom, but he's been charged with sabotage ("Behind the Lines"). Odo, enmeshed in the female shape-shifter's spell, remains incommunicado, ignoring his responsibilities and all the things that once were important to him.

After Weyoun announces that Rom will be executed for attempting to halt Dominion efforts to bring down the minefield, Quark vows to find a way to free him. But Rom says it's more important that Quark complete his work and destroy the antigraviton beam that would eliminate the mines. In a last-ditch effort to save Rom, Kira asks Ziyal to speak to her father about pardoning the Ferengi, but Gul Dukat turns his daughter down, alienating the young girl.

Damar's thrashing by Kira doesn't elicit the response he anticipated from Dukat. DANNY FELD

Meanwhile, Quark learns from Damar that field tests using the antigraviton beam have been successful; the minefield will be down in a week, and Dominion troops will pour into the Alpha Quadrant.

As Quark and Kira try to figure out a way to warn Starfleet, Jake reveals that he knows how to get an encrypted message to his father. Not long after, Morn delivers the information to Sisko. The captain realizes that the time has come to launch the assault, even though some of the needed reinforcements are days away from arriving at Starbase 375. Sisko takes command of those ships that *can* be rallied immediately and prepares to lead the fleet to DS9. As the ships head out, Nog receives word that he's been made an ensign.

Tracking the movements of the Federation fleet, Dukat and Weyoun realize that Starfleet is planning something big. But Dukat is nearly as concerned about reconciling with Ziyal, who refuses to see him. The Cardassian leader sends Damar to get her to speak to him, but Damar is unable to convince the girl. When he tries to strong-arm Ziyal, Kira intervenes. The bad blood between her and Damar boils over, and she beats the Cardassian into unconsciousness. Later, Dukat receives an intelligence report that indicates the Federation fleet is heading for the station. He pulls Dominion troops from the front lines to meet Sisko's task force. Dukat is distracted when a bruised Damar asks permission to arrest the major. But Dukat demands to know what Damar did to Ziyal that would warrant such violent retribution from Kira.

Odo has a disquieting conversation with the female shape-shifter, who suggests that the solids need to be broken of their desire for freedom. Troubled, Odo seeks out Kira. He attempts to explain his recent behavior, but Kira lets Odo know that his apology doesn't even begin to bridge the schism that's developed between them.

In space, Sisko's troops suddenly find themselves facing a wall of more than twelve hundred enemy ships. Sisko orders the much smaller group of Starfleet vessels to assume attack formation, and then, noting that "fortune favors the bold," he tells them to move forward.

SACRIFICE OF ANGELS
Episode #530
WRITTEN BY IRA STEVEN BEHR & HANS BEIMLER
DIRECTED BY ALLAN KROEKER

GUEST CAST	
Garak	ANDREW J. ROBINSON
Weyoun	JEFFREY COMBS
Gul Dukat	MARC ALAIMO
Rom	MAX GRODÉNCHIK
Nog	ARON EISENBERG
Martok	J.G. HERTZLER
Tora Ziyal	MELANIE SMITH
Damar	CASEY BIGGS
Leeta	CHASE MASTERSON
Cardassian Officer	DARIN COOPER

AND	
Female Shape-shifter	SALOME JENS

STARDATE UNKNOWN

Sisko and the *Defiant*, along with some six hundred other Starfleet vessels, face a Dominion force that's twice their size, standing between them and retaking Deep Space 9 ("Favor the Bold"). The captain orders the fleet's attack fighters to concentrate their fire on the Cardassian vessels, in the hopes that they will break formation and chase after them, opening a hole in their lines. On the station, Dukat observes the strategy and announces his intention to give Sisko his opening—and then close it on him. Meanwhile, Damar is concerned that Rom's associates—Leeta, Jake, and Kira—may try to sabotage the station to prevent the destruction of the minefield, so Dukat gives Damar permission to hold them "for questioning." Damar is also worried that Ziyal's friendship

The *Defiant* runs the gauntlet back to Deep Space 9. ROBBIE ROBINSON

with Kira may negatively influence her loyalty to Cardassia, but Dukat will not hear of any attempts to abrogate his daughter's freedom.

Out on the battlefield, Sisko's crew notes that the captain's plan seems to have worked; two squadrons of Cardassians have broken formation, leaving an opening. Sisko suspects it's a trap, but he has no choice. He leads a small group through the Dominion lines.

On the station, the female Founder tells Odo that the battle against the Federation is going well. Noting that he doesn't seem pleased with the news, she reminds Odo that his former friends are, after all, only solids—certainly no match for the Link. But Odo remains unconvinced, and the Founder suspects that it's because he still has feelings for Kira. But the major doesn't deserve his loyalty, she points out; in fact, she's been arrested and will soon be sentenced to death. Odo is stunned by the revelation.

The space battle is intense, and soon the *Defiant* is the only ship moving through the lines. Three Jem'Hadar vessels lock onto the ship and just as it seems they're about to destroy her, Klingon reinforcements arrive and clear a path for Sisko. On the station monitors, Damar notes that the *Defiant* has broken through their lines and is heading straight for them. Weyoun and he want to send ships to stop it, but Dukat tells them to leave the *Defiant* alone. Sisko is no match for the station, he says. If the captain wants to commit suicide, let him.

Down in Security, Quark and Ziyal mount a bold prison break to rescue their friends. Weyoun informs the Founder and Odo that Kira's group has escaped,

and the Founder heads for Ops. However, Odo chooses to stay behind, and a short time later he rescues Kira and Rom from Jem'Hadar troops. While Odo sidetracks additional Dominion personnel, Kira and Rom attempt to shut down the power to the station's weapons array, hoping this will prevent Dukat from detonating the minefield. Unfortunately, Rom completes the job a second too late, and the mines are destroyed.

Knowing that thousands of Dominion reinforcements are about to come through the wormhole from the Gamma Quadrant, Sisko orders the *Defiant* to enter the wormhole. As the crew awaits certain destruction, Sisko finds himself transported to the realm of the Prophets. They inform Sisko that he cannot be allowed to end his corporeal existence, that the game must not end. Sisko refuses to allow them to save him. Instead, he demands that *they* save Bajor from the onslaught that is about to arrive. After all, he challenges, haven't they claimed to be "of Bajor"? The wormhole aliens admit that they are indeed of Bajor, but Sisko's attempt to control "the game" must be penalized. They inform him that he, too, is of Bajor, and he will find no rest there.

Before he can ask what they mean, Sisko finds himself back on the *Defiant*, awaiting the attacking Dominion fleet. He tells his crew to prepare to fire . . . but suddenly, there's nothing to fire at. The enemy ships have vanished.

Dukat is shocked when he sees the *Defiant* emerge from the wormhole—alone. But there's no time to figure out what's happened. The *Defiant* is firing on the station, and thanks to Rom, the station's weapons are off-line. What's more, some two hundred Federation ships are headed their way. The female Founder decides to evacuate the station and orders her troops to fall back to Cardassian space. Damar urges Dukat to evacuate with the others, but Dukat, stunned by the sudden turnabout in his fate, refuses to leave without Ziyal. He wanders through the deserted station, finding his daughter in the habitat ring. Ziyal tells her father that she won't go with him and leave her friends. In fact, *she* helped Kira and the others escape, thus helping to bring about his downfall. Yet she still loves him.

Dukat moves forward to embrace Ziyal; he can't hate her. But before he reaches Ziyal, a phaser blast kills her. Damar has executed Ziyal for her traitorous behavior, yet he still wants to save Dukat. Devastated, Dukat remains with the body of his daughter, and Damar escapes.

Sisko and his crew retake the station and rejoice over their victory and their reunion with family and friends. For Garak, there is little joy in returning to the station once he learns of Ziyal's death. Dukat, convinced that Ziyal is still alive, barely notices when he's captured. He returns Sisko's baseball and allows himself to be led away, noting in passing that he forgives the captain as he forgives his daughter.

THE FIRST SIX EPISODES

Building a Story Arc—The Concept

"This was big," says Hans Beimler, "a really big thing for us. Because even though we had done some strange things over the course of the show, we never had attempted a six-episode arc. In the history of *Star Trek,* it never had been done. None of us came from series where you did that, so it was a new experience for all of us, and there was a learning curve. But it showed us the possibilities and the excitement that could be garnered, and in the end, we liked it so much that we decided to do the ten-episode arc at the end of the series."

"The initial thinking was that we would end Season 5 on a cliff-hanger with the Federation plunged into war, and then we would come back and do a multi-episode arc," Ron Moore explains. "And

The writers crafted the relationship between Dukat and Weyoun as one of equals. ROBBIE ROBINSON

the war would last that long. Of course, later on we decided that we'd get the station back by the end of the last episode in the arc, and then we'd see how long the war ran after that."

"The initial hill that we had to climb was how many episodes would be required in order to tell this particular story," states Ira Behr. "It started out as four, then I said, 'Well, we need five,' and then I went back and said, 'You know, to really make this work, we're going to need six.' The truth is, we easily could have done ten, but I think that six was okay. There was some hesitation over whether it was a valid direction for us to take, about whether we were pushing the envelope a little too far. But ultimately everyone agreed that it was tremendously successful, and one of the best things the show ever did."

Behr and his staff were nothing if not ambitious. The six-episode arc was not only a challenge to dramatic tradition, but also to the very nature of the traditional *DS9* writing process. "It changed the dynamics of the way we work and it changed the kind of involvement that everybody had," asserts Beimler. "Because René [Echevarria] or Ron would go away to work on an episode, and discover something in the writing process that was going to change everybody *else's* script. One of them would be coming back all the time, saying, 'You know what, guys? We need to rethink.' And then we'd call in all the troops and rethink the storyline."

"It was very hard," confirms Echevarria. "It was very tricky. We made some mistakes along the way. Everyone was working at the same time, and it was 'No, no—*you're* supposed to be doing that B-story, but wait a minute, this isn't established yet.'"

"The *breaking* of the stories was not that difficult," Behr observes. "The *writing* of the scripts seemed to be *very* difficult. I mean, Hans and I had it fairly easy. We did episode one, which was easy to follow through on from 'A Call to Arms' at the end of Season 5, and then we did the final two episodes of the arc, 'Favor the Bold' and 'Sacrifice of Angels.' It was the episodes in between that caused a lot of problems. The guys were coming in saying, 'What are you writing?' 'Are we gonna do this?' 'Where's Kira at right now?' 'What's Odo doing?' There were a lot of phone calls, a lot of running into each other's offices, a lot of 'Should this go before this?' and 'Wait a second—does this track?' The fact is, the show isn't geared to work like that. But here we were and we hadn't set anything up to help the process along, so we really had to stumble through it."

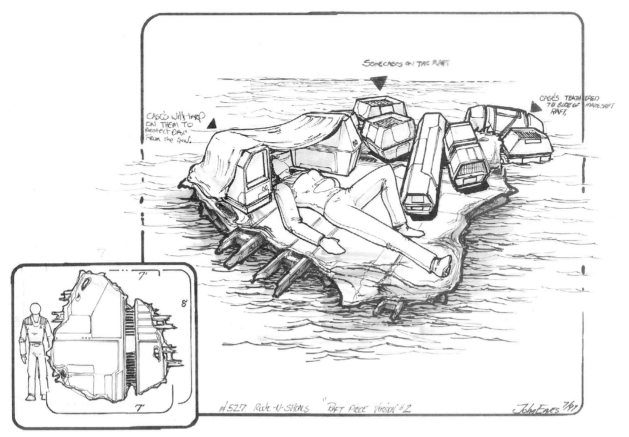

Dax's raft, "made" out of a piece of the crashed Jem'Hadar ship. JOHN EAVES

By the time the actors received the scripts, of course, most of those problems had been squared away. But if the writers had found it difficult to keep the myriad plot threads of the episodes separate in their minds, the actors found it twice as hard. To most of them, the arc itself was just one big episode. "For the most part, I honestly can't remember which one was which," admits Nana Visitor. "But the fact that we were going to have an arc, that a section of the season was going to be one piece, was actually pretty interesting to me. Particularly Kira's role, heading up the station. It was an interesting position for her to be in. Kira's maturity had to kick in, because she couldn't just react the way the younger Kira would. There was too much at stake. There was too much to lose. So even though it wasn't as much fun to play, I found that it was an important growth point."

Armin Shimerman, too, relished the opportunity for growth that the arc provided—even though he's not exactly sure which episode spawned that opportunity. "I don't know which part of the arc it was in," Shimerman says with a shrug, "but they gave me a

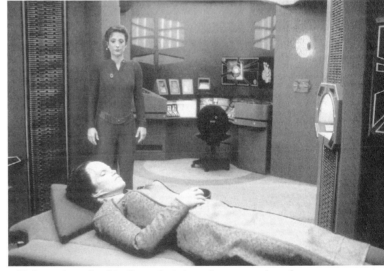

Kira's reaction to her friend's murder is in stark contrast to how she would have reacted six years earlier. ROBBIE ROBINSON

speech for which I am very grateful. Quark says, 'You know, this occupation isn't all that bad.'" The Ferengi was contrasting it, Shimerman reflects, to the previous Cardassian Occupation, in which "there was slave labor and the people were treated like animals. But he soon learns that although things may appear to be good under Dominion rule and life is pretty good, they still don't have liberty, and you've got to fight for it. Quark was one of those deluded people who thought, 'This is fine—we all get to do what we want to do,' and didn't realize that liberty was more important than creature comforts. But he *learns*, and I was very appreciative for that aspect of the arc. Like any Everyman character in literature, Quark has to go through some turmoil before he realizes the truth."

Other actors were a bit uncertain about the direction in which the arc seemed to be taking them. "When we started the arc, it was one of the few times that I have ever called the writers to try and get a sense of where it was going," recalls Rene Auberjonois. "I didn't mind the fact that Odo was going to 'the dark side'—I thought it was interesting that they were doing that—but I felt I needed a little information about where it was headed and how it was going to resolve itself."

Filling the Canvas—The Writing

The writers thought they had a pretty good idea of where they were going after the initial break sessions. "We wanted to do one show about the war, so we all sat and watched *None But the Brave,* the 1965 Frank Sinatra movie," Behr recalls. The film, which deals with the interactions of the crew of a downed American plane and a Japanese army patrol during World War II, bears "certain similarities," he allows, to the team's planned ground war episode, "Rocks and Shoals." Beyond that, he says, "we knew that 'Favor the Bold' and what became 'Sacrifice of Angels' were going to be the big broad-canvas shows. And we knew that we wanted to do 'Behind the Lines,' which would be a show about being on the occupied station."

"Sons and Daughters" had a strong A-story concerning Klingons. As such, it was the closest thing to a stand-alone episode in the batch. And "A Time to Stand," as Behr noted earlier, had the advantage of being a sequel, of sorts, to the previous season's finale. Plus, it had the Jem'Hadar vessel from "The Ship" providing the producers with the extra bonus of a ready-made model and set.

"When I'd bought the pitch for 'The Ship,'" relates Beimler, "from the get-go, Ira and I could see the possibilities, that it would be something we could use for other episodes."

Ironic that a Klingon story focused on family relationships rather than war. ROBBIE ROBINSON

"It seemed like a cool idea to use it here," Behr observes. "There's always something nice about stories that deal with characters sneaking behind enemy lines in an enemy ship, and to show them learning the ins and outs of piloting and steering an enemy craft."

As the season starter, much of the focus of the first episode was on crowd-pleasing themes of action and suspense. Nevertheless, Behr and Beimler made sure that the human heart also received its due. "We knew that going into the war would make it easy for us to fall into the 'hero' trap, where you concentrate on *Star Wars*–type heroic space battles and stuff like that," Behr says thoughtfully. "But we really wanted to keep the *human* aspect of the pain of war. So we included a human moment: the concerned father talking to his son." In this case, that meant Joseph Sisko relating to son Benjamin, rather than the more traditional dynamic between Ben and Jake. The writers also took time to show viewers a warm moment between Worf and Dax, to remind them that a wedding between the pair, hastily promised in "A Call to Arms," had not been mere lip service, although Behr admits that there was a bit of an ulterior motive there.

"We knew that there was going to be a certain letdown after the sixth episode," he says. "How could we top it? We decided that the only thing we could put in immediately after the arc was the wedding. So we were letting the viewers know, 'Hey, there'll still be stuff going on later on.'"

One more heartfelt touch was the episode's dedication to Brandon Tartikoff, the recently deceased

A promise there would be a wedding, soon. ROBBIE ROBINSON

television executive who'd been in charge of Paramount at the time *Deep Space Nine* was being developed. "I think everyone felt that he was a strong force for good in the TV business," says Behr, "so a tip of the hat was warranted."

"Sons and Daughters" was the second episode to go into production, although its storyline actually *followed* that of the third episode, "Rocks and Shoals." "We shot 'Rocks and Shoals' third for production reasons," explains Ron Moore. "We wanted to go out on location for it, and it just worked out better in the schedule for us to shoot it third but air it second."

Predictably, this played hell with the already nerve-wracking writing process. "In a way, it made it easier for me," chuckles Moore, who penned "Rocks and Shoals," "but harder for Brad Thompson and David Weddle [who wrote the script for "Sons and Daughters"]. I had more time. But it complicated things for me too, because the station storyline on 'Sons and Daughters' changed while *they* were doing it, which meant that my station-based storyline had to reflect that change.

"By the time they got around to shooting 'Rocks

and Shoals,' René [Echevarria] was working on the next episode, 'Behind the Lines,' and that's where we *all* got really confused," adds Moore. We couldn't keep it straight in our heads, and we kept stepping on each other. Had something already happened, or was it happening the following week? It became very difficult to get the whole thing under control."

"It *was* difficult," says Weddle, "because [prior to Season 6] Brad and I had been working as freelancers, doing stand-alone scripts. And suddenly we were trying to adapt to being on staff, and at the same time creating a show that was going to have runners to the other five episodes, and trying to make sure the continuity works and that the characters are in the right place emotionally. Everyone else was doing that, too, but they were more experienced than us."

But confused or not, Weddle and Thompson plunged into the writing wholeheartedly. Both Weddle and Thompson recall sitting at lunch with the rest of the writing staff and being asked, essentially, if they wanted to take a crack at writing *The Guns of Navarone* or *Rio Grande*.

"At the time," explains Thompson, "show number five—'Favor the Bold'—was about a mission to blow up another ketracel-white facility [*The Guns of Navarone* was about a mission behind the lines to destroy German guns]. Ira offered us the choice of doing that or a father/son show about Worf and Alexander that we likened to *Rio Grande*, where the commander of a fort discovers that one of his new recruits is the son he hasn't seen since he got divorced from the boy's mother. Since both Brad and I have some issues with fathers and sons," he laughs, "we decided to do that one, which became 'Sons and Daughters.' And then *Guns of Navarone* never happened, since we blew up the white in the first show and figured, why do it again?"

So Weddle and Thompson were given the task of reintroducing Alexander (last seen in *TNG's* "Firstborn") to *Star Trek* audiences. Alexander had previously experienced an amazing growth spurt between his introduction as a toddler in *TNG* Season 4's "Reunion" and his return as a child who looked much closer to seven or eight in *TNG* Season 5's "New Ground," but here the writers had to bring him all the way up to fighting age—presumably at least eighteen.

"Yeah, he did grow up awfully fast," says Thompson. "We took a little dramatic license and said, 'We really have no idea how quickly Klingons grow up, so let's push him to maturity.'"

Concept for the ketracel-white facility. JOHN EAVES

"Yeah, yeah, we had all those boring discussions about his age," Ira Behr acknowledges wearily. But the bottom line, he says, was that "Klingons are not humans, and our human failings and limitations need not always be pressed on other aliens."

Other considerations also were factored into the decision about setting Alexander's age. "The role demanded a lot of time on the set," says Co-supervising Producer Steve Oster. "And the amount of time you have with a minor is very restrictive. Add to that the fact that Klingon actors need to go through three hours of makeup in the morning, and suddenly you have very little time with your actor. So his age was important. Also, we kept in mind the fact that if the actor was too young, Worf would seem too harsh. He'd come off like an abusive father, rather than a father who wants the best for his son."

Filling in the gaps in Worf's relationship with his estranged son was intriguing for the writers. "We all thought that the idea of Worf the failure as a parent, the guilty father who isn't comfortable with his own child, was a very painful subject," observes Behr. "And anytime we can take Worf into an emotional area is worth doing, and setting it against the background of war worked nicely."

"Alexander was a Klingon, all right, but he sure wasn't what Worf would have asked for in a son," adds Thompson. "And we enjoyed playing against expectations. We didn't end it with 'Well, I showed my dad that I'm a great warrior,' but we did have him show his dad that he has guts."

Although Alexander would return a few episodes later in "You Are Cordially Invited," the writers didn't anticipate needing him beyond that. "The relationship between him and Worf was more or less resolved by the end of 'Sons and Daughters,'" observes Thompson. "We would have had to come up with a very compelling reason to bring him back, because the dynamics were resolved."

For the distaff component of the titular characters, however, it was a different story. "At the point we were working on 'Sons and Daughters,' we suspected that we were going to kill Ziyal," says Behr. "When we talked about the arc, we knew that there was going to have to be a price to be paid. And then we went through all the names. Were we going to kill Nog? Were we going to kill Garak? What would be the emotional cost if a character was killed? And then it occurred to us that the strangest thing would be to kill the *villain's* daughter. So we set out in this arc to

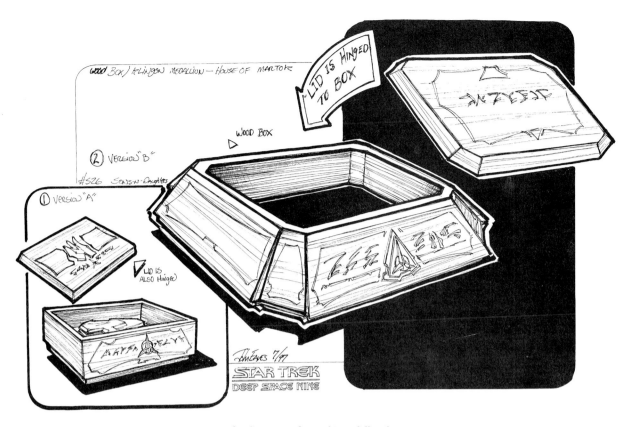

A starting point for the House of Martok's medallion box. JOHN EAVES

make her the pure innocent, to make the audience invest emotion into that innocence."

"We had to get her to a point where it would matter to the audience besides mattering to Dukat," adds Weddle. "So we began to work with Ziyal, to try to make her a better puppy, as it were," the idea being, of course, that the surest way to trigger an audience's emotions is to threaten a puppy.

Third up, but second aired, was "Rocks and Shoals," a title that Moore explains is a slang term for British military justice—although that isn't why he chose it. "It's just a phrase I've always liked," he says. "The specific in this episode was my feeling that some of the characters had run onto the rocks and others were just in shoal water. That's all."

The episode had more than its share of action, which Moore initiated right in the teaser, where he wasted no time at all getting Sisko and company in deep trouble with the Jem'Hadar. "The last time we saw them ['A Time to Stand'], they were stranded and didn't have warp drive," he says. "I made a choice here to just cut to the chase and put them on the run. I didn't see the need to connect the dots of how we got from there to here."

But danger doesn't preclude humor; Moore

Dukat, *Deep Space Nine*'s personification of evil, is undone by his love for his child. DANNY FELD

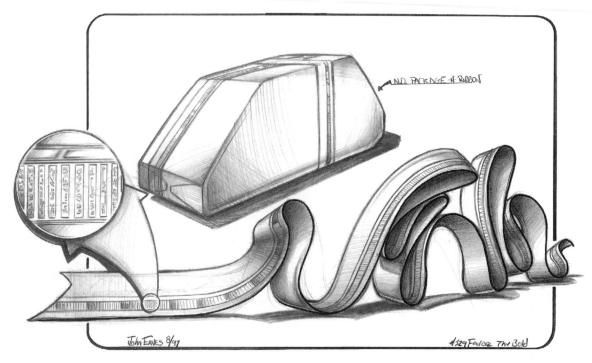

Jake sends a message to his father via a ribbon wrapped around a present for Morn's mother. JOHN EAVES

inserted light moments, such as Nog's emulation of O'Brien's cursing during the heat of battle. "I was trying to play the grace under pressure moments," he relates. "Humor, to me, comes out in most moments of stress. And yeah, it's a dangerous situation, but that doesn't mean you can't put in little witticisms or humanizing character moments. One of my favorite moments is when O'Brien tears his pants. It's just the absurdity of the whole thing, after all that's gone on, you tear your pants and that's what you're upset about. But it's such a human thing to do."

Back on the station, Moore was leading Kira into some dark territory. "I wanted her to have to face that she was becoming a collaborator without realizing it, and how easily that can happen to somebody in that position. She's got Jake asking her very pointed, very legitimate questions about what they're doing, and her getting furious about it, but at the same time allowing things to happen on the station. I knew it would take a fairly dramatic moment to kind of wake her up about what she was doing." Hence, the dramatic suicide of Vedek Yassim, an act of civil disobedience that Behr likens to those of the Buddhist monks who set themselves on fire decades ago to protest the war in Southeast Asia.

By all accounts, the fourth episode in the arc, "Behind the Lines" (originally titled "Life During Wartime"), was the toughest one to write, and the one that went through the most changes. "Poor René," says Behr. "He was really behind the eight ball on that one, going around to each of us, asking 'What are you doing?' 'What are you doing?' 'What are you doing?' He was suffering, and it was a very painful experience, but ultimately the show worked. It's amazing that it turned out as good as it did because usually when shows have that painful a birth, they usually show it on-screen."

"It was probably the hardest show I ever wrote," confirms Echevarria. "The most grueling birth I've ever been through. I don't know if it's because it was part four, but that was part of it."

Key story points would go through drastic changes before filming began. "The original concept," Echevarria relates, "was that Odo would become so invested in his relationship with the female Founder, and that this Founder instinct he's always had, the innate need for order, would become so pronounced that he would try to actively put a stop to the distasteful chaos that humanoids cause. He actively arrests Rom in this version."

The other storyline came to *DS9* by way of a movie from the 1930s called *Dawn Patrol,* in which a tough commanding officer is forced to send green aerial recruits into battle. Says Echevarria, "Sisko gets promoted, but that means suddenly he's not the guy out there flying the missions. He's the guy who has to

Handwritten on image: this is to be the size of a coke can

BURNT OUT PHASER CONDUIT

#528 "BEHIND THE LINES"

John Eaves 7/97

STAR TREK DEEP SPACE NINE

Possible design for a depleted phaser conduit. JOHN EAVES

send them out on the missions. And they're telling him, 'We can't do it, it's crazy, we tried,' and he keeps sending them back to the same target. And it's tearing him up inside."

Initially, Echevarria recalls, he thought things were going swimmingly. "I had more time than usual, so I turned in a first draft a good two weeks before prep, and got the other writers' notes and polished it. I thought I was done, and then, to my utter horror, Ira says, 'This doesn't work for me at all.' I couldn't believe it! It was the second draft! And he was telling me it didn't work?"

The Sisko storyline, at that point representing about a quarter of the script, was too short. "It should have been a two-hour movie, not the B-story of one episode," admits Echevarria.

"We liked the idea, but we only had six episodes to play with," comments Behr. "If we'd had a seventh . . ."

"It couldn't be delivered in the page count we had," Echevarria continues. "So we came up with a new B-story to fit into those twelve or fifteen pages. This was about Dax getting command of the *Defiant* and realizing how much she loves the fighting. She comes back after the mission and confesses to Sisko, 'And I liked it. I *liked* it.'"

"It stirs her in some way because she's in com-mand of this ship at a time of war," explains Moore, "touching on all these experiences that the symbiont's had over the years. She gets into it too far and becomes Patton."

But that, too, wasn't to be. "I could never feel it in my heart," says Echevarria. "I tried to execute it, but we couldn't spend much on the B-story, so we wouldn't have even been able to show her fighting the war. It was all sort of off-screen.

"So we reinvented it yet again, making it a much smaller, quieter little story, where you're just asked to put yourself into Sisko's shoes and see how hard it must be for him to have to sit back and send his friends to war."

For all that *Sturm ünd Drang* over the B-story, the main problem with the script was actually with the Odo story. "Ira told me that he didn't buy it, that I hadn't built to it, and that Odo wouldn't do this yet," Echevarria remembers. The irony was that Echevarria had never quite bought into the premise either. "I had never believed that Odo would get to that place. I think I was even resistant to the idea during the break session. I could never see this innate need he had for order as a character trait. I didn't *feel* it."

Echevarria confessed to Behr that he was stumped. He didn't know how to get the changeling to the point where he would betray his friends, and there was very little time to figure it out. "We were in *prep,*" says Echevarria, which meant it was only a matter of days before the cameras would begin rolling.

Then Echevarria had an odd thought—but at this point, any thought was worth voicing. "I told Ira, 'The only way I could buy it is if Odo's behavior was a sin of omission, not a sin of *commission.*'"

Echevarria smiles. "The old Catholic maxim," he explains. "A sin of omission. Out of Odo's carelessness and his obsession with the female shape-shifter, he doesn't deliver on what he's supposed to do. And when he's confronted with it, he realizes that he really doesn't care that much. It doesn't seem important.

"And Ira looked at me and said, 'I buy that.' So I sat down and very quickly began to rewrite." He sighs. "That's the thing. I always try to get back in and start the scene fresh and make it more than just 'TV.' You've got to get back in the saddle and deliver."

Behr tends to think of "Favor the Bold" and "Sacrifice of Angels," written by Hans Beimler and him, as a two-parter, even though they're also parts five and six of the arc. The two scripts are difficult for him to separate, which is understandable, considering the fact that "Favor the Bold" was once scheduled to be the *last* of only five interconnected episodes.

"When we did the break session for the arc, it was the last one," Thompson reveals. "On the beat board, we had each of the episode titles listed, like milestones. And under 'Favor the Bold,' it said, 'We retake the station.' And then suddenly it turned into, 'We can't get all of this done in one show.'"

So suddenly Behr and Beimler were writing one hundred twenty pages, rather than sixty—not an easy thing, by any means, particularly not in a short period of time. "It changes your life," intones Beimler. "The physical toll is really hard. You become exhausted. It's like writing a screenplay in three or four weeks. But it does help when you're doing it with someone else."

But surely the process became easier as they were reaching the home stretch of the arc?

"Definitely not," states Behr. He chuckles as a memory surfaces. "Actually, the story document for the last part got distributed with a typo on it. It was 'Sacrifice of *Angles,*' which is a title that I loved. I don't know what the hell it means, but somehow, that's the way I'll always think of the episode."

Because everything is so twisted around?

"Yeah!" he says enthusiastically. "You know?"

"Weyoun is like an artichoke," says Ira Behr. "All those layers of prickly leaves." ROBBIE ROBINSON

There was a lot of territory to cover in the two episodes: Odo's return from the dark side, Quark's heroism in the jail break, Ziyal's split from her father, her death, and a major space battle between Starfleet and the Founders. But it's the character nuances that seem to stick in the writers' minds.

Weyoun's desire to be able to carry a tune, for example.

"We have this *endless* fascination with Weyoun," Behr confesses. "We enjoy exploring the little facets of his character. There's a price to being Weyoun, just as there's a price to being a Jem'Hadar (not eating, sleeping, nor making love). The idea that so much of life is just out of his range of understanding—appreciating a painting, or whatever—is interesting to play. Plus the fact that I never know when Weyoun is telling the truth or when he's B S-ing you just to run a number on your head. I can't tell."

And if the executive producer doesn't know, no one does.

One character he *does* know is Dukat. By the end of "Sacrifice of Angels," some viewers might have been tempted to believe that the archvillain's love for his daughter was so great that her death drove him mad. But according to Behr and Beimler, he was already well on his way.

"Anyone who could be the head of the Occupation ain't all there," Behr declares. "Insanity, like genius, is the ability to keep two opposing points of view in your head at once. The difference between Dukat and someone like Sisko—it's one of the ultimate differences of this show . . ." He pauses thoughtfully, then starts again. "A healthy human being like Sisko knows himself. That doesn't mean he doesn't have limitations. It doesn't mean he doesn't make mistakes. But he knows himself. Dukat is a totally self-deluded person. He's a deeply, deeply screwed-up Cardassian who doesn't understand his own motives."

As for his relationship with Ziyal, Behr adds, "He loved Ziyal, but like the true sociopathic personality he is, he wasn't above using her, or lying to her."

Beimler wouldn't even go that far. "It's not that he really loves her," he says, passion in his voice. "He feels guilt about her. *Guilt!*" Beimler slaps the surface of his desk to emphasize the point. "He's a bad guy."

As for Sisko, he's a good guy, obviously, and he wins the day. But he has to argue with the gods to do it, and the gods tell him that he'll pay a price.

"It's the burden of what you take on," comments Beimler. "It's tragic hero stuff. A hero takes on things for others, but doesn't necessarily find any peace himself in the result."

Behr cites examples, both sacred and, well, cinematic if not profane. "Moses wasn't allowed to enter the Promised Land," he says. "And at the end of *The Searchers,* John Wayne's character restores the family unit, but he cannot enter the house. Everyone else enters the dark, comforting house, but he has to turn and walk back into the desert. Because there's no place for him there."

As for the resolution of the episode, Behr is incensed by suggestions that having the Prophets get rid of the Dominion ships was the ultimate cop-out. "I felt that it was the perfect next step in the evolution of the relationship between Sisko and the Prophets that began in the pilot," he says emphatically. "Hearing people refer to it as some dopey deus ex machina is really annoying, because I would think they'd give us more credit for being on the ball. We didn't *have* to end it like that, we *chose* to end it like that. Because we wanted to say that there was something going on here. And ultimately that would lead to our finding out that Sisko is part Prophet ['Image in the Sand']. They wouldn't have done this for just *anyone.* This was the man going out into the wilderness and demanding his God to interfere, to do *something,* for crying out loud. The corporeal characters had done so much in this episode; surely, they'd earned the help of the gods."

The revelation that Sisko was part Prophet was many months away, so Behr had to hope that the audience would give the writers the benefit of the doubt and have faith in the virtues of good writing.

Hitting Their Marks—Acting!

The arc gave all of the regular actors more than enough to keep them busy, and it gave most of the recurring characters juicy responsibilities as well. This was an opportunity for everyone to shine, and no one appreciated it more than Aron Eisenberg, who had once believed that Nog's ticket to Starfleet Academy would lead to a quick trip to the unemployment office for the actor.

"They started giving me all these responsibilities on the *Defiant,*" he says happily. "I thought it was so funny that the least experienced crewman was handling a ship that was full of the most experienced officers!"

Some of the established feature players in the series found that the arc brought their characters some interesting twists. Quark, for example, becomes a hero in "Sacrifice of Angels."

"He's a reluctant hero," observes Armin Shimerman. "It's not in his nature to do it, but his brother is very close to him, and sooner or later you have to take a stand. That's what oppression does to people. It forces them to become accidental heroes. I mean, it's easy for a Starfleet person to be a hero. It's what they do. But my character isn't bred for it; it's something he has to be educated to do, and it's much harder for him."

As tough as Quark is, Shimerman explains, he's

The fatal flaw—overreaching confidence will be the downfall of the Dominion–Cardassian alliance. ROBBIE ROBINSON

The most respected admiral in Starfleet—Barry Jenner joins the cast.
JERRY FITZGERALD

go through tissues," Beimler laughs. "Tissue after tissue had been discarded. We could never find the right person. They were either too strident or too difficult or too unbelievable. But when we found Barry, we knew we had found someone that we could develop and use on the show. He gave us the right attitude—that *admiral* attitude—that was really intelligent. He seemed like someone who could be Sisko's boss, although not his superior, obviously, because the show is about Sisko."

"He seemed like a good foil," concurs Echevarria. "Light and droll and all the things that we wanted an admiral to be."

Jenner was unaware of the kudos he was receiving behind the scenes. He was just happy to land the first episode. "At a casting session, you get one shot," he says. "So I just decided to play Ross as someone who was very straight, very military, but as I always do with a character, I tried to give him some sense of humanity. Because otherwise you're merely fulfilling a function, particularly on a show like this."

Jenner got his first hint that he'd be coming back from the series' lead actor. "I was standing outside and Avery Brooks came over and introduced himself and shook my hand. And he said, 'So you're going to be Admiral Ross.' And I said, 'No, I'm only here for today.' And he said, 'No, you're going to be around a lot. You'll be back, you'll be back.'"

Brooks was right. "After 'A Time to Stand,'" notes Behr, "we said, 'Hey, this guy's okay. We should give him another shot.' And then after we did one or two more with him, it suddenly dawned on us that Barry

never killed anyone. "That's why he's so shocked after he kills the two Jem'Hadar," he says. "Again, that's something that comes easy to Starfleet people with their phasers. But I didn't want it to be easy for Quark."

A host of new characters were introduced during the arc, and some of them were lucky enough to join the ever-growing repertoire of recurring actors. Barry Jenner, introduced in "A Time to Stand," would be called back again and again to play Admiral Ross. He was thrilled to be accepted as part of the family, but he had no idea that he was bucking a long-entrenched *Star Trek* curse.

"Traditionally, admirals in *Star Trek* have never come off very well," says Echevarria. "Most of them seem shifty or untrustworthy." Or, at best, a pain in the butt for the captain of the ship. This was often the case back in the era of the original series, and things didn't get any better in *TNG* or *DS9*.

"Finding an admiral for either show has usually been both a joke and a horror," states Behr. "Because what we basically get at casting sessions is either *gruff!* or bland. Gruff or bland."

"We went through admirals the way some people

"I was thrown into this not knowing what was going on," says Marc Worden. ROBBIE ROBINSON was a solid actor. He brings a *gravitas* to the role, and yet you can see there's a man behind the uniform. I think that Barry Jenner is one of the unsung heroes of the show, one of the pieces of the puzzle that might not be readily apparent to the audience. But he's part of the glue that makes our job easier."

Another newcomer to the show was Christopher Shea, who was cast as the Vorta Keevan for "Rocks and Shoals." "He came in to audition for a different role, a Romulan, and he wasn't right for that, but he had a certain look in his eyes that we noticed," recalls Steve Oster. "He's a wonderful man, but he could give you this very unsettled feeling just by looking at you. After we saw him, we all looked at each other and said, 'We need to bring him in as a Vorta!'"

Shea was cast as Keevan on his birthday, a happy coincidence for him. "I read the script and just loved it," notes Shea (who is *not* the actor who voiced Linus on the *Peanuts* specials). "It was a dynamite role, and so well written. It reminded me of Shakespeare in many ways. A lot of the actors on the show are classically trained, and the writers give you so much to work with."

Just as the captured Jem'Hadar vessel from "The Ship" made a return appearance in "Rocks and Shoals," Shea's captured Dominion representative would be back in "The Magnificent Ferengi." Unfortunately, both came to a sorry end, with the ship biting the dust—or rather the salt water—in "Rocks," and Keevan getting in the way of an errant phaser blast in "The Magnificent Ferengi."

Mark Worden, who won the opportunity to play Worf's estranged son Alexander, also appeared in two episodes: "Sons and Daughters" and "You Are Cordially Invited." Cast for the role at the last minute, Worden recalls much of his experience on the set as a blur—except for the Klingon makeup, of course. "The day after my call-back I was rushed in to do a fitting for my teeth. That was a *very* strange experience," he laughs. Although Worden found himself hurried onto the soundstage almost immediately after that ("the very next day," he says), he feels that the time spent in the makeup chair actually helped prepare him for the role psychologically. "It took about three hours," he says. "But what's great about it is that it allows you to just step on set already in character. So much work has already gone into creating the illusion of this being."

Phil Morris had experienced the same thing when he was cast as a Klingon in "Looking for *par'Mach* in All the Wrong Places," but he found that

"It was the hottest day in ten years," says Phil Morris. By the end of the day many Jem'Hadar extras were insensible from the heat.
ROBBIE ROBINSON

the Jem'Hadar he played in "Rocks and Shoals" was an entirely different animal. "Klingons are formally type-A personalities," he says with a grin. "That's how it was explained to me when I auditioned. They're macho. They talk about how bad they are. But the Jem'Hadar *are* the baddest boys in the bar, so they don't *need* to talk about it."

Although the Jem'Hadar are, indeed, the bad boys of *Deep Space Nine*, the writers periodically have introduced some honorable individuals: Goran'Agar ("Hippocratic Oath"), Omet'iklan ("To the Death"), Ixtana'Rax ("One Little Ship"), and Morris's ill-fated character, Remata'Klan. "I likened him to a samurai warrior who is loyal only to his feudal lord," says Morris, "and that's how I played him. The Jem'Hadar are predisposed to have that loyalty; it's bred into them by the Vorta." His willingness to die, despite Sisko's offer of an alternative, he says, "is Remata'Klan's most honorable moment."

Morris remains excited about his ties to *Star Trek*. The prosthetics, he admits, can sometimes be a pain, "but you know what?" he says. "I would do it again. I would do an episode of *Star Trek* tomorrow, because it is one of the greatest opportunities for an actor in television."

The opening arc also brought several recurring characters into major prominence.

Glinn Damar had been introduced in fourth season's "Return to Grace" for what actor Casey Biggs expected to be a short-term job opportunity. "My lines were, 'We're in range—fire,'" he jokes. "And now I'm the leader of the Cardassian Empire! I don't know how the hell the writers figure these things out, but it gave me a whole hell of a lot to do, and more interesting stuff, too."

"I knew Casey from his role as Travis in the IMAX movie about the Alamo," says Ira Behr with a smile. "So when he came in to read for Damar, I thought 'Oh, that's good.' He was right for Dukat's sidekick, and I just knew he was going to develop and that he could play someone a little more thuggish than a plain ornery Cardassian. Of course," he chuckles, "little did we know at the time that he was going to become the savior of Cardassia by the end of the series."

"I created the character of Damar in my teleplay for 'Return to Grace' because I wanted someone for Dukat to talk to," says Hans Beimler. "He was a minor character, but he developed, partly because Casey was such a good actor."

The writers decided to make Damar a drinker in the opening arc, a trait that would become even more pronounced the following season. "Like all well-developed characters, he has a flaw," Beimler explains. "It was Ira's idea to make Damar flawed. By this time, he's become a real bad guy, but he's drinking, and you want to know why. He's not drinking because he's an alcoholic. He's drinking because he has a conscience. There's something he doesn't want to deal with. He knows Dukat's deal with the Dominion is wrong, wrong, wrong. And so he's drinking."

"I think they liked the way I looked in Quark's bar," Biggs coments. "I had a couple of scenes with Armin in the bar, and I heard that the producers liked the way I played the scenes, so they just wrote the drinking in more and more."

Some of Damar's activities in the arc amazed Biggs. "When I read the script where I kill Dukat's daughter, I was really surprised. They could easily have killed my character off at that point, but they didn't. Then, the next time they called me in ['Statistical Probabilities'], I had this big speech to the Cardassian nation where I was talking about being their leader. I had no idea of that until I got the script."

Salome Jens, whose real face is unknown to many *Star Trek* viewers, was similarly uninformed about the course of her character, the female shape-

"She assumed his shape to find a way to get through to Odo," says Salome Jens. ROBBIE ROBINSON

shifter. Although she had played the unnamed Founder since Season 3 ("The Search," Part I), "I didn't know I was a villain until now!" she laughs. "I knew that she was a part of the Great Link, one of the many, although she seemed to assume responsibility for all of it. Even when there were other shape-shifters with her, she was the one leading the pack. So I knew that she, as I like to say, walks with a lot of power. But I didn't know that I was a bad guy."

Jens's surprise at her villainous nature may be due to the subtleties of the scripts for the episodes she's appeared in. There's a rational explanation for each of her actions, and Jens can understand why Odo would continue to trust a person who had "lied to you, tricked you, and sat in judgment of you," as Kira points out.

"I have a true sense of where my character has come from because I've learned all of her lines and they're inside of me, and I have established my own logic for them," explains Jens. "My character believes that the inhabitants of these other worlds are insane and that's not the way to live," she says. "She doesn't think of herself as bad. I don't think that she wants to purposely make people suffer. She gets angry at the people around Odo, at the stupidity of those people, and she's in the Alpha Quadrant primarily to bring Odo back into the fold."

In the six-episode arc, the female Founder resorts to Mata Hari tactics to win Odo's soul. "Odo is more important to her than winning the Alpha Quadrant," says Behr. The sexually suggestive nature of their links, however, isn't entirely deliberate. "We didn't quite see it as sexual at the beginning," he admits, "but now we get that it makes a certain amount of sense. I don't think that we write it that way, but that's how it plays."

"Those were love scenes," states LeVar Burton, director of "Behind the Lines." "Absolutely. Because she was seducing him. Straight up. Plain and simple."

"We've had many discussions about the Link," says Beimler. "It's not sexual in the way we know sexuality, although it may be sexual in the sense that something that is intimate is sexual," he offers.

"I think it has some kind of sexual implications," says Rene Auberjonois, "although in Season 7 when Odo links with Laas ['Chimera'] it sort of begs the question. But I think that it definitely is a very sensual experience. For Odo, it is absolutely the consummation of a kind of peace that he can't have."

"Ecstasy is ecstasy," shrugs Jens. "When they move into the Link, I think they are moving through the universe, they're moving into a free space. It's possible that men go immediately to the sex thing," she chuckles, "but my bent is that they're moving into oneness, into freedom, into the wind, into space."

In the Trenches—Behind the Scenes

With all of the storylines running through the first six episodes, it's ironic that the single most vivid memory anyone has of filming the arc is the temperature during the location shooting for "Rocks and Shoals."

Remember the old adage that "Everybody talks about the weather . . ."?

On location the sea looks more like an overgrown puddle; the ocean effects would be added in postproduction. ROBBIE ROBINSON

"Oh my God, it was *so* hot!" says Aron Eisenberg.

"I understand it was one hundred and eight degrees," notes Gary Hutzel.

"One hundred and twenty degrees at the bottom of the pit," conveys Laura Richarz.

"My whole crew was fainting," Jonathan West reports.

"It was just blistering, baking hot, and the makeup was melting on-camera," Ron Moore groans.

"Actually, the surface temperature outside the pit was one hundred and eighteen degrees," recalls Steve Oster. "Inside the pit was a hundred and twenty-eight. I have a pair of hiking boots that I bought specifically for that location. The rubber soles are burnt."

It's no wonder that Oster's first reaction when asked about the episode is, "Aaaaaaggghhh! The rock pit show!"

In other words, it was a typical *Deep Space Nine* location shoot.

"For several weeks, we looked for locations at an ocean shore," Oster relates, "but within easy reach of the studio, there was no location that would work for all the elements of the story. We needed a big wide-open battlefield situation, with a beach that would be safe for the actors to wash ashore on. And we needed a three-hundred-sixty-degree view. We finally ended up in a rock quarry north of L.A., in Sun Valley. It had the view and there was water in the bottom of it, a small lake, and we created the ocean optically, in postproduction.

"We were going to start shooting on a Monday, and when we did the final checks on Friday, it was eighty degrees and kind of breezy," he continues. "Then on Saturday, it went up to ninety-five degrees. Sunday, one hundred and five degrees. And then Monday . . ." He groans. "It was like an oven."

"Those guys suffered out there," sympathizes Behr. "Particularly the Jem'Hadar. The next time you watch it, look at their eyes. They're red from the sweat dripping into them from beneath their masks."

"It was almost unbearable," confirms Phil Morris. "The hottest sequence of days in ten years. And we're out there in prosthetics and neoprene, the same stuff that dive suits are made out of."

The production crew, which was suffering through the same conditions, did what they could. "They kept the vans standing by at all times," Morris says. "They were air-conditioned, and we could jump in them to cool down. And I remember there was this guy whose entire job while we were there was to stand over me with an umbrella between takes, and hand me water."

All went as well as can be expected, given the circumstances, until the crew ran out of light on the third day.

"From a cinematographer's point of view, location shooting is always problematic," observes Jonathan West. "Any time you go outside you lose a lot of control with your environment, because you're dealing with the sun and it's constantly moving."

"We hadn't shot the last scene in the script, where Worf shows up to pick up the crew on the Klingon ship, which is where they are in the start of the next episode ['Sons and Daughters'], says Oster. "But we didn't have enough light. There was no time to shoot it. So at that point, all I could do was tell the crew, 'Well, it is what it is. We'll have to figure it out with the writers later on.'"

Ron Moore picks up the story. "So the director, Mike Vejar, and the editor looked at the footage and told us, 'We don't think we need to go back and shoot that ending.' And our first response was, 'What do you mean? How do you end the show?' And then they showed us their cut of the episode, which ends on a close-up of Sisko's face as he looks out at Keevan and all the dead Jem'Hadar. And we realized that it was perfect. We didn't need another thing. And that's where the show ends. We figured the audience could fill in the blank between the two episodes and assume that O'Brien gets the communications system working. Even the Vorta know that Starfleet engineers can do just about anything. It wasn't too much of a stretch."

However, a line was added to the teaser of "Sons and Daughters," where Sisko thanks Martok for picking them up in the *Rotarran*. On the viewscreen in front of the two men is Starbase 375, first seen in "A Time to Stand." Astute viewers may have noticed that the station bears a distinct resemblance to the Regula I Space Laboratory from *The Wrath of Khan*. In fact, it is Regula I, with a few modifications. "All the lower tanks were removed, and it had been refurbished by Gary Hutzel and Tony Meininger," notes David Stipes, who shot the revitalized station for "Sons and Daughters."

"I had seen it in storage," says Hutzel. "We brought it back because it was such a cool model, a really beautiful miniature."

For "Sons and Daughters," Stipes notes that he "did a nice little reveal shot where the bird-of-prey whips past the camera and then heads toward the station. The station is kind of canted over because

"Klingons operate on an extreme level of behavior," observes J.G. Hertzler. ROBBIE ROBINSON

whenever possible I try to do these sort of odd angles, just to show that space isn't necessarily up and down."

One of the problems in shooting models is dealing with differences in scale. A bird-of-prey is supposed to be a fairly large ship, but in Stipes's episode, the three freighters that the *Rotarran* is escorting are supposed to be a lot larger. "The idea was that they were supposed to be huge and Martok's ship is tiny compared to them, so I was constantly playing with the concept of big to small. I also was trying to visually reinforce the kind of futility of what was going on. The *Rotarran* was out there all by itself with these ships, so I wanted to make it seem big and strong when it swoops by in the beginning of the shot and yet kind of insignificant by the time it meets up with the freighters."

The script called for the freighters to be Klingon vessels, but Stipes's team didn't have any models that would fit the bill. "We actually wound up using Cardassian freighters that were modified by Tony Meininger, which didn't seem all that implausible, considering all the fighting that had been going on between the Klingons and the Cardassians. We painted them Klingon colors, as if they were the prizes of war."

was to remind us of Sisko's presence," says Behr, even when Dukat was in command of the station.

"We see Dukat playing with the baseball all the time," says Beimler. "The ball is everything. The ball is the station, his job, his responsibility, the burden, command—everything. When Dukat is thinking about that, he's concentrating on the things that matter to Sisko. It's very important, considering the resolution of the arc, or the last sequence of 'Tears of the Prophets.'"

In the end, Dukat fails, and the baseball is returned to Sisko.

"It was a great moment," smiles Behr. "The baseball didn't work for him. There was no mojo in that baseball for Dukat."

As Dukat, Alaimo often fondled the baseball, as if his character thought the human's token would bring him luck. DANNY FELD

The space battles for the arc's final episode, "Sacrifice of Angels," were carefully researched. "We talked to Dan Curry, and Brad Thompson, who is a pilot, and to some war and military experts," notes Behr. "We wanted to do a different type of space battle, a more military one, with specific strategies."

The sequences called for by the writers were much too extensive for the visual effects team to rely on motion control photography. "The problem is that motion control is about shooting one ship at a time, one pass at a time," says Stipes. "There was just no way we could have done it. We just didn't have enough time or money. So we ended up having Digital Muse and Foundation Imaging do the 23 shots in CGI. Digital Muse was responsible for the first half, with the strafing runs and the orbital platforms, and Foundation did the second part, where the *Defiant* is breaking through the lines and being chased, and then the Klingons finally show up."

In the props department, Sisko's baseball may have been the item that was most likely to be needed on the set on any given day during the arc. "The ball

YOU ARE CORDIALLY INVITED

Episode #531

WRITTEN BY RONALD D. MOORE
DIRECTED BY DAVID LIVINGSTON

GUEST CAST

Martok	J.G. HERTZLER
Alexander Rozhenko	MARC WORDEN
Sirella	SHANNON COCHRAN
Leeta	CHASE MASTERSON
Nog	ARON EISENBERG
Rom	MAX GRODÉNCHIK
Lt. Manuele Atoa	SIDNEY LIUFAU

STARDATE 51247.5

A week after the triumphant return of Federation and Klingon forces to Deep Space 9 ("Sacrifice of Angels"), the mood remains celebratory, despite the fact that war continues to rage throughout the galaxy. The station now has been designated headquarters for the Alpha Quadrant's Ninth Fleet, and, following Sisko's recommendation, Martok has been named Supreme Commander of that fleet. Martok asks that Worf be allowed to continue to function as his principal intelligence officer, and Sisko agrees.

In Quark's bar, Worf and Dax enjoy drinks with the Klingon's son, Alexander ("Sons and Daughters"), who informs Worf that he's been transferred from the *Rotarran*. He'll be shipping out at the end of the week. Realizing that with the war on, it may be a long time before Worf and Alexander see one another again, Dax suggests that she and Worf get married immediately. The wedding will be held on the station, rather than on the Klingon homeworld as they'd

After swallowing her pride to win favor with Sirella, Jadzia is welcomed into the House of Martok. ROBBIE ROBINSON

planned, and Alexander will serve as *Tawi'Yan*—the Klingon equivalent of best man.

To prepare himself for the joining, Worf invites his closest male associates—Martok, Alexander, Sisko, Bashir, and O'Brien—to join him in *Kal'Hyah*, a ceremonial bachelor party that runs for four consecutive nights. In the meantime, Dax will be spending her time in a different Klingon ceremony, enduring the traditional evaluation by the mistress of her future husband's house. Since Worf is now a member of the House of Martok, the evaluation will be conducted by Sirella, wife of General Martok.

Dax doesn't anticipate any problems; as Curzon Dax, she was well-known and respected by most Klingons. But Sirella is a difficult woman to please, and she immediately lets Jadzia Dax know that a non-Klingon such as herself is unlikely to win her favor. Upon learning that Sirella is opposed to Worf's marriage with Jadzia, Worf asks Martok to intervene. But the general refuses to interfere in his wife's domain.

On the first night of the *Kal'Hyah*, Worf's acquaintances learn that a Klingon bachelor party bears no resemblance to a human one. The setting is a holosuite replica of a blisteringly hot cavern on Qo'noS. There's food—but the guests are not allowed to eat it. In fact, they're not allowed to eat anything at all until the wedding. And fasting is only the first of the six trials they'll be required to face over the next four nights. Yet to come are blood, pain, sacrifice, anguish, and death.

Dax's ceremony is equally taxing. No matter how well she performs the tasks Sirella assigns, they are never done correctly in the mistress's eyes. Sirella urges Dax to give up, noting that she never will be truly accepted as a member of a Klingon house. But Dax refuses, and manages to exact a little revenge on her taskmistress when her research discloses that, contrary to accepted belief, Sirella's ancestry includes no imperial blood; she is, in fact, descended from a concubine.

Deciding that she deserves some fun, Dax decides to throw *herself* a pre-wedding party, and this one is filled with drinking, debauchery, and Samoan fire dancing. The noisy party draws Odo's attention as the station's peacekeeper, but Kira assures him that the festivities have the authorization of the station's first officer—her. He's about to leave when Kira invites him in; the two have been avoiding each other since the Dominion cleared out, and Kira feels it's time they discussed what happened during the period the female Founder was on the station ("Behind the Lines"). The two of them spend the rest of the night talking in the only quiet place they can find—Dax's closet.

The party is in full swing when an uninvited guest shows up. It's Sirella, and she demands that Dax join her for yet another ritual. Dax refuses and orders Sirella to leave. Harsh words are exchanged, and Sirella attacks Dax. The Trill responds by decking her, and Sirella angrily declares Dax an enemy of her House.

The next morning, Worf informs Dax that Sirella has forbidden her to join the House of Martok. He asks her to go to Sirella and beg forgiveness, but Dax refuses to humiliate herself just so Worf can have a traditional ceremony. Stung by the thought that Jadzia doesn't take his culture seriously, Worf suggests that perhaps Sirella's right; there shouldn't be a wedding. Jadzia says that's fine with her.

Later, Martok convinces Worf that he's made a mistake. If he loves Jadzia, he should be with her. Worf apologizes to his *par'machkai*, but is shocked when she refuses to change her mind. Sisko goes to talk to his old friend, and Dax explains that there's no way the person who negotiated the Khitomer Accords with the Klingon Empire is going to beg for Sirella's forgiveness. Sisko reminds Jadzia that it was *Curzon* who negotiated the accords, and that she can't expect Sirella to treat her like Curzon. To Sirella, Jadzia is just a young woman who needs to prove her worth, and if that means getting down and kissing Sirella's boots in order to honor Klingon tradition, she ought to do it—assuming that she truly loves Worf.

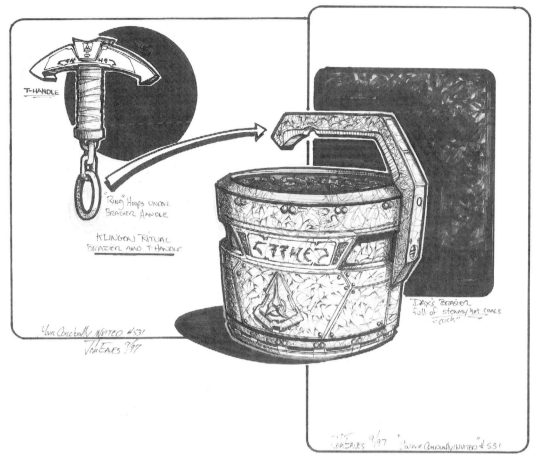

Labels within image:
T-HANDLE

"RING" HOOPS UNDER BRASIER HANDLE

KLINGON RITUAL BRAZIER AND T-HANDLE

DAX'S BRASIER full of steamy hot coals "ouch"

You are Cordially INVITED #531
John EAVES 9/97

John Eaves's design for the braziers that hold "steamy hot coals ouch."

A short time later, a traditional Klingon ceremony takes place in Quark's bar, with Sirella officiating. She recites the story of the Klingon heart, noting that when two such hearts beat together, no force can oppose them—not even her, she adds softly. The vows are completed, and Sirella welcomes Jadzia to the House of Martok as her daughter.

"I specifically tagged the wedding show as *mine*!" Ron Moore states enthusiastically. "On *The Next Generation*, I had tried to get us going in the direction where we could marry Worf and Troi." Following the "heaviness" of the war arc, Moore says, he found the opportunity to revisit that idea—with a change in bride—in "You Are Cordially Invited" (formerly known as "Once Upon a Wedding"). "We wanted to do a lighter show, and I thought that doing a big Klingon wedding would be a blast!" Moore grins.

"There was a reason for keeping the wedding episode light," expains Ira Behr. "We wanted to stay away from what I call 'The *Bonanza* Syndrome.' On *Bonanza* a guy would get married and at the end of the episode the woman would be killed so everything could revert to normal. Little Joe gets married, she's killed; Hoss falls in love, she's killed; Adam falls in love, she's killed; Ben falls in love, she's killed."

And that wasn't the only way the writers chose to upend viewers expectations. "I wanted Worf to be the one who's more obsessed with the wedding details and the wedding he's planned his whole life," says Moore, "kind of giving him the traditional female role."

Which, of course, left Jadzia with the traditionally male role. "That made sense for her," Moore observes. "She'd been through it before, so she would take more of a live-and-let-live approach to it. She could have a party with guys around and drinking and doing that whole routine before she got married. But Worf's bachelor party was not going to be a barrel of laughs. It was going to be *very* serious, and it was going to be this kind of trial by fire for the guys shanghaied into it."

The wedding also gave Moore the opportunity to correct an unfortunate impression of Klingon society that he himself had instigated years earlier. "I realized that by bringing Jadzia into the House of Martok, I could address the question, 'What's the role of women in Klingon society?'" Moore explains. "We'd seen them as warriors, but we had no idea if they would have some other role within the structure of the great houses.

"I'd inadvertently shoved Klingon women aside in some of the episodes I'd written, particularly on *TNG,* and looking back on it I didn't think that was a good decision," he continues. "Not letting women sit on the High Council was done for a specific reason way back in the 'Redemption' arc because I'd needed a plot device to make the story work. But the fallout from that was that the role of Klingon women got much smaller, and I hadn't intended to do that. It was a real disservice. So I figured that if men run the Council and rule the Houses, maybe women rule the social structure, and within that structure the mistress of a great House wields pretty much unchallenged power. Even Martok isn't gonna mess with his wife in her domain," Moore laughs.

"Martok is *such* a Klingon," Behr chuckles. "And the idea that this guy would be cowed by this woman was just great. I thought that Sirella was a *hoot!*"

And so did the actor who plays Martok, J. G. Hertzler. "Sirella and Martok were basically like Beatrice and Benedict, from *The Taming of the Shrew,*" Hertzler says. "When I heard that Shannon Cochran was going to play her, I said, 'Perfect!' because she has a Shakespearean background and I knew we could really feed that into the two characters' relationship."

Hertzler and Cochran had become friends when each played a role in the film version of *Treasure Island* that plays twenty-four hours a day at the Las Vegas hotel of that same name. "Anthony Zerbe is Long John Silver and I'm the pirate, Black Dog, and Shannon plays the mother of young Jim Hawkins," Hertzler says. "And when we shot it, Shannon and I really hit it off."

The Klingon wedding ceremony was to be held in Quark's bar, and that required decorating it in an appropriate manner. "The script said that there were vines and flowers hanging down all over Quark's," Laura Richarz says. "Now, when you think of vines and flowers you think of softness, but these are people who eat heart of *targ.* We'd never seen this particular side of them before. We had to think in a differ-

Jadzia's wedding gown from the House of Blackman. ROBBIE ROBINSON

ent way until we found an appropriate combination of vegetation."

Designing Worf and Jadzia's wedding clothes was equally challenging, but Bob Blackman ultimately fell back on a concept based on previous Klingon designs. "The wedding garb was my interpretation of the original Klingon clothing that Robert Fletcher designed for the *Star Trek* motion pictures [I-IV]," says Blackman. "And there was an element that had an Elizabethan doublet look to it." While most Klingon gear is black leather, that clearly wouldn't do for a big celebration like a wedding. White didn't seem right either, but one look at Jadzia in her stunning red leather trousseau should be enough to convince viewers that it was the only way to go.

While the wedding would seem to be the natural focus of the episode, ultimately the two bachelor parties took center stage. Moore's script gave the male side of the wedding party a series of challenges to overcome. "Fasting, blood, pain, sacrifice, anguish, and death!" Moore recites. "That was as many as I could come up with that sounded good."

Shooting the male party would have been as torturous for the actors as it was for the characters, if

Director David Livingston hadn't relented in some of his plans. "Originally I'd wanted to hang Sid [Alexander Siddig] and Colm [Meaney] off the ground for one long shot, where we'd see that their feet weren't touching anything, and then push the camera in slowly for the close-ups. But that would have forced them to be hanging up there for a real long time, and I couldn't do that to them."

But changing that shot didn't make the actors' work in the scene easier. "I had to get them as close to that fire pit as I could, because we wanted to take advantage of the interactive lighting," Livingston notes. "But that made it very hot for them, and it was very smoky. I don't think the actors liked working in those caves at all."

Jadzia's party, of course, was much more fun. But where on Earth did the idea of a Starfleet Samoan fire dancer come from?

"I had taken a vacation in Hawaii and Tahiti," admits Moore. "I have a fondness for Polynesian culture, and I thought it would be fun and different to bring some of that to her bachelor party. We're always doing alien claptrap that doesn't mean much to anybody, or else it's violins and clarinets, and I wanted something that spoke to another culture. A fire dancer just leapt to mind."

To establish that a Samoan fire dancer and drum band would be in the vicinity of the station, Moore opted to make them crew members on the *Starship Sutherland*, which briefly had been Data's ship in "Redemption, Pt. II." "We'd been talking for a while about making the *Sutherland* the 'party ship' of the fleet," Moore says. "Whenever the *Sutherland* pulled

into town, you'd know that it would be the wild ship. And once we'd seen the Samoan dancers, we were going to keep using it that way. I kind of regret that we never got around to following up on it."

But the *Sutherland* wasn't the only reference to elements of the wider *Star Trek* franchise that was discussed as the guest list was put in order. "We also talked about bringing the *Enterprise* crew in," Moore laughs. "I thought it would be kind of cool if we could convince the *TNG* guys to come in for a cameo. They could just stand in the room, wear the uniform, and smile. That would have been great, but there was no way that we were going to get the entire crew." And although LeVar Burton and Jonathan Frakes had offices on the Paramount lot at the time, the *DS9* producers decided against inviting only two members of the command crew. "It was all or nothing," Moore sighs.

Casting the fire dancer turned out to be easier than anyone had expected. Comments Steve Oster, "We put out a casting call, saying we needed someone of a specific physical type who could fire dance and who had to be a member of the Screen Actors Guild and had to be able to act. And we got twelve of them! It's a wacky business." Out of that dozen, the producers found one actor with the perfect combination of talents, and Sidney Liufau was cast as Lieutenant Atoa.

"Usually when you're filming a party scene, it's hard to get energy and vitality going," says Livingston, "but I felt that we pulled this one off successfully. There was a lot of energy. It wasn't just people standing around having cocktails."

To accomplish this, Livingston made some very atypical decisions. The standard way of filming scenes where music is playing is to have a prerecorded tape of the music start, then have the people begin their activities, dancing, conversations, etc., and then to cut the music while the background players continue to mime those activities. That allows the cameraman and the sound recorder to concentrate on the key actor's dialogue while the background still appears to be active. The music, of course, is then added during postproduction. But to make *this* party more lively, Livingston opted to have the drummers playing live—even during the dialogue. "I wanted them to play *loud*," Livingston notes. "That way I could have people talk *loud*. With that drumming in the background, they had to be more active, they had to deal with it. If I'd have had them stop playing, the people would have toned down their performances."

Livingston found another way to keep that energy up—by requesting an unrehearsed performance

The only way to film a great party is to *throw* one. The still photographs show that it *was* just as fun as it looked. ROBBIE ROBINSON

To his surprise and delight, Aron Eisenberg found he was the center of attention. ROBBIE ROBINSON

from a very surprised Aron Eisenberg. "I didn't have any lines that day, so I thought I'd just be mingling in the background," says Eisenberg. "All of a sudden David says, 'Okay, Aron, at the top of the scene Nog is going to be dancing.' My jaw dropped, and I went, '*What?*' He said, 'You're gonna lead the scene, so I need you to be dancing.' And I thought, 'Oh, my God, how the *hell* does Nog dance? He's a Ferengi, so I can't dance like Aron, but how do *Ferengi* dance?'"

"I just told him, 'Make it as goofy as you want and I'll tell you if it goes too far,'" Livingston laughs.

"I was really stressing out," Eisenberg continues, but inspiration struck as he began talking to Nana Visitor about it. "I said, 'You know what? I'm gonna do this!' And I put my hands out kind of like a cat, and I did a catlike growl: 'Gaaaaaggghhh.' Then I leaned forward and growled again, 'Ggggaaaaag-gghhhhh.' I jumped to the right and brought my arms in and shook my butt and then jumped to the left and shook my butt, and then I went 'Ggggaaah, gggaaahhhh.' I decided to call it the Ferengi Love Dance, because I was trying to win Nana over.

"And Nana just laughed and said, 'Yeah! Yeah! Do that!' She was great, because I looked like a freak and

she was acting like I was the most adorable thing in the world. So I did it for David and the rest of the crew and everybody was on the floor dying! I mean, the crew was *laughing*, and if you can make the crew laugh you know you're doing all right.

"And *then*," Eisenberg adds, "at the end of the scene Dax grabs me and does the dance with me. Well, that was never in the script. Terry Farrell just thought the dance was hysterical, so she joined in."

Not all of the actors felt as good about their character's actions in the episode. "Kira feels betrayed by Odo after what happened with the female shape-shifter," explains Rene Auberjonois. "But the resolution between the two of them was turned into a scene that never occurs on-screen. Kira and Odo go into a closet at the wedding party and when they come out of the closet the next morning, they've solved all their problems," he says, shaking his head unhappily.

Visitor concurs. "I would like to have heard what Kira and Odo were saying in that closet instead of it happening behind closed doors," she says. "I'd like to know how they resolved their problems."

"That was a bad mistake," Ira Behr confesses. "It's

a scene that I wish I could take back, because I'd definitely do something about that. It just did not work."

So how did something so important slip through the cracks? Ron Moore volunteers to clear up the facts. "It's one of those things that I've wanted to explain," he admits. "Here's what happened. We had originally planned that in this episode we were going to start having Odo lock himself away, refusing to mingle with anyone else on the station. The events of 'Behind the Lines' and 'Sacrifice of Angels' had really shaken him and made him wonder, 'What am I doing, where do I belong, look what I almost did.' So he was going to show up at the wedding and make an unexpected announcement. He would say, 'I've decided I can't be friends with any of you anymore, because clearly you can't trust me, so I need to go my own way. I'll do my job but that's it and that's all that's ever going to be.' And then he would walk out again. And the people there were going to go, 'Whoa, what does this mean?' Then we were going to play Odo completely different for the rest of the season.

"I was in the middle of writing the beginning of that arc, when Rene called Ira and Hans and me. He had some problems with that direction. It felt like we were going to alienate his character and we then wouldn't have a good place to take him after that. Where could you go once you took him in that direction? None of us had really looked down the line to where it would go. So Rene was right. It felt wrong to take him out of the mix and alienate him from everybody without a clear idea in our heads about why we were doing it. Finally the decision was made, 'Let's not do this.'

"So that all got pulled out," Moore says, "and I just had to find something to do with him, so I decided that clearly Kira and he had a lot to talk about based on the last couple of episodes. And I felt like, 'Just say that they've talked. Put them in the closet at a party, which *does* happen to people, and after they've talked until morning, somehow they've worked it out.' It's a total cheat and I know it's a cheat, but at least it was addressed in some way.

"I know Nana and Rene don't like it and some of the fans don't like it and I don't really like it," Moore says. "It's just one of those things that we had to do because we were out of time, and I felt that I had to do *something* so that it didn't seem as if we hadn't even touched on it. I felt like, 'well, at least here's a way to *imply* that they worked it out.'

"C'mon," Moore asks with a smile, "can't we all just get along and move on with the story?"

RESURRECTION

Episode #532

WRITTEN BY MICHAEL TAYLOR
DIRECTED BY LeVAR BURTON

GUEST CAST

Vedek Ossan   JOHN TOWEY
Bareil Antos   PHILIP ANGLIM
Security Guard   SCOTT STROZIER

STARDATE UNKNOWN

Like newlyweds the galaxy over, Dax is eager to share her domestic bliss by inviting friends to dinner with her and her husband. Kira graciously accepts the invitation, but she puts her foot down at Dax's suggestion that she bring a date, particularly when she hears Dax's candidates: transparent-skulled Captain Boday, three-eyed Dr. Trag'tok, or Odo. The first two don't appeal to Kira at all, while the thought of dating Odo is something for which neither of them is ready.

Kira discovers that the mirror image of Bareil is not the gentle man she knew. ROBBIE ROBINSON

Kira has barely had a chance to take a sip of her morning *raktajino,* when Ops becomes a flurry of activity. Although there are no ships within transporter range of the station, someone is attempting to beam aboard DS9. Suddenly, a crouched figure appears on the Ops transporter platform. When Kira moves forward to help the man, who seems to be injured, she finds herself facing his disruptor. But more shocking than the man's weapon is his face; he looks exactly like her dead lover, Vedek Bareil Antos.

The intruder takes Kira hostage and demands transportation. Sisko offers to provide him with a runabout in exchange for the safe return of the major. As kidnapper and hostage head for the runabout pad, the intruder reveals that he's from the mirror universe ("Shattered Mirror"), and that he's trying to escape from the Alliance, the powerful political coalition of Klingons and Cardassians that controls that region. When they reach the docking ring, Kira overpowers her captor, and Odo arrests him. The mirror Bareil tells Kira that he doesn't care how they choose to punish him, so long as they don't send him back. Kira asks Sisko to release Bareil and allow him to remain. Sisko complies, despite the fact that he thinks she's allowing herself to be influenced by her feelings.

A thief in his universe, Bareil finds it amusing when Kira reveals that his counterpart was a religious leader. Although he's never been inside a temple, Bareil joins her at services, hoping, he says, to gain a little spiritual guidance for his new life. During the ceremony, Kira points out the Orb of Prophecy and Change, and tells Bareil about the Prophets that her people worship. As they prepare to part, Kira impulsively invites Bareil to join her for dinner at Dax's and Worf's quarters. The evening is a resounding success, and Bareil ends up spending the night with Kira.

The next day, Kira encourages Bareil's exploration of Bajoran spirituality by arranging for him to be exposed to the powers of the Orb. He seems both moved and exhausted by the experience. Going to his quarters to rest, Bareil is surprised to discover the intendant—Kira's amoral counterpart from his own universe—waiting for him. The intendant kisses him and asks how their plan is going. Resisting her advances, Bareil admits that despite the fact that he wasn't expecting her to show up this early, everything is going smoothly.

The intendant is pleased, but she quickly picks up on the fact that Bareil has fallen for Major Kira. Bareil admits that he thinks Kira's wonderful, but

insists his feelings won't interfere with their scheme to steal the Orb and take it to their universe. Once there, they plan to use it to unite the Bajoran people in a war against the Alliance.

The next day, a troubled Bareil has a few drinks at Quark's. Later, Quark tells Kira that her new boyfriend seems "tormented," a description that surprises her. But she's even more surprised when Quark lets her know that Bareil appeared to be casing the Bajoran shrine.

That night, Bareil deactivates the security protocols surrounding the Orb chamber. But before he can take the sacred relic, Kira shows up to stop him. Seconds later, the intendant arrives, pointing a phaser at the startled major. Kira appeals to the decency that she believes is within Bareil; he may have come for the Orb, but his experiences here have shown him the truth about himself. He *can't* entrust the intendant with the Orb.

Kira's words touch Bareil, and he stuns the surprised intendant with a phaser. He tells the major that he'll return home with the intendant, and *without* the Orb. Then Bareil reveals what he saw during his Orb experience: Kira and him, together on Bajor, raising a family. But he feels his past ultimately would come between them; he's a thief and he belongs with the intendant, not Kira. The pair beam back to their own universe, leaving Kira to ponder Bareil's fate.

"I knew we were going to get smacked for *whatever* show we came up with after the war arc and the wedding episode ['You Are Cordially Invited']," says Ira Behr. "People were going to say, 'This is what you're doing next?' It's that feeling of letdown after you've done something big. It was bad timing, and it probably shouldn't have been a relationship show, but I felt we needed one for Kira. And actually, I think it was one of our better romantic shows."

For the male component of the ill-fated relationship, Behr decided to resurrect the dead, mirror-universe style. "I thought it would be interesting to see the mirror Bareil," Behr confirms, although he knows Nana Visitor felt that throwing Kira into the arms of her late lover was a little strange. "I think Nana was past the whole Bareil thing, but she did a great job, all the same."

It wasn't that Visitor disliked the character. It was *her* character's behavior that she disliked—specifically, Kira's rather impulsive decision to become romantically involved with a man she barely knew. "It both-

"All I had to do was add water and there she was," Visitor says of the persona she created for Kira. ROBBIE ROBINSON

ered me," Visitor admits. "But it's tricky stuff. If you love someone madly and lose him, and then you see his double, I think it's safe to say you'd be thinking, 'It's hard to resist this. I want it to be so. I want him to be like the other one. Maybe I'm delusional, but God, I just want to *feel* this for a moment.'"

To be fair, some scenes that were cut from the episode's teaser did set up Kira's desire to be reunited with shades from her past. Although viewers at home saw the episode begin with Dax and Kira in midconversation in one of the station's corridors, it originally started in Kira's quarters, which are filled with Ziyal's paintings. Dax observes that Kira still misses Ziyal, to which Kira responds, "I'll get over it. Death and I are old friends." To which Dax, ever the enemy of solemnity, replies, "Maybe *he* can be your date tomorrow night."

And, in a way, he was.

Although the end product of writer Michael Taylor's labors would be classified as a romance, it didn't start out that way. The overworked staff needed an extra hand to get started on an episode while

they were completing the season's complicated opening story arc and the wedding show that followed. Taylor's exact assignment, however, was left a little vague.

"The producers brought me out to California to write a military adventure that was sort of based on *The Guns of Navarone*," Taylor laughs. "But after I got here, that concept didn't seem to be that interesting to anyone. That's when we started talking about doing another mirror episode."

However, the mirror universe had been bypassed entirely during the seven-year run of *The Next Generation*. When LeVar Burton was asked to direct "Resurrection," it was, says the *TNG* actor, "My first exposure to the alternate universe."

Burton had little trouble finding his way, however, thanks, in part, to the producers' decision to keep the action at home for their fourth episode about the mirror universe. "We wanted to bring them to us," recalls Behr. "We thought that the next time we did it, whatever the story was, it would take place over here. It would give us a different spin on the whole thing."

The only aspect of the mirror universe that might have been a challenge for Burton—the scenes in which he directed Nana Visitor interacting with Nana Visitor—was actually old hat. "My very first episode as a director was 'Second Chances,' on *The Next Generation*," he notes. "That was with Riker and Riker. It was a really intense first episode to be assigned, and it completely and totally immersed me in visual effects photography. It took enormous planning and preparation, but I walked out of that experience knowing that, 'Hey, I really can do this.'"

For "Resurrection," Burton chose to use a computer-controlled camera to capture Kira's scenes with the intendant. First Visitor went through her cues as Kira while the computer memorized each pan and tilt called for by the director. Then, as the camera went through an identical set of moves, Visitor performed as the intendant, tailoring her perfomance to accommodate the established setup.

"She had to hit each of her marks at a specific time," says Jonathan West. "She was great."

Although the station's Bajoran temple had been seen before, with so much of the plot centering on action that takes place within its walls, the set had to be expanded. That didn't surprise Randy McIlvain. "We've kind of changed the temple every time we've seen it on the show," he admits. "We've continually created new rooms or different sections of the same room. We've essentially kept the architecture the same, but we've changed it every time because we don't have storage space available to hold on to the entire set. We do store certain recognizable pieces, like columns."

Director Burton loved shooting in the temple. "It was a memorable episode for me," he says, " because it was the first time we had the opportunity to shoot a Bajoran religious ceremony. I'm a big fan of ceremony, and actually conceiving what a Bajoran religious rite would feel like was exciting."

Creating the Bajoran rites was a joy for Taylor as well. He remembers working on the episode in the fall, during the Jewish high holidays of Rosh Hashanah (the Jewish New Year) and Yom Kippur (the Day of Atonement). Not surprisingly, Taylor decided to focus the Bajoran ceremony around the use of a musical instrument, similar to a shofar: a wind instrument carved from a ram's horn that has been used in Jewish religious services for more than three thousand years. "It seemed appropriate, being a story of atonement and all," Taylor remarks. "It was fun thinking about the ceremonial song and this strange instrument."

The instrument, referred to in the script as a

An amazingly close body double for Visitor. ROBBIE ROBINSON

T'fan, appears for only a few frames of the final episode, and the sweet sound it produces differs quite a bit from that of an actual shofar, which can play only two harsh notes. "We dropped a lot of it," Taylor says, "but at least I got to call up the new set."

Bareil's first name, Antos, comes not from tradi-

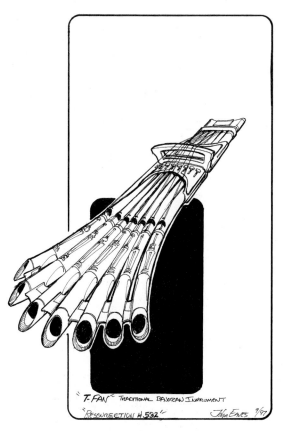

Percussion and wind instruments. JOHN EAVES

tional Bajoran, but is of Polish origin, by way of Broadway. "It actually came from 'Anton,' which was Tony's real name in *West Side Story*," Ira Behr says with a laugh. "I just thought the romance here was that kind of *West Side Story* thing. Of course, we couldn't use Anton, so Hans suggested 'Antos.'"

STATISTICAL PROBABILITIES

Episode #533

TELEPLAY BY **RENÉ ECHEVARRIA**
STORY BY **PAM PIETROFORTE**
DIRECTED BY **ANSON WILLIAMS**

GUEST CAST

Weyoun	JEFFREY COMBS
Jack	TIM RANSOM
Dr. Karen Loews	JEANNETTA ARNETTE
Lauren	HILARY SHEPARD-TURNER
Patrick	MICHAEL KEENAN
Damar	CASEY BIGGS
Sarina	FAITH C. SALIE

STARDATE UNKNOWN

With the secret of his genetic engineering now out in the open ("Doctor Bashir, I Presume?"), Starfleet asks Dr. Bashir to work with a group of genetically modified individuals who, unlike Bashir, are incapable of living outside of an institution. There's manic, hyperactive Jack; Lauren, who exists in a constant state of sensual overdrive; timid, childlike Patrick; and the ghostlike Sarina, who is totally withdrawn and apparently out of touch with her surroundings. The four are sent to spend some time with Bashir on Deep Space 9, in the hopes that meeting someone who's like them but lives a normal life, will have an impact.

Bashir's initial meeting with the group in a refurbished Cargo Bay is somewhat disturbing—he knows that in the hands of a less skillful doctor he easily could have been a misfit like them—but a dinner engagement with his regular friends on the station is not much more comforting. As he listens to Sisko, Worf, and the others discuss the rationale in restricting genetically enhanced individuals from entering into certain activities, Bashir can't help but feel as out of step as the group in the Cargo Bay.

Bashir returns to the misfits, and together they watch a broadcast of a speech being delivered by Gul Damar, the new head of the Cardassian government

Bashir finds it difficult to get through to a group of genetically enhanced savants. ROBBIE ROBINSON

in the wake of Dukat's breakdown ("Sacrifice of Angels"). Damar's address to the Federation appears to be an entreaty for peace, but Bashir is shocked when Jack's group comes up with an amazingly accurate analysis of the events that led to Damar's rise in power—just by observing the Cardassian's body language, tone of voice, and choice of words. Curious about the extent of their abilities, Bashir asks Sisko if he can show the group a recording of an upcoming meeting between the captain and Dominion leaders Damar and Weyoun. Sisko agrees. Bashir tells Jack and the others, and the doctor notes that their focus on the subject seems, at least temporarily, to ground them in reality.

The session goes better than Bashir could have hoped, with the group again discerning vital information from almost imperceptible clues. Although the Dominion representatives appear ready to concede some territories, the savants determine that what they really want is a neighboring star system whose planets contain the raw materials for ketracel-white, which they need to control the Jem'Hadar. Jack and the others also arrive at a dizzying series of projections and predictions regarding the course of the war. Impressed, Sisko sends the analyses to Starfleet Command, which responds by giving the group access to classified information on its battle readiness.

Neither Sisko nor Starfleet are happy with the long-term projection that the group provides. There's no way the Federation and its allies can win the war. Fighting the Dominion will wrack up hundreds of

Keenan expresses a childlike response to disappointment. ROBBIE ROBINSON

billions of casualties, and the Alpha Quadrant will be lost. The group recommends surrender, which will produce the same bleak outcome but without the loss of life. Sisko declares that surrender is out of the question, and that the Federation will go down fighting. He agrees to forward the strategy to Starfleet, but refuses to endorse it; predictably, Starfleet rejects the recommendation.

Jack refuses to accept the situation. He suggests they send the Dominion the classified information that Starfleet has provided; that way, the Alpha Quadrant will fall within a matter of weeks with far fewer casualties than in a drawn-out war. Bashir warns Jack that it's that kind of rationale that makes the outside world fear genetically altered individuals, but Jack doesn't care. When Bashir tells him that he won't go along with the plan, Jack knocks him out and sets up a meeting with Damar and Weyoun.

Bashir awakens in the Cargo Bay, bound to a chair. Only Sarina remains in the room with him. With his communicator removed, he's unable to warn Sisko about where Jack and the others have gone. But Bashir manages to get through to Sarina, convincing her that if she doesn't help him, Jack and the others will be convicted of treason and she'll never see them again. After being released by Sarina, Bashir heads off

her three companions before they reach the Dominion representatives. Odo informs Damar and Weyoun that their meeting has been canceled.

Sisko opts not to press charges, and Bashir informs the group that they'll be returned to the Institute. When Jack attempts to take out his frustration on Sarina, Bashir points out that their projections might have been wrong; after all, they couldn't predict that one person—Sarina—would choose to throw a wrench in *their* plans. They could be wrong about the outcome of the war.

Jack poses a question: If they can come up with a way to beat the Dominion, will he listen? Bashir assures them he will, and the group of misfits peacefully leaves the station.

"If people need to ask, 'Was that a comedy or a drama?' you know it was probably one of my favorite shows," admits Actor Alexander Siddig. "'Statistical Probabilites' was like that, not quite one thing or the other. The humor came out of the misery and angst captured by those wonderful actors. And I enjoyed the fact that Bashir served as a kind of pinball throughout that show. He was just being battered about."

The spark for the show was the producers' decision to delve a bit more into Bashir's past, specifically, the fact that he'd been genetically enhanced. "'Doctor Bashir, I Presume?' was a terrific episode," comments Ira Behr, "but I was never totally comfortable with [our discovery of] Julian's genetic engineering. It was one of those revelations that did not seem quite authentic to me. We'd had to work backward to get it. So I felt we needed to do something to help that idea along."

Former *Deep Space Nine* Intern Pam Pietroforte provided the opportunity for that "something" when she pitched the idea of sending a "think tank" comprised of genetically engineered savants to the station. "The break premise was essentially 'What happens when you can predict the future?'" recalls David Weddle.

"That was kind of a riff on 'cycle history,' from Isaac Asimov's *The Foundation Trilogy*," explains Bradley Thompson. "The idea that you can predict the future based on the movements of history. Like, 'In ten years the Dominion is going to turn into this and then we'll probably have a revolution in seventy years and then . . .'"

Starfleet had put together this group of geniuses and assigned Bashir to run it, explains René Echevarria, who wrote the teleplay. "They'd been invited to the station by Starfleet for the express purpose of helping us with this analysis. But that didn't really work. The crazier we made the characters, the more ludicrous it became that they would have been sent here, so I jettisoned that premise."

Thus the jumping-off point for the story became the fact that the savants were being sent to the station for a bit of counseling that only someone like Bashir could provide. In the process, the sympathetic Bashir found himself identifying more and more with the eccentric geniuses' point of view. "We could see coopting Bashir into becoming 'One of us! One of us!'" chuckles Thompson, quoting from the famous scene in Tod Browning's *Freaks* in which a beautiful circus performer is transformed into one of the sideshow oddities.

An early draft of the script began with Bashir being informed that the group was coming, followed by a dry explanation of their genetic backgrounds, but Echevarria eventually decided "to start the show cold," he says, "with the savants already on the station, talking about how they don't want to meet Dr. Bashir. That allowed me to immediately tell the backstory of these people in a fun way," by allowing them to demonstrate their personalities for the viewing audience.

Choosing the personalities for "the Jack Pack," as

Siddig and Shepherd-Turner are both talented actors—not dancers.
ROBBIE ROBINSON

they were dubbed, made the break sessions fun. Jack, for example, had noteworthy literary roots. "In the break session, we thought of the Jack character as Neal Cassady, the hero of Jack Kerouac's novel *On the Road* who talks a mile a minute and quotes philosophy by heart," says Weddle. "The final character that René developed is quite far from that, but that's one of the basic ideas he started from."

Some of the other characters were holdovers from the old think tank premise. "We'd had an astrophysicst who couldn't talk in that mix," Thompson recalls.

"Then there was the woman for whom everything was filtered through sex," says Echevarria, describing Lauren.

"That came from Ira," says Weddle. "And we all wanted to be in the casting sessions for her."

Playing sexy Lauren was a distinct change of pace from Actor Hilary Shepard-Turner's previous *Deep Space Nine* appearance. Viewers can be forgiven if they don't recall her face from fifth season's "The Ship." She played Hoya, the Benzite who was blown up along with the runabout.

"Lauren was the most brilliant woman in the universe *and* a nymphomaniac. My husband says she's the complete opposite of me!" laughs Shepard-Turner. "She was described as being obsessed with Bashir, and very *va-va-va-voom*, but I decided to make her a little bit Hannibal Lecter–ish as well." It was Director Anson Williams's idea, she says, to never let Lauren stand up. "The only time I ever stood was when I danced with Bashir."

And that, she admits, might have been a mistake. Williams had in mind a much more elaborate dancing sequence than appeared in the final episode, but he was foiled by his actors. "Both Sid and I are the biggest klutzes," Shepard-Turner admits. "They had this whole overhead camera crane shot set up, but they had to kill it because we were stepping all over each other. Laura Behr is a fabulous choreographer and she was just saying, 'Ay, yi, yi!' in exasperation. Finally they just had us keep our upper bodies looking like we knew what we were doing," Shepard-Turner laughs, "but if you'd seen our feet, you'd have known we were just stumbling all over the place."

Stage actor Michael Keenan found his characterization of Patrick right there in the writing. "It was pretty specific," he says. "I mean, he's essentially a child, so I just played him that way. Children have instant access to their emotions and they don't filter anything, so that's what I did."

Keenan literally talked his way into the episode. "It was really kind of funny," he says, giggling. "I'd already done *The Next Generation* (as Governor Maturin in Season 7's "Sub Rosa") and *Voyager* (as King Hrothgar in Season 1's "Heroes and Demons"). So as a joke, I went into [Casting Director] Ron Surma's office and said, 'Hey Ron, I've gotta do the Triple Crown.' Ron laughed, and the very next week he called me in for 'Statistical Probabilities.'"

In contrast, Actor Tim Ransom, who's appeared in *Courage Under Fire,* and dozens of television shows from *The X-Files* to *The Practice,* had a tougher time getting his foot in the door. "I'd been auditioning on and off for *Star Trek* for years and had never been booked," he comments. "In fact, I had read for the part of Bashir way back when."

When he got his latest opportunity to audition for *Star Trek,* Ransom gave it his all. "The producers had told me that Jack was a bit manic, so I figured he's the equivalent of a guy who drinks forty cups of coffee a day. I brought that energy into the room and I think that's what got me the job."

As the most active of the Jack Pack, Ransom notes that it was fortunate he's a bit of an athlete. "But not nearly so much as Jack," he laughs. "Particularly not in tight pants. Those things, man! It was hard enough to stand up straight let alone to do all of that bending around and other stuff. And I *didn't* do the backflip. I wish I could lay claim to that and I hate to destroy the illusion, but that was a stunt double."

Being cast as the silent Sarina was a good-news, bad-news break for Faith C. Salie. "When I audi-

tioned for the part, I had four lines of dialogue in the pivotal scene where I decide to untie Bashir. And, in fact, that's the way we filmed it," Salie says. "So it was much to my surprise when I sat down with my family at Thanksgiving to watch it and discovered I'd turned into a mute."

Unfortunately, Salie's only speaking scene had landed on the cutting room floor. "The episode was long, so we were looking for cuts," says Echevarria. "And it just played better when Bashir made his case to this woman and you didn't know what she would do until the next scene, when you discovered Bashir had been freed. So we cut Sarina's dialogue in the editing room. I remember thinking, 'Oh God, this poor woman. She's probably told everybody she knows about this scene.'"

Ironically, if they'd allowed Sarina to speak in "Statistical Probabilities," the writers never would have had the incentive to do "Chrysalis," an episode that focused on the evolution of Salie's character.

One of the reasons the cuts worked so well in the episode was the fact that although they'd initially thought Sarina would speak a few lines, Salie had been directed to behave for most of the show as if she couldn't. "I was told to behave pretty much catatonic," the actor says. "Anson told me, 'There's a lot going on in your mind, because you're genetically enhanced and you're brilliant, but you can't facilitate it because your body doesn't know how.' I don't want to make it seem like some terribly difficult actor's moment, but I did work on it. I created a switch in my brain that I could turn on and off to make everything become hazy around me, so that it seemed as if an amalgam of voices and senses were coming at me and that it was overwelming. Of course," she chuckles, "sometimes it was as simple as trying not to blink! In most of my scenes, I kept myself busy by focusing on the wall and touching it. Michael Keenan kept making jokes about my playing the wall. He said, 'I'm so glad those wall lessons your parents gave you paid off.'"

Originally the scenes were supposed to be in the station's Wardroom. Steve Oster comments, "To have five or six people in a room where a lot of activity is taking place, well, we just didn't have room in any of our quarters or even the Wardroom." The Cargo Bay seemed like it might serve the production's purposes, but its use created an interesting philosophical dilemma. "We wondered what we might be saying about Starfleet's treatment of these people if we put them in the Cargo Bay," says Oster. "We went back and forth on that."

In the end, size won out, and that decision

worked to the episode's advantage. As Siddig points out, the treatment of people who are different from you is very much an underlying theme. "The episode touched on a couple of political issues in terms of whether or not you can incarcerate people like this," he says. "I think the commentary that came out of Bashir's mouth was right and called attention to the fact that double standards happen in society. We *do* put good people away, like the Japanese-Americans placed in internment camps during World War II. The group in this episode seemed like lovely people, and Bashir showed some vulnerability in the fact that he understood their plight. They might not have been misfits if they had not been put away for such a long time," Siddig adds thoughtfully.

And yes, Director Anson Williams is indeed the same person as Actor Anson Williams, otherwise known as "Potsie," from the sitcom *Happy Days.*

When Moogie is abducted by the Dominion, Quark recruits a band of Ferengi for a rescue. ROBBIE ROBINSON

THE MAGNIFICENT FERENGI

Episode #534

WRITTEN BY **IRA STEVEN BEHR & HANS BEIMLER**
DIRECTED BY **CHIP CHALMERS**

GUEST CAST

Brunt	JEFFREY COMBS
Rom	MAX GRODÉNCHIK
Nog	ARON EISENBERG
Ishka	CECILY ADAMS
Gaila	JOSH PAIS
Keevan	CHRISTOPHER SHEA
Leck	HAMILTON CAMP
Leeta	CHASE MASTERSON

AND

Yelgrun	IGGY POP

STARDATE UNKNOWN

As Quark unsuccessfully attempts to thrill his customers with heroic tales about earning a profit, he receives some alarming news from the grand nagus. His mother, Ishka or Moogie, has been captured by the Dominion, and the nagus—Ishka's secret lover ("Ferengi Love Songs")—wants Quark to rescue her!

While neither Quark nor his brother Rom are particularly interested in risking their lives by going up against the Dominion, Zek's offer of a sizable reward convinces them to do the right thing. They realize, however, that they won't be able to accom-

plish this task on their own. Quark puts together a Ferengi commando team consisting of Nog, his cousin Gaila, an assassin named Leck, and *ex*-Liquidator Brunt.

But even with his team in place, Quark realizes their prospects are grim. Battle simulations in the holosuite prove that they have no hope of taking Ishka by force, so Rom suggests they take advantage of their own particular strength. Ferengi are negotiators, not commandos; they should make a deal for Moogie. The idea seems sound—but what do they have to trade that the Dominion would want?

After being prompted by Kira, who owes Quark for having rescued her from the Dominion ("Sacrifice of Angels"), Sisko talks Starfleet into providing the Ferengi with a marketable commodity: Keevan, the Vorta who surrendered to Starfleet ("Rocks and Shoals"). The Ferengi take Keevan to the abandoned Cardassian space station Empok Nor ("Empok Nor"), where the prisoner exchange is to take place. The team is feeling pretty good about its prospects until Keevan, who anticipates being killed by his people after a long, unpleasant interrogation, informs the team that the Dominion is unlikely to allow them to live.

The nervous Ferengi prepare for the Dominion's arrival, leaving Gaila to watch over the prisoner. But Gaila falls asleep, and Keevan gets away. Fortunately, Quark had the foresight to have Rom disable the impulse engines of their ship, leaving Keevan without the means to leave the station. He's quickly apprehended and returned to their base camp, just as dozens of Dominion troops arrive.

Leaving the others to watch Keevan, Quark, Rom, and Nog go out onto the Promenade to meet with Yelgrun, the Vorta in charge. Yelgrun has Ishka with him, and he wants to conduct the exchange immediately. But Quark has taken Keevan's pessimistic predictions to heart and come up with safeguards that he hopes will protect all the Ferengi, including Moogie. Yelgrun is to send all but two of his Jem'Hadar soldiers back to Dominion territory. That effectively will strand the Vorta long enough for Quark and his cronies to make their getaway.

Yelgrun isn't happy about Quark's conditions. He'd kill the three Ferengi now and forcibly take Keevan, but Quark guarantees the other Ferengi would kill the captured Vorta. Since Yelgrun wants him alive, he agrees to Quark's ultimatum. The exchange will take place in thirty minutes.

The relieved Ferengi return to base camp, where Rom inadvertently reveals the fact that he and Quark are holding out on some of the reward money. A fight ensues, and in the confusion Keevan accidentally is killed. Nog concocts a desperate, last-ditch solution, and wires a series of neural stimulators to Keevan's body. The stimulators allow the ensign to animate the corpse, making Keevan appear to walk under his own power. The deception works just long enough for Rom, Brunt, Gaila, and Leck to get the drop on the Jem'Hadar soldiers. The group heads back to Deep Space 9 with Yelgrun as their prisoner. Ishka is safe and sound, and Quark is a genuine hero.

For an executive producer, a visit to the set during shooting is a rare event. Faced with the ticking clock and the never-ending list of responsibilities that come with the job description—planning, writing, supervising, viewing, casting, listening, pinching pennies . . . you name it, he does it—it just doesn't happen very often. "I can't," laments Ira Behr. "None of the writers can, really. I can't tell you how badly I want to be there for any given scene, but chances are I won't be." But Behr made an exception during *DS9*'s sixth season, and no one who's known him for more than a few days was surprised to see him hanging around the set the week they were filming "The Magnificent Ferengi."

What drew him to the set?

"Iggy was here," he says simply. "For Iggy, I would not be denied. *I would not be denied!*" Behr's voice takes on a gleeful tone. "Not only that, but I

Casting for episodic television is not simple; sometimes it's a matter of luck and timing. ROBBIE ROBINSON

had all my Ferengi! I had Nog and Rom and Quark, whose joint presence is worth a million bucks for me, anyway, and on top of that I had Jeff Combs back as Brunt, Josh Pais as Gaila ("Business as Usual"), Hamilton Camp, whom I *loved* from his Second City days, playing Leck ("Ferengi Love Songs"). And Chris Shea ("Rocks and Shoals") was back as a wonderful Vorta. *And Iggy Pop*. I was a happy boy."

"Ira was thrilled!" laughs Hans Beimler. "For cryin' out loud, Iggy Pop has been a hero of his for years. I've *heard* about Iggy Pop since I've known him. I've *seen* Iggy Pop posters in his home. What can I say? The man was in heaven."

Behr had attempted to book the busy rock 'n' roll star/actor before, for roles in the *DS9* episode "Past Tense," and in his previous series, *Fame*. But Pop's schedule never had been in sync with Behr's. However, the musician had dislocated his shoulder during a performance several months prior to the filming of "The Magnificent Ferengi." The injury forced him into an extended period of recuperation and made him available for a short acting gig. Behr was ready with the role of Yelgrun, although he admits it wasn't the best match with Pop's well-known persona as an unrestrained stage presence.

"I knew that the role was going to be tough for

"I really had to be on my toes," Adams says, "because everyone was magnificent." ROBBIE ROBINSON

Iggy, because he's a very kinetic performer," Behr comments. "His physicality is certainly part of who he is, and unfortunately we cast him as a Vorta, one of the most immobile of characters."

In a way, it's just as well that Yelgrun wasn't a physically demanding part. "Iggy was still suffering from the effects of his injury," Behr notes sympathetically. "You could see that he clearly was uncomfortable for all the hours he had to be there on the set, but he never complained. And he really got that demented quality the Vorta have, like Weyoun has—think Caligula! He was just a delight."

Considering the number of tributes to classic films that Behr and company have done over the course of *Deep Space Nine,* it would be natural to assume that "The Magnificent Ferengi" is an homage to *The Magnificent Seven,* or to that film's original inspiration, *The Seven Samurai.* However, it would be wrong.

"'The Magnificent Ferengi' is a good title, but we never really thought about *The Magnificent Seven* at all when we were writing it," remarks Behr. "It has nothing to do with that film in terms of plot *or* structure. Nothing."

Unfortunately, Behr neglected to tell that to his cast. "Armin and I looked at the movie," confesses Max Grodénchik. "I guess I thought of myself as a wimpy Steve McQueen. And Armin [Shimerman] was Yul Brynner, which seemed right because he and Yul Brynner have the same kind of head."

"We thought about it and tried to make it a sort of pastiche of that movie," confirms Shimerman, who enjoyed performing in the episode. "I just loved being with all those Ferengi. I tend to think of myself as the overactor on the series—the ham, if you will. But," he adds with a laugh, "there were so many hams on that episode that I decided to step back and enjoy myself and let them have a good time. They were brilliant."

"They're all quite talented comics," agrees Director Chip Chalmers. "I had no trouble whatsoever getting absolutely magnificent comic timing out of each and every one of them. For instance, when they're sitting in Brunt's ship and Keevan pipes up from behind them, 'You're all going to die anyway,' they all turn and look at him, and then they all turn back to the front of the ship at *exactly* the same time. It wasn't planned. It was just something that happened. I knew they were going to turn but I didn't know that they'd do it together. It was magical."

Although "The Magnificent Ferengi" was Chalmers's first *DS9* episode, he was no stranger to *Star Trek*, having previously directed four episodes of *The Next Generation*. He also directed "Captain's Holiday," which featured an appearance by Max Grodénchik as a Ferengi, but Chalmers wasn't familiar with *DS9*'s take on the species. He brushed up on his Ferengi etiquette by reading *The Ferengi Rules of Acquisition* and *Legends of the Ferengi*.

The story went through some minor changes before Chalmers got to the soundstage. "Originally they were going to have the Dominion kidnap the grand nagus," Chalmers recalls. "But Wallace Shawn wasn't available." The script was rewritten, making Ishka the victim, and Cecily Adams happily made her second appearance in Moogie's makeup.

Adams *loves* Moogie. "She never backs down," Adams says proudly of her character. "Here she is in this episode, giving financial advice to her captor! I feel very fortunate to play her. She's made me grow as an actor *and* as a person."

Nog is another Ferengi with backbone. Although he occasionally showed classic Ferengi behavior, it was typical, in the last two seasons of the series, for Nog to volunteer for the most dangerous tasks, for example, checking to see if the Jem'Hadar have arrived at Empok Nor. "We put this guy into *Starfleet,*" says Behr. "We had to believe he had 'the right stuff' or we wouldn't have done that. If we'd just put him into a Starfleet shirt and he'd turned out to be Jerry Lewis, that would have been making needless fun of the Ferengi."

Not that *every* Ferengi can rise above the stereotype. Just ask Jeffrey Combs. "I learned something about Brunt in this episode," he says. "When it comes down to physical demands of bravery, he is an absolute coward. Whenever something bad happened, he was the first one out of the room. So I had a lot of fun, showing that behind all of his bravado and rudeness is a chickenheart."

"The whole thing about heroism in this episode," Behr observes, "the questions of 'What is a hero?' and 'What value does that have?' basically had to do with the fact that the Ferengi needed to show that they *could* be heroes, but after they showed they could, it was like, 'Well . . . now we don't have to do that anymore.'"

If the episode wasn't meant as an homage to *The Magnificent Seven,* it *did* include a tip of the hat to another film. The teaser begins with Quark opening a shipment of syrup of squill, while the fifth act includes a scene where Moogie discusses the value of hypicate root futures. Both terms originated in the classic W.C. Fields movie *It's a Gift,* according to Behr. "They're from a scene where Fields is trying to sleep and a little girl keeps waking him up by yelling at her mother, 'What do you want me to get, Mom, syrup of squill or hypicate?'" Behr recites from memory. "Squill," he chuckles. "I just love that word."

WALTZ
Episode #535
WRITTEN BY RONALD D. MOORE
DIRECTED BY RENE AUBERJONOIS

GUEST CAST

Weyoun	JEFFREY COMBS
Dukat	MARC ALAIMO
Damar	CASEY BIGGS

STARDATE 51408.6

Traveling aboard the *U.S.S. Honshu* toward Starbase 621, where he will testify before a Federation Special Jury convened to investigate Dominion war crimes, Captain Sisko meets with his old nemesis, Gul Dukat, who is being held in the brig. Dukat, the subject of the investigation, knows that Sisko will be testifying for the prosecution, but he seems unperturbed. His Federation doctors have declared that he has recovered from the breakdown suffered when his daughter died ("Sacrifice of Angels"), and he seems to be at peace with himself. Suddenly, the *Honshu* is attacked by a wing of Cardassian destroyers. In the confusion of the evacuation, Dukat is freed from his cell. He rescues a seriously injured Sisko and takes him to a shuttlecraft. The two get away just before the *Honshu* blows up.

Awakening in a makeshift campsite inside a cavern, Sisko finds the left side of his body bandaged, and his arm immobilized in a metallic cast. Dukat offers him some water and relates how he got their shuttle to a nearby planet. Unfortunately, the engines were damaged by the shockwave from the *Honshu*; they can't take off again. However, the shuttle's distress beacon seems to be operating, so it's only a matter of time till someone—be it Dominion or Starfleet personnel—comes to rescue them.

Dukat tells Sisko that he's going to search for local sources of food and water. But as he travels through the tunnel that leads to the planet's inhos-

Declared recovered from his breakdown, Dukat is still taunted by visions of people who *aren't* there. ROBBIE ROBINSON

pitable surface, he encounters Weyoun, who questions his intentions. Dukat impatiently informs the Vorta that he has a great deal to discuss with Sisko, but Weyoun wants the Cardassian to kill him right away. When Dukat resists, Weyoun belittles him, reminding him of the pathetic, sobbing ruin he was at the Federation hospital. Dukat fires a phaser at his tormenter, who disappears.

The next day, Dukat tries to solicit Sisko's opinion of him by engaging the captain in light conversation. But Sisko isn't very forthcoming, which irks the Cardassian. When Sisko asks why it matters *what* he thinks, Dukat observes that it matters what old friends think of each other. Sisko points out that they aren't old friends; he's grateful that Dukat saved his life, but that's all. Dukat isn't satisfied with the response, but he's distracted by some noise that only he can hear. When he leaves the cavern to check it out, he encounters Damar, who urges Dukat to stop wasting time. And although the presence of Damar is a hallucination, just as Weyoun's was, Dukat feels obligated to explain his intentions: he needs to find out if Sisko respects him; he needs to hear him admit it.

While he's gone, Sisko crawls over to the survival kit to retrieve some water and notices that the distress beacon is off-line, even though it looks like it's func-

tioning normally. Since this could be an honest mistake on Dukat's part, Sisko tests the Cardassian by asking him to double-check the system. Dukat investigates and says that it's fine—which tells Sisko all he needed to know.

Meanwhile Worf looks for Sisko with the *Defiant.* It's a race against time; Worf knows that he must abandon the search to rendezvous with a Starfleet convoy in a matter of hours. Although he manages to find a number of survivors from the *Honshu,* Sisko is not among them.

The next time Dukat wanders off, Sisko uses a small sliver of metal to repair the beacon. When Dukat returns, Sisko pretends that everything is normal. Once again the Cardassian attempts to get Sisko to elicit a positive opinion about him, but Sisko is reticent about participating in the conversation. Dukat's hallucinations grow worse; now he sees "Kira" in the cavern with them. She taunts Dukat, noting that Sisko feels that the Cardassian is the same evil, sadistic man he always was. When Dukat begins responding to the phantom in Sisko's presence, the captain realizes that something is very wrong. He decides to humor Dukat and tell him what he wants to hear— that the Cardassian has been judged unfairly, that he had good reasons for the murders he committed.

Sisko's words seem to placate Dukat, but "Kira's" words destroy any sense of peace that they bring. She assures the Cardassian that Sisko is only patronizing him, and that he's going to make a fool of him when he escapes. Infuriated, Dukat begins firing at "her" with his phaser, forcing Sisko to scuttle out of the way to escape injury. Suddenly, Dukat notices a fork with a missing tine lying near Sisko's former resting place. On a hunch, Dukat checks the beacon and realizes that Sisko has repaired it by using the tine as a tool. He destroys the instrument and then pummels the defenseless captain, noting that he despises betrayal.

Later, Dukat tells a battered Sisko that he brought his punishment upon himself. Sisko painfully comments that Dukat probably felt that way about all of his victims. Realizing at last that Dukat has been seeking his approval for his past behavior, Sisko decides to lead him to the truth. He gets the Cardassian to talk about his experience with the Bajorans during the Occupation, how every kindness he extended to them was rewarded with treachery, how their stupid pride kept them from understanding that the Cardassians were their superiors. Sisko comments that Dukat must have hated them for their behavior. Dukat says that he did, and admits that he should have killed every last one of them.

Surrounded by a phantom chorus that eggs him on relentlessly, Dukat is so overcome by his passions that he fails to notice the captain has moved directly behind him. Sisko strikes the Cardassian over the head with a metal bar, knocking him senseless. He hurries to the shuttlecraft outside the cavern, but is overtaken by Dukat before he can get away.

Sisko expects Dukat to kill him, but instead the crazed Cardassian tells him he has unfinished business with the Bajorans, whom he intends to destroy. And this time, he says, their Emissary won't be able to save them. Dukat takes off in the shuttle, but before he leaves the system, he alerts Sisko's rescuers as to the captain's location. The *Defiant* picks up Sisko, Bashir treats his injuries, but the captain remains deeply troubled by the encounter. He vows to protect Bajor from the evil that Dukat represents, noting that from now on, "It's him or me."

"**D**ukat is the hero of his own story," Ron Moore explains with a grin. "He definitely thinks that he's on the side of the angels, and he doesn't understand why everyone else doesn't see that."

The writers, on the other hand, see Dukat as the personification of evil, and "Waltz" was their way of getting him to face that ugly fact. "I wanted us to come away from this show with Dukat finally having faced who the hell he is and what he's done," states Ira Behr. "To get him to finally admit that he hates the Bajorans and he wishes to kill them all. And he does."

If there's a tone of self-satisfaction in Behr's voice, it's understandable. Like the rest of his team, he knows that Dukat has become a very popular character with the fans. That's all well and good—a well-defined villain is often far more interesting than the hero of a piece. But Dukat is not just any villain. Not to Behr. And not to the other writers.

"I'm always a strong proponent of giving characters' personalities multidimensional aspects, and portraying someone in shades of gray rather than black and white," Behr explains. "But you know, being human, I can't help but sometimes react to the feedback we get. And the fact that Dukat has become *such* a popular character, and I've read things on the Internet where people actually talk about the fact that 'only five million Bajorans were killed during the Occupation—that's not such a big deal.' It's just so . . ." Behr sighs. "Anyway, I make an exception in Dukat's

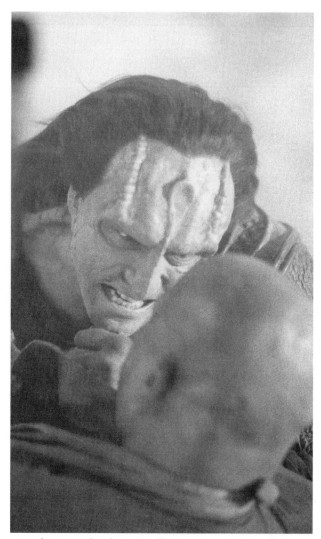

Dukat craves the admiration of his enemies, and he'll resort to violence to get it. ROBBIE ROBINSON

case. Evil may be an unclear concept in this day and age. But Dukat certainly has done evil things. And since he refuses to admit to them, we then have to simplify things, deconstruct things, until we get to the most simplistic level. Which is: 'He does evil things, therefore, *he is evil.*'"

Structure-wise, the episode wasn't quite as clear-cut.

"We started out wanting to do 'inside Dukat's head,' in the same sense that we had done 'inside Bashir's head ['Distant Voices'],'" recalls Behr. "I just thought that would be an interesting place to go."

"We called it 'Dukat's Head' for quite a while," confirms Moore, who pulled together both story and teleplay. "The idea was that Dukat is crazy and Sisko goes to see him in the mental hospital. Sisko's sitting outside of his cell talking to him, and Dukat's inside, catatonic, and the camera pushes in on Dukat's face and we go into his mind and see what he's thinking. It's this fantasy of himself running the station again, being in charge, with Kira as his wife. Then the fantasy starts unraveling and we find all these internal demons in his mind. We find out about the Bajoran woman, Tora Naprem ['Indiscretion'], who was Ziyal's mother, and what happened to her and why it was a twisted relationship.

"We all kind of liked the idea, but it was hard to structure and make sense of," Moore admits. "The more we talked about the episode, the more we kept saying, 'Yeah, and after this fantasy sequence, then he and Sisko have this scene together.' Finally, we realized that the show was focusing more on the reality scenes between Sisko and Dukat than it was on Dukat's fantasy. So we discarded the whole fantasy element and went for just a two-man show, with them marooned together, and Sisko slowly realizing that Dukat is completely insane."

"I loved the fact that Dukat's insanity was written as a 'Roman Polanski' kind of crazy," comments Director René Auberjonois. "It comes as a surprise to the audience how psychotic Dukat really is," he says.

"Marc Alaimo really had a handle on it,"

Auberjonois notes admiringly. "He was in touch with where it was coming from in his own psychology and where it was going. And that's the way a good actor plays a villain, by finding ways to rationalize what he's doing. No one knows more about a character than the actor playing him."

After the "head" scenario was tossed, the episode was primarily written for two actors on one set. "That played into whatever strengths I have as an 'actor director,'" Auberjonois comments. "'Waltz' was a stage piece, and it dealt with acting, acting, acting all the time. The challenging part was to keep it *visually* interesting." For that, Auberjonois had to rely on the periodic appearances of Dukat's "ghosts," positioning them in interesting and occasionally surprising places. The phantom Kira, for example, cozies up to Sisko as she taunts Dukat. And in the sequence where all of Dukat's ghosts appear at the same time, smiles Auberjonois, "I put them all on a rock, like birds of prey!"

Auberjonois worked closely with Jonathan West on choreographing the scenes with the phantoms. "Because the ghosts were appearing and disappearing, we had to light the set with their presence in

A first step, with suggestions on where pieces of this prop could be found. JOHN EAVES

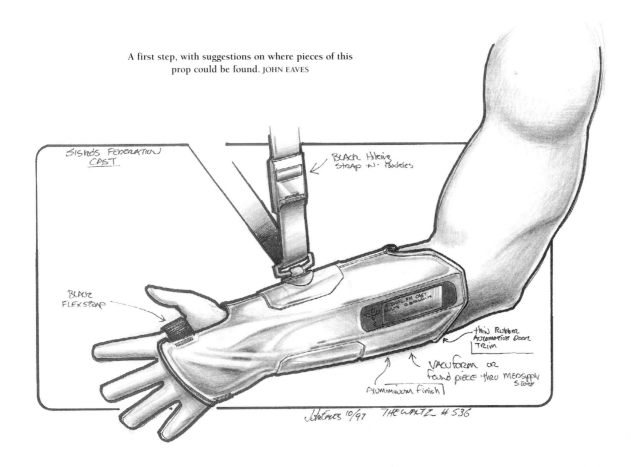

Cardassian's parting shot to Sisko is a chilling warning that Sisko will "learn what it's like to lose a *child*." But that idea fell by the wayside before filming began.

"It was such a specific threat," explains Moore. "It was hard to see where to go from there. Sisko would come back to the station and he'd have to protect Jake. He'd have to send him to Earth, or put him under twenty-six-hour guard. It would have been an awkward thing to have to work into every episode—Sisko always watching Jake, wondering if they have enough people around him. That would have been a pain."

The writers realized the story should be as much about Sisko as it was about Dukat's insanity. ROBBIE ROBINSON

mind even if they weren't in the shot," says West. "That way, we wouldn't have a big light shift when they entered."

Behr liked Moore's use of the ghostly chorus. "We actually thought about bringing them back, so that the next time we saw Dukat he'd still have those characters with him," chuckles Behr. "But we decided against it because that seemed a little silly, and this show really gave them to us enough."

The episode's B-story, with Worf searching for Sisko in the *Defiant*, was, according to Moore, "a riff on a plot that's been done several times in *Star Trek,* where the lead character is told that he can't look for his friend or missing crewman longer than X amount of time because of this important mission. And usually Lead Character breaks orders, saves his friend anyway, and is forgiven by Starfleet. But this time I thought, well, let's set it up the same way but not *play* it the same way. So Worf does not disobey his orders, even for Sisko."

An early draft of the script featured a different conclusion to the verbal match between Sisko and Dukat. Instead of delivering his pronouncement that "Bajor is dead and not even its precious Emissary will be able to save its populace this time," the

WHO MOURNS FOR MORN?
Episode #536
WRITTEN BY **MARK GEHRED-O'CONNELL**
DIRECTED BY **VICTOR LOBL**

GUEST CAST

Hain	GREGORY ITZIN
Krit	BRAD GREENQUIST
Larell	BRIDGET ANN WHITE
Nahsk	CYRIL O' REILLY

STARDATE UNKNOWN

Quark's delight in his new hologram—a lifelike, albeit silent, holographic version of Morn that the bartender plans to activate whenever his Lurian customer is out of town—evaporates when Sisko and Dax break some bad news: the real Morn is dead, killed in an ion storm. Quark offers the use of his bar for a memorial service, which, not coincidentally, offers *him* the opportunity to make some profit by selling the mourners offerings of food and drink for the deceased to take with him into the afterlife.

Sisko interrupts the service to inform Quark that Morn left everything to the Ferengi. Quark eagerly reviews the Lurian's financial records and is horrified to learn that Morn was broke. He's inherited only the assets of Morn's shipping business—a cargo bay full of overripe beets—and the contents of Morn's quarters on the station: a matador painting on black velvet and a hot tub filled with mud.

A closer investigation of the hot tub proves rewarding. Holding her breath beneath the mud is Larell, a beautiful humanoid female who claims to be Morn's ex-wife. She reveals that Morn had a substantial retirement fund consisting of one thousand bricks of gold-pressed latinum. For a ten-percent share of

In addition to Morn's estate, Quark inherits his partners.
ROBBIE ROBINSON

the take, she promises that she *won't* try to tie up the estate in court. Quark agrees, even though he hasn't a clue where to find the latinum.

Later, Quark returns to Morn's quarters to search for clues and finds two new visitors, brothers Krit and Nahsk, who refer to themselves as the Lurian's "business associates." The pair tell Quark that Morn owed them one thousand bricks of latinum. After haggling briefly, and having Morn's matador painting smashed over his head by Nahsk, Quark agrees to give them fifty percent. When the brothers leave, Quark discovers a claim slip for one of the station's storage lockers concealed in the ruins of the painting. As it turns out, the locker contains only *one* bar of latinum—but that bar is inscribed with a message indicating the remainder is in the Bank of Bolias.

Quark hurries to his quarters to contact the bank, only to encounter yet another stranger. This one is a human male named Hain, who claims to be a Lurian security officer. Hain explains that Morn was Luria's crown prince, and that the money, a bequest from Morn's parents, is government property that must be returned. When Quark mentions the presence of Morn's alleged ex-wife Larell, Hain reveals she's a criminal and offers Quark a reward for her capture. That's better than nothing, figures Quark. He points out that there also are two brothers looking for the latinum, and Hain instructs him to have the bank deliver the latinum to the station; he'll catch *all* the crooks when they try to grab the loot.

A short time later, Quark finds a fearful Larell waiting for him in his quarters. She thinks someone's

following her. When Nahsk and Krit show up, Larell hides. As Quark tries to deal with the brothers, another caller arrives, and the two aliens hide in a different spot. When Hain enters, however, everyone comes out, weapons in hand. Quark learns that *all* their stories have been lies. The four of them robbed a bank on Lissepia with Morn's assistance. The take was one thousand bars of gold-pressed latinum, but the Lurian ran off with the money and stashed it away. Now that the statute of limitations on the booty has expired, they've come to collect.

Yielding to the logic of the situation, the thieves decide they'll split the latinum when it arrives. They'd prefer to eliminate Quark from the equation, but they need him to take delivery, so it will have to be a five-way split. Once the crated latinum arrives, greed rears its ugly head and the thieves attack each other. Quark dives into the crate to get out of harm's way and a few minutes later, Odo arrives to arrest the four crooks. But Quark's relief turns to despair when he realizes that someone has extracted the latinum from the gold. His haul is worthless!

The next day, as Quark reflects on his misfortune, Morn shows up, alive and well. He had faked his own death and left Quark to deal with his former associates, knowing that eventually they'd turn on each other. When Quark points out that he could have been killed, Morn sheepishly offers Quark a bit of consolation. He regurgitates a small amount of liquid latinum from his second stomach, where he's been storing the precious substance for years. The offering is the equivalent of a hundred bricks of the substance, and it's all Quark's, making the entire experience profitable.

Many had tried—and failed—to successfully pitch a story about *Deep Space Nine's* resident barfly, Morn. The show's producers had no proviso against such stories. The pitch letter that they sent out to aspiring freelance writers contained no warnings about Morn in the ominous paragraph titled "What We're NOT Looking For." But Morn's character *did* have one very basic curse, and that curse had a tendency to trip up almost everyone who tried to write about him. He couldn't speak on-camera.

Of course, everyone who's ever watched the show knows that Morn *can* speak. According to the other characters, he apparently speaks way too much. But the conceit of the series was that the viewers would never *see* Morn speak, just as television audi-

Keeping the characters true to their center, Quark strives for profit, while Morn is silent. ROBBIE ROBINSON

The story essentially revolved around the idea that Morn had disappeared from the station, thus providing a fun way to demonstrate to the other characters that "they don't really know anything about him," says Gehred-O'Connell.

The producers didn't really know that much about Morn, either, admits Ira Behr, "So we saw this as a chance to have some fun. I mean, if Morn can have a licensed *action figure,* he might as well have a backstory too," he laughs. "So we gave him some backstory."

Gehred-O'Connell was pleased to be responsible for a part of that backstory. He was allowed to establish that Morn's species was Lurian. And he also got to reveal that Lurians have two stomachs. "I can't say for sure how that idea got in there," the Wisconsin native says with a chuckle, "but I *do* live in cow country."

But not every aspect of his script would remain intact.

After Gehred-O'Connell turned in his script, the refinements began. "Mark did a good job," René Echevarria says, "but the comedy was too broad. Ultimately, it wasn't a Morn episode; it was a story about Quark. And the most common mistake people make in writing Quark is to make him transparently greedy. On paper, that's very funny, but Armin [Shimerman] doesn't play Quark that way. Armin plays it real."

The freelancer's first draft of the script had involved the show's regulars in the detective work. "One by one, Quark had to let the others in on his secret, and before you knew it, the entire cast was in on this search for Morn's fortune," says Gehred-O'Connell.

Echevarria took away the detective duties from the main cast and brought in four new characters. He also polished the humor, amusing himself with subtleties, such as calling the characters of Krit and Nahsk twins. "It was just stuff," Echevarria laughs. "For whatever reason, I just thought it was funny."

The makeup for the twins helped get Michael Westmore nominated for another Emmy award. "Those two green-headed guys that acted like Jack Nicholson were about the only new aliens we had that season," says Westmore, so they hold a special place in his heart. His inspiration, he admits, was not particularly complex. When the script came in, he says with a laugh, "I thought, 'We haven't had a green one in a long time, so let's grab a head and some faces and paint them green.'"

Sexy Larell's makeup was simple, although help-

ences would never see Niles Crane's ex-wife Maris on *Frasier.* It just wasn't going to happen.

But freelancer Mark Gehred-O'Connell really wanted to do a Morn episode. By Season 6, Gehred-O'Connell already had worked on three *DS9* episodes ("Second Sight," "Meridian," "For the Cause"), which gave him a little insight into the producers' minds. "I knew that at this point the guys were willing to do a little crazier things with the characters. But I also knew that if I pitched a story about Morn, he wouldn't be able to talk."

And that, he admits, sank a lot of his ideas. "Then one day I realized, 'Wait a minute—we can do a story about Morn where Morn isn't there!'" he says. "So I pitched an idea to Ron for a story in which Morn disappears in the teaser. Ron seemed to get a real kick out of it, and he told me, 'You know, we've heard a lot of Morn stories, but this is the only one that I think can really work.'"

Unlikely as it seems, these two were the only "new" aliens in this season. ROBBIE ROBINSON

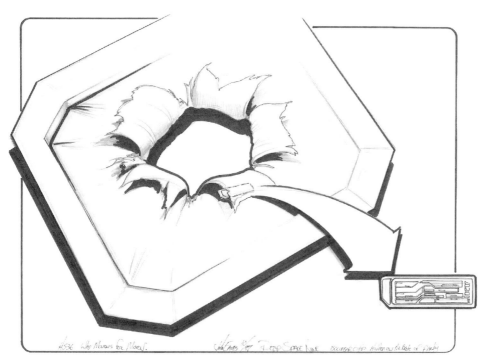

Morn's painting. JOHN EAVES

ing the actress to keep it on wasn't. "She had a rubber headpiece on, and we really had to seal her in, because moisture could get behind it when she got into the mud bath. If the glue had lifted once they started filming, we'd never have been able to glue it down again. We'd learned that lesson years ago on *The Next Generation* when they dunked some other alien in mud."

And what did they use for mud? "We used," Gary Monak says with a smile, "what the mud wrestlers use! It's a powder that's called 'driller's mud,' used in oil drilling," he notes. "That's what we mixed up in the hot tub. Engineers use it to seal lakebeds so they don't lose their water, and it's also used as a makeup base." The latter use seemed fortuitous. "The actress had to be in it, on and off, for about eight hours, but she came out okay," Monak observes. "She didn't wrinkle up too bad."

The show also established that latinum is a liquid. "I'm proud to say that that was mine," Gehred-O'Connell admits. But in making the valuable commodity a liquid, he had to find a way to deal with the series' oft-used term "gold-pressed latinum." Simple. The script explained that the lucrative liquid was stored in pieces of "worthless" gold.

The plot of "Who Mourns for Morn?" concerned a great deal of gold-pressed latinum, and there was a need for a large quantity of gold. Up to this point, gold-pressed latinum had been referred to only in slips, strips, and bars. But Morn's treasure trove was so large that the Property Department had to make something new to accommodate it: bricks. They also had to make a crate that was large enough to hold both the bricks and Quark. Fortunately, says Laura Richarz, "we'd had this rolling janitor cart that we'd used to store tribbles in fifth season. It was very big and made out of this great plastic, so we turned it upside down and took the wheels off."

Another important prop in the show was Morn's treasured matador painting. The original version, seen in "In the Cards," had been rented. So how did the filmmakers dare smash it over Quark's head? Stand-ins. "I painted ten duplicates of the one that Joe Longo rented," reveals John Eaves. "I painted

them all day and all night. Then we scored them so they'd rip when they hit Armin."

Despite the indignity of being whacked with a matador painting, Shimerman enjoyed the episode. "I had two old friends on the set," Armin Shimerman relates. "I've known Gregory Itzin ['Dax'] for fifteen years. And the director, Victor Lobl, is someone I worked with for six and a half years on *Beauty and the Beast*." Lobl would return to helm "In the Pale Moonlight" later in the season.

Although Morn did not utter a word in the episode, he wasn't entirely silent. There was that . . . well, let's call it a belch, even though that's not really what it was. First of all, it didn't emanate from Actor Mark Shepherd's throat. The gurgling sound that the audience heard actually originated in *DS9*'s Special Effects Sound Department. "We combined a number of audio elements for that sound," explains Supervising Sound Editor Mace Matiosian. "We knew that this would not be the sound of a normal human bodily function. For one thing, the substance that comes up is latinum, not water, and not saliva. So it has a certain weight. *And* it comes from Morn's second stomach, an area of his body that . . . well, we don't even know where it is," he admits.

"We started with tracks of a sound element we call 'slime,' a somewhat organic element that we developed for other purposes on the show," Matiosian explains. (Among those other purposes: it's one of many sounds combined to provide a soundtrack for Odo's morphs.) "And we added a processed, pouring sound. Then we did a Foley session, and recorded verbals and some vocalizations to enhance those other sounds and give them a sense of coming out of the body. The final burp was a very complex combination of sound elements."

While the gurgle took about one second of screen time, Matiosian notes that the Foley session took half a day and that his team spent five or six hours editing the new and previously recorded elements. "The man-hours do add up," Matiosian says.

So wouldn't it have taken a lot less time to just record a belch?

Matiosian shakes his head. "To just have an actor belch would be very un-*Star Trek*-like."

ONE LITTLE SHIP

Episode #537

WRITTEN BY **DAVID WEDDLE &**
BRADLEY THOMPSON
DIRECTED BY **ALLAN KROEKER**

GUEST CAST

Nog	ARON EISENBERG
First Kudak'Etan	SCOTT THOMPSON BAKER
Second Ixtana'Rax	FRITZ SPERBERG
Gelnon	LELAND CROOKE
Third Lamat'Ukan	CHRISTIAN ZIMMERMAN

STARDATE 51474.2

The *Defiant* is captured by the Jem'Hadar. ROBBIE ROBINSON

As part of an investigation into a rare subspace compression phenomenon, Sisko sends Dax, Bashir, and O'Brien into the anomaly's vortex, while the rest of the crew observes from the *Defiant*. Information from previously launched sensor probes has suggested that the *Runabout Rubicon* will shrink when it enters the phenomenon, and that the effect will be reversed once the runabout leaves. Sisko plans to keep the *Defiant*'s tractor beam on the ship to stabilize it within the anomaly, but that tether is broken when the battleship comes under attack by a Jem'Hadar vessel. Suddenly the *Rubicon* is on its own.

The runabout manages to escape from the anomaly. But because the ship's external sensors are down, and blast shutters can't be opened; they're flying blind. They follow the *Defiant*'s transponder signal and hope for the best until the chief gets the shutters open—but even then the trio can't immediately make sense of what they see outside of the runabout's windshield. It looks like a big white metallic wall.

Suddenly they realize that it's a small section of the *Defiant*. It *looks* gigantic because the runabout is only six-and one-half centimeters (two-and-one-half inches) long. They haven't returned to normal size—the result, Dax observes, of exiting the anomaly via a different path than they entered. To regain their size, they'll need to reenter the anomaly and follow their original trajectory out, but they'll need the *Defiant*'s help to do that. With communications also down, O'Brien suggests that the best way to contact the crew of the *Defiant* might be to enter the ship via a plasma vent, and they attempt to find their way through the conduit.

Unknown to the *Rubicon* crew, the *Defiant* has been captured by Jem'Hadar troops and its command crew locked in the ship's mess hall. When his own men are unable to restore the *Defiant*'s badly damaged

warp drive, Kudak'Etan, the Jem'Hadar first, orders Sisko to guide them through the repairs. The second, Ixtana'Rax, feels this is a grave miscalculation, and that Sisko will use the opportunity to retake the ship. But the first refuses to heed his more experienced second's warning, even when Sisko asks for additional crew members to be released from the mess hall to help him. Feeling confident about his decision, Kudak'Etan tells Gelnon, the Vorta in charge of the Jem'Hadar attack vessel, that the *Defiant* will soon be operational, and Gelnon leaves.

As Sisko's crew begins working on the repairs, the *Rubicon* makes its way into engineering, after narrowly escaping being vaporized by superheated plasma coming from *Defiant*'s impulse engines. It doesn't take long for the *Rubicon*'s crew to realize that the battleship is under Jem'Hadar control. They can see that Sisko is trying to retake control of the ship from an engineering console, and that Worf is covering Sisko's tracks. Nog is attempting to override the bridge lockout that is blocking Sisko's efforts, but O'Brien doubts that the Ferengi can do it from engineering. It's up to them to get to the bridge and do the work from there.

Reaching their destination, O'Brien realizes that they won't be able to release the control lock from inside the *Rubicon*. O'Brien and Bashir must leave the ship and do the job manually, from inside the circuit housing. But because the oxygen molecules outside the *Rubicon* are too big for their bodies to assimilate, Dax beams a bubble of compressed oxygen into the housing ahead of them. They'll have twenty minutes before they run out of air. Unaware of their crewmates' presence on board, Sisko orders a computer virus planted in the warp plasma subprocessor. If his plan to regain control of the ship doesn't work, the *Defiant* will blow up when it reaches warp one.

O'Brien and Bashir have a difficult time releasing the controls, but they manage to do it just before they run out of air. Down in engineering, Nog is surprised but grateful when he notices that command functions have been transferred to engineering. Unfortunately, before Sisko can do anything about it, the Jem'Hadar figure out that the crew has been stalling, and that the repairs are complete.

Kudak'Etan tells his crew to prepare to bring the warp drive on-line, but before they can, the *Rubicon* takes out a number of Jem'Hadar with tiny photon torpedoes, providing Sisko's team with the distraction they need to gain control of the situation in engineering. Kira disables the computer virus while Sisko floods all the other areas of the ship with anesthezine gas. After repairs are completed on the *Defiant*, the ship returns to the anomaly and successfully restores the runabout and its crew to full size.

"I put in a call to Andre Bormanis and said, 'We want to shrink the runabout,'" recollects Bradley Thompson. "And Andre said, 'I've been dreading this call for years.'"

"It's true," admits Bormanis. "For years I'd been dreading the day the writers would decide to do some version of *Fantastic Voyage*," he says, referring to the classic science fiction film about a medical team that's reduced to microscopic size and injected into a human body. The prospect of coming up with some technically feasible rationale for such an implausible premise worried Bormanis. "I didn't know whether I'd want to ask for a credit or a disclaimer on the episode!"

But there was no way to avoid it. "It was the sixth season, so why *not* do it?" observes Ira Behr, providing all the rationale the writing staff needed. "How many series can do a salute to *Land of the Giants,* to *The Incredible Shrinking Man*?" he demands. "We *had* to do this show! We owed it to all the schlock science fiction that had come before us. If we hadn't done it, it would have been a crime—a creative crime, and, dare I say, a crime against humanity itself. And it just became clear to me, you know? Maybe that tumor moved a silly centimeter in my brain. But we just *had* to do it. And that was that."

Not that this homage to "sci-fi" was Behr's idea in the first place, nor even that of the episode's writers, David Weddle and Bradley Thompson. No, the spark for this visual effects–driven bit of fun came from a staff member better known for some of *Star Trek's* most sensitive character pieces.

"It's a story that I'd wanted to do for years," René Echevarria states enthusiastically. "In fact, I wrote a version of it as a *TNG* spec script, way back before I sold the producers my first episode ['The Offspring']." Echevarria admits that he never sent that spec script in while he was freelancing, but he never forgot about it. It was only after he'd been brought on staff as *The Next Generation's* story editor during that show's sixth season that he broached the subject. "Jeri Taylor (then *TNG's* supervising producer) looked at me like I was out of my mind," he chuckles. And later on, after he moved to *Deep Space Nine,* "Ira looked at me like I was out of my mind."

Echevarria notes proudly that he "worked on them for years. Every now and then I'd say, 'We can always do the shrinking show!' And after a while, whenever we got stuck, Ira would say, 'We could always do that stupid shrinking show.' And then one day we were really stumped. We didn't know what we were going to do for the next episode. I walked out of the room for ten minutes, and when I came back, Hans [Beimler] said to me, 'We're gonna do the shrinking show.'"

Echevarria could scarcely believe it. But apparently the word had come from the series' executive producer, who'd just had an in-car epiphany. "I was driving and I suddenly thought, 'It's time to do the little ship show,'" Behr relates. "I came in and I told the guys and they thought I was kidding, because I'd been saying, 'No, no, no, no, no,' for years. But I assured them, 'It's no longer an issue to be discussed. We're just doing it.'"

Okay. They were doing it. But just because they were doing a story that *sounded* silly (the phrase "Honey, I shrunk the runabout" made the rounds behind the scenes) didn't mean the episode actually had to *be* silly. Hence the call to Andre Bormanis, motivated by a need for some scientific terminology that would make the premise of shrinking a ship seem feasible.

Putting aside his reservations, Bormanis did some serious brainstorming with Weddle, Thompson, and Behr. The writers already had decided that the ship would be miniaturized on purpose, as part of a scientific mission, rather than the result of some stereotypical accident. "We were trying to develop

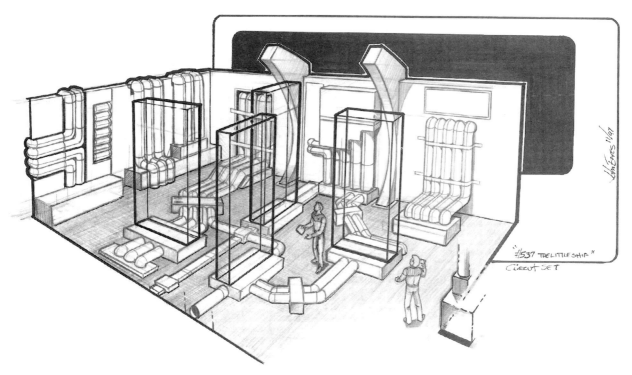

The Art Department suggested how to position Bashir and O'Brien inside a maze of chips. JOHN EAVES

this notion of getting into a layer of subspace, kind of by folding dimensions," Bormanis remembers. "Some physicists today contend that there are actually eleven dimensions—the three spatial dimensions that we experience in our everyday lives, and then time, which is a dimension, and then seven other dimensions that are compacted into a realm that is sub-sub-sub-microscopic. They're too small for human perception, and that's why we're not aware of them. Physicists use the term 'compactification' in discussing them," he says, "but the writers didn't like the phrase 'subspace compactification.' It just didn't seem to roll off the tongue. They thought 'compression' might be more accessible to the audience, so we used 'subspace compression anomaly.'"

Bormanis will stand behind the quasi-scientific elements woven into "One Little Ship." "Usually I'll defer to the producers on whether a point of technology or science is needed or if it can be ignored," the science advisor says. "I told them that if they were going to shrink the runabout, they'd have to shrink all of the air inside of it too," he says. "And they'd have to make it clear that the crew couldn't go outside of the runabout without environmental suits or a force field, because the air molecules would be so much bigger than the crew, they wouldn't be able to breathe them in."

The writers complied, which allowed them to acknowledge the scientific point so important to Bormanis, *and*, he notes, "a great ticking clock, because the crew could start passing out before they finished their job."

Now they had some scientific validity. But the writers knew that there were still likely to be some snickers from the audience, and they decided to deal with that possibility head-on. They would show that even the crew of the *Defiant* knew how wacky this ride was.

The writing of a *DS9* script is frequently a collaborative process, and "One Little Ship" was no exception. "René said, 'We've got to get the audience from the very beginning, we've got to have a character laughing at this,'" recalls Ron Moore. So Moore contributed a scene to the teaser in which Kira can't even talk about the mission without breaking into laughter. "It *is* an absurd premise," smiles Moore, "and Kira's reaction acknowledges that. It's like a signal to the audience: 'This is kinda silly, folks, and we know it's kinda silly, but try to run with us on this one.'"

Which isn't to say that Moore took the show a whole lot more seriously than Kira. "We were doing the story break in René's office," says David Weddle. "Ron wasn't at the break session, because he was in his office working on 'Waltz.' So we're sitting there

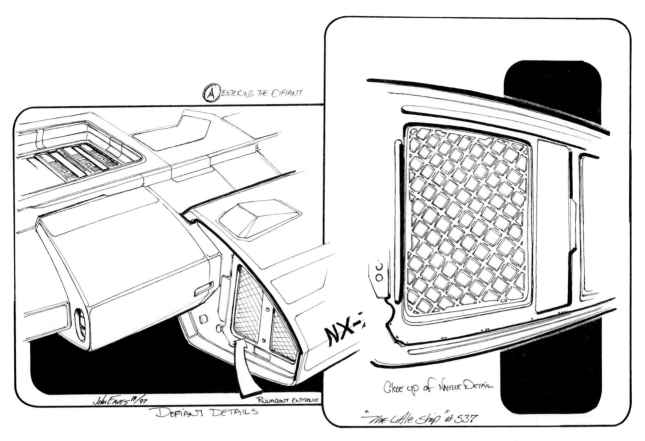

Where the *Rubicon* could enter the *Defiant*. JOHN EAVES

talking and suddenly we hear some tapping on the window. The back of René's chair was blocking the view out the glass, so he finally turned around, wondering if the tapping was from a bird. He looked around for a minute and suddenly saw a tiny plastic ship, hanging on the end of a string."

The other end of the string was up on the building's roof, in Ron Moore's hand. "He came in later," laughs Weddle, "saying, 'Hi, guys. How's it going?' We all just about died laughing."

Although the "little ship" premise hadn't originated with them, Weddle and Thompson went all out to do it justice. Knowing that the runabout essentially would be the main character in the episode, and that the director and the visual effects department would have many questions about what that character was doing at any given moment during the action, the writing team spent many hours on the sets of the *Defiant,* choreographing shots. "It was just Bradley and me in the engine room with a little model ship," Weddle says. "We took turns being a Jem'Hadar and figuring out how the ship could be positioned so it would not be seen."

"We blocked out all of the shots for Act 3 and put all the actors' marks on a floor plan with stick pins," Thompson adds. "It was like, 'We'll put Kira over here and Nog over there, so now we can move the ship over *here* and the Jem'Hadar will see this but not *this.*'"

"Prepping this show was a process of evolution," notes Director Allan Kroeker. "The writers and Gary Hutzel and I would go to the set and talk. David and Brad had written it very specifically, but there were still little logistical things to work out with visual effects. We'd talk about angles while Gary shot video of a tiny ship on a stick, roughing in the sequences."

"Normally the first time I see a script is the day before the first preproduction meeting, but in this case, they called me in advance to discuss some of the potential problems," says Hutzel.

During principal photography, Hutzel digitally recorded data on all of the camera moves. "First we'd stage a scene with a little four-inch ship standing in for the real runabout, performing the action," he says. "That let us know what size the ship had to be in the frame. Then we'd shoot a plate *without* a ship in it,

Fortunately for our heroes, John Eaves has provided clues as to the dangers they could face.

and take that plate back to the motion control studio, and use the data recording information to duplicate the motion while we photographed the real ship."

The real ship was a six-inch miniature runabout built by Tony Meininger. "Tony built it with exactly the same lighting setup as our nineteen-inch model," Hutzel says. "It was just beautiful, an exquisite little model."

"The visual effects guys were terrific," Kroeker says with admiration. "They always worked very closely with me, so I never felt I was in the dark. I had considerable faith in Gary. If he said, 'Yeah, I can pull this off,' I'd say, 'Great!' and then I could sleep."

In the end, Echevarria was very pleased with what his "little ship" idea had turned into, although he does have one regret.

"I think the Jem'Hadar were the wrong villains for the show," he sighs. "We needed more comedic villains. I remember during prep I started saying, 'We should have used someone like the Pakleds, from *TNG*.'

"Then Ira got into it and said, 'No, not the Pakleds—someone like Harry Mudd, from the original series. He's a real villain, but essentially a comic character, and that would make the two sides of the story match up.'"

It was, however, too late in the process to make a drastic change like that, so the possibility of reintroducing Harry Mudd died a quick death . . . except in one writer's imagination.

"After we'd been shooting for a couple of days, Hans stopped me in the parking lot," smiles Echevarria. "He told me he'd figured out the perfect ending to the Harry Mudd episode, one that seemed to reflect the spirit of the original series. Once Harry realizes he's been foiled, he steals a runabout and tries to make his escape from the *Defiant*. And of course he gets pulled into the anomaly and it's about to close up forever when we beam him onto the ship, and he's only *this big*." Echevarria imitates the gesture Beimler showed him, holding thumb and forefinger a fraction of an inch apart. "And Odo says, 'Well, at least we won't have to feed him very much!'"

FAR BEYOND THE STARS

Episode #538

TELEPLAY BY IRA STEVEN BEHR & HANS BEIMLER
STORY BY MARC SCOTT ZICREE
DIRECTED BY AVERY BROOKS

GUEST CAST

Joseph Sisko/Preacher	BROCK PETERS
Weyoun/Officer Kevin Mulkahey	JEFFREY COMBS
Gul Dukat/Officer Burt Ryan	MARC ALAIMO
Martok/Roy Rittenhouse	J.G. HERTZLER
Nog/Vendor	ARON EISENBERG

AND

Kasidy Yates/Cassie	PENNY JOHNSON

STARDATE UNKNOWN

Although the Federation scored a major victory when its forces retook Deep Space 9 from the Dominion ("Sacrifice of Angels"), the war is far from over. Squadrons of Jem'Hadar fighters hover near the Cardassian border, and the latest victim of their vigilance is the *U.S.S. Cortez* and its full complement of four hundred, including Captain Quentin Swofford, an old friend of Captain Sisko's. The war effort is beginning to take its psychological toll on the commander of DS9. Visiting his son's station for the first time, Joseph Sisko observes that it seems like the weight of the Alpha Quadrant is on Ben's shoulders.

The disheartened captain admits to his father that it may be time for someone else to take over his position and "make the tough calls." Joseph says that Ben has some thinking to do; he'll support whatever decision his son makes. But before the captain can allow his thoughts to travel in that direction, he sees a man dressed in a twentieth-century business suit walk past the door of his office. Sisko is bewildered by the experience, and even more surprised when, a few minutes later, he's greeted by a man in a baseball uniform. This time, he decides to get to the bottom of his apparent visions, and he follows the baseball player through a door . . .

. . . and into twentieth-century Manhattan! As Sisko stares around himself in astonishment, he's clipped by a cab and knocked to the ground. He awakens to find himself in DS9's Infirmary, surrounded by his loved ones. Dr. Bashir tells Sisko that he's exhibiting the same unusual neural patterns that he experienced the previous year ("Rapture"). Bashir hands Sisko a padd so the cap-

tain can review the results of his examination for himself . . .

. . . and suddenly he finds himself back in 1950s Manhattan, staring at the cover of *Galaxy*, a science fiction pulp magazine. This time, however, Sisko isn't surprised by his surroundings. In fact, he's no longer Captain Benjamin Sisko. He's Benny Russell, a writer for *Incredible Tales* magazine, *Galaxy*'s key competitor.

Benny heads to his office and greets his fellow writers: Albert Macklin, an absentminded mechanical engineer turned writer; Julius and Kay Eaton, a married couple who write under one—male—name; and Herbert Rossoff, an opinionated, feisty author with leftist leanings. The magazine's editor, Douglas Pabst, is a cost-conscious man who'll do whatever it takes to keep his publication on the newsstands. Each of Benny's co-workers resembles one of Ben Sisko's associates on Deep Space 9.

Pabst hands out the coming month's story assignments, which are inspired by illustrations produced by Roy Rittenhouse, the staff artist. Benny chooses an illustration of a distinctive-looking space station.

There's an uncomfortable moment as Pabst announces that the publisher wants pictures of the writers to appear in the next issue—although there will be no photos of Kay or Benny. The publisher

In an apparent vision, Sisko finds himself living the life of Benny Russell, a 1950s pulp science fiction writer. ROBBIE ROBINSON

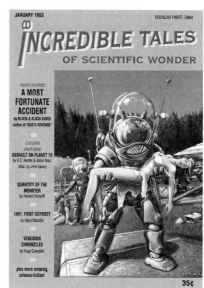

Covers of the magazines that were "edited" by Pabst.

feels that letting the public know that there are a female and a Negro writer on staff would be disconcerting to readers.

As Benny leaves the office, a sudden gust of wind blows Roy's illustration of the station from his hand. It winds up at the feet of plainclothes cops Ryan and Mulkahey. After giving Benny a difficult time, the pair reluctantly return his drawing, and Benny heads uptown to Harlem. As he makes his way home, he encounters an elderly Negro street preacher. Although Benny has never seen the man before, the preacher seems to know Benny. He urges Benny to write the truth that's in his heart, in the hopes that his words will open the eyes of others. Benny goes to his apartment and that night begins writing a story about Captain Benjamin Sisko, a Negro man who commands a powerful space station. As he works, Benny sees a disconcerting vision of himself as Sisko. He shrugs it off and continues working.

A few days later, the story is finished. Benny tells his girlfriend Cassie about it, but Cassie is more enthusiastic about the possibility of the two of them buying the coffee shop where she waits tables. Benny points out that he's a writer, and that his future doesn't lie in a coffee shop. Suddenly Willie Hawkins, a Harlem local who made good by getting into professional baseball, stops by the shop. He flirts with Cassie, but despite her frustration with her boyfriend, the waitress has eyes only for Benny.

A street kid named Jimmy enters the coffee shop and tries to sell Benny a stolen watch. Benny express-es concern about the teenager's future, but Jimmy feels this is the only way to succeed on his own terms; he's not about to settle for a menial job in the white man's world. Trying to break through Jimmy's self-defeating attitude about his birthright, Benny tells him about the story he's just written. "I'm writing about *us*," he says. Amused by the idea of "colored people" in space, Jimmy allows that he might read the story after it's published.

At his office, Benny's fellow writers agree that the story, called "Deep Space 9," is excellent. But Pabst refuses to publish a story whose protagonist is a Negro man; he's too worried about the repercussions. Back in Harlem, Jimmy cynically observes that things will never change in the way Benny foresees, and Cassie, although sympathetic, feels that the rejection could be a sign that Benny should change his career. But Benny refuses to give up on his dream—which seems to be encroaching on his reality. He sees visions of Kay looking like his fictional character "Major Kira" and Willie looking like a big Klingon warrior named "Worf."

That night, Benny again runs into the preacher, who urges him to walk with the prophets and "write the words" that will lead his people out of the darkness. He returns home and writes another story about Ben Sisko, forgetting all about a late-night date with Cassie. Later, she arrives at his apartment and invites him to dance with her. As they sway to the music, Benny has a disorienting vision of himself as Sisko, dancing with Kasidy Yates in Sisko's quarters on Deep

Space 9. Rattled, Benny tells Cassie that he feels as if he's becoming Captain Sisko.

But he can't stop writing. A few weeks later, he shows up at *Incredible Tales* with even more stories about Deep Space 9. Pabst thinks Benny's insane, but the other writers want to see the stories published. They suggest that Benny make the ending of "Deep Space 9" a dream, the dream of a young Negro man's vision of a better future. Benny is willing to accept this compromise, and surprisingly, so is Pabst. Benny goes home to celebrate with Cassie, but the night turns ugly. The two of them run into the preacher, who warns that the path of the prophets sometimes leads into pain. Moments later, the sound of gunfire draws them to a nearby crime scene. Ryan and Mulkahey have shot and killed a teenager who was attempting to break into a car. Benny is horrified to see that it's Jimmy. He lunges at one of the cops, giving them the excuse to beat him mercilessly.

Weeks later, Benny is still suffering from the aftereffects of that dreadful night, but he goes to the office to pick up a copy of the latest issue, which will contain his new story. To the surprise of Benny and the rest of the writers, Pabst announces that there will be no issue this month; the publisher has had the entire run destroyed. What's more, the publisher has ordered Pabst to fire Benny. The news pushes Benny to the breaking point. Sobbing in frustration, Benny tells the group that they may be able to deny *him*, but they can't deny Ben Sisko. Sisko's life, his station, his friends, his *future*—they all exist. The future is *real*, Benny declares defiantly, because he's made it real.

Not long after, an ambulance arrives to take the shell-shocked writer away. During the trip to the hospital, Benny realizes that the preacher is riding with him. He looks down and sees that he's dressed in Sisko's uniform. "Who am I?" Benny asks the preacher in confusion.

"You're the dreamer," is the reply, "and the dream."

Benny closes his eyes, trying to make sense of it all . . .

. . . and then opens them to find himself back in the Infirmary on Deep Space 9. Bashir reveals that Sisko was unconscious only a few minutes, and that his neural patterns have returned to normal, which is welcome news to his family.

A few days later, Joseph prepares to go back home to Earth. He asks his son if he's made his decision, and Sisko says that he will stay on the station to finish the job he's started. As he and his father stare

out the window of the station into space, Sisko wonders if his dream of Benny was really a dream. Perhaps they're all just figments of Benny's imagination, he says, and maybe somewhere, far beyond the stars, Benny Russell is dreaming their story . . .

"'Far Beyond the Stars' presented a page of our history, from a time when science fiction was becoming a part of the mainstream," observes Director Avery Brooks. "And when we talk about those writers, we're talking about the reason that we're even *here!*" he laughs, gesturing at the *Deep Space Nine* sets, located on a soundstage at Paramount Pictures.

"The people we saw in that office each had a very specific identity," Brooks continues. "I wanted to see who those people were, in order to investigate one of the most oppressive times of the twentieth century. They were living with McCarthyism and the atomic bomb and the Red Scare." He nods thoughtfully. "I mean, that was a *very* interesting period."

The idea that set in motion one of *Deep Space Nine's* proudest hours came from a pitch by Marc Scott Zicree. Zicree's story focused on Jake Sisko's experiences as he appears to time-travel back to the 1950s, where he meets a group of science fiction writers. "But it turns out that he didn't really go back there," recalls Ira Behr. "It was some alien trick to find out something from Jake. It felt a little bit like a gimmick. There was no 'bottom' to the story, and at the time I said, 'No, I don't think so.'"

Still, says Behr, "It was a great backdrop—1950s science fiction writers—and *that* interested me. So months later, I was driving in my car and it suddenly hit me that a story in that setting should be about *Benjamin* Sisko, and racism, and what is reality and what isn't."

In an unusual break from the norm, "We had lunch with Zicree and basically pitched that idea to *him*," Behr says with a chuckle. "He wrote a story that we broke with the writing staff."

After the story break session, Behr and Hans Beimler wrote the first draft of the teleplay. Traditionally, scripts go through several drafts, with scenes shortened, lengthened or deleted altogether in an attempt to reach perfection (or at least "final shooting script" status), but this first script "was as close to the show that aired as any I've ever seen," remarks Bradley Thompson. "They came *that* close."

The fictionalized portraits of the *Incredible Tales* staff—tributes to the hardworking people who worked in the 1950s pulp magazine publishing business—came easily. "The characters just fell into place," Behr says. "So it became a very exciting show to write."

When the actors received their scripts, they were all struck by the honest and straightforward depiction of racism—both overt and subtle—at the heart of Benny Russell's story.

"It was a wonderful, gripping episode, beautifully conceived," says Rene Auberjonois, who portrayed Douglas Pabst—an "unenlightened white man," says Behr—and the ostensible villain of the piece, since it is Pabst's refusal to stand up to the publisher that pushes Benny over the edge. "Ira was very concerned about how I would react to being the only one of the principal characters to be, essentially, a bad guy," Auberjonois relates. "But I *loved* the part. And I don't necessarily see Pabst as 'the bad guy.' He was a peripheral character, and the only one, aside from Benny, whose viewpoint went through a whole process. His character is the conflict for Benny and the world Benny lives in, and I was delighted to play it." Clearly, Auberjonois had no problem separating Pabst from Odo in his performance choices for the episode. The other actors had a similar experience, to lesser or greater degree.

"Personally, I felt like Eve Arden, and it didn't feel good!" Nana Visitor laughs, referring to the wisecracking star of the classic 1950s television series *Our Miss Brooks*.

"At first I wondered where I could find Weyoun

"It was fun to see Armin and all the others finally free of all that rubber," Nana Visitor says. ROBBIE ROBINSON

in this guy," Jeffrey Combs says of his character, the openly racist undercover cop Mulkahey, "but then I realized that his status as a suppressing authority figure is the synthesis for Weyoun in Benny's mind. So I approached him as a completely different character."

Armin Shimerman concurs. "Herb Rossoff was not an extension of Quark," he says. "He was a communist"—which is about as far from a Ferengi as you can get—"and he was the only one of the characters to stand up for Benny, not enough, obviously, but he did stand up for him."

On a more mundane level, the fact that they were going to be seen on camera sans prosthetic makeup (or spots, or uniform), also made a big impression. "Being out of makeup was slightly off-putting," confesses Shimerman. "I've grown accustomed to the Quark mask being a mechanism for support. That face describes who I am as an alien character. And also, while many actors worry about how they look on camera, I don't, because *my* face isn't *on* camera. So it was bizarre to be bare-faced on a *Star Trek* show. I never had been before."

J.G. Hertzler had never appeared sans prosthetics on the show either, but playing the role of staff artist Roy Rittenhouse "was like falling off a log for me," he laughs. "Because I really do draw and paint. So when I was sitting there drawing, I literally *was* drawing the cast."

"It was very strange," comments Combs. "Everybody was out of makeup and we were standing on a back-lot New York street. It was just a totally different world."

It was a different world for Dean Jones as well. "The makeup trailer was a *lot* less busy while they worked on that episode," Jones says with a grin. "It was a cakewalk, it was so easy."

But easy is the *last* word you'd use to describe Avery Brooks's duties in "Far Beyond the Stars."

"I was talking to Steve Oster and I said, 'This is going to be a tough show to direct,'" notes Behr. "And he said, 'What about Avery?' I said, 'Well, he's going to be in every scene, but he has the passion for it, so he'll do a great job.' We offered it to him and he said, 'Yes.'

"We discussed the possibility of Avery directing, knowing that he was going to be in every frame of film," Steve Oster acknowledges. "We don't like that combination, because it's very hard to direct yourself. However, this was a story about racism and prejudice and we felt very strongly that it would be wrong if it came from a bunch of people who didn't necessarily

Jeffrey Combs (left) and Marc Alaimo, still cast as the villians of the piece. ROBBIE ROBINSON

know about that experience. We knew that it was imperative to the story and imperative to the integrity of television for it to be done right."

Sad to say, Brooks did know about that experience.

"If we had changed the people's clothes, this story could be about right now," Brooks states. "What's insidious about racism is that it is unconscious. Even among these very bright and enlightened characters—a group that includes a woman writer who has to use a man's name to get her work published, and who is married to a brown man with a British accent in 1953—it's perfectly reasonable to coexist with someone like Pabst. It's in the culture, it's the way people think. So that was the approach we took," Brooks says. "I never talked about racism. I just showed how these intelligent people think, and it all came out of them."

Brooks is proud of the massive combined effort that went into the episode. "I fought very hard to make sure that everybody in every single department was on the same page, and that part of it I really enjoyed," he say. "Everybody was very, very meticulous and worked to make this 1953 reality as exact and precise as he or she could."

Turning a section of the Paramount back lot into an exact replica of 1953 New York represented a considerable amount of that work. Herman Zimmerman designed and constructed a full coffee shop set, inte-

rior as well as exterior, on the back lot rather than on the soundstage to provide the extra touch of realism that the sight of vintage automobiles passing outside of the window of "Eva's Kitchen" would bring to the production.

While the interior offices of Stone Publishing were on Stage 18, several scenes called for an exterior door to the "Trill Building." That, too, was filmed on the back lot. And, of course, any astute New Yorker is aware of the well-known Brill Building, located in the heart of Manhattan. Pun intended.

Brooks specifically asked that the cafe, the street, the offices and Benny's apartment all be decorated to fit the personalities of the people who frequent them. Therefore the walls of the coffee shop are adorned with a number of celebrity photos, including one of Michael Dorn as baseball star Willie, and Benny's apartment is filled with books, a piano, and a rich collection of native African artifacts.

In creating such set decorating minutiae, the film makers find material where they might, and that's sometimes in the darkest recesses of their active minds. Thus it should come as no surprise that posters outside of the Rendezvous Dance Club list such featured acts as "The Tom Arp Trio" (named for the series' construction coordinator) and "Phineas Tarbolde and the Nightingale Women" (a reference to a poem quoted in an original series episode).

The full name of the magazine that Benny Russell writes for is "Incredible Tales of Scientific Wonder." The cover design is modeled after that of an actual 1953 Gernsback publication, the most well-known of that era's publishing firms. One of the items on Herbert Rossoff's desk, a rocket ship–shaped trophy, is a Hugo Award. It is awarded annually by the Science Fiction Writers of America, and named after Hugo Gernsback. The prop is an actual Hugo, loaned to the show by its owner, Senior Illustrator Rick Sternback, who won it (and another) as "Best Professional Artist."

Pinned above every desk are humorous and pertinent drawings, notes, newspaper articles, and assorted toys. Most of the drawings were done by Doug Drexler, John Eaves, and Jim Van Over, although a few are actual sketches by Matt Jeffries, production designer for the original series.

Visible everywhere are pinned-up memos from Mr. Pabst. One memo to Albert Macklin advises him that "four laws of robotics is too many," and suggests that he lose one. The memo brings to light the similarity between Albert and famed science fiction writer

Isaac Asimov, who wrote a series of novels in which robots operated according to three "Laws of Robotics." Asimov's groundbreaking novel *I, Robot* was published by Gnome Press, as was Macklin's first novel. Another Pabst memo, this one to Herb Rossoff, advises that "no one would believe that a cheerleader could kill vampires." This inside joke works on two levels, given that Rossoff's counterpart, Armin Shimerman, appeared for several seasons on the series *Buffy, the Vampire Slayer.*

The other elements that provided the episode with the correct look conveyed a much more serious message. For instance, the 1947 ambulance that carries Benny away at the end is old, dirty, and in poor repair, because, as Brooks notes, "That's what they would have sent."

The episode didn't highlight much in the way of visual effects, but the Special Effects Department had some fun. Benny's first run-in with the bigoted cops occurs when his drawing of the space station blows down the street and lands near the foot of one of the officers. Getting the sketch to follow those stage directions was Gary Monak's job. "I tied a big helium balloon to the drawing with a monofilament on a fishing pole," Monak says. "The balloon was just off-camera. I had to yank the drawing out of 'Benny's' hand and direct it toward Marc Alaimo, the cop, so that he could put his foot on it. *And* it had to land with the picture in the right direction for the camera," Monak laughs. "It was one of those gags that we could have done three hundred times and it wouldn't have worked out. We actually did it twice and it worked great."

Brooks's interest in period authenticity didn't end with prevailing attitudes and the visual look of the episode. He carried his involvement all the way through postproduction. "Avery came to the music spotting session," says Dennis McCarthy. "That's the first time that any of the actors have come to a spotting session except for LeVar Burton, who came once when he directed an episode of *The Next Generation.* We had long discussions about what kind of music Benny and Cassie would dance to, the style of music coming out of the clubs and the style of the scoring."

Brooks's performance as Benny was, of course, impressive to his fellow actors. "Avery was spectacular, in front of the camera and behind it," says Combs. "There was a scene toward the end where he falls apart with the camera right in front of his nose.

Out from behind the Klingon makeup, Michael Dorn as a New York Giants ball player. ROBBIE ROBINSON

It was just riveting." Members of the cast and crew fortunate enough to witness that scene, where Benny insists, "The future is real—I made it real!" state without hesitation that they witnessed an Emmy-caliber performance, and that the tears Brooks shed were genuine.

"Avery did an unbelievable job," Ira Behr states. "This was the closest we'd worked together in the whole six years. I mean, obviously we work and talk on a regular basis, but this was a very intense couple of weeks that we spent together, and it had a big impact on me. It certainly strengthened the bond that I feel toward Avery. Just his stamina, and the pressure of being on New York street filming those scenes . . . they were *so* well done!"

And how does Brooks himself feel about the finished episode? "Actually," he says with a smile, "it should have been a two-parter."

HONOR AMONG THIEVES

Episode #539

TELEPLAY BY RENÉ ECHEVARRIA
STORY BY PHILIP KIM
DIRECTED BY ALLAN EASTMAN

GUEST CAST

Chadwick	MICHAEL HARNEY
Krole	CARLOS CARRASCO
Flith	JOHN CHANDLER
Vorta	LELAND CROOKE
Raimus	JOSEPH CULP
Yint	BRAD BLAISDELL

AND

Liam Bilby	NICK TATE

STARDATE UNKNOWN

In order to infiltrate the Orion Syndicate, O'Brien gets into Bilby's good graces. ROBBIE ROBINSON

On the gritty, industrial planet of Farius Prime, three petty criminals bide their time in a disreputable bar, unaware that they are being observed by the scruffy human seated on the other side of the room. When Krole, one of the trio, walks over to a combooth and tries to use his dataport to get some food, the human stranger surreptitiously aims a small device at the combooth. Suddenly, the booth overloads, and Krole is nearly fried by an arc of energy that runs from the comunit into his dataport. But before Krole is seriously injured, the stranger jumps to his feet and saves him.

Krole examines a piece of his dataport in dismay. It's fused, and he can't afford to get a replacement—which means that he and his two cronies could be in deep trouble with their boss, Raimus. But the human comes to the rescue once again, noting that he might be able to repair it. Bilby, the superior of the other two men, takes the stranger up on his offer, and tells him to have it fixed by the next day.

The human leaves and goes to a nearby alley, where he rendezvous with a Starfleet Intelligence officer named Chadwick. He updates the officer on his recent encounter and Chadwick congratulates him; he didn't think it was possible to make contact with members of the Orion Syndicate so quickly. But the human, Miles O'Brien, tells Chadwick that he *wanted* to make contact quickly. He's anxious to complete the mission and go home. He's not cut out to be an undercover operative for Starfleet Intelligence.

Chadwick assures O'Brien that his recruitment for this assignment was necessary. The Syndicate seems to be on to Starfleet Intelligence's web of undercover operatives; five have been killed in the past year. Once O'Brien finds out the name of the Starfleet informant who's helping the Syndicate, Chadwick will put the chief on a transport back to DS9.

That's not nearly soon enough for members of the crew back on the station, who are having a difficult time coping with the hybrid Federation-Cardassian equipment in O'Brien's absence. What's more, Bashir is concerned about his friend's sudden disappearance, and Sisko can't reveal any details to reassure him—other than the fact that he's convinced the chief can take care of himself.

O'Brien brings the three Syndicate members the repaired equipment. He learns that Bilby already has checked his story. Connelly, the chief's cover identity, is a down-on-his-luck fix-it man. Bilby gives him one additional test, asking the chief to take a look at some faulty Klingon disruptor rifles that he's supposed to deliver to Raimus. O'Brien quickly spots the problem and agrees to repair them. Bilby is so taken with O'Brien's skills and apparent honesty that he decides to take him under his wing, much to the displeasure of Krole and his cohort Flith. But although O'Brien now has the dubious distinction of being a trusted insider, he can't relax for a minute. He's unnerved when Bilby kills a man right in front of him, despite the fact that the man was an unscrupulous arms dealer.

Later, Bilby explains that he will do whatever it

takes to protect what he has. Bilby's obvious fondness for his family, who live off-planet, resonates with the chief, but he won't allow himself to forget what he's there for. He eventually gets Bilby to reveal just enough about the identity of the Starfleet informant to satisfy Chadwick's needs, but before he can deliver the information, Bilby takes him to meet Raimus.

At the meeting, Bilby "witnesses" for O'Brien, putting his own life on the line by vouching for O'Brien's trustworthiness. But for the moment, O'Brien is more surprised by the presence of the Vorta who accompanies Raimus to the meeting. What could this mean?

When O'Brien gets together with Chadwick, he lets him know about the apparent connection between the Orion Syndicate and the Dominion. Chadwick extends O'Brien's assignment long enough to find out what's going on between the two groups.

O'Brien ingratiates himself with his little group by helping them to rob a bank via Krole's dataport. His sense of camaraderie with the criminals, particularly Bilby, surprises him, and he begins to worry about what will happen to Bilby once his assignment ends. Will the Syndicate kill him for trusting a Starfleet operative? Chadwick tries to assure O'Brien that if Starfleet gets to Bilby first, he'll be safe in a Federation prison. But O'Brien is troubled by the idea of betraying his new friend, particularly when Bilby confides that he thinks he's finally going to be moved up in the organization.

The next time O'Brien and the others meet with Raimus and the Vorta, Flith is executed for conducting business on the side. Raimus tells Bilby that he's fortunate he never opted to witness for Flith, or he'd be dead, too. Before O'Brien has the opportunity to reflect on this, the Vorta gives Bilby's group an assignment. They're to assassinate the planet's Klingon ambassador, using the disruptors that O'Brien repaired earlier. O'Brien realizes at once that this will make it look like the ambassador was killed by a rival Klingon House. The Vorta explains that the ambassador has been advocating that the Klingon Empire break off its alliance with the Federation, something Chancellor Gowron adamantly opposes. It will therefore be assumed that Gowron is behind the assassination. The ambassador's cause will gain strength and the Klingon alliance with the Federation will come to an end—giving the Dominion one less enemy to worry about in the Alpha Quadrant.

O'Brien passes the information on to Chadwick, who says that he'll warn the Klingons. O'Brien is hor-

rified; he knows that the Klingons will kill Bilby and his men. Chadwick tells O'Brien that isn't his concern; he's going back to DS9. Unfortunately, O'Brien feels it *is* his concern. He knocks out Chadwick and hurries to Bilby's apartment to stop him from going on the assignment.

Unable to come up with a convincing lie that will keep Bilby home, O'Brien finally confesses that he works for Starfleet. Bilby is crushed, and he lets O'Brien know that he's done him no favor by coming to warn him. If Bilby doesn't go through with the assignment, then the Syndicate will think he's in league with O'Brien—and Starfleet. And if they can't get Bilby, they'll go after his family, to make an example of what they do to traitors. The only thing he can do to protect his wife and children is to allow himself to be killed by the Klingons. He asks O'Brien to take care of his cat, Chester, and the two men part. O'Brien returns home with Chester and tells Bashir what happened. Despite Bashir's attempt to reassure his friend that he was only doing his duty, O'Brien remains troubled by his memories of Farius Prime.

"I really didn't approach 'Honor Among Thieves' any differently in terms of acting," observes Actor Colm Meaney, "but it was structured very much like a mystery, and I imagine that the writers approached it differently than they normally would." That's true enough, although it wasn't entirely deliberate on their part. In fact, if the shortest distance between two points is a straight line, then the writer-producers of *Deep Space*

The Orion Syndicate finally acquires a face. ROBBIE ROBINSON

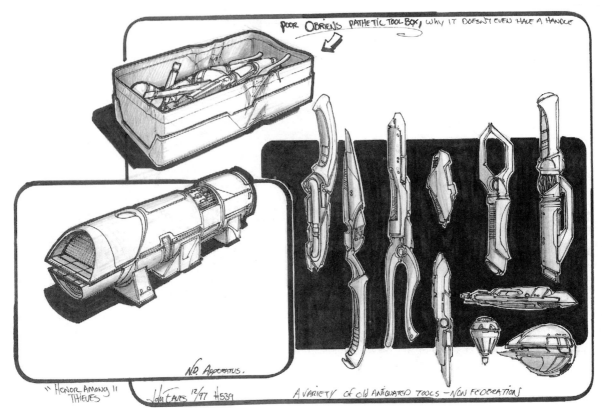

Handwritten annotations on image:
POOR OBRIENS PATHETIC TOOL BOX, WHY IT DOESN'T EVEN HAVE A HANDLE
"HONOR AMONG" THIEVES
N.D. APPARATUS.
John Eaves 12/97 #539
A VARIETY of OLD ANTIQUATED TOOLS — NON FEDERATION

Connelly's—O'Brien's—"pathetic" equipment. JOHN EAVES

Nine twisted and turned many light-years out of their way before arriving at the final version of "Honor Among Thieves."

"It started out as a really light-hearted story about Jake and Quark," reports Philip Kim, who was a *DS9* production assistant (P.A.) when he pitched the idea to Ron Moore. "Jake saves the life of a girl whose father turns out to be the head of the Orion Syndicate, and as a result of this selfless act, he gets all these new, questionable friends. For a while, it's an eighteen-year-old's dream. Anything Jake wants, these guys in flashy suits get for him, and it's really cool. But then things start to take a frightening turn. Jake has a small public argument with Nog on the Promenade and the next thing he knows, Nog is in critical care in the Infirmary. That's when Jake starts wondering what he's gotten himself into.

"While Jake is trying desperately to get *out* of this situation without offending anybody or getting himself killed, Quark is trying just as desperately to get *into* the situation," Kim continues. "Quark sees it as his big opportunity to ingratiate himself with these extremely powerful, very wealthy people, so all of a sudden he's made himself Jake's best friend. But finally Jake and Quark both realize they're being used by a third party who's trying to ascend to the leadership of the organization."

Kim chuckles. "Obviously, it turned into a much deeper and much darker episode," he says. Although he knew all of the *DS9* writers in his capacity as a P.A., Kim found himself on a different footing in his pitch session with Moore. "Ron was a very imposing presence for a first-time pitch," Kim recalls. "He just sat there with not one change of expression the entire time. When I walked out of there, I thought, 'Well, that was an experience—but there's was no way I made a sale.'"

Over the next six months, Kim was allowed to pitch numerous other stories (one of which would inspire seventh season's "Treachery, Faith, and the Great River"). Nevertheless, he was surprised when the producers invited him to a meeting and told him they were interested in buying his first story idea. "I had forgotten all about it," he says. "And suddenly Ira [Behr] was saying, 'We want to do this with O'Brien, and we think O'Brien should betray this guy . . .' I just sat there, nodding my head, convinced that they were talking to the wrong person. Because the story they were talking about, I didn't recognize at all!"

As it turned out, what had inspired Behr and the

others was Kim's mention of "the Orion Syndicate," the criminal organization previously alluded to in "The Ascent" and "A Simple Investigation." Although the writers themselves had invented the Syndicate, they hadn't thought of doing a story about its members until Kim brought the name up in his pitch session. They told him where they wanted to go with the story. "I went home and wrote a treatment based on our discussion, and the final script that René [Echevarria] wrote was very similar to the treatment," he says happily.

"We'd been looking for an O'Brien show, because it had been a while since we'd done one," says Echevarria. "I'm not sure we found a level to this that made it truly an O'Brien show, or even truly a *Deep Space Nine* show. The story's a little familiar. Every television detective series has done a story about the crime fighter going undercover, getting involved, and coming to kind of respect the code of the bad guy. So it wasn't a resounding success for me. But O'Brien is our Everyman, and if O'Brien can find himself sympathizing with a gangster-thug-killer, then anyone should be able to."

"It was meant to be a character study about two men, one who has to betray the other," Ira Behr says. "We wanted to put Colm Meaney against another actor and just let them hold the screen for forty-two minutes, and within this science fiction setting make you care about the humanity of these people. That was the intent. It was a fragile thing. The episode's success was totally dependent on that relationship. If the relationship sinks, then the whole episode sinks. If the relationship is okay, then the whole episode is okay. And I think that's what we had. We had 'okay.'" If Behr can't quite bring himself to see the episode as something that's more than "okay," it's because he still can't separate what *is* from what might have been.

One of the most important aspects of dramatic presentation is casting. Ideally, during the casting process, the producers will find an actor who fits a character perfectly. For the role of Orion Syndicate operative Liam Bilby, they found two such actors. Director Allan Eastman, who had worked with Producer Hans Beimler on *TekWar,* suggested Nick Tate. Ira Behr suggested veteran character actor Charles Hallahan, who'd most recently appeared on *NYPD Blue* and in the feature film *Dante's Peak.*

"This is a very complicated and sad story," Eastman says. "The casting decision really came down to Nick and Charlie. But what Ira and I found interesting is that there was a kind of physical resem-

The writers continued the thread of Bilby and his family into a final-season episode. ROBBIE ROBINSON

blance between Charlie and Colm, so that you could almost believe that Charlie was Colm's father. And we thought that would have been very interesting to work with, so that tilted the balance. We went with Charlie, and I told Nick about our reasons.

"Charlie was very excited to do the show," Eastman continues. "But before we got into production, he had a heart attack and died. It was very tragic, losing such a gentleman and an actor of that quality, a very, very sad circumstance, but we had to go to camera in two days. So I suggested that we go ahead and call Nick. It felt quite odd asking him to come and do the part in that situation, but he took it with a great feeling of wanting to do it in honor of Charlie's memory."

Tate was excellent in the role, all agree, but it changed the tilt of the relationship between O'Brien and Bilby. "We played it a little more on the basis of friendship," says Eastman, "given the way that Nick and Colm matched up. But we lost the possibility of the father and son relationship."

"I still have trouble watching the show because I still always see Charlie in it," admits Behr. "As a character, O'Brien is so genuine and so trustworthy, and there's no guile in him. And for me, Charlie was the perfect guy to play Bilby, because he had what O'Brien has. It would have been reflections of two guys who were a lot alike, and Charlie would have broken your heart."

In order to infuse Bilby with what Eastman calls "an emotional goodness of the heart, in spite of what he does in his job," Echevarria gave the character a cat. And then, as he had done when he invented Dr. Bashir's teddy bear ("The Quickening") he tried to give it a unique name. This time, however, Ira Behr opted to nip the impulse in the bud.

"He tried to do it to me again!" the executive producer pretends to fume. "He gives this Orion Syndicate guy a cat! And then," Behr continues in disgust, "he tries to name him '*Sweet Pea.*' I just put my foot down and said, 'No. *Kukalaka* is bad enough, but this guy does *not* have a cat named *Sweet Pea*. Only you, you twit, would have a cat named Sweet Pea, thank you.' And *then,*" Behr shakes his head in feigned frustration, "in the end the cat goes to *O'Brien.*"

O'Brien—or rather Colm Meaney—wasn't much happier about inheriting the cat, now named Chester, than Behr was.

"I'm not a big cat man," admits Meaney. "Dogs are fine, but cats are mean. But this cat was good. You know—it was an acting cat. It knew its place."

CHANGE OF HEART
Episode #540
WRITTEN BY RONALD D. MOORE
DIRECTED BY DAVID LIVINGSTON

GUEST CAST

Lasaran   TODD WARING

STARDATE 51597.2

Worf doesn't know much about *tongo*, but he has infinite faith in his wife, Jadzia Dax. And although Quark is currently in the midst of a *tongo* winning streak (206 straight games in the past month), Worf bets Chief O'Brien that Jadzia will break that streak. But while Jadzia is a skilled player, Quark tops her with a full consortium and wins his 207th game.

Though Worf now owes O'Brien a bottle of scotch whiskey, he is unconcerned. As he tells Jadzia, he would rather lose a bet on her than win on someone else. The two settle in for a cozy evening together, but their sleep is disturbed by a summons to the captain's office. Sisko informs them that they're to travel immediately to a specified point near the Badlands. There, they'll receive an encrypted transmission from Lasaran, a Cardassian double agent who's been supplying Starfleet with military intelligence reports.

As the runabout heads toward their destination,

When Jadzia is wounded, Worf must choose between saving her life and their mission. ROBBIE ROBINISON

Jadzia and Worf discuss locations for their long-delayed honeymoon. Worf is leaning toward somewhere rough, but Jadzia wants pampering and room service. To Jadzia's surprise, Worf yields to her desires; as a married man, he explains, he's decided that he should make some adjustments in his lifestyle.

When they reach the coordinates, they're contacted by Lasaran, who presents them with an interesting proposition. The double agent believes he's about to be discovered, and he wants to defect to the Federation. He's willing to provide vital strategic information about the Founders *if* Dax and Worf can transport him to safety immediately. The hitch is the rendezvous point Lasaran specifies: Soukara, a planet located inside Dominion-controlled space. It won't be easy for the two officers to get there. It will be even more difficult for them to get Lasaran off the planet, since it's covered with transporter scramblers. They'll need to land their runabout and meet him in the planet's jungle, a two-day walk from the landing site. With no other alternative, Dax and Worf agree.

On the station, O'Brien sets his mind to breaking Quark's winning *tongo* streak. He asks Bashir to help him practice, but quickly realizes that it's *Bashir* who should compete against the Ferengi after all, he's the one with the genetically engineered brain. Bashir and Quark square off at the *tongo* wheel, and the *hew-mon* does well, at first. Then Quark begins talking about Jadzia—how wonderful her smile is, how odd her choice of husband was. Before long, Bashir finds himself thinking about how he may have allowed true happiness to slip through his fingers when he stopped pursuing the statuesque Trill—instead of about his next move in the game. Quark's winning streak remains intact.

The trip through the jungles of Soukara proves almost as strenuous as a Klingon's idea of a honeymoon, but Worf and Dax make good progress until they run into a small group of Jem'Hadar. They manage to kill the soliders, but not before Jadzia is injured. The blast leaves an anticoagulant in her bloodstream, and Worf can't stop the bleeding. For a while, Jadzia manages to keep pace with her husband as they make slow progress toward the rendezvous point. But despite frequent injections of plasma, the blood loss eventually takes its toll and Jadzia collapses. She urges Worf to go on without her. As a Starfleet officer, that's his duty, and Lasaran's information could be invaluable to the war effort. Reluctantly, Worf agrees, promising to return for her the next night. He knows there's little chance that she'll survive that long.

As Worf hacks his way through the dense jungle, he seems to hear the sound of his heart beating. The farther he gets from Jadzia, the louder the sound becomes. At last, it is deafening, and he finds he must stop—and make a decision. Suddenly, he turns and heads back the way he came.

He takes Jadzia to the runabout and returns to Deep Space 9, where Bashir saves the Trill's life. Sisko informs Worf that Lasaran was killed when he returned to the Dominion base from the jungle. The captain is angry. What was Worf thinking? Lasaran's information could have saved millions of lives.

Worf reminds Sisko about the story Sirella recited at his wedding ("You Are Cordially Invited"), about the first two Klingon hearts, and how nothing could stand against them once they were united. He explains that he never understood the story until he found himself standing in the jungle, listening to his heart pounding—and he realized that even *he* could

not stand against his own heart. He had to return to his wife, no matter what the consequences.

Sisko tells Worf that as his captain, it's his duty to inform him that he made the wrong choice, and that the incident will go in his service record. Starfleet will probably never give him a command of his own.

However, as a man, Sisko admits, he doubts he could have left his wife behind either.

Typically, a television series will do a story that probes the depths of love that one character feels for another *before* it marries off the two characters. But the courtship of Worf and Dax was somewhat truncated by the war arc, and quickly followed by their wedding. So the subject didn't come up until the writers were nearly two-thirds of the way through the sixth season.

"We'd married these two characters and we really hadn't played them very much since, so we thought we'd do a show about their relationship," Ron Moore says.

Considering the fact that Worf is a Klingon and his wife is an expert with a Klingon *bat'leth*, it goes without saying that a Worf and Jadzia "relationship" episode *has* to involve a life-and-death struggle. "We talked about doing it like *The Green Berets*," admits Moore, "with the two of them going behind the lines to kidnap an enemy general. That's why we got into this whole thing about the jungle."

It seems to be a rule for the writing staff: a romance story must include jeopardy. ROBBIE ROBINSON

"This was the episode that was going to show that the love Worf has for Dax goes beyond his Klingon upbringing, and even beyond his Starfleet training," states Ira Behr. That was a bold step to take with a character who had previously been defined by those very two elements.

"While we were breaking the story, I felt very strongly that we shouldn't let Worf off the hook when he's faced with a tough choice. So often in a story like this a character will get to have it both ways—his wife lives *and* he accomplishes the mission. They always cheat it somehow. But," Moore asserts, "Worf was just not going to let Jadzia die out there in the jungle, so we decided to let him fail, to let that guy die and to let Worf take that hit. It represented a more interesting choice, and an unexpected decision on the part of the character."

While Behr is frequently one of the series' harshest critics, he was quite pleased with "Change of Heart." "I thought Terry Farrell gave us one of her best performances," he states admiringly. "And Michael [Dorn] was very good. It was a nice show, and [Director] David Livingston did a great job," Behr adds, "in spite of the fact that the set was about as big as my office!"

Which is not, contrary to public expectations, very big.

A jungle setting would seem to call for a location shoot in a place that's filled with lots of trees and exotic vegetation, such as Griffith Park's Fern Dell section, or the nearby Angeles National Forest. But after the season's effects-heavy opening arc and detail-driven episodes like "Far Beyond the Stars," the only practical choice was to shoot at the studio. When the usual "swing set" area on Stage 18 was deemed too small, the Art Department had the Greens people assemble all of their flora on Stage 5, a larger area that has been used for big pieces of the *Enterprise* in various films.

"Because so much of the show took place trekking through the vegetation, we built the jungle like a big doughnut," explains Steve Oster, "with a circular pathway running though it, forming an island in the middle."

While the end result looked incredibly realistic, it quickly became apparent that form had outpaced function. "It was almost impossible to shoot in there," sighs Randy McIlvain, shaking his head. "We had too much stuff. We had designed small platforms to put all these trees on, so that the filmmakers could move the platforms out and get into the jungle area to

The Greens Department did amazing work on the episode.
ROBBIE ROBINSON

shoot. But they added more and more plants, until we couldn't move the platforms! The plants and vines were all intertwined," he laughs. "So they ended up having to shoot a lot of it at the periphery of the jungle, rather than going inside of it."

"It got so difficult," confirms Oster with a chuckle, "that we might as well have been on location. We had a whole back half of the jungle that we never even photographed, because we couldn't get to it. Best laid plans," he says with a shrug. "We kind of outsmarted ourselves there."

By necessity, the script was short on dialogue; Jadzia and Worf were trying to be quiet, after all. So David Livingston's main job was to make a lot of walking through the woods seem interesting. "Every shot that you see has something occur in it," he points out, "some piece of activity. It just wasn't shoe leather for shoe leather's sake. Either there's a relationship piece, or Jadzia starts to slow down a little bit, or her condition gets worse. Every shot had a purpose and a reason."

Livingston modestly credits the writing staff for the carefully described visual montages that convey Jadzia and Worf's passage through the jungle. They gave Livingston a clear, concise path to follow. "This episode was pretty heavily scripted, and those shots really tell the story," he says.

In fact, the "traveling" sequences scattered through the script are unique as compared to the series' other scripts. While scenes traditionally are numbered in sequence for easy reference by cast and crew members, the traveling scenes in "Change of Heart" carry an additional number. For example, scene 50 includes a montage of shots that are designated EXTERIOR JUNGLE #13–19. The visuals include Worf hacking away at foliage, Dax struggling to keep up, Worf changing Jadzia's dressing, Jadzia plunging through a thick patch of bushes, Worf checking their progress on a padd, and so forth.

The structure of the script is also unique in the way it deals with the episode's B-story. Typically, scenes will alternate back and forth between A and B lines. But in "Change of Heart," the B-story, in which O'Brien and Bashir try to beat Quark at tongo, ends just before the episode's halfway point; the rest of the story is spent in the jungle with Worf and Jadzia. "I wanted to wrap the B-story up so we could just concentrate on the serious story," Moore notes. "After Jadzia gets hurt, it gets so intense that we didn't want to break out and be cutting back." Moore knows how jarring such shifts can be in a highly dramatic story. He was responsible for the teleplay to "Life Support," wherein gripping scenes of Bareil's slow demise were interspersed with a light B-story about Jake and Nog on a double date.

The B-story for "Change of Heart" initially revolved around Nog and Rom. "Nog's mother had come to the station," Director Livingston reports. "The situation sounded hilarious, and the mix of really low-brow comedy with high tragedy would have provided quite a contrast." But Behr didn't like the basic concept for it. "It was about Rom being hoodwinked by this woman all over again," he says. "But it just did not work. Not at all."

So Moore replaced that subplot with the one about the tongo game, which was inspired, Behr says, by an experience that he had in a bar on Long Island. "I was listening to two guys pump themselves up about some competition that one of them was going to enter, some 'strong man' thing, and the other guy was going to be his coach," he relates. "And just by listening to them talk and talk and talk and talk, I knew by the end of the night that these guys were never going to do this thing, even though it meant so much to them at the time.

"Our take on that was this whole idea of wanting to beat Quark, needing to beat Quark, and this friendship thing between the guys, O'Brien and Bashir," Behr explains. "It didn't quite work, though. It never made it anywhere, the script didn't delve into it enough."

It did reintroduce the idea that Quark and Bashir were still crazy about Dax—more so now that she was really unavailable. "It played off obvious stuff that had been in existence since the beginning of the show," says Behr. Clearly they both had been pining for her all along, but we hadn't done much with it recently, and it seemed like an interesting way to go. Now that she was married, it was like, when you can't have someone, that's when you really want her. All of a sudden you're obsessed about this person who you know you cannot have." This subplot would run through the rest of the series, and eventually pay off with Bashir getting a second chance at the girl of his dreams, albeit in a new package.

Trills don't like heat, which is the operative explanation for why Jadzia begins to shed pieces of clothing the minute she sets foot on Soukara. "It gave the viewer a sense of the heat they were experiencing in the jungle," explains Moore. "And I think that Terry looks better out of that uniform," he admits. "It's just not very interesting."

Behr backs up Moore on both points. "It was really hot!" he asserts. "We wanted her to appear miserable and also to show the passage of time. And obviously when you have somebody as beautiful as Terry, it's easy to do something like that. We never miss an opportunity"—he pauses and breaks into a grin—"to make our cast as beaten up, dirty, and dusty as we possibly can!"

WRONGS DARKER THAN DEATH OR NIGHT

Episode #541

WRITTEN BY **IRA STEVEN BEHR** &
HANS BEIMLER

DIRECTED BY **JONATHAN WEST**

GUEST CAST

Kira Meru	**LESLIE HOPE**
Gul Dukat	**MARC ALAIMO**
Basso Tromac	**DAVID BOWE**
Legate	**WAYNE GRACE**
Halb Daier	**TIM DeZARN**
Kira Taban	**THOMAS KOPACHE**
Scavenger	**JOHN MARZELLI**
Gul	**MARC MAROSI**
Station Computer Voice	**JUDI DURAND**

STARDATE UNKNOWN

Kira travels into the past to learn about her mother. ROBBIE ROBINSON

Dax is understandably curious when she observes an unusual sight: Quark presenting Kira with Bajoran lilacs. Giving in to the Trill's relentless questioning, Kira explains that they aren't a gift; she ordered them herself, to commemorate her mother's birthday. Her father, Taban, had told her that lilacs were Meru's favorites, but Kira knows little about her mother. She died in a Bajoran refugee center when Kira was three, and according to Taban, she was the bravest woman he knew.

That night, Kira's sleep is disturbed by an incoming message from escaped war criminal Gul Dukat. Dukat says he wants to help her clear away the "self-deceptions" that may be controlling her life. He's chosen this day to contact her because it is Meru's birthday, and he wants Kira to know the truth about her mother. Kira Meru was his lover. And she didn't die in the refugee center. She left Kira at the age of three—in order to be with Dukat!

Kira doesn't want to believe her old enemy, but she's disturbed by statements that she can't disprove. She goes to Sisko and makes a request of him in his capacity as her people's Emissary: let her go to Bajor and consult the Orb of Time, so she can witness the truth for herself. Sisko worries that she'll interfere with established timelines, but Kira assures him that the Prophets won't allow anything to happen that shouldn't.

Reluctantly, Sisko agrees and Kira soon finds herself in the past, at the Singha refugee camp. She quickly locates Taban and Meru, who are struggling to find enough food to sustain their three children . . . including three-year-old Nerys. When a scavenger tries to steal what little they have, an angry adult Nerys steps forward and defends them, winning the gratitude of her parents, who don't recognize their grown-up daughter.

Realizing that she can't refer to herself as Nerys, Kira introduces herself as Luma. But the strange reunion doesn't last long. Troops arrive to round up "comfort women" for the Cardassians who serve on the new ore processing center that orbits Bajor. The families of the women who are chosen will receive extra rations of food and medicine, although that's small comfort to those deprived of loved ones, including Taban's family, which loses Meru. Kira, too, is chosen, and taken to the facility known as Terok Nor, where she promises Meru that she'll help her escape.

But while Kira finds it easy to focus on resisting the Cardassians, her mother seems overwhelmed by the surfeit of food laid before them. Meru's delight in partaking of this bounty is tempered only by her sorrow that she can't share it with Taban and the children, but she convinces herself that the Cardassians will make good on their promise to take care of them. Later, Meru is singled out for special attention by Dukat, then prefect of the space station. When he notices a scar on Meru's otherwise beautiful face—the result of an earlier brush with Cardassian cruelty—Dukat calls for a dermal regenerator and eliminates the disfigurement. Kira is concerned when she sees that Meru is deeply affected by this apparent show of kindness.

Sent to entertain high-ranking Cardassians at a party, Meru confesses to Kira that she always has dreamed of having enough food to eat and pretty clothes to wear, but she never thought that her dream would come about in this way. Her beauty attracts the unwanted attention of a boorish gul, but suddenly Dukat appears and forces the man to unhand her. Again, Dukat impresses Meru with his gentlemanly behavior, but a Cardassian legate at the party lets Kira in on the fact that Dukat's gracious "performance" has been played out many times, with many different women.

Later, when Kira returns to the quarters she shares with Meru, she's told that Meru has been invited to live with Dukat. Suspecting the worst, Kira forcefully demands to be taken to Meru, but her actions land her in the station's Bajoran ghetto. Now she'll be treated like a common laborer and forced to work in the ore processing center.

Weeks go by, and Kira befriends Halb, a member of the Bajoran resistance, who gives her updates on Meru. Halb wants Kira to help the efforts of the resistance, but Kira hesitates, knowing that her involvement could affect the timeline. Before she can reply, however, she's summoned to meet with Meru. Kira is surprised how quickly her mother has adapted to a life of luxury. Instead of despising Dukat, she seems to genuinely care about him. Meru knows nothing of the harsh way he treats the laborers and believes that Dukat actually wants to help her people. Kira tries to get her mother to see the truth, but when she fails, she angrily accuses Meru of being a collaborator.

Returning to the ghetto, Kira tells Halb she'll help the resistance. When Halb asks her to set off a bomb in Dukat's quarters, Kira agrees, even though there's a chance the blast could kill her mother. Pretending to have a change of heart, Kira goes to see Meru and apologize. Her mother is delighted to see her and Kira feigns affection, despite the fact that she still feels betrayed by Meru. She furtively slips an explosive into a potted plant and is about to leave when she hears Taban's voice eminating from a prerecorded message that Dukat has obtained for Meru. Taban wants his wife to know how grateful he is to her for her sacrifice. Thanks to her, the children are thriving. Life is still difficult, but they're back at home together, with enough food to sustain them all. Taban bids her peace in her new life, and lets her know that he will always love her.

Kira stares at the grief-stricken Meru, who is sobbing over the life she knows she can never return to. Taban's unaltered affection for his wife makes Kira realize that she should yield to similar generosity of spirit. It's too late to deactivate the bomb, so Kira warns Dukat and Meru to leave. The three of them escape into the corridor seconds before the bomb goes off. But when the smoke clears, Dukat and Meru see that Kira has vanished . . .

. . . and returned to her own time. As Kira tells Sisko about the experience, she notes that she's always despised collaborators, and that she grew up thinking that her mother sacrificed her life for Bajor. Sisko gently reminds her that her mother did what she felt she had to in order to save her family, but Kira still doesn't feel that made her actions *right*.

And yet Kira saved her life. Sisko wants to know why. Kira has been wondering the same thing. At last she admits that no matter what Meru did, she was still her mother. And that seems reason enough.

As most viewers know, the character of Kira Nerys isn't the most even-tempered individual in the world. Her passions are extremely close to the surface, and she's tremendously easy to provoke—and sometimes people take advantage of that sensitivity.

The *DS9* writers, for example.

"We asked ourselves, 'How can we take Gul Dukat and bond him closer to Kira in a way that would just make her *insane?*'" recalls Ira Behr.

"We thought, 'What if Dukat had been making it with Kira's mother?'" adds Bradley Thompson. "We ran and got the *Star Trek Encyclopedia* and discovered that there was a perfect opening in Kira's backstory to do something like that—and suddenly we had the premise for a great story."

Is it any wonder that the major gets a little testy now and then?

The original premise for the episode dealt with wrongs that were even darker than those of Dukat's.

The producers chose Canadian actress Leslie Hope to play Kira's mother. ROBBIE ROBINSON

It was a story, Behr says, "about the ghosts of Bajoran children appearing on the station, the result of the efforts of a Cardassian scientist back in the Occupation. The Bajorans thought that this scientist was someone like [Nazi Germany's] Dr. Mengele, but what he really was doing was sending these children into the future. Well, we tried to work that story out, but it was very difficult. We never could get it to sustain. It just wasn't working. Finally, in a fit of pique, I just declared, 'We're not doing this show!'"

"We'd gotten halfway thorough the break session," confirms David Weddle, "and we quit and started talking about Kira's history."

"We'd always talked about Kira's mother internally," Behr continues, "and what kind of figure her mother had been. So we decided to do a show about her role during the Occupation, and whether she actually had or hadn't been a hero—you be the judge."

The decision to avoid making an editorial judgment call on Meru's behavior made for powerful drama, but left the lead actor without adequate emotional closure. "I think that Nana's performance was incredibly truthful from an emotional standpoint,

with the anger toward her mom [in conflict with] her love for her mom," comments Weddle. "That's very real. It was a muddy issue—did her mother do the right thing, or not? Or was it just a choice of survival for a Bajoran?"

"Nana had a hard time with it," Behr notes. "We went over the ending many times, especially those last few lines that she says when she's back with Sisko. Because, you know, there's a part of Nana who wanted to blow her mother up," he adds with a chuckle. "It was a very tough choice for Kira."

"The writers originally had Kira feeling much more sympathetic toward her mother in the last scenes of the show," Nana Visitor remembers. But that wouldn't have been true to the Bajoran character that she's worked so hard to create. "Maybe Kira could be sympathetic about the subject in twenty years," reasons Visitor. "But at the time, it was hard for her to deal with the fact that she hadn't killed her."

Visitor often has noted that she has a much different personality than that of Kira, but it's amazingly easy for her to get into her psyche when she puts on Kira's clothes. "I have a good imagination," Visitor says, "so I've sort of lived through certain scenes of Kira's life, of being brought up by my father and wondering about my mother, thinking that she's dead and then learning the truth. It's very hard for me to think those thoughts and not have a physical reaction to that kind of . . . betrayal. And betrayal is a very weak word for it. A *very* weak word."

Still, Visitor admits that she's finally able to see that it was for the best that the major did not kill her mother. "In the end, it *is* her mother," she says. "And Kira believed that the Prophets were guiding her, so I imagine that she believes not killing her mother was in response to the Prophets telling her it was wrong. And anyway," Visitor concludes, "she wasn't supposed to mess with the timeline."

But if Visitor is at peace with Kira's decision about her mother, it's harder for her to rationalize allowing Dukat to survive the blast. "That was very, very hard to accept. Kira can never forgive Dukat," Visitor says. "I think it's been made very clear in the show that she's past the racist aspects of hating Cardassians. This is truly about Dukat, the individual. He's like Hitler to Kira, and there's no forgiving. She can never let go."

Behr tends to agree, and he suggests that the title, which Hans Beimler appropriated from Shelley, seems aimed more at Dukat than at Meru. "It's a great

It just looks as if Blackman has very little on Visitor. ROBBIE ROBINSON

Thus the common practice of using twins and triplets, which allows a director to stretch the period of time he or she has with a juvenile character. In "Wrongs Darker Than Death or Night," a set of triplets alternated as Baby Reon, and a set of twins shared the role of two-year-old Pohl. Still, Director Jonathan West had to invest a lot of energy into finding a way to get the work with the children completed in the allotted amount of time.

"I had to do everything with the kids right away, completely out of order," West explains. "Usually we try to complete all of the angles of a scene during the same period of filming. But because of the kids, we'd do just one angle of a scene, and then one angle of the next scene, and then later in the day, after we'd sent the kids home, we'd do the reverse angles on all those scenes."

Worried that cast and crew might become confused by the untraditional separation of related shots, West opted to invest time in order to save it later on. "I brought the cast in (sans children) and we rehearsed the entire sequence," he says. "That way everybody knew where they were going to be for all of the different parts of the entire day's work. It took almost an hour in the morning to do that seven-page rehearsal," West says, "but we all learned what we were going to do, and it saved us in the end."

Over in wardrobe, Robert Blackman was given the task of creating a look for the Cardassian "comfort women." That meant making them look sexy, but sexy within the parameters dictated by television. The line between sanctioned-for-general-viewing and destined-only-for-cable-access, the costume designer notes, "was about the same as the one I draw for the dabo girls—in other words, whatever I can sneak by. They were meant to look like glamorous harem girls or call girls, but because of the dramatic storyline about Kira and her mother, there was a certain dignity that had to be maintained, or it would undercut the end of the episode. We couldn't use plunging necklines, because that would be too tawdry. It's better to just have a nice long slit in the skirt and see a leg and some shape, which gives the impression that it's all very sheer," Blackman says. "It's easier to play with that line when you're dealing with background people rather than principal players," he admits, but he was ultimately pleased with his sexy but not *too* sexy "daboesque kind of Bajoranesque kind of Cardassianesque dresses."

title," Behr smiles. "What could be wronger than death or night? It would have to be Dukat, because he *is* a wrong darker than death or night."

Beyond its darker themes, the episode establishes a few firsts. During a rather inconsequential discussion under the episode's opening credits, O'Brien broaches the subject of Earth's glorious battle of the Alamo with a skeptical Bashir, representing the first mention of a subject that would continue to preoccupy the two friends until the end of the series. And at the Singha refugee camp, viewers get to meet Kira's two brothers, previously mentioned in "Shadowplay," and learn that their names are Reon and Pohl.

Although the two boys are on camera for a very brief period of time, they caused their share of problems for the production team. Because of strictly enforced labor laws, producers are allowed to utilize children on a film set for very limited periods of time.

INQUISITION

Episode #542

WRITTEN BY **BRADLEY THOMPSON** &
DAVID WEDDLE
DIRECTED BY **MICHAEL DORN**

G U E S T   C A S T

Weyoun	JEFFREY COMBS
Lieutenant Chandler	SAMANTHA MUDD
Lieutenant Kagan	BENJAMIN BROWN
Station Computer Voice	JUDI DURAND

S P E C I A L   G U E S T   S T A R

Sloan	WILLIAM SADLER

S T A R D A T E   U N K N O W N

Bashir is the subject of a bizarre investigation by Deputy Director Sloan. ROBBIE ROBINSON

The night before he's scheduled to leave the station for a medical conference on Casperia Prime, a harried Dr. Bashir attempts to finish up some work in the Infirmary. He's interrupted by an emergency visit from his friend O'Brien, who's dislocated his shoulder kayaking in the holosuite.

At last Bashir retires for the night, but morning comes before he knows it. Dressing quickly, he gathers his things together and prepares to leave for the conference. But before he can get out the door, he's ordered to report to Ops, along with the rest of the senior staff.

When he arrives at Ops, Bashir is surprised to see several Internal Affairs guards. Their leader, Deputy Director Sloan, informs Sisko and the others that Starfleet Intelligence believes there's been a security breach aboard the station, and that someone is passing information to the Dominion. Following standard procedures, the senior officers are relieved of duty and confined to quarters, where they're to wait until Sloan contacts them for questioning. Sloan informs Bashir that he won't be attending the conference on Casperia.

As he waits impatiently, Bashir tries to order breakfast, but the replicator refuses to respond. A few minutes later, a guard escorts him to see the Deputy Director. Sloan's demeanor is casual and friendly during the interview process. He asks Bashir a few innocuous questions about recent events in the doctor's life, then sends him back to his quarters. Before he leaves, Bashir mentions that his replicator isn't working. Sloan admits that he's had all the replicators taken off-line as a precaution. However, he'd be happy to have some breakfast sent to the doctor. Bashir eagerly takes him up on the offer.

When breakfast arrives, Bashir discovers he's been sent the wrong order—a plate of *gagh,* meant to be delivered to Worf. Deciding it's a little early in the day for live serpent worms, Bashir resigns himself to his hunger and tries to get some work done. But as he looks around his quarters, he realizes that his possessions have been moved, albeit just slightly. The obvious conclusion is that his room has been searched, although he can't imagine why. While he's puzzling that out, he receives a surreptitious message from O'Brien, who tells him that Sloan grilled him for two hours—and all the questions were about Bashir.

The guards return to Bashir's door. Sloan wants to talk to him again.

This time Sloan's questions aren't so innocuous. He goes over the details of Bashir's capture by the Dominion the previous year ("In Purgatory's Shadow"), questioning apparent inaccuracies in Bashir's account, and the fact that his eventual escape was suspiciously easy. Sloan suggests the possibility that Bashir's genetically engineered brain may have made him uniquely susceptible to engramatic dissociation—that, in fact, the Dominion brainwashed him while he was imprisoned, but his well-disciplined mind has compartmentalized the information and suppressed it. An incredulous Bashir denies the possibility, and Sloan, now openly hostile, has the doctor manacled and taken to a holding cell.

Incensed, Sisko demands to sit in on all further interrogation sessions. As the next round of questioning begins, the deputy director picks apart questionable decisions the doctor has made over the past few years. He reminds Sisko of an incident at Bopak III, where Bashir and O'Brien were captured by Jem'Hadar ("Hippocratic Oath"); the doctor was more interested in curing his captors than escaping. Then there was Bashir's recent attempt to convince Sisko that Starfleet should surrender to the Dominion ("Statistical Probabilities"). Finally, Sloan presents the most damning evidence: Bashir had been concealing the truth about his background for years ("Doctor Bashir, I Presume?"). In the course of covering up his illegal genetic enhancement, he's repeatedly lied to Starfleet, and to his commanding officer, Sisko.

To Bashir's dismay, Sloan's attack seems to have undermined Sisko's support. The captain wonders if Sloan's theory about engramatic dissociation is possible, and if Bashir only *thinks* he's innocent. Later that night, Sloan tells Bashir that he's removing him from Deep Space 9 for further questioning. But before Sloan can take him away, Bashir suddenly finds himself transported out of his cell and onto a Cardassian ship. There, he's met by Weyoun, who greets Bashir like an old friend.

Weyoun asserts that Bashir was broken by the Dominion, and they've had many covert meetings. Each time, the doctor denies that he's a Dominion operative. Eventually, he breaks down the walls to his suppressed memories and realizes the truth. As Weyoun tries to get Bashir to remember, it occurs to Bashir that both Weyoun and Sloan are trying to convince him of the same lie. They must be working together, he deduces.

Suddenly, Weyoun's ship comes under attack by the *Defiant*, and Kira and Worf beam aboard to rescue Bashir. But after the three officers return to the Federation vessel, Bashir once again finds himself the subject of suspicion. When Bashir brings up his theory that Sloan is working with the Dominion, Sisko becomes angry and accuses the doctor of attempting to shift the focus of the investigation in order to exonerate himself. To Bashir's surprise, his other friends unite against him, even O'Brien. But then he notices that O'Brien shows no sign of the shoulder injury Bashir recently repaired. What's more, it's clear he doesn't remember the accident that caused it.

Just as he realizes that he's surrounded by imposters, the *Defiant* fades around him—and he finds himself in a hologrid. Once again he faces Sloan, but this time Sloan identifies himself as an operative of Section 31, a secret division of Starfleet Intelligence that seeks out and identifies potential dangers to the Federation. Sloan explains that he had

Bashir beamed into this holodeck program while he was asleep, and has subjected him to a series of highly stressful situations in order to test his loyalty to the Federation—which, he admits now, seems to be above reproach. If Bashir had turned out to be an actual Dominion agent, Sloan suggests, he would have been dealt with . . . quietly.

On the heels of this pronouncement, Sloan reveals another equally chilling motive in testing Bashir: he wants to recruit him as a member of Section 31. Stunned, Bashir turns down the offer, but Sloan asks him to keep it in mind when he returns to Deep Space 9. With that, he has Bashir drugged and returned home.

Later, Bashir reveals the whole disturbing story to Kira, Odo, and Sisko. The captain notes that when he asked Starfleet Command about Section 31, they didn't acknowledge the division's existence—or deny it, either. Unsettled, Kira suggests they try to track Sloan down, but Sisko points out that there's no need. Sloan asked Bashir to think about joining the secret organization, which means he'll be back. Next time Sloan asks Bashir to join, instructs Sisko, he's to say "Yes."

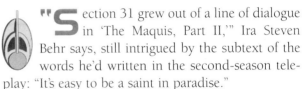 "Section 31 grew out of a line of dialogue in 'The Maquis, Part II,'" Ira Steven Behr says, still intrigued by the subtext of the words he'd written in the second-season teleplay: "It's easy to be a saint in paradise."

"It came from my growing realization that we could do more with the *Star Trek* franchise than we'd initially thought we could. It was the idea of culpability, the idea that we should avoid knocking the Federation and we should avoid knocking Starfleet, but we could knock *elements* of them."

The theories behind Section 31 are diabolical. "Why *is* Earth a paradise in the twenty-fourth century?" Behr asks. "Well, maybe it's because there's someone watching over it and doing the nasty stuff that no one wants to think about. Of course it's a very complicated issue," he adds. "Extremely complicated. And those kinds of covert operations usually are wrong!"

When Behr saw an opportunity to explore the dark side of paradise, he took it. The result was "Inquisition." Of course, as one would expect from the executive producer's creative mind, he found that opportunity in the most unlikely of places, in what Bradley Thompson calls "a cute little romp about dealing with the Department of Motor Vehicles on a Sunday."

That "cute little romp" was one of many story ideas purchased from freelancers over the years. In this one,

For just one fleeting moment, Weyoun nearly convinces the audience that Bashir is a spy. ROBBIE ROBINSON

"Bashir went to a planet to do something really nice, like saving the lives of everyone on the whole planet," Thompson says. "He parked his runabout in orbit, and when he finished doing this wonderful thing, he found out that his runabout had been towed and he had a parking ticket! So he had to go up against the bureaucracy. It was the ultimate genetically engineered human against the ultimate bureaucratic red tape."

"When Brad told me about that story, I said, 'That's Franz Kafka's *The Trial*, with Bashir,'" comments David Weddle. "*The Trial* has always been one of my favorite novels. Then we went to lunch with Ira and told him about it, and he immediately spun it into the concept that you see in the episode, with this secret organization in Starfleet that's interrogating Bashir through a holoprogram that he doesn't realize is a holoprogram. And that's where we started writing."

"Suddenly it stopped being a romp and it became this nightmare," Thompson laughs.

"I wanted to do something with spies and Bashir in the real world, after doing it in the holosuite so much," Behr explains—although, ironically, the story still wound up taking place in a holosuite.

"The idea of establishing a behind-the-scenes, shadowy organization was very much Ira's thing," notes René Echevarria, who provided input on the script, "but we have to thank Brad and David for the work they did with Sloan as the inquisitor. They did a lot of research and managed to put together a very compelling case for Bashir in fact *being* what Sloan was saying he was. They found things that could be

construed as suspicious in 'Statistical Probabilities' and all the way back in 'Hippocratic Oath.'"

"One of the great things about *Star Trek* is that there's such a tremendous backstory on the characters," Weddle says. "We just took the scripts, put ourselves into Sloan's paranoia, looked for all the things in Bashir's past that don't add up, and just started questioning him. But the 'funnest' part for us was figuring out what, in his heart of hearts, Bashir might feel guilt about."

"We had to torpedo the relationship between Sisko and Bashir and still keep Sisko believable," Thompson adds. "So it was fun having Sloan ask, 'When did you tell the captain that you were genetically enhanced?' Bashir admits that it was after he got found out, and Sloan says, 'Would you ever have told him otherwise?' We could torture Bashir and push the other characters outside of the envelope."

"The episode was very dark!" Alexander Siddig says, admitting that what Echevarria refers to as a "fantastical situation" affected his approach to the episode. "I had to work hard at trying to make sense of things from my character's point of view, to exert myself trying to make sense of what I thought was illogical. It wasn't, of course, it was perfectly logical."

Sleep deprivation was one of the techniques that Sloan used to make Bashir lose his sense of reality, but playing that wasn't hard for Siddig at the time. "I didn't have to prepare for that," he says, chuckling. "It was very easy for me to be entirely tired. I had a one-and-a-half-year-old baby at the time, so I just went into 'dad mode.'"

According to Siddig, he did not go into "genetically engineered mode." "I just ignored the genetically engineered thing and dealt with the situation as it came up," he says.

And that was okay with Behr, even when Sloan hits Bashir with the argument, "You're a spy and you don't even know it." "We could believe that his mind could hold those two thoughts at once, so that was one of the few times being genetically engineered helped us in the story-telling," Behr admits. "But ultimately we don't use it too much. It's too powerful a weapon."

"The character name of Sloan came from the 1963 Samuel Fuller film *Shock Corridor,* about a guy who goes undercover in a mental institution to try and solve a murder," Thompson reveals. "It happened to be playing down the street, and Ira took us all to see it. After that, we decided to call our inquisitor 'Sloan.'"

"But then Avery Brooks asked us 'What's his first name?'" Thompson laughs. "It's not in the story—he just

The producers had considered Martin Sheen for the role of Sloan before they decided on William Sadler. ROBBIE ROBINSON

'Inquisition,' Ira asked for dark black, severe, hostile looking garments. Well, that's black leather."

The viewers are used to seeing "establishing shots" of the station or the *Defiant* or a planet surface between scenes. These shots assist in telling the viewers where that next scene is taking place. But because 'Inquisition' essentially takes place in a holosuite, the editors dropped that stylistic norm for the episode. "We had to stay true to being in a holosuite, so we could never step outside," points out Steve Oster.

"Even when Bashir was on the Dominion ship, which was being blasted by the *Defiant,* we resisted cutting to an exterior shot," Oster says proudly. "Instead, we showed it on a monitor in the room Bashir's being held in."

"Inquisition" is Michael Dorn's second episode as director. "Michael is just straight ahead as a director," Thompson enthuses. "He told the story economically and built this real nice sense of paranoia as he went through it, without trying to do any bizarre camera angles or any of that kind of stuff. He did a great job on that show."

wanted to know something about the character that nobody else knew. So David came up with a first name."

Weddle christened the character "Luther," but that would remain his and Brooks's secret until the episode "Extreme Measures" aired a year later.

Although Sloan didn't need a first name for this episode, he did need a face. Ira Behr suggested William Sadler. "I'd seen Bill in a lot of stuff," Behr says. "But the thing that I really liked him in is a movie that my buddy Dick Miller also was in, *Tales from the Crypt Presents Demon Knight.* We needed someone who had real power as an actor, who could keep you from jumping to a final conclusion about his character.

"When we were shooting that last scene, I told Bill, 'You've got to play Sloan totally straight. Sloan is giving information, but he cannot have too much of an attitude about it because it's up to Bashir to do what he wants. And I just thought Bill was great."

Even Sloan's wardrobe was designed to fit his personality. "We design a lot of Gestapo/S.S./Naziesque outfits for our villains," Bob Blackman comments. "And when they're really the *ultimate*, like the Section 31 people, we immediately go that way to make them look like storm troopers, because that's an imagery that works best, not only for the viewers, but for the producers. For

IN THE PALE MOONLIGHT

Episode #543

TELEPLAY BY **MICHAEL TAYLOR**
STORY BY **PETER ALLAN FIELDS**
DIRECTED BY **VICTOR LOBL**

GUEST CAST

Garak	ANDREW J. ROBINSON
Weyoun	JEFFREY COMBS
Damar	CASEY BIGGS
Grathon Tolar	HOWARD SHANGRAW
Vreenak	STEPHEN McHATTIE
Station Computer Voice	JUDI DURAND

STARDATE 51721.3

A troubled Captain Sisko sits in his quarters, recording a private log entry. He needs to talk about the events of the past two weeks, but he can tell no one. Perhaps by laying it all out in his log, he says, he'll be able to figure out where things went wrong, and where *he* went wrong . . .

It began in the station's Wardroom, with the posting of the weekly casualty list: a growing roster of Starfleet personnel killed, wounded, or missing in the war against the Dominion. Included that week were

Sisko risks everything in order to boost Starfleet's chances against the Dominion. ROBBIE ROBINSON

the names of crew members from the *Cairo*, a starship that disappeared near the Romulan Neutral Zone. Most likely the Federation vessel had been caught off guard when a Jem'Hadar ship crossed over the Romulan border and attacked it. That never would have happened if it weren't for the nonaggression treaty between the Romulans and the Dominion.

If the Romulans could be persuaded to join Federation and Klingon forces against the Dominion, Bashir had pointed out, the tide might be turned. But there's no reason for the Romulans to do that, Dax had replied. They have more to gain by just sitting back and watching their enemies duke it out.

At that moment Sisko made a fateful decision. He would bring the Romulans into the war.

It wouldn't be easy—he knew that. The only thing likely to move the Romulans to the Federation's camp was evidence that the Dominion was plotting to invade Romulus. Sisko was confident that this scenario was likely to take place eventually, but if evidence to that effect existed, it would be buried somewhere on Cardassia Prime—which meant that he needed the services of a man who was an expert at retrieving classified information from dangerous places.

Sisko went to Garak, the station's lone Cardassian resident, and asked him to use his contacts on Cardassia to obtain the evidence he needed. Garak agreed. Despite his good intentions, Sisko notes in retrospect, it was the first step on the road to hell.

In three days, Sisko went to Garak for an update. The tailor reported that he'd found some former associates who would have been willing to help. Unfortunately, they'd all been killed within a day of speaking to Garak. But the former spy had a suggestion. If Sisko needed evidence of a Dominion plan to attack the Romulans, he and Garak should manufacture it themselves.

Sisko's instincts told him to reject the suggestion. But with recent news that the planet Betazed had fallen to Dominion forces, he was desperate to find a solution. He agreed.

Garak laid out the plan. They would need to convince an influential Romulan senator named Vreenak of the threat to Romulus. As an ardent supporter of his world's link to the Dominion, Vreenak's opinion was the one they needed to sway. With Vreenak scheduled to attend a diplomatic meeting with Dominion representatives in ten days, it would be an optimal time to convince him to make a side trip to Deep Space 9 so that he could be presented with the manufactured evidence. To produce that evidence, Garak told Sisko, he would need to employ the services of a master forger, a man named Tolar who was awaiting execution in a Klingon prison.

Sisko obtained the man's release and brought him to the station, where complications immediately set in. A drunken Tolar stabbed Quark, but Sisko was forced to instruct Odo to cover up the crime. Further, he had to bribe Quark in order to keep the Ferengi from pressing charges against his assailant.

Pushing aside his doubts about continuing with the plan, Sisko continued to tread moral terrain he'd never crossed before. In order to obtain the necessary Cardassian optolythic datarod for the forgery, Sisko arranged for biomimetic gel, a rare and dangerous medical substance, to be given to the rod's supplier. With the rod in hand, Garak and Tolar created a holographic program of a fictional meeting between Weyoun and Damar, wherein the two discuss the impending invasion of Romulus. After Sisko okayed the program, Tolar recorded it onto the optolythic rod, and Sisko prepared to convince Senator Vreenak that a lie was the truth.

Vreenak proved to be an arrogant, condescending man who was certain that the Federation would soon fall to the Dominion. Sisko's suggestion that the Dominion was planning a sneak attack on Vreenak's homeworld put a dent in his confident veneer, but the senator demanded proof. Sisko showed him the recording of the "meeting," and then allowed Vreenak to examine the datarod.

Sisko had been counting on the fact that Vreenak could be convinced that the recording was real. If he couldn't, the captain knew the incident had the potential to push the Romulans even further into the enemy camp. He was horrified, therefore, when Vreenak declared the recording to be a fake. Furious, the Romulan departed from the station vowing to expose Sisko's "vile deception" to the entire Alpha Quadrant. But before he could do that, his shuttle exploded, killing all aboard. An initial investigation conducted by the Romulans seemed to suggest sabotage, with the Dominion the primary suspects.

Sisko's crew was ecstatic over the thought that the Romulans might turn against the Dominion. Sisko was furious. He went immediately to Garak's tailor shop and confronted the Cardassian. Garak admitted that, yes, as a fallback position in case the datarod didn't pass muster, he *had* placed a bomb on Vreenak's shuttle. What's more, he'd killed Tolar as well. But it was all worthwhile, he assured Sisko. The Romulans would complete their investigation and find the remnants of the datarod, damaged but viewable after some painstaking forensic work. They would believe the recording to be real, and think that the Dominion had killed Vreenak to prevent him from revealing the truth to his government. The Romulans would join forces with the Federation against the Dominion, just as Sisko had wished. The cost of that wish, Garak had pointed out, was quite low: the life of one Romulan senator, one convicted criminal, and the self-respect of one Starfleet officer.

As Sisko concludes his log entry, he reflects on the outcome of his actions. The Romulans have formally declared war against the Dominion. They've already begun attacking Dominion bases along the Cardassian border. It's a big victory for "the good guys."

A guilty conscience, he concludes, is indeed a small price to pay for the safety of the Alpha Quadrant, and one that he'll learn to live with—because he must.

He then deletes the entire log entry.

While creating the premise for *Deep Space Nine*, Rick Berman states, "the biggest challenge that Michael Piller and I had was trying to come up with an idea that would not break Gene Roddenberry's rules." Those rules,

The episode comes close to breaking most of *Star Trek*'s rules.
ROBBIE ROBINSON

observed so specifically on *The Next Generation*, seemed to imply that Starfleet officers were like Boy Scouts—trustworthy, loyal, helpful, friendly, courteous, kind, obedient, cheerful, thrifty, brave, clean, and reverent.

By Season 6 of the series, however, with interstellar war being the main focus not only of Starfleet, but of the Federation as well, such idealistic rules were bound to be bent, if not broken. Thus, we encountered Captain Benjamin Sisko, conspirator, in partnership with suspected Cardassian spy Elim Garak, manipulating a deadly game by tricking potential players into choosing sides.

With such subversive goings-on, it is no wonder then that fans refer to "In the Pale Moonlight" as the "darkest" episode of the series, and, indeed, in all of *Star Trek*. But curiously, rather than being offended by Sisko's heretical actions, viewers embraced the episode. At the series' end, a survey conducted by *Sci-Fi Entertainment* magazine proclaimed "In the Pale Moonlight" *DS9*'s "highest-ranked episode." And *The Star Trek Communicator* recorded that members of the Official *Star Trek* Fan Club voted the episode in the series' Top Ten.

Andy Robinson, the actor who plays the Cardassian Garak, casts his vote somewhere in the middle. "'The Wire' still is my favorite episode," he says. "Right after that is the two-parter with Garak and Odo, 'Improbable Cause' and 'The Die Is Cast,' and then comes 'In the Pale Moonlight.'"

Robinson, of course, likes the fact that it is his character who takes charge in the unholy alliance between Garak and the captain. "There was a payoff at the end

The list of casualties includes Art Department personnel, security guards, production assistants, and the author and editor of this book.

of 'In the Pale Moonlight,'" Robinson says. "Garak teaches Sisko a very important, very hard lesson: You don't go to bed with the Devil without having sex."

"'In the Pale Moonlight' showed how *Deep Space Nine* could really stretch the *Star Trek* formula," says Michael Taylor, who received teleplay credit on the episode. "It pushes the boundaries in a realistic way, because the decisions Sisko makes are the kinds of decisions that have to be made in war. They're for the greater good."

But while Taylor appreciates his involvement with the episode—"I thought it was a brilliant show," he says—he also acknowledges that the script he turned in was very different from the final show, and that much of the credit for the filmed episode should go to Ron Moore.

"In the Pale Moonlight," originally titled "Patriot," traveled a long and winding road before the cameras began rolling. It started with discussion of the events that shaped the Vietnam War, from the Gulf of Tonkin incident (in which North Vietnamese gunboats reportedly attacked U.S. naval vessels), which led to increased U.S. military involvement in Vietnam, to the Watergate Hotel break-in a decade later. With those historical events in mind, the staff contacted former writer-producer Peter Allan Fields, who came up with a tale.

"'In the Pale Moonlight' began life, believe it or not, as a story about Jake 'Watergating' Shakaar," Ron Moore chuckles. "Jake finds out some nasty secret about Shakaar that would bring down the whole Bajoran government if word got out. Sisko tries to stop his son from publishing it. We developed that for a while, but it didn't quite work. We felt that it would be a better story if Jake were Watergating his own father.

"And that's the version that Mike Taylor wrote," Moore continues. "It started with Jake trying to get an interview with Garak for the Federation News Service, because he thinks Garak is an interesting guy. But Garak won't give him the time of day. Through some machinations, Jake realizes that Garak is up to something, and then Sisko steps in to tell Jake to leave it alone, which, of course, Jake doesn't. He ultimately discovers that Garak and Sisko are planning to completely pull the wool over the Romulans' eyes and drag them into the war.

"It became this whole thing about Sisko telling Jake, 'I won't let you publish this story no matter what,'" Moore says, "but that just didn't work. It was really no contest between Sisko and Jake, because as much as we want to, it's hard to get those two characters into conflict with each other. So it didn't really ring true. Jake was so young and Sisko was so experienced, you didn't really believe the central conflict of the show.

"We came in and started rebreaking the story, still with Jake," Moore continues. "We spent a day at it, went home, came back the second day, erased everything, started again, went home, came back the third day, erased everything, started again, just trying to make this show work. We lost Jake and tried to make it just about Sisko, but we couldn't make this stupid thing work. So the fourth night I was home watching TV, drinking scotch, and I got this idea—what if we told it in flashback for Sisko's log, with Sisko starting the show talking to the camera about this thing that's happened, and then telling us the story all through this scenario. The next morning, I pitched the idea, everybody liked it, and then we broke the show that way. So the script was reworked, and that's the version that ultimately aired."

"Making it a Sisko/Garak story was a wise decision," Taylor comments approvingly. "I thought it was really cool to see Sisko battling with these very real concerns."

In the final script, the point of no return for the captain's involvement is when he hears the news that the Dominion has invaded Betazed. "We wanted a moment that would really galvanize Sisko," Moore explains. "Just when he's starting to waver on his involvement in this plot, war news comes that makes him willing to go to the mat. So we needed to have a familiar world fall, and it was either Vulcan, which none of us really wanted to use because it just carried *too* much weight, and other than that it was . . ." Moore pauses to chuckle, "well . . . Betazed. What else could it be that has some sort of meaning in the *Star Trek* universe?"

Having the story narrated as a log entry, with Sisko talking to the camera, was a new structure for *Star Trek*, an innovation that Director Victor Lobl recognized as an added responsibility. "I choreographed all of the sequences that involved Sisko talking to the console in that room quite specifically," Lobl says. "So Avery's movements were almost exactly what I had put down on paper before we started to shoot. The thing about Avery is that he will say, 'Just tell me what you want,' and he'll do it for you exactly that way. It's wonderful working with him. And of course, in this

Sisko is willing to pay the moral price for making a decision that sets him apart. ROBBIE ROBINSON

instance I think he anticipated that it would be deadly if he just sat somewhere, so he was ready to hear my intentions.

"There were some very specific transitions that we had to make from scenes that involved him in that room talking, to other scenes," the director says, "so exactly where he was in the room was really critical. In some instances there were time lapses, or the transition was as critical as a head turn. so we would get that specific.

"Because of that, we shot it in sequence," Lobl recalls. "We did each scene virtually in continuity, so then I knew exactly how I could cut it. On set, I would walk with Avery to his mark and say, 'When you get to this line,' or 'On this word, you need to make a turn and start walking away from the camera.' And Avery was right there for that.

"Usually there's flexibility," Lobl points out, "but in this instance I shot it very tight, and I did not have many editing options once I committed to the shot. I had to know the A side and the B side of every cut very specifically."

One concern that actors always have is what to do with their hands while spending a lot of time on a single set. In this case, the script gave the stage direction that Sisko was drinking, an indication of the character's discomfort with his recent actions. "Originally he had a lot more to drink during the course of the script," Lobl laughs, "He powered back quite a bit of drink, whatever it was. And as we approached the shooting day, I kept thinking that somebody was going to pull the plug on that concept. But they never did. They just said, 'Be judicious about it.' I felt that if we just let him get more and more relaxed in his *clothing* that would help us," the director says. "And since we shot it in continuity, we just kept letting him strip down a little bit." Thematically, of course, that also indicated that the character was baring his soul. "That was the intent," Lobl confirms. "But with that uniform, there's just so much that we could strip him of."

For the final scene, Lobl did have Sisko just sit someplace—on his couch. "It just seemed to me that that would give us the physical repose of his arriving at a place where he's accepted this whole experience," the director says. "If he were standing, I think, because of Avery's physical presence, it would still leave a kind of question."

Ira Behr chose the final line that Sisko says, "I can live with it," as a tribute to another film hero. "That was my *The Man Who Shot Liberty Valance* homage," Behr says. "John Wayne's character kills Liberty Valance, and that makes the career of James Stewart's character. The Wayne character, all bearded and looking terrible, tells the story in flashback, and then, at the end when they cut back to real time, he says, 'That's right. It was murder. But I can live with it,' and you know that he can't. That's what I wanted in the scene. I wanted Sisko to say 'I can live with it,' and see that vulnerabilty."

HIS WAY

Episode #544

WRITTEN BY IRA STEVEN BEHR & HANS BEIMLER
DIRECTED BY ALLAN KROEKER

GUEST CAST	
Melissa	DEBI A. MONAHAN
Ginger	CYNDI PASS

SPECIAL GUEST STAR	
Vic Fontaine	JAMES DARREN

STARDATE UNKNOWN

Dr. Bashir is eager to show off his new holosuite program—a charismatic Las Vegas lounge singer, circa Earth's 1960s—to the station's senior staff. Their response to the setting isn't quite as enthusiastic as Bashir had hoped, but they're quite impressed with the crooner, Vic Fontaine. Vic is unlike any other hologram they've encountered. He's self-cognizant and strangely perceptive, particularly about affairs of the heart. Vic seems to have some special insight into the personality of everyone he meets, even Odo—but for some reason, he chooses not to reveal his insight about the changeling.

A short time later, Odo is shaken when he learns that Kira is going to Bajor to visit her ex-boyfriend, First Minister Shakaar. Knowing of Odo's fondness for Kira, Quark chides the changeling for waiting so long to ask her out. If he's smart, he'll forget about her, suggests the Ferengi. After all, he's not exactly a lovable guy.

As far as Quark is concerned, the conversation is over . . . so he's surprised when Odo calls him back, and even *more* surprised when Odo asks if he can use the new holosuite program.

Activating the program, Odo asks Vic what it was that the singer noticed about him the night before. Vic

Vic Fontaine pours champagne as Odo unsuspectingly practices romancing the real Kira. ROBBIE ROBINSON

doesn't mince words: Odo is clearly crazy about Kira, but afraid to do anything about it. And Kira thinks of Odo as a friend. However, he adds, women have been known to change their minds, given a reason.

Odo tries to shrug off the suggestion, noting that Kira prefers Shakaar. But Vic points out that Odo's primary obstacle isn't Shakaar—it's Odo. He keeps his emotions so tightly under wraps that he appears cold to others. But Vic thinks he knows a way to turn up the heat.

First he suggests a change of clothing. Odo obliges by morphing his uniform into a tuxedo. Then Vic gets him to fill in for the pianist in the lounge's holographic combo. Odo's not clear what good this will do him, but he eventually finds himself enjoying this bit of playacting. After their set, Vic takes Odo on a double date with a pair of beautiful holographic showgirls. Again, Odo doesn't understand the point, but Vic convinces him that he has to go through a "trial run" before he considers taking on the real thing.

As Odo's visits to Vic continue, the "therapy" slowly begins to have an effect. But after a week, the changeling confesses that he still has no idea what to do about Kira. Trust in Uncle Vic, the hologram tells him. Then he introduces Odo to the lounge's new chanteuse, Lola Chrystal, a sexy hologram who looks exactly like Kira. Vic successfully teaches Odo to flirt with an appreciative Lola, but the constable can't bring himself to kiss her. She may *look* like Kira, but she doesn't act anything like the real thing. What's more, Odo is certain that once he's faced with the real Kira, he'll revert back to the same cold fish he's

always been. Sure enough, when the major returns to the station, Odo can barely speak to her.

Deciding that Odo needs a little help, Vic takes matters into his own hands. He visits Kira in her holographic meditation program and tells her that Odo would like her to join him for dinner in the holosuite. Intrigued by both the unorthodox visit and the dinner invitation, Kira accepts.

Now Vic has to make sure that Odo will be there. Patching into Odo's comline, the hologram explains that he's completely overhauled the Lola program. She now acts *exactly* like Kira. He invites Odo to come and meet her that evening.

The date starts off perfectly. Odo is "wearing" his tux and Kira is dressed to the nines. Vic serves an elegant meal with champagne, and the couple find it surprisingly easy to chat. Thinking he's dining with a facsimile of Kira makes Odo more confident and open, and the change in his personality makes a favorable impression on his date, the real Kira. As Vic sings a romantic song, Odo invites Kira to dance. Everything goes well until Kira realizes that Odo is under the impression she's a hologram. At that point, Vic sheepishly admits to Odo that she's the real McCoy. Realizing that they were both tricked, the couple stare at Vic accusingly. But Vic points out that he's brought them together—and isn't that what counts?

Feeling like a complete fool, Odo abruptly leaves the holosuite. But Kira is feeling something different—regret that a lovely evening turned out so badly. Later, Vic tries to tell Odo that it's clear from the way Kira acted on their date that she *really* likes him. But Odo refuses to listen.

Meanwhile, Kira has been thinking about the evening, and about her feelings. Suddenly she reaches a decision and approaches Odo on the Promenade. She wants to talk about what happened at Vic's. Odo doesn't. Kira insists, so Odo suggests they discuss it later in his office. Kira suggests they discuss it over dinner. Odo suggests that Shakaar might not approve. Kira says that Shakaar has nothing to do with this; he's just a friend. Her trip to Bajor was strictly business. That catches Odo off guard, and he's not sure what to say. His emotions are chaotic.

"Are they going to have dinner or not?" Kira wants to know. "If they do, then what?" Odo parries. "Maybe dancing," Kira retorts. And after that, Odo accuses, she'll "probably expect him to *kiss* her."

Kira admits that it's possible.

"Then who needs dinner?" says Odo, taking her into his arms and kissing her.

And although the Promenade is crowded with people, suddenly it seems as if there's only two.

"'Far Beyond the Stars,' 'Duet,' 'In the Pale Moonlight,' and a lot of other episodes I could mention, are quality shows, terrific shows, wonderful shows on a whole lot of levels," Ira Behr states assuredly. "And those shows are easy to point to: each has the theme, each has the stuff. But let me tell you something. To do a show like 'His Way' and have it turn out as successfully as it did, is *twice* as difficult as doing those other shows. It just takes so much effort. To do a nice romantic comedy without a lot of clichés, to be clever, to not over-do it, and to have emotion rather than sentimentality, empathy rather than sentimentality, is *incredibly difficult*. Especially in a series like *Star Trek* that isn't geared to that kind of stuff.

"The quality of the show is not apparent to everyone, and that's really, really sad. Because that show is as perfect an episode as we ever did. You would be hard-pressed to find moments that don't work. It does exactly what it's supposed to. As looney as the show might seem, it's a real triumph. I'm not saying it's the only triumph by any means, but it's the one that's most masked, I guess, the one that's toughest for the audience to recognize. And that makes it dear to my heart."

Las Vegas is home to some of the glitziest entertainment productions ever staged, and that makes it Behr's kind of town. "I go to Vegas every six months or so," he says with a smile.

He'd been wanting to do an episode that touched on the Vegas magic for a long time, something that would incorporate memories of the "Rat Pack" era—a period in the 1960s when Frank Sinatra and his pals Dean Martin, Sammy Davis, Jr., Peter Lawford, and others ruled the strip. For years Behr had been talking about bringing a new recurring character to *Deep Space Nine*—a Rat Pack type who would dispense advice to the lovelorn. But devoting an entire episode to such a character hadn't been part of the plan until he decided that he wanted, at long last, to bring Kira and Odo together.

"'Children of Time' basically gave us the impetus to do it," Behr says. "We'd pulled on that thread for so long without really doing anything with it, and we were running out of time. I already knew that at the end of the series Odo would be going back to the Founders to become goo. And even

Nana Visitor fulfills a childhood dream. ROBBIE ROBINSON

though I didn't know the title 'What You Leave Behind' yet, I knew Odo had to leave something behind of real value. And it just seemed to me that Kira was that value.

"Of course, we could have stayed with the unrequited love thing, which would have made the actors happier," Behr notes.

As Nana Visitor and Rene Auberjonois have mentioned, the prospect of romance between their two characters was not a favorite of theirs.

"Nana and I always had thought that it would remain an unrequited love," Auberjonois says. "We didn't really know that they would actually become a couple until they handed us the script to 'His Way.'"

Visitor, in fact, actually had tried to discourage the writers from pursuing the romance. "I'm not much of a fan of Kira and Odo being together," Visitor remarks, "but they found a way to make it all make sense. I've always felt that I have to open my mouth and pick my fights. And even though I know that there's a certain amount of fights that I'm going to lose, I always do it anyway. That was one that I lost," she laughs. "But moments are more important to me than big storylines, so I can make the leap that these things happen, because God knows that in my *own* life things have happened that I'm surprised have happened!"

What surprised everyone when it happened, from the real-life audience to the fictional crowd on the Promenade, was Kira and Odo's first kiss. It was memorable, but not in a romantic way.

"It was funny," grins Auberjonois, "because we shoot things out of order. And the kiss was very early in

"They used the first take of the kiss," Visitor says. "It really was the best one." ROBBIE ROBINSON

the shooting schedule, one of the first scenes we shot for that episode. So we did it even before we had a chance to work on the show and find out how we would get to that point. I remember the day we were rehearsing it that both Nana and I were very nervous. I looked at her at one point and said, 'C'mon, we're pros, we can handle this.' We rehearsed it once, just marking it, but not going through it, you know. We'd walk down the Promenade for the camera, getting the marks, and then we would sort of indicate that we would kiss. Then we did sort of a final dress rehearsal before we actually shot it so we were sort of doing it more up to speed, but we hadn't ever really done the kiss.

"And so we were in it, and we started the scene and when we got to the mark, boom, we kissed each other. When they yelled cut and we stopped, I looked at Nana and her face was sort of orange and weird, and Dean Jones, my makeup artist, looked at me and went, 'Oh, God.' We had been so anxious about it we just sort of went 'Khuh. . .'" Here Auberjonois lurches forward and makes a crashing sound, ". . . and kissed, and my makeup got all over her face and I

tore my mask! Now when people ask, 'Well, what was it like to kiss Nana? I say, 'The definition of safe sex is this latex mask. It was the most unsensual kiss I've ever had. I didn't feel anything!'"

"Listen," Visitor adds with a giggle. "I'll be the one to say this, because probably nobody else will. The rubber is *really* smelly. It gets a sulfurous egglike smell after a while. And Cardassians are the *worst!*" she laughs.

While the kiss may not have been Visitor's most pleasant memory, "His Way" did allow her to relive a wonderful old one. She got to sing the classic pop song "Fever."

"I chose the song because I've always loved it," the actress says happily. "I have this childhood memory of my mother's dear friend Doris Duke singing that song." Duke was the heiress to the American Tobacco Company fortune and the daughter of the founder of Duke University. She was the wealthiest woman in America when she died in 1993, and was an ardent supporter of the arts around the world. "My mother was a dance teacher, and one of Doris's forays was dance," Visitor explains. "So she and my mother became friends. One of my childhood memories is going to her house in Somerville, New Jersey, where she had a theater with a stage. She'd sit at the piano and sing and we'd listen. She did 'Fever' with this very breathy quality to her voice, and I remember thinking, 'Oh, that's a real sophisticated woman.' I was about eight or nine years old at the time.

"So that was a personal connection for me," Visitor concludes. "It was a memory from when I was a little girl of what I thought a woman should be like—and I got to be that woman."

"'Fever' was Nana's choice," Behr acknowledges. "We had chosen another song, and she said, 'How about "Fever?"' As soon as she said that, we agreed. We knew that if she wanted to sing 'Fever,' she must have known that she could give us a great 'Fever.'"

Rene Auberjonois got to display his musical aspirations in a much different way. "I've never played a musical instrument," he says, with regret in his voice. "But all of my life I've loved to sit down at pianos and *pretend* to play, to the point where people say, 'Stop doing that! You don't know how to play!' And so to get to pretend, as goofy as it was, was just a blast for me. We used a silent piano that didn't make any noise, and I worked with a man who knew where my hands should be at what time. It was so much fun."

"By now we had met with Robert Goulet and had tried to get Steve Lawrence, and Tom Jones, and Jerry Vale, so when Fred comes back I say, 'You know, I'm doing a show on *Deep Space Nine* about a Vegas lounge singer and that might be the guy. I'm gonna go talk to him.' And Fred says, 'You can't talk to him here!' I say, 'What do you mean I can't talk to him here? You just talked to him about his *spaghetti sauce*.' Fred says, 'He's gonna think you're a mental patient!' I say, 'He's gonna think *I'm* a mental patient?' He says, 'You can't do it here.' I said, I have a business card. I'm legit.' He says, 'No, no, no, you can't do it here. Go to work on Monday, talk to your casting guy, and do it that way.' So I don't do it. I listen to Fred.

"So on Monday, I talked to Ron Surma. And Ron sent Jimmy the script. A few days later Ron says, 'You know, Jimmy's been directing for fifteen years, but he's gonna come in. We're not gonna have a whole casting session, he's gonna come in alone, and we don't know if he's gonna read.'

"So the other writers and I go out to lunch. And sitting there at lunch, in our favorite sushi restaurant, I'm telling the guys that Jimmy Darren's coming in. To which they want to know, 'Who's that?' I say, 'Moondoggie.' No response. 'Moondoggie, from *Gidget*. No response. I say, 'The *Time Tunnel* guy.' Nothing. 'Remember the guy with the turtleneck in the *Time Tunnel*? Not really. Vaguely.' 'Okay,' I yell, 'William Shatner's sidekick in *T.J. Hooker*.' 'Oh!! Yeah!! Sure!!'

"These people have *Star Trek* on the *brain*! It's like, you can't . . . it all has to come back to *Star Trek* in some way, shape or form.

"So Jimmy Darren comes in, and he's talking about how he

ROBBIE ROBINSON

owns a pair of Dean Martin's shoes, and he knows where to get the right tuxedos, at Sy Devore's store, and all of that stuff, and he's being great. We're all listening to him. And suddenly he starts talking about him and Frank and Dean and gambling and making all this money, and suddenly we realize that he's doing the part. It catches us totally by *surprise*. We're sitting there with the script pages and don't even realize it.

"He had gone right from being Jimmy to being Vic—without a beat. After he did that, we said goodbye, and I started freaking out that he was great. But then I started to say, 'Well, maybe we should see some other people, just to be on the safe side,' and Hans Beimler just said, 'Are you out of your mind? What are you talking about? Vic Fontaine was just in the room! There's no question, there's no question! He's the guy!'

"And he was."

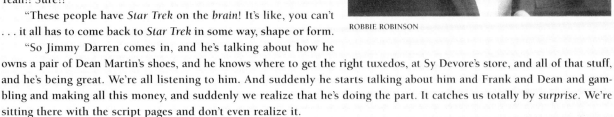

"When Rene was playing piano, faking his way through the song," recalls Director Allan Kroeker, "the musicians played wonderfully with him. They were even offering him encouragement every now and then, just like real guys doing a gig. I'd wanted to incorporate them in a real way so that they weren't just background guys, and they weren't—they were foreground guys."

But if Visitor and Auberjonois were fulfilling daydreams, James Darren, who at one time had been a junior member of the Rat Pack, was experiencing genuine déjà vu. "When I read the script, I thought to myself, 'God, I've lived this thing before,'" Darren laughs. "I used to go down to Vegas just about every

weekend with Nancy Sinatra and Frank Sinatra, Junior, and a bunch of friends. It was usually on Frank's plane. We'd go to the Sands Hotel, and of course, being with Nancy, we had front row center."

When Darren, as Vic, delivers the line, "I remember that weekend with Frank," he's not kidding. "Vic is Frank *and* Dean," the singer laughs. "And having idolized both of those guys, talking like them and being like them and using the expressions they used was quite easy."

Says Behr, "I looked up some of those expressions, and some of them I'd heard, so that was a lot of fun. Anytime you'd see Dean Martin, he'd call someone 'Pal' or 'Pallie' or something like that. And

The final mural.

in one of Sinatra's live versions of 'Come Fly With Me,' he adds the word 'Clyde' into the lyrics."

It was easy for Behr to choose a repertoire of great songs for the episode. What wasn't so easy was clearing the rights to use some of those songs. "We were still picking tunes on the way to the recording studio," says Jay Chattaway. "Because so many of them were cleared at the last minute, I couldn't really do full arrangements of them in advance, so I only wrote generic intros and endings. I didn't know what the rhythm was going to be, or the key, but when the tune did get cleared I'd just say, 'Okay, we're going to use intro number two,' and I would quickly rearrange it for the tune in the studio."

Chattaway thinks that perhaps the loose method they used to finalize the songs added to the authenticity of the period sound they were looking for. "If I would have written the music out too much, maybe it wouldn't have had the magic of a lounge band," he says. "Our musicians were improvising as if they really were combo players."

"We tried to make the choice of instruments authentic to the period," Chattaway points out, "including the right kind of hollow-body electric guitar and the right kind of drum set. Of course, the size of the bandstand had something to do with it too," he laughs, "because that's as many people as we could get up there at one time."

On a practical note, the small size of the bandstand was all that would fit in the limited space on the soundstage. But just as important, it was authentic to the era being duplicated in the episode. "We knew that we'd need a stage and performers, but the producers hadn't given the look of the lounge much further thought," says Randy McIlvain, who served as production designer while Herman Zimmerman worked on *Star Trek Insurrection*. "Nowdays we think of Vegas as bigger than life, but in the fifties and sixties it was pretty tame and kind of drab. The colors used were grays and browns and the walls were done in big sheets of paneling. So I asked Ira, 'Is this really what you want?' I suggested that we give the back of the bar a good visual that would be more exciting than curtains. So we designed a mural."

The task of painting the mural fell to acting Art Director Andrew Reader and Scenic Artist Assistant Anthony Fredrickson. Together, they designed it with images that they found on a fifties-era cocktail napkin: champagne glasses and dancers. "And then I did these sort of period shapes," Fredrickson adds. "They look like slices of liver," he laughs.

"Allan Kroeker has to take a lot of the responsibility for the success of this show," says Behr, "because he understood it, and he gave it a wonderful, wonderful, wonderful, wonderful look and feel. And the actors were fabulous. Nana was fabulous. Rene was fabulous. Jimmy was fabulous."

Kroeker thoroughly enjoyed directing "His Way." "Before I ever directed an episode of *Deep Space Nine*," he says, "I'd had the producers send me a bunch of episodes and I crammed, grabbing any information that I could. And of course, I was quite impressed with what I saw. But the show that I thought was the killer episode among the ones they sent was 'Crossfire,' where Odo can't speak his love for Kira. That was one of my favorite episodes of all time, so I was delighted to finish that story. I had a marvelous time on 'His Way.' It probably should be illegal to have that much fun."

THE RECKONING

Episode #545

TELEPLAY BY **DAVID WEDDLE &
BRADLEY THOMPSON**
STORY BY **HARRY M. WERKSMAN &
GABRIELLE STANTON**
DIRECTED BY **JESÚS SALVADOR TREVIÑO**

GUEST CAST

Koral	JAMES GREENE
Kai Winn	LOUISE FLETCHER
Station Computer Voice	JUDI DURAND

STARDATE UNKNOWN

Sisko receives a brief respite from the tensions of the war when archeologists at Bajor's B'hala dig summon him to see an unusual religious artifact they've unearthed. Along with Major Kira and his son, Jake, the captain goes to B'hala. They are shown a stone tablet, inscribed in ancient Bajoran. Although much of it is difficult to translate, two words are immediately recognizable to Sisko and the Bajorans present at the dig: "Welcome, Emissary."

Suddenly, Sisko finds himself in the presence of the Prophets, who, as always, speak cryptically. Now that the Emissary has come, they say, the Reckoning must begin. Much will depend on his actions. The Sisko will bring the Reckoning, and it will be the end . . . or the beginning.

When Sisko revives from his trance, he asks the monk in charge of the dig about "the Reckoning," but neither he nor Kira have ever heard of it. Sisko feels

that it's important to figure out the rest of the inscription on the tablet. The ranjen allows him to take it back to the station, where Dax can work on the translation.

The removal of the tablet from Bajor brings Kai Winn to the station. Although she hides her feelings under a thin veil of civility, Winn is incensed that Sisko took the artifact without first consulting the Vedek Assembly. The captain tells her that he believes he's doing what the Prophets want, and he'll return the tablet as soon as he finishes studying it. An unsatisfied Winn lodges a formal protest with Starfleet, which sends Sisko a directive: Return the tablet.

Sisko resists and pushes Dax to work harder. He feels the artifact has something to do with the penance the Prophets said they would exact after he called on them to stop the Dominion fleet ("Sacrifice of Angels"). The tablet is the key. But Dax's computer has decrypted only a portion of the inscription, which notes that during the time of the Reckoning, the Prophets will weep, and their sorrow will consume the gateway to the Celestial Temple—which Dax takes to mean Deep Space 9.

A sense of uneasiness settles upon the inhabitants of the station. It's made worse when the wormhole, known to the Bajorans as the Celestial Temple, unaccountably begins to open and close. The instability of the wormhole affects the nearby planet of Bajor, causing earthquakes, floods, and tornadoes. The kai tells Sisko that the damage is being caused by the Prophets, who are angry that he has taken the tablet from the planet. Again Winn demands the return of the artifact—and now she has a request from First Minister Shakaar seconding her request. Not wanting to damage relations between Bajor and the Federation, Sisko promises to return it in the morning.

Kira tells Sisko that she thinks the kai is jealous of Sisko's relationship with the Prophets. After all, Winn is the spiritual leader of Bajor, and they don't speak to *her*. Instead, they've chosen an outsider to be their Emissary. That's something for which her eminence can never forgive Sisko.

That night, Sisko finds it hard to sleep, as does his son. Jake is concerned about his father's role as the Emissary. Twice in the past year, Sisko's visions have landed him in the Infirmary ("Rapture," "Far Beyond the Stars"); Jake is afraid that one day his father won't recover. Sisko tries to comfort his son, but admits that whether he asked for it or not, he *is* the Emissary.

When Kai Winn triggers the chroniton generator, the beings inhabiting Jake's and Kira's bodies depart. ROBBIE ROBINSON

The captain goes to the Science Lab to examine the tablet one last time. He's tired of riddles, he tells the Prophets, and he wants them to tell him what they want him to do. Suddenly, he's overwhelmed by an impulse to throw the tablet to the floor. After it shatters, Sisko stares at the wreckage in disbelief. What has he done? Then, something even stranger happens, as two strands of energy rise from the fragments of the artifact and shoot up through the ceiling of the room.

The next morning, Dax and Odo can find no sign of the energy discharge Sisko witnessed, although there *is* an unexplained drain in the station's power supply. Whether there's a connection or not remains to be seen, but Sisko is suddenly certain of one thing: he did what the Prophets wanted. Kai Winn doesn't see it that way, and she tells Sisko that the populace of Bajor, devastated by the planet's continuing environmental disasters, will wind up paying the price for his act of sacrilege.

Their meeting is cut short when the station's power winks out. Sisko receives an urgent call from Odo, asking him to come to the Promenade. There Sisko finds a strangely transformed Kira, her entire being ablaze with an unearthly blue luminescence as it seems to draw power from the station. As she approaches Sisko, he realizes that this being is no longer Kira Nerys. She is a Prophet, occupying Kira's body. The Prophet/Kira tells Sisko that the time of the Reckoning has come, and that she awaits "Kosst Amojan."

Sisko doesn't recognize the term, but Winn does: the Evil One, a Pah-wraith banished from the Temple. The Prophet announces that the battle will take place on the station when the Evil One chooses a corporeal form. Winn is thrilled; according to one of the prophecies, the defeat of the Evil One will usher in Bajor's golden age—a thousand years of peace in a world where the Prophets and the people will be as one. Except that there's no guarantee that the Kosst Amojan *will* be destroyed. It could be the station that's destroyed.

Dax and Bashir rig a device to drive the wormhole beings from the station by flooding the Promenade with chroniton radiation, but Sisko tells them not to use it. Instead, he orders the station to be evacuated. He won't stand in the way of the Prophets.

The residents flee the station, leaving behind only a skeleton crew. Then the Kosst Amojan chooses its host: Jake! The battle commences, and Sisko watches in helpless anguish as the alien beings in Kira's and Jake's bodies shoot deadly bolts of energy at one another. Dax urges Sisko to trigger the chroniton generator, knowing it could save Jake's life. In his heart, Sisko believes the Prophets will protect Jake, and that even if the being in Kira destroys the Kosst Amojan, Jake will be spared. With the station in danger of exploding, the rest of the crew clears out. But Sisko stays behind to see the outcome of the battle. The kai pretends to leave with the others, but sneaks back to Ops, and just as it seems that the Prophet is about to vanquish the Pah-wraith, she triggers the radiation.

The two alien beings evacuate their humanoid hosts and leave the station, their prophesied battle uncompleted. Kira is unharmed and Jake is left battered, but not permanently injured. As life on the station returns to normal, Kira escorts the kai to her transport. Winn tries to take credit for preventing the destruction of the station and saving both the Emissary and his son, but Kira won't hear of it. Winn didn't do it for Sisko, or even for Bajor, which has returned to normal. She defied the will of the Prophets because she couldn't stand the fact that a non-Bajoran had more faith in them than she did. Because of her interference, the Reckoning was stopped and the Evil One still exists. Who knows what that means for Bajor?

And for once, Winn is left without a response.

"Our feeling after 'The Assignment' was that we had dealt with the Pah-wraiths way too easily," Ira Behr says. "We thought there was more juice that we could get out of them, but we were juggling a lot of balls in the air, and sometimes balls don't drop for a long time."

And then . . . they do.

"We were looking for the ultimate battle between good and evil," Bradley Thompson says. "We thought, 'Let's put a Prophet up against a Pah-wraith and deal with some deep stuff.'" When they brought up the idea, other members of the writing staff realized that it was similar to a pitch they'd heard from freelancers Harry Werksman and Gabrielle Stanton, so they purchased the older premise and moved forward with the concept.

During the story break session, the writers decided to have Kira possessed by the Prophet and Kai Winn possessed by the Pah-wraith. With the combatants identified, they next looked for a logical location where the two Bajoran religious entities would first appear. The legendary sacred city of B'hala

Winn's deep envy of Sisko's connection with the Prophets motivates her to defy them. ROBBIE ROBINSON

("Rapture") seemed to fit the bill. With the story opening in an ancient archeological site and leading up to a battle between the gods, Thompson recalls, "Ira said, 'It's Godzilla versus Mothra, with a mummy movie opening.'"

Thompson and writing partner David Weddle took Behr's description to heart. "We did a mummy movie type of beginning," Thompson laughs. "And we went a little further with it than we'd planned."

The duo's first draft started with a vedek discovering an ancient casket, opening it, and releasing the two mysterious entities. "The battle between them had been going on for centuries," Thompson says. "Open the box and it starts again! The vedek had a heart attack, and we even had big ugly birds sitting on the tops of the walls. It was *way* too mummy movielike.

"And then, after the entities possess them, we had Winn and Kira stalking each other throughout the whole station, throwing fireballs at each other, and just ruining the place," Thompson continues. "Finally it got just too complicated, and when René joined us, he was very instrumental in smoothing it out."

René Echevarria, who had missed the story break, returned just as Weddle and Thompson were nearing completion on their first draft. "They had Winn and Kira running around throwing lightning bolts," he says, shaking his head. "When Steve Oster looked at it, he said, 'Hey guys, this is a fifteen-day shoot!' And," Echevarria confides, "it was very silly."

"It definitely had the potential to come off like a bad old outer-space serial," concurs Oster.

"It took us a while to figure it out," Echevarria says, "because the original idea had been that Sisko was going to stop this great battle. He was going to choose to protect his station and his people rather than side with the gods. But then it hit us that this was exactly the opposite of what it should have been. It wasn't that Sisko should put a stop to it, it was that Sisko should be the *last man of faith*. And if that was the case, then the combatants were wrong. Jake should be one of them, because Sisko would be like Abraham being asked to sacrifice his own son." With this serious turn, suddenly the story was no longer B-movie material.

Director Jesús Treviño, thinking both about the production and what was produceable, "was the one who came up with the idea of doing the battle as if it were more of a one-on-one contest of wills rather than a lot of running and jumping," says Echevarria.

"It goes back to the Old West," comments Thompson. "You stand out there at opposite ends of the street, draw, and shoot."

While that change made Steve Oster happy on the postproduction budgetary front, he was still a bit concerned about the shoot itself. "It was very hard to imagine what this was going to look like on the set," he admits. "I had a little joke going that when Nana [Visitor] came out on the Promenade for the first time as the Prophet, she could do a Wonder Woman stance. That would have been a cheesy way to do it, and I was hoping we would not cross into that territory."

Visitor, too, had worries about the scene, but for a different reason. "I was trying very hard not to laugh at Cirroc [Lofton]," she chuckles. "He is the funniest of young men, and he was being totally irreverent. I really had to call on my powers within. It was very challenging."

It's hard to blame Lofton for going for laughs. To anyone watching the two actors perform, without the benefits of the postproduction visual effects, it did look a little . . . well, silly, as Dennis McCarthy can testify. When he received a copy of the footage to facilitate the scoring process, the big contest of wills wasn't very dramatic. "They were just standing there looking weird, like they were at the dentist's office, thinking of their upcoming root canals," McCarthy chuckles.

The idea that the Prophet and the Pah-wraith were released from something found at B'hala stayed

Sisko's reaction to the tablet is not a measured, scientific one.
ROBBIE ROBINSON

Kira's words to Winn, "You defied the will of the Prophets . . . you're confusing faith with ambition," were harsh enough. "I know that the writers want Kira to give Winn respect because she's her spiritual leader," Visitor states, "but I can't accept the fact that she would be my leader. I think Kira would say, 'Not this woman.' I understand the need to toe a line, but if I were writing this, the language would have been a *lot* stronger."

in the story, but the box they had been entombed in became the stone tablet that Sisko smashes on the floor. The Property Department assigned John Eaves to design the tablet. "I based it on the Bajoran symbol," he says, "but I altered it a little because it was from an ancient time. Instead of a circle in a bigger oval, I made it more of an egg shape." The tablet then was carved out of foam so that it would have a "rock-like" texture, and a mold was made. "The final piece was cast from a mixture of plaster and silicone, so that it would be fragile and break in pieces easily," Eaves says. "We actually made weak points by putting scribe lines where we wanted it to break."

Having the Pah-wraith that escapes from the tablet inhabit Jake Sisko's body rather than Kai Winn's gave the writers the opportunity to put Winn back on a path she'd veered from a season earlier. "In 'Rapture,' she seemed to be coming around to Sisko's side a little bit," points out Echevarria. "But here she just cannot stand to see that once again he's going to steal her thunder. That was the biggest dodge we did, because we didn't really explain why she had a change of heart, but it set up what we needed to do with her later on in the series."

"'The Reckoning' really gave us a more multidimensional Kai Winn," Behr says. "We had lost sight of what to do with her for a while. We loved having her as a villain, but this really made her a tragic figure. It made her a totally *screwed-up* figure, and we now understood her."

Visitor doesn't think the writers made Winn feel her tragedy enough, and she *really* doesn't feel that

VALIANT
Episode #546
WRITTEN BY RONALD D. MOORE
DIRECTED BY MICHAEL VEJAR

GUEST CAST

Nog	ARON EISENBERG
Tim Watters	PAUL POPOWICH
Karen Farris	COURTNEY PELDON
Riley Aldrin Shepard	DAVID DREW GALLAGHER
Dorian Collins	ASHLEY BRIANNE McDONOGH
Parton	SCOTT HAMM
Computer Voice	MAJEL BARRETT

STARDATE 51825.4

When Odo notes that Quark seems to be having a bad day, the Ferengi complains that the bar's drink replicator is down and Nog hasn't come by to fix it. Suddenly Dax shows up, tool kit in hand. Nog had an opportunity to take a trip to Ferenginar, she explains, so she's covering for him. Surprisingly, this doesn't serve to restore Quark's spirits. Mechanical labor is beneath Dax, he comments. Her hands weren't meant to be poking around inside a filthy drink replicator. Odo is amused. It's clear to him that Quark is still in love with Dax, despite the rattled Ferengi's statements to the contrary.

In the meantime, Nog is en route to Ferenginar to hand-deliver a diplomatic message from the Federation Council to the grand nagus. Accompanying him in the runabout is Jake, who sees the trip as an opportunity to get an exclusive interview with the nagus for the Federation News Service. But before they get anywhere near Ferenginar, their runabout is intercepted by a Jem'Hadar fighter and fired upon. Seriously outmatched by the enemy vessel, the pair don't think they have much of a chance until a starship arrives on the scene and begins firing on the

Jake tries to convince Nog that his newfound loyalty to Watters is misguided. ROBBIE ROBINSON

most of the crew, Watters has been dosing himself with stimulants to stay awake and ever vigilant against enemy attack.

Nog takes his new responsibilities as seriously as the rest of Watters's crew. He successfully modifies the *Valiant*'s warp capabilities, earning the respect of the captain. He proudly informs Jake of his achievement and shows off his Red Squad insignia pin, but Jake is troubled by Nog's new loyalties. Before they can discuss the matter further, however, the ship goes to red alert. They've found the battleship.

The *Valiant* launches a sensor probe that covertly picks up vital information about the Dominion vessel while the starship remains undetected. Their mission complete, the *Valiant* is free to return home to Federation territory. But Watters isn't satisfied; he feels that the battleship should be destroyed while they have it in sight. The data from the probe has revealed a weakness in the enemy vessel's design that he wants to exploit. Nog points out that the act is risky. Not only would *Valiant* need to manually hit its target, but it also would need to get within a mere three hundred meters of the battleship. Jake speaks up and observes that his father, a seasoned Starfleet captain, never would attempt a maneuver that dangerous with the *Defiant*. But Watters has convinced his crew that Red Squad can do anything, and they plan the attack.

Later, Jake expresses his concern to Nog, only to find that the Ferengi has been taken in by Watters's charismatic command style. Jake reveals that Collins told him the captain has been taking stimulants for months, making his judgment questionable. But Nog can't see beyond the job Watters has asked him to do. Watters, secretly observing the exchange on a monitor, has Jake arrested and sent to the brig.

The battle ensues, and the *Valiant* sustains heavy damage. Following Watters's plan, the crew launches a specially rigged torpedo at the Dominion ship. But to their horror, the enemy vessel is unscathed by the attack, and it moves in to destroy them. In the chaos that follows, the majority of the crew is killed, including Watters. Soon, Nog and Collins are the only two left standing on the bridge, and Nog makes a life-or-death decision: abandon ship! They hastily free Jake from the brig and exit the ship in an escape pod moments before *Valiant* explodes. Their distress signal is picked up by the *Defiant,* and the three are rescued.

As they return home, Nog summarizes the experience for a story that Jake plans to write: a good ship with a good crew that made a mistake by blindly fol-

Jem'Hadar. As the runabout takes a serious blast, the two young men are beamed aboard the starship, a *Defiant*-class vessel, the *U.S.S. Valiant*, which destroys the Jem'Hadar ship.

Jake and Nog are surprised to discover that the *Valiant* is crewed entirely by members of Red Squad, an elite group of Starfleet Academy cadets. Their commanding officer, who received a battlefield commission from the vessel's late captain, is a twenty-two-year old cadet named Tim Watters. Jake and Nog learn that the *Valiant* originally was on a three-month training cruise when the war broke out. The starship was trapped in Dominion space and damaged by enemy fire. The regular officers were killed in that initial attack, but the cadets managed to repair the ship and have kept it safe behind enemy lines for eight months. Although Starfleet is unaware of the situation, Watters is trying to complete the late captain's mission to gather data on a new Dominion battleship. Caught up in Watters's fervor, Nog agrees to join the crew as chief engineer.

While Nog and Watters hit it off, the young captain is less enamored of Jake, the only civilian on the ship. When Dorian Collins, a young member of the crew, becomes melancholy after Jake talks to her about home, Watters orders him to stay away from her. Jake agrees, although he's concerned that the captain equates a conversation about home with a threat to the ship's security. After Jake leaves Watters's quarters, the captain swallows a pill; unknown to

lowing its captain over a cliff. Unable to separate logic from loyalty, Collins disagrees, but Nog refuses to back down. Watters may have been a hero, he says, but in the end, he was a bad captain. And he gives Collins his Red Squad pin.

"We were talking about war stories that we could do," Ron Moore reminisces, "and we thought of coming across a ship that's been behind the lines since the beginning of the war, with a crew that has gotten rowdier and more ragged and embittered—a wild-eyed bunch of crazies that have been lost and out of contact for a long time. Then I said, 'It would be interesting if they were cadets, if it was a whole ship of kids that had been lost behind the lines.' And Ira said, 'Yeah, that'd be great. We could use Red Squad.'"

The elite cadet group, Red Squad, had been introduced in the fourth season episodes "Homefront" and "Paradise Lost," but, Moore says, "we hadn't talked about them for a long time."

Oddly enough, although Nog was the primary to interact with Red Squad in the past, Moore left him out of the original story. "In the first draft, it was Kira and Jake that were picked up by the *Valiant*," says Moore. "It had almost the exact same plot, but it didn't work because you couldn't believe that Kira wouldn't kick every one of their asses and take the ship back single-handedly. It occurred to us that if we put Nog in there we'd have a character who could buy into what Red Squad was doing. And Jake was a character who could stand back from it. That worked a lot better."

"I've always thought of Nog as a very ambitious creature," says Eisenberg. ROBBIE ROBINSON

Still, it wasn't entirely clear sailing from there. "It was a tough show for Ron to write because I couldn't get him to let Watters make the mistakes he had to make," Behr chuckles. "It went against a lot of Ron's *Star Trek*-Horatio Hornblower type of childhood dreams."

"Nog's dilemma in the episode was, 'Should I do the right thing? Or should I grab the opportunity to do what I've always wanted,' which is to become an officer," comments Aron Eisenberg. The actor takes his character's responsibility as the first Ferengi in Starfleet very seriously—so seriously that he easily can provide a thumbnail sketch of Ferengi psychology and how it relates to Nog's career path. "When a Ferengi sees what he wants, he doesn't let anything get in his way," Eisenberg expains. "He has all these rules for obtaining money, and that's the center of his life. Nothing really deters him from that goal. Nothing clouds that vision. A Ferengi won't allow it.

"So I applied that same mentality, those same philosophical ideas to Nog's desire to be a Starfleet officer," Eisenberg continues. "After he joined Starfleet, I turned all that attention to the one goal of succeeding in Starfleet and not failing, not letting anything deter him from that goal. So I started to play Nog as very, very, straitlaced, a perfect military guy.

Trapped behind the lines, the cadets of Red Squad hear only the beat to quarters. ROBBIE ROBINSON

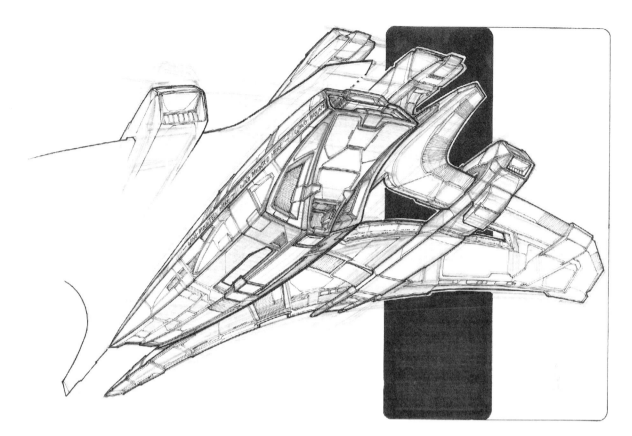

Early sketch showing the "weak spot" on the Dominion ship. JOHN EAVES

"In 'Valiant,' somebody was offering Nog a chance to be an officer and he could justify it, even if those justifications weren't correct, as Jake pointed out. He wasn't going to listen to anybody except for his captain. That's what made that show so powerful for me—the fact that Nog realizes when it's almost too late that he's made a horrible, horrible mistake. I thought it was great that the writers let him make the wrong decision. But then he was man enough to admit it too. And in the end scene, he gives back his prized possession, the Red Squad pin, which symbolizes what he wanted so badly." Eisenberg concludes, "I think Nog grew tremendously in this show."

The lesson that Nog learns in the episode is one that the producers also hoped viewers would pick up on. "I felt that after the war arc we needed a dose of reality," Behr says. "I just was afraid that people might be watching the war stuff and getting off on it. But I wanted them to know that it's not that simple, that life isn't really like that."

As strong and simple as it seems, that theme did not gel until halfway through the final draft of the script, according to Behr. By that time, of course, the show already was in production. "The rewrites on the ending took forever," he says. "We wanted to show that Watters was a hero but that he was a bad captain. And that finally summarized the whole."

"Casting this show was critical to its success," comments Steve Oster. "It was a story that had to be carried off entirely by young people. We had a young regular cast member, Cirroc, and a young recurring cast member, Aron, and an all guest cast of young people. And for the most part, it's very hard for seasoned actors to pull off Starfleet military roles, so for young actors to pull it off is an enormous feat. We saw lots and lots of kids for every role, and we called them all back two or three times."

"The young actors were not indoctrinated in the ways of Starfleet," notes Jonathan West, "so everyone had to teach them things that we take for granted at this point, like Federation posture and how to move their hands on the controls, because the controls aren't just typewriters."

The character of Collins was created to give Red Squad a face the audience could relate to. "She was a little softer than I would have liked," Behr observes. "She didn't quite strike me as 'Starfleet Cadet' enough, but it worked out all right. In a way it's scary that *she's* the one to still be waving the flag at the end of the show. Even with all that's happened, she still doesn't get it."

Setting the episode on a *Defiant*-class ship was a practical idea that allowed the staff to turn their regular set into a brand-new ship with very little work. In fact, the set decorators made only one distinctive change. "The panels on the *Defiant* are gray/blue," says Laura Richarz. "We reupholstered them with a deep red, and just made some basic changes like that."

"Using the existing ship set gave us the ability to spend more on visual and special effects," Moore confirms. To Special Effects Supervisor Gary Monak, that meant bigger and better explosions. "We blew up the interior of the ship nonstop for four days," he says cheerfully. "We hung special rafters overhead, just off camera; they were soft so it wouldn't hurt when they fell on the stunt people. And of course, we were particularly careful because the actors were all minors."

For the name of his *Defiant*-class ship, Ron Moore finally was able to use the name he'd originally chosen for Sisko's tough little warship ("The Search, Pt. I").

Lumba hopes to bring Nilva around to "her" way of thinking.
ROBBIE ROBINSON

PROFIT AND LACE

Episode #547

WRITTEN BY **IRA STEVEN BEHR & HANS BEIMLER**
DIRECTED BY **ALEXANDER SIDDIG**

GUEST CAST

Nilva	HENRY GIBSON
Brunt	JEFFREY COMBS
Rom	MAX GRODÉNCHIK
Nog	ARON EISENBERG
Ishka	CECILY ADAMS
Leeta	CHASE MASTERSON
Maihar'du	TINY RON
Uri'lash	SYLVAIN CECILE
Aluura	SYMBA SMITH

SPECIAL GUEST STAR

Zek	WALLACE SHAWN

STARDATE UNKNOWN

Quark isn't happy when his brother interrupts an important meeting with Aluura, a new dabo girl, who, in the bartender's mind, doesn't measure up in a crucial area of job performance. Quark had hoped to improve Aluura's prospects for continued employment by introducing her to the virtues of Oomox *for Fun and Profit,* but

with a frantic Rom refusing to go away, the meeting is postponed.

For a change, Rom's anxiety may be warranted. Ishka is missing, or at least incommunicado, as are Grand Nagus Zek and the entire staff of Ferenginar's Tower of Commerce! Has Ferenginar been invaded by the Dominion? Are they all dead? Apparently not, because a Ferengi ship has just docked at the station, with Zek and Ishka aboard.

The visiting Ferengi bring news from home. Zek has added a new amendment to the Ferengi Bill of Opportunities, giving females the right to wear clothing in public. This means that they'll be able to leave their homes and earn profit. Quark's horror at this shocking turn of events is nothing compared to that of the rest of Ferenginar. Financial chaos has erupted all over the homeworld, and Zek has been deposed as grand nagus, temporarily replaced by Quark's old nemesis, Liquidator Brunt. However, the Ferengi Commerce Authority (FCA) won't confirm Brunt as the official nagus for three days. This gives Zek and the others just enough time to help Zek regain his position—assuming their plan works.

Zek plans to invite every member of the FCA to the station for a meeting, which Ishka will run. They're counting on the fact that Ishka's wealth of financial knowledge and keen instinct for profit will win them over. Zek hopes the end result will be that the FCA will reinstate him as nagus. But after hundreds of transmissions to Ferenginar, only one commissioner agrees to come to Deep Space 9: Nilva, the influencial chairman of Slug-o-Cola. It's an important start. If they can convince Nilva to follow Zek, the other commissioners will follow. But before they can celebrate, Acting Grand Nagus Brunt arrives on the station. He informs the group that no matter what they offer Nilva for his support, he'll double it and make them all paupers!

Later, an angry Quark blames his mother for destroying all of their lives. She is, he says, the worst thing that ever happened to the Ferengi Alliance! Incensed, Ishka starts to respond . . . but then collapses, the victim of severe coronary distress. Dr. Bashir performs a heart transplant and saves her life, but it's clear that she'll be unable to meet with Nilva. How can they introduce him to a Ferengi female who's brilliant enough to convince him that gender equality is a good idea?

Playing upon Quark's guilt, Zek convinces the bartender to allow Bashir to perform a temporary sex change procedure so that he—or rather *she*—can meet with Nilva. Through the miracle of twenty-fourth-century techniques, Quark is transformed into a female Ferengi whom his friends name Lumba. The next few hours are hell for Lumba, as "she" studies Ishka's notes for the meeting and learns to walk, talk, and dress like a female. Unfortunately, Nilva arrives at the station a day early, and although they try to put him off until the next morning, Nilva insists on seeing Zek and Ishka immediately. After Brunt informs Nilva that Ishka is ill, Nog is forced to take the cola magnate to meet Zek's *other* female financial advisor, Lumba. Realizing that Quark is ill prepared for the encounter, Zek attempts to take Nilva to dinner, but Nilva only has eyes for Lumba. He wants to have dinner with *her*.

Rising to the occasion, Lumba turns on the charm and manages to convince Nilva that giving equal rights to females will both expand Ferengi economy *and* increase his own cola profits. Impressed as he is with Lumba's mind, he is far more interested in her body. He invites her back to his quarters for dessert, but quickly reveals that Lumba is the only dessert he craves. The new female is desperately fending off Nilva's advances when Brunt bursts in and declares that Lumba is actually a male! But after Lumba reveals her body to all, Nilva declares that she appears female enough for him. Nilva promises to do everything he can to ensure that Zek remains grand nagus, and leaves the station. With Zek's future secure, Lumba is transformed back into Quark. However, there is enough of a hormonal

hangover to temporarily make him a sensitive, caring male who wouldn't think of taking advantage of Aluura, much to Aluura's—and Quark's—regret.

 It is, perhaps, one of life's little ironies that Season 6 produced both an episode that ranked near the top of everyone's list of favorites ("In the Pale Moonlight") and an episode that ranked at the very bottom.

"Profit and Lace" *could* have been the *Some Like It Hot* of *Star Trek*. The teleplay worked fine. "The script was delightful," states Ira Steven Behr. "[Creative Consultant] Michael Piller's memo on it was, 'This is going to be a classic!'" Instead, the episode had the dubious distinction of appearing on the bottom rung of *Sci-Fi Entertainment Magazine*'s "10 Best, 10 Worst" DS9 episodes list.

It started out innocently enough. "I guess I have to take some of the blame," says René Echevarria. "We were all at lunch, talking about doing an episode about Moogie, the feminist movement, and giving Ferengi women the right to vote. It was a very preliminary discussion, and I said, 'I have this feeling that Quark ends up in a dress. I don't know why, but I think somehow Quark and Rom have to masquerade as women in order to pull something off.'"

It seemed like a good idea at the time. ROBBIE ROBINSON

The script indicated that Lumba cried a lot, but Shimerman didn't like what that said about women. ROBBIE ROBINSON

His co-workers' initial reactions may have been a portent of the future. "Ron hit the person next to him, who hit the person next to him, who hit me, and Ron said, 'Shut up!'" Echevarria chuckles at the memory. "Then we started talking about other things for other episodes, and I forgot about it.

"At the end of the day I was working on something else and Ira walked into my office and said, 'Well! I hope you're satisfied! Because Hans and I have decided to do it!' And I said, 'Really? Quark and Rom in dresses?' And Ira said, 'No, just Quark.' And I said, 'Oh, c'mon—it's *gotta* be Quark *and* Rom.' I still feel that way. Because Max would have played it in a way that would have been very funny."

"The idea was to do a character comedy," Behr says with a sad shrug. "We wanted to take this misogynist character and make him into a woman. But it's very difficult, for a lot of reasons, to get people on board with stuff like this, and when they *do* get on board they tend to go too far, or too broad, or they lose the reality, or they're not comfortable with it." And if any of those things are true, it won't work.

What the writers had in mind was light farce. But what the director, Alexander Siddig, and the main performer saw, at least in key parts of the script, was a glimpse into the darkness of the humanoid soul. "Sid had brilliant ideas, and I had a great time working with him," comments Armin Shimerman. "He wanted to make it less of a comedy and more of an exploration of the relationship between a bickering mother and son. He tried to push the envelope and

take Quark into an area that Quark isn't used to going in. I applaud him for it, although we reshot some of the scenes, like the heart attack, because he had a much darker vision than they'd intended."

Cecily Adams, who made her third appearance as Ishka in the episode, observes that "Sid wanted to explore how people who love each other really can hurt one another. Quark and Moogie have a very complicated, layered relationship, and they each have access to that place in the other where they can cause hurt, and they both use it. The first time we shot the heart attack scene, it was very dark and the pace was slow. It was actually disturbing. We wouldn't have played it any differently had we not been wearing rubber masks. Armin and Sid really liked it, but when I watched it in dailies, *I* didn't like it. Even though it was an interesting exploration of the dark side, I didn't think it was exciting enough. And apparently the producers felt that way too. They wanted it more humorous."

In the end, Shimerman feels that the episode was neither fish nor fowl. "It could have been a more serious dramatic piece or it could have been funnier," he says. "But it was neither one nor the other."

Adams disagrees with that. "I think it had qualities of both," she says. "The way we redid it, there is still depth and reality and pain and the disgust they feel for each other. But it's also funny. I laugh my head off every time I watch Moogie fall over." The argument she and Quark have is still very realistic, she points out, but the addition of physical humor keeps the scene from tipping into tragedy.

Astute viewers may notice that while Siddig had used his given name, Siddig El Fadil, for his director's credit on "Business As Usual," this time his credit was the same as his professional name, Alexander Siddig. While it wasn't his happiest directing moment, he admits, the name change was just a slip. "They forgot what it was the first time and I forgot to remind them," he laughs. "But it really doesn't matter, because the director is about as pale a person on the set as anybody else."

Behind the scenes, the Makeup and Costume Departments gave their all to make Lumba a dish, but it was an uphill battle. Makeup Artist Karen Westerfield started by giving Shimerman a more petite cranium than he normally sports as Quark, using the headpiece that had been molded for Pel in Season 2 "Rules of Acquisition." "They did sculpt a new face for him," Westerfield says, "with a smaller nose and higher cheekbones. And I lightened the color of his skin tone. But actually," she says with a giggle, "he was pretty scary as a woman."

"The makeup didn't bother me," Shimerman says. "I thought that was rather feminine. It was the costume and the fat suit! I don't know why I had to wear a *fat* suit."

Of course, a fat suit to one person is a pleasant package of pulchritude to another. Costume Designer Robert Blackman feels he was acting in Lumba's best interests. "When Moogie was on Ferenginar, she wore these sort of big smock things, which would have been easy to do for Quark," he explains. "But the Ferengi males are all sort of pear-shaped, and I always accentuate their bellies with a pad. So I thought that it would be fun to give Moogie this Rubenesque body with a padded body suit. And once we'd made one for her, we decided to do it for Lumba, too. We gave him the exact same kind of body. Then we made both of them jump suits of stretch velour to wear over the padding."

In spite of his reservations about Lumba's look, Shimerman took great pains to make her properly feminine. "I did research on this part," he says. "I watched *Some Like It Hot* and *Tootsie*. The difference beween those films is that [in the former film] Tony Curtis was always winking at the camera, as if to say, 'I'm playing a woman, but you know I'm really a man.' Dustin Hoffman's performance in *Tootsie* was, 'I'm playing a woman and I believe it.' And I decided I wanted to do the latter. I tried to be as feminine as I could.

"I now have great admiration for women who wear high heels, because they are *truly* a pain," he says. "I don't know how women do it. It was rare that I could navigate across the room without losing them."

Although Rom never got to dress up as Echevarria had envisioned, he did get to demonstrate that he is "in touch with his feminine side." Max Grodénchik chuckles as he recalls his character's demonstration of how to walk like a girl. "I thought about how a [female] friend of mine walks," he smiles. "And the guys helped me out, too. Sid is British, and they have a long tradition of drag humor." Then too, Grodénchik adds, "I think Rom is an observer of people, and he's an engineer—and what better example of marvelous engineering than the female anatomy?"

"He knows more things than people give him credit for, that Rom," Ira Behr agrees. "He's the guy."

In the long run, "Profit and Lace" was just one episode, and there were plenty of others that were critically lauded. Still, Behr is disappointed that it didn't work out. "If you look through the list," he notes, "'Profit and Lace' was really the last Ferengi show. 'The Emperor's New Cloak' is a mirror universe show, and the Ferengi portion of 'The Dogs of War' is only the A-story *or* the B-story," depending on how you look at it, he explains. "So this was the nail in that coffin," he says, tongue not quite in cheek.

Of course, they say that even behind the darkest of clouds there is a silver lining. Jeffrey Combs feels that his character, Brunt, was *very* happy in the episode. "He finally reached the place where he had always wanted to be," Combs says with a grin. "He was *the nagus!*" He pauses dramatically. "For about a minute and two seconds."

TIME'S ORPHAN

Episode #548

TELEPLAY BY **BRADLEY THOMPSON &
DAVID WEDDLE**
STORY BY **JOE MENOSKY**
DIRECTED BY **ALLAN KROEKER**

GUEST CAST

Keiko O'Brien	ROSALIND CHAO
Molly O'Brien (18)	MICHELLE KRUSIEC
Molly O'Brien	HANA HATAE
Pinar	SHAUN BIENIEK
Lieutenant Jones	RANDY JAMES

STARDATE UNKNOWN

Today is a big day for Molly O'Brien. Her parents are taking her and brother Yoshi to a nearby planet for a long-promised picnic. Now that the chief has determined that things are quiet enough to allow Keiko and the kids to return to the station, this seems like a perfect way to celebrate the family's reunion.

The day begins beautifully. The weather is perfect, the children are happy, and the chief is feeling optimistic about their future. As Molly explores some nearby boulders, Miles and Keiko drink in the tranquility of their surroundings. But the pastoral moment is shattered when they hear a scream from Molly. Hurrying over to the rocks, O'Brien finds that his eight-year-old daughter has fallen into a hole in the ground that opens into an underground cave. He can see Molly hanging from a ledge, her feet dangling above a strange vortex of swirling energy.

Molly rejoices when she is given her favorite doll. ROBBIE ROBINSON

Unfortunately, he can't quite reach her, and seconds later, she loses her grip, disappearing into the vortex. Then, the vortex disappears, leaving what appears to be a long-abandoned alien portal.

The chief contacts the station and summons help. Dax determines that the portal is some kind of time machine, built long before the Bajorans colonized this planet. It looks like Molly has been thrown three hundred years into the past, to a time when neither the aliens who invented the device nor the Bajoran settlers lived on the planet. After hours of investigation, they finally figure out a way to activate the vortex and lock onto Molly's DNA signature. After that it takes only a few seconds to beam her out.

Unfortunately, they pull Molly out of the wrong time period. She's no longer an eight-year-old girl; she's an eighteen-year-old—one who's been living like a wild animal, without human contact, for ten years. The experience has left her so traumatized that she doesn't know her parents, and she's lost the ability to speak. With no other alternative, Bashir sedates the terrified girl and they bring her back to the station. To help her acclimate, the O'Briens are allowed to transform a cargo bay into a setting that might feel a little more familiar to Molly, with trees, rocks, and grass. There, the couple begins the painful process of regaining their daughter's trust.

To give the O'Briens the time they need with Molly, Dax offers to look after Yoshi. But Worf insists on sharing the responsibility—indeed, taking on the brunt of it. When Jadzia expresses surprise at how seriously he's taking his role as baby-sitter, the Klingon confesses that he is determined to prove that he can be a good father to their future children.

It's a slow process, but the O'Briens gradually begin to reawaken long-buried memories in Molly. She seems to recognize them as her parents, and is willing to play with them. Eventually, she utters her first word since her return: "Home." The O'Briens excitedly bring her to their quarters and show her the room that used to be hers. But they soon discover that Molly no longer considers this her home. She spots a picture that was taken at the picnic site and indicates that *this* is her home, not the station. Hoping to fulfill her need to return there, the O'Briens recreate the location in one of Quark's holosuites. Molly is ecstatic—until they have to relinquish the spot to other customers. The chief ends the program and tries to get a disoriented Molly to leave the bar. Alarmed by the disappearance of "home" and frightened by the hubbub of the crowd, Molly panics and attacks a customer, stabbing him with a broken bottle. A security guard stuns her, and she's taken to one of the station's holding cells.

Things go from bad to worse when the injured customer opts to press charges against Molly. After talking to a Federation magistrate, Sisko informs O'Brien that his daughter must be taken to a special care facility for evaluation. But judging from Molly's behavior in the holding cell, O'Brien realizes that forcing her to stay inside a confined facility over an extended period of time probably will kill her.

While this drama plays out in one part of the station, another takes place in Worf and Dax's quarters. Kirayoshi has bumped his head while playing with the Klingon, and although Dr. Bashir assures him that the baby is fine, Worf is wracked with guilt. He tells Jadzia that he isn't fit to be a father, and he is unworthy of her love.

With no other solution at hand, O'Brien decides to steal a runabout and take Molly back to the planet. Once there, he plans to send her back through the time portal and destroy it so that no one will be able to find her. Unfortunately, Security is one step ahead of him, and the trio is stopped in an airlock corridor. Odo expresses his disappointment in the chief; surely, if anyone can break a prisoner out of a cell and get him off the station, it's O'Brien! Then, to Miles's and Keiko's surprise, he allows them to leave in the runabout.

On the planet, the O'Briens tearfully send Molly back through the vortex with her favorite doll. But after the eighteen-year-old steps into the past, she hears the sound of a child crying and finds eight-year-old Molly hiding in the cave. Recognizing the frightened child as herself, the older girl hands her the doll and sends her back through the portal. As little Molly is reunited with her startled parents, the older girl winks out of existence, happily murmuring, "Molly . . . home."

When the family returns to the station, Dax delivers Kirayoshi to their quarters. Later, she tells Worf that the little boy kept repeating something she couldn't understand. The Klingon realizes that it's part of a game he taught to Yoshi. Somehow the fact that he made an impression on the little boy during their time together lightens his spirits. Perhaps he isn't as bad with children as he had thought.

Considering *Deep Space Nine*'s usual luck (pouring rain or raging heat) when it comes to location shooting, the crew was amazed by the temperate climate that accompanied the outdoor scenes for "Time's Orphan." It seemed as if Mother Nature had finally decided to smile on the production. Or was she actually laughing at them?

"Has anybody told you about the *snake*?" Rosalind Chao asks. "We were filming the picnic, where everybody's supposed to be happy and laughing and kissing. I noticed that people were talking during my dialogue, and I wondered what was going on, but I just kept going, and when they yelled, 'Cut!' someone whispered, 'Now Rosalind, don't panic.'"

"We were in a big open field," explains Steve Oster, "shooting the master shot with Keiko and Miles and the two children, when we saw something moving in the grass. It was a rattlesnake working its way toward the shot."

"But they kept the camera going!" Chao says, laughing.

"We didn't want to alarm the actors and cause a bigger problem," says Oster. "There were two small children there, and we didn't want them to freak out." Director Allan Kroeker, who was watching the take on a video monitor some distance away from the action, "was unaware of what we were seeing because he was concentrating on the performances," Oster says, "so he didn't call 'Cut!'"

An impromptu discussion took place around the camera equipment—the talking Chao heard—as the crew quickly weighed the pros and cons of halting the action on their own. Fortunately, the snake was moving very slowly and they were right near the end of the shot, so Oster waited a few seconds and then

Location filming has its drawbacks, especially on *DS9*, where a lovely day in paradise must include a snake. ROBBIE ROBINSON

calmly told the actors, "Could you all step this way here?" The snake continued along its way and moved off slowly, pursued by a park ranger.

The picnic scene was shot in Malibu State Park, where such productions as *Planet of the Apes* and *M.A.S.H.* have been filmed, and where the topography gave the *DS9* producers everything they needed, except the alien stand of rocks required by the script. "So we took big fiberglass rocks out there and created our own little Stonehenge," says Randy McIlvain. "Molly plays on them and goes inside. When she walks in, we cut back to the interiors on the Paramount soundstage."

The story for "Time's Orphan," originally called "Out of Time," had been generated years earlier by veteran *Star Trek* writer Joe Menosky "as a way to get rid of Alexander, whom he really disliked," René Echevarria recalls with a grin. "In that story, Worf and Alexander were on a hunting trip and Worf loses sight of his son for a second. Alexander goes through some sort of portal, winks out, and then a second later he walks out and we learn that he's been in a world where fifteen years have passed. He's now a grown man and a warrior and he has great resentment toward his father because he doesn't understand what happened. But we never did that show," Echevarria chuckles, "because Alexander was Michael Piller's mother's favorite character."

"Michael shot it down time and again," confirms Ron Moore, like Echevarria a veteran of the *TNG*

MOLLY OBRIEN

Molly may have the maturity of an eight-year-old, but the producers wanted primitive renderings; John Eaves obligingly brought her artwork down several notches.

years. "Alexander was going to come back as a nasty, scarred warrior."

"After I came to *DS9,* I thought about doing the story with Molly, instead of Alexander," notes Echevarria, "but Ira [Behr] and Hans [Beimler]—not coincidentally, both fathers—just hated the idea of losing their daughter's childhoods. They didn't even want to think about it. It was like, 'No! I don't want to do that! You don't have kids. You don't know how awful that is!'"

Finally, Echevarria was able to list enough positive reasons to do the episode. Behr relented. "It had been a long time since we'd done a science fiction episode, we wanted to do another O'Brien show, and we needed to do something that would be pretty much a bottle show," Echevarria says, ticking off his list. "But it was very clear right from the beginning that the only way we could do it was if we got the little Molly back at the end."

Working with Echevarria, Weddle and Thompson began their first draft, following Menosky's original notion that the time-shifted child had been reared in another culture, in this case, a seventeenth-century farming community where the people treated her well. Molly returned to the O'Briens as a shy alien child who never really got over what happened to her, and who resented her real parents. "But that didn't work very well," Thompson chuckles. "It came across as if she had been sent to a bad summer camp."

"It was full of all this teen angst emotional stuff, and she sounded so damned American," sighs Echevarria. "I must confess that I had encouraged the guys to go in that direction, but the situation was so much more fantastical than that. We really didn't know how to fix the problem until Ira suggested, 'What if she's the 'wild child'?"

The premise of a child raised alone in the wilderness pleased everyone. The writers quickly began doing some research on the subject. "We called on a number of psychologists and clinical social workers to ask them what happens when you put an eight or ten-year-old out in the wilderness for ten years," Bradley Thompson reports. "They all looked at us oddly and said, 'There aren't any studies on stuff like that. How would we do one? Take our own kids out and leave them there for ten years and see what happens?'" Thompson laughs.

Still, they did get some validation on traits they wanted to give Molly, her loss of language skills, for example. "The child psychologist I talked to said that deterioration of verbal skills was a credible reaction," reports Echevarria. "She would be capable of speech, but she hadn't used it for years."

An early draft of the "wild child" script used some of that research in an extended scene in Act 2, where Bashir goes into detail about the extent of Molly's psychological trauma. In fact, a comment Bashir makes about such children coping with their isolation by coming to believe that inanimate objects around them are alive, serves to explain why Keiko and Miles are concerned when Molly begins drawing anthropomorphized landscapes.

When research on human psychology fell short, the writers improvised by looking at other species. Molly's intense fear of being confined was inspired by a syndrome known as "capture shock." "When you capture dolphins, about half of them will die simply from the act of being captured," relates Thompson. "So we didn't focus as much on the possibility that the Federation was going to punish her as we did on

The covers to a pair of Molly's books. DOUG DREXLER

the fact that if confined, she'd have to be sedated the whole time or she would go into capture shock. And we see that she freaks out just from being put in the holding cell."

It's clear that the producers felt this was a key sequence in the script, for one of the requirements in the casting session for the older Molly was for each of the candidates to pantomime being trapped in a holding cell and wanting out. "We also had them do the 'Molly, home,' scene, where she tries to convince her parents that she wants to go home," Echevarria says. "We were very lucky to find Michelle Krusiec to

The expansion of one minor scene created a subplot for another show.
ROBBIE ROBINSON

play Molly. She just blew the other actresses right out of the room."

The Art Department had to recreate Molly's bedroom, which had not been seen for several seasons. "The last time we'd seen her bedroom, Molly had been about a two-year-old," says Laura Richarz, "so we had to rethink it to suit her current age." Molly may be a twenty-fourth-century kid, Richarz notes, "but a kid's mind is a kid's mind—it's just the toys that would be different. Kids are playing with computers now, so Molly would have techy stuff, but she still has to cling to her doll, as well."

The Art Department also made her a dollhouse. "It was beautiful," reminisces Richarz, "with a thatched roof that comes off so you can see all of Molly's toys inside." The dollhouse actually was based on a house design that had been conceived for Season 1's "Progress" but never built. Unfortunately, the beautiful dollhouse was never used for "Time's Orphan," but it didn't go to waste. Less than a year

later, it would be recycled into Sisko's model of his Bajoran house, featured prominently in Season 7's final arc of episodes.

For the "refrigerator drawings" that both Mollies present to Keiko and Miles, John Eaves "drew a whole series of stuff," Eaves says, "from extremely juvenile sketches to more finished renderings. The producers wanted happy faces on the moon and the trees and the rocks." Ironically, for this assignment, research was no help whatsoever. "My daughters were five at the time, but their drawings were too advanced for what they wanted," grins Eaves, "and Ira said his six-year-old's drawings were way too articulate." John used his imagination and pulled the sophistication level down to a three-year-old's work.

To illustrate Molly's psychological growth, Jay Chattaway wrote a four-note melody that developed, along with her communication skills, gradually becoming warmer as she felt warmer toward her parents. By the time the trio got together for a family hug near the end of the episode, the piece had grown into a full orchestral piece. Because this was the story of a child, Chattaway decided to do something brand-new on *Star Trek*: he used a child's voice as a key instrument in the melody.

The B-story for the episode, which deals with Worf's feelings of uncertainty about his merits as a father, came about in an unusual way. While they were shooting the episode, the producers realized that "Time's Orphan" was going to run about nine minutes short. Clearly, a new subplot would need to be inserted to pad the episode. But what?

At the same time, Behr and Beimler were grappling with a problem related to the season finale. "'Tears of the Prophets' represented the last time we would ever see Jadzia Dax, and the last time we'd see the Worf/Jadzia relationship," explains Behr. "So we realized that whatever juice we were going to get out of it, we'd better get out of it *now*." But where to get that juice?

The two problems meshed into one solution. In their episode, Thompson and Weddle already had included a humorous little scene—the "gung, gung, gung" scene, as they refer to it—in which Bashir and O'Brien find Worf holding a rattle and speaking Klingon baby talk to Yoshi. An embarrassed Worf passes off the lapse in his usually stoic demeanor by explaining that he was giving the infant some training in "hand-eye coordination," important for babies who plan to grow into warriors.

All of the writing staff liked the scene, and it

struck a chord in Behr's mind. This was something he and Beimler could build on in "Tears." "It seemed like it'd be nice to show Worf and Dax talking about a future, a future that was never going to be, to demonstrate that this relationship was *solid*," he says.

So Weddle and Thompson built on their "gung, gung, gung" scene and came up with "a whole runner about Dax and Worf dealing with kids, and whether Worf was going to be a worthy father as well as a worthy husband," says Behr.

"That allowed Ira and Hans to build *their* storyline about Jadzia deciding that it's time for them to have a baby, which made her loss even more poignant," smiles Thompson.

The crew of the *Defiant* becomes obsessed with saving the life of Captain Cusak, only to discover that she's already dead.
ROBBIE ROBINSON

THE SOUND OF HER VOICE

Episode #549

TELEPLAY BY **RONALD D. MOORE**
STORY BY **PAM PIETROFORTE**
DIRECTED BY **WINRICH KOLBE**

GUEST CAST

Captain Lisa Cusak	DEBRA WILSON
Kasidy Yates	PENNY JOHNSON

STARDATE 51948.3

On board the *Defiant*, Sisko, his command crew, and Convoy Liaison Officer Kasidy Yates complete an assignment and prepare to head back to Deep Space 9. It's Kasidy's first mission with Sisko, and she's a little confused by his distant attitude, although she understands that he, like the rest of the crew, is weary and anxious to return home. Unfortunately, home will have to wait. The ship has received a distress signal from a Captain Lisa Cusak, whose escape pod has crashed on a remote planet following the destruction of her ship, the *Olympia*. Sisko tells O'Brien to try to establish two-way voice communication with Cusak. In the meantime, he has the crew plot a course for the six-day journey it will take to reach her.

On the station, Jake observes a rather typical exchange between Odo and Quark. Odo tells Quark that his new barstools are dangerous and must be removed. Quark protests that they were expensive and aren't harmful to anyone. Odo rejects Quark's appeal and is about to move on to a new topic of harassment when Major Kira arrives and invites the shape-shifter to lunch. Odo's mood instantly changes

from curmudgeonly to cuddly, a transformation that Quark doesn't miss. He points out to Jake that love is a distraction, and a distracted policeman is an opportunity! Jake is puzzled, but the next time Odo returns to the bar, Quark demonstrates exactly what he has in mind.

He begins his gambit by asking Odo if he's purchased a gift yet. "Gift?" questions the constable, clearly confused. Quark patiently explains that Saturday is the one-month anniversary of Odo's first date with Major Kira, surely an occasion that merits a gift. Somewhat surprised, Odo exits the bar to look for a gift. Jake presses Quark for an explanation, but for the moment, all Quark will say is that the anniversary will be a very special occasion for Major Kira *and* for Quark's bank account.

On the *Defiant*, O'Brien keeps the one-way link with Cusak open while he tries to establish communication. Cusak maintains a constant flow of often humorous chatter to keep her spirits up in the desolate, soggy terrain. O'Brien doesn't mind; he knows she's alone, and he can't help feeling it helps her to listen, even though she doesn't know he's doing it. As he works, Kasidy stops by to talk, but their conversation is interrupted by a cry of surprise from Cusak. She's heard their voices; O'Brien has succeeded in creating a two-way link!

The stranded captain reveals she's been giving herself triox injections to compensate for the excess carbon dioxide in the atmosphere, but Bashir realizes that she doesn't have enough to last until the *Defiant* arrives. He advises her to lower her dosage, hoping that the strength of her cardiopulmonary system will gradually increase and help sustain her. In the meantime, members of the crew agree to take turns talking to her, so she won't be by herself.

Lisa proves to be as good a listener as she is a talker, and her strong sense of humor and refreshingly positive attitude quickly win the affection of the crew. She gives Sisko some sound advice about his relationship with Kasidy, gets Bashir to stop focusing on his work and start focusing on his bedside manner, and helps O'Brien, who worries that his friends will become casualties of war, to cope with his feelings. They're all concerned, however, when they learn that Lisa has run out of triox. Bashir estimates that she can only survive another two days—but the *Defiant* is still three days away.

Back on DS9, Quark finally reveals his plan to Jake. The Ferengi has a shipment of "allegedly" stolen Denevan crystals hidden in one of the cargo bays, and he wants to sell them to an "alleged" criminal who happens to be an acquaintance of his. It's exactly the kind of setup that Odo would be likely to spoil, assuming, of course, that he wasn't distracted on Saturday night. But Quark has managed to maneuver the shape-shifter into making a night of his and Kira's anniversary, complete with an evening's entertainment in one of Quark's holosuites. Everything is going perfectly . . . until Odo announces that he's decided to celebrate on Sunday, the anniversary of their first kiss, rather than Saturday, the anniversary of their first date.

Quark is devastated. He just can't seem to get a break. Odo's going to ruin everything—and after all he's done for him, encouraging him to make his move for Kira, which resulted in their getting together at last. As he bemoans his fate, he doesn't realize that Odo is quietly spying on him and considering the Ferengi's words.

On Saturday night, Quark gears himself for failure—and is startled to see Odo and Kira arrive in the bar, hoping to use that holosuite the Ferengi promised. It seems that Kira agrees with Quark, says Odo; she wants to celebrate the anniversary of their first date.

Now Quark is ecstatic. He's finally won! He's beaten Odo at last. But as Odo escorts Kira to their romantic evening, the changeling reflects that he owed Quark one, and now he's gotten one—but only that one!

Deep in space, Sisko makes the risky decision to deplete the *Defiant's* phaser reserves in order to get

them to Lisa's world before she dies. They reach the planet's orbit just as she loses consciousness, only to realize that there's no way to take the ship through the dangerous energy barrier that caused Cusak's ship to crash in the first place. But a shuttlepod just *might* make it through.

Sisko, O'Brien, and Bashir put their lives on the line to get to the planet's surface. But when they reach the cave where Lisa had taken shelter, they find only a skeleton. Apparently, Lisa has been dead for over three years! O'Brien surmises that somehow the metreon radiation in the energy barrier must have time-shifted their radio signals, so that hers traveled to the future and theirs to the past.

Taking her body back to the station, the crew gives Lisa a proper send-off: an Irish wake filled with good friends and good spirits. And together they lift their glasses to toast Lisa, and the sweet sound of her voice.

"**H**ow do you see the moon?" Director Rick Kolbe asks rhetorically. "You see it only because something else, the sun, puts out light that illuminates it. And in 'The Sound of Her Voice,' a voice illuminates the characters on the *Defiant*. They go into themselves and bring out their own problems, their own baggage, and present them to the other person, so we see *their* reflections. To me, that's fascinating.

"It was a very deeply psychological show, because the characters don't know the person they're talking to," Kolbe states. "I wanted them to bare their souls, to have them tell us their inner feelings through this device of talking to an unknown, unseen person."

The story originally known as "Voice in the Darkness" that developed into "The Sound of Her Voice" is the fourth pitch purchased from freelancer Pam Pietroforte ("Statistical Probabilities"). "Pam's concept was that Sisko is playing around with subspace radio when he picks up a transmission from a woman in 1940s America," says Ron Moore. "He doesn't tell her that he's a captain from the future, so she doesn't know, and they develop a relationship over time."

But there were inherent troubles with that relationship. "They fell in love with one another," Moore says. "It became a sweet, interesting story, but none of us could quite get a handle on how to make it work. Sisko already was involved with Kasidy, which complicated it, and we never found a way to do it.

"After we talked about it, we just decided to take

Kolbe chose to insert a shot of Terry Farrell to accompany O'Brien's comment that someday one of their own might be missing.
ROBBIE ROBINSON

that idea and make the woman a starship captain who's in trouble, and we try to help her, not knowing that she's in the past. And then, as we got into it, I saw it as an opportunity to have each of our characters reveal something about themselves and get into their own personal stories. But," Moore says, "I think it was only partially successful."

Ira Behr agrees with that evaluation. "It was an interesting idea," he says. "Originally this woman was going to affect our people and help them figure out their lives, kind of like Vic Fontaine, but that got diluted a bit and never really made it through the script."

"It's ironic," Moore says, "but when we watch the finished episode it seems to us that the twist, that she was back in time, was just thrown in to make the ending different. But that was the core concept of the pitch."

None of those concerns bothered the director. His attention was on a different aspect of the project. "This was an *acting* show, and they're always fascinating," he says. "I directed another one for them after that, ''Til Death Do Us Part' in seventh season, and I just love those shows. In acting shows," the director states, "the people on stage really have to *act*."

Since the person behind the disembodied voice of Captain Lisa Cusak would never be seen on camera, the producers decided to cast an actress solely on the virtue of her voice, with no thought of physical appearance. For the casting session, Kolbe had each of the potential candidates sit in a recording booth and do her lines. The best of the audition tapes were sent over to the producers. "We didn't want to *see*

them," Moore says. "We didn't want to be influenced by having them in the room at all. We just listened to the tapes and picked a woman purely on the sound of her voice."

The chosen voice—and the acting ability behind it—belongs to Debra Wilson, one of the original cast members of *MAD TV.* "They told me that Lisa was supposed to be a 58-year-old Caucasian Starfleet officer," says Wilson, an African American artist, "but I wasn't really thinking of color or race when I read. I was just thinking about a distressed human being who needed human contact."

The role was actually Wilson's second *Star Trek* audio stint. "You hear my voice at the *Star Trek Experience* [in Las Vegas]. I'm the Starfleet officer who tells you to sit down, buckle up, and please don't take any flash photography!" she laughs.

As for the name of the character Wilson was to play, Moore confesses, "I have a hard time coming up with names, so I tend to pull them out of something sitting on my desk at the moment. I'd just seen in the paper that Joan Cusack had just done a movie, so I chose her last name [after losing he second 'c']. And then I added the simplest first name I could think of at the moment, 'Lisa.'"

In an effort to create an atmosphere that resembled the storyline, Kolbe chose to keep Wilson separated from the other actors. "I didn't want the other actors to focus on her," Kolbe says, "I just wanted to get their performances. So we put Debra as far away as possible, and then we set up speakers in such a way that it sounded as if there was no direct source."

"They set me up in various areas," says Wilson. "When I was talking to Sid, I was on the *Defiant* bridge. When I was talking to Colm, I was in the hallway, next to where he was filming his lines. With Avery Brooks, I was off to the side of Sisko's ready room."

By the time the character, Lisa, appeared on camera, she had been dead for three years, so it became the task of Dean Jones to create her corpse. "I started with a store-bought skeleton and built up a muscle structure from latex and cotton and used generic prosthetic appliances to form the features of a face," Jones says. "Then I painted it all with charcoal tone to make it look rotted," he says, "but I ended up having to use fire to get that real cool charred look."

Jones applied the fire right next to the *Deep Space Nine* makeup trailer. "I was over there in the corner, lighting this body with a blow torch and people were walking by saying, 'What's he doing?'" Jones laughs. "Mysterious things happened near that trailer."

Debra Wilson, with her vocal talents, made Captain Cusak a memorable character. ROBBIE ROBINSON

TEARS OF THE PROPHETS
Episode #550
WRITTEN BY IRA STEVEN BEHR & HANS BEIMLER
DIRECTED BY ALLAN KROEKER

GUEST CAST

Garak	ANDREW J. ROBINSON
Weyoun	JEFFREY COMBS
Gul Dukat	MARC ALAIMO
Letant	DAVID BIRNEY
Martok	J.G. HERTZLER
Nog	ARON EISENBERG
Damar	CASEY BIGGS
Admiral William Ross	BARRY JENNER
Sahgi	MICHELLE HORN
Glinn	BOB KIRSH

SPECIAL GUEST STAR

Vic Fontaine	JAMES DARREN

STARDATE UNKNOWN

Taking a brief break from the horrors of the war, two celebrations are held aboard the station: the annual Bajoran Gratitude Festival ("Fascination") and a smaller ceremony to award Captain Sisko the prestigious Christopher Pike Medal of Valor in recognition of his acts of bravery. After the festivities are over, Admiral Ross tells Sisko that Starfleet Command has decided to take the captain's advice about implementing an offensive strategy against the Dominion. What's more, Starfleet has

To explain the mystery of how radio signals could, as the episode indicated, time-shift, Andre Bormanis suggested that the writers send them through "a weird radiation field. We can slow radio waves down, obviously," he says, "and there is a time delay in the transmission of radio signals, but that doesn't work both ways, so you can't talk to someone in the past as an actual scientific phenomenon. That's why we decided to use fictional metreon radiation."

The writers found a way to bring Kasidy Yates along for the ride as a convoy liaison, but oddly, Jadzia Dax was missing. "Terry Farrell was only available for one day during that shoot, so she's only in the final scene," Ron Moore recalls. "That's because she was getting serious about leaving the show. We were giving her a chance to go to readings," he laughs, "so she was off doing *casting* sessions!"

Although Sisko blames himself for Jadzia's death, he promises her that he will make things right. ROBBIE ROBINSON

chosen Sisko to plan the invasion of Cardassia. After analyzing the situation, Sisko chooses the Chin'toka system, which he feels could be the weak link in the Dominion's defense of Cardassian territory.

Elsewhere on the station, people try to get on with their lives in spite of the war. Odo and Kira engage in their first fight after the security chief arrests a vedek for "fund-raising on the Promenade." Worf and Jadzia decide to have a baby. Bashir reminds Jadzia that, medically speaking, it won't be easy for them to conceive. But Jadzia is unfailingly optimistic about their chances. Quark and Bashir are depressed; this certainly means that the marriage is working out. Any chances either of them ever had of winning Dax's heart are long gone. They visit Bashir's Vegas holosuite program ("His Way") to see if Vic Fontaine can cheer them up. Instead, Vic offers them some sage advice: Move on to greener pastures.

Sisko and General Martok meet with the Federation's and Klingon's new ally, the Romulans, and convince them of their plan. Unbeknownst to Sisko, the Cardassian-Dominion Alliance has been working to deploy hundreds of unmanned orbital weapons platforms around Chin'toka. Once deployed, any vessel that enters the territory will be easily eliminated. And just as bad, Gul Dukat has returned to Dominion headquarters, bringing word to Damar and Weyoun that he's found a way to destroy Sisko and the Federation.

On the eve of the invasion, Sisko experiences a vision of the Prophets. In their usual cryptic manner, they point out that "the Sisko is of Bajor" and warn him not to "leave the chosen path." Troubled, Sisko goes to Ross and tells him that the Prophets have asked him to stay behind. An impatient Ross retorts that Sisko will have to make up his mind. He can be the Emissary or a Starfleet captain—but he can't be both. Sisko makes his choice and tells Ross he'll lead the mission as planned.

Realizing that the combined fleet is rushing toward Chin'toka, Damar's troops hasten to finish work on the weapons platforms. In the meantime, Dukat reveals his plan—gleaned from studying the Bajoran ancient texts—to attack the wormhole aliens. He recites an obscure ceremonial chant and breaks open a Bajoran artifact, releasing a strange energy vortex. The energy enters Dukat's body, and the Cardassian is possessed by the spirit of an evil Pah-wraith, just as he had hoped.

On DS9, Odo and Kira make up, and Kira tells Dax that she's said a prayer for her at the station's shrine. Dax is pleased; maybe this will help her to get pregnant. After Worf leaves on the mission, she visits Bashir, who gives her good news: it appears that the ovarian resequencing enzymes he's given her are working. It looks like she and Worf *will* be able to have a baby.

Sisko and his troops arrive at their target and prepare to fire. Suddenly, the Dominion's defense grid goes on-line and the weapons platforms spring to life. With ships being destroyed all around him, Sisko and his crew desperately search for a weakness in the weapons. Garak, who was aboard providing his unique talents, finds one. The platforms don't have their own individual power supplies. If the *Defiant* crew can find the central source of the power, they can shut down all the platforms at once.

Feeling that she may owe the wormhole beings a word of thanks, Jadzia decides to visit the Bajoran shrine. Unfortunately, the shrine is about to receive another visitor: the conjoined Dukat/Pah-wraith. Jadzia sees him and starts to draw her weapon, but he is faster. He shoots bolts of energy into her body and leaves her lying on the floor of the temple, barely alive. With Jadzia out of the way, he opens the ark that contains one of the Orbs of the Prophets. The energy vortex shoots from Dukat's body into the Orb, which abruptly goes dark.

Outside the station, the wormhole seems to implode—and on the *Defiant*, Sisko staggers as he feels the Prophets reach out to him, and then withdraw. Filled with dread, he barely notices when O'Brien announces that he's found the power source: a facility on a nearby moon. The *Defiant*'s weapons can't get through the moon's defense grid, so the crew uses their deflector array to imprint a Federation warp signature on the power generator. The plan works. The weapons platforms open fire on the generator, destroying their own power supply.

The jubilation over their victory is short-lived as a message comes in from Bashir—and the crew rushes back to the station. The Bajoran people are in a panic. With the wormhole gone and *all* of the Orbs dark, they feel the Prophets have abandoned them. But the crew feels a far more personal loss when Bashir informs them that he was able to save the Dax symbiont, which must be rushed back to Trill, but could do nothing for Jadzia. She survives long enough to bid Worf goodbye, then dies. Devastated, Worf recites a Klingon mourning chant.

Sisko mourns in his own way. As he stands over Jadzia's coffin, he expresses his sorrow that he couldn't protect her, and confesses that he has failed as both the Emissary and as a Starfleet officer. He promises Jadzia that he will make things right—but he knows that he can't do it on the station.

A short time later, he says goodbye to his friends and departs for Earth with Jake. After he leaves, Kira steps into his office and notes with dismay that Sisko has taken his baseball with him—which means that he's not sure if he's coming back to Deep Space 9.

"I didn't want to kill Jadzia," Ira Steven Behr states. "To me, that has very little to do with good storytelling."

It was, however, a dramatic necessity. Terry Farrell had decided to leave the series, and the script for the season finale had to reflect her departure. With the series deep in the middle of the Dominion war arc, there were very few alternatives in terms of dispensing with the character. So death it was.

Of Farrell's decision to leave the show, the actress says simply, "My heart said it was time to move on. After playing the character for six years, there's things I wish we would have done. I wish I would have had at least one fight scene this year. But there's nine major characters, so the writers can only do so much," Farrell admits. "I've had six years and one hundred fifty episodes of experience on this show, so my sadness is more in saying goodbye to the people. I don't feel cheated out of the character in the same way as I would have if the show had been cancelled, because I've gotten the opportunity to play her. And besides," she says, "it's Jadzia that's dying. Dax is living."

But before the writers of *Deep Space Nine* had a free moment to begin thinking about a new Dax, they had to find a way to end Season 6.

Of course, they'd *thought* they had a good concept for the season finale. A *big* concept. Brad Thompson remembers the first time they started talking about it. Behr had gathered the writing staff together and announced: "Okay, don't tell anybody about this, but at the end of the season, we're gonna send Sisko to Earth and all the gods will be dead!"

"I had talked about it with Rick Berman a couple of years earlier," says Behr. "We had certain ideas about how we wanted the seventh season to end," he explains, and keeping the Prophets out of the series for a while would facilitate those plans.

"We began discussing the final episode of the season back in September [1997]," says René Echevarria. "We basically knew we wanted to give Sisko a big setback, and have the Dominion attack the Prophets in some way, shape, or form."

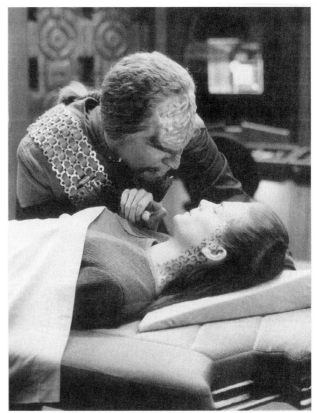

Farrell would have preferred that Jadzia go out fighting.
ROBBIE ROBINSON

But the season finale had taken a back burner to the business of crafting the episodes that came before it. Along the way, certain ideas arose that suggested possibilities for the finale. "Ira kept saying that it would be great if the events of 'The Reckoning' would somehow help us to set up a weakness for the Prophets," says Echevarria. "And in a sense they do, because by the end of that episode, time is sort of out of joint, and things are not as they were destined to be."

"We loved the idea of the prophecy being unfulfilled and that somehow this would play into a later episode," says David Weddle, who cowrote the teleplay for "The Reckoning" with Thompson. "The Pahwraiths weren't defeated, and that enabled Dukat to call upon one later on."

But the announcement of Farrell's departure threw a wrench into their general plans for the episode. "We were in deep waters," says Behr. "We were talking about the death of a lead character on a television show, and how and why this way and not that way," Behr comments. As might be expected, coming up with a story that accommodated both a tribute to Jadzia and the planned story about the perceived death of the Prophets was not an easy process.

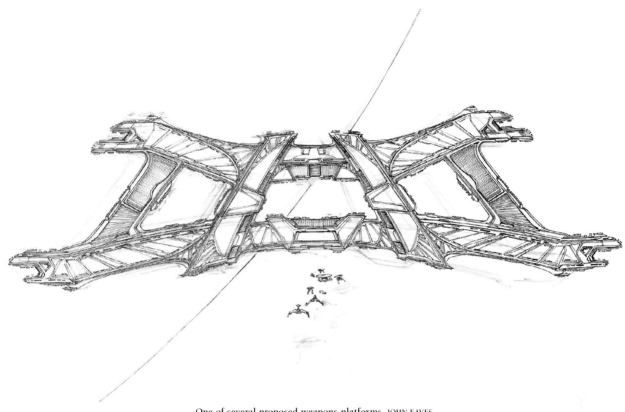

One of several proposed weapons platforms. JOHN EAVES

They had a very rough storyline: Sisko and some of his crew are off-station in the *Defiant*, fighting the Dominion near a biogenic plant that is protected by a defensive grid. Meanwhile, Dukat steals a ship and then steals an Orb of the Prophets. Taking it into the wormhole, he uses a chroniton bomb to blow up the wormhole aliens. Catching wind of Dukat's plan, Jadzia follows him, getting killed somehow in the process.

Jadzia's manner of death stumped the writers for a long time. "We had many discussions about what constitutes a heroic death," says Behr. "There were a lot of clichés to avoid. And some clichés that were necessary. It was a minefield that we had to go through. It's much easier talking about a scene with special effects—you know, why we would choose to shoot a battle scene with these ships rather than those ships."

At last enough of the details were agreed upon for Behr and writing partner Hans Beimler to hammer out the first draft, at the time called "Tears of the Gods." By this point, the chroniton bomb had become a chroniton generator ("The Assignment," "The Reckoning"). And Jadzia would stop Dukat from killing the Prophets, but would herself be killed by a phaser blast.

First drafts are seldom close to the final product, and after the other writers had the opportunity to provide their input on this version of the script, it was back to the drawing board for Behr and Beimler. A key point of contention was the manner in which Jadzia died. Former Executive Producer Michael Piller, now serving as a creative consultant on the series, pointed out in no uncertain terms that the writers had not given Jadzia "a worthy death and a worthy send-off." As Piller recalls, "I felt that they had missed an opportunity for drama and for the emotional impact of her death. It felt rushed, and you really lost the chance for a goodbye scene that would leave the audience choked up."

The decision to add a final scene for Jadzia, allowing her to live long enough to say goodbye to Worf, was an important one. Beimler admits that he was a little worried about it. "I was afraid that we wouldn't do it justice," he says.

And Behr was on the fence. "There was never a total consensus among the writers," he says, "but one of René Echevarria's reasons for existence is because he tends to speak to the softer, gentler side of our natures, and he felt he needed to see her die."

Another important fix had to do with the "clunkiness" of the script. "Dukat had to get a shuttle, a chroniton generator, an Orb," Echevarria ticks off on his hand.

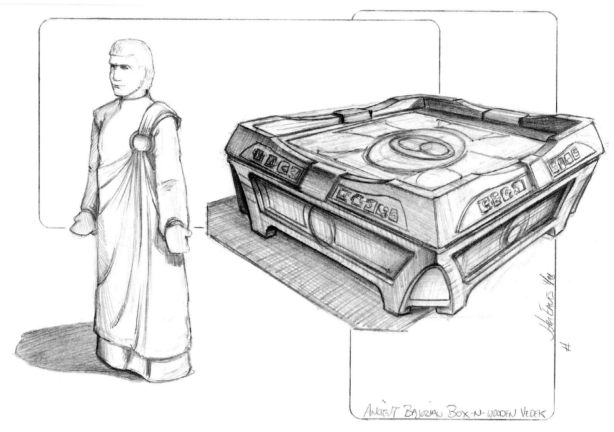

An early design for the Pah-wraith artifact and box. JOHN EAVES

"It was all too mechanical, all comings and goings in spacecraft," says Beimler. "It didn't have the kind of mythic proportions that we were looking for."

Finally Ron Moore suggested, "Couldn't this have to do with the Pah-wraiths? Wouldn't it be much simpler if all Dukat has to do is help the Pah-wraiths get into the wormhole?"

That really pared the story down. After that, says Echevarria, "It was just a matter of asking the right questions." What if Dukat got hold of a Bajoran artifact? What if Dukat let a Pah-wraith into his body? "It tracked better with what we'd seen in 'The Reckoning,'" Echevarria points out.

"And there was something nice about having Gul Dukat, the butcher, be the guy who's suddenly into the Bajoran religion and who learns which little statuette to crack open to get a Pah-wraith to fly up his nose," grins Behr. "Once we went with that, that part of the story just fell together."

Behr and Beimler went back to work. With the inclusion of a goodbye scene, the writers decided to add something memorable for Worf, specifically a mourning chant. The speech was delivered in

Klingon (translation provided by Brad Thompson via *The Klingon Dictionary*) but written in English. Although the scene came across well, Behr couldn't help feeling some regret that the audience wasn't privy to the English translation. "It's based entirely on a Native American chant, 'Only the Earth endures . . .' I like the thought, and it was a nice statement that was lost." Here, for the record, is the entire chant in English:

> Only Qo'noS endures.
> All we can hope for is a glorious death.
> Only Qo'noS endures.
> In death there is victory and honor.

Sisko's goodbye to Jadzia would be recited over her coffin. To emphasize the close relationship between the two characters, Behr and Beimler made the scene a very private one, with only one actor and one prop occupying the screen.

At first, that worried Director Allan Kroeker. "When I first read the script and saw that Sisko has a one-page monologue, I wondered how in the world we were going to put movement into the scene," he

The Pah-wraith prop was inspired by a crude wooden figurine that Beimler had brought. ROBBIE ROBINSON

says. "But then I got inspired. A scene like this breathes life into you, because we're not wading through a lot of technobabble."

"Ira and I wanted to find the anguish of the man and focus on what it really was about," Beimler says. "The scene had to be about some deep lasting inner truth about Sisko. We had a lot of questions to answer. Why is Sisko leaving the station? Why does he feel he has to go home? We felt that if *he* could answer those questions, he wouldn't need to go home, so we had to answer them for the viewer by letting them see through Sisko's eyes without being too specific as to where he is in his mind." Many versions of Sisko's soliloquy were written, and each time something seemed to be missing—until the writers added one final line: "I failed as the Emissary and, for the first time in my life, I've failed in my duty as a Starfleet officer."

"That is a huge and important moment in the show," Behr says emphatically. "It came about because Ron Moore felt the speech was still missing a specific." The original idea for the story was to have Sisko feel crushed by the death of the Prophets. But Jadzia's death had reduced the impact of that tragedy. "So we had to draw back from our original plan," says Behr. "We needed something else. Finally we came upon this idea of acknowledging failure, and Ron immediately said, 'That's it!' At the beginning of the episode, Sisko is a success in both of those things.

He's the Emissary who is bringing children *peldor joi* even while he's the officer plotting the invasion of Cardassia. He's on a roll. But now he feels like a failure. We condensed all of that in a very simple line."

Shooting the scene over the coffin made an impression on everyone, including Avery Brooks. "A loss of someone you love is devastating," he says, explaining the emotions that he tapped into for his performance. "I know about loss. It's one of the things that we experience as a part of living, part of the consequences of living." But part of what made the scene so powerful goes deeper than simple common experience. "It's because we know Terry Farrell," Brooks says. "We're going to miss her. That's what's underneath all the words."

And that's what's behind the images that accompany the words. "Avery had an idea on how to shoot this," Kroeker says. "He stood at the head of the coffin and then he started to come around it as if she were there and he was getting in her face. That gave me an emotional click. And the prop helped, too. Keeping the torpedo in the foreground all the time kept Jadzia present, in a way. I knew the viewers would want that."

The coffin, too, had some historic relevance, although exactly *which* part of history is debatable. When the production staff realized that they'd need one of *Star Trek*'s traditional one-size-fits-all torpedo tube/coffin, Laura Richarz pointed out that the one they had was the same one that had been used for Spock in *Star Trek II: The Wrath of Khan*. The notion pleased everyone—but it wasn't necessarily true.

"We *do* have the prop from the second feature," comments Mike Okuda. "However, Herman Zimmerman had a bunch of new torpedoes made for *Star Trek VI: The Undiscovered Country*, so it's really impossible to say whether the one in this episode is Spock's or not."

In the end, Behr was very happy with the episode. "There's so much going on," he enthuses. "Everything from the invasion of Cardassia to lovely scenes with Weyoun, Damar, and Dukat, to Pah-wraiths and Prophet visitations. All this and Vic Fontaine, too. It's an amazingly busy show that seems to be bursting at the seams. Usually, when we do something like this, it's a setup, and we pay it off later on. This time, because of Dax, in a way, we had to set it up and pay it off all in one episode. But that means you'll get a lot of bang for your buck. I think it's a wonderful entrance into the seventh and final season."

Nicole deBoer is welcomed to the cast as Lieutenant Ezri Dax. JEFF KATZ

SEVENTH SEASON
O V E R V I E W

"A lot of the things we did on <u>Deep Space Nine</u> were not meant to be that way," proclaims Executive Producer Ira Steven Behr. "The show wasn't geared to be what we kept turning it into. That made it very difficult for us, because we had to play it as it lays. We had to kind of do it and hope that it was going to work out. It wasn't like we had everyone saying, 'Oh, good—give us serialized episodes, give us anything.' People had definite opinions about the show. It was a journey into the unknown every time we dared to try something different, even in the seventh season, by which time you'd think that they'd be saying, 'Oh, just go do what you want already.' That never happened."

For example, if the producers had conducted a survey at the end of Season 6, what's the likelihood they'd have received the answer "Go for it," if they stated, "We're contemplating wrapping up the series with ten interconnected hours that must be viewed in sequential order to understand what's going on. What do you think?" Or, "We'd like to end the life of the captain in the final episode, but it's okay, he's going to become a god."

Exactly.

"So we didn't lay it out at the beginning of the year," says Behr. "We planned them as we were doing them. That allowed us to find great stuff, but occasionally it put us into situations where we were saying to each other, 'Well, what do you want to do with Dukat and Winn *now*?' 'I dunno, what do *you* want to do with them?'"

Given the vast pool of characters and the myriad plot threads, the serialization of the last group of episodes was inevitable. "We knew there was no way that we were going to be able to tie this up in one two-hour finale," admits *Star Trek* Executive Producer Rick Berman. "So rather than try to tie up every loose thread in the few hours, we thought, 'Why not look at the last third of the season as a continuing, building conclusion to the seven-year story?' But we also wanted to be certain that it would not feel like you were watching a soap opera, or that people coming into an episode would not feel like, 'Oh God, I just picked up episode three of a five-part miniseries.' We tried to give each episode a beginning, middle, and end, and a sense of totality, despite the fact that we were carrying forward certain ideas."

By this point, it would have been difficult to reverse course and try to put the series on more episodic footing. For the writing staff, the story of *Deep Space Nine* had become much more than the sum of its individual parts. Although nearly the first two-thirds of Season 7 was comprised of stand-alone episodes, there was no way to escape the demands of continuity. "The continuity began closing in earnest at the beginning of Season 6, when we did the war arc," observes Co-executive Producer Ronald D. Moore. "Even though we opened it up again, it never left our minds, and going into Season 7, we knew everything was canted toward the end. We were seeing plot threads and characters and where they were going. Even in the stand-alones, we could see that the tapestry was getting woven tighter and tighter. So we had to be careful, *especially* on the stand-alones. Because on those episodes, I wasn't walking into René Echevarria's office telling him, 'I'm doing this on 'Once More unto the Breach,' and I hope it isn't contradicting something you're doing now.'"

Although the Dominion War was now driving a large percentage of the plot threads, both Berman and the studio had strong feelings about one thing. "They didn't want the final episode to be about the war," notes Behr. "I could see the point. *Deep Space Nine* is bigger than just the Dominion War. So we split it. We had a two-hour episode, which allowed us to give the audience the big battle scenes and all that stuff, but then say, 'Hey, this is the final episode and we have a lot of other stuff to take care of, too!' I think it worked out nicely."

The audience seemed to agree. "Ratings were strong during the final arc," notes Berman happily. The final two-hour episode, in fact, put *Star Trek* in a position it had not held for many years: the top weekly dramatic show in national syndicated ratings. *Star Trek: The Next Generation* had held this position for many years during its reign in television, but *Deep Space Nine* subsequently had faced much stiffer competition from series like *Xena* and *Hercules*. But

"What You Leave Behind" summarily trounced all comers. In terms of the popular vote, following a ballot posted in both *The Communicator* (the magazine for the Official *Star Trek* Fan Club) and the *Star Trek Continuum* (the authorized *Star Trek* website), "What You Leave Behind" was positioned as viewers' second favorite *DS9* episode ever, ranking just behind "Trials and Tribble-ations." And the arc itself fared extremely well in a nationwide poll of fan-run Internet sites that was cited in *Sci-Fi Entertainment*, the Sci-Fi Channel magazine. According to the poll, two of the segments—"The Changing Face of Evil" and "Tacking into the Wind"—made the top-ten list of best *DS9* episodes.

At awards time, the series drew four Emmy nominations for outstanding art direction ("Prodigal Daughter"), hairstyling ("Badda-bing, Badda-bang"), makeup ("The Dogs of War"), and visual effects ("What You Leave Behind"), bringing the series' total to thirty nominations (and four wins) over its seven-year run.

But the prospect of awards, attractive as it is, was never a prime motivator for Behr. As corny as he knows it sounds, working on the series was the biggest reward he could hope for. "I've been around the block enough times to know, as a very wise Cardassian said, 'We live in uncertain times,'" he says, smiling. "And this is a very uncertain business. I hope for the best, I expect the worst. But having something like *Deep Space Nine* in my pocket really takes a tremendous weight off my shoulders. I don't need to worry about finding my great moment, because I *had* a great moment. I had a great moment that lasted seven years."

In the producers' offices at *Deep Space Nine*, the story was always the thing. Season 7 found the writers working harder than ever to bring forth the stories they'd always wanted to tell. The year began with two immediate challenges: replacing the character of Jadzia and defining Sisko's role in the series.

"Terry Farrell's exit was a big low for us," admits René Echevarria, who started the year as co-supervising producer and ended it as a full supervising producer. "Once we knew for certain that she wasn't going to return, we decided to take the opportunity to create a new Dax."

"We knew we needed a female," Behr explains. "We couldn't have Kira Nerys be the only female regular character. So we started the casting process, and all I saw was a lot of people who couldn't play the part. There was absolutely no one in the running."

"Initially, Ira was looking for someone who had a kind of spooky quality," Echevarria comments. "We talked about it several times as a group, and I wasn't quite getting what he was going for. Finally, one day at lunch I said, 'What if we make the character a little more complicated. What if she wasn't an initiate. What if she wasn't planning to be joined, but she was the only one available because of some circumstance. And she was completely unprepared for it.' And Ira looked at me and said, 'Mayyyybe. Let me think about it.' And we all got in our cars—he was in a separate car from me—and went back to the studio. By the time he got there, he had it all figured out! He bounded out of his car and shouted, 'I've got it! She's neurotic! She hears voices! She doesn't know which way is up!' He'd developed a whole backstory from this vague notion and incorporated it into a character in a really delightful way."

"I just loved this idea of joined Trills being basically schizophrenic," Behr says enthusiastically. "We'd never played up the idea in the past, but it made sense. What must it be like to have all those voices and opinions? 'Do I like *raktajino* or do I only *think* I like it?' It would give us all this wonderful stuff to play. And it was an interesting idea that she got the Dax symbiont because she was in the right place at the right time, or the *wrong* place at the *wrong* time, if you prefer."

After that, the casting process became more focused. "We wanted someone vulnerable," says Behr, "because Jadzia, as the show went on, became a stronger and stronger character. And someone young." But still, there were no real contenders until Hans Beimler remembered a young woman he'd worked with in Canada.

"I'd worked with Hans on two shows up there, *Beyond Reality* and *TekWar*," recounts Nicole deBoer. "I knew he'd been a writer on *The Next Generation*. He used to tell me he'd get me on *Star Trek* some day, but I thought he was just being nice. Then one day I got a call from my manager, saying that Hans had asked if I would put myself on tape to try out for a character on *Deep Space Nine*. I used my own little video camera and did an audition for him. Then the producers asked me to come down to Los Angeles."

The producers brought deBoer to the studio to do a test, using a scene that they'd written specifically for audition candidates. "It was long," says Behr, "about four and a half minutes, and it established a lot about who and what Ezri was. We cannibalized the scene later on and used it in 'Afterimage.'"

Although she clearly charmed the producers, the audition is an embarrassing memory for deBoer. "Before I started, they asked me if I wanted some water, and I said 'Sure.' So I took a gulp of water just as they called me in to meet Ira Behr and Rick Berman. Of course, it went down the wrong pipe and I started coughing and turning red and couldn't breathe. They were just sitting there looking at me. Finally, I got into the bathroom, caught my breath, and came out to do the audition. But the whole time I was thinking, 'Oh, I blew it. How graceful of me.'"

"We got a good vibe off of her," smiles Behr. "She knew the part. She *got* it. And that was it."

Sisko's retooling was a little less cut-and-dried. "As the show began winding down, we realized that we wanted to be a bit more specific about the whole Emissary thing, which as an arc had been so interesting to us," says Echevarria. "We settled on this idea that Sisko was, in some way, half man, half god."

That wasn't exactly a traditional *Star Trek* notion, although Behr states that it was the whole *Star Trek* mystique that inspired the idea. "I just felt that all the Starfleet captains are treated like gods by viewers," he explains. "Clearly, the next step was to actually make one of those captains a god, or godlike. I had a chance to do that with Sisko, and the thought appealed to me on many levels."

In the best traditions of classical mythology, the writers decided to make Sisko *half* divine, much like Hercules, son of Zeus and a human woman. "It was dramatically right," Behr notes. "If both parents were gods, then you couldn't relate to him. You can't relate to someone who is a god. He's got to be partly human."

A Prophet took over the body of Sarah, a human woman, in order to seduce Joseph Sisko and conceive Benjamin. "We originally thought that Sarah *was* a Prophet—there was no human woman involved," recalls Echevarria. "But we ultimately nudged the idea into something a bit more oblique, saying the Prophets could take over another person's form. That still had all the right mythic overtones, and it certainly answered the question of *why* Sisko was the Emissary. We were all very excited by the whole notion."

For Behr, the whole thing paid off in a wonderful visual in "'Til Death Do Us Part," where the Sarah Prophet lays Sisko's head upon her breast and for the first time refers to him as "my son." The choreography of the scene was improvised by Director Winrich Kolbe, who emulated the style of German expressionist films to convey the tender moment. "It's typical of something you'd see back in the 1920s," Kolbe states. "It was a very frequent image—the prodigal son comes home and returns to the source of life, the mother."

"It was a beautiful moment," Behr comments approvingly. "I saw it and I went, 'Yeah.' It speaks to the entire seven years of the show, from 'Emissary' to that moment. It just gave me chills."

One other theme that ran through the seventh season was the series' ongoing references to the battle of the Alamo, subtle at first, and then more and more overt. By the time Bashir and O'Brien began playing with a full-scale model of the Texas fort, viewers couldn't help wondering if they were being set up for a massacre at the end of the series, with *Deep Space Nine* overrun by Dominion forces.

But no—it was just Behr and company having a good time. "I guess if people wanted to look at it that way, we already did a show like that in 'The Way of the Warrior,' with the big Klingon attack," says Behr. "But really, it was just one of those things that grew on its own."

It all began with Behr's fascination—some would say obsession—with the events of March 6, 1836, when 187 men lost their lives defending the San Antonio fort against attacking Mexican forces. "Everyone who knows me knows that I like the Alamo," Behr grins. "A few years ago on Alamo Day I even brought in beef jerky and tequila for everyone and we sat around discussing it. Then last season, Hans and I put in one mention of it in a conversation between Bashir and O'Brien ("Wrongs Darker Than Death or Night"). And then Ron picked up on it, and René, and before I knew it, it had taken on a life of its own. But it's just the result of a bunch of guys living and working together for all these years. We've basically gotten insane together and we feed off of each other, trying to crack each other up."

As the season wound down, all of *Deep Space Nine*'s regulars received their due, although the producers' need to cram in as much as possible within a finite amount of episodes disappointed some. "I was a bit frustrated," admits Armin Shimerman. "I had some good episodes, and I was even proud to be in the ones where I didn't have much to do, because the stories were very well told. But I couldn't help feeling that a lot of the time I was in a scene just to serve drinks. It got to be a standing joke between Judi Brown, the script supervisor, and me. 'What drink do you serve in this episode?' she'd say."

"I had a lot of great scripts," notes Rene Auberjonois, "but I remember there was a day when Nicole looked around and said, 'Hey, I'm doing all the work here. Everybody's off doing things.'" He laughs. "And it was kind of true. The writers had a new character to explore, and that gave us a break to go off and work on other projects. But I loved the arc for my character throughout the series," he states emphatically. "Odo began as perhaps the most alien character in the cast, and the one who most resisted the humanizing qualities that came from being part of this 'family' on the station. But by the end, Odo returns to his people in order to carry the message of humanity."

Still, it was clear that time was taking its toll. "After seven years, we weren't happy to see it end, but most of us were kind of looking forward to getting away," says Colm Meaney. "The experience was way beyond anything we could have hoped for, but having said that, seven years is a long time, and we all had desires and plans and ambitions to do other things."

Over in the Makeup Department, there was plenty to do, but much of Michael Westmore's work consisted of "pulling out molds and running Weyoun ears and Worf foreheads," the Emmy award–winning makeup designer says, smiling. In other words, there weren't many new aliens because the series had plenty of established species to keep them busy. And although Westmore had decided, at the time Terry Farrell left, that it was time to stop hand-illustrating Dax's unique Trill markings himself, he wound up "detailing" Nicole deBoer throughout the season (with Makeup Artist Mary Kay Morse maintaining her look for the rest of each shooting day).

Kira's promotion to colonel entitled her to a new uniform, so Costume Designer Robert Blackman created a new look with a high-waisted bolero jacket. The colonel also adopted a new hairstyle, darker, because Nana Visitor had decided she wanted to go back to her natural color, and longer. Reactions among viewers were mixed at the beginning, but by midseason it no longer was an issue. Visitor laughs at the thought that anyone pays that much attention. "It's hard to come up with a hairdo that works for Kira," she admits. "For years she was literally a hand-to-hand combat fighter. She hung out underneath houses and blew things up. I just couldn't see her fussing with her hair back then, so I hacked it all off. But now she's a colonel and she's in a more administrative job. Her hair is more sophisticated, and appropriate to her age and her position. I asked for the costume change, too. I wanted a 'suit' something with a jacket so that if Kira were talking to someone, they'd definitely be looking her in the eye because there was nothing else to look at! Television being what it is, I didn't quite win on that one, but I got my hair," she says, giggling.

Other promotions for real people, as opposed to the characters, included Hans Beimler, who moved up from supervising producer to co-executive producer before the season was over, and the writing team of Bradley Thompson and David Weddle, who went from story editors in Season 6 to executive story editors in Season 7. Camera Operator Kris Krosskove got the opportunity to fill in for Jonathan West as director of photography on a number of episodes, including most of the final arc, while West worked as cinematographer for Director LeVar Burton on *Smart House*, a film for the Disney Channel.

There were times toward the end of the season when Ira Behr wondered if he and Hans Beimler would ever have time to complete the final episode. He wondered if the train that was *Deep Space Nine* was still on track. "There was a lot of anxiety there," he admits. "I wondered if it was moving too slow, if the fans were going to get bored. I wondered if we were giving them enough bang for their buck. Were we connecting too many dots for them, or having too much fun with the characters at the expense of the bells and whistles? Did we need *more* bells and whistles? But that's all part of putting on a series. At the end, you look at it and you say, 'So, given everything, would I do it again?' And you say, 'Absolutely!'"

IMAGE IN THE SAND
Episode #551
WRITTEN BY IRA STEVEN BEHR & HANS BEIMLER
DIRECTED BY LES LANDAU

GUEST CAST

Weyoun	JEFFREY COMBS
Damar	CASEY BIGGS
Admiral Ross	BARRY JENNER
General Martok	J.G. HERTZLER
Senator Cretak	MEGAN COLE
Nog	ARON EISENBERG
Bajoran Man	JOHNNY MORAN

SPECIAL GUEST STARS

Vic Fontaine	JAMES DARREN
Joseph Sisko	BROCK PETERS

STARDATE UNKNOWN

Three months after the death of Jadzia Dax and the departure of Benjamin Sisko from Deep Space 9 ("Tears of the Prophets"), change is in the air at the station. DS9's acting commander, recently promoted Colonel Kira Nerys, feels apprehensive about an impending visit from Starfleet's Admiral Ross. Her sense of unease is heightened by the growing presence of members of the Pah-wraith cult on both Bajor and the station. Kira can see how the disappearance of the wormhole might make some Bajorans feel that the Prophets have abandoned them, but she can't understand why they would turn to the gods' ancient enemies for comfort.

Ross arrives and delivers some unwelcome news.

Three generations of Siskos ponder the mystery of Sarah and her locket inscribed in ancient Bajoran. ROBBIE ROBINSON

Starfleet plans to allow Romulan Senator Cretak to move onto the station, along with the senator's aides and personal guards. Kira isn't happy. The Romulans may be an ally in the war against the Dominion, but that doesn't mean it's a good idea to allow them to establish a military presence on the region's most strategic outpost. But, as Ross points out, the decision already has been made, and Kira will have to live with it.

On Cardassia Prime, Damar celebrates a recent win against the combined Federation forces with a drink, leading Weyoun to observe that the Cardassian leader has become inordinately attached to his *kanar*. Damar ignores him and focuses on reasons to celebrate, key among them the fact that ever since Dukat released a Pah-wraith into the wormhole, the war's momentum has shifted in the Dominion's favor.

On board the *Defiant,* a series of routine convoy missions has made Worf unusually testy. Undoubtedly contributing to the Klingon's foul mood is the fact that he has yet to recover from Jadzia's death. Bashir and O'Brien aren't sure what they can do to help. In fact, the only thing that *everyone* on the station is certain of is that things would be better all around if Captain Sisko were back.

But Sisko hasn't accomplished the task he set for himself when he left DS9. He remains at his father Joseph's restaurant in New Orleans, ostensibly trying to figure out a way to contact the Prophets. However, as far as Jake can tell, his dad has retreated into himself and shows no sign of doing anything to "make things right," as he'd promised months earlier.

Then, abruptly, things change. Sisko has a vision. He sees himself on the arid world of Tyree, digging in the sand. His efforts uncover a shrouded face, made of stone. Then the stone crumbles, revealing the face of a beautiful woman, who opens her eyes to stare at him . . .

Awakening from his trance, Sisko realizes that the vision has come from the Prophets, and that he must find this woman, whoever she is. As he tries to reconstruct a portrait of her face, Jake notes that he's seen the woman in one of Joseph's old photographs. But when Sisko asks his father about her, Joseph angrily refuses to provide any information.

On the station, Kira meets Cretak and finds that the senator is more personable than most Romulans. When Cretak asks if the Bajoran government will allow the Romulans to set up a hospital facility on Derna, one of Bajor's uninhabited moons, Kira facilitates the request. Meanwhile, O'Brien utilizes considerable quantities of bloodwine to get to the root of Worf's unhappiness. The Klingon feels that Jadzia isn't in *Sto-Vo-Kor,* Klingon heaven, because she didn't die in glorious battle. The only way that she'll get there is if Worf wins a great battle in her name. Unfortunately, the only missions he's been assigned to recently have been uneventful convoy runs. He needs a truly dangerous mission.

Bashir and O'Brien talk to General Martok, who offers Worf the opportunity to take on a mission dangerous enough to assure Jadzia a place in *Sto-Vo-Kor.* He is to destroy the Dominion shipyards at Monac IV. Bashir decides to accompany Worf on his quest to honor Jadzia, and O'Brien opts to join them.

On Earth, Joseph eventually yields to Ben's persistent questioning and talks about the woman in the photo. Her name, he explains, was Sarah, and she was Joseph's first wife *and* Benjamin's biological mother. Married for only two years, she disappeared shortly after Ben's first birthday. Joseph never knew why. After years of searching for Sarah, he tracked her to Australia, but learned that she'd died in an accident. Once remarried, Joseph made the decision not to tell Ben that his stepmother wasn't his birth mother.

The revelation surprises the captain, but he's uncertain why the Prophets would send him a vision of this woman. However, when Joseph gives him a locket that once belonged to Sarah, Ben begins to understand. On the locket is an ancient Bajoran inscription; it translates as "The Orb of the Emissary." Sisko reasons that if such an Orb exists, it might be the key to contacting the Prophets. He decides to go to Tyree to see if he can find an answer there.

Kira is troubled by a report from Odo that indicates the Romulans have been arming Derna with plasma torpedoes. When confronted, the Romulans admit that it's true, although they claim they want the torpedoes for defensive purposes only. Nevertheless, Kira orders Cretak to remove them immediately or *she'll* do it for her.

As Sisko prepares to leave Earth, he's stabbed by a Bajoran man, apparently a member of the Pah-wraith cult, determined to prevent the Emissary from finding the Orb. Jake incapacitates the assassin and gets his father to the hospital. Later, a recovered Sisko learns that he'll have some companions on his trip to Tyree; Jake and Joseph have decided that with Pah-wraiths in the picture, he'll need their help. But just as three generations of Siskos are about to depart, a young female Trill arrives at the restaurant and shyly introduces herself . . . as Dax!

"**A**s we started the final season, we made a very bold and perhaps stupid choice," declares Executive Producer Ira Steven Behr, "although I'd do it again. We wrote the quietest opening episode we've ever done on the show. If you look back at the first episode of every season after the pilot, you'll see 'The Homecoming,' which was the first hour of a three-parter, then 'The Search,' 'The Way of the Warrior,' 'Apocalypse Rising,' and 'A Time to Stand.' All *big* shows with a lot of stuff going on. But this time, we decided we were going to play with the audience's expectations and give them something smaller, more intimate, quieter. A reflective breath, so to speak."

But with four intertwining plotlines—Kira standing up to the Romulans, Worf seeking a way to get Jadzia into *Sto-Vo-Kor,* Sisko attempting to resurrect the Prophets, and Damar and Weyoun trading insults back at Dominion headquarters—how quiet an episode could it be?

"Well, we weren't *relaxing*," Behr affirms with a smile. "We just weren't giving the audience the *wham* they expect to get at the beginning of the season."

In truth, while it may seem like there's a great deal going on in "Image in the Sand," much of the hour is devoted to setting up events that will be paid off in the subsequent episode, "Shadows and Symbols." The most striking moment of physical action—the attack on Sisko by a knife-wielding Pah-wraith cult member—occurs within the otherwise quiet, introspective sequence of scenes at the Sisko restaurant in New Orleans. The assault would have seemed violent in any episode, but it stood out as particularly vicious against the backdrop of a location that Sisko had chosen as a place of refuge.

"We wanted it to be nasty," Behr admits, "although it ended up a little nastier than we thought it would. But violence is an ugly thing, and Avery [Brooks] really wanted to convey that."

With all the precautions about what is and isn't suitable for a younger viewing audience, the crew initially was uncertain how much they *could* convey in the scene. "We went around and around on how to treat the knife wound," says special effects head Gary Monak. "It was really a last-minute decision on the set between [Director] Les Landau and Avery Brooks. They wanted him to grab his stomach and see blood come oozing out. So we had to make a tricky little appliance out of a plastic bag and a sponge, and then we stuck that under his shirt so that when he pushed on it, the blood would come out and be all over his hands."

The idea that a cultist commits the violence was another delicate, if deliberate, point that Behr and his writing staff wanted to make. "We wanted to show that, like war, religion can be a dangerous thing," Behr observes. "We'd spent six years portraying the Bajoran religion, celebrating it, in a way, and establishing that there is something greater than technology. And that's good. But [faith] can be subverted very easily. It's what you put your faith *in* that ultimately matters. A lack of faith, I think, is bad. But unthinking religion also is bad. We deal with very volatile topics on this series, but we never want to come down squarely on either side."

Other important details were established in this episode, although they were introduced in a surprisingly matter-of-fact manner. Viewers learn that Kira, for example, has received a promotion to colonel. "I asked for it to happen," says Actor Nana Visitor. "I thought it was high time for it after six years of good service!" she laughs. "Everyone around her had been promoted—Sisko, Bashir, Jadzia, and even Nog—so why not?"

Kira's promotion took place off-camera, but Visitor doesn't mind. "I would have loved a scene, but it was all right as long as I got to be *Colonel* Kira," she says grinning. The promotion is disclosed in the teaser, during a humorous exchange between Kira and Odo that also establishes a somewhat different title—a given name—for one of the show's recurring characters: Admiral Ross.

"Odo refers to the admiral as 'Bill,'" confirms Behr. "And at the time Hans and I wrote the line, we

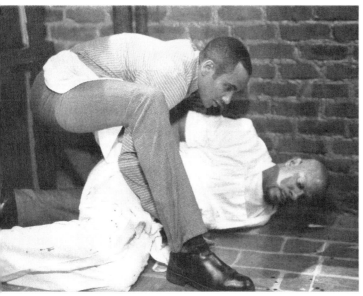

The quiet scenes set in the restaurant served in sharp contrast to the attack on Sisko. ROBBIE ROBINSON

"I didn't know what a Trill was when they called me," says deBoer.
ROBBIE ROBINSON

weren't even sure if that *was* the admiral's name, because Odo was making a joke. But it caught on, and after that, every goddam writer had to put the name in his script. You know: 'Oh, there's Bill Ross.' 'Let's get Bill Ross to perform the ceremony.'" Behr shakes his head, clearly amused. "So he's no longer 'Admiral Ross,' he's Bill."

One person who would have laid odds that Bill *wasn't* the admiral's first name is Ross's counterpart, Barry Jenner. Like many actors, Jenner is always interested in the subtext of the characters he plays. Over the course of his tenure on *Deep Space Nine*, for example, he created a whole personal backstory for Ross to enhance his performance. "He has two children," postulates Jenner, "a boy and a girl, both serving in Starfleet. The young man was lost in battle, but his daughter is still alive, and I think that one of the reasons Ross likes Benjamin Sisko is because he would trust for his daughter to serve under the captain." Given his interest in continuing to develop his character, it should come as no surprise that Jenner has studied the details of the admiral's office at Starbase 375 quite closely. "He has some diplomas on his walls," Jenner grins, "and one of them says that it was presented to 'Admiral *Cliff* Ross.'"

The diplomas, of course, were created during Season 6, and were meant to serve as set decoration that would never be exposed to the tight scrutiny of the camera's eye. The writers didn't think of the prop diplomas when they finally got around to giving Ross a first name. But they did have fun providing a few of the script's other references. The shipyards of "Monac IV," for example, were a tip of the hat to Gary Monak, while O'Brien's mention of Barclay and his holosuite escapades came courtesy of *DS9*'s former *TNG* staffers. And while the name of the planet "Tyree" would *seem*, at first glance, to be a nod to a character in the original series episode "A Private Little War," Ira Behr notes that he actually borrowed it from a character in the film *Major Dundee*.

One of the most important "elements" of the entire episode was established in the very last scene of "Image in the Sand," when an unfamiliar young woman enters Joseph Sisko's establishment and introduces herself as Dax.

"I came in and I had one line—that's it," Actor Nicole deBoer says, laughing. "I hadn't moved to L.A. yet, and I hadn't even found a place to live."

"She was very sweet," says B.C. Cameron, first assistant director (A.D.) for *DS9*'s odd-numbered episodes. "And a little nervous. But she only had to work about a half day for her first episode."

"By my second show, I understood what was going on in the rest of the series," deBoer says. "They gave me some tapes to look at and I watched them. I was hesitant to watch a whole bunch of Jadzia stuff, because I didn't really want to feel like I was copying her or trying to be different from her. But I did watch all the other stuff. They were some pretty neat shows."

Ironically, the all-important titular image from the episode was not filmed during production of "Image in the Sand." Since Director Les Landau needed the shot to match the Palmdale desert location of "Shadows and Symbols," it made sense to shoot it during production of *that* episode. The only complication was that time is always short during location filming, as crew members scurry to get everything done while shooting conditions are optimal. "Everybody was very concerned about getting the work done in the two days we were scheduled to be out there," says Lou Race, first A.D. for *DS9*'s even-numbered episodes. With two directors (Allan Kroeker directed "Shadows and Symbols") striving to capture the light, stake out the turf, *and* utilize the lead actor, competition was a bit hectic. "Les had come up with a fairly involved shot," Race recalls.

"He needed a big dolly track setup because he wanted to crane around as Sisko was digging. Fortunately, we were able to orient the day so that the track was laid and that whole thing was set up over *here*—" Race gestures with one hand, then the other—"while we were shooting over *there*. We were able to avoid shooting in each other's direction."

SHADOWS AND SYMBOLS

Episode #552

WRITTEN BY IRA STEVEN BEHR & HANS BEIMLER
DIRECTED BY ALLAN KROEKER

GUEST CAST

Weyoun	JEFFREY COMBS
Damar/Dr. Wykoff	CASEY BIGGS
Admiral Ross	BARRY JENNER
General Martok	J.G. HERTZLER
Sarah/Alien	DEBORAH LACEY
Cretak	MEGAN COLE
Siana	LORI LIVELY
Bajoran Crewman	CUAUHTEMOC SANCHEZ

SPECIAL GUEST STAR

Joseph Sisko	BROCK PETERS

STARDATE 52152.6

Sisko stares in amazement at the young woman who claims to be Dax. It's true, she assures him, although she's not Jadzia she's Ezri. She has all of Jadzia's memories, as well as Lela's, Curzon's, and all the rest of Dax's previous hosts. Ezri was a Starfleet ensign, an assistant ship's counselor serving on the *U.S.S. Destiny*, when the Dax symbiont was brought on board for its trip back to Trill ("Tears of the Prophets"). But halfway through the trip the symbiont took a turn for the worse and had to be placed into a host immediately. As the only Trill onboard, Ezri was the one viable candidate, despite the fact that she'd never had any of the training or preparation required of potential hosts before they're joined. As a result, she's been going through a rather rough acclimation period. She's so full of other hosts' memories that she barely knows who *she* is anymore. So after requesting a leave of absence, she decided to find Ben Sisko. Something told her that if anyone could help her through this period of adjustment, it was he.

Unfortunately, Sisko is about to leave for Tyree. Fine, says Ezri, immediately volunteering to come

A jealous Worf resents Quark's presence. ROBBIE ROBINSON

along. It'll be just like old times, she assures her old friend. Except . . . different.

Back at Deep Space 9, a solemn Klingon crew plus Bashir and O'Brien prepare to embark on their mission to win a great victory in Jadzia's name, thus allowing her to enter the sacred halls of *Sto-Vo-Kor* ("Image in the Sand"). But before the bird-of-prey can leave, another passenger boards. It's Quark. He cared about Jadzia, too, he admits, and he's willing to pledge his life to their mission. The other warriors accept his presence, and they head for Monac IV.

On the station, a serious situation is developing. Although Admiral Ross claims that the Federation is as upset as the Bajorans are about the Romulan weapons on Derna, they aren't willing to initiate any action to force the Romulans to remove them. But if Ross's hands are tied, Kira assures him that hers are not. She plans to set up a blockade to prevent the Romulans from completing the work that will make the weapons operational. Ross warns Kira that this will lead to a fight that she can't possibly win, but Kira's mind is made up.

Arriving at Tyree, the four travelers beam down to the arid planet's surface. Almost immediately, Sisko begins hearing things—a hospital paging system's persistent calls for a 'Dr. Wykoff'—but he ignores them and starts off in search of his goal, the mysterious "Orb of the Emissary." Jake, Joseph, and Ezri follow, hoping that Sisko truly knows where he's going.

On Martok's bird-of-prey, O'Brien explains their plan to Quark. They'll need to fly extremely close to the Monac sun, then fire an electromagnetic pulse into it. In theory, the pulse will trigger a solar plasma ejection, which will, in turn, incinerate anything within a hundred million kilometers, including the shipyard. It's a dangerous plan, but that's what makes it worthwhile. Even more dangerous, however, are Quark's interactions with Worf. It's no secret that the Klingon has never liked him, but Quark is incensed that Worf is so openly hostile. He should be thanking Quark and the others for risking their lives to help Jadzia, Quark observes. An angry Worf says that he owes them nothing; they're here only because they wish to convince themselves that they're worthy of Jadzia. They should thank *him* for allowing them to come along and pay honor to her memory.

Martok speaks to Worf in private, and reminds him that these men were Jadzia's friends. They honor her with their presence, he says. A chastized Worf realizes Martok is right. He approaches the three non-Klingons and admits that he never liked sharing his wife's affections with them. For that reason, he didn't want them to come on this mission, which was to be his personal gift to her. But he has changed his mind; he's glad they're there.

Kira confesses to Odo that she knows the twelve old Bajoran impulse ships in the blockade will never be able to hold off a group of powerful Romulan warbirds. But she's hoping that the Romulans won't let the situation deteriorate into a firefight; if it does, it could jeopardize their alliance with the Federation. After the Bajoran blockade is set up, Ross warns her that four warbirds are headed her way, but Kira holds her ground. Cretak tells Ross that she's certain Kira is bluffing about firing on the warbirds, but the worried admiral isn't so sure.

On Tyree, Sisko marches relentlessly through the blazing hot sand, ignoring Jake and Ezri's concerns about Joseph's stamina. At last Sisko comes to an area that might—or might not—be the spot. As he considers the possibilities, the captain idly toys with his baseball. Frustrated, Ezri snatches it from his hand and tosses it away. To her surprise, Sisko decides that he'll dig where the ball has landed. Although the others worry that he's lost his mind—something the voices in his head seem to confirm—Ben at last unearths an Orb ark.

As he prepares to open it, the desert disappears around him. Suddenly, he's Benny Russell, severely traumatized by past experiences ("Far Beyond the Stars") and confined to a hospital's isolation ward. And at last "Dr. Wykoff"—a human who resembles Damar—appears and instructs Benny to drop the pencil that he's been using to scribble on the walls.

Benny is torn. He needs to finish Ben Sisko's story. The captain was about to open the Orb of the Emissary, he explains. But Benny also wants to go home, and Wykoff tells him that if he continues to write, he'll be throwing away all the progress he's made at the institution. He'll never get out. Benny hestitates . . .

. . . On Tyree, Sisko's companions see him freeze in front of the Orb ark, seemingly paralyzed and oblivious to his surroundings . . .

. . . In Bajoran space, Kira finds herself facing imminent destruction as the warbirds near her position . . .

. . . And in the Monac system, the crew of the bird-of-prey sweat as the ship moves painfully close to the sun. They fire an EM pulse at their target, but nothing happens. They'll need to make some adjustments—but they've been spotted by Jem'Hadar forces, who are moving in quickly.

In Benny Russell's world, Dr. Wykoff hands his patient a paint roller. He explains that he's giving Benny the opportunity to wipe away all of his mistakes. They're just words, Wykoff says, and if Benny paints over those words, the doctor will allow him to leave. Benny moves the paint roller close to the wall, tempted . . .

. . . And Ben Sisko begins to bury the ark without opening it. But that's not good enough. He has to destroy it! He raises his shovel over his head and prepares to smash it—but Ezri steps in front of him, unwilling to let him complete the destructive act. He promised Jadzia he'd make things right, she reminds him. And now's his chance—open the box!

In the isolation ward, the doctor's face contorts in anger as Benny drops the paint roller and touches the tip of his pencil to the wall. Wykoff tries to stop him, but Benny knocks him to the ground and completes his sentence: *"Sisko reaches for the Orb box and opens it . . ."*

. . . And as Sisko does so, an intense white energy vortex leaps from the box and shoots straight up into the sky. In seconds, the vortex has traveled across space to reach Deep Space 9. To the excitement of the Bajorans standing on the Promenade, the wormhole bursts into view for the first time in months. Waiting nearby in her Bajoran ship, Kira, too, witnesses the phenomenon and sees a stream of red energy expelled from the mouth of the wormhole. With new resolve, she instructs her crew to lock weapons and prepare to fire on the Romulans. Cretak is prepared to battle with her—but at the last minute, Ross takes a stand. The

Romulan ships abruptly withdraw, the result, Ross informs Kira, of his having told Cretak to remove her weapons or Starfleet would do it for her.

In the Monac system, Martok's crew holds off the Jem'Hadar ships long enough for O'Brien to complete his work, and they fire another pulse. This time it works, and the resulting arc of solar plasma destroys both the shipyard and the attacking ships. It is truly a victory worthy of Jadzia and one that is certain to open *Sto-Vo-Kor's* gates.

Sisko has a vision of the woman he saw before. It is Sarah—and yet it isn't. She is an alien, one of the Prophets, but she reveals to Sisko that she once shared Sarah Sisko's corporeal existence, to ensure that Sarah would marry Joseph and give birth to Benjamin. After that, the Prophet left Sarah's body, leaving a confused human woman who had never chosen to be with Joseph. This was why Sarah left him so soon after Ben's birth. Sisko's mind reels as he realizes that he literally exists because the wormhole aliens knew that they would need him someday to defeat the Kosst Amojan. Indeed, thanks to Sisko, the evil entity no longer threatens the celestial temple in which the aliens reside; "Sarah" was able to cast it out. She explains that the Kosst Amojan tried to stop Sisko with false visions, but he succeeded. Sisko has fulfilled his destiny, yet there are more tasks ahead of him, Sarah says.

Sisko and the others return to Deep Space 9, where the grateful Bajoran people greet their Emissary warmly, knowing that he was responsible for bringing back the Prophets. As the happy throng sweeps him and the others along the Promenade, Ezri spots her old friends in the crowd and calls hello to them. Puzzled, Bashir asks Jake who the young woman is. Jake grins and reveals that it's Dax, Ezri Dax. As the others look on in disbelief, a dazzled Ezri takes in her familiar yet unfamiliar surroundings.

"It was very funny," recalls Director Allan Kroeker. "I hadn't been around *Deep Space Nine* for several months, so I came into prep for 'Shadows and Symbols' and asked, 'Who's the new Dax?' And someone tried to pronounce her name for me and said, 'Oh, you'll like her. She's French Canadian.'" His curiosity piqued, Kroeker, a native of Winnipeg who now resides in Toronto, asked to see a photo of the new cast member. "I looked at it and said, 'It's Nicky! Nicky deBoer! And she's *not* French Canadian—she's from *Toronto*. I've done ten shows with her!'"

Kroeker laughs at the memory. He had directed a

Despite the hazards, the location added wonderful scenery and underscored the desolation felt by the Bajorans. ROBBIE ROBINSON

number of episodes of deBoer's previous series, *Beyond Reality*. "I was very happy," he says, "because I knew Nicky was a very serious young actress who knew her stuff and was very easy to work with."

Since Kroeker was about to send deBoer and three other actors on a forced march across the blazing sand dunes of Palmdale, California, "easy to work with" was a definite plus. "It was hard shooting there," the director admits. "I had never drunk Gatorade in my life, but I'll tell you, this was my initiation!"

"It must have been strange for Nicole," observes Lou Race. "She signs on to do *Star Trek* and for her first major episode, she's sent out to do *Lawrence of Arabia!*"

Compared to the previous week, when all she'd been required to do was deliver a few short lines in a controlled environment, this was an initiation by fire. "It was awful out there," deBoer admits. "Really hot and awful, hiking up and down hills all day, for two days. I was glad to get back to the soundstages."

As was everyone else. "We had photo doubles for everybody, which helped," says Race. "So while the main unit team was shooting the uncovering of the Orb box, second unit was out shooting the photo doubles trekking across the sand dunes. About half of the trekking was the doubles. We were all a little concerned about Brock Peters, because he's a bit frail, but he held up well," Race comments. "The fact that Brock was out there willing to work made other people feel the same way."

Considering the fact that even optimal shooting conditions in the desert are never entirely pleasant, wouldn't it have been easier for writers Ira Behr and Hans Beimler to indicate that Joseph stayed behind at the restaurant? "Yeah, it would have been," Behr admits. "But Ben came back home to be with his father, and I just felt that keeping the family together meant something. If it had been my kid going off [on the quest for the Orb], I'd have gone with *my* kid. If it had been *Bonanza,* Ben Cartwright would have gone with Little Joe and Hoss and even Adam."

Which isn't to say that the writers didn't have feelings about submitting their actors to yet another mercilessly hot location shoot. "Hans and I felt so bad about what we were putting the actors through that we drove out to Palmdale, too," Behr says. "To show the flag, you know, and let them know we knew that they were suffering. And it really *was* hot as hell."

Hot, yes. And full of surprises. "We found this natural mound out there, and we decided to use it as the spot where Sisko digs," relates Art Director Randy McIlvain. "And then we decided we wanted to move part of it forward, to enhance it. So the crew started digging—and suddenly thousands and thousands of ants come out from *everywhere.*" McIlvain begins to laugh. "It turns out this mound just happened to be a gigantic ant hill! Fortunately, this was the day before we were set to shoot, and after we disturbed the ants, they went someplace else and didn't come back."

Because Nicole deBoer was somewhat unfamiliar with the backstory of the various *DS9* characters at this point, she had no difficulty expressing Ezri's bewilderment over Sisko's strange behavior in the episode. "I remember thinking, 'I'm never going to get a hold on all this Prophet stuff! This is trippy!'" deBoer says, giggling.

The writers, however, were well-versed in both the behavior of Prophets *and* the characters' backstories — which makes it hard to explain the gaffe inherent in Ezri's plea to Sisko as he's about to destroy the Orb box:

EZRI
(adamant)
You promised Jadzia you'd make things right . . .

Viewers may recall that at the point when Sisko made this promise to Jadzia (in "Tears of the Prophets"), Jadzia was already dead—and the Dax symbiont already was secured aboard the *Destiny,* on the way to Trill. So how does Ezri know about the promise that Sisko made over Jadzia's body?

Behr attempts to explain the unexplainable. "On the trip to Tyree," he offers gamely, "in the ship, Ezri

Caught between two contentious allies, Jenner's Admiral Ross walks the tightrope usually reserved for Sisko. ROBBIE ROBINSON

says, 'So what happened while I was dead? Why are you doing this? Why did you go back to Earth?' And Sisko says, 'While you were lying dead . . .'"

Really?

Behr gives it another try. "But it's obvious. They talked about it. During the flight. What else were they doing? Just sitting there?" Suddenly he buries his face in his hands and sighs. "I don't want to think about this."

Meanwhile, back on the station, the writers had given Kira her own little "Cuban missile crisis" to deal with—at least that's how Behr thought of the colonel's standoff against the Romulan weapons on Derna. "Kira's in command now, and we wanted to show how she would handle a tough situation," he says. "And what we came up with is that she doesn't force the Romulans to back down. She forces the *Federation* to back down. Barry Jenner has made Admiral Ross such a well-rounded character that we realized we could have him back down without making him appear weak, and then we could have *him* put pressure on the Romulans."

Jenner is flattered that Behr and the others have allowed his portrayal of Ross to influence the way they write the character. "It makes you feel good as an actor when you try to bring something to a scene and the writers sense it and use it," he says. "Ira came down to the set and watched as Nana and I went through the scene where Ross tells Kira he won't back her if she goes against the Romulans. Afterward he came over and asked what I was playing there. I told him that I was trying to show that Ross feels regret over his decision because he really respects Colonel Kira. And Ira told me he never thought of putting that into the scene, but he appreciated that I did."

Behr and Beimler added new dimension to Quark's personality in the episode. "Quark's relationship with Worf has been prickly from the beginning," Behr explains, "and Jadzia was always in the middle. Here we use that to have Quark say some very good, logical things in his own unique way."

Actor Armin Shimerman was pleased with the opportunity. "It established firmly in my mind that Quark was mourning the loss of Jadzia, whom he'd always had a fondness for," he explains. "He was distraught over her death, and his feelings later transmogrified into a great fondness for Ezri, in the sense that he was looking for the lost woman in this new Dax."

Worf's tribute to Jadzia included a Klingon chant uttered upon the successful completion of the group's efforts at the Monac shipyards. The shooting script included a translation:

> Open your gates, *Sto-Vo-Kor*.
> Welcome Jadzia to your halls.
> Welcome this honored warrior.
> Welcome her, *Sto-Vo-Kor*, for all eternity.

One thing the script didn't include, however, was a transcription of the Captain Sisko epic that Benny Russell composed in the hospital isolation ward. It mentioned only that the padded walls of Benny's cell "are covered with intricate writing."

"I had to make sure the camera didn't linger on the walls for too long because some aficionado at home was bound to freeze the frame, enhance it, and try to read the history of *Star Trek* there," laughs Kroeker. "Still, some poor guy had to fill those walls with writing."

Make that some poor *guys*.

According to Scenic Art Supervisor Michael Okuda, the entire *DS9* Art Department pitched in to write Benny's story on the wall. "My first thought had been to put some sort of text into the computer and then render it out in a script font," Okuda notes. "But that just didn't look right." It was Scenic Artist Anthony Fredrickson who suggested they try doing it the old-fashioned way, with a number two pencil. "We asked Avery Brooks to write a couple of sentences and then we tried to match his handwriting," recalls Okuda. "But after a while we gave up on that and just hoped that it would look similar. Thankfully, it did." Although Fredrickson started the process, it quickly became apparent that there was too much for one person to do before shooting began. "Pretty soon the whole art team joined in," says Okuda. "Even Lou Race helped."

But just what *were* they writing? "It was supposed to be the story of Deep Space 9, as told by Benny Russell," relates Okuda. Although the words probably wouldn't be legible, it seemed appropriate for the text to contain terms that would reinforce the illusion — like "Sisko" and "Odo" and "runabout." As the source for those words, Okuda turned to a reference tool he

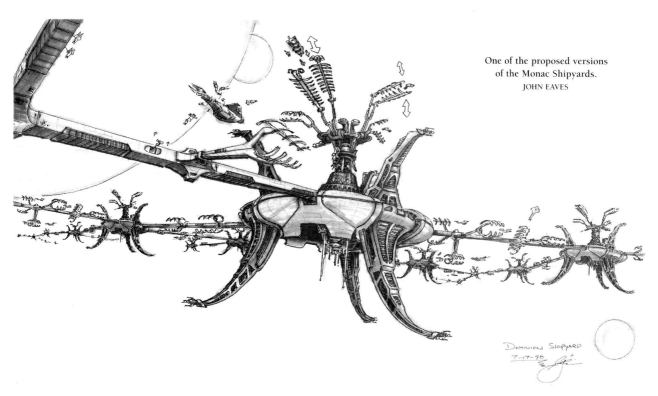

One of the proposed versions
of the Monac Shipyards.
JOHN EAVES

had in his office—an early draft of *The Deep Space Nine Companion*. "We used the synopses of the episodes," he says. Although he no longer remembers exactly which episodes were used, he does remember the one he spent the most time copying out. "Tribbles," he says with a grin. "I seem to remember spending a lot of time with 'Trials and Tribble-ations.'"

Much of the Monac IV sequence, as well as the shot of the ships around the Bajoran moon, were done as CGI by Digital Muse, reports Visual Supervisor David Stipes. Although there's always gratification in knowing that one has done a good job on a difficult task, it's hard not to feel frustrated when, for one reason or another, that good work doesn't get seen by the audience. "We had this wonderful concept laid out for the Monac shipyards," sighs Stipes. "And then the structure of the story got shifted around so that we never had a place to feature it, except on a viewscreen. We'd invested a tremendous amount of time and energy in creating this big, beautiful pull-back shot that would reveal the Dominion ships under construction. I felt bad that we couldn't show off the work that all the guys had done, although I understand that the story comes first."

AFTERIMAGE

Episode #553

WRITTEN BY RENÉ ECHEVARRIA
DIRECTED BY LES LANDAU

GUEST CAST

Elim Garak ANDREW J. ROBINSON

STARDATE UNKNOWN

The day after her arrival on Deep Space 9, Ezri Dax wanders the corridors of the station with a curious feeling of nostalgia. It's all very familiar to her; as Jadzia, she spent six years here. But she's no longer Jadzia, and her run-ins with Jadzia's old friends are strangely awkward, with the exception of Quark, who is as flirtatious as ever. Morn doesn't know her. Kira is polite but reserved. And Worf is unwilling to speak to her. Dejected, Ezri goes to see Sisko and tells him about Worf's behavior. Sisko suggests that perhaps Worf is trying to respect Trill traditions against reassociation ("Rejoined"), but Ezri doesn't believe that. All she knows is that her mere presence seems to be painful to the Klingon. It's a good thing she isn't staying on the station, she says. Sisko notes that he'll miss her when she goes back to her ship, the *Destiny* ("Shadows and Symbols").

When Ezri tries to counsel Garak, the secretive Cardassian actively resists. ROBBIE ROBINSON

In Quark's bar, Bashir and O'Brien discuss participating in a holosuite reenactment of the battle of the Alamo. They ask Garak when he'll be finished with their costumes. A moody Garak reminds them that his shop hasn't been open for some time; he's been busy decoding Cardassian military transmissions for Starfleet Intelligence. Later, Odo goes to Garak's shop and finds the Cardassian on the verge of collapse, the victim of a claustrophobic attack. The changeling rushes him to the Infirmary. Garak explains that he's been claustrophobic for most of his life ("By Inferno's Light"). For some unknown reason, however, the feeling seems to be getting worse. He asks Sisko to free him from his decoding responsibilities until he's up to the task. Knowing how much Starfleet has come to depend on Garak for information about Cardassian military strategies, Sisko asks Ezri to use her counseling techniques to help him. Although her own self-confidence level is at an all-time low, Ezri agrees to try.

Garak is polite but wary when Ezri shows up for their first "session." He eventually reveals that when he was young, his father used to punish him for misbehavior by locking him in a closet. Although Garak doesn't think his father's behavior was inappropriate, Ezri observes that *nothing* a child does can justify locking him in a closet. She suggests that Garak's claustrophobic response might be due to feelings of misplaced guilt over imagined wrongdoing. As Garak mulls over that possibility, Ezri heads back to her quarters and literally runs into Worf along the way. She attempts to make conversation, but Worf tells her that he has no desire to make her acquaintance. His wife is dead and in *Sto-Vo-Kor*, and *she* is not Jadzia.

The next day, Sisko informs Ezri that Garak's problem seems to be under control and that he's gone back to work on the transmissions. The assistant counselor is surprised but happy to hear it. She's even more surprised when Sisko invites her to stay on at Deep Space 9 as a full counselor, with the rank of lieutenant junior grade. Ezri is pleased to know that he wants her to stay, but admits the situation with Worf makes it impossible. Later, the Trill gets reacquainted with Dr. Bashir. The two hit it off nearly as well as Jadzia and Bashir, particularly when Ezri reveals that Jadzia always enjoyed his flirting. In fact, she confides, if Worf hadn't come along and won her heart, it would have been the doctor.

Bashir is touched by the comment, which reminds him how much he misses Jadzia. Ezri takes his hand to comfort him and fails to notice that Worf is watching their interaction. The warm moment is interrupted by a medical emergency: Garak is inside an airlock, trying to open the door into space! Ezri brings Garak to one of Quark's holosuites, hoping that an illusion of wide open spaces will calm him. The peaceful oceanside setting helps for a while, but Garak knows the holosuite is only a placebo. He needs a real solution. Not long after, Bashir receives a visitor in his Infirmary. It's Worf, and the Klingon is furious. He warns Bashir to stay away from Dax.

When Ezri goes back to check on Garak, she discovers that he's left the holosuite and gone to his shop. There she finds him ripping apart a dress and then trying to put it back together. His mood has changed. He's no longer frightened, he's angry, and the insecure Ezri is a very convenient target for his venom. Garak points out that the Trill is too confused about her own identity to help anyone, and tells her to leave, which Ezri is happy to do. Distraught, she offers Sisko her resignation from Starfleet, and tells him she doesn't deserve to have the Dax symbiont. To her surprise, Sisko agrees with her. Dax has had eight incredible lifetimes, he says. So what if the ninth is a

waste. He tells her he'll transmit her resignation to Starfleet Command, and coldly dismisses her.

O'Brien goes to see Worf, hoping to calm the rough waters between the Klingon and Bashir. Worf comments that seeing Bashir treat Ezri as if she were Jadzia dishonors Jadzia's memory. But O'Brien disagrees. Treating Ezri like a *stranger* is what dishonors Jadzia's memory, not Bashir's behavior.

As she prepares to leave, Ezri tells Garak that his decoding work has led to a new assault against the Cardassians. He should be proud, she says encouragingly. But her comments trigger a new attack, leading Ezri to realize what his real problem is. While he tells himself that his actions will end the war, in his heart he feels that he's betraying his people and paving the way to their annihilation. The claustrophobic attacks give him an excuse to stop fighting against his people. But now that Garak realizes the truth, the attacks will end, and he can go on helping Starfleet.

After this small victory, Ezri decides that she wants to remain in Starfleet—but she already has given Sisko her resignation. She asks the captain to have her reinstated, but Sisko admits that he never sent in her resignation. He asks her again to stay on DS9. Not long after, Worf comes to see her and admits that he has not treated her as Jadzia would have wished. If she wants to remain on the station, she should, because Jadzia would not have wanted her to leave. Ezri admits that she does want to stay, and promises to give Worf "breathing room" to adjust to the presence of a loved one who is departed, but not entirely gone.

Ira Behr explains, "We put 'Afterimage' into development before we even saw the dailies on the first two episodes. But we had faith in Nicole. We had a good vibe off of her and the character of Ezri in concept. We knew we had to be bold and not just try to sneak her into the show. Maybe we could have if this had been Season 2 or 3, but [by this point] we only had one season, so we just had to go for it. There was no tomorrow."

Nicole deBoer would have appreciated an extra tomorrow or two. "'Afterimage' was my *big episode*," she says sighing. "I was working *really* hard, going through the lines and thinking about the scenes. I just wanted to do a good job." She takes a deep breath before continuing. "So we shoot for *one day* of my big show and break for the weekend. And over that weekend I go and wipe out on my bicycle! I got this huge black eye and one half of my face was

"I've always worn my hair like this, although for *Star Trek* it's glued down so nothing moves," laughs deBoer. ROBBIE ROBINSON

swollen. It was *awful*! And to make it worse, the studio had scheduled that week for the show's publicity photos, and I'm like, 'No! I'm gonna look weird!'"

DeBoer chuckles at the memory. "It was a bit . . . stressful," she admits. "Fortunately, Mary Kay Morse, amazing makeup goddess that she is, managed to cover it, and you couldn't even tell I had a shiner."

"I used a prosthetic makeup on her, which is thicker than the usual makeup," reports Morse. "And because it was still a little swollen, I shaded her eyes differently, so that the camera wouldn't pick up that one eye was squintier than the other. It worked out fine."

Ezri's *big episode* was assigned to René Echevarria, who also would have appreciated a bit more time. "It was tricky, because Hans [Beimler] and Ira were writing the first two episodes while I was working on this one simultaneously," he recalls. "So while they were sort of discovering Ezri's voice, I was off on my own. I didn't even know what she looked like until I was halfway through my draft. I hadn't seen the actress's face."

Echevarria initially focused on the Garak portion of the story. "In the script's original formulation, Garak's problem was much more intricate and com-

plicated," he says. "He'd gone on a mission at Starfleet's behest, and over the course of that mission, he'd had to lock himself into a torpedo tube—either to hide or to escape, I forget which. And he'd had a breakdown as a result of that, and forgotten the information that he'd been sent to obtain. Ezri had to cure him in order to get this information, which was pivotal to Starfleet's war efforts."

Unfortunately, in order to make such a complicated psychological story work, "Ezri would have to be a very, very effective counselor," notes Echevarria. "And that would make the scenes between her and Garak more about psychotherapy than about Ezri's character. The plotlines were fighting each other. This person who didn't know who she was would not be an effective therapist—and that was a major part of the story. So I radically simplified Garak's problem in my second draft. And by that time I'd seen Nicole, which gave me more ideas. She became more quirky, standing on her head and stuff like that. We decided to let her almost stumble onto the solution to Garak's problem, and allow her vulnerability to bring it about."

On paper, deBoer liked the characterization, quirks and all. But later on she came to regret one aspect of her counterpart's personality. "I didn't think standing on my head would be too bad, except that I might not look that great upside down," she says, laughing. "Nobody looks that great upside down. I remember standing on my head as a kid and I didn't mind it then. But I guess it's been too many years. I found that I couldn't do it for very long. All of a sudden the blood would rush to my head and even my tongue felt like it was filling up! I couldn't even talk!"

The writing staff liked the new spin on the story and Echevarria quickly finished his final script. "Ezri helps Garak sort of by serendipity, and that gives her confidence," he notes. "That was the intent, although I'm not sure we pulled it off. I talked to some professional therapists after they saw the episode and they told me, 'That was just bunk.'" Echevarria laughs and shakes his head. "That was disappointing to hear, that we'd missed the mark. But I still think it was a good introduction to Ezri, and to the whole problem with Worf."

Although he seldom comments on plot, Composer Jay Chattaway is completely behind Echevarria's assessment. "I was very smitten with Ezri in that episode," he smiles. "She struck me as a real girl-next-door type, and I could see a synergy there [with the rest of the actors]. The stuff between her and Worf really worked for me. You knew he was still in love with what was inside of her. You knew they were going to get together. It was just a matter of how long the writers were going to stretch it out before Worf reached out and accepted her."

Traditionally, individual *Star Trek* characters don't get musical themes, but Chattaway did instill Ezri with her own unique melodic essence. "I gave the music a careful but coquettish quality that matched the character. Jadzia was *never* coquettish. I made Ezri more bouncy, not sultry at all."

The difference between Ezri and Jadzia is pointed up in the new host's initial conversation with Bashir. But while Ezri's open admission of Jadzia's feelings for the doctor seem to hint at the romantic relationship the two would develop later in the season, Echevarria says he really didn't have that in mind when he wrote it. "I thought of it more as closure for Julian," he comments. "He'd had that long, simmering crush on Jadzia, and now he was feeling the true loss of a friend. Paradoxically, only by talking to her new incarnation does he get the whole closure. He's very moved when Ezri tells him that Jadzia loved him, and that there was more depth to the relationship than he knew. It was very well played by the actors."

It was the chemistry in this filmed scene and some subsequent ones that led to the later romantic developments, says Behr. "It's always a possibility," he explains. "You see how they play together. You see Odo and Kira. You see Jadzia and Worf. You look at it on-screen and if it works, you go, 'Okay.' If there's no chemistry, no charisma, you don't. If there had been no charisma between Avery Brooks and Penny Johnson, we would have lost Kasidy. But there was, and we said, 'Okay. Here's somebody who can help humanize the captain.'"

While the interplay between Ezri and Garak wasn't romantic by any means, there was a certain amount of volatile chemistry between the two of them that worked to the episode's advantage. Ezri's attempt to foist her services, however kindly intended, on a character who views such efforts as a hostile intrusion isn't a huge stretch from what the two actors were experiencing, to a certain degree, on a personal level. "Nicole was walking into a show that had been going on for six years," explains Robinson. "Everybody really has their characters solidly under control, and they know what the hell they're doing. And she's still searching. And then she walks into a scene like this! That was a challenge for her."

But while Robinson felt for her, he knew that it wouldn't be true to his character—or hers—if he held

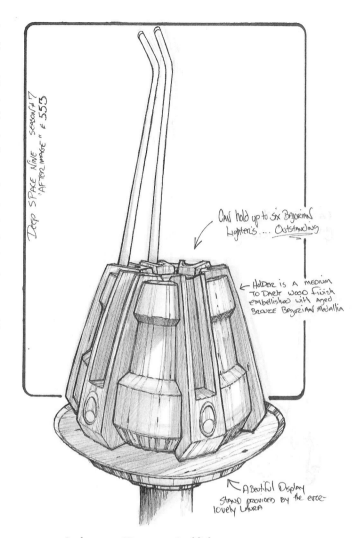

Deep Space Nine Season #17 "After Image" # 553

Can hold up to six Bajorian Lighter's..... Outstanding

Holder is a medium to Dark wood finish embellished with Aged Bronze Bajorian Medallia

A Beautiful Display stand provided by the ever-lovely Laura

In the teaser, Kira uses a ritual lighter. JOHN EAVES

back in the vituperative level of his performance. "I didn't pull any punches, nor would she have wanted me to," he says. "I just gave her my best and she hung in there. She stood up to it. And that does show in the episode."

The viciousness of Garak's response to Ezri's well-intentioned attempts comes, Robinson explains, from his interpretation of Cardassian nature. "Garak is a Cardassian, and I think of them as really working from the reptilian part of their brain. They're very suspicious when anyone tries to interfere or pry or get inside their very carefully constructed perimeters. So although Garak was suffering this terrible anxiety that was affecting his breathing, he was driven to fence with Ezri, daring her to get inside him, and trying to stop her. But finally his anxiety overwhelms him and he realizes that he does need her help. And in the end, he is grateful."

The writers did not create a nice little story to introduce the new Dax.
ROBBIE ROBINSON

flames. The earth salted. Destroyed. It was almost personal."

On a lighter note, Ezri's difficulties with pronouns in the episode were a reflection of similar problems the writers were experiencing behind the scenes, according to Behr. "We were in a situation where we had to figure out how we were going to refer to Dax, how we were going to refer to Jadzia, how we were going to refer to Ezri," Behr notes. Ezri's comment that "these pronouns are driving me crazy," he adds, was Echevarria's personal comment on that situation. "René threw it in because we used to make jokes about 'pronoun trouble,' as in the famous Bugs Bunny cartoon 'Rabbit Seasoning,'" grins Behr.

TAKE ME OUT TO THE HOLOSUITE

Episode #554

WRITTEN BY RONALD D. MOORE
DIRECTED BY CHIP CHALMERS

GUEST CAST

Rom	MAX GRODÉNCHIK
Nog	ARON EISENBERG
Solok	GREGORY WAGROWSKI
Leeta	CHASE MASTERSON
Kasidy Yates	PENNY JOHNSON

STARDATE UNKNOWN

Captain Sisko isn't happy to lay out the welcome mat to the *Starship T'Kumbra*, which has come to the station for repairs. The ship's captain, a Vulcan named Solok, is a longtime rival who shows an un-Vulcan-like predilection for one-upping Sisko whenever he finds the opportunity. And his current reunion with Sisko has provided a perfect opportunity. Knowing that Sisko is a keen fan of the ancient Earth game of baseball, Solok and his senior staff have become experts at the game. The Vulcan challenges Sisko's crew to a game in Quark's holosuite, noting that the *T'Kumbra*'s all-Vulcan crew is the best in the fleet. Sisko takes Solok up on the contest, despite the fact that he has only two weeks to organize and whip a completely untrained team into shape.

The practice sessions are grueling. Only Sisko and Jake have played the game before, and the inexperienced "Niners" are plagued by injuries. But Sisko will let nothing stand between him and a victory over

The idea that Garak's problem is triggered by patriotism may have taken some viewers by surprise—this is, after all, a man who has killed many Cardassians in his lifetime, and who has been ostracized by his homeworld—but it shouldn't, according to both the actor who lives in Garak's skin and the writer. "Again, it's reptilian," says Robinson. "It's that absolute need to defend and be loyal to your own territory. And we know from 'The Wire' and 'The Die Is Cast' how desperately he wants to go home someday."

"Yes, he's killed Cardassians," comments Echevarria, "but he always felt on some level like he was working in the best interest of the people at home, and that sacrifices had to be made along the way. Now his home was occupied and he saw the end coming. He knew where it all was going."

Did the writers know at this point where it all was going?

"Not all of it," Echevarria admits. "But as to the destruction of Cardassia, yes, definitely. That was something Ira specifically wanted. The world in

Resentful of Solok's attitude, Sisko accepts the Vulcan's challenge.
ROBBIE ROBINSON

Solok. When O'Brien is sidelined by a torn rotator cuff, Sisko makes him a coach, then pulls some strings to enlist freighter pilot Kasidy Yates—who already knows how to play—as O'Brien's replacement. Still, the team is rocky at best, and some of the players, Rom in particular, are virtually hopeless. After Solok observes Rom's inept attempt to hit the ball during a training session, Sisko decides to cut his losses and drop Rom from the team.

Although the rest of the Niners threaten to quit over Sisko's callous treatment of Rom, the good-hearted Ferengi urges them to continue without him. He wants to see them win the game, even if he has to do it from the stands. Training continues, and the night before the big game, Sisko finally tells Kasidy why it's so important to him to beat Solok. Their rivalry, it seems, goes all the way back to Starfleet Academy, where Solok first expressed his views that Vulcans were naturally superior to humans and other "emotionally handicapped" species. Back then, Sisko challenged Solok to a wrestling match to prove that humans were every bit the equal of Vulcans. Unfortunately, Sisko lost, and Solok never let him forget about the incident. And now, Sisko growls, he's come to DS9 to attempt to beat Sisko at his own game!

Kasidy relates this tale to the rest of the Niners, who vow to help Sisko win. But Solok's team is as good as he promised. The first Vulcan who steps up to bat slams a home run, and the game goes downhill from there. By the top of the fifth inning, the Niners are losing to the Vulcan "Logicians" seven to zero. When Sisko goes over to argue a play with Odo—who is acting as the game's umpire—he inadvertently touches the changeling, giving Odo the opportunity to throw him out of the game.

Now Sisko has to watch the game from the stands, just like Rom. As the two of them root for the home team, Sisko begins to regret his decision to pull the clumsy Ferengi out of the mix. After all, it's only a game—one that everyone deserves to play. So at the bottom of the ninth inning, with one Niner—Rom's son Nog—on third base, Sisko has O'Brien call a time-out. And a few minutes later, a pinch hitter is sent in for Jake. It's Rom! Although the Niners would like to end the game with at least one run, they all realize how important Rom's inclusion is. To everyone's surprise, Rom hits a perfect bunt, allowing Nog to run home. The Niners go wild and launch a joyous celebration, even picking up and carrying Rom. Solok is highly disturbed. The game isn't over, and the Niners haven't won. *Why* are they celebrating? And then he makes a mistake and touches the umpire . . . and is thrown out of the game by Odo.

Later, the Niners continue the festivities in Quark's bar. Solok still doesn't understand. The Ferengi's bunt was an accident, he protests. The Niners lost the game. And they are attempting to manufacture a triumph where none exists. But there's nothing Solok can say to spoil Sisko's delight in the results of the match, and in the end, it's the Vulcan who walks away in defeat, frustrated by the united front of illogical emotionalism.

Someone once pointed out to film director Howard Hawks that the plotline to his 1970 picture *Rio Lobo* closely resembled that of his 1959 classic *Rio Bravo*. The Academy Award honoree is reputed to have replied, "If it worked once, it'll work again." Let it not be said that Ira Steven Behr doesn't learn from the masters. "I did an episode on *Fame* called 'The Old Ballgame,'" Behr reveals, "and I had a lot of fun with it. So *this* show was an homage to *that* show—which is why I didn't dare write it," the executive producer laughs.

In truth, while the two plotlines have their similarities, they're not identical by any means. "Some of the gags are the same, like the guy not knowing who to tag," Behr comments, referring to Nog's inability to tell which Vulcan had just crossed home plate. "That was a *true* story that happened in the minor leagues," Behr says. "It reminded me of when I was a kid, play-

"A simple little show," Chalmers jokes. "Really, it was one of the most complicated things I've done." ROBBIE ROBINSON

ing baseball in school yards where we didn't always know the kids we were playing against."

The ending is also similar. "In the other episode," notes Behr, "a girl who can't play accidentally helps to win the game. This time we had Rom, the worst player, score a run."

Scoring a run isn't the same as winning the game, but it was all the writers needed. "I wanted us to lose the game," says Ronald D. Moore, who wrote the episode. "I didn't want to do 'the-little-team-that-comes-from-behind-to-win.' That's such a cliché. Keeping that in mind helped steer the story. We would lose the game but eke out a kind of morale victory at the end. I felt that Rom was going to contribute heart to the whole episode. He accidentally does something that gives him a personal victory, and everybody can celebrate his victory even though they've lost the whole shootin' match."

Ironically, Max Grodénchik, the actor who plays the athletically inept Rom, is, in real life, a serious baseball player. "I played with a semiprofessional team in high school," Grodénchik says. "But that was short-lived because I got a hankering for the stage." He wasn't the only cast member skilled in the game. Avery Brooks and Cirroc Lofton led the way in experience, with Armin Shimerman and Aron Eisenberg not far behind. "The joke was that the Ferengi were the worst ball players, but, in fact, we were the ones who really *could* play," Grodénchik says, chuckling. "I had to play left-handed, because that made it easier for me to look bad."

In stark contrast were the skills of Nana Visitor.

"I'd never held a baseball or a bat before in my entire life," she says with a laugh. "They gave me a few lessons. It was pretty thrilling when I actually hit the ball on my first take! The whole crew came around me as if I'd done something extraordinary. I felt like a big hero!"

The fact that some members of the cast were inexperienced at playing America's favorite pastime didn't surprise Behr. "On *Fame*, we had all these dancers who had to play," Behr says. "Some of them were okay and some of them looked like dancers. So this time we just blindly charged into the sound of the guns—*A show must be filmed! Charge!*"

Fortunately, the producers didn't have to go far to find someone who could give baseball lessons to the actors. They simply turned to Joey Banks, longtime member of *Deep Space Nine*'s stunt team and a regular background crew member on the *Defiant*'s bridge. Banks, the son of Chicago Cubs outfielder and Baseball Hall of Fame inductee Ernie Banks, began playing baseball with his father at the age of two. In addition to his stunt work, Banks keeps busy as one of Hollywood's foremost baseball coordinators. "My job was to make the actors look experienced," Banks says. "I showed them everything from the balance of the swing and the fundamentals of throwing to just having them carry themselves as if they had some knowledge of the game. But it was tough because they didn't have a lot of time for training. We could only get together during their leisure time."

The producers also asked Banks to assemble a group of baseball players to appear as the Vulcan team. "Joey brought us some pretty sharp players," Director Chip Chalmers says. "They knew how to swing that bat, and they knew how to throw very, very good."

Why Vulcans as the opposing team? "We talked about who the opponents would be," Ron Moore explains. "Was it going to be a holosuite opponent? Or the Bajorans against the Federation? Then we realized that we should put all of our heroes together on one team and find an opponent that would be easy to dislike. Somehow, the idea of Vulcans came up. There's something about them that ticks you off."

"Vulcans are ripe with comic possibilities," adds Behr. "In fact, if there's anything about the show that I *don't* think was successful, it's that we didn't do enough with the Vulcans. The lead protagonist—who comes in so strong at the beginning—is absent through big chunks of the episode. We didn't realize it until we saw a rough cut of the show, and by then it was too late. So the structure is weird. The thing with Sisko and the Vulcan goes about halfway through the show, and then it becomes Rom's story. And the fact that the show works as well as it does is due to Max, who really makes you care about Rom. So let's take a moment and salute Max Grodénchik."

The episode called for far more camera setups than usual, due to the very nature of baseball itself. As Lou Race explains, "A simple sentence in the script like, 'Kira hits the ball into right field, rounds first base and slides into second,' had to be broken down into one shot of the pitcher throwing the ball, one shot of Kira hitting, one shot of the right fielder grabbing the ball and throwing it, one shot of Kira rounding first, and one shot of Kira arriving on second. That's five setups for *one* sentence." In order to accomplish the amount of work involved, the producers allotted the episode an eight-day shooting schedule rather than the usual seven. "There were thirty-five pages of baseball in the script," Race notes. "We had to spend five days doing that thirty-five pages. That left the other three days for twenty-seven pages of stage work, so there was tremendous pressure. Chip Chalmers and I broke every baseball play down into its cuts. We shot everything that happens on first base, then we shot everything that happens on second base, and so forth." This approach meant that each of the five setups in the example above might happen on a different day. "Fortunately," notes Race, "all of the actors were into it."

"All of the different setups made this a costuming nightmare," recalls Chalmers, "because we had our characters in three different uniforms. They started out with a sweatshirt look, then went to the practice day, and then to the sparkling new uniforms." For the first look, Brooks and Lofton personally chose the baseball caps they wanted to wear: Brooks picked the San Francisco Giants, Lofton, the Atlanta Braves.

Time-consuming makeup needs for some of the characters also complicated the scheduling, so the filmmakers brought in photo doubles for all of Sisko's team, the Niners. "That way, when we were doing a shot of Kira at second base, with Quark out in center field behind her," says Race, "we could use the photo double so Armin didn't have to be out there, and he could pace himself a little."

"My favorite moment was when I found myself sitting down and eating lunch with three Worfs," Chalmers interjects, "a photo double, a stunt double, and Michael Dorn, all made up as Worf.

"Because we were going to keep Odo behind the

In order to accommodate a baseball cap, a piece of rubber was added to the back of Nog's head. ROBBIE ROBINSON

umpire's mask most of the time," Chalmers continues, "we were able to use a photo double for him most of the time. That way we could always have an Odo behind the plate, even when Rene was in the makeup trailer. In fact, the only time we used Rene was when he was supposed to lift up his mask, or when he was arguing with Sisko."

"I didn't have to work very hard on that show," smiles Rene Auberjonois. "I shot everything I needed to do on the field in one day. The rest of the week I was off shooting the film *Inspector Gadget*."

Finding the right baseball field took a little searching. Eventually, a deal was struck with Los Angeles's Loyola Marymount University, a campus facility located near the ocean. For once, *DS9*'s on-location filming did not call down the weather Pah-wraiths. "We had some nice cool temperatures," Steve Oster reports, sounding surprised at his own words. "We were very lucky. The weather held."

"Shooting in that great weather was a really nice experience," says Nicole deBoer. "I like to play baseball, but I didn't get to bat. The writers kept me way out in the field, but it was still fun." DeBoer's alter ego did have one unique shot: performing a back flip while catching the ball. Of course, that wasn't performed by deBoer—nor was the ball performed by, well, the ball. It was added in postproduction by Visual Effects Animator Kevin Bouchez.

CHRYSALIS

Episode #555

WRITTEN BY RENÉ ECHEVARRIA
DIRECTED BY JONATHAN WEST

GUEST CAST	
Jack	TIM RANSOM
Sarina Douglas	FAITH C. SALIE
Lauren	HILARY SHEPARD-TURNER
Patrick	MICHAEL KEENAN
Nog	ARON EISENBERG
Officer	RANDY JAMES

STARDATE UNKNOWN

It's a lonely night for Dr. Bashir. His best friend O'Brien is having dinner with the wife and kids. Kira and Odo are on their way to a night out at Vic Fontaine's—and they don't want company. With no one else to turn to, Bashir decides to turn in. However, minutes later he gets a call from Nog. An "Admiral Patrick" is in the Infirmary, and he demands to see Bashir immediately.

At the Infirmary, Bashir is greeted by three Starfleet officers—or rather, by three people wearing the uniforms of Starfleet officers. Bashir is stunned to realize that his visitors are Jack, Lauren, and Patrick, the genetically engineered misfits he'd attempted to help a year earlier ("Statistical Probabilities"). They've escaped from the institute to bring Sarina, the fourth member of their group, to Bashir for treatment. Bashir is concerned. He'd considered bringing Sarina to DS9 in order to attempt an experimental surgical procedure that might free her from her catatonic state, but he'd never meant for her friends to escort her, particularly not by running away and impersonating Starfleet officers. After speaking to Sisko, who agrees to smooth Starfleet's ruffled feathers, Bashir gets permission from the Institute to perform the surgery on Sarina. Her friends are allowed to remain on the station for a while, in the hope that their presence will make Sarina more comfortable.

Bashir feels that Sarina's catatonia is due to her visual and auditory faculties being out of sync with her genetically enhanced cerebral cortex. Basically,

Dr. Bashir thinks he's found true love. ROBBIE ROBINSON

she can't process the information that her senses receive. To correct the problem, he'll need to design a neurocortical probe capable of stimulating new synaptic growth in Sarina's brain. O'Brien confesses that an engineering feat like that is beyond his abilities; he can't break the laws of physics. But Jack, Patrick, and Lauren figure out a way to *bend* those laws and come up with precisely the tool Bashir needs. Bashir operates, and the procedure seems to go flawlessly . . . except for the fact that Sarina shows no initial signs of improvement. Five days after surgery, a disappointed Bashir is ready to admit defeat. Suddenly, he spots Sarina standing in the center of the Promenade, staring at her surroundings. Puzzled, Bashir asks the young woman what she's looking at. To his profound amazement, Sarina actually responds. "*Everything*," she says, clearly fascinated by the world around her.

Sarina delights in her new ability to comprehend and communicate. Bashir is moved by the sight of the shy woman who is blossoming before his eyes. After a day of exciting new discoveries, Sarina admits she is afraid to sleep; she fears she'll wake up the way she was before. Bashir reassures her that that part of her life is behind her. As they spend more time together, Bashir is impressed by her keen mind. Here, at last, is a companion who can keep up with him intellectually. Hoping to expand her social circle beyond her dysfunctional companions, Bashir invites her out to an evening with *his* friends. Sarina charms the entire group and later confesses to Bashir that she enjoyed being with people who she knew weren't going to behave outrageously or unpredictably. Bashir gently explains that she no longer belongs with her old friends. When the others go back to the Institute, she won't be going with them. As she ponders the life ahead of her, Bashir suggests that she consider staying on the station, and he seals the thought with a tender kiss.

The next day, Bashir tells O'Brien that Sarina is the woman of his dreams. For years, he has longed to meet someone like himself, genetically enhanced but capable of leading a normal life. O'Brien is happy for his friend, but he warns Bashir that things may be moving too quickly. Bashir shrugs off the comment and goes to tell Jack and company that Sarina won't be returning to the Institute.

He takes her out for another evening at Quark's, but this time Sarina finds being the center of attention somewhat disturbing. Later, Bashir suggests that they go away together for a week. She accepts the invitation, but something is clearly wrong. When she fails to show up for dinner the next night, Bashir finds her sitting alone in her quarters, as withdrawn and unresponsive as she was before the surgery. Medical tests fail to establish why Sarina has relapsed, so Bashir turns to her genetically enhanced friends for help. Although resentful that the doctor has taken her from them, they agree to help. After spending some time with her, they tell Bashir that Sarina can still talk—but for some reason, she's afraid to. Bashir goes to Sarina and begs her to tell him what's wrong. At last she confesses that she doesn't know what to do or what to feel. She *wants* to make Bashir happy, because she feels that she owes him everything, but she doesn't know how.

To his horror, Bashir realizes that he's pushed her into accepting a fantasy of his own making in order to assuage his loneliness. What she really needs is the opportunity to discover who she is, so Bashir arranges for her to receive a position at a research center. There, she'll be able to learn how to deal with others at her own pace. Bidding her a reluctant farewell, Bashir sends Sarina on her voyage of self-discovery.

If the *DS9* viewing audience loved the so-called "Jack Pack" of "Statistical Probabilities," the writing staff loved them even more. "We *always* wanted to bring them back," smiles René Echevarria. With the series firmly entrenched in its final season, it was only a question of when—and how.

"Our initial notion was for Bashir and the Jack Pack to go on a mission together," Echevarria says. "It would be a fish-out-of-water story, where they're on a starship and for some reason they have to pose as Starfleet officers. And I wanted it to have something to do with Section 31. A *One Flew Over the Cuckoo's Nest* kind of story. But Ira didn't like that. It wasn't the right tone."

"It was a cool idea, but we're not good at taking cool ideas and turning them into something," Behr comments. "We're better at looking at characters. We'd come up with all kinds of cockamamie plans for these genetically engineered people, but it got complicated and expensive." Besides the expense, the kicker for Behr, as always, was story. "We didn't have a real ending," he says. "The idea just didn't go anywhere."

So it became more of a character story. "It was going to be a 'Jack' show, where we'd do something like *Flowers for Algernon*," notes Echevarria, referring to Daniel Keyes's story about a retarded man who is turned into a genius via a scientific experiment, only

Although Sarina is intellectually advanced, the writers saw her emotional development on a par with that of a child. ROBBIE ROBINSON

to ultimately revert. "Jack would become normal. And we tried for days to break this story. It boiled down to the fact that it was a tragedy that this guy becomes normal, which kind of glamorizes mental illness. That's a very common sort of Hollywood story. 'Oh, aren't they cute—don't rob them of their originality and make them *normal*.' Which is bull.

"So we were stymied," Echevarria continues. "Time was running out and we were just sitting there. And then all of a sudden Hans [Beimler] said, 'What if it's about Sarina? A love story with her.' And *boom*, that was it."

Sarina had been rendered mute when her dialogue was edited out of "Statistical Probabilities." Now that serendipitous fact was about to bail the writers out of their predicament. Echevarria came up with a script that would more than compensate Actor Faith C. Salie for the disappointment she'd experienced the previous season—but only if she was up to the job.

"I had to go through a few hoops," Salie admits. "The producers were concerned because this was such a big featured part and I had not done much in the first episode. Before offering it to me, they auditioned me. But to be fair to them, they didn't call in anyone else."

"We certainly didn't want to recast, but we did bring Faith in to read," recalls Echevarria. "It must have been incredibly stressful for her. She had a role that was hers to *lose*. But within seconds of her reading, we knew she was in."

"We suspected that Faith would be fine," notes Behr. "I'd seen her do some children's theater, and I knew she was a very intelligent woman."

Had they known at the time just *how* intelligent Salie is, they might not have questioned her ability in the first place. The actress had studied theater at Northwestern University before transferring to Harvard, where she earned a degree in history and literature of modern France and England. After that, she was named a Rhodes scholar, an honor that carried her to Oxford University, where she secured her master's degree. Curiously, Salie confesses, she hadn't liked majoring in theater. "It wasn't what I wanted out of a college education," the actor says, laughing. However, it certainly didn't hurt her in the long run!

Although she'd played Sarina before, Salie had not developed a personality for the character. Now the producers had a very specific idea of what that personality should be. "They explained to me that she should have no subtext," Salie comments, "which is a very unusual feature for a character. As an actor,

you're taught to dig, dig, dig, to find what's underneath the lines and to know the backstory, because often a character might be saying something that she doesn't really mean. But with Sarina, there was none of that. She was guileless. She hadn't been around enough to learn about disingenuousness or even flirtation. The undercurrent in almost every scene in film or television between a man and a woman is one of some sort of flirtation or sexual attraction. But I was told specifically to take that out of my scenes with Bashir. In no way was I supposed to relate to him flirtatiously. It sounds like a simple task—'Just say the line and mean it'—but that was hard to play, because we're never trained to take lines at face value."

The scene in which the newly awakened Sarina takes in the sights of the Promenade was much easier for Salie. "The word used in the script's stage direction was 'astonished,'" Salie says. "Well, the way the soundstage was set up, that wasn't hard to play! The Promenade set just bombards you with colors and flags, and I was surrounded by aliens. And," she grins, "it's always very exciting to have the camera right in your face. I'm not over *that* yet."

Director Jonathan West gave her another useful stage direction for the scene. "Jonathan called that shot the 'Maria moment,'" Salie recalls. "The camera was going to zoom down on my face when my mouth was wide open. Jonathan said, 'Just think about Maria on top of the mountain in *The Sound of Music*, twirling around and around.'"

The episode included a first for *Deep Space Nine*—an extended musical sequence. "It was extremely difficult," says West. "Shooting it was kind of like doing a music video. I listened to the music and literally choreographed where the actors would come from and where the camera would move to. I wanted to make it move a lot, and if you look at the sequence, you'll see that I never shot a master of everything that happens. I always have one person leading into somebody else, which leads to somebody else, and then flows with the music."

The music sequence was Echevarria's favorite part of the show, and the one for which he fought the hardest. "When Sarina comes in and speaks to her friends for the first time, everyone gets excited. At first I had them all start to waltz, like they had in the previous episode," he says. "But since I'd already done that, I was bored with it. I decided to try something entirely different." It struck him that Sarina should have a bit of a vocalization problem when she begins talking—but it should be something that he could dispense with very quickly. "That's why I thought they should start singing," Echevarria says. "Now the scene establishes the vocal problem, gets away from it, and shows everybody's joy. And most importantly, we fall in love with Sarina and we certainly see Julian falling in love with her. I was just delighted with the scene in the script, but Ira was skeptical."

Behr admits that he didn't quite get it. "René kept explaining it to me, and showing it to me on paper, but I was still unconvinced." However, it did serve to raise the visibility of the rest of the Jack Pack—something Behr had been concerned about—so he allowed Echevarria to have his way. In the end, Behr admits, "I saw that I had been wrong. When I saw it on-screen, it worked."

The task of writing the musical piece fell to Composer Jay Chattaway. "The producers called me with the assignment on a Thursday," Chattaway recalls with a laugh. "They said, 'You've got two minutes of screen time to take this woman from not being able to speak properly to gradually having her recoup all her intellectual capacity and ultimately become a coloratura soprano in a piece of music that has to represent a genetically perfect society, has to be like a Bach fugue, can only use the Do, Re, Mi syllable scale, can't sound like 'Do, a Deer,' and has to be brilliant. And it shoots next Tuesday!' I said, 'Okay,'" the composer says chuckling.

Chattaway composed the piece as a motet, a vocal form that developed in the Middle Ages. "I recorded a keyboard demo and the producers approved it," he says. "We scheduled a rehearsal for Monday, thinking everything was fine. But when the cast came in, two of them couldn't read music! They could sing, but this piece wasn't like a show tune. It was a pretty complicated deal. So we had to schedule a lot of extra rehearsals, and finally they got it. And they got it with such pride that it was fascinating."

As it turned out, Faith Salie, the performer about whom the producers had worried most, was the most proficient vocalist. "As soon as I read about the singing in the script I was so excited," she says, "because I'm musically trained. I don't think any of the other actors enjoyed doing it as much as I did."

Actress Hilary Shepard-Turner, reprising Lauren, had sung in an all-girl punk band during the 1980s, but she admits that she found this difficult. "I can read music and sing," she says, "but this was really hard. The song stuck in my head for months. I just thought it was very bizarre to be on *Star Trek* dancing in one episode and singing in the next."

"The music was more lovely than I'd imagined it," says Echevarria.
ROBBIE ROBINSON

Michael Keenan, the actor who played Patrick, was philosophical about the musical challenge. "They didn't audition us for the scene; it was just there. So I thought, 'Well, either we do it right or they dub it later,'" he says, bursting into laughter.

The scene presented the biggest challenge for Actor Tim Ransom, Jack. "I'm not a singer at all!" he shouts. "And you can ask the person who had to dub my voice."

Or you could ask costar Shepard-Turner. "Tim! Oh, my God! He's tone deaf and he was singing right in my ear!" she recounts in amusement.

"Faith and Hilary and Michael are singers," Ransom continues. "I, however, am barely comfortable singing in the shower! So that was a frustrating shooting day—but not as frustrating as the looping session when we actually tried to lay the tracks in. The other three had enough talent to do it, so I'm the only one on there who had to be dubbed." In retrospect, Ransom has final thoughts on the whole sequence. "René Echevarria is a good friend of mine," the actor grins. "But I curse his name for writing that scene. That was so frigging hard!"

In spite of Behr's skepticism and Ransom's curse, Echevarria remembers the sequence fondly. "Jonathan did a very lovely job of choreographing it, and doing matching images on Julian and Sarina," he says. "Then he began to focus on her, and the wonderful fact is that she had the best voice in that group. The scene just began to soar. I could not have been happier," Echevarria says ardently. "In fact, it's one of my happiest moments in *Star Trek*."

TREACHERY, FAITH, AND THE GREAT RIVER

Episode #556

TELEPLAY BY DAVID WEDDLE &
BRADLEY THOMPSON
STORY BY PHILIP KIM
DIRECTED BY STEVE POSEY

GUEST CAST

Weyoun	JEFFREY COMBS
Damar	CASEY BIGGS
General Martok	J.G. HERTZLER
Nog	ARON EISENBERG
Rom	MAX GRODÉNCHIK
Female Shape-shifter	SALOME JENS

STARDATE UNKNOWN

Odo is skeptical when he receives a coded message from Gul Russol, one of his most reliable informants. Russol was executed when Cardassia joined the Dominion, or so Odo had thought. Yet now Russol—if that's who it is—is asking Odo to meet him on a desolate moon. It could be a trap, but Odo decides to go anyway, if only to learn the truth. At the rendezvous point, Odo does not find Russol, but Weyoun. It was a ruse, the Vorta admits, but it was the only way he could think to lure Odo to a meeting. To Odo's surprise, Weyoun announces that he would like to defect!

Back on DS9, Chief O'Brien is in dire straits. He's hip-deep in station repairs and Sisko has ordered him to get the *Defiant's* gravity net up and running by the time he returns from a conference in three days. Unfortunately, the graviton stabilizer that O'Brien needs to accomplish the repairs won't be available for three *weeks*. But Nog thinks he can help, if the chief is willing to leave everything to him.

Soon the chief suspects that Nog's help is going to get him in even deeper trouble. After Nog obtains O'Brien's authorization code, the young Ferengi begins wheeling and dealing for the stabilizer in the chief's name. Not long after, Captain Sisko's desk disappears from the station. Nog explains that it's on loan to Al Lorenzo, the chief of operations on Decos Prime, who wants to take a holopicture of himself sitting behind it. In exchange for the loan, Lorenzo will give O'Brien an induction modulator, which O'Brien can trade to the *U.S.S. Musashi* for a phaser emitter. The phaser emitter will go to the *U.S.S. Sentinel*, which has the stabilizer O'Brien needs.

O'Brien is near panic. How does Nog know that

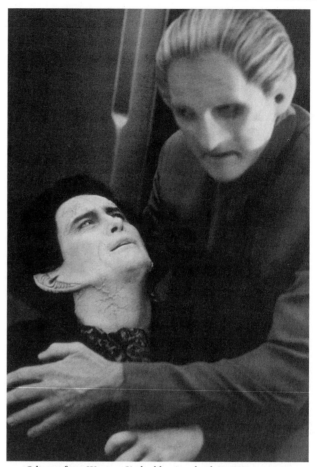

Odo comforts Weyoun Six by blessing the dying Vorta. ROBBIE ROBINSON

any of this will work out? Nog tells the chief to trust in the Great Material Continuum. The Ferengi believe that the Continuum flows through the universe like a river, bringing the items that people have to the people who want them. And the river, Nog explains, will provide O'Brien's stabilizer.

On the barren moon, Weyoun's offer to trade valuable information about the Dominion in exchange for asylum in the Federation is too good to pass up. Odo agrees to take Weyoun back to Deep Space 9, but before they get very far, they receive a transmission from Cardassia. Odo stares at the viewscreen in amazement; the transmission is from Damar *and Weyoun*—Weyoun clone number seven, to be precise. The Weyoun who is seated in the runabout with Odo is Weyoun Six. Apparently the Weyoun that Odo had dealt with in the past—Weyoun Five—is dead, the victim of an unfortunate "accident." Weyoun Six had been activated to replace him, but was judged "defective" because of his lack of faith in the Founders' war against the Federation. Six escaped, and Weyoun Seven was activated to take his place. Now that Seven has found him, he orders Six to trigger his termination implant, something all Vorta clones have within their brains. When Six refuses, Damar vows to prevent the runabout from returning to Deep Space 9 with the errant clone aboard.

Soon a Jem'Hadar fighter appears and begins firing on the vessel, making it clear that Damar is deadly serious. Weyoun Six provides Odo with information about the attacking vessel's weaknesses, allowing him to destroy it. As they continue their journey, the Vorta tells Odo the story of how his people came to be linked with the Founders. They were nothing more than timid, apelike tree dwellers when they saw their first shape-shifter, fleeing from a mob of angry "solids." A family of Vorta hid the changeling from his pursuers, and the grateful changeling promised that someday his people would transform the Vorta into powerful beings that would play an important role in a great new empire. And with the Founders' advanced bioengineering skills, a new species of Vorta was created.

After Odo expresses satisfaction that his people are capable of some degree of kindness, Weyoun makes a startling revelation: the Founders are dying, victims of a mysterious illness that has spread through the entire Great Link. Odo seems to be the only changeling who is unaffected. But even as Odo ponders this information, the runabout is set upon by four more Jem'Hadar ships. He takes the small vessel into an asteroid belt, hides it within a large chunk of ice, and shuts down the power. But within a few hours, the Jem'Hadar have flushed them out of their hiding place and they're on the run again.

Odo evades his pursuers as well as he can, but Weyoun Six can see that their plight is hopeless. Hoping to save Odo's life, Six contacts his counterpart and asks him to call off the attack. Then, as Weyoun Seven watches on the viewscreen, Six activates his termination implant. Satisfied, Weyoun Seven withdraws the Jem'Hadar ships. Six asks Odo to give him one thing before he dies—his blessing. Although Odo despises the idea that the Vorta view the Founders as gods, he grants Weyoun Six's last wish. The Vorta dies peacefully, leaving Odo with the depressing thought that if his people *are* dying, no matter which side wins the war, he's going to lose.

Back on DS9, O'Brien's three days are up and Sisko calls him in for an update. O'Brien approaches Sisko's office with great trepidation, uncertain if it contains a desk. To his great relief, he finds that the missing piece of furniture is back. What's more, Nog has already informed the captain that they have the new stabilizer and are ready to install it. As Nog had predicted, faith in the Great River has paid off.

With the "end-of-the-series" clock ticking ever louder, Ira Behr was determined to bring to fruition every titillating storyline— and every potential team-up—that had been languishing in the writing staff's collective consciousness. Key among those ideas was a personal favorite of Behr's. "I *really* wanted to do an Odo/Weyoun show," he says. "I love Rene and I love Jeff, and I just thought it would be great." The writers had been toying with a concept about sabotaging a Jem'Hadar cloning hatchery since the sixth season. Perhaps *that* would serve? Behr let everyone on the *DS9* staff know of his desire. "I was going around saying, 'Somebody get me an Odo/Weyoun show!'" Behr laughs.

Production Assistant Philip Kim heard about Behr's search. But he was inspired more by the idea of the Jem'Hadar hatchery than he was by a changeling/Vorta team-up. "I pitched it as a Weyoun/Sisko story," Kim notes. "Weyoun approaches Sisko to ask for his help, saying that the Founders are breeding a new race of warriors called the Modain. They would make the Jem'Hadar look like Boy Scouts. Weyoun tells Sisko that the Modain are meant to replace the Jem'Hadar. He suggests that it would be in both his and Sisko's interests to destroy these things. For the sake of the Federation, Sisko very reluctantly agrees to help Weyoun. But after the two of them lay waste to this breeding facility, Sisko discovers that Weyoun's been manipulating him. The Modain were not meant to replace the Jem'Hadar. They were meant to replace the *Vorta.* Weyoun had stumbled upon the blueprints for the phasing-out of his entire race."

Kim's pitch had all of the elements Behr had been looking for—except, of course, for Odo. However, that was an easy fix. The concept of the breeding facility, or "hatchery," evolved into some references to the Vorta cloning process. And the idea that the Vorta are being replaced by the Modain became a plot about Weyoun Six being replaced by Weyoun Seven. Odo may have felt that the universe wasn't "ready for two Weyouns," but Ira Behr was. "The idea of having two Weyouns just sounded nutty," he says. "And it also sounded great, because Jeff Combs would play both of them."

"It was quite fun to have conversations with myself, I must tell you," Combs says. "Both Weyouns

About the name Al Lorenzo, Behr explains, "I wanted a name that didn't sound Starfleet or twenty-fourth century." ROBBIE ROBINSON

knew each other's games, so there was a mutual awareness as well as a mutual disdain. One Weyoun was defective, but that didn't mean that he was weak or that he wasn't manipulative or that he couldn't see what the other Weyoun is doing. Finding the right balance was tricky, so it really was my most challenging show. I would say to myself, 'Okay, now, how would *that* Weyoun say that line and how would *this* Weyoun react to it?'"

Because Combs already knew the original Weyoun personality inside and out, the heart of his challenge was to define the "defective" character. "I tried to make him a Weyoun of a different color," the actor explains, "a Weyoun who could align himself with the Federation and see the flaws in his leaders. This actually appealed to me. I've always thought that Weyoun had some innate goodness in him somewhere. It's just difficult finding it because the Vorta are genetically designed to be loyal. But one person's defectiveness is another person's enlightenment. He was blind but now he could see. And for that, he was labeled a 'problem.' That was fun to play," Combs says. "I thought of each Weyoun as a different slice of

the same pizza. One just didn't have any pepperoni on it."

While fleshing out the idea of an "enlightened" Vorta, Bradley Thompson and David Weddle recognized a contemporary metaphor for the nature of his defect. "In the past, when we've lost a Weyoun, we've gotten an identical one as his replacement, we assume because they download their memories every so often into some kind of 'brain jar,'" Thompson hypothesizes. "It's just like backing up a computer program. You still have what you had the previous time you backed it up. But if you have a bad disk or something like that, it's going to be a corrupted copy."

But coming up with the technological raison d'être behind Weyoun Six was easy. "The difficult thing was to bring a level of depth to his story," David Weddle says. "Ira finally hit upon the idea of telling the story behind how the Vorta formed their alliance with the Founders. It was brilliant. It was the one thing that we needed."

"The episode called for it," Behr says with a shrug. "I like to get the audience thinking one way about a character or a race, making them think that these are definitely the bad guys. Then you slip something like this in so they have to reevaluate the opinion you've already given them. These are still the bad guys, but now, at least, you understand something about why. So I just loved that the Vorta, this calculating, Machiavellian race, started out as Hobbit-like cute little creatures who were genetically altered and directed to do these horrible things."

The Vorta religion, the "faith" reference in the title, carried the most weight in the episode for Behr. "We wanted to have Odo accept on some level that he is a god," Behr says. "And then have Kira, a person whom Odo does give credence to, tell him the same thing at the end of the show. It's kind of mind-blowing for him. You'd think that Kira would support Odo's point of view, but she doesn't because she's another 'true believer.' It's quite complex stuff for television."

By accepting, like it or not, that he plays a role in the Vortas' faith, Odo must accept his identity as a Founder. And with that acceptance, the character took his first step into the writers' ultimate plans for him. "We knew that we wanted Odo to go back to his people," Behr notes. "And giving the Founders an illness seemed to give him a reason to do that. To save them. The idea that the hero goes to save the villain is nicely complicated."

In a completely different way, the episode's B-story was equally complicated. "There was a tragic element to the Weyoun/Odo story," points out Director Steve Posey, who joined the *Star Trek* fold with this episode. "The Nog/O'Brien story was comic, so I guess you could think of it as the B-story. But I think that they are equally important stories. The light story was no less important to the success of the show as a whole."

The B-story, admittedly inspired by *Catch 22*, came about because writers Weddle and Thompson are ardent fans of the famous Joseph Heller novel. "Brad practically can quote *Catch 22* word for word," Weddle laughs. "I had reread it just before we started working on this episode and Ira read it shortly after me. As we were talking about the B-story, Ira said, 'Why don't we do one in which Nog is like Milo Minderbinder.' Of course, Brad and I loved that idea."

Minderbinder, Heller's mess officer turned syndicate boss, runs the entire second World War as a business venture. "We decided not to take Nog *that* far," Weddle notes. "That would have besmirched the character too much, so we reined it in."

Aron Eisenberg, who plays Nog, saw the role as an opportunity to define his character even further than he'd done to date. "This was Nog taking the

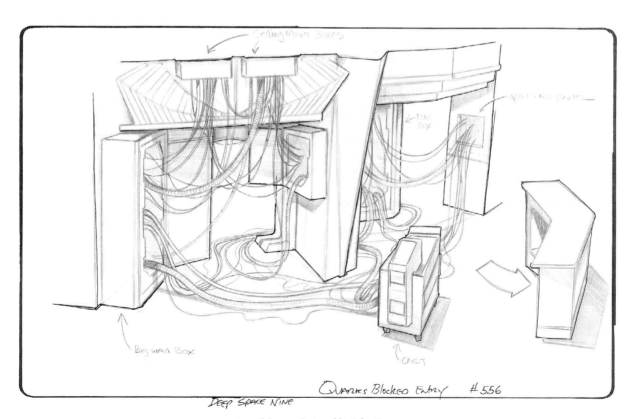

An artful mess designed by John Eaves.

The writers compelled Odo to look at who he was. ROBBIE ROBINSON

GUEST CAST

Kor	JOHN COLICOS
General Martok	J.G. HERTZLER
Darok	NEIL VIPOND
Kolana	NANCY YOUNGBLUT
Synon	BLAKE LINDSLEY

STARDATE UNKNOWN

same energy and Ferengi ideals he'd had before he joined Starfleet and incorporating them into his goals in Starfleet," Eisenberg comments. "What I love about having an honest Ferengi in Starfleet is that he knows how to manipulate the situation. In Starfleet, you go through certain channels to get things done. It's all very official. Nog just feels that you don't have to. You can do it this way and it works just as easily and it's *much* faster. He thinks it's perfectly natural to do this. No one else in Starfleet would have done things this way except Nog. It would be interesting to see Nog as a captain someday, and see how he would use his Ferengi philosophy to deal with a threat. He would deal with it completely differently than Kirk, Picard, Janeway, or Sisko."

For one thing, it's unlikely that any of those illustrious captains would have thought of trading away their superior officer's desk. And, in fact, the writing staff was a little uncertain about how well the idea would play. "I was the only person in the world who thought that gag was going to work," Behr laughs. "It was just a little riff on fandom, on the guy who wants to sit in Picard's chair. Everyone thought I had lost my mind, but I thought it was funny."

While some elements of the B-story fit the classic "torture O'Brien" category of episodes, Behr says that was not the intention. "It's less torture O'Brien than it is torture Colm Meaney," the executive producer says, chuckling. "Colm has a hard time having his character being told stuff by *Ensign* Nog. He's very serious about his role. But he wound up playing it great, and I think it's one of the best B-stories we ever did."

One night at the bar, O'Brien and Bashir are engaged in a friendly debate regarding the death of Davy Crockett. There seems to be no way to resolve the discussion until Worf offers his personal belief that one either believes in a legend or he doesn't. If he does, then he accepts *all* of the details that make the man a legend, and that settles that.

Later, Worf is visited by a Klingon warrior that both he and his late wife Jadzia considered a legend: Kor, the *Dahar* Master. Kor's visit isn't purely social. He has a favor to ask. In the twilight of his years, Kor finds that his services as a warrior are not required, despite the fact that his entire race is locked into a great conflict against the Dominion. He no longer has any influence in the Klingon Empire, and would like Worf to help him find a position where he can fight and die like a Klingon.

Touched by Kor's plight, Worf promises to secure him a commission with General Martok. But to Worf's great surprise, Martok refuses. Years before, the general explains, Kor denied Martok officer status, simply because he was a commoner. Martok eventually won a battlefield commission, but he never forgave Kor. Worf understands the general's feelings. However, he used his own authority to appoint Kor third officer on the *Ch'Tang*, Martok's flagship. The general tells him that what's done is done and that Kor will be *Worf's* responsibility.

Before Kor leaves, he has the opportunity to encounter his old friend Dax, in its new host, Ezri. Later, Ezri tells Kira that a part of her wishes she could accompany Kor on his mission, so that they could be together again. Quark, overhearing the conversation, mistakenly believes that Ezri is talking about getting together again with *Worf*, which the Ferengi thinks is a terrible idea. Eventually, Quark builds up his nerve and

After Kor endangers the Klingon fleet, Martok's crew mocks the aging *Dahar* Master. ROBBIE ROBINSON

tells Ezri that she should forget about pursuing Worf, and leave herself open to *new* relationships. Bemused, Ezri tells him that she isn't interested in another relationship with Worf, but she finds Quark's concern very dear. This wasn't the reaction Quark expected, but he's ecstatic. Clearly Ezri is mad about *him*!

As the *Ch'Tang* prepares to lead a small fleet against the Dominion, Martok's crew learns that Kor will be serving aboard their vessel. Much to the general's annoyance, they treat Kor with deep respect and are enthralled by tales of his heroic battles. But unbeknownst to the crew, Kor is no longer up to such battles. His memory is poor, and he frequently mistakes past for present. During a fierce attack on a Dominion starbase, both Worf and Martok are incapacitated, leaving Kor in command. The old Klingon is more than willing to step into the breach, and he continues the attack in ernest, acting out a battle from the distant past.

Unfortunately, Martok's strategy had called for a hit-and-run attack. The extended battle weakens the Klingon fleet and threatens to destroy the *Ch'Tang*, but Kor fights on until Worf recovers sufficiently to call a retreat. Enraged, Martok banishes Kor from the bridge. Later, Worf tells a devastated Kor that he is no longer up to the challenge of active duty. Making matters worse, Martok's crew taunts the old man. But although Martok has dreamed of seeing Kor friendless, stripped of his rank and title, he admits to Worf that he took no joy from witnessing fulfillment of that fantasy. However, he has little time to ponder this turn of events. Sensors reveal that their vessel is being pursued by ten Jem'Hadar fighters.

The crew estimates that the fighters will catch up to them in two hours, when it is certain they will overpower Martok's small fleet. The combined forces of the *Defiant* and seven other starships await Martok's fleet in the Kalandra Sector, but it will take three hours and forty-five minutes to reach them. Worf notes that if the Jem'Hadar could be forced to drop out of warp for just ten minutes, they wouldn't have time to catch the fleet before its rendezvous with Federation forces. The only way to execute such a plan is to have one of the Klingon ships serve as a decoy to engage the Jem'Hadar while the rest of the fleet moves on. Worf volunteers for the assignment, despite the fact that it means certain death.

Overhearing the plan, Martok's aide Darok, who greatly admires Kor, relates the strategy to the *Dahar* Master. Kor realizes that Darok is offering him the opportunity to redeem himself by saving the others, and to die a glorious death. He intercepts Worf, knocks him out, and beams over to the other ship. As the crew of the *Ch'Tang* looks on, Kor performs precisely as planned, holding off the enemy, ten ships to one, until at last his vessel is overwhelmed. Recognizing his great sacrifice, Martok is the first to toast the old man, and the crew remembers the bravery of Kor, *Dahar* Master.

Heroes. Warriors. Legends. The end of an era. And what better way to tell the tale than to invoke a little Shakespeare in the title: "*Once more unto the breach, dear friends . . . when the blast of war blows in our ears . . .*" (KING HENRY V).

"We'd been talking about the end of the series, and what plot lines and character threads we'd need to tie up," recalls Ron Moore. "We felt that we'd like to see Kor one more time."

And so it was that Moore tackled Kor's last appearance in *Star Trek*—or at least what one can *assume* will be his last appearance if one takes the episode's opening teaser at its word. "At the beginning of the episode," says Moore, "we start out talking about Davy Crockett and the Alamo, and how the debate continues: Did he surrender? Was he executed? Did he die on the Alamo walls, swinging his flintlock over his head? It depends on whether he's a hero or not, or if he's a legend to you. If he is, then he went out a hero. If you don't think that, then he's just another guy and it doesn't matter how he died.

"It felt like we could send Kor out the same way," he continues. "It doesn't really matter how Kor died.

The script jibed with J.G. Hertzler's feelings about why Martok behaves as he does. ROBBIE ROBINSON

It doesn't really matter what he did in those final moments of his life. What matters is the legend."

In this case, the Alamo tie-in was a natural. Some months earlier, Moore relates, "Ira had given all of us a copy of an article that speculated about Crockett's death, with all the conflicting reports and the diaries and the whole debate in academia about whether or not they could determine if he'd died at the Alamo. And it stuck with me. I wanted to work the material into the episode somehow, because I liked what it said about myths and heroes, and how warriors die under mysterious circumstances. As I was approaching the teaser scene, it seemed like such a natural tie-in, that I put it in." Worf's speech about the death of heroes, which mirrors Moore's comments above, serves as a fitting epitaph.

As for the rest of the story, Moore notes that the writing staff "thought that it would be interesting if Kor had a conflict with Martok. I stumbled onto the idea of making it a class thing between them. That just felt right with their personalities. John Colicos always played Kor as an aristocratic and 'to the manner born' Klingon who ruled by 'divine right.' J.G. Hertzler always made Martok seem like a *guy*, like a common soldier who has worked his way up through the ranks. So there was a natural antipathy between the two characters."

"That worked like gangbusters for me," Hertzler says enthusiastically. "I'm basically from a blue-collar family. My father started as a mechanic in the Air Force. He rose to become a colonel, but he still was a director of maintenance. We had a work-oriented home, and I believe that's what Martok's life was like. It was a soldierly, military family that never had any officers. Combined with what I'd already developed in my own mind as backstory, Ron's take all made sense to me."

Needless to say, "Once More Unto the Breach" stands out in Hertzler's mind. "It's my favorite *Deep Space Nine* script," he says. "It was an actor's dream. I got to really let loose my most venomous, vindictive anger at this old man, and just attack him relentlessly. I think that made some of the viewers uncomfortable, because it was hard to like Martok in those scenes, but we all do things that people don't like. It made my character three-dimensional, so I was happy."

And although Kor ultimately proves that he has what it takes to enter *Sto-Vo-Kor*, warrior heaven, Hertzler didn't want his character to alter his feelings about the old man. "I told the producers that Martok shouldn't join in singing the ballad at the end," the

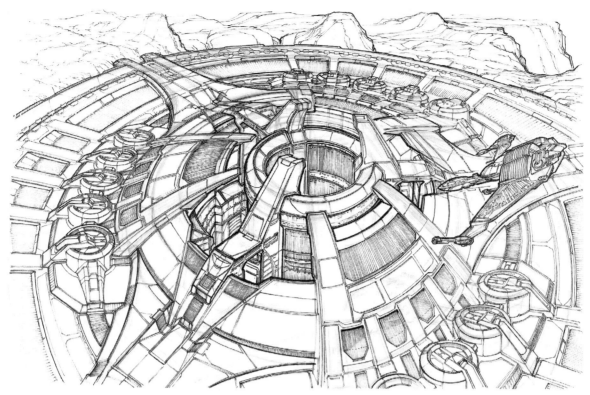

A suggestion of how the strafing run could look. JOHN EAVES

actor comments. "They were worried about that, but I said 'Listen, Martok can give Kor all the due praise, but he cannot sing to him because the hatred is still there, underneath. He does not forgive what that man did.' I thought that was more important for my character than bringing him all the way around. I wanted to leave that shoe unfallen."

For Director Allan Kroeker and Actor Nicole deBoer, working with esteemed fellow Canadian Colicos was a real treat. "I first saw John in *Anne of the Thousand Days* in 1969," Kroeker says. "He's someone that we Canadians are very proud of. I had never met him before, so I was scared! I said, 'Man, he always plays tough guys in movies!' But he turned out to be a real sweetheart to work with."

DeBoer had worked with Colicos on her prior series, *Beyond Reality*. "He remembered me," she says. "At least," she adds with a chuckle, "I *think* he did, unless he was being polite."

Although the episode focuses primarily on the interaction aboard the bird-of-prey, deBoer appears in several scenes, including one where she discusses Kor with Kira. This ties into a later scene in which Quark, under the mistaken impression that Ezri was discussing a different Klingon, advises the young Trill to stay away from Worf. The encounter typified much of Quark's

character arc during the series' final season. "For the most part," says Armin Shimerman, the Ferengi's alter ego, "the season is about Quark either mourning Jadzia or pursuing Ezri." But the actor knew that it was all for naught. "The audience would never accept them as a couple, so there was never a chance for that," he sighs. "So I spent most of the season crying into my own drinks, woeing the fact that I was getting nowhere with Ezri." A touch of the spurned suitor creeps into his voice as he points out that "everybody *else* on the show seemed to get somewhere with her."

In the original version of the episode, Quark really *did* spend some time crying into his drink. "There was a middle scene that got dropped," Moore reveals. "We shot it, but it got cut for time. The bar was closed and for a change, Quark was sitting on a barstool, while Jake was trying to mix Quark a drink. Quark is just pouring out his troubles, going on about, 'Why does this always happen to me? I'm not a bad guy. Now she's with that idiot again.' It was a real 'Woe is me' speech that was a lot of fun. In the meantime, Jake is listening and offering advice, and he keeps screwing up the drink and pouring it out and starting over again. It's too bad that it got cut, because the B-story wound up kind of thin."

Other lengthy speeches did survive the editing

The stratification of Klingon society mentioned here would be revisited later in the season. ROBBIE ROBINSON

kind of standing here on the set.' I told him, 'You're absolutely right and I'm sorry. We'll get you into the year somehow.' And we did," Moore adds happily. "We gave him a whole arc at the end of the series."

One new piece of Dominion technology was invented for the episode: a long-range tachyon scanner to detect the Klingons' cloaked ships. "I had to establish a way for them to penetrate their cloak, otherwise there wouldn't have been much jeopardy for most of the show," explains Moore. Of course, this meant that he and the other writers might have to deal with this new Dominion capability in subsequent episodes if they wanted their facts to be consistent. "It is the kind of thing that gets fans' attention," he admits. "So we talked about it and decided that if it came up later, we could legitimately fall back on the idea that as technologies advance, counter-technologies advance along with them, and then counter-counter-technologies follow. We figured that was a little dance we could have keep going for a long time."

process. "Ron really loves speechifying," Ira Behr smiles. "And he's great at it. We were cracking up while we were watching the dailies, because it's *so* Ron."

Guilty as charged, admits Moore. "I started to notice it in my writing when I did 'The Darkness and the Light,' with Kira sitting in the Infirmary giving this long monologue about how she joined the Resistance. Ever since then I've enjoyed finding places where I can just let the character go on. It's very theatrical, in a way. It's not done a lot on television anymore."

Unfortunately, one character gets shortchanged in the episode, with neither lengthy speech nor great heroics to fall back upon. "Worf is a bit of a third wheel," points out Behr, another charge that Moore agrees with. "That was unfortunate."

"When I was writing it," says Moore, "I thought that Worf was central to the drama, and so I trapped him between Martok and Kor. But he wound up on the short end of the stick, and Michael Dorn called me on it. He pulled me aside down on the stage and said, 'Let me tell you, I love this script. I think it's a *wonderful* script, but it's really not about Worf. I'm just

THE SIEGE OF AR-558

Episode #558

WRITTEN BY IRA STEVEN BEHR & HANS BEIMLER
DIRECTED BY WINRICH KOLBE

GUEST CAST

Vargas	RAYMOND CRUZ
Reese	PATRICK KILPATRICK
Nog	ARON EISENBERG
Larkin	ANNETTE HELDE
Rom	MAX GRODÉNCHIK

SPECIAL GUEST STARS

Kellin	BILL MUMY
Vic Fontaine	JAMES DARREN

STARDATE UNKNOWN

On the eve of an important supply run to the front lines, Dr. Bashir stops by Vic Fontaine's holographic nightclub to pick up an audio recording of Vic's greatest hits. The tunes may be old, Bashir assures Vic, but to the troops at the front, they'll sound brand-new.

The *Defiant* speeds toward its destination, a barren planet known only as AR-558. Accompanying the crew is one unhappy civilian, Quark, assigned by the

As Jem'Hadar troops approach, Sisko and the others await the inevitable. ROBBIE ROBINSON

nagus to analyze conditions at the front from a Ferengi perspective. The trip to the planet, located in the Chin'toka System, isn't exactly quiet. Although the Federation now controls the region ("Tears of the Prophets"), the Dominion is eager to retake it, and Jem'Hadar attacks are frequent.

Leaving Worf in command of the *Defiant*, Sisko, Ezri, Nog, Bashir, and Quark beam down to the small base camp. They're greeted by Chief Nadia Larkin, ranking officer following the deaths of her captain and commander. Tensions run high among Larkin's people, who've been attacked repeatedly by Jem'Hadar soldiers trying to reclaim the former Dominion facility. The shell-shocked troops have spent five difficult months guarding the base's prize: the largest Dominion array in the sector. If Starfleet can figure out how it works, the Federation will be able to tap into the enemy's entire com system. But the Dominion is determined to prevent that from happening. With over two-thirds of the company killed, Larkin is uncertain how much longer they can hold out without reinforcements.

After Sisko's crew unloads some much-needed supplies, Bashir expresses concern over the mental health of the troops. Unfortunately, with Starfleet's forces spread thin by the war, there's nothing anyone can do to help. Sisko's crew learns about a danger as great as that of attacking Jem'Hadar: "Houdini" mines, so called because they "hide" in subspace and appear at random. The insidious devices have claimed the lives of many of Larkin's people.

The captain receives a transmission from Worf,

who informs him that the *Defiant* is under attack by Jem'Hadar ships. At the same time, Sisko learns that Jem'Hadar troops are landing near the base camp, preparing to attack the beleaguered group once again. The captain makes a difficult decision. He tells Worf to take evasive action and get the *Defiant* out of danger. Sisko and the others will be staying on AR-558.

The group awaits the inevitable attack of the Jem'Hadar ground forces. When the enemy soldiers show up, the Starfleet officers begin firing. But they quickly realize that the Jem'Hadar soldiers are only holograms, sent in to draw fire and determine troop strength without risking casualties. After another Starfleet officer is felled by a Houdini, Sisko assigns Ezri and a young engineer named Kellin to find a way to detect and disarm the mines. Then the captain sends Nog, Larkin, and a battle-hardened soldier named Reese on a scouting patrol to pinpoint the enemy's location.

Quark is incensed. Why should Sisko send a young cadet like Nog when there are so many veterans to choose from? The choice is obvious to Sisko. With Starfleet tricorders out of commission—jammed by the enemy—he's counting on Nog's sensitive Ferengi ears to detect the Jem'Hadar. Quark notes that Sisko wouldn't be so quick to send Jake out on the assignment, but Sisko replies that Jake, unlike Nog, isn't a Starfleet officer.

Nog is instrumental in discovering the Jem'Hadar camp, where Jem'Hadar soldiers outnumber Sisko's forces three to one. But as they head back to report their findings, Larkin is killed by enemy fire, and Nog catches a phaser bolt in his leg. Reese carries the injured Ferengi back to base camp, where Bashir tends to his injury. A short time later, Quark angrily informs Sisko that Nog will lose his leg.

The group receives its first bit of good news when Ezri and Kellin figure out a way to make the Houdinis materialize. But rather than disarming them, Sisko has them relocated to a ravine that's located between them and the Jem'Hadar troops. When the enemy passes through, the odds will be a little more in their favor. As the Starfleet officers prepare to face the remaining attack forces, Bashir puts on Vic's music to soothe their nerves. Soon they hear the sound of multiple explosions coming from the ravine, and then a brief moment of silence. Then the main onslaught begins.

All becomes chaos as the casualties quickly mount on both sides. After the Jem'Hadar soldiers break through the main defensive line, fighting becomes hand-to-hand. Kellin dies while saving Ezri's life. Quark kills a soldier who bursts into the makeshift infirmary. Sisko rescues Bashir from a nearly fatal attack, but is himself incapacitated when he catches a rifle butt on the back of his head. When he comes to, Sisko discovers that Starfleet forces managed to retain control of the camp, but at a heavy price. Fortunately, reinforcements have arrived, and the survivors of the battle of AR-558 can leave. A somber Sisko reflects on the toll that was paid to retain control of the outpost, and notes that they must never forget the names of those who died protecting the Alpha Quadrant.

Perhaps no episode stretched the parameters of *Star Trek*'s philosophy of a peaceful future more than "The Siege of AR-558." Certainly Production #558 caused the most discussion behind the scenes at the studio. "A lot of people didn't want us to do the episode, and a lot of people were unhappy as it was being developed," says Ira Behr. "But I felt that we needed to do it. War sucks. War is intolerable. War is painful, and good people die. You win, but you still lose. And we needed to show that as uncompromisingly as possible."

This isn't the first time the writing staff has commented on the cruelty and futility of war, but it is the most overt. "'Rocks and Shoals' was a terrific show," comments Behr, "but I don't think we went quite far enough. The idea there was that war isn't just exploding ships and special effects." This time, Behr was determined to take a more intimate look at combat. "If the viewing audience has become deadened to certain forms of violence, because of the use of weapons like phasers, I would like to think there's still something disquieting about knives. You've got to *stick* a knife in someone to hurt them."

When it came to deciding which characters would come along on the mission to AR-558, the writers chose carefully, making sure that the series' toughest fighters were left out of the combat arena. "If we'd used Kira, Worf, and Sisko, we'd have had *The Dirty Dozen*," Behr observes. "But we wanted guys who are mechanics, not warriors. Sisko was necessary for the story, but we wanted Nog and Bashir and Ezri and Quark to go along with him. We created new characters—Reese, Larkin, and Vargas—for our warriors. Of course, Worf essentially *is* Reese, so we couldn't use him."

By populating the battleground with this new group of seasoned fighters, Behr knew he could com-

By giving death a familiar face, the writers drove home the indiscriminate nature of war. ROBBIE ROBINSON

ment freely on the ravages of combat that go beyond the physical. Only deep psychological wounds could make a tough soldier like Vargas cry over the death of a compatriot whom he'd hated. Reese's injuries were even more subtle. "This guy was wearing ketracel-white tubes around his neck, which was about as grisly as we could get on *Star Trek*," Behr says. "His way of getting through this ordeal was to depend on his knife. At the end of the show we had him throw the knife down. Maybe he doesn't need the crutch anymore, but he's pretty far gone. I think he's going to need some twenty-fourth-century reconditioning."

At the other end of the spectrum was the engineer, Kellin. "I knew Kellin would provide me with the alternative to Reese," Behr points out. "The hard-as-nails guy who gives up his humanity lives, but Kellin, the decent guy, dies. War is very cruel."

Behr offered the role of Kellin to Actor Bill Mumy, a veteran of numerous television series, most notably *Lost in Space*. "Bill is a pal of mine," Behr says. "He's wanted to do the show for a long time, but after wearing prosthetics for years on *Babylon Five*, he didn't want to wear extensive makeup. I'd been looking for a role that would put him in a Starfleet uniform. Even though the part of Kellin isn't huge, I thought he'd be great in it because he can play intelligence and decency."

"Ira had offered roles to me a bunch of times," Mumy says. "I was flattered, but the roles were always aliens of some sort. After forty years in the business, I don't want to get the reputation of the guy who only plays aliens. I'm a fair-skinned kind of guy," laughs the redhead, "and, man, those solvents on my face

A redo of *DS9*'s cave set for the communications relay station. JOHN EAVES

every day make me look like I've been standing behind a 747 getting blasted. So I told Ira, 'It's a prerequisite that I'm a human.' When he sent me this script, I called him back immediately and told him I'd do it. And he said to me, 'Nobody is going to believe that we brought Will Robinson over to *Star Trek* only to kill him.' I loved that!"

The regulars in the episode served a different purpose, serving, in a way, as surrogates for the viewers at home who may never have faced such grim circumstances. Ezri's participation in the story surprised Nicole deBoer. "I was shocked," she says. "When I signed on, I knew I was supposed to be a counselor. I wasn't picturing myself in war scenes. I'm so tiny, and everyone else is so much bigger than me! And I had to fight a Jem'Hadar!" she laughs. "We did this little choreographed stunt where he knocks me out, but I'm sure that in real life he'd have gotten rid of me way quicker than that!"

In a significant conversation with Reese, deBoer's character serves to point up one of the terrible truths about war, as Ezri realizes that the vicious mines they'd once considered weapons only the Dominion would use can seem a lot friendlier once they change hands.

"We were very passionate about this episode," Behr says. "These horrible Houdini mines, these vicious mines—suddenly *we're* using them. The whole idea of 'God is on our side' in war is such a strange concept, but it's used all the time. *Nobody* is clean in war."

The writers opted to include Quark, a civilian, in the story so that he could serve as a kind of Greek/Ferengi chorus. "He served a similar purpose in 'The Jem'Hadar,' in Season 2," notes Behr. "Quark gets to say things that are very truthful, that you don't expect to come out of his mouth. He scores a lot of points in this episode. He's the moral consciousness, and I think it was very important to have him there."

"I'm very proud of this episode," says Armin Shimerman. "*Star Trek* is a franchise about people who, for the most part, belong to the Federation, and it's usually the humans that the show centers on. But in this episode, they allowed me to express an 'other-than-Federation' point of view. I got to do something that was Spock-like, in the sense that Spock, as an outsider, could comment about humanity."

Of course, the most emphatic statement about war came when Nog lost his leg in battle. "We were going to blow off *both* of Nog's legs," Behr admits.

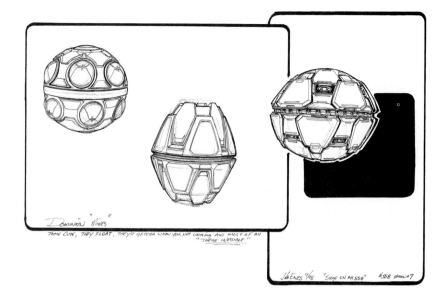

The Houdini mines.
JOHN EAVES

"That would have presented a much grislier image, but it's too strong for *Star Trek*. In the end we had to compromise. Losing one leg is horrible. I'm not making light of it. But we really wanted to say, 'BOOM! This man has been chopped in half by this war.'"

Actor Aron Eisenberg welcomed the direction his character's injury would take him. "Up until this point," Eisenberg comments, "Nog had been a gung-ho soldier who thought nothing could happen to him. He wanted to be Starfleet, and be the best because only the best could become captain. So no matter what he saw, no matter how many people he saw die, he was like a train that just kept going. Then he got hit. I played him as if he were in shock, but the first thought that would have come into his head is, 'Oh my God, I could *die*.' And that's what takes us into 'Paper Moon.'"

The writers picked names for the new characters from among the cast and characters' names in the motion picture *Hell Is for Heroes*, one of their favorite war films. The inspiration for the storyline, on the other hand, came from a more direct source. "My father fought with the Marines at Guadalcanal," David Weddle says, referring to the famous World War II battle. "Ira wanted to do tragic warfare," Weddle notes, "so I said, 'Why not make it like Guadalcanal? The soldiers had to hold on to an area because it was strategically important. It's one of the greatest heroic stories of World War II. Those men and women stopped something incredibly evil," he states proudly, "and when they came back, there was no talk about post-traumatic stress syndrome or therapy groups. They won, but it changed their whole

lives. Ira and Hans really tried to capture the essence of that conflict."

Director Rick Kolbe thought of a different conflict as he prepared for the episode: World War I.

"We wanted Nog's injury to have real consequences," says René Echevarria. ROBBIE ROBINSON

Reese embodied the dehumanizing effects that killing can have on soldiers. ROBBIE ROBINSON

AR-558 to be that type of battleground, a totally non-descript piece of real estate that didn't deserve one drop of blood to be shed for it. It shouldn't say anything to the eye or the mind except that we were there because somebody had decided to put a relay station on this rock."

A Vietnam War veteran, Kolbe also saw parallels to the Battle of Khe Sanh, said to be the most ferocious siege in that war. "I left Vietnam before my division went to Khe Sanh," he says, "but it was another one of those godforsaken places that had strategic value.

"We wanted the siege scene in 'AR-558' to convey the psychological impact, and not come across like a shoot-'em-up," Kolbe notes. "What I remember from Vietnam is sitting in a ditch somewhere and waiting. It is the waiting that drives you nuts. You know they're coming. You can hear them. You can feel them. When you have to wait, your mind plays tricks on you and you hear things and see things, like Vargas, who's about to explode. Once the battle starts, your adrenaline kicks in and you have an objective. But when you have to wait, time just slows down to a crawl."

"The images you see from that are trenches of churned-up dirt," he says. "The battleground always looked like there was absolutely nothing there that anyone could ever want. Yet people were blowing each other to smithereens over this land. I wanted

By varying the rock size and camera angle, a small set can be made to look like a large battlefield. JOHN EAVES

The producers decided to emphasize both the waiting period and the battle itself by setting them against a backdrop of surprising musical choices. Vic Fontaine's rendering of "I'll Be Seeing You"—one of the quintessential ballads of World War II—accompanied the tense wait before the Jem'Hadar attack. "There's a method to our madness," Behr smiles, "even when it comes to Vic Fontaine. You wonder why we have these songs in the series, and then in that moment when they're waiting for death, you hear this music and it's very haunting. This may sound pretentious, but we were trying to give the characters an inner life greater than you would think necessary on a TV show. By doing the music, by seeing the characters' reaction to the music, by telling you what they were thinking before the music started, we're seeing that they are scared, we're showing you a whole bunch of things without dialogue."

Terry Potts and Composer Paul Baillargeon conceived of covering the sounds of battle with a blanket of soft melody. "We knew it was a different approach," Potts says, "We wanted to mix the battle sounds *under* the music, so I went to Rick Berman and told him what we wanted to do. He said, 'Okay, but make it sad.' Paul wrote the piece without looking at any footage. It wasn't about hitting any story points in particular. It was about creating a mood."

"It's a sixteen-bar melodic phrase," Baillargeon says. "I just got up on a Saturday morning, sat down at the piano, and in ten minutes it was done."

"We thought the music was brilliant," Behr states emphatically. "Rather than trying to get everybody's blood boiling with martial music, they went against it with melancholy music."

The title for the episode—a location in space noted only by a few letters, AR for "array," and three numbers—harkens back to *Deep Space Nine's* pilot, "Emissary," and the battle of Wolf 359, where a different war brought Sisko his greatest loss, the life of his wife, Jennifer. Asked why the producers decided to use the episode's production number, 558, as the three numbers, Behr simply replies, "Because we could."

COVENANT
Episode #559

WRITTEN BY **RENÉ ECHEVARRIA**
DIRECTED BY **JOHN KRETCHMER**

GUEST CAST

Gul Dukat	MARC ALAIMO
Vedek Fala	NORMAN PARKER
Benyan	JASON LELAND ADAMS
Mika	MAUREEN FLANNIGAN
Midwife	MIRIAM FLYNN
Brin	MARK PIATELLI

STARDATE UNKNOWN

Returning from a service on the nature of forgiveness at the station's Bajoran temple, Kira joins Odo and her friends at Quark's. Odo wistfully comments that he wishes they could attend services together, but Kira points out that he wouldn't get much out of it since he doesn't believe in the Prophets. Odo muses that it must be very comforting to believe in something more powerful than yourself.

Late that night, Kira receives a surprise visit from Vedek Fala, the monk who was her childhood instructor in the Bajoran faith. After reminiscing for a moment, Fala gives Kira a gift—a crystal that begins to glow . . .

. . . And suddenly Kira finds herself transported to Empok Nor ("Empok Nor"), a long abandoned Cardassian space station located far from Bajoran space. Kira is surprised to see that the station is now occupied by members of the Pah-wraith cult ("Image in the Sand"), and even more surprised when she meets their leader—Dukat.

It makes sense that the cult would choose the Cardassian as their leader, observes Kira, since Pah-wraith followers worship evil. But Dukat points out that Kira doesn't understand him or his followers. The Prophets are the ones who are evil; they stood by and did nothing while Cardassia took over Bajor. It's the Pah-wraiths who are the true gods of Bajor, cast from the Celestial Temple because they wanted to take an active role in Bajoran life. As for himself, Dukat continues, he's a changed man—the Emissary of the Pah-wraiths. He's built a community on Empok Nor so that the group can purify itself in preparation for the day the Pah-wraiths reclaim their rightful home in the wormhole. And he's brought Kira to that community so she can see at last that they're bound together by destiny. She belongs at his side.

Kira is shocked to learn that Dukat's Bajoran followers would defend him with their own lives. ROBBIE ROBINSON

Back on Deep Space 9, Kira's friends realize that she's missing. O'Brien finds clues that lead him to believe she's been transported somewhere via use of a long-range Dominion transponder. She could be as far away as three light-years. But they have no idea where to begin looking for her.

On Empok Nor, Fala comes to see Kira. He admits that he's been a member of the cult for many years, and he tries to explain that Dukat brought her to them because he cares about her spiritual well-being. Kira reminds Fala of the millions of Bajorans that Dukat murdered during the Occupation, but Fala emphasizes how important it is to forgive. Although the lesson is similar to the one she recently heard on DS9, Kira tells Fala that there are some things that *can't* be forgiven.

Hoping to convince her that there's nothing to fear from the cult, Fala introduces Kira to some of the station's residents, including Mika and Benyan, a married couple who were given Dukat's special permission to conceive a child. Although Kira finds this very odd, the Bajorans accept Dukat's rules as if they were gospel. She learns just how deep their devotion

to him is when she steals a phaser and takes aim at Dukat. One by one, his followers step between her and their "Master," shielding Dukat with their own bodies. Defeated, Kira lowers her weapon and is knocked unconscious by one of the followers. Kira awakens to find Dukat at her side, tending to her injury. Repelled, she lambasts him for his behavior during the Occupation, working people to death and forcing Bajoran women to share his bed. She's surprised when Dukat expresses regret over doing things that caused others pain, and disturbed when he tells her that she embodies everything he admires about the Bajoran people. If he can open *her* heart, he says, he knows that he can open the heart of any Bajoran to his cause.

The discussion is cut short when word arrives that Mika is in labor with the station's first child. They arrive at her side right after the baby is delivered. To nearly everyone's surprise, Mika's baby is half-Bajoran and half-Cardassian. Dukat proclaims that the infant is a miracle, a living symbol of the covenant that he's made with the Bajoran people. But Kira can see from both Mika and her husband's expressions that this isn't the truth. She's certain that Dukat fathered the child. Kira speaks to Fala about the baby's obvious paternity, but he tries to convince her that her hatred of Dukat is preventing her from seeing the event as the miracle it is. A subsequent conversation with Benyan triggers the young man's ire but fails to make him reject Dukat. Thinking that Mika may have a different point of view, Kira goes in search of the new mother.

Meanwhile, Mika secretly meets with Dukat in one of the station's airlocks. Dukat apologizes for what happened between them "that night" and asks if she's told anyone the truth. Mika says she hasn't, but admits that she isn't sure that she can keep lying to her husband. Telling her not to worry, Dukat leaves the airlock. Then he locks her in and opens the outer door to the vacuum of space. Kira happens upon the airlock just in time to save Mika. Although she doesn't see Dukat, it's clear to Kira how this alleged accident happened.

Realizing that his secret will soon be revealed, Dukat comes up with a plan. Calling all of his "children" to prayer, he announces that the Pah-wraiths have spoken to him and asked the group to join them—by abandoning their corporeal bodies. To Kira's horror, she realizes that his followers are willing to obey his bidding and commit mass suicide. Dukat has Kira locked in her quarters so she can't interfere, but she manages to escape. She arrives at the temple just as Dukat and his followers are about to ingest poisonous capsules. She knocks him to the ground, along with a ceremonial stand containing the capsules. Dukat drops the capsule he was holding in his hand and it disappears among the others.

Noting the look of panic on his face, Kira reveals to the group that Dukat never planned to die with his followers. He's a fraud who would allow them all to die so they'd never find out the truth about Mika's baby. The crowd turns against their former Master, and Dukat beams away from the station, to parts unknown.

Unable to deal with this betrayal of his faith, Fala swallows one of the deadly capsules before Kira can stop him. After the *Defiant* arrives, Kira tells Odo that what really frightens her about Dukat's behavior is that he seemed convinced that he was doing what the Pah-wraiths wanted. And that makes him more dangerous than ever.

The twists and turns of Dukat's mind gave him the tools he needed to prey on his flock. ROBBIE ROBINSON

A funny thing happened on the way to the final season. As the Dominion War began to figure more and more prominently in *Deep Space Nine*, the man responsible for bringing Cardassia into that war seemed to recede into the background. "We felt that we'd lost Dukat," René Echevarria says. "He's a wonderful character and well liked by the audience, but he'd become a very peripheral villain after the six-episode arc at the beginning of Season 6. We'd done two shows with him after that ['Waltz,' 'Tears of the Prophets'], but now he had no role to play."

So the writers very deliberately began crafting a new role for Dukat, one that would return him to his rightful position as the series' premier villain. "'Covenant' brought him back into our story," Echevarria continues. "Somehow it seemed like it was going to help us put him into conflict with Sisko. But we didn't really know much more than that: Pah-wraiths versus Prophets, Dukat versus Sisko."

It felt right, even if the producers weren't entirely sure of what the end would bring. "I always knew that the ultimate challenge would be Dukat, and not the war," states Ira Steven Behr.

Initial discussions for the episode begat an idea that Dukat would set himself up as the leader of a new race of aliens. Development of that idea was assigned to Echevarria, who ultimately came up with something far more intriguing. "I said, 'I'll tell you what would be really twisted: Dukat becoming the leader of some *Bajorans*.' Ira said, 'That's the most

ridiculous thing I've ever heard—what kind of Bajorans?' I said, 'Pah-wraith cultists.'"

The idea clicked with the entire staff. "It gave us a chance to ask ourselves, 'What is Dukat's craziness, and how is it manifesting itself now?'" observes Brad Thompson. "We could touch base with him and show that he's really getting hooked into these Pah-wraiths. And that would help us set up the end of the series."

At the time, the news was full of stories about Heaven's Gate, the San Diego–based cultists who recently had committed mass suicide. Investigative journalist David Weddle had written stories about various cults for *The L.A. Weekly* and the *San Jose Mercury News*. "I've always been fascinated with them," Weddle admits. "I'm interested in that hunger to find something to believe in that's bigger than the viewable reality. The desire to find heaven on earth often ends up leading people down a very twisted, paranoid road. Fundamental human longing can be twisted by a cult leader, because he can never really deliver on his promises of bringing about a golden utopia. Then he has to come up with reasons why, and it's always that there's a conspiracy out there, that something or someone is conspiring against the group. That's when paranoia gradually overshadows the whole thing," he explains. "I brought a lot of that stuff to the table while we were breaking the show."

The episode's Vedek Fala, he notes, is a good example of a typical follower. "He's someone who desperately wants to believe," Weddle says. "When you study cults you find a lot of people who were brought up in traditional religions and who had a strong faith when they were young. But they became disillusioned with that faith when they saw hypocrisy. They cast aside the faith they were brought up with, but they still have the need. The hunger is still there. At the end, when Dukat turns out to be a total charlatan, Fala can't handle it. He would rather die still trying to grip the illusion than go on living."

But the biggest revelation in the episode, observes Writer Echevarria, is the fact that Dukat himself is actually a true believer. "He is sincere," says Echevarria, with just a touch of surprise in his own voice. "That wasn't clear in the first draft, not even to me. But then I came up with the idea of having him pray alone. He's not performing for anybody. In his own twisted, self-aggrandizing way, he genuinely would prefer to send these people to their makers with their faith intact than allow it all to fall apart."

In order to visually sell Dukat as the Emissary of the Pah-wraiths, "We took a very theatrical approach," relates Kris Krosskove, who served as the episode's cinematographer. Perhaps nowhere is this more evident than in the teaser, when Dukat reveals himself to Kira. "He's in black with a very strong backlight," Krosskove explains. "I asked my crew to rig theatrical lighting up in the rafters. It was exactly as if we were doing a Broadway show, with a strong pin-light as a spotlight. I really took it to the limit. I even allowed the film to white out in certain areas," he adds, chuckling. "That's very unusual for *Deep Space Nine*. We took some artistic license." The result was startling, to say the least, with the overexposed area above the top of the Cardassian's head producing the unsettling effect of a halo crowning the self-proclaimed religious leader.

But as powerful as Dukat's newfound faith is, it can't overpower Kira's belief in the Prophets. Early in the episode, the pair have a lengthy verbal duel. The scene, which runs for nearly the entire first act, was crucial to pointing up their individual convictions. Director John Kretchmer recognized the importance of the six-and-a-half-minute duet, and he enlisted the assistance of the actors in staging it. "Blocking that scene out," Kretchmer recalls, "was very much a collaborative effort between Nana Visitor and Marc Alaimo. From an emotional standpoint, this was about two people who were coming together, although for an entirely weird reason. Kira and Dukat are locked together like two cats in a bag." To create

Fala's desire to believe in something—or someone—made him an easy mark. ROBBIE ROBINSON.

tension in the scene, Kretchmer had the camera push in very slowly on the characters until, at the end, they're caught in a tight two-shot. "I felt that was much more effective than the typical coverage of close-ups would have been."

If the writers were confident of Kira coming out on top in this standoff, Actor Visitor was even more so. She knows her character's past as well as they do. Kira never loses confidence, despite the nightmarish quality of her situation. "For Kira, the only alternate to *not* being confident would be to slip up for a second and die," Visitor states with conviction. "So the terrorist thing kicks in. If a door of opportunity closes, Kira quickly looks for another one, or maybe a window, or even a place in the dirt where she can tunnel out. She just does *not* accept defeat. She has to find a way to get out of this. In this case," Visitor smiles, "she knew Dukat's psychology well enough that she understood that *it* was her way out."

For the people behind the scenes, however, Dukat was not the most frightening presence on the station. That distinction fell to the so-called "Baby from Hell."

B.C. Cameron rolls her eyes as she remembers the moment she learned about the existence of the creature. "The script was distributed, and we all began reading it," she recalls. "When I got to the part about this half-Cardassian, half-Bajoran baby, I stepped out of my office and saw Steve Oster coming down the hallway with the open script in his hand. And just then, Bobby della Santina came out of his office with the open script in *his* hand. We all looked at each other and said, 'A newborn baby? Half-Cardassian and half-Bajoran? How are we gonna do *that*?'"

The problem, Cameron explains, is that you can't put prosthetic makeup on an infant, which would make it difficult to convey the apparent hybrid nature of the child. In addition, child labor laws require that an infant can be on the set only twenty minutes at a time, for a total of one hour's work spread over a half-day. "Steve said, 'We're going to have to make an animatronic baby,'" says Cameron, "so he got hold of the people who made Chucky."

Yes, *that* Chucky, star of the film *Child's Play* and all its horrific sequels. "We didn't have a lot of research and development time," Oster explains. "So with all respect to the people who created the mechanical puppet, it was *too much* of a good thing."

"The doll was *huge*," says Echevarria. "It was the size of a three-year-old! It was just ridiculous."

"It looked like Chucky with a Bajoran nose," Cameron says with a shudder. "His eyes were blinking, and he was *really* spooky looking."

The filmmakers knew they were in trouble from the moment the Baby from Hell arrived on the set, but they went ahead with production all the same. The result, laughs Behr, "was one of the greatest days in dailies of all time! This animatronic baby was moving its head, and Marc Alaimo was holding it up for the camera, playing the scene for all it's worth, even though it *looks* ludicrous. It looked as if he were proclaiming to the world, '*Take a look! This is a phony baby! You can get one at Toys "R" Us! Thirty-four dollars and ninety-five cents!*' We were howling with laughter and crying in frustration at the same time. The day will live in infamy."

It was clear that they would have to reshoot the scene. Quickly revisualizing the sequence, the director shot most of it using a doll the size of a normal infant, which was wrapped in a blanket. "Then we went ahead and cut the show, so we'd know exactly what else we needed to sell the scene," Oster says.

As it turned out, they decided that they would require only a single close-up to reveal the baby's racial mix to the audience. That was good, notes Oster, "because we wouldn't have to keep a real baby for long." The Makeup Department resorted to the same technique they'd used for the infant playing the Jem'Hadar in "The Abandoned," using a small amount of K-Y jelly to hold in place a tiny prosthetic rubber appliance.

IT'S ONLY A PAPER MOON
Episode #560
TELEPLAY BY RONALD D. MOORE
STORY BY DAVID MACK & JOHN J. ORDOVER
DIRECTED BY ANSON WILLIAMS

GUEST CAST

Nog	ARON EISENBERG
Rom	MAX GRODÉNCHIK
Leeta	CHASE MASTERSON
Kesha	TAMI-ADRIAN GEORGE

SPECIAL GUEST STAR

Vic Fontaine	JAMES DARREN

STARDATE UNKNOWN

Following treatment at a Federation hospital for the injuries he received on AR-558 ("The Siege of AR-558"), Nog returns to Deep Space 9. His friends and family are happy to see him and eager to help him forget the fact that he lost a leg in the battle. But Nog *can't* forget. He claims that his biosynthetic leg—which is functioning perfectly, according to the doctors—hurts. He's tired of people telling him the problem is all in his head. Ezri attempts to counsel him, but their sessions go nowhere because Nog is sick of talking about his feelings. Ezri suggests to Sisko that they leave him alone for a while and see what he does.

Unfortunately, what he does is . . . nothing. He sleeps eighteen hours a day, skips physical therapy, and plays one Vic Fontaine recording over and over, driving roommate Jake crazy. Finally, Jake puts his own foot down and tells Nog that if he wants to listen to the song again, he'll have to do it in the holo-suite. Nog hobbles off to do just that, entering the holographic world of Vic Fontaine's Las Vegas nightclub, circa 1962. Vic's easygoing, matter-of-fact style makes Nog feel better. Impulsively, the young Ferengi asks Vic if he can spend some time living in the holo-

When traditional therapy fails to help him, Nog finds what he needs at Vic's. ROBBIE ROBINSON

gram's world. After all, he's officially on medical leave and he's allowed to choose his rehabilitation facility. Why *not* Vic's program? Vic doesn't have a problem with it, so Nog moves in to the singer's holographic hotel suite.

Although Rom is concerned about his son's decision, Ezri supports Nog's desire to escape from reality for a short period of time. She briefs Vic on Nog's condition and explains that although Nog seems dependent on his cane, he really doesn't need it. Vic figures out a way to wean the Ferengi off his psychological and physical crutches. He gives Nog an elegant walking stick as a gift, but warns him that it's fragile and won't be able to support his whole weight. Nog allows that he won't need to put his whole weight on it, which Vic takes as a positive sign.

That evening, Nog is less than happy when Jake and Jake's girlfriend Kesha decide to sit with the Ferengi at Vic's show. In no time at all, Nog manages to hurt Kesha's feelings, offend Jake, and punch his old friend out. Vic breaks up the fight and kicks Nog out of the club, although not out of the holosuite itself. Nog goes back to Vic's hotel suite and apologizes when the singer comes home from the club. Noting that Vic is having some difficulty balancing his books, Nog volunteers his services as an accountant. Vic gratefully accepts. The next day, Ezri comes to the nightclub to discuss Nog's altercation with Jake. Ezri feels that it's time for the Ferengi to leave the illusory holosuite environment. Nog informs the counselor that if she forces him to leave, he'll resign

his commission. What's more, he and Vic have big plans. Nog is going to help the holographic singer to build a new casino.

Nog remains in the holosuite, helping Vic plan the new club and enjoying the ambience of Vic's world. Ezri visits periodically, discreetly observing the Ferengi from a distance. She notes that he's no longer limping and that the cane has become a showy prop and nothing more. He's also much more upbeat, and genuinely friendly when Rom and Leeta come to visit. Ezri congratulates Vic on Nog's progress. Then, turning the conversation around slightly, she compliments him on his clever ploy to boost Nog's spirits by getting him involved with the new casino. Soon the Ferengi will be able to leave the holosuite, she says, and go back to his family and friends, who miss him greatly.

Vic picks up on Ezri's cue and gently tells Nog that it's time to go back to reality. When the Ferengi protests, Vic gives him a stronger "nudge" by deactivating his own program. Nog tinkers with the circuitry for a while, trying to get the program running again. But O'Brien informs him that Vic's matrix is different than that of the standard hologram. If he wants to stay off—he's off. A few minutes later, Vic appears to talk to the unhappy Ferengi. Nog pleads with Vic to let him stay, and finally admits that he's afraid to go back into the real world, where he could die at any moment. Vic assures him that if he remains, he'll die anyway, little by little. The only thing to do, Vic says, is to play out the hand life has dealt him — winning a few, losing a few, but staying in the game.

Nog goes back to his former life, but returns a few days later to thank Vic for all he's done and to give the singer a gift. Nog has made arrangements with Quark to keep Vic's program running around the clock, which will give the lounge singer a "real" life of his own.

When members of *Deep Space Nine*'s production staff read the script to "It's Only a Paper Moon," they were shocked. "There were virtually no principal players in the story," recalls Costume Designer Bob Blackman. "It only had two guest stars. It blew me away. I actually called Steve Oster and asked him if we really were doing that. And Steve said, 'Yup.'"

A *Star Trek* story with no principals? What were they thinking?

"It was never meant to be," Ira Behr sighs. "It was *supposed* to be a show with three storylines, all of

It seems only natural that a Ferengi would be attracted to Las Vegas.
ROBBIE ROBINSON

them taking place in Vic's. Vic was going to be involved in all of these different stories, and Nog was going to be in *one* of them."

Although he had become a familiar face around the station, Aron Eisenberg's Nog was only a supporting character, and *Star Trek* episodes aren't built around supporting characters. The presence of James Darren as Nog's main costar didn't help to alleviate the problem; Vic Fontaine was a supporting character, too, and a recently added one at that.

"Doing an entire show with supporting characters is asking a lot," Behr says. He sighs again. "I had no choice."

"I told Ira, 'You're very brave,'" James Darren chuckles.

It's not as if the freelancers who'd pitched the story had twisted anyone's arm. Ron Moore had received the pitch from freelancers John Ordover and David Mack ("Starship Down") in 1995. It was, to say the least, a very soft sell. "Basically, we said, 'You guys could do an entire episode on a single set if you wanted to,'" Ordover laughs. "That was it! Our notion was that the most attractive pitch would be something that was as cheap for them to produce as possible. Well, that would be an entire episode that had no visual effects, very little makeup, and only one set to light."

Ordover and Mack had proposed one way to do it. They suggested setting an episode in Quark's bar on some kind of holiday, when it would be the only establishment open for business on the Promenade. The setup would allow for a number of stories to take place in the bar simultaneously. "We called it 'Everybody Goes to Quark's,'" Ordover says, a tip of the hat to *Everybody Goes to Rick's,* the stageplay upon which the film *Casablanca* was based.

"It was an idea I always liked," Moore says, "a great high-concept show. But we could never get a handle on it. We could never find a frame, what the holiday was, what the whole thing said about Quark. So we abandoned it. Then one day, we were having a meeting and Ira said, 'You know, we could do it all in Vic's.' And my eyes just lit up. Having 'Everybody Goes to Quark's' at *Vic's* was a whole different ballgame and sounded like a lot of fun. We sat down to break the idea, which immediately became 'Everybody Goes to Vic's.' We decided that we were going to need a whole bunch of plot threads, different little things that were happening on the station, with Vic finding out about them as the patrons come and go."

With the central premise tilted toward comedy, Moore adds, "we decided that one of the plotlines should be a little serious and have some weight to it. It shouldn't all be fun and games." As the rest of the staff toyed with the premise, Behr and Hans Beimler went back to working on "The Siege of AR-558," which was about as far from fun and games as one could get. After hearing that the pair were planning to blow off both of Nog's legs (later modified to *one* leg), Moore notes, "We said, 'Well, we could follow that up. Nog will be dealing with artificial limbs. That could be the heavy thread, and we could develop a relationship between him and Vic.' We kept working on it, and it was such a heavy storyline that it started to dominate everything else."

"Finally," continues Behr, "it got to the point where I said, 'Fellas, I have to tell you. Nobody's going to like hearing me say this, but this is a Nog/Vic show. You can throw out everything else, because nothing else works. We're going to have to make this a Nog/Vic show.'"

The thought of doing an episode that primarily would feature guest stars was startling. "It was *remarkable* that we decided to do it," Moore says with a pleased smile. "We didn't even do a B-story with it. As the show developed, Ira really got into it, and he kept shaking his head and saying, 'God, if I'd had any idea that we were going to do this kind of a show, we would have cut off *O'Brien's* leg in that other episode.'" Moore laughs. "And then O'Brien and Bashir would have been doing this episode in the holosuite with Vic. But it was too late. He'd already

The power of the story gave the producers no choice: Nog would take the lead. ROBBIE ROBINSON

made the decision and the show had sprung forward. Actually, it was nice that it worked out this way because it gave us a chance to explore Nog as a character on a very deep level, in a way that we already had explored O'Brien."

The episode that aired was so different from Ordover and Mack's original pitch that the writing team wondered why they were given story credit. "We really would have never guessed that it was from the same thing," admits Ordover. "So we were very thankful when they called us."

But for Moore, there was no question of giving credit where credit was due. "The truth of the matter is that they pitched what we started with," he says. "As a producer, you draw those lines. We all have a sense of where a story comes from. And this is one of my favorite shows."

If Moore was pleased with the final episode, imagine how Aron Eisenberg felt. "I was *honored*," the actor says. "It was my biggest episode in all seven seasons. I was working every day, and I was in almost every scene. I had a ball! They *trusted* that James Darren and I could carry an episode, and I gave it everything I had."

The production certainly put him through his paces. "We ran Aron pretty ragged by the time we were done," notes Steve Oster. "He had three hours to get into makeup and an hour to get out of it every day, and twelve to fourteen hours on the set."

Eisenberg didn't mind. It helped him to focus on the character. "I played Nog differently than I had before, because he was in a different place in his mind. He wasn't the gung-ho soldier anymore. Now his goals were blurred, and he was on this downward spiral because of his fear." Eisenberg's favorite scene is the one he worked at the hardest. "It was the one where I had to cry," he says. "It wasn't written that way. The script just said that Nog gets emotional. When we were ready to shoot I realized that I *had* to cry. It was the defining moment of what the episode was all about. You finally see what's inside that's gotten Nog to this point. Up until then, you didn't know why he was behaving that way.

"I grew that day as an actor," Eisenberg says. "Before that I'd always been afraid that I couldn't get myself to cry on camera. It's very hard." To draw the tears, he brought a painful memory to mind: as a teenager learning to drive, he'd accidentally knocked down his mother with the family car. "I was wracked with guilt," the actor says. "It wasn't until years later that I cried and forgave myself. Well, Nog was constricted with this fear of dying that he'd never dealt with before. When stuff like that is locked inside and then you let it out, emotion is going to come through with it." Eisenberg's best reward for his hard work came from the combat veterans who wrote and told him that he'd done a good job. "That was the best compliment," he says, "because those guys have lived through the stuff that we were playing."

James Darren also used a bit of method acting for his character's part in the scene. "I played it as if I were disciplining a child," he says. "When you love a child you have to put on a little front and be really firm. Afterward you feel bad, but you know it had to be done that way."

As in all of the period-specific Vic Fontaine episodes, careful attention was paid to detail. Clothing, furnishings, and even television programming were carefully chosen. And although both Nog and Vic prefer *The Searchers* to *Shane* (as does most of DS9's writing staff), the latter was a Paramount film, which made it somewhat easier to clear the clips that were used.

Once again the episode includes a reference to Davy Crockett, this time in a conversation between Ezri and Quark. One might wonder how and why a Trill and a Ferengi would be discussing a nineteenth-century frontiersman. But Behr knows. By this time, he'd become convinced that the show's writers knew all they had to do was throw an Alamo reference into a scene and their boss, the Alamo aficionado, would be far less critical of their work. "This proves it!" Behr cries in triumph. "Moore knew that if he put that name in the script I wouldn't look at it closely, because I'd get such a kick out of just seeing it there. You see how they took advantage of me?"

PRODIGAL DAUGHTER

Episode #561

WRITTEN BY **BRADLEY THOMPSON &
DAVID WEDDLE**
DIRECTED BY **VICTOR LOBL**

GUEST CAST

Norvo	KEVIN RAHM
Janel	MIKAEL SALAZAR
Bokar	JOHN PARAGON
Fuchida	CLAYTON LANDEY

SPECIAL GUEST STAR

Yanas	LEIGH TAYLOR-YOUNG

STARDATE UNKNOWN

Sisko is furious when he learns that O'Brien has vanished while on a secret trip to New Sydney to locate Liam Bilby's widow. Bashir reveals that because the chief still feels responsible for Bilby's death ("Honor Among Thieves"), he's been keeping close tabs on Bilby's wife, Morica. At least, he *had* been until Morica disappeared. After failing to turn up a lead through official channels, the chief opted to follow up on his own. Now they're *both* missing.

Knowing that Ezri's mother owns a major mining operation in that region of space, Sisko asks the young Trill if her family would be willing to intervene with the local authorities. Ezri's mother, Yanas Tigan, is willing, but only if Ezri comes home for a long-overdue visit. Although a trip home is the *last* thing Ezri wants, she agrees for the sake of finding O'Brien.

At her mother's home on Sappora VII, Ezri is reunited with her domineering mother and her two brothers, burly Janel and gentle Norvo. Although both brothers work in the family business, Norvo, an artist, is clearly miserable with his lot in life. Ezri realizes that nothing has changed since she last saw her family, and she encourages Norvo to leave. But he's still under Yanas's thumb, afraid to break free and do what he wants with his life. When Norvo gets drunk and destroys one of his paintings, Yanas accuses Ezri of triggering the destructive behavior. Ezri points out that Norvo is expressing his frustration with *Yanas*, not her.

The argument is interrupted when Fuchida, an officer of the New Sydney police bureau, shows up at the door with a bruised and battered O'Brien in tow. Fuchida explains that he managed to wrest O'Brien from the clutches of the Orion Syndicate, which O'Brien had begun investigating after he found

Ezri makes a trip home to see her dominating mother, Yanas, and her brother, Norvo. ROBBIE ROBINSON

Morica dead. He is convinced that the Syndicate killed her, and that he would have obtained the proof if the police hadn't intervened. But Fuchida says that if he hadn't intervened, O'Brien would be dead. The officer doesn't believe that the Syndicate killed Morica; its members would never kill the widow of one of their own, he says.

Yanas asks the Chief to utilize his engineering skills and take a look at an inoperative piece of equipment in the mines. While he's gone, Ezri invites Norvo to return with her to Deep Space 9. Although tempted, Norvo is evasive. There are things going on in the company that he can't walk away from right now, he explains. In the mines, O'Brien quickly figures out the equipment problem, and Janel realizes that it's the result of sabotage. Moments later, Bokar, a self-described "commodities broker" shows up and suggests that Janel might not be having problems if he hadn't recently fired a member of his crew. After sending O'Brien away, Janel tells Bokar that sabotage won't convince him or his family to rehire the crooked crew member or to do more business with the Orion Syndicate. But Bokar is on to a new topic of conversation. He's recognized O'Brien, and he tells Janel to make the engineer leave the system quickly, before something happens to him.

Sensing that Bokar may be a member of the Syndicate, O'Brien gets Ezri's permission to check the mining company's financial records for clues. What he finds shocks him. Morica Bilby was on the company's payroll when she died. Because only Yanas, Janel, or Norvo could have authorized her payments, one of them may have been involved in the death.

Ezri and O'Brien confront the three of them with the information, and Janel admits that he hired Morica to repay a "favor." Unbeknownst to Yanas, the Orion Syndicate had once bailed the company out of financial difficulties. Later, Bokar asked Janel to hire Morica and pay her a salary. Janel complied, but Morica soon began to ask for more and more money.

Janel claims he doesn't know how Morica died, but Yanas suspects that her oldest son had the woman killed. Norvo quickly jumps to the defense of his brother, but Yanas ignores him and continues to accuse Janel. Ezri realizes that something is tearing Norvo apart, and she begins to question him. At last Norvo reveals that he tried to talk to Morica about her escalating demands, but she wouldn't listen to reason. It occurred to him that if she were dead, all of their problems would go away.

There is dead silence in the room as everyone realizes what Norvo is saying. Both Yanas and Janel had always thought he was too weak to deal with the tough problems, Norvo says bitterly. But they were wrong. He handled it.

The police arrive and take Norvo away. Ezri stays for the trial, and Norvo is sentenced to thirty years for his crime. When she returns to the station, Ezri tells O'Brien that she can't help blaming herself for what happened. She was so anxious to get out of her mother's house that she never thought about what was happening to Norvo, left behind. O'Brien protests that she's not responsible, but Ezri refuses to believe it. She should've gone home a long time ago, she says. And nothing will convince her otherwise.

Ezri Dax, Mafia Princess. It has a tantalizing quality to it, a "must see" kind of come-on. And it *almost* happened.

As American poet John Greenleaf Whittier put it, "For of all sad words of tongue or pen, the saddest are these: 'It might have been!'"

"There's plenty of blame to go around on this," Ira Behr admits with a rueful smile. "First of all, it was my idea. And I still think it's a valid idea. *Deep Space Nine* is a character-based show, and this had all the makings of a classic drama. But the script never came together."

The biggest problem seems to have been that there was no time to do justice to anything the writers came up with for this particular slot in the season. Ironically, time is what the episode was originally supposed to be about.

"This was going to be the series' last great time travel story," reveals Brad Thompson. "We were going

The writers felt viewers needed to know more about the new Dax.
ROBBIE ROBINSON

to have Sisko battling Sisko, with the Sisko from the future coming back and telling the Sisko of the present, 'You can't do this, because nasty things are going to happen.'"

But the ambitious idea never made it out of the gate. "David [Weddle] and I got a great teaser out of it, and then we realized that the story went nowhere," Thompson admits. "There was nothing to say beyond the fact that these two Siskos have a great struggle. There was no bottom to the show." Unfortunately, by the time the writers realized that there was, as they say, no *there* there, the episode was a mere two weeks from the start of production. "We didn't have an idea, and finally Ira suggested that we do an episode that would reveal Ezri's backstory."

"I just wanted to see where she came from," Behr says. "We hadn't needed to know about Jadzia's family, because we'd dealt with her past in 'Equilibrium.' In a way, Jadzia's family was Curzon." But now they had a new host, and Behr felt that viewers would be interested in *her* family. And it was Behr who came up with the intriguing notion for what her family was. As the writers feverishly began to spin ideas about life at the Tigan residence, Behr tossed the phrase "Ezri Dax, Mafia Princess" into the mix.

"I just thought, 'Cool!'" recalls Ron Moore. "We were going to find out that Ezri's family is in the Orion Syndicate. Ezri would be like [*The Godfather's*] Michael Corleone, the child who went off into the service and then came back to the family."

"We began playing around with the idea that Ezri's mom was powerful in the Syndicate," Thompson comments. "We created the family from hell! Mom says to Ezri, 'How do you think you got that worm, anyway? Why do you think that worm was shipped on the *Destiny*?'"

It was daring, all right—a little too daring. "We structured the whole story to be like that," says Moore, "but ultimately had to lose it."

Why? "It seemed a little too sleazy to suggest that Starfleet could be manipulated like that," sighs Thompson. With only days left before shooting was to begin, the writers were told to start over. To save time, they tried to keep whatever elements they could: the notion that Ezri was going home, and even that the family somehow was involved with the Orion Syndicate. But that would work only *if* they could find a viable reason. Behr suggested that bringing Miles O'Brien into the story would allow them to pay off the O'Brien/Bilby story from "Honor Among Thieves," while at the same time giving them room to explore interpersonal dynamics at the Tigan homestead.

"Trying to marry those two stories was really difficult," Moore says. "It was just a mess." Moore speaks from firsthand knowledge. Because the writing staff was in a bind, he offered to help out, and went directly from his final draft of "It's Only a Paper Moon" to helping out Weddle and Thompson with "Prodigal Daughter." "The show was already in prep," he notes, "so it was a case of 'First thought, best thought.' Just throw it down and move on, because we've gotta get ten pages out today. So *boom*! You just blaze through it."

"It was written so fast," Thompson concurs. "David and I were writing chunks of it, and Ron was writing chunks of it. There were enough ideas in there, and interesting places to go, but we were at the point where we had to start shooting, so we didn't have the chance to get to those ideas and places. We needed one more draft to swirl all of it out."

In the rush, many of the writers' favorite ideas were left behind. "We were going to go into Ezri's old bedroom and see all of the spaceship models that she's had since she was a kid, because she'd always wanted to be in Starfleet," Thompson says. "Ron had this great idea for remote-control starships that would be hanging in the air without wires, because they'd have these little anti-gravity gizmos on them that would keep them up there."

Production sketch for the Tigan home. JOHN EAVES

"We'd have liked to see O'Brien wandering around in the streets, tracking down Bilby's wife," notes René Echevarria. "But once you started to chip away at the story, you realize that you couldn't go out into the streets. It all had to take place in the house, or in the caves. None of O'Brien's story could happen on-screen, so there was no investigation. The story got so diluted that it felt like a soap opera."

In fact, the soap opera correlation became so widespread that crew members behind the scenes began to call the episode "Audra Goes Home," a tongue-in-cheek reference to *The Big Valley*–like aspects of the story (rural homefront where Momma rules with an iron fist). Nevertheless, Nicole deBoer took the atypical feel of the story in stride. "I knew when I started working on *Deep Space Nine* that it had more of a serial feeling than any of the other *Star Trek* shows," comments deBoer. "I thought that maybe this was the norm, that now and then we'd have a straight drama." She chuckles good-naturedly. "Ira *apologized* to me for the episode afterward."

It didn't feel like the norm to Director Victor Lobl either. "I kept trying to get a handle on it in terms of

the *series*," he says, "but other than the trappings, it never felt part of *Deep Space Nine*. It seemed like O'Brien had been brought in just to bear witness to these events more than anything else. But that only got us to a location, and then we just watched things unfold. The feeling across the board was there was nothing very powerful driving it, although obviously everyone did the best work that he could."

"We're not mystery writers," Moore says with a shrug. "Mysteries are a difficult genre, and for some reason, they've been hard to do on all of the *Star Trek* series. Whenever we've attempted to do one, it never quite works."

With soundstage space always at a premium, it was uncertain where they'd be able to construct the few new sets required for the episode. "Finding the space and the time to build the Tigan home presented a quandary," explains Steve Oster. "Herman Zimmerman finally came up with the wonderful idea of turning Vic Fontaine's lounge into the living room. So after we wrapped 'It's Only a Paper Moon,' we didn't rip out the entire set or the lighting. Instead, we reskinned the lounge. Back where the fireplace is, with the windows behind it, had been Vic's stage. If you look closely, you can see that the basic geography of the room is more or less the same as the lounge. The Art Department did a terrific job of converting it."

The producers had requested that the visual establishing the Tigan home on Sappora VII suggest a "ranch-style" house. However, after matte-artist Sid Dutton noted in the script that the house was "sited upon the crest of a bluff," he suggested another direction. Simulating the Prairie Style of acclaimed twentieth-century architect Frank Lloyd Wright, Dutton rendered an oil painting that pays homage to Wright's Pennsylvania masterwork, Fallingwater. The final visual, which later was scanned into the computer for last-minute touches, appears to hang over the bluff the way Fallingwater nestles above its waterfall, and brings to mind yet another American landmark, as reflected in the name Dutton chose for his work: "Wright meets Mt. Rushmore."

Quark learns that the mirror version of Ezri is full of surprises.
ROBBIE ROBINSON

THE EMPEROR'S NEW CLOAK
Episode #562
WRITTEN BY IRA STEVEN BEHR & HANS BEIMLER
DIRECTED BY LeVAR BURTON

GUEST CAST

Garak	ANDREW J. ROBINSON
Brunt	JEFFREY COMBS
Rom	MAX GRODÉNCHIK
General Martok	J.G. HERTZLER
Maihar'du	TINY RON
Leeta	CHASE MASTERSON
Helmsman	PETER C. ANTONIOU

SPECIAL GUEST STAR

Zek	WALLACE SHAWN

STARDATE UNKNOWN

A jealous Quark watches in disgust as Bashir and Ezri enjoy each other's company in the bar. He pays little heed when his brother Rom rushes in to tell him that Grand Nagus Zek has disappeared. The nagus left a note for their mother Ishka, telling her he was going on a business trip to open new territories for financial exploitation. However, he's been gone twice as long as he projected, and no one has heard from him. Quark dismisses Rom's fears, noting that Zek probably stopped off at Risa for a little "rest and recreation."

That night, Quark pays a traditional bribe to the Blessed Exchequer in the hopes that the sacred Ferengi deity will bless him with wealthy, thirsty customers . . . and a chance to get closer to Ezri. Seconds later, Quark is both shocked and delighted to see Ezri at his door. Dressed rakishly and brandishing a knife, Ezri seems a different woman. She is. She's the Ezri from the mirror universe ("Shattered Mirror"), and she's brought some disquieting news. The nagus is being held prisoner by the Alliance in the mirror universe. However, Regent Worf is willing to send Zek home in exchange for a ship's cloaking device, since that technology doesn't exist in the alternate realm. Zek is counting on Quark to bring the device to the regent within three days.

And if he doesn't? asks Quark.

Then the nagus will die, responds Ezri.

Quark enlists Rom to help him steal a cloaking device—while it's cloaked—from a Klingon bird-of-prey that is docked at the station. They bring it to one of the cargo bays, where the mirror Ezri awaits. Rom worries that the regent won't live up to his promise and return Zek, so the two brothers accompany Ezri to Terok Nor in the mirror universe. They arrive just in time to witness an altercation between the Bashir, who's part of the rebel resistance against the Alliance, and Vic Fontaine. Rom and Quark are surprised to see that in this universe, Vic isn't a hologram. He's a living being . . . at least he is until Bashir kills him. Unfortunately, since Ezri is working for the Alliance, Bashir is her enemy. He quickly takes her prisoner, along with Quark and Rom.

The captives are interrogated by O'Brien's counterpart, Captain Smiley, who decides that the cloaking device must remain with the rebels. He's willing to let the Ferengi go back to their own universe, although Ezri will remain a prisoner. Smiley leaves the three of them in a cell overnight, so that Quark and Rom can make their decision. Quark tells Ezri that they can't go home without Zek, and explains to her that the grand nagus is the head of the Ferengi Empire. Ezri, a mercenary who works for the side that can pay her the most, is impressed by Quark's account of Zek's wealth. A short time later, there's a commotion outside their cell, and the mirror version of Brunt bursts into the holding area. Unlike their Brunt, Quark and Rom discover that this one is actually a nice guy. He's also a good friend of Ezri's and has come to get her off the station. Together they retrieve the cloaking device, and the four of them head for the regent's ship, while Rom attempts to figure out which people in this universe are "alternate" and which are not.

Zek's confinement on the regent's flagship hasn't been unpleasant. He's been sharing a cell with Intendant Kira, who is quite adept at *oomox*. The intendant is in a good mood. It was her idea to get the cloaking device, and the regent has promised to release her, along with Zek, once it's delivered. The mirror Garak, who is the regent's right-hand man, reminds Worf that it took two years to track down the intendant. She's far too dangerous to release, he warns. But the regent, who's rather fond of the intendant, hasn't made up his mind what to do with her.

After Quark and Rom turn over the cloaking device, which will give the regent the ability to crush the rebellion, it becomes clear that the Alliance has no intention of releasing Zek—or them. Ezri receives a very warm greeting—in the form of a kiss—from the released intendant, which alerts the two Ferengi that her loyalties certainly aren't to them. Worf has them thrown into Zek's cell while he decides what to do. Brunt asks Ezri to convince the intendant to release the Ferengi. Unfortunately, the intendant hears the conversation and doesn't like it. She kills Brunt before Ezri's horrified eyes, telling the Trill that she was certain he was going to betray her.

Garak has difficulty bringing the cloaking device on-line, so Ezri tells Worf that Rom knows how it works. Worf sends Ezri to deliver Rom to the device, and the Trill tells a dubious Quark that she's trying to help them. However, as soon as Rom finishes working on the cloak, Worf orders Garak to kill the three Ferengi. Fortunately, the mirror Garak isn't nearly as bright as his counterpart on Deep Space 9, and the prisoners are able to delay the execution by telling the mirror Cardassian stories about *their* Garak.

Aboard the *Defiant*, Captain Smiley wonders if they'll be able to catch up with the Ferengi before they hand over the cloaking device to Worf. For all they know, the regent's flagship could be right behind them, with the device installed and activated. Unfortunately, he's right. The flagship decloaks and prepares to fire on the hapless rebel vessel. Suddenly, Worf's ship suffers a primary systems failure. Rom had the foresight to sabotage the flagship while he was working on the cloaking device. Just as Garak is about to execute the Ferengi, Ezri shows up and uses Garak's weapon—a hypo containing a deadly virus—on the Cardassian. After she frees the prisoners, Quark expresses bewilderment at Ezri's sudden change of heart, but she doesn't explain it.

The crew of the *Defiant* figures out that the flagship's power grid is off-line. They begin firing on Worf's vessel, a sitting duck that can't even raise its shields, and force the regent to surrender. The intendant searches for an escape shuttle and runs into Ezri in one of the corridors. The two women study each other distrustfully, then Kira invites Ezri to come along with her. Ezri declines, noting that the intendant shouldn't have killed Brunt. But despite her newly developed conscience, Ezri allows Kira to escape. Afterward, the rebels capture the Trill along with the regent's crew. Quark, still smitten with Ezri, offers to stick around for a while, but Ezri seems more interested in one of Smiley's crew, a mirror version of Rom's wife Leeta! With that final surprise, the three Ferengi are more than ready to go home.

"Yes, *Star Trek* is great drama, and yes, there are great *serious* episodes, but every now and then we have to do something that says something else," Ira Behr says, grinning. "The Emperor's New Cloak," he explains, allowed the writers to address those people in the viewing audience who tend to "point fingers at us and say, 'You guys think you're *so* serious, but deep down inside, *Deep Space Nine* is a pretty silly show,' and we got to respond, 'Hey, you know what? We're both!'"

What's more, Behr continues happily, "We finally got to question the whole lunatic idea of the mirror universe," albeit via one of his favorite Ferengi. Unlike the rest of the *DS9* regulars, who've simply accepted the bizarre events and personalities in the

The dark, grim mirror universe take on a different slant when seen from the Ferengi perspective. ROBBIE ROBINSON

alternate plane, the analytical but easily befuddled Rom keeps trying to make sense of it throughout the episode, only to come to the inevitable realization that "it just doesn't make any sense."

Timing was one of the primary motivators in returning one last time to this fascinating terrain. "We knew that we had a huge block of shows coming up to end the series, and we wanted to do something with Quark and Rom before the going got hot and heavy," Behr says. "The mirror universe was due for a Ferengi show. That gave us a chance to present another example of the Ferengi having to face adversity and danger, and Quark having to rise above himself a little bit. It also gave us the opportunity to deal with the Quark/Ezri relationship, which we knew we weren't going to be able to advance in terms of the real Ezri Dax," he adds.

A bit more than a year after he'd last set foot on the *DS9* sets ("Resurrection"), Director LeVar Burton returned to shoot his final episode for the series. "It was the mirror universe again," Burton says, recalling his previous encounter with the intendant. But it wasn't until he began working on "The Emperor's New Cloak" that he saw the entire scope of *Deep*

Space Nine's mirror characterizations. "What's memorable to me about the episode is that Michael Dorn was having so much fun," Burton says, chuckling. "He has a wonderful sense of comic timing, and he's the sort of actor who can get very big and very broad, to wonderful effect. Seeing him play the regent is a perfect example of that. He is *great* as the regent!"

Burton hadn't had the opportunity to work with Nicole deBoer prior to the episode. And even during "Emperor's" production, he didn't have much of an opportunity to work with the familiar Ezri Dax. *Mirror* Ezri was the identity he was dealing with. "And a very interesting identity she was," Burton smiles broadly.

"Nicole's performance gave me a real appreciation of her skill as an actress," says Lou Race. "She wasn't just playing 'Cute in Leather.' She became a much more sinister and driven, harder-edged character." Apparently, he adds, she enjoyed the performance. "Afterward she said, 'Can I play this character all the time?'"

"I knew right away what I wanted to do with the role," deBoer says, "so I just came in and did it. After playing sweet Ezri, I thought, 'Yeah! This is gonna be fun!' Not that Ezri is *too* sweet, but this was just really fun to do. I liked seeing everybody else's take on the mirror characters, particularly Nana's."

"I was pleased with that show," Nana Visitor says. It's the first time I thought that I got the intendant right. She can become a 1940s movie queen—overly campy—so quickly, and I never thought that was effective. I've always wanted for her to be laughable, but then the minute you start laughing you realize that she's done something absolutely horrifying. So I thought what they wrote this time was nice. The intendant was as complicated as she should be, but she was also pathetic, the way self-obsessed people who come from an ego-based existence and who live 'in the now' are."

As for that kiss between the intendant and the mirror Ezri, Visitor notes, "I never take scenes like that personally. If it had been Kira, it might have been a whole different thing, but as the intendant, I kick into a whole different place in myself. Of course," she reveals, "I never intended for the intendant to be bisexual. I think that was an assumption that everyone, including the writers, made after the character fell for Kira in 'Through the Looking Glass.' But that had been total narcissism on her part. It had nothing to do with sexuality. I never liked that people took her for bisexual because she's an evil character. There are so few gay

"I knew Jadzia had kissed a woman," says Nicole deBoer. "This was different." ROBBIE ROBINSON

characters on TV, and we really don't need an evil one" to play to some people's negative stereotypes.

"Doing the scene didn't bother me, but I was a little surprised that the producers would write it!" deBoer says. "I hadn't kissed anyone else on the show at that point. Luckily, I got to kiss someone who didn't have big, gnarly teeth that would cut me, like Quark or Rom. It was very nice. Nana can kiss very honestly," she laughs.

While the episode was written by Behr and frequent collaborator Hans Beimler, several suggestions offered up by René Echevarria during the story break made it into the final episode. "I'm proud to say that stealing the cloaking device *while* it's cloaked was my gag," Echevarria says happily.

Armin Shimerman and Max Grodénchik, the actors who would have to perform the gag, immediately recognized several challenges. In order to make carrying an invisible object seem realistic, the object must appear to have weight. That, obviously, would be the responsibility of the actors "carrying" the object. In addition, the actors would be required to keep a constant distance from one another, and to keep their own hands a set distance apart, so that the object would not appear to get longer or wider as they moved down the corridor. "Max and I practiced for three days, carrying something that wasn't there," Shimerman says. They received a welcome assist from the effects crew when they finally got to the set. "They gave us a rectangle of transparent filament that was connected to four dowels. So when we picked up

the invisible object, we actually picked up the dowels." With the filament taut between them, the actors never got too far apart.

Unfortunately, the filmed scene didn't play very well "as is." "We thought we'd have to cut it way, way back, and we didn't want to do that," Echevarria recalls. "I'm proud to say that I had a second brainstorm. I asked, 'What if we make it fritz?'"—that is, add an occasional visual-effects energy crackle that would briefly reveal the shape of the cloaking device. The idea worked for everyone, although it did cause some complications. The scene hadn't been designed with a visual effect in mind, so the actors hadn't maintained a precise 90–degree rectangle between their four hands as they went around corners. Nevertheless, Visual Supervisor David Stipes and his crew managed to finesse the effect to the point where the gag worked just the way Echevarria had imagined.

Jeffrey Combs was recruited to play the mirror version of Brunt, but although the actor has a lock on exactly who Brunt is in our universe, "the 'good Brunt' was hard to get to," he relates. "Our Brunt is just out and out tenacious, mischievous, and mean. So for the mirror Brunt, I just decided to be me in a good mood. He was this guy who's willing to help out in a pinch and not out to hurt anybody." Unfortunately, "None of the Ferengi from the alternate universe seem to survive," Combs sighs. "His death was par for the course."

"It was a necessity," notes Behr. "We needed to kill off a Ferengi to keep our streak going." Brunt's death marked a turning point in the story, he explains. "His death impacted both Ezri and Quark, and that stuff was important."

Several other mirror characters also bit the dust. The mirror Garak, for example, also drew his last breath. But that didn't bother Andrew Robinson. "I was really, really, *really* happy about it," Robinson smiles. "I never liked those alternate universe shows because that Garak was just a stupid bad guy. The thing that's great about *our* Garak is that he has subtext. There's a lot going on beneath the surface, and if you don't pay attention, then you're in trouble because he's *got* you. But the mirror Garak had no subtext. He was just a toady opportunist." Robinson did, however, find a way to enjoy his final performance as the toady. "I made him much more theatrical," he says. "In fact, I went a little overboard with that. But I had a *good* time doing it."

Behr admits that he had a secret agenda in killing off the Cardassian. "As the series drew to a close, many

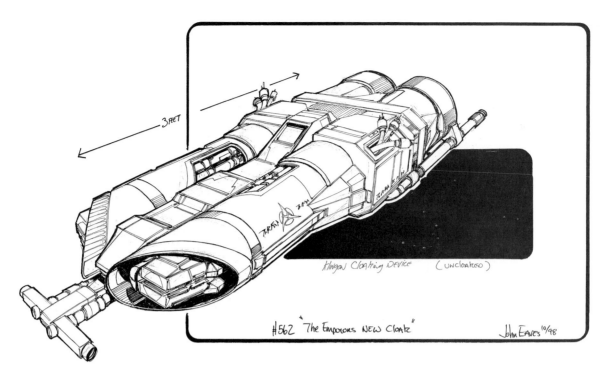

Klingon Cloaking Device (UNCLOAKED)

3 FEET

#562 "The Emperors New Cloak" John Eaves 10/98

An uncloaked Klingon cloaking device. JOHN EAVES

fans seemed to think that Garak was one of the characters who had a target painted on his back," Behr explains. "But I've never wanted to kill Garak. By killing the mirror Garak I gave those viewers their cake without quite letting them eat it," he says laughing.

Even more surprising, perhaps, was the death of the counterpart of a character who isn't even alive in the regular universe: everyone's favorite hologram, Vic Fontaine. James Darren—who played the uncredited role—relished both the opportunity and the fact that for once he wouldn't be playing a hologram. "I couldn't wait," Darren says excitedly. "I said, 'Let's make him evil! Spike my hair!'" That was exactly what the producers had in mind. "Ira met with the hair people," recalls Darren, "and he said, 'He can't be combed— that would be silly. Make him look like he's just nuts.' And then my character tries to kill Bashir, the man who brought him to Deep Space 9 in our universe," Darren continues enthusiastically. "That was *perfect*."

It was a brief bit, but it satisfied everyone. "We just wanted to get Vic into the episode," comments Behr. It added, he says, to the aforementioned lunatic nature of the mirror universe.

Vic's death scene was a new experience for Darren. "My characters have died before, but never on-screen," he explains. "Usually it's from lead. This is the first time it was from a phaser blast!"

The episode includes the usual complement of

Robinson didn't shed any tears when the mirror Garak met an untimely end. ROBBIE ROBINSON

intriguing references for viewers who notice such things. We learn that the mirror Jadzia has recently died in the alternate universe, just as her counterpart has in our own. Quark's entreaty to Ezri to call him "Shmun," from *Vulcan Love Slave,* is drawn, once again, from Behr's book *Legends of the Ferengi.* And Quark's prayer to the Blessed Exchequer is accompanied by a physical gesture—wrists pressed together with palms apart—that Shimerman has used more than once on the show. "It was one of the first things that Terry Farrell and I started doing years ago to tease one another on the set," Shimerman says. "I've been a *Star Trek* fan since the sixties, and I know that the Vulcan hand sign is universally recognized. I thought, 'Let's see if we can find something like that to do. I used it as a form of respect, rather like a Japanese bow, and it also can mean hello or goodbye."

The producers dedicated the episode to Jerome Bixby, well-known science fiction writer and the man responsible for creating the mirror universe in the classic original series episode, "Mirror, Mirror." "He'd passed away that year," Behr recalls. "He was a respected writer and certainly had done good things for *Star Trek.* Our show was about to end, and it just seemed that we could give one more tip of the hat to the origins of the whole thing."

Ezri consults with an earlier host, Joran, to catch a murderer. ROBBIE ROBINSON

FIELD OF FIRE

Episode #563

WRITTEN BY **ROBERT HEWITT WOLFE**
DIRECTED BY **TONY DOW**

GUEST CAST

Ilario	ART CHUDABALA
Chu'lak	MARTY RACKHAM
Joran	LEIGH J. McCLOSKEY

STARDATE UNKNOWN

A spectacular debut as helmsman of the *Defiant* is just cause for a celebration in honor of Lieutenant Hector Ilario at Quark's bar. The regulars toast the piloting skills of the new arrival, a recent graduate of Starfleet Academy. Before the evening's over, young Ilario has gotten a little tipsy on Saurian brandy, so Ezri walks him to his quarters. The next morning, she's shocked to discover that someone has killed Ilario just ten minutes after she left him. The method of murder was quite unusual: he was shot with a tritanium bullet, fired from a projectile weapon. Since virtually no one uses

such weapons anymore, the bullet's composition is an important clue. Sisko and O'Brien recall that Starfleet developed and tested a rifle, the TR-116, which fired titanium bullets. However, it never got beyond prototype stage. Only Starfleet officers would have access to the files that would allow someone to replicate a TR-116. Could the murderer be someone in Starfleet?

Another strange clue is revealed. Sensor readings show that the bullet traveled only a few centimeters—yet Ilario's body bears no sign of the powder burns that close-range gunfire would produce. Perplexed, Sisko orders Odo to launch a thorough investigation into Ilario's friends and potential enemies.

That night, Ezri, Bashir, and O'Brien ponder Ilario's murder and wonder if they could have done anything to prevent it. Later, as Ezri walks through the Habitat Ring, she finds Odo leading a manacled prisoner. The shape-shifter tells her that he's caught Ilario's killer. But the man in the restraints is actually Ilario. After Odo leads the man away, Ezri realizes that her hands are covered in blood. A second later, she's confronted by Joran Dax ("Equilibrium"), one of the Dax symbiont's former hosts and a three-time murderer. Joran tells Ezri that he can help her find Ilario's killer. All she has to do is perform the Trill Rite of Emergence and ask for his help. Ezri wants no part of Joran, but he assures her that he knows how the murderer thinks. And with that, Joran throws Ezri and himself over the railing of the Promenade, but before she hits the ground, she awakens. Seconds later, she receives a call from Sisko. There's been a second murder.

The latest victim is a science officer who's been stationed on Deep Space 9 for three years. The cause of death is the same as that for Ilario: a tritanium bullet fired at close range. Again, there are no powder burns. Other than that, there appears to be no connection between the two victims. O'Brien deduces the reason for the lack of powder burns and provides a demonstration for Odo and Ezri. He dons an exogenic targeting sensor that can scan through bulkheads and attaches a micro-transporter to the muzzle of a TR-116. Then, when he fires the weapon, the bullet is beamed to the location he scanned, where it continues its trajectory and hits the test object. Odo admits that it's an ingenious weapon; whoever came up with the method is obviously quite intelligent.

With no leads, Ezri decides that her dream was right. Summoning forth the consciousness of the murderous Joran is the only way to get inside the mind of the station's killer. The ritual is successful, and Joran begins to offer advice. Ezri must learn to think like a killer if she wants to catch one, he advises. Joran urges her to handle a TR-116 and look through the targeting display. He walks her through the process of picking a target and locking the sensors onto her prey. Finally, though, Ezri finds that path of investigation too disturbing to continue.

Next they head for the victims' quarters, but a search through their personal belongings proves futile. As Ezri sits in Quark's, pondering her next move, she sees a Starfleet officer being pursued by security. When the fleeing man passes Ezri, she trips him and tries to prevent him from getting up. In the heat of the confrontation, Joran urges her to find a weapon and use it. Without thinking, Ezri grabs a knife from one of the tables and raises it threateningly. Odo intervenes before she can use it, leaving a surprised Ezri shaken by her own actions. She's even more rattled when she discovers that the apprehended suspect is innocent. He's guilty of accessing the classified replicator patterns for the TR-116 without authorization, but he wasn't on the station when the first murder occurred. Deciding that it's too dangerous allowing Joran to influence her behavior, Ezri prepares to reverse the ritual that brought his personality to the surface. But she's interrupted by a call from Odo. A third victim has been found!

After investigating the dead officer's room, Ezri discovers the link between the three. Each had a photo on display in his or her quarters, showing the victim laughing with family or friends. For some reason the killer hates laughter. Ezri surmises that the murderer is a Vulcan, a species that is conditioned to find displays of emotion distasteful. Something happened to the killer, something so emotionally painful that it's made him lose control, she says. When he looks through the sensor and sees laughter, preserved forever in a photo, it triggers his violence. As Ezri begins to draw up a list of potential suspects, Joran spots a Vulcan science officer and studies him closely. Then he tells Ezri that he's certain it's the killer.

Ezri identifies the Vulcan as Chu'lak, and learns that he recently survived a devastating massacre by the Jem'Hadar. Ezri puts on the targeting device so she can see what Chu'lak is doing. She watches as he looks up *her* service record and then picks up a rifle. Joran urges Ezri to shoot the Vulcan before *he* has a chance to fire at her. At last she does, and Chu'lak falls to the ground, injured. Ezri heads for the Vulcan's quarters and elicits a confession while Joran urges her to finish the job and kill him. Instead, Ezri summons medical aid. Then, with the case closed, Ezri completes the ritual to rebury Joran's memories, knowing that he will always be a part of her, with his consciousness as much a part of who she is as any of Dax's other hosts.

David Weddle, Bradley Thompson, and Ron Moore were attempting to iron the kinks out of the troubled script for "Prodigal Daughter," which was about to go into production. Nearby, Ira Behr and Hans Beimler were deep in the throes of writing the following week's episode, "The Emperor's New Cloak." Down the hall, René Echevarria was developing a story for which he felt a strong affinity—the upcoming "Chimera," which was scheduled for three weeks hence. But what would they shoot in *two* weeks? Behr had an open slot and no available staff writer. It was time to call in a hired gun. Behr contacted former *DS9* Producer Robert Hewitt Wolfe.

"Ira called and said he had an idea about a sniper who was loose on the station," Wolfe says. "But he didn't know what the sniper was doing and he didn't have a hell of a lot else." One thing the executive producer was specific about, however, was that the episode should work as a stand-alone story, one that wouldn't require in-depth knowledge of the preceding or succeeding episodes. "They knew they were going to be jumping into the heavy continuity stuff real soon," Wolfe comments, "so they wanted an episode of some tension and peril that *wasn't* locked into continuity." This actually made Wolfe's task quite a bit easier; he wouldn't have to catch up on all the

The fact that everyone is so concerned about a fruit's few seconds of screen time speaks volumes about the production staff.
ROBBIE ROBINSON

ongoing storylines. One of the primary things that prompted him to accept the assignment, however, was an element that hadn't existed on the show during his tenure.

"I'd never written for Ezri Dax," Wolfe says. "The staff had been thinking about this as an Odo story, but I felt as if we'd seen the constable investigate this kind of thing before. I wanted to use a character whom we *hadn't* seen spearhead an investigation. That gave me a chance to do something with Ezri."

Wolfe initially developed a draft that was strongly steeped in the mystery genre. "It was like a police procedural, with lots of steps on profiling the killer," he says. "But the staff cut way back on that." However, the producers didn't alter Wolfe's *method* of profiling the antagonist. Noting that Ezri was a counselor, the writer opted to have her use what she knew best: psychology. "I wanted to make the murder investigation really resonate for Ezri, beyond just trying to find the killer. When I pitched that to the writing staff, I suggested that investigating the murder would start bringing out memories of Joran, because obviously there's a resonance there. I didn't know Ezri's character in depth, but she was still Dax, and I knew a lot about Dax. *And* I know Joran. I was there when he was created."

Behr liked Joran's part in the story so much that he expanded it with each draft of the script. In Wolfe's first draft, Ezri creates a hologram simulation of Joran who talks her through the investigation. Instead,

reports Wolfe with a chuckle, "Ira opted to go the Trill mumbo-jumbo route. My original version would have kept him tied to the holosuite, but this let them have him with Ezri all the time. As it developed, Joran just became more and more a part of the story."

Dax's previous host Joran Belar had been created in Season 3's "Equilibrium." The role was originated by performance magician Jeff Magnus McBride. But while that episode had capitalized on McBride's skills with masks, his acting abilities had not been tested. As Behr points out, "We now had a role that needed an actor." When the magician proved to be unavailable, the producers were free to seek out other casting options.

"The casting sessions for Joran were endless," comments Director Tony Dow, who won a place on the director's list following a suggestion to Behr from mutual friend Bill Mumy ("The Siege of AR-558"). "Joran is a pretty complex character. The actor had to play him with a sort of crazed unpredictability, but he couldn't be such a jerk that Ezri would just put him back in the bottle," Dow notes. After an exhaustive search, Actor Leigh J. McCloskey was chosen. "Leigh didn't have the scariness of appearance that we'd initially anticipated," says Dow, "but he's such a terrific actor that it worked out well."

Dow, too, worked out well. He is best known for the years he spent playing Wally Cleaver on *Leave It to Beaver*. Between directing stints, Dow produced several visual effects–oriented features, and worked as a visual effects supervisor. "Ira showed me 'The Darkness and the Light' as an example of what they wanted to accomplish in this episode," the director recalls. "It had the same sort of mystery feeling, with a renegade who kidnaps Kira. Ira told me that it was really the only other show of this type that they'd done. There isn't much personal violence on this series, so when it does occur, it's something to be reckoned with. My objective was to create an atmosphere of apprehension and a bit of panic about what was going on."

To create that atmosphere, Dow fell back upon his visual effects experience. For Ezri's dream sequence, for example, he wanted to create images that would have a dreamlike blurriness. "I shot that segment at twelve frames per second and then had it processed at six frames per second," Dow explains, pointing out that film is typically shot at twenty-four frames per second. "That gave the scene the slow motion and the blurriness. The dream sequence was specifically choreographed so that I could whip-pan

CLIP DETAIL

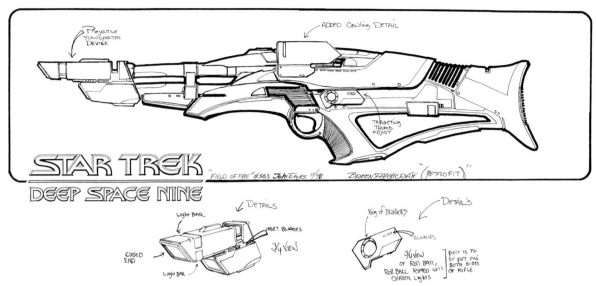

PROJECTILE TRANSPORTER DEVICE

ADDED COWLING DETAIL

TARGETING THUMB ADJUST

STAR TREK
DEEP SPACE NINE

"FIELD OF FIRE" #563 John Eaves 11/98   BREEN PHASER RIFLE (RETRO FIT)

DETAILS

Light Bar

CLOSED END

Light Bar

INSET BLINKIES

3/4 VIEW

Ring of BLINKIES

DETAIL'S

BLINKIES

3/4 VIEW
OF Roll BALL,
Roll BALL RIMED with
CHASER Lights

PIECE IS TO
BE PUT ON
BOTH SIDES
OF RIFLE

The TR-116 rifle is a retrofit of a Breen weapon. JOHN EAVES

(swing the camera very rapidly) off scenes and whip-pan into scenes. Then the editor could make his cut within the whip-pan." The camera and cutting technique gave Ezri's movement from room to room a surreal quality that didn't dip into the show's visual effects budget.

In fact, one of the show's most painstaking effects was a physical effect done during first unit production. "The script said they were going to shoot this big fruit that was going to explode," recalls B.C. Cameron. "I thought, 'Oh man, what a mess that's going to make.' I knew that if we had to do it more than once, we'd have to take the time to clean the watermelon off the walls and the carpet. I suggested that we put it inside a dome, because the gun shoots through walls anyway. But the producers wouldn't go for the watermelon dome. When the time came to shoot the scene, the Prop Department brought in the watermelon, which they'd painted purple." Cameron laughs. "They didn't want it to look like a watermelon. But I pointed out to them that when they blew it up, *everybody* would know it was a watermelon, because that's what it would look like on the inside."

Enter Gary Monak, maven of physical special effects. "I ran to the caterer, got some tapioca pud-

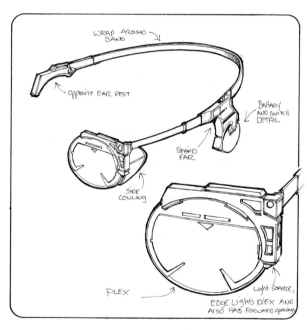

WRAP AROUND BAND

OPPOSITE EAR REST

BAHARY AND SWITCH DETAIL

BEHIND EAR

SIDE COWLING

PLEX

LIGHT SOURCE,
EDGE LIGHTS PLEX AND
ALSO HAS FORWARD openings

The exogenic targeting sensor. JOHN EAVES

ding and died it a real pukey lime-green color," he says with a chuckle. "Then we injected that into the center of the watermelon."

"They made a little hole where the camera wasn't going to see, so they could pump in the tapioca," Cameron interjects. "They had to pump it really *hard*, so it would squash down the melon meat and let the pudding fit in there."

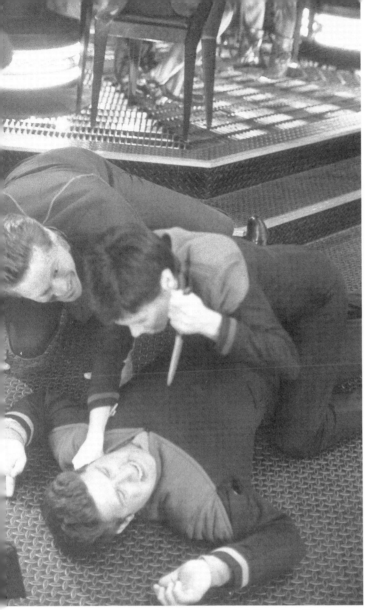

"I liked that Ezri chose to bring out the killer in herself to solve the murders," says deBoer. ROBBIE ROBINSON

"And *that*," Monak giggles, "totally changed the nature of the watermelon. Now we weren't sure what our pyrotechnics were going to do when it blew up, and we couldn't test it. It wasn't dangerous, but you know how the producers worry about the costumes! The actors were standing just a couple of feet away from it." Fortunately, the trajectory of the pukey pud-

ding proved to be nonhazardous to both humans and wardrobe, and the effect satisfied everyone.

Of greater concern to Dow was the technology behind the weapon used by the killer. "When I first read the script, I wasn't sure it was going to work," he says. "I thought it was essential that we really see the insides of the walls—I mean, actually go through a wall so that the audience understood what was happening."

"The magic gun that shoots bullets through walls!" reminisces Gary Hutzel. "But that wasn't the gag so much as that you could *see* through the walls. That drove a whole lot of aspects of the effect. It had to look as if Ezri was looking through a scope toward a target that was a great distance away."

Hutzel's team built a section of wall with its interior wiring and other components exposed. They then shot the prop wall from various angles so it could be used multiple times. Next they rearranged the walls in the set that normally serves as Sisko's quarters, creating a number of smaller rooms. Inside the rooms, they photographed various extras. "In order to get the right appearance, we had a Steadicam operator run sideways past the rooms so that the walls would be foreshortened in the foreground," Hutzel explains. "That gave everything the appearance of extreme distance, and the Steadicam gave it a handheld look, as if Ezri were looking through the targeting display. The operator had to run like nobody's business back and forth across the set and then come to a sudden stop, emulating Ezri's movements. He would run, run, run and stop, run, run, run back and stop," Hutzel smiles.

The killer, it turns out, is a Vulcan. "What would be the biggest surprise to a regular *Star Trek* fan?" Wolfe ponders. "No one's going to be surprised if a Bajoran or a Cardassian or a Romulan is the killer. But a *Vulcan* serial killer? That'll make you sit up and take notice." Wolfe had an additional reason for his choice. "I wanted to show that the psychological strains of the war are far-reaching. If you've got a *Vulcan* who's cracking under battle, that says something."

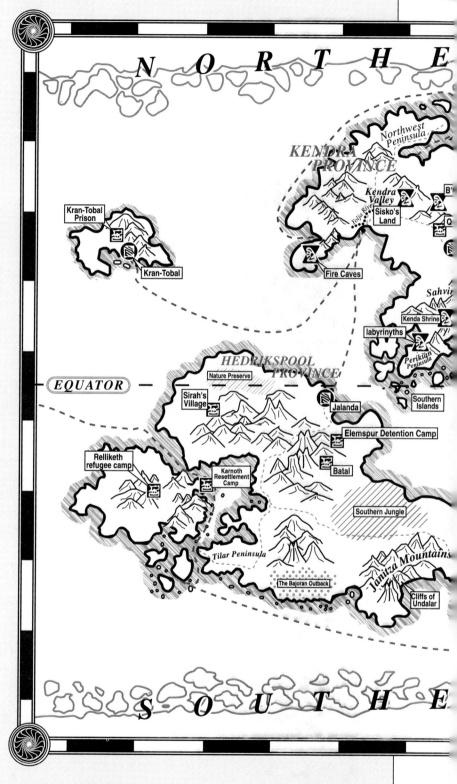

This map of Bajor has been rendered by Alan Kobayashi from a drawing that Robert Hewitt Wolfe executed during his tenure with Deep Space Nine. After Wolfe's departure, the map was continued by Bradley Thompson. Frankly, the editor of this book became obsessed with trying to show this map. It makes you wonder.

"I had a dry/erase board in my office that I theoretically was going to use to break stories," Robert Hewitt Wolfe explains. "But my office during the first season was not big enough to hold more than two people at a time. After staring at the blank board for months, it occurred to me that unlike planets we'd visited on previous *Star Trek* shows, Bajor was there and wasn't going to go away. So I felt like it might be fun to create a map.

"I drew some arbitrary continents, two large land masses and one small one, with an equator down the middle," he laughs. "I thought that probably would do it. The shorelines are fairly random. I tried to put a lot of interesting coastlines on there, but the decision-making process was pretty arbitrary.

"For a long time we put everything in the northern hemisphere. Then I started trying to figure out things to put in the south. If you compared these places with episodes, you'd probably find that the early seasons are on the top and then they start to move lower.

"Basically, the places that Kira had a personal interest in or a personal interaction with during the Occupation, are all clustered in the same general vicinity. I wanted things to be close to where she was working, like the former weapons depot that she raided, or the prison at Gallitep and the Bestri Woods; these are all places that she went to at some point during the occupation.

"Things that Kira didn't have a lot to do with, I put elsewhere. I felt that the Sirah's village, from "The Storyteller," seemed very different culturally from the Paqu and the Navot territories, so I put it as far away from them as possible.

"The map reminded us of places that we'd mentioned before so we could mention them again," Wolfe notes. "It made Bajor more of a physical reality for me. It became a real place."

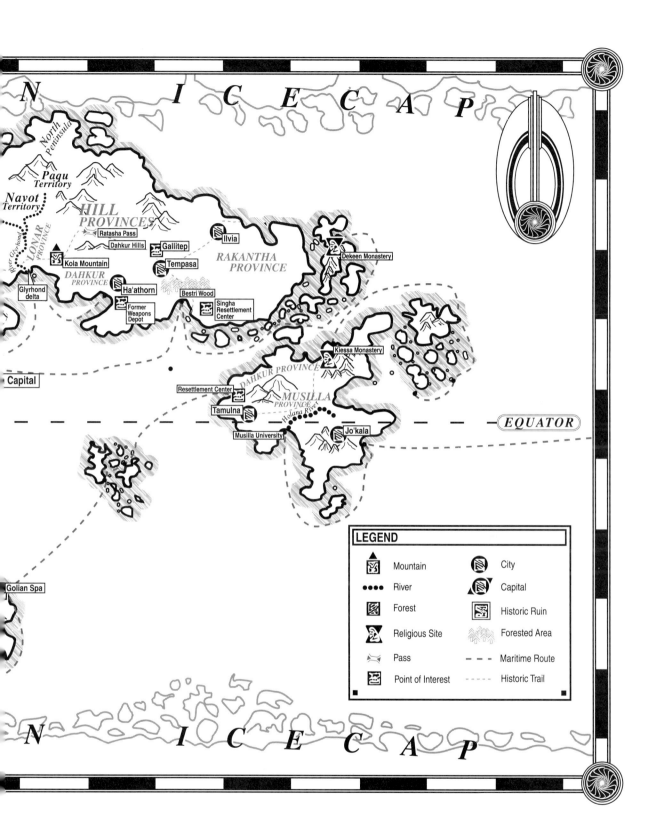

N I C E C A P

North Peninsula

Paqu Territory

Navot Territory

HILL PROVINCES

Ratasha Pass

Dahkur Hills

River Glyrhond

LONAR PROVINCE

Kola Mountain

DAHKUR PROVINCE

Glyrhond delta

Ha'athorn

Former Weapons Depot

Gallitep

Tempasa

Ilvia

RAKANTHA PROVINCE

Dekeen Monastery

Bestri Wood

Singha Resettlement Center

Kiessa Monastery

DAHKUR PROVINCE

Resettlement Center

MUSILLA PROVINCE

Tamulna

Holana River

Musilla University

Jo'kala

Capital

EQUATOR

Golian Spa

LEGEND

Mountain		City	
River		Capital	
Forest		Historic Ruin	
Religious Site		Forested Area	
Pass		Maritime Route	
Point of Interest		Historic Trail	

N I C E C A P

CHIMERA
Episode #564

WRITTEN BY **RENÉ ECHEVARRIA**
DIRECTED BY **STEVE POSEY**

GUEST CAST

Laas   GARMAN HERTZLER
Klingon   JOHN ERIC BENTLEY
Deputy   JOEL GOODNESS

STARDATE UNKNOWN

s Odo and O'Brien head back to the space station after a conference, the runabout's proximity alarm sounds, signaling the presence of something in their immediate vicinity. They're startled when they see a large spacefaring life-form move toward their vessel, and unnerved when the creature slams up against it. And then the thing that was outside the ship suddenly is *inside* the ship, a mass of changeling protoplasm that enters through a vent and reforms into a humanoid shape that is reminiscent of Odo's. O'Brien is wary. What if it's a Founder? But Odo knows that it isn't. He instinctively realizes that it's one of the "hundred" ("The Search, Part II")—one of the hundred infant changelings sent out by the Founders to explore the galaxy.

O'Brien isn't entirely convinced that the changeling isn't a Founder. He feels they should imprison it until they know the truth. Although the changeling doesn't trust humanoids, he's never run into another shape-shifter before, so he allows the pair to take him prisoner. Once they arrive at Deep Space 9, Odo pleads the changeling's case to Sisko. Bashir has scanned the being and found no trace of the disease that's affecting the Great Link, therefore, Odo reasons, he's not a Founder. Putting aside his reservations, Sisko releases the changeling into Odo's custody.

Odo tells the changeling, named Laas by the species who found him, about their people and their war against the humanoids in the Alpha Quadrant. Laas can understand the Founders' distrust of solids; he's had his share of bad experiences with them. Odo tells him that the ones he's encountered are different. They accept him completely. Laas is dubious. He's older than Odo and once found humanoids fascinating as well. But eventually he found their lack of tolerance oppressive. Noting a picture of Kira in Odo's quarters, Laas notes that he, too, once had a humanoid mate. The relationship didn't last because

Odo can't help but empathize with some of Laas's observations about solids. ROBBIE ROBINSON

they couldn't have children. The remark disturbs Odo, because he's often wondered if that factor will affect his relationship with Kira.

When Laas asks Odo if he knows how their people reproduce, Odo explains that in their natural state, they don't exist as separate entities at all. He links with Laas to show him what he means. Moved by the experience, Laas tells Odo that he's given up a great deal to stay among the humanoids. Odo explains that he won't have anything to do with the Founders and their war, but Laas realizes that Odo stays at Deep Space 9 only because of Kira.

When Odo tells Kira that he linked with Laas, Kira is concerned. Odo assures her that Laas isn't trying to lure him to the Dominion. Kira asks to meet the other changeling, so Odo arranges a get-together between Laas and his friends on the station. However, with Laas's antipathy toward humanoids, the encounter goes poorly, with the changeling alienating the entire group. When Odo chastizes Laas about his behavior, Laas explains that he was merely speaking his mind, whereas Odo denies his true nature in order to fit in with the humanoids, who would reject him otherwise. Laas's comments—and his invitation to join him in a search for the rest of the hundred—give Odo much to think about.

When Odo recounts the conversation with Kira, she's troubled by the fact that Odo didn't refuse Laas's invitation outright. Odo assures her that he's happy on the station, and that he loves her. For the moment, it's consolation enough for both. Later, Odo tells Laas that he doesn't intend to leave. However, he invites Laas to stay for a while, and the changeling agrees. Not long after, Odo comes to regret that decision when Laas gets into an altercation with a pair of Klingons who react badly to his shape-shifting in front of them. One of the Klingons draws a knife, and Laas responds by morphing his own hand into a knife. Then the other Klingon reaches for a weapon and Laas stabs and kills him.

Although Odo feels Laas acted in self-defense, Sisko informs him that the Klingon government intends to prosecute. Odo protests that Laas will never get a fair trial on the Klingon homeworld, but Sisko insists that a decision regarding Laas's extradition will be made by a magistrate. Odo can't help feeling that the case is driven by anti-changeling prejudice, and that Laas's paranoia about humanoids might be justified. A subsequent conversation with Quark, who tries to explain how repelled humanoids are at the sight of someone "turning into goo," makes him feel even worse. For once, not even Kira can soothe him. He admits to her that although the months he's spent with her have been the happiest of his life, a part of him wishes that he could be out in space with Laas, searching for the others and living as a changeling, not as a humanoid.

Wanting Odo to be truly happy, Kira helps Laas escape from his cell and tells him to wait for Odo in the Koralis system. Then, while Sisko orders a massive search for the fugitive, Kira tells Odo where to find Laas. Odo goes to Koralis and meets the other changeling, but to Laas's dismay, Odo tells him to go on alone. Laas protests that Kira let him go so he could find out where he belongs. Odo responds that he already knows where he belongs. Back at the station, Kira is surprised but grateful when Odo returns to her quarters. She tells Odo that she hopes she never made him feel that he couldn't be himself with her. She wants to know him the way he *really* is. In response, Odo morphs into a beautiful cloud of golden energy particles and wraps her within the shimmering light, bringing them both to a feeling of communion they've never been able to share before.

W ith the series' final arc looming on the horizon, *DS9*'s writing staff realized that it was time to set up the playing field for Odo's ultimate decision to return to his people. That decision would ring true to the viewing audience only if they learned a bit more about Odo's true nature. "It was our sense that because all of the

Monak supervised the robofogging of the Promenade. ROBBIE ROBINSON

changelings we'd seen were evil, that it was easy for Odo to say that he didn't want to be involved with his people, because they were all bad guys," René Echevarria recalls. "So it was never a fair choice for Odo. He'd never truly faced his own nature. That was the spark: 'What if he meets a changeling who's had no contact with the Founders? That could throw his life into turmoil.'"

The story that the writers broke was very heady, notes Echevarria. It was also very wrong. "It was this strange thing where Odo decides that humans are all a bunch of racists, or species-ists, and Sisko and the others keep denying it and denying it. Finally, Odo decides to go off with this other changeling out of anger. But Sisko goes, 'Okay, dammit, you're right. We are. We can't help it. Human nature is what it is—we shrink from what is 'other.' And somehow"—Echevarria laughs—"Sisko's honesty makes Odo stay. It was preposterous! We threw it out, except for some of Sisko's dialogue, which was recycled as Quark's speech to Odo. After that, I reenvisioned the story as much more of a triangle. It ultimately became an exploration of Odo and Kira's relationship."

Of course, any discussion of a couple's relationship has to include the nature of their sex life. "In the first draft, there was a scene between Odo and Kira, who were in bed together," continues Echevarria. "There was tension between them, because this changeling guy had been around. So they've had an argument, and she's saying, 'Oh, yeah? Well you know what it's like sleeping next to you? You're like a cold fish—you have no body temperature.'" Echevarria begins to laugh. "I don't know where I was going with that. My initial feeling was that Odo was able to mimic the human form, so he was able to please Kira. But on a different level, she couldn't really enjoy it because she knew that *he* couldn't enjoy it the way a human would. He was just performing for her, and she didn't get the satisfaction of giving him pleasure. I did call both Rene [Auberjonois] and Nana [Visitor] separately and talked to them about their characters, and how they envisioned their sex life—which was pretty hilarious. But ultimately there was no way to talk about any of that on a family television show, so all of it fell by the wayside. Later I realized that I'd had it all wrong, that really Kira was unable to give Odo something that was so natural to him. She couldn't share with him in the way that he's capable of sharing, by linking. It's a different kind of intimacy."

By the end of the episode, the couple have decided that they truly want to be together, but Echevarria realized the script was missing something: a scene that would demonstrate Kira and Odo's willingness to try something different that would deepen their relationship. With the help of the Visual Effects Department, that became the scene where Odo morphs around Kira as a ghostlike mist, allowing her to know how it feels to link. "The scene was just magical," smiles Echevarria. "It moved their relationship to a new level, with him not trying to be human like her, and her meeting him halfway. You can see on her face that she is experiencing something special."

It took a while for David Stipes's visual effects team to translate the script's magical closing image into something everyone liked. "At first the producers wanted to have Odo on the sofa, and when he turns to goo, Kira would snuggle into it," Stipes says with a frown. "Everybody thought, 'Ugh. That sounds disgusting.' Then they decided to have snow fall on her. Well, *that* sure sounded warm and reassuring!" he laughs. "Nobody knew what the heck to do. Finally I was talking to my wife, Patricia, and she recounted the story of how she'd first seen the aurora borealis up in Michigan. She said she couldn't believe how beautiful it had been."

The idea resonated with Stipes. "I began to think, 'What if Odo turned into some sort of wonderful, golden color and surrounded Kira in a shimmering curtain of light, like the aurora borealis. That would be warm and beautiful. And that's what we went for. We combined the aurora borealis with a warm and fuzzy feeling. It was a visual expression of love. In a way, the effect was a little present from me to my wife."

Laas doesn't think Kira and Odo's relationship will last—an opinion the writers shared. ROBBIE ROBINSON

To create the "warm and fuzzy" aurora, Stipes contacted designer David Lombardi at the effects company Digital Muse. Lombardi generated a series of animated light elements that resembled the tail of a slowly moving comet. Those elements then were delivered to Davy Nethercutt at Pacific Ocean Post. Nethercutt combined them with numerous layers of light and sparkle elements that had been created by Dan Curry and his staff for previous *Star Trek* effects. Nethercutt and fellow animator Steve Fong made the resulting effect blend from a ghostlike morph into an ethereal and elegant light show, which they then rotoscoped around Kira's form. "We had to cue the movement of the light off of Nana's performance," Stipes explains. That performance was an effect in itself, he says. "She looked so romantic. It was very lyrical."

Visitor's partner in the scene, Rene Auberjonois, was equally impressed. "I was standing off camera watching Nana when she was doing that," he says. "She was essentially acting to nothing. Afterward, I told her, 'God, you make me look like such a great lover!'" he laughs.

The catalyst to all of this drama was Laas, one of the hundred changeling infants sent out by the Founders years earlier. And although the screen credit for the actor behind the tall, soft-spoken shapeshifter reads "*Garman* Hertzler," he was none other than the far more familiar J.G. Hertzler. "I was so happy that they cast J.G. Hertzler in that role," Auberjonois says. "The whole show depended on him to make it work, and he certainly did."

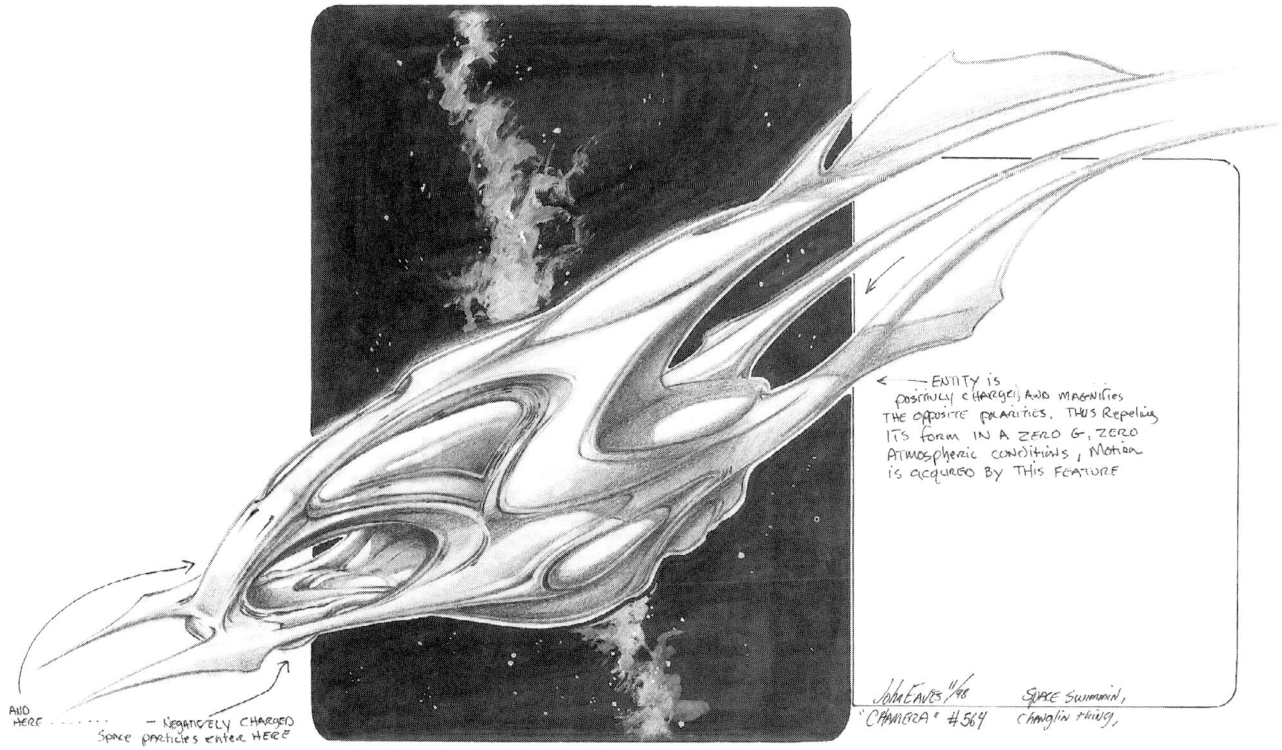
ENTITY is positivly charged, and magnifies the opposite polarities, thus repeling its form in a zero G, zero atmospheric conditions, motion is acquired by this feature
John Eaves 11/98
"CHAMERA" #564
Space swimmin, changlin thing,
AND HERE
- NEGATIVELY CHARGED Space particles enter HERE

John Eaves's concept for the "space swimmin' changelin' thing."

But why *Garman*? J.G. Hertzler laughs at his private little in-joke. "I spread the rumor that Garman was my reclusive brother from New York," he grins. Of course, Hertzler doesn't *have* a brother, but he *does* have an alter ego of whom he's just as protective. "When they talked to me about doing the role, they were worried that Laas would be too much like Martok," the actor comments. "And frankly, I was worried about damaging the image of Martok, since Laas kills a Klingon in the show." The dilemma reveals a lot about Hertzler's seriousness as an artist. "I don't like watching myself on film," he says. "But I really do enjoy watching Martok. I didn't want to do anything that would compromise the reality of *that* being. I felt that if it was known that the same actor, J.G. Hertzler, could do something else, then Martok wouldn't be as real. That was my concern."

With such concerns on all fronts, why did the producers decide to use Hertzler for the part? "We needed an actor who could stand up to Rene, because Rene is so good," comments Ira Behr. "We had to give him the best. We saw lots of actors, but none of them were doing it for us." The producers started thinking about the character actors they put the most stock in. Coincidentally, they were all currently under *DS9*'s employ. "We kicked around the idea of using Jeff Combs for a while," Behr grins. "We also talked about using Andy Robinson, but his voice is just so recognizable. Then we said, 'How about J.G.?' I'm just a huge fan of his, but we weren't sure. We brought him in and he auditioned for us."

Despite some initial concerns that he might sound too much like Martok, "Garman" did just fine. In fact, his characterization was so distinctive that few recognized him. Nor did they recognize the source of his characterization. "I wanted to find a way to keep this character sort of annoyingly judgmental, because of his politics," Hertzler reveals. "He felt that these humanoids were so far beneath him that it was like talking to dogs. His proenvironmentalist point of view, feeling that humanoids *ruin* things, seemed like almost a passionate adherence to the Prime Directive. And that reminded me of James Kirk. William Shatner has a theatrical way of delivering lines by taking breathing pauses and holding onto the ends of words. I thought, 'That would work for Laas.' So that's where the voice came from. It's me doing my best imitation of somebody else doing William Shatner doing Kirk!"

As for the genesis of the changeling's name, not

even René Echevarria remembers how "Laas" came to be. "I wanted his name to be something really strange and unusual," the writer remarks. "Ira kept making fun of it. Whenever we would talk about the story, Ira would say, "And then the Swedish guy comes in . . .'"

Hertzler had his own interpretation. "Laas has these wonderful speeches that question the very foundation of the Federation, where people of all religious and racial backgrounds come together to live in peace and harmony. Basically he was saying, 'Forget about it. It's not possible. It violates the laws of nature.' To me, his name was *laws*."

The name of the episode, "Chimera," reflected Laas's contention about the impossibility of racial harmony. The term, from Greek mythology, carries two meanings: "an imaginary monster" and "an unattainable dream." Echevarria felt the second meaning fit the love story between Odo and Kira. "In my first draft, the possibilitiy of Kira and Odo really coming together was somewhat unattainable," Echevarria says. "That part changed, but I kept the title."

As for the imaginary monster, the episode begins with Laas appearing as a fishlike life-form, swimming though space. To save on the budget, they considered reusing some footage of the whalelike life-form that appeared in the *Voyager* episode "Elogium." In the end, however, Senior Illustrator John Eaves created a new design, which was then rendered in CGI.

At the time "Chimera" was produced, the writers had not yet completed their throughline about Odo carrying the disease that threatens his people. That leaves one unanswered question about Laas: Did Odo infect him? "I've thought about that many times," Hertzler says. "Laas is out there, and I don't know what his story is."

"One of the things I regret is not having time to bring Laas back," Behr states. "That has nothing to do with whether he was sick or not. I just liked the character. Believe me, it even came up while we were breaking the final show," he sighs. "But with everything that we had to tie up, we just couldn't."

INTER ARMA ENIM SILENT LEGES
Episode #565
WRITTEN BY **RONALD D. MOORE**
DIRECTED BY **DAVID LIVINGSTON**

GUEST CAST

Garak	ANDREW J. ROBINSON
Cretak	ADRIENNE BARBEAU
Koval	JOHN FLECK
Admiral Ross	BARRY JENNER
Neral	HAL LANDON, JR.
Wheeler	CYNTHIA GRAHAM
Hickam	JOE REYNOLDS

SPECIAL GUEST STAR

Sloan	WILLIAM SADLER

STARDATE UNKNOWN

The day before Bashir's departure for a conference that will take place on the Romulan homeworld, the doctor goes to the Replimat with Garak. Bashir explains that he will be participating in talks about Dominion biogenic weapons and ketracel-white, subjects that Garak finds rather dull. But the Cardassian offers the opinion that Starfleet Intelligence will probably send along someone to gather information on more interesting subjects, like Romulan intelligence and military capabilities. Bashir scoffs at the notion; the Romulans are, after all, their allies. Garak merely smiles and notes that the doctor is, as always, the eternal optimist.

That night Bashir awakens to find a visitor in his quarters. It's Sloan, the Section 31 operative who previously tried to recruit the doctor for that shadowy organization ("Inquisition"). Sloan informs Bashir that he has an assignment for him. He wants the doctor to gather data on the Romulan leadership. Bashir makes it clear that he doesn't intend to work for Section 31, but Sloan is unfazed. He knows that Bashir will be unable to resist the lure of secrecy and intrigue. After Sloan disappears, Bashir reports the encounter to Sisko, who tells the doctor to carry out Sloan's assignment. Starfleet Command has done virtually nothing to investigate Section 31 since Sisko and Bashir informed them of its existence the previous year. The captain is concerned that someone in Starfleet may be protecting the organization. If Bashir plays along with Sloan, they may get some useful information about the organization and its connections.

On the *U.S.S. Bellerophon*, the *Intrepid*-class starship

Bashir is bemused by Sloan's appearance en route to the conference on Romulus. ROBBIE ROBINSON

that is transporting the attendees to the conference, Bashir enjoys a drink with Admiral Ross and Romulan Senator Cretak ("Shadows and Symbols"). The doctor is shocked when they're joined by Sloan, who is posing as a Federation cartographer. Bashir advises Ross that Sloan is on board. Obviously there's more to this assignment than the simple intelligence-gathering mission that Sloan had described to Bashir. Bashir wonders if they should remove him from the conference. Ross considers and then decides to let Sloan play out his hand. Otherwise, they'll never know what he's up to.

Later, Sloan briefs Bashir on the mission at hand. He wants the doctor to diagnose the health of Koval, chairman of the Tal Shiar. Koval is a powerful figure on Romulus, and he opposes the government's current alliance with the Federation. Sloan explains that Koval is said to suffer from Tuvan Syndrome, a degenerative neurological disease. Although Sloan won't reveal why he needs Bashir's confirmation of Koval's ailment, Bashir suspects that Section 31 will use the information to keep the Romulan off the Empire's powerful Continuing Committee. Sloan admits that if someone like Koval does rise to power, it could be a disaster for the Federation. It would be better if Cretak received the position.

Bashir meets Koval shortly after arriving on Romulus. He lets Sloan know that the Romulan *may* have Tuvan Syndrome, but if so, it's in the very early stages. Koval could function normally for another fifteen years. After Sloan asks if there's anything that could trigger the acceleration of the disease, Bashir

becomes convinced that Sloan is plotting to murder Koval. He expresses his concerns to Ross, who says that he'll have Sloan confined to his quarters immediately. But Bashir worries this may not be enough. If Sloan has an accomplice on Romulus, which Ross thinks likely, he already may have set his plan in motion. They need to warn the Romulans, Bashir says. But Ross refuses to allow Bashir to act. Ross will tell Starfleet Command about the situation. In the meantime, Bashir is to do nothing.

Not long after, Bashir hears that Ross has been felled by an aneurysm. With the admiral incapacitated, Sloan is still at large, free to carry out whatever plans he has in mind. With nowhere else to turn, Bashir decides to confide in Cretak. He tells her about the plot to assassinate Koval and asks her to get him a copy of Koval's personal database, which may provide leads as to Sloan's accomplice. Sloan tells Bashir to get a sample of Koval's skin cells so that he can confirm the diagnosis. However, when Bashir meets with Koval, the Romulan lures *him* into an interrogation to find out why Bashir is on Romulus and who he's working for. When the doctor refuses to respond, Koval resorts to painful scanning techniques, which don't work on Bashir's unique brain structure.

The Romulan brings him before a meeting of the Continuing Committee, where Bashir discovers that Cretak has been arrested for attempting to access Koval's database without authorization. In Bashir's mind, there's only one thing to do. He tells the committee everything—about Sloan, Section 31, and the assassination plot, and about his effort to get Cretak to help him. After Bashir finishes his story, Koval has another prisoner brought in. It's Sloan, and to Bashir's surprise, the operative looks like a beaten man. Koval relates that he has used his scanning devices on Sloan as well as Bashir. In Sloan's case, however, they were effective, and Koval has discovered that there is no Section 31. Sloan is *not* the master of a "rogue agency." He's just an agent of Starfleet Intelligence who decided to take justice into his own hands when his superior, a Starfleet admiral, died, allegedly at the hands of the Tal Shiar. He invented Section 31 so that Starfleet Intelligence would be held blameless when Sloan assassinated Koval, the head of the Tal Shiar.

Koval's findings clear Bashir, although Cretak's involvement, however well intentioned, gets her convicted for treason. Suddenly, Sloan attempts to grab the weapon of one of the guards. Reacting quickly, Koval vaporizes Sloan with a phaser. Bashir is returned to the *Bellerophon*, where he goes over all the pieces of the puzzle until they fall into place. Confronting the "recovered" Admiral Ross, Bashir demands to know the truth. He's realized that it was Ross who led him to believe that Sloan had an accomplice, and Ross who prevented him from contacting either the Romulans or Deep Space 9. When Ross had his aneurysm, the only person left for Bashir to turn to was Cretak—which was obviously what Ross and Sloan wanted him to do. Bashir is positive that Sloan is still alive.

Ross admits that Sloan was supposed to be beamed away a split second before Koval's phaser beam hit him. And Koval has been a mole for the Federation for over a year. The removal of Cretak from her position has left Koval in a very secure position within the Romulan government, giving the Federation a friend in a very high place who will make sure that the Romulans don't switch sides in the middle of the war.

Bashir is furious. Ross has allied himself, if only temporarily, with Section 31, an organization that tramples the beliefs of the Federation. Ross's only reply to Bashir is a quote from Cicero: "*Inter arma enim silent leges*—in time of war, the law falls silent." Depressed, Bashir returns to DS9, where he isn't at all surprised to receive another nighttime visit from Sloan. The operative has dropped by to thank Bashir for being the decent human being Section 31 thought he was. Only a man of conscience would have performed to their expectations for this assignment, and Bashir didn't let them down. Sloan bids Bashir sweet dreams and disappears, leaving a troubled Bashir unable to sleep.

The most obvious question, of course, is where did Ronald D. Moore get that title? "I think Ron was trying to get even with Hans and me for 'Wrongs Darker Than Death or Night,'" chuckles Ira Behr. "Or maybe he was looking to top everyone else, so he thought, 'Latin!'"

Not so, says Ron Moore. "I got the title at a book store," he explains. "I was browsing through the new stuff, and there was a copy of William Rehnquist's new book. It was about habeas corpus in American law and how Abraham Lincoln had suspended that writ during the Civil War, along with some other civil liberties. On the book jacket, there was a blurb that said Lincoln's suspension of *habeas corpus* was a classic case of the old Roman dictum *Inter arma silent leges*— 'In times of war, the laws fall silent.' And I looked at it and said, 'Hey!' because I was working on this episode and it was all about Section 31 and this

Given a choice between self-righteousness and self-recrimination, Behr would have chosen the latter for Bashir. ROBBIE ROBINSON

espionage thing and how the law *was* going to fall silent because of the war. It was *perfect*!"

Moore sent the phrase over to the show's research consultant, who provided a somewhat longer version for the writer's use. "The word order was different from the original quote, but she told me that word order doesn't matter in Latin so I could arrange the words however they looked best," he says. "So I arranged them in a way that looked and read best to me."

Because Ross has to deliver the line at the end of the episode, the phrase received a special notation in the script's pronunciation guide (a regular component of all *Star Trek* scripts). For those who want to impress their friends, the correct pronunciation is EN-ter ARM-ah EYE-nim SEE-lent LEH-ges.

Moore also tossed in a bit of ancient Greek with the name of the *Intrepid*-class ship that takes Bashir to Romulus: *Bellerophon*. Moore blames the British for his inspiration, though. "The *Bellerophon* was a ship on which Lord Nelson sailed," he says. "That's where I plucked the name from." Interestingly, the mythic character of Bellerophon rode the winged horse Pegasus, which happens to be another name that Moore used for a starship, this one in *The Next Generation* episode of the same name. "Yeah, someone pointed that out to me after the fact, but I wasn't trying to draw a connection between the two," Moore laughs. Nor was he trying to draw a connection between Pegasus's master and the Chimera, the legendary beast slain by Bellerophon (and coincidentally the name of the preceding episode). "I didn't even *know* that," he admits.

Sometimes coincidences *are* just coincidences. However, the idea of bringing back Section 31 and Sloan was quite deliberate, notes Ira Behr. "We'd had that idea since the end of 'Inquisition,'" he says. "We wanted to bring them back. We just needed to find a spot for it when Bill Sadler would be available."

"'Inquisition' demanded a follow-up," confirms Moore. "It ends with the idea that this will happen, and that we're going to let Julian be a spy for real after all those fantasies of his. The trick we came up with here was to really lead him along and make it look to the audience like he's ahead of the game. Make the audience believe he's figuring it all out and then telling them, 'No—they've figured *him* out.'"

"It's an excellent show," says Behr, "but it doesn't have all the levels it should have. We thought we'd do a show about the compromising of Bashir. Unfortunately, it doesn't do that. At the end, Bashir winds up making this angry, pointed speech to Ross, which is a lot less interesting than the situation at the end of 'In the Pale Moonlight.' There a man is trying to deal with his own culpability. And this is a show that demanded, I felt, Bashir's culpability. And he gets to walk away clean, with him being the one pointing the finger. It takes the show down a notch, and keeps it from reaching the level we wanted."

Actor Megan Cole, who had played Cretak in the first two episodes of the season, was unavailable for "*Inter Arma,*" which forced the producers to cast their nets for a replacement. They chose Adrienne Barbeau, perhaps best known to audiences for her roles in the film *Escape from New York* and the long-running sitcom *Maude.* "She'd been in before to read for *Star Trek,* and this time she nailed the part," notes Director David Livingston. "She brought a lot of humanity to it, which made Cretak a very rich character. She had the strength of a Romulan but a great deal of emotional depth."

"Adrienne was great," agrees Moore. "She brought something different to the role, a certain sympathy and vulnerability that worked for the character in this episode. You *wanted* to like Cretak more in this than you had in the other two. And that made you feel bad that she was going down at the end.

Cretak was the only Romulan the writers tried to flesh out.
ROBBIE ROBINSON

Cretak was much harder in the two-parter because she was there to serve a different purpose. She hadn't been designed with this episode in mind."

Admiral Ross, too, seemed to go through a shift in characterization, even though Barry Jenner once again filled his shoes. "He'd do anything to save the Federation," Jenner says of his character. "And here he puts so much value on the success of the war efforts that he's willing to do things that might not be thought of as honest and aboveboard. He was willing to bend some rules behind the scenes and go through some soul-searching to defend the integrity of the Federation."

In that sense, he's not all that different from Sisko, whose efforts to get the Romulans into the war the previous year were almost worthy of an amoral operative like Sloan. "Ross is a compromised guy, just like Sisko," observes Behr. "But it's not like he's a double agent. If he were, we'd have never allowed him to marry Sisko and Kasidy." Behr pauses and shakes his head, bemused. "It's so spooky talking about this stuff. It almost sounds heretical. Compromised heroes! Compromised supporting characters! It's wonderful, isn't it? I'm very proud of what we've been allowed to do."

The *Intrepid*-class *Bellerophon* is, of course, the same class of vessel as *Voyager,* which allowed the producers to utilize a very convenient look-alike on a neighboring soundstage for some of their sets. "When we started structuring the show," says Moore, "I called Rick Berman and [*Voyager* Executive Producer] Brannon Braga and [*Voyager* Supervising Producer] Merri Howard and said, 'I'd really like to use the

Voyager sets on this.' We could have reused the *Defiant* sets once again [as in 'Valiant'], saying the *Bellerophon* was a *Defiant*-class ship, but I didn't want to. I thought that using a bigger starship with a different look would make the mission seem bigger and more important. And we could save a lot of money if we went over and used their existing stuff, rather than building a new ship."

"We wound up using their conference room and their mess hall," says Livingston. "We scheduled it for a day when the *Voyager* crew was working on a different soundstage."

The *DS9* crew also made use of some items from the most recent *Star Trek* film, *Insurrection*—specifically, the new dress uniforms created for that movie by Bob Blackman. As they had with the new duty uniforms created for *First Contact*, the producers had adhered to an unofficial embargo on debuting the costume on *DS9* until after *Insurrection* was in theaters, and held them until this episode.

Sisko agrees to help Vic by playing the high roller in the crew's carefully constructed caper. ROBBIE ROBINSON

BADDA-BING BADDA-BANG

Episode #566

WRITTEN BY IRA STEVEN BEHR & HANS BEIMLER
DIRECTED BY MIKE VEJAR

GUEST CAST

Kasidy Yates	PENNY JOHNSON
Mr. Zeemo	MARC LAWRENCE
Tony Cicci	MIKE STARR
Frankie Eyes	ROBERT MIANO
Nog	ARON EISENBERG
Countman	BOBBY REILLY
Guard	CHIP MAYER
Al	JAMES WELLINGON
Blonde	ANDREA ROBINSON
Croupier	SAMMY MICCO
Dancer	JACQUELINE CASE
Dancer	KELLY COOPER
Dancer	MICHELLE JOHNSTON
Dancer	MICHELLE RUDY
Dancer	KELLY SHEERIN

SPECIAL GUEST STAR

Vic Fontaine	JAMES DARREN

STARDATE UNKNOWN

Bashir and O'Brien are disappointed when Vic Fontaine turns down an invitation to join the pair in their "Alamo" holosuite program. He doesn't look good in buckskin, he explains. To cheer his friends up, he begins to croon

a tune about Texas, but during the song, something strange happens to Vic's program. It destabilizes for a few seconds. Then, suddenly everything's fine—except for the fact that the lounge has been transformed. It's darker, smokier, and filled with a much rowdier crowd, primarily made up of tough-looking guys in cheap suits. Vic attempts to finish his song, only to be pushed offstage by a group of showgirls. As if that isn't bad enough, Frankie Eyes, an old crony of Vic's, shows up in the club, accompanied by his bodyguard, Tony Cicci. There's no love lost between Vic and Frankie, and Frankie wastes no time in telling Vic to take a powder—from both the club and from Vegas. It seems that Frankie has bought Vic's hotel and as far as he's concerned, Vic is history.

O'Brien's not about to let Vic take that kind of abuse, so he attempts to delete Frankie and Cicci from the holosuite program. To his surprise, nothing happens. Nor can he freeze the program. Uncertain what to do, O'Brien suggests that they could shut down the program manually and reset it. But Bashir points out that this would mean wiping Vic's memory. He'd forget everything that's happened to him since he was first activated ("His Way"). The doctor recommends an alternate plan; he'll call his friend Felix, the man who designed Vic's program. But the news that Bashir receives from Felix isn't good. It seems that the programmer incorporated a "jack-in-the-box" in Vic's program—a surprise to keep things interesting. But Vic's friends liked the program the way it was. Bashir reports that the only way to get the program to reset is to get rid of the Frankie Eyes character. There's a catch, though. The program is period specific, so they'll have to eliminate him in a way that would make sense in 1960s Las Vegas. And they'll have to keep Vic safe from Frankie and his mob pals while they do it, because if anything serious happens to Vic, his matrix will be eliminated from the program—permanently.

Vic's friends band together with Bashir and O'Brien to try to figure out a way to help him. Odo, Kira, and Nog all feel indebted to Vic for his help in dealing with personal problems, while Ezri and Kasidy just enjoy going to his club. Worf, however, feels that a hologram is a hologram. Vic is entertaining, but he isn't a real person. And Captain Sisko is strangely uninterested in having anything to do with Vic or his club.

The stakes grow higher when Bashir and O'Brien visit Vic's holographic hotel suite and discover that Vic has been beaten up by Tony Cicci. The abuse was clearly a message from Frankie: Vic shouldn't waste time clearing out. O'Brien and Bashir tell Vic that they're working on a plan to help him. In fact, at that very moment, Odo and Kira are in the lounge, checking up on Frankie Eyes and looking for the mobster's weak spot. Dressed elegantly to fit the era, the pair split up, and Odo gets to know Tony Cicci while Kira flirts with Frankie. Before long, Odo has become part of Cicci's close circle of friends and Kira has become the apple of Frankie's eye. Together they gather enough information for the group to begin plotting.

Frankie works for crime boss Carl Zeemo, who apparently fronted Frankie the money for the hotel in exchange for a healthy percentage of the casino's take. According to what Frankie told Kira, Zeemo will be coming to see the place soon, to pick up his first payment and to take a look at his newest acquisition. As the group ponders what would happen to Frankie if he didn't give Zeemo his "skim" of the gambling proceeds, they realize that *that's* the answer. They'll have to rob the casino to make sure that Zeemo doesn't get his money. After that, they won't have to worry about Frankie, because Zeemo will take care of him.

The plan is set in motion. Kira continues to flirt with Frankie, at the same time gathering information on the casino's safe. Kasidy befriends the security guard at the door to the countroom where the safe is located, while Odo uses his connections with Cicci to get Ezri a job as a waitress. In the meantime, Vic convinces Frankie to let him bring his high-rolling contacts into the casino.

Back in the real world outside of the holosuite, Sisko is annoyed with Kasidy for taking part in the scheme. Kasidy doesn't understand, until Sisko explains that in the Las Vegas of circa 1962, people of his and Kasidy's color would not be permitted in a nightclub—not as guests. Kasidy explains that she's always been welcome at Vic's, as has Sisko's son Jake. Racial prejudice is the one aspect of Vic's that isn't really period specific. It may not be an accurate representation of how things were in 1962, but it demonstrates the way things *should* have been. Sisko contemplates Kasidy's words and later volunteers to play the role of the high roller who's pivotal to the plan.

Vic walks the crew through the complex scenario, one that allows them only eight minutes to pull off the heist. Kira will keep Frankie Eyes away from the casino and the countroom, while Sisko and Vic lay down enough money at the craps table to draw a crowd. Bashir will spike a drink with ipecac, which Ezri will serve to the countman, while Kasidy and O'Brien will distract the guard watching the countroom by staging an argument in front of him. The countman, made ill by Ezri's drink, will race from the countroom, allowing Nog to get in and use his sensitive Ferengi ears to figure out the combination to the safe. Odo will help Nog get the money out of the room.

It all sounds perfect, but on the night of the actual robbery, there are several glitches in the plan, most notably when Nog realizes that the safe has an auto-relock tumbler that will make his job much more difficult. While he struggles to crack the lock, Zeemo unexpectedly shows up a day early, eager to pick up his cash. Vic does his best to stall the kingpin, the other crew members ad-lib their way through enough distractions to give Nog time to finish his job. Odo and Nog make their getaway with the money, and when Frankie opens the safe for Zeemo they discover it's empty. Moments later Frankie and Cicci are led away by Zeemo's thugs. The minute they step out of the lounge, Vic's club resets to the ambience that everyone on DS9 knows and loves. The group toasts their achievement with champagne, and to the delight of the crew, Sisko joins Vic in crooning a rousing rendition of "The Best Is Yet to Come."

The season's sixteenth production would be DS9's last stand-alone episode. With the series about to enter into the final arc, the writers decided to go out with one big, fun adventure. "We'd wanted to do a caper show for years," says Ira Behr, "but we'd never been able to pull it off."

The scene where the crew watches Frankie Eyes leave was shot against two different backgrounds to accommodate visual effects.
ROBBIE ROBINSON

It was now or never—and with Vic Fontaine and a holosuite version of Las Vegas within reach, all the elements seemed to be in place.

The premise that would set the complicated caper in motion was surprisingly simplistic. Vic needs help. Only his friends on the station can provide that help. That's it. "It didn't matter to us that the regular characters weren't in jeopardy," Behr states. "None of us wanted to do the old 'The-holosuite-is-malfunctioning-and-we're-all-gonna-die' thing. We just wanted to do a show about helping this holo-gram." It didn't seem unrealistic to assume that people like Odo and Kira and Nog would want to help the "lightbulb" who'd helped them in the past, he explains. "So in the same way that viewers have invested in the artifice of *Star Trek* and care about characters who aren't real, *we* decided to do a show about our characters caring about Vic."

Of course, Behr knew that there were some people in the *Star Trek* viewership who weren't particu-larly enamored of the whole holosuite/Vegas milieu.

But he had a plan for that, too. "By making Sisko the naysayer in the group, the one who's saying, 'This is ridiculous,' we could address all the viewers who felt that way about Vic. And once we won Sisko over, we figured that would give the audience the leeway to say, 'Okay, just go with it.'"

Behr used Sisko's skepticism to make a cultural statement as well. "We didn't want the audience, espe-cially the younger audience, to think that 1962 Las Vegas was a place where you had a lot of black people sitting in the audience at a nightclub, or enjoying themselves at the hotels and casinos," he says. "That just didn't happen. So by having someone of Sisko's historical understanding questioning that fact, we could clarify before we got him to Vic's that he's well aware that Las Vegas was very, very, very white."

With their plans for fun, adventure, and assorted political statements all in line, the writers were ready to flesh out a story. "We needed a scam that was easy to produce, that used a lot of our characters, and was very simple in terms of the things that went wrong—

again, to make it easy on the production." Behr explains. "We decided that the best way to convince the audience that the little screwups were something that had some tension behind them was to show the whole thing through once where it all worked perfectly. Then they'd understand the significance of those little things going wrong."

Not that doing things twice simplified it for the behind-the-scenes staff. "They robbed the casino *twice*," Lou Race laments. "We had to be very logistically hip to what was going on because we were doing two different versions of the same caper. We made charts and I hired an extra assistant director, because we had a lot of extras and a lot of costuming, two big new sets, music and dancing—and we did it on either side of the Christmas hiatus when nobody was focused on doing the show! We broke the sets into four areas, the crap tables, the roulette tables, the blackjack tables, and the slot machines. Then I broke the extras into two groups. I called them, 'The Fantasy Robbers' and 'The Real Robbers.' Then I'd tell them, 'The Fantasy Robber guys are always in the blackjack area and these other guys are always in the roulette area. Then for the *real* robbery we switched it around. It was a difficult show."

"The casino set is one of the largest we ever built for the series," says Bobby della Santina. "The walls were nearly twenty feet high, to give them some scope and to accommodate the high crane shots."

As research for the appearance of the casino and its patrons, Behr suggested that the production personnel watch the motion picture *Ocean's Eleven*, a 1960 film that follows the exploits of Frank Sinatra's legendary Rat Pack on a Vegas caper of their own. "I think that was just an excuse for Ira to make us all look at the movie," Ron Moore suggests with a chuckle.

Regardless of Behr's intentions, the department heads all took the research to heart. Art Director Randy McIlvain acknowledges that the show's casino was based on the look of the film, although he admits to having watched *Viva Las Vegas* as well. As for the costumes, "They were all rented, and matched the original look of *Ocean's Eleven*," Bob Blackman confirms.

"I *loved* my dresses," Nana Visitor smiles. "It was fun to dress up like that." While the idea of Kira Nerys playing the seductress in the caper's cast may seem a little out of character for the straightforward colonel, Visitor says that it wasn't hard for her to imagine Kira in that kind of role. "She must have done it with so many Cardassians when she was doing terrorist work. I mean, as a terrorist, a woman

Darren was inspired by Vic Fontaine to record a CD.
ROBBIE ROBINSON

would have to get used to the fact that using her sexuality to charm men and to trick her way in was one of her strengths. That's a reality. I had no trouble thinking that Kira would be a good actor."

Nicole deBoer had no trouble with her role either. "I've actually played a cocktail waitress for Hans Beimler before," she says, laughing. "And it was on a science fiction show too. Hans just does that to me, I guess." DeBoer enjoyed the episode's distinct change of pace. "It was fun because by that point I'd become really comfortable with everybody at work. It was just a fun one to do."

Rene Auberjonois also enjoyed himself, for similar reasons. "This is the show where Aron Eisenberg and I really became good friends," Auberjonois states. "I mean, I had known him all this time, and I liked him very much. But it's only when you get to stand around on the set for hours and hours on end that you actually talk. I really became so fond of him."

There were a few interesting surprises among the guest cast. When Ezri enters the money counting room to give a drugged drink to the casino employee named Howard, she is surprised to find a different employee, identified in the script as "Countman #2." Viewers may be equally surprised to find that the actor who played Countman #2 has been associated with *Star Trek* since the fourth season of *The Next Generation*. The actor's billing probably didn't help— he went by the name "Bobby Reilly."

"A lot of the fans don't recognize me out of Klingon makeup," laughs Robert O'Reilly, who normally portrays Chancellor Gowron. "So Ira and I thought this would be fun to give them one shot to see me as me. I asked them to bill me in the credits by the name I had back in 1962, the era in which the story was set. My stage name is Robert O'Reilly, but my childhood name was Bobby Reilly. Not many people got the joke, but I found it great fun."

Behr's fondness for casting familiar faces netted him Marc Lawrence as Mr. Zeemo. "We wanted an actor who would carry the weight of history to any film buffs who were watching the show," Behr says. "Marc did a million film noir gangster movies. And he was *perfect* as the character. He's not physically threatening, but he made you realize that this guy is as cold-blooded as Weyoun. Plus," the executive producer says, sounding much more serious, "he had been blacklisted in the fifties. I feel that it's always great to give work to a guy who had been blacklisted."

One additional role, this one behind the scenes, was even more personal for Behr. His wife, Laura, once again served as choreographer for the dance scene in the lounge. "We had dance auditions, and Laura called in some people she knew," Behr notes. "One of the dancers, Michelle Rudy, had worked with us on *Fame*, so that was a blast from the past," he adds with a smile. "We needed to do something sexy but confined, because the stage wasn't very big. It looked pretty good having all these sexy dancers," he laughs. Unfortunately, after Vic's holoprogram was "debugged," the sexy dancers disappeared. Still, they left some pleasant memories. "There was one great moment, when the dancers all did the 'Badda-Bing,' and they all pointed their fingers like guns as Frankie Eyes comes out with Zeemo to 'go for a ride.' That was a nice piece of the dance telling the story," Behr says.

This time, Behr took the opportunity to insert his own mention of the Alamo and Davy Crockett. In the teaser, Bashir and O'Brien invite Vic Fontaine to join them in their Alamo holosuite program. "The idea of trying to convince a hologram to go into another holographic program really appealed to us," Behr chuckles. "Bashir and O'Brien *finally* consider letting someone else into their program, and it's a hologram! These guys have been under a lot of stress, obviously."

The executive producer also ordered up a special song for Vic's opening number. "This show was Ira's baby," Jay Chattaway observes. "He told me, 'We need a vocal about the Alamo that Vic can sing. It can't be a country song and it has to mention San Antonio and Davy Crockett.' This was on a Thursday, and they were shooting on Monday. I had to write six instrumental tunes for the band *and* an original song with

lyrics. I came up with a song done in a Sinatra swing style, about losing the battle of the Alamo, and 'Davy Crockett never really got it right' as one of the lyrics."

One other song was even more memorable, particularly for its unique teaming of vocalists. "I suggested the song 'The Best Is Yet to Come,'" James Darren says. "I already had a chart for it, and that's what we used on the show. The difference between Avery's voice and mine made it that much better. I knew what a good actor Avery was, but I didn't know he was a wonderful singer. And he's an incredible piano player, too."

"I've wanted Avery to sing on the show for seven years," Behr notes. "I just never could justify it. But when we did 'His Way,' I *knew* that I was going to get him to sing. It's just jaw dropping how good he is. And the song, 'The Best Is Yet to Come,' worked on a lot of levels," Behr says happily. "Especially with the last ten hours of shows coming up with a true badda-bing, badda-bang."

PENUMBRA
Episode #567
WRITTEN BY RENÉ ECHEVARRIA
DIRECTED BY STEVE POSEY

GUEST CAST	
Kasidy Yates	PENNY JOHNSON
Weyoun	JEFFREY COMBS
Gul Dukat	MARC ALAIMO
Damar	CASEY BIGGS
Sarah	DEBORAH LACEY
Female Shape-shifter	SALOME JENS
Saghi	MICHELLE HORN
Federation Computer Voice	MAJEL BARRETT
Cardassian Computer Voice	JUDI DURAND

STARDATE 52576.2

Sisko revels in his purchase of twelve hecapates of land in Bajor's beautiful Rakantha province. He plans to start building a home there as soon as the war's over, and someday, he tells Kasidy, he'd like to retire there. It wasn't part of his master plan to become so attached to Bajor and its people, he says, but it clearly was his destiny. Kasidy notes wryly that when your mother turns out to be part wormhole alien, words like destiny are important.

Elsewhere in the station, Bashir expresses annoyance when Ezri mentions that she's gotten reacquainted with Captain Boday, the Gallamite with the

Sisko slips a rubber gasket from his model onto Kasidy's finger and proposes. ROBBIE ROBINSON

an escape pod fired from the doomed vessel. Arriving at the position where the pod would have entered the Badlands, Ezri cuts her engines, hoping that the plasma stream will carry her runabout in the same direction as Worf's pod. After a dangerous, bumpy ride, Ezri spots an escape pod tumbling through the turbulent region. She locks it in a tractor beam and transports the pod's occupant onto the *Gander*. It's Worf—and he's alive!

A worried Sisko can't sleep, so he occupies himself by working on a model of the home he hopes to build on Bajor. When Kasidy joins him, he tells her about his plans for the layout, then allows that he wants it to be *their* house, not just his. He asks her to marry him, and Kasidy happily accepts.

At Dominion headquarters, Damar complains about the tremendous casualties that Cardassia has suffered in the war effort, but Weyoun notes only that their sacrifices won't be in vain. Damar attempts to drown his troubles in a glass of *kanar*, and comments on the fact that the female Founder hasn't looked well lately. Weyoun avoids commenting on the topic. Later, he meets with the Founder and informs her that the Vorta doctors haven't yet formulated a cure for her ailment. The Founder tells Weyoun to eliminate the doctors and activate their clones. Perhaps a fresh perspective will hasten the results.

Space is limited on a runabout, and for the first time since Ezri came to Deep Space 9, she and Worf are forced to spend time alone together. Although Worf tries to busy himself with the vessel's controls, Ezri insists on making conversation. Unfortunately, the conversation always seems to return to memories that relate to his relationship with Jadzia, which make Worf uncomfortable. The two begin to bicker but are interrupted when two Jem'Hadar fighters launch an attack against the *Gander*. Since the runabout can't outrun or outshoot them, Worf takes the *Gander* into the atmosphere of a planet in the nearby Goralis system. The Dominion ships aren't designed for suborbital flight, so Worf's tactic works and the fighters give up the chase. Unfortunately, their attack has damaged the runabout's thrusters, and they can't pull out of their dive. They'll have to abandon ship. Grabbing weapons and emergency backpacks, Worf and Ezri beam to the surface of the planet and watch as the *Gander* blows up. But before they can congratulate themselves on their good luck, they realize that neither one of them thought to bring communications equipment from the vessel. They're stranded with no way to call for help.

While Sisko and Kasidy would be more than

transparent skull whom Jadzia used to date. But the banter between them ceases when Kira reports that Worf's ship was ambushed by a Dominion patrol near the Badlands. Although several emergency pods were retrieved, Worf wasn't aboard any of them. Sisko takes out the *Defiant* to hunt for additional survivors, but after three unsuccessful days, Sisko tells Ezri that he'll have to call off the search. There are too many Jem'Hadar ships in the vicinity.

Troubled, Ezri goes to Worf's quarters and finds herself overcome by Jadzia's memories of life with Worf. Recalling her predecessor's vow to stand with Worf against all opposition, Ezri feels that it is her duty to find the Klingon. She takes the *Runabout Gander* from the station without authorization and heads for the Badlands, ignoring Sisko's orders to return to DS9.

When Ezri reaches the region in which Worf's ship was lost, she deduces the probable trajectory of

content with a small, simple wedding, they haven't taken into account the aspirations of the Bajoran people, who've learned about the coming nuptials. The Emissary is getting married—definitely not a small and simple event in their lives—and the Bajorans are looking forward to a lavish ceremony.

On Cardassia Prime, Damar receives an unexpected visitor in his quarters. Dukat has come to request a favor. Damar agrees to help his former mentor in whatever way he can. He's surprised, however, when Dukat asks him to use his connections to find him a surgeon who can transform a Cardassian into a Bajoran.

Ezri and Worf try to make the best of living conditions. Worf enjoys the thrill of the hunt while Ezri attempts to create a comunit by combining parts of her combadge and tricorder. The bickering between the pair—which covers a growing feeling of sexual tension—intensifies, particularly after Ezri mentions that she dined with Captain Boday before she left the station. Worf's long-simmering jealousy of Jadzia's relationship with the Gallamite boils over, and the pair launch into a huge fight, which culminates in an explosion of long-repressed mutual passion. Later that night, the couple are awakened by Breen soldiers, who confront them at the campsite. Before Worf can reach his weapon, the Breen fire their weapons, and the two Starfleet officers fall to the ground, unconscious. They awaken in a cell aboard a Breen ship, wondering why they've been taken prisoner by a species with whom the Federation is not at war.

On the station, Sisko experiences a vision of the Prophet he's come to know as "Sarah," and who is, in a very real sense, his mother ("Shadows and Symbols"). Sarah warns Sisko that he must accept his destiny—and marriage to Kasidy is not a part of that destiny. He must walk the path alone, or he will know nothing but sorrow. His greatest trial is about to begin . . .

'TIL DEATH DO US PART
Episode #568
WRITTEN BY DAVID WEDDLE & BRADLEY THOMPSON
DIRECTED BY WINRICH KOLBE

GUEST CAST	
Weyoun	JEFFREY COMBS
Kasidy Yates	PENNY JOHNSON
Gul Dukat	MARC ALAIMO
Damar	CASEY BIGGS
Admiral Ross	BARRY JENNER
Sarah	DEBORAH LACEY
Nog	ARON EISENBERG
Solbor	JAMES OTIS
Female Shape-shifter	SALOME JENS

SPECIAL GUEST STAR	
Kai Winn	LOUISE FLETCHER

STARDATE UNKNOWN

Jake is perplexed when Sisko informs him that the Prophets—or rather, one particular Prophet—told him he shouldn't marry Kasidy ("Penumbra"). Sisko confesses that he hasn't yet had the opportunity to tell Kasidy about his conversation with Sarah, and Jake wonders how his father is going to break the news. But before the pair can discuss the matter any further, Sisko receives word that Kai Winn has arrived to see him. Her timing, as always, is impeccable.

Dismissing Jake, Sisko greets the kai, who offers congratulations on his engagement and volunteers to assist in the preparations for the momentous wedding. Sisko debates whether or not to tell her about Sarah's message, and finally mentions only that the Prophets have warned him that he's going to have to face a great trial. Although envious of Sisko's relationship with the Prophets, Winn says that she's certain he'll be willing to do whatever they ask.

As she steps from Sisko's office, Winn seems to experience, at long last, a vision from the Prophets. They tell her that the Sisko has faltered and that it will be up to her to bring the "Restoration" to Bajor. A guide will reveal the way. Winn asks how she'll know this guide, and the Prophets state that he will have "the wisdom of the land."

On the Breen ship, Ezri and Worf try and fail to escape from their cell. The two are more comfortable together since they gave in to their physical desire for each other in the Goralis system, but Ezri begins to

Worf and Ezri are imprisoned by the Breen. ROBBIE ROBINSON

suspect that Worf sees her as a replacement for Jadzia. She has little time to dwell on that, as the Breen drag Worf out for some brutal interrogation that leaves him weak and shaken. Shortly after they return Worf to the cell, they remove Ezri for similar treatment. When they bring her back, she's disoriented and semiconscious. As Worf tries to make her comfortable, she rambles deliriously, tossing random comments at Garak, her brother, Joran, and Worf. Then, to Worf's shock, she declares her love for Julian Bashir.

Damar's drinking has taken its toll on him. He can barely stand to look at himself in the mirror, let alone drag himself to his duties each day. Even Dukat, for whom Damar has provided identity documents that match his new Bajoran appearance, notices the change in his old friend. He urges Damar to reach inside himself and find the brave leader that Cardassia needs. Damar takes strength from Dukat's words, and bids his former leader goodbye.

When Kasidy returns from her most recent cargo run, she finds Sisko in a somber mood. He tells her about the visit from Sarah and the warning she gave him. Kasidy is devastated when Sisko tells her he can't go against the Prophets; he can't marry her. She leaves his quarters without another word. Later, a troubled Sisko tells Kira what's happened, and she supports his decision.

In another part of the station, Dukat arrives in Bajoran guise, ready to set forth on the path to his own destiny. He goes immediately to the quarters where Winn is staying and asks for an audience. Introducing himself as Anjohl, Dukat describes himself as a farmer, a "simple man of the land," who desires her blessing. The phrase strikes a chord with Winn, who remembers what the Prophets told her. Could this Bajoran be the guide that they mentioned?

She invites him to dine with her, and asks him to tell her about his farming. "Anjohl" relates a story about a blight that affected his crops the previous year. He dealt with it, he explains, by burning his fields to destroy the contamination. Then he let the land lie fallow for a season, to allow for the restoration of the soil. To Winn, Anjohl's tale is a metaphor for the "Restoration" of Bajor that she is to bring forth. Now she is convinced that Anjohl is her guide, and she joyfully informs him of the role he is to play in their planet's future. Anjohl accepts this honor with great humility. Later, Winn casually probes his feelings about Bajor's Emissary, and is delighted when Anjohl confesses that he doesn't really understand why the Prophets chose an outsider to be their liaison to the Bajoran people. His revelation that she inadvertently had a hand in saving his life during the Occupation further cements her belief that their fates are linked.

As Kasidy prepares to leave the station, Quark brings Sisko the diamond wedding ring that the captain had ordered for her. Noting that the item is non-refundable, Quark suggests that it would be a shame to let something so beautiful go to waste. Already conflicted about his decision to cancel the marriage, the incident serves to remind Sisko that losing Kasidy would be much more of a waste. He rushes to the loading docks and catches her before she leaves. He doesn't care what the Prophets want, he tells Kasidy. He loves her and wants to marry her. They can worry about the rest later. To confirm that he has no intention of changing his mind again, Sisko hustles her off to the Wardroom, where Admiral Ross waits to join them in marriage. Sisko's friends are happy about his decision, but Kira worries about the Emissary's decision to go against the Prophets.

Her concerns are well founded. Even as Sisko places the ring on Kasidy's hand, he receives a vision from Sarah, warning him that the union is not meant to be. Sisko tells Sarah that he's made his decision and will live with it. His love for Kasidy is too strong to deny. Surely Sarah's brief experience as a corporeal being gave her some idea of what love is. The Prophet does seem to understand Sisko's actions, but she warns that she cannot change the sorrow that is to come.

Elsewhere on the station, another couple is united when Anjohl goes to Winn's quarters to report the miraculous growth of his newly planted crops. Winn tells him that it is a sign from the Prophets that he should remain at her side. Certain that the Prophets have brought them together, Winn seals their fate with a passionate kiss.

On the Breen ship, Worf confronts a recovered Ezri with her feelings toward Bashir. Surprised, Ezri denies that her ramblings meant anything, although she's not really certain if that's true. Moments later, the two prisoners receive an even bigger surprise when the Breen transport them to the bridge of a Jem'Hadar ship, where they are handed over to Weyoun and Damar. A gleeful Weyoun tells the pair that they should feel honored. They are witnesses to a historic moment: the birth of an alliance between the Dominion and the Breen!

STRANGE BEDFELLOWS

Episode #569

WRITTEN BY RONALD D. MOORE
DIRECTED BY RENE AUBERJONOIS

GUEST CAST

Kasidy Yates	PENNY JOHNSON
Weyoun	JEFFREY COMBS
Gul Dukat	MARC ALAIMO
Damar	CASEY BIGGS
General Martok	J.G. HERTZLER
Solbor	JAMES OTIS
Female Shape-shifter	SALOME JENS

SPECIAL GUEST STAR

Kai Winn	LOUISE FLETCHER

STARDATE UNKNOWN

After Weyoun's stunning announcement about the Dominion–Breen alliance ("'Til Death Do Us Part"), Worf and Ezri are taken to a cell on the Jem'Hadar vessel, which is headed for Cardassia. Hiding the increasingly obvious signs of the disease that afflicts her people, the female Founder greets Thot Gor, the Breen leader, and prepares to launch into discussions that will culminate in a signed treaty between their two factions. Damar is uneasy. He hasn't seen the treaty and has no idea what the Founder is offering to the Breen. His suspi-

Dukat's disguise as a Bajoran farmer fools Kai Winn. ROBBIE ROBINSON.

cions are confirmed later on, when he discovers that the treaty calls for Cardassia to make certain "territorial concessions" to the Breen. Weyoun attempts to placate Damar, noting that after the war is over there'll be plenty of territories to compensate for the loss of a few minor planets in the Cardassian Union. Damar is furious, but Weyoun makes it clear that since all Cardassian territory already belongs to the Founders, there's nothing he can do but sign the treaty. Humbled, Damar asks for help dealing with Klingon troops that have landed on Septimus III. Weyoun tells Damar that the situation will be dealt with and that Damar's outnumbered Cardassian soldiers will not die in vain.

On Deep Space 9, General Martok assures Sisko that his troops will take Septimus III within a week. Then, putting the subject of the Dominion war aside, he counsels Sisko on the war that he will soon be fighting with Kasidy—the eternal battle that has existed since the dawn of time between husbands and wives. Sure enough, Sisko is soon engaged in the first battle with his new wife when she refuses to officiate, in the capacity of the Emissary's wife, at a Bajoran blessing ceremony.

When the Jem'Hadar ship reaches Cardassia, Weyoun and Damar visit the two prisoners in their cell. Weyoun notes that they have two choices. They can cooperate and provide information that will allow the Dominion to end the war quickly, or they can refuse to cooperate and be tried and sentenced to death as Cardassian war criminals. Weyoun suggests that it would be a shame if Ezri died without telling Dr. Bashir how she felt about him. The comment proves to be a major tactical error on the Vorta's part. An incensed Worf steps forward and breaks Weyoun's neck, killing him instantly. Damar can't help but find the incident amusing. He knows the Founders will activate another Weyoun clone to replace him, perhaps one that's not quite so overconfident. Nevertheless, he reminds Worf and Ezri that they have two days to make up their minds. After that, they'll be executed.

Now involved in an intimate relationship, Winn and Anjohl—the surgically altered Dukat—vow to bring about the Restoration. Nothing will stand in their way, not even the Emissary. Later, Winn receives another vision and learns the terrifying truth about the entities who are now guiding her fate. They *aren't* Prophets; they're *Pah-wraiths*. The kai is the person they've chosen to help restore them to their rightful place in the Celestial Temple. Winn awakens from the vision in a state of utter panic and demands that her aide, Solbor, bring her the Orb of Prophecy from the station's shrine. She must bare her soul to the Prophets and beg their forgiveness, she says. But when Winn looks into the Orb, she sees nothing. The Prophets have forsaken her because she's been in communion with the evil ones, she laments.

At this point, Anjohl/Dukat makes a "confession" to Winn. He first came to see her because he had a vision from the *true* gods of Bajor, the Pah-wraiths, who asked him to serve them. *They* led him to her. Winn is aghast. She refuses to listen when he tries to tell her that the Prophets have done nothing for her people. Only the Pah-wraiths care about them—and her. Turn away from the Prophets, he advises, or live forever in Sisko's shadow. Devastated, she throws him out, then turns to Colonel Kira, the only person she feels will be honest with her. Without mentioning the Pah-wraiths, Winn tells Kira that she has strayed from the path the Prophets meant for her to follow. She admits that she's given in to the temptations of power and that she wants to earn the Prophets' forgiveness. Touched by Winn's sincerity, Kira tells her that it's never too late to seek redemption. She's certain that Winn will find her way after she steps down as kai.

Suddenly Winn's demeanor changes. Step down? Why would she step down? Bajor needs her, she says. When Kira realizes that Winn isn't willing to do what it takes to find her way back to the Prophets, she leaves the kai alone to figure out her own solution.

Damar's amusement over the dispatch of Weyoun Seven ends abruptly when he learns that his successor, Weyoun Eight, has given Thot Gor complete access to the entire Cardassian military database.

What's more, the Founder has decided that henceforth all of Damar's military recommendations should be submitted to Thot Gor, who will pass them on to her. Damar begins to realize that his position as leader of the Cardassian Union is becoming a joke. Worf and Ezri feel equally impotent when their escape attempt is thwarted before they get more than a few yards from their cell.

Meanwhile Quark's daily ritual of pouring a drink for the missing Ezri gets on O'Brien's nerves. He finds it morbid, but Quark thinks of it as an optimistic gesture. When Ezri comes back, she'll find her drink waiting for her. Sitting nearby, a moody Bashir seems barely aware of the conversation as he waxes nostalgic over Ezri's endearing nature.

Damar is horrified when he discovers that Septimus III has fallen. Five hundred thousand Cardassian soldiers have been wiped out. But when he asks Weyoun what happened to the help that the Vorta promised, Weyoun points out that he never said he'd send reinforcements, only that the situation would be dealt with—and it was. He allowed the Klingons to commit valuable resources to capture a strategically worthless planet. The sacrifice of Damar's men was not made in vain, at least, not from Weyoun's point of view. Feeling utterly betrayed, Damar goes to his quarters to pour himself a drink—and then stops, suddenly pensive.

In the Cardassian holding cell, realizing that they're on the verge of death, Ezri confronts Worf about his feelings for her. He's been trying to convince himself that he loves her, but the truth is that he loves Jadzia. Perhaps they both made a mistake back on Goralis III ("Penumbra"), she suggests. After mulling this over, Worf admits that she's right, that he let himself see the part of her that was Jadzia when he made love to her. Ezri admits that she fell prey to the same emotion, and allowed herself to be close to him because that was what Jadzia wanted. She also reveals that she had no idea how she felt about Bashir until she confessed her love for him in Worf's presence. The two make peace with each other and vow to be friends—for as long as they have left to live.

When Damar comes to their cell, Worf and Ezri figure their time is up. But to their surprise, Damar kills the two Jem'Hadar guards and provides the prisoners with an escape route back to Federation space. He asks only one thing in return: Tell the Federation that it has an ally on Cardassia.

Sisko is pleased when Kasidy agrees to preside over the blessing ceremony. Elsewhere, O'Brien pays a visit to Bashir in the Infirmary and confesses that because of the time he spent with Ezri on Sappora VII ("Prodigal Daughter"), he feels protective of the young Trill. Therefore, he feels bound to warn the doctor that if he plans to romance Ezri, if and when she returns, he'd better treat her right—or else. Bashir promises to do so.

In another part of the station, Winn has come to a decision about her future. Calling Anjohl/Dukat to her quarters, Winn explains that despite a lifetime of dedication, the Prophets have never offered her their guidance, have never trusted her with their wisdom. She's run out of patience and will no longer serve gods who give her nothing in return. She will walk in the path of the Pah-wraiths, with Anjohl/Dukat at her side. Together, no one will be able to stand in their way.

The Founder allows the crew of the *Defiant* to escape after the Breen destroy the ship. ROBBIE ROBINSON

THE CHANGING FACE OF EVIL
Episode #570
WRITTEN BY IRA STEVEN BEHR & HANS BEIMLER
DIRECTED BY MIKE VEJAR

GUEST CAST

Weyoun	JEFFREY COMBS
Kasidy Yates	PENNY JOHNSON
Gul Dukat	MARC ALAIMO
Damar	CASEY BIGGS
General Martok	J.G. HERTZLER
Nog	ARON EISENBERG
Admiral Ross	BARRY JENNER
Solbor	JAMES OTIS
Gul Rusot	JOHN VICKERY
Female Shape-shifter	SALOME JENS

SPECIAL GUEST STAR

Kai Winn	LOUISE FLETCHER

STARDATE UNKNOWN

Worf and Ezri's return to Deep Space 9 after their imprisonment by the Dominion ("Strange Bedfellows") is an occasion for much rejoicing among their friends, particularly Bashir. However, the mood becomes somber after Sisko receives a report that the Breen have attacked Earth. It's their first action as part of the new Dominion–Breen alliance. Although Starfleet was able to destroy most of the attack force, the Breen wreaked havoc on Starfleet Headquarters in San Francisco. The strike was a shockingly bold move, one which underscores the enemy's confidence.

Weyoun and the Breen commander, Thot Gor, congratulate themselves on the success of the attack, while Damar plots with a trusted comrade, Gul Rusot, to free his homeland from Dominion occupation. On Bajor, Winn clears her calendar and cancels a scheduled appearance before the Vedek Assembly, surprising her aide Solbor. Feeling like a hypocrite in the trappings of the kai, she expresses her impatience to "Anjohl," unaware that her ally is Gul Dukat. Anjohl/Dukat tells her that the true gods, the Pah-wraiths, will be ready to embrace her once she frees them from Bajor's fire caves. Anjohl/Dukat's advice takes Winn aback. The prophecies say that the release of the Pah-wraiths will mean the end of Bajor. But Anjohl/Dukat assures her that a new Bajor will rise from the ashes of the old one. Only the worthy will be left to enjoy the Restoration—and Winn will rule that new paradise. But first she must release the Pah-wraiths, and to do that, she needs to consult the ancient text of the Kosst Amojan, a book that all but the kai are forbidden to open.

At Quark's, Bashir and O'Brien distract themselves from the Breen threat by working with a model of the Alamo. Although Quark doesn't understand the preoccupation, the two men are determined to figure out how they can win the battle that was such a devastating defeat for the Texans who defended the fort. Worf and Ezri observe the pair from a table on the second level. The Klingon feels that Ezri deserves better than a man who gets excited playing with toys, but if Bashir is the man she wants, she should tell him. Elsewhere on the station, the captain and his new wife have a disagreement about Sisko's desire to keep Kasidy out of harm's way. The captain is concerned about her going out on cargo runs while the war is heating up, but Kasidy makes it clear that she wants to continue to live her own life on her own terms.

Solbor brings Winn the text of the Kosst Amojan, but not without expressing his concern over the request. The knowledge contained in the book, he says, is very dangerous. Anjohl/Dukat attempts to dismiss Solbor's fears, and says that he will make sure no harm comes to the kai. But Solbor doesn't trust the man who has become Winn's closest advisor. He's certain that this stranger is the one who gave her the idea to consult the book. But Winn refuses to consider Solbor's fears. She sends him away and unlocks the book, only to find that the pages are blank. Anjohl/Dukat feels that it's a trick. Winn, however, believes the words are actually there, but hidden. It's up to them to find them.

After noticing that Ezri has been avoiding him, Bashir decides to approach the Trill and ask if he's done anything to offend her. Ezri assures Bashir that he hasn't and tries to explain her feelings. Unfortunately, Bashir gets called away to the Infirmary before she can get very far. A short time later, Admiral Ross informs Sisko that the Breen have launched a counteroffensive against the Federation's lone foothold in Dominion territory: the Chin'toka System. Sisko and his crew take the *Defiant* to rendezvous with Federation ships in the region. Along the way, O'Brien chews out Bashir for losing one of the little figures that populate their model of the Alamo. Worf takes the opportunity to tease Ezri once again about the fact that her "intended" plays with dolls.

Once the Federation fleet reaches the Dominion–Breen lines, the battle is engaged. But moments into the fighting, the *Defiant* is hit by a blast from a Breen weapon. The discharge turns into a strange force field that engulfs the starship, shutting down almost every major system—weapons, communication, primary computer systems, and helm control. The defenseless ship is pummeled by enemy fire and suffers hull breaches on multiple decks. With no other options

left open, Sisko makes the only decision he can and orders the crew to abandon ship. As they evacuate in escape pods, the *Defiant* explodes behind them. From his position on a nearby Jem'Hadar vessel, Weyoun cheerfully observes the destruction and prepares to destroy the pods. But the Founder stops him, noting that the survivors will spread the word about this stunning defeat, demoralizing Federation troops throughout the quadrant.

On Bajor, Solbor rushes in to the kai's office to reveal something he suspected all along. The man Winn trusts above all others is a fraud. The real Anjohl Tennan died years earlier. This "Anjohl" is not a Bajoran at all—his DNA shows that he's a Cardassian. And Solbor knows exactly *which* Cardassian he is: it's Winn's old enemy, Gul Dukat!

Winn backs away from Dukat, picking up a knife from her dinner tray and holding it out to protect herself. But Dukat stays where he is, smiling calmly. Solbor doesn't understand the love of the Pah-wraiths, he tells Winn. Suddenly Solbor realizes why Winn has been trying to study the text of the Kosst Amojan. He accuses her of betraying her people *and* the Prophets, and threatens to stop her. Desperate, Winn tries to prevent Solbor from leaving. When she fails, she plunges the knife into his back, killing him. Shocked by her own behavior, she turns to the book, feeling she must destroy it. As she reaches for it, a few drops of Solbor's blood fall on the blank pages—and suddenly the ancient text appears!

Dukat takes advantage of Winn's surprise and tells her that the Pah-wraiths have judged her worthy. Their secrets are now hers. They are offering her their power! Winn hesitates, then begins to read the text.

Back at the station, Sisko speaks sadly of the ship he's lost, and Ross vows to get him a replacement. For now, they need to figure out a way to neutralize the Breen weapons—and that means they'll need to buy some time. But how? The conversation is interrupted by Kira, who reports an important transmission they're receiving from Cardassian space. It's Damar, declaring that he has broken away from the Dominion and launched attacks on key Dominion outposts. He urges his fellow Cardassians to drive the Dominion from their homeland. As Sisko listens, he realizes that the Dominion will now invest all of its energy on tracking Damar down, which may buy the Federation some of the time it needs. Damar could be the key to saving the Alpha Quadrant. The Federation will need to find a way to help him.

CLOSE-UP: The Changing Face of Visual Effects

"When we started *The Next Generation* in 1987, computer graphic imaging (CGI) was available to us, but much of it looked corny," *Star Trek* Executive Producer Rick Berman states. "The images were just not acceptable for *Star Trek*." Although there were proponents of CGI at the time, Berman admits, the best-looking effects were those produced using highly detailed physical models, carefully lit and shot via motion-control photography.

"We were a hard sell on computer animation," confirms Visual Effects Producer Dan Curry. "On *TNG*, some of the earliest morph effects that we created were hand-painted, frame by frame. And, in fact, one hundred percent of the space shots were photographed with motion-controlled models. But motion-control, like hand-painting, is very time-consuming. If you're lucky, you might be able to shoot three ships in one day. But for a very elaborate maneuver, it might take three days to do one ship. The time factor was one of the main reasons that computer animation became attractive."

When *Deep Space Nine* debuted in 1993, "we continued with motion-control work," says Berman. "Over the years, slowly but surely we found that certain effects being created digitally were becoming much better in quality. When we could, we used them, but where it was either financially or creatively beneficial to stay with models, we did." As the series progressed, CGI became more and more competitive in both areas. As a result, *DS9*'s Effects Department embarked on a transition that was so seamless, most viewers were unaware of the change. "By the last season of *Deep Space Nine*, instead of being ninety-nine percent motion-control photography to one percent CGI, it was one percent to ninety-nine percent in the other direction," Berman comments.

Curry attributes much of the transition to Visual Effects Supervisor David Stipes, who worked with Curry on *TNG* and later replaced departing supervisor Glenn Neufeld at the end of *DS9*'s fourth season. "David showed us that if you closely monitor the art direction and work very carefully with the computer graphic animators, you can approximate the highly realistic look of models."

"I prefer to use whichever technique gets the job done," David Stipes confesses. "I'm not enraptured with any one technique. But the problem we were having is that the shows were getting more demanding. When I had to shoot the Dyson Sphere for the *TNG* episode 'Relics,' I immediately realized there was no physical way to do it with a model. That's when I really started pursuing CGI as an alternative."

Although CGI technology initially "was incredibly expensive," according to Stipes, the burgeoning digital revolution quickly brought prices down and artists' expertise up. The balance in cost-effectiveness came about just in time for *DS9*'s Effects Department. With the advent of the Dominion War plotline, the writers were turning out scripts that seemed to call for the near impossible. By the time "A Call to Arms" went into production, motion-control work was no longer cutting it. "We shot motion-control for weeks on that, running into trouble and not getting the shots," recalls Stipes. Dolly tracks, and indeed the soundstages themselves, literally were too short to provide the appropriate perspective in shots that required multiple ships.

"Sometimes we would resort to drastic measures," Curry adds. "Like using *Star Trek* Christmas tree ornaments in the background of a shot, to fake the perspective. It was very hard to program each ship individually, so a huge amount of labor would go into large-scale shots." With scenes that involved fifty to one hundred ships becoming more likely, straight motion-control became impossible. "We started doing only the foreground ships in motion-control and the background ships in CGI," says Curry. "Then, as software continued to improve, we began to segue into only CGI. It's still an open debate as to which has the superior look, but for the most part, it's difficult for the audience to tell."

Hardware advances accompanied those in software, and desktop computers became an integral part of the process. "We often take work that's created on a lower-end platform and recomposite it on heavier high-powered equipment," Curry notes.

These days, people hoping to break into the visual effects industry can actually start out in the comfort of their own home. "It's rapidly becoming a cottage industry," Curry admits. But he still feels a serious candidate needs more than good computer skills to become a computer graphics *artist*. "Technology is no substitute for artistry," he says. "Just as owning a camera doesn't make someone a good photographer, owning a piece of good software doesn't make someone an artist. Obviously, you have to keep abreast of the technology or you'll be a harness-maker in the age of the Model T. But on the other hand, the young artist who bypasses training in traditional fine arts media will be handicapped in the business.

"Visual effects technology is still in the pre-embryonic stage," Curry concludes. "It's hard to predict exactly where it will go in the future, other than that it will be very, very different and much more evolved. As the home viewing experience evolves, as screen definition improves and sound systems become more sophisticated, entertainment will become very different from what it is today."

WHEN IT RAINS . . .

Episode #571

TELEPLAY BY **RENÉ ECHEVARRIA**
STORY BY **RENÉ ECHEVARRIA &**
SPIKE STEINGASSER
DIRECTED BY **MICHAEL DORN**

GUEST CAST

Garak	ANDREW J. ROBINSON
Damar	CASEY BIGGS
Gul Dukat	MARC ALAIMO
General Martok	J.G. HERTZLER
Admiral Ross	BARRY JENNER
Gowron	ROBERT O'REILLY
Gul Rusot	JOHN VICKERY
Hilliard	SCOTT BURKHOLDER
Velal	STEPHEN YOAKAM
Seskal	VAUGHN ARMSTRONG
Ensign Weldon	COLBY FRENCH

SPECIAL GUEST STAR

Kai Winn	LOUISE FLETCHER

STARDATE UNKNOWN

Martok is taken aback when Gowron announces that he will replace the general as commander of the Klingon forces. ROBBIE ROBINSON

In the aftermath of the battle at Chin'toka ("The Changing Face of Evil"), O'Brien has made a very important discovery. Like the *Defiant*, some 311 ships—Federation, Romulan, and Klingon—lost power when the Breen engaged their energy-dampening weapon. However, one didn't: a bird-of-prey called the *Ki'tang*. The only thing that was different about that vessel was the fact that just prior to the engagement, *Ki'tang*'s engineer had adjusted her fuel intermix to compensate for a problem in the warp core. Hoping that they're on to something, all Klingon ships will make the same adjustments to their ships. Unfortunately, since Starfleet and Romulan ships are of a different design, they can't use this technique and are still vulnerable to the Breen weapon.

While Romulan and Starfleet scientists continue to work on the problem, Klingon vessels will move to the forefront of the Federation's attacks on the Dominion. With luck, between them and Damar's resistance movement, they'll be able to keep the Dominion off balance and prevent them from launching an offensive. But Damar will need help. He's a by-the-book soldier who has little experience with the kind of small-scale hit-and-run strategies that can work for a rebellion. That's why Starfleet decides to send him someone who does—Colonel Kira. To Kira, the irony is blatant. She's being sent to teach the resis-

tance strategies that once defeated the Cardassian forces occupying Bajor to those very forces. The captain tells her to put aside her personal feelings about the Cardassians in general, and about Damar, the murderer of Ziyal ("The Sacrifice of Angels"), in particular. Knowing that Garak still has many useful contacts on Cardassia, Sisko asks Kira to make him a part of her team.

Odo will also be a member of Kira's team. Before he leaves, however, Bashir asks the changeling to assist in his medical research by loaning him a cup of "goo." The constable reluctantly cooperates, noting that he'll want it back when he returns. In the meantime, Garak successfully locates Damar and offers Kira's services. Despite the antipathy that he and Kira have shared in the past, Damar agrees that her skills are needed—but he points out that many of his men would never accept taking orders from someone in a Bajoran uniform. Ross and Sisko get around this hurdle by giving Kira a Starfleet commission of lieutenant commander.

On Bajor, Winn covers up the death of Solbor and reevaluates her relationship with "Anjohl," whom she now knows to be Dukat. Although he claims to have been changed by the Pah-wraiths, Winn cannot forgive the way he treated the Bajoran people during the Occupation. Still, their destiny is now one, and she resigns herself to make the best of it while she searches the text of the Kosst Amojan for the answers they need to complete their task. Winn's research goes slowly, and Dukat begins to suspect that she is withholding secrets from him. He decides to take a look at the book himself. Sneaking into her office, he stares at the pages. Suddenly, a tendril of energy snakes up from the book and lances him in the eyes. Dukat howls in pain, bringing Winn on the run. Realizing what happened, Winn coldly reminds him that the text of the Kosst Amojan is for the eyes of the kai alone.

After Kira and the others depart, Martok nervously prepares for the arrival of Chancellor Gowron, who is coming all the way from Qo'noS to induct the general into the Order of Kahless. The ceremony is conducted, and afterwards a traditional celebration is held aboard the station. In the midst of the revelries, Gowron makes a stunning announcement. He's decided to assume direct command of Klingon forces, replacing Martok. Although he claims that he's made the decision for Martok's benefit, it is clear that what he really wants is the widespread admiration that the general's victories have inspired among the Klingon people. Martok is seen as the savior of the Empire, and that's something that Gowron cannot tolerate. Despite the fact that Gowron doesn't have Martok's military expertise, Martok decides that it would be in the best interests of the Empire to support Gowron.

Bashir once again tries to have a meaningful conversation with Ezri, this time summoning her to the Infirmary under the pretext of discussing the results of her last checkup. As Bashir runs a morphogenic enzyme analysis of Odo's "donation," he and Ezri awkwardly resume their previous attempt at conversation, with Bashir asking why she seems to be avoiding him. Ezri begins by telling him how the time she recently spent with Worf brought up a lot of old feelings, and how one thing led to another . . . Bashir immediately jumps to the conclusion that Ezri has fallen in love with Worf, but before Ezri can correct that impression, Bashir is distracted by the results of his lab analysis. He contacts the runabout in which Kira, Odo, and Garak are traveling to give them the devastating news: Odo is infected with the same disease that's killing his people.

Although shaken by Bashir's findings, Odo insists that he and Kira continue on the mission. Bashir contacts Starfleet Medical to get the results of the tests they ran on him the last time he was on Earth ("Homefront"). The doctor is surprised when his request is denied. The files, he's informed, are classi-

fied. Later, Sisko uses his higher clearance to request the records for Bashir.

At Damar's rebel outpost, the Cardassian staff bristles at some of Kira's strategic advice, which calls for the resistance movement to attack Cardassian garrisons when necessary. Still, Damar recognizes the logic to Kira's suggestions and sides with her against the opinion of his trusted ally, Gul Rusot. His officers, however, are not happy with Damar's decision, and they try to provoke Kira into a fight by picking apart Odo's record at Terok Nor. "Was her lover a collaborator?" they ask. Kira resists and goes on with her job. In the meantime, Odo recognizes the first signs of the deadly Founders' disease in himself.

As Bashir goes through the information in the files that Sisko obtained, he and O'Brien discuss the doctor's brief conversation with Ezri. O'Brien tells Bashir that he must have misunderstood Ezri. Worf has told the chief that he and Ezri are just friends. While Bashir ponders this possibility, he realizes that the information in the Starfleet files is fake. Someone has gone to a lot of trouble to make him believe that it's real. O'Brien can't believe that Starfleet Medical would be that underhanded. Grimly, Bashir agrees, knowing that the only other possibility is that Section 31 is behind the fakery.

Winn informs a now blind Dukat that the doctor can find nothing wrong with his eyes. Obviously, the Pah-wraiths have taken his sight as punishment for his arrogance. Only they can give it back. The kai observes that a lesson in humility would probably help him. And with that, she turns him out into the streets of Bajor to beg for food and shelter.

On Deep Space 9, Martok is shocked when Gowron comes up with a strategy that will make *him* look bold, but needlessly waste the lives of hundreds of Klingons. In the Infirmary, Bashir figures out that Odo wasn't infected by the female shape-shifter, as he'd originally suspected. The disease showed up in his system long before that. He pinpoints the date and realizes that Odo was infected *while* Starfleet Medical ran the tests on him. Clearly Section 31 created the virus and decided to use Odo as a carrier to the other changelings. When Odo linked with the female shape-shifter, he passed the disease on to his entire race. Bashir vows to get hold of the cure that he feels certain Section 31 has in its possession.

TACKING INTO THE WIND

Episode #572

WRITTEN BY RONALD D. MOORE
DIRECTED BY MIKE VEJAR

GUEST CAST

Garak	ANDREW J. ROBINSON
Weyoun	JEFFREY COMBS
Damar	CASEY BIGGS
General Martok	J.G. HERTZLER
Gowron	ROBERT O'REILLY
Gul Rusot	JOHN VICKERY
Female Shape-shifter	SALOME JENS
Luaran	KITTY SWINK
Vornar	J. PAUL BOEHMER

STARDATE UNKNOWN

Following a mission to destroy a Jem'Hadar fighter, Kira takes Damar's men to task for failing to follow their instructions. Yes, they managed to blow up the enemy vessel, but they set their explosives in an obvious hiding place. If the Jem'Hadar had not been sloppy in their security measures, the mission would have failed. The ten-sion level between Kira and Gul Rusot rises, but Damar refuses to discipline his close friend.

Odo returns from a mission of his own, a successful raid on a Dominion shipyard. Although she doesn't mention it, Kira can see that the Founder disease is taking its toll on him, so she suggests that he rest in the bunk room. Once there, Odo drops his stoic front and allows his body to revert to a pain-wracked, desiccated shadow of the being everyone knows. Garak happens upon him in this form and is surprised at how quickly the illness has incapacitated Odo. The shape-shifter notes that changing form seems to accelerate the disease's progress, and over the past few weeks, his missions have required dozens of changes. Still, he refuses to simply lie in his bunk and wait to die. And he refuses to let Kira know his true condition. Garak promises he won't say anything to Kira, but as it turns out, Kira is quite aware of Odo's state. But she's also aware of the fact that Odo doesn't want her to know, so she says nothing and allows him to continue going on missions.

On Deep Space 9, Bashir works around the clock trying to find a cure for Odo, to no avail. O'Brien observes that the only option left is to get hold of

Odo poses as the Founder to help Damar gain control of a Jem'Hadar ship. ROBBIE ROBINSON

someone in Section 31 who may have knowledge of an antidote to the disease they created. Bashir rejects the idea, concerned about alerting Section 31 to the fact that people are on to the agency's involvement with the Founders' disease.

Gowron attempts to blame Martok for a failed attack on a Dominion stronghold. An angry Sisko points out that both he *and* Martok had previously informed Gowron, who ordered Martok to lead the mission, that the attack was ill-advised. Seven Klingon ships have been destroyed, and five others are heavily damaged, while Martok himself is in critical condition. Sisko implies that Gowron is solely to blame for the situation, but Gowron allows Sisko's thinly veiled accusations to roll off his back. He tells the captain that he will continue to command the soldiers of the Klingon Empire as he feels appropriate.

At Dominion headquarters, the female Founder expresses dissatisfaction with the lack of progress that Weyoun has achieved in quashing the Cardassian rebellion that Damar has incited. She orders the nervous Vorta to redouble his efforts and tells Thot Pran to step up his efforts to install the deadly Breen energy-dampening weapons ("The Changing Face of Evil") aboard all Dominion ships. At the same time, Kira and Garak begin plotting to get hold of one of the ships equipped with the Breen weapon, so that Starfleet can figure out how to defeat it. Rusot tells Damar that they should be working to free Cardassia from the Dominion, not helping Starfleet. But Damar realizes that they're all in the battle together. What helps Starfleet will help Cardassia. He agrees with Kira's plan, which calls for them to sneak into a Cardassian repair facility and steal a ship. Later, Rusot tries to provoke Kira into a fight, hoping that it will give him an excuse to kill her. But Kira overpowers Rusot and warns him to back off. Observing from the shadows, Garak advises Kira that the time is coming when she'll need to take care of Rusot permanently. She needs to kill him before he kills her.

Sisko meets with Worf to discuss Gowron's behavior, which threatens to destroy the Federation's entire defense posture. Worf fears that Gowron cares about only one thing right now—humiliating Martok in the eyes of the Empire. It would not be the first time a Klingon chancellor has put his own interests ahead of the greater good. Sisko tells Worf that something must be done—and he's counting on Worf to make sure that it happens. Worf goes to the recovering Martok and urges him to challenge Gowron, to prevent the chancellor from leading the Empire to

ruin. But Martok refuses to defy the ruler of his people. Later, Worf confesses to Ezri that he may have been wrong to ask Martok to revolt against Gowron. But Ezri disagrees. Corruption within Klingon leadership is epidemic and goes against the esteemed ancient traditions of honor and integrity, she observes. But if no one is willing to take a stand against it, if even Worf, one of the most honorable men Ezri knows, is willing to tolerate corrupt leaders, then there is no hope for the Empire.

En route to the repair facility, Damar receives word that Dominion forces found his wife and son and put them to death. He angrily wonders what kind of state would order the murder of innocents, leading Kira, who lost friends and family during the Cardassian Occupation of Bajor, to pose the same question to him. Damar stalks away in disgust, leading Kira to regret her quick tongue. But Garak points out that if Damar is the man to lead a new Cardassia, he needs to face the sins of the past as well as the trials of the present.

At the Dominion repair facility, Damar, Rusot, and Garak escort Kira, supposedly a Starfleet prisoner, onto a Jem'Hadar ship that's been equipped with the Breen technology. The Cardassians go to the bridge, where they present their prisoner to the Vorta in command for interrogation. The Vorta is suspicious; she's heard nothing of this prisoner transfer. Suddenly, the female Founder enters the bridge, cowing the Vorta and the Jem'Hadar who surround her. The Founder pretends to inspect a weapon, then tosses it to Garak, who mows down all of the Dominion personnel. The Founder then morphs into Odo, and the group prepares to leave with their prize. But Garak discovers that the crew hasn't finished installing the Breen weapon.

Kira refuses to go until the weapon is hooked up. After Odo collapses, Rusot panics, feeling the whole plan is coming apart. Aiming a weapon at Kira, Rusot demands to leave. Kira refuses, and Rusot prepares to kill her. Garak responds by pointing a weapon at Rusot, while Damar, noting that the workers have finished installing the weapon, tries to talk everyone into dropping their weapons. But Rusot refuses. He still wants Kira dead, and he urges Damar to kill Garak as well. Forced to make a difficult decision, Damar kills Rusot, explaining that Rusot's Cardassia is gone, and won't be coming back.

Aboard the station, O'Brien suggests that Bashir send a message to Starfleet Medical saying that he's found the cure. Bashir agrees, realizing that this will certainly lure someone from Section 31 to the station —and that person will either know what the cure is, or know someone who does. They prepare to lay a trap for the operative.

With Ezri's words still fresh in his mind, Worf listens as Gowron plans to announce yet another futile stab at the Dominion, one that's sure to waste more lives and lay more humiliation at Martok's feet. But Worf is no longer willing to put up with Gowron's madness. He accuses Gowron of ruling without wisdom or honor, words that he knows will provoke a fight to the death. He and Gowron grab their *bat'leths* and engage in a fierce battle, which Worf ultimately wins. With Gowron dead, the Klingons gathered declare Worf leader of the Klingon Empire, but Worf declines that honor. He declares that Martok, already a hero to the Klingon people, is the man to lead the Empire to a new era of honor and dignity. Later, at Quark's, Worf drinks a toast to Chancellor Martok, while Ezri proudly toasts Worf's brief but noble reign as chancellor.

Bashir and O'Brien decide they must go inside Sloan's mind to obtain a cure for Odo's illness. ROBBIE ROBINSON

EXTREME MEASURES
Episode #573
WRITTEN BY BRADLEY THOMPSON & DAVID WEDDLE
DIRECTED BY STEVE POSEY

GUEST CAST

Garak	ANDREW J. ROBINSON
Jessica	JACQUELINE SCHULTZ
Nurse Bandee	KATE ASNER
Operative	TOM HOLLERON

SPECIAL GUEST STAR

Sloan	WILLIAM SADLER

STARDATE 52645.7

Kira and Garak bring Odo back to the station for treatment by Bashir, but there's little the doctor can do, other than alleviate the shape-shifter's pain. Knowing that he has only a week or two at most, Odo asks Kira to go back and continue assisting Damar's rebellion. Kira doesn't want to leave, but Odo insists. He knows she watched Bareil die ("Life Support"), and he doesn't want her last memory of *him* to be witnessing his death. Kira yields to Odo's request, tells him that she loves him, and kisses him goodbye.

After she leaves, O'Brien and Bashir tell Sisko about their suspicions that Section 31 infected Odo

("When It Rains . . ."), with the idea that he would infect others in the Great Link. They explain their plan to lure someone from Section 31 to the station so they can find out if there's a cure. Sisko isn't happy about the scheme, but he knows that at this point, it's the only hope Odo has. Later that night, O'Brien finds Bashir playing darts at Quark's. The doctor can't sleep, and he can't read either. He tells O'Brien that he keeps reading the same page of *A Tale of Two Cities* over and over again. But his preoccupation isn't Odo—it's Section 31. Bashir feels that the insidious organization must be destroyed. O'Brien agrees, but suggests that Bashir stay focused on Odo for now.

Bashir returns to his quarters and finally falls asleep, but a short time later, he's awakened by the realization that someone is in the room with him. Sure enough, it's Section 31's Sloan (*"Inter Arma Enim Silent Leges"*). The operative tells Bashir he has an assignment for him, but Bashir counters by saying *he* has an assignment for Sloan. The doctor stuns the agent and brings him to the Science Lab, where he's met by O'Brien. When Sloan comes to, he finds himself in a bio-bed, restrained by a force field. Bashir tells Sloan that he intends to find out what the agent knows about the Founders' disease—and he's prepared to use a Romulan mind probe to do it. But after Bashir places the device on Sloan's temples, Sloan attempts to commit suicide by activating a neuro-depolarizing device in his own brain.

Bashir manages to stabilize the agent, but the device has done its work. Sloan has suffered irreversible brain damage and will die within the hour. But Bashir is determined to retrieve the vital data that he knows is inside Sloan's mind. He directs O'Brien to create a multitronic engrammatic interpreter, which Bashir says will allow him to link his mind to Sloan's. The doctor assures O'Brien that he'll be able to automatically break the link when he wants to, but the engineer worries that Bashir will lose his way, or be trapped when Sloan dies. He insists on going along on the trip through Sloan's mind, and Bashir includes him in the link.

To the two Starfleet officers, the interior of Sloan's mind resembles the interior of Deep Space 9, from a turbolift that takes them on a wild ride, to endless corridors. To their surprise, Sloan—or an abstraction of him—appears and greets them. When they ask him for the cure, Sloan obligingly recites its components, but his words sound garbled. Sloan apologizes, explaining that a part of him doesn't want them to know until they accompany him to the "Wardroom." With no other choice, they follow him to the large meeting room, where a party is in progress. The room is filled with Sloan's friends and family members, and the agent makes a speech, telling his guests that he's sorry for all the years he let his duty come before them. Sloan's wife, "Jessica," steps forward to kiss her husband, and gives him a padd that contains the information about the cure. But just as Sloan is about to hand the padd to Bashir, he's shot in the back by another Sloan, who leaves with the cure. Bewildered, Bashir and O'Brien attempt to follow Sloan down a long, winding corridor with locked doors on either side.

Meanwhile, in the Science Lab, Sisko and Ezri find the unconscious bodies of O'Brien, Bashir, and Sloan and send for a medical team to see if they can be revived. Inside Sloan's mind, the two officers run into another Section 31 agent, who refuses to let them proceed. When Bashir attempts to force his way past, the agent shoots the doctor with a phaser, and O'Brien as well. Bashir tries to break the link and awaken them both, but he fails. Believing they're about to die, the two men express their affection for each other, and decide that they may as well die like Travis and Crockett, the heroes of the Alamo, doing their duty to the end. They stagger toward one more door, thinking that perhaps this one won't be locked . . .

. . . But before they can open it, they awaken in the Science Lab, revived by Bashir's medical personnel. Bashir insists they must reenter Sloan's mind to obtain the information, but it's too late. Sloan dies, despite Bashir's best efforts to keep him alive a little longer. Knowing that Odo's last chance has died with the operative, a depressed Bashir heads back to his quarters and tries to distract himself by reading. He picks up his copy of *A Tale of Two Cities* and begins to read, then stops as he notices something peculiar. The book stops abruptly and starts over again on page 294. He quickly gets hold of O'Brien, and explains that he thinks they're still in Sloan's mind. Sloan is drawing on their memories to make them *think* they're back in the real world. The book was the clue. It seems unfinished because Bashir's never read the whole book. The pair realize that they must have been very close to the answer when Sloan resorted to this last trick.

O'Brien and Bashir return to the corridor they were in before they were "revived" and try the door they'd been heading toward. It opens, and they find themselves in a room crammed with all kinds of information. Sloan sits in a chair at a desk and greets them. He's weak, but he refuses to tell them where to look for the cure. As the two officers search, Sloan sidetracks Bashir by pointing out files that contain documents of political intrigue, information that could destroy Section 31. But O'Brien, who finds what seems to be the components of the cure, realizes that Sloan is trying to detain Bashir so that the two of them will die when the agent does. Alerted to the trap, Bashir breaks the link, pulling himself and O'Brien out just in time. Bashir rushes to surgery and injects Odo with what he hopes is the cure. To everyone's relief, Odo is restored, and Bashir thanks O'Brien for being the one random element that Sloan didn't anticipate.

THE DOGS OF WAR

Episode #574

TELEPLAY BY **RENÉ ECHEVARRIA** &
RONALD D. MOORE
STORY BY **PETER ALLAN FIELDS**
DIRECTED BY **AVERY BROOKS**

GUEST CAST

Kasidy Yates	PENNY JOHNSON
Garak	ANDREW J. ROBINSON
Weyoun and Brunt	JEFFREY COMBS
Rom	MAX GRODÉNCHIK
Damar	CASEY BIGGS
Admiral Ross	BARRY JENNER
Ishka	CECILY ADAMS
General Martok	J.G. HERTZLER
Leeta	CHASE MASTERSON
Nog	ARON EISENBERG
Mila	JULIANNA McCARTHY
Maihar'du	TINY RON
Female Shape-shifter	SALOME JENS
Broca	MEL JOHNSON, JR.
Seskal	VAUGHN ARMSTRONG
Velal	STEPHEN YOAKAM
Jem'Hadar	PAUL S. ECKSTEIN
Broik	DAVID B. LEVINSON
M'Pella	CATHY DEBUONO
Lonar	LEROY D. BRAZILE
Federation Computer Voice	MAJEL BARRETT

SPECIAL GUEST STAR

Zek	WALLACE SHAWN

STARDATE 52861.3

Excitement runs high on the station as Sisko receives Starfleet's replacement for the destroyed *Defiant* ("The Changing Face of Evil"), a brand-new *Defiant*-class starship called the *U.S.S. São Paulo*. As Admiral Ross transfers command of the vessel to Sisko, he points out that Starfleet has granted special dispensation to change the ship's name from *São Paulo* to *Defiant*, a change that the crew appreciates. They also appreciate the modifications that Starfleet has made to the new *Defiant*'s shield generators. This ship won't be vulnerable to the Breen's energy-dampening weapons.

Spirits are similarly high on the ship carrying Garak, Damar, and Kira to Cardassia. Damar has convinced Gul Revok and Legate Goris to bring their respective troops over to his resistance efforts. With half a million men, they should be able to make a considerable dent in Dominion forces. But after the

Brunt grovels to ingratiate himself with Quark, the man he believes will be the next nagus. ROBBIE ROBINSON

three beam down to the agreed-upon rendezvous point, they realize something is wrong. Jem'Hadar soldiers are killing everyone at the site. Revok has betrayed the rebellion. Kira tries to contact Damar's ship so they can make a quick getaway, but the vessel has been destroyed in orbit. Trapped on Cardassia, the trio make their way to the planet's capital, where Garak leads them to the home of his father, the late Enabran Tain ("In Purgatory's Shadow"). There, they are hidden in the cellar by Mila, Tain's housekeeper ("Improbable Cause").

Quark is surprised when he receives a static-filled message from the grand nagus. Zek is coming to the station to announce his retirement and to name his successor. The conversation is a little difficult to follow, and Quark is more than a little surprised when he realizes that Zek intends to name *him* the new grand nagus. In the Infirmary, Bashir gives Odo a final checkup and declares him completely recovered from the changeling disease. Bashir feels compelled to tell Odo the complete truth behind the ailment. He was infected by Section 31 so that he would transmit the disease to the Founders. When Odo turns to Sisko for an explanation, the captain explains that the Federation was unaware of the rogue organization's actions. However, now that they've been made aware, Sisko admits, they are unwilling to provide information about the cure to the Founders. Odo points out that this means Sisko's virtuous Federation is abetting genocide. Sisko can't deny that, but he notes that the Founders were the ones who started the war, and no one can afford to give them any advantage that would strengthen their hand at this point.

In the Replimat, Ezri and Bashir awkwardly agree to have lunch together. They finally admit their mutual attraction to each other, but then decide that they don't want to risk their friendship over it. It's a resolution that isn't very satisfying, but it makes sense to both of them. At the bar, Quark daydreams about his future in the Nagal Residence. To his surprise, he receives a visit from his nemesis, Liquidator Brunt. For a change, Brunt isn't there to cause trouble. He just wants to score points by sucking up to the nagus-to-be.

From their cellar hideaway, Kira, Garak, and Damar listen as Weyoun broadcasts an announcement to the Cardassian people. The Vorta states that Damar and his cohorts were killed when Dominion forces blew up their ship. The good news is that Jem'Hadar forces won't be looking for the three of them. The bad news is that the Dominion has managed to eliminate all eighteen rebel bases—and that there's no way for Kira and the others to call for help or get off occupied Cardassia without being spotted by the Dominion. Unless they can think of something, they may wind up spending the duration of the war in a cellar! The trio's dismay turns to hope when they learn that Damar's alleged death has catapulted him to the status of legend. The organized resistance may be gone, but the Cardassian people are fed up with Dominion occupation. If Damar appears in public and asks for their support, he may be able to incite a revolution.

To get into the nagus-to-be's good graces, Quark allows Brunt to present him with a sizable bribe. He is horrified by Brunt's news of the changes that await him on Ferenginar. In recent months, Zek has instituted a progressive income tax, which was necessary to pay for the planet's new social programs, such as wage subsidies, retirement benefits, and health care. Quark realizes that Ishka has gotten Zek to turn the greed-worshipping society he loves into a democracy, but there seems to be little he can do about it. He complains about the changes to Rom, who doesn't find them all that terrible. Looking out for his own future, Rom is more interested in getting Quark to sell him his bar. Quark decides that he needs to take a stand on the terrible "disease" that's affecting the very fabric of Ferengi society. If Zek wants him to be nagus, he'll have to allow Quark to do things his way—the traditional way—or he'll turn down the job.

At Dominion headquarters on Cardassia Prime the female Founder learns that the Federation has developed a countermeasure to the Breen weapon. She orders a strategic retreat of Dominion forces to Cardassian space, where they'll be able to concentrate their forces and hold off attacks while they build new ships and create more Jem'Hadar. In the same city Kira and the others launch their insurrection, with Garak slipping into some Jem'Hadar barracks and planting a bomb. But when a Jem'Hadar guard prevents Garak from leaving the immediate area, the revolution is in danger of ending before it can begin. Observing from a distance, Damar and Kira realize that the bomb could go off at any second, killing Garak. Damar creates a distraction, allowing Kira to remove one of the guards and Garak another. After the explosion, Damar steps forward to address the Cardassians who witnessed the scene, and encourages them to rise up and join him in fighting the Dominion. His speech galvanizes the crowd, exactly as they'd hoped.

On Deep Space 9, Ezri and Bashir meet by chance on a turbolift and note how happy they are that they had their little conversation. By the time the turbolift arrives at Ops, however, the pair are locked in a passionate kiss. O'Brien and Worf observe that the couple seem to have worked things out. Meanwhile, Zek and Ishka arrive at the station, and Quark launches into his speech about needing the freedom to do things his way as Nagus. To his surprise, Zek says that he never had any intention of making Quark the Nagus. Apparently, the static was so bad during their communication that he mistook Quark for Rom—the *real* successor that Zek has chosen. The new Ferenginar needs a new kind of nagus, Zek explains, a kinder, gentler nagus. Offended, Quark declares that as far as he's concerned, the Ferenginar that he once knew no longer exists—*except* on Deep Space 9, in his bar. He asks Rom to sell him back his establishment, but Rom graciously gives it to him as a present.

In the Wardroom, Sisko discusses the Dominion's retreat with Chancellor Martok, Ross, and Romulan

Commander Velal. But although they know that it would take a major offensive to break through the Dominion's new defense perimeter, the group agrees that it makes more sense to attack than to allow them to refortify their fleet. As Sisko returns to his quarters, he finds Kasidy waiting up for him. When she tells him that she's pregnant, Sisko is surprised, but delighted. Kasidy is happy too, but she's concerned about the warning that the Prophets gave Sisko prior to their marriage ("Penumbra"). Could the sorrow that Sarah spoke of have something to do with their baby? Sisko assures her that everything will be fine, but in his heart, he's not really certain.

Getting a handle on it

They'd done it before. Together they'd tackled a multi-episode arc in which every member of the writing team was responsible for certain segments—contiguous episodes that would wind up making sense and tracking correctly and even sounding pretty much like everyone knew what he was doing, despite some comments to the contrary. Could they do it again?

Sometimes, ignorance is bliss. When the writers had jumped into the six-episode arc that launched Season 6, they hadn't known what they were in for. But this time . . .

"It *was* frightening," admits René Echevarria. "And I've got to say there were moments in which I was afraid we weren't going to pull it off. Moments when I thought that we'd backed ourselves into a corner. It wasn't until we had broken the last episode that I finally said, 'You know what? I think we did it.'"

"It was definitely hard," comments David Weddle, "but it was 'good' hard. It was 'exciting' hard. We had a lot of balls to juggle. A lot of stories to keep going. You really got a sense of how *big* the story was becoming. That was fun, but we had so many balls in the air, and so many questions about how we could service each story and each episode."

"We had graphs and charts," Brad Thompson says. "We knew what we *wanted* to do, and we had a kind of wish list of what we were going to try. As for how we were going to get there—we had no clue. Of course, when I say 'no clue,' I'm speaking for David and myself. Who knows what was going on in the back of Ira's head? But the break sessions didn't feel like, 'Well, yes, we'll just do this and then this and then we do this. That is definitely *not* what they felt like."

A sample of the pages from the ancient text of the Kosst Amojan.
JOHN EAVES

"We knew where all the characters were going to end up," explains Ron Moore. "We had talked specifics: Odo goes to the Great Link; Sisko goes over to the Prophets; Kira gets the station; O'Brien goes home. We had gone through them all. We knew that we had to wrap up the war. The war was going to end, and all these people were going to meet their fates. We had stroked out some very general stuff about the arc. 'This should happen. We'd like it to be a classic three-act structure. The episodes should be in this order.' But the discussions just kept getting more complicated. We'd sit in the room and try to keep it all straight as one big piece, and it got very difficult. At some point, Ira just said, 'Look, we're just going to start. Let's start breaking the first one and keep it going.'"

"The basic overall structure was there," states Ira Steven Behr, "but the details had to be filled in on the run. It was a journey into the unknown. We took a lot of risks. We ran the risks of taking missteps and falling on our faces. And the only thing we had that would convince people that we were doing the right thing was the quality of the episodes. We had to keep everyone interested in order to keep doing what we wanted to do. That was our one fallback position. People might have hated the fact that it [these eight episodes] was serialized. They might have hated the direction that the show was going in, but they *had* to admit that the episodes were pretty good."

Finding the words

"It was one of the most intense times," Ron Moore reflects. "I'd say that the arc we'd done in Season 6 was a little tougher, because we weren't prepared for all the continuity problems, and didn't realize just how closely we'd have to work together. But the 'machine' was definitely working at this point. So what we primarily were feeling was pressure from within, our own pressure to make it work, to make it as good as we could. We all heard a lot of 'This isn't good enough. How can we make it better?'"

But even a well-oiled machine needs *all* of its parts in order to function properly, and the best-laid schemes, as Robert Burns said, "gang aft agley." When Ron Moore's wife gave birth to son Robin a month ahead of schedule, that wasn't in anyone's plans. "I was in the middle of the rewrite for 'Strange Bedfellows' when my wife called and said she was leaving for the hospital and to meet her there," Moore

The writers found a way for Worf to deal with his memories and feelings for Dax. ROBBIE ROBINSON

Now that Ezri was comfortable with being the new Dax, the writers had to make Worf as comfortable. ROBBIE ROBINSON

notes. "I told the guys, 'I gotta go,' and I was out for the next week. But you know, the team was such that everybody was working in concert. They kept it going and never missed a beat. That's how tight the staff was at that point."

Which isn't to say that his absence didn't create a little stress around the writing offices. "Hans [Beimler] and I were working on the following show, 'The Changing Face of Evil,'" recalls Behr. "Then all of a sudden Ron wasn't around, we had to do some of those scenes, and René had to do some rewrites. It got very hectic." Before long, he says, he realized that he was going to have to give up on fulfilling "the dream."

"I had this dream," Behr explains with a sigh. "I knew it was going to be very hard to achieve. I'd told Hans that we were only going to write *one* show in the arc leading up to the final episode. That's because we were going to take our time on the last episode, 'What You Leave Behind,' and really do it right. It was a *drag* knowing that we were only going to write one show. I wanted to write a lot more. But I said, 'We're only going to write one. That's one of the things we're going to have to suck up in order to have the privilege of writing the last *Deep Space Nine*." He pauses, smiling ruefully. "But then Ron went out, and other things happened and it got worse and worse. So eventually we ran out of time, and the last episode was written in a rush of white heat that was *unbelievable* in terms of its pain and agony."

This time around, René Echevarria, who'd been given what turned out to be the toughest episode in the previous season's arc ("Behind the Lines"), got the plum assignment: first up. "I started the ball rolling with 'Penumbra,'" he says. "It was a lot easier than the ones I worked on later, like 'The Dogs of War.' The first one doesn't have to be a self-contained story with its own self-contained arc and self-contained payoff, which can be extremely challenging." It did, however, contain just as many plot threads as the subsequent episodes.

The unusual title was his idea. "Penumbra means a region of half-shadow, half-light," he says. "I knew the word from the Supreme Court decision that says, 'the right to privacy casts a penumbra that includes the right to abortion.' It's kind of a spooky word, and the episode was about a shadow, the beginning of a spooky, difficult time."

With that title set, Weddle and Thompson, who were scheduled to write the next episode, decided to call their story "Umbra," an area of much deeper shadow. The third part, assigned to Moore, would be called "Eclipse." In theory, it all made sense, and it made for interesting imagery. In practice, "it was deeply confusing to everybody," Moore says, laughing. "We were getting confused ourselves, and then there was a point when Ira and Rick Berman were debating some story point, and they were saying 'Penumbra' when they meant 'Umbra' and it just became maddening. It was, 'This cannot be! We have to change these damn titles!'"

As Behr relates one of those maddening conversations, it begins to sound like Abbott and Costello's classic "Who's on First?" routine: "We were saying, 'That's in "Eclipse." 'No, it's in "Umbra."' 'No, it's not "Umbra." It's "*Penumbra.*"' 'Not "Umbra"?' 'No, "Penumbra."' 'So it's in "*Penumbra*"?' 'No, no— "Eclipse"'! It just drove us insane! We needed titles where we would know what the hell show we were talking about, and that would tell us what happened in the show. Changing the titles helped."

One of the first plot threads Echevarria began developing was Ezri's attempt to find Worf. "We needed to address the Dax/Worf relationship,"

The simple solution. ROBBIE ROBINSON

says Behr. "We really wanted Ezri to wind up with Bashir, but we couldn't just jump into having her involved with him, because then we'd have to go back and deal with the Worf stuff. She had to get old business out of the way before she could go on to new business."

There was another reason for sending Ezri out on a wild Worf hunt. "This was our way of putting them behind enemy lines," Echevarria points out. "They would be the ones who bring us to the plot about the Breen, who we'd decided would jack up the war stakes when the Dominion loses the Romulans as an ally. It was a very roundabout way of getting to a larger geopolitical point."

However, it was a point that would not be fully developed for several episodes. "We were flying by the seat of our pants with this," says Behr. "We knew that bringing in the Breen would up the stakes. But we didn't have the whole thing worked out, so we weren't sure how much we'd learn about the Breen in the long run."

To get Ezri (and ultimately Worf) into the hands of the Breen, Echevarria put the Trill in a runabout, where the Badlands' currents would carry her to the missing Klingon. "I wanted her to do something risky," he explains. "It needed to be something that Sisko *couldn't* have done in the *Defiant*, not something that he didn't do because he gave up too soon. The *Defiant* is so big that even if he'd thought of what she tries, the ship never would have followed the same path. It was a practical solution, and not too tech-y."

What turned out to be a lot *more* tech-y—or at

least more of a technicality—was the name of Ezri's runabout. Echevarria had decided to put her in the *Ganges*, and his script reflects that decision. "Then some smartass said, 'That one was destroyed ["Armageddon Game"].' And I said, 'Oh, yeah? Well, this is a *new* one.' And the discussion got all the way up to Rick, who said, 'It was destroyed. We need a new one.'" Clearly, it would have been simple for Echevarria to come up with the name of a previously untapped river, but he was feeling feisty. "My feeling was, 'So what if it was destroyed?'" he says. "That was five years ago. This is a new one. How many *Galileo*s have there been?"

Ultimately, the majority ruled and the runabout was christened *Gander*, after a Canadian river. The name debate proved to be much ado about not much, since the vessel is destroyed in the very same episode. It lasts just long enough to get Ezri and Worf to a planet in the Goralis system, where they're captured by the Breen. Before that happens, however, they get to spend one romantic night together and, in the best tradition of general television practices, they wake up fully clothed. That decision had less to do with moral standards—Ezri and Bashir are clearly not clothed when they awaken together in "What You Leave Behind"—than it did with Klingon anatomy. "It was this whole production question," reveals Behr. "What does a Klingon look like under his clothes? It was just too complicated to think about."

Complicated doesn't begin to describe what the writers had in mind for Gul Dukat. If viewers still don't know what Cardassians look like under their clothes, they *do* know what Marc Alaimo looks like under his prosthetic makeup. "Turning him into a Bajoran made sense," Echevarria admits. "How else could he interact with Winn? He had to have the surgery."

"The story dictated it," Behr agrees. "The way Dukat was going, getting involved with Bajoran religion, the next step would be to go to Bajor, and to Winn. Bringing together two of the best villains ever and giving them this intricate relationship was truly *Shakespearian* in its scope. The lust. The hate. The manipulation. It was just *fun!*"

Less fun was the development of the Sarah Prophet's pronouncement that if Sisko marries Kasidy "he will know nothing but sorrow."

Echevarria sighs. "It never quite paid off," he says. "The idea was that the Prophets knew Sisko was going to die. He should begin disassociating himself with things of this world, because that relationship ultimately would be painful to him. Believe it or not, Sarah originally was going to tell him, 'Don't build this house on Bajor.'" In the following episode, Echevarria explains, Sisko would talk to Kasidy about marriage, and in the third installment, Moore would be responsible for joining the two of them in matrimony. But that didn't quite work for Echevarria. "I realized, 'Why don't we skip all this and have the Prophets say, 'Don't get married' instead of 'Don't build a house.' Because who cares about the house?"

Echevarria relayed his concerns to the other writers. "We were working on all three of the episodes simultaneously," notes Thompson. "So René comes in and says, 'I can't really lead to this unless you guys get them married in the second show.' And suddenly it's, 'Oh, sorry, Ron. You can't get them married because that's going to happen in the *second* hour now.' And Ron is going, 'Aarrrggh! Then what's going to happen to *my* show?' So scenes moved from our show to René's, and from Ron's show to ours, and so forth."

But while the assorted shifts seemed to work to everyone's satisfaction at the time, the long-term repercussions of Sarah's comment would come back to haunt the writers later on.

As with the previous year's arc, Weddle and Thompson were second at bat, this time with "'Til Death Do Us Part" (formerly known as "Umbra"). The episode includes an important wedding, the creation of a powerful political alliance, and one of the most perverse pairings in *Star Trek*. "The idea of Dukat wooing Kai Winn appealed to

"Putting Dukat and Winn together gave us so much to play with," says Thompson. ROBBIE ROBINSON

"One of the most pleasant duties of a senior officer is the privilege of joining two people together in matrimony." ROBBIE ROBINSON

us on a very twisted level," grins Thompson. "Our two bad guys were going to mate! We were howling with glee at the idea."

How did it come about? "Ira had said, just as a throwaway kind of thought, 'It's too bad we can't get Winn and Dukat in bed together,'" recalls Moore. "And I said, 'Well, why can't we do that?' And everyone just stopped and said, 'Wait, that's a *great* idea.'"

"The two characters are so worthy of scene after scene after scene," Behr rhapsodizes. "And when we decided that they actually were going to have a physical relationship, it was just dementedly wonderful."

"The whole thing worked *really* well," says Echevarria. In fact, compared to the struggles that the writers had with some of the other plot lines, there was only one problem with the Dukat/Winn story. "We started it too soon and we ran out of story for them," he notes. "Suddenly we realized that we didn't need them again until the final episode."

"We had to find a way to get the audience to stop thinking about them for a while," continues Behr. Which led to another example of what Behr considers to be the series' unofficial motto, particularly at the end of the final season: "Make it a virtue!"

"Every time we got stuck and something wasn't working, we'd say, 'Let's make it a virtue!' We should have had T-shirts made up," Behr grins. "So that's what we did. We blinded Dukat and had Winn send him out begging. It was the same situation with Sisko's quick wedding. The captain keeps changing his mind. This is a guy with indecision. Well, make it a virtue. Have the wedding be an impromptu thing."

"The wedding was like, 'We've got to do it and we're going to do it *now*,'" says Thompson. "Sisko has jerked her around. It has to happen right away, and whoever can be there is there."

There was a virtue in doing it as a small ceremony, too. "It didn't have to compete with the big Worf/Dax wedding we'd already done," notes Behr.

If Admiral Ross's words to Ben and Kasidy sound familiar, it's because they follow a *Star Trek* tradition. "Ron had written the speech that Captain Picard delivers when he married O'Brien and Keiko in *TNG* ['Data's Day']," explains Thompson, "and he based that on a speech that Kirk gives at a wedding in the original series. David [Weddle] and I looked at both of those episodes, and then modified it a little. We took the tradition and improvised on it, because the words don't actually come out of a book. You can say whatever you want. So they're similar but not identical to what Kirk and Picard say."

While the ceremony was relatively simple, the scene where Ezri learns from Worf that she loves Julian was a lot tougher. "That scene came up in the break session, and we wondered how we could do it without resorting to some painful soap opera-ish kind of twist," recalls Weddle. "René suggested that we do a dream sequence, where Ezri has some kind of dream and tries to tell Worf about it. Brad doesn't like the idea of dream interpretation, but I do, so we decided to make the scene about our feelings. Then we came up with the idea of Ezri being chased by a Breen, and he takes off his helmet and it's Julian."

At the close of "'Til Death Do Us Part," Weyoun announces the birth of the alliance between the Dominion and the Breen, noting that it "changes everything, doesn't it?"

The very next episode would show just how much it changed things for the character of Damar, making him one of the very "Strange Bedfellows" of the title. Although some viewers may not have anticipated Damar's potential for genuine heroic behavior, the executive producer had.

"Ira has really good instincts, even when he doesn't know *why* he wants to do something," says Hans Beimler. "It was his idea to make Damar a drinker, but he didn't know back then that he wanted to make him a hero. It was answering the question 'Why is he drinking so much?' that led us there. Damar had a conscience, and that ultimately told us where we needed to go."

By this time, Damar's drinking had carried the character's development as far as it could. "It was so wonderful at first," says Behr, "but now we'd gotten to the point where *we* were getting disgusted with the character in the same way that he was becoming disgusted with himself. We wanted him to put down that bottle."

"As soon as Damar stops drinking, his conscience comes to the forefront and takes command," continues Beimler. "He takes hold of himself and goes through an incredible character arc."

"They started to turn me into some kind of comic book hero," Casey Biggs says, laughing. "I got to step out of the shadows and save the day."

While Ron Moore constructed the basic bones of the episode, the other members of the staff made some interesting contributions in his absence. Sisko's

Damar evolved from Dukat's lackey to the savior of Cardassia.
ROBBIE ROBINSON

conversation with Martok about the battlefield that is marriage, for example, is the product of Behr and Beimler. "The series was getting so fragmented that we wanted to remind people that Sisko had gotten married in the preceding episode," explains Behr. "At the same time, we felt that Martok had been lost from the series for a while, and we wanted to bring him back in."

Martok's scene prefaces one in which Sisko asks Kasidy to fulfill a function of her new role as the Emissary's wife by performing the annual blessing of the station's hopeful Bajoran mothers. Kasidy turns him down, noting that she doesn't even believe in the Prophets, leaving Sisko to mull over Martok's prophetic words. Two related scenes, however, are missing from the aired episode: one in which Kira tells Kasidy that her father, although not a religious man, used to attend services every day because he had loved Kira's mother; and another in which Kasidy surprises Sisko by taking over the blessing ceremony in midstream. "Both scenes were filmed, but we were short on time," Echevarria says regretfully. "Kasidy walked in and said, 'All right, let's see a show of hands—who wants boys?' It was very charming."

Weddle and Thompson added some amusing subtext to the scene where Weyoun tries to convince Damar that granting the Breen some territorial concessions would be a good idea. "He tells Damar that he should spend some time with Thot Gor, because he's really quite personable once you know him," smiles Weddle. "That went back to something that Ira was always telling us—make the character smart. In the first draft, Weyoun was just putting Damar down.

"The scene wasn't so much about Worf breaking Weyoun's neck as Damar's reaction to it," Behr points out. ROBBIE ROBINSON

one level, could seem very cruel and dismissive," Behr explains. "She's not giving this woman anything to hold on to, really. But at the same time, you have to understand that Winn is a total loss, that she just doesn't get it. She *thinks* she's going to get it. That's the key! It's intricate stuff. You think *maybe* she's going to get it, but she just can't. She's blind."

"'The Changing Face of Evil' was the culmination of the first four episodes, in a lot of ways," Echevarria states. "Damar launches his rebellion, Winn is completely on board with Dukat, Ezri and Worf have decided not to be together, and Sisko and Kasidy *are* together."

Beimler and Behr were careful to include details from "the Sisko homefront" right along with the ostensibly more interesting scenes from the war. "We liked the idea of showing the domestic life," says Behr. "In the midst of all the pressures that Sisko is under, he still has issues at home. He's still a human being. Kasidy burns his peppers. That hurts! Life is hard, but you should not have to have your peppers burned!"

Some things hurt even more than that, such as watching the *Defiant* be destroyed. "We knew we couldn't kill anyone," Behr notes, "but we wanted to do something that would be painful and gut-wrenching to everyone. And it worked very well. It wasn't the *Enterprise*, it wasn't *Voyager*, and it wasn't the basis of the show. But still, the ship had become a character that had caught on in people's hearts and minds.

But when we stopped to think about what the smart thing would be for him to do, we realized that Weyoun would want to *sell* Damar on the idea."

"That's the used car salesman in Weyoun." Jeffrey Combs grins. "He slips into that persona easily. 'Look, don't worry about the details. I'm on your side here. I want you to have this car at a good price. Just sign here. You have nothing to worry about. You can trust me.'"

Some of the best touches, however, remain Moore's, such as the demise of Weyoun Seven. "I just knew it was going to be a fun moment," Moore chuckles. "Weyoun would just get a little too close and say the wrong thing—and Worf would break his neck. And then Damar would laugh. It was gold."

The scene where Kira suggests that Winn step down from her role as kai wound up in Moore's hands as well. "That was a very tough scene," says Behr. "It came about late in the process, and Ron took a lot of passes at it." Tone was the elusive quality the writers sought. "Kira had to do something which, on

Even though her soul is on the line, Winn refuses to give up the power she craves. ROBBIE ROBINSON

Even though we're not a *Star Trek* series that takes place on a ship, when the *Defiant* went down, that hurt."

Pain isn't necessarily relevant to the villains. Winn, who had her chance for atonement in the previous episode, plunges headlong into sin here, kills Solbor, the true believer in her camp. And still, says Behr, she doesn't see the light. "She experiences self-loathing, and loss, and you wonder, 'Okay, does she get it *now*?' No, she doesn't. As soon as Dukat explains to her that she can cover the murder up, it's clear that *she's* the only thing she's worried about. It's always her. It's a very shocking, scary, pathetic moment that shows that power isn't a wonderful thing. Power can only twist."

Of course, Behr smiles, despite all of Winn's horrible behavior, "when the smoke clears, she's *still* less tainted than Dukat. Dukat is still the master, the manipulator, the liar. They're quite a team."

Although Dukat was still the master, he would have the wind knocked out of his sails in the following show, "When It Rains . . ." Dukat is blinded by the Pah-wraiths. Martok's command of the Klingon forces is wrested away by Gowron. Odo learns that he has the Founders' disease. Bashir learns that Section 31 has launched a plan to commit genocide. Kira is sent on a mission to teach the Cardassians the exact skills that allowed her people to defeat them years earlier. No one is particularly happy with his lot in this episode.

The primary source of Dukat's injury was the fact that the writers had nowhere to take his or Winn's characters for the subsequent three episodes. "I was told, 'Find a way to stall,'" says Echevarria. "I needed to leave them in a place where the audience would feel, 'Okay, they're doing this, but I don't need to see them do it.' And I came up with the idea of blinding Dukat. Now, truth be told, I didn't really have a specific intention when I wrote that, but I can justify it after the fact. The Pah-wraiths knew that they needed to maneuver these two people to get them into the caves. They needed her to get *him* there, and they needed him to die there, so that they could use his body. If he had read in the book, 'You will be killed and be reborn,' he might not have gone for it." Thus, the Pah-wraiths blinded him, and Winn was given a few weeks to read the book in peace and quiet.

The idea of sending Kira to help Damar's forces originated with Ron Moore. "The initial idea was that Damar would function as a double agent through the

Odo's disease makeup was easy on Auberjonois. "I didn't have to worry about it cracking or pieces falling off." ROBBIE ROBINSON

last part of the war. I wasn't very happy with that," Moore recalls. "I began insisting that some of the regulars had to join Damar. It was important. We had to get some of our players over to that side of the story or we'd never wind up visiting it again. He would just leave the bunker and drop out of the story. I kept fighting for this, and finally Hans said, 'It sounds like you're arguing for us to turn Damar into Spartacus.' And I said, 'Yes! That's it! Damar is Spartacus! That's the story we need to tell. It's the slave revolt!'"

The rest of the team went for the idea and began plotting it out. "First we said, 'Okay, let's get Kira over there,'" says Moore. "But then someone said, 'Well, we can't separate Kira and Odo for this whole chunk of time. That's no good. They're a couple, and this would split them up till the very end of the show.'" But how could Odo go with Kira when plans already were in the works to have him track down Section 31's involvement with the Founders' disease?

Fate stepped in, in the form of a plot twist that Echevarria decided to introduce in "When It Rains . . ." "When I began working on it," he explains, "the idea we'd plotted out was that Odo would learn that Section 31 had used him to give the disease to the Founders. But he was not going to get sick, just as Typhoid Mary never got sick. She just spread the disease. But as I got into it, I began thinking, 'So what? So you find out something that's happened in the past. There's nothing to be done about it.' And I was a good fifteen, twenty pages in when I made the realization that Odo *had* to get sick. Ron already was working on 'Tacking into the Wind,' and when I told him, he flipped his gourd. He said, 'No! You'll ruin everything!'" Echevarria laughs. "But we hashed it out, and he agreed that in order for this to be an ongoing storyline that mattered, Odo needed to get sick."

Which meant that Odo would go with Kira on her mission—and get sick while he was out there—and Bashir would have to be the one to follow up on Section 31 *and* to find a cure. "We had to make that choice," says Moore. "Odo couldn't serve both stories."

At this point, the writers also began pushing Bashir and Ezri together in earnest—although their mating ritual seemed to have a lot more downs than ups. Why the need for the tease? Behr seems to become the protective father. "We didn't want Ezri to be that *available*," he says, laughing. "So this was a *courtship*, in a way. A wacky courtship. A *Deep Space Nine* kind of courtship, where people don't even know they're courting. Or how to court."

Ron Moore's role in *Star Trek* history as "the Klingon guy" came full circle in "Tacking into the Wind," as he executed a popular character he'd helped to create nearly a decade earlier, and delivered sharp commentary on the state of a society he'd helped shape. "The first draft of this episode was quite different," he explains. "The initial thought was that Worf would talk Gowron down from his position and make him face what he was doing to the Empire purely for his own selfish reasons. And then Gowron would promote Martok to field marshal and go back to Qo'noS.

"And then Michael Piller, who [in his capacity as creative consultant] writes a memo on every episode, said that he thought Worf should *kill* Gowron, and either take over the Empire himself or give it to Martok," Moore continues. "I read that and thought, 'Wow! That's a *much* better idea.' I went to Ira, and he agreed, so on my second pass, I sent the arc in that direction. This whole idea of the Klingon Empire and

what it's become hadn't even come up until I was working on that pass. That's when I realized that this was my last opportunity to do anything with the Klingons, these aliens that I had been involved with for a long time," Moore relates. "I wanted to view the Klingons in a different manner, and look at what I'd created with the same cold eye as Ezri. Yeah, these guys *are* corrupt, and Worf *has* put up with that for a long time. They talk a good game about how honorable they are, but they're not capable of living up to their ideals. I thought, 'That's an important thing to say, so let's say it.'"

It was nearly as important to bring Kira Nerys full-circle, to show what made her the person she ultimately became. "It was always hard to do that on the show," says Moore. "The backstory is that she's a terrorist who's become part of the establishment. There had never been a comfortable way to make her a terrorist again, although we'd had a few shows where she'd go off and do things. But to bring her back to a 'blows-up-buildings-terrorist' would have been hard to justify. We finally were able to justify it here through circumstance."

Although Moore had become reconciled to the idea that it would be Bashir, and not Odo, who tracked down the culprits in Section 31 who were responsible for the Founders' disease, he still had a tough time setting up the plot for its payoff in the next episode, "Extreme Measures." "The first thought was that Bashir and O'Brien would leave the station for their pursuit. Bashir was going to come up with a clue and they would leave at the end of my episode. It'd be something like, 'The answer's over there, Miles—on Planet X.' And then in the following episode they'd be off the station on that adventure. But by this time, the budgets were getting out of hand and we had to save some money. We already had all these sets up: Dominion headquarters and the *Defiant* and the caves. All this stuff was cramming *our* soundstages, so we would have had to rent another one. It just wasn't possible. We made the decision to lure Section 31 to the station instead."

Like "Rocks and Shoals" before it, Moore opted to give "Tacking into the Wind" a title with a nautical flavor. The expression defines a process by which a ship follows a course against a gale via a series of directional shifts. "It's a very slow, arduous process," notes Moore, "and I felt that it was appropriate. All of the characters were making progress, but it was very difficult."

By all accounts, "Extreme Measures" was "the hardest show of the whole run," Moore states.

"Brad and I did a draft that wasn't very successful," David Weddle says, sighing. "We tried to put two stories together: a conclusion of the Bashir/Sloan storyline, and also a last great adventure for Bashir and O'Brien. We knew that we didn't have many episodes left, so we all thought, well, we'll try to wind up *two* things here. But we'd have been better off trying to do one or the other."

"Ira wanted one last O'Brien/Bashir adventure, a stand-alone show that would give the audience a break from the multi-continuity," comments Moore. "It seemed like that would be nice, because there was so much to keep track of at this point."

"Of course, we needed an adventure for O'Brien and Bashir," continues Weddle. "But Sloan's relationship to Bashir is *so* loaded that it almost demands a story in itself. And with the focus so split, it just didn't work, conceptually."

It could have been even *more* split. The writers originally had thought that Odo's mentor, Dr. Mora, was the person who invented the Founders' disease for Section 31. "He'd never intended to get Odo sick," says Echevarria. "He'd been recruited."

What would have happened next is a little unclear. The characters were going to go into Mora's mind. Or they were going to go into Odo's mind. Or . . . "It was going to be a journey into *someone's* mind," says Behr, "which we'd enjoyed doing years earlier with Bashir in 'Distant Voices' and which we'd thought about doing with Dukat in 'Waltz.' Finally we decided to go into *Sloan's* mind."

Mora's involvement was dropped entirely, and Thompson and Weddle set out to pit Bashir and O'Brien against Section 31's finest. As Weddle stated, the first draft needed some help, so Moore was asked to add his input to the teaser and Acts 1 and 2, while Behr and Beimler took on Acts 3, 4, and 5. Key among the changes was a decision to get O'Brien and Bashir into Sloan's head much sooner—in Act 2 rather than at the end of Act 4.

"The way we'd originally had it, there wasn't much of an opportunity to use O'Brien," says Thompson. "We'd spent a lot of time early on with Sloan and Bashir talking."

"It was a very serious exploration of the moral implications of what Sloan had done, played against Bashir's willingness to cross the line himself to pull the information out of Sloan's head," Weddle

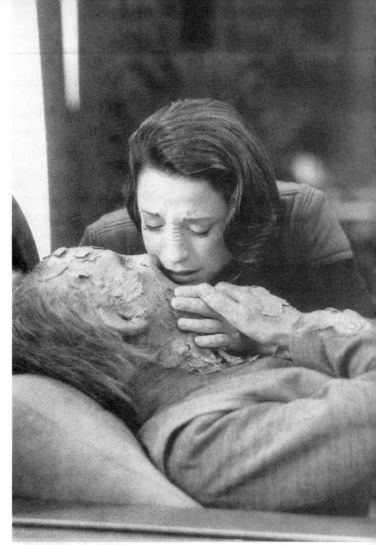

Auberjonois equates Odo's feelings to "learning you're terminally ill and deciding how you deal with it." ROBBIE ROBINSON

explains. "That much was great, but it didn't work at all with the tone of the second part of the story."

"We owed the Bashir and O'Brien relationship," says Thompson. "We needed to see the two guys together. And the scenes that the other guys added played beautifully, particularly the one with the two of them in the hallway, with the light coming and them thinking they're about to die."

"That was one of my favorite scenes *ever*," laughs René Echevarria, "with the two guys sitting there going, 'You love her, but you like me more.' It was Ira's ultimate statement of male bonding."

"That scene became the focal point for the whole show, in terms of the series," Behr says with a grin. "It was the scene that everyone wanted to protect. We knew that the final episode was going to be good-byes, so this was the last chance to look over this long relationship. The two guys are in a ridiculous situation and they think they're going to die. O'Brien got into the situation out of friendship. So it was time to take the bull by the horns and say this thing that they dare not say. Bashir admits that he loves Ezri but he likes O'Brien better and it's *funny* that O'Brien doesn't want to admit his feelings. These guys are best friends. If we made the audience believe that they really care about each other, we did a good thing."

The rest of the episode, including the long, uncharacteristically sentimental speech that Sloan delivers to his friends and family, "either works for you or it doesn't," Behr says, smiling. In that particular case, he says, "I felt that we had built up an audience expectation about Sloan. I liked the actor and I wanted to give him a speech that was totally un-Sloan-like."

But was Sloan being honest and genuine?

"Could be," Behr says mysteriously.

The final show in the octet that precedes "What You Leave Behind" is "The Dogs of War." Echevarria notes, "Writing it was very, very challenging because we were simultaneously breaking the final two-hour show and certain things needed to be in place." Compounding the challenge was the sudden realization that *Deep Space Nine* was nearly over. Former producer Peter Allan Fields helped out by formulating a story document for the episode. Then Echevarria sat down to write the first draft of the teleplay. As he discussed the episode with Ron Moore, Echevarria recalls, he noticed that his co-worker was very glum. "Ron was . . ." Echevarria pauses and smiles. "Frankly, he was very sentimental. He said, 'I can't believe I've just written my last *DS9* script.' So I said, 'Well, help me with mine. I'll do the first draft and then you jump in and help me.' So for that last feeling of camaraderie and fun, we did it together."

"I *was* kind of bummed," confirms Moore. "I hadn't realized that 'Tacking into the Wind' was my last episode, because I went from that to working on 'Extreme Measures.' But that was going to be it for me. And then René very graciously said he could use some help on 'The Dogs of War.' So I came in on the second draft. Then he offered to share the credit with me. I was very touched."

Ironically, Moore already had written much of the episode's teaser. "The arrival of the new *Defiant* was originally supposed to be in 'Tacking into the Wind,'" he explains. "I'd written that teaser and then it didn't quite fit there and the episode was too long, so I set it aside and held on to it. I gave it to René."

"It had a nice sense of reality to it, in terms of official military protocol—stuff that Ron knows a lot about," says Echevarria. Ross transfers command of the *U.S.S. São Paulo* to Captain Sisko, then informs him that the Chief of Starfleet Operations has granted special dispensation to rename the vessel *Defiant*.

"I chose *São Paulo* not as homage to the Brazilian city, but to the ship in *The Sand Pebbles*," says Moore. "And, in fact, when Sisko is left alone with his ship, he says, 'Hello, ship,' which is a riff on a Steve McQueen line in that movie. Just a little salute."

Why destroy the *Defiant* just to reintroduce it a few episodes later?

As Behr has explained, the destruction of the ship made as deep an emotional impact as the death of a regular crew member. It did something else as well. The writers "wanted to kill *Defiant* as a statement on how tough the Breen were. We thought that would rock the characters and the audience," says Moore.

"We'd needed to show that the Breen were formidable, so we came up with the idea of this special weapon," adds Echevarria. "The death of the *Defiant* was quite striking—but at the same time, we didn't want to keep it dead forever."

"There was no way to do the final big battles without it," says Moore. "Not unless we shot on the *Voyager* soundstages all the rest of the time, and *that* wasn't going to work." He laughs. "So we brought it back and 'made it a virtue.'"

In a way, Kasidy's pregnancy, introduced in this episode, was also a case of "making it a virtue." The idea that Sisko would "know nothing but sorrow" if

Kasidy's delicate condition ultimately would lead to sorrow among the writers. ROBBIE ROBINSON

After they decided to make him nagus, the writers worked to create a Ferenginar that Rom *could* rule. ROBBIE ROBINSON

"He really made the Ferengi work." Ira Behr stands behind his creations. ROBBIE ROBINSON

he married his beloved had yet to pay off. "We'd done this whole thing about the 'sorrow' and the warning from Sarah," says Echevarria. "I think the audience was expecting Kasidy to die in the final episode. For a while, I thought she might, too."

But the group had no intention of doing away with Kasidy. So what exactly *was* the sorrow going to be? Echevarria felt the need to define it. "I remember saying to the others, 'Okay, what's the "sorrow," guys? When Kasidy burns the peppers? Is that it?' Because I just didn't see it. 'Is it because Sisko's going to become a Prophet?' And the others said, 'Yeah, can't you see that's really sorrowful?'" But Echevarria reminded them that they'd tied Sarah's warning to the fact that Sisko wanted to get *married*. And while one could make a case for the idea that Sisko's having to leave his new wife *would* be a sorrowful thing, there were some flaws in the logic. "Sisko was going to have to leave *Jake,* too," he says. "So how was the sorrow marriage-specific? And even if he hadn't married Kasidy, he'd still be leaving her and Jake behind."

Echevarria decided on something that would do more than pay mere lip service to the concept of sorrow. He got Kasidy pregnant. "For me, that resolved the question of why the Prophets were warning him about marriage," he says. "They knew it was going to lead to a child, and it would be truly sorrowful for Sisko to have to leave that behind."

Kasidy's condition also allowed Echevarria and

Moore to introduce the forward-thinking notion that men will be much more responsible for birth control in the twenty-fourth century than they are today. "René loved the fact that Sisko forgot to take *his* injection," Moore says, chuckling. "We had to invent some sort of explanation, and that was a nice way to do it. It served two masters: one, it was a cool little fact about the twenty-fourth century; and two, it was amusing enough that it drew your attention away from the fact that Kasidy would probably have some form of birth control, too. I mean, wouldn't they all?"

While the episode includes a lot of interesting action on Cardassia, including an edited scene that had Kira, Garak, and Damar getting drunk in Tain's basement (Kira still can be seen toying with the label on one of the wine bottles), the writers were most pleased with the Ferengi storyline. "It's the one that changed the most and worked the best," says Echevarria. The premise, which Behr attributes to a Paramount exec, was "Wouldn't it be nice if Rom became the nagus?"

"Lots of people like Rom," says Behr. "I thought it was a really good idea. Obviously, we'd played around with the idea of Quark becoming nagus, but that was wrong. Quark had to be in that bar at the end of the show. I felt that the audience needed that continuity even more than whoever was going to run the station. Quark is the center of the station—and *I* needed that center. So we couldn't make Quark nagus. And I didn't feel that we could leave Zek in the office, because we'd put him through all kinds of changes in the past few years, including the Ferengi version of Alzheimer's disease."

Although the suggestion about Rom interested Behr, "the fact that it was a cool idea wasn't enough to base a story on," he says. "We had to figure out what would have had to happen to Ferengi society that would enable Rom to become the nagus."

"There had to be a reason for it," comments Moore. "We were in love with the idea, but Rom wasn't up to being the nagus of the old Ferenginar. They'd eat him alive. But to oversee a *new* Ferenginar that had a heart and compassion and was trying to be more progressive—well, Rom has those qualities. He's an idiot half the time, but he's got heart."

"To some extent, we'd laid some pipe in that direction with Moogie's influence on the nagus," says Echevarria. "The audience had accepted the leap Moogie had accomplished for females, so we figured they'd be able to make this leap. I started writing and came up with this fun thing, all light and frothy. Quark wants to become the nagus, and in the end he doesn't get it—Rom does. There was a lot of really great stuff in the episode for Rom to do, and some lovely scenes between the two brothers. And in the end, the joke's on Quark.

"Ron and I were working on it, and all of a sudden he said, 'You know, this is really fun and I like it—but it's our last Quark show and it's not about Quark. It's about Rom.' And he was right. We'd gotten so enamored with the idea that Rom was the nagus that we'd forgotten about Quark. So the two of us sat back and asked ourselves, well, where do we want him to end up? We developed this completely different take, where Quark actually turns *down* the position. And then we establish him as the last great Ferengi, which is much more honest and true to his character. I'm very grateful to Ron for putting the brakes on the earlier version and saying, 'I know we're making a lot of work for ourselves, but we owe it to Quark.'"

Although he didn't mention it at the time, Moore's impulse came as a huge relief to Armin Shimerman. "I was very unhappy with the first version of the script," he admits. "It's not that I felt Quark should become nagus. He wasn't smart enough, sinister enough, or cold-hearted enough. If I had to decide, I'd have chosen either Moogie or Brunt, both of whom have the makings of a nagus. But the first time around, it didn't make sense for Rom to be chosen. All the stuff about Ferenginar becoming a kinder, gentler place was added later on. Before that, the decision was kind of akin to making Jake the head of the Federation!"

Shimerman was much happier with the final episode, which positions his character exactly as Behr had wanted. "Quark *is* the station," states Shimerman. "He is as much a part of the station as the carpets, the pylons, and the transporters. Everybody goes through Quark's. Everybody deals with Quark."

And, of course, if Moore hadn't pushed for the changes, the writer never would have been able to give Shimerman the opportunity to do his dead-on impersonation of Patrick Stewart.

Moore grins. "It *was* my idea to put in, 'The line must be drawn *here*,' to mock the speech that Picard delivers in *First Contact*. I just didn't realize that Armin was going to *go* for it. And he did it really well!"

Saying the Words

"Creating characters is fun," says Ira Behr. When Behr and the other writers created a character, they looked for an actor to fill that character's shoes. If the character (or the actor) exceeded expectations, he or she was featured more prominently on the series. But, of course, with a large regular cast and the huge extended family that the series had accumulated over the course of seven years, there wasn't always enough prominence to go around. Still, the writers were well aware that Season 7 would be the last opportunity to gift the talented performers, particularly the increasingly important supporting characters, with as many bits of business as possible.

"One of the great things about the series is how certain characters evolve," says David Weddle. Case in point, he explains, is Winn's longtime aide, Ranjen Solbor, introduced in "'Til Death Do Us Part." "We wrote a scene in his first episode where he serves tea to Winn and Dukat. And Dukat says he's hardly worthy to be having tea with the kai and to be served by a ranjen. We noted in the script that Solbor's expression

After Damar gave up drinking, the actor was lit differently, giving him a more "human" look. ROBBIE ROBINSON

should show that he agreed with that. We gave him a little attitude. The actor just played it so well that we all started laughing when we were watching dailies."

"I just fell in love with Solbor, and with James Otis, the actor who plays him," enthuses Behr. "He was exactly what I wanted: a true believer. He was just meant to be your typical lackey, but the actor came in playing this kind of shaky, emotionally constipated guy who radiated fierce devotion. He delivered his lines in a way that showed multiple levels. He was a hoot! As soon as I saw him in dailies, I said, 'Get him for two more episodes!'"

Casey Biggs's Damar fulfilled every expectation the producers had ever dreamed of. "Casting is very important," says Beimler. "When we decided on Casey, we cast somebody who was better than the role. That meant we could expand the role from what originally was there."

"It was an ego trip for us," Behr admits happily. "The fact was that we could take this character who started out with two lines, and over the course of a few years, turn him into a complicated character with the weight of the universe on his shoulders. We knew Casey could pull it off. He puts down the booze, saves Ezri and Worf, and starts his underground resistance movement. And as soon as he does that," laughs Behr, "he slips right into the character of William Barrett Travis, the character that Casey played in the IMAX Alamo movie!"

No one was happier than Biggs when Damar finally put down the booze. "Poor Casey!" says B.C.

Cameron. "When the producers started this thing with *kanar*, they wanted it to look different from anything else. They decided to use Karo syrup, because it would pour real thick. Then when they made Casey's character an alcoholic, he had to drink it constantly. I felt so horrible for him."

Not as horrible as Biggs, obviously. "I *hated* the stuff they made me drink," he says emphatically. "The Karo was just disgusting. Then they changed to a sugar-free pancake syrup, which wasn't quite as bad, but after you do a number of takes, it's *still* pretty disgusting. One time we did so many takes that I got quite sick by the end of the day. I'm *very* happy that Damar stopped drinking!"

Plotting out the paths of their dynamic repertoire of side characters made the final arc exciting for the producers. "We knew that Marc Alaimo would get turned on by playing the seemingly kind, sweet Anjohl in the scenes with Winn," says Behr. Throughout the seven years of the series, the executive producer adds, Alaimo never faltered in his belief that Dukat was, at heart, a good guy. "In Marc's mind, I believe he felt his relationship with Winn was legitimate in some way, and that, in some wacky fashion, it was Dukat's bid for legitimacy. I mean, Marc actually was upset when we had him hit Solbor. Until the very end, he wanted Dukat to be the hero of *Deep Space Nine*."

One thing that Behr regrets is that he never had the opportunity to do an episode that he refers to internally as "Fun in Hitler's Bunker," that is, a look at the final days of the war from the point of view of the bad guys. "None of our regulars would have been in the entire episode, except maybe once at the beginning," he explains. "We'd do the whole show in the bunker—the Dominion briefing room and then just show the machinations between Damar, Weyoun, and the female shape-shifter. Just them. Ultimately we did something even better than just one show; we did *ten* hours where we could just riff on scenes of showing what the villains were doing. That really gave us a chance to make them shine. Dukat, of course, always got a lot of stuff to do. But if you look at the female shape-shifter, and Kai Winn, and Weyoun, and Damar—they've never been better. Because we had the chance to give them so many different levels to play. I mean, Louise Fletcher just kicked ass in that last arc."

It's clear that the producers got the biggest charge out of their bad guys. When it came to casting Rusot, Damar's second-in-command, they chose John

"Garak always had respect and empathy for Odo," Robinson says, "They were both strangers in a strange land." ROBBIE ROBINSON

Vickery, whom Behr had seen perform in the Tom Stoppard play *Arcadia*. "He turned out great," Behr smiles. "We'd needed another Cardassian. We kept running out of evil. Dukat and Damar had become so multidimensional. We needed someone who was just bad. And for this particular arc, we needed someone who would highlight Damar's strength, by putting Damar in a position where he'd have to hold this tiger by the tail and keep him in line."

Watching Vickery, Biggs, and Andy Robinson work together was a real treat, reports Lou Race, particularly in Vickery's last episode, "Tacking into the Wind." "The rehearsals were a crack-up," he says. "They're all good actors, and they were just ping-ponging off each other's lines. And then when Rene Auberjonois got into the mix, it was like watching four pros going through a theatrical rehearsal. They were having fun, finding little ways to upstage each other. It was a pleasure to work with those guys. They had so much enthusiasm—despite the fact that they were working in rubber heads!"

Some character actors—particularly the ones in rubber heads—never get their day in the sun. But "The Dogs of War" gave many of those familiar faces

their due at last. Case in point: Tiny Ron, who'd silently played Maihar'du, faithful servant to Grand Nagus Zek, for seven years. "In the scene where Zek comes in and hands over the nagus-ship to Rom, we had twelve principal actors on the set," recalls Race. "Avery Brooks was directing, and trying to keep track of all that choreography was a job in itself. But while Quark is giving his big speech about how Ferenginar will exist in his bar forever, Avery was doing a reaction shot of Tiny. Tiny doesn't talk on the show, but he's a remarkably reactive actor. So we start rolling, and Armin Shimerman does his speech and Tiny really starts to get into it. He's listening, he's agreeing, he's swelling up, feeling proud of Quark, just going through all of this stuff. And Avery was at the monitor, enthralled. He was just mesmerized by what Tiny was doing. And after it was over he went over to Tiny and took time out of the production just to talk to him and tell him how great he was.

"Max Grodénchik did some incredible stuff in that show, too," Race continues. "In the scene where Quark is saying that everything on Ferenginar is going to hell, and Rom is trying to buy the bar, Max's readings of the much-repeated line, 'So what are you going to do with the bar?' were just *amazing*, and totally unexpected. Max is incredible."

He's also amazingly humble. "I think I cried when they told me Rom was going to be nagus," Grodénchik admits. "Just the thought of it, the idea of where this character has come from and what he's become was overwhelming." It's only fitting, he says, that the last line he recorded in the episode—and on the series, since Rom isn't in "What You Leave Behind"—was a from-the-heart response to both his and Rom's good fortune. "The camera was on me for a reaction shot, and there was nothing in the script for me to say. I assumed the editor would wind up cutting away from me by this point, so I felt free to do what I wanted since it wouldn't be used. And I said what I thought Rom would say: 'Wow.'" The ad-lib was so in character that the producers chose to keep it in the episode. They also allowed two of the bar's veteran employees—Cathy DeBuono, dabo girl M'Pella, and David B. Levinson, as Broik—to finally deliver lines on-camera. "That was René Echevarria's doing," says Behr. "He wanted to give *everybody* lines. This costs money," he adds, adopting a Scrooge-like countenance. "No good deed goes unpunished!"

In addition to their established characters, both actors had performed double duty as stand-ins for the leads: DeBuono for Terry Farrell and Levinson for Quark. In fact, DeBuono continued to stand in for Farrell on the sit-com *Becker*. Both were ecstatic with their "gift," according to Armin Shimerman. "It was really nice of the producers," he notes, "because they'd been around forever."

"That was also the episode where we had dueling Jeff Combs," Race laughs. "We'd never had Brunt and Weyoun appear on the same show before, and this time we did. I tried to never schedule both characters for the same day, but one day it couldn't be helped. It's easier to go from Weyoun to Brunt, so we started with Weyoun. Then we pulled off the ears and popped on the head."

Despite the extended periods in makeup and hair trailers, Combs loved "making *Star Trek* history" by playing both of his characters in the same episode. "A lot of people on the crew were unaware that I played both characters"—he chuckles—"because Weyoun looks nothing like Brunt. So when I walked onto the set after the changeover, all these guys did double takes and said, 'Wait a minute—you're that guy *too*? It was great."

Since one of his personae was a clone, Combs also had the unusual opportunity to play innumerable incarnations of the same character. "I think that

Weyoun died five times in the show—and that's only the ones we saw or heard about," he says. During the seventh season alone, he died four of those times, once off-screen (the "accidental" demise of Weyoun Five, noted in "Treachery, Faith, and the Great River"). Without a doubt, his most memorable death was at the hands of Worf ("Strange Bedfellows"). "Weyoun just gets a little too cocky and a little too close," Combs adds, chuckling.

"I thought it was hysterically funny," enthuses the episode's director, Rene Auberjonois. "We played it like Weyoun was an arrogant lion tamer who makes the mistake of forgetting he's in the cage with a very dangerous animal. Jeffrey was *so* sanctimonious and smarmy, and he walks past Michael Dorn, who's just standing there like a big lion, looking at him. And then Michael just reaches up like he's doing nothing and—*bomp!*—he's gone. It broke me up. Every time I watched it, in the dailies, in the cutting room, I would just laugh. They were so fabulous."

"Really, it was just two actors being able to do their stuff," says Combs modestly. "We didn't really talk about it. Michael just knew what he was doing and I knew what I was doing. He put his hands there and I just yanked my head, turned it to the side and back to center, and fell. We just kind of went with it."

The character of Gowron also met his noteworthy end during the multiparter ("Tacking into the Wind"), something that didn't surprise Actor Robert O'Reilly. "While I was working on 'Badda-bing, Badda-bang,' they hinted that I might be back," he says. "And then when they called me, I assumed it would be for 'the killing fields.'"

The killing fields?

O'Reilly laughs. "A lot of us died during the final arc," he observes. "Dukat died. Weyoun died. It was like '*Deep Space Nine* Kills the Villains!' So I expected it. Actually, I'd expected to die a couple seasons earlier, with the 'Gowron is a changeling' thing. Then the day we filmed my death scene, Michael Dorn — whom I've known for something like twelve years— came in and said, 'I didn't do it! It wasn't my idea!' And I said, 'Michael, I don't blame you.' It was okay with me, actually. I was resigned to it."

The death scene was shot late in the day (or early in the morning, depending on your point of view) on a Friday night. The carefully choreographed fight between Gowron and Worf, and the volatile debate that precedes it, had taken the entire day. "After Worf kills Gowron, he gives this speech," relates Lou Race. "It was about 12:30 A.M. and Michael was absolutely

Gowron brought on his downfall by placing his personal ambitions above all else. ROBBIE ROBINSON

While the writers tried to create scenes that would address nearly every unresolved issue for the characters, it was inevitable that some would fall by the wayside. Andy Robinson, for example, was disappointed that Garak and Damar didn't have a substantive scene together in "When It Rains..." that would deal with their feelings about the death of Ziyal. "The writers didn't give Garak a lot of room to adjust or react initially to Damar, given that Damar had murdered Ziyal," Robinson says. "It essentially went unresolved, and I had to squeeze some subtext into the beginning of the first scene between them. Garak says that they must put aside the murder in order to focus on the main project. He's talking to himself as much as to Kira or anyone else."

"René Echevarria was a big advocate of dealing with the Ziyal thing up front," points out Ron Moore, "and I thought he was right, but it was one more big piece of backstory in a very complicated tale. So we just tried not to go there. It was too much."

Kira deserved the confrontation as much as Garak, says Echevarria. "Ziyal was her friend. I wanted to put Kira into a conflict situation with Damar, get it to where they come to blows and pull weapons on each other. It worked on a lot of levels, but Ira pointed out that on a larger level, it didn't help either of them. We'd been trying to turn Damar into this new type of figure, and this would be a step backward. So we decided to focus more on Damar, because he's the one torn between his Cardassian comrades and their feelings and dealing with Kira. It was the right choice."

In one case, two actors took a proactive stance to ensure that an important storyline didn't get shortchanged. Rene Auberjonois and Nana Visitor were determined to make sure that "the scene in the closet" didn't happen again. "We didn't want to see important aspects of our characters' relationship left unresolved," Auberjonois says. "The writers had acknowledged that putting Kira and Odo into the closet to resolve their differences in 'You Are Cordially Invited' was a cop-out. So late in the final arc, when Nana and I began to have questions about what was happening to our relationship, and how Kira should react to the fact that Odo has this terminal illness, Nana called René Echevarria. She told him, 'We just don't want it to be another situation that's dealt with off-screen. We want to know how we work this out.' And he said, 'No, no, I promise. That won't happen again.'"

And it didn't.

exhausted when he did it. He thought he had done a very bad job on it, but the fact that he *was* exhausted played into it beautifully."

Dorn wasn't the only tired person on the set. "After Michael killed me, I stayed there, lying on the floor," says O'Reilly. "They continued the scene and finally they finished. And I couldn't get up. In these Klingon outfits, you sort of waddle like a turtle, and once you're on the ground, you're still like a turtle. It's very hard to get up. You just sort of roll around. So I called, 'Michael, can you help me up? Michael? *Michael?*' I didn't know he wasn't standing right nearby anymore, and he didn't know where the sound of my voice was coming from, because he couldn't see me. So I said, 'Boy, once they kill you off, they forget all about you!'"

Behind the Scenes

"Each piece of the arc was like a boxcar, and we were all here watching them go by," says Lou Race. "Each boxcar had some machine parts in it, some toys, some clothing. And each show brought a little more clothing, a little more machine parts, a little more toys. And the challenge was to figure out how each small story fit into the bigger story."

Race worked on only the even-numbered episodes, and his counterpart, B.C. Cameron, on only the odd. So at any given time, Race could really see only half of the train. Pity the poor person who *didn't* have the big picture, who simply tried to make sure that his small piece of the puzzle would lock into the next piece, the director-for-hire, for instance.

"I'd talk to other people about the next piece,"

says Steve Posey, who directed "Penumbra" and "Extreme Measures." "But from my point of view everything was pretty much a loose end. When I directed the first part, I didn't know what was going to happen with Worf and Ezri. I didn't know if they were going to get together, or stay together. I didn't know whether someone was going to end up dying. I guess I tried to deal with things the same way each of the characters did—as it was happening."

"In the production meetings, we'd discuss only the episode that we were working on," says Cameron. "The only conversation that would come up about future segments would be the pertinent questions, like the Art Department wanting to know if we were going to see a certain set again—should they store it or leave it up? Or the Wardrobe Department asking whether they were going to need a garment later on. But to be completely honest," she says in a conspiratorial tone,

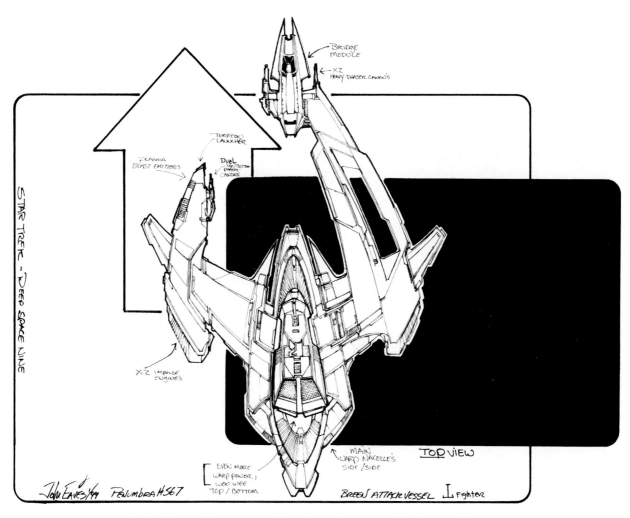

An early sketch hints at the asymmetrical shape the producers wanted for the Breen ship. JOHN EAVES

"we never had a script until we were practically in production. So I'm not convinced the writers really had a clear vision of where everything was going to go."

"I figured that if they wanted us to think about what goes on very far in the future, they'd kind of give us clues," offers Jeffrey Combs. "We could ask, but they wouldn't tell us. They wanted to keep it a secret. The more people that knew, the more likelihood that it was going to get out. So I just had to play fast and loose, like I was up against a batting machine and didn't know when the next ball was coming."

In truth, while the people who made the decisions weren't playing it quite *that* fast and loose, they frequently *were* responding to balls lobbed in from left field. Questions would come in, and they'd provide answers on the fly.

Why isn't the new Defiant, *introduced in "The Dogs of War," called the* Defiant-A, *like the* Enterprise *that replaced the original one in* Star Trek IV?

Moore sighs. "Well, technically, *I* think it is. I fought quite a bit on this rather minute point, because I'm a *Star Trek* aficionado and I feel strongly about these kinds of things," he admits. "I drove Ira up the wall on this 'A' business, trying to get 'A' onto the model. But it was a money issue."

"Obviously it's money," Behr confirms with a shrug. "We would have had to redo all the stock visual effects shots we had of the *Defiant*. So we had to bite the bullet. We didn't have to end the series without the ship—we gave them a new one—but we weren't going to build a new ship at the end of the show, and we weren't going to change the decals [on every frame of stock footage]."

To be fair, the production did give the *interior* of the new ship its own identity. A new paint job. A new wall plaque. A new carpet. Bashir's throwaway comment about hating the carpet, in fact, was Moore's way of drawing attention to the detail changes on the bridge.

Why does the inside of Sloan's mind (in "Extreme Measures") look like the standard interiors of the space station?

According to Sloan, it's because the Section 31 operative wanted to make Bashir and O'Brien "feel at home—comfortable." But would you believe a man who conspired to commit genocide? "We always thought that it would be a series of rooms," says Brad Thompson. "We all have little compartments in our minds, and that was a convenient way to show it. We had the whole rationale for it. Bashir's mind would be interpreting another through its own frame of reference.

The clutter that Laura Richarz scattered in Sloan's office represents the jumbled state of the thoughts in his mind. ROBBIE ROBINSON

We figured that Sloan's brain would be full of labyrinths and corridors where he could hide things from himself."

Unfortuately, that didn't work. "It was one of those times where we ended up fooling ourselves," Moore says, sighing. "We told each other, 'That sounds like a great idea. We'll do a surreal journey inside of one man's mind.' But the production realities slapped us in the face. We had to find a weak excuse to use the *DS9* sets again, and then we said, 'Well, we'll make the corridors all dark and spooky.' And then we saw them and they were brightly lit and they looked like every other corridor and there was nothing spooky about them."

The problem arose precisely because the scripts were being written so late in the game. "In the beginning," explains Director Posey, "we planned to have a real *Alice in Wonderland* kind of experience in Sloan's mind. It was very surreal, and the Art Department and I were very excited about redressing the sets, and repainting some of them in a psychedelic style. But then the writers threw in this plot twist where Bashir and O'Brien think they're out of Sloan's mind and back on the station. That meant we had to make everything *in* Sloan's mind look exactly like it did in reality. If we hadn't, it would have been obvious that we were still in his mind. That took some of the fun out of it, at least in the visual sense."

What's underneath those Breen helmets?

"I always figured they must look like Donald Duck," smiles Race. "You know—because of the beak."

"I don't really know," says Michael Westmore, "but I actually had an unused head in the lab that

Not quite as dangerous as they look. ROBBIE ROBINSON

would have been great. I thought we could put a little bit of a snout onto it, so we could justify the snout on the helmet. But we never had the opportunity to show one of them," he notes regretfully.

Is there a small continuity problem here?

In "'Til Death Do Us Part," Worf notes that "no one has ever seen [a Breen] and lived to speak of it"—but viewers who recall "Indiscretion" know that both Kira and Dukat must have gotten a look at the Breen whose uniforms they stole. To compound the problem, Kira would dispatch yet *another* Breen—again for his uniform—in "What You Leave Behind." So . . . ?

"It's just one of those things," sighs Moore. "There's too many details to keep track of."

But Behr has a simpler explanation. "There's *nothing* in those helmets," he says. "I don't think there's a guy in there, which is something we never got around to saying." He pauses for a moment. "Or maybe there's a little slug, some tiny little creature in there. I never wanted them to be humanoid in any way."

So, what's really underneath those Breen uniforms?

That's easy. Really uncomfortable actors.

"Prior to seventh season, we'd only used the Breen a handful of times," explains Cameron. "But as of 'Penumbra,' they became major players. The prob-

lem was, the people in the costumes cannot see, they cannot breathe, they're wearing big, clumsy boots, and their outfits are layered like an armadillo, making it very hard for them to move."

"The helmets are complicated to take on and off," continues Steve Oster. "They're held together with magnets and they fall off any time someone bumps them. And before we redesigned them, the switches for the little blinky lights were on the inside of the helmet, meaning you had to take them off every time you wanted to turn the lights on. And for some reason we never did figure out, the nine-volt batteries only lasted minutes before they burned out."

"The biggest problem with the Breen mask is that there's only a little hole in the beak," says Todd Slayton, a stand-in and stunt double for Cirroc Lofton who also appeared as Thot Gor as well as a variety of background Cardassians and Jem'Hadar. "The hole sits about eight inches away from your nose so it's a little difficult to get air in and out. The lens that we look out of is also in the beak and it steams up pretty quickly."

How do you defeat the Breen?

Make him cross the room. "We were working on 'Strange Bedfellows,' and it was the last scene of the day," relates Cameron. "Everybody was tired. We were shooting on the Dominion ship's bridge, and the female shape-shifter was supposed to walk in and be introduced to the Breen commander. So I went over to the Breen background extras and told one of them —a great guy named Wade Kelly—to walk across the set and go out the door when we start rolling." Cameron pauses, looking sheepish. "But the minute we rolled camera, I realized I'd made a terrible mistake. Poor Wade couldn't see, but he was determined to give it a shot. Sure enough, he gets to an angled piece of the wall that was sticking out and trips, hitting the wall with a big clunk. Then he tries to see if he can find a way past this thing. But he just keeps going *clunk, clunk, clunk.* I'm thinking, 'Stop, Wade. Just stop.' But he keeps going and finally he gets past this piece of wall and heads for the doorway. And he forgets there's a threshold there, trips over *that*, grabs the walls, trying to hang on, *finally* gets out the door. By this time, I can't see him, but I can hear this huge noise, like he's ricocheting off the walls out there . . ."

". . . Like the ball in a pinball machine," Rene Auberjonois, who was directing the scene, says, laughing. "He sounded kind of like the Tin Man falling over in *The Wizard of Oz.*"

"Finally, I couldn't hold it in anymore," continues

Cameron. "I just burst into hysterics and I couldn't stop laughing. It was the funniest, most embarrassing moment of the entire series for me."

What do the Breen (almost) have in common with Lou Reed?

"We wanted to give these guys something special," states Behr. "I couldn't make them the toughest guys in the galaxy—that's the Jem'Hadar. Or the most arrogant guys—that's the Cardassians. Or the most untrustworthy guys—that's the Vorta. So we decided to make them the most *mysterious* guys in the galaxy, with voices that really grate on the audience. Like Lou Reed's *Metal Machine Music* album, which is basically two hours of feedback, guaranteed to drive you insane." At Behr's suggeston, the postproduction sound staff listened to Reed's album while they created the alien electronic crackle. "It's not what we wound up with, of course," the executive producer says. "But that's what I wanted."

Where did the Alamo model come from?

"First we called the gift shop at the real Alamo and asked if they had any models," reports Laura Richarz. "But they didn't. We found two tiny little models elsewhere, but they wouldn't work for us."

After searching for weeks, the producers were on the verge of having an expensive scale model built from scratch. The prop shop was prepared to build it from plans Production Designer Herman Zimmerman provided. Then the show experienced an unexpected shift in the shooting schedule. Avery Brooks had come down with a bad case of the flu, so certain scenes had to be moved up—including the scene in "The Changing Face of Evil" that features the model—to replace the ones in which the captain was to appear. "There was no way the prop shop could build it that quickly, but there was nothing else that we could shoot," says Script Supervisor Judi Brown. "So they got on the phone and started calling every toy store and hobby shop in the area. And they finally tracked down a model kit that had been sitting on a dusty shelf for twenty years. It was huge! It was wonderful! And it only cost fifty dollars!"

WHAT YOU LEAVE BEHIND
Episode #575-576
WRITTEN BY IRA STEVEN BEHR & HANS BEIMLER
DIRECTED BY ALLAN KROEKER

SPECIAL GUEST STARS IN ALPHABETICAL ORDER

Keiko O'Brien	ROSALIND CHAO
Weyoun	JEFFREY COMBS
Female Shape-shifter	SALOME JENS
Kasidy Yates	PENNY JOHNSON
Garak	ANDREW J. ROBINSON

GUEST CAST

Damar	CASEY BIGGS
Gul Dukat	MARC ALAIMO
Nog	ARON EISENBERG
General Martok	J.G. HERTZLER
Admiral Ross	BARRY JENNER
Sarah	DEBORAH LACEY
Mila	JULIANNA McCARTHY
Molly	HANA HATAE
Broca	MEL JOHNSON, JR.
Ekoor	GREG ELLIS
Ginger	CYNDI PASS
Jem'Hadar	KEVIN SCOTT ALLEN
Jem'Hadar First	CHRISTOPHER HALSTED
Cardassian Computer Voice	JUDI DURAND

SPECIAL GUEST APPEARANCES

Vic Fontaine	JAMES DARREN
Kai Winn	LOUISE FLETCHER

STARDATE UNKNOWN

On Deep Space 9, the crew makes special promises to their loved ones as they prepare to depart for the attack on the Dominion defense perimeter. Ezri and Bashir, who've finally spent the night together, make a pact to come home alive. O'Brien promises Keiko and Molly that as soon as the war ends, he'll accept the teaching position he's been offered at Starfleet Academy. And Sisko promises that he'll return from the battle to Kasidy and the child she carries ("The Dogs of War"). Then he boards the new *Defiant* and orders the ship to join the huge combined fleet of Federation, Klingon, and Romulan ships that are headed for Cardassian space.

At Dominion headquarters, Weyoun informs the female shape-shifter that the joint invasion fleet has left Deep Space 9. They'll reach the Cardassian border by the next evening. The Founder, whose health is rapidly deteriorating, declares that the outcome of

Benjamin Sisko prepares to face his greatest trial. ROBBIE ROBINSON

the impending battle will determine the outcome of the war. Legate Broca, the newly appointed leader of the Cardassian Union, reports that Damar isn't dead after all. Word is spreading that he's on Cardassia Prime, in the capital city. In the cellar of Enabran Tain's former residence, Garak and Damar tell Kira that the plan to unify the planet's populace against the occupying forces is working. Damar's followers will soon begin sabotaging power, transportation, and communication facilities worldwide. The Dominion fleet will be cut off from all ground support and will have to face the invading forces on their own.

On Bajor, Dukat, who has been surgically altered to appear Bajoran, regains his sight ("When It Rains . . . "). He goes to Kai Winn to learn if she's deciphered the secrets of the Kosst Amojan. Winn admits that she has. She knows how to release the Pah-wraiths from the fire caves, but needs Dukat's help. The Cardassian willingly offers his assistance, and together they vow to help the Pah-wraiths destroy the Prophets. As for the Prophet's Emissary, Dukat promises to take care of Sisko on his own.

The Cardassian people are as good as their word. They sabotage nearly every Dominion installation on their homeworld. When the female shape-shifter learns of the damage, she's furious. The citizens of Cardassia must be severely punished for their actions. Moments later, Dominion troops level a major city, killing two million men, women, and children. Weyoun delivers a planetwide address to the planet's inhabitants, warning that for each additional act of sabotage, another city will be destroyed. After Kira, Damar, and Garak watch the chilling speech from their cellar hideout, Kira decides they must attack Dominion Headquarters. But it won't be easy to get inside, Damar explains. They'll have to force their way in somehow.

Garak prepares some explosives while Mila fixes them a meal. But not long after, Dominion forces find the hideout. A group of Jem'Hadar and Cardassian soldiers kill Mila and incapacitate the three fugitives. When she learns of their capture, the Founder tells the soldiers to execute the trio immediately. The Jem'Hadar in the group raise their weapons—but at the last minute, the Cardassian soldiers fire on the Jem'Hadar, killing them. Then they join forces with Damar and the others.

At the border of Cardassian space, the combined Federation forces engage the Dominion forces of the Jem'Hadar, the Breen, and the Cardassians. The *Defiant* takes heavy fire, as does the rest of the Federation fleet. But just as it seems the Federation assault is doomed, Cardassian ships begin attacking the Jem'Hadar and Breen vessels. The revolt has spread to the battlefield! When the female shape-shifter hears of this betrayal, she calls for the complete extermination of the Cardassian population. She then orders Dominion forces to pull back and regroup at Cardassia Prime. Heartened by the Cardassian about-face and the stealthy departure of the Breen, Sisko, Ross, and Martok decide to press forward to Cardassia and end the war, once and for all.

Kira and the others find themselves facing an insurmountable problem. The doors to Dominion Headquarters are made of neutronium, which means that Garak's explosives won't get them inside. They try to come up with an alternate plan. Their problem solves itself when the cargo door opens and a pair of Jem'Hadar soldiers escort Legate Broca outside for execution as a potential traitor. Kira and the Cardassians race inside before the door can close, but Damar is killed before they reach the main briefing room. Kira and Garak rally the others. They find little opposition, since Weyoun has sent most of the

Captured, Damar, Kira, and Garak receive unexpected help.
ROBBIE ROBINSON

Jem'Hadar soldiers out to eradicate Cardassians. In minutes, they're inside the heart of Dominion Headquarters, facing Weyoun and the female Founder.

Garak kills Weyoun—the last of the Weyoun clones—after the Vorta makes an unfortunate comment about Damar and the decimated remains of Cardassia. Kira raises her weapon and orders the Founder to have her ships stand down. The shape-shifter refuses. She knows now that the Dominion cannot win the war, but she is determined to make the Federation's victory a Pyrrhic one. They will lose so many ships and so many lives that their success will feel like defeat. Kira contacts Sisko on the *Defiant*, informing him of her status and the dying Founder's lack of cooperation. Odo suggests that he might be able to reason with the shape-shifter, and beams down to try.

Although the Founder is happy to see Odo, she informs him that she won't surrender her forces. If she did, it would be seen as a sign of weakness, an invitation to the solids to cross into the Gamma Quadrant and destroy the Great Link. Odo insists that the Federation, for all its flaws, wouldn't do that, and it wouldn't allow the Klingon and Romulan Empires to attack either. But the shape-shifter refuses to trust the solids. Finally, in the hope of changing her mind, Odo asks her to link with him. Kira and Garak are alarmed. Both think that it's a very bad idea, and Garak threatens to shoot Odo. But Odo

asks Kira to trust him, and to trust that he knows what he's doing. She tells Garak to lower his weapon. Odo morphs his hand around the Founder's, and slowly her body begins to regenerate. She is completely healed—and it's clear that the experience has profoundly changed her. She steps over to a console and orders the Jem'Hadar to cease fire. What's more, Odo tells Kira, she's agreed to stand trial for what she's done. Kira is surprised. She would have thought the Founder would insist on going back to the Gamma Quadrant to cure her people. But Odo explains that won't be necessary. He'll be going in her place . . . and rejoining the Great Link.

The devastation on Cardassia turns the stomachs of the Starfleet crew members who arrive on the planet. There are eight hundred million known dead, and more casualty reports coming in. In the Dominion briefing room, Garak bids a bittersweet farewell to his old friend Bashir, noting that his long years of exile are finally over. He's returned home—to what's left of home, at least.

On Bajor, Winn and Dukat enter the fire caves. Winn reads from the book of the Kosst Amojan and ignites the abyss before them. Then she prepares to bring forth the Pah-wraiths themselves. She pours a flask of wine into a ceremonial goblet and chants from the book. When she finishes, she prepares to drink from the cup, but then offers the first sip to Dukat. Dukat drinks, then hands the goblet back to Winn . . . who pours the rest of the wine onto the ground. Dukat keels over in pain and looks up at Winn in confusion. Winn smiles, explaining that the Pah-wraiths required a sacrifice, someone worthy of them. Who better than Dukat?

As Winn offers Dukat's life to the Pah-wraiths, the Cardassian falls to the ground, dead, and Winn prepares to complete the ceremony.

When the *Defiant* returns to the station, the Founder signs the official surrender documents and allows herself to be taken away by Starfleet officers. Then the crew prepares to celebrate at Vic's nightclub. Before the festivities begin, Sisko, Martok, and Ross approach Worf with a proposition. They'd like him to become the Federation Ambassador to the Klingon Empire. Although Worf argues that he isn't a diplomat, Martok counters by pointing out that *he* isn't a politician. But the Empire needs Worf, and so does Martok. Similarly encouraged by Sisko and Ezri, Worf accepts. Elsewhere on the station, Kira suggests to Odo that he could return after he cures his people. But Odo gently points out that while his feelings for

Garak is alarmed when Odo offers to link with the Founder.
ROBBIE ROBINSON

Kira will never change, his people need him. They need to learn what he's learned from living among solids. It's the only way they'll ever be able to trust them. Kira accepts Odo's decision and asks one favor. She wants to take him home, so they can spend a few more days together. Odo happily agrees.

At Vic's that night, the crew share old memories and talk of future plans. Sisko toasts them all—the best crew any captain ever had—and tells them that no matter where any of them go from here, a part of them will remain on Deep Space 9.

In Bajor's fire caves, Winn's chanting finally seems to bring forth the Kosst Amojan. But rather than joining her spirit, as she'd expected, a bolt of energy strikes her, knocking her to the ground. Then, to her horror, she sees another bolt of energy enter Dukat's inanimate body. Suddenly Dukat comes to life, his eyes the bloodred color of a Pah-wraith, and

his face is transformed from that of a Bajoran to a Cardassian.

In the midst of the celebration, Sisko feels that something is wrong. Suddenly, he knows what he has to do, what the Prophets have always intended for him. He tells a frightened Kasidy that he must go to Bajor's fire caves, alone.

Taking a runabout, Sisko heads for Bajor. He arrives in the caves to see Dukat taunting Winn, laughing at the notion that the Pah-wraiths would choose her to be their Emissary. Dukat turns to face Sisko and uses his powers to force the captain to his knees. Sisko tells Dukat that he'll stop the Pah-wraiths from conquering anything, be it Bajor, the Celestial Temple, or the entire Alpha Quadrant. Dukat laughs. How can Sisko do that when he can't even stand?

"Then I'll stop you," says Winn. She stands at the edge of the abyss, prepared to toss in the book of the Kosst Amojan. With a wave of his hand, Dukat pulls the book away from her and into his hands. A tendril of energy snakes out of the abyss and wraps itself around her. Winn bursts into flames and dies. But her sacrifice was not in vain. Sisko uses the brief distraction to tackle Dukat. Both of them fall, along with the book, into the infinite depths of the flaming caverns . . .

. . . And suddenly Sisko finds himself in the white limbo of the Prophets. He's greeted by Sarah, who tells him that he has completed his task. The Pah-wraiths have been returned to their prison within the fire caves, along with Dukat. The book was the key to a door that can never be opened again. Sarah tells Sisko that his trial is behind him, and he needs to rest. Sisko responds that he intends to do just that, once he returns to Deep Space 9. Sarah tells him that won't be necessary. He's with the Prophets now.

The crew finds Sisko's runabout orbiting Bajor, although there is no trace of Sisko at the fire caves, or anywhere else on Bajor. No one is prepared to give up the search. Kasidy tells the others that she fears something's happened to Sisko, something bad. The Prophets warned them . . .

. . . And Kasidy finds herself within the Celestial Temple, standing next to her husband. Although she's relieved to see Sisko, she's frightened by her surroundings. She asks Ben to come home with her, but Sisko says that he can't—not now. The Prophets saved him, he explains. But he's still their Emissary, and there's a great deal for him to learn, things that only the Prophets can teach him. Kasidy asks when he'll be back, and her husband admits he doesn't

Dukat is delighted when Winn calls forth an inferno in the Bajoran fire caves. ROBBIE ROBINSON

Odo agrees to Kira's accompanying him when he returns to his people. ROBBIE ROBINSON

know. Time doesn't exist in the Temple, he tells her. It could be a year. It could be yesterday. But he *will* be back, he promises. Kasidy takes reassurance in his ·promise, and tells him that she'll be waiting for him . . .

. . . And then she's back on Deep Space 9, looking at Jake and the others. She tells them that she was just talking to Benjamin. With Sisko's fate in the hands of the Prophets, his crew moves on to their new responsibilities, with Worf heading for the Klingon homeworld, O'Brien leaving for the Academy, and Kira and Odo about to leave the station for the Founders' world. Odo tells Kira that he doesn't want to say goodbye to the people on the station, noting that he's not very good at goodbyes. Quark, knowing the shape-shifter's nature, is unwilling to let Odo leave without a parting word. He catches up with them, and asks Odo if there isn't something the changeling would like to say to him before he goes. Odo confesses that there isn't. And with a final dismissive glance at Quark, he steps into the airlock. Kira looks at Quark sympathetically and tells him not to take it so hard, but Quark breaks into a grin and tells her that it's obvious the man loves him. It was written all over his back.

Kira and Odo travel to the Founders' planet. It looks much the same as the last time Odo saw it ("Broken Link"), except now the vast gelatinous sea is discolored, symptomatic of the illness that's affecting the entire Great Link. Odo asks Kira to tell the others that he's going to miss them all, even Quark. Then, knowing that she liked the way he looked in it, Odo

morphs himself into a tuxedo, so that Kira can remember him that way. They kiss and say goodbye, and Odo walks into the sea of his people. As he morphs into his gelatinous state, the ocean around him begins to change color, regaining its healthy golden tone.

Returning to Deep Space 9, Colonel Kira gets on with the business of running the station. She congratulates Nog on his promotion to lieutenant—one of Sisko's last official acts—and fingers Sisko's baseball as she looks out at Ops and her crew. Bashir invites Ezri to join him in a holosuite program—not the Alamo—while Quark starts a betting pool on who's going to be named the next kai. After Kira reprimands him for conducting betting activities on the station, the bartender cheerfully notes that the more things change, the more they stay the same. Kira walks onto the Promenade and sees a somber Jake, staring out the window at the wormhole. She steps up behind him and puts her arm on his shoulder, letting him know that he's not alone. The two of them continue to stare outward at the stars that fill the heavens. Deep Space 9 is itself a bright but distant star in the vast cathedral of space.

For seven years the members of *Deep Space Nine*'s writing staff had, more often than not, shared their lunches together, chewing over story points along with their food. The period preceding the two-hour finale was no different. The break session for "What You Leave Behind" was complex, and some aspects of the story took longer to gel than others.

"We were eating Peruvian food," René Echevarria remembers. "And the *other* thing that was on the table was the idea that Sisko was going to die in the Dominion War and then be resurrected by the Prophets on some level, or maybe go into their world to do battle with the Pah-wraiths. But nobody was really satisfied with that. We'd been talking about it for several days, but suddenly we realized that he *couldn't* die in the war. He had to go into battle with the Pah-wraiths and give his life in *that* battle. That's the mythic structure. The Prophets had created this man as their champion in the *material* world. If he had died and gone into *their* realm in order to fight, why did they need him in the first place?"

Echevarria credits Michael Piller and Rick Berman for their intuition and foresight as storytellers. "This Sisko as Emissary thing from the pilot was something that intrigued them on some level, and Michael worked it into that first script. I don't think he ever imagined that we would make as much of it as we did. It became this huge thing to be mined."

The final script would mine that element extensively. However, first it had to be written. "It was very hard because we weren't quite looking forward to ending the series," Behr admits. "Every morning Hans [Beimler] and I would come in and feel that if we didn't write that day, then the show wouldn't get written, and the show would not end, and it could all continue." He chuckles. "We were so pressed for time that when we finally finished the first draft of the script, we didn't crack open a bottle of tequila or do a victory dance or anything. We literally just looked at each other, clapped our hands for a second, and went right back into it. There was no feeling of triumph, and that kind of helped us, because we still had a lot to do."

That's an understatement. There was a war to be

The writers agreed to send O'Brien home; only Moore felt that it was time for Bashir to leave the station. ROBBIE ROBINSON

won, after all, and any number of people to do away with. Among the primary characters, the first to be killed was Cardassia's new leader, Damar. "Damar had to be the first to die, because Casey Biggs played Travis in the IMAX Alamo movie, and Travis was the the first guy to die at the Alamo," Behr says, laughing. Not long after that, Weyoun Eight was executed by Deep Space 9's resident exile. "In the end, Garak wasn't a tailor," Behr points out, "he was a killer. His instinct was to kill. Not to hit. Not to knock him down. Not to chide him most fiercely. But to kill Weyoun."

"Jeffrey [Combs] was not pleased," says Andy Robinson, the actor who pointed the phaser. "We were on the set and he said, 'I don't want to die like this. I thought I'd get involved in a big struggle and have a *grand* death.' But giving him that abrupt end," Robinson adds, "was perfect for Garak."

In spite of the female shape-shifter's declaration that he was the last Weyoun, Combs refuses to believe it. "In 'The Dogs of War,' the writers tried to convince us that there were no more clones," scoffs Combs. "But I said to Ira, 'If you think that the Vorta have all their clones in one basket, you've got another think coming. How many times have I died, Ira?' I don't think there's any question that there's some Weyoun clones hidden away in a cave somewhere."

Another character to bite the dust was Mila, Enabran Tain's housekeeper—and possibly something more, at least in Andy Robinson's imagination. "I think that Mila was one of the major relationships of Garak's life," the actor says. "Way back in 'Improbable Cause,' when Garak contacted her because he'd gotten a message from Enabran Tain, I started thinking, 'Well, she's Garak's mother.'" Robinson was so convinced that he incorporated it into the backstory he'd created for his character (in fact, it is a major story point in his novel *A Stitch in Time*, allegedly based on Garak's secret journals).

Any account of the final episode's casualties, of course, has to include the inhabitants of Cardassia. More than eight hundred million were destroyed in the last days of the war, and while the Cardassians, over the course of the series, were never portrayed as particularly *nice* people, the virtual annihilation of their civilization was a subject that the writers felt compelled to comment on within the script. While Sisko and Ross find themselves unable to drink over the bodies of the dead when they arrive on the conquered world, Martok has no such problem. "That showed the difference between humans and Klingons," observes Behr. "Martok enjoys the victory. He enjoys the bodies. He enjoys the triumph. And in some ways, he's right. The Bajorans would have called those deaths poetic justice, and that's something we wanted to remind the audience about. But we humans see things in complicated ways. It's tough being a human. It's much easier being a Klingon. I told J.G. Hertzler, 'Give me a smile in that scene. Martok is having fun. To him, this is good. It's satisfaction.'"

"I thought it rang absolutely true," concurs Hertzler. "It takes a certain amount of intellectualization to say, 'War is wrong.' Klingons are not able to do that. And the fact is, the Cardassians brought it upon themselves. So Martok just enjoyed that one moment of, 'We won.'"

Of course, one also could come to the conclusion that the Founders brought *their* defeat upon themselves in their callous disregard for their partners in the war effort. The female shape-shifter thought nothing of treating the Cardassians like pawns while they were supporting her, and after Damar betrayed her, she decided that a show of brutal strength would turn things around. "The idea that your enemy is not worthy of you is a common attitude in war," explains Behr. "Everyone underestimated the Viet Cong. Custer underestimated the Indians at Little Big Horn. The Founders are like that. They don't consider the Cardassians to be a threat. They're to be used, and that's all." To be fair, he allows that the female shape-shifter was feeling pretty ill by this point, and that

influenced her judgment. "She's sick and dying. She's ticked off that she's been hanging around with solids for so long, and this whole thing hasn't turned out the way she wanted it to. And under those circumstances, people do pretty extreme things. But they're still not nice people."

There were a few other significant deaths in the episode. Gul Dukat's for one. "I was so mad that I didn't get to kill him," says Nana Visitor, sounding far more like her alter ego, Kira Nerys. "I mean, it was *my character* that he tortured all those years!"

Ira Behr sighs. It seemed clear to him that Sisko, as the show's primary hero, and Dukat, as its primary villain, *had* to square off in the end. However, not everyone saw it that way. "*Everyone* wanted to kill Dukat," he says. "And Jeff Combs wanted to kill Damar. And Casey wanted to kill Weyoun. They cracked me up." Behr lifts his voice in a nasal whine. "'*Why* didn't I *get to kill Damar?*' '*Why didn't I get to kill Weyoun?*' I felt like saying, 'Hey, why don't you guys just meet outside your trailers?'" he laughs. "But really, with the exception of Dukat and Sisko, I wasn't really into who was going to kill whom if characters had to die. I didn't think that Kira needed to blow Dukat away in cold blood."

On the other hand, he jokes, "Dukat *had* to kill Winn, because they had sex. And we all know that if you have sex in movies, you have to *die*. Look at *Halloween*. Look at *Scream*."

As for Sisko—is he dead or isn't he? Well . . . that depends on whether you're going by the shooting script or the final version of the episode. The writers initially had planned to allow Sisko to fulfill his destiny by becoming a god and living with the Prophets forever. They discussed Sisko's fate with Avery Brooks and wrote a scene where Sisko says goodbye to his wife.

KASIDY
But you won't be with us, will you?

SISKO
I'll be closer than you think.

But then an unplanned complication arose. "René got obsessed with explaining the 'sorrow' that Sarah had warned Sisko about," says Behr. "And he came up with the idea that Kasidy was going to have a baby . . ."

And suddenly things seemed different. The above scene was shot, but later Avery Brooks confessed that he was troubled by it. In the twenty-fourth century, the situation conveyed only sorrow. However, in the twentieth century, there was a secondary social issue that had particular resonance in Brooks's mind. A black woman was going to be left alone to raise her child.

After talking to Brooks, the producers made a small modification to the scene and the actors went back and reshot it. Now, instead of facing the fact that her husband isn't coming back, Kasidy asks him *when* he'll be coming back.

> KASIDY
> When will you be back?
>
> SISKO
> It's hard to say. Time doesn't exist here. It could be a year.
> It could be yesterday.
> (definitively)
> But I *will* be back.

"We changed that one scene," says Behr. "One scene. It didn't hurt the show. We left it open for interpretation."

Dukat's fate, however, is a lot clearer. "I think he belongs in hell," Behr says firmly.

The road to hell, however, isn't easy to film. Just ask B.C. Cameron. "Reading about the Bajoran fire caves made beads of sweat come out of my forehead," she says, shuddering. "Of all the scenes I've read over my years in this business, nothing struck fear in my heart like that scene. I looked at Steve Oster and said, 'Falling into the abyss of flames? How are we gonna do *this* one?'"

Once again, the series' oft-used cave set—recently expanded when it was used to film part of *Star Trek: Insurrection*—was pressed into service. "We added some stalagmites and stalactites to give it a creepier feeling," Art Director Randy McIlvain says.

After members of the Art Department completed their preparations, Director Allan Kroeker took over. "Shooting the live action was pretty straightforward," says Kroeker, "but that's only because we had no idea how it was going to fit together. There were certain rules, and we obeyed them. [Visual Effects Producer] Dan Curry would watch me shoot a scene and he'd say things like, 'It will be easier for us if you can do this part of the scene against the cave wall.' Together we explained these things to the actors. We told Louise Fletcher that the Pah-wraiths were going to

come out of the canyon and wrap around her like a serpent. Then she reacted in such a way that would help sell the effect."

Some effects were relatively simple—for example, making the book of the Kosst Amogen disappear from Winn's hands. "Dan thought it would look better as a practical effect than as an optical," Kroeker says. "We asked Louise to lift the book over her head as the camera moves up to her face. Suddenly she reacts and brings her hands down empty. I thought it was ingenious. It only took us about ten takes to get it." And where did the book go? "One of our grips, the guy with the longest arms, clambered up on the rocks, reached down and just grabbed it from her hands," Kroeker laughs.

Showing Sisko and Dukat fighting as they fell through the fire was more problematic. One shot, which takes just one and one-half seconds of screen time, required several days using the combined efforts of the Visual Effects Department, the Special Effects Department, and the live-action filmmakers. "I didn't want to put the actors on wires, which would have been the obvious choice," Dan Curry explains, "So I put Marc Alaimo and Avery Brooks on a turntable that would allow them to revolve around a pivot point halfway between them. Each actor stood on a track, like a skateboard, so that the grips could push them back and forth, and the track also worked up and down, like a see-saw. When you see Sisko pushing Dukat away, Avery is actually pushing Marc and Marc is physically rolling backward." Since the actors had to stay vertical during this circus-worthy stunt ("They had safety belts on that held them in place," Curry notes), the camera crew had to turn the camera on its side in order to show the characters falling while on their sides.

"When the two of them are supposed to separate and fall apart, we had to rotate the whole rig and lower Marc's see-saw, so that it gave them the illusion of spinning," interjects Gary Monak. "It was quite an elaborate rig for a couple of seconds of film."

"It had to be photographed in a very smooth, very controlled manner," adds Kris Krosskove. "We put the camera on a dolly track. It was hard to focus, because the actors were coming at the camera as the camera was moving toward them."

To complete the shot, and others in the Fire Caves, notes Curry, "We mapped real fire elements into a computer and built the fire around the actors. When they go over the ledge into the fire, we mounted the camera up on a platform and had the stunt

VIEW LOOKING THRU AND UNDER WALKWAY   JOHN EAVES 3/99 FIRE CAVES #575 #576

One final redo of Stage 18: Bajor's fire caves. JOHN EAVES

people jump off a piece of the cave set into the fire pit. Of course, *all* the fire was created in postproduction." Only the sharpest eyes could tell that the fire had been seen before on the series. "We used one of the columns of fire that Gary Monak created for the Badlands," Curry smiles.

The most unexpected moment during the entire seven seasons of shooting *Deep Space Nine* occurred during the Sisko/Dukat enounter. The shot called for Sisko to swing two punches at Dukat. In theory, it was an easy fight gag, with the camera positioned over one actor's shoulder where it couldn't see the trajectory of the swing. Sometimes, however, "in theory" and "in practice" are entirely different animals.

"Avery has done this sort of thing a million times, so it's never a problem," says Cameron. "I was kind of watching the monitor with one eye and watching the actors with the other. Avery swung at him the first time, and Marc snapped his head back and then brought it back up, the way he was supposed to. And then Avery swung the second time, and suddenly Marc just disappeared from the monitor. For a second I thought, 'That isn't part of the scene,' and then it hit me what had happened and I took off for the set."

What had happened, as footage from that day later revealed, was that Alaimo had brought his head

a bit too far forward prior to the second swing. "It was one of those things where, in retrospect, you realize it could have been worse," Kroeker says.

A studio nurse arrived to examine Alaimo's nose. "After we peeled off the Cardassian makeup," Cameron says, "we were able to determine that Marc didn't need an ambulance, so we got the van and took him to the hospital."

"Alaimo was a real trooper," says Behr, shaking his head. "He wanted to come back just a few days later, but we told him to wait until Thursday."

Because Brooks was scheduled to leave town for a few days, the crew went ahead and filmed his portion of the scene. Alaimo returned a week later, as good as new, to film the scenes where he and Brooks fall into the abyss.

Elsewhere a number of goodbyes needed to be written, including one added rather late in the production. "We had a lot of discussion about whether or not to include one between Garak and Bashir," Behr reveals. "A lot of people thought that their relationship had been forgotten and we didn't need to give them a goodbye scene, that the important thing was Bashir and O'Brien. But I felt that we needed it. For seven years, this guy has been wanting to get out of exile, and he helps free his planet, helps his people

After seven years, the series' hero and main villain in a fight to the death. ROBBIE ROBINSON

do the right thing, and finally he gets to go home to ruins. Bashir gives us this human, kind of well-meaning but not really helpful response to all that's happened, while Garak has his eyes wide open."

"Sid and I didn't discuss how we'd do that scene," Robinson comments. "That was the beauty of working with him. However it came out, it was simply because of our personal chemistry. And I found that final scene to be very satisfying."

There was another final moment for Julian Bashir, with Miles O'Brien. "That relationship means a lot to me," Behr explains. "It's one of the great unsung things about *Deep Space Nine*, relationships like that. People might think that a *Star Trek* series doesn't need relationships like that, but I think it does. As an audience member, I enjoy seeing it. It gives the show meaning, and it certainly gave the final episode a lot of meaning."

While Odo and Kira had a touching farewell before the changeling rejoined his people, the constable refused to offer Quark the satisfaction of some sentimental parting words. Quark seemed to take something positive from their parting all the same, as did Armin Shimerman. "Odo knew exactly what Quark was looking for, and he was damned if he was going to give it to him," he grins. "And Quark appreciated the fact that there was no resolution to their game. That meant the game was still afoot."

Aron Eisenberg was extremely pleased that his character didn't have to say goodbye. "They could have just as easily sent Nog back to the Academy to finish his training," he says. "But they didn't. Instead,

he got another promotion, to lieutenant. That means he's moving up. I hope that means that someday we'll see more stories."

While Sisko was able to bid farewell to his wife, Jake was left without a parting word from his father, something that some viewers sorely missed. "A lot of people thought that was a problem," Behr admits. "But at some point I realized that the last shot of the show, which I'd *thought* was going to be in the bar with Quark and Kira, should be this image of the kid standing there, waiting for his father. And missing him. Is his father ever going to come back? The son yearning for his father was like the audience yearning for the show. As we push back from the image of him, push back from the station, farther and farther away until it's gone, it was just like, *boom,* right on that road we came in on. So no, there is no goodbye between father and son, but to me, the idea that Jake's waiting for Ben is better than any goodbye we could have had."

More painful than separation—the unsaid goodbye. ROBBIE ROBINSON

Now that the characters had said their goodbyes to one another, the producers wanted to allow them to say goodbye to the viewers as well. While Beimler and Behr were writing the teleplay, David Weddle and Bradley Thompson were given an assignment. Search through the episodes and suggest scenes for a montage representing each character's time on the station. "We picked out eighty-five or ninety clips, and then the Editorial Department chose and assembled them," Weddle explains. "We just looked at specific relationships and their evolution."

"The montage was a total killer," Behr says. "Certainly the easiest one to do was Jake growing up. We knew that one was going to be a heartbreaker. O'Brien and Bashir was pretty simple. Actually, it was all pretty simple to do." Well, with one exception.

Unfortunately, the producers were unable to use clips of Terry Farrell.

The producers considered numerous title possibilities before they settled on "What You Leave Behind." Finally, they culled a title from an obscure quote: "All that you take with you is what you leave behind." "I thought it was pretty good," Behr smiles. "And it's true."

It also contrasts interestingly with the title of *The Next Generation*'s finale. "'All Good Things . . . must come to an end' is a statement," Behr observes. "It tells you that the preceding seven years were all good things. 'What You Leave Behind' is a question, a challenge."

It's one that Behr hopes the show's audience will ponder for a long time.

The Last Day on the Set

Tonight is a very special night for some friends of mine. They've been together a long time. But like the man said, nothing lasts forever.

VIC FONTAINE, "WHAT YOU LEAVE BEHIND"

At 8:00 A.M., April 20, 1999, the Cargo Bay area on Stage 4 looks more like "Norma's House of Hair" than it does a space station facility. Customers wait in line while three hairdressers race them in and out of the chairs, giving them cuts or wigs, enhanced with greasy oils or big bouffant fluffs. "I love it," each customer repeats in turn, as the work transforms them from '90s-era actors, writers, and office assistants into 1962 Las Vegas prowlers.

Just outside, in the makeup trailer, Michael Dorn, transformed into Worf for the final time on *this* series, rises, just as Executive Producer Ira Steven Behr arrives to be made up as a patron of Vic's Lounge.

It's the final day of shooting on *Deep Space Nine*.

Looking oddly reminiscent of their high school yearbook photos, the six members of the writing staff gather on Stage 7, the current site of Vic's. The crowd grows—Jeffrey Combs with human ears, J.G. Hertzler with a very un-Klingon mane of white hair, Russ English (security guard for *Star Trek* since 1988) in street clothes—Max Grodénchik, Aron Eisenberg, Casey Biggs, human all—Robbin Slocum (*DS9* production assistant), Lolita Fatjo (script coordinator), each too young to remember the hair-sprayed dos that tower above them—Chase Masterson, who won't appear but just wanted to be here.

By 9:45 A.M. the crowd has grown, filling the soundstage between the Vic's set and the twin-peaked fiberglass Founders' planet island standing unlit across the way. At B.C. Cameron's urging, the "patrons" step into Vic's to dance and drink. The work of an extra is long and hot, but everyone here wants to be part of the last visit to the holosuite. Most feel it would have been harder to stay away.

Behr originally had envisioned this scene much more simply: the writing staff would be sitting on a row of stools talking to Quark. "We were always going to do that," Behr says. "But then I realized that the shot would stick out like a sore thumb at the end of the series. It would have been a 'Brrr-rump-bump' where we didn't need a 'Brr-rump-bump.' So I decided that was a mistake."

Behr moved the scene into Vic's, where the staff could mingle with the crowd. "We were going to be down there watching the filming anyway," he says. "So it became obvious—why not put the monkey suits on." As for inviting the rest of the crowd—

"That was just me being my sentimental silly self," Behr says with a grin. "So many of the supporting people seemed to care about the show as much as the regulars, that I wanted to give them the opportunity to come out of make-

LEFT TO RIGHT: Ira Steven Behr, Hans Beimler, Ronald D. Moore, Bradley Thompson, David Weddle, René Echevarria (kneeling). ROBBIE ROBINSON

David Levinson (Broik) shares a joke with James Darren. ROBBIE ROBINSON

up if they wanted to." With no prompting, Vic's drew a full house.

"It wasn't like Ira was asking a favor of us so much as he was including us in a very, very special time," Cecily Adams says "I felt honored that they included me. I was thrilled to do it."

At 10:00 A.M., Cameron calls "Action!" for the first shot of the day. Russ English enters the lounge, escorting Robbin Slocum on his arm. "That's it," Allen Kroeker calls to the dapper couple, "You're a million bucks looking for change."

The next shot is as much fun. As Vic steps forward to greet Quark, a crowd enters behind them: Ira Behr in his signature sunglasses, Bradley Thompson, Lolita Fatjo, elegant in green, Hans Beimler, Ron Moore followed by David Weddle. For the next shot, the camera is panning along the bar, allowing each of the key characters to deliver a line of dialogue. In the background, two guys in gray seem to be everywhere. They could only be Jeff Combs and Casey Biggs. "We stop at all the right tables," Combs laughs. "Casey and I always make sure that we get our faces in the background as much as possible. Like, if we're gonna be extras, we're gonna be *good* extras."

While filming goes on, still cameras appear as crew members take snapshots. Some of their shots include images of Robert Picardo, *Star Trek: Voyager*'s Emergency Medical Hologram. "It's my day off," he says, laughing, as he enters the set. Picardo stands on the sidelines for hours, watching, and signing the dozens of scripts that are being passed around for autographs.

"So, do you know somebody on the show or something?" David Weddle asks the woman in the red dress seated next to him. "I'm Moogie," Cecily Adams answers, grinning at the lack of recognition. "That totally cracks me up." Weddle laughs as he shakes her hand.

The camera is rolling on Alexander Siddig and Colm Meaney when a tall, white-haired extra slips past behind them. "How the mighty have fallen," J.G. Hertzler whispers when the director yells cut. "One day you're chancellor of the Klingon Empire, and the next day you're background."

"It's a harsh reality," Ron Moore answers from a nearby table.

Andy Robinson steps in, just visiting, as James Darren and the band step onto the stage to rehearse the song sequence. "I was all choked up," Darren will say later. "They picked this great song, 'The Way You Look Tonight.' All of the lyrics have a double meaning." In fact, the lyrics may be too meaningful. As Darren steps toward Nana Visitor during the first take and sings ". . . and that laugh, that wrinkles your nose," Visitor begins to cry. "I told Ira afterward," Darren continues, "from now on, whenever I sing that song, I won't be able to think about this night, because I'll never get through the song."

At 4:00 P.M., the filmmakers break for lunch. A catered meal waits across the alley in *Voyager*'s cargo bay. A row of Borg regeneration chambers lines the wall, and *Deep Space Nine* film clips are running on six video monitors placed about the room. The group eats, eyeing the monitors. Gowron fights with Martok, the diners lay down their utensils and applaud; Sisko learns that the Klingons have joined against the Federation, everyone claps; Kira is stabbed, no one eats. The earlier feeling of sadness visibly turns to exuberance. The Ferengi slap their heads in front of the American military

FAR LEFT: Robbin Slocum, assistant to Ira Behr.
ROBBIE ROBINSON

Script Coordinator Lolita Fatjo stops by the VIP table, in the background (left) is J.G. Hertzler. ROBBIE ROBINSON

"Deep Space Nine was blessed to have such a great cast," says Darren. ROBBIE ROBINSON

in Roswell, New Mexico and the room swells with laughter. These aren't just clips—they're the personal memories of everyone present.

The video ends, and Ira Behr climbs to the top of a twenty-foot ladder to address his appreciation to the crowd. His speech ends with lines from the script, "As the captain said, this is the best crew ever. This may be the last time we're all together, but no matter what the future holds, no matter how far we travel, a part of us, a very important part, will always remain here—on *Deep Space Nine*." The cast and crew rise to give *their* captain a standing ovation. Over the applause, Behr says, "Okay. Back to work!"

At 6:00 P.M., B.C. Cameron calls for the set to quiet. Many of the day's camera angles are completed, and she makes the first of a series of important announcements. "Ladies and gentlemen, she says, "This is good night—and goodbye—to Aron Eisenberg." The words bring a shock of emotion to all present. This is a commonly heard phrase; it is said each time a visiting guest actor completes his or her days on an episode. But Aron is not a visitor. Aron is family. Everyone applauds for a full minute.

7:18 P.M., Cameron again calls for quiet. "Ladies and gentlemen, this is good night and goodbye to Jeffrey Combs." The emotion is palpable; the applause meaningful. Everyone realizes that the biggest goodbye of all is near.

8:37 P.M., and it happens. Cameron's eyes circle the room as she matches names to faces.

"Ladies and gentlemen, this is good night and goodbye to Mr. Avery Brooks."

"Ladies and gentlemen, this is good night and goodbye to Nana Visitor."

"Ladies and gentlemen, this is good night and goodbye to Colm Meaney."

"Ladies and gentlemen, this is good night and goodbye to Siddig El Fadil."

"Ladies and gentlemen, this is good night and goodbye to Rene Auberjonois." The actor sticks his right hand under the layer of rubber covering his face, and with one gentle twist, Odo is gone.

"Ladies and gentlemen, this is good night and goodbye to Michael Dorn." Dorn, too, pulls the prosthetics from his face.

"Ladies and gentlemen, this is good night and goodbye to Penny Johnson."

"Ladies and gentlemen, this is good night and goodbye to Cirroc Lofton."

"Ladies and gentlemen, this is good night and goodbye to Nicole deBoer."

"Ladies and gentlemen, this is good night and goodbye to the background players."

Hugs. Kisses. Sadness. Joy. The height of mixed emotions. The evening's filming is not yet complete, but neither the producers nor the director ask that the work begin anew. This moment is far too important. "My emotional catharsis was that

Cast and crew say goodbye to Avery Brooks. Cecily Adams, Moogie, is on the left. ROBBIE ROBINSON

Penny Johnson hugs Cirroc Lofton. ROBBIE ROBINSON

A moment of applause for Armin Shimerman. ROBBIE ROBINSON

Auberjonois removes his mask as the crew applauds Penny Johnson. ROBBIE ROBINSON

last day of shooting," Ron Moore says later. "It was a full day, but it went really fast. People from all over the studio kept coming in to say goodbye. And then when everyone gathered together to say 'Goodbye and good night,' it all landed on me right then. Boom! When I walked off the set, it was all over."

"For days I'd been saying things like, 'Good night and goodbye to the Promenade,' and 'Good night and goodbye to Stage 17,'" Cameron reminisces. "But when we actually finished with the entire cast . . . that was hard. It's just so sad."

9:00 P.M. The grips resume working, despite the many cast members lingering about. The final sequence to be shot has Quark and Vic sitting alone and playing Go Fish.

"This is the best," Darren says, happily. "The writers told me, 'You're going to be in the very last scene of the very last episode ever shot on *Deep Space Nine*. I'm privileged to have this. Armin and I had this honor."

"It's marvelously metaphoric for me," Shimerman adds. "Quark always has been outside of the group. Now the group is leaving, and here I am. That is just right."

Kroeker has planned part of the scene as an overhead crane shot, so the setup time is considerable. At 10:35 P.M., the stage is quiet. Most of the visitors are gone, save for Chase Masterson, a visiting Lou Race, and a few studio employees. As the camera rolls, Ira Behr sits nearby, eyes on the monitor, showing no signs of leaving.

Race walks up to Behr. "What was the first thing that was filmed on the series?" he asks.

"I came down to the set to see Sisko's office with Kira screaming at him on the monitor," Behr recalls. "She was just screaming. We also shot Dukat and found out that we had to recast. That's when Marc Alaimo said, yes. And the other thing I remember is that the first set of dailies had no sound. We all said, 'What a great way to start, boys.' We had to wait until the third day before we could watch dailies."

11:15 P.M. "I think this is the martini shot," Cameron announces, meaning, in movie jargon, the final one. "Lou," she calls to Race. "Would you like to call the last shot?" "No, I don't think so," he answers.

11:26 P.M. The camera rolls. Take One. Take Two. Kroeker and Cameron look at the replay on the monitor. It's fine. 11:48 P.M. "That's a wrap."

"Ladies and gentlemen, that's a good night and goodbye to Armin Shimerman."

"Ladies and gentlemen, that's a good night and goodbye to Jimmy Darren."

The grips begin to dismantle the crane and camera. The electricians start to roll up their equipment. Kroeker and Cameron walk out of the Lounge along with members of the band. Ira Behr stays seated for a moment, in no apparent hurry to depart.

"I have many years to not be here," Behr says, as the set lights go out and the stage lights dim.

Ira Behr says thanks to Cirroc Lofton.
ROBBIE ROBINSON

Michael Piller, Ira Behr, and James Darren chat with Rick Berman. ROBBIE ROBINSON

ROBBIE ROBINSON

A P P E N D I X

A C K N O W L E D G M E N T S

As a child, my favorite story was that of the good Samaritan, the biblical parable about a man who selflessly gives of his time and efforts to help another. Throughout my life I have met individuals who exemplify the hero of that story, but it was not until I wandered into the *Star Trek* production offices and soundstages that I met an entire assembly of people who would invite me into those offices and into their homes, sacrificing lunch hours, late evenings, and parts of their precious weekends to answer my unending questions about their work. I've learned from them how it feels to be on the receiving end of that parable. The least I can do in return is say "Thank You."

First and foremost, I wish to thank Paula M. Block for knowing the right stuff to say and the right way to say it. She also brews the best cup of coffee in this town.

This book would not have been possible without the encouragement, cooperation, and direction of Ira Steven Behr. He is a gentleman of the first order, despite his having grown up on a Bronx street corner. Thank you, Ira.

My very special thanks to Rick Berman, Michael Piller, Hans Beimler, René Echevarria, Peter Allan Fields, Peter Lauritson, David Livingston, Joe Menosky, Ronald D. Moore, Steve Oster, Dave Rossi, Jeri Taylor, Bradley Thompson, David Weddle, and Robert Hewitt Wolfe, as well as Monique Chambers and Robbin Slocum.

For caring enough to give the very best, my thanks to Avery Brooks, Rene Auberjonois, Nicole deBoer, Michael Dorn, Terry Farrell, Cirroc Lofton, Colm Meaney, Armin Shimerman, Alexander Siddig, Nana Visitor, Cecily Adams, Marc Alaimo, Michael Ansara, Susan Bay, Majel Barrett, Casey Biggs, Billy Burke, Rosalind Chao, Jeffrey Combs, James Cromwell, James Darren, John deLancie, Cliff

DeYoung, Aron Eisenberg, Louise Fletcher, Max Grodénchik, J.G. Hertzler, Famke Janssen, Salome Jens, Barry Jenner, Michael Keenan, Kenneth Marshall, Phil Morris, Bill Mumy, Robert O'Reilly, Robert Picardo, Tim Ransom, Andy Robinson, Tim Russ, Faith Salie, Wallace Shawn, Christopher Shea, Hilary Shepard-Turner, Kitty Swink, Debra Wilson, and Mark Worden.

At Paramount, my thanks to Andrea Hein, Terri Helton, Pam Newton, and Tim Gaskill, Gary Holland, Harry Lang, Phyllis Ungerleider, Guy Vardaman, and Jennifer Weingroff.

For taking care of me on the soundstages, the backlot, the postproduction facilities and the telephone, thank you to Ruth Adelman, Corey Allen, Gavin Ames, Tom Arp, Hilary Bader, Jolynn Baca, Charles Bazaldua, Reza Badiyi, Paul Baillargeon, Joey Banks, David Bell, Tom Benko, Kurt Michael Bensmiller, Earl Binion, Jr., Bob Blackman, Tamu Blackwell, Cliff Bole, Jerry Bono, Andre Bormanis, Mary Ellen Bosche, Kevin Bouchez, Anthony Bro, Adam Buckner, LeVar Burton, Judi Brown, Bob Burns, Zayra Cabot, Camille Calvet, B.C. Cameron, Valerie Canamar, Joe Candrella, Carol Carpenter, Jeanne Carrigan-Fauci, David Carson, Gloria Casney, Sheila Cavanaugh, Chip Chalmers, Jay Chattaway, James L. Conway, Nell and William Crawford, Barbara Covington, Paul Coyle, Dan Curry, Doug Davey, Maril Davis, Robert della Santina, Samuel Diaz, Jimmy Diggs, Tony Dow, Doug Drexler, Dragon Dronet, John Dwyer, P.J. Earnest, Allan Eastman, John Eaves, Judy Elkins, Russ English, Bob Fambry, J.P. Farrell, Lolita Fatjo, Al Ferrante, Jerry Finnerman, D.C. Fontana, Jonathan Frakes, Kim Friedman, Steve Fong, Carl Fortina, Anthony Fredrickson, Brian Fuller, Steve Gausche, Michael Gerbosi, Julie Gesin, Alan Gitlin, Bill Gocke, Nicole Gravett, Don Hahn, Chris Haire, Mark Gehred-O'Connell, Morgan Gendel, Robert Gillan, Lumas Hamilton, Jr., Barbara Harris, Chandler Hayes, Mike Hemingway, Ellen Hornstein, R.J. Hohman, Adam Howard, Adrian Hurley, Gary Hutzel, Dennis Ivanjack, Clynell Jackson III, Phil Jacobson, Gregory Jein, Dean Jones, Penny Juday, Philip Kim, Carlyle King, Lisa Klink, Alan Kobayashi, Winrich Kolbe, John Knoll, Ronnie Knox, John Kretchmer, Allan Kroeker, Kris Krosskove, Carol Kunz, Paul Lawrence, Adam "Mojo" Lebowitz, Robert Lederman, Don Lee, Norma Lee, Robert Legato, David Levinson, Stuart Lippman, Victor Lobl, James Lomas, Joe Longo, Brad Look, David Mack, Dennis Madelone, Molly Mandell, Paul Maples, Jim Martin, Mace Matiosian, Dennis McCarthy, Randy McIlvain, James Minor, Mike Mistovich, Gary Monak, Mary Kay Morse, Richard L. Morrison, Pat Moudakis, Kenny Myers;

And for being in the second half of the alphabet: Davy Nethercutt, Glenn Neufeld, Josee Normand, Michael Okuda, Denise Okuda, John Ordover, Mark Overton, Bill Peets, Richard Penn, Lemuel Perry, Paige Pollack, Steve Posey, Terri Potts, Lou Race, David Ramirez, Frederick Rappaport, Judith and Garfield Reeves-Stevens, Lisa Rich, Laura Richarz, Tim Roller, Josh Rose, April Rossi, Steve Rowe, Marvin Rush, Kevin Ryan, Gerry Sackman, Robert Sheerer, Gary Schwartz, Naren Shankar, Mark Shepherd, Jill Sherwin, Alexander Singer, Todd Slayton, Rick Sternbach, Eric Stillwell, David Stipes, Greg Smith, Heidi Smothers, Evan Carlos Somers, Ron Surma, David Takemura, Michael Taylor, Willie Thoms, Jim Trombetta, James Van Over, L.Z. Ward, Paul Wertheimer, Jonathan West, Karen Westerfield, Robert Weimer, Scott Wheeler, Natalie Wood, Michael Westmore, Fritz Zimmerman, and Herman Zimmerman.

For constantly carrying those cameras and aiming them at the right places, my thanks to Robbie Robinson, Kim Gottlieb-Walker, Julie Dennis, and Danny Feld, as well as Gale M. Adler, Carin Baer, B.J. Cohen, Jerry Fitzgerald, Michael Grecco, Jeff Katz, Wren Maloney, Lynn McAffee, Barry McLaughlin, Gregory Schwartz, Barry Slobin, Gene Trindl, Ron Tom, Randy Topper, and J. Viles for the great selection of photos.

For their contributions to this project and humanity in general, thank you to Steve Aboulafia, D.V.M., Gary Berman, James, Maria and Matthew Block, Louis and Hattie Block, Wade Brown, Sean Burgeson, Gordon Carleton and Lori Chapek-Carleton, Mike Colby, Susan Comara, Cyra and Michael Cowan, Vincent Eugene Craddock, Hua and Devin Curry, Florence Erdmann, Gordon Erdmann, Joyce Kogut and Jeff Erdmann, Denise Greenawalt, John Harper, Judi Hendricks and Robb Stotts, Charles Hardin Holley, Joyce Jasinski, Richard Jordan, Alan Johnson, Devra Langsam, Lilianna Laouri, Randy and Jean-Marc Lofficier, Dan Madsen, Lori and Adam Malin, Dave McDonnell, Germaine Morgan, Jim Oldsberg, Riley Newton, Steve Palmer, Ellen Pasternack, Kurt Piar, Amanda Ruffin, Marcia Olarsch, Rex Ressler, Joan Rosenberg, Paula Smith, Jackie and Tom Truty, Bob Wald, Jeff Walker, KathE and Steve Walker, Steve Wroe, and Joyce Yasner.

I thank too, Margaret Clark at Pocket Books and Paul Ruditis at Paramount Pictures for your diligence, attention to detail, and moral support. All of your work makes mine seem to shine, as does the artistry of book designer Richard Oriolo and cover designer James Wang. Also at Pocket Books, thank you to Judith Curr, Kara Welsh, Scott Shannon, Donna O'Neill, Donna Ruvituso, Penny Haynes, Brian Blatz, Lisa Feuer, Twisne Fan, Marco Palmieri, and Jessica McGivney.

Finally, thank you to DeForest Kelley, without a doubt the sweetest man ever to be associated with *Star Trek*. We all miss you.

TERRY J. ERDMANN
Hollywood, January 2000

The author with some aliens. He's the one in the middle.
ROBBIE ROBINSON